#558 of 1000

PLEBE

A TRILOGY OF NOVELS

For: Tom Wilson
From: Steve

Best Wishes! Enjoy

HANK TUROWSKI

USNA CLASS OF 1971

PARADIGM PRESS

KENT, WASHINGTON

AUTHOR'S NOTE

Annapolis has the most charming and impressive campus in the nation. The scenery and buildings described in this book exist. The routines and customs described are also accurate for the time period. Although many changes have occurred since the Vietnam era, zealous plebe training remains high on the list of midshipman responsibilities. There was a "Tiger" Company, and the indoctrination as described was mostly true based on my personal experiences, direct observations, or information provided from my companymates. Being a midshipman was -- and still is -- intended to be ultimately challenging, but those midshipmen who persevere, discover their extreme physical, emotional, and moral limitations. Service academy graduates provide the leadership backbone for the greatest and most professional military organization in the history of the world.

The characters in these novel are completely fictitious. Any resemblance to real people exists only in demented fantasies, overdeveloped egos, and blatant lies. No one I ever met was as cruel -- or as heroic -- as the young men described in these pages, although some came very near each mark. Plebe Year is designed to be tough, but despite what any graduate -- who may happened to be your spouse, parent, child, friend, or companion says, -- nobody ever had a Plebe Year like Tommy Poole.

ISBN Number **0-9656146-0-3**
Library of Congress Catalog Number Pending

Published by Paradigm Press, PO Box 5248
Kent, Washington

Additional copies of this book or the art work may be obtained by contacting the publisher or by using the order forms in the back of this book

Printed in the United States of America by Book Crafters, Chelsea, Michigan.

Cover design and architectural sketches by Eileen Wilson Turowski of The Design Forum
Interpretive Tracings by Andy Dunloy

DEDICATION

In loving memory of :

Henry and Catherine Turowski

In sincere appreciation to:

Eileen Wilson Turowski
Mike and Sandy Hallahan
Josh and Twyla Whitmore
John and Fran Gladden
Rita Happy
Andy Knowles

In Acknowledgment to:

The U.S. Naval Academy Class of 1971
Every alumnus who had a Plebe Year
(or thought they did)

THE QUALIFICATIONS OF A NAVAL OFFICER

It is by no means enough that an officer of the Navy should be a capable mariner. He must be that, of course, but also a great deal more. He should be as well a gentleman of liberal education, refined manners, punctilious courtesy, and the nicest sense of personal honor.

He should be the soul of tact, patience, justice, firmness, and charity. No meritorious act of a subordinate should escape his attention or be left to pass without its reward, even if the reward is only a word of approval. Conversely, he should not be blind to a single fault in any subordinate, though at the same time he should be quick and unfailing to distinguish error from malice, thoughtlessness from incompetency, and well meant shortcoming from heedless or stupid blunder.

In one word, every commander should keep constantly before him the great truth, that to be well obeyed, he must be perfectly esteemed.

From a composite letter of John Paul Jones compiled by Augustus C. Buell in Reef Points

BIOGRAPHIES

Hank Turowski grew up in an ethic neighborhood in Baltimore, Maryland. He attended Parochial school and the Baltimore Polytechnic Institute before being appointed to the Naval Academy. He graduated from Annapolis in 1971 with a degree in Mechanical Engineering and in 1980 received a Master's Degree in Financial Management from the Naval Postgraduate School in Monterey, California. After graduation from Annapolis, Hank served on the USS Rupertus, DD-851 in Vietnam and Westpac, then attended Flight School in Pensacola, Florida. In 1973 he transferred to the Civil Engineer Corps, and performed various engineering and construction responsibilities throughout the world, including, the Naval Station at Guantanamo Bay, Cuba; the Weapons Station at Yorktown, Virginia; the Public Works Center on Guam, Marianas Islands; the NATO Naval Air Station in Sigonella, Sicily; and Engineering Field Division and the Naval Base in San Diego, California. He retired from the Navy in 1991.

Following military retirement, Hank managed construction projects in Saudi Arabia for three years. He presently writes and works for a the environmental remediation subsidiary of a major construction company. He has two sons: Hank Junior, a computer whiz, is a student and entrepreneur in Washington State; and Patrick, who presently lives in Maryland, and is equal parts vagabond, poet, and troubadour.

POSTSCRIPT: The author was a mediocre soccer player at Annapolis. He skated his first set and bagged Plebe Year whenever he could. (But he still had a better Plebe Year than his roommate.)

The artist grew up on a farm in rural Tennessee. She studied art and art history at the University of Tennessee and is an Industrial Design graduate of Auburn University. She has designed personal computer housings, and holds several patents for airline food service containers. Eileen has worked for several large architectural companies and has lived throughout the United States and in the Middle East. She also has more than 20 years domestic and international experience as an interior designer for major office, religious, retail, educational, and family living spaces.

She has two children, Andrew and Scott, both students, living with her in Washington State.

USNA SEAL

The Academy seal features a hand holding a trident, two opposing torches, and a shield with the images of an ancient oared ship of war and an open book. Below in Latin is written, "Ex Tridents Scientia" which translates as "From Knowledge, sea power."

TABLE OF CONTENTS

LIST OF ILLUSTRATIONS

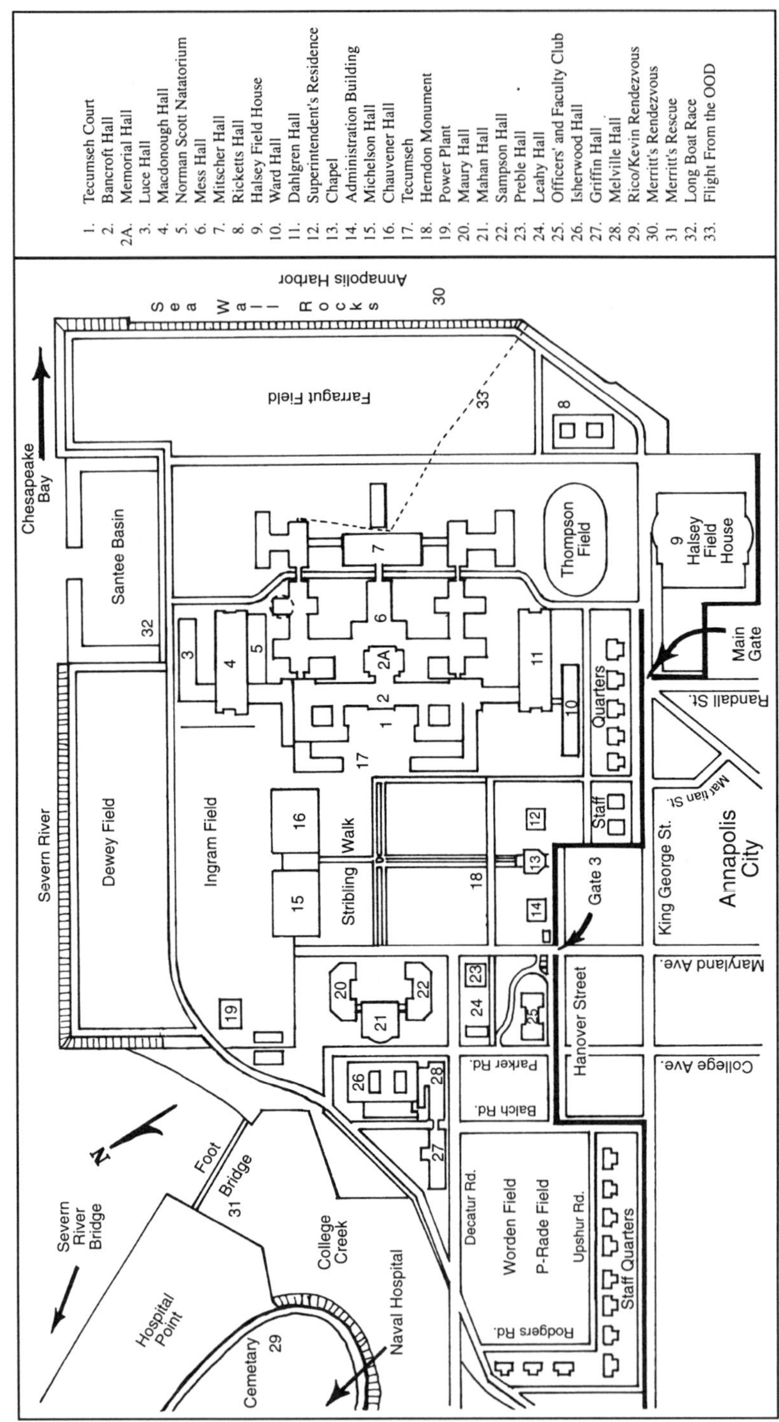

THE ACADEMY GROUNDS

This map shows the building and important features of the Naval Academy, particularly as they relate to the story.

PLEBE

SUMMER

A NOVEL OF THE NAVAL ACADEMY

HANK TUROWSKI

USNA CLASS OF 1971

PLEBE SUMMER

CHAPTER 1

PROLOGUE

Herndon Monument looked exhausted and embarrassed. The late morning sun that peeked through the branches of the enormous poplar trees on either side dappled the incredible scene in a rhythmic sway of shadow and color. The once shiny marble sides of the monument were coated with a mixture of various slimes -- both manufactured and human. Streak and smear marks traversed the mess, along with an assortment of deeply embedded finger trails. The precisely crafted pointed top was marred by the shredded remnants of material -- once part of a midshipman's hat -- which had been glued in place earlier that morning, but which had been rather hastily ripped away just moments ago.

The area surrounding the monument looked like the scene of a battle. The once meticulously groomed lawn was chewed into unrecognizableness and transformed into a mud patch. The mud was littered with muddy and sweaty white gym shirts -- some ripped into shreds -- all of which had been shed during the recent melee. And a solitary gym shoe stood toe-first in the middle of the muck, looking almost like a miniature representation of the obelisk. There were blood stains on the monument almost ten feet up where someone had accidentally broken a nose in their haste to climb. There was a vomit puddle almost at my feet. This was a remnant from one of my more athletic classmates who unthinkingly hurled himself into the mass of young humanity that plastered itself against the obelisk, and who had been crushed sick into the ensuing swelter.

An enlisted medical crew worked nearby on one of several newly promoted plebes who had been overcome during the crush of the ceremony. I could see smiles on the faces of the corpsmen. I knew they thought we were stupid to have so enthusiastically performed a ritual so fraught with peril and so seemingly stupid. I smiled secretly at them. They would never in their wildest dreams understand the motivation that went into the climbing of the Herndon Monument -- an act that signified the official end of Plebe Year for me and slightly more than a thousand of my classmates. I wasn't even sure of the reasons.

I looked down at my hands, which were grubby and slime covered like everything else nearby, but which also held a treasure unlike anything I had ever held. It was a hat -- a filthy hat -- but not just any hat. It was *the* hat. The one that had mocked the plebe class from its perch atop the monument, and which had been ripped away by one of my companymates just moments earlier. Of course it had to be my company that gained the prize. We were the *Tigers*! The company of companies. The ones every other midshipman hated -- and secretly envied.

I lifted the hat into the air and held it aloft. I could feel a tear starting to run down my left cheek. Where had that come from? I began to laugh loudly. My laughter startled the corpsmen, who stared at me as if I were a lunatic. Maybe I was. I didn't care. It was finally over. No more plebe insanity. No more pushups till my arms gave out. No more running and vomiting and running some more. No more "How's the cow?". No more chopping in the passageways. No more square meals. No more chow calls. No more bracing up. It was finished, and I had survived.

A few minutes earlier nearly every other classmate had raced to Bancroft Hall to clean up for liberty and brief summer vacations, and the hundreds of visitors who had witnessed our triumph had dispersed -- some to wait for their sons at the statue of Tecumseh, others to wander the campus. I was almost alone -- almost.

Across the way I saw a familiar figure staring at me. I was slightly startled. I hadn't noticed until now he was there. The man wore a brilliant white officers' uniform complete with choker collar, sword, and white gloves. It was a Marine Corps uniform, and the gold bar signifying his rank as a fresh Second Lieutenant sparkled in the sun. He smiled at me, almost gently. I stared in return. I could never be as elegant and poised as this individual. At one time I hated him with a passion. Now -- I wasn't so sure.

I lowered the hat, feeling somewhat silly for my euphoria. The figure across the way smiled more broadly, than snapped his right hand to the brim of his cap in a perfect military salute. The kind reserved for senior officers, dignitaries, and pretty females. He held the salute. I suddenly realized that I had never been saluted before. Wow! It made me feel strangely powerful. I hesitated only briefly. I knew I wasn't supposed to salute dressed as I was, however, I couldn't *not* do this. I raised my own hand in a much less perfect version of his salute, than dropped my hand quickly. He dropped his in return, smiled again, then turned smartly and strode away, no doubt anxious to be off to Quantico and his Marine Officer Basic Training -- and finally to some steamy jungle battleground. God help the enemy he faced.

I watched him as he went, feeling a strange sense of pride in the fact that I had known an individual like Rock Stone. Immediately I caught myself. Was I actually proud of Rock and his *Tiger* mentality? My brain whirled in confusion at that concept, which would have been totally foreign just days ago, but which now amused me. What had happened to me? Had I changed so much in the last year that my entire social frame of reference had shifted almost diametrically? I considered this deeply for a long moment, looking down at the hat as I did so. But after a long consideration, I could find no shame in admiring Stone, and no self mutiny in being proud of him and my own new found status. Maybe I had changed, and maybe that was a good thing. Maybe Rock Stone was okay, and maybe I could find a place to accept his philosophies. Maybe, I realized with acceptance -- and a little fear -- I had finally become what the system wanted me to be after all. I really was a midshipman and a naval officer -- even if pinning on the Ensign shoulder boards was three years away -- and I was proud of that. I was amazed at myself. How had I gotten to this momentous point in just a fleeting year? What a story that would be! Where and how did it start?

ARRIVALS

Later, when I tried to remember the details, I discovered the first several days of life as a military school student a confusing blur of intense physical pain, severe mental pressure, and almost overwhelming emotional turmoil. I suppose the almost overwhelming flood of new experiences caused a kind of temporary sensory and psychic overload that I was totally unequipped to handle (at the time). It's funny though how quickly we all adapted. At least most of us did. It was only years later, recalling the initial experiences as I began the mental process that would lead me to the word processor, that I felt the specifics reluctantly emerged from the subconscious niches where I had unceremoniously stuffed them in the confusion. But from the safe perspective of more than twenty-five years, as I now strain to get it all straight, I am convinced that nothing could have prepared me adequately for the bewilderment and chaos of Plebe Year at Annapolis.

Of course it wasn't just any Plebe Year, mind you. It was 1967 -- not a particularly good year to be a military school initiate. Camelot had recently crumbled, and residual bitterness hung like a dirty cloud around us. The country was embroiled in a confusing and messy war that we seemed to have no real intention of winning. Young American men of every race and creed died before our horrified eyes every evening on national television. Protests raged. Civil Rights fervor and violent response swept the nation. The British had invaded the rock and roll scene with a painful and head throbbing intensity, which at the time I didn't find so objectionable. America seemed lost -- without manifest destiny -- for the first time in its history. Yet, all the furious external energies of the entire universe faded into absolute obscurity on the morning of June 7, 1967.

I remember standing in the warm June sun just beside the passenger door of our old green Nash Rambler, one hand poised on the pitted chrome front door handle holding it open as my mother and young brother climbed from the cramped back seat. I wore a brand new dark blue sport coat, purchased expressly for this occasion. Only half noticing my family, I gaped at the scene that confronted me. It was the first of many gapes during that and the succeeding summer days.

Large puffy white clouds slowly traversed above the campus on their inevitable way down the Chesapeake Bay. The Severn River, which I could see not a hundred yards south of where we had parked, was alive with stark white sails, billowed and straining to exploit the slight, balmy, breeze. On the nearby rock seawall several young men in uniform sat calmly, dividing their time between the confusion in the parking lot and the gorgeous view to seaward. The spacious parking lot around us on all sides was a constant, jockeying swirl of motion, as other cars arrived -- each loaded with a perspective Naval officer and several close relatives -- and still others departed, one confused passenger lighter. People surged toward and from the direction of the Naval Academy Field House. Two cars away a young man approximately my age was entangled in an impossibly passionate embrace with a pretty young lady while several embarrassed relatives looked pointedly away. Nearby a tall blond boy nervously retrieved a suitcase and guitar from the truck of his family Buick. Our eyes locked for an instant and I answered his confused entreaty with a smile and a shrug. He smiled in return before his family swept him away.

The scene must have mesmerized me far longer than I realized because when I glanced back toward the car, I found that my family had long since exited. They stood nearby staring silently and intently at me, almost as if they were seeing me for the first -- or the last -- time. I was somewhat taken aback by this sudden notoriety. As I looked closely at each of them in turn, I realized (somewhat prophetically) that this day began a new phase in O'Reilly family relations. Maybe their unspoken fear was that once I disappeared into the bowels of whatever awaited, I would emerge a far different person from the Kevin O'Reilly that entered.

My mom wore a nervous smile, and I could see tears glistening in her dark green eyes as she huddled my ten-year-old brother Sean protectively to her side. But I knew instantly they were good tears. Sean buried his head with its pile of bright red hair against the soft ample warmth of her cotton blouse. As I looked at the two of them, I suddenly remembered mom's earthy smell of fabric softener and cooking foods with just a hint of perfume and how her smell always delighted me when I was his age and still willing to cuddle with her in the evenings before bed.

My father -- also a Kevin -- now stood before me, smiling awkwardly. Once a flaming redhead, the same as Sean and me, his own hair had dulled with the years and now showed considerable gray despite his relative youth. He held my small brown scuffed leather suitcase at his side, its plastic handle swallowed up by his massive fist. Despite his formidableness and still somewhat muscular bulk he seemed uncomfortable and embarrassed, and I became instantly disconcerted. I rarely saw dad confused. In fact, he had always been a kind of bigger-than-life hero to me. Everything seemed so effortless for him. He made friends easily, and people listened to him. He told jokes with natural grace. And he had a devilishly twinkling smile that could light up a room in an instant. In short, he was much I was not, and I had always wished I could be less awkward and more like him. But, as he told me a thousand times, being the life of the party had its drawbacks, and besides, I had talents in other areas. I could run like the wind, carry a tune, tinker with machines, and play a very good game of chess. I also had a minor talent for math and the sciences that had led to my being actively recruited by several colleges, including Annapolis.

The decision of which school's offer to accept was a tough one, but as always it was my father's advice that carried the day.

"Son." He said, "you can get a decent education at any one of those colleges, but I suspect the Naval Academy will give you more of what you need for life." With that sage advice dutifully considered, I declined all the offers except the one from Annapolis.

But now dad stared at me as if he might have regretted his advice.

"What's with the big guy?" I thought. "Did I make the wrong choice after all?" I hesitated, staring at him for a long moment. Then dad suddenly brightened, and that famous smile of his enveloped his face. He reached over and put one massive hand on my shoulder.

"Son," he said, chuckling. "I envy you your adventure."

Instantly everything was okay, and I relaxed. Realizing that I had unconsciously held the car door open for several minutes, I smiled awkwardly and quickly recovered my dignity. I closed the door, and Dad guided me, hand still on my shoulder, toward Sean and Mom, who waited apprehensively near the rear of the car.

"Ready?" Dad asked as I took the suitcase from him, intent on handling the situation on my own, at least as much as I was able.

"As I'll ever be," I bravely answered, staring off into the confusion that swirled near the entrance of the Field House. But as I watched, I realized that what I initially sensed as confusion was in fact a choreography of registration, assignment, and circulation the likes of which I had never experienced to that day.

As we slowly neared the front of the building, Dad still clutching my shoulder with pride, and mom and Sean flanking me on the opposite side, a man in a crisp white uniform approached us, smiling broadly. He had a chest full of ribbons and two large gold stripes on his shoulder boards. He walked with a loose confidence that I instantly envied. His name tag indicated his name was Bill Large. We stopped and waited for him.

"Do we have a new midshipman in the group?" he asked warmly, looking at me. His eyes had a devilish twinkle.

"Yes," I said before either of my parents could answer for me.

The man looked at me closely, still smiling broadly.

"Wonderful," he said directly to me.

To my family he continued. "Listen, your son is going to be incredibly busy for the next few hours. It would be best if you said a short goodby here and let him get registered. At 1600," He looked at me, still smiling, "That's four p.m. -- there will be a formal Oath of Office ceremony in Tecumseh Court. Afterward you'll have a few minutes to say a proper farewell."

He waited while we looked at each other.

"Well," I said to the family, "I guess I'll see you at four . . . " I looked quickly back to Bill Large and said, "1600." He laughed genuinely; then he looked more seriously toward Mom and Dad.

"Don't worry a bit," he said. "Your son will do fine. I have a feeling about these things." With that he strode smartly off to greet the next confused family. Dad watched him leave, plainly impressed with his style and demeanor.

For several seconds we huddled quietly at the corner of the building. Then Dad broke the spell by grabbing me in an enormous bear hug that almost squashed the breath from me. His huge hands gently patted my back several times as we embraced. Then he kissed me on the cheek lightly, and I could feel the raspy stubble left from the morning's shave. When he drew away, smiling, all teeth and freckles, I saw tears welling up in his deep blue eyes. My dad hadn't kissed me for longer than I could remember, and I almost bawled in front of everybody I was so suddenly consumed by familial bliss. But one hug was all he had in him. He quickly recovered, held out his hand, and crushed mine in a farewell grip.

"Good luck, son," he whispered as he struggled with his own emotions.

I turned toward my mom and found her smiling broadly while at the same time weeping unabashedly. She gently dropped my brother's hand and walked with quiet dignity to where I stood.

"Give me a hug, Kevin," she said, and as I leaned over to embrace her, I heard her say quietly, "We're all so very proud of you."

"I know, Mom," I answered with equal dignity, prolonging the touch. She didn't seem willing to let go, and I allowed the hug to continue for several long, warm seconds. Finally I noticed Sean waiting nervously, slightly detached from the three of us. He was also crying silently, and I knew how much the tears meant because he always made a point of not ever being a crybaby or a sissy. I let Mom go, kissing her on the cheek as I did so.

"Can I have a farewell hug, Sean?" I asked.

Sean glanced nervously at his feet, and shifted his weight from leg to leg. His straight carrot-colored hair hung almost to the bottom of his eyes, and it swished from side to side as he shifted.

Then he looked up at me with an enormous smile, a smile so very much like my dad's, and said, "I guess so -- as long as you don't tell anyone."

"I promise," I replied, and he walked slowly toward me. I smiled at my mom, slowly let go of her hand and walked three steps toward Sean. Kneeling down on the asphalt, I opened my arms. He responded, and we held each other for a long while. I could hear and feel him crying on my shoulder as we embraced, and through the sniffling he said, "I'm gonna miss you, big brother."

"Me too," I replied, and we separated. Standing, I turned toward my parents.

"Well," I said. "Time to go." I picked up my suitcase from where I had placed it and smiling at my family turned toward the front of the Field House.

Almost instantly we noticed another family headed away from the building, passing very near to us. It was impossible not to notice. Two extremely agitated parents flanked a short, chunky dark-haired boy about my age as they hurried away from the building. The father was a dark, ruggedly handsome man who wore tall polished boots, a large white cowboy hat, and jeans with a huge silver belt buckle.

"I told you! I'm not going through with it!" the boy shouted as they passed. His mother was a very pretty and petite blond woman who also wore jeans and a plaid embroidered shirt. Her long hair hung loosely down her back, streaming behind her from side to side as she ran to keep up.

"But you haven't even tried," his father implored in a deep Texas accent. "How do you know it's going to be so bad?"

"I've seen enough," the boy replied. "It was your idea to do this, and I don't want to be here. I'm not going and that's final!"

"But, son . . . ," his mother began in a sweet drawl, "can't we talk this over?"

The boy stopped and almost collided with his parents as they struggled to keep up. He turned toward his mother and I could see a frightened and exasperated look on his face.

"Look, Mamma," he said, "all my friends are going to be starting at the University of Texas next semester. I've got a scholarship, so it won't cost you anything. I never liked the military. And you know Carol Ann isn't going to wait for me if I'm here." Before his father could protest, the boy continued, this time speaking directly to his father. "Besides, Dad, this place doesn't even have a decent football team." As if that were the final nail in the coffin, he turned and again strode toward the family car. His parents gave each other exasperated looks and hurried off after him.

I looked over at my family. My mother was shaking her head sympathetically; her own neatly-coifed dark hair didn't move so much as an inch. My brother stared in disbelief, but my father was silently laughing and, judging by the look on his face, also admiring the way the woman filled out her jeans, (which wasn't bad for an older lady). Then he looked at me, suddenly serious.

"You can leave any time you want to, Kevin," he said. "It's up to you."

"I know," I replied. Then I laughed. "I think I'll give it more than a few minutes, okay?"

"Great," he said. Then turning toward the direction of the crowd, he continued, "you better be off. You're almost late."

"See you at 1600," I said laughing. Hefting the bag, I turned the corner and walked toward the registration area.

Twenty rectangular metal tables had been set up in front of the Field House. Each table was covered with a white tablecloth which, draped over the front, reached precisely to the concrete sidewalk. Seated behind the tables were young-to-middle-aged women who greeted and directed incoming plebes. Behind each woman stood a large metal pedestal with a sign that designated specific letters of the alphabet. I selected the line 'M - P' and waited with three other young men. As I waited, I noticed for the first time a large blue banner that spanned the front of the Field House. On it, in bright gold letters was the message. "WELCOME - CLASS OF 1971"

"Nice touch," I said to the boy in front of me.

"Huh?" he replied, noticing me for the first time.

I indicated the banner with a nod of my head.

"Oh, yeah," he answered absentmindedly, then returned to whatever thoughts consumed him.

I found myself at the front of my line almost immediately encountered an elderly woman.

"M through P?" she asked, smiling kindly.

"O'Reilly," I answered, smiling in return. "I guess that fits."

"It certainly does," she said as she consulted a computer listing in front of her. With a few seconds she looked up. "Okay, Kevin. Just a moment and I'll have you on your way." She opened a folder with the letter "O" boldly lettered on its front and quickly found my file. She pulled it out and handed it to me.

"Here's a file of general information for you to read and your copy of *Reef Points*. You've been assigned to the Twenty-third Company," she said. She pulled an index card from the folder and handed it to me. "This tells you your Company, room number, and identification code, all of which you should memorize immediately." She pointed toward the oval track across the street. Inside the oval several lines of young men waited nervously in the hot June sunshine, suitcases on the grass beside them.

"Go over there to the track. Find your Company. Then wait in the correct line. Someone will be along shortly to escort you to your Company area." As I took the card and folder, she smiled. "Good luck," she said.

"Thanks," I replied, and headed quickly across the street. As I hurried toward the track, I noticed for the first time the enormous light stone building almost immediately on the opposite side of the track. The empty windows seemed to stretch forever toward north and south.

Rope barricades in the middle of the oval delineated thirty-six precisely equal spaces. Long wooden poles with small dark blue pennants suspended at each top had been planted in front of each area. The flags were numbered consecutively from one to thirty-six. I quickly found the flag that indicated the twenty-third, and moved to the back of a short line of six other boys. The boy at the end of my line turned to me as I put my suitcase on the grass beside me.

"Hi," he said. He had a slight accent that hinted of the south somewhere. "The name's Jim Merritt. What room are you assigned to?"

"5405," I replied, looking down at my index card.

He quickly turned to the others.

"See," he said. "It's like I told you. We are reporting by room numbers."

He turned back toward me, smiling.

"I got here early this morning to wander around the campus, and I've spent the last hour watching the registration procedures. Our welcoming letters told us to report at exactly ten o'clock, and I'll bet yours did too." I nodded in confirmation. Merritt smiled knowingly.

"I think they can only handle so many new faces each hour, and if our group goes the same as the last one, at exactly ten thirty a man in uniform will be here to take us to wherever we're going inside the dormitory," he said. "Also, the fact that the seven of us are assigned to the same two rooms tells me this isn't a random process. They probably process eight new recruits an hour, and I'll bet we're going to be living four-to-a-room, for a while at least."

"What do y'all mean for a while?" asked a squat, massive boy who had been listening from front of the line.

Jim Merritt turned to him.

"Well it stands to reason. This place has an incredibly high drop-out rate, so while we may start out with four roommates, I'll bet we don't end up that way." Merritt turned back to me, and I quickly held out my hand.

"Kevin O'Reilly is my name," I offered.

"I'll bet your nickname's 'Red'," said Merritt. "Let me introduce the gang, if I can remember them all." He turned again toward the rest of the group and held out his arm to point to each in turn.

"Up front is Joe Ramsey," he began, but before he could say another word, "Joe" spoke up.

"Ah'm *Jubal* Hunter Ramsey," he said in the thickest accent I had ever heard. "Jubal is short for "Jubilation" which is an old family name. -- Don't ask!"

"Jubal, it is," said Merritt, laughing. "Jubal's from High Point, Alabama. His father was in the Army. And he's here to play football."

"I should hope so," I said looking at Jubal. While he was slightly smaller than my own six feet two inches, he was built like a fireplug, and every inch of him looked solid. He had a nose that bent slightly in several directions, indicating that it had been broken repeatedly over the years. His light brown hair was very short, almost crew-cut, and his ruddy complexion and thick bull neck seemed out of place in his coat and tie. He was obviously suffering in the hot sun. Sweat ran down his face, and just looking at him made me wish I had on a more sensible shorts and T-shirt ensemble.

Merritt continued, "Next we have one of your roomies, Rico Guevarra. Rico is from Brooklyn -- where else?" Rico proved to be a quiet, darkly handsome boy who turned a devilish smile in my direction.

"I know I'm going to like it here," he said without a trace of an accent. "I arrived last night with my parents, and during a stroll around the town I met several nice young local ladies. I have their numbers right here." He patted his shirt pocket and beamed a knowing smile in my direction. "They wanted me. Imagine what I'll be able to do in a uniform." I laughed, envying his smooth charm.

"Next," Merritt continued, "we have my roommate Jeffrey Polk. Jeffrey's from New Hampshire."

"You can call me Jeff," Polk said, smiling slightly, but offering nothing further. Jeff was several inches shorter than I, and probably weighed no more than 150 pounds. He had a pleasant, friendly face and dark, curly brown hair. I leaned over to smile at him.

"Go, Red Sox," I said loudly. "I'm from Boston." Jeff smiled in return.

"After Jeff is Donny Delmont, another of your roommates. Donny is from Idaho, and his father's a rancher."

Donny, a thin, dark-haired, plainly nervous youth, smiled but said nothing.

"This bean pole next to me," Merritt continued, "is Anthony Grizwald. Anthony hails from San Jose, California. He's your roommate, and he's a musician."

Anthony stood an awkward and angular six and a half feet tall, but couldn't have weighed more than 160 pounds. He had longish blond hair and a very toothy, lopsided smile.

"I play the oboe," he said proudly.

Merritt then indicated himself with a flourish.

"As I said, I'm James Wesley Merritt. You can call me Jim. I'm from Amarillo, Texas. I don't have a thick accent because my mother trained me to *enunciate.*" He said the word slowly, smiling. "I play a little football, and to tell the truth I'm excited as hell to be here." Jim then looked at his watch.

"It's almost ten thirty," he announced, "and unless I miss my guess, someone will be along to pick us up in just a few minutes." He looked around at the general scene and at approaching recruits. "But we're still missing someone," he said. "There should be eight of us."

We engaged in general banter for the next five minutes until several midshipmen began emerging from various doorways in the enormous nearby building. They were identically dressed in pressed white uniforms. Black vinyl hat brims and brass belt buckles sparkled in the sunlight as they approached. Each was military trim and walked with an arrogant swagger that I immediately envied. One of these midshipmen stopped in front of each line and began addressing groups of recruits. As we waited expectantly, a tall, very thin, light-haired individual headed in our direction. As he approached, he examined us curiously and smiled knowingly to himself.

"So this is the next batch of Twenty-third Company rejects," he announced disgustedly in a raspy nasal twang as he stopped in front of our line. "Jesus, where do they drag you guys up from?" He then looked at each of us closely for a long moment, then, with a sad shake of his head, began speaking in a serious and lecturing voice.

"My name is Midshipman second class Maxwell," he began, eyeing each of us individually, "but you can call me *sir*. I'll be one of your two squadleaders for the next two wonderful months. You'll meet Midshipman Battle soon enough."

At the front of the line Jubal reached a large hand toward Midshipman Maxwell. "Glad to meet you, sir," he said earnestly.

Maxwell stared at the beefy hand that reached toward him as if it were infected with some hideous disease. He drew back instantly, stopped, looked closely at Jubal, then laughed.

"Nice try, douchebag, but I don't spoon anyone so easily."

Jim turned toward me with a puzzled expression. "Spoon?" he whispered quietly. I shrugged.

"You seem to be missing one of your classmates," Maxwell continued. "Does anyone know where he might be?" When no one answered, he shook his head disgustedly. "That figures," he said. "Well, time and tide wait for no man. Let's shove off, shall we, ladies?"

At almost that precise moment I sensed a disturbance behind us. I looked back as a slightly rotund boy hurried up, awkwardly lugging an enormous suitcase with both hands. He was an absolute mess. His sport coat was undone and flapped at his free side, and his thin black tie was badly askew. His hair was mussed, and he was flushed and out of breath from the jog across the street. He seemed almost about to cry. To complete the disheveled image, the shirt flap on the side away from his suitcase had pulled from his pants, and in manhandling the suitcase, his shoes had become covered with grass clippings and clumps of brown soil. He seemed extremely confused and out of place.

"Excuse me," he asked to no one in particular. "Is this the Twenty-third Company?"

Maxwell looked him over with a glare of absolute disgust. "One of my children, are you?" he asked. "Are you sure you're in the right place?"

"Ah, I am if this is Twenty-third Company," the newcomer answered, panting heavily.

"It is," Maxwell answered, repulsed. "Get in line and follow me." The young man almost waddled to the rear of the line and stood panting behind me. I picked up my own suitcase and glanced back at him.

"Hi," I said. "I'm Kevin O'Reilly."

"My name is Thomas Henry Poole," he answered. "Sorry I'm late. My dad had car trouble."

"Don't apologize to me," I said smiling. "I think it's the guy up front that really matters."

"Okay ladies, let's get started," Maxwell shouted in a grumble we would soon dread hearing. "We have a lot to do today. Follow me! Stay in a single file if you can." With that Maxwell spun about smartly and headed off toward the enormous light-stone barracks buildings which loomed in the foreground. We followed, each moving in his own individual style and thinking his own private thoughts.

We accumulated information about whom we were and what was expected of us piecemeal over the next several months, so I'm jumping ahead of myself here, but let me explain about that imposing structure we headed toward. The building is named Bancroft Hall after an early Secretary of the Navy, George Bancroft, who founded the Naval Academy in 1845. Bancroft is a very important person insofar as naval history is concerned, and hence the largest and most important building on the academy grounds bears his name.

Bancroft Hall is constructed in eight approximately equal-sized wings, each having a thick light-colored granite facade and a verdigris copper-clad roof. The wings are connected by broad corridors on each of the four floors and are oriented to the north on a large, ornate, and quite beautiful rotunda and formal reception area. The four northernmost wings almost totally encircle Tecumseh Court, the center of all official midshipman activity. It is the largest dormitory building in the world, containing more than 4.8 miles of corridor, 33 acres of floor area, and living space for more than 4,000 students. The students are called "midshipmen," an archaic term borrowed from the days of wooden sailing ships when the junior most sub-officer would stand duty *amidships* doing whatever junior naval officers did in those days. The proper modern slang term for a prospective naval officer, we soon found out, is "mid." It's improper to call Naval Academy midshipmen "middies." As I read in my Reef Points, *"Middie is an odious term for midshipmen sometimes used by mothers and newspapers."*

But as I studied the stately and imposing building, I experienced a sudden feeling of deep dread. The hundreds of windows in the wing facing the track seemed to be watching us, and the darkness behind the glass felt somehow uninviting. Even the bright sunshine couldn't dispel the discomfort. I shuddered.

Inside Bancroft Hall are the thirty-six company areas, separated by communal toilets and punctuated by Company offices and Wardrooms. The quarters themselves each come equipped with a sink and shower and are sized to fit two, three, or four individuals in somewhat Spartan comfort. I didn't think much about it while I was a "mid," but I suppose the facilities compare favorably with most other colleges and universities. My only complaint -- a significant one -- was that the building has no air conditioning system. This was normally not a problem since midshipmen are seldom home in the summer months, but plebes are, and the summer of 1967 nearly overwhelmed us with the most miserably hot months I could ever remember.

At precisely 10:40 that morning, thirty-six groups of eight-man snakes headed toward Bancroft Hall. Because of Poole's late arrival our group was the last of the snakes, and we moved at a hurried pace as Maxwell strained us to catch up with the others. It was not to be, however. We hadn't gotten more than 50 yards when I heard a dull thump and an exasperated sigh from behind me. I turned around quickly to see Poole sprawled across his oversized bag, which somehow had exploded open and spilled his considerable possessions across the asphalt parking area along which we now hustled. I stopped, momentarily unable to decide whether to keep up with the group or to stop to help Poole in his predicament. I turned back toward the main group and found to my dismay that they were now twenty meters ahead of me, and the gap was opening quickly.

"Wait!" I yelled. "There's a problem back here."

Maxwell turned to look at us without slowing. Even at this distance I could see his face redden.

"God dammit!" he yelled, stamping his foot. He quickly followed the first exclamation with a loud, "Squad halt!" That command told me two things. First that our little snaky group was called a squad; second that Anthony Grizwald, who might well be the best oboe player in America, did not acquire any significant motor skills during his years in marching band.

Considering that we had never had any military training, I thought we actually did pretty well. There were two collisions, but only Grizwald bit the dust, unable to stop his long legs as he plowed into Donny Delmont from behind. Donny would also have gone down had it not been for Jeffrey Polk, who, sensing the impending chaos, dropped his suitcase, braced himself for a collision, and held Delmont in place by extending his arms outward and behind him. Jubal Ramsey, a participant in countless football drills, stopped on a dime and waited. Rico Guevarra, who had been strutting behind him, yelled something in colorful in Spanish and avoided colliding with Ramsey by leaping gracefully to his right, still holding his bag. Only Jim Merritt and I were unscathed, but I had those 20 yards of open distance to use to my advantage. Merritt didn't miss a beat and reacted instantly to help Grizwald to his feet.

I found myself unable to contain a laugh. Maxwell, who was passing me at that exact instant, stopped dead in his tracks and turned to glare at me.

"Do you think this is funny?" he barked at me. His pale blue eyes held the promise of something unpleasant as they locked on mine.

"Well, -- yes, sir," I answered, smiling, and choosing the wrong of two possible answers. Apparently neither the humor of the situation nor the sincerity of my smile impressed him.

Maxwell quickly took the one giant step necessary to stand exactly in my face. His brightly polished white shoes almost touched my own brown loafers. He was that close. Even though I was taller, he seemed to tower over me. His pale, slightly squinted, eyes locked on mine vengefully.

He spoke in a quiet sneer. "What's your name son?" As he spoke, I could see that the nostrils on his thin nose flared slightly, and that his two bottom front teeth were slightly crooked. When he talked, he pursed his bottom lip so that the two crooked teeth protruded somewhat, making for a very menacing appearance. I was immediately scared senseless.

"Kevin O'Reilly," I answered, absolutely intimidated. For a second I thought I was going to wet myself in fear.

"Well, Kevin," he said in a jeer. "Later today I'm going to wipe that silly-assed smile off that comical Howdy-Doody face of yours. Do you think you'll be smiling then?"

"I'm sure I won't be, sir," I stammered.

"You're damn right you won't," he said. "Now get over there and help your effeminate girlfriend pack her things, and do it quickly before I get really angry."

I hurried over to help Poole. Maxwell turned to the rest of the group.

"Anybody else think this is funny?" he yelled. No one answered. Apparently they were all smarter than I was.

"Good," he said. He pointed to Ramsey. "How much can you bench press?"

"Three hundred pounds, sir!" he answered, puffing out his chest.

"Very impressive, scum bag," Maxwell observed. "Now get your fat ass to the end of the line and carry the girl's bag for her."

"Excuse me, sir?" Jubal sputtered.

"You heard me, fatso. Carry your friend's bag for him. Otherwise, we'll never get done today."

"Yes, sir," Ramsey answered, clearly deflated. He trudged to the rear of the line and grabbed the handle of Poole's suitcase, which we had only just finished repacking. He glared at Poole, hefted the bag easily, and returned to his place at the front of the line.

"Is everyone ready?" asked Maxwell. "I'm not going too fast for you, am I, girls?" He didn't wait for an answer. Instead he raised a hand above his head.

"Forward . . . march!" he commanded, and with a downward sweep of his hand, we started off again. I had no idea how he intended to punish my laughter, but I was sure I wasn't going to like it.

We trudged away, setting an even faster pace as we entered the building complex. Soon I was completely lost. Bancroft Hall is that enormous, and every section seemed exactly like the others. We entered through a lower level door, moved past a huge laundry facility and several darkened maintenance offices, then scurried up a small circular staircase and emerged in the barracks proper. We made a hard right turn, passed a group of similar newcomers being led by their squad leader in the opposite direction, and traversed some long broad corridor past innumerable rooms. None of these rooms seemed occupied, but the sounds of our various shies clapping on the tile floor, and the sight of the long row of thick, official-looking dark hardwood doors intimidated me slightly. After the long passageway we emerged through a set of heavy metal double doors into the Academy rotunda. I could hear several murmured exclamations from my squad mates as we glimpsed the tall ceiling and the ornate beauty. Merritt turned toward me as we neared the center of the domed area.

"Wow! This is great, huh?" he said, clearly awed.

"Very nice," I answered quietly. It wasn't that I couldn't appreciate the majesty and grandeur around me, but ever since our ignominious delay in the parking lot, I hadn't been able to get my mind off Maxwell's threat. "What a way to start my life as a prospective naval officer," I thought to myself while the others oohed and aahed.

We traversed the rotunda, which was alive with groups of new recruits and with visitors, then turned left onto a broad stairway and climbed upward past the second and third floors to the fourth -- and final -- floor. Four floors are not so many, and by the end of that first summer I could sprint from the rotunda to my fourth floor room and not even break a sweat. But on that first day the upward distance (30 steps per floor) seemed daunting. Poole almost didn't make it. By the beginning of the third flight of stairs I could hear him laboring behind me even though he didn't have a suitcase to contend with. I looked back and saw that he had placed a hand on the railing and was hauling himself along. His face was red with effort, and his breath came in labored gasps.

"Are you okay?" I asked him. His only answer was a strained nod of his head.

At the top of the fourth flight of stairs we turned left and passed through another set of double doors into a different but identical barracks area. Several of these rooms were occupied, however, and Merritt, checking the room numbers, which were stenciled on a brass plate in the center of each heavy wooden door, turned to me again.

"This must be our area," he said. "I'm in room 5404." He pointed to a door to our left which had that number on it. "You're in 5405." He pointed to a room across the hall on our right. As I found out repeatedly that year, James Wesley Merritt was seldom wrong, and almost immediately after his pronouncement Maxwell growled a "Squad, Halt!" To our credit no one fell down this time, although Grizwald did brush against Delmont's backside with his right knee.

We stopped, most of us out of breath, and put our bags unbidden on the tiled corridor floor. Maxwell came back to stand in front of the center of the squad. As he did, I noticed several fresh faces attached to shiny bald heads emerge tentatively from two nearby rooms. None of these faces was smiling. Maxwell also spied the spectators.

"Do you have all your gear put away?" he yelled at the nearest room. I heard a meek "No sir," from somewhere, and the shiny heads disappeared as one. Maxwell turned to us.

"You have your cards with the room assignments?" he asked of no one in particular. Merritt held his aloft. "Go to your assigned rooms, select a bunk, and get the toiletries and other personal items from your bags. Put those items on your racks. Do not unpack your civilian clothes." He smiled broadly, then continued. "You won't be needing them for a long while. Next, close your bags and put them on top of your rack. Select a locker and a desk, and temporarily store your personal things. Once you are finished come out into the passageway and stand against the bulkhead until Midshipman Battle returns with the last batch of your classmates. Then I'll tell you what to do next. You may talk among yourselves, but there will be no horseplay or commotion. Am I understood?" Everyone murmured assent.

"Then get moving!" Maxwell yelled. "And hurry up!"

I almost collided with Poole as I turned toward my room, eager to be the first to pick a bed and desk. Poole, still panting from the long hike, walked to where Ramsey had unceremoniously deposited his bag. Hefting it with two hands, he lumbered to his room.

I was first inside the room, and what I saw was not particularly complicated. The room was a large one. Ahead, a wide double window framed a view of the enclosed area between the east and west wings of Bancroft Hall. Below I could see the roof of a building I was later to learn was the Dining Hall. Four gray metal desks clustered in the center of the room in sets of two positioned front-to-front. On the right was a sink with mirror and medicine cabinet, and a small shower stall. On the left was a series of four small lockers recessed into the wall, each with a wooden sliding door. A small closet area for storage and hanging coats was built into the far left corner. Bunk beds stood against the walls on either side of the room. I hurried to the right side of the room and claimed the lower bunk and a desk by the window. Delmont followed me and took the top bed.

Grizwald put his bag on the bottom bed across from us, but before he could begin unpacking, Guevarra stopped in front of him and said, "Tony, do you mind taking the top bunk. I'm afraid of heights." He said it with such complete seriousness that at first I thought he was being honest.

"Oh, sure," Grizwald answered, quickly removing his bag and oboe case from the lower bed and slinging it up onto the upper.

"Thanks a lot," Guevarra said, turning toward Donny and me. Hidden from Tony's view, his face lit up into an enormous smile. I smiled in return and shook my head.

I didn't bring many personal items, a few science fiction books -- mostly Andre Nortons -- a Red Sox pennant, a pair of soccer cleats, a baseball glove, and a picture of my last girlfriend. I had recently broken up with her but I figured the picture would make me seem more like one of the guys. For toiletries I had a toothbrush, a half tube of Colgate toothpaste, some Mennen stick deodorant, a small bottle of English Leather cologne, and a black comb. A half hour later I realized how silly and vain that last item was. As a matter of fact it remained practically unused the entire year. Within five minutes I had unpacked and prepared my things exactly as Maxwell had recommended.

I walked to the doorway and peered tentatively outside. Merritt stood quietly against the far wall examining the corridor with curiosity. He noticed me and smiled.

"Come on out, the water's fine," he said. I peered cautiously outside and, not seeing Maxwell, stepped into the corridor. I stood quietly against the opposite wall and smiled at Merritt.

Maxwell, who had been using the communal bathroom in the center of the hall, suddenly strode into view. My heart sank.

"O'Reilly!" he yelled. "Get your redheaded ass over here!" I cursed to myself and ran toward him, wondering briefly about the anatomical possibilities his order implied.

"Where is everyone?" he yelled. "I thought I said for you to hurry up?"

"I did, sir." I replied. It was my second wrong answer of the morning.

"When I say *you*, asshole, I mean all of you. When one of you is late, you're all late. When one of you screws up, you all screw up. Now get your butt down the passageway and hurry up your sissy classmates. If you aren't ready when Battle arrives, *you* -- and I mean ***all*** of you -- will be very unhappy."

I sprinted back to my room and checked inside.

"Hurry up," I said desperately. "Maxwell's gonna kill us."

"Tell Maxwell to calm down," Guevarra said seriously, feigned concern apparent on his dark handsome face. "Stress can lead to a heart attack."

I started to reply to that unbelievable statement, when Guevarra suddenly broke into a devilish grin. His white teeth flashed, and his eyes twinkled with mischief.

"Go hurry up the other room," he said. "I'll help get things organized here."

I ran across the hall, but Merritt already had responded. He and Polk were stuffing Poole's suitcase haphazardly as I entered.

"We've got things under control here, Red," Merritt said calmly. "We'll be out in a second."

I raced across the hall to check on my roommates, but they exited the room just as I arrived. Soon all eight of us waited expectantly against the corridor walls. Maxwell, emerging from a room near the center of the corridor, looked at us.

"Well, well," he said. "I didn't think you fairies would be ready so quickly. Maybe we should play some games while we're waiting."

I didn't like the sound of that, but luckily, at that moment the double doors burst open and a shiny-bald, much shorter squadleader emerged, followed by eight, identically-bald young men. The group lugged beige canvas duffel bags crammed to overflowing with various gear. The weight was substantial and I wondered how Poole was going to hold up. Ramsey must have wondered the same thing because I saw him glance briefly at Poole with a not altogether friendly glare.

As the new group approached us, its leader shouted, "Squad, halt!" The group stopped without incident, and I was instantly jealous. The squad leader smiled at Maxwell then laughed out loud.

"Ain't they pretty?" he asked, chuckling.

"I'll say," Maxwell answered, also smiling. Turning toward us, he continued, "Get a good look at each other, gentlemen; then look at your classmates here. This will be your new hair style for the next year, unless of course you're insane and want to be a Marine Corps officer when you graduate like classmate Battle. Then you might choose this particular coiffure for the next four years, and ad nauseam thereafter."

Battle turned toward his group.

"All of you into my room right now," he growled. "I'll show you how to stow your gear." The group trotted off down the hall.

Maxwell didn't wait for us to observe the newcomers.

"Okay, ladies," he yelled. "Form a straight line behind me and hurry up!" We raced to comply. I purposefully watched Tommy Poole to see where he would position himself in the line, and I squeezed in several people behind him. I didn't want to take any chances with drawing attention to myself again. Maxwell made sure we were reasonably ready and barked out another "Forward . . . march!"

We exited our company area through the double doors and hurried down the same stairs we had recently ascended. This time we didn't stop at the rotunda but instead descended another level into the basements and proceeded along a broad passageway past several offices and storage rooms until we came to an obviously well-used section of the building. Hundreds of our classmates streamed in and out of the area or waited at various gear issuing stations for whatever was in store.

Maxwell marched us to the far end of the corridor. We halted outside a massive barber shop.

"Fall in behind that last group," he announced. We complied.

A steady stream of "customers" entered and left the barber shop. The entering recruits sported hairdos of varying lengths and styles. What exited was a line of mostly bald, mostly shocked, and mostly very unhappy young men. As each squad completed the hair cut phase and began to mill about outside, squadleaders quickly assembled them and marched them off to the next hurdle.

We seemed to enter the shop all too quickly. Inside were more than twenty chairs, each with a grinning civilian barber. The floor almost overflowed with hair clippings of various colors and textures. The haircuts themselves were little more than ten swipe affairs using the closest possible setting on the clippers. I timed one poor lad, who spent a total of 30 seconds in the chair, all the while staring sadly at the cascades of luxuriant blond hair that drifted to the floor. His barber removed the drape with a matador's flourish and flapped it in the air with a loud snap.

"Next!" he announced with much too sadistic gusto.

I took a deep breath as my turn neared.

"This won't be so bad," I thought to myself. "After all, everyone is going to be in the same boat." Well, almost all. As I waited to be shorn, a recruit from another squad sauntered up to a barber and pointed to his head, which sported hair as long as any I had seen today.

"I was in a motorcycle accident," he said smiling. "I've got scabs on my head. Go easy, huh?"

"No problem," the barber replied. Thirty seconds later my classmate was as bald as the next guy except for ten thick tufts of hair that marked the location of his scabs. He looked like a refugee from a nuclear accident site or maybe the victim of some cruel wasting disease.

The barber spun him around in the chair -- something I hadn't seen done with any other recruits, and the classmate gaped at the sight he had become. Before he could protest, the barber took scissors and deftly trimmed the patches so that ten dark stubbly spots remained.

"Come back when the scabs fall off," the barber announced removing the drape. "Next!"

It was my unfortunate luck to be the next victim of that same barber. He smiled as I approached.

"How do you want it cut?" he asked sarcastically.

"I like what you did to that last fellow," I replied sitting gingerly, "but a few more patches would be better. Maybe you could make my head into a checkerboard and my classmates and I could use it to entertain ourselves."

He considered the suggestion, looking closely at my head from several angles as he did so.

"Wouldn't work," he finally said.

"How come?" I asked, truly puzzled.

"The pieces would fall off," he announced, bursting into a deep, throaty belly laugh. My cut took less than fifteen seconds, and if possible I was even balder than the rest of my classmates.

Outside in the corridor my squad mates stared at my head in amazement, which immediately blew my theory about being in the same boat. All heads are not created equal, and while the lack of hair was actually becoming to some of the squad members -- which of course included Merritt -- my ruddy complexion and wealth of freckles made my head look more like a dull apple with worms. I was quite a sight. But I wasn't the worst-looking mug by far. Poor Poole was a phrenologist's dream. I had never seen or imagined that a scull could be so variously contoured and landscaped. From behind he looked like a relief map of the moon except that *his* lunar cranium had had a collision with some other celestial body which caused a deep indentation on one side, making his whole head appear nubby and off centered.

"Form up!" Maxwell announced, laughing at our obvious discomfort. Soon we headed off in the opposite direction into the crowd. What awaited us was an incredible series of gear-issuing stations. First we received identical duffel bags, which we carried to the adjacent skivvies-issue station where we received five pairs of boxer shorts, five v-necked T-shirts, and five crew-necks -- all white. Next came three pairs each of thin white and black socks, followed by shirts of various styles, pants and jumpers, and five pairs of shoes -- two black, one white, one brown, and a pair of hideous-looking high-topped tennis shoes. We also added a metal lockable box, several jock straps, three caps -- two combination caps and a white sailor's "dixie cup" cap with a blue stripe at the top of the brim -- and a shaving kit complete with razor, toothbrush, comb -- obviously a joke -- Kiwi shoe polishes (white, brown, and black), and generic spray deodorant.

By the time we arrived at the tailor shop, we had loaded our bags to capacity, -- except for Poole. He couldn't seem to fit it all in, and carried several shoe boxes while dragging the bulging duffel bag behind him. Most of the others slung the bags across their backs by stretching the one thick strap over the neck and shoulder. I had tried that, but the strap dug too deeply into my shoulder. Instead I hoisted the bag up onto my shoulders behind my neck. Holding the bag balanced with both hands, I trudged, bent over like a beast of burden. Ramsey, living up to his bench pressing image, carried his bag leisurely in one hand at his side.

In the tailor shop we were expertly measured by the staff. So many hands touched my crotch that morning that I was never sure what exactly they were calibrating. One elderly gentleman circled my chest with a tape and called out numbers that could not have been my girth at that location. I looked at him skeptically.

"We have to allow a little for growth," he said. Then he taped my waist and pulled the tape so tightly I almost groaned. He looked at me again. "We must also allow for contraction in certain areas," he said.

The entire process of haircut and gear issue took less than a half hour, and soon we had formed up in the hall for the trip back to the company area. Maxwell took stock of us before we left and paused when he came to Poole.

"Why isn't your gear inside the duffel bag, mister?" he asked.

"It wouldn't fit, sir," Poole replied.

"Sure, pal! You have two minutes to make it fit!" Maxwell barked and turned to the rest of the group. "I'm becoming very tired of these delays," he said. "You won't like me when I'm tired. I get very cranky."

I nudged Polk who was in front of me in line.

"Let's help Poole," I whispered, "before we all catch hell."

Polk looked back at me with a skeptical leer and announced fiercely but quietly, "This is all bullshit, you know."

"Yeah," I said, "I know. But let's do one thing at a time and worry about the bullshit later."

We knelt beside Poole. Tommy tried to help, but Jeff waved him away brusquely. Soon we had his bag unpacked on the terrazzo floor and had placed everything neatly inside. It all fit, and the entire operation took less than a minute.

Merritt, who had changed places with Guevarra to be directly in front of Poole, asked Tommy softly, "How are you doing? Can you make it back up the long staircase?"

"Not with this load," Poole answered quietly. "I don't think so."

"Okay," Merritt said gently, "here's what we'll do. I'll sling my bag over my left shoulder and reach back with my right hand and hold the front of your bag. You carry the back end. That'll reduce your load by half."

"Not exactly," whispered Poole.

"Huh?" Merritt said, slightly dumbfounded.

"Well," Poole replied. "This bag weighs about 120 pounds. I should be okay on level ground carrying 60 pounds, but once we start up the stairs, the center of gravity of the bag will shift to the rear. On a 45-degree slope that will mean that nearly three-quarters of the weight will be on my end. I'm not sure I can handle 90 pounds up those stairs."

Merritt stared at Poole for a moment.

"You calculated that in your head?"

"Yes," Poole answered. "Estimated, really."

"Well, no problem, because Rico and Jeff and Kevin will help on the hard parts, right guys?" Merritt announced smiling.

Jeff and I just nodded. Rico looked at Merritt and Poole seriously.

"Shit, guys. I'd really like to help, but I just got over this hernia operation and the doctor told me to avoid any heavy lifting for a while. You know how it is."

Merritt looked at him and said nothing. Polk blurted skeptically.

"You must have had a hell of a time with your physical?"

Rico smiled disarmingly, looked quickly around, and put his right index finger to his lips in a gesture of silence.

"I know," he whispered conspiratorially. "I'm hoping the brass here doesn't find out about it. They might drum me out."

"No problem," Merritt said, eyeing Guevarra skeptically. "We can handle it." With Polk and me alternating on one side at the rear and Poole on the other, we handled the load. Soon we burst triumphantly through the double doors to encounter another group of fresh classmates lining the corridor. They looked at us as if we were alien monsters -- bald alien monsters.

"Don't they look great?" Battle asked the group in the hall. He seemed genuinely enthusiastic. No one answered.

We halted in the middle of the corridor, and Maxwell examined the squad critically.

"Whoever's in *that* room," he said pointing to 5404, "raise your hand." The four occupants raised their hands reluctantly, and I was secretly thankful that he hadn't picked 5403, although I didn't know why. He looked the four of them over closely for the first time, smiling sadistically.

"Well, well," he said, "we have the lady and the palooka in the same room with a midget and a smack. I think I call 5404 the *goon room*. Any objections?" None came to mind.

"Okay," he continued, smiling devilishly. "I want all eight of you douchebags in Room 5404 immediately. Let's see if I can teach you how to fold your underwear properly." He started for 5404, but when we didn't react quickly enough, he yelled, his face changing instantly to display deep rage.

"Get in there now, God dammit!" We ran, dragging our bags.

Maxwell selected the nearest desktop and grabbed the duffel bag from Ramsey's hands. He plopped it on the floor and looked at Ramsey.

"Which is your rack?" he asked. Ramsey indicated the lower one to the right. Maxwell opened the bag and dumped the contents haphazardly onto the bed. Next he selected a pair of boxer shorts and held them up by the elastic band for all of us to see. They were rather large.

"Jesus, Ramsey!" he exclaimed, "who else is going to live in these things with you?" Ramsey was smart enough not to answer, a trait I hoped I would soon develop.

Maxwell looked at us, scanning our faces as he began talking.

"Before I begin my demonstration, let me say that I haven't the faintest idea why we fold and stow clothing the way we do here, and I don't particularly care either. I also don't care how your mommies taught you how to fold clothes, because the *only* way that's accepted from now on is the way I'm going to show you. Do it exactly as I say and you *might* survive the million locker inspections you're gonna have before the Brigade returns in September." He then looked directly and pointedly at Poole. "Then again, you might not."

What followed was a 20-minute whirlwind demonstration of how to fold everything we now owned from skivvies to jock straps and how to put them in the locker space provided. Each item was precisely folded with exact dimensions and distances being vital. I would not have believed it possible that a stack of underwear could look square, but they did when Maxwell folded them. It also amazed me that socks could be rolled and formed into precise blocks so that the inside sock showed its fabric rows in an exactly vertical direction through a neat rectangular opening in the outer sock. I watched Maxwell, his hands deftly manipulating form and fabric, completely amazed. Midway through the procedure, Jeff Polk looked over at me from across the room and shook his head in disgust. He didn't seem to be getting into the spirit of the exercise.

I could understand intellectually what Jeff was implying by his disapproval. Here were eight, nearly-adult human beings intently observing a young person nearly their own age fold a jock strap into an equilateral triangle. I could see the reason for Polk's reaction. It was very stupid. But on the other hand, it was Academy stupid, and these were skills -- no matter how inane -- I would have to master. I returned to intent observation and realized I had missed the technique that made 45-degree angled corners appear in the sheets and blankets on the ends of the made-up beds. That seemed like an important piece of knowledge to me, so I vowed to watch as my roommates did their beds. When he was finished, Maxwell straightened and smiled.

"Okay," he said, "I want each of you to do exactly as I have done in your own rooms and lockers. Be finished in 30 minutes." He started for the door and we parted like the Red Sea for Moses to let him pass. Midway to the door he halted, and with a devilish smile he turned.

"Almost forgot," he said. Going to Ramsey's locker, he swept all his recent clothes-folding efforts in a heap on the floor, and pulled the sheets from the newly made rack. He smiled at Jubal.

"You wouldn't want an unfair advantage over your classmates would you?" he asked.

"No, sir!" Ramsey answered smartly.

"Sure, pal," Maxwell said still smiling broadly. Then he turned to the rest of us. "Well, get to it," he said, and swept out of the room.

I dragged my bag back to my room and emptied the contents carefully on my desk. Starting with the skivvy shirts, which I thought would be easy, I began to fold and stow in a frenzy. I did a very good job on the skivvies and the linen, but the socks either ended up with the fabric at an acute angle or had an opening that resembled Marilyn Monroe puckering up for a wet one. And I couldn't seem to get the bed corners straight even though I watched Rico neatly and effortlessly make his bed into an almost perfect match of Maxwell's work. But time was of the essence, and I finished quickly enough to help Grizwald -- who had just worked his way through the thin cotton underwear -- with his linen. Just as I finished Tony's last washcloth, I heard the final group of bald recruits return. I poked my head out into the hall to watch as they meandered in a shiny-topped eight-man snake to a set of rooms farther down the hall toward Maxwell's room.

No sooner had my head broken the plane between door and passageway when I heard Maxwell yell. "O'Reilly!"

"Yes, sir!" I answered, copying Ramsey's snappy style.

"Are you finished folding your things?" he asked.

I realized immediately that this was a question with no good answer, and I paused, contemplating. Before I could say anything to embarrass or injure myself, Maxwell continued.

"You had better make sure everything is perfect, pal, because I'll inspect later today."

"Yes, sir," I yelled darting back inside my room and hustling for my *rack*. Grizwald had worked his way up to the gym gear, and Delmont was making his rack when I plowed headlong into the intricacies of hospital corners. Rico, was sitting at his desk reading a book, his feet on the window sill.

I didn't waste any time wondering about Rico's calm, because, except for his marvelous-looking bed, his stuff sure seemed in need of further attention to me.

"Oh, well," I thought, "that's his problem." I had mastered -- sort-of -- the bed making technique, and I was just getting the knack of the vertical sock lines when the latest group raced into their rooms to stow their gear.

Thirty minutes later Maxwell and Battle, standing in tandem in the middle of the hall outside their room, yelled in unison.

"Form up for chow!" Together they moved down opposite sides of the corridor yelling in each room. Lunch sounded like a great idea to me, and I was outside even before Maxwell could roust me. Even though I reacted quickly, Merritt beat me by several seconds. He smiled at me as I arrived beside him, and soon a tide of new faces joined us and jostled for position.

"Face the double doors!" yelled Battle, his beak-shaped nose snapping up and down with each emphasis. We turned with a great deal of confusion.

"Poole!" yelled Maxwell, "what's eight times four?"

Without missing a beat Poole answered, "Thirty-two, sir."

"How can we divide into three, nearly-equal squads?" Maxwell asked again.

Instantly Poole answered, "Eleven, eleven, and ten men each, sir."

"Very good, Poole," announced Maxwell. "That higher math sometimes confuses me."

"Okay, people," Battle announced from a position near the double doors. "You heard Poole. I want you to form yourselves into three squads of eleven, eleven, and ten men -- beginning here!" With a white shoe he indicated a point directly in front of him. We raced to comply, and after a bit of initial confusion, the lines formed. Our efforts obviously offended his sensibilities, because he grimaced when we had finished.

"Now," he said, "arrange yourselves in descending order of height starting with the tallest man at this end of the line." This quickly became an exercise in confusion as many nearly-equal individuals struggled to estimate who was taller.

"Hurry up!" Maxwell yelled as we milled in some confusion. Eventually the lines evened somewhat, and we ended with three squads of stair-step precision tapering off to the rear. Battle looked us over for a moment, was about to make a further adjustment, thought better of it, then turned toward the doors and shouted in a clipped bark, "Forward march!" We exited the area and again turned right (starboard) and went down the rotunda stairs.

Instead of going into the basement, we crossed the rotunda at an angle, passed through a crowd of gaping onlookers, and descended another flight of stairs toward the rear of the facility. We emerged into the Academy Mess Hall.

I may seem as if I'm repeating myself, but *big* is the operative word here also. The Academy Dining Hall -- also referred to as the "Chow Hall" or the "Mess Hall" -- is the largest such facility in the world. More than four thousand persons eat simultaneously three times a day. It is incredibly efficient.

My first view of the facility almost staggered me. The Mess Hall is constructed in a "T" shape with three equal-size wings extending out from a central hub, seemingly to near infinity. We emerged at the top of the central hub of the "T" and so had an immediate view of the officers' and guests' seating area directly in front of us. The ceiling was very high -- more than 20 feet. Amazingly, no columns marred the broad vista. Long wings lined with tall windows extended ahead and to both sides of us. Each wing seemed to be more than 100 yards long. (How long is the Mess Hall? -- That's another story.)

We didn't have much time to enjoy the view. Immediately after entering, Battle marched us straight down a wide central aisle and stopped a middle set of tables on the starboard side of the middle wing. As we hurried along I could see that double sets of large, thick, ten-man tables extended out from the walls on both sides of all three wings. There was still room in the middle for an aisle almost six yards in width. (Like I said, it is enormous.)

Several of the other tables were occupied or being occupied as we arrived. In typically efficient Academy fashion we were assigned tables in order of Company Number. The first through the thirteenth companies of plebes sat in the right-hand wing, we sat in the middle wing with companies fourteen through twenty-six, and twenty-seventh through thirty-sixth companies sat in the left-hand wing. Even with more than 1,300 new plebes eating together, the building seemed almost empty. It was hard to imagine what it would be like with more than 4,000 diners. Our three tables were designated by small blue and gold placards.

"Grab a seat at any chair except those at the bow and stern of the table," Maxwell announced as we arrived. We scurried to comply. Seated, we craned our necks to appreciate the view and waited for the chow. Maxwell chose a seat at the head (bow) of a table on the aisle side, Battle sat at the foot (stern) in the rear of a second table. The third table contained only plebes. I waited to choose my seat, hoping to get at the table without a squad leader, but my hesitation killed me.

"O'Reilly! Poole!" announced Maxwell, smiling broadly, "sit here next to me." He indicated the seats to his immediate right and left, which were both already occupied by unfamiliar faces. I groaned inwardly and walked slowly to the indicated position. Maxwell looked at the plebes who were already sitting and suddenly barked, the smile gone completely from his narrow features.

"Don't ever sit before you're told!" The two classmates leapt to their feet.

"Find a chair somewhere else nearby!" he yelled again, and they scurried away, no doubt relieved to be removed from the source of such commotion.

I moved to the seat on Maxwell's right and put my hands on the chair back. Poole stood behind the left-hand seat. The table was set with utilitarian flatware and Naval Academy plates -- white with blue and gold trim. A dark blue milk carton stood at each end of the table next to a large profusely sweating aluminum pitcher filled with iced tea. There were two plates of hot dinner rolls waiting on each table as well as a large bowl of tossed green salad topped with garnish and three bright red cherry tomatoes. The tomatoes looked inviting, but my math skills are excellent, and I immediately knew I would be waiting a long time before I would be able to taste one of those juicy babies.

Although we were generally subdued and cautious, most of us were also restless and somewhat excited with the newness of the experience. There was a great deal of shuffling, neck craning, and gaping at the surroundings. This general commotion continued until all the companies had arrived and were somewhat settled at their places. Suddenly a bell loudly sounded from somewhere in vicinity of the hub of the "T," and we all turned to see what new thing the sound would bring. A midshipman called the Mess Hall to attention using a public address system, and a chaplain said a short grace. General announcements followed. We learned that the barber shop and gear issue stations would remain open until 1500 -- three in the afternoon -- and that we must be in our places in Tecumseh Court for the swearing-in ceremony at 1530. The announcer then intoned a drawn-out "Brigade . . . seats!"

Most of my classmates scurried to sit, Poole among them. Several reached for the rolls and salad. Maxwell watched the proceedings with an amused grin, and I held my place, watching Maxwell closely. He shot a quick glance at me and smiled more broadly, the effort making his pinched face seem even more thin. But it was a genuine smile that had a you-catch-on-quick message attached, and I felt instantly proud of myself for picking up on the trick of who was the top dog at the table. His smile was a brief one however, and his features became instantly stern as he looked at the rest of the occupants of the table.

"Stand up, all of you!" he yelled. I could hear almost the identical message being delivered simultaneously, and in varying degrees of severity, at every table in the Mess Hall. My classmates stood hurriedly, and every eye at our table and the adjacent one focused on Maxwell -- Battle was performing a similar lecture at his own table.

"You might as well get the eating procedures straight immediately," he snarled. "In the Mess Hall, like everywhere else on the campus, and for the next year, you are all less than scum. You will defer to every individual who is senior to you, no matter how superior you mistakenly think you are. Believe me, every individual who is senior has already made it through a plebe year, a task you are just facing. They have earned the deference you will give them. Today's meals are going to be relatively free from stress, but tomorrow morning, plebe year starts for you, and you will begin bracing up and eating square meals." He paused at this point, considering his next words.

"In the Mess Hall, you will always remain standing at your chairs until the announcements are over and *"Brigade, seats"* is called. Then you will sit only after all the upper-class at your table have seated themselves or unless you are personally ordered to sit by the senior midshipman at the table. Food will not be touched by plebes except to pass it to all other midshipmen in descending order of seniority. In other words you will serve yourselves last -- and you had better leave enough of each item so that all of your classmates at the table get an equal share of what remains. If you want more of any item or if a more senior midshipman so demands, you will hold the appropriate tray or plate aloft until a steward comes to the table. Tell the steward what you want and he will bring it."

"During the meal you will eat looking straight ahead -- or, "keeping your eyes *in the boat*." Do not look anywhere else unless you are directed to do so by an upper classman. If I ask you a question, put down your utensils and swallow your food before answering but continue staring ahead. There will be no general banter except to ask each other to pass food or drink or unless I grant the table a privilege called *carry-on*.

"'Carry-on' means you can act almost as if you were home with mommy and daddy, and you don't have to brace up. We'll tell you all about bracing and chopping and square meals after lunch today." He paused again, clearly enjoying his superior position over us.

"Okay, gentlemen," he continued, "I'm hungry. Let's eat." We sat -- after Maxwell made himself comfortable, of course.

I glanced quickly to my classmate on my left, "Pass the rolls and salad, please," I said somewhat loudly. My classmates rushed to comply, and soon I had handed Maxwell the nearest roll plate, smiling at him in the process. As he took the roll plate from me and I reached to take the salad from my neighboring classmate, I saw Polk scowling at me from his place across the table. Our eyes locked briefly, and I looked hurriedly back to Maxwell, somewhat embarrassed for playing plebe so well.

Maxwell eyed the rolls as if there were an actual difference between the various specimens, then selected one, taking care not to touch the others in the process. He handed the roll plate to Poole, and it began its way down the far side of the table. Within a few minutes I realized why speed in serving may not be a virtue. When the rolls finally came back to me, what remained was a misshapen, shriveled affair that had not been fully baked. And not only did I not get a cherry tomato, but all that was left of the salad when it appeared at my place were a few wilted and soggy leaf pieces in the bottom of the bowl, some celery, and only a few small carrot chunks. I was not disappointed with the remainder of the meal, however. As I sat looking despondently at the soggy salad and doughy roll, the main course -- dinner steaks -- arrived.

Instantaneous meal serving for 4,000 hungry and growing young people is an unbelievably coordinated affair. Large double doors opened along the walls facing the main part of Bancroft Hall in the cross piece of the Mess Hall "T," revealing the interior of an enormous kitchen. Immediately large stainless carts raced into view from the kitchen, each one pushed by several Filipino stewards. Every cart hurried to its prearranged position in the center aisle and the stewards quickly pulled trays of food from the racks on the carts, moving up and down the aisles to bring the food to each table. My mother, and later my wife, always hated to hear this when I told them, but meals at Annapolis were the best I had anywhere, either before and since.

For lunch that day we had steak, a common experience. The steaks were good-sized portions of choice cuts of beef, and everyone -- even me, Maxwell's serving boy -- had a satisfactory portion. In addition to the steaks, the stewards brought steaming bowls of several vegetables. When I held aloft the roll tray, it was instantly snatched from my grasp and replaced with another.

"I sure won't starve to death," I thought happily as I enjoyed the meal, although Maxwell's enigmatic smile made me a bit uncomfortable. Maxwell noticed me staring at him and said, still smiling,

"What are you looking at, O'Reilly?"

"Nothing, sir," I stammered. I had fallen into a classic plebe trap and again had given exactly the wrong answer.

"Are you calling me nothing, O'Reilly?" he asked.

"No sir," I answered, then quickly added before he could jump on me further. "I was wondering why you were smiling like you are, sir?"

He brightened, chuckling. "Sure, pal. I know something you don't know, O'Reilly."

"What's that, sir?" I asked.

"Oh, you'll find out soon enough," he said. "I don't want to get too far ahead of my self. Eat up. There isn't much time."

"Yes, sir," I said. He was correct. I had just finished my steak when a team of stewards arrived and our plates were cleared. Almost immediately large bowls of ice cream appeared on the table, and soon we were spooning down a very creamy and delicious vanilla concoction that I quickly grew to love.

We weren't left any time to savor the food. Almost immediately after my spoon had entered my mouth with the final bite of ice cream, Maxwell, who had finished first, looked at Battle's table.

After confirming that Battle was also ready, announced loudly, "Okay, ladies. Put down your spoons. Take a last swallow of your drinks. And let's get formed up in the passageway."

After a few moments of stumbling, we achieved a pretty close approximation of the formation we arrived in, and Battle, satisfied with our appearance, ordered a "Company . . . Forward, March!" We returned to the Company area without incident.

Arriving in the Company area, Battle ordered a halt, moved to the front of our group, and announced, "Go quickly to your rooms, wash up, and straighten your clothes. If you have to visit the *head*, hurry. Leave your sport coats and ties behind. In five minutes I want you back in this exact location." He paused, looking at us.

"Dismissed!" he barked. We scurried to our rooms.

I was first to the sink, and I quickly soaped and dried my hands on one of the wash cloths from my locker. Next I took off my coat and tie, undid my pants, and carefully tucked in my shirt. When I had finished, I went into the passageway and found my approximate place in the formation. We had all been in formation for more than five minutes when Battle and Maxwell emerged from their room and marched to our position.

"Very good," Battle announced as he moved to the front of our formation, and stood perfectly still, hands behind his back. "I want you all to back up to the far bulkhead and have a seat on the deck." We quickly complied.

"Okay," Maxwell said, taking the lead after we were settled, "it's time to teach you who you are. What I'm going to say is very important, so listen carefully." He shifted into his own lecturing mode, which in contrast to Battle, meant pacing repeatedly and nervously in front of the group as he talked.

"I'm sure you already know that this is Annapolis, and this is a military academy. If you don't suspect that what happens here is far different from your average university, you have no business being here. This is a very difficult program. Not only are the academics among the toughest in the nation, but we will make severe demands on you physically, mentally, and emotionally. Annapolis graduates are naval officers who are immediately responsible for the lives of fellow human beings. You have to be better than your peers and your enemy if you are going to survive in combat someday, and this place will give you the edge you will need to survive." He paused and looked down at us for the first time.

"Some of you will not be around to graduate," he continued, pacing again. "Some of you won't make it through the year. Many will drop before the summer is over. Maybe a few of you won't even take the oath today. That's what I want to talk about.

"The military is not a game, and Bancroft Hall is not a big fraternity house," he went on. "We are involved in the serious business of preparing you for war, and for some your early deaths, in combat or in training. Annapolis is a life's commitment, gentlemen. And it brings challenges very few people can meet. You got this far, so you are probably smart enough, but it takes more than brains to be a good naval -- or marine -- officer. You must take orders immediately and without question. You must learn how to maintain yourself at a peak of physical conditioning and to function under severe pressure. You've got to be intimately familiar with your own leadership attributes and how to use them to your advantage. None of this is easy. As a matter of fact, it's damned difficult, and it's no disgrace to drop out if you decide this is not the life for you. So if you know right this second that you absolutely do not want to be here, let us know within the next two hours and we can make appropriate arrangements.

"As of the instant you take that oath, however, you are committed to allowing yourself to become the lowest of the low in the Academy system," he continued. "You will be officially *plebes*. Everyone and everything outranks you as a plebe, including our mascot Bill the Goat. You will have to refer to all upper-class as *sir* and do everything they tell you to do. Your rooms must be kept spotless at all times. You will have to run in the passageways and square your corners wherever you go in Bancroft Hall except when you are marching. You will also brace up and keep your eyes focused straight ahead. At meals you will sit on the last three inches of your chairs and eat every single bite of food with exaggerated square motions.

"And Midshipman Maxwell and I are not going to be your best buddies for the next two months," Battle continued, his hands still folded neatly behind his back. "We're here to prepare you for when the Brigade gets back from summer cruises. Right now you plebes outnumber the squadleaders seventeen to one, but come September there will be three upper class for every one of you, and the pressure will really be on. We don't have a lot of time to prepare you for that ugly moment, so we're going to be somewhat testy over the next few weeks. As a matter of fact, we're going to run and harass the hell out of you and enjoy every minute of it. You are going to memorize stupid sayings and statistics and spout them off on command. You are going to learn how to wear several uniforms with pride, and believe it or not, we're going to make marchers out of all of you in short order." He paused, then smiled and continued. "On the fun side you are going to learn how to shoot the rifle and pistol, how to sail a knockabout, how to function on a naval vessel, and how to operate a computer.

"When Maxie and I are through with you -- hopefully just before the Brigade returns -- you are going to be completely different persons than the ones sitting before me. You may even like yourselves better for the effort.

"Poole and O'Reilly!" Maxwell shouted, suddenly taking over, "front and center!"

I was shocked out of a deep reverie by Maxwell's summons, but I jumped to my feet and hurried to the fore. Poole had a bit more trouble getting up and moving.

"Tomorrow morning," Maxwell began very seriously, "you will be plebes." Since I was so close to him I had a great opportunity to watch his face as he talked, and I could see in his eyes that he truly believed in what he was saying. His voice and features held such a conviction of purpose that I found it difficult not be caught up in the fervor.

"That means," he said continuing, "you will have certain responsibilities and obligations to yourselves, your classmates, and to the Brigade. To begin with you will 'chop' with your eyes in the boat whenever you are out of your room in Bancroft Hall. Chopping is a short-stepped jog, which you will use as your primary means of transportation from now on. And when you chop, you will square your corners." He looked at me. "Do you know what that means, Mr. O'Reilly?" he asked.

"No, sir!" I answered quickly.

"It means," he said looking at the group, "that you will turn all corners at a sharp 90-degree angle by planting and pivoting on the foot opposite the direction of turn. If you are going to turn port, pivot on your starboard foot, and vice versa." He turned to Poole. "Do you think you could demonstrate what I've just said?" he asked sweetly.

"Well," Poole began, "I've never tried it before, and I'm not exactly certain what you want, and . . ."

"Silence!" Maxwell burst out. He stared at Poole for several seconds, then turned to the group again and smiled. "I must have gotten ahead of myself a bit," he said, smiling sweetly. "Forgive me."

"When an upper class asks you a question, there are only three acceptable answers, gentlemen, -- "Yes, sir," "No, sir," and "I'll find out, sir." When he gives you an order, you say, "Aye, aye, sir." Is that understood?" he asked the group. In response there was a polite smattering of "yes, sirs."

Suddenly Battle exploded forward from his position nearby.

"Listen up, douchebags!" he yelled. He jerked his sharp features at us to emphasize his points as he talked. "When we ask you a question, your answer first had better be the right one, ***and*** second it had better make us deaf for a brief period. And for me that means loud, gentlemen, because I'm already hard of hearing." He stepped back and looked at us, this time with a smile.

"Now," he said. "Did you understand what midshipman Maxwell just said?"

We yelled a booming "Yes, sir!" in chorus. I thought it was pretty loud, but before I could mentally congratulate us for the effort, Battle yelled again.

"You call that loud? I could hardly hear you. Try again!" We did, louder this time. But it wasn't loud enough. We tried again, and again, and again, until Battle was satisfied with the decibel level, or maybe tired of the game. At any rate he finally smiled and said, "That's enough for now."

Maxwell turned to me. "O'Reilly," he said, "demonstrate the "chop" for us."

"Aye, aye, sir," I said. I had been experimenting mentally with the procedures ever since Maxwell first asked Poole to demonstrate, so I thought I knew what to do. I headed off slowly at a jog down the passageway toward the far wing.

"Always chop in the middle of the passageway!" Maxwell yelled at me as I jogged. I complied.

"A little faster!" yelled Battle. I sped up slightly.

"Okay," Maxwell said. "Now stop, turn around, and come back, and when you get to your room, turn and go inside. And always yell "Beat Army" whenever you pivot."

"Aye, aye, sir!" I replied, and coming down the passageway I watched my classmates observing me. They seemed impressed with my instant mastering of the chop, so I stuck out my chest a bit and continued past them. But just as I came level with Battle, he jumped along side and started running with me.

"Didn't we tell you to keep your eyes in the boat?" he yelled.

"Yes, sir!" I answered.

"Then do it!" he yelled again. I concentrated on the double doors at the end of the passageway and continued chopping until I came even with my room -- which was on my port side. Timing the pivot, I turned on my starboard foot, yelled a loud "Beat Army," and jogged into my room. Once inside I stopped and waited for a response from the two squadleaders.

After a moment, Maxwell announced, "Good job, O'Reilly. Now get your ass back out here on the double!"

I ran out of the room and straight to the group.

"God dammit!" Battle yelled moving quickly to stand in my face. "I thought we just said plebes always chop in the passageway."

"Yes, sir!" I answered.

"Then why didn't you?" he asked.

I thought quickly, then answered, "I'll find out, sir!" That satisfied Battle. He smiled, and his eyes crinkled in a friendly but measuring way. It was a look that told me that Battle could be a nice person, if he ever decided I measured up to his standards.

"Okay, ladies," Maxwell announced, "I want you all to practice chopping for the next few minutes. Chop up and down the passageway, keeping your eyes in the boat, and chop into and out of your rooms. No collisions please." With that both Maxwell and Battle stepped back and let us chop to our hearts content. Soon the sounds of shuffling feet, and a continuous chorus of "Beat Armys" echoed in the passageway. Several of my classmates -- Poole included -- had trouble figuring out which foot to pivot on, and the squadleaders quickly and loudly jumped on them. Thankfully, they left me alone.

After several minutes of chopping, Battle and Maxwell consulted their watches and bid us be seated again. This time Battle started the lecture.

"Okay, you know how to chop and keep your eyes straight ahead, but now comes the hard part. You also have to "brace up" whenever you are out of your room. Let's have Poole and O'Reilly front and center again." I scurried to comply.

Battle walked over to where I stood.

"Face the Company," he ordered. I turned. Battle then turned to my classmates, put his hands behind his back, and began.

"To brace up you push your chin into your neck so far that it almost comes out the back side. At the same time you must keep your head and shoulders perfectly straight and of course keep your eyes in the boat and not miss a step. You will brace up whenever an upperclassman enters your room and whenever you enter his. You will brace up while chopping and while eating meals. The only time you do not brace up is when you are in your rooms, outside of Bancroft Hall, in class, or when an upper class says you can carry-on." He turned to me.

"O'Reilly!" he suddenly yelled, "Brace up!" I hurried to pull my chin in, but as I did so, my head sagged toward my chest.

"Get your forehead straight, you stupid shit!" he yelled. I did, but my chin popped out.

Battle grabbed me from the side and shoved my shoulders forward while at the same time pulling my forehead back so that it was vertical.

"Hold that position!" he commanded. I did. Next he put two fingers on my chin and shoved it toward my neck. Out of the corner of my eyes I could see his own dark eyes watching me with a fierce intensity.

"Forehead back!" he yelled as my forehead started to droop chinward in response to his ministrations. I rotated my forehead backward and held my chin against the pressure of his fingers, and he let go. I stayed braced for several long seconds, looking at my classmates. I could see several astonished stares.

"Good, O'Reilly," Maxwell said. He touched my neck gently. "I count three chins, how about you Tom?" he asked Battle.

"Three it is," Battle replied, then he turned to the rest of the group. "All right. All of you get up and stand against the bulkhead behind you." Everyone rose and complied.

"Brace up!" Maxwell yelled when we were reasonably ready, and chins multiplied on bald heads with varying degrees of success. Battle and Maxwell toured the line, yelling and pointing out mistakes.

Suddenly Maxwell roared. "Everyone come here and look at your classmate Ramsey!" I turned starboard toward the sound of Maxwell's voice and soon joined a group of astonished classmates surrounding Jubal's position against the bulkhead.

Joe had sprouted six chins on his thick bull neck. Battle and Maxwell flanked him, counting chins aloud and in happy amazement.

"This," Battle indicated pridefully, "is what it means to brace up." We stared in awe at Jubal, and I could surreptitiously see several of my classmates pulling their chins down and moving their fingers along the bumps of skin in a vain attempt to copy Joe.

What followed was several minutes of practice bracing during which time Maxwell and Battle focused their attention on Poole and several other classmates, much to my inward delight.

Finally Maxwell consulted his watch and announced. "Okay. Enough for now. Everybody sit down." We sat and waited as Maxwell went to his room and returned carrying a large dark blue book. On its cover in oversized golden letters was printed the title, *NAVY SONGS*.

Before Maxwell had returned, Battle began. "Now comes the hardest part of today's training. It's hard for me because I'm tone deaf and hard for Maxie because he can actually sing." He turned to Maxwell, who had just arrived.

"As part of the Oath of Office Ceremony," Maxwell began, "you will be required to sing two famous Navy songs. The first is titled *The Navy Song*, and it's sung to the tune of *Anchors Aweigh*. You all know the tune, so repeat after me." He took us through *The Navy Song* several times with gusto until we had it pretty well memorized -- although I can't vouch for the quality of our little hootenanny since I saw tone-deaf Battle flinch several times as we tried to belt out the lyrics. Maxwell, however, actually had a sweet contralto voice that did not at all match his raspy bellow. When he was satisfied with what we had learned, we practiced another song, titled *The Navy Blue and Gold,* a much slower and solemn piece, which, since it was sung usually after Navy touchdowns, we did not sing very often during the four years of my attendance.

Finally Battle ordered us to stand, and for the next several minutes we practiced the Oath of Office Ceremony with our right hands raised, and we memorized the choreography that would get us to and from our assigned seats. Eventually Maxwell announced that we were as ready as we were ever going to be. Battle checked his watch.

"You have 15 minutes before we have to leave the company area for the ceremony. Go back to your rooms and wait. But be back in the passageway in 10 minutes in the clothes you arrived in. Wash your faces, straighten your ties -- and comb your hair." He looked at Maxwell and they both burst out laughing at the ignominy of the last remark.

"Be formed up exactly as we were for Mess Hall." He looked us over for a moment, them turned to Maxwell and said, as if we weren't there to hear, "This is a sorry-assed group. Do you think any of them will make it through the summer?"

"Some might, but for several others there's not a chance in hell," Maxwell answered. I noticed that Maxwell was staring at Thomas Henry Poole as he made that announcement.

We congregated in the passageway as requested and without too much confusion. Battle and Maxwell emerged from their rooms two minutes early to inspect us. Satisfied, Battle led us through the double doors, down the same ladder, and into the rotunda. This time we followed him through the huge metal double doors that mark the main entrance to the rotunda and out into Tecumseh Court. After so long indoors I squinted into the bright sunlight to see what was prepared for us.

Tecumseh Court had been roped off and cleared of visitors. The area behind the ropes extending out to the statue of Tecumseh and beyond was packed with excited family and visitors, many calling and waving as they recognized -- or thought they recognized -- their friend or family member. At this distance I could not see my family, although I knew they were there somewhere. Directly ahead a flight of broad granite stairs ended in a wide landing. On the end of the landing near the stairs stood a podium and several chairs facing the Court. Below at the bottom of the steps two identical sections of chairs awaited us.

We descended to port on one of the broad curving ramps that flank the main steps, and soon arrived at the seating area. Midshipmen waited near the seats to ensure we entered the correct row. The chairs had been set up in 18 identical rows of 36 seats. A cardboard sign attached near the bottom of the first chair of each row indicated the number of the Company to sit in that row. Companies one through 18 sat on the port side facing the steps, 19 through 36 sat to starboard. Battle led the group into our row and we followed single file. Maxwell brought up the rear.

When we were about half-way down the row, a loud voice from the crowd shouted "Rico! Amigo!" Rico Guevarra, who was several persons ahead of me, stopped, smiled broadly, and waved both arms high in the air. General cheering erupted from a portion of the crowd. When we had all entered the row and arrived at our seats, Battle called out a "Right face!" and we pivoted toward the stairs. He followed with a "Seats!" and we sat down obediently.

Within a few minutes all the new plebes were seated, and immediately several dignitaries emerged from the rotunda area. At the time I hadn't the faintest idea of rank and seniority, but I could tell from the carriage and demeanor of these officers that they were important persons. Hats and shoulders overflowed with gold braid and fancy designs as they moved confidently to their seats, and their chests were resplendent with multi-colored ribbons. The dignitaries sat, and one of their number approached the podium. What followed was an invocation by the head chaplain, followed by a welcoming speech by the Superintendent of the Naval Academy, Rear Admiral Jake Conrad. Although I can't recall the entirety of the talk, I remember distinctly his stressing the qualifications of our group. 50 percent had been varsity athletes in at least two major sports. 70 percent were National Merit Scholars. 80 percent were presidents of their senior class in High School. 60 percent were Eagle Scouts. I was very impressed.

The ceremony lasted 30 minutes, concluding with the Oath of Office, where we pledged allegiance to God, the country, and the president, and sang our rendition of *Navy Blue and Gold*, which didn't sound at all bad. At the conclusion of the ceremony we waited for the dignitaries to depart into the rotunda, and a midshipman approached the microphone.

"Liberty Call commences immediately for the Class of 1971," he announced, smiling. "Assemble in prearranged areas at 1730." We had previously been instructed that we could spend the next hour with our families but that we were not to leave Tecumseh Court. Battle and Maxwell would rendezvous with us at our seats at exactly 1730, and on pain of death, we had better not be late.

The midshipman at the podium dismissed us, and we filed neatly from our seats. Once in the main section of Tecumseh Court "T-Court", we headed for the crowd. Like a thousand other plebes, I had told my family I would meet them at the statue of the Indian, and I soon dismayed that I would ever find them in the crowd. My dad, always the hero, had thought up a solution. As I cautiously approached the pandemonium, I saw Sean, hefted up onto Big Kevin's shoulders, anxiously scanning the approaching plebe crowd.

"Sean!" I yelled, waving an arm in the air. He spotted me and beamed broadly and unbelievingly at my new appearance. I indicated with a wave that they should move clear of the crowd, under the shade of one of the enormous tulip poplar trees that lined the brick walkway, and soon my family unit detached itself from the confusion and approached me cautiously.

"Oh, my God!" my mother said, horrified as she stared at my baldness. Slowly she put a pale hand to her cheek. Sean burst into a deep belly laugh.

"Get a load of that," he said pointing. My father only chuckled, his eyes sparkling with humor.

"Well, Kevin," Dad asked, "how is it so far?"

"Great Dad," I answered, smiling. "So far I've had my foot in and out of my mouth a dozen times, embarrassed myself in front of my peers, and only managed to piss off one of the upperclassmen. -- I'm doing great." Dad laughed.

"Aren't they treating you right, Kevin?" my mother asked seriously.

"Rin," big Kevin said patiently, "this is like a boot camp. They have to be hard on them. It's how they weed out the good from the bad." He looked at me solemnly, and suddenly his eyes welled up with tears. Rather than speak, he turned his head to one side and stared off to infinity. My mom noticed his predicament.

"Your father is so sentimental," she said, smiling like a Madonna in a stained glass window. "He cried during the Oath you said, too." She reached a small hand toward his large arm and patted it gently. "I'm sure Kevin will be fine, dear."

"I know he will," Dad answered, turning toward me again recovered from his near sobbing. "I'm sure of it." We moved off to one side of the crowd and found a spot where we could sit and watch the activity. I explained everything we had done thus far, and they told me about their adventures exploring the campus and the beautiful city of Annapolis. Sean wanted to see me brace up, so I pulled in my chin for the family.

While we were talking I noticed Jubal Ramsey approaching nearby with his mother and several other siblings. I caught his attention and waved. His mother, a petite and attractive brunette, noticed my wave and steered the group in our direction. I stood as they approached, and introduced my family. His mother, May, talked with a gentle and refined Southern accent as she named her children for us. While she talked, she kept one arm firmly and protectively locked around Jubal's arm. Each of Joe's siblings smiled and offered a hand to shake. When Jubal shook hands with my dad, they held their grips appraisingly. Jubal stared appreciatively at the sheer mass of big Kevin, then he looked at me questioningly. I laughed.

"I must have missed out on the family "Hulk" genes," I said. Jubal and his mother laughed.

"Couldn't your dad make it today?" Sean asked innocently.

Before anyone else could answer, Jubal said, "No, he couldn't." The strange way in which he said it, and the sad look his mother gave him in response told me there was a story somewhere that Joe wasn't ready to reveal. We let the subject drop, and in a few minutes the Ramseys politely excused themselves and strolled away.

We traded small talk for most of the hour, and I promised I would write every day -- a promise I would break the very next day. Finally I noticed a general movement in the direction of T-Court and I stood.

"Well," I said "time to go. If I'm late, I'm dead." We exchanged hugs and kisses again, and I gave my dad a firm man's handshake, but this time it was easier to let go than it had been at the Field House. I think the fact that I was now part of a larger group of identical individuals signified that I had taken a major step on the road toward eventually maturity. At least that's what I would have liked to believe as I stood, proud family around me, basking in the glow of their admiration.

Maxwell and Battle waited nearby as when we assembled at our chairs. One of our classmates stood to one side looking down at his feet. After they had counted the last of us, we formed into the three now-familiar squads and prepared to return to Bancroft Hall. Before we departed, however, Maxwell spoke quietly to the embarrassed classmate and pointed in the general direction of the main office. The classmate nodded silently but did not look at us.

Walking in front of the group, Maxwell asked quietly. "Was it sad saying goodbye to your families?" Several subdued "Yes, sirs" came in reply.

"Well," he said, "I have some good and bad news for you." His initial and obviously faked concern then turned to sadistic glee as he announced, "The good news is that some of you will be seeing mommy and daddy much sooner than you think."

"What's the bad news?" asked Battle with feigned sincerity as we digested that piece of encouragement.

Maxwell laughed. "Those of you who don't see them are going to soon wish that you could." With that Battle started us toward the bowels of Mother Bancroft. What followed was my last meal in civilian clothes in the Mess Hall for more than 25 years, and the last meal for several months that wasn't accompanied by intense harassment and grief.

We returned to the Company area just after 1800. Battle halted us in the passageway, and Maxwell went into their room.

"Stand against the bulkhead!" Battle ordered. We moved to obey. Maxwell returned with a chair and several sets of uniform clothes. He placed the clothes on the chair, then scanned the crowd. I slunk into the nethermost regions of the group against the ugly dull-pink tiles that covered the bulkhead. His eye caught sight of me, and I could tell he knew I was trying to hide. He grinned mischievously.

"O'Reilly!" he bellowed. "Front and center!"

I groaned and several of my nearby companymates laughed. Battle pounced.

"What's the matter, O'Reilly, are we making pests of ourselves?"

"No, sir!" I said as I chopped to the front of the group and stopped beside Maxwell. Battle watched me, shook his head, and slowly walked toward me, stopping immediately in front of where I stopped. He was so close I could smell the garlic sauce from the spaghetti we had for dinner still lingering on his breath. He leaned in closer until his nose almost touched my chin. His brown eyes locked on my own in a narrow, emotionless stare which he held for several seconds. I was completely unprepared for his close proximity, and I instinctively drew back.

"What's the matter O'Reilly? Do I have bad breath or body odor?" he asked.

An honest answer was not expected so I quickly sputtered, "No, sir."

"Well then," he continued. "When I talk to you from now on you will remain perfectly still no matter how close I come." He reached out and put his index finger on my chest. "I may even have a reason to touch you during the course of our training. You can understand that can't you?" he asked.

"Yes, sir" I answered hesitatingly, unsure where the conversation was going.

"You wouldn't consider me a faggot if I touched you, would you, O'Reilly?" he asked further. I was very confused. The silence behind me was palpable. I could sense that every person in the passageway, Maxwell included, was waiting to find what Battle was getting at.

"No problem, Sir," I said, coming to an instantaneous decision, "I can't see as how you'd be interested in me that way."

This was not an answer Battle expected. He drew back slightly and gave me a suspicious look. "Why is that, O'Reilly?" he asked.

"Well, you see, sir," I answered smoothly. "I just an Irishman, and everybody knows we have these teeny tiny pencil dicks. So what's the point?" Both Maxwell and Battle burst out laughing, and the group behind joined the uproar. The laughter went on for a long minute. Finally Battle calmed enough to looked at me seriously then at the group at large.

"All right everyone," he yelled. "You've had your little laugh. Calm down." His attention returned to me.

"It's a good thing I have a sense of humor, O'Reilly," he said. I nodded an answer, still smiling.

"And you don't need to worry about the Homo-thing either," he said loudly. "The only time I'm going to touch one of you douchebags is when I kick your ass for not performing."

He looked at the group.

"Is that understood?" he asked. There was a loud general consensus reply.

"Now that we've had our little laugh," Maxwell continued, "I think it's time to begin some more training. He picked up a jock strap and held it aloft.

"This is a jock strap," he said. "I'm sure some of you have never seen one, so let me just say that the fat part goes in front." He looked at me and smiled. "To protect your pencil dick." The group chuckled. He reached down and picked up a pair of navy blue gym shorts.

"These are gym shorts," he said, transferring them to the same hand as the jock. He did the same with a white gym shirt, blue-stripped athletic socks, and the ugly gym shoes. When he finished he was holding all the items aloft.

"Together they make up something called *gym gear*." He looked at me. "O'Reilly, run to your room and put on your gym gear as quickly as possible, then return." I chopped for my room, and was back in less than five minutes

When I returned, Maxwell and Battle looked me over as critically as they could, but after all, I was in shorts and gym shirt, so creases, polish, and alignment were irrelevant. Satisfied, Maxwell turned to the group.

"Okay, ladies," he said. "You see how O'Reilly is dressed? I want you all back here in the identical outfit in five minutes. Get moving!" The herd stampeded to their various rooms.

No sooner had the thunder of departing feet stopped reverberating in the passageway than Maxwell turned to me again.

"Come here, O'Reilly," he said from his position near the chair. As I approached he held up a white jumper and matching cotton pants. "I want you to go back to your room and change into this uniform," he said. "Wear regular underwear, black socks and shoes, and bring your dixie cup. Go!"

I chopped to the room, confused about the necessity for such an exercise, but I complied nonetheless. By the time I returned, Maxwell and Battle had the rest of my companymates standing loosely against the bulkhead and were inspecting the way in which they wore their gym gear. I clomped into the hall in the strange uniform, squared my corners, and waited beside the chair. The other plebes watched , wondering what was in store for them.

Maxwell moved to the center of the passageway and stood next to me.

"Okay," he said. "Believe it or not, there was a reason for this exercise. Tomorrow morning we are going to begin a regular exercise program to get you into shape. Some of you desperately need it, by the way. You will be dressed in gym gear and standing against the bulkhead outside your rooms at 0600. Mr. Battle and I are going to take you on a short three mile run followed by 30 minutes of calisthenics. I don't want any confusion to delay the program, consequently you now know what to wear and how to wear it. After the exercise you will have thirty minutes to shower and change into white works." He pointed to me.

"This is *white works*. Study what your classmate is wearing. Notice he has on regular undies, black shoes and socks, and he has his dixie cup in his hand. Now all of you go to your rooms and get on your white works. Five minutes. Move it!" Again the herd thundered off. Maxwell turned to me.

"Go stand against the bulkhead, O'Reilly," he said.

I could see by the clock across the passageway that it was almost seven in the evening. I said "seven" to myself, then converted the hours 1900. I was exhausted. I had never had a day so full of so much activity or so many new experiences. I yawned loudly. Battle glanced sharply in my direction.

"Tired, O'Reilly?" he asked, not unkindly.

"Yes, sir," I answered.

"Too damn bad!" he barked. "This is not my idea of how to spend the perfect evening either. Playing nursemaid to a bunch of wimps. Believe me, I'd rather be out on liberty or back home with my girlfriend. So spare me your droopy eyes or I'll start your plebe year tonight with about a hundred pushups."

"Aye, aye, sir!" I hurriedly answered.

My classmates began returning within three minutes, wearing various versions of the uniform I had on. Some wore v-neck T-shirts. Some had no T-shirts. Some had no underwear. Some wore the wrong shoes -- or the wrong socks. A few forgot the hat. Battle and Maxwell reacted in an appropriately loud manner.

Thomas Poole was the final midshipman to arrive, and he arrived reluctantly. In his haste he had put on his T-shirt inside-out, which was a barely noticeable error considering that his pants had been incorrectly fitted in the gear issue room, drew glaring attention to the remainder of his apparel. The trouser legs were too narrow for his ample thighs, and the flared bottoms ended several inches above his ankle. The pullover tightly accentuated his overabundant middle. I felt immediately sorry because I knew the two squadleaders would zero in on him as an example of how not to dress. I was right. Although I learned the precise technical word later in the summer, that first day I knew instinctively that Thomas Henry Poole was a perfect "shit screen".

It took 20 minutes for Battle and Maxwell to satisfy themselves that the group could dress itself reasonably well for the first day of plebedom. Afterward Maxwell yelled for us to return to our rooms and instantly reappear in gym gear for the final evolution of the evening. We reluctantly hustled to comply. Maxwell's voice, strained from the yelling and constant jabber of the day, cracked often as he moved from room to room urging us to hurry.

Eventually we assembled, a very tired group of proto-plebes, and he instructed us to sit on the deck. The chair had been removed from the passageway, and he and Battle had also changed from their white uniforms into a casual evening attire. Instead of gym gear, however, they sported various versions of pre-sleep clothing. Maxwell wore a pair of old civilian boxer shorts, bright red hearts emblazoned thereon. He also had on a T-shirt that announced him to be a devoted fan of the Saint Louis Cardinals. Over this he wore a bathrobe, not a standard purplish, Naval Academy issue model like the one that we had been given centuries earlier that day but rather a dull gray affair with an unfamiliar crest on the chest pocket. On his feet were rubber shower shoes affectionately called "clacks" because of the noise they made. He kept his hands in his bathrobe pockets as he waited for us to get settled.

Battle wore a red and gold pair of Marine Corps athletic shorts and a T-shirt with a picture of a hungry buzzard on a dead tree limb and a caption that announced that it was a bad day when you can't kill anything. He also had on a bathrobe, but this one was a very old and significantly faded Naval Academy robe, the back of which sported various letters and the numbers "39" attached in several places. He also wore clacks, but with white gym socks. He stood with hands folded behind his back, and since this was the first time I had seen him without his hat on, I saw that he was going prematurely bald in the back and front of his head.

"Okay, gentlemen. Listen up!" Maxwell began when we had all seated ourselves somewhat uncomfortably on the hard linoleum tile deck. "This will be the final lecture of the night, a fact that I am just as happy about as you are, I can assure you. But this one may be the most important one you will receive the entire summer. We'll go very slowly because this will all be new for you, but what we are about to say is absolutely vital to your survival and to the survival of this institution and the nation."

Many of my classmates murmured disbelief at that last statement, and Maxwell paused for a moment to let the minor commotion die out.

"What I've said is absolutely true." He looked at the group, then quickly pointed to a plebe in the front. "You," he asked. "What's your name?"

"Tony Delvecchio, sir," the short, swarthy classmate answered.

"Why are you here, Tony?" Maxwell answered. Tony paused for a moment before answering.

"To get a good education, sir."

Maxwell pointed to another new face. "You, same question," he said.

This classmate, a lanky, light-haired individual, answered unhesitatingly, "Robert Strong, sir. To fly jets. And maybe be an astronaut."

Maxwell selected the only black member of the company. Growing up in the near-ghetto areas of inner-city Boston, I found nothing surprising about black students at Annapolis, certainly the schools I had attended to this point had all had been racially and ethnically mixed, and I had gotten along rather famously with the black players on my high school basketball team. I also knew that Annapolis students came from every state in the country, and several of my company mates had ethnic names. Rico was obviously Puerto Rican, and an Asian classmate sat against the back bulkhead. I expected diversity. Hell, being ethnic myself, I welcomed diversity. But hearing this particular fellow plebe speak, I began to get a sense of exactly what Annapolis had grouped together in this passageway.

My classmate was a small, very handsome boy, who spoke softly in precise English with a hint of an "islands" accent.

"My name is Wesley Roy Lamont," he said, and immediately sprouted an infectious smile, "and I am here because my father served in the navy during World War II and now runs a small fishing charter in the American Virgin Islands. I have spent a great deal of my life on or near the water. I love the sea and everything to do with it. Where else but Annapolis?"

Maxwell paused and stared at Lamont for a second before selecting Jeffrey Polk.

"Jeff Polk, sir. I'm here because it seemed like a good idea at the time." Several people, including Maxwell, laughed at this. Some obviously found more truth than humor in the comment.

"Sure, pal!" Maxwell replied.

Maxwell stopped at this point and stared hard at the group, then he turned to Battle.

"I've heard enough. Tommy," he said. "Tell them why they are really here."

Battle, who had been patiently standing nearby, moved to the front of the group. He looked us up and down for a moment before beginning.

"Bullshit!" he said loudly. "What I just heard is pure bullshit! You're not here to get an education or to learn to fly or sail the ocean blue. You're here to serve the country and to prepare yourselves to die for your fellow citizens. Nothing more or less is expected from you." He paused to let the point sink in. "You *will*, of course, have to study hard *and* work your asses off for the privilege of serving your nation, but ***that's*** why you are here."

"The Naval Academy was founded in 1848 to train officers to serve in the fleet. Since that time only sixty thousand men have graduated from this institution. That is not a large number, gentlemen. This is a very elite school with traditions that are deeply and jealously rooted in duty, honor, and loyalty; and training new recruits is a very, very serious business. Thousands of those graduates I have mentioned have paid the ultimate price fulfilling the mission of the military of this nation. Very few other schools can make that kind of claim. You may also die as a direct result of your decision to enroll in this institution."

Battle went on, "In combat you will be expected to instantly obey the commands of your superior officers. Your life and the lives of your shipmates will depend on that. That's why midshipman Maxwell and I will accept nothing less than instant obedience on your part. We will tell you to do things that seem senseless. You will be forced to memorize inane banter. Part of what we ask may even be personally humiliating. Tough! But we're not going to ask you to carry a rifle up a hill against an enemy position or drive a ship into hopeless battle, or fly an A-4 against a SAM site. Our little drills may be stupid, but they won't kill you, and you will obey nonetheless because that's what expected of you. If you can't deal with those facts, quit now before we spend too much time training you. There's no disgrace in admitting the error in your decision making -- one of your company-mates has already departed -- and if you are truly not sufficiently gifted to earn a commission from this institution, your decision to leave now may ultimately save the lives of men who would be depending on you in combat."

Battle loosened his posture a bit and paced toward the far end of the group away from the double doors.

"Everyone be quiet for a moment," he said, "and listen." The instant that he ordered attention to the surrounding din was the first time I became consciously aware that we were not the only group of plebes being trained. Down the passageway and around the corner and drifting up from the decks below, I could hear noise from another company, as other squadleaders ranted indiscernibly.

"Even as we speak," Battle continued, "35 almost identical groups of fresh young ugly faces are being assaulted and berated by other squadleaders. And I'm sure that more than one thousand pea-brained plebes just like you are right this very minute wondering what the hell they are doing here."

He suddenly dropped his military guise so instantly and completely that I was slightly shocked. He turned toward us, leaned in closer to the group, and continued, almost whispering.

"You know -- you guys are lucky. Maxie and I are pussy cats compared to some of the other squadleaders on the summer detail. But I'm going to be honest with you; when the Brigade gets back in September, you are going to face the toughest group of first class in the entire Academy. They are a bunch of assholes who call themselves the "Tigers," and they make even the staunchest of my classmates look like Sunday school teachers. Life will not be easy for you poor pukes. Hell, I hate them myself, and I could easily run rings around most of them."

"I happened to be talking to a classmate after dinner today," he continued. "He works as an assistant to the Commandant for the Plebe Summer period. He told me that nearly a hundred of your classmates either elected not to show up today or have already decided to go home. That's almost a tenth of the group the first day. But that's not unusual at Annapolis. This is a special school, and we have special requirements for our students and graduates. Tonight as you prepare for bed I want each of you to give serious thought to whether you really want to be here. If you're not prepared to meet the ultimate challenge, then leave now." He turned to Maxwell. "Did I explain things well enough?" he asked with a smile and a slightly sarcastic edge to his voice.

"Great job," Maxwell answered. "Give him a hand, gentlemen. Tommy here is a truly dedicated professional." We applauded Battle boisterously for more than 10 seconds until Maxwell held his hand up for attention.

"Don't overdo it, guys," he said, then continued. "For my part of the final hour I will do two things. First I'm going to tell you about what it means to be a midshipman. Second I'm going to have one room of classmates introduce themselves and give us all a two minute talk on their background and what they expect from this experience. For the first evening's entertainment I have selected 5404, "The Goon Room". I want the four of you 'goons' to mentally prepare for your presentations while I am talking." Almost immediately Poole pushed a flabby arm into the air. Maxwell acknowledged him.

"The head goon wants to speak. Speak goon," he said

"Sir," Poole began in a very professional tone, "in order to properly prepare, can we go back to our rooms for pencil and paper to outline our talks?"

"Very impressive, Poole. You want to do a good job on your first assignment. What do you think, Tom?" he asked Battle with an anticipatory smile.

"Shit no!" Battle answered immediately. "What are you going to do in combat, Poole, jot down notes before the enemy attacks so you'll know what to do if you face the business end of a bayonet?"

"You heard the man," Maxwell said, "This will be a little impromptu talk." Maxwell turned to the group and cleared his throat with some small difficulty. It was apparent that the day's talking and yelling had taken a toll on his vocal chords.

"There is one concept that forms the basis for everything a midshipman is," he began with a slight croak, "and that is the Honor Code. I happen to be an Honor Committee Representative for the Company, so I am very familiar with the Code and all its nuances. But I can summarize with the words you will find in your *Reef Points*. '*A midshipman does not lie, cheat, or steal.*'"

"It sounds too simple," he added. "It seems unnecessary. It may even insult your personal code of behavior to be reminded of the rules. But I can assure you that the Honor Code is very serious to the Brigade of Midshipmen, and sadly, some of the students of this school violate the Code anyway." He paused for effect. "We midshipmen police the Honor Policy ourselves and are wholly responsible for actions on any reported violations. A few students here are expelled for such violations every year.

"At Annapolis we have a Code that differs from the ones at West Point and at Colorado Springs. Cadets at the "Point" are required to reveal to the authorities whatever they suspect. Cadets at Air Force are only responsible for their own behavior. Midshipmen, however, are allowed broad discretion in how they treat honor violations. This is an important distinction because it not only makes each of us responsible for the actions of the entire Brigade, but it also gives us the ability to apply reason and common sense to whatever actions we take. If I see you violate the Code, I can first talk to you, discover what it is I saw, and ask how you intended your action. If I'm convinced you acted inadvertently or improperly, I can let the matter drop, or I can lecture you and have you make appropriate retribution. If I am sure you violated the Code, I can request that you inform the Honor Committee yourself, or, if the action is sufficiently severe, I can and will report to the Honor Committee myself. Hell, I'd turn my own mother in if I thought it appropriate." I looked at Battle, and he was nodding seriously.

Maxwell continued. "It isn't always obvious that an honor violation has occurred. Sometimes in the heat of a moment you may say something in error that was never intended to be a deception, or you may do something just plain stupid. The system will punish these simple errors in judgment with demerits and not dismissal. However, if there is no doubt in the Committee's mind that you have lied, cheated, or stolen, you will be dismissed in disgrace.

"Over the next several days I will entertain questions regarding Honor policy, and I will give you some horror stories about midshipmen who thought they were too smart for the system. By the end of the summer you will have a very good idea of what the Honor Code means to each of us." With that he stopped and took a deep breath.

"Now," he continued, "Mister Battle and I will go to our rooms for chairs, and when we return the Goon Room will tell us all the sordid details of their past lives. Wait quietly, children. We'll be right back." Maxwell and Battle departed.

Jim Merritt immediately stood up and searched for his room mates.

"Who wants to go first?" he asked. Nobody answered.

"Okay, I will," he said. "How about if you go second, Tommy, with Jeff third, and Jubal last?" He smiled at Joe. "I'm sure you have the best story anyway," he said. Nobody objected.

Merritt continued, "I intend to talk about my family background, brothers and sisters, where I went to school, sports, and generally about my interests. I think we should keep it light. No religion or politics. Everyone agree?" Again there were no objections. Merritt smiled and sat down.

Almost immediately Maxwell and Battle returned carrying the light-weight metal desk chairs from their room. They sat them off to one side.

"Okay," Maxwell said,. "One at a time, I want the goons to get up in front of the group and tell their sad life story. Who's first?"

Merritt rose quickly, smiling, and moved to the front of the group. "I am, sir," he said. Then he turned to us classmates and began with an ease and natural flair that I instantly envied.

"My name is James Wesley Merritt," he began. "You can call me Jim. I was born in Amarillo, Texas on June 15, 1949. My father, John, is a junior manager with Gulf Oil Company. My mother, Martha, is a housewife. I am the oldest of five children. I have a brother Samuel who is fifteen, another brother Houston who is twelve, and sisters Monica and Merri who are ten and six. I attended Sam Houston High School in Amarillo, where I played three seasons of football and two of track. I was the reluctant president of my class. I like music and sports, and I have a sweet girlfriend back home named Lynda. I'm very excited to be here, and I want very much to be a Navy pilot and astronaut." With that he finished, and turned to the squadleaders. "Questions, sirs?" he asked.

"Anybody have questions for classmate Merritt?" Maxwell asked the group. Nobody did. "Sit down, Merritt. Next!"

Tommy Poole reluctantly stood, straightened his gym shirt down over his belly, and walked to the front of the group. He looked at the squadleaders. Maxwell nodded his head. Poole turned toward the group.

"My name is Thomas Henry Poole," he began nervously. "I was born in Flint, Michigan on August 22, 1949. My dad works at the General Motors Plant in Flint. I attended St. Ursula's High School in Flint, and I was president of the Debate Society and the Physics Club. I was also a member of the Drama Club, Chess Club, and National Honor Society. I enjoy sports but I didn't letter except as manager as the hockey team. I also like music, especially the Beatles, and I can play piano a little. I am looking forward to the challenge Annapolis will surely bring." He smiled. "Questions?"

"Any sisters?" asked Battle. When Maxwell looked at him strangely he said. "I'm thinking of dating a woman with brains instead of the usual big-titted babes that hang out in town. Maybe Poole has a likely prospect?" The group laughed loudly at that comment.

The idea of Battle dating his fictional sister was almost too much for Tommy, who stammered a hasty "No, sir. No sisters." Immediately, however, Poole paused and tears came to his eyes.

"I had an older brother who was killed in an accident several years ago," he added, almost to himself. The group quieted immediately upon hearing that news.

"You can sit down, Poole," Maxwell said. Tommy stepped gingerly over classmates and found his way back to his place.

Before Maxwell could call for the next goon, Jeff Polk rose and moved quickly to the fore. He turned immediately toward the group and began in a deep nervous voice.

"Hi," he said with a crooked smile. "I'm Jeffrey John Polk. I don't have much of a story. I grew up in Derry, New Hampshire. My dad works at a paper mill. I have a younger brother. I play baseball and a little guitar. Any questions?"

"That's it?" Maxwell asked. "Your whole life in under ten seconds? Doesn't that make you feel a little sad, Polk?"

"No, sir," Jeff answered.

"Well then, sit down, pal," Maxwell ordered, "because I don't know about you Tom, but I'm more than anxious to hear from the human tree stump."

"Yeah," Battle answered, "me too!"

Jubal Ramsey recognized the cue and stood. Because of his unusual size, several of my classmates had to squeeze sidewards to let him get through. Joe took it all in stride. He sauntered to the front, faced the squadleaders, bowed gracefully, then turned toward us.

"Hi," he said in that unbelievable accent. "Ah'm Jubal Hunter Ramsey, and ah'm from High Point, Alabama, which, in case you cain't guess, is deep in the heart of Dixie. I love the military. My daddy went to West Point. I have a brother, Mason, two years younger, who's bigger than me. And two sisters, one Becky who is three years younger and almost bigger than me, and Melinda, who is only ten and ain't fully grown yet. I love football, and I hope to play here."

"Why didn't you go to West Point?" Battle asked.

"Sir," Jubal answered, "my grades weren't up to snuff during High School and I had to attend Alabama University for a year. No West Point appointments were available when I reapplied. But ah'm sure I'll like it here. You fellas seem real nice." The group laughed, and the squadleaders couldn't tell if they were being had.

"Your fat ass will see how nice we are in the morning, pal," Maxwell observed. "Sit down."

Maxwell then stood and moved to a place opposite the center of the group.

"Well," he said, "that concludes today's festivities. You can return to your rooms, but be absolutely quiet. Lights out at 2100. Set your alarms for early, and do not fail to be ready at precisely 0600. Any questions?" I had so many I couldn't frame them all in time to respond. I'm sure the rest of my classmates felt the same.

"Good night, ladies," Maxwell said, and with that he and Battle returned to their room. I eased myself up off the deck and stretched my arms high over my head. I looked around my company mates who were also mostly looking around at each other. Then almost without consciousness, we headed slowly toward our individual rooms.

Inside I neatly prepared my gym clothes and white works for the morning. Then I folded my civilian clothes and put them in my suitcase. Finally I prepared to take a shower. While I was puttering about I noticed Donny Delmont sitting quietly at his desk. Without a word he rose and left the room.

Once he was gone, Rico looked at me and said. "He's not long for this place."

"What makes you think so?" I asked.

"He's got the look," he answered. "Wait and see." With that prophecy, he returned to calmly reading a book he had brought.

"I suppose it's all right to go to the bathroom?" Grizwald asked me in a shaky, nervous voice as he emerged from the coat closet where he had just placed his suitcase.

"Sure, why not?" I answered, and he too left the room.

"He'll be next," Rico said after he was gone.

"What?" I asked.

"Grizwald will be the next to go," Rico stated.

"He's got the look, too?" I asked skeptically. Rico only nodded, then returned to his book. "What about me?" I asked. "Am I destined to soon depart these hallowed halls?"

"No. You're what they call a *lifer*," he answered, smiling knowingly. I wasn't exactly sure what that meant, but at least from the standpoint of Rico's crystal ball I was safe for the time being. For some strange reason, it reassured me.

Grizwald returned fairly quickly, but Delmont was gone a long time. I had finished my shower and put on my bathrobe when he finally came back to the room. He didn't look at any of us but went straight to his locker and silently put away his things. I could see Rico surreptitiously watching him from his position across the room. Delmont quickly undressed and climbed into the bunk above mine. He slid himself as far against the wall as he could, turned his body away from the room, and lay silently. Rico looked at me from over the top of his book. He nodded and winked at me knowingly.

For a moment I considered saying something to Delmont, but I was unsure what to say, or even what was wrong. Instead I walked to the doorway and peered outside. I wondered if I should inform the squadleaders. Across the passageway I could see activity in Merritt's room. They appeared to be getting along famously. As I watched, Jim Merritt appeared in the doorway, smiled at me, and quickly headed down the passageway toward the head facilities. I hesitated for a second and followed.

Navy communal facilities are called "heads" for some reason that was never explained to me. The heads in Bancroft Hall were clean and spacious. Against one wall was a bank of five white porcelain urinals, separated from a series of three equally white sinks by a splash partition. Across the room were four green metal stalls. I selected a urinal next to Merritt.

"You lied to Battle today, you know," he said to me in a serious voice soon after I had begun my business. My heart instantly sank and momentarily I lost control of my aim. Instantaneous visions of Honor Committees and dismissal in disgrace flooded my thoughts.

"What?" I asked incredulously.

"You lied to Battle. You don't have a pencil dick," he said grinning, his head indicating the activity in my fixture. I was instantly overcome with relief, and it took a second for me to laugh.

"That was a terrible thing to say," I replied after a moment, still smiling. He apologized sincerely.

"What do you think of everything so far?" he asked me.

"The jury's out," I answered. "Listen," I immediately continued, "my room mate Delmont is acting strangely. Rico thinks he's quitting already. Should I do anything?"

Merritt thought for a moment.

"He's gonna quit, huh?"

"It seems like it. He's sure acting strangely, but I'm not sure what's 'strange' after today," I answered.

"If he quits, he quits," Merritt answered. "He's old enough to make decisions on his own. Maybe you could get Delmont to talk to Poole about leaving. I have a bad feeling about him. He doesn't seem suited to the environment, and his screw-ups are going to get all of us in trouble. There's already friction between him and Ramsey because of the suitcase. And Ramsey has made it very clear to us that the Navy is sub-par and that he would rather be at West Point. And Polk has a bad attitude about what he calls the "Mickey Mouse" rules. I expect fist fights before too long. I'm not sure I want to be in the Goon Room. Want to change rooms?"

"Maybe I'll have to," I answered, "because Delmont's going to leave, and according to Rico, Grizwald will be next. Soon I may be alone in my room, and I don't think I could handle that." Merritt thought for a moment.

"Listen," he said. "You're a steady influence on the group. You've got a good head on your shoulders. And you're funny. Why not act as the peacemaker for my room. Come visit. Draw the others out into conversation. Get them to reveal things and maybe start depending on each other."

"Can't you do that?" I asked.

"Maybe," he answered. "But if I suddenly try to assume a leadership role, they'll probably resent it and clam up even more. No, what we need here is an outsider. Someone they know but not too well. You're perfect for the role." He looked at his watch. "There's still almost an hour before lights out. Come visit." With that he left the head and ambled toward his room.

Still considering what Merritt had asked, I returned to my room. Delmont remained pressed against the wall. I didn't think he was asleep. Grizwald was in the shower. Rico hadn't moved from his seat. He looked up when I returned. I winked at him, then went over to his desk, drew up Grizwald's chair, and sat down. He put his feet down from the desktop, placed his book on the desk, and looked at me, expectantly. I started to speak, noticed something peculiar about the book he was reading, and reached over to examine it. It was the kind of book we used to pass around in the locker room at high school, one with passages guaranteed to excite young hormones. The title was *Sex Spy,* and the cover showed a scantily clad young lady wearing a heavy fur Russian military cap and lying on a polar bear skin rug, thick lips parted and leering seductively at the reader.

"You actually read this stuff?" I asked incredulously.

"It's a technical manual of sorts," he answered half-seriously. "You can never have enough ideas about the different ways to please a woman. I consider it research."

I laughed. "Listen," I said, "I'm going across the passageway to visit the goons. You want to come along?"

"No, not tonight. I'm going to shower after Grizwald and hit the sack. I have a feeling that tomorrow will come very early."

"Okay," I said. "I won't be long."

He smiled. "I'll leave a light on for you," he said.

First checking the passageway to make sure it was empty of squadleaders, I hurried across to Merritt's room. Inside there was still considerable activity. Ramsey was in the shower. Polk was stacking laundry in his locker. Merritt was wiping down his desk top. And Poole was sitting at his desk trying to precisely fold his skivvy shorts.

"You guys look busy," I said as I entered. Poole and Merritt looked up and smiled, and Polk nodded but did not smile. I went over to one of the desks and sat on the smooth top. "You guys ready for tomorrow?" I asked.

"How could we be when nothing they do makes any real sense?" asked Polk quickly. "They'll probably have us digging and filling latrines and call it a strategic exercise. Or maybe we'll sing songs and march around campus to impress the tourists. And have any of you looked at that stupid little book called *Reef Points* yet? Wait until you hear some of the insanity they expect us to memorize." Merritt looked at me.

"Well, you know, Jeff," I said, "it seems to me that all the nonsense has a purpose. It's like the initiation for a club -- something you have to do to pay the dues so to speak. And it is one way to learn self discipline."

Polk looked at me skeptically. His dark eyes narrowed. "It's still bullshit," he said.

"No doubt about it," I replied, "but all the complaining in the world isn't going to change it or make it any easier. Maybe not dwelling on the bullshit will lessen the burden. It can't hurt to at least give it a try." I lowered my voice. "I've got two room-mates who Rico Guevarra swears will be gone in a week. If that's true, then they don't seem to be willing to give the place a decent chance. That's what I'm going to do. I'll wait and see, maybe through the summer. If I don't like it, then I'll go to MIT or Georgia Tech."

Poole interrupted, his interest perked.

"You had acceptance from MIT?"

"Conditional. My verbal scores weren't outstanding, but my math scores were in the low 700s. How about you Tommy. What were your scores?"

Poole hesitated. "I had 800," he answered.

"Wow!" I said, "that's a perfect score. Was that math or verbal?"

"Both," he answered quietly. Ramsey had just emerged from the shower when Poole made this pronouncement.

"You maxed out the SATs?" he asked incredulously. Poole nodded. "Then what the hell are you doing here?" Ramsey asked. "Y'all don't belong in military school with us dumb-dumbs."

"I want to be here," he said. "Maxwell didn't ask me, but I came to serve my country."

"This place is gonna eat you up and spit you out, boy," Ramsey said. "Look at yo'self. I'll bet you cain't even do one push up. How you expect to keep up with us?"

"If I had known we were supposed to arrive in shape," Poole answered, "I would have prepared better. I thought the purpose of the summer training was to get us into shape."

"My daddy used to tell me stories about what it was like at the Point," Jubal replied. "I think y'all gonna get the lot of us in trouble." Merritt looked at me again. I was beginning to resent acting as his sounding board.

"Well," I said, "I suppose if we all act together, it'll be better than getting angry at one another. We're supposed to be a unit."

"Tell me that tomorrow after you have to do extra to make up for some people," replied Jubal. I had no answer for that. I didn't want to do extra work because of anybody's deficiencies. I'd just have to wait and see.

"Well," I said, "I'm really bushed. I think I'll get some sleep. See you bright and early tomorrow." With that I left the room, my stint at peacemaking not entirely successful.

Back in the room Rico had climbed into bed. Grizwald was snoring loudly. Delmont was deathly silent. I took off my robe and hung it up, turned off the lights, and lay in bed. For almost a whole minute I lay on my back considering the swirl of the day's events. For some strange reason,I found myself slowly and quietly whispering the Oath of Office as my brain slowed it previously frantic pace. I realized for the first time that I had assumed an awesome responsibility and I hoped I could honor my part of the bargain with Uncle Sam. As the last words of the Oath vibrated in my brain, I fell into the deepest sleep of my life.

"I Kevin Patrick O'Reilly, having been appointed a Midshipman in the United States Navy, do solemnly swear that I will support and defend the Constitution of the United States against all enemies, foreign and domestic; that I will bear true faith and allegiance to the same; that I take this obligation freely, without any mental reservation or purpose of evasion; and that I will well and faithfully discharge the duties of the office on which I am about to enter; so help me, God."

CHAPTER 2

CUSTOMS AND ROUTINES

The lights flashed on. I had been sleeping on my back in exactly the same position as when I had fallen asleep just five minutes ago. Only it wasn't five minutes.

"Jesus, guys!" announced Merritt in a ferocious whisper from just inside the doorway. "It's 0545! You should have been up a half hour ago. Move your asses or you'll be in big trouble!" With that he hurriedly left the room, no doubt to check the other plebe rooms for slackards and ne'er-do-wells.

I exploded out of bed, as did Rico and Tony. I had left my gym gear where I could easily reach it. I hastily threw off my bed clothes and began dressing.

"Donny!" Tony said loudly, "Hurry up!"

Delmont rolled slowly over and looked at us. There was something in his eyes that told me he was avoiding us, reluctant to speak. He fumbled for words.

"What's the matter? Don't you feel well?" I asked, giving him an out if he wanted it. He looked at me gratefully.

"Yes," he mumbled. "I don't feel well at all. I'm not up to this running."

"I'll tell Maxwell if you want," I offered.

"Okay," he said slowly. "Please do that." He continued watching us as we hurriedly donned the necessary items. I was dressed within two minutes. Rico within five. Anthony took the entire time as he groggily got shirt and shorts mixed up, and even held his jock strap up for a long moment plainly considering what to do with the obviously alien thing.

"The other end goes in front, Tony," Rico offered, laughing.

"Huh?" Tony said in a daze, then slipped into the garment, his long bony legs tripping over the first strap in the process. Eventually he was ready, and we slipped quietly into the passageway. I turned out the lights as I left, glancing back at Delmont, who was still silently watching us from his top bunk perch. Something was definitely wrong with the guy. I winked and smiled.

"Wish us luck," I said as I hurriedly departed.

The passageway was dark with only a single bank of lights illuminating the entry to the heads. I never discovered how the passageway lights went out each night, but they did -- almost by magic. And now the corridor walls were alive with the dark and shadowy figures of my company mates as they waited nervously for Maxwell and Battle to visit pre-dawn physical activity onto our young bodies. Across the passageway I could see the Goon Room occupants nervous and restless. Merritt waved to us slightly.

"Thanks," I whispered. He nodded and checked his watch.

At 0605 the door to the squadleaders' room opened slowly and Maxwell's disheveled head emerged. He looked up the passageway at his expectant charges, groaned loudly, then disappeared inside. We plebes exchanged glances and nervous giggles and waited.

Two minutes later the two of them emerged, dressed in their own versions of gym gear. Battle was red-and-gold resplendent in a Marine Corps gym outfit. Maxwell wore a pair of old civilian YMCA shorts and a torn USNA T-shirt. Both had on sports shoes, but neither pair were the Academy issued garbage we wore. They looked us over as they walked toward the double doors, although in the dark the most they could do was count noses.

"Everybody here?" Battle asked when he came even with our room.

"No, sir," I answered. "Donny Delmont doesn't feel well. He's still in the room."

"Check that out, would you Maxie?" Battle asked. Maxwell, who still hadn't said a word or made a sound, soundlessly entered our room. He returned a minute later.

"Midshipman Delmont won't be joining us," he announced in a groggy voice.

"Okay, scum bags," Battle began, warming to the event ahead by windmilling his arms vigorously. "Let's start Plebe Year right with a little morning run. Line up in exactly the same formation we used for chow." We scurried to comply. But obviously not fast enough to suit Battle. "I said hurry, douchebags. Now we'll have to speed up the running to make up those lost seconds."

Soon we were in formation.

"Follow me," Battle said, "and be quiet in the Rotunda area." We exited through the double doors, descended the familiar broad ladder, and entered Tecumseh Court through personnel doors adjacent to the main doors of the Rotunda. We followed Battle down the wide granite steps and into Tecumseh Court proper. Once out in the center, Battle stopped us. No human beings moved on the main campus. It was quiet, almost reverent, and actually quite beautiful. I had always loved the early morning, although, truth be known, I rarely rose early enough to enjoy it. But now as I tasted the cool air and noticed the pinkening sky, I was moved. I inhaled deeply, exhilarated.

"What are you doing, O'Reilly?" Maxwell asked loudly in my ear from a position just to my rear. How he had sneaked up on me unawares I had no idea.

"Admiring the morning, sir," I answered.

Maxwell looked out at the huge trees and the silhouettes of massive academic structures. He smiled wistfully.

"It is beautiful, isn't it?" he asked almost reverently.

"Yes, sir," I answered. He turned to me with a smile.

"Do you think you'll feel that way after our little work out?" he asked sarcastically. In truth I wasn't particularly afraid of a run and some exercise. I had been in excellent condition during basketball and track seasons, and running had never been a problem for me. For the last two weeks prior to reporting in I had also been doing my own exercising. I was as ready as I could be for the physical aspects of what awaited -- or so I thought.

"Maybe, sir," I answered boldly. Wrong answer again.

"Sure you will, pal," Maxwell chuckled. Turning to Battle he said. "Tom, O'Reilly thinks this morning workout stuff is all a piece of cake."

"He does, does he?" Battle asked. "Well let's get Mr. O'Reilly up front with the top performers so I can admire his prowess." I hesitated. Maxwell looked at me and smiled.

"He probably didn't say anything -- he's very modest, you know -- but Tom was captain of Navy's plebe cross country team, and a strong member of last season's varsity. He'll be anxious to have you challenge him. Up front, O'Reilly. Don't keep Mr. Battle waiting." I walked to the front of the group, where Battle waited, smiling broadly. He looked me over, then he spoke to the group.

"Anybody else think they can keep up with me?" he asked.

"Yes, sir," came two replies. One bold challenge came from a fellow plebe I didn't know as yet. The other challenger was Merritt, who had said he was a distance runner for his track team. "Come forward, by all means, and let's see what you've got," Battle announced. Soon I was flanked by Merritt and a small classmate named John Pirelli. Pirelli looked like a runner. He had that lean, graceful look and the hungry, cadaverous eyes I always associated with "serious" runners. I decided I'd put my money on Pirelli, no matter what Battle's qualifications.

Battle and Maxwell checked the remainder of the squad for positioning. Merritt turned to me.

"I didn't know you were a runner?" he asked.

"I'm not," I replied quietly. "I ran a little track, but I never lettered; and besides, I was a sprinter not a distance man. This is all Maxwell's idea of a joke."

"I see," Merritt answered, smiling. "Well, good luck. He held out his hand to me. We shook, then did the same with Pirelli.

"Kick Battle's ass," I whispered to Pirelli. He nodded, deadly serious. I became immediately concerned about my unsmiling classmate Pirelli. I silently hoped he wasn't the type who had an overpowering need not only to compete but also to win. Those kind of zealots always scared me. Victory is fine but sometimes mere survival is sufficient.

Morning runs came to represent a subtle metaphor in military personality. Some midshipmen plodded along not doing the best they could, never really reaching for the maximum. Those classmates didn't last very long. Others ran strongly but easily, keeping up with the pack, doing whatever was expected but never pulling ahead to break the tape. Some few others ran every step intending to be the first to finish. Jim Merritt fit into that category. He wore his destiny for all to see. He would be a success no matter what he tried.

But there were others, like Pirelli, for whom winning wasn't the final goal. Mere winning wasn't enough. Their goal was setting the record, being better than anyone had ever been. These guys became perfect jet pilots or boat skippers, and believe me we can all sleep well at night knowing that the system cranks out officers like that, because if the big one ever goes down, I know for a fact that the fleet is manned by professionals who will do whatever it takes not only to win but also to annihilate whoever has the unfortunate distinction to be the enemy at that particular time. These guys are insanely dedicated, and when all is said and done, those people will usually tie their eventual success into the fact they had a Plebe Year.

Satisfied with the preparations, Battle stood beside the group, put his hands behind his back, and said. "Today we're only going to run three miles. We'll start here, head down the path along Bancroft Hall, and run on the field out to Hospital Point." As he talked he pointed down toward the Severn River, then along the river toward the bridge at the far end of Academy grounds.

"On Hospital Point we'll stop," he continued, "do some light exercises, then return to the fields below. The run out and the calisthenics there will loosen us up, so don't overdo it. On the run back, however, I want to see what you've got. We'll run in formation on the way. Step to the pace I call out. Coming back, those of you who finish in the top third can rest easy." He paused, looked at us, and laughed. "The rest will have additional exercises to do. By the end of the summer you will all be performing in the top third." While I was trying to digest the logic of that remark, he spun forward, and with a "Forward . . . March!" started us toward the entry to T-Court and the famous smiling statue.

"Left, right, left, right," he sang out as we moved. I found it easy to get the hang of marching.

When we emerged from the Court he ordered a "Right Turn, March!" and we turned almost as a group toward the river. Turning as a group was the wrong thing to do in a "right turn" maneuver. Only the front rank was supposed to turn immediately. Battle didn't care. Maxwell ran along side and herded us back into proper ranks.

"Marching starts tomorrow," he said, groaning. "Just follow the man in front of you."

We *marched* down a flight of stairs along the second wing of Bancroft Hall, and into a parking lot. Once we were all safely on the asphalt, Battle looked back and announced a "Double Time... March!" With that he picked up the pace, and we began a slow trot out onto Dewey Field, an enormous open area that sat between the academic buildings and the Severn River.

Immediately the evolution began to deteriorate. Within seconds, I could hear Maxwell yelling at classmates in the rear to keep up with the others. I heard the name "Poole" followed by profane expletives almost constantly during that going-out exercise. I kept up with the front rank without a problem. Keeping up with the group was never a problem for me.

The jog out along the river face was nice. The sun had just peeked over the eastern horizon, and the lazy Severn River was quiet and creamy in warm morning haze. The summer air, floating gently but humidly in from the water, brought exotic smells and tastes. I breathed deeply, and Merritt, running steadily next to me, nudged me and smiled. I winked in reply. As we ran effortlessly along the river, I noticed other groups of plebes and squadleaders running in other various strung-out formations along the water. Most seemed headed for the same place we were. We followed the contour of the water for almost a half mile, eventually curving back toward the campus along an inlet in the river. Halfway along the inlet was a narrow wooden bridge. This was the bridge to Hospital Point.

The bridge and I would develop an intimate familiarity during the next two years, especially in the time before I could legally have an automobile and when dating ritual required some out-of-the-way location to which to bring a young woman for the opportunity to "go-the-distance", or more accurately in my case to try desperately to go the distance but usually to end up far short of success, disturbed by intrusions or moans from other groping couples or by the occasional watch officer who got his jollies from coitus interruptus.

But so much for Hospital Point. As we moved steadily along the bridge, its wooden deck planks sang dull reverberative notes. It was a tune that old bridge must have played tens of thousands of times over the years. We had to fudge the formation, however, since there wasn't really enough room for us to go three abreast. We exited on the other side and quickly reformed whatever loose rank remained. Following Battle, we jogged to near the very opposite end of the "Point". There were several groups already in place when we arrived. Vigorous exercise regimes were strenuously ongoing, accompanied by equally vigorous verbal abuse.

"Squad, Quick Time… March!" Battle yelled, and I braced myself as we slowed. As far as I could tell there were no collisions, but I think that was more because we had spaced ourselves considerably during the run. As a matter of fact, I surreptitiously glanced back to observe our progress and found that the worse group stragglers, Poole among them, were being herded by an irate Maxwell more than 100 yards to the rear.

"Squad,...Halt!" Battle yelled. He turned and glanced rearward. A look of absolute and abject disgust played across his face as he watched the approaching mess. He looked at us.

"Anybody tired?" he asked irritated. I wasn't, Merritt wasn't, and Pirelli wouldn't admit it if he were about to have a heart attack. Behind us in the main body no one else said a word, although I could hear loud huffing and wheezing from several classmates.

"Spread out in ranks of six facing the bridge," he said indicating the Severn River Bridge just ahead. We formed the required ranks. I was in a front rank with Merritt and Pirelli. They looked loosely comfortable with the front rank notoriety; I definitely was not.

Eventually the others caught up with us and entered the back ranks. Poole wasn't the worst of the new arrivals, although he was nearly so. Immediately after stopping, one other very overweight and out of shape classmate bent over and began heaving on the grass. Battle was absolutely disgusted. He looked at us.

"Jumping Jacks! Begin!" He extended arms and legs in the classic sweeping and jumping motion and we followed him. He counted us through 50.

"Push-up position!" he next yelled. We got down on the recently-mowed grass. The smell of chlorophyll was strong. He assumed an arms-extended position I would soon learn was called "leaning rest", and looked at us expectantly. I copied his pose.

"Straighten your backs! Look at me!" he yelled. He counted us through 30, but very slowly. On my own at home I could crank out 50 push-ups with no problem. At the end of 30 slow ones, however, I was beginning to feel the strain. Merritt and Pirelli hadn't even broken a sweat.

"Get a partner! Sit-ups!" Battle yelled. He looked around the group for a partner, and naturally his eyes immediately focused on my bald, red, noggin.

"O'Reilly! Get your ass over here!" he yelled. I hastened to comply, wiping grass clippings from my hands as I approached him. I held his feet down, while, with knees deeply bent and arms behind his head, he counted us effortlessly through 50 sit-ups. Many of the group could not do 50, however, and Maxwell's voice rose to cacophony in response as he moved within the body of the company. Battle and I then switched positions, and he counted for me while I did my 50. He didn't notice the ease with which I breezed through. His focus was on the rest of the group, particularly the falterers.

After sit-ups we did what was to become for me the most hated "legal" exercise of his repertoire, a torture named "squat-thrusts". For this we stood, backs straight and hands-on-hips in anticipation, then quickly dipped down and placed our hands on the ground next to our legs. Next we thrust our legs out and back behind us so that we ended up in a leaning-rest position. Then we did the reverse, and ended up standing, hands-on-hips again. After ten of these monsters I began to tire. At 20 I was ready to stop. Luckily Battle stopped at 20.

"All right ladies," Battle said, windmilling his arms and twisting his body. "Form up. We're going to run back to Bancroft Hall the same way we came. Stay in formation until we get out onto Dewey Field, then you can open it up if you want. We'll finish even with the parking lot. Anyone who beats me," he added smiling, "can relax at breakfast. It's something we call *carry-on*. You'll eventually be willing to die for it."

I didn't know at the time what *carry-on* was exactly, but it sounded like a great idea. I intended to beat Battle if I could. We formed up in a squad. Merritt and Pirelli looked loose and ready. Battle glanced back at us and smiled, and with a "Forward... March!" we started off.

Within ten meters we had begun a double-time jog, which we continued up to and across the bridge. By the time we hit the opposite side of the bridge and I glanced rearward, the squad was already strung out over a 100 yards and the distance between the front and the last ranks was rapidly expanding. Battle then picked up the pace, running easily in front. The first four rows of plebes matched his pace.

Battle looked back and smiled. With some surprise, I realized I found the experience exhilarating. We raced in formation, our pace strong and steady and our feet slapped the ground in identical thrumps. It was heady. When we reached the Dewey Field, 200 yards separated us from the finish. Battle picked up his pace to a near sprint, and from behind several classmates broke ranks and began to pull up even with him. One lanky plebe pulled quickly ahead. Merritt and Pirelli also stretched out their pace and evened with Battle. I moved to the very outside and matched Battle. I had no intention of outdoing any classmate except to top Battle -- if I could.

At approximately 100 yards from the goal -- my high school sprint distance -- Battle and I both opened the pace. I was slightly behind to begin, but I quickly caught up and passed him. I also passed Merritt and Pirelli, and we all gained rapidly on the plebe who sprinted passed earlier. He was quickly running out of steam. Soon Battle and Pirelli both caught up with me, and Pirelli pulled slightly ahead. Battle actually smiled at me as he came even, which deflated my spirits somewhat. I wondered what he knew that I didn't. He then tried to pull in front, but as I said, I had been a sprinter -- not a particularly good one in a school district dominated by inner city black athletes -- but my best times were respectable. Battle did not pass me, although a determined Pirelli continued to nose ahead with twenty yards remaining. I could also hear the sound of several sets of feet pounding behind us. Some were gaining. I still didn't care about them. I focused on Battle. I smiled back. At 20 yards from the finish Battle began an all out sprint, and we both passed the front-running classmate, but I hadn't hit my maximum, and I kept Battle slightly in the rear even when he increased his speed to near my limit.

The end came quickly. We never caught Pirelli, but one other classmate passed me with a final burst of speed, and Merritt caught up to Battle at the wire. Battle didn't stop at the finish line, however. The tird continued to sprint. But I kept going also. We soon passed Pirelli, who shouted and began to sprint again to catch up. 10, 20, 30 yards we continued. I wouldn't let him pass. But then I began to wonder if I wasn't carrying the exercise a bit too far. I slowed ever so slightly and Battle caught up to me. The bastard was still smiling. I let him pull ahead, and he pretended to break a finish tape several yards ahead of me. I copied his effort.

He slowed considerably, threw his hands into the air in a mock victory signal, and rounded his finish, whooping and beaming broadly at me, arms still aloft. I tried to look more exhausted than I was as he passed me jogging slowly back toward the finish line. I turned and started back, not as quickly. On the way we passed Pirelli, who was retching on the grass. He looked up at us with a "that-wasn't-fair" expression. Battle laughed. I shrugged and continued my trudge.

Despite our extra sprint and our slow return, more than a third of the squad still hadn't ended when we returned to the imaginary finish line, although I did notice both Ramsey and Polk recovering. Neither seemed particularly strained. Some of my classmates were overtly sick, however. Many of the others were bent over, hands-on knees, gasping for air. Battle looked at them all with a prideful disgust. I was also winded, but I had drawn deep breaths on the way back, so I didn't feel the need for any public display of my exhaustion. As I came to the finish line I could hear Maxwell yelling loudly to the approaching final group of seven classmates, which included Poole and to my surprise also contained Grizwald.

"Any of you who don't beat me will have hell to pay!" There was no way most of the final seven could finish without slowing to a near walk, much less beat Maxwell. He knew that. Only one of the group could muster a semi-sprint, but Maxwell would not let him win. The group finished in a bedraggled and pathetic mess.

As they passed among us I watched their faces. "Agony" would be the operative word for what I saw. These guys had obviously not led an athletic existence to this point, and beginning their new lives with a three-mile sprint seemed too much for them to handle. All except for Poole, that is. I saw in his eyes, perched behind the pain, a kind of grim determination. He wasn't the fastest of the group by a long shot, but he wasn't the slowest either, and the fact that he had finished at all was obviously a source of pride to him.

His pridefulness was short-lived however.

"None of you scum sucking bastards will last a week here!" Maxwell screamed at the last finishers. "You're pussies! You're worthless! You're a disgrace to this institution! Go home to your mommys now before the training gets really tough!"

Battle ordered us into formation again, and we complied. When we were ready he turned and came down the line.

"Who beat me to the finish?" he asked. Pirelli, Merritt and one other plebe raised their hands instantly. I also raised mine, but not so quickly. "You four, huh?" he asked. He looked at Pirelli. "You were number one weren't you?" he asked.

"Yes, sir!" Pirelli answered proudly.

"Well how come you quit so early, pussy?" Battle announced. Pirelli started to answer, but Battle became instantly angry.

"Do you have something to say to me, asshole?" he asked moving in front of Pirelli.

Pirelli swallowed, then answered. "No, sir!"

"Good!" Battle stated. Then he looked at the group. "The only one who had the guts to go the distance with me was O'Reilly here. Right, Kevin?" he asked smiling and putting a hand on my shoulder.

"Yes, sir!" I answered loudly.

"That's pretty impressive for a scum bag like you," Maxwell said as he stood beside Battle.

"Thank you. sir!" I answered, again loudly. I had discovered instinctively that noise is the bastion of military discipline. From the first day onward, whenever I was asked a question by an upperclassman, even if I didn't know the answer, I always answered as loudly as I could. It seemed to satisfy some primal leadership need. Battle gripped my shoulder tightly.

"But who actually won the final sprint, O'Reilly?" he asked so that everyone could hear.

"You kicked my ass, sir!" I replied in a voice that must have carried all the way back to Massachusetts.

"Damn right I did!" Battle answered proudly. He dropped his hand and addressed the group. "The four douchebags who finished ahead of me today will be granted carry-on for the breakfast meal. O'Reilly here can have carry-on for noon meal too. We're going to play this carry-on game every day but not necessarily for every exercise and training period. Sometimes we will announce when the contest is on; sometimes we won't. When we don't, it's up to you to guess correctly." He turned toward the front of the group. "Let's eat!" he announced, and we started back to Bancroft Hall.

We returned to our rooms and immediately began showering and changing. Delmont was not in his rack. Rico shook my hand once we were inside.

"That was great, redhead" he said enviously. "I came a scrot hair from beating him myself. If this carry-on shit seems like a good deal, I may join the ranks of victors tomorrow."

"I wonder where Delmont is?" I asked no one in particular.

"Probably in the head," a very tired looking Grizwald answered.

"We won't see him again," Rico stated prophetically. He was right. Grizwald looked troubled. But we didn't have any time to worry. Our immediate need was remembering how to dress in white works.

There are three meal-time perspectives for a plebe at Annapolis. The first is the standard "brace-up" "end-of-your-chair" "eyes-in-the-boat" experience that is just one small step away from living in hell. I certainly had my share of those meals. The second, and far more desirable, meal-time is an almost human "carry-on" meal, where most of the pressures are relaxed. I had a few of these meals, mostly later in the long year when many of the psychological pressures had been relaxed and the upper-class were more interested in graduating or summer cruises than harassing plebes.

The third option, which is considered plebe paradise, is athletic training tables where plebes are insulated from the company and actually protected from harm by their fellow jocks. I had a brief shot at paradise while I was desperately trying to ensure a spot on the plebe basketball team. I fell short of the promised land.

We marched to the Mess Hall following the same path we had yesterday, and proceeded to our places. After Battle dismissed us, I joined the general mad scramble to get a seat at the third and still leaderless, table. I was not successful, but I did manage a seat near the far end of Maxwell's table. He didn't ask for me by name this time.

Once we had all selected chairs, Battle announced cheerily, "Plebes, Brace-up!" I pulled my chin in and waited. We stood rigidly while announcements were made. At the call of "Brigade Seats" from the midshipman at the microphone, both Maxwell and Battle sat down. We waited. They looked us over. Finally Maxwell said, "Plebes. Seats!" and we complied. Battle then came around to each table and pontifically touched the select four on the shoulders and intoned a solemn "carry-on." I was the final honoree.

I cautiously looked around the table. At the head, Maxwell smiled at me. One of my classmates also gave a curious glance around, but Maxwell saw him.

"What's your name, mister!" he asked loudly.

"Steinway, sir," he answered, dipping his head slightly and swallowing loudly. Ronald Steinway was a slight, pallid boy, no more than five feet four inches tall. He had pale blue eyes that darted around the table nervously as Maxwell verbally accosted him. He also had an enormously protruding Adam's apple, the largest I had ever seen.

"Steinway, do you know what it means to get your eyes in the boat?" Maxwell asked.

"To stare straight ahead, sir," Steinway timidly answered.

"Then do it, damn it!" Maxwell yelled. Steinway centered his eyes for a moment, but his head vibrated in a slight spasm, and I could see his eyes wavering as if some psychic pressure was forcing his view to one side or another. No way was he going to be able to hold that pose very long.

"All right, everyone," Maxwell continued. "I want you all to begin by sitting on the last three inches of your chairs." My classmates and I scurried to comply. "Not the dummies with carry-on," Maxwell continued looking at me. "But you lazy assholes better observe closely, because your turn is coming very soon." I slid back against the back of my chair and watched.

"Straighten your backs!" Maxwell yelled. "Eyes in the boat! Brace up, god-damn it!" I could see my classmates straining to comply. As I found out that evening, it takes a bit of coordination to successfully complete an Annapolis plebe meal of the *braced* variety. For one thing sitting on the last three inches of a chair is no easy matter.

"I said the last three inches, Poole!" Maxwell yelled at poor Tommy, whom he had personally selected to sit permanently on his left hand side. Poole slid down farther toward the end of his chair.

"Three inches, not twelve!" Maxwell yelled again. He rose and came around behind Poole. Putting a finger on the chair seat behind Poole's ample rear to indicate position, he said, "Stand up, Poole!" Poole stood. Maxwell then took a small ruler he had carried in his hat, and measured the distance from the end of the chair to his finger.

"Four stinking inches, Poole. Try harder! All of you try harder!" he yelled. "Straighten those backs!" Plebes slid out precariously and firmed up their spines.

Maxwell then came around the table, and one by one jiggled the chairs. Rico Guevarra, who was sitting next to me, toppled onto the floor when Maxwell moved his chair.
"What's your name?" Maxwell asked.

"Guevarra, sir!" Rico answered.

"Good job! Sit down, Guevarra. Repeat exactly what you just did to perch on the edge." Maxwell faced the group. "That's what it means to sit on the last three inches, gentlemen. You should be so close to the edge that any motion knocks your ass on the deck. That's what I want to see from now on. Now get out on those final three inches!" He returned to his place as my classmates squinched and squirmed their bottoms out to the brink of collapse.

Maxwell reseated himself, then looked around the table with sadistic satisfaction. His eyes locked on mine. He smiled.

"God I love this," he said, laughing slightly. To the table in general he said, "Brace up! Eyes in the Boat!"

"Now," he continued, "about the meal. Plebes ensure that all upper class select their portions first, starting with the seniors who are 'first class' midshipmen, and who usually sit together at the bow of the table where I am. Next come the juniors who are *second class* midshipmen or secondos. That's what Battle and I are, by the way. We usually sit at the stern. The sophomores are called *youngsters,* and they sit along the sides with the plebes, get the food next. Plebes, being lower than pond scum, pick last." He sat back smugly. "Serve the food!"

Plebes reached diligently for the bread and scrambled eggs, and in short order it appeared in front of Maxwell.

"You're going to have to be a lot faster than that, " he said. "If you want to eat, that is." He picked a roll and scooped eggs onto his plate, then he handed the plates to the plebe on his right. The plebe held the plates, unsure what to do. Maxwell looked at him.

"Are all the upper class at this table served the bread and eggs?" he asked sarcastically.

"Yes, sir," my classmate answered cautiously.

"Who eats after the upper class?" Maxwell asked.

"Plebes, sir," came the response.

"Are you a plebe?"

"Yes, sir."

"Then begin eating for Christ's sake," Maxwell yelled, "or we'll never get through the meal!" My classmate quickly selected a roll and passed the bowl, then dumped a load of eggs on his plate. Maxwell, watching carefully, became instantly angry. He slammed his hands down on the tabletop, causing silverware to hop into the air and come tinkling to rest. He jumped up from his seat, and leaned across the table toward the classmate.

"You scum sucking pig!" Maxwell yelled. The plebe was startled into complete silence by Maxwell's violence. His mouth gaped open in astonishment. "How many of your classmates are there at this table?" Maxwell asked loudly.

The plebe started to look around, thought better of it and asked, "Request permission to count them, sir."

"Go ahead, shit-for-brains, count," Maxwell growled. The plebe turned his head, quickly added up the total and turned to Maxwell.

"Nine, sir!" he announced.

"Look at your plate, mister," Maxwell continued, still angry. "Do you remember how much egg was in the bowl when you served yourself?"

"Approximately, sir," the plebe answered.

"Well," Maxwell said, "if everybody takes an egg portion as large as you just did, how much will remain for your classmates at the other end of the table?" The plebe quickly did a mental calculation.

Sheepishly, he replied, "Nothing, sir."

Maxwell exploded again. "You're god-damn right, nothing! If there's one thing that will not be tolerated from anybody at any table -- and that goes for firsties, secondos, and youngsters as well as plebes -- it's hogging more food than you deserve. *Everybody* gets an equal portion. And you had better get used to figuring out exactly how much to take, because you'll get your young ass reamed if you ever do that again. Is that understood?" The plebe nodded acknowledgment.

"I didn't hear that answer, mister" Maxwell said loudly and threateningly.

"Yes, sir! I understand, sir!" the plebe yelled.

Maxwell looked at the rest of the occupants of the table.

"Do all of you understand that?" he asked. A chorus of "Yes, sirs," boomed in response.

"Sure, pal," Maxwell said as he sat. "Continue the meal."

Almost immediately Filipino stewards brought forward large stainless steel trays from the serving carts in the middle of the center aisle. The trays contained plates of bacon, potatoes, and pancakes. They presented them to the plebes at the sides of each table. Rico reached out quickly and grabbed the plates one-at-a-time and passed them hurriedly toward Maxwell, and the process of pass-and-serve began again. Soon the rolls and eggs reached me, and I put a portion on my plate. I did the same with the other food a minute later. I looked around. No one had eaten as yet, afraid to make some ritualistic error. It was a good thing we waited.

"Okay, douchebags," Maxwell said. "Look at me for a moment, but do not relax your posture." Everyone turned. He picked up his fork. "This is what it means to eat a *square meal* at Annapolis. Watch closely." He forked a small portion of his potato and looked at us. "When you eat, you will only eat in small portions. The food, however, will not travel by the most direct route from plate to stomach. Instead you will lift the fork or spoon vertically until it is exactly even with your jaw." He picked up his fork to demonstrate.

"Then you will square the corner and bring the utensil horizontally to your mouth," he continued, and again he demonstrated in a swift motion. "Put your utensil on your plate while you are chewing, but do not dawdle. Chew your food quickly, swallow, then get another bite." He paused, then added further, "And do all this braced, on the ends of your chairs, and eyes where, Poole?"

"In the boat, sir!" Poole answered.

"Sure, pal," Maxwell said, smiling. "You may begin eating."

We plebes dove into the meal with gusto, and soon small elevator utensils were lifting tiny portions of egg and meat tentatively into the air to eager young mouths. During plebe year, mealtime was a focus of concentrated tension and abject terror for me. I hated almost every moment I spent at the Company tables, constantly waiting for the next question or demand. And I wasn't especially picked on.

After a minute, and once the table had settled into an eating routine, Maxwell put down his fork and said, "Steinway?" I looked across at Ronald. He had just ingested a bite of bacon, and his fork was still in his mouth when the question came.

"Yes, sir," he answered, his fork poised in the air, food unchewed in his mouth, and consciously struggling to keep his eyes from leaping in the direction of the question.

"Damn it, Steinway," Maxwell said. "Didn't your mother tell you not to talk with your mouth full?" Ronald took a moment to consider, and quickly began chewing his bacon.

"Three-chews-and-a-swallow, Steinway," Maxwell announced. Ronald nodded, his jaws worked like crazy. After almost 15 chews, he swallowed vigorously. I watched his Adam's apple bob like a fishing float when the line is struck by a big one.

"Yes, sir?" he asked.

"Put your God dammed fork down, Steinway!" Maxwell said loudly. Ronald complied quickly. "Put your hands in your lap, Steinway. And when I say three-chews-and-a-swallow, that's exactly what I mean. You chew the food three times, and send whatever's left in your mouth on its way to your miserable stomach." While Ronald readied himself, Maxwell addressed the table. "That's how to properly answer an upper-class question during meals. Is that understood?" There followed a moment of intense action as the remaining 10 plebes rushed to swallow, put forks down, and place hands on laps.

"Yes, sir," came the chorus moments later.

"Good," Maxwell said. "Begin eating. Steinway?"

"Yes, sir."

"How's the cow?"

Steinway, along with the rest of us, was instantly confused. "Excuse me, sir?" he asked.

"How's the cow, Steinway?" Maxwell repeated. Steinway thought furiously. Soon I could see a light of inspiration come on in his head.

"I'll find out, sir!" he announced with a smugness.

"Good, Steinway," Maxwell said, "You do that! Before evening meal." He looked around. "All of you do that by evening meal," he said.

Plebes scurried to swallow, put utensils and hands down, and answer with "Aye, aye, sir!"

"Plebe on Steinway's right," Maxwell continued. "What's your name again?"

Maxwell had selected Wesley Lamont who was seated directly across from me. Wess hurriedly prepared himself, then answered.

"Wesley Lamont, sir," in his precise accent. It might have been because of the contrast with his dark complexion, or maybe it was genetic or some magic ingredient in the island diet -- hell, maybe his uncle was an orthodontist -- but whatever it was, I noticed almost immediately that Wesley Lamont had the straightest, whitest teeth I had ever seen. They actually sparkled in his mouth as he talked.

But it wasn't only his teeth that were perfect. His face was as smooth as silk. There were no ravages of the usual teenage fight-to-the-death with acne, no moles, no blemishes, no unusual protrusions or even the slightest disfigurement. It also didn't even appear that he needed to shave, or if he did, the process didn't irritate his skin the way it did my sensitive epidermis. Even his hair -- what there was of it, anyway -- was perfectly centered and without irregularity on his dark head. He certainly didn't look at all like most of the African Americans I had known in Boston. In fact he was so perfect I envied him. I pictured him in a native loincloth loitering on a white shady beach in the shade of a tall palm. He was smiling with a dazzling display of dentition and several young lovely women rushed to please him. He accepted the attention. It probably was natural for him. It sure had never happened for me.

"Lamont," Maxwell said, "What time is it?"

The Mess Hall had any number of clocks, and Maxwell wore a black-strapped diver's watch prominently on his left wrist. The question was obviously a trick one. Lamont was ready, however. He smiled, sparkling.

"Sir," he said intoning in a lyrical sing-song voice which immediately started me thinking, Christ, the bastard is also probably a gifted singer. "I am greatly embarrassed and deeply humiliated that due to circumstances beyond my control, the inner workings and hidden mechanisms of my chronometer are in such in accord with the great sidereal movement with which time is generally reckoned that I cannot with any degree of accuracy state the correct time sire. But without fear of being too greatly in error, I will state that it is about 0721, and fifteen seconds, sir!"

What the hell was that about, I wondered? His answer certainly wasn't on the approved-response list. I could tell that everyone at the table was flabbergasted -- at least we plebes were.

Maxwell, however, beamed. "Well done, Lamont! You did your homework." he paused, considering. "Shit, Lamont, you can carry-on for the rest of this meal." Lamont grinned directly at me and relaxed. Maxwell addressed the table, still smiling.

"What Lamont just did, gentlemen, was to show unusual initiative. He memorized one of the plebe rates without being told. I like that in a plebe. It's one of the traits you had all better develop dammed quickly or else you'll be out on your sissy asses before you know it. And, Lamont?" he continued, his smile gone.

"Yes, sir!" Lamont answered.

"Don't get cocky, pal. There's a lot of Plebe Summer remaining."

"Yes, sir," Lamont answered, winking surreptitiously at me.

Maxwell looked around at us, checking chins and eyes and chairs and backs with a quick sweep of his vision. He watched amused as my classmates lifted and shoveled tiny morsels of food at ninety degree angles into their waiting mouths. It was a ridiculous sight, and I wondered how Polk was taking it. I looked around but he must have been sitting at the table behind me; because I couldn't see him.

Because of the three-chews-and-a-swallow rule, the bites we took were much smaller than any of us were used to. Food had to be eaten quickly; otherwise the meal would be over and a gnawing hunger would remain. I found that out during the first week and quickly adjusted. A square mea' was therefore also a rapid one, and some of my classmates, Ramsey among them, moved food from plate to palate so quickly as to be almost a blur of motion. Maxwell watched it all briefly. Satisfied that all was relatively well, he diverted his attention to his own food. Soon a general quiet descended over the table. Not so at other tables nearby, however. The process of plebe indoctrination continued unabated in other companies, and the noise of screaming and panicked response was continuous.

There is no such thing as a leisurely meal at Annapolis. The time the staff announced "Brigade Seats" to when the Mess Hall emptied usually encompassed a period of less than forty minutes. Breakfast, the most hasty of the meals at 30 minutes, continued rapidly and included a breakfast desert of ice cream, which I found extremely unusual but which I never once complained about in four years.

Twenty minutes into the meal Rico Guevarra reached across the table, picked up a plate that had previously held potatoes, and lifted it into the air. I had seen other plebes around the Mess Hall do the same thing, but no one had asked Rico to order seconds. When I looked at his plate I noticed that he still had food waiting to be consumed, so I was initially puzzled.

"Guevarra, isn't it?" Maxwell asked him.

"Yes, sir!" Rico answered, assuming a picture perfect brace position.

"Why are you holding that plate up?" Maxwell asked.

"Sir, I thought you might like some more potatoes," he answered.

"How did you know I needed more potatoes?" Maxwell asked, his voice narrowing slightly. I could see where this was leading, and so could Rico. He obviously couldn't admit that his eyes had wandered. He thought quickly.

"I just assumed that since most of my classmates were finished, you would be too, sir," he answered. It was not the most believable of answers, and Maxwell didn't buy it.

"Sure, pal," he said skeptically, drawing the statement out in a nasal whine. He turned to Tommy.

"Poole," he said. "Go down there and give Guevarra a punch on the arm."

"Excuse me, sir?" Tommy asked, puzzled.

"Go punch Guevarra on the arm. Hurry up!" Maxwell ordered. Poole rose slowly and moved to a position adjacent to Guevarra. He poked him slightly on the upper arm.

"Did that hurt, Guevarra?" Maxwell asked.

"No, sir!" Rico shouted.

"Hit him again, Poole! Harder!" Maxwell ordered.

Tommy hit Rico again, slightly harder. He pretended to put his weight behind the punch, however, and it appeared that he had really belted Rico, but he actually pulled the punch at the end of his thrust. Rico rocked to one side in response.

"Did that hurt, Guevarra?" Maxwell asked.

"Yes, sir," Rico lied.

"Sure, pal," Maxwell replied skeptically. "From now on all of you better not order extra food unless you yourself are still hungry. And don't ask for anything you can't eat, understood?"

We blurted out a general "Yes, sir!"

"As for taking care of me -- my friend Poole here . . ." He reached over and put a hand on Tommy's shoulder, "and whoever sits in the other chair," -- he indicated the chair on his right -- "will see that I eat properly and well. Right, Poole?" he said turning to Tommy.

"Yes, sir!" Tommy answered enthusiastically.

"Why did you hit Guevarra, Poole?" Maxwell asked in a serious-sounding voice. Tommy was confused by this question.

"Because you asked me to, sir," he responded tentatively.

"No, Poole, you weenie!" Maxwell shouted. "You hit Guevarra because he tried to steal your job. It's your responsibility to keep me fed, Poole, and you have to show your classmates that you're willing to fight for that privilege."

Maxwell took his hand away from Tommy's shoulder. "Now, Poole, why did Guevarra ask for more food?" he asked. Tommy looked at Maxwell's plate.

"Because your plate is empty, sir?" he asked questioningly.

"You're god-damn right it is!" Maxwell exploded. "How dare you let a classmate cover for you like that! You should be ashamed of yourself, you momma's puke. Apologize to Guevarra for hitting him!" Tommy took a breath, obviously as confused as the rest of us.

"Sorry, Rico!" Tommy announced.

"You don't address your buddies by first name while you are braced, Poole!" Maxwell blurted, leaning over toward Tommy. "Say "classmate" from now on in public."

"Aye, aye, sir!" Tommy responded. He paused. "Sorry classmate!"

"Now, Poole, since you shirked your duties and let a classmate be punished for your error, I want you to get down on the floor between the tables and give me twenty push-ups. Hurry up!" Tommy rose and moved to a position behind me. As Poole prepared for his latest torture, I could see Maxwell looking nervously at the head table. It seemed from his expression that maybe exercises of the Mess Hall floor were an aspect of training he was supposed to avoid.

Tommy slowly bent over and knelt on the hard floor, still obviously sore from the morning exercises. He assumed leaning-rest and began trying to comply with Maxwell's request.

"Count them out, Poole. I can't see you from here," Maxwell requested.

Tommy strained through a "One, sir," and a "Two, sir," and a "Three, sir" before faltering. Number four took several seconds.

"Four!" Maxwell exploded. "That's all you can do? Four?" By this time Poole finished the next.

"Five, sir!" he said, clearly straining.

"Poole you are the biggest pussy I have ever seen. I am disgusted by your effeminate body and your momma's boy attitude. Do you want to be a man some day, Poole?" Maxwell asked. He didn't wait for an answer. "Get back here and sit down." Tommy slowly rose to his knees. I looked back at him in sympathy. His eyes met mine then he quickly looked away ashamed.

"O'Reilly," Maxwell asked, noticing that Tommy and I had exchanged glances. "Aren't you disgusted by your classmate Poole?"

What a question? "No sir," I answered, thinking that to be the most correct of several unattractive responses.

"You're not!" Maxwell yelled. "You're a liar, O'Reilly! How can you not be disgusted? Poole is the saddest excuse for a human being I have ever seen. Give me 20 for lying, O'Reilly."

"Aye, aye, sir!" I yelled. I jumped up from the table and moved quickly to a position behind my seat. I hurried into leaning-rest on the cold deck and began quickly cranking out push-ups.

"One, sir!" I yelled especially loudly. "Two, sir! Three, sir!" I could hear Maxwell rise quickly and come around to the aisle to watch. "Eight, sir! Nine, sir!"

"Not so loud, O'Reilly!" Maxwell whispered fiercely, glancing toward the head table.

"Aye, aye, sir!" I yelled even louder, then toned down the noise for the remainder of the push-ups. At 20 I stopped. Maxwell still watched from the head of the aisle.

"One more to Beat Army!" he demanded.

"Aye, aye, sir!" I responded. I did a final push-up and added a "Beat Army, sir!"

"Okay, O'Reilly. Sit back down," he ordered. I complied. Maxwell returned to his seat. "Anybody else not personally disgusted by your classmate Poole?" he asked the table.

A general quiet followed for several seconds. Then Rico and John Pirelli blurted almost simultaneous "Me, sirs!", followed almost immediately by Lamont. Maxwell looked at them and smiled wickedly.

"Twenty! All three of you!" Rico, Wess, and John jumped up simultaneously and began push-ups, including one to "Beat Army". Maxwell didn't watch them. Soon they had returned to their seats. A full twenty seconds passed.

Most of us had hastily returned to eating, when Steinway blurted out a tentative "Me, sir."

Maxwell looked up from his ice cream. "What, Steinway?"

Ronald took a deep swallow. "I'm not disgusted by classmate Poole, sir," he said.

"Are you shitting me, Steinway? Why the hell didn't you answer with the rest of your brave classmates?"

"Sorry, sir. I'll find out, sir" Steinway answered.

"You, are an idiot, Steinway!" Maxwell blurted shaking his head. "Poole's probably disgusted with you." Steinway sat expectantly, but Maxwell returned to his ice cream.

Almost immediately Battle and his table passed beside us on their way to the center passageway. Maxwell took a final scoop of ice cream and put down his spoon.

"Time and tide wait for no man, gentlemen," he said dropping a piece of nautical wisdom on us. "Meal's over. Let's get moving." We rose to leave while Battle rousted the remaining table. Once we had formed in the center Battle looked us over.

"Those of you who fought for and won seats on the leaderless table will sit at my table for noon meal and at Maxie's for evening meal," he announced with a smile. So much for that small piece of refuge.

"All except my friend Poole," Maxwell continued, smiling. "We've become such good buddies that I can't bear to be parted from him. Right, Poole?"

"Yes, sir!" Tommy answered not altogether enthusiastically. Maxwell and Battle laughed loudly at Tommy's discomfort. "Forward . . . March!" Battle commanded.

When we returned to the Company area Maxwell announced, "Your next evolution is a lecture by the Commandant of Midshipmen, Captain Mack Hallahan, in Mahan Hall at 0900. We will leave here at zero-eight-forty-five, and we will be marching, God help us." He looked at his watch. "You have precisely 20 minutes to clean up whatever messes you've made and return to this exact spot. Be here on time. Dismissed!"

We scurried to our rooms, chopping and squaring corners on the way. As we did, the slip-slap sounds of our new black shoes shuffling on the tile deck, and the booming yells of "Beat Army, sir" as we sharply turned corners echoed in the previously quiet passageway.

Entering our room, I paused just inside the door looking toward Delmont's bed. Guevarra and Grizwald almost collided with me as they entered. They also stopped and stared speechless. Delmont's rack was devoid of bedding. His desk was bare. And I was certain that if we opened his locker, we would find it empty. Delmont was gone. None of us ever saw or heard from him again. I strained for a moment to remember what he looked like, or what he had said or done that first -- and last -- day, but I had difficulty doing so. Despite the fact that we had not exchanged more than ten words with Delmont, I felt a loss at his passing. It seemed almost as if he had died. (It was weird!)

"Shit!" I said to no one in particular.

"Do you think he's gone for good?" asked an incredulous Grizwald.

"Of course he's gone for good," answered Rico with a touch of sarcasm. "Do you think he decided on his own to move to another Company or maybe to a room down the passageway?" Tony stared at Rico but didn't say anything. I could understand Tony's reluctance to admit that Donny had quit after only one day. His departure was like a blaring alarm to each of us. If he could leave, then any of us could.

Silently we straightened our things, considering our own mortality. So far I didn't have any problem with what had transpired. I could handle the physical aspects of the training without too much trouble -- as long as I avoided those damn squat-thrusts -- and the emotional pressure hadn't been more than I had experienced on the basketball court or avoiding groups of hostile marauding rivals on my way home from school or the movies. Of course there were only two squadleaders now and more than 30 of us plebes to divert their attention, and guys like Poole and Steinway took up a large portion of their focus. What would happen when the Brigade returned was another matter. But, hell, so far it wasn't so bad. Why would anyone quit? Did they have some precognitive foreknowledge I lacked?

I revived from my reverie and found myself staring out the window. Rico was watching me from across the room.

"No big deal!" he said quietly but firmly. When I looked at him quizzically, he added, "This Delmont thing. No big deal! He didn't like it here and decided to leave. Let him go. It's none of your concern. Worry about O'Reilly. I know I'm taking care of Guevarra first." I nodded and returned to my cleanup.

I decided that my skivvies needed refolding, and I worked on them to what I considered perfection.

"No need to do that," Rico offered from across the room. I had wondered why he was so cavalier about his own locker.

"Why not?" I asked.

"This is a training exercise," he answered. "It doesn't matter a fart in a windstorm how good you make your locker look. They're just gonna come around, call it crap, knock everything on the floor, and make you do it over. After a couple weeks they'll slack off. Then you can store the skivvies with the skid marks on the outside and they won't care. Once they finish their little game I'll fold it all perfectly."

What Rico said made strange and perfect sense to me, but I still devoted some extra attention to the creases in my undershirts. Maybe I'm stupid. Maybe I'm a closet perfectionist. Maybe I have an underwear fetish. Whatever the reason, I've always been orderly, and at Annapolis I enjoyed the neat perfection of a well-organized closet and the comfort of an organized life. It's something that carried over into my later life and career.

We chopped out into the passageway with two minutes to spare. Most of our company-mates were waiting.

"Delmont is gone," I whispered to Merritt as I passed him. He nodded sagely. A minute later Maxwell and Battle approached.

Battle stood near the center of the Company, and, hands-behind-back, he announced in a smug voice, "It is with deep regret that I wish to inform you that your classmate Donald F. Delmont is now an ex-classmate. Mr. Delmont is one of more than 50 of your group that did not make it through the first twenty-four hours. Adding that to the 100 or so that quit yesterday or didn't even show up, and you can see that your class is dropping like flies. You've been decimated in a classical sense. But don't worry, (he added, with a smirk) I guarantee that there are still many of you standing here that will not be here at the end of the summer. As a matter of fact, most of the future dropouts already know who they are.

"Classmate Maxwell and I would like to think that we will provide the impetus for many eventual decisions to quit this institution. It's our job this summer, and we're proud of what we do. But it's also a waste of our precious time, so for those of you on the fence about staying here, please save us the trouble of running you out. If you know you aren't suited to the lifestyle, quit now." He paused and looked at us more informally. Then he smiled.

"You know," he continued, "Maxie and I were discussing the prospects of this group just a minute ago. We've made a list of ten of you we doubt will be here long, and certainly won't make it through the year. Of course, it wouldn't be proper for us to tell you whose names are on the list, but I can say that the seven slackards from this morning who couldn't even run a mile without crying for their mommies figured prominently in our discussion." He reverted to his military pose.

"Okay gentlemen. We're going to be going out into public, and that means that we'll be observed. It also means that any screw-ups will reflect badly on Maxie and me. So you're just not going to screw up. Is that understood?"

"Yes, sir!"

"Good," he continued. "I've already mentally performed the exercise of getting from here to Mahan Hall and returning, so I know it can be done without too much preparation, but here's what I want." He stopped and turned toward the double doors and used his arm to point in theoretical directions. With each individual instruction he added emphasis with a wave or chop of his arm. "We're going to exit Bancroft Hall the same way we did this morning. Then we'll form up in T-Court facing the statue of Tecumseh. I will lead the group. We'll march in step straight down the Stribling Walk toward Mahan Hall. Mr. Maxwell will count cadence. At the end of Stribling by the Macedonian Monument, we'll turn left. For that complicated maneuver (he added sarcastically) I'll order a 'Left turn, March!'" He looked at us closely.

"I'll give the command on the left foot. In order to turn port, we'll pivot on our right feet in two consecutive steps, just like squaring a corner. However," he said loudly, "for a left or right turn in formation we do not all turn together. Instead only the front most rank will pivot on the first right foot after the command. All other ranks will continue straight ahead until it is their time to turn. The second rank will pivot on the next right foot after the first rank. The third rank will pivot on the third right foot and so on." He moved to the front of the formation.

"I want this first rank of midshipmen to turn around so that you face in the opposite direction," he said. I was in that rank. We turned. "Now I want you to walk forward 30 paces, stop, and turn to face me." We marched forward and turned as instructed.

"Good," he said when we had finished. "Now, when I give the order I want you to march forward until you come to me. When you get here I'll order a left turn, and you will do a two-step pivot one-after-the-other into this room." He pointed to my room which happened to be exactly even with him and on our port side.

"Remember, only one person pivots at a time." He looked at us, shook his head slightly, then barked, "Squad... Forward...March!"

We began well enough, heading straight toward the group. Maxwell sang out the "Left, right" cadence we would all come to hate. As we approached Battle's position, he took a breath and barked, "Squad...Left Turn...March!" Chaos ensued.

Being tall and therefore near the front rank, I didn't have a view of everything that happened, but I could hear the immediate slap-skid sound of two classmates behind me turning prematurely. How they decided to turn early was beyond me, but they weren't the only screw ups. Two people in front, Anthony Grizwald tried to pivot on his left foot and almost fell over as he tried to compensate for the fact that his feet became hopelessly crossed and his body leaned to the port side in response to the command. He stumbled, recovered, and took two large steps to bring himself back into formation. I could also hear similar shuffling behind me as the two other miscreants hurried back into line.

I had lost count of steps by the time my turn came. It didn't matter. Battle was furious at our confusion. He had left his position at the front and run to a place behind me to scream at one of my classmates. I glanced at the doorway, timed my pivot, and followed the plebe in front. We entered the room without any trouble. Grizwald had apparently kicked his left calf with his opposite foot during the confusion, and he hobbled to his deck to nurse the proto-bruise. The other three plebes stood facing the door waiting for the wrath of Battle to descend.

Maxwell came over to the doorway after the final squad member had entered. He was smiling and looking down the passageway. Outside we could hear Battle screaming insanely at someone. The invective was both creative and unprintable. Rico Guevarra, who had followed me in, smiled at me from across the room. I raised my eyebrows in astonishment. He smiled again.

"Okay douchebags," Maxwell said, jerking his thumb over his shoulder, "out in the passageway. Now!" We reluctantly chopped outside and returned to the formation. Battle had the two clumsy classmates braced against the bulkhead. His face was contorted and red with effort. As he screamed, turning first one way then the other to confront the plebes, I could see tiny globs of spittle fly from his mouth. Several struck the unfortunate plebes, one of whom was Tony Delvecchio, in their fresh young faces. I cringed at the thought of this unexpected salival shower. I could see Tony flinch as each ejaculated bubble-glob arched its way toward him. He was desperate to leap aside before the slobbery impacts, but discretion kept him firmly glued in place, albeit wetly.

Battle inserted Grizwald and the two smaller classmates into the middle rank of the Company on the theory that they would be protected from their own coordinational stupidity. He then patiently explained the theory of the "Right Turn", which was the mirror opposite of the "Left Turn" maneuver. He used the far right rank to demonstrate, and either that group was far superior to mine in a physically coordinated way, or fear of reprisal is a mighty powerful tool. They performed the maneuver with only minor problems.

So now we could do the turning necessary to get to the lecture, sort of, but it was too late to worry if we couldn't. Battle quickly marched us out of Bancroft Hall and into T-Court. Since there were many visitors gawking at us, he must have felt verbally restrained. But before he started us forward on our way to destiny, Battle looked at us. He didn't say anything. He didn't give any demonstrative hand signs. He didn't even spit. He merely looked, hard and long, and every one of us knew that whoever screwed up on this march had better fling himself quickly off the Chesapeake Bay Bridge. His chances of survival would be better in the Bay.

We started. I discovered immediately that Battle was a *hot dog* squad leader. He strutted, chest puffed out twice its normal size with his head, beak and all, poised slightly skyward. If it wasn't for the fact that Maxwell was watching us like a hawk, we might have laughed at the spectacle of Battle in command.

The straight ahead part came off without a problem. As we marched down the long, broad, brick paved, tree-covered lane we were observed by several groups of tourists who ogled impressively at us. One group of three young ladies gave us the eye in a purely physical way, and I was elated. Although 1967 was supposed to be centered in the very heart of the sexual revolution, and I had heard that the motto of all red-blooded college students was "Free love for all", somehow the Age of Aquarius had bypassed the ethnic neighborhood where I grew up. Girls in South Boston still didn't even allow groping on the first date -- sometimes never -- and sex was a fantasy that had altogether eluded my fervent grasp to that point.

I also found my own chest expanding as we passed the girls. They cheered us, and I felt special. But then again they also cheered every group of plebes that passed -- all thirty-six Companies.

The test of the left and right turns came and passed without incident. The group mentality prevailed, and we turned more or less correctly, although I watched as Ramsey surreptitiously grabbed Grizwald from his position on the right side and held him firmly in place until it was time to turn. Soon we entered Mahan Hall and made our way to a row of seats prepared for us. Guess which row? Twenty-third of course. Sitting, I noticed an interesting contrast. I assume that every Company started with the same number of plebe novitiates; however, some of the Companies had significantly fewer members than we had. Several rows in front of us in what must have been fourteenth row, only twenty plebes sat. I didn't think I was the only one who noticed this fact.

At the beginning of the lecture, the midshipman speaker at the microphone yelled out an "Attention on Deck!" and the Commandant entered from stage left. The audience sprang to attention. The sight of a thousand recruits leaping to their feet almost in unison was very impressive.

The Commandant of Midshipmen, Captain Mack Hallahan, gave a speech. He was a personable speaker who talked to us almost as if he were our father. He seemed genuinely interested in our success and well-being, and I liked that. He welcomed us aboard again and told us to be good boys. He talked for ten minutes; then a younger officer came to the podium and the lights dimmed. The second fellow briefed us on the academic merits of the institution. According to him, we were fortunate. Our class was the first Annapolis class that would graduate with accredited degrees. Previously graduates received a degree in general engineering, but in order to further their education at some other institution they would have to finish first a year of undergraduate work. We would have degrees just as those from good as any other school, and in many ways our degrees would be better.

According to the young officer, the typical academic semester consisted of 16 or more credit hours. If these were solely devoted toward the major, the load would be heavy. But in addition to the purely academic load, midshipmen were expected to complete courses in seamanship, navigation, leadership, military history, weapons science, and tactics. And this would be in addition to the requirement for parade practices, evening lectures, and mandatory afternoon sports participation. And, he reminded us with a chuckle -- the first year (when the load was heaviest) would also be our Plebe Year -- the year from Hell. By graduation, the lecturer continued, the typical midshipman would accumulate more than 160 credit hours. The speaker intoned about each major and its requisites and explained the academic policy on changing majors. It was an almost frightening academic prospect.

The lecture ended with my having more questions than I had when it began. But I figured that all my questions would be answered eventually (so I decided to bide my time.)

We snapped to attention again at the end of the lecture and soon afterward filed out of our seats -- by Company, naturally. Battle formed us to his satisfaction, and we marched toward Bancroft Hall. Maxwell must have been in a pretty good mood that morning, or maybe the sight of the female pulchritude that lined the walk buoyed his spirits. Whatever the reason, he suddenly burst into song.

"Around her neck she wore a yellow ribbon!" he began, keeping the beat in time to our steps (and like I said earlier, he had a good voice.) When he came to the last line, however, he changed the words to indicate that the woman waited for a midshipman who was "far, far away". After he finished -- with a flourish that absolute delighted the observing young ladies who giggled and looked at him like he was a god-figure -- he turned toward us and bellowed, "All together!" and on the next left foot we began to sing exactly what he had sung. We started tentatively at first, then picked up the volume and intensity. He led us through several verses. By the time we entered T-Court, we had that song down pat.

Battle halted us in the passageway in our Company area. Maxwell moved down the ranks and stopped at the front of the formation.

"Okay , ladies," he said. "That wasn't bad for a first march. This afternoon we'll have additional practice." He looked us up and down. "Who here knows how to sing?" he asked. One or two tentative hands -- including Ramsey's, much to my surprise -- went into the air. Maxwell looked at the singers.

"Good," he said. "You people heard other Companies singing songs. I want each of you to find out the exact lyrics of those other songs. We may not end up being the best military marchers, but by God you ladies are going to be the best singers. I want you each to be ready to demonstrate your songs for the group on Friday at the first "P-rade" practice."

Battle next addressed the group.

"Your next event starts at 1000," he announced. "It's a period of physical training in Macdonough Hall. This week you will get an introduction to wrestling. Next week is swimming evaluations. The following week you get a chance to box each other, God help you. The week after are gymnastics evaluations. In July there will be two weeks of track and field, a week each of soccer and softball, and a week of touch football. In August you'll have golf, tennis, squash, fieldball, and basketball." He smiled.

"That's quite a schedule, gentlemen," he continued. "No other college or university provides such a training regimen. Over the next four years --assuming of course you make it that far -- you will also be exposed for much longer periods to the same sports opportunities. You'll even be tested and evaluated on many of them. And it won't be easy, take it from me. I'm a terrible swimmer and I spent my plebe year on the sub-squad catching up to classmates such as Maxie here, who can swim rings around me." He looked at his watch. "Be back in formation, in white works Charlie in ten minutes....Dismissed!"

We chopped to our rooms and hurriedly began the process of changing from one uniform -- white works "bravo" which was the white jumpsuit with white undershirt and black military shoes -- into one that was almost totally different -- white works with the complete gym outfit underneath. This rapid and hysterical clothing on-and-off process soon became an integral part of Academy life.

We returned to the passageway within the allotted time and waited at braced attention. While we stood, I heard a minor whispered commotion behind me. Suddenly Tommy Poole bolted from ranks and raced into his room. As he pivoted for the turn, I could see that he had mistakenly put on his black uniform shoes. The rest of us wore Academy-issue tennis shoes. It seemed impossible to me that he could change shoes before the squadleaders returned. I was right. Maxwell and Battle beat him by less than ten seconds.

"Poole! What the hell are you doing?" yelled Maxwell.

"Sir! I had on the wrong shoes. I went back to change them," Tommy answered chagrined.

"Hit it for ten, Poole, you idiot!" Maxwell shouted. "And make them ten good ones." Tommy dropped to the deck. "One, sir! Two, sir! Three, sir!" he began. At five, however, he tired.

"Come on Poole, you pussy. Five more good ones!" Battle yelled. Tommy tried, but there was no way he could do them. "You are the most disgusting sack of shit I have ever seen, Poole!" Battle yelled. He glared at the rest of us.

"All of you look at poor Mr. Poole," he demanded. Battle walked over to where Tommy had just gutted out a weary number six. "This asshole, and several like him, is slowing up the group. They will draw you all down, cause the group to falter, and make you look foolish in front of your superiors." He looked down at the exhausted Poole. Tommy had paused in leaning-rest position. His arms shook from the effort, his back sagged, and his ample middle drooped till it was almost touching the tile deck. Battle emitted an exclamation of absolute disgust.

"Poole! Stand up!" he yelled.

"Aye, aye, sir!" Tommy responded weakly as he struggled to his feet and stood braced and staring ahead

"In order to make up for the weak links in the chain, all of you have to be stronger gentlemen," Battle said smugly. "Therefore I want all of you on the deck this instant. Every one of you give me ten good pushups for Mr. Poole. Poole, watch as your classmates do what you were supposed to do." We hit the deck and instantly thirty-odd voices began singing out numbers. When we finished, we sprang to attention. I noticed that some of my company-mates didn't exactly spring up. Some had as much trouble as Poole finishing ten push-ups. Battle watched, disgusted at them for a moment. Then he looked at Poole.

"How does it make you feel, Poole, having your classmates do your work?" Tommy watched as the remaining plebes finished and struggled to their feet. He swallowed hard and the look of grim determination returned to his face.

"It makes me feel bad as heck, sir," he announced.

"Bad as *heck*!" Battle exploded. "Bad as heck?" Battle moved to one side of Tommy's head near his right ear. Maxwell moved to the left side.

"You shouldn't feel bad as *heck*, Poole, you miserable shit," Battle yelled. "You should feel like you want to crawl in a deep hole and bury yourself. You should want to die, Poole!"

"What the hell is wrong with you, Poole?" Maxwell screamed from the opposite side. "You are the most disgustingly screwed-up embarrassment I have ever seen. I'm supposed to be impersonal, but I'm beginning to hate you, Poole. I want you to quit this place right now. Get out of here. Save your classmates the pain of having you for a classmate. Do you hear me, Poole?"

Tommy swallowed hard again.

"Yes, sir!" he yelled.

"Are you going to quit?" asked Maxwell.

"No, sir," Tommy replied timidly.

"Why the hell not, Poole? You don't belong here. Don't you understand that?" Maxwell continued.

Poole stared ahead grimly.

"I can do this, sir," he said, but not altogether convincingly.

"You *can't* do this, Poole, you stupid shit-for-brains!" yelled Maxwell whose face was now bright red and contorted with emotion and whose language became more colorful as his anger increased. I was shocked, not so much by the language, which, while colorful, was no worse than some of the stuff I heard in my hometown neighborhood. But vernacular not withstanding, Maxwell was absolutely out-of-control enraged, and this scared me to death.

Battle had calmed and was staring at Maxwell. Even he seemed concerned.

"Okay , Poole," he said slowly, "back in ranks. We'll deal with you later."

Tommy scurried back into the relative safety of the formation. We stood far more rigidly now than we had earlier. I wanted desperately to leave the Company area. I could sense that several other of my company mates were frightened by Maxwell's anger. Battle looked us over.

"Does everybody have the correct uniform?" he asked. No one responded in the negative. He turned toward the double doors, and in a calm voice, commanded, "Forward...March!" We started forward, eager to be away.

To get to Macdonough Hall we marched along the same path we had taken not three hours ago on the way to the morning run. Instead of continuing out onto Dewey Field, we turned to starboard and approached a huge old brick building that was connected to Bancroft Hall by a covered passageway. This was Macdonough Hall. The upper portion of the Hall served as a large open physical education area. Gymnastics gear had been set up along one wall. Ropes and pulley arrangements hung from the ceiling. Exercise machines stood against an opposite wall. A huge expanse of mats covered a large portion of the floor. In the basement of the same Hall, I soon found out, was a large swimming pool. I swallowed a great quantity of water in that pool, over which hung suspended the dreaded platform from which every midshipman was required to leap frightened into the frigid water 40 feet below.

Some midshipmen swore to me that civilian work crews arrived poolside early each morning to dump truck loads of ice into the water to cool it down for our hot young bodies. Most mornings I believed the stories, as it seemed impossible that a body of water that large could maintain near freezing temperatures, particularly in the midst of a sweltering summer. (at least not without some external agency stealing the precious calories from the molecules).

But today we headed topside to the matted area for general instruction in wrestling. This week-long training was supposed to familiarize us with the basics so that, come the start of academic year, we could embrace the real wrestling classes with gusto. Actually, except for the swimming -- which I had never completely mastered to the Academy's satisfaction -- I liked the general physical training classes. They weren't particularly difficult; and being a minor athlete, I didn't have any trouble with the various techniques.

We doffed our white works in neat piles and sat on the mats facing the small office. We were one of three Companies that had wrestling training the first week. I later found out that all the Companies rotated through the various classes during the summer. While we were wrestling, other groups of classmates were engaged in each of the other sports.

A trim civilian physical education instructor entered the area from the office. He was one of at least a hundred, several for every sport, and many, many for the "manly" and alumni-supported sports like football, basketball, and baseball. He went immediately to the center of the mats and faced us. He smiled. It was a real smile. It was refreshing. He seemed human.

"How is everybody today?" he asked in a friendly tone.

"Fine, sir!" three Companies responded simultaneously. "Whoa, whoa," he said laughing and holding his hands over his ears. "There's no need for that plebe baloney here in this facility, understood?" Did we ever. He looked us over. "Good," he continued, "let's get started."

What followed was a week of fairly intense wrestling training. It was easy. It was fun. And I actually enjoyed it. Soon it was time to depart this brief island of sanity and return to the company area. It was shoe shine time in Bancroft Hall.

We returned to the Company area immediately . Battle held us in the passageway for a moment.

"Third period is company training time," he said. "Today's lesson is how to spit shine your shoes properly. If you think you already know how, forget it. I guarantee you don't do it good enough to satisfy Maxie and me. Everybody get your black shoes and your *black* shoe polish and return immediately to the passageway." When he emphasized the word *black* he stared hard at Tommy Poole.

We chopped to our rooms. I gathered up my shoes and polish, and prepared to leave when Rico stopped me.

"What did you think of Maxwell's little act?" he asked.

"You mean with Poole?" I asked.

"Yeah," he replied. "What he did with Poole."

"I don't think it was an act," I said. "He seemed pretty much out of control." Rico stared at me for a second.

"Why was everybody so frightened?" he asked. "I could sense it."

"Jesus, Rico," I said a little fiercely, "do you want him to do that to you?"

"It's just words, Kevin. They can't hurt you."

"But what if he actually loses control? *That* could hurt you." Rico looked at me closely.

"Listen Kevin," he said. "No one here is allowed to hurt you or me or anyone else for that matter. All they can do is yell or make you do exercises or some stupid embarrassing act. They're not allowed to touch, push, kick, or punch; and if they do, they're fair game as far as I'm concerned."

"You'd start a fight if they hit you?" I asked incredulously.

Rico paused and smiled.

"Do you how much trouble they'd get into if it came out they used physical punishment on a plebe?" he asked. "They won't do that. And I can personally handle an awful lot of psychological abuse. But if they push me past my physical limit and use violence against me -- stand by. I can take care of myself."

I looked Rico over closely. "I'll bet you can," I said.

We returned to the passageway, arriving in formation immediately before Maxwell and Battle exited their room. Maxwell carried two pairs of shoes. Battle carried a chair, which he placed on the deck in front of the Company. Maxwell sat down. One pair of shoes was covered by individual chamois pockets. He put those shoes reverently on the floor beside him and looked up at us. He was smiling. Seemingly he had forgotten the incident with Poole.

He held up the other pair of shoes so that we could see them. They gleamed nicely in the fluorescent passageway lighting. "These are my *everyday* shoes," he said. "Notice how they shine?" He said this with such obvious fondness that I began to suspect him of a foot fetish. But I soon learned that shoes were a source of pride to most midshipmen, mainly because of the amount of effort that went into making them presentable.

He rotated the shoes so that they caught the light from all directions.

"I polish these shoes every day," he said with pride. "Now hold up your own shoes." We did. There was no comparison to the gleaming brightness he held. But then we hadn't applied a single coat of polish to ours.

"This is how I want your shoes to look before Sunday evening," he continued. "And they will if you follow my instructions to the letter."

What followed was a 15 minute lecture on the fine art of spit shining. I learned that actual spit is involved in the process. There must be some special enzymatic ingredient in saliva because, according to Maxwell, ordinary tap water will not do for a proper spit shine. He also said that those of us whose mamma's told us to avoid expectoration better kill their fears immediately, because it usually takes a gallon of slobber to bring out a proper gleam from the black unpolished leather.

Maxwell took out a well-used can of black Kiwi polish. A gleam of metal from the bottom of the can indicated that this can had seen plenty of use. The process of spit and dip and rub began. Soon he had coaxed a brighter shine from the shoes. He held them up, smiling broadly. They gleamed, no doubt about it.

"See what a little care and attention can do to a pair of shoes?" he asked the group. I don't know about the rest of my company mates, but I was impressed. Then he reached down and carefully lifted one of the covered shoes. He held it reverently on his lap, almost as if he were about to unveil a holy relic from the sacristy of a church. He gingerly slid the chamois wrapping from the shoe, being careful not to touch the shined top. He held the shoe up for all to see.

"These are my good shoes, my "grease" shoes," he said. "I only wear them to evening meal and watch formations."

I learned another piece of Academy jargon with that statement. The term "grease" is used to refer to any item that is top-of-the-line or saved for special occasions. We were supposed to maintain and reserve separate shoes, hats, and uniforms, whose quality and appearance immediately announced their 'grease' function. Also, a midshipman might date several girls in town during the four years he's a resident of Bancroft Hall, but his girl-back-home is always his "grease" girl.

The process by which midshipmen accumulate leadership points and the grades that rate how well they adapt and adopt the Academy system is also referred to as grease. So far so good, but a midshipman who mindlessly adopts the teachings of the Navy, however can sometimes be called a "greaser", which is not good. Never in my four years at Annapolis did anyone even think of calling me a greaser. I'm kind of proud of that.

Maxwell held up his grease shoe. I could hear a collective gasp. A crown jewel had been exposed to public view. His sacred footwear shone in the light almost as if it emitted its own black rays. It was dazzling as he rotated it slowly first right then left. It gleamed equally well from all directions. I was immediately covetous. I wanted that shoe with a passion, even if it didn't fit me. (Maybe I had a secret foot fetish.)

"By the end of the week," he said slipping the holy shoe into its protective pouch, "your shoes had better look like this." He held one of the now ordinary shoes aloft. He looked at his watch.

"Go back to your rooms and start shining," he said. "Be back in the passageway ready for noon meal at exactly 1220. Dismissed!"

Back in our room, I sat at my desk and opened the polish. I suddenly realized that no one had issued us a polishing cloth. Maxwell had used what seemed to be a piece of torn-off T-shirt. Should I do the same, I wondered? I looked over at Rico. He was reading his book again. I was beginning to hate that Russian bitch on the cover. I'll bet sex with her wasn't any good -- but then again, how would I know whether sex with anyone was good or bad? I sure as hell wanted to find out though.

I looked over at Anthony. He was about to dip the end of a bath towel into the polish.

"Wait, Tony," I said hurriedly. He stopped and looked up at me.

"Rico?" I asked questioningly. He put down his book and looked at me.

"What should we use to polish the shoes? They didn't issue any cloth for that."

Rico thought for a moment.

"Max used a piece of T-shirt," he said. What a guy -- he actually called the human terror by a nickname. He stood and went to his locker. Before either Tony or I could object, he took one of his T-shirts and ripped it down the middle with a loud, sharp sound. Then he further ripped it into three pieces. One he gave to Grizwald, another to me. He kept the third for himself.

"I suppose I should at least try this polishing thing," he said, clearly disappointed to be considering divorcing himself from Olga or Ivana or whatever the hell the name of that communist sow was. In the end his sense of duty compromised with his lust and he propped the book on his desk with his metal lock box while he absentmindedly worked polish into the hungry leather.

After ten minutes Rico held up his shoe to the light and frowned. He held it toward me.

"What do you think?" he asked. It looked like hell. Smears and streaks crossed and crisscrossed the top of the shoe haphazardly. "Maybe I used too much polish?" he asked.

"I have no idea," I responded. I held my own up. "Yours looks about the same as mine." I turned to Anthony. "How are you doing," I asked. There was no response. "Tony?" I asked a little loudly.

He looked up distractedly from what must have been absolute concentration. It was a musician's gift that I hadn't been aware of previously. He could totally immerse himself in any activity and could not be disturbed short of by nuclear explosion, and even then it had better be a near hit or Grizwald wouldn't notice.

"How are you doing, Anthony?" I asked.

He looked at me for a long moment, not completely understanding my question. Eventually the lights came on behind his eyes.

"Oh," he said. He looked down at his shoe. "Pretty good. What do you think?" He held up the shoe he had been working on. It gleamed perfectly in the light.

"Jesus, Anthony," I exclaimed. "How the hell did you do that?"

He looked down at the shoe and answered with a shrug.

"I don't know," he said. "It seems pretty easy."

"Anthony," Rico said from his desk, "I'll give you ten dollars if you'll get my shoes to look like yours before Sunday." Ten bucks seemed like a lot of money. If I could polish like Anthony I would have accepted in a second. Anthony hesitated. Rico took that to mean that negotiations were underway. "Fifteen, and I'll fold your locker for you."

"Well, my locker already looks good," Anthony said. That was the truth. In his free moments he had molded and cajoled the items in his locker into a very orderly arrangement.

"I'll make you bed for you the rest of the week," Rico offered. He indicated his own rack, which was impressively tight. Anthony considered.

"Well, I guess I could," he said.

"Great!" Rico said enthusiastically. He stood and retrieved his wallet from the lock box and removed 15 dollars from a very impressive stack of greenery. He handed it to Anthony, along with his shoes, and immediately went over to Anthony's rack. I watched as he pulled and straightened and tucked and smoothed. Within less than a minute Anthony's rack looked as good as Rico's. This wasn't good.

My rack now stood out like a festering sore -- a lumpy, bumpy, festering sore. Rico saw my look and smiled. He raised his eyebrows questioningly. The bastard wanted to get his 15 dollars back from me. No way! I groaned, stood, and turned toward my bed. Kneeling on the floor I attacked the problem of rack tightness with a scientific vengeance. Soon I had nearly matched Rico's efforts. Of course, it took me five times as long and it still wasn't quite as good. I had to do better.

I returned to my shoes with the same concentration I had used on my rack, while Rico went back to imaginary escapades with the frigid Ruskie. After what seemed only a few minutes, Merritt poked his head into the room.

"Time for chow," he announced. We stopped what we were doing and stood. I noticed that my hands were black from the polish, and I moved quickly to the sink.

Merritt shook his head at us.

"You'd better move your asses," he said. "The uniform is white works." I looked down at myself. I had on white works already. "Without gym gear underneath," he continued. Oh shit, he was right as always. "Five minutes, guys!" he announced, then departed to warn the other rooms.

Torn between dirty hands and uniform dismantling I decided correctly that I had better have clean hands before I touched my "white" works. Anthony did not reason as well as I did. In his blind panic, he immediately grabbed the front of his blouse and smeared a large black stain prominently across the belly area. He groaned loudly, and looked at me as if he were about to cry. Tears actually appeared in his eyes for a brief moment.

"Hurry, Anthony!" I said. "Wash up!" He looked at me thankfully. He needed guidance.

I splashed water on my hands and applied soap with a fierceness. Grizwald worked feverishly beside me. Two minutes of scrubbing were not enough to remove the stains completely, but I had them down to a nearly manageable level. I gingerly removed my blouse and pants, quickly exchanged gym gear for underwear, and donned the same clothing. Suddenly I realized that black shoes were going to be a problem. I had diligently worked to smear the hell out of my right shoe, but the left one was still virginal in its dullness. I couldn't wear those shoes.

We had been issued a second pair of black shoes, but I hadn't even laced them. Sensing impending doom, I hesitated only briefly. I dove into my locker for the second set of shoes, as I watched Rico depart the room. I wasn't sure I would make it. I raced. I missed several of the holes with the laces, but the pants would cover that up for the most part. By the time I was ready to exit, I only had seconds remaining. Anthony still wasn't completely dressed, however. He looked at me in a panic, obviously remembering what had happened to Poole this morning and desperately needing guidance. My heart sank.

I'm not really a son-of-a-bitch, but I sure felt like one; and Anthony probably has never forgiven me to this day, but . . . I gave Anthony a final panicked look, shrugged, and darted from the room. My reasoning was that even with my help he never would have made it to formation on time, and it was better -- at least as far as I was concerned -- if only one of us caught hell. Anthony's Bambi eyes held me pleadingly for a moment before I left the room. He was close to tears again. I felt like hell, but I was soon safely tucked in formation.

To his credit, Anthony wasn't the only person who was late. He wasn't even the latest. But late is late. Battle and Maxwell, somehow sensing that some momentous screw up was in progress, approached the formation with a look of anticipatory glee. I could hear rustling and shuffling within several rooms. No sooner had the two squadleaders settled themselves silently in front of us, then Grizwald emerged from the room. He forgot to chop. He forgot to brace. He forgot to square his corners. Maxwell pounced happily.

"Hit it for a million, Grizwald!" he yelled, laughing slightly at the sight of Grizwald in such a panic. Anthony tried to stop to comply but instead tripped over a shoelace that wasn't tied. He fell forward in slow motion like some giant redwood toppled by a logging crew. He thrust his hands out to slow his fall but only partially succeeded. His right arm struck the deck dead-on with a resounding "crack." He emitted a strange squeak as he continued to fall, and his forehead struck the unforgiving hardness with a dull thump. I could see Maxwell and Battle look at each other in concern. Battle ran to Grizwald and bent over to help him up. Grizwald rose groggily.

"Are you okay ?" Battle asked. It was obvious Grizwald was not okay . His arm hung at an unusual angle, and a large lump formed on his forehead. Battle helped him over to a place against the bulkhead.

"Sit here!" he commanded. Grizwald slid down the wall, holding his arm gingerly. "Stay there!" Battle turned.

"Pirelli!" he yelled.

"Yes, sir!" Pirelli answered from the rear of the formation.

"Front and center!" Battle commanded. John Pirelli ran to the front in a perfect chop. Battle looked him over. "The main office is directly below us on the first deck. Run down there as fast as you can and tell the Watch Officer to call for an ambulance. Tell him we have a midshipman with a fractured arm and a possible concussion. We'll bring Grizwald right down behind you. Return immediately! Go!" Pirelli streaked away.

In the meantime another late classmate arrived. Maxwell pounced even harder in an effort, I think, to impress us with the fact that the show must go on.

"Give me 100 push-ups!" he yelled. The classmate dropped immediately to the deck without incident and began yelling out numbers in time with his up and down motion.

"Who's still missing?" Battle asked the group over the number noise.

"Terry Patterson, sir," came the response from somewhere in the ranks.

"What room is Mister Patterson in?" asked Battle.

"5409, sir!"

Battle went quickly down the passageway to room 5409. He stood in the doorway.

"Patterson?!" he asked loudly, his voice becoming gruff, "are you joining us some time this century?"

"Yeah," came the tired and incorrect answer. Battle exploded.

"What do you mean, yeah?!" he screamed, advancing on the room.

"I said, yeah!" the hidden classmate repeated with conviction. "You guys win! I quit! This place stinks! Leave me alone!" Battle immediately softened.

"Come to lunch with us then, " he said. Then he laughed. "You can even have carry-on."

"I'm not ready," Patterson answered, a bit subdued. Battle turned to the formation.

"Take your time. Come to the table whenever you're ready." He walked back to the group, looking at the still groggy Grizwald. "Ramsey, O'Reilly! Front and center!" he yelled. We hurried to the front.

"Take your classmate to the Main Office and wait with him until the corpsmen arrive. Once he's on his way to the Hospital, come down to the Mess Hall." We answered with identical "Aye, ayes!" Ramsey reached down with surprising softness and grabbed Grizwald under his good arm. Almost without conscious effort, Ramsey hefted Anthony into the air so that he stood, still groggy, against the passageway wall. Grizwald moaned slightly as he leaned backward.

"Is my arm broken?" he asked incredulously.

"Sho' looks it," Ramsey laughed in a friendly fashion. "Don't ya'll worry. We'll get you to the Office -- no problem." Ramsey lifted Anthony's good arm so that it was around his broad shoulders. "Lean on me," he said, softly. Grizwald held his broken arm gingerly, and Jubal turned them toward the double doors. We began moving slowly along the passageway just as the Company departed the area.

I ran ahead of the two of them and pushed open one of the heavy doors. I held it while they exited and walked ahead of them down the ladder, clearing an imaginary path. I felt extremely helpless, as well as guilty about my earlier desertion. At the first landing I turned back.

"Anthony," I said, "I'm sorry about running out on you."

He looked at me like he was seeing me for the first time.

"What do you mean?" he asked, quizzically.

"I mean about not helping you just before meal," I replied. "There was no time left."

"Don't worry about it," he said in a not totally convincing fashion. I groaned inwardly and returned to my leading duties. Within a few minutes we had Grizwald at the office. Almost immediately an ambulance arrived outside and corpsmen rushed into the office. They examined his head, wrapped it in a bandage, put the arm in an immobilizing sling, and whisked Anthony out the doors. Once they drove off I turned to Jubal.

"What will happen to him?" I asked. Jubal pondered.

"Nothing much," he replied. "A broken arm ain't nothing. I wonder how he's gonna finish plebe summer with a busted arm, though."

"According to Rico," I interjected, "he won't finish."

Jubal nodded his head several times. "I thought so. He ain't got what it takes. And neither does Poole. I hope he quits soon. Ah'm gittin mighty tired of pullin' his weight."

"Maybe if we all helped him more, he could make it," I offered. I didn't say anything about my own feelings in the matter. Jubal snorted.

"Not a chance," he spat emphatically. "He's a complete waste. He's no military man." We wandered slowly down into the Mess Hall, where announcements had just finished. Several unfamiliar squadleaders stared at us menacingly as we passed leisurely down the passage.

At the Company tables Maxwell had saved adjacent seats for us with him, which I didn't think was a completely fair reward for our humanitarian services. We sat. I was still supposed to have carry-on, but I was afraid to push the issue. I could see Jeff Polk across the table staring at me, the question of whether I was going to stand up for my rights clearly on his mind. I wasn't. I was a coward. Hadn't the episode with Grizwald just shown that? I stayed braced for the entire meal, and neither of the squadleaders said a word.

The meal was somewhat subdued. No one -- not even Poole -- got yelled at. I could imagine what Battle and Maxwell must have been thinking. Having to explain an injury to a plebe entrusted to them -- even if it was his own clumsy fault -- couldn't have made them comfortable.

That afternoon just after noon meal we had our first real experience with military marching. It was quite an experience. Prior to the auspicious event, Battle marched us over to Dahlgren Hall, which is on the opposite side of Bancroft Hall from our wing. Dahlgren Hall was another older building used primarily for group functions such as intramural basketball competition and tea dances. It had a large open bay nearly 50 yards in length and 20 wide. The ceiling was more than 15 yards high. The only light came from a continuous row of dingy windows that lined an upper mezzanine which completely circled the building and from a completely inadequate set of hanging incandescent lamps. Along the walls of the upper mezzanine under the windows stood racks with row-after-row of old M2 rifles. That's where we headed. We reported to a group of enlisted personnel who carefully issued each of us a weapon and bayonet. They noted the serial numbers of the rifles we were assigned, I suppose so that none of us could steal one of the old, heavy things. It wasn't something any sane individual would have considered, especially considering that the firing pins had been removed.

Armed with non-lethal weaponry -- unless you incorrectly consider the dull bayonet a dangerous weapon -- we descended the ladders of Dahlgren Hall into the open area below. Battle halted us in the middle of the open space at nearly the middle of a well-used basketball court and gave us quick instructions on how to affix the bayonet to the barrel of the rifle. We did this without anyone cutting or maiming himself, and soon we marched out the far lower doors onto Farragut Field for parade practice.

Farragut Field is nearly a mile long, and stretches flat and green from near the Field House at the far western end of Academy grounds all the way to the Severn River, -- the far eastern boundary. Wings seven and eight, which are the farthest parts Bancroft Hall from the rotunda, flanked the northern side of the field, while the Annapolis inlet of the Severn River lay to the south.

As our three clumsy ranks clumped their way toward Farragut, I felt a minor sense of concern. I had never marched before but then again, how hard could it be? Battle halted us just after we entered the field area. He moved to the center of the group.

"Company . . . .Left, face!" he barked in a nasal cough I would soon be able to translate. I say translate because when he ordered the left-face, he didn't actually say those words. What he barked sounded more like "Comp'ny . . . Le'l houghaaa!" Most of us associated the command with the necessity to watch him while he explained the intricacies of marching, and we shifted our weight in a leftward direction. A good many others waited a millisecond to see what the majority would do, then also turned. The remainder shifted and rotated in various directions before coming to rest in a somewhat matching alignment. Battle groaned.

"Oh, Jesus!" he intoned, "why me?" Maxwell laughed.

Battle walked briskly to the front rank and stood in front of Ronald Steinway.

"Is that piece heavy?" he asked. "Ah, ha," I thought, "piece equals rifle." I filed that information away in whatever newly formed memory section of my brain that now stored Academy-related trivia. I fervent hoped my brain would never reach nautical overload and begin dumping obscure but-possibly-relevant data.

Steinway hesitated, a trait that caused him no end of grief.

"Well Steinway! Is it heavy or not?"

"No, sir," Steinway mumbled, then quickly changed his mind. "Well, yes, sir, sort of," he said, very unsure of himself. Battle reached out for the "piece" and snatched it roughly from Steinway's shoulder. Ronald winced but didn't protest. He stood confused and afraid, waiting for the abuse we all knew would soon rain down.

Battle shook his head in disgust.

"You're a god-damn girl, Steinway," he said. "Do you know that? Never let anyone take your piece away." He looked nervously around the field. "Go stand behind the Company and give me twenty push-ups, Steinway! Hurry!" Ronald scurried in a kind of loping tiptoe shuffle to the rear of the group and began push-ups without much enthusiasm. The noise of Steinway yelling numbers brought a momentary smile to Battle's face. At least until Steinway faltered at number 15. Battle looked to heaven, then quickly toward Maxwell.

"Maxie, would you bring the young lady back?" he asked sweetly.

"Of course, classmate," Maxwell answered with equal sweetness. He walked unhurriedly to the rear of the formation. "On your feet, douchebag, and hurry back into formation," he said, very unsweetly. Steinway scrambled back into line, wiping grass and soil disgustedly from his hands as he returned.

Battle demonstrated the entire standing-still repertoire of "left face", "right face", and "about face", and we watched intently. For the following several minutes we practiced without incident. Afterward we right-faced into marching readiness and Battle started us forward.

"Follow the beat of the drum with your left feet!" he commanded as we moved in unison toward the inner parts of the enormous grassy tract. Several other Companies also practiced on various parts of the field.

Until he said the word *drum* I had been unaware except in some vague subconscious way that a drum pounded nearby, although nearby isn't the proper word. Out in the very center of Worden Field, more than several hundred yards away, stood a lone enlisted drummer, a kettle drum strapped over his shoulder. He beat a steady and repeated *thrum-thrum-thrum-ta-ta-tum* that we were supposed to used as an aural guide to pace our progress. I wondered what kind of terrible duty that must have been, standing for hours in the hot summer sun, beating a never-changing tattoo on a heavy drum. Maybe it was a kind of musician's plebe year for enlisted troops. At any rate it must have been horrible for the poor guy. Thrum-thrum-thrum-ta-ta-tum, over and over and over.

But compassionate thoughts were fleeting at best that summer, and soon Battle began barking out marching commands in the same alien language he used earlier for the facing commands. We learned the right and left turns, which were easy; then he dared to attempt us in a "to-the-rear" movement, and I thought surely we would take casualties. Some plebes turned on their right feet, some on the wrong feet, some pivoted to the left, some to the right. A few hesitated and continued forward into their turning classmates. A chaos of collisions, stumbling, bumbling, and incredible confusion followed, punctuated by the yelps of frightened young men, the flash of sunlight on bayonet, and the anger of the two squadleaders.

"All of you!" Battle yelled. "Give me 20!"

"Ah, Tom," Maxwell immediately interjected. "Do you think that's wise?"

"I don't give a shit," Battle answered. "These pukes are the most pathetic bunch of screw ups I have ever seen, and I'm going to teach them how to march even if it kills them." While they discussed the propriety of public discipline, we fell to the ground and began the ordeal. I had done more push-ups that day than ever in my life, and I found that my chest and shoulders tired quickly. After five I began to feel sore. Almost instantly, however, the sound of Ramsey's accented voice rang out above all the others as he did his push-ups in time with the beat of the drum. It heartened me. Soon others joined in the vocal rhythm, and by the time we finished ten the entire group -- less the several who had to stop at ten -- were counting identically. The sound of voices raised in unison of purpose echoed over the huge field, and I found the soreness lessening as I tried to shout louder than my classmates, and adrenaline pumped through my system. Maxwell and Battle stopped their discussion and watched us in amazement. Battle actually smiled.

"Ramsey!" he yelled, laughing, if you survive this year intact, I'm going to make a Marine out of you!"

Jubal answered with a loud "Aye, aye, sir!" between push-up cadence.

That evening after meal Maxwell's lecture dealt with plebe "rates". This jargon term however, had nothing to do with rights or privileges. "Rates" instead explained the requirements of the plebe system. In a nutshell, we were slaves. We must do -- within reason and short of violating public law, human morality, or placing our lives in danger -- anything an upper-class asked. He also explained that plebes were not to be personal servants to any upper-class but that we had better carefully consider before refusing favors or requests because the resulting discipline could be severe. Then he talked about the difference between discipline and *hazing* -- a thin and confusing distinction.

We could do pushups until our arms fell off and run back and forth in the passageway until we passed out or puked on the deck, and that was allowed because those were permissible exercises recognized by the Academy as discipline enhancers. However, we not supposed to be forced to do something called a "dead horse" or be placed in the "thinking position" during exercising. At meals "rigging"' pitchers and "locking on" to the table were also forbidden. Maxwell said this all in a thoughtful voice that indicated he himself had been the target of these academy inducements, and that he truly didn't believe they would do us any harm.

"Christ, they make it easy on you pukes," he said. "When I was a plebe . . ."

He then proceeded to happily tell us how miserable and painful his own plebe year had been, and he wistfully recounted all the horrible things that had happened to his classmates. He said it with such reverence and fond nostalgia that it was obvious he wanted us to experience the same painful manly training he had endured. Symbolically at least, no "dead horses"' meant no plebe year for us, and that was a shame (at least as far as he was concerned.) The thought of dead horses made me nervous, however. I decided I would be perfectly happy with the push-ups, thank you.

Plebe Year stories -- next to tall tales about sexual prowess -- are the most often heard boasts at the meal table. Plebe year is the academy badge of courage. It's the ticket, the dues, the testing that separates the men from the boys, although what they call it now that women attend I don't know. Women at Annapolis. It sure can't be plebe year like I knew it. Why, when I was a plebe . . .

"O'Reilly!" The sound of Maxwell's shout broke my reverie. "We need someone to demonstrate the illegal exercises -- for informational purposes only, you understand."

"Of course, sir," I replied laughing as I rose smiling from my position on the floor and hastened to the front of the group. Maxwell smiled in return at me in his somewhat evil fashion and turned to the group.

"Mr. O'Reilly is now going to demonstrate two of the illegal exercises so that you will know what not to do when the Brigade returns in September. First you will see the classic and ever popular "dead horse."" He turned to me.

"O'Reilly, lie on your back!" he ordered. I lay down, facing the suspended ceiling.

"Raise your arms straight into the air, O'Reilly," Maxwell ordered. I did so. "Good! Now raise your legs the same way." I lifted my legs into the air, but flexibility not being my strongest asset, they only came up to a 60 degree angle, then stopped.

"All the way up, O'Reilly!" Maxwell yelled. I rotated my legs backward by lifting my lower back slightly off the ground. My legs got closer to vertical but still fell short of a right angle, and I held this position.

"Can't you do any better than that?" asked Maxwell.

"No, sir," I replied.

"Well hold that sissy position for a moment, pal," Maxwell said. Then he turned to the others. "Can anyone do better than this pussy?" Merritt and Lamont raised their hands simultaneously thereby raising serious questions in my mind about their sanity.

"You two get up here and show us," Maxwell said. I was confused as the two of them rushed to the front and assumed identically perfect dead horses. I held my position stoically, strangely angry that their dead horses were better than mine. So far holding the position had been easy. I focused on the ceiling, and saw for the first time the metal ceiling grid and the lenses that covered the banks of fluorescent lights. The plastic lens covers had been manufactured with a small raised diamond pattern that sparkled and flashed if I turned my head slightly. I experimented with the glittering while I waited. It was almost psychedelic, although never having had any experience with drugs -- mind altering or otherwise -- I could only guess at this premise.

"O'Reilly!" Maxwell said from his position near Merritt. "How are you doing?"

"My horse is dead, sir," I answered. I figured a little humor couldn't hurt the situation. Maxwell and Battle both laughed.

"Yours is the worse looking dead horse I have ever seen," Battle added with a chuckle.

"I'll take that as a compliment, sir," I added, my sense of humor on a roll. After another minute however, my legs began to sag-- along with my sense of humor. I straightened. After half a minute my legs lowered again, and I had to strain to get them back up. My arms began to tire as well. Within another twenty seconds I could not get my legs back up. They began slowly to droop toward the floor. I hunched my shoulders to relieve some of the pressure that was building there. Shit, this was hard. I groaned as I repeatedly tried to adjust position without success.

"What's the matter, O'Reilly? Getting a teensy bit difficult?" Maxwell asked, laughing.

"Yes, sir!" I answered honestly.

"Do you find anything funny now, O'Reilly?" asked Battle.

"Not as funny as a minute ago, sir," I answered.

"Everyone stop!" Maxwell ordered. We did -- gladly. I lay on my back and watched the ceiling as I recovered. I didn't like the sparkling lenses anymore either.

"O'Reilly! Roll over!" Maxwell ordered. I did. "Lock your hands behind your head!" he demanded. I did. "Rotate you elbows inward until they are directly beside your head!" he commanded. Again I did what he said, although I didn't like the direction this particular "exercise" was going. "Lift yourself up so that your weight is resting on your elbows and toes!" he directed. I lifted.

The linoleum tile used in the Academy decks is a creamy white with specks of brown and green imbedded in the color. The tiles themselves are standard eight inch squares set onto the under deck with black adhesive. Years of wear and the tromping of young feet had worn several shallow grooves into the tile directly beneath me. The deck is also extremely hard. My elbows dug painfully into the tile as I held myself aloft. Sweat immediately popped out on my forehead. I tried to adjust position without success. I groaned aloud.

"Painful, O'Reilly?" asked Maxwell.

"Extremely so, sir," I answered.

"Hold that for another minute, asshole, if you can," he said. "I used to able to hold the thinking position for five minutes without tiring."

"A remarkable achievement, sir," I answered, knowing I was a little out of line.

"Shut-up, O'Reilly!" Battle ordered. I did.

Almost exactly at that moment the double doors at the end of the passageway opened. I glanced in that direction and saw an officer enter, accompanied by two plebes. My body was slightly shielded by Merritt's. Without thinking I ceased my "thinking" and changed to a push-up position.

"One, sir! Two, sir! Three, sir!" I began, yelling loudly.

"Attention on Deck!" Battle shouted. We sprang to attention. Maxwell looked at me closely while the officer approached. His eyes told me nothing. I winked.

"Carry-on," the officer said smiling when he reached us. Battle snapped into a parade-rest position. The rest of us relaxed somewhat. The officer wore a freshly pressed tropical white uniform. His shoulder boards indicated he was a lieutenant, a stratospheric difference in rank from Midshipman Fourth-class.

"A little push-up training, I see," the officer started, still smiling.

"Yes, sir!" I answered for the group. Maxwell looked at me again.

"How many can you do, plebe?" the officer asked. I hesitated before speaking.

"This morning sir, I could do close to 50," I began. "Now however I'm almost push-upped to death." He laughed resoundingly.

"Well," he said, "by the time I finished my plebe year I could do more than 100 good ones. That'll give you all something to aim for."

"Aye, aye, sir!" Battle answered. The officer then continued down the passageway. I could see Battle and Maxwell look at each other for a moment.

"Time to post road guards?" Battle asked. Maxwell nodded.

Maxwell turned to the group. "You know that everything we do here is for your own good, right?" he asked. We all answered with affirmative "yes, sirs!"

"Good," he continued. "Sometimes the Academy doesn't understand the need to take the training beyond recommended levels -- for demonstration purposes of course." He looked at me. "In order to stay out of possible conflict with the authorities -- something I'm sure you can all understand -- we're therefore going to establish a careful guard on some of the things we do." He pointed toward the double doors. "When we deem it necessary, one of you will stand at those doors, and another down there at the passageway intersection." He pointed in the opposite direction toward where the officer had recently turned on his way to visit other Companies.

"At any sign of an officer," he continued, "or any visitor you do not recognize, the guard will drop to the deck and begin yelling out his push-ups. And I mean yelling."

Maxwell looked at me. "O'Reilly. Back into formation!" I complied.

Maxwell explained about the duty plebe room, whose responsibility was to perform "chow calls" for the Company. A chow call consisted -- so we were told -- of loud public announcements at ten, five, and two minutes prior to every meal, of the meal's menu; the appropriate uniform; the Officers of the Watch; the movies currently playing at the local theaters; and finally the number of days remaining until the next vacation period, various other important events, and the Army-Navy game. Why these particular tidbits of information were vital I never learned. But I did learn quickly that the information announced in the chow call was part of the plebe rates. Learn it or face severe retribution.

Members of the duty room would post themselves at strategic locations in the passageway to make the announcements, chopping hurriedly back to their rooms between the ten and five minute call but going directly to formation after the two minute announcement. Room 5401 would begin the chow call process on Sunday night, and the duty would last a week, shifting to 5402 the following Sunday.

For a closing activity that evening Room 5401 introduced themselves. Those classmates consisted of George Thomas Abbott from Tea Neck, New Jersey, whose father was an advertising agent and whose mother was a first grade teacher. George was a tall, brawny, good natured, individual with very dark eyes, a pronounced shadow of beard on his face, and dark stubble already sprouting profusely on his head. George would have to shave twice or more every day of plebe year to avoid the wrath of upperclassmen. George was an only child who had been an All-State soccer defender at a Catholic High School, and his thick muscular legs identified him as a formidable kicker. He looked tough, but he spoke with a soft, sing-song femininity that belied his physical capabilities. I certainly didn't want to meet George on the soccer field -- or any field for that matter.

Henry John Butkowski spoke next. Hank was the largest of my classmates, standing well over six feet four and weighing I would guess close to 250 pounds. He had laughing blue eyes and prominent facial bones which matched his large arms and legs. But despite his formidable size, he was plainly nervous, and he spoke haltingly. He came from Jeanette, Wisconsin, where he played football, obviously. Hank's father ran a local lumber company, and he had three brothers and three sisters, all older than him.

"Did Coach Snelling contact you about pre-season practices?" asked Maxwell.

"Ah, yes, sir," answered Butkowski. "They are supposed to start next week in the afternoons."

"I guess that means we have to dismiss you from the marching and from the morning workouts?" asked Battle sarcastically.

Butkowski, unaware at that moment of the status granted footballers, stammered nervously, "I think so, sir, but I don't mind the extra workout. I could come along in the morning."

"You come along, pal," said Maxwell, looking at Battle closely. "We'll try not to run you too hard."

Next came Tim Butler from Modesto, California. Tim was a small, medium build, regular looking, nondescript, plain sort of person. I'm sure his hair, when it grew in, would be standard American mouse brown. He seemed to be the kind of individual who could inhabit a crowded room for hours, and invariably be forgotten. He might even forget himself. Tim spoke in an ordinary, unpretentious, unaccented voice about his parents, one of whom was head librarian at the county library, the other was a homemaker. Tim had no siblings, or if he did he probably forgot.

Bill Allen was the last member of 5401 to introduce himself. I liked Bill immediately. He had a constant smile, an extremely easy-going personality, and a smoothness of speech and manner that made it obvious he could get along in any situation. He stood about six feet tall, was moderately thin, and judging by his ample eyebrows, would be very blond when his hair grew back. His parents were both engineers, which I found interesting. They ran their own consulting firm in Denver. Bill announced that he had two younger sisters, both of whom were eligible and very attractive.

Maxwell dismissed us to return to shoe shining and other plebely duties. It was close to 2100, and he reminded us that lights out would again be at 2200.

Inside my room I approached Rico.

"What do you think about Anthony?" I asked. Rico thought for a moment. "I think he'll use this as an opportunity to quit," he answered. "It's a perfect out. But I'm more concerned about one other thing.".

"What's that?" I asked.

"Is he going to shine my shoes, or do I get my money back?" he said in perfect seriousness. I was mildly surprised, but I supposed it was a valid concern. I took out my own shoes for polishing. The one with the polish looked better in the fluorescent lighting, but it was still horrible. I attacked both shoes with a vengeance, and at the end of thirty minutes I had polish smartly smeared on both shoes. Now both shoes looked like hell, but at least they matched. I began thinking that my spit lacked some critical enzyme. Maybe I needed a medical examination. I could go to Sick Bay in the morning -- if I could find out where that was -- and hock one for the doctors.

At 2130 I decided to give up on my shoes and go visiting.

"Going to the Goon Room," I announced. "Want to come along?" Rico agreed to the change of scenery, and we cautiously glanced into the passageway. No squadleaders were in sight, and we hurried across the passageway.

Things were quiet in 5403. Too quiet. Each of the goons sat grimly at his desk polishing shoes. I could sense tension.

"Hi, guys," I said, trying to sound as bright and chipper as I could. "What's up?"

"This place sucks!" said Polk with vehemence, looking up briefly from his work.

"I hate it too," said Poole with a determined sadness. His shoes sat on the desk in front of him. They looked worse than mine, and that made me strangely satisfied.

"Ah'm tah'rd of classmates who cain't pull their load," said Ramsey looking at Tommy. Jubal had brought a nice shine up on his shoes. He was holding them up to the light as we entered. They looked halfway decent. Now I was jealous. Merritt looked at us.

"And don't you just love my happy roommates," he said, laughing. One finished shoe rested on the floor beside the desk. Naturally it looked perfect. He was just glossing his second shoe. Now I was livid with envy.

"I see you guys all have your shoes in better condition than mine," I observed. "How about one of you coming over and polishing mine so I can watch your technique?"

Poole looked up from his polishing. He held up one badly done shoe.

"Yours are worse than these?" he asked incredulously.

"Orders of magnitude, my friend," I answered. "How do you do it?" Tommy looked at me, then at his shoe.

"I don't know," he said, and continued polishing with renewed vigor. Merritt looked at him for a moment, then nodded his head toward Ramsey. I sensed that the task for this evening was to soften up Jubal.

"Just how big *are* your sisters, Joe?" asked Rico suddenly. I was shocked. Ramsey looked up quickly, staring with narrowed eyes at Rico.

"What kind a question is that?" he asked loudly and somewhat angrily. Rico threw his hands out in front of him and laughed.

"I'm serious," he said. "I've always had a thing for southern women. Are your sisters like, really big, or are they just a little chunky?" Jubal considered the question, then laughed.

"They're really big," he said. "They could easily have played be'sahd me on the High Point football team."

"That's too bad," Rico said seriously, "'cause I do love southern women." We all laughed together.

"How do your arms and legs feel, Tommy," I asked. "You had a tough day."

"He's a sissy!" added Jubal with unveiled antagonism.

"Hold on there, Jubal," I interjected, trying to sound reasonable. "If you had to do as many push-ups as Tommy here, you'd be tired too."

Ramsey looked at Tommy's back for a moment.

"Maybe," he said, "but he don't belong here."

"Let the system decide that, Jubal," I offered. "In the mean time we all have to work together."

"You know," Jeff suddenly offered from the opposite side of the room, "what you say is okay, but the damn system doesn't make much sense. The physical workouts are okay , if all they do is exercise us, but I can see why they outlawed those tortures Maxwell had you demonstrate. You can hurt yourself doing those, and what's the sense in that? And what the hell does memorizing the answer to "How's the cow?" or the names of the sorry-assed movies in town have to do with being a good naval officer?" He swiveled in his seat and faced the room more directly. Everyone watched him intently as he preached.

"And then, assuming we all make it through the next four years, what's in store? There's a war going on you know? People are dying, and that includes graduates of this place. What are they dying for? I don't understand."

"Jesus, Jeff, make some sense," Jim Merritt answered. "Government policy is none of our business. We'll go where we're told and do whatever job is required. If you're afraid of dying, maybe this isn't the place for you."

"It's got nothing to do with dying!" Polk burst out. "I'm not a coward! But I want to understand why I might have to die or why I might have to kill someone else."

Ramsey jumped up from his desk.

"Listen you bastard!" he said fiercely. "We're in Vietnam because the president said so, and y'all are here because you joined the military. If you cain't follow orders, quit! There's too many good men puttin their lives in danger every day. I don't want to hear your complaints, especially about Vietnam. So shut up right now!"

Polk stood up quickly.

"Make me, asshole!" he said.

Ramsey moved quickly from behind his desk and advanced on Polk. Instantly Merritt and I jumped between them and held Ramsey back. Rico moved to where Jeff stood, took him by the arm, and turned him forcefully away from Ramsey. He didn't object. Poole sat and stared open-mouthed at the activity. I doubt he had ever seen anything like that on the chess team.

"What's the matter Jubal?" asked Jim Merritt. "Why did you get so angry?"

"'Cause if I believe that bullshit, then everybody who died in Vietnam died for nothing. I won't have it! He better just keep quiet about it, that's all." I watched Jubal's face as he talked. Beneath the anger was something else, and he was near tears when he finished.

"Want to talk about it?" I asked sincerely.

He glared at me. "No, Yankee, I don't want to talk about it, so leave me alone." With that he spun away from us and hurriedly left the room. We stared at the empty doorway for a moment before anyone moved or spoke.

"Wow!" said Merritt. "I wonder what's with him?"

"I don't know, but something," I added.

"Whatever it is, you can tell he feels it's a good reason," added Rico. He looked at Jeff, whose arm he still gripped. "I think it would be a good idea if you didn't say anything anti military for a while," he said quietly.

Polk nodded, still staring at the door, then added, "I wonder if I should do anything?"

"Maybe apologize," added Poole from across the room. We had momentarily forgotten about Tommy.

"Yeah," Jeff said after another moment, "maybe I should."

"That's enough excitement for one night," said Rico smiling. "This room sure seems to be the focus of controversy. I think I'll visit whenever I'm bored." He let go Jeff's arm. "Sorry about that," he said nodding his head at the finger marks, still visible on Polk's upper arm. Jeff looked down absentmindedly.

"No problem," he said, "thanks."

I announced my own departure, and scampered across the passageway, but not before Merritt admonished us to get up on time the next day. We laughed. There was no way I wanted to repeat this morning's near disaster.

I watched Rico as he pointedly set a small alarm clock for 0515. He sat the clock on the middle of his desk, then quickly undressed and climbed into bed.

"I'll join you in just a minute," I said.

"No hurry," he replied. "I could sleep through anything."

I spent the remainder of my free time writing a single-page letter to my parents, bringing them up to date on my experiences. I had just finished the most active, unusual, and physically and emotionally demanding two days of my life. A whole summer -- hell, a whole year -- of the same lay ahead. I already felt like a veteran of combat. In my letter I summed it up in one word -- incredible! That night as I lay in my rack counting my bruises and nursing my sore muscles, I wondered again if I had the mettle to finish. It was a bedtime thought I would repeat every night for a very long time.

USNA CHAPEL EXTERIOR

One of the original buildings of the Naval Academy complex, the chapel has been the source of moral comfort for more than a century. It is one of the most beautiful and awe-inspiring of the Academy structures. In the lower crypt is the coffin holding the last remains of John Paul Jones.

CHAPTER 3

CONFLICTS AND CONFUSION

The lights flashed on in the room at 0545. "Jesus, guys!" Merritt said fiercely. "This is getting to be a very bad habit. Fifteen minutes. Hurry!"

"God-damn!" Rico yelled as he and I reacted simultaneously. With an angry groan, he leaped from his bed, grabbed the alarm clock from the desk, glared at it for a short moment, then threw it energetically out the window. I stood at my bedside amazed at what he had done, watching him for several long seconds.

He looked at me, then and said sheepishly. "It must have been broken." I laughed. Almost immediately we heard the sound of the clock splintering on the hard red-tile walkway four floors below.

"If it wasn't, it is now," I said.

We hurried into our gym gear and out into the passageway. We arrived with nearly two minutes to spare. Merritt stared at us from his position across the passageway and shook his head, amazed.

"So we like sleeping in," I whispered. He chuckled. This morning everyone was prepared prior to the workout, and we departed without incident. I found myself in a cheerful mood. My legs felt fine. I was ready to win more carry-on. But there were no physical contests that morning or any of the next three. I was disappointed.

As I jogged almost effortlessly along the seawall, I carefully observed what transpired. With only two squadleaders and 30 plebes, it seemed impossible for Max and Battleaxe to observe everyone all the time. In fact, during the runs their attention was almost continually focused on the stragglers. Those of us at the front were free from scrutiny. And even as we exercised, I could see classmates surreptitiously watch the squadleaders to see where their heads were pointed. Whenever attention was diverted, the quality of the exercise would slacken. Rico, I soon discovered, was an expert at faking it. He would watch for any opportunity and immediately seize it. If the break came during push-ups, he would rest his stomach on the grass, smiling and shouting the numbers along with the rest of us. During sit-ups he would rest on his back. Once or twice he glanced at me during his rests. I would labor away, afraid to stop for fear of being caught. He would smile or wink. He loved playing the game.

But cheating on a few push-ups didn't motivate me. In fact, as the days passed and my physical strength increased, I began basking in the endorphins and relishing the physical training. I was being turned into a machine, and I liked what was happening to my body.

At the same time, however, I almost unconsciously began to feel my attitude toward my classmates change, and to resent the fact that we could slacken at all. Gradually I came to accept that this deficiency in the plebe training process was because of our more backward classmates. Poole and several others were "shit-screens." Some were so badly out of shape and so unused to discipline that during every evolution they drew attention to themselves. So long as the two squadleaders were yelling at other plebes, they left the rest of us alone. Therefore, I reasoned, it wasn't necessary to excel to survive. All I had to do was keep up with the majority, and I guess for that we all owed Poole a debt. I decided to use that argument on Ramsey. Maybe it would soften him up, although it seemed ironic to me that I might survive my plebe year, not because of the forward thrust of my own personality, but rather due to the backward drag of the non achievers like Tommy Poole. I chuckled inwardly at this interesting twist, and I wondered if the Academy suspected as much.

Later that first week Battle lectured us on the finer points of formations and inspections while Maxwell inspected our rooms. I could hear Max humming as he went from room to room, loudly accompanied by the sounds of sheets being pulled up and various gear falling on the deck from our lockers. This was the evening for our room to introduce itself. Anthony was still a no-show, which seemed strange since all he had done was break his arm, so Rico and I talked.

"Hola," Rico began in a thick accent as he faced the group. "I'm Enrique Jose Guevarra from Brooklyn, New York." For a moment I was observing a character from *West Side Story* rather than the articulate, educated person I knew him to be. "My parents, they come to this great nation from Puerto Rico," he said heavily accenting the words "Puerto Rico". "My padre, he's a grocer. He has a small store and cantina. My momma, she helps with the sales. I haf two seesters, mucho pretty -- but not for sale." I laughed as did several of my classmates. Maxwell looked at me, then at Rico.

"Okay, Pancho, knock it off," he said.

"Si, senor," Rico answered, smiling. Before Max could react he continued, changing his demeanor completely.

"I attended Brooklyn Polytechnic High School. I played varsity baseball and basketball and was a member of the National Merit Society." He paused and looked down at his feet. "I was also president of my senior class." He smiled disarmingly and returned to his spot on the floor beside me. I rose and came boldly forward.

"Wow," I said turning to the group. "What a resume! Let's all give Rico a big hand and welcome him." I started clapping, and my classmates joined in, at first hesitatingly then with gusto. Cheers erupted. After several long seconds I raised my arms in the air to signify silence and the group quieted. I could see several classmates looking from me to the squadleaders, wondering what would happen next. They didn't have to wait long.

"Give me 20, O'Reilly!" Battle barked, in a not totally unfriendly fashion.

"Aye, aye, sir!" I yelled and dropped to the deck and began counting.

"O'Reilly!" interrupted Maxwell.

I stopped and rested my belly on the deck.

"Yes, sir!" I answered.

"Since you seem to be such a clown, why don't you make your presentation in leaning-rest?" he said. "Maybe it won't be so funny then."

I looked over at him.

"Would it help to remind you that leaning-rest is a *forbidden* exercises, sir?" I asked.

Maxwell laughed. "No, pal, it wouldn't," he answered.

"Aye, aye, sir!" I replied. I raised myself up off the ground and addressed my companymates.

"My name is Kevin O'Reilly," I began. "I come from Boston, Massachusetts, where I played basketball and ran a little track for my high school. My dad works on the Boston waterfront; my mom hangs around the house and takes care of my younger brother." I paused. I had rehearsed the speech, so I kind of knew what I wanted to say. "I may not be as gung-ho as Jimmy Merritt or as formidable as Hank Butkowski or as well endowed as Rico Guevarra, but I want you all to love me anyway. After all, I'm your classmate." I paused. The group laughed.

"Why do you say that about your classmate Guevarra?" asked Battle, falling for the bait.

"Sir, I've seen him naked," I replied. "Horses would be jealous." Everybody laughed, Rico most of all. In fact what I said was true, the guy was enormous, and yes I was jealous.

"Okay, O'Reilly," Max said. "Take your place next to your enormous classmate." As I returned to my place, Battle brought out a pencil and paper and addressed the group.

"Gentlemen," he said, "I have a little contest going with the nineteenth through the twenty-fourth companies. I want each of you to announce you verbal and math Scholastic Aptitude Test results. Merritt, come here and jot them down. After you record them, calculate the average for me." Jim rose and went forward. He took the pad from Battle.

"Let's begin," Battle said. He pointed to each of us in turn and we sang out our scores. I was very surprised at the range. There were only two classmates with either score in the 500 range, and several with one or more 600. Most had a combination of six and seven hundreds. Three classmates had 800 in one category. Amazing Tommy Poole was the only one with double perfect 800s. Maxwell whistled.

"Double 800s. Wow! Poole you're a certifiable genius!"

"Have you gotten the average yet, Merritt?" Battle asked after a few seconds. "I'll bet Poole could do it faster.

From deep within the group Tommy Poole announced sheepishly, "1,346, sir."

"What, Poole?" asked Maxwell.

"The average, sir. It's 1,346."

"Are you shitting me, Poole?" asked Battle.

"No, sir. Not if I heard the numbers correctly."

Battle looked at Merritt, "Well, Merritt?" he asked. Jim had just finished. He looked up.

"Classmate Poole is correct, sir. 1,346 is the average." Soon afterward we returned to our rooms to clean up the messes, and I was too busy that night to visit the Goons.

At nearly midnight that evening urgent rumbling signals from the nether regions awakened me, and I climbed from my bed to visit the head. Since I didn't exactly know the rules about leaving the room after lights out, I crept cautiously down the passageway in the weak light. Once in the head I avoided turning on the lights, selected a dark stall, and got down to business with a vengeance. God it felt good. I lingered. Five minutes later someone else quietly entered the darkness. He stood uncertainly in the doorway for a moment, then went to the sink. I could hear the sound of running water and something else -- faint sobbing.

I instantly felt like an intruder. The water sounds ceased after a minute, but the tears did not, in fact they increased in volume for what seemed a very long time. I froze, dreading the possibility that I would make a noise to announce my presence. I waited until the sadness abated, but the visitor didn't depart immediately. Instead he went to the wall, quickly flipped on the lights, and hurried to the sinks again.

With the lights on I was afraid he would see my feet under the partition door. I raised them slightly. But now I could also see a portion of his body in the crack between the stall door and the partition wall. I didn't recognize him at first because the space through which I could view was very small. Then he leaned in closer to the mirrors to check something on his face, and in the mirror I could see him plainly. It was Pirelli -- Pirelli the tough man -- Pirelli the machine -- Pirelli the invincible. "Super-plebe" himself was crying in the dark. Jesus, did that shake my confidence. I waited in the dark for a full five minutes after Pirelli departed, pondering that unexpected turn of events uneasily.

A not so quiet truce prevailed in the Goon Room for the rest of that week. The morning workouts continued unabated, with Tommy Poole, Ronald Steinway, and two others suffering the greatest wrath from Max and Battleaxe. On Thursday Rico and I returned to our room after the morning wrestling class to find that all traces of former classmate Anthony Grizwald had vanished from the room. I felt strangely sad again. Rico, however, was pissed.

"He stole my 15 bucks!" was all he could say. I guess Rico would have to learn how to spit shine.

Thursday evening Room 5402 had their turn in the limelight. First up was a classmate named Charles (Chuck) Chalmers. Chuck was a medium height, very thin, individual who had suffered the ravages of acne recently. His face was moderately scarred as a result. He also had a case of nervous jitters and could not remain still while he talked. Chuck's father was a police detective in Cleveland. His mother a housewife. He had two older brothers, one of whom had graduated from Annapolis four years earlier. He didn't say anything about his other brother. Chuck had played tennis in High School.

The next speaker was Daniel Carl French from Chicago, Illinois. Danny was a short, handsome, outspoken, son of a city councilman. His laughing blue eyes and devilish smile indicated a mischievous nature. He had an older sister who was already married, and a younger brother still in grammar school. He lived with his mother because his parents had divorced several years earlier and had decided to split custody. Danny, a wiry individual who could do push-ups from morning until well after dark, had been an All-State wrestler.

Barton Hardesty was next. I took an immediate dislike to good old Barton. He was an average looking individual who came from Memphis, Tennessee, which was okay in itself, but he declared himself a rabid fan of Elvis Presley, which was not so good to a modern rocker like myself. Barton's father was a minister of some Protestant denomination I didn't recognize, something that sounded like "The Friends of the Evangelical Church of Almighty Light", and he himself professed to all of us with fervency that he had been reborn into Jesus only recently -- which seemed inconsistent for an Elvis fanatic. I looked at my classmates while he talked, and I noticed several skeptically raised eyebrows. Barton was a tall, very thin person, much like Anthony Grizwald was. -- Was? I was already thinking about poor Anthony in terms of death. But Barton's eyes were what scared me the most. They seemed to shine with an inner light that to me signified either divine inspiration or near insanity. Troubled myself by questions about life and death and deities, I decided I would avoid Barton's intensity whenever possible.

The final occupant of the room was Anthony James Delvecchio. I already knew that Tony was here to get an education. He had announced that plan the first evening. I also knew that Tony was a pretty fair athlete; he was solidly muscled and had played lacrosse in high school. He had also been my wrestling partner that morning and had neatly pinned me twice. Despite the fact that he talked with a distinct mumble that was difficult to discern, I found out that his dad was a stock broker in San Francisco, and his mom was an attorney. He loved the mountains and the seashore and had several siblings.

That evening Ronald Steinway sought me out after dismissal. He entered the room so quietly that if I hadn't happened to look up by accident from my shoe shining -- which was not going well despite more than eight hours of spit-and-rub -- I never would have noticed he was there. He looked at me, embarrassed to be intruding.

"Hey, Ronald," I said brightly. "What brings you here?"

Ronald looked from me to Rico and back again. Finally he came over to my side of the room and sat in Donny's now-permanently-vacant chair. He folded his hands together in an absentminded gesture of supplication, placed them in front of him on the desktop, and stared at me for a moment from across the two desks. His Adam's apple bobbed several times vigorously, and I stared fascinated at the undulations while I waited for him to speak.

"I want to talk to you about what's going on here," he said. I was taken aback. What was going on here?

"Sure go ahead," I replied cautiously. I could see Rico sitting up a little straighter in his chair as Ronald prepared to speak. He was obviously listening. A smile played briefly across his face. He was enjoying my position as the great mediator.

"Well," Ronald began. "I don't like it here very much."

"No problem there, Ronald," I quickly interjected, "but nobody likes it here. Hell, you'd have to be crazy to like what we've been through so far."

"Yes, yes. I realize that," Ronald quickly returned. "But it's more than that for me. You see, my parents are very proud of my getting into this place. They were immigrants from Russia just after World War II. I'm the first of the Steinways to get to college, and they are counting on my success. I can't quit. It would break their hearts." He paused.

"But Maxwell and Battle won't let up on me," he continued. "I never seem to have a moment's peace. I can't think straight. What should I do?"

His last few sentences came out in such an excited rush that I had trouble keeping up with it all. And I was also partially distracted by his damned Adam's apple, which jumped up and down so much during his agitation that I had trouble concentrating on his words. I sat back in my chair. For an instant I was annoyed that he was even here. I wasn't anyone's father-confessor. I had my own misgivings about the place. I paused, hoping something would intervene, but common sense and my sometimes-irritating benevolence won out.

"Look, Ronald," I said. "You're in an unenviable position, because you're slightly behind the rest of us physically. You've become a target, and Max and Battle have good aim. They know exactly what to do to get to you. It would be damned near impossible for any of us to endure what you and Tommy have had to go through -- I'm serious about that. But, the way I see it, they can't really do anything to you that you can't handle. They're not going to beat you up, or throw you in a cell, or hold back on your meals. It's just a matter of attitude. If you think they can win over you, they will. If you convince yourself they can't beat you, they won't." I paused a minute thinking about Pirelli.

"Believe me, "I continued, "this place affects even the staunchest of your classmates. I know that for a fact. I go to sleep every night wondering if I'll make it through the next day. In case you haven't noticed, my defense is humor. Once they deprive me of my ability to laugh at them and at myself, I'm lost. You need to develop a defense." I stared at him at length. I could see he was considering what I had said.

After a long moment, he looked up at me, swallowed with an enormous bob, sighed, and said, "Thanks Kevin. You've been a real help." With that he rose from his seat and headed for the door. Before leaving, however, he turned toward me.

"I can't let my parents down," he said. "I have to make it."

After he was gone Rico put down his book and looked at me.

"You should have been a priest," he said with a smile. "No way," I thought to myself, smiling. Rico looked at my grin with a puzzled expression as I continued my musing. I have too many thoughts about sex to be a good priest. Besides, I wanted to run my own life, not be responsible for the lives of others.

"What do you think about Steinway?" I asked Rico.

"He needs help," he replied. "He's a very troubled lad." He looked at me with a unusually pensive look. I could sense that Steinway bothered him. "Who the hell is here because of their parents anyway?" he asked. Recognizing the rhetorical nature of the question, I stayed quiet. He continued. "Ronald's got to learn to be a man and lead his own life."

Sick Bay is a Navy term for the medical clinic. During that first week every plebe received a base-line physical and too many immunization shots to count. I felt like a pin cushion.

Part of the testing included a routine eye examination. After a petty officer corpsman dilated all the plebe eyes in the Twenty-Third Company, we waited in a darkened room for the medicine to take effect. Twenty minutes later we took turns in three examination chairs as doctor officers peered into our eyes through strange instruments.

Having watched the procedure being performed on my classmates, I had an idea how long the "look" should take. Mine took much longer. Eventually the doctor grunted, told me to sit still, and left the examination room altogether. He returned shortly with a more-senior officer who introduced himself as the head optometrist. He also stared into my eyes for an extended period. Finally he sat back on his stool and looked at me curiously.

"Wait here," he said. "I'm going to get the head of the department." Meanwhile my classmates were zipping through their own exams and staring at me curiously. I saw Rico wink at me when his exam was finished and he prepared to depart the room. I smiled in return, but very weakly. I began to worry.

Soon an older, gray-haired gentleman came to my chair, escorted by the other doctors. He introduced himself, but I wasn't listening at that point. I was worried. The doctor began his own examination. Eventually he finished peering into my baby blues, and by that time I was bursting with curiosity. He gave me no information, and he and the younger doctors disappeared into his office for consultation. I waited outside, enduring the questioning stares of my classmates.

I shrugged to Jim Merritt who came over, put a hand on my shoulder, and said, "You look worried. I'm sure everything will be fine." I nodded in affirmation, not feeling at all sure.

After several minutes, the young doctor returned and ushered me into the boss's office. The senior doctor asked me to sit, and I could tell by his tone that something was wrong.

"Son," he began, "we don't want to frighten you, but if what we fear is true, you may have a rare eye disease." He spouted out a Latin name, but I did not really hear or listen at that point. "If you have this condition, unfortunately, you will end up partially blind in your right eye within a year." Holy shit! What kind of bedside manner was this!

I had no sense that there was anything really wrong. My vision had always tested 20/20 or better, so I had the feeling their concern was much ado about nothing, but . . .

"Since we don't have the proper equipment at Sick Bay," he continued, "I'm going to recommend further examination by a doctor in the main Naval Hospital. Good luck." With that I was ushered from the inner sanctum of Academy medicine. Before I left the area the corpsman scheduled me for the test. He could see I was worried.

"Hey," he said, grinning at me, and obviously lying, "don't worry. They've sent more than a hundred persons for the same test this week. It's nothing. They just want to be sure."

"Then how come they didn't say that?" I asked him. He gave me a shrug that indicated that officers were another breed altogether. That morning I had to agree.

The unusual events did not stop there. I joined my classmates just as the last group was starting the hearing exam. I had never had a hearing test. I had imagined it might be something like reading an eye chart, except you would stand at a certain distance from a tester and try to discern the whispers and noises he emitted. Annapolis, is very high-tech. We entered large sound-insulated booths in groups of eight. It was a very strange feeling. Almost no outside noise came through the thick walls. The walls also prevented the internal noise from echoing. The corpsman in charge had us put on headphones and grip a small button device in our right hands.

"Whenever you hear a sound," he announced in a bored voice, "I want you to press the button. Let up on the button when you don't hear anything anymore." With that pronouncement, he departed, shutting the heavy door behind him. I could see he was in a hurry, and we were his last group.

As I soon found out, the operative word *anything* can be confusing. I still wasn't sure what to expect, since this was my first hearing test, but I held up the button poised and ready, and stared ahead at the wall. I concentrated and waited and waited.

Even though it was a soundproof room and I wore headphones, I could still hear things faintly. I heard rustling from a neighboring classmate, the tapping of a foot against the wall, coughs and throat clearing, and other unidentifiable faint noises. And still I waited. Eventually a tone, clear and sharp, sounded in my ears and I hurriedly pressed the button in response. I could hear the button click. Another tone quickly followed, a little less audible, and I pressed again. I could hear faint clicking sounds from the booths around me, not all of which seemed to coincide with mine. I began to worry, wondering if they were hearing the same tones I was. The sounds and the clicking continued.

Then there came a pause in the process. Either the tones had stopped or had reached a level I couldn't decipher -- kind of like when a dog responds to a whistle too high-pitched for humans to hear. I strained to listen.

Then I heard a creaking noise that sounded like one of my body joints rubbing, and I couldn't be sure this wasn't a new "tone," so I pushed my button. Almost instantly I decided that I shouldn't have done that. Christ, what if some abnormality in my knee joint just caused me to fail the hearing test? Hand poised, I strained harder to ensure I heard the correct noises.

In the vacuum of the moment my ears and mind were instantly ready to pounce on every sound. And suddenly an entire universe of sounds began to rush at me. Plucked unintentionally from the surroundings and from the far off reaches of my head and body, I began to hear tones. Shrill whistles, faint squeaks, dull rumbles, and sharp pops, all vied for my attention along with what I was sure were the valid tones. I hesitatingly pressed the button, my brain whirling at every noise to be sure what I heard wasn't indigestion or a neighbor's fart. Soon I pressed in a frenzy as my brain madly tried to separate manufactured symphonies from the sounds of biology. I began to sweat profusely, thinking that this couldn't really be what I was supposed to do -- but I couldn't stop either.

Finally the door to the booth opened and the technician came in. As I looked around I realized to my chagrin that the test had been over for several minutes, but a quick check with my senses indicated that the errant tones were still running rampant in my head. I put up the headphones and button, shook my head violently to clear it, turned on the stool, and waited.

"Everybody please come outside," the technician ordered. Then he looked at me strangely. "Had a little trouble didn't you, number four?" I moaned, realizing I had screwed up. Now for the consequences.

"I did have some trouble with false sounds," I said timidly.

The technician looked at my worried features and smiled.

"Well," he said. "I figured as much. You passed -- but barely. Next time don't panic. The tones are easy to hear if you stay calm." He released the group to our next appointed encounter with naval medicine, an invidious probing that I instantly hoped I would never experience again. After more than four hours of poking and prodding and sticking, we trudged wearily back to our rooms. I was exhausted.

The next night the squadleaders' lecture concerned the wearing of the winter uniforms. We raced back and forth into our rooms for the better part of an hour changing into Service Dress Blues and working blues. Strangely, these "blue" uniforms were not blue, but actually a deep, very dark black. No way would a sane person call any of those things blue.

Room 5409 was featured next. After Patterson's hasty departure, only three people remained in 5409. John Pirelli was the first speaker. He was short, dark haired, and looked around with an intensity I found uncomfortable. He confidently strode to the fore and addressed us. I watched him closely. I felt powerful. I knew something about Pirelli no one else would ever suspect. He would never be a god-figure to me.

"My name is John Pirelli," he began confidently. " I was raised in Bangor, Maine. My father is a fisherman. He owns his own boat," He said with obvious pride. It sounded fine to me.

"My mother is a supervisory bank clerk," he continued. "I played football and ran cross country in high school. I was president of my class and a National Merit Scholar. I have three brothers, all younger."

Next up was a classmate I had not talked to as yet.

"I'm Patrick Mulvaney," he said in a very clear voice with a distinctive Midwestern drawl. Patrick was a medium build, dark haired, individual who had not particularly excelled during the mornings, but who was not in the straggler group. "I grew up on a small farm in Dubuque, Iowa. My father is obviously a farmer. We raise corn and soybeans and run a few head of cattle. My mom helps around the farm and runs the business end of the operation. I didn't play any sports in high school, but I did act in several plays, and I was a state finalist in debate. I have six brothers and three sisters, and it would take all night to name them and give their ages. But none of the girls is eligible. My mom makes the best cookies, especially chocolate chip ones, and I brought some with me. They're delicious. I'll share them later."

The final occupant of 5409 was Wesley Lamont. Wesley strode to the front, equally as confident as Pirelli. I could see that there would be conflict and competition in that room. I pitied poor Patrick, but maybe with that many siblings, he was used to competition.

"Hi," Wesley began in his musical accent, smiling easily at the group. "Most of you know me already. As I said previously, I'm from the American Virgin Islands. My father runs a fishing and sightseeing charter, and my mother is organist for the Baptist Church. I attended a private high school that did not offer American football, but I played soccer and gymnastics. I was Islands mens' champion on the parallel bars for two years. I have a lovely younger sister who is presently fifteen, but hands off -- my father won't hear of her dating before she is seventeen. I also have an older brother who helps my father." He looked at Pirelli. "I guess that makes John and me fellow sailors," he said, finishing smoothly.

Once Lamont had returned to his place on the floor, Maxwell addressed the group.

"Gentlemen," he said. "You have just completed your first week of training. You have many, many more to go before you are qualified to call yourselves midshipmen. Tomorrow we will exercise as usual, and all meals will be braced. However, since it's Saturday, there will be no training in the afternoon. That will be free time. You may visit quietly among yourselves, shine shoes, stow your things, or just relax. You may not sleep, however, except after lights out. You also may not explore the grounds -- you're not ready for that yet. And under no circumstances are you allowed to fraternize with any females until Parents' Weekend, and then only with your families."

"On Sunday," he continued, "you are all required to attend the chapel of your choice. I have posted a list of times and assembly places on the bulletin board. On Sunday there will be no morning workout unless you choose to do so on your own. If you do, stay out of T-Court and the main campus in gym gear. Exercise on the athletic fields only. Also on Sunday there will be no brace-up at morning and noon meals. Sunday evening, however, plebe year will return with a vengeance, and you had all better have memorized your rates and the other little ditties we requested."

"Since this is a weekend," he continued with an almost evil smile on his face. "Tom and I have alternate liberty, and we will be exploring the evening's possibilities, or we may be resting. Playing nursemaid to a bunch of sissies is hard work. Do not disturb us unless an actual emergency arises; otherwise you will suffer a severe penalty."

He looked at us for a long moment, then became serious.

"The time for play is finished, gentlemen. Over the weekend I want you each to think about what you really want to do with your lives. The Navy is a lifetime commitment, and Annapolis is much more than a civilian university. Although you may not believe it, up to now we've been slack. Come Sunday evening things are going to get really tough. But I promise they won't be half as tough as September when the Brigade returns. Then you'll wish longingly for plebe summer and your old friends Maxie and Tom." He stared into the eyes of several classmates, and of course Tommy Poole was prominent among them.

"Some of you do not belong here," he continued. "Don't make it too hard on yourselves. Quit now and save us the trouble of running you out. Dismissed!" We scurried off to our rooms, where I spent another half hour unsuccessfully smearing polish on my shoes while Rico read another technical manual.

At twenty-one thirty I chopped across the hall to visit the Goons. Rico chose to remain behind. I think he was embarrassed about possibly having to stand up and reveal where his thoughts had been. The Goons were quiet when I entered. Poole was shining his shoes, and I'll be damned if his didn't look better than mine.

"Poole, you bastard. You'd better hide those shoes," I said.

"Huh? Why?" he asked.

"Because they look so good I'm liable to steal them when you're not looking," I replied. He beamed. "Thanks," he said genuinely.

"Anybody want to sneak out into town for some pizza?" I asked. Everyone looked up at me simultaneously. Poole and Merritt were absolutely shocked. Ramsey and Polk were giving the idea serious consideration.

"Just kidding," I said quickly.

"It happens, you know," Ramsey said seriously after a moment.

"What?" I asked.

"Sneaking into town. My daddy talked about his days at West Point. He said you get so stir crazy that you take major risks to get free for a while. Ah'm not ready yet to risk the wrath of Maxie and Battle, but soon, soon, ah think ah will be."

"Well count me out," said Merritt immediately.

"Me too," Tommy added timidly. "I'm in enough trouble as it is. God, I ache!"

Ramsey looked at Polk, who stared back.

"Maybe," was all Jeff said. Ramsey then looked at me.

"Let me know when," I said smiling. "I'll check my social calendar."

"That's just what we need, you know," Ramsey said. "A little balls in the Company."

"There are balls in the Company, Jubal," I replied. "It's just that Max and the Battleaxe have a strong hold on them."

"We'll see," he said smiling.

Suddenly Jim Merritt jumped to his feet and braced up.

"Attention on Deck!" he shouted. I had my back to the door, so I couldn't see what was happening. But I braced rigidly anyway, as did the rest of the room. After a second Battle walked into my field of vision. He was wearing civilian clothes -- very unstylish civilian clothes. He looked at me for a second and continued over to where Ramsey stood braced, his six chins happily smiling. But Battle wasn't interested in Jubal's six magnificent chins. He obviously had other business in mind.

"Carry-on, Ramsey," Battle said quietly. Jubal unbraced -- but so did Tommy Poole. I don't know why. Battle whirled on Poole.

"Who told you to carry-on, Poole, you stupid smack?" he yelled. Tommy immediately realized his mistake and rebraced.

"Sorry, sir!" he yelled.

"You're goddamn right, you're sorry!" Battle yelled. "You are the sorriest-assed excuse for a human being I have ever seen. I am going to personally see to it that you either quit or die, Poole. Count on that!" Tommy wisely didn't reply, but I could see his shoulders sag slightly.

Battle then turned to Ramsey and stared at him for several long seconds.

"I found out about your father just a few minutes ago, Ramsey. I am deeply sorry. You must be very proud of him -- and he of you. Come see me on the morning of the day the Brigade gets back, and our relationship will change. Until then I will treat you like any other plebe, understood?"

I could see Joe's face from where I stood nearby. He looked at Battle, plainly upset.

"I had hoped no one would find out, sir," he said quietly. Battle looked at him a moment, then shook his head slowly.

"I understand," he said. Then he turned on the rest of us.

"If any of you breathe so much as a word of this to anyone, I'll see that you suffer grievously. Am I understood?" he asked.

I had no idea what he was talking about.

"Yes, sir," I said in time with the others. Battle looked at us for another moment.

"Good," he said, and left the room.

We unbraced the second he departed. All of us stared at Jubal. Ramsey remained quiet.

"Joe," I said when I realized he wasn't going to offer anything on his own, "if you don't tell us what it is we're supposed to be quiet about, we may say something inadvertently." Jubal considered my point. Finally he sat at his chair and looked at us. He took a deep breath.

"Okay," he said. "I'll tell." I moved over to Merritt's side of the room and sat on the edge of his desk. Jubal waited until I was seated.

"My daddy was killed in Vietnam two years ago," he said calmly. "Ah didn't want anyone to know."

"Jesus, Jubal, I'm really sorry," said Jeff Polk from across the room.

Ramsey took a breath.

"It's okay." he said. "No problem." Now of course we were all deathly quiet, staring at Ramsey and no one knowing exactly what to say or do.

Jubal looked at us, and said angrily, "I said it's okay Let it drop, ya hear?"

"How do you feel tonight, Tommy?" I asked, trying valiantly to change the subject.

Tommy took several seconds to pull out of his meditation. He looked at Jubal with sympathy.

"I lost my brother a few years ago," he said, "I know how difficult it is."

"Damn it!" Jubal exploded. "I don't want sympathy. I don't want apologies. I don't want to be buddies. Just leave me alone, okay?" He got up from his chair, checked his watch, slipped on his tennis shoes, and departed without another word.

"Wow!" said Jeff Polk. "Boy, do I feel stupid."

"So that's what's put the chip on his shoulder," said Merritt. "It all makes sense now. The question is, what do we do about it?"

"What do you mean?" Jeff asked.

"Well," Jim began. "Even though he's troubled and he says he wants to be left alone, we can't change our lives and tiptoe around all the issues that concern death and Vietnam. He's going to have to accept the fact that his father's dead and get on with his own life. I propose we act as if nothing has happened and continue discussions of whatever concerns us -- tastefully of course. If he's offended, he can leave the room, or change the subject, or, better yet, join in the discussion and get the weight off his shoulders."

"Good idea," I said.

On Saturday morning Tommy Poole beat both Ronald Steinway and Nathan Spielenberg to the finish line. That fact did not in the least decrease the number of push-ups Tommy had to do. But he did make it to ten without stopping once.

Nathan Spielenberg was the next to go. Nathan was an interesting character, I have to admit. I did not for a second understand how "Big Nate" got accepted into Annapolis. But someone must have called in a major marker.

Not only was he significantly shorter than the rest of us, he was also fat -- not chubby, or stout, or pleasingly plump. Nathan was fat. His flesh hung over his waist in a pink wave of grossness. His arms and legs jiggled, and he waddled grotesquely wherever he went.

Nathan could not complete the morning run even halfway without stopping to wheeze, and as for exercises, he was totally inept. The first morning he struggled to finish even a single push-up, and it was impossible for him to rise off the grass to sit-up with the rest of us. By the end of the week he hadn't improved even a little, and the talk among the Company was that he didn't really care to try. Needless to say, Big Nate was another shit screen, but I didn't feel much sympathy for him. He seemed to pretend to try when everyone else was straining.

But what eventually did him in was food. Nate was constantly hungry that first week and complained incessantly to anyone who would listen that he was starving. When he brought this complaint to Battle, Tom complained in return him that his presence made him physically ill. He demanded that Nathan hide his grossness in his locker for an hour. According to his roommates, Big Nate continued to complain about his hunger even from the depths of his dark closet. Battle also made him pledge that he would stay out of his field of vision at all times or else risk having him vomit on his shoes -- Spielenberg's shoes polished up nicely, by the way. But still Big Nate was hungry, and nothing was going to come between him and the next meal.

On Wednesday evening, Nathan Spielenberg sneaked down into the common area of the Rotunda and made a low-voiced phone call to his mother. Apparently, when she heard about his rough treatment, she was angry. When she heard that he wasn't allowed to eat enough, however, she was incensed. The next day Mrs. Spielenberg phoned her Congressman to report the ghastly treatment the Academy inflicted on her precious son. She demanded action. The Congressman -- constituent interest always a primary concern --personally called the Secretary of the Navy that same evening, who promptly relayed the "hot potato" down through the chain of command to the Commandant of the Brigade of Midshipmen, Captain Mack "Greyhound" Hallahan, who was a handsome, articulate, ex-nuclear surface warfare commander, with striking charisma and a wonderful speaking voice. Rumor had it that his reply was characteristically unprintable, but Academy wheels were set into immediate motion nonetheless.

Thursday evening, in response to the Spielenberg "hot potato," Midshipman Second Class Battle gave Big Nate his first taste of carry-on and also ensured that he ate to his heart's content -- to the detriment of his classmates, whose portions had been reduced to compensate for Big Nate's gluttony. Big Nate didn't care. He was ecstatic. Near the end of the meal, seeing that Nate's plate was finally empty, Battle rose and went to a neighboring table, returning with a bowl of food.

"I know you've still got room," he said after he returned. Smiling, Battleaxe stretched the front of Nate's uniform shirt forward, and spooned the morning's "hot potato", along with several dozen mashed companions into the opening. Nathan sat, dumbfounded. Tears welled up in his fleshy eyes.

Then Battle leaned over and said into Big Nate's chubby ear. "Had enough?" Without waiting for an answer he reached over and pressed a hand down on Nathan's ample middle, smashing the potatoes.

"You may not have had enough, Spielenberg you disgusting puke," Battle continued vengefully, "but I have. From this day until the instant you waddle out the Rotunda door in civilian clothes, you are going to be my favorite target. And I promise to make your life miserable." Tears rolled freely down Nathan's cheeks. His shoulders shook and his stomach quivered as he began to sob openly. I watched, but I did not in the least feel sorry for Nathan Spielenberg. I must be a real fascist.

Battle became even more angry when he saw the tears.

"Stop that baby-assed blubbering, you sissy. Do you really think you could ever be a naval officer if you can't take a teeny bit of pressure without bawling." Battle straightened and turned away from Spielenberg. "You disgust me!" Sitting, he looked again at Nathan.

"Well," he said, "Look around! Your mommy's not here in this Mess Hall, fatso. Nobody's going to save you." Nathan sobbed louder.

Nathan survived Friday without being killed, although I'm sure he hoped for death on several occasions. He also finished the Saturday run, sort of. On Saturday afternoon Nathan Spielenberg packed his few personal things, put on his civilian clothes, and waddled out the door of his room. His roommates asked him repeatedly what he was doing.

"I'm going out in town for something to eat," he replied. When asked why he needed a suitcase for a meal he replied, "I'm really hungry."

It was totally out of character for Big Nate to exhibit any semblance of humor, so the roommates in 5413 initially, albeit skeptically, believed him. However, when he had not returned at thirty minutes before the evening meal, Bob Strong called on the squadleaders. After doing 50 push-ups for disturbing Maxwell's beauty sleep, he reported Spielenberg's absence. The entire remaining membership of Room 5413 had to do 50 extra push-ups in formation before every meal for the next week for not speaking up sooner. Battle probably wanted to personally escort Big Nate to the door.

I wish I could say that my first taste of semi-freedom that Saturday afternoon was spent in worthwhile activity, but actually I sat at my desk, bored to tears, trying to write a letter home for an hour. Then I tried to read a science fiction novel I had brought, but with no success. Finally I took my evil shoes from the very rear-most recesses of my locker where I had disgustedly put them, and I tried again to spit my way to shiny success.

Rico, in the mean time had discovered a wide ledge and gutter that ran along the outside of our window. He went outside on the ledge just after noon meal, took off his shirt, and sunbathed while reading another technical manual. I could see the heroic CIA spy happily blazing away at an enemy of our nation while a totally unclad and rather enormous young lady clung to his muscular arm.

Midway into the afternoon, Ronald Steinway entered the room. He looked very unhappy. He explained the departure of Spielenberg, and I indicated skeptically that the chances of our seeing Big Nate again were rather small. Steinway agreed. He was more concerned with his own survival. He took a letter from his back pocket.

"Here," he said. "Read this."

I opened the envelope, which had been folded over several times so that it would fit in his pocket without showing. It contained a short letter from his father that was written on the afternoon of the Oath of Office Ceremony.

"Dear Ronald," it began. *"You don't know how proud it made your mother and me, seeing you recite the pledge today. This is like my wildest dreams come true. The neighbors back home are so envious. You a midshipman! No one's child has ever done so much. I know you'll do well, you have good blood in your veins. And I am counting on you. Be safe. I love you."* It was signed "Pappa." I returned it to him, waiting for a clue as to what he wanted from me.

"What am I going to do, Kevin?" he asked me. "I hate this place, but I can't quit. My parents would die."

He was obviously serious about this, and I wanted to help, but I still wasn't sure what to say. I hesitated.

"Your parents won't die, Ronald," I finally began. "In my opinion they're putting impossible expectations on you. It's your life. You're old enough to make your own decisions. Why stay somewhere if you're miserable? Write your father and tell him how bad it is here; and, believe me, it *is* bad. Keep doing that for a couple weeks, and maybe he'll accept the idea you'd be better off where you are happier. He might even ask you to come home."

Ronald looked at me for another moment, then looked down at his feet.

"I don't think that would work," he said.

"Then stay here, Ronald, if you have to," I said getting slightly perturbed. "It doesn't seem like you've given yourself any middle ground on this issue." Steinway turned away from me.

"I just don't know what to do," he said.

At that moment Rico crawled in from the ledge, hot and sweaty.

"Where have you been?" Ronald asked. Rico looked at him as if he were stupid.

"Well Ronald," Rico said. "I've been out on the ledge contemplating the possibilities of a swan dive off the roof." Ronald looked at Rico closely.

"I don't think you should kill yourself," he said very seriously.

Rico pretended to be shocked.

"No shit, Ronald?" he said. "Well thanks. I appreciate your help."

Ronald suddenly realized he had been the brunt of a joke. He laughed. Then he walked over to the window and stuck his head out into the hot sunlight. He looked up and down the ledge for a long moment before bringing his head back inside.

"That's pretty neat," he said. "A person could hide out there." He walked to the door just as an idea sprang into my head.

"Ronald?" I asked quickly.

"Yes," he said, stopping.

"What size foot does Big Nate have?"

He looked at me like I had completely lost my mind.

"I don't know, but they seemed pretty small to me."

"Would it be anywhere close to a size nine?" I asked hopefully.

"I doubt it," he answered. "Nathan has tiny, but very wide feet. Why do you ask?"

"Never mind. Just an idea," I answered, deflated slightly. Ronald continued to look at me for a puzzled moment, then he departed.

"What the hell do you want with Fat Nathan's shoes?" Rico asked immediately after Steinway was gone.

"He may be quitting," I said. "And his shoes look better than mine."

"Shit, Kevin," Rico answered, picking up his book. "You must be desperate." He was right about that.

Saturday early evening eight of us asked Maxie for permission to play basketball on one of the outdoor courts. Chuck Chalmers had brought a ball. How he fit it inside his luggage I wasn't sure. Maxie agreed, providing he could play with us. He didn't seem to me he could possibly be an athlete, and he certainly didn't have the physique for basketball, but we agreed.

The outdoor courts were over by the Field House, a fairly long distance away. This was the first time we had been able to wander loosely anywhere around the yard, and the long walk around the rear of Bancroft Hall in the warm evening was enjoyable. As we passed quietly along the outside of the fifth and seventh wings we could hear Plebe Year ongoing in several areas. Maxwell laughed at our discomfort.

"You guys didn't believe us when we said we were pussy cats, did you?" he asked. "As you can hear, some of my classmates are true assholes." He then shook his head sadly. "And when we told you about the "Tigers" we weren't kidding either. Those guys are insane. They scare even Tom, and he's about as tough as they come. You guys are in for absolute hell when the Brigade gets back." With that jolly thought of future pain firmly in our minds, we continued on silently.

The scrimmage was successful in that for an hour I did not think about Annapolis, the "Tigers," or about those unshiny shoes lurking in my locker. I did rather well, and so did Chalmers. Maxwell wasn't really too bad either. Jubal Ramsey also was impressive, but I thought he played basketball too much like football, as my bruised ribs later indicated.

It was Maxwell who finally broke the game up. It was his night for liberty. We returned to the Company area in far better spirits than when we had left, and I found myself restless. After taking a long shower, a luxury I hadn't had the entire week, I wandered from room to room.

I stopped for the longest time in 5413. Maybe I was worried about Ronald. Maybe I wanted to be social. Maybe I just wanted to get a glimpse at Fat Nathan's shoes to make sure they really wouldn't fit. Anyway, inside the room Willy Simpson had pulled out his guitar and was singing in time to his gentle strumming. He wasn't bad. Being an old Peter, Paul, and Mary fan, I hummed along for a few songs. In the next few minutes more of my classmates wandered in. I noticed the Steinway had disappeared, and on a hunch I went to the window. Sure enough Ronald sat outside in the now dark night, staring at the moonless sky.

"What's up, Ronald?" I asked.

"Just thinking," he replied. I reached toward him and patted his shoe.

"It'll be OK, Ron," I said. "Just hang in there." He smiled but didn't answer, and I left him to his thoughts. I was still restless when I reached the Goon Room. Inside the four happy roomies were going about their business silently.

"Hey," I said. "Simpson's got his guitar out and there's a regular song fest going on in 5413. You guys should go check it out." No one seemed in the mood. I noticed that Joe had gone into his closet and was putting on gym gear.

"Where you going?" I asked.

"You don't want to know," he answered. I looked at him for a moment.

"Do I sense adventure?" I asked, becoming excited.

I am usually not an adventuresome person. I had gone through high school without once speeding my father's car. I was scared to death of sex. And I was absolutely convinced that even being in the near vicinity of a dangerous drug like marijuana would cause me to commit violent murder. But suddenly I was feeling brave. After all I had just completed a week of plebe training. What else could life do to me?

"Come on Joe?" I asked. "What's up?"

He looked at me for a moment.

"Ah'm gonna do a little reconnoiter, that's all," he said. "I want to see what it's like around here at night."

"Want some company,?" I asked.

He looked at me for a minute. "We could get into trouble if we're caught," he said.

"I beat Battle to the finish line," I offered. "Who's gonna catch *me*?"

Joe laughed.

"Okay, classmate. Let's do it! Put on some different clothes and meet me in the head in five minutes." I hurried to my room, one part of me excited, the other wondering what I was doing.

Dressed identically to Jubal in long gray matching sweatshirt and sweat pants, I arrived in the head exactly five minutes later. Jeffrey Polk was also there.

"Is this going to be a trio?" I asked smiling.

"Yeah," he answered, "but I never figured you for this sort of thing."

"Never be predictable, that's my motto," I answered.

Jubal looked at us.

"Okay, here's the ground rules," he said. "We go out together along Dewey Field in back of the academic buildings; at the wooden bridge to Hospital Point we cross into the main grounds and explore. Be careful not to be seen. If we get spotted, run like hell. If anybody gets caught, we don't turn the others in. Agreed?"

"Sure," we both said.

"Okay," Jubal continued. "Follow me, and be quiet until we're out of Bancroft Hall."

We made our way cautiously down the passageway deeper into the recesses of Bancroft Hall, stopping occasionally in communal heads or quickly descending ladders whenever activity ahead made passage difficult. In this manner we passed through the plebe indoctrination portions of the Hall into the darkness of unoccupied areas. At the ladder, we descended to the ground floor and passed through a set of fire doors into the darkness outside. Jubal wedged a small wooden doorstop under the door to prevent it from locking us out, then straightened and checked the surrounding area.

We had emerged from a side door in the seaward side of the seventh wing. The area was deserted. With Jubal in the lead, we cautiously crept along Bancroft Hall toward the main yard. At the northeast corner of Bancroft Hall near where the construction of new academic buildings Michelson and Chauvenet Halls was underway, we stopped and cautiously peered westward toward T-Court. There was a great deal of activity in the vicinity of Tecumseh as second class squadleaders and their dates met and departed gaily for town. We raced quietly across the open space to the construction site, the darkness concealing us somewhat. No one tried to stop us. We followed the back walkway of Chauvenet and Michelson Halls and cautiously continued toward Hospital Point.

So far we had not seen anyone else on the Severn River side of the grounds, but as we turned west toward the officers' quarters, we noticed two couples strolling toward us about a block away. In keeping with the Academy regulations forbidding public displays of affection, the midshipmen and their dates maintained a polite separation from each other. We pulled back into the shadows of a group of trees while they passed. As soon as they started on their way across the foot bridge to Hospital Point, I guessed what they were going to be up to in a very short period of time. So far we had not said a word except in low, quick, abbreviated whispers. But now Jeff watched the departing upperclassmen with envy.

"Lucky bastards!" he whispered fiercely. We shushed him.

Scanning the surroundings once more, we hurried across the street to the parade grounds. Moving stealthily in the darkest shadows of the trees framing the parade grounds, we approached officer's quarters and the wall separating the Academy from the outside world. The wall, an eight-foot brick structure, was Jubal's destination. We reached it and he began to survey along it.

"What are we looking for?" I asked.

Jubal looked at me like I was crazy.

"Tell him Jeff," he said to Polk.

Jeff leaned over toward me and whispered. "A safe place to come and go." He examined the length of the wall with Joe.

"I see," I said, but not really seeing.

We crept along the wall in the dark and found two spots that were both hidden and scalable. Jubal chose one spot and looked at us.

"Give me a boost," he said. "I want to see what's on the other side."

Placing my back against the bricks, I faced Joe and made a foothold with my hands. Ramsey put his hands on my shoulders, and quickly boosted himself up so that he could see over the wall. He looked up and down the street on the other side for a minute and climbed down, which was a good thing because he was very heavy. The combination of his bulk, the extreme humidity, and the tension made me sweat profusely. Once down, he leaned toward us.

"This is a perfect spot," he whispered. "The other side is a small side street with almost no traffic."

I stepped back and surveyed the wall. It would take some effort to get over, but I was sure I could make it. In Boston I had been a member of the downtown YMCA for a short period, and the indoor basketball court there occupied a space that was exactly the correct length for a court but left no room for out of bounds at the ends. The backboards were actually built into the end walls. Because of this unusual space restriction, the end walls were also considered in bounds, and it was possible to get well up into the air for a slam dunk by planting one foot on the wall and springing upward. I knew I could easily do this with the Academy wall. How Jubal would manage to raise his heavy frame up that wall without assistance was another matter.

Satisfied that he had identified an escape route, Ramsey turned toward the main part of the yard. We carefully skirted the Officers' Club. What kind of punishment would be in store if you didn't stop when the Superintendent yelled out a "Plebe Halt!"? I didn't want to find out.

We made our way cautiously among the old academic buildings that lined the street and walks in this area. I couldn't help but feel a slight awe as I gazed at these grand old buildings. How many thousands of midshipmen had studied in these halls? What classes would I take here? How well would I do? I began to understand the reverence our squadleaders felt for the institution as I observed the solid, comfortable, places of learning. I could quickly get captured by the mystique if I wasn't careful.

My companions were also mesmerized by the locale, because when we turned a corner to return toward Michelson Hall, we almost stumbled on a squad leader and his date as they sat nestled on a dark bench near Mahan Hall. We froze. The couple hadn't noticed us, but we were awfully close to them. Jubal put out a beefy arm to stop us, and waved that we should retreat. We did, very cautiously. As we backed I watched the couple enviously. What a juicy kiss! I wanted one. I began to flush. It wasn't the first time in my life I ever felt horny, but I still didn't like it.

We cautiously backed around the corner but rather than being safe, we were in bigger trouble. Two more sets of second-class and their dates headed our way, and they had seen us.

"Hey!" one of them yelled. "Plebe Halt!" No way!

We ran hastily in the direction from which we had just come. The startled secondclassman on the bench was just emerging from his love coma when we passed. He stared at us but didn't say a word. He seemed comatose, and his date was no better off. What had they been doing? I wanted to stop and ask, but streaked passed instead. The other squadleaders pursued.

We raced along the walk between Mahan and Michelson Halls toward the construction area. One of the pursuers yelled an almost continuous string of "Plebe Halts!" as he followed. At the back corner of Michelson we turned toward Bancroft Hall and picked up speed.

"Just like a morning workout!" Polk yelled, laughing slightly, as we paralleled each other. Ramsey had been in the lead from the beginning, but he soon began to tire and we caught up to him. I could hear the sounds of footsteps behind us as the squadleaders followed. I glanced back, hoping it wasn't anyone as fleet of foot as Battle. One pursuer, a tall, skinny individual, was not more than 50 yards behind. The other had stopped at the corner of Mahan Hall. That was a good sign, especially since the one still running had on civilian clothes, which included a sport coat and tie and hard street shoes that were sure to slow him down. It couldn't be easy to keep up his effort. It wasn't. At the junction of the construction area, he also stopped.

"I'll get you little bastards!" he yelled at us as we continued, slightly less fast, down the walkway.

We hurried to the corner of Michelson Hall, checked the open area for watchers, then ran to the side of Bancroft Hall. Within two minutes we had slipped back inside our departure door and were snug in the arms of "Mother B". Another five minutes found us safely in our rooms.

"Had an adventure?" Rico asked as I entered, still sweaty and flushed with excitement.

"You might say that," I replied.

"Well," he said. "Battle hasn't been around yet, so you're probably safe."

I hurried into the shower and cleaned myself.

I showered quickly, put on different gym clothes and sat at my desk to recover. Recovery on a humid Maryland August night is virtually impossible, however; as I sat, I continued to sweat. Rico watched me with raised eyebrows until my breathing had slowed. I smiled at him but didn't offer anything. I wasn't sure if his knowing would put him in a bad position.

At 2145, Tommy Poole entered carrying his shoes. He looked at me and grinned a very lopsided smile.

"I figured it out," he said.

"What?" I asked.

"How to make these damn things shine," he replied. "It's easy. Let me have one of your shoes." I hurried to my closet and removed one offending shoe gingerly. There was so much polish on it that even being in its close proximity would guarantee a black stain. I handed it to him by a shoestring.

He took it to the sink and turned on the hot water. I watched, amazed. Once the water was as hot as it could get, he inserted his hand into the shoe, and plunged the shoe under the near-scalding water. Watching closely, I could see the heat melting off layer after layer of polish. Tommy waited until the shoe was almost down to the original leather, then removed it. He shook the excess water into the sink, and went to my side of the room. He sat in my chair and took a cloth from his shorts pocket. Rubbing in small circles, he began to buff the toe area.

"The heat makes the pores open and accept the polish," he said. "Otherwise you have to work too hard to bring up a shine." Within a minute that shoe shined far better than it ever had after several days of my efforts.

"Where does the spit come in?" I asked.

"It doesn't!" he replied with a laugh. "That's just a myth. A little bit of polish, a little bit of water, and small easy circles will do it." He held my shoe up to the light. It sparkled. I was beginning to like this guy.

"I'll pay you ten bucks to do mine," Rico said from across the room.

"No thanks," Tommy replied. "But I'll help you with them if you'd like."

"Great!" Rico said. "They're in the closet. Bring them back before noon meal tomorrow."

"Rico!" I said loudly. "Tommy offered to help, not to do all the work." Rico smiled disarmingly.

"Just kidding," he said. Tommy was confused.

"I will help," he offered again.

"Come back in the morning after church," Rico said, "and I'll gratefully accept." Tommy went to the door.

"Almost time for lights out," he said.

"Hey, Tommy," I said just before he left. He stopped "Thanks," I said.

He smiled weakly.

"God, I'm tired," he said, sighing as he departed.

It was considered a "Class A" offense to have alcohol inside Bancroft Hall. It probably still is. "Class A" offenses are major, meaning so many demerits that an inmate in solitary confinement in Turkish prison has more privileges. But while alcohol in the barracks was considered God-awful serious, being drunk in the barracks was not. We didn't know that. Saturday night around midnight Midshipman Second Class Maxwell returned from liberty weaving happily along the passage, awakening most of us by loudly singing an interesting and bawdy version of *What do you do with a Drunken Sailor?* Don't ask! I rose and went to the door to see what was making that awful sound. Maxwell's normally fine tenor was distorted and strained by the alcohol. Merritt stood in the opposite door.

"O'Reilly, Merritt, you douchebags!" Maxwell shouted. "Hit it for 100!" I stared at him for a moment, groaned loudly, and dropped to the deck in the doorway and began shouting out numbers. Maxwell stood swaying in the middle of the passageway watching and smiling. As other heads poked into the dark passageway, Maxwell ordered additional pushups until more than ten of us were simultaneously yelling different numbers. Maxwell turned a slow, unsteady circle to watch.

By the time I had reached 50, Battle entered the passageway from his room. His short hair was disheveled, and his robe hung loosely oven one shoulder. He looked very tired. He walked to Maxwell and put a hand on his shoulder.

"Come on Maxie," he said. "Let's get you to bed." He steered his roommate awkwardly down the hall toward their room. At the doorway he paused and looked over his shoulder at us.

"Knock it off and go to bed!" he said loudly. "And forget this happened!" After the two of them disappeared into their room, my classmates and I exchanged smiles and head shakes, then returned to our own beds. The next morning a huge, stinking, puddle of vomit lay on the passageway floor near the entrance to the head. I guessed that Maxwell didn't make it.

Tommy Poole who was also a Catholic and who -- more importantly -- had an operating alarm clock, woke us at 0800 for Catholic services. The uniform was Tropical Whites -- the uniform the squadleaders and officers usually wore. We had practiced how to rig the combination cap and shoulder boards, studied the proper alignment of the shirt and pants, and learned how to give ourselves a proper "tuck." Several days previously we had polished our belt buckles to a fine white-gold glossiness and whitened our shoes. Polishing the white shoes was as simple as dabbing liquid white stain from a polish bottle onto the nap. It didn't take me long to ready myself, and soon Rico and I joined Tommy and several companymates in the passageway for the walk for formation in T-Court. We inspected each other quietly and agreed we looked great. I doubted Battle would have agreed, but luckily he wasn't going with us. At 0845 we left the company area and descended the ladder into the rotunda. Once there we joined a throng of classmates headed outside.

Formation for the various services took place on one side of Tecumseh Court. A S-econdclassman stood quietly at the bottom of the steps and directed us. He looked tired -- from last night's liberty, no doubt -- and didn't bother us at all. Catholic formation was directed by another secondclassman. Nearby several smaller groups formed for their walk to services in the city. We formed ranks as we arrived, and at 0850 we marched to chapel.

The main part of the Annapolis campus is bounded by five imposing structures. On the south side toward the Chesapeake Bay is enormous Bancroft Hall, its northernmost wings circling T-Court and fronting the baleful statue of Tecumseh. To the north, more than 200 yards away and separated by enormous and beautiful trees and impeccably maintained grounds, is the old and impressive library building, Mahan Hall which sports a clock tower. To the east toward the Severn River are identical academic buildings, Chauvenet and Michelson Halls. The jewel of the entire campus scene, however is the chapel, which graces the western side.

The chapel at Annapolis may be the most beautiful of its kind in the nation. Possibly only Saint Patrick's in New York can rival its effect on a visitor. The main entrance is through huge brass doors opening onto a wide vestibule. The vestibule leads directly into the church proper, which is shaped like an exclamation point with the entry being at the top of the straight section. A long wide wing flanked by wooden pews leads to the circular dome. The dome, more than 30 yards high, canopies the altar.

The interior stonework and dome are magnificent, and the stained glass windows which surround the upper portions of the dome have been specially crafted to depict four famous naval scenes. What may lift the Academy chapel above the likes of Saint Patrick's is the music. I had to wait until the Brigade returned and midshipman structure was reestablished to appreciate it; but when the Annapolis choir sang in that chapel, it was almost like being in heaven with the angels. I've always enjoyed music, and that was the perfect place for it.

We marched into the chapel and down the main aisle to the dome. I don't remember much about my first Annapolis mass because I spent so much time looking at everything else -- sorry Father. Mass was not a long affair, and soon we marched back to Bancroft Hall. Outside the chapel quite a few tourists watched us and made comments about how wonderful we looked. I felt that way. It was a new feeling for me.

Sunday morning breakfast was paradise compared to meals we had recently experienced. There were no specific company areas. Tables in one prearranged wing were served as midshipmen arrived. What few squadleaders were there didn't care about plebe rates or bracing or squared meals. As a matter of fact, the table where Rico, Tommy, and I sat was populated solely by plebes. We ate, chatted, and felt human again.

The company area was quiet when we returned. Many of our classmates were attending Protestant services, either the main event, which almost immediately followed Catholic mass in the chapel, or with various smaller denominations which met in churches in town. We retired to our respective rooms to change clothes.

Tommy Poole, dressed in gym gear, visited us several minutes later. He sat in an empty chair as I showed him how my shoes were coming along.

"Guys," Rico said from across the room, "continue talking, but I have to excuse myself. I have something important to do." With that statement he turned away from the open doorway, propped a book on his lap, and leaned on one arm. Pretending to read, he soon fell deeply asleep. The ability to doze on a moment's notice and under unusual circumstances is a habit most midshipmen quickly learn. During later years I would happily walk ten minutes to my room to lie down for thirty minutes between classes.

Tommy looked at Rico and laughed quietly.

"He's quite a person," he whispered.

"Yeah," I answered, "but don't tell him that. His ego's already big enough."

"Well," Tommy said, looking at his body. "I'm going to work out a little and see if I can get the soreness from my legs and arms. What are you going to do?"

"I don't know," I answered. "I think I'll write letters and read for a while. After lunch I'm going to try to roust out enough players for a basketball game."

Tommy looked at me and said, "I really envy your athletic abilities."

"It's nothing but practice, Tommy," I replied, lying slightly. Practice is important, but in most sports, you've either have the talent or you don't.

Tommy left the room, heading for Dewey Field, and I pulled out paper and pencil to write a longer letter to my family.

A soft, friendly whisper tickled my ear.

"O'Reilly," it said sweetly. "Wake up, dear." The voice must have coincided with a dream I was having because I smiled as I woke and stretched lazily.

Woke! Instantly I realized I had been sleeping. I had no idea how I had fallen asleep. I jerked my head to the left to see the perverted whisperer and I stared straight into the smiling face of the Battleaxe. My heart sank, and my face instantly and forcefully flushed. I sat bolt upright, then stood quickly, knocking the chair backward in the process.

"Attention on deck!" I yelled over the crashing commotion.

It was too late. Rico already stood at attention on the other side of the room watching me with a slight smile on his face. Apparently Battle had caught him as well, but didn't allow him to make any noise to waken me. As I pulled in my chin to brace I realized that I had slept for some indeterminate time with my head well over to one side. A tremendous cramp in my neck caused me to flinch, and prevented me from achieving full "chin-dom". I groaned.

"Uncomfortable, huh?" asked Battle, feigning concern.

"Yes, sir!" I answered, waiting with apprehension for the punishment to begin. Battle looked at the two of us with glee.

"This is wonderful," he said with sadistic gusto. "I needed two strong men to demonstrate a "comearound" this evening after meal. It looks like you'll be them." He smiled broadly as he headed for the door. "Come around!" he said.

"Aye, aye, sir!" we both shouted to the now empty doorway.

After the noon meal, which was also more like a brunch than a standard Academy affair, the Company split into two distinct groupings. One group, which included Jim Merritt and John Pirelli, welded themselves to their desks and busily memorized plebe rates and other required data. The other group searched for distracting activities. Some jogged. Others read books or wrote letters. Rico and Wesley sunbathed just outside our window. Tony Delvecchio studied the academic catalog. Barton Hardesty meditated with his bible. Willy Simpson played his guitar. I led a group of wishful athletes to the basketball courts for a pick-up game. I wanted to ask Maxwell to accompany us to pick up some brownie points, but Battle met us at the door and declined for his roommate -- still hungover no doubt. Interestingly, Tommy Poole went along to the courts and stretched and exercised while we played. I was beginning to like that guy. He had guts -- no, actually he had *a* gut -- a large gut to be sure -- but he also had character.

We returned to our area two hours before meal. Rico was reading from *Reef Points*. If he had begun preparing for the meal maybe I should too I thought, beginning to feel panic. I quickly showered and joined him in study. If nothing else, years of Catholic education imparts a student with one extremely useful attribute -- the ability to memorize and recite. Even after more than 30 years I still remember much of the altar boy responses -- in Latin.

I did fairly well on the rates, but there was an incredible amount of information to memorize. I realized almost instantly that I needed to spend much more than an hour to properly learn everything. But I did the best I could. A half hour before meal formation I worked on my shoes and checked my uniform. When everything was as good as I could do, I dressed and reviewed my rates while I waited nervously. The anxiety was contagious. Even Rico hustled about the room and recited quietly in a dull murmuring voice to himself.

Ten minutes before formation excited plebe voices shouted from four locations in the passageway, "Sir, you now have ten minutes to evening meal formation! The uniform for evening meal is Tropical Whites. The menu for evening meal is tossed green salad, grilled New York steak, mashed potatoes and gravy, sauted vegetables, bread, milk and butter. For dessert Apple Brown Betty. The Officers of the Watch are: The Officer of the Watch is Lieutenant Thompson. The Assistant Officer of the Watch is Lieutenant Leet. The Midshipman Officer of the Watch is Midshipman Second Class Pera. The movies in town are: At the Capitol, *True Grit;* at the Strand, *Cleopatra;* at Parole Plaza, *Easy Rider*. The days are: There are 66 days until Parent's Weekend, 68 days until the Brigade returns, and 169 days until Navy beats Army! Sir, you now have ten minutes, sir!"

Wow, I thought. Whoever stood at my end of the passageway did a pretty good job. I glanced outside; it was Bill Allen. He smiled at me as he chopped into his room. Five minutes before the appointed time the call was repeated, and immediately afterward I could hear plebes chopping to their places. I stood.

"Well," I said. "This is it." Rico nodded distractedly, still trying to memorize something.

At two minutes before formation the duty room sang out for the final time. "Sir, you now have two minutes before evening meal formation!" After reciting the meal menu they finished, " Time, tide and formation wait for no man. I am now shoving off. You have one minute sir!" The duty room members chopped quickly to formation and joined us in ranks.

Almost immediately Battle and a still-shaky Maxwell exited their room. Battle strode smartly toward us. Maxwell sauntered slowly. Tonight was to be our first true uniform inspection. We opened ranks on command to allow the two of them to view our identical white ensembles. I was in the third rank therefore my turn to be viewed came later in the exercise. I secretly watched the squadleaders as they proceeded down the front of the first rank and up its back and repeated the process with rank number two.

They were very serious that night. There was no smiling and no banter as they proceeded from plebe to plebe. Every individual received some corrective comment. Many received several comments. A few individual appearances made the squadleaders angry and those classmates were asked to comearound the next evening. One classmate in the front rank had his shirt pulled from his pants and was ordered to return to his room for a retuck. Maxwell purposefully scuffed the tops of Chuck Chalmer's white shoes, leaving prominent dark marks.

"Your shoes look like hell," he said. "This is incentive to do better, pal." They both stopped at Tommy Poole's location which was in front of me and slightly toward the rear. They checked his shoes and belt and I heard him get at least two comearounds. Then they came to his hat. They stared, puzzled for several seconds. Battle reached up and adjusted the alignment of the cap, stepped back, shook his head and tried again.

When the second adjustment didn't suit him, he leaned in toward Poole and said, "Your hat's on crooked, Poole!"

Tommy didn't flinch.

"No, sir!" he answered. Both Battle and Maxwell stepped back and re inspected Tommy's hat. Battleaxe looked at Max, who shrugged.

"Your hat's on crooked," Battle said again.

"No sir," Tommy answered.

Battle stepped up until his face was less than an inch from Poole's.

"If your hat isn't crooked, asshole, then what's the problem?" he asked fiercely.

"Sir, my head is crooked, sir!" Poole answered in a perfectly serious manner. Battle was astounded but didn't laugh. Several of my nearby classmates did laugh, however, for which they received an instant comearound. Battle took Poole's word at face value, however, and checked the position of his eyes and ears.

"Christ, I think he's right, Maxie," he said after a minute. He leaned in again toward Poole. "You're a freak, mister. Did you know that? You're a god-damn genetic mutation. You are also one of the damned ugliest people I have ever seen. Genius or not, you've got to go, Poole." I was convinced he meant every word, and with that he moved on to the next plebe.

All too quickly it was my turn. I took a deep breath and pulled in my stomach as Battle stopped in front of me. I could see only the top of his white cap as he bent his head to view my shoes. Slowly he raised his head to check my pants creases and lineup.

"Thumbs along the seams of your trousers!" he ordered. I had thought they were, but I quickly adjusted. His head continued to stare downward at my middle for longer than he had with most of my classmates, so I knew he was checking something.

"Did you polish the top of your belt buckle?" he asked. My brain whirled, considering whether I had or not.

"No sir!" I answered with the truth.

"Why the hell not, O'Reilly?" asked Maxwell, who was now standing next to me, flanking Battle.

"I'll find out, sir," I answered.

"Comearound, asshole," Maxwell said as he and Battle moved on to the next victim.

Mealtime was absolute hell, the worst meal yet. I was so busy passing food, sliding further and further out onto the edge of my seat at Maxwell's urging, and responding to repeated questions that I didn't eat very much. Luckily, Ronald Steinway chose to sit next to me. I think he felt somehow protected in my shadow. He couldn't see that the very opposite was true. Maxwell pounced on Steinway unrelentingly. Steinway recited rates, answered innocuous questions, and must have earned 20 comearounds before the meal was over. In his desire to *train* Steinway, Maxwell even left Tommy Poole alone for the most part.

The only rate I had to recite was. "*How's the cow?*"

I answered with a boisterous and smiling. "Sir! She walks, she talks, she's full of chalk, that lacteal fluid extracted from the female of the bovine species is highly prolific to the fifth degree, sir!" -- "Fifth" indicating that there were approximately five glasses of milk in the nearest container. -- Pretty stupid, huh? Then how come I enjoyed reciting it?

At the table next to us I could hear Jim Merritt and John Pirelli having a virtual rate battle. Every question Battle asked, they answered quickly, efficiently, and joyously. They were clearly overdoing the plebe routine, and I was a bit uneasy. Did I sound like that when I answered? Across the table Jeff Polk stared at me during one of Pirelli's forced but enthusiastic diatribes. Jeff answered my question with a silent but resounding "Yes!"

I felt immediately resentful. Who the hell was Polk anyway? He wasn't my mother or my conscience. If I wanted to feel good while forcing my chin tightly and painfully against my neck and balancing myself precariously on what had to be a quarter inch of seat, while at the same time carefully and squarely lifting individual single gram bites of food to my mouth and yelling to a twenty-year-old college student about bovines and lacteal fluids, what business was it of his? Yeah, what business?

I was exhausted at the end of the meal, more so than after the morning exercises. I retreated to my room to change into gym gear for the evening's training. I wasn't looking forward to this.

"Who are my comearound guinea pigs?" Battle asked the group after we had dutifully assembled for the evening's training. Guevarra and I reluctantly raised our hands. So did Willy Simpson and Ronald Steinway.

"Step out here, gentlemen," Battle demanded. We stepped. I was beginning to feel a little better. I was sure I could outrun the group; and although Rico was stronger than me, we had Ronald in the foursome. The shit-screen theory was going to save me again. Wrong!

"All right, everybody else back up against the bulkhead and watch," barked Battle. "You four stand down the passageway even with the head doorway and face me." We started chopping down the passageway.

"Move your asses!" he yelled. We sprinted. "When I say go I want you to sprint to the double doors. Hit the doors with both hands and sprint back. The winner does nothing. The losers do ten pushups. Ready, go!"

We sprinted. The distance between the heads and the double doors was about 50 yards and I knew the race would be between Rico and me. I beat him to the doors by a full second, and won by the same margin. This wasn't going to be so bad. I hadn't even hit full speed. Rico dropped to the deck and had shouted out two push-ups before Simpson finished. Rico was standing when Steinway crossed the line. Maxwell ran alongside Ronald yelling in his ear. Ronald was already tired.

They didn't let Ronald do his push-ups.

"Save it for later," Maxwell ordered. "Line up!" We readied ourselves for a second run, which I again won easily, but I was beginning to feel sorry for my roommate. During the third race I let Rico pull ahead at the finish, and I dropped for 10. As I stood I looked at Rico and winked secretly.

"Nice job, Guevarra," shouted Battle from his position near the rest of my classmates. "You beat the rabbit. What's the matter, O'Reilly, getting tired?"

"No, sir!" I shouted.

"Lose again, asshole, and you'll do 20 push-ups!" Battle added. My spirits and Rico's flagged appropriately.

We ran twice more, and I won both times. Then Battle called a halt. "Okay, gentlemen," he said. "Now that you're warmed up," he said loudly, "we're going to begin bear-crawls!" When we didn't respond he yelled, "Down on your hands and knees!" We dropped to the hard tile deck.

"Raise yourselves up on your hands and feet," he yelled. We did. He smiled. "Now try the same race in that position. Ready, go!" We started awkwardly forward. Within 10 yards I knew I hated bear-crawls. I could feel the slapping of my hands against the cursed deck all the way up through my shoulders. The awkward motion also instantly made my leg muscles ache, and the friction from the tiles rubbed my hands. I decided instantly I really hated bear-crawls. Unfortunately for me, both Rico and Willy were ursine Olympians, and I suffered through three consecutive losses and the resulting push-ups.

"Stand up!" Battle yelled to us. We stood. I could have kissed him for ending the torture.

"Now we're going to do crab-crawls," he said with obvious glee.

"Sit on the deck facing away from me," he yelled. We sat. I didn't like where this was leading. "Lift yourselves up on hands and feet with your bellies in the air." I lifted myself but it was a very awkward position.

"Now," he said. "Same race course! Go!" We went, although significantly slower. I stumbled twice on the way down the passageway and twice on the way back. It didn't matter. I was not the best crustacean in the group either. Maxwell paced me, yelling the entire three races. Push-ups followed.

"Stand again!" Battle yelled. We stood, but I had trouble lifting myself off the deck. "Back to regular wind sprints!" Battle yelled. Good. This I could do. I won the first one by several seconds, and as I watched my three company mates pushing up, I was secretly happy. To hell with bears and crabs, let's keep up this man's exercise.

"O'Reilly, are you tired?" Maxwell asked. Shit, yes I was tired!

"No, sir!" I answered bravely. Max turned to the Battleaxe.

"Tom, this isn't fair. O'Reilly's too damned fast. He's bilging his classmates. We should adjust the course."

Battle smiled at me.

"You're absolutely right, Tom," he said. "Steinway come up here and stand by me!" Ronald hurried to Battle's position more than halfway to the double doors. "You start from here, Ronald."

"Thank you, sir!" Ronald blurted. Battle didn't like this answer.

"What! Thank you? You douchebag! Hit it for twenty!" Steinway collapsed on the deck and began struggling. Battle didn't say a word until Ronald finished the push-ups.

After Steinway was again braced and facing the double doors, Battle stood just inches from his right ear and said. "I don't like you, Steinway. You're one of the ones who doesn't belong here. I will never intentionally do anything to help you, is that understood?"

"Yes, sir," Steinway stammered.

"Good!" Battle answered. "Remember that from now on." Battle turned to the three of us. "Simpson, stand ten meters closer to the double doors. Guevarra, stay where you are. O'Reilly, take three giant steps backwards."

"Mother, may I, sir?" I asked. Why did I say that? Battle hesitated but didn't crack.

"Give me 20, O'Reilly," he said calmly. I did. God were my arms tired.

The race was much closer. I caught Steinway just after the double doors, and Simpson ten meters from the heads on the way back. I beat Rico with only a half meter to spare. Yes, I did sprint.

"Good job, O'Reilly!" Maxwell said boisterously. "Let's try again, Tom." We ran again, and again, and again. Each race they adjusted positions to make the outcome closer. Each time I sprinted, becoming more and more tired. I didn't win them all.

"Okay," Battle said. "Last race. The winner doesn't have to comearound in the morning and gets carry-on at breakfast. Losers do 50 pushups." They adjusted positions again. "Go!" Battle yelled.

I was last at the double doors by a goodly margin, but I figured the others were tired. Maybe as tired as I was. I sprinted. I could feel my system reacting to the strain, and I was reminded of a similar reaction I had when I overexerted myself during track practice. I kept it up, passing Steinway and Simpson at the ten meter mark.

I almost caught Guevarra. Something else caught up with me, however; and immediately after the sprint I raced into the head. I made it as far as the sinks and began vomiting.

"What are you doing, O'Reilly?" asked Battle. He couldn't hear my retching from his position down the passageway. I had made quite a mess on the floor and edge of the first sink.

I turned on the water, took a deep breath, and between heaves I replied loudly, "Barfing my guts out, sir!"

"Clean up any mess you make, you pussy. And hurry up out here. We can't wait just because you get a little sick." I was almost angry enough to say something about the speed with which Maxwell adjusted to last night's reverie, but I held my tongue in check.

I used paper towels to clean up the still-warm remnants of dinner, quickly wiped my face, and hurried back to formation. I must have looked as bad as I felt because several classmates had distressing grimaces on their faces as they stared at me. Maybe it was the chunks of dinner splattered on my shirt that repulsed them. Most however, avoided staring at me altogether.

"Sit down!" Maxwell ordered. After we had settled he addressed us, smiling slyly. "First I want to thank the volunteers for participating in tonight's practice comearound. As you can see, it takes energy, stamina, and guts to be successful in this institution. Some of you don't have those qualities and never will. Some of you need the gentle molding and encouragement we provide to help you eventually be your best. Some of you already have what it takes but need seasoning to steel your characters. Tomorrow you will all begin comearounds to Mr. Battle and me -- except for classmate Guevarra, of course. You saw what happened out there tonight. If you are not willing to give 100 percent -- even to the point of puking -- then you're not giving it all. We won't accept that. Is that understood?"

Everyone answered with a loud simultaneous "Yes, sir!"

"Is room 5410 ready for introductions tonight?" asked Battle. "Let's get to it."

Tim Richardson led off. Tim was a tall, blond, striking, athletic-looking young man. He smiled and seemed perfectly confident.

"I'm Tim Richardson," he began. "My father is in the Navy, so I moved around a lot when I was growing up, but I guess you could say that Jacksonville, Florida is my home."

"What does your dad do?" Maxwell interrupted.

"He's a Captain. He's Commanding Officer of the Naval Air Station in Jacksonville." Richardson smiled when he said this, knowing that he had laid a very high card on the table. I thought maybe he played it too early, unless he was holding something better in his hand.

Richardson continued. "I attended Jackson High School. Played tennis and volleyball. My mother is usually busy with Wives Club functions. I have an older brother who plays football and is presently a First Class in Eighth Company." -- trump card -- "and I have two very pretty younger sisters." Smiling comfortably, he sat.

Next was a quiet boy named Aaron Rose. Aaron was an average young man, dark-haired, not particularly tall or athletic looking. "My name is Aaron Rose," he started in a quiet voice. "My father runs a beef export business in Omaha, Nebraska. I attended B'nai B'rith school in Omaha. I played no sports, but I was a National Merit Scholar, and valedictorian of my class. I have a brother who is a doctor, and two older sisters, each married." He quickly took his place.

The third classmate stepped forward. He was stocky, almost fat, and had large lips and prominently dark bushy eyebrows that clumped in the center of his forehead so that the separation between them was indistinguishable. He also had a very feminine voice which was pleasant to listen to. He could be a good public speaker. Except he couldn't seem to carry through a complete thought. He jumped nervously from topic to topic with no organization whatsoever.

"Ah -- I'm Steve Rogers. No sisters. I played some Pony League baseball for a while -- catcher. Born in Detroit. I have a younger brother and my dad's an engineer with the city. Mom's dead." We stared at Steve as he regained his place. I watched Maxwell. Behind his slanted eyes I thought I could see him mentally add Rogers to his list of maybes.

The final occupant of Room 5410 was a very interesting individual. He approached the front of the group almost aristocratically. He was tall, blond haired, and very thin. His face was almost cadaverous, and his eyes a pale and very attractive blue. His cheekbones stood out on the sides of his face like the bony plates of a triceratops. He also had a magnificently hooked nose. I didn't envy that, however. Being a flaming redhead I knew what a target a physical abnormality like his nose must have been for him.

"My name is Hans Roudolph," he said. Hans, what a great name. I wondered briefly if he could skate.

"My parents came to the United States from Switzerland soon after World War II." -- He probably could skate -- " I was born in Albany, New York. My father is a banker. My mother is head nurse at the VA hospital. I played tennis in high school, was ranked third in the state. I was also president of the Chess and Astronomy Clubs and the debate team. I have a sister who is one year older and another sister who is two years younger. Both are blond and very attractive." Staring at that magnificent proboscis, I had my doubts about that last statement.

After Hans sat down, Maxwell addressed us again.

"Tomorrow we will begin splitting up the comearounds. Tom will take half of you for a nice leisurely run in the morning air while I manage the fun exercises in the passageway. In the evening, exactly one hour before meal we will all meet here for a joint comearound. The following day you will change routines. Questions?"

"Sir," said Tim Richardson. "What happens if we injure ourselves during the exercises? What do we do?"

Maxwell stared at Richardson for a moment.

"Listen up, pal! If you're seriously injured, stop whatever you are doing and tell us immediately. We'll get you to the Clinic instantly if it's life threatening, or allow you to go to Sick Call later if it's minor."

Battle interrupted. "Why, Richardson? Are you hurt?"

"No, sir!" Tim answered confidently. "It was a hypothetical question." Battle continued to stare.

"Dismissed!" Maxwell announced. We chopped to our rooms.

Almost immediately Rico turned to me, obviously concerned. "Jesus, Kevin," he said. "I'm sorry about your being sick."

"No problem," I answered. "I just got carried away with the thought of carry-on. It was stupid. I'm never doing that again."

He looked at me all-knowingly.

"Yes you will," he said. Although I outwardly protested his prognostication, inwardly I knew he was right again. He must be part gypsy.

When I finished my shower, Jim Merritt was sitting at my desk.

"What's up?" I asked.

"I don't know what to do," he said. "Ramsey and Polk are driving me crazy. A few minutes ago Jubal threatened to strangle Tommy if he didn't quit immediately. He said we'll all be run to death -- kind of like you were tonight -- if Poole and Steinway, and a few others don't leave the Academy soon. And Polk's constant harangue against the system is getting really old. And Tommy Poole is about as depressed as a human being can be."

"Sorry, Jim," I said. "That sounds like a load. But we'd need an army of psychologists to tackle all the problems. And Poole's an enigma. I've only been a midshipman for a week, and already I'm getting protective of the place. I'm not sure that Maxwell isn't right. Do you really think Poole will make a good officer? Maybe he *should* quit."

"Maybe he should," offered Merritt. "But it's Maxwell's and Battle's job to force him out, not ours. Poole and Steinway are our classmates, and it's our responsibility to help them if we can. If we don't stick together, we're going to be in serious trouble later when it really matters."

I thought about what Merritt had said.

"Maybe," I answered after a moment. I could see that Jim expected more.

"The Polk problem is easiest," I suggested changing the subject. "Tell him to keep his mouth shut if he can't contribute to the general harmony of the group."

"He's hiding something," said Rico from across the room. We both turned simultaneously.

"What?" I asked.

"Nobody protests that loudly unless they've got another secret somewhere underneath," Rico said. "I think he's scared to death he won't cut it here, and he's setting himself up to quit. If he doesn't adjust, he'll eventually convince himself that the place is so horrendous he has to leave to satisfy his invented principles."

"What about his anti-war attitude? That seems genuine enough," Merritt offered.

"Of course it is," Rico answered. "I don't know about you guys, but I don't want to die in some stinking jungle. The war doesn't make sense to me either. We all know that intuitively. But the difference between reasonable men like us and unreasonable ones like Polk is we accept the decisions we've made. If we don't want to fight, we can quit and go to Canada. So can Polk. He stays because he's really not sure and he's seeking reinforcement for his doubts. Do what I do. Ignore him. If you don't answer, he'll give up the complaining."

"Do you really think so?" Merritt asked.

"No doubt about it," Rico answered confidently. Jim looked at me skeptically. I smiled.

"Trust Rico. The bastard hasn't been wrong about anything yet." Jim and Rico both laughed. Then Merritt looked at Rico more seriously.

"What about Poole and Ramsey?" he asked. "We can't ignore them."

Rico thought about the answer to that question. "Listen," he said. "Tonight when Kevin here was kicking my ass in the wind sprints, he let up a bit to let me win a few so I wouldn't kill myself. No offense, but that was stupid. Maxie and Battleaxe knew what he was doing, and look what they did to poor Kevin." He paused then adjusted himself in his seat.

"I think that when we're marching or acting as a group against some other group, we've got to stick together. But when it comes to comearounds, it's every man for himself. No offense, Kevin, but there's no way I'm not going to win any event I can, even if you're about to die. It's a matter of self preservation."

"Fair enough," I said. I smiled. "Just don't fault me for my compassion." Rico smiled.

"You can give me all the comearound compassion you want, my friend. I'll accept it happily. I just won't give it back."

"Why the hell not?" asked Merritt, slightly angry.

"Look, Merritt," answered Rico. "I'll tell you a little secret. I may act extremely self confident, but I'm not sure I can hack this place academically. You may not have listened the other evening, but my SAT scores are about the lowest in the Company. I have serious reservations about my longevity once the studying starts. I need every edge I can get, and that means cutting corners and saving my energy when I can. It also means staying in the group that doesn't get noticed. I'm sorry, but that's the way it is."

I was shocked. Rico was articulate, self-confident, and wise beyond his years. He had also graduated from one of the best schools in the country. I could not believe that his SATs properly measured his capabilities. His statement shed new light on Midshipman Guevarra.

Merritt stared at Guevarra for a long time, clearly in thought.

Finally he straightened in my seat and said. "What you say makes a strange kind of sense, Rico. I think I'll come to you from now on when I want philosophical advice." I was immediately upset. Rico had usurped my role as mentor and sounding board. Jim turned to me.

"But I'm coming to "Barfman" when I want action," he said, laughing. I felt relieved.

"Barfman?" I said.

"Everybody needs a nickname." he replied. He stood and went to the door. On the way out he pointed to my recently-stained gym shirt which I had left on the floor by the sink cabinet.

"Do something about that," he said. "It stinks."

"Spaghetti with meat sauce," I said as he left the room. That was our dinner entree.

I picked up the sweat and food-stained shirt gingerly, turned on the sink water full blast and hot, and soaked the shirt, washing out all the chunks and strands and energetically rinsing the stains from the fabric. I wrung the shirt and lay it outside on the window sill to dry, although in this breeze less humidity the chances of it doing so before August of next year were slim at best.

While I was at the window, breathing the moist air deeply, I could hear the plaintiff twang of a sad song Willy Simpson was plucking several rooms away. The notes seemed to hang in the thickness and oppression of the dark, moonless night. Pausing, I looked around at the evening activities framed in the bright windows that faced the inner courtyard. I felt like an outsider, peeking with hidden camera eyes into the secrets of a hundred other young men. Plebes in other Companies were going about their lives much like we were. Some polished shoes. Some cleaned desks and floors. Others sat engaged in vibrant discussion. One other individual leaned out his window in the sixth wing two floors below. We noticed each other simultaneously and waved acknowledgment. Another spy.

As I swept the dark with my secret gaze, I also could see the silhouette of Ronald Steinway. He was sitting in the deep shadows just outside his room, his backside against the metal roof panels, arms wrapped around his legs, staring into the evening sky. I thought about calling to him, thought better of it, and retreated feeling slightly voyeuristic. When I turned toward the room proper I could see into the Goon Room across the passage. On the deck, practicing push-ups but not looking particularly good, was Tommy Poole. He saw me watching and smiled, strain plainly etched on his face. I nodded encouragement then left him to his exercises.

I hate swimming. That may sound incongruous for a potential Naval officer, but it's an undeniable fact nonetheless. Growing up in inner city Boston, I never had ready access to water -- at least not clean swimming water -- and the ocean off Cape Cod is so damn cold I shrivel to the size of raisins in important places. I think I have always been secretly afraid that if I stayed too long in the cold water off Cape Cod, my sex organs would eventually disappearance.

So I didn't swim very often, and I felt uncomfortable in any pool. Unfortunately, swimming evaluations were the second week's physical training exercise.

The water off Cape Cod is God-awful cold; yet it started as the tropical and luxuriant Gulf Stream, so it's not actually icy. The water in the Academy natatorium, however, is piped directly from Antarctica. The big toe on my right foot touched the surface of the pool briefly the first morning of swim class and I let out an involuntary yelp. I suddenly wanted to be out the morning sunlight. Being a plebe, I couldn't flee. Instead I stood shivering in frosty anticipation on the tiled edge of the old pool, looking at my equally-uncomfortable companymates. All of us wore identical blue-with-gold-striped Academy-issue swimming shorts. It was the first time I had seen most of them in any stage of undress.

On the positive side, George Abbott, Danny French, Mike Wojeck, and of course Wesley Lamont looked like young Adonisses. Abbott and Wojeck in particular bulged with muscle, and French and Lamont had sculpted contours over their entire physiques. I secretly looked down at myself. I was not impressed. I had no visible fat, but I was not "developed" like those guys, and I was jealous.

On the negative side, many of my classmates were flabby. It actually hurt my eyes to look at Tommy Poole. He was a corpulent nightmare. Folds of flesh hung on his middle in waves. But he wasn't the only chuncker. Ramsey was no Tarzan, and Butkowski -- even though he was huge -- also could have stood to lose a few hundred pounds -- or more. Tony Delvecchio, Douglas Goto, and Steve Rogers were not thin either. I had an instantaneous thought that it was good that Nathan Speilenberg hadn't returned. He was even worse than poor Tommy.

We had waited only a few minutes before a very bored instructor arrived.

"Good morning, gentlemen," he said. "Hot enough for you?" That line, was a typical Maryland summer greeting much like "How do you do?" He didn't want an answer.

"This week," he began, "we'll be testing your swimming abilities. The Navy, as you can well imagine, has some strict requirements that its officers and men be able to swim. Every year you will have at least one semester of swimming instruction, culminating senior year with a one-mile swim in this pool. You will also jump from the tower above us." We looked up in awe at a metal platform suspended what seemed miles above the water.

"But mainly this week," he continued, "we'll concern ourselves with your more basic abilities. Please stand at poolside. Space yourselves so you don't collide."

Hesitantly I rose and walked to the edge of that hateful body of water. Extending our arms to separate ourselves, we waited.

"Let's start with just a good wetting down," the instructor said. "Jump in, soak up, and return to your places here on the edge." No one moved.

"Please, gentlemen," the instructor said, chuckling. "The water won't hurt you. Jump in. Cool off."

Merritt dove cleanly out over the water and entered with a bare splash. Others followed quickly. But some instinct for self-preservation held my feet glued to the edge. I could not jump even though I wanted to comply. Eventually everyone other than Simpson and me had entered the water. Several were plainly unhappy with the frigid conditions. Willy and I looked at each other, saw identical fear etched on our faces.

"Jump I said!" yelled the instructor suddenly from a position not three feet away.

As my feet came unstuck with a sucking sound, I saw Willy jump. He chose an interesting method of getting wet without getting cold. He jumped vertically outward, then turned completely around so that he faced the side of the pool on his way down. Throwing out his hands, he grabbed at the pool's edge as his feet entered the frigid water. I could see a look of agony spread over his face as his legs disappeared. Still in mid-leap I saw his arms tense on the pool's edge. As his head disappeared from view, his arms flexed mightily, and he immediately propelled himself out of the water. The force of his desperate avoidance of the cold sent him high into the air -- So high that he merely stepped forward and was safely on poolside. I liked his method.

Unfortunately, I had chosen to leap out, not up. As the Arctic wet rushed up to meet me, I decided the only way to save myself would be to try to run across the pool on the near freezing surface. I began to bicycle my legs frantically. I swear I actually made it five steps before gravity sucked me down into the cold cruel depths. My toes curled involuntarily against the undersides of my feet. My legs felt as if they were on frigid fire. Raisins? Shit, my gonads instantly crawled up inside my body and hid. For a week, I had to coax them out gingerly.

I screamed, but the water prevented sound. And my open mouth provided a funnel for tons of icy water to enter. I sank to the bottom, ten feet below thinking that drowning wasn't the worst way to go. But I wasn't finished yet. My curled feet, once in contact with the hard tile deck of the pool, reacted with vigor. I flexed my legs and sprang upward. I left the water, reaching into the air almost as high as Simpson had. I tried to run back to the side of the pool. Two steps later I sank again.

But it wasn't all fun that morning in the pool. Eventually I entered an uneasy truce with the cold and actually swam a warm-up lap. I found out that I wasn't the worst swimmer either. My arms and legs were long and strong enough so that I could overcome, however barely, my lack of technique. After we had warmed up, it was time for practice testing. The first morning we would swim only a lap. The instructor would time us. If we finished within a minute, he assured us, we would pass Friday's real test. Those who did not pass would be required to spend afternoons on swimming sub-squad until they could pass. It was not a good prospect.

Wesley Lamont finished almost before I had reached the far side of the pool. Jim Merritt wasn't far behind. I finished the practice lap in slightly over a minute. Close enough to feel that I could gut out the final test. Ten of us were initially deficient. Five of those would never make the minute mark on Friday. Tommy Poole, to add to his troubles, was a non-swimmer.

The instructor dismissed us with more than 30 minutes to spare, just as Maxwell returned.

"How'd you do?" he asked. Most answered "Fine, sir!" but he could sense that we had a little trouble.

"Who didn't pass the preliminary test?" he asked. The ten of us raised our hands. He looked us over, and his eyes paused when they found me.

"O'Reilly's not a swimmer, huh?" he said to no one in particular.

"Tell you what," he said. "We've got some time, and I want to try a little positive leadership. We'll do the test again, just among ourselves. Anyone of you ten who passes this one has carry-on at noon meal. What do you say? Line up!" We went to the pool's edge.

"Okay," he said. "Swim to the other side and back in less than a minute. Christ, that's easy. Ready, go!" I dove, trying to hit the water cleanly. I also prolonged my time under the surface because my splashing, struggling surface style only seemed to slow me down. Eventually, I broke the plane of the water and struggled forward. I could hear Merritt calling out times as I flopped about, basically moving ahead.

I touched the far wall in under thirty seconds. Instead of instantly starting for the other side, I drew my legs under my body and placed them against the wall of the pool. I thrust away from the side with thirty seconds remaining. It was going to be close. Pumping arms and legs furiously I splashed across the pool. I almost collided with Tommy, who, coming the other way, had somehow gotten his trajectory misaligned and was moving mostly sideways across the pool. He saw me, stopped, adjusted himself, and continued on.

With ten yards remaining I decided not to breathe again. I took a large gulp of air, held it, and churned furiously. In this manner I desperately splash-slapped my way to a fifty-nine second victory. Maxwell smiled at me when I finished.

"O'Reilly, you puke-faced bagger. You get carry-on, but if you don't beat 50 seconds on Friday, you'll have ten instant comearounds. Is that understood?" 50 seconds? Not a chance!

"Aye, aye, sir!" I sputtered, severely depressed.

I couldn't lift myself out of the water. My arms were too tired. Jim Merritt nudged Hank Butkowski, and together the two of them came forward and each grabbed an arm. Butkowski was strong! He lifted me effortlessly and deposited my tired body poolside. I sat near the edge with four other of my non-swimming classmates, who had already finished and were sitting beside me. Three more finished together as I turned to watch the remainder. Tommy Poole was more than 20 yards behind the others. Maxwell became impatient.

"God-damn it!" he yelled. Then he turned to us. "If shit-bag Poole doesn't finish within another 30 seconds, you all will have comearound to me tonight, and I won't be as easy as Tom was yesterday." Classmates began yelling to Tommy to hurry, but how can you hurry someone who's already doing the best he can?

With 20 seconds remaining, Poole was still ten yards from the edge, and faltering quickly when he suddenly sucked some water accidentally, and his face registered panic. I wasn't the only one who noticed. Out of a corner of my eye I saw Jim Merritt explode from among the crowd and dive cleanly into the pool. Wesley Lamont wasn't far behind. Even Ramsey, who had only finished a minute ago, reacted. He plopped his substantial bulk into the pool at the water's edge, grabbed the side of the pool, and reached outward toward Tommy. That narrowed the remaining distance considerably.

Things happened quickly. Merritt and Lamont reached Poole almost instantly. They turned Tommy and kicked toward the waiting Ramsey. Within seconds Jubal had grabbed Tommy and pulled him to poolside. Hank Butkowski lifted Tommy as easily as he had me, and soon Tommy stood bent over on the side of the pool, coughing up water.

Maxwell surveyed the scene, unable to decide what to do.

"Okay," he finally said, "you guys did good. Poole was saved and so were you. Get dressed and let's get moving." We hurried into the locker room to change.

For parade practice that afternoon Jubal Ramsey taught us how to sing, "*There's a 'skeeter on my peter,*" which is sung to the tune of *She'll be Coming Round the Mountain.* I was shocked. Were we expected to yell obscenities during marching drills? As it turned out, yes we were.

That evening's comearound was strenuous, but not sadistic like Sunday night's. I lost a couple races on purpose to save classmates the pushups, but I never came close to winning a crab or bear crawl.

Room 5413 was next up. There were only three people in the room now that Big Nate had gone his chubby way. Robert James Strong was first. Robert was a light-haired, medium tall individual who spoke with intensity. He was serious about himself.

"My name is Bob Strong," he said. As he spoke, his gaze moved from classmate to classmate, spearing us with his ardor. "I grew up in San Diego, California. My father is a manager at a ship repair facility near downtown. My mother works in an insurance office. I attended Patrick Henry School where I played soccer and baseball and surfed. I was president of my class. I have three younger brothers."

Next came poor Ronald Steinway. Ronald had obviously practiced his speech, because he seemed less nervous than usual. He even smiled and kept his Adam's apple under control.

"Hi," he said sincerely. "I'm Ronald Steinway, but you already know that because you've heard my name yelled so often." We laughed politely. "I was born in Ontario, Canada, but my parents decided it would be better to die of heat exhaustion than frostbite, and they moved to Phoenix, Arizona when I was a baby." We laughed again. He was doing well.

"I attended Santa Lucia High School in Phoenix. I was president of the Chess and Metallurgy Clubs, and played the trumpet in the State Champion marching band, but don't ask me to sing because I can't carry a tune. My father is a shop keeper. My mother works for the head of Clinical Psychology at Arizona State University. I'm an only child." He looked up smiling. I began applauding. He deserved it, and several classmates joined in.

The final occupant of the room was Willy Simpson. Willy was okay. He didn't exactly seem an ideal midshipman, but I liked him nonetheless. He was slightly taller than me but thinner, and he was exceedingly awkward, always tripping and falling over things or dropping implements or food trays. He had fair skin and a mouth full of oversized teeth so large that it seemed hard for him to bring his lips together. But he smiled so often, he seldom had reason to close his mouth.

"I'm Willy Simpson," he said in his slow, bashful, Southern style. He looked frequently at the deck and shuffled his feet. "I'm from Greenville, South Carolina. My father is chief of police. My mother is a housewife. I went to Blackridge High School. Didn't play any sports, although I'm pretty good at most things. I have a very pretty twin sister who is presently dating the ex-captain of our school's football team. If any of you want to steal her from her boyfriend, my dad would be very happy. He doesn't like him very much, and neither do I."

Willy started to sit, remembered something, then burst into a broad, contagious smile.

"I also play a little guitar, in case you haven't heard." We laughed and again applauded. He returned to his place awkwardly, clearly torn between pride and embarrassment.

That evening Tommy Poole visited the room. He entered, plainly distressed.

"Hi, Tommy," I said in greeting. "Have a seat. I'd offer you a drink, but after this morning's pool incident, I'll bet you won't be thirsty again for a long time." Both Rico andTommy laughed.

Tommy Poole sat cautiously in Donny Delmont's ex-chair.

"What can we do for you?" I asked. Tommy hesitated.

"You know for sure I'm having big problems," he said, pausing. "Maxwell and Battle are out to get me, and I don't know if I can measure up. Do you have any ideas about how I can turn them off? Because, I'm starting to think about quitting, and I promised myself I wouldn't do that."

I didn't hesitate before answering.

"You can't do anything, Tommy," I offered. "At least not until you improve yourself physically. It's their job to weed out whoever they consider misfits, and you are a perfect target. You're going to have to accept it."

"But what can I do?" he asked. "They're going to kill me and I have to stay."

"Oh, no they're not!" said Rico forcefully from across the room. Tommy turned quickly toward him, hope mirrored on his face.

"What do you mean?" he asked.

"They're not going to kill you, Tommy," Rico said. "Use that enormous head of yours. This is still America, and even though Maxie and the Battle act like the Gestapo, they only have the power you give them."

"I don't understand," said Tommy confused.

"Look," Rico said. "They can't beat you up, or imprison you, or withhold food. And all you can do in response to their demands is the best you can. If they're not happy, the worst you get are a few push-ups and a good screaming in your ear. That's not so bad. What do you think they would do, if you suddenly stood up and walked away from them?" I was just as anxious as Tommy to hear Rico's answer.

"I'll tell you," he said. "Nothing! You have complete control. If you really want to make it through the summer, you can."

Tommy considered Rico's words. "Maybe you're right," he said. "So you think I should defy them?"

"No, no!" Rico answered quickly. "You don't need to defy them. Just keep improving, do the best you can, and ignore the insults. They really can't force you to quit. They know that, but they don't let on. Just hang in there, one day at a time like Kevin and me."

Tommy's face lit up, and he relaxed visibly.

"You know, I think you're right," he said.

"Good," replied Rico, "because good advice is not free." I narrowed my gaze at Rico, trying to figure out what he was getting at.

"What do you mean?" asked Tommy.

"Just remember this when I need help with my homework," Rico said, smiling.

"No problem," replied Poole. "I'll be your tutor."

"It's a deal," Rico said, extending his hand. Tommy walked over to Rico's desk and shook hands with him, then he turned so that he could see the two of us.

"You guys have a good room. I wish I lived over here." After that statement, he turned and departed.

Tuesday night, after another moderate comearound and another hectic dinner, the final plebe room introduced itself.

"My name is Douglas Goto," the first occupant introduced himself, emphasizing the name Douglas. I had not heard Doug say more than two words except when screaming in reply to the squadleaders, except for a curious incident that happened several days earlier when I introduced him as "Doug" Goto. He told me politely that the name "Doug" was not his name, which was the wrong thing for Goto to say to Kevin O'Reilly. From that day forward I called him "Doug", sometimes even "Douggy." No matter how often or how boisterously he protested the nickname stuck. Eventually he adjusted. His yearbook even refers to him by that nickname.

At more than six feet in height, Doug Goto was tall for an Japanese American. He was also muscular, and walked with an athletic grace. He had the typical Asian ruddy complexion, but no trace of an accent. He also had the laughingest pair of eyes I had ever encountered. I liked Doug Goto. He always seemed ready to burst into a booming grin, even when things were not going well. Doug was about as American as any of us -- even more so than many.

"My grandparents came to the United States from Japan at the turn of the century and settled in Baltimore. They run a small restaurant downtown. I attended Baltimore Polytechnic Institute. I played golf and the tuba, and was in charge of the marching band. I was a National Merit Scholar and president of the Electronics Club. I have two very small -- and very pretty -- sisters named Christina and Jennifer."

Next was B. J. Wilson. B. J. was short and somewhat small framed, but very handsome in a feminine way. He had perfect features. Eventually he would sport mounds of dark, wavy, hair. He had piercing blue eyes and incredibly white, straight teeth. I was also willing to bet that no pimple had ever dared to invade that perfect face.

"My name is William Janus Wilson," he said. "I was born in Manhattan. My father is executive producer for several television sitcoms. My mother is an ex-actress." It was his superior attitude that earned him the nickname "BJ" -- which was not an affectionate moniker, and which stuck to him even tighter when we found out he didn't like nicknames. "BJ" was one of those people who somehow pissed me off in almost everything he did, even when he meant well.

"I didn't have time for any sports in High School," he continued. "and my private school offered only squash and fencing. I also have an older sister who is a fashion model."

The third roomie in 5414 rose.

"I'm Michael Donald Wojeck," he said, introducing himself. Mike was a medium tall, stocky boy with a square jaw, prominent facial features, and thinning reddish hair. He was extremely easy going and reveled in social interaction, and when he smiled his light blue eyes narrowed into thin slits.

"My father is also in the Navy. He's a mustang Commander. Right now he's retired and the family is living here in Annapolis. I attended Annapolis High School. I Played a little football and threw the shot put on the track team. I wasn't president of anything, but I did join quite a few organizations in school. I have a sister and a brother, both unmarried."

The final member of the room stepped forward. I didn't know much about him. He had been very quiet thus far in the summer.

"My name is Elliot Mark Zimmerman," he said in an accent that was almost British-New England. Being from Boston I immediately recognized the Beacon Hill in Elliot. He was of medium height and unmuscular, with dark brown, very intense, eyes, and pleasant features. He was also soft spoken, self assured, and probably very wealthy.

"I was born in Boston," he said, "and attended Phillips Exeter Academy in Andover Massachusetts. I played tennis. My father is an investment banker. My mother is an attorney. I have no siblings."

CHAPTER 4

SURVIVAL AND THREATS

Day followed day with almost no letup. We marched, we polished, we recited, we ran, we coped, and as the muggy, grueling days plowed relentlessly one-after-another into deepest Eastern summer, we also sweated. It was physically and emotionally difficult, but I couldn't really complain. Even after working off the ten comearounds to Maxwell for my 57 second swimming record that second Friday, I didn't feel particularly victimized.

Tommy Poole and Ronald Steinway were victims. I watched in amazement as Maxwell and Battle ran the absolute piss out of them. They couldn't recover from any group of exercises before the next batch started. Somehow, however, they kept plugging along. By the end of the second week Tommy could struggle through 20 push-ups, which was absolutely amazing considering he could barely do one to begin with. Ronald had left the straggling runners and joined the middle pack.

I myself was feeding on endorphins. I out sprinted Battle every chance I got, and I improved my own strength so that I could do 71 push-ups -- plus one to beat Army. I was never asked to do more than that number at any one time, but I could eventually do more than 100. But just when I thought I had it all down pat -- about midway through the summer -- the focus of the squadleaders training shifted slightly That shift exposed ugly personality flaws in some of my classmates.

B. J. Wilson was a smack. He wasn't the only smack, but he was by far the worse one. A smack is a plebe who curries favor with the upper class in a disgustingly obsequious way, sometimes at the expense of his classmates. Maybe it was because BJ grew up in an "I-love-ya-baby" entertainment atmosphere, where boot licking and butt kissing and sucking have distinct advantages. Not being a fantastic athlete or the most charisma-laden individual, he may have seen smack-dom where as the only way he could excel. -- Or maybe he was a natural son-of-a-bitch. I'm sure the smacky things he did were not motivated by any amount of goodness in his black heart.

"Wilson!" Maxwell asked one evening meal during the third week.

"Yes, sir?" BJ replied in a sickeningly sweet voice, smiling while he braced.

"Are you serious about the tickets for the theater in October?"

"Yes, sir," answered BJ. "The Brigade will be in New Jersey on the seventeenth for the Cornell game, and the last bus won't leave for the return trip to Annapolis until midnight. Father has arranged for the limo to pick me up at the stadium and take me to the apartment for a few hours. I'll ask Alfred to drop you and your dates off at the early show and to pick me up on the way back to Cornell afterward. We should make it in plenty of time."

"How about the tickets, pal?" asked Maxwell skeptically. "Those are expensive."

"No charge," BJ offered. "My mom can get as many as she wants for free."

"Well, okay, Wilson," Maxie replied, "but don't expect any special treatment for this."

"Of course not, sir," BJ replied smiling. Across the table I could see Polk raise his eyes heavenward. Next to him Rico's face held an enigmatic smile.

That evening Rico and I visited the Goons before lights out. Poole was not there. He was visiting Battle for a special motivational comearound.

“Isn’t BJ Wilson a smack?” asked Jeff Polk almost immediately after we were settled.

“He sure is,” we all agreed.

“Did you know that he offered the tickets to the squadleaders but hadn’t said a word to his roommates or to any of his classmates?” asked Polk. “And he told Doug Goto that he’ll be moving to another room come academic year. He says he wants to surround himself with the up-and-comers.”

Jeff looked at Jim Merritt and said, not altogether in jest. “That probably means you, Jim.”

“Shit,” I said, warming to the controversy. “What an asshole.”

“Up-and comers, huh?” said Jubal Ramsey in a quiet voice from across the room. “He’ll get his comeuppance all right.”

“What should we do?” I asked. “Short-sheet his rack?”

Both Jubal and Jeff laughed like I had made an intentional joke. I hadn’t. Short-sheeting was about the extent of my practical joke experience.

“No,” Jubal said slowly, “I think this may call for more direct action.”

“Like what?” I asked naively.

“The fewer people who are in on it the better,” said Jeff. “That way if a squad leader asks, you can honestly say you don’t know anything.”

“Maybe if somebody spoke to him and told him to let up some on the brown-nosing?” suggested Merritt.

“It wouldn’t help,” said Rico with authority. “He’s just a born smack. He intends to get advantage over as many people as possible however he can. He *is* an asshole.”

“Hardesty is a smack too, and so’s Lamont,” added Ramsey, almost as an afterthought. That comment brought almost instant reaction from us.

“No, Joe, not Lamont. I’m sure of it,” I said. Jubal didn’t respond.

“I think Kevin’s right, Joe,” added Rico. “Lamont is like Merritt here and Pirelli too. They enjoy this shit and get their jollies from being the perfect plebe. Lamont’s no smack. He pitches in with the best of them. Wilson never does, and Hardesty is too god-damned self righteous. He thinks he has all the answers.” Jubal didn’t answer.

“You even have to admit that Poole is showing real improvement,” I said changing the subject. Jubal looked at me and shook his head slowly.

“Poole and Steinway both have got to go,” he said.

I don't see it, Joe," I answered. "He's doing everything we are and then some. I'm rooting for him." I looked around the room for support, but it was thin. Even Merritt looked skeptical.

"Poole won't last the summer," predicted Jubal. Rico didn't object to Joe stealing the prognostication role, so I decided that meant either Jubal was right or Rico wasn't sure yet about Tommy's fate.

Rico chose an interesting way to bring BJ Wilson down to size, although I'm not sure he did it intentionally. The revenge happened after a weekday evening meal during the third week of Plebe Summer.

One of the favorite evening pastimes of the squadleaders was bracing plebes against the passageway wall for mischief. They would mostly ask us plebe rates interspersed with sports, political, or historical questions. It was like an early version of Trivial Pursuit -- except for the pain, of course.

That particular evening Rico was having a terrible battle with stomach distress. We had eaten greasy -- but absolutely delicious -- pepperoni pizza for dinner, and it hadn't agreed with him. In fact, my own piece sat as an uncomfortable lump in my middle, reminding me with every unintentional burp of its spicy contents.

As I stood next to Rico in the passageway, I could hear the dull rumblings and grumblings of gastric turmoil within him. He shifted and moaned several times in obvious discomfort. On his left side, BJ Wilson was too busy bilging classmates with volunteered answers to notice Rico's distress.

Rico finally leaned toward me slightly when the squadleaders' attention was focused elsewhere.

"Kevin, stand by," he barely whispered. "I have *got* to cut one." I heard the strain in his voice, and I could sense that despite the delicate nature of our present predicament, he absolutely had to let go.

But he knew he couldn't just pop for fear the noise would draw attention to himself. Plebe survival equates with being unnoticeable. Despite the obvious pain, Rico showed exceptional restraint and cunning. He waited. He let the event brew a little, he nursed his innards, eased the inevitable along, and eventually let something emerge silently, following it with an enormous sigh.

Relief obvious in his new stance, we waited for our next question. But he had forgotten a very important fact. The particular type of gas that now floated freely in our vicinity, when allowed to accumulate in the nether regions of the human body, will often develop a distinct and somewhat unpleasant odor.

Oh, what an odor! The staunchest swamp dweller would have gagged at the smell. Rico "noticed" it first. I inhaled the aroma an instant later. Rico immediately nudged me.

"Fart, move right, hurry! Pass it on!" he whispered desperately. I needed no encouragement. I nudged the plebe on my right and repeated Rico's request. The word quickly and quietly spread, as did the smell, and everyone to my right quickly shifted almost six feet until we were out of the danger zone. There was now a gap in the ranks to Rico's left -- but his 'gift' drifted left also, and soon there were mutterings as plebes on the other side staggered under the almost physical impact of the gas. A commotion ensued. Several plebes muttered, "Oh, my God!" The line also started shifting to the left.

All except Wilson, that is, who either had no olfactory sense or else had been living in New York City for too long. He remained dutifully in his place on Rico's left, smack dab in the middle of the noxious cloud, now separated from his classmates on either side by six feet. Maxwell and Battle, seeing and hearing the confusion, stopped their merriment and tromped down the line. As they approached, they could see BJ, isolated and confused.

"Hey, pal!", began Maxwell as he approached. "What the hell is up with you?" The smell hit him like a 2" x 4". His eyes expanded in his head like two suddenly inflated balloons. He staggered, almost falling in the process, let out an incredibly creative curse, and backed hastily out of range. "You rotten, bilging douchebag!" he yelled, after taking a deep breath of fresher air. "I can't believe you did that. Hit it for 100!" His arm waved vigorously in the air as he retreated.

BJ Wilson hesitated, torn between the wrath of Midshipman Maxwell and the need to explain He opened his mouth to speak, obviously ready to shift the blame to someone else. Battle didn't let him.

"Did you hear what Maxie just asked you to do?" he screamed. "If you're not on the deck in less than a second, I'll see that your death is slow and painful." Wilson had no choice. He dropped to the tile and began cranking out pushups, reluctantly singing out the numbers in time to his up-and-down motions. Maxwell had backed himself against the far wall of the passageway and was gulping down deep, cleansing breaths to rid his lungs of the contamination. He was too overcome by the fumes to notice how many of BJ's classmates sported secret and heartfelt smiles at his predicament. Everyone but Rico and me thought that Wilson had brought about his own fate, and we weren't about to admit otherwise. It remained our secret. Why didn't Rico confess and save his classmate the unwarranted exercise? He's not stupid, that's why!

BJ's scatological downfall was the initial topic of conversation that evening in the Goon Room, where there was universal lack of sympathy for Wilson the smack. Even Tommy Poole admitted that he thought Wilson was a shit-head. These were strong words from Tommy, who blushed at each "f-word". Tommy blushed a great many times that summer. But tonight Poole was finally one of the guys, and he reveled in the camaraderie. He also said "shit-head" a lot.

Soon thoughts of BJ Wilson disappeared as we discussed the major event of the week, the upcoming "white glove" inspection on Saturday afternoon after meal. Our rooms had been "inspected" by Maxwell and Battle several times already, and most of our clothing had tumbled to the deck so many times that floors outside our lockers was brightly polished. But this inspection was to be special for two reasons. First, it would mark the first time the squadleaders dared risk a white glove on our clean-up efforts, and second, it would be our first encounter with our Company Officer, Marine Captain Rusty "Bull" Dillingham.

Both Maxwell and Battle had mentioned the "Bull" several times during the preceding days. Maxie called him "one crazy-assed Marine." Battleaxe didn't appreciate Maxie's reference to "crazy" and "Marine" in the same sentence but did allow that Captain Dillingham was "an interesting character." We plebes had speculated among ourselves concerning this unknown factor in our survival, and none of us was particularly happy to be led by someone who was gung-ho, crazy, or both.

Preparations for the formation and inspection began Friday evening. Rico and I divided the room into cleaning zones. I was responsible for the sink, the shower area, and the closet. Rico would do the main area. We each were responsible for our own beds, desks, and lockers.

Dividing up the room cleaning was the wrong thing for us to do. Rather it was the wrong thing for *me* to agree to. Friday night after meal I attacked my zone with a vengeance. I spent an hour naked in the shower, scrubbing down the walls and floors, and drying everything carefully with towels. I also scrubbed the sink and faucets tirelessly, even going so far as cleaning inside the faucet spout. Jim Merritt had made a list of obscure and unlikely places to clean where the inspection team would surely elect to put the white glove, and I copied his list, intending not to forget a single cleanable spot.

While I worked my ass off, Rico read another of those damn sex novels. I could see the ridiculous spy hero on the cover, smiling, a naked buxom blond holding tightly to each arm, as he karate kicked a black-clad opponent, obviously thinking wistfully ahead to whatever anatomical feats the young ladies were about to perform for him. I quickly became nervous about the amount of time remaining and Rico's apparent lack of concern.

"Rico," I said after I finished in the shower, "don't you think you better start cleaning? It'll take at least an hour to wax the floor."

"No sweat, Kevin. I'll get it done"

A half-hour later I had finished the sink, and Rico still hadn't stirred.

"Rico," I said, desperation creeping into my voice, "when are you going to start?"

Rico put down the book and looked up at me in exasperation.

"Look, Kevin," he said. "I'll get it done. If you're not satisfied with my efforts, why don't you do it yourself?"

"What?" I exclaimed. "We're supposed to be helping each other."

Rico stared at me, decided I was serious about the cleaning, then said. "Okay, you do the floor on your side of the room, and I'll do mine. Next inspection I'll do the shower and sink." He returned to his reading.

I thought about his offer. I instantly knew the arrangement wouldn't work because of the fundamental personality differences between us. I didn't want to get into any trouble and wanted everything perfect. Rico was able to settle for the minimum. He'd never be able to do the floor to my satisfaction, and I'd worry constantly that we would get into trouble because of it. And since a few push-ups didn't bother him in the least, he'd always think I was putting too much effort into the clean-up. His cost-benefit ratio was completely different from mine.

I grunted, got out the mop and wax, and started on my side of the room. I quickly mopped the entire floor, carefully cleaning the mop in the shower so that it didn't splatter the now-shining walls. Next I waxed the deck according to the instructions on the bottle. An hour later I had finished the entire room. The only help Rico had given me was to lift his feet when I waxed under his desk. I watched him reading as I worked in his area. He was smiling. He knew it would come to this. Sometimes Rico's gift for understanding human nature pissed me off.

I had just seated myself wearily at my desk when Ronald Steinway entered and walked haphazardly across my newly-waxed floor.

"Ronald! Stop!" I yelled without thinking. I hoped that Maxwell hadn't heard that -- we were supposed to be very quiet in the evenings.

Ronald saw the distress on my face and came to an immediate dead stop and looked at me questioningly. On stocking feet, I glided easily to him and checked the floor behind him for scuffs or mars. None were apparent.

"Jesus Ronald," I said. "I just waxed the floor."

Ronald looked around sheepishly.

"Sorry," he said. "We're waiting until the morning. We were going to do it after morning meal and let it dry while we're at lectures." I dropped down onto my hands and knees and put my right cheek against the tile. For several seconds I scrutinized the deck where Ronald had trod. Satisfied, I stood.

"Take your shoes off before you take another step," I admonished. Ronald complied, holding my back for balance as he unshod himself. Afterward he sat at Delmont's desk and pulled a letter from his pocket.

"My parents again," he said, handing it to me.

"If this is personal . . .?" I asked, holding the envelope.

"No, no. Read it," he said.

He pulled out a letter written in wonderfully sweeping cursive strokes -- a talent I could never master despite eight years of penmanship parochial school. This letter had come from his mother. It was dated last week.

"*Ronald,*" it said. "*So glad to hear from you. I'm happy that everything's fine. I told Professor Riggins the other day about how well you are doing, and he's offered to have you speak in his Modern Sociology class about military training and its effect on the human psyche. I hope you don't turn bloodthirsty on me (joking, love). I am so proud. You'll never know how wonderful it makes me feel. Love you Always, MOM*"

I handed the letter to Ronald who was looking at me expectantly.

"Shit, Ronald. Did you tell them this was a country club or something? They think you're happy here."

He stared at me for a long time.

"I can't leave here, Kevin. I have to stay."

"Well, if you do, you do. But prepare yourself for more pain. It's coming, you and I both know that. Once the Brigade gets back, there'll be no let up."

Steinway nodded his head sadly.

"I know," he said. "But I have no alternatives."

"There are always alternatives, Ronald," I said.

Ronald looked up quickly.

"You think I should quit, don't you?" he asked, his feelings somehow hurt by my lack of sympathy.

"Not unless *you* want to, Ronald," I replied. "It's *your* choice. But everybody can see that you're not happy. Hell, you're depressed all the time. Why stay here and be miserable? It doesn't make any sense."

Ronald turned his head and stared out the window.

"You don't understand, Kevin. I have to stay. My parents are depending on me."

"Then have your mom run the morning comearounds and your dad do your push-ups. It's not their place to put that kind of pressure on you."

Ronald stood up, not saying another word, took his shoes in hand, and departed.

After Ronald was gone, Rico looked up from his book. He had a strange look on his face. His handsome features seemed softer, almost glowing. He sighed and then glanced down into his lap and smiled broadly.

"Christ, Mr. Ed is awfully horny," he said. "I have got to get laid soon or my nuts will burst."

"Fat chance," I replied. "No girls until Parents' Weekend. That's still more than a month away."

Rico smiled wistfully.

"Kevin," he said. "Come on, amigo. Don't you want to see your girlfriend naked right now? Can't you imagine yourself doing sweet things with her?"

I could tell from the way Rico talked that he wasn't bullshitting me. He was "experienced." I was jealous of him again. But I wasn't about to tell him that I had no girlfriend and that I had never seen any girl naked or done anything particularly unusual during my brief periods of clothed contact.

"Yeah," I replied. "I think about all those things, but wishing isn't going to make it so."

Rico smiled devilishly.

"It will for me. Want to bet "Mr. Ed" gets laid before Parents' Weekend?"

"No way," I said stupidly.

"Ten bucks says so," he said smugly. "Is it a bet?"

"How you gonna prove it?" I asked.

"Don't worry, I will." I accepted the bet.

We had been specifically instructed by the squadleaders to wear a fresh set of tropical whites for the Saturday uniform inspection prior to noon meal. Captain Dillingham was inspecting. As I critically examined myself in the mirror over the sink, I was impressed. I looked great. Four weeks of exercise had eliminated every inch of spare body tissue and had nicely hardened and contoured what remained. With my shirt blazingly white and tucked expertly, my brass belt buckle -- top included -- gleaming, and the brim of my combination cap pledged to a black brilliance, I had no doubt I was a studly young man. Even the red stubble that was boldly sprouting on my naked skull looked great.

Noon formations on the weekend were now outside in Tecumseh Court, and we didn't have to chop in public, so after exiting the Company area, Rico and I leisurely strolled down the stairs to the Rotunda. Awestruck crowds wandered the broad multicolored terrazzo floor, viewed the many "Go-Navy" displays, and visited the sample midshipman room. The whole setup was geared to generate admiration and support, and I could feel eyes on me as we began our strut across the Rotunda floor toward the doors. Some of those eyes were female, and some of those eyes were beautiful, and I was immediately horny.

In truth, however, Rico was the center of gravity for the attention focused toward us. As we walked to the exit doors, heads turned and young bodies moved almost unconsciously in our direction. I swear I could hear splatters from females drooling on the terrazzo as he passed. And Rico was really sucking this up. He had a quality about him that was absolutely irresistible, and he knew how to use it. I began to worry about my ten dollars.

Almost at the moment that we reached the exit doors, a flock of young lovelies who were also exiting, blocked our path. One particular blond beauty looked at Rico, and I swear he stabbed her with his gaze. She almost staggered. Rico reached out to help her steady herself, and I could see him secretly place something small and paper in her hand. He held her hand for a moment, squeezing the hand with the gift shut tightly.

"Are you okay?" he asked. Teeth flashed in his brown face. His Hispanic eyes sparkled. His voice held promise. Why couldn't I do that? The girl smiled sweetly and Rico released her hand, and we soon passed out into Tecumseh Court. Rico never looked back.

"What was that all about?" I asked as we strutted down the steps.

Rico reached into his pocket and pulled out another note -- one of several. He handed it to me. I looked around carefully, and read it.

"I've been watching you. You are the most beautiful thing I have ever seen. I think I'm in love. Let's talk. Leave a message for me at the Main Office with your name and phone number." It was signed Rico Guevarra, Room 5404.

I handed it back to him, and he precisely replaced it in his pocket, careful not to mar the sharp, flat outline of his pants. "Do you think that will work?" I asked.

Rico gave me an "are-you-shitting-me?" look, then smiled.

"Watch and learn, red head!" was all he said.

Many of our companymates were already waiting when we arrived. As was customary in the few minutes before the squadleaders arrived, we inspected each other with a desperate intensity, adjusting uniform line-ups, blowing the fuzzy dust from fellow shoulder-boards, and correcting cap placement to satisfy our own demanding standards. When Chuck Chalmers, who usually stood in front of me in the outdoor formations, turned so that I could view him from the rear, I noticed one of the dreaded "Irish pennants" hanging loosely from his shirt collar. Unless I could do something quickly, this was cause for panic

"Stand still, Chuck," I warned. "You have an Irish pennant back here."

"Shit!" he exclaimed. "I checked before we left the room." I reached out and tried to get a solid grip on the small thread. "Irish pennants" are any loose threads that extend even slightly from the fabric, and are usually found along seams or wherever any sewing took place. You'd be surprised how many there are on a typical shirt. Usually we removed them with a pair of scissors. Chuck had carefully examined the shirt before he put it on, but Irish Pennants sometimes spring from the material of their own volition, particularly during the period between final checking and uniform inspection. Anyway, he missed one.

I grabbed at the thread end carefully with the tips of my thumb and forefinger but couldn't get enough of a grip to be able to yank it out. I tried again but still could not get any purchase on the damned thing.

"I can't get it, Chuck," I said. "I'll try to push it up under the ends of your collar to hide it."

"Thanks," he replied.

I worked on the thread for a moment until I had it bent over and tucked precariously under his shirt collar. It would stay -- maybe -- until the end of formation.

"Form up!" Battle ordered. I quickly forgot about Chuck's pennant and concentrated on my positioning within the Company so that a straight line could be drawn between the tips of the toes of all the feet in my rank, and so that my head was precisely behind Chuck's. I also adjusted my foot placement so that exactly 90 degrees separated my feet. Then I waited with the rest of the Company for the big moment.

Battle stood at the front of the formation and scanned down each rank, calling out minor adjustments. Maxwell quickly moved along the ranks, checking our uniforms. There was no time to change anything except cap placement, and Maxie knew this. That didn't stop him from calmly and liberally handing out comearounds for every minuscule violation of the Maxwell Uniform Code. He couldn't find anything wrong with me. I smiled at him. I got one comearound on general principles. I winked at him He smiled and shook his head in return, and gave me another comearound.

Before Maxwell could finish with us, there came a sudden hush in the surroundings. I sensed that something was happening. Maxwell looked frightened for a moment and hurried to the end of the formation to stand with Battle. Battle sang out!

"Midshipmen Second Class Battle and Maxwell reporting, sir! Twenty-third Company plebes are ready for inspection, sir!" I could hear feet approaching to our rear. From the sound of the clip-clomping, they must have been enormous feet. The feet-sounds suddenly stopped, and a crisp, professional voice sounded out.

"Very well, Mister Battle. Let's review the troops."

Next followed a scuffling as Battle and Maxwell pivoted and scurried to follow the stranger to the front of the first rank. From where I stood, if I twisted my eyes in my head so that they almost peeked out of my ears, I could just barely see the figures begin the inspection. Battle led. His head moved slowly up from toe to cap on the first plebe. When he finished inspecting he pivoted smartly, took a single forward step that brought him exactly in front of the second person, and pivoted again to face the next victim. Each time he pivoted he brought his heals together with a sharp click. It was very impressive.

But I said "victim" and that isn't exactly true. I could see Battle's face from where I stood, and he wasn't concentrating on his inspection at all. Rather, he surreptitiously watched Captain Dillingham as he inspected. Battle was plainly nervous about the impression the inspection would have on the Company officer. The plebe in front of Battle could have been wearing a red shirt, yellow pants, and a baby blue hat, and I don't think he would have noticed. This was very interesting. Tommy Battle lived in awe, or in fear, of another human being. I recorded this fact in my memory for future reference.

Did I say human being? When I caught my first glimpse of the "Bull", I wasn't sure. The person who followed Battle was *that* different. Captain Rusty "Bull" Dillingham seemed an anachronism, an obvious throwback to more primitive times. I could feel my eyes widen as a watched, and Rico, who stood next to me, grunted almost imperceptively. He was impressed also.

Bull was enormous; very tall and prominently boned and without a visible once of fat. In height he must have been at least six feet six, and I'll bet he weighed 230 pounds. He had no hair -- by choice. Judging from the way the sunlight reflected from the part of the taut skull that showed beneath his cap, he also polished his bald head. Even his ears were enormous. Dumbo would have been envious. But Dumbo would never have mentioned anything to the Bull about his ears. I'll bet no one did.

He had somewhat Cro-Magnon features. His facial bones and eye ridges protruded, his chin jutted forward almost aggressively, and his skin was pulled tightly over his face. His lips were full and wrinkly and covered large almost-predatory teeth, and his blue eyes inspected the uniform and personage of every plebe with a fiery intensity. Under his starched green Marine Corps uniform shirt I could see muscles ripple as he moved. His arms bulged in his sleeves. Holy shit, what a monster! No wonder Battle feared this guy. I almost wet myself just watching him.

Bull carefully checked each plebe as the inspection moved down the front rank. Sometimes he would bend over from his lofty heights and put his face almost on top of some aberrant abnormality in a plebe uniform. Once he focused for nearly ten seconds on the brim of Doug Goto's hat. Without saying anything, he passed on to the next plebe. Maxwell whispered a quiet "comearound" to All as he passed.

Bull didn't say much. He was too busy being professional. He only became confused was when he came to Tommy Poole. He stared at Tommy's head for a long moment, then reached out and "adjusted" Tommy's cap. Leaning back slightly, he stared at the revised placement, frowned, and readjusted the cap. After several of these corrections, he became clearly frustrated and moved on to another plebe. But before he started on the next person, he glanced back toward Tommy, started to say something, shook his caveman head in perplexity, and continued inspecting. Maxwell gave Tommy ten comearounds.

In less than three minutes the inspection team had finished the front of the first rank and started their march up the back side of the first rank. I remembered Chuck Chalmer's Irish Pennant problem. I concentrated on the spot where I had hidden the thread, and to my amazement I could see the bent-over end quiver in anticipation, almost as if it had been stirred by a breeze. But there was no breeze. I watched in fascination. As the group approached, the thread slowly peeked from under the collar. When Battle reached the back of Chuck's head, I swear it sprang out and tried to trip him.

In the dark recesses of the under-collar, the Irish Pennant must have sucked sustenance from surrounding material, or maybe it underwent some type of molecular mitosis at the cotton-cell level. It now seemed enormous as it waved briskly in an imaginary breeze. Battle spotted it immediately. He couldn't have missed it. It nearly slapped him across the face. He paused in his forward movement, unsure what to do. Finally he whispered a quick couple comearounds in Chuck's ear and hurried on, hoping, I'm sure, that Bull wouldn't notice. No such luck.

Dillingham paused at Chuck's backside and pointed to the thread, which now seemed to me three times its normal thickness and to stretch almost to Chuck's waist. Bull frowned, shook his head, and went on to the next person. Maxwell gaped at the now python-sized pennant. He grabbed and pulled it backward. It didn't give up easily. Chalmer's head snapped back, pulled by the force of Maxwell's sudden jerk. Maxwell tried again, but the super thread mocked him and stayed comfortably in place. Maxwell handed Chuck an additional ten comearounds. I could hear Chuck moan involuntarily.

Now it was my rank's turn. I mentally checked myself. Slowly I pulled my hands backward. With my thumbnails, I located the seems of my trouser legs. I placed my thumbs exactly along those seems. I looked down at my feet to ensure I had not somehow lost my perfect ninety degrees. I hadn't. I squared my shoulders and pulled my head back. As Battle moved to Willy Simpson on my right, I slowly sucked in my gut and puffed out my chest in anticipation.

Battle glanced at me without seeing anything. His eyes, as they passed in front of me on their memorized journey from bottom to top, didn't even register on who I was. I could have crossed my eyes and stuck out my tongue and it would have had no effect. I didn't. Battle pivoted and departed smartly -- then the sun dimmed. No, that's not exactly true. An enormous shadow passed across the sun. The eclipse was Bull Dillingham.

From my eyes-in-the-boat vantage point all I could see of Bull was the top of his uniform shirt which held about ten rows of multicolored ribbons. This guy was a hero, no question about it. I had been taught to recognize the major awards, and on this muscular chest I could see from the tiny bronze stars on his Vietnam Service and Campaign Ribbons that Bull had been to the land of steamy jungles on four separate occasions. He had also won three Navy Achievement Awards, two Commendation Medals, *three* Purple Hearts, a Bronze Star, and something I thought was the Silver Star. Holy shit! It didn't matter any more to me what size he was. This guy had my instant respect and admiration.

Bull inspected me briefly; and because of the height disparity, I never saw his warrior's face over my cap brim. I must have met his standards, because he quickly moved to the next plebe, Rico, and I let out a slow sigh of relief. Soon the inspection was completed, and Dillingham moved off toward Bancroft Hall to await us at our Company tables for noon meal. Once Bull had left earshot, Battle moved to the front of the formation.

"Okay, assholes," he said just quietly enough so that the civilians standing at the entryway to T-Court couldn't hear, "most of you were barely acceptable. Some of you were not and will be punished appropriately. Captain Dillingham will be joining us for meal, and at precisely 1300 we will begin our room inspections. You had better be ready."

With that he turned to face the entry to T-Court and the summer Second-class Brigade staff which had formed up there. The Midshipman Brigade Commander gave the command for the plebes to come to attention and to march into Bancroft Hall to chow. We marched off in precision. The crowd cheered! -- Just kidding.

Luckily the Bull chose to eat with Battle, and I was spared reciting plebe rates for his benefit. Merritt and Pirelli were in their full glory, however. Maxwell pretty much left us alone, and I was grateful for that small favor.

On the way back to our rooms I accompanied Rico to the Brigade Offices where he asked confidently if he had gotten any phone or other messages. The plebe on duty sorted through the boxes until he came to Twenty-third Company and pulled out a note to Midshipman Rico Guevarra.

"A very pretty young blonde left this," he said jealously.

Rico took the note, glanced at it briefly, then handed it to me. Cindy Stanver had written the note and left her number. She wanted Rico to call immediately.

"See you upstairs," Rico said as he headed off toward the phones.

I gave our room a once-over, recleaned the sink from the pre-noon-meal wash-up, and waited for Rico When he did, he was beaming. "Mr. Ed is throbbing in anticipation," he said, "of *tonight's* rendezvous."

"Tonight?" I blurted. "How are you going to arrange that?"

"Kevin," he said seriously. "You've basically got no huevos, compadre." That wasn't true. It had been two weeks since swimming evaluations, and I was just fine now. "I talked to Cindy, my dream girl, and she's going to meet me this evening at ten o'clock after lights out. We'll take a leisurely drive in her car over to Hospital Point and get acquainted there."

"How the hell are you going to get from Bancroft Hall to Hospital Point in a car with a girl without being seen, smart guy?" I asked. Rico only smiled.

"Where there's a will, there's a way," he said wistfully. I laughed. I saw what Rico meant. He had real *balls*, mine were pre-shrunk gonads.

Room inspection began exactly at 1300 as scheduled. Captain Dillingham was an absolute stickler for promptness. The three of them began on the far side of the passageway with Room 5401. I heard Hank Butkowski yell out an "Attention on Deck!" as they entered. The inspection lasted ten minutes. I stood in our doorway with my back pressed against the wall so they couldn't see me, and I strained to hear what they had "discovered" wrong in 5401. I couldn't hear anything significant, although at one point I did hear a dull thump that could only be a chair being replaced in a desk indentation. After Room 5401 they moved down the passageway to 5403, the Goon Room.

Since 5403 was directly across the passageway from our room, I quickly slipped out of the doorway and out of sight. But I still listened. Jubal Ramsey did the announcement honors for the Goons. Because they were significantly closer, I could hear more, but what I heard was general banter. Bull asked the Goons questions about their backgrounds and interests while Maxie and Battle checked the room. There were no yells or thuds or thumps of any kind. 5409 was next.

Curious about the chair sound, I went to my desk and pulled out my chair. Gingerly I reached my hand under the desk top and felt around. I found out two things: first that the damn thing had sharp corners, but second, and more importantly, as I pulled my hand away to wipe off the now-welling wound, I saw dust and dirt mixed with the redness. Was that what they had done?

Quickly I wrapped a tissue around my finger and grabbed a dust cloth from under the sink. Hastily going from desk to desk -- much to the delight of Midshipman Asshole Guevarra -- I fumbled under each desktop -- except Rico's -- until I had cleaned the small rim that formed the front brace of the channel-shaped support structure. Then I cleaned the tops of each drawer. Satisfied, I deposited the cloth under the sink and returned to my listening post while Rico read a technical manual in anticipation of the evening's escapade.

It was almost an hour later that the inspection team approached our room. During that period I had contacted the Goon Room by sliding a penny across the passageway floor into their room. Merritt and Ramsey came to the door. I looked at them questioningly, and they gave me a thumbs-up sign. Merritt indicated that we should check under the desks for dust bunnies, and Ramsey pointed to the top of the door. I nodded and cleaned both spots.

Rico looked at me and nodded gently before the inspectors entered, indicating that I was to be the spokesman. That was fine with me. As Captain Dillingham's first huge foot broke the plane of the doorway I boomed out an "Attention on Deck!" aimed at deafening anyone within ten feet.

Rico and I snapped to instant rigidity. The three of them entered and looked around. Bull looked at me.

"Why are there only two of you?" he asked in a surprisingly gentle voice.

"Sir," I said quietly, taking my cue from his style. "The other two classmates have left the Academy."

"I see," he said. "Who are you?"

"Midshipman Fourth-class Kevin O'Reilly, sir!" I answered. Maxwell and Battle went about the room wiping white gloves across various pieces of furniture and fixtures as Bull quietly questioned us. We remained at attention and braced throughout the process. He asked birthplaces, sports participation, and future academic and career goals. After he had gleaned a small amount of information from each of us he looked at Battle.

"Everything Okay?" he asked.

"So far, sir" Battle answered smartly. He went to the door and wiped his hand across the top. It was clean. He looked at me, impressed. Smiling slyly, he went to Delmont's desk. Pulling out the chair, he felt up inside the desktop. His hand came away clean.

He looked at me again, smiled again, and walked over to my bunk. Taking the mattress by the middle with both hands, he lifted it, exposing the enclosed but previously inaccessible, area underneath. He looked inside.

"You didn't clean inside here, did you, O'Reilly?" he asked, his head still peering into the stygian depths.

"I didn't know there *was* an inside there, sir," I answered, a bit dismayed.

Dillingham noted my disappointment.

"Don't despair, midshipman. This has been the best room yet. But a good trooper must be prepared for any eventuality. It will keep you alive when you really need it." As he said this his eyes glazed over slightly in obvious memory retrieval, and I knew he really meant what he said.

"Aye, aye, sir!" I answered. The group turned to go.

As Battle passed me he said quietly, "Good job, gentlemen. Two comearounds a piece for unpreparedness." I later found out that we had gotten fewer comearounds than any other room, which made me weirdly proud. Maybe I *was* becoming the smack Rico constantly implied.

That afternoon the usual group played basketball, and I had a pretty fair first game. I was beginning to think I could make the varsity team if I tried hard enough. I mean, there did seem to be a fair number of white guys here. I dribbled and passed well, but couldn't jump for shit. And maybe I could overcome my shooting deficiency by practicing more with my left hand. I decided to try only left-handed shots in the second scrimmage that afternoon, but several errant shots later, gave up any hopes of being an Academy super jock.

Evening meal was a quiet affair. I think everyone, including the squadleaders, was thankful that the ordeal of the inspections was over. I fully intended to get to sleep early. I spent an hour in the warm early evening writing letters while sitting out on the roof deck. That night's sunset was spectacular. Ronald Steinway came out on the roof from his room 30 minutes afterward. He saw me, smiled and waved, and resumed his familiar pose as night sentinel of the Company. I left him to his reverie. I was writing a serious letter to an ex-girlfriend.

As I wrote, I considered feminine companionship and my lack thereof. I knew Merritt and Polk had serious relationships. They talked about their far away loves almost constantly. Even Tommy Poole had a girl back home that was crazy about him. Listening to all that mooning, I had begun to wonder if there wasn't something seriously wrong with me. I decided to remedy the companionship situation by rekindling a relationship with a girl I had dated when I was a junior, and who I recently heard from friends might have gotten a little "loose."

My letter to her told briefly about the hardship of being a midshipman and how I missed my friends. Then I mentioned that I had been thinking about her recently, asked if she would like to correspond, and suggested we see each other when I returned during Christmas vacation. Satisfied with what I had said, I then decided to write almost identical letters to three other girls I knew from school or other social activities. None of the girls knew each other; and I figured that if only one responded, I could satisfy the love interest requirement and maybe add sexual excitement to my life.

At 2000 I visited the Goons to swap inspection stories. Everyone had gotten off easily except poor Tommy, who now had enough comearounds to last until Christmas leave -- 1985. He was keeping track in a small black vinyl notebook he kept in his top right desk drawer. He pulled it out to show me. On the first page at the top center in bold letters he had written the name Maxwell. Underneath he had ticked off comearounds in groups of five. He canceled out completed comearounds with a pen stroke. The list of Maxwell comearounds almost filled the page. I turned the page to see Battle's list. It was almost twice as long. I groaned and returned the book, mustering my most sincere look of empathy.

"I got a letter from Kate today," said Polk laughing. "She's not happy about what goes on here. She told me to quit and come home. She says she's saving a place for me at the local small college where we can study philosophy together, protest the war, smoke grass, and make love all night. God, is it tempting."

"Go ahead and quit!" Ramsey offered. "Go back to your pot-smoking friends and the anti-war rallies."

"Hold on Joe," Jeff protested. "I never participated in an anti-war rally. I have reservations about Vietnam, that's no secret, but I also have a sense of duty. If I have to go, I'll go, but I don't have to like it." Joe didn't reply.

Jeff continued,"She also says that if anyone wants to come back to New Hampshire with me on vacation, she'll fix them up with a date. She know lots of eligible young ladies."

"Maybe she can fit one in a box and send it down here for me," I offered. "I could use a little companionship right about now."

"What's the matter, redhead, getting a little restless?" Merritt chided. "Me too, but I'm saving it all up for Parent's Weekend. Lynda will be here, and my parents know we'll require a little privacy. -- I can't wait."

"So you're horny too, butt-head," I said. "You just have a specific goal in mind. You don't have to wait to develop a shallow relationship so that you can strike paydirt. I feel like a god-damn hermit."

When I returned to our room, just prior to lights out, Rico was already gone. I checked outside the window. Ronald was still contemplating, but Rico was absent. I stood in the dark and stared outside for a long time, watching the lights go out in rooms all around the courtyard. After the last room went dark, I stared at the stars for several minutes. I decided I was very lonely and that I should go to bed immediately.

I crawled into my rack, severely depressed but not sure why. I lay on my back for a long while, staring at the bottom of the top bunk overhead. I had no particular fantasy in my head and my thoughts drifted aimlessly. Suddenly, and without any warning, I began crying silently in the dark. I didn't understand it at all, but I knew I couldn't control it either. The tears rolled slowly down the sides of my head as I shuddered in the darkness. I forced myself not to wipe them away. I felt the cold, wet drops touch my ears. Some of the liquid pooled inside my ear cavities. Most dripped from my lobes to the pillow. Was this what had happened to Pirelli, I asked myself? I fell asleep, still crying, the pillow on either side of my head wet from my tears.

About an hour later the door to the room opened silently. I woke instantly. I have always been a light sleeper.

"Rico?" I whispered.

"No, it's me, Jeff," came the reply. "Time for some mischief. Want to come?" I didn't hesitate.

"You bet," I said springing out of bed and reaching for my gym gear.

Jubal Ramsey was once again the perpetrator of the stunt. Our goal for the evening was to get to as many Company areas as possible and "borrow" the company guidon from its usual perch outside the squadleaders' room.

"What are we going to do with them once we have them?" I asked.

"We'll line them all up in the grassy area at the inside entrance to T-Court," Joe answered. "We'll plant them just before dawn. It'll make quite a sight to the early church formations."

Merritt and Poole accompanied us -- much to my surprise -- as well as all the occupants of 5401. The nine of us split into four groups and quietly made our way to the company areas. My "team" consisted of myself, Tommy Poole, and Bill Allen. We were the only group of three, and I was the team leader. I was proud. We were to try for the pennants from the Thirty-First through the Thirty-Sixth Companies, which were located in the fifth wing, not far away. Jubal had drawn a rough map of where he had reconnoitered each Company guidon to be. We studied the map in silence.

"Okay," he said. "Let's not take any chances. If you can't get a flag, don't worry about it.

We started out at about twenty-two-thirty. I led my group quietly through our now-darkened Company area. On the way down the passageway we passed the head and startled Steve Rogers who was just emerging when we raced by. We didn't stop to acknowledge him, and I could see puzzlement on his face.

We ran silently, almost tip-toeing to avoid making any noise in our passing. I knew the best way to the fifth wing because I had traversed the same path during my romp with Jubal and Jeff.

We stopped on the landing of a small set of steps at the end of the third wing and discussed our strategy. We decided we would start on the bottom floor of the fifth wing and work our way up. Only Bill and I would make the grab for the pennants since we could run swiftly and hopefully could escape if challenged. After we gathered in a flag, Tommy would carry it back to his room. We sneaked down the stairs to the ground floor, and stealthily crossed the passageway connecting the third and fifth wings. We spotted a guidon in the main passageway. It seemed to be inviting us, daring us to try what we intended. The dark area was very quiet. With Tommy and Bill scouting opposite ends of the passageway, I moved down the broad passageway, hurrying but not running, my eyes incredibly alert for any sign of activity. I approached the pennant cautiously, looked around quickly, and snatched the pole from its leaning-rest position, turned, and sprinted as silently as possible from the area. My heart pounded so strongly in my chest I thought it would surely awaken the occupants of the rooms I glided passed. I was high on adrenaline and endorphins by the time I entered the ladderwell for our prearranged rendezvous. A quick check discovered we had taken the guidon from the Thirty-Sixth Company. Tommy looked from the flag to me and back to the flag. I handed it to him almost reverently. He took it carefully and began to ascend the ladder for his trip back to our Company area, careful not to bump the pole on the terrazzo steps. Bill and I scouted the next deck.

There was no guidon outside any room on the next deck up, so we moved up one more deck, where Bill took the flag from the Thirty fourth Company. Tommy had returned by then, and he carried off the next flag to his room. The next two decks went almost as easily, but we couldn't find a flag for the Thirty-First Company and decided to return to our Company. Four flags out of six seemed like a good night to me.

We were the first group finished. Rico still had not returned. We waited in the Goon Room for the others. Tommy Poole, who probably had never done an illegal thing in his life, was particularly elated. He giggled with delight as he recounted his trips with the guidons. I withheld my own excitement but secretly I was also proud.

We knew the penalties for discovery and apprehension were potentially severe. Jim Merritt had reminded us before we started that being out of the room after lights out was a 10 demerit offense. Being out of the Company area without authorization was worth another 20 demerits. And when we went outside Bancroft Hall later to plant the flags, we would be courting another 20 demerits. That added up to a Class A offense, and that was big time punishment for stealing some stupid flags. I realized that if I thought about it that way, it almost wasn't worth it. However I couldn't let the Company down, and not participate, could I?

Most of the other groups elected to bring all the captured flags back at the end of their raid. As the other groups returned, the number of dark lumber poles and gold pennants gradually accumulated in the Goon Room until the final group returned at nearly midnight with its three flags. In total we had collected 25 of the 36 guidons.

"The last upper-class are supposed to be back in their rooms by midnight, but they'll be sneaking in until after one," Merritt said, " I suggest we get some sleep and go out at around four in the morning to put the guidons up. Anybody that finds us at 0400 probably won't say a word about it." We agreed to that plan and quietly returned to our rooms. Rico still was not in his rack.

I quickly lay down. The excitement of the evening's activity had released the tension from my nervous system, and I didn't feel at all like crying any more. But I *was* tired. I closed my eyes and fell instantly asleep.

Rico returned an hour later. I heard him open the door and slip into the room. He hesitated for a moment, went to the sink area, and turned on the small fluorescent shaving light. I rolled toward him and stared.

Rico had the biggest smile I have ever seen in any individual. I knew instantly he has been successful. I also noticed that he was holding something behind his back.

"Mr. Ed's very happy," he said. I laughed.

"I can tell, you rotten so-and-so," I replied.

"You wanted proof, Kevin? Here it is," he added, bringing his hands out from behind his back. In one hand he held a pair of small, delicate pink panties high in the air with the tips of two fingers, the grin not wavering for an instant.

"So?" I said. "What's that prove. She could have brought an extra pair from home." Rico laughed quietly.

"I'll bet she wished she had," he said. He walked over to my bedside and hung the panties near my face. I inhaled copious pheremones, and I knew instantly Rico wasn't lying.

"I'll pay you in the morning you lucky bastard," I said.

"You don't have to pay me, Kevin. You can do me a favor instead."

"What's that?" I asked cautiously, thoughts of shoe-shining or rack-making springing into my brain.

"Cindy's got a friend," he replied.

Anyone who has ever heard those dreaded words will understand why I immediately paled. There is a universal truth that pretty girls are always attended by not-so-pretty ones. On the few occasions I had helped my neighborhood or school buddies by double dating a "friend", I had been "disappointed". On one occasion I excused myself from chubby clutches to visit the men's room at a local drive-in during a showing of *The Creature from the Black Lagoon* -- which is one of my all-time favorite horror movies, by the way. Once safely inside, I climbed out the back window and walked three miles home in the dark. I knew what the words "she has a friend" could mean.

Rico sensed my hesitation, or maybe he saw my gag response initiating.

He quickly added, "No, no, Kevin. This will be okay. I promise. Cindy can't get the car next Saturday night, but she has a friend who can. Cindy guarantees the friend is good looking and that she's a hot number."

Hold on! What was that? A hot number? My curiosity -- among other things -- was aroused.

"Tell me more." I said cautiously.

"I don't know too much," he replied. "But I promised to bring a good-looking friend if she could arrange another rendezvous, and she swore her friend Brenda was very pretty." Rico thought I was good-looking, huh? Or was he trying to scam Cindy. No, that didn't seem right. Especially when sex was on the line.

"Okay," I said. "Sounds good." I watched Rico as he went to his bed and undressed quickly. He was humming inanely. Before climbing into the rack, he took a deep and obviously satisfying look at his trophy, tucked it under his pillow, and happily settled himself under the covers.

"The gang will be active later this morning. Want to participate?" I asked. He didn't answer at once.

"Kevin," he answered, "I don't think so. I've got to recharge my juices. Maybe next time." We slept.

At precisely 0400 Jim Merritt shook me awake.

"Time to go," he said. "What about Rico?"

"It's a long story," I replied. "He's tired. Next time."

I dressed and hurried across the passageway to the Goon Room. On the way I noticed that the area near the head door was free from Maxwell leavings. It mustn't have been a big night for Maxie.

Merritt and I were elected scouts for the trip out to T-Court. I would reconnoiter far ahead, and Jim would stay just in front of the main body while Bill Allen served as rear-guard. The twenty-five guidons were divided among the remainder of the group. We discussed the plan before we left, intending not to say a word the entire trip out or back unless we ran into an emergency.

Our path to glory this morning would take us through the rotunda area, practically under the noses of the watch staff. I descended the stairs to the main deck and peered cautiously around the corner at the office area. There were several plebes and a second-classman on duty inside but no activity whatsoever. I motioned to Merritt that it was okay to come forward, and I scurried to the main outside doorway. From the dark recesses of the big brass doors, I carefully checked the surroundings. Every room that fronted T-Court was unlit. No sounds interrupted the slumber of the Plebe Summer Brigade except normal night noises and quiet music from a radio in the Main Office. It seemed perfect for what we were attempting.

Cautiously I hunched over and exited Bancroft Hall, moving stealthily onto the wide landing at the top of the steps. I checked to ensure that no one in the Main Office could see me without coming to the window and leaning out. By now Merritt and the group were waiting near the doors. I motioned them outside as I descended the steps and quickly transited T-Court, my eyes on the Main Office during the entire passage.

I stopped in the grassy area on the west side of the entry to T-Court, ducked down behind the short architectural wall, and carefully checked the area. No one walked, sat, or stood anywhere nearby or as far as I could see in any direction. I stood and motioned to the group, who now waited on the landing for my signal. The first flag carrier started forward. It was Hank Butkowski carrying the first five poles in his two hands. Each person carried consecutive numbers. He hardly made a sound as he ran across the stones. He looked like a legendary Greek spear carrier. I indicated the place where he was to stick the flags into the soft earth, and silently he began planting. While he worked, I checked everything again and signaled for the next runner.

Jeff Polk brought four guidons, and soon he and Hank were planting together, carefully spacing each flag exactly two Hank-steps apart for uniformity. I signaled the next runner as Jeff moved out onto the campus and positioned himself near an enormous tree, where he could see more of the campus and be our long-distance sentry.

Tim Butler brought four more flags. Three of those we planted on the west side with the others; the other began the flag formation on the east side of T-Court. Jubal brought four more without incident, as did George Abbott. The last flag carrier was Tommy Poole, who now waited nervously on the landing. I signaled. He started down, immediately tripped, and sprawled on the hard granite steps. Everyone let out audible gasps.

Luckily Tommy had enough sense not to let go of the poles, but the noise of several wooden shafts striking the steps seemed incredibly loud in the dark, still, silence. Jim Merritt immediately sprang down the steps and grabbed both Tommy and the poles, pulling him out of sight behind the short wall that frames the steps. I saw Bill Allen duck quickly inside Bancroft Hall, presumably to warn us if someone from the Main Office came to investigate the noise. We flag planters dropped to the ground behind various bushes and shrubs and waited.

Tommy lay still for several seconds. From where I lay I could see him clearly. He shook his head groggily several times while Jim held him steady. His head-down position was precarious, and he was still in some danger of tumbling further. I could also see the window to the Main Office. The noise had alerted someone. From this distance I could see a second-classman framed in the brightness, staring out into T-Court. I adjusted my position to minimize any chance of being seen. The figure in the window continued to stare, his gaze shifting up and down the Court for nearly a half minute. Eventually he turned and disappeared from view. I stood and signaled Jim to be ready.

Jim and Tommy got to their feet slowly, careful not to make any noise with the poles. They each carried two poles. A full minute passed. Finally Bill Allen emerged from the doorway and signaled that all was well. I stared at the bright window for another ten seconds and signaled them to come across. Tommy went first and Jim followed him closely. They made it with no further problems. I could see Ramsey glare at Tommy as they arrived. He snatched the poles from Tommy's hands and quickly handed them to Hank. Within two minutes they were embedded in formation with the others. Our prank looked great.

We assembled in the grassy area, and I signaled Bill Allen. Bill went inside and almost immediately returned. He signaled that all was well, and Tommy sprinted across the courtyard. Quickly the others followed until only Jeff and I remained. I waved to Jeff, and he started toward me backpedaling, his attention on the campus area. As he neared the grass he suddenly stopped, a look of horror on his face as he stared in the direction of the Severn River. From nearby, I heard a voice.

"What are you staring at, you miserable ass licking plebe?"

I was horrified. We had been discovered. But how had the person whose voice I heard gotten where he was without our seeing him? Taking a chance, I slipped closer to Jeff and looked at where his gaze had frozen. At first I didn't see anything, then I saw movement in the dark, almost at ground level.

A second-classman sat sprawled against a large tree. One leg was drawn up almost against his chest; the other stretched in front of him. He had been drinking. He had been drunk. He had been sick. I knew this because of the smell of alcohol that clung to him like a cheap perfume. I also knew it because of the dark stain on his shirt front and lap where he had vomited, too incapacitated to turn his head.

With one hand he tried to smooth his shirt front, but he only further smeared the vomitus mess. Pausing, he stared at his now-moist hand uncomprehendingly, and wiped it on the red brick walkway. He tried to stand but fell over on his side.

"Do you need help, sir?" I asked. My voice startled him.

"Shit, no!" he answered looking up at me with sad, unfocused eyes. "Do you think I'm helpless?"

"No, sir," I answered. The squadleader valiantly struggled to his feet and wavered unsteadily as Jeff moved to a position beside me.

"Say," he said. "What are you guys up to anyway?" He stared around as best he could, eventually saw the poles behind us, and looked up. His eyes traveled down the line of poles to the second line across the entryway. He chuckled.

"How many?"

"Twenty-five," I answered.

"That's just great," he said, clearly excited. "Did you get Thirty-third Company?"

"Yes, sir," I answered. I had gotten that one myself.

"Well, lemme have it," he said. Jeff started toward that pennant.

On a hunch I blurted, "Sir, that would mess up the formation." Jeff stopped. The squad leader pondered. Somewhere in the dark recesses of his alcohol-soaked brain he saw the very fuzzy logic of this.

"You're right," he slurred. "Leave it as it is for prosperity." I think he wanted to say "posterity" but I wasn't about to correct him.

Gripping the end of the wall, he turned toward Tecumseh Court and started staggering forward. I reached across the wall and grabbed his arm.

"Sir," I said, "If you go that way someone is sure to catch you out this late. Wouldn't it be better to go the back way?" I pointed toward Dewey Field and the side of Bancroft Hall. He pondered again.

"You're absolutely right," he said, a little too loudly. Jeff and I quickly glanced toward the Main Office. When nobody showed a head for several seconds, I signaled Jeff to go. He sprinted off. By now the others knew something was wrong and had disappeared into the building.

"Do you need any help getting back?" I asked the now departing midshipman as he began wavering down the walk.

"No," he replied. Then he stopped and stared again at the flags. "I wish my asshole plebes had balls like this," he said wistfully. With that he continued staggering down the dark walk. I silently hoped he made it back.

I watched the departing figure for several further long seconds, then turned toward Bancroft Hall. There was no activity in the Main Office window. I began my sprint. Ten steps out into the open, however, a white-uniformed figure appeared in the bright window. He saw me instantly. The figure was about to turn and say something. I waved my arms violently across my front, palms outward, in a gesture to wait. The figure paused. As I neared, I could see it was a fellow plebe. Relieved, I reached the steps I put my index finger to my mouth in a signal for silence and I sprinted up the granite stairs. Inside Bancroft Hall I paused. If the plebe had given an alarm, the watch squad would soon come pouring from the office and cut me off before I could make the stairs. I counted to ten slowly. Nothing happened.

Deciding I was safe, I hurried to the stairs and ascended. I didn't realize until I had gotten to the next floor that I had been holding my breath. I inhaled deeply in a huge stress-relieving sigh and continued upward toward safety. Pausing outside the Company area to ensure no one was watching the passageway, I silently pushed open the door and slipped inside. Instead of going directly to my room, I stuck my head in the Goon Room. Polk and Merritt were still up, quietly talking at a desk in the dark. Ramsey and Poole must have been in their racks.

"All's well," I whispered, and returned to my room. I got absolutely zero sleep in the time between when I lay down and when, two hours later, it was time to get ready for mass.

I was tired when I finally dragged myself out to formation. Even the sight of the 25 pennants hanging limply in the humid morning air did nothing to perk me up -- not until a group of watch squad plebes rushed down the steps toward our flag formation. I chuckled and nudged Tommy Poole who smiled in return. We had a secret. Under the direction of the second-class watch officer, the guidons were removed from the loose earth and carried to Bancroft Hall for later distribution to the appropriate companies. As I waited in Catholic formation, I wondered what the retribution for our stunt would be if they somehow caught us, but I didn't have a great deal of time to ponder. Soon we headed off to chat with our Maker.

I would never normally consider intentionally sleeping during mass. In parochial school the nuns instilled a sense of reverence and respect in me that prevents even the thought of such a thing. At Annapolis, however, three factors temporarily changed my attitude about slumber and sacrilege. This change had nothing to do with the church setting, which was awe inspiring. Nor was it related to the priests who said mass in the chapel. They were always dynamic leaders and captivating speakers. And I loved the choir and the organ music.

My attitude wavered because of three disparate factors that completely overrode the music, the venue, and the environment. First, I was God-awful tired the entire four years I was a midshipman. The academic, physical, emotional, and social schedules were completely overwhelming; and any reprieve from the pressure found me automatically dozing off. Second, attendance at church was mandatory. I never liked to be told what to do, especially where religion is concerned, and many midshipmen consequently resented the Academy church process. The third reason, however, was "Sleepy Hollow."

The chapel dome has a wide balcony along a portion of both sides. Midshipmen always sit in the forward-most sections downstairs. Guests sit in the main aisle and the balconies. The areas under the front balcony have several long side-facing rows of pews affectionately called "Sleepy Hollow" by midshipmen.

Our squad leader that Sunday was a very tired second-class. His eyes were bleary, his voice gravelly. And he trudged to chapel rather than marched. After he insured that we were properly seated in the center section, he immediately went to the area under the balcony and selected a position in the middle of one of the back rows. Because those seats faced sidewards I initially thought he sat there to watch us plebes better. However, after the introductory portion of the mass I noticed his head slowly disappear from view.

At first I thought he was tying his shoe or adjusting his kneeler, but five minutes later while we were standing for the gospel, he still hadn't emerged. I knew something portentous was happening. Deductive reasoning, coupled with the fact that if I listened hard enough I could hear the sound of deep steady breathing coming from his vicinity, led me to decide that he was either lying prostrate on the kneelers praising the lord in a continuous rumbling nasal chant, or else he was asleep. I opted for the later.

Initially I was disgusted. How could anyone come to church specifically to sleep? Didn't he know this was the house of God? Why didn't someone turn him in? What kind of place was this anyway? I was still indignant several minutes later when the plebe on my left side -- who luckily happened to be Tommy Poole -- nudged me awake. My head had fallen over so far to the left that it rested painfully on his shoulder. I wondered briefly if he thought I was being fresh. I shuddered quickly awake, straightened in my seat, and looked around. No one had noticed my siesta. That was because most of the plebes were themselves in snoozeville, although none had been so bold as to use his neighbor's shoulder as a pillow.

I glanced in the direction of Sleepy Hollow. It was still noisy, but seemingly devoid of population. It wouldn't always be so. During academic year Sleepy Hollow was a very popular place for slumber seekers. Some first-class would bring plebes along to act as lookouts, which would be fine if the plebes themselves weren't droned to sleep by the sound of so much snoring. Sleepy Hollow would be populated in a classic plebe-big space-plebe-big space-plebe-big space arrangement all midshipmen recognized.

However, in the face of all the hypocrisy and negative motivation to the contrary, I can honestly say that I never intentionally slept during chapel. The operative word here is "intentionally."

But I sure needed sleep that morning. I ate my breakfast in an absolute daze, and crawled into my rack for a two hour nap before noon meal.

On Monday morning during the run, Battle let the better runners scamper ahead while he ran alongside Poole, taunting him mercilessly. The things he said were creative and incredibly disgusting, and I could hear them clearly all the way from my position near the front of the pack. Tommy responded with renewed effort. He ran strongly -- if not quickly -- through most of the race. I watched from the finish line as he approached and spurred by the "urgings" of Battle, began to sprint. I cheered for him as he gutted along, but I was almost alone in my encouragement. He faltered as he neared us.

Tommy's face spoke of absolute agony, and his breath huffed in labored gasps as he approached. His once pudgy but now rapidly tightening legs pumped wobbly in exhaustion, the new thigh muscles straining to keep up the pace. He was doing well considering the sorry state he arrived in, and even Battle stopped his harassment momentarily to watch the gutsy effort.

"Keep it up, Tommy!" I yelled. "You're doing great!"

Twenty yards from the finish, I saw a surprised look spread oven Tommy's face. Is eyebrows arched high on his face. He opened his mouth widely and gasped. His pace dropped to a quivering plod. He wretched noisily, and almost immediately collapsed, vomit gushing from his mouth as he fell.

On the way down he reached out with one stubby arm to push himself away from a grassy nose-dive. Unfortunately for Tommy that arm landed in the very center of a puddle of fresh mess. His arm slipped along the grass. He tried valiantly to pump his legs and regain verticality, but he couldn't. Instead he sprawled forward and landed with a plop on his gradually-flattening-but-still-somewhat-disgusting stomach. I could hear the wind whoosh from his lungs, and see small globs of undigested stuff spit outward onto the nearby grass.

I doubt in all his life that Tommy Poole had ever had the wind knocked out of him. He didn't know what to do. He panicked as he desperately sought to return air to his lungs. His ample weight, pressing on those very lungs, made that task difficult.

A shrill wheezing sound emerged from his widely-opened mouth. His expression became desperate. His eyes bugged outward. Remembering Merritt and the pool, I reacted. I ran forward to Tommy and quickly turned him over. I looked into his frightened eyes. I think he must have decided he was going to die and wanted no part of it. He reached upward toward me, wide-eyed, almost like a sinner on Judgment Day. His look said, "Please Kevin. It's not my time yet. I still owe Maxwell a million comearounds."

"Easy, Tommy," I said. "You're only winded. Relax and it will be okay." Taking his two legs, I lifted them high into the air to move some of his blood back toward his heart. After a few panicked seconds his lungs opened, and the air rushed back inside. He sucked down several grateful gulps, relief visible on his face.

Satisfied that he was recovering, I reached down.

"Okay Tommy," I said. "Let's get up." I helped him slowly to his feet. He staggered slightly as his now-exhausted frame tried to support his weight. I put an arm around his shoulder and began helping him to the finish line. Surprisingly, no one else had come forward. When I looked up, I could see why.

Every plebe face was turned toward Battle, who was livid. I could not remember seeing him this way previously. His face had turned deep red, and I could see veins sticking out on his nearly-bald forehead. He stared at the two of us, speechless for the first time this summer. I realized I was in big trouble, but I wasn't sure why. Tommy and I crossed the line, and let go of Tommy. He bent over at the waist to regain his composure. I looked up. Nothing happened for several long seconds.

I stared at Battle. He wasn't watching Tommy. His madman's eyes bored double searing holes into my skull. I held my own gaze, holding a blinkless stare until my eyes began to water. I had seen his look before on the basketball court, and for a moment I thought he was going to start a fist fight. I quickly sized up the encounter. I was bigger and maybe stronger, but he had better endurance and was a crazy bastard, which could mean a lot in a fight. But I had been in fist fights with crazy bastards before. Hell, I had even been knocked unconscious once by a punch I didn't see coming, so I knew what could happen if we mixed it up. I decided I wasn't afraid of this puke-faced shit-head at all. And I told myself that what Midshipman Tommy Battle didn't know was that when I get angry I get really mean. And just staring at him was starting to rile me. Shit, I might just go after him myself right now. I sure would feel good if I did. Suddenly I decided to kick his ass all the way back to the Company area, and maybe beyond. I began to step forward.

Mike Wojeck "innocently" stuck out his foot slightly before I could complete that fateful first step and then pretended that I had somehow collided with him. He fell in front of me, blocking my path.

"Watch it, Kevin!" he shouted angrily at me.

"Huh?" I said emerging from my warlike trance. I looked down at Mike. His face was hidden from Battle's view. His eyes entreated me to calm down.

I suddenly realized what I had been about to do. Holy shit! I must be crazy. I helped Mike to his feet.

"Sorry," I said to him, not looking at Battle. "I must have lost my balance for a moment." I straightened and looked up. Battle's back was suddenly turned toward me, and he seemed to be staring placidly down Dewey Field toward the old Severn River Bridge.

"O'Reilly," he said calmly without turning. "Give me 50."

I dropped to the grass and began screaming out the push-up count. Battle continued to stare off into the distance until I had finished. "Stay in leaning rest, O'Reilly," Battle said as he turned toward us. He addressed the group. "O'Reilly just screwed up, big time, gentlemen, and I'll bet no one here knows why."

"Because he helped Poole, sir?" volunteered BJ Wilson.

Battle momentarily renewed his anger. He snapped.

"Do you know what a rhetorical question is, Wilson?"

"Yes, sir," BJ answered tentatively.

"Well, smack, the question I posed was just that. Rhetorical! I didn't ask for an answer. I didn't want an answer. I don't even like your answer. Give me 20 for being a bilge." Wilson dropped to the grass, his feelings hurt by Battle's anger. I was still at leaning rest, my arms beginning to weaken.

"Gentlemen, O'Reilly's heroism in Midshipman Poole's behalf was out-of-place." He looked at Tommy. "Poole, front and center!" he said.

Tommy scurried wearily to a position in front of Battle.

"Your good buddy, O'Reilly is in trouble because he didn't let you suffer, Poole, you miserable twit. Does that sound crazy to you, Poole?"

Tommy didn't answer. He was probably as confused as I was. It did indeed sound crazy to me. I waited for enlightenment, my arms straining. Battle continued.

"You've never puked like that before, have you Poole?"

"No, sir."

"You've never lost your wind before, have you Poole?"

"No, sir."

Battle smiled and stared off into the distance at some point above Tommy's head.

"This is a tough life, Poole. But people in the military are expected to overcome severe challenges. More than most civilians can ever dream of." He paused, still staring far away.

"Sometimes we have to die in the service of this country. Nobody wants that, but it's a fact of life. Did any of you know that even in peacetime the military is the most hazardous occupation in the world?"

Before the now-rising Wilson could volunteer an answer, Battle interjected, pointing at Wilson. "That's another rhetorical question, asshole." BJ wisely remained quiet. Battle continued. "You joined the world's most dangerous profession." He turned to the rest of us.

"If you graduate -- a fact which is in absolute question for some of you -- you will return to your tenth reunion to find that several of your classmates are already dead. By the time you retire the number of deceased will be significant. The chances are good that one of your Twenty-third Company-mates will not live to retire."

"To gain the best chance for survival in this very dangerous business," he continued, "you have to learn to test and exceed your limits. The only way to do that is to experience the edge, to live on it." He stared deep into Tommy's eyes.

"You didn't just face the edge, Poole. You ran smack into it head-on. And you didn't like for an instant what you saw there. I could read that all over your face. In combat there won't be any mommy to help you out and dry your tears, and there may not be any O'Reilly to get you back on your feet. You have to learn to do it all on your own, because *you* are the only person in the world you can count on completely."

Battle turned to me. By now my arms vibrated, ready to collapse. My stomach sagged uncontrollably almost to the grass. I hunched and jiggled my shoulders to relieve the pressure. It didn't help.

"You've got to learn not to be such a good classmate, O'Reilly. I fully intend to run Poole's ass until he quits, and if I can't do it this summer, then God help him when the Brigade gets back, because the "Tigers" will. I don't want any more interference from you or your classmates in my handling of Mr. Poole. Do nothing to assist him unless his life is in danger; otherwise, I'll run your ass out along with his. Understood, O'Reilly?"

The pain in my arms was so intense that I would have agreed that my mother had once been the queen of England -- although if she knew I would have considered associating her with anything British, particularly the queen, she would have made me feel far worse than a little leaning-rest.

"Yes, sir!" I blurted out.

"Good," he said, recognizing my severe discomfort with a sadistic gleam in his eyes. "Now get up so we can return to Bancroft Hall in time for formation." I rose unsteadily and shook out my arms to restore circulation. I could see Tommy Poole staring at me from 20 feet away. I winked at him to let him know I was fine, although, to tell the truth, my arms and I were beginning to have doubts about the wisdom of helping out classmate Poole.

Battle led us back to Mother Bancroft at a slow jog. He was very quiet during the trek. I took that as a good omen. Maybe he was considering my actions in a different light and his conscience was beginning to hurt him. I hoped so, but somehow I doubted it.

That evening Battle had a special comearound for Poole, Steinway, Hardesty, Rogers, and me. He positioned the five of us at varying distances along the passageway, with me always the farthest contestant from the finish line. Then he gathered the others along the passageway wall to watch. Before each race he had my classmates place push-up bets on the winners. If they picked correctly, no penalty; if not, push-ups. For further incentive, anyone who picked ten winners would get carry-on at evening meal. We runners could get carry-on by winning ten events. The competition was incredibly intense. I wasn't sure about the others, but I would just about kill for carry-on. I had no intention of losing if I could help it. Most of the early betting was on me, and the crazed screams from my classmates as I sprinted up and down the passageway were almost deafening. It was certainly unnerving to me to be the center of so much attention and pressure, and I was angry the entire evening about being the performing monkey -- but I really wanted that carry-on.

I glided to three fairly easy victories before the squadleaders wised up and adjusted the spacing to the point where I didn't think I could catch the front runner. Before every race Rico looked at me, and I would indicate with a nod or a shake whether I thought I could win. Consequently, the Puerto Rican Rasputin carried on at dinner.

I didn't like listening to my classmates and supposed friends as they rooted for someone else to beat me. I knew this didn't make sense. They wanted a chance to relax as much as I did. But it still pissed me off. I vowed to show the bastards who could run, but unfortunately the distances between myself and the other runners was daunting. I didn't win as often as I wanted.

Midway through the "entertainment" Maxwell upped the stakes and lengthened the course, which was to my advantage. I immediately won twice more for a total of five victories. Hardesty and Rogers had accumulated three apiece, and Poole and Steinway had two. At the same time he announced that as an added incentive, anyone who lost would now get an extra comearound. I signaled Rico that I couldn't win the next two races, and I didn't. Surprisingly, Tommy Poole did.

Then Ronald Steinway did something that sealed his future as a midshipman. During the third-to-last run, as I sprinted on the return leg, trying desperately to catch the leaders, I saw Ronald, who was ten yards ahead of me, wobble on his thin legs. He moaned and slowed up considerably just as I evened with him, and he dropped in a heap as I passed. I didn't pause. I caught and passed the leader, Steve Rogers, at the finish line -- my eighth victory. However, as I turned and headed toward the starting line, I noticed that, while I could hear the squadleaders yelling insanely, the crowd noise was subdued. I knew that something significant was up, and I stared down the passageway at a scene that has been indelibly etched on my subconscious ever since.

Ronald Steinway lay sprawled on the tile floor on his belly. His legs, slightly parted, pointed down the passageway toward the double doors. One arm stretched in front of him, hiding his face from view. The other lay underneath his body. He didn't move except for the rasping breaths that wracked his frame.

Maxwell knelt on one side of Steinway, Battle on the other. They were not there to help Ronald to Sick Bay. Instead, they both screamed at him unmercifully.

"Steinway, you pussy!" yelled Maxwell. "That was the most pathetic feint I have ever seen. Get up and get ready for the next run!"

"So help me God, Steinway!," added Battle. "If you're not on your feet in three seconds, you're as good as dead!" I watched amazed. I hadn't seen Ronald fall, but he looked out of it to me.

His two tormentors didn't let up. The abuse and promises of torture continued for several seconds, increasing in volume and escalating in scope. I secretly hoped Ronald had the sense to stay on the deck. Now that he was there, it was the only logical thing to do. Then Battle pulled a dirty trick on poor Ronald.

"Steinway," he said in a relatively calm voice. "You can't fool me. I know you're faking to get out of exercising. That's a form of deceit you know? And that makes what you're doing an honor violation. If you don't get up this instant, I'll haul you before the Honor Committee, and you'll be out of here in a week. Time's running out, Steinway. Make up your mind."

Steinway stirred. I almost shouted to him to stay on the deck. Battle couldn't prove that Ronald was faking, and there was no honor violation without proof. But if he got up, he would be admitting that he tried to deceive the squadleaders. In my brain I yelled repeated "Stay downs!" to Ronald. He didn't hear me.

I could see him waver on the verge of a momentous decision. His arm moved under his chest. He slowly pushed himself up off the tiles, shaking his head groggily. But even from my distant vantage point I could see that Ronald *was* pretending. He looked like a really bad actor playing an exhausted human being preparing to gut out a final physical effort. He was just too dramatic, and his scene was too *staged* to be real. Despite his pretenses of confusion and swoon, his eyes, which darted from side-to-side in his typical nervous mannerism, were alive and frightened. He knew he had been caught. He stood, pretended to recover, and jogged unsteadily to his starting place.

Every eye was on Battle. Neither he nor Maxie had said anything when Steinway had gotten to his feet. Now they both stared at Ronald malevolently. I realized in that instant that any chance Ronald had of making his parents happy had ended. The squadleaders were going to kill Steinway.

The lull in the racing was to my advantage. I kept warm by jiggling my thigh muscles and swinging my arms, and actually I was still upset at having to demean myself for the benefit of two post-pubescent males hardly older than I was. I also think that the Steinway incident took the fight out of the other competitors. I won the last two races easily. The monkey had gotten his banana.

My big rendezvous with a supposed nymph named Brenda was fast approaching. As the days passed, my thoughts focused more and more on the upcoming event and on women and girls in general. It will come as no surprise when I say that female companionship and sexuality were prime plebe topics of conversation. For most of my classmates getting good sex would have been infinitely preferable to getting good grades. Some got neither.

In that regard I suppose that midshipmen are like other red-blooded males when it come to relationships, however, the monastic isolation at Annapolis infuses a unique intensity in the midshipman dating process that can be and often is overwhelming. Few midshipmen survive the four years of sociological turmoil and remain faithful to their girl back home. Most lose their virginity as students at Annapolis, either on the wet grass at Hospital Point, in a bedroom at a June Week cottage, or in a house of ill repute during summer cruise. The temptations are too all-powerful, the needs too all-consuming, and the uniform and its associated mystique too empowering.

Some of my classmates inherently recognized the sexual energy they exuded and wielded it in a fun-loving way, never promising their partners anything more than companionship and intense physical contact. Rico was foremost among them. He was the best "swordsman" I have ever known, and I never once heard any of his conquests complain about a second's worth of time they spend in his arms. But there were others, like Danny French, for whom the uniform and the power were means to a not-so-glorious end.

In other respects Danny French was a perfectly ordinary midshipman who participated in the process as energetically as any of the rest of us. But when it came to dealing with women, he was immature, scheming, insincere -- and worse yet -- a braggart. Danny, being handsome and athletic and having a father who was a City Councilman, already knew how to wield power, both politically and sexually. Being all of the above plus a midshipman made him dangerous to any female who happened to come within the range of his charm.

To borrow a pre-World War II phrase, Danny French was a cad. He wasn't the only cad among us, but he was the most blatant and unrepentant. Danny bragged often during the summer about how he and four friends formed a club in High School, the sole purpose of which was to deflower unsuspecting young ladies. According to Danny, he was club president and head deflowerer. Six virgins already had fallen for his charms; and according to Danny his parents were bringing another unsuspecting victim to Parents' Weekend, when he was certain to add another girl to his trophy case. With Danny sex was never a question of feelings unless you counted his own primal urges as meaningful.

But while Danny's lack of sexual conscience was the epitome of crass manipulation, none of us except George Abbott seemed immune to the temptations of sex. Big George had met his sweetie pie, Diane, during their freshman year in high school, and the two of them instantly knew they were made for each other. George carried her picture in his hat, had her portrait on his desk, and kept another photo in his shirt pocket next to his heart. As for sex, George was strange. Despite four years of dating, George bragged that he and Di had never had sex, and had vowed they would wait until they were married before experiencing the big act.

The only glimmer of weakness George even admitted was that he once peeked down Di's blouse as she was bending over to pick up a book she had dropped. He shamefully confessed this immoral act to Diane immediately, but rather than chain him to a tree and beat him with a catechism -- an act I'll bet Big George secretly would have enjoyed -- she forgave him and took to wearing turtlenecks. I guess she didn't want to tempt the demons within poor George. At the time we thought George was naively stupid. In retrospect, I envy George's restraint, if not his complete sexual abstinence. At the time, George must have thought us heathens.

I say all this because in the preparation for the big night, I had no plane of reference with which to compare what I wanted to happen with what I fantasized might happen. I found my self stuck between Danny or George. On the one hand the thought of seeing this girl solely for the purpose of getting her skirt off appalled me. On the other hand, I sure wanted to see what was inside that mythical skirt.

I was in a quandary as to what to do about preparing for the encounter. Rico and I had agreed not to say a word to anyone about our plans. You never know when a classmate will turn screw, particularly if a little carry-on is on the line. So I couldn't just ask for classmate advice, and I also couldn't let on to Rico the extent of my inexperience. I didn't want to disappoint him. So I did the next best thing. I borrowed one of Rico's "training manuals." He understood immediately.

"Getting yourself revved up, huh?" he asked. I agreed.

It was not a difficult book. I finished it in under an hour. Of course, I only skimmed the dialog, deciding it would be meaningless except to provide me with a good base from which to develop my sexual vocabulary. I was wrong about that by the way. How many times in your life can you find the opportunity to use a phrase like "throbbing love muscle" in casual conversation? Besides, I discovered that in the heat of passion I usually become incoherent.

I decided to study the steamier scenes intensely -- from a purely technical standpoint of course. I finished the book in under an hour, amazed that two people could physically do the things suggested on those pages. I also noticed that a great deal of my blood seemed to be concentrated in one particular area. No wonder Rico didn't want to be disturbed when he was reading one of these things. If his "Mr. Ed" reacted like my "Master Eddie," a standing Rico would surely have fainted from the volume of the blood collected in his throbbing love muscle. -- What do you know? I did use that phrase.

Armed with the information imparted from that one book, I felt ready for my encounter with Brenda. Of course there wasn't much blood left in my brain at the time, so I suppose any thoughts of sexual prowess should be forgiven.

That Saturday was significant for two reasons other than the impending date with sexual destiny. For one thing Patrick Mulvaney got a "Care package" from home. Most of us from time to time received boxes of goodies, which usually included a few cookies, maybe a piece of a sibling's birthday cake, and a copy of a local newspaper. But when Pat received a package, several grown men had to carry it.

Living on a farm with ten other people, I suppose the Mulvaneys learned to do things in a bigger way that most of us. But this was bigger than big. Mrs. Mulvaney must have enlisted all the sisters and several neighbors full time to bake the prodigious amounts of cookies that came Pat's way. His favorite, we all soon found out, were of the chocolate chip variety.

Just after noon meal, while I was trying to decide if I should reread Rico's "technical manual" in case I had missed some subtle points, I had a sudden, almost uncontrollable urge to visit Room 5409. Maybe the sound of tearing paper and ripping cardboard gave me a clue. Maybe the smell of chocolate wafting down the passageway perked my senses. Maybe it was the sight of the long line of classmates forming up outside Pat's room that alerted me. Suddenly I knew was that I had to visit my old friend Pat -- with whom I hadn't had more than five minutes conversation in the last six weeks. As a matter of fact, except for showing up like a vagrant at a soup kitchen whenever he got a package, I'm not sure Pat and I ever had a conversation that didn't include the word "cookies."

The second and far more momentous event of that day was a surreptitious visit by three first-class midshipmen who would all too soon become our Company leaders. It happened just after evening meal while the fried chicken and baked potato dinner still sat undigested in our young stomachs.

"Plebe Ho!" yelled a gruff and unfamiliar voice from the passageway after we had settled ourselves in our rooms. I had removed my shirt and shoes and was in the process of taking off my pants when the voice called out. At first I was startled. I reacted slowly, unsure whether to go into the passageway in this stage of undress lest it be an officer who had called us forth. I wasn't sure yet about the protocol with officers.

But I could hear other classmates scampering into the passageway, and I decided that hesitation might hurt me worse than indiscretion. I ran outside, Rico immediately behind me, and braced myself along the bulkhead just outside the room and yelling out my identity simultaneously with my other company mates. In the confusing moments between my exit and my bracing I noticed three individuals in civilian clothes standing arrogantly in the center of the passageway. They looked around as we surged forth, obviously checking us out. Our voices echoed down the previously silent passageway.

"Well, well. What do we have here?" said one of the group after we had all assumed our positions. "Our new plebes. Aren't they cute?" Keeping my eyes in the boat, I couldn't see who was talking or who the talker was referring to.

"Give us 20 push-ups, all of you!" said another harsh voice. We dropped to the deck and started singing simultaneous numbers. During the push-ups I glanced quickly at the newcomers to see who they were. I had no idea, and Neither Maxie nor Battle were in attendance, which also confused me.

"All right, pussies, on your feet," the tallest one yelled. We quickly stood.

"At ease!" the first one snapped. We relaxed and stared in their direction.

The first speaker, the shortest of the group, sported a Marine Corps close-cropped haircut took the lead. His clothes weren't half bad looking. -- He should give Battle lessons on how to dress.

"My name is Sidney Littleton," he said from his parade rest position. "I will be your Company Commander for the second set this coming winter. Since I happened to be in the area between summer cruise and vacation, I thought I would stop by and introduce myself and kind of let you know what you can expect from my classmates and me come September." He indicated the tall, dark-haired individual to his left. "This gentleman is Dale Micklewski." Micklewski smiled sardonically but said nothing. He seemed to be sizing us up. I didn't like his look at all, and I shuddered; several of us did. Littleton sensed our reaction and laughed.

"On my other side is my good friend and roommate Peter "Wild-man" Kopciak", Littleton continued. "He's a pussy cat." I stared at the "Wild-man", and something told me Sidney was lying. He chuckled again. I decided I didn't like Sidney. There was something about him, besides his stupid name, that was at the same time both arrogant and unredeeming. Maybe the humanity had been ground from him by the Academy crucible, and all that remained was his baser side. He turned slowly, keeping his hands precisely positioned behind his back, which seemed very affectatious in civilian clothes.

"You are going to be part of the Twenty-Third Company Tigers," he said with some pride. "We are the meanest, toughest, most gung-ho Company in the Brigade, and we're proud of it."

He snorted, then indicated his companions with a nod of his head.

"*We* had a Plebe Year. You can count on that. None of this sissy stuff you've experienced so far, and a whole lot worse than the worst we can do to you and stay within the rules."

He stopped and stared wistfully at us, and he continued with absolute sincerity.

"I wish we could show you a real Plebe Year. By not having one, you will miss out on the greatest challenge in the military." He paused, then continued in a sad tone, "It's too bad." I happened to glance across the passageway at Merritt. He was staring at me, dumbfounded. Apparently he agreed that Sidney was not to be believed.

"But," Littleton continued, perking up a bit, "we fully intend to give you the best Plebe Year we can within the limits the Academy sets. It's the least we can do for you and for this institution. So don't worry. You'll have a Plebe Year. You just won't have a real Plebe Year." There was no question in my mind about his seriousness. I began to worry. Up to that point I didn't really believe that the return of the Brigade would be so bad. I mean, everybody had to study , didn't they?

"I suppose "Big Jim' Daly is the worst of us for training plebes," he continued. "Pray you don't get in his squad. But Dale here is also a plebe killer. He gets pretty intense sometimes." Dale Micklewski smiled broadly, and Littleton continued. "And I also have a reputation. It's completely deserved, believe me; but if you survive, you'll one day thank me for my special attention." He and his companions had turned so that they were now facing completely away from us. I looked at the Goon Room. Polk shook his head in disbelief. Ramsey stared at the backs of the three first-class, sizing them up. Poole looked terrified. Merritt seemed angry for some reason.

I found myself a bit angry too. How dare they insinuate that what we had experienced thus far wasn't a Plebe Year. It sure felt like a Plebe Year to me. Besides, I bet I could outrun any of them. I also bet myself that I could handle anything they could dish out -- although I really wanted to avoid the dishing.

My irritation was broken when Maxwell and Battle entered the area through the double doors. They apparently hadn't returned after dinner. They stopped and stared. Maxwell was openmouthed. Battle narrowed his gaze at the trio.

"Where the hell have you been?" asked Littleton gruffly.

"We stopped by the Main Office to pick up a note for midshipman Maxwell," Battle replied boldly. "While we were there we talked to the duty section about scheduled activities."

"You know that you are not supposed to leave the plebes alone at any time?" asked Littleton.

"We were in the Main Office," answered Maxwell unsurely. "We weren't there more than 10 minutes."

"That's no excuse," said Littleton officiously. "Put yourselves on report for not following correct procedures, and you can bet I'm going to let Rock Stone know about this."

I was shocked. Littleton was putting our squadleaders on report. Hell, none of us plebes had received any demerits as yet. This was incredible.

To his credit, Battle didn't flinch.

"May I remind you, Sidney," he said slowly, "that you are not allowed to be in this area. This wing is strictly set aside for plebe training, and that means only the second-class assigned to the plebe detail. Shouldn't you put *yourself* on report for not following correct procedures?"

Littleton stared at Battle for several long seconds, then smiled, nodding his head slowly and regarding Battle with open malevolence. That same look radiated from Michlewski's and Kopciak's ugly faces.

"Touché, Midshipman Second-class Battle," Littleton said. "We'll be going now." Then Littleton did a quick circle and laughed cruelly, "See you guys come September!" His companions also laughed, and the three of them quickly disappeared around the corner and down an unused passageway.

Battle and Maxwell exchanged glances, then Maxie spoke.

"All right everyone. The fun's over. Back to your rooms." We hastened to comply, while the squadleaders hurried to their room. I could hear them whispering furiously.

Once safely inside, I said to Rico, "What did you think of that?"

"All crap," he said.

"You think he wasn't serious?" I asked.

"No," he replied, "Littleton was serious. But he spouted shit."

"What about the thing with Battle?" I asked.

" Battleaxe just went up a notch in my estimation from asshole to just plain ass," replied Rico. "Come on Kevin, lighten up. We've got better things to think about."

Rico was right as usual, but before I completely calmed, I decided to visit the Goons.

As I entered, the goons looked up and became instantly silent. They had obviously been discussing something they didn't want an outsider to hear. The question was, did they consider me an outsider?

"What's up?" I asked as I entered.

"Plenty!" answered Polk.

Jim Merritt looked at his roommates before speaking. When no one objected, he continued.

"We're discussing our future," he said. "Tonight's incident throws new light on everything."

"How so?" I asked.

"Are you shitting me, O'Reilly!" said Ramsey fiercely. "We just met the midshipman from hell, and you ask what's changed? Maybe you didn't see that gleam in Micklewski's eyes, but I did. The guy is insane."

I looked at the others, and I could tell from their expressions that they agreed.

"Let's not panic yet," I said. "It could be that the whole thing was staged to scare us."

"Well, it worked," said Polk. "And besides, that little confrontation between Battle and Littleton was not staged. They hate each other. And all three of them hate plebes. This is going to be one miserable year, my friend. Is it worth it?"

I thought he was asking himself that question, so I didn't immediately answer. Tommy Poole had been strangely quiet to this point, and I watched him as he stared out the window, deep in thought.

"Look, fellas," I said, trying my best to sound reasonable, "let's take this one day at a time and see where it all leads. Besides, look at Tommy here." When he heard his name, Poole turned toward me. I don't think he even knew I was in the room until that instant.

"Nobody has caught more shit than Tommy, and he's doing just fine. No way can what they do to us come academic year be any worse. By God, if Tommy can hack it, so can we all." Tommy's eyes narrowed and he stared at me for a long second before speaking.

"Tommy's not doing so well," he said sadly. "Tommy's tired. Tommy's in constant pain. And Tommy's sick of the humiliation." Poole turned back toward the window.

"That's what we were discussing when you entered," offered Jim Merritt. "Tommy said he's thinking about quitting, and some of us are trying to talk him out of it."

"And some of us still think it's a great idea!" added Ramsey with more vigor than necessary.

I watched the four of them for a second. Whoever assigned roommates could not have put four more different personalities into the same small space. This was a perfect microcosm of the stresses we all suffered, and to see how the pressure changed people, and brought out the best -- and the worst -- in all of us.

"Tommy! Listen!" I said. "You can't quit. If you do, you acknowledge everything Maxwell and Battle said. You *will* be a pussy to them. And how's is it going to affect you? After you leave, are you going to start believing that crap they spouted here. That decision could affect your future in ways you can't know."

"Y'all are so full of shit, your eyes should be deep brown," said Ramsey leaning back in his chair. "Where did y'all get your psychology degree, and what makes you think you know everything? Come down to earth red head, and stop living in your fantasy."

"Maybe you're right Joe," I replied a little angrily. "Maybe I *am* the biggest bullshitter in this Academy. Christ knows my mother accuses me of that often enough. But I'll tell you something: Tommy Poole has more heart and guts than the best of us. I hope that if it ever gets too hard for me, I can remember what he's had to suffer and will continue to suffer. He's a genuine hero in my opinion."

Tommy turned again toward me. He eyed me skeptically for a moment, then turned his head back toward the darkening window.

"I'm going to discuss everything seriously with my famiily and make a decision during Parents' Weekend," he said sadly. "I don't want to quit, but God, this is the hardest thing I've even done." No one said a word for a long time. I could sense that their private moment with Kevin O'Reilly was ended and that I was an outsider again. I turned toward the door, and discovered that the excitement had made me horny.

"Well, guys, the read head has better things to do this evening. See you later."

Rico was brushing his teeth in anticipation when I entered.

"Hustle, Kevin," he said. "They'll be here in 30 minutes."

"No problem," I answered. "I'll take a quick shower; then it's just another uniform race."

I turned on the water. While it warmed I went to the window and gazed outside. The night was humid and moonless and no breeze stirred the dark masses of trees. But life went on in the courtyard windows around me. The myriad fluorescent rectangles seemed unusually bright in contrast to the darkness that gripped the Academy. Or maybe my mood made it seem that way. The visit by the "Tigers" must have had a profound effect on the entire Company . No music issued forth from Simpson's guitar, and the usual subdued but intense grab-ass and friendly banter were also missing. I turned toward Simpson's room, fully expecting to see Ronald Steinway perched on his favorite spot. He was. I was about to shout a word or two of encouragement, but I could hear a soft sobbing sound drifting my way on the still dark air. I quickly ducked my head inside.

I finished my shower, shaved, brushed my teeth, and got dressed in fresh gym gear within fifteen minutes. Rico checked us out before we departed.

"What about this white shirt," he said. "It shows up too easily in the dark."

"We could were sweat-gear. It's gray," I offered. Rico smiled.

"That would take too long to get off, Kevin. I don't think I can wait. I am ready for action."

"Me too," I added, and I was proud of myself for that admission.

"Follow me," I whispered to Rico as we exited the room toward the heads. "I know some secret ways to the outside." We jogged stealthily along dark unused passageways and down narrow stairways until we came to the exit door I had used with Ramsey and Polk several weeks previously. Once outside, we rigged the door for easy entrance later, crept in the darkness toward the parking lot of the Midshipman's store, and waited hunched over in the shadow of a bush for my destiny to arrive.

We didn't wait long. Not more than five minutes later a large dark late model automobile pulled around the corner from the direction of the yacht basin and turned into the parking lot. Without hesitation it drove to a point directly in front of us and stopped. Its headlights went out immediately. I could see two shadows inside. The shadow in the front passenger seat turned, knelt on the seat, and reached back to open the door behind her. The lights came on inside the car. A very pretty blond girl -- Rico's Cindy, obviously -- knelt on the passenger seat, looking expectantly in our direction. My attention, however wasn't on the passenger. Instead I strained my eyes to see the driver, but my view was blocked by Cindy's body. Rico nudged me.

"Let's go," he said.

We crept from behind the bushes. Carefully checking the surroundings, we sprinted for the back seat. Rico piled in first, and I was close behind. Cindy shut the door almost immediately, and it bumped my backside slightly as it closed.

"Get down in the wheel-well and cover yourselves with the blanket," she said.

A large dark blanket lay in the back seat. Rico reached for it as we slid down.

"Wait," said the driver, "let me get a look at my date first." She turned on the overhead light, turned around, and faced me.

Being hunched over on all fours on the floor of an automobile, I was not exactly the position I would have chosen for an introduction. We stared at each other for a long second. I felt like that monkey again. In the few moments that we had to look at each other I caught a glimpse of a hard but pleasant face, dark eyes, no obvious deformities or scars, and an enormous head of hair, piled up on her head in a bee hive. She was also chewing gum furiously. Not exactly the type of girl I would have picked for myself, but I was not complaining. Besides I wasn't even sure what my type of girl was yet. This was the time for experimentation.

"Hi," she said, smiling. "My name's Brenda."

"I'm Kevin," I replied. Brenda turned toward Cindy, smiling. "He'll do," she said, and they both tittered as Brenda turned out the light, started the car, and quickly turned toward the yacht basin.

Luckily it's possible to get from Bancroft Hall to Hospital Point and not leave the grounds. Going through the gates with a dark, covered lump in the back seat might have posed a problem. At least I thought so at the time. That was before I got to know the civilian gate guards, who we affectionately referred to as "Jimmy-legs."

Being mostly older gentlemen and Federal government employees, they lacked any type of military zeal. I believe their standing orders were to keep outsiders out rather than escaping midshipmen in.

During my second-class year, when it was "illegal" for me to have a car at the Academy, I struck up a friendship with a friendly black jimmy-legs guard who usually stood weekend duty on Gate Number Three. His name oddly enough was Jimmy. Jimmy didn't care what time I crept in, what clothing I had on, or what condition I was in. Consequently I would always enter through Jimmy's gate. During first-class year Jimmy even let me smuggle my brother Sean, -- who was as big as some of my classmates by then -- onto the campus late the night before the Army-Navy game so he could spend the night with me and get a taste for the military life. I even "borrowed" a uniform from a plebe about his size and brought him on the bus with us so that he could participate in the march-on and the hat trick. Without any practice whatsoever he still marched better than some of my plebes -- who did *not* have a Plebe Year like mine, by the way

We drove slowly through the dark campus, Cindy giving directions. To tell the truth, I felt pretty silly hiding under a blanket in the rear of a car, but it had to be done for this potential moment of glory. Besides, Rico was also huddled in the identical predicament, and misery loves company.

The ride to Hospital Point took about ten minutes. Brenda stopped the car along the road adjacent to the hill leading up to the Academy cemetery.

"Stay down while we check the area," Cindy said, and I could hear her and Brenda shifting in their seats as they looked in all directions. "I think it's all clear," she finally announced.

Rico straightened in his seat, reached over, and opened his door. Cindy and Brenda exited from their own doors, and I slid out the same side Rico had used.

"Bring both blankets," Cindy said as she came around to our side. Rico already had one. I reached inside and grabbed the other.

Cindy clutched Rico's arm as they turned toward the hillside.

"Let's move uphill away from the car," I suggested, "in case someone sees it and checks nearby."

"Good idea," Rico replied. We started for the hill.

Brenda moved alongside me and held my arm with her hands. "May I?" she asked, smiling in the dim streetlight.

"Absolutely!" I answered. She squeezed my biceps and I flexed in response.

The grassy hill leading to the cemetery is fairly steep in places, but we soon found as we ascended that there are level plateaus where trees, decorative bushes, and a few ex naval officers are planted. Rico and Cindy selected one spot under a large spreading tree whose drooping branches hid any view of the road. Brenda and I picked a similar location several yards away and nearly in the "shadow" of a large granite headstone. Light filtering from a streetlight down the hill revealed that we were near the resting place of Captain Benjamin Fromme. I hesitated, shuddering slightly. After a moment's consideration, however, I assumed that Fromme, who must have once been a midshipman himself would have no objections to my dallying nearby, in fact he might even approve. Brenda didn't even notice the stone.

I spread the blanket and Brenda sat in the dark, holding her knees with her arms and watching me. She had on a pair of tight short pants, and in the dappled dimness that filtered into our dark niche from a streetlight 30 yards away, I could see she had good, strong-looking legs. I sat down next to her and boldly put an arm around her shoulders. She leaned in toward me and rested her head against my chest.

"Nice night," I whispered, not knowing what else to say.

"Uh, huh," she replied quietly. We sat in the dark for several long seconds.

"Is anything wrong?" I asked.

"No," she answered. "Just a little nervous."

"How come?"

"I don't know. You seem nice enough. But I don't really know you at all."

"We could talk," I said. "Get to know each other a bit." She thought for a minute.

"Kevin?" she said. "Would you think badly of me if I didn't want to talk -- if I just wanted you to kiss me."

Was she crazy? I was instantly excited in a powerful way.

"That would be fine," I stammered. She turned toward me and pushed me down onto the blanket. Then she climbed slowly up on top of me and settled herself precisely against me. She felt my arousal.

"Oooohhh, Kevin," she said slowly and provocatively. She leaned down and pressed her breasts against my chest and kissed me.

The kiss lasted more than a minute, our passions compounding all the while. She pressed against me powerfully and I pushed against her equally. I was in immediate danger of losing control. She saved the day.

Moaning, she straightened and sat on my chest. She pulled off her blouse and reached behind to unfasten her bra. Large, firm breasts spilled out from her lingerie. She sighed and bent over toward me, smothering me with her flesh. I didn't complain for an instant. I would have welcomed death had it come that way.

Before I gotten the hang of it, she straightened again.

"Ohhhh, Kevin," she said, kissing me passionately.

Pushing against my chest, she stood and looked around. I could see her breasts jutting forward like two dark projectiles. Satisfied that the coast was clear, she dropped her shorts and undergarment. Hesitating only slightly, she knelt between my legs and grabbed the waistband of my gym gear. Deftly she tugged my shorts off.

"Ohhhhh, Kevin," she moaned again. I pulled off my own shirt and waited. She straddled me, knelt down, and suddenly every nerve in my body was on fire. I felt things I had never suspected were possible. Brenda moaned again -- she did that a lot -- and rocked back and forth. I moaned. I guess I did that a lot too. Then she began motions designed to drive me wonderfully insane. I moaned again, and again, and again.

To a casual listener we must have sounded like rutting animals. Since I had no experiences to relate to, I decided that I was just along for the ride. After what seemed like only a few seconds, I exploded. At first I thought I had injured myself: the intensity was that great, and it continued for a long, long time.

Eventually Brenda's motions subsided, and she moaned a final time before settling against me. I enjoyed her softness against my chest. Her head settled on my shoulder, facing away from Rico and Cindy. Unfortunately, her beehive -- which had the consistency of thirty-day concrete -- pressed against my nose and mouth and distracted me from the afterglow. I turned my head in Rico's direction, and for the first time could hear the commotion ongoing on their blanket. They certainly sounded as if they were enjoying themselves. I know I was, cotton candy hair notwithstanding. I felt like a stud.

Brenda and I lay still for several minutes. After a minute she looked down at me.

"Get on top for a while," she said huskily.

We rolled over and adjusted positions and soon were moaning again. After 15 minutes of this, Brenda finally stopped gyrating. She was plainly exhausted.

Unfortunately our reverie was broken by Rico and Cindy, who had finished and dressed.

"Hey stud," whispered Rico from his blanket, "time to go." Brenda straightened, patted me a final time, then reached for her garments. I did the same.

As she was about to slip into her undies, however, I said, "Brenda, could I keep your panties as a remembrance?"

She hesitated.

"Kinky, huh?" she asked.

"Sort of." She looked at the dainty, lacy object in her hand, almost as if seeing it for the first time. It was so dark I couldn't see her expression. I did see her shrug. She handed me the panties and continued to dress. Soon Rico and I were back in the rear seat of the car and headed toward the Academy proper. In the parking lot we uncovered, sat up, and looked around. All was quiet. Before we departed, Cindy reached back and grabbed Rico's arm. "I love you," she said sweetly. Rico was a bit taken aback.

"Me too," he said uncomfortably. "I'll call you."

Solemnly I reached up front-ward and touched Brenda's massive hairdo.

"And I love you, Brenda," I said tenderly. She twisted around quickly and gawked. Every eye in the car watched me as I continued to pat her rigid coif. Then I smiled and gave her an exaggerated wink. Obviously relieved, she laughed.

Rico and I hastily exited and returned to our place in the bushes. After the car turned the corner, we began to make our way stealthily toward the waiting door. When we passed under an exterior light I stopped to examine my shirt. It was severely wrinkled and moist in several places. Rico watched me closely. I looked at him, broke into an enormous grin, and displayed my pink, frilly, trophy. Rico slapped me on the back and laughed.

" O'Reilly my man," he said. "You're a true stud."

Silently we made our way back to the Company area. Almost immediately I sensed something was wrong. Instead of deathly quiet, as we glided along the passageway, I could hear mumbling noise from several plebe rooms. I looked at Rico, who only shrugged.

No sooner had we entered our room than the door of the Goon Room flew open. Merritt looked across at us. He sprinted across the passageway.

"Steinway has disappeared," he said.

"What do you mean?" I asked.

"He isn't in his room. Simpson said Ronald was sitting at his desk writing a letter home in the light of a tensor lamp when he left for a minute to go to the head. Strong was already asleep. Anyway, when Simpson returned, Steinway was gone. Simpson waited several minutes, checked the head and the other company rooms but no Ronald."

"He seemed pretty sad after dinner; maybe he went for a long walk to clear his mind?" I offered.

"Maybe he pulled a "Speilenberg" and we'll never see him again," offered Rico.

"Simpson doesn't think so. Ronald can't bear the thought of quitting, and he never wants to even bend the rules. He's scared to death of any attention." I went to the window and checked outside. I didn't see Ronald, but I also didn't have a good view of the entire roof.

"Let me check something," I said, and I climbed out onto the dark roof.

"Where are you going?" asked Merritt.

"Ronald liked to sit out on the roof and meditate. I'll check around out here."

"Be careful," Merritt warned. "It's awfully dark out there."

I carefully stood and began walking with my feet placed carefully one-foot-in-front-of-the-other in the copper gutter and one hand on the tilted roof, leaning in an exaggerated angle away from the edge. It *was* precarious in the dark, and I've always been a bit acrophobic -- some condition for a future jet pilot, huh? In this shaky manner I moved slowly toward Ronald's room, checking up and down the roof as I went. I couldn't see anything. After a minute I arrived at Ronald's room and peeked inside. Merritt and Rico were there, along with several other classmates. Merritt turned to me.

"Should we wake Maxwell?" he asked. "They got in trouble before for not reporting Speilenberg's absence, but if Ronald is only out somewhere for a stroll, he'll be in serious trouble when he returns."

"Let's think for a minute and develop a plan," I said. "We should probably conduct our own search first. Maybe he's got a bad case of diarrhea and he's been in a stall in the head all this time."

"I already checked," said Willy in his slow drawl.

"I'll gather the others," said Merritt and departed.

I stayed on the roof, looked out into the dark, and tried to analyze the situation. Where would I go if I were Ronald Steinway? -- I decided I wouldn't go anywhere. After all, I had my lonely perch if I wanted solitude, so there was no reason for meandering around Mother Bancroft -- that would only invite trouble I wanted desperately to avoid. I was a prime target for the squadleaders, and I couldn't afford any more pressure, because I was already at my limit. I had been crying this evening on this very spot because the interruption by Littleton and his cohorts promised more trouble. I couldn't quit because my parents were counting on me, and I couldn't disappoint them because they were so proud. But I couldn't stand this place another minute, and I was desperate, so I had to do something. . . .

I suppose the solution to Ronald's problems had been with me the entire time I had sat there rambling to myself in the dark. The thought had been poised just beyond my consciousness. I hadn't chosen to recognize it because it frightened me. I had pushed it away repeatedly and tried to avoid it. But my brain reached the inevitable conclusion and decided there was only true possibility of escape for poor Ronald.

I sighed loudly. I rationalized that it wouldn't get any easier the longer I waited. I slid on my rear down into the gutter. Placing one hand on the roof, and the other firmly gripping the edge of the gutter, I leaned out over the black void.

I became immediately disoriented. The shadows swirled wildly beneath me and I pulled back. But in that instant of swimming vision I saw an indistinct lighter blob among the dark plant shadows four floors below. That blob seemed deathly still.

I whirled around away from the roof's edge and sprawled on the tile facing the window. For an instant I thought I was falling over the edge, and I reached out with open hands and gripped the roof tightly. I became lightheaded. I moaned loudly, my left cheek pressed against the roof tiles.

"Ooooohhhhhh, Jesus! Mother of God! No!" I began to hyperventilate. Bob Strong came to the window. He looked at me and saw the distress on my face. He turned pale. He didn't say a word, but his eyes asked the question. I nodded quickly, gulping air.

"Oh, no, Ronald, no!" he said loudly with a shrillness that sent chills down my already weakened spine. I grabbed harder at the tile and I could feel the fingernail of my right ring finger peel back painfully. I didn't let go.

Jim Merritt jumped out of the window onto the roof and scampered over me to the edge of the roof. I watched him as he peered over. He wasn't afraid of heights, and I was irrationally angry. He stared for less than three seconds then hurried inside the room. He even said "excuse me" when he bumped against my hand on his way past. I raised my head to watch him.

"Strong," he asserted, taking charge, "you and Simpson race down to the Main Office and get an ambulance over here immediately. Tell them someone has fallen from the roof. Ronald's directly below your room in the bushes. Pirelli, you and Ramsey find Ronald and see if you can help."

"What, from four floors up?" asked Jubal sarcastically. "We won't be any help at all."

"Maybe the bushes broke his fall?" offered Simpson.

"Yeah, and pigs can fly," offered Ramsey.

"Hurry Jubal!" said Merritt. Ramsey didn't object further, and he and Pirelli followed Strong and Simpson out the door.

"Rico, you and I had better wake Maxwell."

"Let's get Kevin first!"

Silence followed. Rico came slowly to the window. He stared at me for a moment then reached out and touched my hand gently, much as I had Ronald's shoe several weeks ago. I shuddered.

"You okay, Kevin?" he asked softly.

I stared at his hand, suddenly frightened. I jerked my hand away from the contact and moaned again, much louder than previously. Loud enough to wake the dead -- maybe that was the reason. The sound of my cry echoed in the courtyard eerily and sent renewed shivers down my spine. I'm sure I woke every plebe whose room bordered the courtyard. I began to cry loudly and uncontrollably. My body racked with convulsions. I shook my head to stop the tears. They immediately ceased and I became lightheaded again, then incredibly angry. Almost instantaneously however, I calmed. Rico reached out a hand.

"Come on Kevin. It's not safe out there, and you've just had a massive shock."

I felt suddenly drunk. "That's two shocks in one night," I said, now laughing uncontrollably. "One was good, but this is not so good, Rico. Ronald's dead."

"I know, Kevin. Come on in. We've got to report this." He leaned out, grabbed my arm in a firm grip, and began pulling me in. I took a deep breath, and my senses cleared almost instantly. I felt the tension wash from my body in a gushing turbulence that left me feeling strangely renewed.

I leaned toward the edge and Rico jerked me quickly back toward the room. I looked at him calmly.

"I'm okay now, Rico. I have to look one more time. I'm afraid if I don't, I won't ever be the same again. The universe just changed, and I need to see this in perspective."

Rico looked at me skeptically. He must have decided that I was okay, because he let go reluctantly. I leaned over the edge and looked down into infinity -- poor Ronald's Infinity. Jubal was right. Ronald didn't survive the fall; I could see that from here. Ronald was broken. No doctors were going to help him, and all the King's horses and all the King's men couldn't put this fragile Humpty Dumpty together again.

Sighing, I turned toward Rico and nodded. I crawled away from the edge and back into the relative safety of the room -- Ronald's ex-room.

Jim Merritt was waiting quietly at the doorway. A crowd of plebes had gathered in the passageway. They had heard but had not believed the words. The three of us walked slowly to Maxwell's door. We looked at each other. I decided to take the lead. I didn't hesitate. I knocked. There was no answer. I knocked again, louder, but still no one acknowledged us. Looking at Merritt, I pushed the door open and turned on the overhead lights. Merritt and Guevarra followed me inside.

My first reaction was, "what a pigpen!" In fairness to Maxwell and Battle there was almost no clutter and no dirt in the room, but a few things were strewn around near the sink where Battle had prepared for his departure on liberty, and one of the desks was covered with an open newspaper and several novels. We plebes could never get away with this. I glanced around the second-class inner sanctum. One rack was made-up but empty. In the other a form under the covers stirred slowly. Maxwell must have been a very heavy sleeper. I calmly walked over and shook him.

"Sir!" I said. "You need to get up. Something's happened."

Maxwell stirred and turned groggily. He focused on me with great difficulty. I thought at first he had been drinking. "What the hell do you want, O'Reilly?" he asked sitting up in bed. " You had better have a good reason for this!"

"Yes, sir!" I said. "There's been a bad accident. Ronald Steinway may have been killed."

"What!" Maxwell leapt from his bed. "What happened? When? Where?" he yelled reaching for his B-robe. He donned the robe and raced passed Merritt and Guevarra out into the passageway. Pausing, he looked up and down for Steinway.

"Where is he?" he asked.

"Sir," Jim said. "He fell from the roof outside his room, but we don't exactly know when. We've sent for an ambulance, and two classmates are down there with him now."

Maxwell brushed Jim aside and ran into Steinway's room. "Let me see," he said.

We watched as he went to the window leaned out, then crawled slowly, to the roof's edge.

"Don't touch him!" he yelled to someone below. "You might injure him further." He continued staring at the scene below for almost a minute, then pulled back inside and came into the passageway.

"I'm going down to check," he said. "You people stay here."

"What about Battle?" I offered. Maxwell stopped and stared at me, thinking furiously. He hurried into his room and returned with a slip of paper. He scribbled on the paper, and looked up.

"Pirelli!" he yelled. John Pirelli came forward. Maxwell handed him the note.

"Call this number. Ask for Tom Battle. Tell him about Steinway and to get back here ASAP. If you can't reach him, put on gym gear and go to that address. Knock until he answers. Carry your ID. Run like hell. If you get stopped, tell the gate guard there's been an emergency and that the Duty Office authorized your trip." Pirelli started to speak.

"Don't ask questions, damn it! Get going!"

After Maxwell had hurried out the double doors, the rest of the company crowded around to hear what we had to say. I let Jim and Rico tell the story. I was beginning to get the shakes again. I trudged to the nearest bulkhead and sat slowly down, hunching my knees closely to my chest. After a minute, the loud noise of ambulance arrival sounded shrilly in the T-Court area, and the entire plebe Brigade came awake. Excited shouts and loud questions seemed to emanate from all directions.

I stood slowly and walked through the double doors to the balcony overlooking the rotunda. I watched the frantic activity below. Plebes in rooms across the way saw me and did the same. Soon the balconies filled with classmates and second classmen, everyone wondering about the commotion.

It didn't take long for the ambulance crew to get what was left of Ronald loaded onto a gurney and rushed through the rotunda into the waiting jaws of the ambulance. They seemed in an awful hurry for a lost cause. Soon the only sound was the murmur of excited voices echoing in the rotunda. A midshipman watch officer came out into the center of the rotunda and shouted. "It's all over. Get back to your rooms immediately."

"What happened, Phil?" asked a second-class from across the way.

"Not sure yet," the watch officer answered. "But a pretty severe accident."

While we stood on the balcony, Maxwell came up the stairs flanked by an officer in crisp tropical whites. We began snapping to attention and yelling but the officer cut us short. "None of that bullshit tonight, okay?" he said. He looked at us for a moment, then said.

"Let's go back inside the Company area." He herded us through the double doors. Once isolated from the rotunda he said.

"Okay, everybody relax. Sit on the floor, please." We sat.

"Guys," he said, speaking to us as equals -- something that hadn't happened thus far this summer. -- "I'm really sorry to inform you that your classmate and friend, Ronald Steinway, is dead. There'll be an investigation to determine what happened and to prevent future accidents of this sort, but from what we can tell he was crawling along the roof in the dark and slipped. He broke his neck in the fall, and his death, thankfully, was instantaneous." The officer paused, staring at the deck and twirling his hat nervously in his hands.

"Who were his roommates?" he asked. Strong and Simpson raised their hands.

"Who was with him at any time this evening?" he asked. Patrick Mulvaney raised his hand.

"Who discovered the body?" I raised my hand.

"Who assisted in the notice to the Main Office and the vigil by the remains?" I didn't like the way he said that "remains" word. I shivered again. Jubal and John Pirelli put their hands up.

"Anyone else involved in any way?" Maxwell nodded toward Jim, Rico, and me. "These three plebes and I organized the response, sir," he said. It wasn't lost on us that he was taking credit, but that was fine with me. Hell, it was his job to take care of us, and that probably included reacting to our untimely deaths.

"Okay," the officer said. "Get some sleep if you can. Tomorrow morning sometime before noon I want each of those persons who were identified just now, plus anyone who might have additional information that could shed some light on this tragedy, to come by the Main Office and give a statement. That should be about all. Again, I am truly sorry for this unexpected sadness." With that he turned and walked slowly out the double doors.

We hesitated. Maxwell stood, thinking for a long moment.

"Everybody, when you give your statements tomorrow, tell the absolute truth," he eventually said. He was troubled by something, however, and I knew what it was.

"What about Littleton's visit?" I asked, voicing the subject that was troubling him. He looked at me. He could be in serious trouble and he knew it. It was almost a no-win situation. He became irritated.

"What about it?" he asked.

"Well," I said, "I'm sure it doesn't relate to what happened to Ronald, but if the visit become general knowledge, it could mean trouble to all of us." I had lied slightly about the relationship between tonight's visit and Ronald's leap to destiny. I did think the visit might have been the final straw for Ronald. I didn't for a second think Ronald had fallen from the roof. But I couldn't prove anything, and besides what purpose would voicing my opinion on that matter serve. No one could do anything now to save Ronald, and a fall was certainly a more noble death than a suicide -- that is if any death can be noble. There didn't seem to be any sense in bringing it up if we could avoid it.

Maxwell thought about the situation, then addressed the group. "Okay," he said. "Tell the absolute truth in your statements, but do not mention the visit by Littleton *unless* . . ." He emphasized the word strongly. "you feel it has a direct bearing on the accident. Getting Littleton in trouble, despite the fact that he is an asshole, will not do a thing to help Ronald, and will only cause complications for you later. I say again, I am *not* ordering you to say nothing about Mr. Littleton, just use discretion and common sense."

"Okay," he said reassuming his squadleader guise. "Get to your rooms and get to sleep!" The Company rose slowly and began wandering toward their respective rooms.

"I said now!" Maxwell exploded. Some of my classmates immediately braced and chopped hurriedly away, others did not immediately react.

"Mulvaney! Goto! Give me 20!" Neither reacted.

"Now!" Maxwell screamed.

I don't know why, but I reached out and grabbed Maxwell firmly by the arm. I then turned him around so that he was facing away from the rest of my classmates.

"Maxie," I said in a fierce hush. "Jesus man! One of our classmates is dead! We're all shocked. This is no time to pull the squadleader bullshit. Take it easy. Show some compassion."

Maxwell stared at my hand where it rested on his arm for several seconds considering. Then he gently shook my hand away. He turned toward the Company.

"I have been reminded that the events of this evening have been a shock to us all. That's true for me too. I'm sorry. You all have carry-on until further notice. Now please get some sleep if you can." Without a further word Maxwell turned and went to his room.

I suddenly found myself very tired. I began walking slowly in the direction of my own room. Jim Merritt stood in front of me. He raised his eyebrows. "Maxie?" he asked quietly. I smiled.

"*He who will not risk, cannot win*," I said, quoting Reef Points. "It worked."

Rico was also hovering nearby.

"You got huevos the size of cannonballs amigo," he said. As I came closer Jim wrinkled up his nose questioningly.

"You also smell funny, O'Reilly," he said.

I smiled and lifted the front of my shirt to my nose and breathed deeply.

"I do don't I?" Rico laughed. Jim was confused, but I provided no enlightenment.

The next morning after chapel I gave my statement to the Officer of the Day and then said good-by to Aaron Rose and Bill Allen, both of whom had decided to depart Annapolis for greener, and hopefully less dangerous, pastures. I bought Bill Allen's nicely polished shoes even though they were a half-size too small.

CHAPTER 5

PAIN AND SUFFERING

For the next week things were very quiet in the Twenty-Third Company. We attended lectures, practiced on the rifle range, and marched as usual. We even participated in the plebe Company marching competition and came in ninth -- There must have been some very inept plebes in the Class of 1971, because I thought we stunk. But Maxie and Battle momentarily forgot we were plebes. We endured no comearounds, no early morning runs, and no bracing at meals. It was almost heaven -- yet somehow I felt cheated.

I reported to the Main Office on Sunday and gave my verbal report on the events of the previous evening. I studiously avoided mentioning the visit by Littleton and my escapade on Hospital Point. Apparently everybody left out the part about Littleton, because nothing ever came of the incident.

The Academy's Accident Investigation Report was issued within three days and declared that Steinway's death was an accident caused by a misstep on a dark evening in a place he should not have been. To avoid any repetition of the same event, the Superintendent issued a memo to all midshipmen forbidding any excursions onto the roof. That was fine with me. For the rest of that year I could not look outside at night and not expect to see troubled Ronald sitting in the dark, contemplating his future. If ever a spot were likely to be haunted, it would be that lonely stretch of roof outside Room 5413. But I didn't intend to verify my ghostly suspicions.

Monday evening the entire Brigade of plebes attended a special memorial service in the chapel. Twenty-Third Company sat up front, just behind Ronald's parents, who were flown in from Phoenix to meet with the Superintendent and bring Ronald home to rest. It was a wonderful ceremony. Rear Admiral Conrad's speech was emotional and uplifting. Ronald's mother wept quietly the entire service, and his father comforted her stoically. The military has had a great deal of practice over the years in honoring its fallen heroes, and Ronald certainly left the Academy in style. I'm sure it made his parents proud. At the end of the service when the congregation sang the Navy Hymn -- which is one of the most touching and beautiful tunes ever written -- and we sang the part about "*those in peril on the sea,*" I cried too, and I wasn't the only classmate in tears. Ronald was certainly in peril. I just wish he could have chosen a different escape, God rest his troubled soul.

We lost three classmates that hectic and unfortunate week, which was very depressing. Aaron Rose was a borderline midshipman, struggling with his place in the military system. I was reasonably certain he only wanted a good excuse to depart, so I wasn't particularly surprised by his leaving. I did regret Bill Allen's decision, however. I considered him one of the best people we had in the Company.

With all the posturing and pretense going on that summer it was hard for me to tell who was being himself. I never had that problem with Bill. I liked his smile. I liked his sense of humor. And I especially liked his ability to see through the baloney and view the system in comfortable perspective. I hardly knew him, but I was sure we would have become good friends, and I regretted his departure.

I felt the same regrets many times during my career. The constant shuffling of jobs and duty stations made it almost impossible for me to have close friendships. It seemed that just when I had decided that a contemporary was a likely friend, it was time for one or both of us to leave for opposite ends of the earth. I had never experienced anything similar during my childhood. Ethnic neighborhoods never change, but the military certainly does. I find it exceedingly funny that supposedly educated people accuse the military of inflexibility. Nothing could be farther from the truth. Military life and work create a constant broil of motion, adjustment, and readjustment, and most successful military leaders learn to adapt to turmoil.

It was Jubal Ramsey who crashed us through the seemingly impenetrable barrier that Steinway's death erected and brought us back into Plebe Summer where we belonged. It happened on the Friday of the week after Ronald's demise, one of the hottest and most humid days of that longest of all summers.

We had been very depressed, including Maxwell and Battle, with no sign of let-up. The squadleaders led us to events but without their original vigor. They inspected us but missed discrepancies that would have meant major punishment only days earlier. Meals were dormitory affairs with no questions asked and no three-chews-and-a-swallow hassles. It was good for us, but it was also not good for us at the same time. There was no fun -- or pain -- any more.

On Friday morning we had attended a final academic lecture in Sampson Hall, where we selected majors, chose classes, and received our tentative schedules for the first semester. On the return march down the walkway toward Bancroft Hall a very lethargic Battle, noticing that a flock of young lovelies hovered expectantly along the walk, perked ever so slightly, turned toward us, and said over his shoulder in a very uncommanding voice.

"Ramsey, how about leading us in a song?"

"Aye, aye, sir!" came the response, followed by a pause, followed by a deep breath, followed by . . .

"There's a skeeter on my . . ."

Before Ramsey could belt out the next word, a surprised Battle spun around, tripping and almost falling to the bricks in the process. He yelled.

"Ramsey! Knock it off!" Straightening, and continuing to march backward, Battle eyed Ramsey for several seconds, his eyes wide as basketball hoops. He smiled.

I had never seen Tommy Battle actually smile before. It wasn't a bad smile; and, best of all, it was a genuine smile. He followed the genuine smile with a genuine laugh, which Maxwell echoed and which we all soon imitated.

It felt good to laugh after nearly a week in the doldrums. That combined laugh drove away the last residue of Ronald's death. We were plebes again, and Battle and Maxie were our squadleaders. In that instant I loved those guys -- but I must admit I was a bit caught up in the emotions of the moment.

"Ramsey!" Battle yelled, still smiling. "Give us a song. But make it appropriate or I'll personally boil you in oil."

"Aye, aye, sir!" Jubal responded, and immediately began a stirring but not so tuneful rendition of *She Wore a Yellow Ribbon* for the girls. They loved it.

The Saturday afternoon after Ronald's death we had a meeting with Captain Dillingham. The squadleaders wouldn't tell us what it was to be about. Bull lined us up against the passageway wall, fully braced, while he conducted the meeting. I decided this was a sign that Plebe Summer would continue.

"Gentlemen," Dillingham began, "in three weeks the Brigade returns, and things will be very different around here. I want to make sure that you are prepared, and I have discussed your individual progress with Midshipmen Maxwell and Battle. There's good and bad news to report." He paused before continuing.

"The good news is that every one of you qualified with both rifle and pistol. Seven of you were double experts. That's excellent. You also finished ninth in the Marching Competition, which is good considering the recent tragedy. I also thought you did a good job on your rooms and uniforms for the last inspection. Keep up the good work."

"But," Bull continued, slapping one hand palm up on the other to emphasize his points as he walked in front of us, "I am disappointed with some other results of your training thus far." I could see him as he approached my position, and I noticed how much his enormous biceps muscle bulged as he slapped. I figured this was an intentional show of prowess designed to intimidate us. It did me.

"First," he continued, "the squadleaders have given me their evaluations of your individual performance, and only a very few of you reached the highest category. Work harder. There's a great deal of room for improvement.

"Second, I have noticed that several of you still do not carry yourselves like potential officers in the Unites States military. Some of you remain disgustingly fat, slovenly, and in far from perfect condition. That must also improve.

"Third and most important, I had a long talk with your squadleaders earlier this morning, and I discovered that several of you continue to hold back the development of your classmates despite ample evidence that you are not suited for this institution." He paused and his eyes narrowed. "I don't like that at all." Bull's voice, normally gentle, rose in volume and timbre as he continued. "I told Midshipmen Battle and Maxwell that I want my Company lean and mean, and I have asked them to work harder to weed out the non-performers. If you fall into that category, please do your duty and go home."

Bull stopped in the center of the passageway midway down the line, and turned smartly toward us.

"One final point, gentlemen," he said. "Your peer evaluations must be given to the squadleaders by evening meal today. Fill out the evals privately. Do not consult among yourselves. I expect we will be able to draw some interesting conclusions from this first evaluation." I wasn't sure what he meant by that remark, but I dutifully retreated to my room after he dismissed us and filled out the evaluation form. I ranked myself an honest number three, behind Merritt and Wojeck. Rico was my number four.

Comearounds returned with a vengeance the next week. Battle and Maxwell redoubled their efforts to steel our characters and to remove Tommy Poole and the bottom dwellers from our ranks. It was not a pretty sight or experience.

"God-damn you, Poole!" Battle yelled during an evening comearound early the next week when it became clear that Steinway's death was having no effect on Poole's resolve. "You're a pussy! You're bagging it! I know you can move faster than that. If you don't beat Butler this next time, every plebe in the Company does 50 push-ups." He also set an impossible task for Tommy, who lost the race as expected, and dropped to the deck for push-ups.

"No, Poole!" yelled Maxwell. "You relax, just like you've been doing during comearounds. Your classmates will do the work for you." Tommy stood in the passageway while the rest of us yelled out the 50 numbers, plus one to Beat Army and one for Ronald Steinway. Tommy was embarrassed and angry, and so were several of my classmates.

I was also angry, more at Battle than at Tommy. Besides, push-ups were nothing -- the first time. Two minutes later after Poole lost the next impossible race, it was harder to crank out 50. The third time they were damn hard and very irritating. The fourth time they were almost impossible. Most people could not finish. The fifth time my arms gave out after ten, and only Rico, French, and Lamont finished. The sixth time I hardly lifted myself from the cold deck, and even Lamont strained. There was no seventh time -- at least not that day.

The push-up punishment continued over the next two weeks, and anger accumulated.

"Son of a bitch!" I announced to Rico and Merritt later that week during an evening visit in our room. "This push-up shit is pissing me off."

"Better to be pissed off than pissed on," replied Rico, laughing, and not at all acknowledging the seriousness of the matter.

"Come on, Rico," I said. "What Tommy is doing to us is pretty bad."

"Poole isn't doing anything to you, Kevin," Rico answered.

"Then what do you call these aching arms that I can hardly lift?" I asked.

"Come on, Barfy," Rico said sarcastically. "Even you can see that your aching arms are part of a little game Battle and Maxie are playing to put peer pressure on Tommy and some others. It's not Poole who's the villain here; it's our glorious squadleaders."

I hesitated before answering. At heart I knew what he said was correct, but it seemed to me that no matter who was the actual culprit, my arms would not be aching so much if Tommy were not still a midshipman.

"What you say may be true, Rico," I answered. "But even *you* must admit that Poole doesn't belong here." Jim Merritt sidled up next to me when I said this to lend support to my statement.

"Jesus Christ, Kevin!" Rico said, startled. "Listen to yourself. Just two weeks ago you were calling Tommy Poole the biggest hero since Audie Murphy. Now he's suddenly a worthless douchebag who doesn't measure up to *your* standards. What's happened to you?"

"I don't know," I replied smugly. "Maybe I'm just seeing the light."

Rico shook his head sadly. "I liked the old Kevin better than "greaser" Kevin." he said slowly. "I hope you see your error soon."

"Wait a minute, Rico," added Merritt. "I like Tommy. But it seems to me that his staying slows the rest of us down and prevents us from moving ahead." I smiled. Good old Merritt. That was a good point. Tommy *was* hindering our progress.

"Moving ahead?" asked Rico incredulously. "To what? Better rack-making? Straighter formations? Shinier shoes? Give me a break. I personally would not choose Tommy Poole for a close friend, but he's not my enemy either, and I for one am focusing my resentment where it belongs -- right on the heads of two assholes who are supposed to be leaders but who are really children playing silly games with people's lives."

Neither Jim nor I had a reply to this argument -- probably because we both knew Rico was right. I wasn't yet ready to admit it, however, and I lapsed into an immediate funk that lasted an entire day. I didn't like being forced to take a moral stand on the issue I had considered settled in my mind. I began to consider and reconsider other issues.

Plebe Summer had a strange effect on me. Like a quiet evening rainstorm, the Academy sneaked up on me and thoroughly drenched me with its outpouring. And once the traditions and ceremonies soaked in, I found I could not and would not separate myself willingly. One bright, hot morning nearly at the end of Plebe Summer I awoke and discovered that I was no longer a civilian proto-plebe. Suddenly -- and surprisingly -- I found myself a full-fledged, heart-and-soul, into-the-breach, damn-the-torpedoes member of the Brigade of Midshipmen. Kevin O'Reilly had joined the fleet.

With that change, however, came certain responsibilities and certain, fundamental shifts in my logic process. During the first part of the summer it didn't really matter to me who made it through the torture and who didn't. We were, after all, companions in confusion, partners in pain, teammates in torture, sidekicks in sadism. We were equals in the same miserable boat. But as the summer wore on, my young body firmed, my shoes achieved a mirror finish, and my marching became crisp and precise, I began not to adapt but rather to adopt. It became *my* Academy rather than *the* Academy. I began to esteem the place and accept it as a bastion of brave and honorable history, an institute of noble and August tradition, a school of the highest moral and ethical standards. And I accepted my part of it and charged myself with its protection. I didn't want the image -- which was now *my* image -- tarnished in any way.

But that admission of reverence and adoption had a darker side. Its very exclusivity meant that not everyone could necessarily be worthy members of the club. And I began to wonder things -- like what was Barton Hardesty still doing here? He was more interested in God than the military. And Doug Goto studied far too much. And good-old-boy Willy Simpson preferred singing over sailing. Why were those people still here? They were different -- maybe too different. They didn't fit the Academy image at all.

And Tommy Poole? What made him think he would ever make a good naval officer? He looked terrible in his uniform, he couldn't march for shit, and he didn't know the winner of the last World Series. -- He didn't even care. Why *was* he staying? Maybe Bull Dillingham's inference was correct, and it would be better for the Academy -- and my sore arms -- if he and some of the others quit.

My intolerance for Tommy and the other "marginal" plebes seemed to rise almost in lock step with the intensity of the physical exertion we underwent, which is why Rico's admonition troubled me. Just when I thought I had it all figured out, he came along and confused me.

But my resentment focused not only on the "misfits," wishing them uncomfortably away, it also elevated itself to the Plebe "greasers" who had settled themselves smugly at the other end of the social and leadership spectrum. *Greaser* is a term I had never heard before I attended Annapolis. A classmate who views the Academy as the ultimate test of his own ability to succeed, particularly at the expense of others, and who goes out of his way to show the upper-class or the officers that he is the perfect midshipman is termed a "greaser." Grease was also the name of the rating system used to evaluate an individual's adaptability to the military and the Academy. Every midshipman receives a semester grease grade from his superiors and peers that reflects his "Annapolis-ness."

Having superiors evaluate performance and aptitude is a necessary part of life, inescapable except for the out-of-work or self-employed. I could accept that. But at Annapolis we also secretly evaluated the grease of our own Company classmates, rating them by name from first to last. I never liked the peer review process; it always seemed somewhat Nazi to think that my classmates were tallying mental points for and against me that they would use in their secret evaluations. It was almost like turning in a relative for not supporting the system.

The results of the first peer review -- the one Dillingham wanted finished so badly -- were posted outside the squadleaders' room on the Monday following Bull's pep talk. Wojeck and Merritt were first and second -- just as I had predicted. I came out number 10, and Rico was 15. Someone obviously made a mistake in the ranking or the calculations.

It wasn't that 10 was a bad number. Considering the talent and capabilities of the competition, I supposed it was pretty good. I just felt I would rank better among my classmates. After all, I was a fairly nice guy. I avoided controversy. I did more than my share of work. And I considered myself well-liked. Apparently I wasn't as good as I had thought. I wondered why.

I studied the names of the classmates who made the top to determine what it was that put them there. And I suppose I also secretly wondered what I could do to join them. I expect the Academy wanted me to do exactly that, but as it turned out, it didn't work that way with me. Surprisingly, when I applied my own patented O'Reilly logic to the process, I found that I didn't particularly like what floated at the top any more than what groveled at the bottom.

John Pirelli was far too intense and unpersonable for my liking. Tim Richardson was much too self-assured and arrogant. Bob Strong had a single-mindedness that scared me. Mike Wojeck was the nicest of the greasers, but he was too gruff and unpolished. Even Jim Merritt, who to my way of thinking had the best leadership qualities, showed a certain eagerness to please that begged belief. And how the hell did BJ Wilson out-grease me? And why did I even care?

I don't want to be second best. It's human nature. But I'm also a Irish realist, and I have always tried to be aware of my many shortcomings. It helps me keep life in perspective. I quickly accepted the truth that, despite their faults, the best in the company was better than me. I was never going to be able even to hold the door open for the Chief of Naval Operations, much less lead the Company through a parade. I wasn't a born leader. I didn't have the inherent charisma. That was that. Case closed. Time to move on to other pursuits.

On the evening after posting the grease results, the squadleaders called a surprise general meeting. Rico and I chopped to the assembly area across the passageway from the squadleaders' room and waited, braced against the wall. Maxie and Battle emerged together. They looked us over briefly from their position in the center of the passageway.

"Carry-on, gentlemen," Maxie said in his mischievous voice. "Have a seat." We sat on the tile deck and waited. Ever since the resumption of hazing, I had developed a dislike for the way the two of them were treating us. It seemed as if they were being childish and petty. I watched them skeptically as they conferred quietly for a moment.

Maxwell walked to the bulletin board, and pointed to the grease list.

"Has everyone seen this listing?" he asked. Of course everyone had. It had been *the* topic of discussion all day.

"Well," Maxwell continued, examining the list with feigned interest, "it does indicate some very interesting things about you guys. Let's see." He looked more closely, then settled his gaze on the bottom of the list. He pointed to the names and called them out.

"Poole? No surprise there. Butler? Ditto. Hardesty? Agreed. Rogers? Yes there too. Chalmers? Sure thing. Simpson? Maybe so. And Polk? Now that's a surprise. I wonder what he did to piss off his classmates." He then straightened up and turned toward us.

"Okay. Let's have those gentlemen out here, front and center please," he said. The aforementioned plebes rose and trotted reluctantly to the fore.

"Face your classmates, gentlemen," Maxwell said in his most sarcastic sneering whine. "Let them get a good look at you." They turned. All except Tommy Poole were plainly embarrassed. Poole stared at us defiantly. He caught my eye. I winked at him. He smiled briefly. I also tried to signal reassurance to Jeff Polk, but he stared resolutely at the deck as he shifted nervously from foot to foot.

"This is the bottom of the barrel, gentlemen," continued Maxwell while pointing to the classmates standing in front of us. "These are the lowest of the low.--- They are the dregs. The waste. The scum." Some of us murmured uncomfortably and Maxwell stopped.

"Don't be angry at me," he said in mock indignation. "It's not my list -- even though I might agree with it. No, you guys developed it yourselves by your grease selections." Maxie strolled in front of the group, shaking his head and pointing to the unfortunate selectees with a raised palm as he walked.

"These are the classmates you feel are not adapting to the Academy system. These are the classmates you believe are not coping with the pressures. These are the classmates you say are not leaders." Maxwell paused and turned toward the group. "I can't say as I blame you," he said. "They are a very depressing collection of misfits, whiners, and non-performers." He again turned toward us.

"For the rest of the summer I will refer to these people as *The Magnificent Seven.* They don't belong here, and I think we all know that. We'll be counting on the more responsible members of your group to help us convince the misfits either to improve drastically or hit the road. Hopefully, by the time the Brigade returns, there'll be no more *Magnificent Seven* left for any of us to worry about."

"Now," Maxwell continued. "I want you *Magnificent Seven* to look at your classmates. Can you see the disgust on their faces? Can you see the disappointment in their eyes? Your classmates think you suck, guys. Isn't that reason enough to quit? Why not make it easy for everyone and get out now. Don't waste our time any more. I'm tired of being a nursemaid for a bunch of sissies like you."

Maxwell paused and looked at us. I was dumbfounded and offended. This was degrading.

"I want the rest of you to wave good-bye to the *Magnificent Seven.* Help them on their way, gentlemen." Some of my classmates immediately began waving at the unfortunate group. Others stared at each other in disbelief. A few openly refused to participate.

"Wave good-bye! All of you!" Maxwell screamed. Many more classmates began waving. Maxwell caught my eye. My hand wasn't yet in the air, but it was creeping upward slowly. Suddenly Jubal Ramsey flipped over and began loudly counting out push-ups. I stared at Joe, unsure what he was doing.

"Ramsey," shouted Maxwell. "What the hell are you doing?"

"Push-ups, sir!" Joe answered.

"Why, Ramsey?"

"Because Ah'm not going to wave like you want, and I thought I'd just start my punishment without being asked." The passageway became absolutely quiet except for the sound of Ramsey's counting. Maxwell was enraged. His face reddened, his eyes bugged, and I could see him ball both hands into tight fists. I looked back at Ramsey and caught Merritt's eye. He nodded to me. I knew what he wanted. I nodded in return. Simultaneously he and I flipped over and began push-ups. Within a few seconds every plebe who had been seated on the deck was shouting numbers.

"Stop immediately!" Maxwell screamed. We didn't.

Maxwell was still too emotional to utter more than a croak of frustration. Battle stepped forward calmly.

"Stop this disobedience or you are all on report." he announced. Several plebes paused, but the majority continued. "That's 5 demerits." No one stopped. "That's 10 demerits." No one stopped.

From their standing position, both Polk and Poole dropped to the deck and also began push-ups. The other five former standers followed suit. Soon the entire Company was shouting and moving rhythmically up and down.

"15 demerits!" said Battle. "20!" Still no one stopped.

"If you don't stop immediately, you can forget about Parent's Weekend," added Maxwell, who had calmed sufficiently to be coherent. Most of the plebes immediately paused for an instant. The suddenly stuttering voices of twenty-five plebes caught between doing what was right and losing what was important, added a disharmony to the previously boisterous cacophony. I immediately lost my feeling of primal elation and became enraged. I wasn't the only angry plebe.

Tim Richardson stopped his push-ups. I could see that his face was flushed with ire. He stood, brushing dust from his hands, and turned toward the squadleaders.

"No way are you going to take Parents' Weekend away," he said defiantly.

"Who gave you permission to speak, asshole?" Said Maxwell.

"I gave myself permission, asshole!" replied Richardson. We all stopped pushing up to observe and listen.

"What did you say!" screamed Maxwell.

"I said you're an asshole!"

"Not only did you just lose Parent's Weekend, mister, but you just committed a Class A offense. You won't have any liberty for two months."

"I don't think so," said Richardson, calmly.

"Oh, really? Why?" asked Battle.

"Because you're way out of line, and you know it. If I have to call my father and tell him to cancel his leave from Jax because I won't be able to see him and Mom, he's going to want to know why. And when I tell him how you violated the regulations, then punished us for refusing to cooperate, he's going to want to have a heart-to-heart talk with his classmate, the Superintendent. After I explain to them what's been going on, I'll bet there will be two second classmen who won't be on liberty for a long time either."

"Are you threatening me, you son-of-a-bitch?" asked Maxwell, advancing on Richardson. Tim braced himself, clearly ready for a fist fight. Ramsey and Butkowski jumped in front of Richardson and prevented him from moving any closer to Maxwell. Battle stopped the confrontation by stepping in front of Maxie and restraining him with an outstretched arm. Maxwell paused, staring hard at Richardson, who mirrored his gaze.

"Okay," said Battle after a tense moment had passed. "Everybody sit down and we can settle this."

We collectively paused, shocked, as we realize what had almost happened. I could hear several long and exaggerated outflows of breath from classmates who had tensely stopped breathing during the confrontation. Ramsey and Butkowski helped Richardson to his place on the deck, and Battle let go of Maxwell. Battle then stepped forward.

"There seems to be a misunderstanding." he said. "The peer grease list on the wall is important for several reasons. It tells the senior midshipmen how well the plebes are performing among themselves. It gives each of you an opportunity to see what your peers think of you. It also gives everyone a chance to improve. Most important of all, however, it should open up your minds to the thought that some of you may be wasting your time and ours. There are certain qualities a good naval officer must possess in order to succeed. Some of it can be trained. Some of it can be learned. The rest is natural. -- You either have it or you don't." He paused, and his quiet voice took on a questioning tone.

"Why would anyone want to stay here knowing that they won't be successful in the fleet? It doesn't make sense." Battle paused again and turned toward the *Magnificent Seven.*

"Some of you will not -- cannot -- be good officers. That's just the way it is. You might as well accept it. Tom and I love this place. We don't want to see anyone unhappy, but we are also committed to doing the best we can this summer, and that means training you for your responsibilities once the Brigade returns. That also includes motivating the poor performers into giving up on a senseless dream.

"About tonight," he continued. "It's possible that we may have gotten a bit overzealous, and we apologize for that. But we cannot allow any of you to get away with open defiance of our authority. Your classmate issued a threat to us this evening. He may be serious about he says he will do, but so are we about what we do. If it means doing some extra restriction to see that discipline is maintained, Tom and I are ready for that challenge. However, what I suggest is that you forget about what might be considered inappropriate treatment of your classmates, and we will reduce the demerits you receive to 10 . . ." There was a general grumbling at this statement, and Battle held up his hand. ". . . which we will hold in abeyance until the return of the Brigade. If there are no repetitions of tonight's mutiny, then we'll forget about the demerits. Fair enough? Good, that's settled. Get back to your rooms and get ready for lights out."

I returned to the room. Rico flopped at his desk and laughed.

"Richardson sure put out Maxwell's fire didn't he?"

"I'll say," I replied. "I was obviously wrong about Tim." Rico laughed.

"No you weren't, Kevin. Richardson's didn't act out of concern for his fellow plebes. He could give a shit. He's still too arrogant and self interested, and he thinks his dad and brother will protect him when the chips are down. I think he's wrong. He played a big card tonight, and he won. But his victory's only temporary. He's a marked man from now on."

"What do you think Max and Battle will do come September, swami?" I asked.

"They'll forget the whole thing happened if we do."

"What about Richardson?" I asked. "Do you think he will?"

"I'll bet he was scared shitless. He'll forget."

"How did Polk get on the bottom part of the grease list?" I asked changing the subject. "I didn't vote him there."

"Well, Kevin," Rico replied. "I think most of our classmates are tired of listening to the complaints. He'll have to keep his negative comments to himself."

"But criticism is healthy."

"Sure -- for you and me, but not for some of our classmates. They're too insecure as it is, and they don't want to hear any of Jeff's cryptic sarcasm. His ranking is a signal to knock it off for a while. I'll bet it won't matter next year. We'll be youngsters, and our enemy won't be physical exercises or the squadleaders; it'll be the system. We'll all be complaining among ourselves next year just like Jeff, wait and see."

"I guess so," I answered skeptically. Rico smiled.

The squadleaders had really upset me with their humiliation of Poole and the others, and I wasn't happy about the added physical attention we all were getting either. I didn't cooperate with my usual gusto for several days, even in the aspects of the system I enjoyed.

The two most important books in a plebe's reference library are his *Reef Points*, and a copy of the latest version of *The Guinness Book of World Records*. The first contains every bit of information a plebe must know to survive the almost constant grilling that goes on during meals and comearounds. The second book is important because a great many midshipmen play at being either athletes or intellectuals -- sometimes both -- and they often expect their plebes to be a portable version of *Guinness*.

"How many medals did Jessie Owens win in the 1938 Olympics, Merritt?"

"Sir, Owens won three medals at the Berlin Olympics. A gold in the 100 meters, another gold in the mile relay, and a gold in the long jump. And the year was 1936, sir, not 1938."

"Nice work, Merritt", Maxwell replied. "How are the Saint Louis Cardinals doing in the pennant race, Lamont?" He picked Saint Louis because he was a native of that fair city. To survive as a plebe, you had to know these things and anticipate.

"Sir, Saint Louis is presently in second place with a critical series coming up in Pittsburgh this weekend."

"Good. Hardesty, who is Johnny Unitas?"

Barton paused, considering, and when he could not find the name under his mental file of biblical references, said, "I'll find out, sir!"

"Comearound, Hardesty!"

Being a consummate Red Sox and Celtics fan I already knew a great deal of sports data, and having had a memorization fanatic named Sister Dorena as my eight grade principal, I could learn almost anything instantly. I did okay with this trivial pursuit process -- actually I found it kind of fun. I also enjoyed the mealtime newspaper debates.

Every plebe read the newspaper before morning formation -- usually the Washington Post or the Baltimore Sun -- and had to be ready to speak about any topic. Squadleaders would ask, "What's going on in Europe?" or "When's the next NASA launch?" or "Who won the mayoral election in Atlanta?' and the designee would give a brief report. I was never so informed on the status of the world as when I was a midshipman.

Battle was in a pensive mood. He always seemed to get this way when the morning discussions concerned the topic of the War in Southeast Asia. The summer of 1967 was a grim and thought provoking period.

"Delvecchio, what's the latest body count?"

Tony, one of the intellectuals of the plebe group, immediately answered, "as of this morning 31,000 brave young Americans have paid the ultimate price, sir." This was a question that Battle asked often, and this was the only acceptable way to answer. Battle, being a potential Marine Corps officer, was interested in strategy and body counts.

"What's the enemy body count?" he asked further.

"Sir, as of today the enemy has lost 250,000 brave young men."

"Goto, what's your analysis of the situation?"

Douglas Goto was probably the most analytical of us all. He always seemed to recognize aspects of any situation that we had overlooked.

"Sir, if we accept Westmoreland's theory that a kill ratio of 10:1 is necessary to successfully defeat a guerrilla opponent, then we are short of that goal. However, the enemy efforts are presently stalled in the northern jungles, and we have made recent progress in several areas."

"Wojeck, what do you think we should do?"

Mike Wojeck was the Company hawk. He had a voice that was as forceful as his personality, and he almost seemed out of place among his more-refined classmates.

"Sir, the war has drug on for too long, and the death toll is far too high. I think we should nuke 'em into the Bronze Age."

"That's pretty god-damn drastic, Wojeck. It was already suggested and denied in Korea. How do you think the rest of the world will respond?"

"Sir, who cares? We made a commitment to aid the nation of South Vietnam. Either we do it 100 percent, or there's no sense in being there."

"So you think we should either destroy the enemy or get out?"

"Sir, if we're not going to fight to win, than what's the use in fighting at all?"

"How would you win the war, Polk?"

Jeff Polk struggled with the morality of the war the entire four years. Partly it was because he had an overactive sense of justice and partly because he felt frustrated and inhibited in the Academy system.

"Sir, I wouldn't. I don't see any sense in being in Vietnam. There's nothing to gain. Our allies are repressive and backward and in some ways no different from the communists. We have no reason to be there. I say get out now."

"What about dominoes, Mr. Polk?" asked Battle.

"Sir, the Domino Theory is wrong," Jeff said, getting revved for his favorite argument. "Nations become communist not because of military intervention and suppression but for economic reasons."

"You think the communist system is better than ours?" asked Battle in pretended skepticism.

"Of course not, sir. But we are a developed nation. Hardly anybody here has to worry about their next meal -- except of course for plebes." Battle didn't laugh.

"What are you going to do if you get sent to Vietnam after graduation, Polk?"

"I'll go where they send me, and do what I have to do. But I don't have to like it, sir." Jeff answered with such conviction that he drew the silent attention of Tom Battle for a full ten seconds. This kind of answer did not endear Jeff to Battle or to any of the other potential Marines -- many of whom were totally committed to the support of the president and the nation, and understood the grim possibility that the course of the duty they selected may add their own names to the body count.

"How do you feel about the protesting going on at home, Wilson?"

I didn't like anything about BJ, particularly his left-wing attitude, so naturally, anything he said I would disagree with.

"It's everyone's right to protest, sir. This is a democracy."

"What about when the protests could cause serious harm to our troops?"

"If you're asking about the Jane Fonda thing, sir, I think she's got to follow her own convictions."

Battle didn't like that answer.

"What about if her actions give aid and comfort to the enemy cause?"

"Sir, if that's what she believes, then more power to her."

"Wojeck? What do you think?"

"Wilson is full of shit, sir!" Most of the plebes at the table agreed with Wojeck, and even from a braced-up position we nodded assent or grumbled support.

"How about you, O'Reilly? What's on your mind about this?"

I wished he hadn't called on me.

"Sir," I said. "It's all very confusing to me, and I hate the thought of the slaughter on both sides. I also think communism is totally wrong, and Jane Fonda and friends can kiss my ass. My intuition tells me that my leaders have made the best decisions they can, considering the circumstances."

Battle was quiet for a long time.

"Carry-on, everyone, and look at me," he said with a sobering seriousness. We turned, surprised. The Battle sat patiently with his hands folded neatly in front of him. He stared at all of us for a moment.

"Time for another lecture," he said. "This one is vital."

"The three most important words you will learn here at Annapolis are the ones that the Academy code is based upon -- duty, honor, and loyalty. This institution is an arm of the military of the Unites States, and you are potential officers in that military. Wherever duty calls, you must go. Your service must be with the utmost honor. *And* you must follow the orders of your superiors implicitly.

"But this is not Nazi Germany, gentlemen. You are not required to follow an immoral or illegal order. In fact, you are forbidden to do so. We don't kill prisoners or shoot civilians. If you are ever asked to do immoral things, you must refuse. But you may indeed be asked to kill the enemy. That's what war is all about. You cannot refuse that order, because by doing so, you will endanger your comrades.

"You also can't refuse to fight and call it an immoral war. The issue of whether a war is valid is one that the government and the population must decide. You are all soldiers of our nation, not any faggot Jane Fonda fans. If you want to protest the war, do so with your ballot. You will be punished if you do not support the will of your president.

"So let me make myself clear on this. You can talk all you want. Your opinion is valid, no matter how misguided. But what you feel must stay an opinion. No overt action or protests are allowed here. If you can't live with that, resign now. I promise you'll get even less sympathy when the Brigade returns. A great many of the midshipmen come from military families or have relatives who have served in combat or who are in Vietnam now. You will be in serious trouble if you don't watch what you say on this issue. Is that clear?" He didn't wait for an answer.

"All right then. Brace up! Hardesty, who's Mickey Mantle?"

"I'll find out sir!"

"Comearound, Barton, you god-damn pussy!"

I returned to the room that morning after breakfast full of thoughts about war and death and honor. I wished I could be sure about things like Wojeck and Polk, but I kept coming up against ideas that seemed too profound for me to handle and too complicated for me to fully grasp. Vietnam was one of those issues.

When I entered the room, I found a note on my desk that said I had a message waiting in the Main Office. I hurried downstairs to pick it up. The message was a baby blue letter-sized envelope that had been hand-delivered this morning. It smelled really good, and I could see that the plebe on duty was jealous. I smiled knowingly at him and hurried to my room to savor the experience. My first love letter.

As soon as I opened it, I saw Brenda's signature in neat cursive at the bottom. I smiled to myself in anticipation. The note was a single page. It was a single paragraph. It was almost a single sentence, and not a very good one at that.

"Dear Kevin," it said, *"I had a wonderful time last Saturday, but we can't meet any more because I'm married. My husband is a union carpenter and I have two wonderful children that I don't want to disappoint, so I'm sorry. You were a great lover, and it was fun.*

That was it? I had been kissed off, dumped, jilted, and abandoned by my first love interest. One part of me was devastated. It had been a thoroughly enjoyable experience that I really wanted to repeat. The other part of me was shocked. Holy shit! I did the big act with a married woman. Christ I could've gotten into serious trouble. God-damn labor unions are always screwing things up. Then there was a third part of me that was proud. Great lover, huh?

I put the note down on my desk top and noticed Rico staring at me. He raised an eyebrow.

"Brenda says I'm a great lover," I said, not quite willing to divulge the entire contents of the note.

"That's nice," replied Rico, obviously waiting for the rest.

"Okay, Rico," I said. "What do you know?"

"About Brenda's children or about her being unavailable for further poking?" he asked.

"Both," I answered.

"I found out about her family two nights ago when I was talking to Cindy. As a matter of fact I urged Cindy to convince Brenda to knock it off with you."

"What?" I blurted. "How could you?"

"Kevin, Kevin," he replied imploringly, "stop thinking between your legs, amigo. The consequences of seeing a married woman are too great to consider. She was using you, and I probably just saved your life. But don't worry. Cindy's got other friends."

I was content with the bone Rico offered, and I said nothing further. As a matter of fact I gained a bit of Company notoriety for being the first classmate to get a "Dear John." I tacked the letter to my bulletin board, displaying it like a badge of honor. "See," it said, "Kevin O'Reilly is human enough to be hurt, but man enough to make light of it." I wonder what George Abbott would do if his precious Di told him she got secretly nailed by a union carpenter?

Another week passed, and it became obvious that Maxwell and Battle were focusing their almost exclusive and unmerciful harassment on the *Magnificent Seven* with each of the rest of us serving as secondary characters in the drama. I was a very tired secondary character. The rest of us began to wager on the outcome. Barton Hardesty was the reluctant front runner in the betting race on the next classmate to go permanently out the rotunda doors. He didn't help himself with his unworldliness.

"Hardesty, you fart-sniffing puke. Christ, don't you know anything?" Battle was pissed at Barton as usual. I had sprinted past the bent over and retching form of Willy Simpson that morning to earn carry-on at breakfast, and Hardesty sat directly across from me, so I had a front row seat, so to speak, for the morning's demoralizing entertainment.

"No, sir," Hardesty answered. A frustrated look passed across Barton's face as he answered.

"Did your god-damn high school offer any sports, asshole?"

"No, sir."

"Did you ever watch news or sports on television, you shit-for-brains?"

"No sir."

"Where did you go to school, anyway, numb-nuts?"

"I went to Memphis Christian Academy," Hardesty answered.

"Well, you may be smart, Hardesty. But your education leaves a god-damn lot to be desired. You don't know shit about anything important."

"Request permission to speak freely, sir?" Barton asked. Hardesty had been increasingly uncomfortable under the grilling, and I could see him preparing to make a statement of some kind.

Battle paused, considering the audacious request.

"Okay, pal. Speak up!"

"Sir," Hardesty said. "I am deeply offended by your language. It is not Christian to take the Lord's name in vain. It troubles me. Please stop."

I looked at Battle. He winked at me. Why? I don't know.

Then he shouted to Maxwell's table, "Tom, Hardesty here says my language offends him and I should stop using bad words. I think we hurt his feelings. Do you think we should respect his wishes?"

Maxwell smiled and pretended to think. He stared up at the ceiling for several long seconds, then looked at Battle seriously.

"Fuck no!" he replied loudly. Several of my classmates tittered. I was slightly shocked at the amount of off-color language flung about. I could never get away with even thinking some of those words around my mother, and my father -- even though he worked in a very rough environment -- rarely cursed. I suppose when you're that big you don't need colorful language to get attention. But I also hadn't been sheltered from the nastier elements of the English language. I certainly heard my share of colorful epithets on the basketball court and on the neighborhood streets, and technical manuals like Rico's had many interesting words and phrases. But I had always been uncomfortable using them. I still am. But I was also smart enough to know when to protest and when to bite the bullet.

Battle looked at Hardesty and smiled wickedly.

"Sorry pal. This ain't the Boy Scouts. Salty language is part of the fleet. You'll just have to train your shit-stained ass to put up with it." I could see Hardesty wince under the blow of another off-color word. I also think he must have realized that it would be a lot worse for him, language-wise, from now on.

Tommy Poole still caught the worst of it physically, although his performance was improving. He could sometimes beat Rogers and Butler in the morning runs, and he equaled Chalmers and Butler in push-ups. But I've never seen anyone retch as often as he did during the physical exercises, so I knew that his efforts must have been quite a strain and that he really was putting everything he had into succeeding. Two weeks before Parent's Weekend, after watching him pass out during an evening comearound -- this was a legitimate feint because I could see and hear his head strike the tile floor as he fell -- I began to admire Tommy again. I realized how silly my short-lived superior attitude had been. But for the remainder of the summer I never once lost a race on purpose if I could help it. I would have done anything to avoid the pain or the physical attention.

The week before Parents' Weekend we selected roommates for the upcoming academic year. We would be moving to the first deck of the fourth wing for the academic year, and we had to consolidate. I hadn't realized that Rico and I would have to acquire new roomies, but plebes don't live two-to-a-room, and the departure of seven classmates made a few gaps in the Company ranks.

This presented a problem because, truthfully, I didn't want another roommate. Rico and I were getting along just fine, and I'm more the hermit than the socializer. The thought of putting up with another set or two of problems was almost too much to consider. Jim Merritt took the decision away from me.

On the morning of the room selections Jim chopped into our room just prior to morning formation.

"Guys," he said. "Have you decided on your new room additions?"

"No," I answered. "Not yet."

"Well listen, can I join you?"

I looked at Rico. We both liked Merritt, so I didn't see it as a problem.

"What about the rest of the goons?" asked Rico.

"Tommy Poole wants to move in with Butler, Butkowski, and Abbott. They said it would be okay. Polk wants to room with Simpson, and Strong wants to stay with Willy. So either Jubal or I have to go. I decided it would be me."

"It's fine with me," I said. Rico nodded concurrence. Then Merritt hit us with the kicker.

"'BJ' Wilson wants to room with us too. Is that okay?"

No, it wasn't OK. Not for me anyway.

"Well . . . ," I began.

"Yea, it'll be fine," answered Rico for the two of us. I felt betrayed. I turned to look at Rico. He smiled and nodded encouragement. His look said, "trust me again, Kevin; you'll see." I looked back to Jim.

"I guess so," I said reluctantly. What else could I do?

The approach of Parent's Weekend brought up another problem for me. While everyone else was dreaming about seeing their favorite girl from back home, I still had not been able to arrange for anyone feminine to tag along with my family. None of the girls I had originally written to had replied favorably to my letters. One didn't remember me at all; that hurt. Two were already connected to someone "wonderful," and I could tell by the tone of their letters, they had marriage plans swimming around in their empty heads. The last one wrote me a very nice note, but informed me she was preparing for college and didn't have time for a relationship. I seemed to be the only plebe with no plans for wanton sexuality that weekend. I missed Brenda. At least I missed what Brenda did for -- and to -- me.

My mother, bless her misguided heart, sensed my frustration, probably because I whined so much about being companionless in the weeks preceding their visit. In a letter I received a month prior to the big event she informed me that she had asked several of the mothers in the neighborhood if their daughters would like to come along on the trip to keep me company. Particularly she was focusing of Sarah Connelly, a girl I had known since parochial school.

The instant I read that statement I put the letter down unfinished and hurried to a phone. Jesus, what was my mother trying to do to me? If in the heat of passion I had tried to touch one of the neighborhood colleens, I would be persona non grata in South Boston for the rest of my life. I immediately had to squelch any ideas she had about me and any neighbor's homely daughter.

Luckily she hadn't quite completed plans for Sarah Connelly to accompany them. I was relieved. In fact Sarah was kind of cute, but she had the personality of a rock and had an older brother Patrick who was big as a truck. Rather than have mom's detective work go to waste. I did ask her to accumulate a list of potential dates for when I returned at Christmas time. She agreed, mildly amused at my reaction. I think she and dad must have been talking about his own boot camp frustrations.--- But not with Sarah, mom! I had to have a heart to heart talk with Big Kevin real soon, and since I would be alone Parents' Weekend, I decided that would be the best time.

I was very surprised to find out that Rico wasn't even going to see Cindy that weekend. His parents were bringing down a "friend" named Rosa from Brooklyn.

"It was arranged long ago, Kevin," he said. "I told Cindy I wanted to spend the time with my family, which is the truth, sort of. She understands."

"Does Rosa have any friends?" I asked half seriously. Rico laughed but didn't offer any help.

The incident of the Company guidons had become a topic of conversation among the squadleaders. Battle and Maxwell mused about what group of brave young men had the gonads to pull that off -- certainly not us they agreed. Immediately afterward, the Companies took to hiding their banners in a select plebe room overnight. If the flag turned up stolen, God help the plebes whose responsibility it was to guard it.

The guidon incident ignited a rash of evening sorties. Some nights there were more plebes running around campus than there were asleep in their racks, and the thunder of young footsteps along the night passageways seemed almost constant on the remaining weekends. One Sunday morning we woke to find that someone had painted the statue of Tecumseh blue on one side and gold on the other. I liked it that way. It gave the beaked-nosed Indian a certain character lacking in his normal bronze motif. Another time one of the display fighter aircraft -- which must have weighed several tons -- was moved nearly a quarter mile to the entrance to the Field House.

Two weekends prior to the visit of the parents, Twenty-Third Company, under the mischievous leadership of Jubal Ramsey, relocated several small cannons from their stands in the yard to the very center of the Rotunda floor.

The late night activity was not without its risks, however. As the big weekend approached, plebe antics became more pronounced. Several groups were caught in the act of mischief, and only the direct action of the Superintendent prevented them from losing all privileges for Parent's Weekend. In an act of unusual kindness and understanding, he postponed the punishment of anyone apprehended in an unauthorized evening's event until after Parent's Weekend had concluded.

On the Wednesday night prior to Parent's Weekend I visited the Goon Room to ask about their plans for the weekend. Several of us had discussed the possibility of getting all our families together for a dinner out in town on Saturday night. When I arrived, their room was dark. Only Merritt and Ramsey were awake, and they were each reading by the light of their desk tensor lamps. Polk was snoring loudly on one side of the room, and Poole was curled up in a lump against the opposite wall, also deeply unaware.

"Have you guys thought about the Saturday night dinner idea?" I whispered.

"Yes," Merritt answered immediately. "My parents think it's a great idea."

"My momma's still considering," Joe answered cautiously. "I'll let you know."

"What about Jeff and Tommy?" I asked.

"Don't know about Tommy yet," Jim answered, "but Jeff said his parents might want to spend a quiet evening with him, and he had plans with Kate."

"I'll bet," I answered, trying to keep the jealousy from my voice. "What about you and Lynda?"

Merritt smiled. "We'll work something out. Don't worry."

"Attention on deck!" The sound exploded on us from somewhere nearby and reverberated loudly around the room. We immediately sprang to attention in the dark and braced in anticipation. Jubal almost tipped over his chair in the process. Jeff Polk snapped immediately awake and dropped his covers on the floor as he leaped down from his rack in response to the command. Within two seconds we stood alertly, waiting for whatever was going to happen next. I was more worried than the others because I wasn't supposed to be visiting at this hour.

Nothing happened for several seconds, and the room became deathly quiet. I suddenly realized that I hadn't heard the door to the room open, but it was possible that someone had sneaked in while we were talking and was waiting just inside the door. But somehow I thought not. Slowly I twisted my head in the direction of the doorway and found that the room was empty of anyone except for four braced plebes and one still-sleeping classmate. I relaxed and stared at Tommy's inert form for a moment. Then I began to laugh quietly. At first the others didn't realize what was funny.

"Tommy just had a comearound dream," I said. "Poor guy. He can't escape the system even when he's zonked out." The others relaxed. Jim and Jubal readily appreciated the humor of the situation. Jeff was still groggy. He grumbled for a second and tumbled back into his rack.

We sat down again and Joe outlined what was to be our last bit of mischief before the Brigade returned. I suspect that Battle and Maxie expected something, and maybe an act of some kind was traditional. They threatened us with bodily harm if we did anything to them before the Brigade returned; and they became more and more nervous as their last days approached. I immediately became swept up in conflicting emotions. I had tired of the unrelenting discipline of the past months, and I needed either rebellion or release to put it all in perspective. We decided the act would take place on the Friday night before the beginning of Parent's Weekend. That way, the squadleaders would have almost no time to react. On the following Monday their harassment would end, and the "Tigers" reign of terror would began. Friday I went to bed exactly at lights out; the excitement of the impending activity churned in my mind.

At 0200 a soft tap at our door announced that the company was assembling in the passageway. Rico and I dressed quickly and identically in shorts and gray sweats, pulling hoods down over our faces for disguise. We congregated outside the squadleaders' room, quiet but tense with excitement. Four plebes went ahead to scout our route. The passageway was just dark enough that I could not recognize the majority of my classmates in their hooded garb, but I could sense they were ready for action.

At Jubal's signal, we stormed into the room, divided into two equal groups, and raced for the beds. Battle and Maxwell didn't have a chance. What followed was less than 60 seconds of confusion, muffled cries, and struggling bodies. We subdued the two of them, and hoisted them into the air, several of us on each arm and leg. Battle, who was dressed in only his skivvies, took it all calmly after he realized there was no chance for escape. Maxie, in shorts and Saint Louis Cardinals T-shirt, struggled and tried to yell. We gagged Maxwell with a washcloth and raced out of the room with our two burdens. I could almost taste the adrenaline that pumped forcefully throughout my system as I carried my part of the burden -- which happened to be a lower piece of Maxwell's' left leg -- out into the passageway.

Companymates stood watch at all key intersections as we hurried down the dark passageways and ladders, and proceeded outside through a normally unused set of doors leading into T-Court. The night was moonless and deathly still and humid beyond belief. Not slowing a step, we moved like two racing amoebas pushed out by frantic struggles and pressed back by our own momentum. Our progress carried us toward the Severn River and the dark Yacht Basin.

As Maxie -- whose skinny leg I held tightly at the ankle -- sensed our destination and our probable purpose, his struggles increased. Once, while gingerly tromping down the exterior stone steps between Bancroft and Michelson Halls, we almost tripped and went down. I thought to myself that it was pretty stupid for Maxwell to struggle so much, particularly when if he did get loose, he would land painfully on the hard ground. But he didn't escape, and I don't think anything could have stopped us that evening. We had taken control of our own destinies in a mini-mutiny and had united in a common purpose. Maxwell be damned! We surged on.

We arrived at the Yacht Basin within minutes. We were far enough from Bancroft Hall to ungag our prey and savor the "conversation." The expletives coming from Maxie's mouth were exquisite. We laughed. Maxwell still continued to struggle as he yelled, while Battle calmly accepted his fate. Maxie, however, wasn't being a good sport.

One of us checked the water for obstructions; but since it was nearly pitch black, the surveillance was cursory at best. Battle was first to meet his fate.

"Any last words?" someone asked him.

"No," he replied. "Just hurry up and get this over with so I can get back to sleep."

The first group stood back from the edge of the pier, swinging Tommy Battle by his arms and legs, ready to let him soar into the night. "One, Two, Threeeeeeee!" Marines can't fly.

Out into the black, humid night he sailed, limbs flailing until we could no longer see him in the darkness. After a short pause we heard a loud splash. Someone checked to ensure he came up for air; then my group readied Maxwell for his toss.

Back and forth we swung him, still struggling violently and yelling and cursing us all. He was acting stupidly considering how we were now in complete control of his fate. I looked across at Hank Butkowski and nodded rearward. We backed up to make the throw more exciting. Maxwell yelled louder.

"One!" He jerked.

"Two!" He wiggled.

"THREEEEEEEE!" He pulled and pushed and . . . was airborne. Maybe it was his struggling at the exact instant of our toss; perhaps we had too much confidence in Hank Butkowski's strength; or maybe the frustrations and angers of plebe summer made us all want to punish Maxie a bit. I'm not sure if any or all of those reasons motivated us, but, Maxwell flew out along the wooden pier into the dark, facing up into the starry night, screaming and waving his arms and legs as if he could climb his way back to earth. As I watched, laughing along with my classmates, I suspected that his trajectory was not exactly what we had hoped. He disappeared in a blur of motion. Then we heard. "Bump . . . Bump . . . Kerploosh!"

"Shit," I said too loudly. "I hope we didn't kill him!" We waited in the dark, holding our collective breaths. We didn't kill him. We didn't even slow him up.

Within seconds he sputtered to the surface, yelling louder than ever, and the spell of remorse shattered. As a group we turned and raced for the relative safety of Mother Bancroft, feigning sleep the rest of the night. Battle and Maxie returned several minutes later, loudly sloshing their way down the passageway.

"You almost broke my ass you miserable bastards!" Maxwell yelled as he sloshed down the passageway passed our room. I imagined I could hear a limp in the wet sounds.

"The Brigade's almost back and you still can't do anything right!" Battle added. I caught a slight hint of amusement in his voice.

"I'm going to murder every one of you!" Maxwell yelled just before he closed his door, and I realized that I had just learned a valuable lesson.

I now understand how pranks can trap a person in their momentum, and make reason and sensibility sometimes disappear. It isn't easy to resist a group, a mob, or a gang, and maybe it doesn't matter if the intention is fun or violence. There is something of the mob or the pack in all of us, and there is probably something of Maxwell still embedded in the Yacht Basin pier.

Maxwell didn't murder us on Saturday morning, although he did give us a final desperate running in the passageway which made me very tired and which made Tommy Poole puke his guts out again. The morning was devoted to the administrative preparation for the return of the Brigade. We moved our things from Room 5404 to Room 4024, which was across T-Court from where we had been trained and conveniently on the ground floor. This was Twenty-Third Company's assigned area. Our new room faced an enclosed alcove of T-Court. Directly across the wide passageway from us was Room 4025, which housed Ramsey, Polk, Strong, and Simpson.

The setup of the rooms along the ground floor was interesting. Those with windows opening on the outside world had a deep moat-like trench directly below them. This moat prevented excursions through the windows. We plebes would have to sneak out by the doors -- if we could sneak out at all with an additional 3,000 yes watching us.

These rooms were large enough so that the four of us had racks mounted on the deck, a vast improvement over bunk beds. Rico and I were first in the door, and we selected opposing racks on the starboard side of the room, Merritt and Wilson took the other side. I still wasn't happy with the idea of rooming with BJ, but I decided I would make the best of a potentially bad situation. He probably wasn't happy with me either; after all, I wasn't a high greaser, my family had no money, and I didn't particularly like New Yorkers -- but than again who does?

After stowing the gear, we marched to the Academy Midshipmen' Store for book and study equipment issue. Each midshipman receives a monthly salary of one-half an ensign's pay, which is pretty good money for a cloistered novitiate. From this the Academy deducts charges for laundry, books, and meals, and anything we bought in the Midshipman's store could be charged to our personal account. What remained at the end of the month wasn't much, but it provided spending money. Actually it was more cash than I had ever consistently had in my possession, and it was difficult to decide what to do with all the loot. I let most of it accumulate in a home town bank account, only cashing 20 dollars a month for various sundry items. My first major procurements were a clock radio and a desk tensor lamp.

Parents' Weekend began at precisely 1300 hours, immediately after noon meal. The formation for meal was as loose as any we had ever had. Every one of us was anxious to get away, however briefly, from the bosom of Mother B and be human again. Mom had called me from the hotel and left a message that they had arrived and would be waiting by Tecumseh for me. I was excited. It had been only three months since I last saw them, but those three months amounted to a universe of emotional and psychic distance. I wasn't the same Kevin O'Reilly they left at the Field House, and I was anxious to share my metamorphosis. I think my parents suspected great changes but were a bit afraid of who might meet them at the stoic statue.

Hundreds of people witnessed the noon meal formation that day. Most were parents, relatives, and friends of the Plebe Brigade. We turned crisply and marched especially tall that day. The spectators applauded, and it made us all feel very special.

Meal was a hurried carry-on affair. Maxwell and Battle were as anxious to be rid of us as we were to get away. They also had plans. For this special occasion we would be allowed to ride in cars during liberty hours, and there would be no evening meal formation. Liberty expired at midnight, which sounds like an early night for a typical eighteen and nineteen-year-old; but to a plebe who has just spent three months forced to turn lights out at 2100 or face the consequences, it was daring and mature.

The only significant restriction for the weekend was that we would have to wear our uniforms in public. After three months of nothing but uniforms, I would rather have worn civilian clothes. But a later poll of the mothers present at the company dinner revealed that uniforms were the clothing of choice for them. They universally agreed uniforms made us all look very handsome. I suppose I could understand that. We did look damn good.

We talked excitedly among ourselves during noon meal and made final arrangements for the evening congregation. Jim Merritt had called an Italian restaurant in town and made reservations for 25 at 1800. At the last minute Jeff Polk had decided to be included. BJ Wilson, whose parents had to stay in New York to make preparations for the upcoming television season, would tag along as a solo.

At precisely 1300, doors in all parts of Bancroft Hall opened with identical whooshes, and ecstatic plebes rushed outside into the hot September afternoon. The sight of hundreds of startlingly white uniforms hurtling down outside stairs and charging headlong across the tile courts was nearly overwhelming. The smiles on those hundreds of excited faces rivaled the sun that blazed overhead. My smile was foremost among them. Soon the entire vicinity of Tecumseh Court was alive with excitement, and even the usually sullen bronze gaze from Tecumseh himself seemed to have been developed a knowing and enigmatic twinkle. Everywhere the greetings were effusive, as parents and relatives embraced and kissed their plebes, who kissed and embraced energetically in return. It was a wonderful scene, and I paused slightly as I approached the appointed rendezvous to smile at the surrounding peace and contentment. I saw my own family, waiting near the statue in the shade of a huge old elm.

There is nothing more warm and secure than the hug of a mother who has been separated from a child for an extended period. Mom's hug was great. Even Big Kevin's bear-like grip was very satisfying.

"It's good to see you guys!" I exclaimed as the greetings concluded. I pulled back slightly from them, trying to see how much they had changed since I last saw them. I saw with some surprise that they hadn't changed, not a bit -- at least that's what I first decided. But on further examination I noticed that Big Kevin and Sean were different somehow, and I was surprised. At first I couldn't decide what it was, and I suppose it was very unobservant of me. They both looked at me, smiling, waiting for me to discover whatever secret I was supposed to notice. I looked more closely, frowning. Suddenly it came to me in a flash of revelation.

"Your hair!" I exclaimed.

They had both gotten their hair cut very short. Why, I wondered? I must have looked puzzled.

"We wanted you to feel more at home with your own short hair, Kevin," Dad said. This was a completely unexpected surprise. Being surrounded by a thousand identically shorn young men, I hadn't given my hair a single though since the first day. Apparently my family thought the short hair was a big deal to me. It was very touching.

I laughed and pointed to Sean's head. "You let dad talk you into that?"

"It wasn't easy," Big Kevin answered.

We paused, and I could see them examining me critically. Judging from the way my family examined me, I must have seemed completely different, -- but not bad different. I could tell that from the gleam in mom's eye -- she was near tears -- good tears. And I had never seen Big Kevin's massive chest swell the way it seemed to that afternoon. They liked what they saw, and I was glad.

"We sure missed you, big brother," Sean burst out.

"Yeah," I said. "I missed you too."

"Well, there's a lot to catch up on," Mom offered sweetly. "What would you like to do?"

"How about if I give you a quick tour of the campus. Then we can go to the hotel for a swim in a real pool?" I offered.

"Real pool?" asked Sean, frowning.

I laughed.

"I'll tell you all about it later."

"The tour sounds great, son," said Big Kevin, putting two huge hands tenderly on my shoulders and squeezing slightly. I had never seen him so outwardly affectionate since I was very small. I stared at him for a moment, smiling, and he drew back, somewhat surprised at himself.

"Sorry, Kevin. We're just so very proud of you."

"No, Dad," I answered. "It's okay. Touching parents is allowed. We're not supposed to show any public affection with unrelated females while in uniform."

"You mean like that?" asked Sean laughing. He was pointing to a classmate who was partially hidden behind a huge elm tree. The plebe was engaged in a prolonged and passionate kiss with a person who was obviously not a relative; or if she was, their family had a different idea about closeness than mine.

"Probably a "cousin" from Tennessee," joked Dad. We all laughed.

"We could have brought Sarah Connelly to keep you company," Mom offered when she saw how my glance quickly became a stare.

"Mom," I said laughing. "Can you picture Sarah and me doing something like that? I wouldn't want to melt the ice queen, and if I did I wouldn't want Patrick to kill me either."

Mom didn't seem convinced.

"I don't think Sarah's cold at all. She's grown up quite a bit lately, and she's become very popular. You just have to get to know her better. She's really very nice."

"I'm sure she is, Mom. But you can't tell me that her brother has suddenly seen the light and become docile." Patrick Connelly had been an outstanding linebacker on his high school football team, and he had also been outstanding at breaking furniture and people when he was angry. And Patrick was very protective of his baby sister.

Mom laughed. "No, Kevin, Patrick's still a problem for poor Mrs. Connelly."

We started toward the chapel, walking slowly on the wide brick walkway under the enormous trees. Sunlight piercing the thick foliage high overhead made the white uniforms all around us blink in dazzling flashes as plebes strolled with their families. It was a warm and humid day -- the radio had predicted a record -- and I could immediately see that Big Kevin, who was a furious sweater, would suffer if we stayed outside too long. I gave them the abbreviated tour.

We walked first to the chapel, and I showed the family where I usually sat and explained the protocol of Sunday mass at Annapolis. I didn't mention Sleepy Hollow. My parents were suitably awed by the grandeur. After several minutes of silence we went into the basement area under the chapel to view the tomb of John Paul Jones and listened with a hundred other visitors as the civilian guide explained about John Paul and his importance, identified the various woods used in the coffin, and extolled the contents of the many displays that lined the walls of the dark circular vault. Like every attraction at Annapolis, the crypt and its accompanying inset display cases were meticulously and professionally presented. Everything the Academy does it does with style and aplomb, except maybe Plebe Year, where gusto and intensity are the key elements.

After the chapel we visited the Academy Museum and strolled the grounds between Mahan and Bancroft Halls. As we walked, Sean quizzed me on the significance of every statue and memorial, most of which I could remember from my study of *Reef Points*. Sean was impressed. Finally we went into Bancroft Hall and saw the displays and sample room. The entire tour took about an hour. Mom, the family shutterbug, took seven rolls of Instamatic pictures.

"Well, how about a dip in the pool?" I asked as we walked down the steps leading from the huge ballroom in the rear of the rotunda. "Dad looks as if he could use one." Big Kevin was very damp by this time, and he grunted affirmation. On the way down the broad stairs we passed Maxie and his date going up. Our eyes met, and he halted.

"Midshipman O'Reilly," he said pleasantly. "Are these your parents?"

We stopped on the stairs.

"Yes, sir," I said. "This is my mom and dad and my brother Sean." Then I indicated Maxie and said to my family. "And this is Midshipman Second-class Maxwell, one of our cream puff squadleaders." Maxwell laughed loudly.

"This is my friend, Rebecca," Maxwell said indicating a petite blond who stood awestruck and admiringly at his side. Then he noticed Big Kevin and was suitably impressed.

"You have a good son, Mr. and Mrs. O'Reilly -- even if his sense of humor leaves a bit to be desired sometimes."

"Thank you," Mom replied. "We think he's great."

"About my being a "good son" or my strange sense of humor?" I asked her half-seriously. She laughed.

"Both!" Big Kevin stated with emphasis. Maxie laughed.

"Has Kevin given you a tour?" Maxwell asked.

"Yes, he has," Mom answered. "It's a wonderful campus."

"We like to think so," Maxie answered, swelling up with pride. For an instant I thought he was going to cry.

"Well, sir," I said, "we're off to where I can immerse myself in a pool devoid of icebergs."

Maxwell laughed again.

"You think the natatorium is cold, huh? Well, to tell the truth, so do I. It makes me shiver just thinking of it. I hate whenever I have swimming for physical training." Wow, Maxwell had a human side. Maybe he wasn't so bad after all? I decided to reserve judgment on Maxie.

The drive to the Holiday Inn on Ritchie Highway took more than 30 minutes. "I know the hotel is far from Annapolis," my mom said apologetically, "but it was the closest one we could afford."

"Did you know that the ones in town wanted to charge almost 100 dollars for one night?" Big Kevin asked incredulously. I whistled. That sounded like a lot to me.

"God, dad, that's incredible."

"Yeah," he said, "even *this* hotel costs more than a day's take-home. Plus the gas for the drives down and back, plus meals and souvenirs. It can really add up." I knew my dad worked outdoors at a backbreaking job for a few hundred dollars a week, and I also knew that he was constantly worried about money. But Sean and I never had to worry about toys or sports equipment. Dad always found the money for us, even if mom had to wait an extra year for the new electric range or if we all suffered an additional winter with a furnace that badly needed replacement.

I hadn't thought much about it before, but at that moment I realized that my attending Annapolis must have been a godsend for Big Kevin. He and mom had always been determined that I would get an education; and if I had elected to go to a local college and hadn't gotten a scholarship, they would somehow have found the money, but it would have meant deep sacrifices. Now all they had to worry about affording was an occasional trip to Annapolis to visit. I was saving them money and I felt good about that. I was finally making a contribution to the family.

It took me less than five minutes to shed my uniform and get poolside. There must have been other parents that shared my dad's view about costs because several plebes were already in the water. Some of those plebes had sisters. Some of those sisters were cute. I strutted to the edge of the pool and surveyed the area coolly. I noticed the stares of some of the sisters, and I stuck out my bulging chest and pulled in my washboard stomach. Then the mood shattered.

Preoccupied with the choreography of my entrance, I had forgotten about Sean, who came silently up behind me and shoved me headlong into the pool. I yelled, terrified, forgetting for an instant where I was and preparing myself for glacial immersion. I landed with an undignified splash and immediately reveled in relative warmth. My terror disappeared with the feeling of comfort and release the pool provided. I rose slowly and contentedly from the water, at first intending to deal with my brother in a physical way, but titters from the girls around the pool calmed me. Instead I splashed water in Sean's direction.

"Nice dive, big brother!" he yelled from the relative safety of my parents' doorway.

Fifteen minutes later my parents emerged from the room and selected a place at a nearby table. I watched from my position at the side of the pool. My mother, always uncomfortable about the dangers of sunburn on her freckled and sensitive skin, immediately slathered lotion on her extremities. Afterward she did the same to Big Kevin.

As she spread the white liquid on Dad's back I noticed with some surprise that he rippled and jiggled. That was surprising to me. Apparently when I wasn't looking my father had lost his muscle tone and had become somewhat -- perish the thought -- fat. And Mom, who was never the skinniest of women, also seemed plumper and more matronly. Could it be that my parents were getting old? How old were they anyway? I found to my surprise that I hadn't the faintest idea. I didn't even know the exact dates of either of their birthdays. That upset me. I should have known those things.

I did a quick mental estimation based on their approximate ages at marriage, added a year for mom's pregnancy, then added my age, and I found that my parents must have been at a minimum 41 to 43 years old. Why didn't I know exactly? I made a mental note to find out more information about them.

At that moment, Sean, who was an even worse swimmer than I, leaped into the pool over my head and swam splashing and flailing to my side.

"How's the water, big brother?"

I smiled.

"It's wonderful, Sean, a big change from the Academy pool. The water there is so cold it hurts."

"Shrivels your pecker, huh?" Sean asked. I was shocked. I did a double take.

"Where'd you hear that?" I asked, slightly taken aback.

"Hey," he replied soothingly, "I'm almost 11 years old. I know a lot more than you think."

I stared at him for a moment.

"Maybe so," I said. "I hope you don't say things like that around Mom and Dad."

"Are you kidding?" Sean asked. "Mom would die, and Dad would kill me." We laughed together. He was right on both counts.

When I turned to watch the activity in and around the pool, I noticed a young lady in a very black bikini staring at me unabashedly. She was lounging on a reclined deck chair on her belly with her head facing the pool. She had lifted herself slightly to get a drink from a Coke on a table next to her. As she lifted I saw that she was very well built and quite pretty, and I estimated her age at about 17. I smiled at her. She smiled in return. Sean hit me on the arm.

"Great tits, huh?" he whispered, giggling slightly.

"Hey, knock it off!" I said.

"No time for girls, big brother."

"There's always time for girls, Sean," I replied, laughing. I decided to handle this the way Rico would. "Check this out."

I took a deep breath and ducked under the water. Bending my knees, I used my legs to push off in the direction of the young lady. I made the distance in one breath, and surfaced just in front of her location. "Hi," I said as I burst from the water and put my arms on the pool deck in front of her. I flexed my biceps slightly, hoping she would notice. She did.

"Hi," she said in return.

"My name's Kevin," I said. "I'm a plebe at Annapolis."

"I'm Kathy," she replied. She had a Midwestern accent. "My brother is also a plebe. We came from Omaha to visit."

I looked around.

"Where's your brother?"

"He and my parents went out to buy some groceries. They'll be back any minute. Then we're going to visit Annapolis and have dinner. We're coming back here afterward for a while, then take Billy back to school before eleven."

"We have almost the same plans," I said. "I'll be back here about nine."

"Kathy!" came a woman's voice from a balcony nearby. "Time to go, dear!" Kathy looked up and over my shoulder, and I turned to see a plump woman standing on the third floor balcony. I waved at her, and she smiled tentatively and waved in return.

"Okay, Mom," Kathy said, and she rose from her lounger. I almost choked. Kathy was very, very nicely built. I must have stared too obviously. She looked down at me and smiled smugly.

"See you later, Kevin?" she asked with raised eyebrows.

I thought quickly. "How about 2130, sorry, 9:30 this evening right here?" I asked. I hoped the drool wasn't showing. She thought for a moment, then smiled.

"Okay, 9:30. See you then." She walked away and I stared at her as she went. She knew I was watching. I could tell by the way she walked. After she disappeared into the stairwell, I turned to Sean and swam back to him. He looked at me disapprovingly.

"Still driving the girls away, huh?" he said. I laughed.

"I have a date with that young lady for later."

"With her?" he asked incredulously. "No way!"

"Yes way, Sean," I said smugly. "Your big brother's growing up too."

Sean and I roughhoused in the pool for about fifteen minutes; then my mom called to us.

"You boys better get over here and put some lotion on. You'll burn for sure." I was exasperated. Mom was entirely right, but I wished she wasn't such a mom sometimes. Sean rose from the water and I followed him. We sat at the white metal table. Mom handed us the *Sea and Ski*, and I quickly applied a light coat. Sean followed suit. Dad had disappeared inside the room and emerged carrying a six pack of *National Bohemian Beer*, a brand I was not familiar with. He picked a chair and plunked the beer down on the table. The beer had been iced in a chest they had brought along for the trip. It looked deliciously cold. My dad sighed as he popped the tabs from his and Mom's cans.

He and Mom were both beer drinkers. Dad was a straight-from-the-can kind of guy; Mom used a glass and ice. She was the only person I ever saw that drank beer on ice. Dad hesitated then pushed the now four-pack toward me.

"Have a beer, Kevin?" he asked.

Wow! This was the first time he had ever offered to share alcoholic imbibement with me except for the traditional Christmas toast of flavored brandy. He knew I had experimented with drinking during high school. I had even been sick inside his old '57 Chevy one terrible night -- which hadn't exactly made him happy. But this was a coming-out for the two of us. He was accepting my near adulthood and seemed to be offering a sudsy toast to acknowledge my new status.

I accepted with a smile, and soon cold National Bo slid its way deliciously down my throat. I immediately decided that I liked it. It had a texture and smoothness like no other beer I had yet tasted -- both of them -- yet it also possessed a subtle boldness that spoke of buxom women and brawny men. And it had no aftertaste, a fact I discovered a few seconds later when the frosty liquid made me belch involuntarily. I had no concept of the quality of any of the beer I had tasted previously. The sole reason for drinking previously had been to get loaded and act silly. But this beer met two critical criteria: it was cold, and it was wet. I took several slugs without speaking.

"Take it easy, Kevin," said Dad. "It's your first drink in a long time, and you're not used to it."

"Sure Dad," I said, putting the beer on the table. I sighed and looked. "This is great!"

"Glad to be away from the Academy?" asked Mom.

"You can't imagine," I replied.

"Want to talk about it?" asked Dad seriously. "I've been asking around down on the waterfront and I've heard that these places can be physically hard."

"You don't know the half of it, Dad," I said.

"If you want to leave, Kevin," said Mom. "it's okay. We don't care a bit if you stay or not." I knew she meant that, but she obviously didn't understand what the challenge of the Academy was all about.

"Mom," I replied, "don't worry about me. I can hack it. You're going to meet a guy tonight who's had it ten times as hard as me."

"Have they treated you badly, Son?" she asked again, being motherly.

"No worse than anyone else, Mom," I said. "I'm okay, really."

Dad changed the subject slightly.

"Well, you've filled out nicely," he said.

I looked down at my body.

"That's from about a million push-ups and two million miles of running," I said laughing.

"It looks good on you," Mom said. I glanced at Sean.

"I'll bet you never thought you'd have a muscle man for a brother, did you?" I raised my arms into the sun and flexed my biceps. The stark sunlight exaggerated the bulges nicely. Sean reached up and grabbed my right biceps and squeezed.

"Wow!" he said. "Pretty good, big brother."

"When do classes start?" Dad asked.

"On Monday. I have all the typical freshman courses in the engineering curriculum, except I'll be in advanced math and chemistry. I also decided to take German as a language, plus an additional environmental science course. I'll be carrying sixteen credits."

"That's great. How do you think you'll do?"

I laughed.

"I've never had any problems before, and I looked at the books already. The material seems straightforward. I'll be fine."

"Good," he said, getting serious. "Now how do you like it there?"

That seemed a strange question. I had always thought you went to college to get an education, and that being happy was secondary. I answered cautiously. "It's good. I wasn't sure at first if I would enjoy the military, but I fit in pretty well; and some of the discipline and tradition is kind of fun. I feel almost at home."

Dad seemed relieved, but Mom was still skeptical.

"You still have a home, Kevin, and lots of friends who are always asking about you."

"Like Sarah Connelly?" I asked, laughing. Mom ignored me.

"If you ever get tired of this, you'll always be welcome," Mom said, very seriously.

"Do you have the hots for Sarah Connelly?" asked Sean incredulously.

"Sean!" said Mom. "Kevin doesn't have "the hots" for anybody, and Sarah is a nice girl." She looked at Big Kevin and continued, "where does he get those ideas?"

Dad shrugged.

"Don't know, hon," he said half seriously. But there was a twinkle in his eye when he said it. I could see he enjoyed Sean's pre-teen blurtings.

"Kevin has a date ," Sean said. "For tonight. With a girl he met at the pool just now."

"With the one I just saw you talking to?" asked Mom disapprovingly. Big Kevin however, looked at me with his best devilish twinkle. *He* did not disapprove.

"Yeah. For around nine-thirty. We'll just talk and exchange addresses so we can correspond."

"You gonna kiss her?" asked Sean, laughing.

"Sean," I said, faking moral outrage, "how could you insinuate that I would do such a thing?" Then I leaned in closer to him and whispered, just loud enough for my parents to hear. "If she'll lets me, you're damned right!"

The three of them laughed with me, then Mom said. "You know you don't have any time to be serious about anybody! Studies come first!"

"Not even Sarah Connelly?" I asked half sarcastically. "You've been pushing Sarah at me. Are you sure you wouldn't like me to start dating her?"

"You can date her, but I don't want you getting serious about anyone," she said with finality.

"Tell Mrs. Connelly that I'll be writing to sweet Sarah, and maybe we'll have a date or two when I'm back for Christmas leave. And I promise not to ravage her." I leaned over and whispered to Sean again, "unless she lets me, that is." They all laughed again.

"Which I doubt," said Sean.

"You got that right," I answered. "I'll bet she's colder than the Academy pool." Dad and Sean laughed.

"Kevin!" Mom said. I could see she was genuinely offended.

"I'm sorry," I said honestly, and we let the subjects of the girl at the pool and Sarah Connelly drop.

For the next hour we traded friendly small talk about life at Annapolis, happenings in the old neighborhood, and the Red Sox, who as usual were blowing a late season lead to the nearby team from Baltimore. Mom and Dad especially liked my bragging about our late night escapades.

I did *not* mention my trip to Hospital Point. Mom never would have understood, and I think even Dad might have been a bit shocked to discover the nature of my first sexual experience.

"Is there anything you need from home that we can send you?" Mom asked.

"You know what? I've been thinking about that very thing," I answered. "If you could make be a batch of your Christmas cookies and send them in late November, I think it would really endear me to the upper-class." My mom made the best Christmas cookies in the world, which is quite a statement from someone who had never been out of New England before coming to Annapolis.

But I had tasted neighbor's cookies, and relatives' cookies, and friends mothers' cookies, and store-bought cookies; and my mom's were absolutely the best. They were something to die for, and I seriously didn't see how anyone could do better. I knew that if my squad mates ever got a taste, I'd be in good with them all forever. They'd be begging me to ask Mom for more. Mom's oven would blaze in sugary glory, and her cookies could be the ticket to my Plebe Year salvation. Years later, after she passed away unexpectedly while I was stationed overseas, Sean and I searched the old house for an entire day trying to find her recipes; but they were missing from her kitchen recipe collection, and from the reams of other nearly insignificant documents and mementoes she kept in a thousand places all over the house. With her death the most wonderful Christmas cookies ever baked would never again slide happily down my ecstatic throat, and Christmas would never be the same.

"Of course, Kevin," she said. "I can do that. But why?" she asked.

"Because your cookies are the best in the world," I answered incredulously.

Mom looked at me strangely. "You've never said that before," she said.

"I haven't?" I hadn't? Why not? "They are, trust me!" I replied.

"Then you'll have them," she said. I could see she was really pleased by my statement, but I wondered why I hadn't ever said that I adored her cookies. My God, I usually ate a thousand every holiday. Then I wondered what other similar gaps I had left in my home life.

"How many dozen do you want?"

"Several," I said.

I could see her making mental preparations to dive into her kitchen immediately after their return to Boston and begin planning the cookie barrage she would send. Good, let her send a million cookies. If the upperclass didn't like them, I'd eat every one.

"What are your plans this year?" I asked Sean, who was going into his seventh grade at the same Catholic school I attended for eight years. Our Lady of Good Counsel seems like a strange name for a school; but that's what it was, and I didn't think much about it at the time.

"I'm gonna play soccer again," he said, "and try to hide from the nuns." I laughed. I could understand his attitude. Nuns and I didn't get along very well in grammar school, as my still-aching knuckles and backside would attest. Actually, the brothers at St. Catherine's High School weren't much better, just more devious in their tortures.

I had played a bit of soccer in grade school -- most East Coast parochial school boys do -- and my skills were fair, but Sean was an outstanding player. He had a natural talent for the game, and already several high schools in the Boston area were recruiting him. I secretly hoped he would choose St. Catherine's, but the better soccer players went to Saint Henry's across town.

"That's great," I said. "Did you play in the summer league?"

"Of course," he said proudly. "I was scoring champion again."

"How did I know you would be?" I asked, patting him on the arm lightly.

"Any other news from the home front?" I asked the three of them.

"Sarah Connelly says 'hi'," my dad offered, laughing devilishly. Sean and I also laughed. Mom did not.

"Okay, Kevins," she said firmly. "That's enough about Sarah." Sensing the finality of her remark, we shut up obediently. It's not wise to mess with Mom after she says a subject is closed.

At 1700 we went inside to dress for the meal. Mom put on nice church clothes and dad wore a coat and tie -- something he rarely did except for weddings and funerals. Despite vigorous protests to the contrary, Sean also put on a sport coat and tie. I told him he looked good, which was a big mistake. He turned toward Mom.

"It's too hot for this, Mom," Sean said in a child's whine which reminded me more of the Sean I remembered from several months back. I looked at Big Kevin, who I could see completely agreed with Sean about the attire but who also knew better than to argue with Mom when she had her mind made up.

"Stop complaining, Sean," he said, running a finger along his shirt collar to ease the tension. "If I have to suffer, so do you." Mom gave Big Kevin an exasperated looked but said nothing.

I showered and dressed quickly in my whites. They gaped at how quickly I was ready.

"You sure look good," Mom said, her eyes sparkling again with tears.

The drive to Annapolis was uneventful. The section of Ritchie Highway leading in to Annapolis is lined with deep deciduous forest and scenic rolling hills. I spent a few quiet minutes gazing out the open window and soaking in the peacefulness. It was quite an emotional change from the hectic activity inside and around Bancroft Hall. We exited at the convergence of Route 50 and Ritchie Highway where the sign indicated Annapolis lay 5 miles ahead, and stopped for a few minutes at the scenic lookout just east of the Academy across the Severn River. In the early evening, with the sun just descending toward the western horizon almost exactly behind the big dome of the Academy chapel and the river sparkling in a soft rippling orange glow, it was a very stirring sight. I looked at Dad, who leaned his two big arms on the stone railing to enjoy the view.

"Pretty impressive, huh dad?" I asked quietly. He grunted an affirmative reply, which was usually as enthusiastic as he got.

While the rest of us admired the view in quite contemplation, Mom took pictures of everything around us. I often wondered if Mom ever saw any of the sights we visited because she was always so busy recording events for posterity. But she thoroughly enjoyed the photography, even if the quality of her old Kodak Instamatic left a lot to be desired. A new camera was another of the expenses Big Kevin and she had decided to forego. Mom fussed at us, arranging us for posed pictures along the stone wall with the Academy in the background. I didn't have the heart to tell her that at this distance it would be very difficult for anyone to recognize the buildings in her pictures. So I posed for her -- standing at attention, standing at parade rest, saluting, cap on, cap off, and sitting on the stone wall. She loved it. I didn't complain.

The Restaurant was called *La Tratoria*. It was a somewhat dingy three-story brick-faced building in the middle of a row of other establishments on Main Street. Only a hand-painted sign in the small dark window indicated that this was indeed the place we sought. From the street it didn't look like much, hardly big enough to seat our party. We paused outside, unsure what to do next. I looked up and down the block. We were ten minutes early, and I didn't see anyone else I recognized among the throngs that lined the narrow cobblestone street. There was a great deal of activity in the small city that evening as plebes and their families strolled, shopped, and enjoyed each others' company.

We had found a parking space with some difficulty about a quarter mile away, and the walk in the humid near-evening had already caused Big Kevin to sweat profusely. He was terribly uncomfortable in the coat and tie. Sean whined through the entire walk. Only Mom held up stoically; that was her nature.

Sensing that action was required, I pushed open the glass door and held it for my family. The interior seemed dark, particularly after the evening brightness on the street. It was also warm and heavy with the pleasant smells of cooking. An elderly woman approached, holding several menus to her bosom, and smiling broadly.

"Welcome," she said. "How many in your party?" She had a trace of an accent I assumed was Italian.

"Jim Merritt made reservations for us," I told her. "There should be about 20."

"Oh, yes," she said, "the Merritt party. This way please." She led us through the narrow main restaurant toward a back section. Most of the tables were set up for four persons, and each was covered with a red and white checked tablecloth. A small candle set in a red glass container burned on every table, and every table also held a tiny bud vase with a single red rose. I liked this place, and I turned and smiled at my parents. Kevin nodded approval, Mom smiled, and Sean didn't know what to think. We didn't eat out very much at home. And, although they didn't know it, I had 50 dollars in my pocket to pay for their meal. I was going to do this right.

At this early hour we were almost the only ones in the restaurant. A young civilian couple sat in a corner by the window. One other plebe family sat at a table against the wall. I smiled at him as we passed, but he was focused on his father, who was lecturing him on the latest events in Little Rock, Arkansas. I swear I heard the father say "Them there Razorbacks" in the brief period when we passed.

The matron led us through an arch into another part of the restaurant. Without the bulk of the kitchen to take up space, this back area was much wider. And the back was apparently all ours. Jim Merritt and his family were already there, sitting at the large wooden table facing the entryway. It was just like him to get here early and make sure everything was ready. He smiled as we entered and rose quickly, as did his father. Jim came hurriedly around to the front. "Kevin," he said warmly, shaking my hand, "glad you could make it."

He turned toward the table.

"This is my father and mother, Mr. and Mrs. Michael Merritt, and this is Lynda, my 'sister'." He winked at me. Lynda was very pretty. Jim and his parents laughed. Lynda looked up at me, feigning indignance.

"I am *not* his sister," she stated firmly.

"Jim, Mr. and Mrs. Merritt, Lynda, this is my family," I said. "My dad, Kevin. My mom, Maryne, and my brother, Sean." Jim shook hands with everyone, as did Mr. and Mrs. Merritt. Jim returned to his seat, and we selected chairs facing them across the table.

Mr. Merritt stared at Big Kevin. "Everybody calls me 'Happy'," he said. "My God, you are a biggun. Ever play football?" Dad laughed.

"I've always been a bit large," he said. "And yes, I did play football for the Army team in the Pacific during the War. I was a fullback."

Mr. Merritt stared at Dad. "And then some," he said. I stared at dad too, slightly open mouthed. He had never said he played football for the Army or for anyone. That was interesting. I had to start talking to him more.

"Are you comfortable dressed like that?" Mr. Merritt asked my dad, indicating the coat and tie. Mr. Merritt had loosened his tie considerably and his jacket was draped over the back of his chair. "Come on. Get comfortable. We're all friends here." Dad looked down at Mom, who thought for a moment before indicating approval with a slight nod of her head. Quickly he and Sean were coatless and open-collared. They both looked considerably more at ease.

Mr. Merritt was a slightly rotund, older gentleman, who had a jovial and entertaining personality. Soon he was regaling Dad with stories of Texas and the oil industry. Mrs. Merritt, who had obviously heard the stories several times before, began a quiet conversation with my mom. I couldn't hear what they were saying, but they glanced lovingly in the direction of Jim and me and smiled several times.

I watched Jim and Lynda, who held hands tenderly across from me. Lynda noticed me staring and smiled.

"I'm jealous," I said.

She looked puzzled. "Of what?"

"Of Jim. You're much too attractive and nice for this country clod. Are there any more at home like you?" She and Jim laughed.

"Kevin doesn't have a girlfriend," Jim said.

"That's too bad," Lynda answered, "because you're a good looking man." Man? I liked this girl. "But I'm sorry," she continued. "No sisters."

"How about your mother?" I asked. They both burst out laughing, as did Sean, who was listening from his seat next to mine.

"She's married," Lynda said.

"Happily?" I asked questioningly. They laughed again.

"Kevin is the Company jokester," Jim said.

"I can see that," Lynda said, still laughing.

Within a few minutes Jubal Ramsey and his family showed up and introductions were made again. Joe was right. His sisters *were* big, and the oldest kept staring boldly at me. But Joe's mom was the star of the show. She was a dark-haired and wonderfully articulate woman who had lived in several exotic places around the world, and she could tell a story beautifully. I could see immediately where Joe got his personality. She was also very pretty -- a trait that had apparently skipped Jubal. And she wasn't married. -- I stopped that train of thought immediately.

No sooner had the Ramseys settled across the table to my left than the Pooles and Polks arrived almost simultaneously. Tommy was looking nervous as he introduced his parents and his pleasant looking girlfriend, Sara. She hung on Tommy's arm, obviously impressed with her newly sculpted he-man. I couldn't blame her -- if she knew the half of it. His family sat on our side of the table at the end next to my mom. I quickly lost track of the names. The Polks sat across the table on the other side of the Merritts. Tommy's parents were typical middle-class people, very nice, and obviously proud of their son. Jeff's parents were more down-to-earth and homey. I also liked Jeff's girlfriend, Kate, who was a petite and very pretty blond with a perky nose. Her long hair hung down her back to her waist. She sat next to Lynda, and soon the two of them were trading stories about their plebes.

I exchanged small talk with the Polks for a minute, but even surrounded by so much enthusiasm and good spirits, I was feeling a bit lonely and sorry for myself. Then Rico showed up.

Rico was by far the handsomest man in the room and in the restaurant and probably on the planet. He shone like a brilliant sunrise in his white uniform and his parents hovered proudly nearby like attendant planets. I immediately decided that the Guevarras were outstanding people: happy, fun loving, and garrulous. And Rosa was the most beautiful creature I had ever seen. She had long, lustrous black hair, almost as long as Kate's, but so straight and shiny it sparkled. Her complexion was pale and flawless, and her eyes dark and smoldering. She had full red lips, a perfect nose, and shapely breasts. In the dark miniskirt she had chosen to wear, I could see she had the most perfect set of long legs I had ever set my eyes on. Conversation at the table stopped when Rico introduced his family and Rosa. Christ, no wonder Rico had decided to forgo Cindy's pleasures. I would be satisfied just staring at Rosa, much less doing some of the things I'm sure Rico had in mind. What a lucky bastard!

And Rosa sat next to me, ha, ha. I held out her chair before Rico had the chance to offer. He looked at me from behind Rosa's back, his eyes alive and mischievous. He smiled, totally unjealous and sure of himself. What a guy! Rico took the seat at the end of the table so that he faced Jubal. Maybe he wanted to watch Rosa and make sure I stayed a gentleman?

I soon discovered that Rosa had one glaring flaw, however. When she opened her mouth to talk and words began to flow past those perfect teeth and lips, she had the most thick and grating New York Brooklyn accent I had ever heard. I had expected to hear Katherine Hepburn or Elizabeth Taylor, but instead out came the Bowery Boys. But she was as boisterous as the Guevarras and a great deal of fun to talk to, and I soon forgot her speech idiosyncrasies and fell victim to her charm. Rosa also liked to touch, and when she rested her hand on my arm to emphasize a point, it was electric. I would have done anything for this woman Even Kate and Lynda were outclassed and they knew it.

BJ Wilson showed up ten minutes later, just as we were about to order.

"Sorry I'm late," he said with his usual charm. "I had a phone call from Dad, and he and Mom wanted me to tell you how much they wished they could be here. Dad's feverishly working on the *Bonanza* editing for next week's season opener."

"*Bonanza?*" asked Mr. Merritt.

"Yes," answered BJ. "My dad is the producer for the television series, and my mom runs a fashion studio in Manhattan. This is a very hectic time of year for both of them."

"I'm sure they wanted very much to be here, dear," said Mrs. Poole. BJ smiled at her.

"Yes ma'am. They did."

Everybody on Jim Merritt's side of the table adjusted seats so that BJ could sit between Lynda and Kate. Poor Lynda and Kate. They'll have to listen to BJ's insufferable stories. He immediately focused on Rosa, however, who was now almost directly across from him. I looked quickly down at Rico. He smiled and winked knowingly at me. He wasn't worried. But *I* was a bit peeved because I had been doing a pretty good job of occupying lovely Rosa. Now, with BJ spouting stories of Broadway and Hollywood, I was thoroughly outclassed. I quieted and engaged in conversation with Kate and Lynda.

We ordered our food, and BJ suggested a wine which had no price on the list. That probably wasn't a good sign for my wallet. When always-frugal Big Kevin began a protest, BJ waved him quiet.

"Trust me," he said, smiling knowingly, and Kevin's objection died aborning. Soon the meals had arrived with a flourish and such a clamor of warmth and garlic and cheesy smells that I was momentarily overwhelmed. I had become so used to Academy food -- which as I said is very good -- that I had forgotten other tastes existed. My lasagna was delicious and seemed to melt in my mouth. I was in epicurean heaven for the next 30 minutes as I hungrily dived into my food.

Except for some wonderfully told stories from Mrs. Ramsey -- I wonder how old she is anyway? -- and some interesting oil tidbits from Mr. Merritt, the meal was very quiet. Once, following a hilarious joke by Jim's dad, Rosa leaned against me, overcome by laughter. When she leaned, she exposed a great deal of pale and delicious-looking cleavage almost in my surprised face. No one at the table missed the show, and I was extremely embarrassed. I could feel my face redden. I looked at Rico, who was laughing so hard at me he had doubled over. I put my arm around Rosa's milky white shoulder and sneered humorously at Rico.

"Do you have any sisters, Rosa?" I asked. Everyone laughed.

By the time the meal ended and our desert plates were cleared, we had consumed four bottles of the wine plus enough food to feed a small army. It was such a pleasant unhurried affair, so different from the slam-bam Academy meals, that I was overcome with respect for my classmates and admiration for their families and friends. Of course I had also drank three glasses of that delicious wine. I leaned back in my chair and let out a huge contented sigh. Jim and Lynda looked up from their muted conversation and smiled at me. I smiled at them. Then I winked at Jeff and Kate. Then I grinned at Rico. I even tried to peek surreptitiously down Rosa's blouse, but Rico caught me and laughed. I didn't care. Life was great, and everybody, including the normally obnoxious BJ Wilson, was getting along famously.

I listened in on surrounding conversations, almost in an out-of-body condition. Mr. Guevarra was telling Mr. Polk about the grocery business, emphasizing a point with his unused dessert spoon. Mrs. Ramsey was telling my mom and Mrs. Poole about life in China before the war. -- She couldn't be any more than forty years old. -- Jubal's sister, Belinda, was watching me. I smiled at her. She smiled in return. She had a nice smile.

Big Kevin was telling Mr. Merritt about how he almost invested in a mahogany farm in the Philippines after the War. Mahogany? The Philippines? I really had to talk to Dad. He had a secret life I knew nothing about. I was worried about my $50, but stoically decided that I could survive without any cash until the next payday. Near the end of the meal BJ excused himself and disappeared into the restaurant proper. He returned a few minutes later just as several of the ladies excused themselves to "powder their noses."

The parents began exchanging addresses and promises to write and send Christmas cards. We also exchanged mutual invitations of visitation rights. Finally Mr. Merritt said.

"Well it's about time for the checks."

"No need," 'BJ' Wilson said with a charm and a flourish I envied. He stood. "Ladies and gentlemen," he began. "You will be pleased to know that although my Dad could not be here, he sends his greetings -- and his Diner's Club Card number." BJ laughed. "The dinner is on him. He says he hopes you enjoy it and that he and Mom have already made plans to be here June Week when we scale the Herndon Monument. He raised his wine glass, which still had a swallow in it.

"To the Class of 1971!" he said. We all raised our glasses, except me. Mine was missing momentarily until I saw that Sean had "borrowed" it for the toast. I borrowed it back. Jim Merritt stood.

"BJ," he said. "Please tell your parents thank you from all of us. It was a very pleasant meal and I enjoyed all your company. To the Twenty-Third Company!" We drank again.

Joe quickly stood and raised his glass.

"To the Brigade of Midshipmen!" We sipped again.

Rico stood next.

"To our wonderful parents, without whom we never could have made it this far!"

Jeff stood awkwardly and said in a soft voice as he stared down at Kate.

"To our sweet and lovely female companions, whose support we so desperately need."

Tommy Poole stood next.

"To Ronald Steinway!" he said sadly. We drank a solemn toast. Everyone looked at me. In my contented stupor I didn't realize that my classmates had alternated toasts. It was my turn. My brain quickly fumbled. My buddies seemed to have covered everything possible. I stood slowly, trying to be dramatic, but in reality searching desperately for something appropriate to say.

I raised my glass.

"Three months ago the seven of us fresh-faced and innocent young men began an adventure." I liked what I had said so far. Now what? "The adventure has not been without its pain." I raised my glass to Tommy. "And its losses." I lowered my head and paused. Everybody at the table was staring at me enraptured. I was on a roll. I continued. "But we made it, despite the odds, despite the stress, despite the fact that it would have been far easier to be somewhere else. There are heroes in the making at this table, and I'm dammed proud to be counted among them. To us!"

My six classmates stood and raised their glasses with me. I finished my wine with a flourish. I thought briefly of throwing the glass against the brick wall but decided that I had been dramatic enough. I sat. Everybody smiled at me. Rosa gave me a special look. I winked at Rico.

Dinner broke up soon afterward, and we were in great spirits as we exited the restaurant into the warm moonless night. Overhead the stars blazed, and I felt as if I were blazing just as brightly. Mom held my arm as we strolled down a rapidly quieting Main Street toward our car.

"That was a nice speech, dear," Mom said.

"Did you practice it?" Sean asked.

"Actually I made the whole thing up as I went," I said. Sean looked at me skeptically. "It's true." He wasn't convinced.

As we drove away from the city I glanced at my watch. It was 2030, an hour until my rendezvous with Kathy of the marvelous body. I smiled to myself. I was feeling invincible. What a hero! What a stud! Maybe things would be more satisfying later?

Back at the Holiday Inn dad pulled a fresh six-pack from the cooler, and we settled down around a small round table to talk.

"What's this about football in the Army and mahogany in the Philippines?" I asked. Mom answered.

"Oh, don't listen to that talk, Kevin. Your dad was just bragging about nonsense."

"That's okay," I said I want to listen.

"It's nothing really, son," Dad said. "I played a little football for the Army team during the war. A scout for the University of California even talked to me about a scholarship. But I'm not a California person, and I had to get back to work after the War because my family needed the money. And the mahogany thing was an idea me and several unit comrades discussed. We even calculated how much we would each need to invest to make it work. But too many of us dropped out of the venture as the war ended and we forgot about it."

Wow, my Dad was almost a college football star and an entrepreneur. I was impressed.

"Those were very nice people we met this evening," Mom said.

"Yeah they were, weren't they?"

"I had a nice time," she continued. "How about you, Kevin?" she asked Dad.

"It was fun," he said.

"Sean?" she asked.

"Me too. Wasn't that Rosa lady beautiful?"

"I'll say," I answered.

"She was hanging all over you, Kevin," Sean observed, nudging me with an elbow.

"I wish," I said. "But she wasn't at all interested in me. She's Rico's girl."

"He's a handsome young man," Mom said, "but not as handsome as you, dear." I looked at her disbelievingly. I could see she was serious. Moms, don't we love them?

We talked until almost 2130 when mom yawned.

"Go on your date, Kevin," mom said. "I'm tired. I'll get ready for bed. Dad will drive you back."

"Okay, Mom. Good night and I'll see you tomorrow." I kissed her on the cheek and hurried into the bathroom where I changed into my swim suit and a T-shirt. Then I started for the door.

"Be back here at exactly 1115," Dad said sternly as I opened the door to depart. I acknowledged him with a wink and grabbed two beers from the table.

There were a few young children at the pool when I opened the short fence and went inside the pool area. I selected a pair of lounge chairs and pulled them far from the water -- out of sight of my parents' room -- and settled back and waited. I could see Kathy's room from where I sat, and within a minute the curtain opened just a bit and someone peeked out. Less than a minute later she exited the room, waved at me, and came quickly down the stairs. She had on her bathing suit, but over top she wore a T-shirt with a Mickey Mouse logo on it.

I stood as she neared and indicated the chair next to me. She looked up at her room.

"Can we move them over some more?" she asked. "I don't want my parents spying." I readily agreed, and soon we had cozily settled ourselves side-by-side in a far corner of the pool area.

I popped a beer for her and she took a deep drink. Then she rolled onto her side, just inches from me and said sweetly.

"Tell me about yourself, Kevin." I outlined the life of Kevin O'Reilly in about sixty seconds. I was still feeling the influence of the wine and the beer, and I was definitely amorous. I reached over and brushed a strand of hair from her face.

"There," I said. "Perfect."

"Do you think so?" she asked demurely.

"Absolutely," I answered.

"Thank you," she answered as I took her hand and brought it to my mouth and kissed it.

"That's nice," she said. I leaned in to kiss her, but she pulled away and turned over onto her back. I moved after her but she held up a hand.

"Not here," she said. "Too many people around."

"How about if I borrow the car and we find a more secluded spot?" I asked. She thought for a minute.

"Okay," she said. We rose from the lounge chairs, and I went to my parents' room and entered. Mom was in the bathroom. Dad sat at the table. Sean was in bed watching TV. Dad and Sean looked up.

"That was quick," Sean said.

"Dad? Let me borrow the car. Kathy and I are going down the road to a McDonalds." Dad looked very skeptical. "I'll be back on time. I promise," I said holding my right hand up in an oath position. He still hesitated; then he reached into his pocket and withdrew the keys. He held them aloft.

"Eleven-fifteen, Kevin. No later."

I grabbed the keys and hurried outside. I had neglected to tell Dad about the driving restriction for midshipmen other than first-class within seven miles of Annapolis, but what the heck. Kathy was waiting near the end of the block by the parking lot. This was great. She seemed as anxious as I was to get down to it. I jogged to her, took her hand, and led her to the Rambler. Soon we had exited the parking lot and turned north toward Baltimore. She slid over next to me and held my arm while I drove. I flexed for her.

At the first narrow cross road, about a quarter mile north of the motel, I turned right. Following the road for less than a minute we came to a parking area for what appeared to be an abandoned church. This seemed perfect. I pulled into the parking lot and stopped.

"There," I said, turning toward her. She smiled up at me and reached up with a hand to my face. She slid the hand behind my head and pulled me toward her. We kissed, at first tentatively, then with greater passion. She was a good kisser.

I slid my right arm around her and pulled her toward me. I could feel her ample chest against me, and it felt good. I slid her down onto the seat, but the front of a Rambler is not very spacious and obviously wasn't built for snuggling. The steering wheel interfered with my legs, and one foot seemed stuck in the vent window slot.

"Damn!" I said.

"What's the matter?" she asked looking at me demurely. Then she lifted her arms over her head and stretched. I almost had a heart attack as her chest bulged toward me.

"Let's get into the back seat," I said quickly. "It'll be more comfortable." She giggled, and without a word scurried over the seat into the back. I did the same, flopping awkwardly next to her. We laughed at the ridiculousness of the situation for a moment, settled onto the seat next to each other, and began kissing again.

She had a very sweet kiss, and her arms held me tightly against her. After five minutes I was incredibly excited. I pressed involuntarily against her and moaned in pleasure. We moved together for a minute, until I was ready to explode. I slid my right hand up into her shirt until it settled itself comfortably on her bikini top. She didn't resist. Her breasts seemed to overflow the material, and I squeezed gently and moved my hand lightly over both of her incredible mounds. I could feel hard lumps plainly inviting me, and I thought about Brenda and Rosa and Sarah Connelly all in a sudden rush of desire.

I tried to slide my fingers under the bottom elastic strap of her top, but it was too tight and I couldn't do more than wiggle in a few inches before I was stuck. I quickly extracted my fingers with a snap of elastic and tried to insert my whole hand down into her bikini bra from the top, but because my position next to her made us almost level, I was no more successful with a top down attack. Damn but I really wanted to get my hand in there somehow. I could almost hear her breasts calling softly, "Kevin, Kevin. Come get us." I almost screamed but what came out of my mouth was a croak of frustration.

Thinking quickly I slid one shoulder strap down along her arm, but this seemed to awkwardly pin her arm to her side, and she shrugged the strap up above her elbow. She just wasn't cooperating at all. So I squeezed and rubbed through the fabric while we kissed. After another minute she removed my hand with one of her own, gently placed it on her arm, and kissed me passionately as if in compensation. All say one thing, that girl liked to kiss.

Her arm was fine, but I still wanted more. I moved my hand back where it felt most comfortable, but she returned it to her arm. I tried again with the same result. We did this back and forth exercise several times before I suddenly realized that she was playing out a scene she had practiced in the back seat of other cars many times in her young life. I guess that's the price a girl pays for such overt nobility, but that was high school thespianism, and I wanted no part of it. I stopped kissing and lifted myself up onto an elbow. She tried to pull me down, but I resisted.

"What's the matter?" she asked sweetly.

"I'm terribly frustrated, Kathy," I said. "You keep stopping me from doing anything."

"Don't you like to kiss?" she asked.

"Of course I do," I answered. "And you're a great kisser, but you are driving me insane. Do you realize how beautiful and sexy you are? You're not in high school any more, you know? You should stop playing games with me and grow up a little." What possible connection her school status had with her cooperative actions in the back seat of my father's Rambler was very tenuous at best, but it was the best argument I could think of at the time. But then, since I didn't even know her last name, I couldn't very well tell her that I loved her and wanted to seal our relationship for eternity. And since the chances of my being shipped out to war in the morning were rather slim, I couldn't use that argument either. But telling her I was desperate to see what she had inside that bikini seemed a bit crass. I guess you go with what seems best at the time.

"I really like you, Kevin," she said sweetly. Ah, that was something to start with.

"I like you too, Kathy," I said, and immediately inserted my hand into her bikini top all the way to paydirt. She looked at me and didn't do anything to stop me. Apparently my argument worked. I smiled and I opened my hand and found her soft and warm. She still didn't respond, and I was confused. I tried to smile at her.

"What's the matter?" I asked sweetly as I began moving my fingers against her nipples.

Still she didn't say anything, and I noticed in the dim light from a nearby parking lot light that a glimmer of a tear had formed in the corner of one eye. I suddenly felt like a real ass. My God, what was wrong with me? I was being Danny French, the guy I ridiculed. I quickly removed my hand and stared at it for a moment. I felt really bad about myself, and I realized that my passion had died.

I turned around in the seat and faced the front.

"I'm really sorry," I said. "I tried to take advantage of you, and you didn't deserve that." She didn't answer. I could hear her crying gently, and I felt even worse. I turned around toward her and put a hand gently on her cheek.

"What's wrong?" I asked tenderly. She continued crying. I lay down next to her and held her, patting her head and saying "It's all right" over and over in her ear.

"I didn't want you to do that," she finally said.

"I didn't know," I said apologetically. "I'm sorry."

"I'm sorry too," she said. "Take me home."

I tried to kiss her but she avoided any contact. We sat up and climbed into the front seat. No laughter this time. When she was settled, I started the car and drove out onto the highway heading north and looking for a turnaround. At the next intersection I saw a McDonalds, and I pulled in.

"Let me buy you a Coke," I offered. We ordered Cokes and fries from the drive-through window, sat in the car in a secluded corner, and ate and drank in silence.

"Are you okay?" I asked, touching her on the arm. She didn't answer. I was really confused and a bit angry. I didn't really do anything did I? It wasn't like we had sex or anything like that. Why was she so hurt? I decided to chalk it up to weird feminine idiosyncrasies.

We were quiet the entire way back; but she did sit next to me and hold my arm, and I decided everything was fine again. We parked in the same spot we had vacated just an hour previously. Boy, it sure seemed like more than an hour. We sat for a minute, staring out the windshield and holding hands. I reached over, opened the glove compartment, and pulled out a notebook Dad always kept there. I opened it, tore out a page, and quickly scribbled my address at Annapolis for her. I handed it to her, and she held it in her hand tightly.

"What's your address?" I asked. She told me and I wrote it down. I put her address in my swimsuit pocket.

Then I turned toward her and put my right arm around her shoulder and my left hand on her chin. Gently I turned her face toward mine and kissed her. After a few seconds she responded and soon had her arms tightly around me. She sure liked to kiss. We stayed that way for five minutes, until I broke contact.

"I have to go," I said. She nodded, but didn't make eye contact.

"Will I see you tomorrow at the pool?" I asked.

"We'll be out all day," she said.

"Will you write me?" I asked. "Please?"

She smiled and finally looked at me. "Okay," she said. Then she kissed me again passionately but quickly. I helped her out of the car and walked with her slowly, hand-in-hand, to the end of our hotel wing.

"Stay here," she said. "I'll go on ahead alone. She turned and put her arms around my waist and hugged me. "Good-bye, Kevin," she said. I didn't like the finality of that statement.

"Write me," I said as she started down the concrete walkway adjacent to the building. She didn't answer.

She hurried down the walkway and turned the corner into the stairwell. I remained where I was for more than a minute, then walked slowly to my parents' room and entered quietly. Dad and Sean were waiting inside. Mom was asleep in the bed farthest from the door. I could see from the surprised look on Dad's face that he was surprised that I had gotten back early.

"Did you get kissed?" asked Sean.

"Maybe," I answered.

"Get anything else?" he asked tittering.

"Wouldn't you like to know?" I said, smiling broadly. I think my smile deceptively indicated more than actually happened, but I didn't correct his perceptual error. I quickly dressed in my uniform, and the three of us left the hotel for Annapolis. Even with the additional visitors for Parents' Weekend, traffic was light, and we arrived ten minutes early. I spent a few moments hugging Sean and Dad in the parking lot of the Midshipman's Store and told them about the Yacht Basin incident. They enjoyed the story. Then I raced up the steps and through T-Court to the fourth wing and my new room.

I arrived two minutes early. Merritt and Wilson were there. "How was your evening, Kevin?" Jim asked.

"Interesting," I replied. "How about yours?"

"Great. We took BJ along with us to the hotel and sat talking by the pool all evening."

"What about Lynda?" I asked.

Jim looked confused. "She was there," he said.

"I mean," I continued. "What about you and Lynda and . . . being together?"

Jim laughed. "O'Reilly, you poor sad thing," he said. "There's more to life than sex. It was wonderful to see her and touch her. I'm perfectly satisfied."

"Merritt, you're not shitting anyone," said a voice from the doorway. Rico had arrived. "Rosa and I had steamy, exhausting sex for two hours this evening while my parents were in Annapolis shopping for souvenirs. It was great, and I'll bet she won't walk straight for a week. No way is just looking as good." Rico turned to me. "Rosa says hi, by the way. I'm going to have to keep an eye on you from now on. I think she was interested in you. It must be your tragic Irish charm."

"When you finish with her, let me know," I said. "I'll gladly take seconds." Rico laughed.

"I don't know when I'll finish," he said. "She's a hot number. She almost wore me out."

Because this was a special night, Maxwell and Battle held a muster in the passageway at precisely 0030. We braced outside our rooms while they called the roll to ensure we were all there. We weren't. Both Richardson and Mulvaney were missing. Mulvaney arrived during the muster, Richardson showed up an hour later. Both of them were written up for their tardiness, and now faced weeks of Restriction musters to work off their 25 demerits.

After the muster we to bed. Liberty would start on Sunday after a special 1300 parade for the parents.

As we prepared for sleep I remarked to the room. "I had a great time tonight at the dinner. All the families were wonderful people."

My family had awakened early to come to Annapolis for mass. They stood outside watching as we marched up the chapel steps and into the church. They waved and smiled. They repeated the greeting as we departed. That morning after mass and meal I straightened my things in preparation for the Brigade's official return later that evening. Upper-class would be returning individually and in small groups after 1500, and the entire Brigade would be assembled at the 1800 meal formation. I began to feel a sense of apprehension. I didn't want to go through the plebe shit again. I had completed Plebe Summer hadn't I? Shouldn't that be enough?

The day was another sunny, hot, and humid one. Luckily, our parade for the parents was an abbreviated affair on Worden Field. The 36 small groups marched out onto the field led by the squadleaders and halted in precise locations indicated by markers set into the grass. We did the manual-of-arms, and the Superintendent spoke about how proud he was of us and what an adventure we had ahead. Within 30 minutes we marched the pass-in-review for Jake Conrad, the dignitaries, and our parents, and marched back to Bancroft, anxious to be away from the Academy.

As we marched along the street toward Bancroft Hall I heard Rico remark quietly, "Look at those tits!" All heads swiveled toward Rico's side of the formation, which luckily happened to be mine as well. Ahead was a girl and her family watching the groups pass. The girl was extremely well developed and attractive. It was Kathy.

She was scanning the companies and looking at the guidons. She was looking for me. She knew what Company I was in from my note. As we neared, I leaned outward to get her attention. I was on her side of the formation, and with my red hair shining from under my cap, I am usually easy to find in a group. She saw me. I smiled. She smiled in return. She raised her arm slightly and waved at me. She didn't want her mom and dad to see that she knew any midshipmen other than her brother. Maybe they were protective.

"She knows you, Kevin?" asked Rico incredulously from his position behind me.

"It's Kathy," I said. "I met her yesterday."

"And already she's giving you that look? You lucky bastard. Did you . . . ?"

"Not saying." I answered.

"Holy shit!" he exclaimed. "You stud! I'm not letting you within a mile Rosa from now on!" We laughed. Naturally I didn't let on.

I was dressed in my tropical whites and out the door in ten minutes. My family waited in the parking lot for me. We repeated the hugged greetings, and soon headed to the hotel.

My family and I relaxed at the pool for an hour. I shared their beer with an unaccustomed gusto. We were pals. As the beer mellowed me, I began to relate some of the more unusual experiences of the summer. For the first time I talked about Ronald Steinway and Tommy Poole. When I recounted Ronald's last moments, I felt tears forming involuntarily in my eyes. I finished the story, teary but not weeping. Mom however was crying.

Dad laughed. "That poor dear," she said. "I feel so sorry for his parents."

"I feel sorry for his classmates," said Dad. What a strange thing to say.

"What do you mean?" I asked.

"You're the ones who have to cope with what happened. He's out of it now." I hadn't thought of it quite like that, but I could see that Dad was right. Ronald would be a cloud that hung over us for a long time to come.

"It was like that during the war," he continued. "Every time we lost a buddy it was really hard to go back into combat again. But you do what you have to do. You too, Kevin. Do what you have to do."

We made plans for Christmas and I informed Mom that I would indeed be writing to Sarah Connelly, Patrick Connelly be damned. Mom seemed pleased. All too soon it was time to leave. I hadn't even caught a glimpse of Kathy the entire afternoon, and I was disappointed; but I'd write her too and make things better.

The drive to Annapolis was silent and uneventful. We said tearful good-byes in the parking lot and my parents promised to watch for me during the evening meal formation. I hurried inside -- and confronted utter bedlam.

The previously deserted passageways and rooms were teeming with strangers, every one a potential enemy. I immediately decided I didn't like the look of most of them. Gear was being stowed, and loud greetings exchanged. The clamor of so many people rushing to prepare for formation was almost overwhelming. I was nearly frightened to death. I could imagine how poor Tommy Poole must be feeling just now. The fun was only starting for him. I wonderered briefly how his conversation with his family went.

I chopped quickly to my room, chins tight against my neck and my eyes unwaiveringly in the boat. I didn't want any trouble just yet. I was the first one back. There were 15 minutes to formation. Merritt and Wilson showed up almost immediately after me, and Rico followed them by five minutes. As we prepared, Tommy Poole appeared in the doorway.

"Talked it over with my family," he said, his voice assuming a steely quality I hadn't heard before. "I'm staying!" We each congratulated Tommy, and he hurried to his room. I began to woory about how prepared I was for this.

"I don't even know which platoon we're in," I stated.

"It must be posted," said Merritt. "Who wants to check?" No one volunteered. The flow of human tide outside the room was almost frenzied. I didn't want to be caught up in it.

"Kevin," Rico said, "you deal with these people better than us. You go." Where did he get that idea?

Maybe the beer still had me emboldened. I accepted the challenge. I hurried outside and chopped to the Company bulletin board outside the Company Office. There was a crowd milling nearby, checking the Company information. I inserted myself into the group and scanned the list hurriedly. So far no one had noticed a plebe in their midst. I found our names: second platoon, first squad. I turned to go, and almost collided with Midshipman First-Class Raymond "Rock" Stone, our Company Commander. I almost wet myself. He knew I was a plebe: he could smell my fear.

"What the hell are you doing here, plebe?" he said.

"Checking the formation listings, sir!" I yelled.

"You should have done that about two hours ago when they were posted. You're blocking the view of the upper-class. Give me a 100 -- but over there out of the way."

"Aye, aye, sir!" I chopped to a position against a far wall and started loudly cranking out push-ups. At 100 I leaped to my feet and hurried down the hall. I was not amused by the time I entered the room.

"So much for your my ability to deal with people," I announced angrily. "That little trip cost me 100."

"Sorry, Kevin," Rico said, smiling broadly and not at all repentant. "So what platoon and squad?"

"Two and one," I replied.

Evening meal formation was a confusing affair of hunt-your-place, and there was no time for any special attention for any of the plebes, which was good. The meal was a similar affair, as the upper class attention was more for their classmates than us plebes. We made it back to our rooms without incident. God, was I relieved. I really didn't want to be doing this; I wasn't prepared.

We began to ready our things for the start of academics in the morning. I was turned toward the window dividing my books into stacks when a voice announced from the doorway.

"Excuse me. Which one of you is Kevin O'Reilly?" I turned. A strange plebe stood in the doorway. He wasn't someone I had ever seen before.

"I am," I replied. He looked me over as I walked toward him. Relieved that the visitor had nothing to do with them, the others went about their business. "What can I do for you?"

"You can stay away from my sister!" he said loudly. "She told me about last night. She's only 16 years old you know?"

I started to speak. Sixteen? But she told me she had graduated from high school, hadn't she?

"Listen . . . ," I began. It was the last thing I said clearly for several days.

I saw him move, and I saw a momentary glimpse of something about fist-sized coming quickly at my head. I was completely unprepared. I had no time to react. Everything went black.

I awoke on the floor of the room seconds later. My mouth was full of blood. By probing my tongue, I could feel that my two front teeth were loose and that my lip was split on the left side. Rico stood in the doorway staring down the passageway. Merritt knelt beside me. Wilson sat still at his desk, staring uncomprehendingly at the scene.

"Are you okay, Kevin?" Jim asked, very concerned. I tried to answer, but my mouth was full of blood and my lip was quickly swelling. I mumbled and tried to sit up. Jim went to the sink, got a washcloth from the rack, and soaked it in cold water. He brought it to me. I wiped my face, but I still had the blood in my mouth. Jim and Rico helped me to my feet. I spit what seemed to be an enormous quantity of blood into the sink. It splashed the entire sink and mirror with bright red dots.

I rinsed my mouth for a minute until the bleeding stopped. Rico and Jim still hovered nearby.

"Do you want us to help you go to Sick Bay?" Jim asked, and for some reason I became angry.

"Naaaaaa, Ah don won ta goh ta Sk By!" I said loudly. At least that's what came past my injured and swollen lips. Jim and Rico stepped back, as flecks of bloody spit sprayed from my mouth in all directions along with the incoherent words. Jim looked concerned.

Rico understood, however. He laughed almost uncontrollably, and Jim looked at him as if he were insane.

"Sixteen, huh?" Rico said. "Christ, O'Reilly, you really run the gamut, don't you? Do you know any women your own age?" I saw his point and tried to smile but it hurt to do that. It was funny in a strange and tragic way. I had to do something about this Irish curse that seemed to follow me.

I staggered to my desk and tried to clean myself. I had experienced split lips before from elbows to the face during basketball games, so this wasn't a new experience. It still hurt though. Jim Merritt sat in his chair. For the first time I could see a taint of strain on his normally stoic face. I could also see that BJ Wilson was definitely regretting being roomies with Kevin O'Reilly the wondermid. Only Rico was unperturbed. He enjoyed this.

"Christ, Kevin," Jim said. "What next?"

Almost immediately a stranger entered the room, and we snapped to attention. He walked to my desk and put a pair of grubby black shoes down in front of me.

"Okay, Howdy Doody," he said. "I need these shoes looking good before morning meal." With that he turned and departed.

I stared at my roommates incredulously. Jim and BJ seemed discouraged. Rico was still smiling. "I guess now we know that the Brigade's back," he said.

"Ye weh dah," I said.

THE STEPS TO MEMORIAL HALL

At the south end of the Bancroft Hall Rotunda are these wide stairs leading to Memorial Hall, where displays honor alumni killed in action.

THE BRIGADE

A NOVEL OF THE NAVAL ACADEMY

HANK TUROWSKI

USNA CLASS OF 1971

THE BRIGADE

CHAPTER 1

ARRIVALS

It was unbelievable! The passageways of Bancroft Hall teemed with upper-class midshipmen returning to Annapolis from cruises or summer leave. Animated conversations and loud music reverberated from every bulkhead. This was a far cry from the last three months of training, where only two second-class (junior year) midshipmen supervised the activities of more than 30 of us (first year) plebes. We had some safety in numbers then. After today there would be three upper-class for each plebe. We would be hopelessly outnumbered. It was put-up-or-shut-up time, and that was a very scary proposition, one that many of my classmates had been dreading for several weeks. But not me so much.

I peeked again from my Naval Academy room doorway, careful not to draw too much attention to myself. But the upper-class seemed more concerned with the logistics of their return rather than the harassment of lower-than-dirt plebes. They probably knew there would be plenty of time for hazing later. Still, the ongoing activity itself was amazing. Twenty-third Company area was alive with motion and emotion as classmates and company mates greeted each other boisterously and exchanged stories, all the while lugging suitcases and armloads of gear into their rooms. I smiled to myself. It was quite a sight. I was strangely proud to be a small part of it, although I realized that as a plebe, I was nearly insignificant.

Today was the last day of Plebe Summer Parents' Weekend. Mom and Dad had dropped me off more than two hours ago in the parking area near the chapel, where we had said our goodbyes amid the clamor of the returning Brigade of Midshipmen. Parents' Weekend marked the official end to a physical and emotionally demanding phase of training called Plebe Summer, where newly arrived Annapolis recruits experienced their first taste of military discipline, learned to march and wear uniforms, and generally got the hell run out of them. I loved every minute of it, and that's the truth.

As we had watched the hundreds of upper-class resolutely heading toward their dormitory rooms in Bancroft Hall, I knew that my parents were concerned about my well-being, but they also sensed my supreme self-confidence and my pride at being part of this wonderful place and a member of one of the most elite groups of young men on the planet. They knew I would succeed no matter what. That was my nature -- and I had told them so repeatedly during the past weekend.

What I hadn't told my parents, -- because I didn't want to hurt their feelings -- was how completely at home I felt within the brick walls that surrounded the campus. In some ways I was more "at home" here than at home with them. Annapolis, the Navy, military life, the system, the camaraderie -- I loved it all. This was what I was meant to do. I was positive about that. And I would do well. No question of that either. I already had it all figured out. I even had a four-year plan which I had developed in my head over the past hectic months of Plebe Summer -- I've always been good at planning. I was determined to lead the Brigade and its midshipmen during my senior year. How's that for self confidence?

First I had to survive the rest of Plebe Year -- no easy matter, particularly in the Twenty-third Company, the "Tiger" Company, where each succeeding batch of first-class (seniors) prided themselves on being tougher than the last. It would be extremely difficult, but I could handle it. I could handle anything. Plebe Summer had been a picnic, and I would manage the academic year just as easily.

Still smiling, I returned to my locker area confidently. Already I had neatly packed away the civilian clothes I used on Parents' Weekend, readied my tropical white uniform for the upcoming meal, and set out the "white works" uniform for tomorrow's classes. I had straightened my locker, adjusted the hospital corners on my bed to absolute perfection, and cleaned the area around my desk. My text books for tomorrow's classes sat precisely in a neat pile in the upper right-hand corner of my desk, arranged by academic period. My class schedule was posted both on my small bulletin board and in my notebook. I had studied the "rates" for the evening meal and for breakfast tomorrow. All in all, I was ready, and I knew it. I smiled to myself. Let's get this thing started.

I looked at my three new roommates as they prepared for tonight and tomorrow, each in his own unique style. Except for Rico Guevarra, the others seemed exceedingly concerned about the upcoming turmoil of the first meal with the full Company assembled and particularly worried about this evening's "Hell Night" activities. Enrique Guevarra sat at his desk reading a smut novel, one of several he kept in his locker. I had heard about his "collection" during the summer from other plebes; but I hadn't borrowed any, and I didn't intend to. Those sex books were garbage as far as I was concerned, and I had no time for them. Rico seemed oblivious to the clamor in the passageway, which amazed me. He was not at all prepared for the ordeal that awaited us. His locker needed arranging, his bed and desk area were slightly messy, and he needed a shave. Yet he didn't seem to care, and I couldn't figure that out. Guevarra was the enigmatic roommate. I like to know exactly where everyone stands and what to expect from them. I was going to have to study Rico Guevarra more closely.

Rico had definite assets. He was a dark, devilishly handsome, and very intelligent Puerto Rican-American from Brooklyn, New York. He had inherited his parents' spontaneous gaiety and pragmatic acceptance of fate. He was an athlete who could out-run and out-exercise most of his classmates -- myself excepted -- and he had a natural charm that was hard to resist. Rico had done exactly what was necessary to get by as a plebe this past summer. In Academy lingo, Rico "didn't sweat it," and maybe he felt that he didn't have to sweat it.

William Janus "BJ" Wilson sat directly across from me at his own Academy-issue gray metal desk. He was busily polishing his white shoes in preparation for evening meal formation 30 minutes from now. He had a look of intensity on his handsome face, and his almost-startling blue eyes flashed as he concentrated on coating the white shoe nap with a uniform covering of liquid polish. I say BJ was handsome, but actually he was "pretty." BJ Wilson lacked the ruggedness and the virility usually associated with movie stars. BJ's features rather were perfectly sculpted and totally without a blemish -- the genetic product of mating between a famous high fashion model and a handsome TV executive.

BJ had spent his entire life in Manhattan, growing up in an apartment high above Central Park -- not exactly a spawning ground for pioneers, dragon slayers, or naval officers for that matter. I wondered again why he was here at all. With his parents' money and influence he surely could have attended any college or university in the nation. That was another question I would have to find the answer to.

BJ's hair, which had grown in thickly during the summer, was dark, wavy, blue-black, two inches in length. Not one hair was out of place. Somewhat slight of frame, he had filled out nicely. As

I watched him, I realized that he reminded me of what I always thought the Greeks had in mind when they personified their ancient gods, except I don't think Greek gods polished shoes very often.

Then there's my other roommate, Kevin -- Kevin Patrick O'Reilly -- the redheaded, sassy, incredibly complex, Boston-Irish boy-clown of our Plebe Company. I laughed to myself thinking about him. Kevin had more bizarre personality traits than any ten people I had ever met, but he was completely honest, devoted, and likable. He had almost singlehandedly made Plebe Summer bearable, just by being Kevin. I felt confident I would eventually figure out Rico and BJ, but I wasn't so sure with Kevin. He was *that* different.

Kevin was busily arranging and rearranging the things in his locker, attempting to ensure that every item was placed precisely in its regulation position. Annapolis published a manual that described in painstaking detail how every item of clothing was to be folded and where each item was to be stored or displayed in the locker or closet. I watched Kevin, smiling again as every few seconds he looked up, distracted by the commotion outside the room. Kevin was dreading the return of the Brigade.

Some background is in order at this point. Rico, BJ, Kevin, and I are plebes at the United States Naval Academy, Annapolis -- Class of 1971. We reported aboard on June 27, 1967, along with more than thirteen hundred of our classmate recruits. The Academy is divided into 36 Companies, and we plebes (fourth-class midshipman) were divided among these Companies. Twenty-third Company -- ours -- started summer training with 32 plebes. Seven of that number are no longer with us, succumbing to various pressures, fears, or intimidations. One of them, Ronald Steinway, died in a sad "accident" several weeks ago. Twenty-five plebes remain in Twenty-third Company to face the rigors of academic year -- and the wrath of the returning "Tigers" who clambered outside our rooms.

Why is the Brigade returning? Where's it been? During Plebe Summer two second-class midshipmen had complete control of our training. That was their summer duty. The rest of the Company and the Brigade, was away on vacations and training cruises. Today, Wednesday, September 6, 1967, each Company reunited itself as a new entity. Everyone who had been here at the end of last year had moved up a notch in rank, and we plebes were now the lowest caste in the system. Next in importance -- which wasn't saying much -- were the sophomores (third-classmen), also called "youngsters," followed by the juniors (second-classmen), and finally the godlike seniors (first-classmen), who actually ran the Company and the Brigade itself. The Naval Academy is the ultimate in student government, and it works like a well-oiled machine. I smiled again, thinking of myself as a cog in that wonderful machine.

My name is James Wesley Merritt. My friends call me Jim. I was born in Amarillo, Texas, eighteen and a half years ago. My father is a low-level manager in a well-known oil company. My mom works around the house, taking care of my two brothers and two sisters, all younger than me. I'm a Texan and proud of it, but I'm not stereotypical. I can't ride a horse. I don't know how to roll a cigarette -- I don't even smoke. And I don't particularly care for country music. I stand six feet one inch tall. I'm thin and in great shape -- thanks primarily to Plebe Summer. Usually I'm a dusky blond, but with my hair this short it's hard to notice my hair color. I played football and ran track for a medium sized high school in Amarillo, but right now I have undefined collegiate athletic ambitions. I want to adjust to this place first, then decide. I have a wonderful girlfriend named Lynda who came to Annapolis with my parents to see me this past weekend. We had a wonderful time together, and I'm not saying what that means. We talked quite a bit about our future, Lynda and me. I really love that girl.

I snapped out of my reverie and checked my watch.

"Time to start getting ready for meal, guys," I said with authority. I had decided to assume a leadership role for the room and the plebe cadre in the Company, and it was best to assume that position immediately. I didn't think anyone in the room would mind. Some of them, including Rico and Kevin, needed leadership.

"Has anybody looked to see what Platoon and Squad we're in?" asked a very nervous Kevin O'Reilly. Only 20 minutes remained before the evening formation. I was actually ready to do just that.

"I checked on the way in, but nothing was posted yet," I answered.

Kevin stopped arranging his locker, turned, and looked at me.

"Well, someone has to find out so we know where to go," he said.

"Good idea!" said Rico, not looking up from his book. "Hustle down to the bulletin board, will you Kevin?"

"Wait a minute!" Kevin said quickly. "Why me?" As he asked, he glanced nervously out the doorway at the bustle and commotion.

"Kevin," Rico said patiently, looking up at him, "you deal with these people better than any of us. We all know that. You're the perfect candidate." Where did Rico get that idea about Kevin? Kevin O'Reilly usually fumbled his way to success, and I certainly wouldn't say that interpersonal relations were one of Kevin's best qualities. Rico winked at me while Kevin was looking away, and then I realized that Rico was playing directly on Kevin's inability to resist a challenge even when he knew the results might be painful.

Kevin looked nervously at us, working up the courage for the possible passageway gauntlet. Then he took a deep breath and nodded at me, smiling slightly in his twinkly lopsided way.

"Okay, I'll go," he said, "I can handle this." He hurried outside into the passageway, chopping in the short crisp-step-and-squared-corner choreography that plebes must use to navigate the passageways of Bancroft Hall.

I followed him to the doorway and watched as he turned smartly in the center of the passageway, yelling a loud "Beat Army" in time with the turn. He chopped toward the bulletin board outside the company office, where an upper-class crowd was milling. He inserted himself into the group without any trouble, and I turned to the room and met Rico's gaze.

"O'Reilly's quite a guy," he said chuckling. "He'll do anything to prove his character. He's the ultimate midshipman as far as I'm concerned."

I frowned at Rico. What did he mean by that? O'Reilly was a great guy and a perfect team player, but he would never be a leader of the Company. He was too comical and unsure of himself. Rico stared at me, still smiling. He could sense my skepticism.

"He's the only person in this Company I would trust with my life, Jimbo. That says everything to me."

I smiled and nodded. He had a point. Kevin was like that -- completely trustworthy. I returned to my desk area and began dressing for formation. Rico rose and went to the sink to wash up and shave, while BJ put down his shoes and hurried into the shower.

Kevin was not amused by the time he returned to the room ten minutes later. His ruddy face was flushed with exertion, and his baby-blue eyes flashed briefly with anger. He was an emotional lad, this Kevin. He hadn't yet learned to go with the flow. I could help him there.

"So much for your idea about my ability to deal with people," he announced to Rico only half angrily as he hurriedly threw off his gym clothes and put on his uniform.

"That little trip cost me 100 push-ups."

"Sorry, Kevin," Rico said, toweling his now-perfect face and smiling broadly, not at all repentant. "So what platoon and squad?"

"Two and one," Kevin replied in a mumble, his head buried in his white V-neck undershirt.

"Did you notice who our squad leader is?" I asked. Kevin looked at me strangely, pausing for a moment in buttoning his crisply pressed, white uniform shirt. The stripeless black shoulder-boards stood out starkly in contrast to the bright whiteness of his shirt. As did the black name-tag which read "O'REILLY '71" in yellow letters, and the three colored ribbons Kevin wore above his right uniform pocket. The red and yellow striped one was worn by all active duty personnel for National Defense. The two blue-with-thin-gold-striped ones were for rifle and pistol expertise. Kevin had been a double expert -- as had I -- and his marksmanship ribbons each had a brass "E" placed in their centers.

He obviously questioned why I would ask about squadleaders. He began stepping gingerly into his equally white and stiffly pressed pants, careful not to drag them on the deck.

"No," he answered. "How come?"

"You have to know who you're dealing with, Kevin," I replied patiently.

"We'll find out soon enough," Rico laughed. "There's no sense in worrying needlessly. And besides, we have no control over which squad or which squadleader." Kevin seemed to accept Rico's logic, and he carefully stepped into his white shoes.

I thought about explaining how valuable foreknowledge was; but I decided Rico would just brush off the comment, and Kevin wouldn't understand. BJ Wilson, who had absorbed some of the wiles of the business world from his parents, would understand. That's why I chose BJ for a roommate after I split up from my Plebe Summer "Goon Room" classmates. Of all my classmates in the Company, he had developed a philosophy closest to mine, even though I found him much too ingratiating and eager to please the upper-class. But he was wealthy and probably had powerful family friends, so he was a good person to know for future reference. Neither Kevin nor Rico understood this. I could tell they were surprised by my pairing off with BJ. By now Kevin had tucked his shirt precisely in his pants so that not a wrinkle marred either front or back view. He checked to ensure his bright brass buckle, shirt edge, and fly were exactly in line. He looked up smugly and nodded to me. He looked great in his uniform.

The "Goons" had split up after the summer. Jubal Hunter "Reb" Ramsey and Jeff Polk roomed directly across the wide passageway with Bob Strong and Willy Simpson. That was a good mixture. Bob Strong was a leader and a moderating force who had grown up in the Navy town of San Diego. He would keep them in control and provide the voice of reason when things got too tough. Willy Simpson was a low-keyed South Carolina boy who was quite an accomplished guitar player. It would be hard for Ramsey and Polk to get him involved in any of their heated discussions, and God, did the two of them love to argue.

Reb Ramsey was an opinionated southerner from Alabama, the son of a West Point graduate who had been killed two years ago in a Vietnam helo accident. The name "Jubal" was a shortened form of "Jubilation," an old family name, which Reb sternly informed us we had better not use. Jubal was also a large ex-football-lineman who had a bull-like intensity but who was also extremely fun-loving and incredibly mischievous. However, nicely he could become sullen in an instant.

Jeff Polk, a hardheaded New Englander, was a rebel and a questioner. He considered himself a free-thinker and seemed to be constantly embroiled in the negative aspects of politics, the Academy system, the world situation, or anything that was controversial. I had found much of what he said to be counterproductive and not conducive to good discipline, but he seemed sincere in his views. And like the rest of us, he had come to Annapolis to succeed, and I couldn't fault him for that.

The other ex-"Goon," Tommy Poole, had moved up the passageway with George Abbott, Hank Butkowski, and Tim Butler. I think he figured that staying in the shadows of the super jocks would shelter him from the upcoming turmoil. I wasn't sure that was true. George Abbott and Hank Butkowski were varsity-level athletes -- Abbott in soccer and Butkowski in football. Since those were first season sports, they would miss many Company evolutions and military drills and would be eating at training tables. Their coaches would also demand they remain free from unnecessary hassles, and I think that's what Tommy was counting on. He desperately needed a place where he could retreat and be safe for brief periods from the terror he knew he would suffer during the remainder of the year. The "Tigers" were going to zero in on Tommy for sure.

Poor Tommy was neither a perfect plebe nor a classic midshipman. In an institution that prides itself on its superiority over other academic establishments, that was a cardinal sin. He was short and squat -- but not obese; quite homely -- but not uncomfortably so; extremely unworldly -- but who isn't at 17; and he was geekishly intelligent -- a bonafide genius as a matter of fact. He also looked terrible in his uniform -- an unpardonable sin at Annapolis. To top it off, he had reported aboard in such disgusting physical condition that he drew immediate attention to himself. Tommy was one of the first plebes the second-class had targeted, and he had suffered an extraordinary amount of physical and emotional abuse during the summer training. The squadleaders had made it their public policy to try to run Tommy out of the Academy, stressing repeatedly that he didn't have the right material to be a good naval officer. But I had to hand it to him: Tommy eventually prevailed and survived the summer harassment, although I don't think he really understood the squadleaders' motivation.

I liked Tommy Poole, but I personally thought the system was right about him Tommy didn't really belong at Annapolis. He wasn't the right caliber. He'd never look good in a uniform or be able to mold himself into a leader, and he'd always have trouble fitting in with the rest of the officers, whether on a ship, in a cockpit, or in a contracting office somewhere stateside. But that was a problem the upper-classes had to deal with, and his being in another room meant more time for me to study and prepare myself for the academic year.

I finished dressing before the others, just as the duty plebe room shouted out the five minute chow call from the nearby passageway intersection. We listened, mentally reciting the "rates" along with our classmates.

"New York cut steaks for dinner!" Rico exclaimed when they had finished. "I can't wait!"

"If we even get a chance to eat," offered Kevin as we chopped out the door, squaring our corners one-after-another in precision and heading outside into Tecumseh Court for formation. The summer squadleaders had posted a chart to show where the academic year meal formations would be held, both outside and in, and we had a good idea where to go. Just prior to returning to our room I had scouted Tecumseh Court to familiarize myself with the approximate location. I led the others. I liked doing that.

Tecumseh Court is a wide expanse of flattened stones that serves as the outside centerpiece of the Annapolis campus. On three sides the Court is framed by the gray, five-story granite walls of the midshipmen's dormitory, Bancroft Hall. With its eight sprawling wings are rooms for more than 4,000 students. Bancroft Hall is the largest dormitory building in the world. The centerpiece of Bancroft Hall is the rotunda, a wonderful domed area adjacent to the Academy's Main Office, and where displays depict the historic valor of the Navy and the traditions of the Academy. Wide granite stairs lead from Tecumseh Court to the Bancroft Hall rotunda. On the north side of Tecumseh Court directly opposite the rotunda lies the main Annapolis campus with its quiet red brick herringbone walkways shaded by enormous tulip poplar and oak trees. Facing Bancroft Hall is the famous bronze statue of the Indian *Tecumseh* after whom the Court is named. Under the watchful eye of the old Indian, hundreds of visitors daily view the comings and goings of the Brigade and the pomp and circumstance of meal formations. It is a truly wonderful setting and about the most perfect campus I could imagine. I became excited every time I walked out into T-Court.

"The Company should stand about here," I said indicating the location with a wave of my hand. From a visitor's perspective Twenty-third Company formed up on the right, or starboard, side of T-Court in the center. We were somewhat out of sight, but the fact that we formed up in T-Court at all was special since only 12 of the 36 Companies could fit there. The others were assigned formation locations in various other outdoor areas around the eight wings of Bancroft Hall.

"First Platoon will be about there." I indicated a position toward the center of the Court. "Second Platoon will be about here." I indicated the paving at our feet. "And third platoon farther west." We milled about nervously, waiting for the rest of the Company to arrive. Plebes are expected to be in formation and ready by the time the firsties put in their appearance.

Within a minute a strange midshipman came up to us. By the single slanted gold stripe on his shoulder-boards, I could see he was a youngster. Last year had been his turn to suffer plebedom. He looked at us, and we shifted uneasily on our feet. We didn't have to brace up or yell for upperclassmen in public, and none of us was sure yet how to react to the second-year students. He stared at us for a moment.

"Twenty-third Company?" he finally asked.

"Yes, sir!" I answered for the group.

"Okay," he said, smiling. "I'll give you some pointers." He moved off to the front of us and stared at the walls of Bancroft Hall and the paver lineup in Tecumseh Court. Satisfied, he looked at us. "The Company should line up about here." He waved his arm in a line only slightly different from the one I had indicated. "First platoon, second platoon, third platoon." He indicated positions with a chop of his right hand. Again I was very close. "Let's see," he continued and he moved to inspect the pavers near my feet. About a foot to my right, and slightly in front of me was a faint "V" drawn onto the tile with a magic marker.

"Hey," he said, laughing, "it's still here." He looked up. "Okay, this is what you need to do. Stand where I said by platoon and squad, facing the visitors. Then wait for the rest of the Company to show up. Once everyone is here, you'll line up according to height in your squads. Then "Rock" Stone, the Company Commander, will call us all to attention. Next he'll "dress up" the Company so that you line up precisely with the midshipmen to your right and in front. Once you've reached that final position, memorize it. Count the bricks, study the various aspects of Bancroft Hall, triangulate from the rotunda -- do whatever you need to do. If you're smart, you'll come back here later and mark the spot where you stood so that you can go directly to it each formation. It'll be one less thing to worry about. The Company will form up based mostly on where the plebes are standing when the upper-class come out. If there's too much confusion getting settled, there'll be hell to pay." He looked over our shoulders.

"Looks as if the rest of the upper-class are starting to wander out. Get into your platoons. Hurry up!" he whispered fiercely. We scurried to comply.

Evening meal formation began as a confusing affair of hunt-your-place. I had to move several times as upper-class arrived, estimated their height in relation to others, and inserted themselves brusquely into the squad. Because we were almost identically tall, Rico Guevarra and I stood together near the middle of the squad. Kevin, slightly taller, stood second in line, and BJ was three to the rear. There was no time or interest in devoting any special attention to the plebes during formation, which disappointed me. I was crisply and sparklingly ready. No one introduced themselves either, although a short, very diminutive, first-classman briefly checked our uniforms. He greeted several of the underclass by name but didn't say a word to any plebe.

Two minutes before formation "Rock" Stone moved to the front of the Company and turned toward us. He was more than 6 feet tall, ramrod straight, and well developed. His uniform was perfect -- almost as perfect as mine. His facial features were pleasant, and his head sported the shiny-bald I'm-gonna-be-a-marine look. He seemed incredibly self-assured, and his steely blue eyes twinkled with an arrogant glint and self-superior attitude. I could immediately tell he was proud of the fact that he was in charge. He seemed the perfect midshipman.

"Company, . . . Attention!" We snapped to attention.

"At a close interval, dress right, . . . Dress!" We snapped our heads to starboard, slid our left arms up onto our hips and pointed our elbows precisely at 90 degrees to our bodies. Elbows out, we adjusted position so that we were exactly one bent-elbow's distance from the midshipman to our right and so that the tips of our shoes lined up exactly with the tips of the shoes of our squad mates. After three seconds of this adjustment, Stone barked, "Cover!" We dropped our elbows and snapped our heads frontward. Since I was in the first squad, the command to "Cover" didn't affect me, but behind I could hear minor scufflings as the Platoon adjusted position to line up exactly behind the midshipmen in front.

Stone looked us over for a moment, grunted noncommittally, then turned toward T-Court. Soon the Brigade Commander called the brigade to attention in a loud voice and ordered us to march off to chow to the beat of a single drummer who stood at the top of the rotunda steps. We marched toward the center of the Court, then turned and marched up the wide side ramp into the rotunda. We crossed the rotunda, descended the rear stairs, and entered the Mess Hall, heading for our company eating area.

Now that the entire Brigade had assembled, I had my first opportunity to see the Mess Hall as it filled with midshipmen. Midshipmen poured inside from all directions. It was an impressive sight. The Annapolis Mess Hall is also said to be the largest in the world. It is an enormous T-shaped affair that allows four thousand people to eat simultaneously. Our Company area had changed from the Plebe Summer position in the leg of the "T" to one near the far end of the left arm.

We followed Stone as he turned starboard when we reached the center of the "T" and headed in loose formations down the starboard arm. The Company sat at tables number 261 to 271 out of what must have been 350 tables altogether. Each squad had a separate 12-man table assigned. The leader of our squad went immediately to Table 264, which extended outward from the wall. He selected a seat facing the center aisle. Kevin automatically chose the seat to his right. I moved to a position behind the left seat and did the same. I winked quickly at Kevin, who was very nervous, and he acknowledged me with a brief nod.

Most of the squads had two first-classmen, and the non-squadleader in our squad sat in the seat next to mine. Without even an "excuse me," he nudged me out of the way as he passed. I could see Kevin staring wide-eyed at the new arrival. He didn't look too happy. Of course I couldn't see the surly newcomer because I was constrained by being braced up and by keeping my eyes in the boat.

Bracing is a painful posture. To brace a plebe stands or sits rigidly at attention and pulls his chin in as far as possible against his neck, while at the same time keeping his head vertical. The more "chins" that show during this process the better. Plebes "brace up" out of their rooms or in the presence of any upper-classman or officer. Thankfully bracing is not permitted outside the confines of Bancroft Hall. Being somewhat thin, I could manage only three folds of skin when my chin crushed itself against my neck. Kevin matched my three, and Rico, who didn't really strain, could produce two. Jubal Ramsey could squash out six chins on his massive neck, and he was the Company record holder. Second-class midshipmen visited the "Goon Room" from other Companies during the summer to see Reb's six chins.

*Eyes-in-the-boat*is another Academy-specific phenomenon. Whenever a plebe is braced, he must not look anywhere but directly ahead. I don't know why we had to practice this restriction, but it certainly improved my peripheral vision. A plebe caught with wandering eyes is punished.

I stared straight across the table, focusing on the infinity just above the head of the unknown youngster who stared at me calmly in return with a slight smile on his ugly puss. He knew exactly what was in store for me during the upcoming academic year because he had survived an identical indoctrination. As a youngster he had graduated from the bracing and eyes-in-the-boating, and he would never have to eat a "square meal" again either. "Square meals" upset me more than anything else.

Square meals are braced, eyes-in-the-boat affairs in which a plebe sits on the last three inches of his chair with his back rigidly straight. To eat a single minuscule bit of food, a plebe must raise fork or spoon vertically until it is on the same level as his mouth, then move the food horizontally into his eager maw. He then returns the fork or spoon to the plate by the same right angle, time-consuming route.

And God help the plebe who takes more than a tiny bite at a time, because the other mealtime rule is *Three-chews-and-a-swallow*. Whatever a plebe puts into his mouth had better get into his stomach pretty darn quick in case someone asks a question. Sadistic upper-class actually counted jaw movements to ensure plebes don't waste any precious harassment time in such silly pursuits as eating properly.

Plebes also kept upper-class plates and glasses full and served themselves and ate last. And whenever someone needed seconds, plebes ensured the food got there quickly. Sounds pretty gruesome, huh? It was. Plebe year meals were the least enjoyable times of my entire life. Most plebes lost weight for lack of food and because of the incredible amounts of energy expended waiting on everyone else and playing mind games with the upper-class. I was constantly hungry Plebe Year. That's one of the prices of admission into a service academy. It's a rite of passage into the elite ranks of the officer corps.

However, this evening's meal was a surprisingly relaxed affair. Upper-class attention focused more on classmates than on plebes, and the talk centered on exotic ports, fascinating sights, and female companionship. At the head of the table, Kevin and I orchestrated food service for the first-class -- in between microbites. Rico and BJ, at the foot of the table, did likewise for the second-class. We passed food, ordered seconds, and filled glasses with plebe-like haste and efficiency, and no one complained or asked us any rates. I almost ate my fill -- even if it was one culinary molecule at a time.

Back in our room, we hurriedly undressed and put on gym gear in preparation for whatever might come. This was the beginning of *Hell Night,* the dreaded evening of mischief when upper-class introduced themselves to their new plebes in various nefarious ways. It was a night we had all been dreading, and I could sense the discomfort in the atmosphere of the room, particularly from Kevin, who worried about everything.

Five minutes later, after I had begun sorting and labeling my notebook dividers by subjects, a strange plebe chopped into our doorway. He was still in his white uniform.

"Excuse me," he announced in a troubled voice. "Which one of you is Kevin O'Reilly?" I looked up, confused. Plebes were not generally allowed to visit other Companies, so the visit was decidedly unusual. The plebe didn't seem happy either, and I could sense something was wrong. I started to rise just as Kevin turned and walked toward the stranger.

"I am," he replied with a smile. "What can I do for you?"

"You can stay away from my sister!" the plebe said loudly. "She told me about last night. She's only 16 years old you know?"

Kevin stammered and shifted uncomfortably on his feet. His face and neck turned instantly red, and he focused on the deck. He started to speak.

"Listen . . . ," he began, but the strange plebe swung his right fist from down near his waist and struck unsuspecting Kevin squarely in the mouth. Kevin flew backward and fell like a stone onto the hard tile deck. His head struck with a dull thud. The plebe sneered at the fallen form, turned quickly, and chopped away.

Rico ran to the doorway, intending to follow and confront the classmate, but the passageway was alive with upper-class. In their own gaiety and confusion no one had noticed Kevin's predicament. Rico hesitated too long to give effective pursuit. I moved toward Kevin. BJ Wilson sat rigidly at his desk, far too shocked at what had just happened to be of any assistance to Kevin. His handsome mouth hung widely open, and his eyes had a startled appearance. I'll bet he never saw anything like that at any of his private schools. I knelt beside Kevin just as he lifted himself groggily from the floor and perched on his elbows. He looked like hell.

I stared at poor Kevin. His mouth was rapidly filling with blood, his lower lip was split on the left side, and I could see him probing for loose teeth with his tongue. The blow had also burst his tear ducts, and his eyes were wet and reddened. He shook his head to clear his thoughts.

"Are you okay, Kevin," I asked? He tried to answer but only mumbled something incoherent. He struggled to sit up. Rico knelt next to him on the other side and gripped his arm, supporting him, while I went to the sink to get a washcloth from the rack. I soaked it in cold water for a moment and brought it to Kevin. He took it and wiped his face. BJ still stared at us. Rico and I helped Kevin to his feet, and he went to the sink where he spit blood into the bowl, splashing the entire area, including the mirror, with bright red dots.

Kevin rinsed his mouth -- thoroughly but painfully -- while Rico and I looked at each other. I raised my eyebrows questioningly at Rico and he shrugged.

"Do you want us to help you to sick bay, Kevin," I asked? Kevin became angry at that question. He turned on us.

"Naaaaaa, Ah don won ta goh ta sik bay!" he mumbled loudly and mostly incoherently. Rico and I quickly jumped back to avoid the flecks of bloody spit that were spraying from his mangled mouth in all directions along with the incoherent words. Rico smiled at the spectacle and began to laugh almost uncontrollably. I looked at Rico as if he were insane.

"Sixteen, huh?" Rico said. "Christ O'Reilly, you really run the gamut, don't you? Do you know any women your own age?" I was confused. This was some private joke between Rico and Kevin. After a few seconds of glaring Kevin apparently saw Rico's point, and tried to smile but he was obviously in pain. Looking at Kevin's now-swelling lips and seeing the twinkle in his red eyes, I suddenly also saw humor in what had happened. I began to laugh with Rico. I looked over at BJ, but he still didn't comprehend.

We helped Kevin stagger to his desk and sit gingerly. He used the washcloth to blot and swab his wounds. I could see that his mouth hurt, but I could also see that he was under control. Kevin O'Reilly was nothing if not a trooper. I returned to my chair and tried to look sympathetically at Kevin. What the hell did he do to that girl anyway? Rico Guevarra continued chuckling. He enjoyed this kind of thing. For a moment I envied the closeness between the two of them. We never achieved that sort of bonding in the Goon Room.

"Christ, Kevin," I said after a moment. "What next?"

I hadn't finished that question when a strange upper-classman entered the room.

"Attention on deck!" I yelled, and we snapped to attention and braced. Almost by cruel coincidence, he walked directly to Kevin's desk and put a pair of black shoes down in front of Kevin.

"Okay, Howdy Doody," he said. "I need these shoes looking good before morning meal." With that he turned and departed.

I was instantly irked. We weren't servants, and personal favors were strictly forbidden by the rules. It was bad enough being a plebe and coping with the usual routine of plebe rates. I sighed as I unbraced and slouched into my chair dejectedly. Rico was still smiling.

"I guess now we know that the Brigade's back," he said.

"Yea we dah," Kevin said from across the room, still smiling despite his physical impairment.

By 2000 we had prepared for the upcoming day and had just begun began to relax when the parade started, almost as if heralded by some unheard signal. First two, then three more, then an additional four midshipmen entered our room. It seemed suddenly crowded and I could see from Kevin's troubled face that he was dreading whatever came next.

"Attention on deck!" I yelled, and we braced.

"Carry-on!" the lead-most stranger said as he reached the center of the room. We relaxed as the crowd grew. Soon 12 midshipmen of various sizes and shapes stood in the room with us. I stepped forward.

"Midshipman Fourth-class Merritt, sir," I said in the standard greeting.

I now recognized the stranger as the youngster who had instructed us on the formation set-up. He was a tall, dark, thin individual who seemed extremely friendly and immediately likable. He smiled at me and his eyes danced with merriment.

"Merritt, huh? Great! I'm Jack Collins." He stuck out his hand in greeting. I hesitated for an instant. "Go ahead," he said. "I don't bite!" I reached out quickly and shook his hand, thereby accepting a "spoon" from my first upper-class. Jack and I were now on a first name, no brace-up, basis. We were almost equals. I smiled.

"My name's Jim," I said.

Jack turned toward the others.

"These are some of my classmates," he said, and a rash of introductions and hand shaking began. Soon we had been spooned by every one of the 12.

"We asked Maxie which room would be the best to start with," Jack continued, referring to one of our second-class squadleaders, Mike "Maxie" Maxwell, "and he suggested this one. He said you were the best group of plebes he had seen all summer. So we decided to start spooning here." We were the best, huh? That was encouraging. I noticed Jack staring at Kevin, and in particular his now-enormously-swelled-up mouth.

Jack then turned toward one of his classmates.

"Eddie Christensen here is in your squad," he said indicating the youngster who had sat across from me during dinner. Eddie smiled that same "I-know-something-you-don't-know" smile. "He'll help you all he can to adjust to the "Tigers.'"

While he was talking, Jack continued to stare at Kevin from across the room. He frowned.

"What happened to you, anyway?" he finally asked. "You weren't messed up like that at evening formation."

"Rin intah a dor," Kevin said, his mouth still hurting. Jack didn't understand. He looked at me. I chuckled.

"Kevin said he ran into a door," I translated. Jack laughed somewhat suspiciously as he looked from roommate to roommate.

"Door, huh?" I could tell he didn't believe O'Reilly. "Probably W. T. Door," he said laughing and referring to the fictional generic midshipman the Academy used as an example on all its forms. Collins probably decided we had a fist fight and was trying to decide which one of us did the damage to Kevin's face. He stared the longest at Rico.

Rico smiled back.

"Don't look at me," he said, shrugging and indicating his chest with his hands. "I couldn't be a door because I don't have the knobs for it."

"No matter," Jack replied, laughing further. "What happens between you and the doors is your own business." He paused. "Any of you have any questions about the academic year?" he asked.

"Yes," I said. "Tell me everything you can about our squad leader and the second-class."

"Good question," Jack replied. "Have a seat." We sat at our desks while the youngsters arranged themselves around the room. Rico offered to let several sit on his bed -- an act strictly forbidden to plebes. O'Reilly did the same. I hesitated. I had worked hard to achieve a tight smooth finish on my covers, and I felt that my rack's pristine and unruffled condition announced boldly that I was an up-and-comer. But this was a question of priorities and necessity. Several youngsters looked at me questioningly.

"Go ahead," I said, smiling broadly, "Please. Sit."

When everyone was comfortable, Jack continued.

"In a way you're both lucky and unlucky," he started. "Your squad-leader is Henry Brandis. He's not so bad for a "Tiger" -- so long as you perform. But if you screw up, he'll jump right down your throat. It's the other firstie you have to really watch. That's "Mugsy" McGinley. He's a certifiable crazy asshole. He's also a Brigade middleweight boxing champion. What's so weird about him is that he's not a "sweater" like most of the other "Tigers." He doesn't keep his uniform neat. His room's a mess. He always needs a shave. And he ridicules the Academy system every chance he gets. But he's hell on plebes if he doesn't like them. He gets a sadistic satisfaction out of running them till they drop. Whenever you "comearound" to him, pray for death if he's made you a target. He'll also offer an open challenge to each of you to take him on in the ring. If you beat him, he'll spoon you. But don't take him up on that. You won't beat him. He's an absolute animal, and he just keeps coming at his opponents until he wears them down and pounds them into jelly."

"I'll bet Kevin could take him," Rico offered. He seemed perfectly serious. Kevin's mouth fell open, revealing a bloody mess inside. He stared at Rico, incredulously. Rico looked at him. "You could do it, Kevin. I'm sure of it."

No one spoke for a moment; then Kevin shook his head.

"Yur crzy, Rico," he said.

"You could do it, Kevin," Rico repeated. "You're the redheaded wondermid." Kevin continued to shake his head in disbelief, but I could see an idea forming in that Irish brain. Maybe he thought he could do it. Then again maybe the evening's punch loosened something in his thick Irish skull.

"Okay," Jack continued, snapping the spell. "Your second-class are Joe Mahoney and Billy Bob Clanton. They're not so bad, although I wouldn't trust Mahoney for a minute. Billy Bob's a good guy though, even if he is a little bit dense. Just keep the food flowing to Mugsy and don't make fools of yourselves, and everything will be fine the first set. Any other questions?"

"Ys," asked Kevin, flexing his arms and smiling slightly despite pain. "How tuff iss Mugs agin?" I could tell he was only joking. Most of the others could too. Everyone laughed.

"All right, Kevin!" Rico said enthusiastically. "Go for it!"

The youngsters soon left the room and headed across the passageway to spoon Room 4025. Within five minutes another group of youngsters entered and spooned us. We were feeling pretty good. This *Hell Night* stuff wasn't so bad after all. Then Henry Brandis and Mugsy McGinley entered. We snapped to an immediate braced-up attention.

Brandis and McGinley calmly looked each of us over for several seconds. They both wore Academy-issue bathrobes with T-shirts and gym shorts underneath. Henry Brandis was a very short, extremely thin individual who had an unusually high forehead and enormous ears which stuck out from his head like pink signal flags. His close-cropped brown hair actually exaggerated the size of his aural appendages. Brandis, we later found out later was a Dean's List scholar who was presently being considered for a Rhodes Scholarship. His voice was soft, and his eyes were a pale, listless blue.

Mugsy McGinley was a total contrast to Brandis. He was very dark complexioned, and swarthy. Never once in the year did I ever see him when it didn't appear that he needed a shave -- badly. His white T-shirt was torn raggedly under one arm, and his shorts were ripped in the crotch area so that as he walked I could see a dark, hairy thatch of hair and an occasional glimpse of something else peeking out. I quickly averted my glance, not wanting to imagine what lurked in the darkest places inside those grubby shorts.

Mugsy's body was thickly muscled and he had the coarsest crop of black body hair I had ever seen. Even the areas on his shoulders and back were completely covered with hair. It was almost comical to see how the black forest on his body ended so abruptly where it was shaved just three inches from the neck of his T-shirt. It looked as if a giant ugly troll was peering out of the Schwartzwald looking for victims to devour. In keeping with the rest of his persona, Mugsy's eyes were deep black; and his nose, which had obviously been broken several times, was squashed against his face at an odd angle. He didn't look anything like my picture of a midshipman, but, boy, would he fit the hit-man stereotype perfectly.

Brandis asked us to introduce ourselves, and we did each in turn. McGinley looked us over closely as we yelled.

As luck would have it, McGinley chose to view O'Reilly last. He stared closely at Kevin's split lip for a moment and shook his head. Then he reached out and gripped the lower lip, pulling it back to view the gums and teeth. Kevin winced.

"Hurt?" McGinley asked with feigned concern.

"Na sr," Kevin mumbled. McGinley stared into Kevin's mouth for another moment then released the lip and wiped his hand on Kevin's shirt.

"You'll be okay," he said. "I've had about a thousand of those in my career. You shoulda ducked." He laughed loudly, then noticed the worn black shoes sitting near Kevin's desk. He stared.

"These yours?" he asked.

"Na, sr," Kevin answered.

"Whose are they?" he asked.

"I'll fnd out, sr," Kevin replied, invoking the standard reply for ignorance.

"Don't know, huh?"

"Na, sr."

"Well, when he comes to retrieve them, you tell him to come see me first. Got that?"

"Ys, sr," Kevin answered.

"Okay, plebes," Brandis began, stealing the stage from McGinley, "we'll begin a regular series of morning comearounds tomorrow at 0630. I'll run you in the passageway for about 15 minutes. That'll give you plenty of time to shower and be ready for 0700 breakfast formation. Wear gym gear, and don't be late. If you do fine we'll keep it to a tough fifteen minutes, if not, we'll meet earlier and make it tougher. Questions?" On one spoke.

"Good," Brandis said. "See you tomorrow." They turned to depart and as they headed out the door Mugsy turned to Kevin and smiled sadistically. "Don't forget," he said. "Send him to me."

After they had gone, Kevin turned to Rico. Rico stared at him with raised eyebrows.

"Na dam wy!" Kevin muttered emphatically. So much for the big fight.

Immediately after the first-class departed, two unfamiliar midshipmen arrived. We braced up again and waited as they sized us up. I could sense BJ and Kevin's exasperation. This visitation was getting old.

"You!" one of them said, pointing to BJ. "Go to room 4033. Ask for Shithead Shantz. Tell him he blows. Then run your ass back here. Got that?"

"Yes, sir! Shithead Shantz in Room 4033," BJ replied, smiling. He chopped from the room. We remained braced.

When BJ returned the same midshipman said. "Okay. Who's the push-up champion of the room?" We looked at each other for a moment, then Kevin mumbled.

"Rico, sir!" nodding toward Guevarra.

"How many?" the upper-class asked.

"A hundred, sir!" Rico answered. The upper-class wasn't particularly impressed by this, and frankly neither was I. He shook his head, shrugged and departed. Hell, I could do 100, if perfection didn't count for the last few. Kevin looked at Rico.

"A hundred?" he asked.

"I didn't want to put myself on the spot," Rico answered. Kevin looked at me.

"I personally saw Rico do 200 in a row, and he wasn't particularly straining." Now 200 *was* impressive, even for a plebe.

Thirty minutes before lights out Jubal Ramsey boldly chopped across the passageway into our room. He was smiling broadly, obviously pleased with something. "Hey, Reb!" I said. "What's up?"

He looked around the room, still smiling smugly.

"Guess what just happened to me, ya'll?" he asked in his thick Alabama accent.

"Wht?" Kevin asked in return, trying to smile but wincing when his thickened lips expanded. Reb began to speak, then noticed for the first time Kevin's condition.

"What happened he'ah?" he asked.

"Kevin's been giving lessons in how to get along with our classmates," offered Rico.

"Did ya'll win?" Reb asked laughing.

"Kevin didn't even know he was in a fight until it was all over," added Rico with a chuckle. Kevin tried to laugh at this but his lip prevented more than a cursory smile.

Reb stared at Kevin for a moment, smiling to himself. Finally he shook his head and returned to the subject of his visit.

"Ah was spooned!" he said proudly.

"Big deal!" Rico returned. "About 30 nobody youngsters just spooned us too."

"Not by a youngster," said Reb with a chuckle. "Ah was spooned by none other than the Tommy Battle himself." Tommy Battle had been one of our hard-as-nails proto-Marine squadleaders this past summer. The thought of him being friends with anyone -- much less with a plebe -- was a shock.

"No sht?" Kevin exclaimed. "Wht fr?"

Jubal was mildly taken aback. "Because he was so impressed with my leadership qualities and Marine Corps potential," he said.

"More likely those famous six chins of yours," said Rico. Then changing the subject quickly, Rico continued.

"Okay, Jubal. You got spooned by a living legend; that's wonderful. But I've got to ask you about something else far more important. I could see that she had the hots for Kevin, but what about fixing me up with your sister Betty June anyway?" Everybody paused, trying to gauge whether Rico was serious. Reb was a big guy, but his sister, who we had met just last evening at a group dinner, was enormous -- very cute and incredibly sweet in a southern way but enormous nonetheless, and certainly not Rico's type.

Jubal laughed.

"I noticed your date," he said. "My sister's not your type, and I wouldn't trust you within 10 feet of her. But Kevin, on the other hand . . . " he said facing O'Reilly. "She said you were as cute as a little o'l puppy dog and she just wanted to hug you to death." I tried to imagine Becky's massive arms around poor Kevin, and I realized that she might well be able to live up that promise. Kevin paused, torn between not wanting to hurt a classmate's feelings and not wanting to commit to anything.

Finally he asked Jubal in a very serious if somewhat garbled manner.

"How old *is* yr sistr, Reb?"

"Eighteen."

Kevin thought for a minute. "Sorry. Too old fah me." Those of us who had witnessed Kevin's recent confrontation with the unknown brother understood his question. We laughed. Even BJ Wilson got *that* joke.

Jubal stared at us for a second through squinted eyes trying to decide if he had been had or if his sister's southern honor had somehow been besmirched.

"It's a long story, Jubal," I said, still laughing. "I'll explain all about it tomorrow on the way to class." Jubal and I had Psychology 101 together first period, so we could discuss our impressions of the first evening with the Brigade.

"Well, . . . okay," Jubal said. "See you guys at comearound in the passageway tomorrow morning." With that he turned and chopped across to his room. I looked at my watch. "It's almost time for lights out," I announced. "We should probably all get a good night's sleep. Tomorrow will be a long day." BJ Wilson nodded and immediately put down this letter tablet. He stood, stretched, and went to the sink to wash up. Kevin looked around the room for a moment, and went to the window. He stared outside for a long time while BJ busily and noisily brushed his teeth. Finally Kevin drew himself in from the humid night air and looked at me strangely.

"I'm really glad we're not up on the third wing, fourth deck anymore," he said, speaking slowly so that his words came out pretty close to normally. "I was almost afraid to look outside my window for fear I would see Ronald sitting out there in the dark. But it's kind of a shame there's no ledge to crawl out onto." He didn't wait for a reply. Instead he went to the door, checked the passageway, and chopped quickly toward the communal heads. Kevin was a very complicated guy.

Rico stood up slowly and walked to the shower. He reached inside and turned the water on. Then, just as BJ began his incredibly noisy gargle, Rico pinched him on the butt, causing BJ to cough and spit mouthwash all over the sink area and mirror.

"What the hell?" BJ sputtered, spinning around and staring wide-eyed at Rico's reflection in the mirror. "Why'd you *do* that?"

Rico looked at BJ seriously.

"Sorry, BJ. I couldn't help it. You've got the cutest little ass I've ever seen."

BJ was speechless for a moment.

"Well," he said indignantly. "Don't do that again." Rico didn't acknowledge BJ, however. Instead he dropped his shorts to the deck, took off his shirt, smiled at us, and stepped into the shower. I remembered Kevin's comment during the summer that a certain part of Rico was enormous, and I could see what he meant. Rico Guevarra was certainly larger than average -- and Rico obviously knew it.

Before he closed the curtain, Rico looked at BJ sternly.

"Don't you dare peek at me while I'm in the shower," he said with mock seriousness. BJ had no reply, and Rico began to draw the curtain. "Remember," he repeated. "No peeking!" He closed the curtain with a flourish. Soon we could hear loud Spanish singing echoing from the shower stall. I didn't recognize the song, even though I had heard a great deal of Hispanic music during my life in Amarillo.

BJ looked at me.

"He's quite a character," he said, still a little uncertain about what had just happened. I nodded agreement.

Kevin returned while Rico was still singing.

"Everything come out okay?" I asked him.

"Yeah," he replied, wincing and smiling his toothy grin at me, He paused to listen to Rico croon. The shower water stopped, and Rico continued humming.

"He doesn't sound half bad," Kevin said, trying hard to speak normally. "You know, the Academy Glee Club has tryouts scheduled for Sunday afternoon. I think I'll give it a shot. I heard that being in the Glee Club is almost as good as being on a sports team. You get lots of time away from the Company, there are travel opportunities, and you get to mingle with outsiders -- some of whom are young and female. Besides, I have a good voice."

"O'Reilly," said Rico as he emerged from the shower, "your voice sucks. You have as much chance of making the Glee Club as I have of taking Merritt's Brigade Commander job away from him first-class year."

Brigade Commander?

"How did . . . ?" I began, but Rico just stared at me with a give-me-a-break look. Was I that obvious?

Kevin shook his head sadly.

"Puerto Ricans have no musical appreciation," he said to no one in particular. "But luckily for me the Glee Club doesn't sing cucaracha music. This is serious vocal art, and I have a voice like an angel. Ask my mother."

"You have a voice like an untuned diesel engine," said Rico. "You'll be lucky if the Choir Director doesn't give you a comearound just for having the nerve to try out."

"The Choir Director is some sweet old matron lady who's always smiling and offering the midshipmen cookies and lemonade," said Kevin smugly.

"She won't be smiling once you open that mouth," Rico observed.

"We'll see, Rico."

"Yeah we will."

BJ and I had been chuckling during this good natured exchange. Rico and Kevin seemed to enjoy putting on a show for everybody else.

I went to the sink to wash up for bed. BJ and Rico had already climbed into their racks by the time I finished. Kevin was at the window again, staring into the dark night. I checked my watch again.

"Two minutes to lights-out, Kevin."

He turned toward me. "Thanks, Jim. I was waiting for you to finish." I climbed into bed as he went about his own sleep preparations. I watched him as he gingerly brushed his teeth and rinsed his gums. I could tell his mouth was very sore. He saw me watching in the mirror reflection and smiled, shaking his head at his predicament. Then he turned out the room lights and climbed into his own rack. I liked the layout of this plebe room better than the one we occupied plebe summer. It was large enough to fit four single beds on the deck -- two on each side of the room -- rather than forcing us to adapt to the nuisance of bunk beds. There wasn't much room between the racks, but I didn't expect that BJ and I would be playing too much kneesies anyway. What Kevin and Rico did was between them.

"Did you set your alarm?" Kevin asked from across the dark room.

"No sweat, Kevin. It's all taken care of. We'll rise and shine at 0530."

"You know what, Jim?" Kevin asked.

"What's that?"

"I hate comearounds!"

"Me too, Kevin, but remember that what doesn't kill you can only make you stronger."

"Yeah? Well the problem is that sometimes death seems preferable to bear crawls."

"Christ, I hope you didn't say that to Steinway!" said Rico. I thought he had already fallen asleep. Kevin groaned.

We were quiet for several minutes and I had just begun drifting off to sleep when Kevin whispered, "Poor Ronald." No other sounds disturbed me that night.

CHAPTER 2

FIRST DAY

Comearound the next morning started exactly on time. We had heard that Midshipman first-class Brandis was a stickler for precision, and I had no intention of being late. Rico and Kevin rose without any trouble at 0530 when my alarm went off. I was afraid I would have trouble with them in the mornings They tended to sleep to the last second during the summer, and it made me nervous if everyone wasn't up and ready well ahead of time. While we dressed, we read the morning paper aloud to each other and studied our "rates" for the day. That meant memorizing the menus for the three meals; the names and jobs of the watch officers; the number of days remaining before Thanksgiving vacation, the Army-Navy football game, Christmas vacation, and first-class graduation; and the movies playing out in town. It sounds like a lot of information, and I remembered how impressed my parents had been when I recited my "rates" for them during Parents' Weekend. Actually the memorization was easy once you trained your mind to lock onto the right facts.

Brandis' room was around a corner from the main Company passageway in a narrow, secondary passageway. No other first-class had rooms nearby, so things were quiet as we waited outside braced against the bulkhead. Reveille had gone off at 0600 as we studied rates, and I could hear movement inside Brandis's and other rooms. Someone was up and about.

At exactly 0630 the door opened, and a groggy Henry Brandis stepped outside. He was bare footed and his B-robe sat haphazardly across his shoulders like a cape. He hadn't washed, and the hair on the right side of his head stuck up at an odd angle. He yawned and wiped sleep from his eyes as he looked us over. Then he noticed our careful scrutiny and he laughed.

"Okay," he said, chuckling. "I'm obviously not a morning person, but I don't need to be to run plebes." He stretched. "I want you to take a fast lap around the wing following the inside passageway. Stay in the Company area, and when you return give me 20 push-ups . . . Ready, go!" We sprinted down the passageway as a unit, Kevin slightly to the front.

"Slow up, Kevin!" Rico whispered fiercely as we turned the first corner. "He didn't say this was a race, just a fast lap. Let's don't show him too much too quickly." I didn't exactly agree with that logic. I thought we should go all out every time we ran. But Kevin accepted Rico's plan, and soon he slowed us to a moderately fast run rather than an out-and-out sprint. I decided not to argue. I had learned painfully several times during the summer that I could not hope to compete against Kevin the redheaded wonder-mid in a sprint. Even in medium distance runs he could hold his own. I let Kevin take the lead on this as we headed around a corner into the commotion of the main passageway.

We raced single-file down the center of the wide main passageway, passing other groups of plebes at comearound. The main company area was clogged with classmates running, exercising, and yelling responses. Several times we had to sidestep fellow plebes to avoid collisions. Passing the Company Office, I saw Midshipman First-class Stone observing several plebes, one of whom was the poor, Tommy Poole. Stone stood calmly nearby, muscular arms folded across his broad chest, a sneer on his ruggedly handsome face, and his crew cut bristling menacingly as Tommy and Tim Butler strained to pump out push-ups. Dale Micklewski was bent over the hapless pair, yelling words of discouragement.

"Do you know why you're in this particular squad, misters Poole and Butler?" Micklewski yelled as we neared.

"No, sir!" Tommy yelled.

"Because I'm the only one around here who can make your life so miserable that you'll quit, that's why! I'm gonna run your sissy butts out of here and be a hero for doing it. You are both miserable, disgusting excuses for . . . " By that time we had passed out of earshot and headed around the third corner. Why didn't Poole just quit? I didn't understand what kept him here.

But compassionate thoughts have no place during comearounds. Survival is of the utmost importance. Soon I had forgotten completely about Tommy, and we turned the final corner and sprinted to the door of Brandis' room. Kevin picked up the speed at the end to make the run seem more stressful than it was, and both he and Rico wheezed unnecessarily after the running ended. Brandis was inside when we arrived, which seemed initially puzzling. In fact the entire passageway was without life or sound. We tromped to a halt and looked at each other briefly. Shrugging, I dropped to the deck, and the others followed suit. We yelled out our push-up count simultaneously.

Within ten seconds Brandis pushed the door hurriedly open and came outside, plainly agitated.

"Quiet for Christ-sake!" he said fiercely. "Do you want to wake up Mugsy? Believe me, you won't like it if he gets pissed. In this passageway everything you do in the morning will be done quietly. Is that understood?"

"Yes, sir!" I whispered for the group. No one was supposed to be asleep after reveille, so this fact about McGinley's being a slug-a-bed was a revelation.

Brandis seemed satisfied.

"Okay," he said. "On your feet! Another lap. Go!"

"This is too easy!" Rico said after we had turned the first corner. "Evening comearounds must be the pits."

As we turned the corner into the main area, I could see Tommy Poole lying on his back, arms and legs extended straight in the air in a posture suspiciously similar to the forbidden "Dead Horse" position. Tim Butler braced bent-kneed against the bulkhead, arms extended his back and head firmly planted against the wall. He looked as if he were sitting without benefit of a chair, and I could see considerable strain on his face. The smaller of the two squadleaders did leisurely push-ups in a position between Tim and Tommy while Micklewski continued to yell like a maniac. Stone pointedly faced away from this "illegal" activity. He had a faraway, almost dreamy expression on his face, and looked like a field general surveying the troops. As we neared, I could see that Tommy's arms were shaking and his legs had begun to droop.

"Keep those arms and legs up, you fat fart!" Micklewski yelled in Tommy's ear as we passed.

Stone noticed us and yelled, "Plebes halt!" We stopped immediately, our rubber-soled tennis shoes screeching loudly, and waited rigidly. Stone approached with an arrogant, swaggering gait. "You guys are Tigers aren't you?" he asked.

"Yes, sir!" we yelled in unison.

"Why are you just taking laps? Who's your squadleader?"

"Midshipman First-class Brandis, sir!" I answered for the group.

"Why aren't you over at his room? Who's supervising your activity?" Stone seemed upset. I guess we were having too much "fun" and needed a squadleader to direct it personally.

Before I could answer with an "I'll-find-out-sir," Micklewski looked up.

"Mugsy's the reason, Rock," he said. Stone paused in his anger sufficiently to consider the circumstances, then nodded.

"Continue," he said, waving us away. Mugsy must carry some weight around here for Stone to be afraid to confront him.

We halted outside Brandis' room and did our pushups. Henry stuck his head outside for an instant.

"One more time. After your push-ups return to your room and get ready for chow." We ran. Wow! I hoped that every morning comearound was going to be as easy.

Rapid uniform changing is an almost constant aspect of life at Annapolis. There are a thousand confusing uniform variations. At 0630 we had waited in the passageway outside Henry Brandis' room in gym gear -- blue shorts with gold stripes along the side, white T-shirt with the Academy seal emblazoned over the heart, white socks with blue and gold stripes, and white, ill-fitting tennis shoes. We ran our laps, did our 60 push-ups, returned to the room, showered, changed into "White Works," and made it to morning formation by 0655.

"White Works" is a loose white jumper-style uniform with a wide, open collar in front and a flap that hangs midway down the back of the jumper top. It looks similar to the classic navy enlisted uniform. The matching pants are button-flied, string wasted, and bell-bottomed for easy removal during gym period or if you happen to fall overboard during a seamanship exercise in the Severn River. White Works "Alpha" includes a black, navy-style neckerchief with a perfectly sculpted rectangular knot hanging exactly at sternum level, and with tapered and equally long ends reaching precisely to the waist. Black shoes, a traditional navy black-brimmed combination cap, and white underthings round out the ensemble.

To confuse the uniform picture -- something the Academy staff must love to do and something that always seemed a mockery of the word "uniform" -- morning formations during warm weather specified a modified version of White Works without the neckerchief. This was White Works "Charlie." But midshipmen headed to morning gym class could forgo the combination cap for a round navy cloth "Dixie Cup," -- which at Annapolis has deep blue top trim -- and wear gym gear, including tennis shoes, under the whites. That was White Works "Bravo." There were also White Works "Delta" and "Echo" variations, which I won't attempt to describe. Rico and Kevin wore "Bravo" that first morning. BJ and I wore the "Charlie" version.

Morning formations were always grumpy affairs. The first-class were generally tired and surly, the under-class usually uninterested, and the plebes exhausted and flushed from comearounds. Uniform inspections almost never happened; at least that's the word we had from the youngsters. However, I could hear loud comments from Dale Micklewski concerning Tommy's sloppy appearance. I had roomed with Tommy during the summer, and I knew that he usually devoted a great deal of time to looking proper, and did a pretty fair job of it. Although I admit, he still fell short of the sharp midshipman's appearance most plebes could achieve.

While I waited in ranks for Stone to command us to attention, Mugsy passed in front of me headed for his usual place at the second position in the line. Instead of continuing directly to his spot, he stopped in front of O'Reilly, and I listened surreptitiously as he leaned in close to Kevin. I also noticed that Mugsy's uniform was wrinkled and unkempt, his cap was cocked at an odd angle on his head, and he hadn't shaved. I'll bet he hadn't brushed his teeth either, something Kevin must hate right about now.

"You didn't come to me yet with the name of your shoeshine visitor," he said to Kevin.

"No, sir. Whoever it was must have come by while we were out at comearound and picked up the shoes."

"Did you shine them?"

"Yes, sir."

"Why the piss did you do that?" Mugsy grumbled loudly. Mugsy was plainly unhappy.

"Sir, I wasn't sure what you wanted, so I decided to play it safe."

"Safe, huh? What's your name anyway?" Mugsy asked.

"Midshipman Fourth-class O'Reilly! Sir!"

"O'Reilly, you just screwed up, and I don't like screw-ups. Do you understand that?"

"Yes, sir!"

"Okay, O'Reilly. I'll be watching for you from now on."

I could hear Kevin groan from my position several men to the rear. Luckily Mugsy didn't seem to notice. Rico, who stood next to me, quietly chuckled at Kevin's predicament. Poor Kevin wasn't the take-charge type. He didn't like attention and avoided most kinds of notoriety like the plague. Being the recipient of special notice from a character like Mugsy would really upset him. I guess I wouldn't be too happy either if it were me.

Rock Stone stepped to the front of the Company, interrupting my thoughts.

"Attention to orders!" he said, looking up and down the three platoons with obvious pride. He clasped his hands behind his back and spread his legs slightly in the classic Marine Corps parade-rest style. A similar morning-orders process happened in every other of the Thirty-six Companies, but no one loved it as much or did it as professionally as Rock.

"Today is the first day of academic classes for all midshipmen. If there is any confusion about schedules, please see your Academic Advisor or Majors Department immediately." Stone paused, then he laughed slightly. "Today was also the first day of Brigade training for the new plebes, and I was pleased to see all the bright young faces straining in the passageway. Keep up the good work, classmates."

Stone's face changed as he continued. His features became sterner and far more serious.

"However, some of the plebes are not prepared for the stress of Academic Year training, and I suspect that several will be leaving us soon for greener pastures. Listen up, plebes! This is a tough place. There's no disgrace in not measuring up. Very few people can. You made it through Plebe Summer, which is commendable; but now the serious stuff starts, and there'll be no slacking off. The slackers have got to go." That was obviously a reference to poor Tommy.

"I also noticed that Chow Calls this morning were not loud and clear," Stone continued. "Work harder. I want to be able to hear the call clearly from one end of the passageway to the other. Today will also be our first noon meal formation together, and I want everyone shining. I will personally inspect one squad each noon meal. That inspection will be on a random basis, so stay alert." Stone paused, smiling again. The guy was completely at ease with his leadership. Even if he was completely insufferable, I liked his style. He was born to command.

" One final thing," he continued. "Flu shots are this afternoon after sixth period. Muster indoors at 1630 and no excuses." I could hear several audible groans. Stone laughed. "Company, attention!" he snapped and returned to the front of the formation. Soon we marched off to morning chow.

Mugsy McGinley grabbed Kevin as we arrived at Company tables and steered him to the seat next to his.

"Have a seat, O'Reilly." Kevin stood rigidly braced behind the indicated chair, while I stood behind the one next to Henry Brandis. We faced each other across the table and Kevin raised his eyes slightly toward the Almighty. I didn't think any divine power was going to intervene, but I winked encouragement anyway.

"What's the menu for this meal, O'Reilly?" asked McGinley with a sneer.

"Sir the menu for morning meal is breakfast steaks, golden baked potatoes, scrambled eggs, toast, butter and jelly, sir!"

"How about noon meal?"

"Sir the menu for noon meal is Italian spaghetti with meat sauce, green beans, Julienne potatoes, dinner rolls and butter, and Apple Brown Betty, sir!"

McGinley groaned.

"I hate Apple Brown Betty!" he said. "You can have mine, O'Reilly."

"Aye, aye, sir!"

"But you'd better eat it all. What about evening meal?"

"Sir the menu for evening meal is barbecued spareribs, mashed potatoes, golden corn, dinner rolls and butter, and chocolate ice cream, sir!"

McGinley thought for a moment, seemingly no easy task, and turned toward Brandis.

"Sounds like Animal Night to me." "Animal Night" was a special occasion when the plebes were required to eat whatever food was served without utensils. Ice cream was the worst. Brandis considered Mugsy's suggestion.

"No," he said. "It's too early for playtime. Let's test the plebes some before we slack off."

Mugsy leaned toward O'Reilly.

"I want to amend my offer, O'Reilly. I'll trade my Apple Brown Betty at noon for your chocolate ice cream tonight. How's that sound?"

"No, sir!" Kevin answered, shocking everyone at the table.

"What!" McGinley shouted. "What did you say?"

"I said, no, sir, I do not want to trade my chocolate ice cream, but I'll let you have my spareribs tonight for extra potatoes from both meals -- and the Brown Betty, sir."

McGinley was stumped. O'Reilly's mind was too bizarre.

He considered the complications of the transaction for a long minute before asking. "Why extra potatoes, you douchebag?"

"Sir, I'm Irish!" O'Reilly said sounding offended.

"Oh," Mugsy answered, unsure what Kevin meant. "Now the deal is . . . ," he began hesitatingly, "that you'll give me your spareribs tonight if I give you my potatoes at noon and tonight plus my Apple Brown Betty at noon?"

"Which you hate, sir!" Kevin added boldly. Several of the upperclass at the table, including McGinley, laughed.

"Okay, O'Reilly. You've got a deal. How many days until I graduate?"

"Two hundred sixty-five, sir!"

"That's 265 too god-damn many!"

Kevin and I did a bang-up job during the meal keeping everyone fed and happy. McGinley was quite an eater, and he went through two seconds of the steaks. Of course Kevin and I were lucky to be able to eat even a small portion of the meal. Twice Brandis called on me to perform. The first time I was asked "How's the Cow?" which is a rate from the Plebe Bible, a small blue book titled *Reef Points*. The question elicits a guess from the plebe of the number of glasses of milk remaining in the nearest blue and gold Naval Academy Dairy milk carton. Rather than answer with a direct "Three glasses, sir," the expected Academy response was "Sir, she walks, she talks, she's full of chalk. That lacteal fluid extracted from the female of the bovine species is highly prolific to the *third* degree, sir!" "Third" in the response is an indication of the number of glasses.

My second challenge was to summarize the contents of the morning paper concerning the war in Vietnam. Next to sex and sports, Vietnam was the topic most often discussed during meals. The young men sitting at the head and foot of the table would all too soon be sailing off the sandy coast, tromping through the muddy paddies, or flying low over the steamy jungles of Vietnam. I'm sure their pending personal involvement in war was a scary prospect, but it was also one most midshipmen accepted without complaint. I gave my summary, and quoted an anti-military commentary from Jack Anderson's column I knew would inflame the table. McGinley raised his arms and pretended to sight down a rifle barrel.

"Jack Anderson," he said and pulled an imaginary trigger. "Oughta be a dead man!"

Later in the meal McGinley turned to O'Reilly who had just squared a fork of eggs into his mouth.

"What time is it?" he asked. Kevin took the requisite three chews, swallowed, and began to recite the *Reef Points* answer about sidereal movements, but before he could say more than a few words, Mugsy interrupted him with a punch on the arm -- not a light one.

"I don't give a shit about *Reef Points,* O'Reilly. All I'm concerned about is food, the days until I leave this hell-hole, and whether or not "Big Nose Brian LaPointe" has the duty. You just stick to those three things and I'll be perfectly happy."

"Big Nose still after you?" asked Eddie Christenson, and several of the midshipmen at the table laughed.

"Yeah, the bastard." He looked at Kevin and put a big hairy arm around his shoulder. Kevin, being braced and sitting on the last two inches of his chair, seemed an inappropriate recipient for Mugsy's confidences. "See, O'Reilly. There's this Lieutenant Commander who works as the Academy Laundry Officer or something like that, and he's the biggest asshole ever created. When he has the duty he goes on a rampage, frying everyone he can. He's not happy unless he can put at least 50 midshipmen on report. He got me twice for sleeping in last year. So whenever he's the Duty Officer I have to be very careful. The prick always checks my room in the mornings."

"Why do they call him "Big Nose," sir?" Kevin asked with his typical boldness.

"His real name is Brian LaPointe," replied McGinley completely unfazed by Kevin's question. "And he's an old mustanger who looks like hell in a uniform -- even worse than me. Mugsy and Henry laughed. "His hat flops down on both sides of his ugly head. His uniforms are never pressed. And I swear he still wears the same pair of black shoes they issued him when he was a midshipman about a hundred years ago. But the worse thing about him is his god-damn nose, which is bumpy, bulbous, and red as a beet on its tip. And his nose hair is so thick and long, the inside is like a bugger jungle. He's disgusting, and he loves to make life miserable for us poor midshipmen. Your job is to warn me whenever he's on duty."

"Aye, aye, sir!"

Mugsy returned to his plate, polishing off the last of his toast.

"Sir, 0736, sir!" Kevin blurted almost immediately and seemingly without provocation. I looked at Kevin. His eyes sparkled. He was up to something. Everyone was shocked.

"What?" asked McGinley.

"The time, sir!" Kevin announced with a slight smile.

"Oh, yeah," McGinley replied looking at Kevin closely. "Thanks."

There isn't much time between the end of morning meal and the beginning of classes at 0800. We chopped hurriedly back to our room, straightened our individual areas, readied our noon-meal uniforms, swept out the room, and chopped out of Bancroft Hall to class. Sweeping out the room with a dust broom was a required morning occurrence. I was the only person who took that responsibility seriously. I don't think Rico ever touched the broom the entire year. -- That pissed me off. -- He was perfectly content to let the dust accumulate until it blocked the doorway, even though we could get into trouble. And Kevin wasn't much better about room responsibilities. He would do a cursory sweep of the main floor. And I had serious doubts that BJ could identify the correct side of the dust mop to use. So the morning sweep generally fell to me, although Kevin and BJ did contribute occasionally if I razzed them about it.

Every morning after chow I grabbed the dust mop and swept the room, particularly under the desks and in the corners. Then I pushed the day's dust into a pile just outside the door and shook the mop thoroughly. Later a janitor collected the leavings from outside each room.

I once asked Rico why he never helped with the morning mopping. He told me I was too thorough, that the minuscule amount of dust that collected each day could not be seen by a casual observer, and that anyone who came to the room to find discrepancies could invent plenty if they wanted. So why bother sweating needlessly, he asked me? I thought his philosophy was stupid, but I also knew he was serious and no amount of logic or cajoling would convince him otherwise, so I assumed the room sweep responsibility stoically, but resentfully.

I was surprisingly eager to get started in class. My grades in high school back in Amarillo had been respectable, and my College Board scores had been high enough so that entrance to Annapolis was not a problem, but I had never really felt taxed in high school. I was anxious to experience higher education, especially here where the reputation for scholarship was so high.

I met Jubal in T-Court just outside the fourth wing in our prearranged location. My morning classes would consist of psychology, calculus I, and chemistry. In the afternoon I had physical education, military leadership, and English literature. My total credit load was 18 hours, which was about average. In my current curriculum, Naval Architecture, I would need to accumulate 140 hours before I graduated four years from now. It wouldn't be easy, but I didn't choose Annapolis because I wanted anything easy.

Reb was not as anxious for the academics to begin. He had not had such an easy time with high school studies, and even though he selected the easiest of the curricula -- Management -- he felt he would still have to struggle to graduate. While we roomed together, I had noticed that Reb possessed a substantial inherent intelligence that he seemed to belittle. I was sure he would do well, and I reassured him as we walked.

The first thing I noticed as we headed to Mahan Hall was that no upper-class took any notice of us like they would inside the confines of Bancroft Hall. Academics obviously occupied a separate universe at the Academy -- like varsity athletics.

"What do y'all suppose they'll have us do the first week in class?" Jubal asked.

"Not much, I'm sure. Just get acquainted with the text and the plan for the semester."

"I hope so. I'm not ready for a huge study load."

"You'll do fine, Reb!" He didn't seem convinced.

"What's your squad like?" I asked to change the subject.

"Half and half," he answered. "Big Jim Daly is the squadleader. He's an ex-footballer who hurt his knee last year and can't play any more. He's intense but okay. Harvey Linehan, on the other hand is a puke who I would dearly like to strangle already. He thinks he's a little god, and he stands out in the passageway during comearound looking like Napoleon. I'd love to give him his Waterloo. The second-class, Weatherby and Phegler, are okay, especially since Battle let it be known that he spooned me. Plus Willy Simpson is a natural shit screen, bless his hillbilly heart. So, all-in-all, I'm gonna be fine. How about you?"

"Well," I said, "Henry Brandis is okay so far. This morning's comearound was a cinch. But I don't trust Mugsy McGinley. He's crazy and I intend to stay as far from him as possible. Luckily Kevin draws attention to himself, so I should be fine too."

"What about Guevarra? Is he gonna survive? I don't like that guy. He's jist too greasy."

"Well, Rico does have his drawbacks, but so far he's been fine."

"He's not "American" like you and me," Reb observed. "You're from Texas, you know what I mean."

I knew that he wanted me to validate his bigoted attitude about foreigners. I guess he thought I'd be sympathetic because of my country background. But I don't buy that segregation business, and I had been happy it had been firmly dealt with by the government."

"Come on, Reb," I replied. "Rico was born in New York City. That makes him as American as we are."

"Maybe so," he answered, "but he still seems foreign to me. Like that Lamont guy." Wesley Lamont was a black plebe in our Company who came from the American Virgin Islands. During the summer he had proved himself to be friendly, energetic, and helpful. He even had a delightful Islands accent I wished I could imitate.

"Hey Reb!" I said immediately. "Wesley's a good man."

"Did you know he dated a *white* girl for Parents' Weekend?"

"So?"

"That doesn't bother you?" he asked me incredulously.

"No," I answered honestly.

"It would if it were your sister," he said with finality. Would it? I wasn't sure. To tell the truth, I hadn't given the matter much consideration.

Because Annapolis is a military school, the academic environment, while ostensibly free and open, does have some restrictions. A midshipman class leader takes daily muster to ensure every student is there and on time. Being tardy or missing a class meant demerits. Many of the professors were naval officers whose military duty was to teach midshipmen. They were very competent, but it was extremely inadvisable to show even the slightest disrespect to an instructor who may outrank you by five or more military levels. The final difference was that the system didn't brook any slacking. If you had homework, you'd better do it correctly and on time or else face possible disciplinary action. Bad grades carried their own punishment -- like flunking out. And failure in the last two years at Annapolis meant spending time in the fleet as an enlisted man to pay Uncle Sam back for the expense of the training already received. Being civilian was preferable to being enlisted. Nobody wanted to fail once second-class year started.

Academic year started with an 18-credit rush. I'm no genius, but I have always been able to succeed when I put my mind to it. I planned to take copious notes, ask insightful questions, and do every piece of homework. It was a plan I scrupulously followed, except in calculus, where the solutions to some of the more difficult problems seemed to pass high over my head. I even started plebe study groups in each subject to take advantage of my classmates' substantial capabilities. After the first week I knew without a doubt that I would do well as a student.

Noon meal formation that first day also went extremely well. Rock Stone picked our squad for his first inspection, and he carefully examined everyone, including the first-class.

I heard him talking quietly for several moments to McGinley, who answered with a somewhat loud and sarcastic, "No big deal, Rocky my friend. No big deal!" Stone continued down the line. He made several comments to Kevin, which O'Reilly answered with his usual brashness, and soon he stood in front of me.

I focused my eyes on the horizon and stood rigidly as his eyes traveled slowly from my wonderfully shined black shoes, to my crisp white pants, to my perfect neckerchief, to my immaculate shave, and finally to my polished cap. He didn't say a word the entire viewing. He read my black and yellow name-tag and looked at me with a smile.

"Nice job, Merritt," he said with conviction. I instantly decided that I *did* like that guy, and I marched to noon meal feeling high on my own shining qualities. During the meal I answered every question with confidence and accuracy, even when Brandis tried to trick me with a "How Long is the Mess Hall?" -- an obscure plebe rate not in *Reef Points*.

"No, sir," I answered with aplomb. "How Long is a Chinaman!" Brandis was impressed. Tally one point for Jim Merritt. I would have this system down pat before too long. I could handle anything they dished out and then some.

I felt almost invincible later that first day when the Company assembled to go to Sick Bay for annual flu shots. Flu shots at Annapolis are mandatory. Immediately after the final class of the day Rock Stone -- my new idol -- mustered the Company in the passageway outside the Company Office.

Muster did not go well. Many of the upper-class were slow to form up.

Stone yelled for everyone's benefit, "Listen you douchebags. I don't have all day. The sooner we get started, the quicker we'll be back. Take a muster of your squads. Whoever's missing can tell Captain Dillingham why." Within a minute we had settled down, counted heads, and started off toward Sick Bay, leaving several people behind, one of whom called out from the recesses of the communal head facility as we passed.

"I'm taking a shit for Christ's sake, Stone. Give me a break!"

We weren't the only Company assigned to get flu shots that afternoon. When we arrived at the middle of the sixth wing, a long line snaked its way into the lower levels. Several "Tigers" groaned at the prospect of a long wait. Stone planted us in single file formation at the end of the line and went ahead to reconnoiter the situation. He returned within a minute.

"It's not as bad as it looks. There's a shot station on the landing leading down to Sick Bay, and they're moving pretty fast. In five minutes we'll be there." He then took his place at the front of the line.

He was as good as his word. The line moved quickly. Soon I was at the head of the stairs watching the flu shot operation on the landing below. Two enlisted corpsmen handled the process. One prepared the shot doses, the other wielded the "gun" with a steady hissing bang. In front of me was a second-class I didn't recognize. Rico was behind me. I watched as Rock Stone took his shot first and stepped to a corner of the landing to watch his Tigers. The first platoon finished without incident. I saw Kevin O'Reilly get his shot. He yelled in mock pain after the hiss; then pranced away as the corpsman took a playful swipe at him. Stone glared at him.

I hadn't noticed until just before my turn came, but the second-class in front of me was very nervous. I saw the corpsman take hold of his arm, turn it, then shake it slightly to try to loosen up some of the muscle tension. He paused and looked at the unknown midshipman.

"Take it easy," he said. "I've done a thousand of these. It doesn't hurt. Relax your arm, and it'll be over in a second." The second-classman wasn't convinced. He tightened his arm muscle again as the gun touched his skin. "Easy!" the corpsman repeated. "I promise it won't hurt."

The second-class relaxed somewhat for an instant, but just as the corpsman squeezed the trigger, he flinched. I was watching from no more than two feet away when he jerked, and I had a perfect view. The shot entered the midshipman's upper arm at a severe angle and traced a white line along the inside of the skin for an inch or so. The shot next exited the arm by making a second puncture hole and sprayed blood and serum on a nearby bulkhead. It made quite a mess. The second-class took a long look at the sight and gasped. His eyes rolled up into his head. He fell loosely toward the deck in a swoon. I grabbed his stricken arm as he fell, but my hand slipped on the liquid mess. He ended up lying against my legs -- out cold. The other corpsman rushed over to help ease the midshipman to the tile deck, and the first one looked disgusted.

"Move him over against the wall and let him recover there," the corpsman with the gun said. "There are lots more shots to give." I helped the other corpsman and Rock Stone slide the unconscious second-classman to a place against the bulkhead. Stone looked at the Company and reacted.

"Some of Bilecky's god-damn classmates had better get their asses down here and take care of him, or there'll be hell to pay." Three midshipmen sprang forward. I stood to one side unsure what to do. Stone touched me on the shoulder.

"Get back in line, Merritt. Show them what a trooper you are." Wow! He remembered my name from noon meal.

"Aye, aye, sir!" I responded, moving quickly back into line.

The first corpsman looked at me when I took my place as the next recipient of the gun's load of medicine. "You okay?" he asked.

"Sure, fine." I answered boldly.

"Jim Merritt is a stud," said Rico from behind me, putting one hand on my shoulder. "Do him twice and see what I mean." I was in a really good mood at this point.

"Yeah," I said with a sneer, holding both arms out toward the gun. "Do me twice!" I heard Stone, my hero, laugh at my boldness.

Evening comearound was harder than the morning circle-the-company-area run. Brandis and McGinley both doled out the verbal motivation, but McGinley -- the crazy bastard -- participated. He lined himself up in the passageway alongside us for every sprint and gutted out each and every push-up. O'Reilly and I beat him easily in the runs, but the son-of-a-gun could do push-ups 'til the cows came home, rivaling even Guevarra. That first evening we must have done ten sets of 30, with Mugsy yelling and gloating the entire time that we were pussies. He could even do one-handed push-ups, a feat I never did master.

"That was a great little workout!" Mugsy exclaimed when we had finished and stood braced against the bulkhead. "O'Reilly, you and Merritt be outside this room tomorrow at 0530 for a little five-miler. Henry here can handle the others for the morning exercises. If we have fun, we'll do it once or twice a week."

"If you can get up on time," offered Brandis with a hint of sarcasm. McGinley turned on Brandis smiling.

"Why, Henry," he said. "I'm looking forward to it. I think I may be training the next Brigade boxing champs." I groaned inwardly. O'Reilly might be crazy enough to entertain the idea of voluntarily stepping into the ring and being struck on the face and head by someone else, but I didn't want to be a boxer. During summer indoctrination we had a week of boxing training, and I hadn't cared at all for the feeling even a well-padded fist makes when it comes in forcible contact with the human nose. I stared in dismay at McGinley's own multidirectional protrusion and tried to imagine my own looking like that. Mugsy laughed delightedly while staring into my stricken eyes.

We returned to our room with barely enough time to shower and prepare for formation. I hustled so quickly that I didn't stop sweating until I was in line and waiting for Stone to address us. Most nights it went that way. But once at attention, I knew I was perfect. Mentally I dared anyone to inspect me and find something wrong.

Evening meal was another grueling, edge-of-the-chair, rigidly braced, infinitesimal-bite affair. We passed food, answered questions, recited rates, and ate very little. Nobody seemed to notice how little food we ingested. That night immediately after we returned to the room I wrote two quick letters, one to Mom, and the other to Lynda, begging each to send a "Care Package" with plenty of high-energy junk food. Good old Lynda, my sweetheart, she'd come through for me. She wrote me almost every day, and her letters were a source of strength. During some of the quiet time we spent together during Parent's Weekend, we even talked about the possibility of eventual marriage. She'd make a great wife and mother.

I had come from a room where talk of special girlfriends was touching and almost constant to one where talk of sex was paramount. In the Goon Room of the summer, Jeff Polk continually raved about how his girl Kate was the greatest thing ever, and I had vigorously proclaimed the virtues of my Lynda. Even Tommy Poole had a girl named Sara at home. Reb Ramsey, always the quiet one where personal issues were concerned, also wistfully mentioned a girl back home in Alabama named Martha. We were each in love in our own wonderful ways.

Rooming with Guevarra, O'Reilly, and Wilson was definitely different. Guevarra was obsessed with sex. He had that stupid slut-book library that he was constantly reading and rereading. And when he discussed his dating habits, it wasn't fondly but rather with animal lust. I saw him once put several scrotal hairs into an envelope addressed to some local girl named Cindy. I had no doubt that he was as successful as he said. He had a definite animal magnetism that affected even Lynda. And he and O'Reilly traded secret looks and smiles at the memory of some Plebe Summer escapade they had pulled off.

O'Reilly was a much sadder case. He told us that he had only dated casually in high school, and he must have been a late bloomer. He had never had a steady partner, and I don't think he had ever been intimate with anyone. He was desperate for female companionship and was beginning to develop a Guevarra-like interest in things base and sexual.

BJ Wilson was experienced -- no question about it -- but he approached sex and companionship with a how-will-it-benefit-me attitude. In his inherited position near the peak of the entertainment power ladder, he had access to people and situations I could only imagine. He told me during the summer that an attractive co-worker of his father, who was in her late twenties, had offered him sex in exchange for information about an upcoming television deal. He had accepted the sex and afterward told his father what the person wanted. His father had encouraged him to take advantage of the woman's favors while doling out selected bits of planted information. BJ accepted this behavior as normal. He said the sex was great. I wasn't interested in sex-for-sex-sake.

So I was the only normal one in Room 4024 in so far as relationships were concerned, and I had my Lynda to rely on. I felt convinced that I had the better of the womanly deal.

Soon after I had sealed my second letter, Eddie Christenson entered. I almost snapped to attention, forgetting that he had spooned the room yesterday. He smiled at us.

"I noticed that you guys didn't get much to eat today, so I borrowed some extra dinner rolls and four pieces of fried chicken from a neighboring table. Here you go." He held out a small paper bag whose bottom was grease-soaked. Kevin sprang from his chair to accept the food offering.

"Thanks!" he said. "I'm starving!"

"No problem," Eddie replied. "How's everything going so far?"

"Okay, I guess," I answered. "Comearounds have been easy enough, and there've been no surprises at mealtime."

"Tomorrow we have to run with Mugsy," Kevin said. "What do you think?"

Eddie laughed.

"You'll find out for yourselves. Mugsy's a wild man. He destroyed his opponent in the Brigade Boxing Finals -- showed no mercy at all. Last year he also chased a first-class out of his room for trying to wake him before he was ready. And he told you about his ongoing battle with "Big Nose." But, boy, if you can get on his good side, you're in like flint."

Kevin passed a piece of chicken and a roll to each of us. It was illegal to bring food from the Mess Hall, but many midshipmen did it anyway. We ate quickly and put the remnants into the paper bag.

"I'll dump the bag in the shitcan in the head," Eddie said as he departed.

"That was nice of him," Kevin observed.

No sooner had Eddie left than Mugsy poked his head into the room.

"The four of you in the Wardroom. Now!" he ordered.

Every Company has a TV and conversation room patterned after a ship's Officers' Wardroom. Generally it contains several couches and easy chairs, a few small tables, a book shelf and wall unit with a TV, and, of course, a refrigerator. Only first-class midshipmen are allowed to use the Wardroom, but usually not during weekday evenings, so Mugsy's invitation was a complete surprise to us. I don't think any of us had ever been inside an Academy Wardroom before.

We chopped into the main passageway. The Wardroom was next to the Company Office where our Company Officer, Marine Corps Captain Rusty "Bull" Dillingham, held court each day. Mugsy must have been inside already, but still we hesitated, braced uncertainly in the center of the passageway. The others eyed me for leadership, so I stepped forward and pushed the door open. We entered in a rush and immediately braced against a bulkhead. McGinley sat at a table, piles of bread and luncheon meats spread out in front of him.

"Carry-on, damn it!" he said. "No plebe shit in here. This is business."

We unbraced and looked around curiously.

"Get over here!" he commanded. We hurried to positions surrounding where he sat. He looked up at us.

"Didn't eat much tonight, did ya?" he asked.

"No sir!" we answered as a group. He smiled.

"Well, you guys are plebes. You can't expect to get a lot to eat. But I have the solution, plus a way to make a little money on the side." He paused. "At least for me to make a little money. Here's what we're gonna do."

He indicated the piles of food with a wave of a hairy arm.

"Welcome to McGinley's Sandwich Mess," he said. "Every night just after meal you guys are gonna come here and prepare sandwiches from the list I give you and deliver them to your classmates and to other hungry midshipmen." He consulted a penciled price list. "All sandwiches come with two slices of whatever. Cheese sandwiches are a buck. Baloney is a buck twenty five. Pimento loaf and salami are a buck and a half. Combinations are two bucks. One with the works is three bucks. Pickles are a quarter extra, but all other condiments are free."

He went on. "When you go to each room announce yourself as representing McGinley's Sandwich Mess. Deliver the sandwich, collect the money, take tomorrow's order, and come by my room and give me a financial report. I'll replace the supplies every week, but you tell me if you start running out of anything. Questions?"

"Yes, sir," I said. "Am I to understand that you want us to do this without your being here in the Wardroom?"

"That's right," McGinley answered. "Right after evening meal. Can't you handle a simple thing like that?"

"Yes, sir," I answered, slightly offended. "But what if somebody comes in here and sees us?"

"Just tell them who you represent, and everything will be okay. And tell me if any of the customers give you a hard time. Any other questions?"

"Yes, sir," asked Rico. "What's in it for us?"

"For you?" asked Mugsy with a smile. "Excellent question. You can each have one free sandwich a night, but not a double or a deluxe -- that you have to pay for."

"Sir?" asked Kevin questioningly. Oh shit, I saw Kevin's eyes twinkle momentarily, he was up to something.

"If we can have a regular sandwich for free and that usually has two slices and unlimited condiments, couldn't we have a "special" with one slice of everything for free and only pay if we had extra pickles, or maybe skip the condiments and have an extra slice of baloney or cheese or a half slice of each, but without the pickles?" I could see that McGinley was as confused as I was, but he didn't want to admit his confusion, and Kevin was so serious looking that Mugsy couldn't be sure he was being had.

"Yeah, whatever," he said with an irritated wave of his hand. "Just get started." With that he stood and strode from the room.

Rico immediately burst out laughing.

"O'Reilly, you are amazing!"

We looked at the piles of bread and food. I picked up the list and began tallying. Rico immediately began making a sandwich.

"Let's see," I said. "We need six cheese, ten baloney, two pimento, and three salami, plus one deluxe for Mugsy himself." I looked at Rico, who hadn't listened to a thing I said. He had piled three slices of baloney and two slices of salami on a piece of bread and covered that with a slice of cheese and a pile of pickles. As I watched, he lifted the huge construction to his mouth and took an enormous bite.

"Rico!" I said incredulously. "What are you doing?"

"Making my sandwich first," he mumbled, crumbs falling from his too-full mouth.

"Three chews and a swallow, plebe!" Kevin announced with a chuckle. Rico laughed and mumbled a "Eat shit, O'Reilly!" then took another enormous bite. I hesitated only briefly.

Rico's idea was a good one. I was still hungry from the day's activities, and that tiny piece of chicken hadn't satisfied me at all. Kevin, BJ, and I looked at each other for a second. Then Kevin gave us one of his smiles, and we all ate, although we didn't have Rico's balls when it came to sandwich size.

It took about five minutes to make the sandwiches and decide who would deliver to whom. We left in two groups -- safety in numbers I suppose -- with BJ and me being paired. We worked opposite sides of the passageway, careful to chop down the center and square corners precisely as we went.

Our first room was a youngster room. Jack Collins looked up as we entered.

"Mugsy's Sandwich Mess," I said, opening the bag and removing the required items. "Let's see, that's one baloney and one cheese, correct?"

Jack didn't look happy, but he paid me, as did his roommate, Lester Crump.

"What's the matter?" I asked. "Not what you ordered?"

"No," Jack replied. "I ordered the sandwich, but under some duress. I suppose it's better than making a gedunk run every night."

"Gedunk?" I asked. There was a word I hadn't heard before.

"Gedunk is a generic name for snack food or candy," Jack answered. "McGinley sold us on the Sandwich Mess because we wouldn't have to go down to the Steerage and wait in line. He inherited the Mess from a firstie who graduated last year. I understand the sandwich concession made the guy enough in one year to buy a brand new Corvette. What do you guys get?"

"Just a free sandwich," I said. Jack laughed.

"Well, it's better than nothing -- which is exactly what my classmates got last year for doing all the work."

"Same thing tomorrow?" I asked.

"I guess so," he answered. We turned and left.

The next room was a second-class room. It also happened to be Maxwell's. His roommates for academic year were Tommy Battle, whom we knew from Plebe Summer as a tough-as-nails proto-

Marine, and a tall thin midshipman named "Happy" Houseman. Midshipmen seem to favor nicknames. Happy was a varsity fencer, and with those long arms and legs, I could imagine it would be hard to score a touch on him. They both looked up, surprised, when we entered and braced up just inside the door.

"What the hell do you want, Merritt?" Maxie began.

"McGinley's Sandwich Mess!" I announced.

"Oh, yeah." Maxwell reached for his wallet as I readied the order.

"Two baloney sandwiches. That'll be two dollars," I said. Maxwell walked over to where we stood and checked the sandwiches. He shook his head.

"This is it? Just two slices?"

"Orders, sir!"

"A buck is robbery for two slices," he said, but paid me, as did Houseman.

"Same thing tomorrow?" I asked.

"Why not?" Maxie answered. We left hurriedly.

The rest of the deliveries and collections went well, and soon we entered McGinley's room with the money and braced against the bulkhead.

"How'd it go?" he asked.

"Fine, sir," I answered.

"Let's have the money and tomorrow's list," he said. I gave it to him. He sorted through the money, did a quick mental calculation to ensure we hadn't short changed him, then sat back in his chair, smiling at the small stack of money on the desk in front of him.

"America," he said. "The land of opportunity." We waited to be dismissed, but McGinley did nothing. Brandis was too busy studying to notice us. Finally Mugsy looked up.

"Where the piss are your classmates?" he asked, irritated.

"I'll find out sir!" I answered in the standard plebe response. McGinley started to rise, but almost immediately Guevarra and O'Reilly burst through the door. Rather than stop and brace, Rico went directly to Mugsy and handed him the money and the next day's list.

"Why ain't you braced, and where have you been?" Mugsy asked. Mugsy's demeanor didn't faze Rico.

"Sir, as you said, this is business." I could see McGinley begin to get angry, but before he could say a word, Rico continued. "And we took the liberty of stopping by every youngster and plebe room in the Company to get their orders for tomorrow. We figured you didn't have a chance to ask everyone. So, I have in my hands orders for 15 more sandwiches starting tomorrow."

The thought of additional revenue immediately calmed Mugsy. He smiled.

"Nice work, Guevarra and O'Reilly." He took the money, counted it all again, and held it aloft. "God I love free enterprise. Just think what I can buy by the end of the year. Maybe I'll have enough for a down payment on a house in California. How about Hollywood? I always wanted to move out there."

"Yes, sir," Kevin said, twinkling again. "I agree. Move away from here. I think California is the place you ought to be. Swimming pools and movie stars, sir. Maybe someone will star you in a show. How about *The Beverly Hair-Billy?* " Brandis and Guevarra laughed. McGinley looked up from his monetary reverie and stared at Kevin, dumbfounded.

"O'Reilly," he said. "You are one strange midshipman."

"Aye, aye, sir!" Kevin answered with a resounding snap. McGinley only shook his head.

"Outta here. All of you. See you in the morning."

Immediately after we returned to our room O'Reilly said to me, "Jim, when we were in Butkowski's room, Tommy Poole asked for you to stop by tonight. He has some news."

"For me? How come?"

"Don't know, but I'll go along. I want to hear how Tommy's squad is." Kevin and I chopped to the main passageway and entered Poole's room. The entire complement of occupants was at home.

Hank Butkowski sat at his desk reading a textbook. Hank was the biggest plebe in the Company. He was almost the biggest human being I had ever known, but one of the most gentle. He stood a solid six feet five inches and more than 240 pounds. He had been an All-State lineman in Jeanette, Wisconsin, and had been recruited for football. During the summer he had missed some of the afternoon plebe exercises so that he could attend special practices with the varsity. Now he was the darling of the Company and several prominent varsity football players had already been by to spoon him. Butkowski was now in protected status, and he knew it.

Across the desk from Hank was George Abbott, another jockstrapper. George had been an All-State soccer defender from Tea Neck, New Jersey. He was an up-and-comer with great promise for the varsity, and he had also been prominently spooned. In addition, George was a formidable person whose swarthy features and stocky build promised severe punishment for those opposing forwards who dared invade his territory. Both George and Hank sat on training tables rather than eat with the Company, and I envied them for that.

Training tables were select tables set aside in one far corner of the Mess Hall where the athletes ate their special high-energy food in portions worthy of a medieval banquet, and where Plebe Year was suspended under the guise of athletic camaraderie. The chances of my ever participating in the paradise at the training tables were remote, so I only wondered about how wonderful it would be to act like a human being at meals. Maybe I would try out for the plebe track team.

Tim Butler sat across the room at his desk. Tim was a startling contrast to the Hank and George. He was small framed, nondescript, quiet, and his mannerisms were almost feminine. Both his parents were librarians in Modesto, California, and I don't think Tim had ever participated in an organized sport before he came to Annapolis. He was extremely intelligent, his brain power paling only when compared to Tommy Poole's.

Tommy sat across from Tim. Tommy once told me during a quiet period in the Goon Room routine that he had graduated from high school in Flint, Michigan without ever opening a book. I believed him. Tommy had earned perfect scores in both verbal and math on the Scholastic Aptitude Tests and could do problems in his head that I couldn't do with a calculator.

Neither Tommy nor Tim was popular with the upper-class. Despite their shining intellects and pleasant personalities, I could completely understand why. -- It had been explained to us enough times during the summer by the squadleaders and by the Company Officer. Annapolis is responsible to graduate naval officers, not nice guys and not Einsteins either. In order to be successful in his future career, every midshipman must possess a combination of plentiful raw intelligence, dynamic personality, unrelenting drive, athletic ability, and copious leadership potential. The Academy doesn't aim to produce captains of industry or science, although many of its grads become major business players and researchers. Annapolis-trained naval officers are required to lead men -- sometimes into battle and sometimes to their deaths. To ensure success in battle, a special kind of military man is needed. The best leaders are cool under severe pressure, and can fight all day, love all night, and inspire confidence in those around them. Our Company Officer, Rusty Dillingham, had those qualities. Rock Stone also had them, and so did I to a lesser extent. I just needed training and practice.

But neither Tim nor Tommy measured up to those standards. Both had reported aboard severely out of shape. Tim was almost a scarecrow in body-type; Tommy was severely pear-shaped. Even after three months of several-workouts-a-day, both lacked the necessary stamina to keep up with the pack. In addition, neither was particularly military in appearance. When Tim wore a uniform, it always seemed about to fall down around his knees. Tommy bulged in places. Neither marched well either, and both seemed to stumble through life rather than stride with confidence. I certainly wouldn't want to follow either into combat. When the squadleaders declared that Poole and Butler didn't belong, I completely understood and sympathized.

Tommy had been expecting us.

"Hey Jim, Kevin!" he said. "How's everything going?"

"Just fine, Tommy," I answered. "How are things with you?"

"Well," he said dejectedly, "they could be better, but I'm surviving." He looked over at Hank and George, then lowered his voice to a bare whisper. "I hated to split up the 'Goons', but moving to this room was the best thing I could have done. So far my evening has been quiet." He looked at Kevin and smiled. "Except for the ingestion of some very needed nourishment brought by my dear friend, Kevin, I've been left alone."

I looked at O'Reilly. Poole's name wasn't on the original list. Kevin smiled and shrugged.

"I made an extra," he said. O'Reilly the humanitarian. He'd never learn. He had gotten in serious trouble with Battle during the summer for helping Tommy during a morning run. O'Reilly actually found Poole something of a hero for his ability to endure severe humiliation and punishment. I liked Tommy well enough, but he really didn't belong here, and I was surprised Kevin had such trouble seeing that.

"How's your squadleader treating you?" I asked Tommy.

"Dale Micklewski? He's worse than both Maxwell and Battle combined," offered Tim Butler. "He's almost sadistic."

"He's also operating under the direct orders of Rock-head Stone," said Tommy. The other room members laughed at Tommy's bold attitude. Kevin also joined in, but I wasn't about to demean the good nickname of my idol.

"Attention on Deck!" George yelled from across the room as Rock Stone entered -- almost on cue. We immediately braced and yelled out our names.

I had my back to Stone. I could hear him as he stepped smartly into the room, his shower shoes (clacks) slapping loudly against his bare feet.

"Jesus Christ, a mutiny!" he said half in jest. "Who doesn't belong here?"

"Me, sir!" "Me sir!" Kevin and I answered. Stone came around to look at us. "What the hell are you two doing here?"

"We came to discuss tomorrow's classes, sir!" answered Kevin with a little lie.

Stone looked closely at O'Reilly.

"You have a class with genius Poole?" he asked incredulously. Kevin doesn't seem smart on the outside, but I knew that he had turned down a partial scholarship to MIT to come to Annapolis.

"Yes, sir. Advanced chemistry." Kevin answered. Stone's eyes narrowed.

"Well, where's your book?" he asked.

"Just some general questions, sir," answered O'Reilly without missing a beat. No way could Stone outsmart O'Reilly. He could think on his feet faster than any person I had ever met.

"I see," Stone said, accepting defeat. He turned to me. "What are you doing here, Merritt?" He said it as if he were disappointed in me. I felt as if I had let down my father.

"I'll find out, sir!" Stone shook his head.

"Comearound tomorrow, both of you!" he ordered.

"Sir!" O'Reilly interrupted. Stone turned on him.

"What is it, wise ass?"

"Sir, we have a personal comearound tomorrow morning with Midshipman First-class McGinley."

Stone thought for a moment. "You do huh?"

"Yes, sir!" said O'Reilly with a slight smirk. Stone saw the look and smiled.

"We'll see about that," he said. Then he turned to the others. He stared at Hank Butkowski. "You must be the football player?" he asked.

"Yes, sir!" answered Hank smartly.

"So no comearounds for you this set, huh?"

"No, sir!" Stone smiled devilishly.

"I'll make sure you're in my squad next set," he said.

"Plebe Indoor Track, sir!"

"What's that mean?"

"Sir, I throw the shot put for the indoor track team in the winter!"

"So no comearounds then either?"

"Hopefully not, sir!"

"And you'll be working out with the varsity footballers in the spring, won't you?"

"Yes, sir!"

Stone paused. When he continued, he sounded genuinely sad.

"That means you're not going to have a Plebe Year, Butkowski. Doesn't that make you feel bad? Thousands of your predecessors graduated from this institution after paying a very heavy price during their Plebe Years. They worked hard. They sweated and overcame tremendous obstacles. And you get through without so much as a proper comearound. You'll go through the rest of your life wondering if you have the right stuff. I feel sorry for you."

"Yes, sir!" Butkowski answered. Thinking about it, I realized Stone could be right. Plebe Year is a big part of the dues every midshipman pays for the privilege of wearing the Academy ring. What kind of naval officer would Hank make if he never paid the price the rest of us did?

Stone looked at George Abbott next.

"The soccer player?" he asked.

"Yes, sir!" George answered.

"Let me guess. Plebe fencing? Wrestling? Gymnastics? What's your excuse to bag Plebe Year?"

"No winter sports, sir!" Abbott answered, but I could see his brain calculating the possibilities of all the sports Stone had mentioned.

"Good!" Stone said happily. "I'll at least make sure you're in my squad next set." Then he turned toward the rest of us. He looked at Tim Butler for a long moment. "You're Butler, aren't you?"

"Yes, sir!" Tim squeaked. I flinched. Butler had never learned how to "knock 'em together" when he answered. His voice sounded like a little girl's. Stone leaned inward until his face was only an inch from Butler's ear.

"You're kind of a sissy, aren't you?" he asked.

"No, sir!" Tim squeaked again. I could see Tim's face. He was terrified.

"You sound like a sissy!" Stone hissed in Tim's ear. "You don't ever have "funny" thoughts about the men around you, do you?" he asked.

"Sir?" Tim asked, clearly confused.

"You're not a homo, are you?" Stone shouted so loudly that Butler flinched and almost toppled sidewards.

Tim quickly straightened.

"No, sir!" he said with a bit more emphasis.

"Good! Because we don't allow that shit here, Butler. If you are and you're caught, you go out on your ass in disgrace."

"Aye, aye! Sir!"

Stone slowly looked at Tommy Poole.

"And then we have Midshipman Douchebag Poole," he said. "The girl who doesn't belong, but won't get the message." Savoring every second, Stone strolled around the desks to where Tommy stood braced. He stopped beside Tommy and leaned in so that his mouth was next to Poole's ear.

"I've read the file," he whispered fiercely. "It's quite a reading. Did you know it is the largest of the plebe files? -- except for the one on a plebe named Ronald Steinway, who isn't here anymore. And besides, most of the stuff in Steinway's file was medical injury and death reports. Why do you suppose *your* file is so thick, Poole?"

"I'll find out sir!" Tommy shouted. Tommy didn't have any problem with vocal volume or forcefulness.

"You don't have to find out, Poole you fat shit, because I'm here to tell you. Your file is crammed with negative material about your fitness for duty. You're the sloppiest looking of the plebes. In fact you may be the worst looking plebe I've ever seen. You can't march for shit. Your locker is always screwed up. Your shoes are horrible. You can't do 20 push-ups without crying. You can't run a mile without falling down. The only thing positive your file says about you is that you're smart as hell. Well, smart doesn't hack it for you, Mister Poole, because you got nothing going for you besides the smarts. I put out the word on you to all the upper-class. You are to be run out of here as soon as possible. So you might as well face the inevitable and quit now, because your life is going to be hell on earth. Have I made myself clear?"

"Yes, sir!"

"Based on what I just told you, are you considering quitting?"

"No, sir!"

"Why the hell not!"

"Because I can hack it, sir!"

Stone's face became red. He leaned in closer to Tommy and said loudly.

"No, you can't hack it, you miserable, disgusting, puke! I will personally see to it that you don't last a week! Avoid the pain, Poole!"

"No, sir!" Tommy answered boldly. I had to hand it to Tommy. He had balls. But he *was* stupid. Stone and the Tigers would kill him. Some of Stone's accusations were not strictly true. Tommy didn't fit in a uniform very well, but he had nicely shined shoes, and his locker was fantastic. He could do 30 push-ups fairly easily, and could run a mile without too much trouble. In fact Poole beat two of his companymates in the final morning run of the summer. But the handwriting was on the wall for Tommy. Why *didn't* he quit?

Stone starred at Tommy's ear for a long moment as he calmed. Then he straightened.

"Well, no matter. Just remember where you put your suitcase, Poole, cause you're out of here." Stone turned toward Kevin and me and looked hard at O'Reilly, who had an I'm-rooting-for-Poole look on his face.

"I don't like you, you redhead sack of shit. I don't like the way you look. I don't like the way you act. And I especially don't like the way you talk. You're a smack, and I intend to destroy that wise-ass attitude of yours. Does that bother you, O'Reilly?"

"Yes, sir!" Kevin answered honestly.

Smiling, Stone pounced. He leaned in toward Kevin the way he had with Butler and Poole. His chest and forearms swelled as he flexed his ample muscles.

"I scare you, don't I, O'Reilly?"

"No, sir!" Kevin answered.

"Bullshit!" barked Stone, popping an ample biceps in Kevin's face. "Are you telling me I don't scare you at all?"

"Not a bit, sir!"

"O'Reilly, be honest. I can run you 'til you drop. I can give you push-ups until you collapse. I can make you hate me, can't I?"

"Do you want me to be honest, sir?"

Stone hesitated, then he smiled and looked around the room.

"Sure, O'Reilly. This is for posterity, so be honest." Oh, Christ. Kevin was going to get himself into trouble again. He never knew when to keep his fat-lipped Irish mouth shut.

"Sir," Kevin said, speaking slowly and precisely since his lip was still recovering. "You can do everything you said, but I'm never going to be afraid of you. You're just not that scary, and we both know that there's a line you can't cross without serious consequences."

"Are you threatening me?" O'Reilly.

"No sir! I'm just not afraid of you."

Stone's eyes narrowed.

"You think you can take me, don't you?"

Kevin didn't even flinch. "It would be a close call, sir, but, yes, I do."

Stone laughed and looked at his muscles again.

"Not a chance, O'Reilly. Not a chance."

"We'll never know then sir, will we?" Holy shit! Kevin just challenged Rock Stone -- who must outweigh him by 20 very solid pounds -- to a fist fight. If the results of the one short fight I saw Kevin in are any measure of his abilities, Kevin would get himself clobbered. He was absolutely crazy.

Stone looked at O'Reilly for a long moment. "Naaaa," he said, "it wouldn't be in keeping with my position."

"Well, maybe next set when you're only a squadleader, sir?" Jesus, Kevin! Shut up! Stone only laughed at that and leaned in closely again so that his face was separated from Kevin's by only a few inches. He put one finger on Kevin's chest and shoved slightly. Kevin didn't flinch.

"You got balls, O'Reilly. I'll give you that. But no fight. And I'm still gonna run your ass. That's just too bad, huh O'Reilly?"

"Yes, sir," Kevin said slowly and with such deliberation that Stone's smile instantly faded. In that fleeting instant I saw Stone experience shock. Something in Kevin's eyes must have worried him. He stared at Kevin for a moment longer, and turned toward the rest of us.

"Those of you who don't belong better get out as soon as you've conducted legitimate business." Stone then click-clacked out of the room.

After Stone departed, no one spoke for a long moment. Every eye in the room was on Kevin O'Reilly.

"O'Reilly, you're one crazy asshole," said George Abbott. Hank Butkowski shook his head in disbelief. Tim Butler stared open-mouthed. Tommy Poole on the other hand looked at Kevin with narrowed eyes.

"What's your plan, Kevin?" Tommy asked.

"Plan?" I interjected.

"Yeah. Kevin was feeding Stone what he wanted? What do you think he'll do, Kevin?"

"He'll probably spoon me in the morning," Kevin said with his usual fake seriousness. Everyone in the room thought he was being serious except Tommy and me.

"He'll probably kill you in the morning," I said.

Kevin laughed.

"Yeah. That's the other possibility."

"You really think you can take him?" George asked.

"Not a chance," Kevin replied. "But I knew he wouldn't accept the challenge. If he did and beat me, he'd look like the bully he is. If he did and lost, he'd lose his tough-guy image. I put him in a lose-lose situation and he realized it."

"Why did he seem so afraid of you at the end?" I asked.

Kevin laughed.

"I gave him the patented O'Reilly I'm-really-an-ax-murder-disguised-as-a-midshipman look. It gets them every time. He'll probably go to sleep tonight with his door locked and wake at every sound thinking the mad Irishman is creeping up on him preparing to slit his throat. -- It's not really such a bad idea, you know."

"What isn't?" asked Abbott.

"Slitting his throat. Stone is one crazy son of a gun. I'd probably be doing humanity a favor." I kept quiet. This probably wasn't the time to tell Kevin that I thought Stone was a genuine hero.

"We'd better be getting back, Kevin," I said instead.

"Yeah" Kevin turned toward the door and we prepared to leave. Quickly he spun around and addressed Poole. "How do you like our chemistry instructor?"

"He's fine, I guess," Tommy replied, puzzled at the question.

O'Reilly chuckled.

"Just asking general information in case Stone grills me tomorrow." Poole laughed.

"Good idea," he said.

We departed and returned to our rooms. It was almost 2000, which left only an hour to study before lights out. I hurriedly pulled out the books for the next day's classes and reviewed notes, then did the assigned homework. Since the academic year was only one day old, the amount of homework was small -- a fact that would soon change for the worst.

CHAPTER 3

ROUTINES

Kevin and I were outside McGinley's room at 0530 the next morning as requested. The main passageway lights don't come on until reveille at 0600, and everything was very quiet -- almost eerie. We waited silently in the near darkness braced against the bulkhead; although, since the possibility of discovery was minimal, I wasn't completely rigid. We could hear movement inside the first-class room, and at 0535 McGinley emerged, looking none too happy. He looked us over with a scowl.

"It's too damn early for this," he mumbled.

"We could go to our rooms and wait for you to be ready, sir?" Kevin offered quietly. McGinley didn't recognize the borderline insubordination.

"Nah. I'm up. We might as well get it over with. Let's go." We began chopping behind him as he trudged down the passageway toward the outside door. Our tennis shoes made squeaky sounds as they patted out rapid tiny steps. After ten feet Mugsy stopped dead in his tracks and turned to us. We hastily stopped, narrowly avoiding a collision with him.

"Let's get one thing straight right from the start," he whispered fiercely. "When we work out, we're "almost" equals. No plebe shit. Is that clear?"

You bet it was! "Yes, sir!" we answered simultaneously -- but quietly. We both unbraced and matched Mugsy's stride down the passageway. As we neared the doorway to Tecumseh Court, another first-class emerged from a room, obviously on his way to the head facilities. He stopped when he saw us, and stared particularly hard at Kevin and me. For a moment he wasn't sure who we were.

"Morning Mugsy," he said carefully, still looking us over. "What's up?"

"Taking some plebes for a run," McGinley answered.

The firstie, who I now recognized as one of the trio who had visited us illegally one Plebe Summer evening, addressed Kevin suddenly.

"Brace up, plebe!" he snorted in a Midwestern nasal twang. Kevin immediately snapped to attention and pulled in his chin. So did I. Mugsy reacted however.

He held out an arm between the firstie and the two of us and said, "Carry-on!" We unbraced. Then Mugsy turned to his classmate.

"I'm taking these gentlemen on a run this morning. We don't do plebe shit when I'm in training." The classmate paused.

"Stone's not going to like this," he twanged.

"Who's gonna tell, Sydney?" asked Mugsy in a belligerent tone, emphasizing the firstie's name with derision.

Sydney, whose last name I later learned was Littleton, backed up a pace. He whined again.

"You know people talk, Mugsy. He always finds these things out. The Standing Orders are that plebes must brace up at all times in the Company area unless Stone or Captain Dillingham orders it otherwise. You're asking for trouble."

"Well, if Stone the Pussy wants to make trouble let him come down to my room and start something. Any of you Tigers think you can mess with 'ol Mugsy, are welcome to try. I'd enjoy pounding some of you assholes into pudding. It might teach you a lesson about real life, not the kind of horseshit you learn in this Mickey Mouse outhouse of an institution. Tell Stone *that,* you miserable pissant."

"We'll see," Littleton said confidently as he barged passed us on his way to the head.

We exited dark passageways of Bancroft Hall and walked across Tecumseh Court toward the wide stone stairs that lead down into the Dewey Field area. The morning air was warm and slightly damp, and the eastern sky was lightly tinged with pink as the sun labored its way upward toward dawn. It was going to be another hot and humid Maryland day. Birds in several of the enormous poplar trees didn't seem bothered, however. They chirped out a vigorous reveille as we passed. Everything else was exceedingly quiet. I took a deep breath. The air was sweet with early September scents of pending autumn.

"Excuse me, sir," O'Reilly said, interrupting my love affair with the Maryland pre-dawn.

"What!" McGinley snapped. He obviously didn't want to be disturbed either.

"Sir, this brace-up stuff is no big deal to us. We don't want you to get into trouble. We'll happily do the plebe routine while we're inside." Good idea, Kevin. I wasn't happy about Stone's noticing me too many times in the first week. It might bode poorly for the future.

McGinley thought for a long moment as we walked.

"What's the matter O'Reilly? Are you afraid of what Midshipman asshole Stone might do?"

"Frankly, sir. Yes."

"Too bad," Mugsy answered, smiling. "This is a matter of principle, gentlemen. Most of what these assholes do here in the Tiger Company has no effect on leadership. They're just too stupid to recognize that. If a man can't stand up for his principles, what else is left in this life?" Holy shit! Under his tough guy guise Mugsy was a philosopher!

I knew several Annapolis "characters" like Mugsy who I would have sworn were terminally stupid. But military academies don't admit stupid people. They have nearly the highest entrance requirements of any schools in the country. McGinley's acting as the Company palooka was therefore a fraud -- part of his mystique. It was very convincing but a fraud nonetheless. I had better keep reminding myself of that if I wanted to survive Plebe Year intact.

"Know any Shakespeare, O'Reilly?" McGinley asked. No way! This couldn't be broken-nosed Mugsy speaking? More McGinley surprises.

"Some, sir," O'Reilly answered. Another surprise! Kevin O'Reilly quoting the Bard? Amazing Kevin!

McGinley raised a finger to the morning sky.

"This above all. To thine own self be true, O'Reilly."

Kevin smiled and pointed his own finger skyward.

"And it shall follow as the night the day. Thou canst not then be false to any man, sir!" he said finishing the quote. "Hamlet. Polonius to his son Laertes, sir!" Wow! McGinley chuckled. O'Reilly and McGinley made quite a pair of frauds.

At the bottom of the steps McGinley suddenly began jogging. We caught up with him easily and soon moved smoothly, stride for stride, across the dew-wet "Dewey" field. I always loved early morning running. At Annapolis, when the morning is fresh and the air is slightly cool, there is no place better to run. I felt instantly exhilarated. Bring on the Brigade!

McGinley kept up an easy pace for the first mile. We crossed the small wooden foot bridge leading to Hospital Point, our feet pounding out a trio of wood-songs on the decking. The light from the east traced mottled pink patterns on the inlet as we crossed. It was quite lovely. Once over the bridge, we turned north and headed along the sea wall toward the Old Severn River Bridge. The water was very still and smelled somewhat exotic -- certainly different from the smells I was accustomed to in Amarillo. I loved it. At the end of Hospital Point we made a great circle and started back toward the wooden bridge along the roadway, running easily in the deep shadows under several huge trees. As we ran, I noticed Kevin looking up into the trees and smiling. He caught my stare and winked. Another O'Reilly mystery.

Instead of running us to death as I feared, McGinley continued the easy pace across the bridge and along the sea wall paralleling Dewey Field. Soon we passed the Yacht basin, where the Annapolis sailing fleet is berthed, and turned westward along the rock sea wall toward the Field House. Mugsy hopped up onto the rocks and expertly leaped the uneven surfaces. He had obviously done this before. It didn't look too safe, particularly in the proto-light of near dawn and with the rocks wet with dew. Almost immediately O'Reilly jumped up next to him and began hopping the stones in parallel with McGinley. I felt left out and not at all leader-like. I jumped up behind Kevin and joined the rock hopping. It required a great deal of concentration, but it *was* exciting. I became a rock running convert.

We stopped, stretched, and exercised briefly near the Field House. The sun was fully up by the time we had finished two sets of 30 push-ups, sit-ups, and jumping jacks. We headed back to Bancroft Hall by the same sea wall route. Mugsy never sprinted or even pushed the pace, but we had worked up a wonderful sweat. At the entrance to T-Court McGinley halted.

"That was great for a first time!" he said happily. He was plainly excited by the effort. "No run tomorrow. But we'll go again on Thursday and Saturday mornings. Each time a little faster, and a little tougher. Go immediately to your rooms and get ready for chow!" With that he strode into Bancroft Hall.

Kevin and I remained outside to stretch out our legs. I looked at him while he pulled one foot back and held it tightly against his butt.

"Shakespeare?" I asked.

"I was lucky," he replied. "He picked a quote I knew." He smiled broadly. "But damn! I was impressive, wasn't I?"

Plebes crowded the main passageway, engaged in various forms of exercise and humiliation as we turned the corner and headed for our room. We hurried past the activity. Wilson and Guevarra were already in the room when we arrived. BJ had a worried look on his face.

"What brings you back so early?" I asked.

"Trouble!" BJ exclaimed.

'What kind?" Kevin asked Rico.

Rico shrugged. "Brandis gave us the same around-the-area comearound we had yesterday, and Stone was none too happy. He spent at least 20 minutes in Brandis' room, and their voices were raised." Rico smiled mischievously. "Although, try as I might, I couldn't make out the words. When Stone came out, he smiled at us as if he knew something was going to be painful -- for us."

"Oh, well," I said trying to sound as pragmatic and unconcerned as possible. -- the mark of a good leader. -- "There's nothing we can do about it. No sense in worrying." Kevin and I hurriedly undressed and prepared for the morning meal.

Everything went well until we arrived at our tables. Both Brandis and McGinley seemed distracted. Then Stone arrived suddenly, and stood behind me. He put a hand on one of my shoulders. I could hear a strange gaiety in his voice.

"Who's it gonna be, Henry?"

Brandis looked at Stone with a scowl.

"Merritt," he said, "go with Midshipman First-class Stone and help at his table. O'Reilly, you have the noon meal duty. Wilson, evening meal. And Guevarra tomorrow morning. Continue that rotation until further notice." I watched McGinley. Mugsy glared at Stone with such intensity that I was sure he had something bad planned. I didn't understand what this was all about, but being a plebe, I didn't question either. It was apparent there was trouble brewing in the Tiger Company.

I followed Stone to his table -- also Poole and Butler's, and I realized immediately what was happening. Since Butkowski and Abbott were on training tables, only two plebes remained at Micklewski's table. It was too much for Tommy and Tim. They needed help in serving the upper-class. That made sense. I selected a seat next to Stone's and braced rigidly. Dale Micklewski sat next to Stone, grilling Poole about some aspect of the morning paper. Tommy stood braced on the other side. Beads of sweat stood on his forehead as he answered. Tim Butler, at the second-class end of the table, endured a similar grilling.

I cautiously inspected the table, making sure I knew exactly where the milk, coffee, juices, and syrups were. Micklewski's other first-class sidekick, Dick Salenger, a short, prematurely bald individual with a hooked nose and piercing blue eyes, who now sat directly across from me, caught me checking out the table.

"What's your name, plebe?" he yelled.

"Midshipman Fourth-class Merritt, sir!"

"Do you know what it means to keep your eyes in the boat?"

"Yes, sir!"

"Then why were your eyes all over the table, asshole?"

"I'll find out, sir!"

The firstie leaned toward me. He put his two tiny hands, palms-down, on the table.

"Are all your classmates so screwed up, Merritt? I thought we had the worst of the lot. But I can see I was wrong. What's the menu for morning meal, douchebag?"

I spouted off the menu with no problem. He followed my answer with questions on each of the standard plebe rates, which I also handled flawlessly. The third degree was interrupted, thankfully, by the Brigade Commander, who called us to attention and commanded the meal to begin. I immediately grabbed the milk and coffee and ensured that Stone had the first crack at those items. Tommy did the same with Micklewski and Salenger.

Simultaneously with the announcement "Brigade Seats!" various doors accessing the enormous Annapolis pantry opened and hundreds of naval enlisted stewards rushed into the Mess Hall, pushing large stainless carts heaped with trays of steaming food. This was an exercise that never ceased to amaze me. Instantly the Mess Hall became energized with the smells of food. I began to involuntarily salivate as I heard the carts clanking smoothly into position nearby. I was hungry. No sooner had the carts assumed their positions in the center aisle then the stewards grabbed trays and brought them to the tables. Plebes grabbed the plates eagerly from the trays and passed the food immediately to the firsties, then to the other classes of midshipmen in descending order of rank.

Once everyone else was served, I put some scrambled eggs and bacon on my plate. I saw that Micklewski, who was somewhat pudgy and unathletic looking, was out of eggs already. I quickly passed eggs in his direction.

"More eggs, sir?" He looked at me with surprise, and he turned toward Tommy.

"Did you see what your classmate just did, Mister Poole? He saw I needed eggs and got them for me. Why haven't you been able to master such a simple thing?"

While he was talking, Stone finished his orange juice. I refilled his glass. Stone made no comment. When I replaced the juice pitcher on the table, I saw Tommy glance at me. I could tell from his look that he wasn't angry at me. Good! I didn't need his approval to do my job. I just happened to do it better than he did.

The food passing and the grilling continued throughout the meal. The firsties soon decided they weren't going to catch us on our standard rates -- Tommy Poole and I were flawless and unflappable. They started on the Guinness Book drills.

"What was Ted Williams highest batting average, mister Merritt?"

"What's the tallest building in the world, Poole?"

"Name all the combat aircraft in the fleet!"

"What's the composition of a Marine Combat Squad?"

"Who's the Secretary General of the United Nations?"

"Name every member of the President's Cabinet!"

Most of the midshipmen at the table, regardless of their seniority, could answer any of those questions. The extracurricular educational process, particularly for the plebes and for the upper-class who trained them, was as rigorous as the actual studies themselves. Most midshipmen become involuntary intellectuals to compliment their athletic abilities and burgeoning self confidence.

Morning meals end strangely. Midshipmen wander back to their rooms whenever they finish, beginning immediately after "Brigade Seats!" Micklewski and Salinger left after 20 minutes. Stone followed suit five minutes later, once he had his own chance at Poole. After Stone departed, one of the second-class near the foot of the table asked us questions until he too tired of the games and left. I glanced at the wall chronometer and saw that we had five minutes remaining before we had to leave the Mess Hall. I also realized that neither Tommy nor I had eaten a single bite, and that upset me. I picked up my fork.

"Poole, Butler, Merritt!" I put down my fork and stared straight ahead. The voice had come from my starboard side and I had no idea who had called to us.

"Sir!" we all answered.

"Carry-on. All meal restrictions are relaxed at this table. Eat quickly!" I unbraced and glanced gratefully down to the end of the table. A single third-class remained. It was Jack Collins. He smiled at me. "Hurry up! Eat!" he commanded. We ate quickly and in large bites.

Eating one meal in four with some of the biggest assholes in the Brigade was not such a big deal. I could hack that. I explained what had happened when I returned to the room. What I didn't expect was the other part of the deal Stone had arranged with Brandis.

Guevarra explained it.

"It seems that meal times aren't the only periods when Stone-the-asshole wants company for Poole and Butler. He told Brandis he wasn't happy with his Henry's comearound routines. Apparently they aren't what the "Book" defines as motivational enough. So from now on we'll do our comearounds with Stone himself. Great, huh?"

I may have thought that Rock Stone was a great leader, but I wasn't stupid enough to relish the pain I was sure accompanied coming around to him either. I groaned.

"What did McGinley say?" I asked.

"Mugsy told us that on mornings we would continue to run with him when he wanted a workout and that Stone could kiss his ass." I went to class that morning not at all happy about this turn of events.

It's amazing how quickly a person can fall into a routine, even a painful one. Comearounds to Stone *were* painful, but luckily they were a once-a-day affair. Rock was careful not to give us any "forbidden" exercises, but, Jesus, he ran us up and down the passageway mercilessly. He was an expert at comearound torture. The first week ended with further incident, but I was very sore.

On Friday night I chopped down to the telephone banks and called home to let my family know I was surviving and to emphasize my request for food donations. It was good to hear my parents' voices. I really missed them. I also missed Lynda, and I called her immediately after Mom and Dad. She was waiting for my call, and her voice flowed with sweetness and life and hope for the future. The longer I was away from her, the more I realized how deeply I felt. We pledged undying love before we hung up.

On weekends after noon meal, plebes have liberty in town, which lasts until evening meal formation. The four of us decided to visit the city of Annapolis to show off our studliness and get something to eat. Even though we weren't allowed to speak to a female, Rico intended to use the city visit as an opportunity to meet some young ladies, and Kevin wholeheartedly supported him. They could take that risk, but I wasn't interested. I had my Lynda back home. I didn't need any other women in my life.

Jack Collins had told us about a great submarine sandwich shop on Main Street, and I had repeated salivating visions of eating one with the "works." BJ and I'd stick to subs while the other two went "trapping for beaver" as Rico so indelicately put it.

The uniform for town liberty was Tropical White Long, which was an actual naval fleet uniform composed of starched white pants, matching, perfectly pleated white shirt, black shoulder-boards -- without any stripes since we were only plebes -- a white belt with gleaming gold buckle, polished white shoes, and combination cap.

We inspected each other before we left the room. We looked great. Rico was positively oozing male sexuality and he was raring to go. The walk to Annapolis proper is as easy as exiting at the Field House gate, turning to port, and continuing for two blocks in a westerly direction. The downtown area bustled with tourists, midshipmen of various ranks, and hordes of young ladies anxious to meet midshipmen of any rank. We noticed several appreciative stares from young and old ladies alike as we swaggered toward Main Street, laughing and jostling as we walked. God, were we studly!

Once on the main drag, which happens to be named Main Street, Rico stopped us to look around.

"Okay," he said. "I see several likely prospects. Who's with me?"

Kevin immediately volunteered. BJ hesitated.

"How do you intend to do this with all these upper-class around?" he asked.

"Very carefully, but with style," Rico answered. Rico turned to me and took out his wallet. "Get me a meatball sub with lots of sauce and onions," he said handing me a five-dollar bill. "I'll meet you in front of the old market in a half hour." Next, Kevin took out his own wallet, and gave me a five.

"Make mine a hamburger sub. Hold the onions," he said. I looked at BJ who still hesitated torn between the emptiness in his stomach and the call of the wild. Then he extracted his own wallet.

"Pastrami, tomatoes, lettuce, and lots of mayo," he said.

I laughed good-naturedly.

"You'll probably all get caught and sent back to Bancroft Hall," I said. "It's a long walk. I might get hungry."

"No sweat," Kevin said. "Just save me half of mine."

They wandered off toward a group of attractive young ladies who were staring and giggling to each other at the sight of Rico and BJ. Kevin, I figured, was along for the leftovers, but he could be awfully charming when he wanted to be. I crossed Main Street and headed for the sub shop. Before entering I glanced back and saw that the girls had followed Rico and his "trapper trainees" into an antique store. I opened the door and entered culinary paradise.

Inside the sub shop the smell of delicious foods warred with each other. I took a deep satisfying breath, and my stomach rumbled in anticipation. I moved quickly to the end of a line of about 10 people -- all civilians. I immediately noticed that the person directly in front of me was a very pretty girl about my age. She had dark, Italian features and a very nice figure, which looked wonderful in the tight white miniskirt she had chosen to wear. Her hair was thick, long, and straight and hung midway down her back. She glanced at me when I moved into line behind her and smiled sweetly. I smiled in return.

Once while we were first dating, Lynda had explained some of the techniques girls pass on to each other about making themselves more attractive to men. The young lady in front of me had been a very good student. As I glanced appreciatively at her, trying hard not to stare, she rose on tiptoe, ostensibly to check the menu board that hung over the counter. The motion made her already fine legs seem longer and more shapely. Then she turned slightly so that I could get a side view of her bust line, which was ample and nicely formed. Then she flicked back her hair so that it swished and shimmered from side to side. She was good, really good! Once she was certain she had my attention, she twisted toward me. Leaning in close so that I could smell her provocative perfume, she smiled again and asked. "Can you see the menu board?" I smiled in return.

"Sure!"

"What's the price of the foot long luncheon meat sub?" I checked the menu

"Three dollars."

"I've never eaten here before," she said changing the subject. I knew she hadn't been at all interested in the cost of baloney. She knew that I knew. "Do they make good subs?"

I checked quickly to see if any upper-class were in the shop. There weren't any. I then gave her a jolt of Texas charm.

"Well, ma'am," I said. "To tell the truth, this is my first time here too. I guess we're both winging it."

She smiled again and turned completely toward me. She was very attractive -- as pretty as my Lynda but rather more exotic.

"Are you a middie?" she asked. I laughed.

"Never say "middie." It's an insult. We are "mids" or midshipmen. And, yes, I am one."

She laughed sweetly, and I noticed that she had very white, straight teeth and full lips that invited kissing.

"Sorry," she said. "I didn't realize."

"You're not from around here?" I asked.

"No. I was born in Richmond and grew up there. Now I'm going to college near Washington, D.C. I drove down here to see the sights."

"I hope you like what you see so far," I said in an obvious but casual flirt. As I made the statement I began to feel a little bit uncomfortable about "cheating" on Lynda, but I was only talking to this young lady. What harm was that?

She reached out and offered her delicate hand.

"I'm Leslie Taylor Wallace," she said with just a hint of an accent. That was quite a name. I liked it. It spoke of Southern refinement and good breeding.

"I'm James Wesley Merritt from Amarillo, Texas," I said, taking her hand and holding it far longer than I would have for a casual introduction. "It's very nice to meet you, ma'am."

"Yes it is," she said. By this time we had reached the front of the line, and she ordered. I also noticed that two second-class midshipmen had entered and now stood at the rear of the line. One looked at me suspiciously -- and jealousy. Leslie's order arrived. Leslie paid her bill, reached into her purse, and pulled out a small notepad. As I waited for my orders, she scribbled her name, address, and phone number on a piece of paper and handed it to me.

"Unfortunately I don't have time to chat now. I came here with two friends who are waiting to meet me, so I've got to run. Call me, please," she added the "please" with emphasis and smiled an incredible smile. She liked me, no doubt about it. She hurried out of the sub shop.

I studied the note and found to my surprise that the prefix matched my birthday and the last four digits of her phone number was the numerical opposite of my parents' number in Amarillo. I put the note into my pocket, keeping my back firmly toward the upperclass. I paid my tab, and with the four subs tucked under my arm, I headed quickly for the door and exited.

Unfortunately so did the second-class who had watched my interchange with Leslie.

"Plebe halt!" he said with a loud sneer. Several tourist families stopped to watch as he approached me. Luckily I did not have to endure the humiliation of being braced up in public.

"What was that conversation all about, plebe?" he asked.

"Sir. She asked me if I could read the menu for her. I did."

"And then did she write the prices down so you wouldn't forget them?" he asked sarcastically.

"No sir!"

"Let's see the note plebe!" He held out a hand almost in my face. He was definitely sneering at my discomfort. The tourists watched intently.

I hesitated. He pounced.

"If I don't have that note in my hand in one second, I'm going to put you on report for fraternization. You don't want that do you, plebe?"

"No, sir!"

"The note!" he said again. I took the paper from my pocket and reluctantly handed it to him. He opened it and read it.

"Contraband," he said, smiling. "I'll have to keep this."

"Sir?"

"You heard me. I'm keeping this. Consider yourself lucky I'm letting you go so easily. Beat it!"

I stood my ground for a moment, actually thinking about my chances of escape if I decked the jerk and ran for the hills -- grabbing the note in the process, of course. Then I remembered that I had my Lynda, so I didn't need the information on the note. I wasn't intending to do anything with it, was I?

I turned, endured the sad stares of several nearby adults and the sarcastic comment of a hippy in a denim jacket embroidered with flowers, who laughed and said. "What kind of Admiral are you? I thought they taught you guys to be killers? You shoulda punched him out." The rest of the audience laughed. I was humiliated.

I crossed the street and went to the Market. I began fuming. I waited outside for several long minutes. Deciding that the others had forgotten our rendezvous, I started back toward the Academy. As I turned, I heard a voice from across the street yell.

"Jim! Over here!" It was Kevin beckoning from the doorway of the antique shop. I crossed the street, still upset.

Inside the shop was dark. Several pieces of heavy wooden furniture and a dusty window blocked a clear view of the interior. After entering I saw Rico and BJ talking to three giggly young ladies. Kevin stood watch by the door while he conversed with another girl.

"Jim, come over here and meet someone special!" Rico said. Immediate calculations showed four girls, and now, four plebes. Rico needed me to round things out. I wasn't in the mood for this, but I went anyway. The girls all seemed nice enough but they were clearly high school aged, and high school was a long way from college -- for us one year -- and that seemed almost infinity. These girls certainly weren't mature like my Lynda or cultured like Leslie. Leslie? What brought her to mind? I had no designs in that regard. But at least the girls were pretty and nubile, so I decided not to act like I felt. I engaged in animated conversation. The proprietor of the store said nothing as we exchanged pleasantries. He must witness an identical scenario every weekend. Maybe he was just a nice guy interested in the fate of the downtrodden. Maybe the flow of plebes and young ladies into his store brought other curious customers. Maybe he was a voyeur, taking note of how virile men like us handled our affairs of the heart.

Rico introduced me to the group. He had already "trapped" one for himself -- surprisingly not the best looking. She was certainly the most sensual of the group, however. I guess that fit Rico's plans. BJ had paired himself off with the long-haired blond beauty of the four. The one that remained for me, another blond, while not unattractive, seemed almost overeager to get to know me better.

Annapolis has a strange effect on young women. I was flattered by the girl's attention but she reminded me of a young Lynda, so I was slightly put off. I remained charming, and I thickened my Texas drawl to add to my mystique. Conversation continued for a few more minutes, and soon we exchanged addresses. These four young ladies lived not far from Annapolis, in the Severna Park area -- wherever that is -- and yes they were in high school. I wasn't interested in further contact, but it was nice to be the center of someone's interest for a few minutes. And this was twice in one day. I am a true midshipman stud, no question about it!

We ate our sandwiches outside near the boat basin sitting on a set of wide stone steps facing the activity in the harbor. Annapolis' harbor is beautiful, and multitudes of sailboats berthed nearby. Out in the Severn, and farther out in the Chesapeake, I could see a rainbow of multi colored sails painting the blue waters with splotches of brightness. I could also hear the sounds of laughter and the snapping of luffing canvas from several nearby boats. A breeze had picked up, and the water farther out was white-capped, but the bright sun sparkled off the calmer harbor water. The harbor air brought smells of life and adventure to those of us landlocked on the wooden harbor deck. I loved the water and the idea of a life at sea. I raised my nose to the air and took a deep breath.

"Stinks, doesn't it?" Rico observed from his seat across from me.

"What?"

"The damn water stinks. Smells like dead slimy things."

"If you think this is bad, you should smell Boston Harbor," Kevin added, laughing. "The smells there make me gag."

"That's nothing," added BJ with a chuckle. "I know a stretch of Manhattan where the river stinks so bad even the fishermen retch."

I was confused because they seemed to be serious. But I didn't find the smell distasteful at all. In fact, it was exhilarating. Cattle smelled bad. Crude oil smelled worse. Some of the migrant workers who frequented the downtown area of Amarillo were unbearable. But not this. This was wonderful. I breathed deeply and savored the various flavors as we ate. The sub was delicious, even slightly cold, and only Kevin managed to spill any of the various sauces or juices on his white uniform, but we all expected that -- even Kevin, who laughed it off, but who would worry until we returned that some upper-class would punish his clumsy eating mistake.

The plebe conversation centered on the Academy and sex, not particularly in that order. I didn't say a word about what happened to me, but the others talked about their female conquests of the afternoon, and Rico explained sotto voce in detail what he intended to do with his young lady.

"There's no liberty away from Annapolis until Army-Navy and Thanksgiving," I said. "How do you plan to make good on your promise?" Rico laughed and looked at Kevin, who twinkled in return.

"I have my resources," he said. "Want to make a bet that I have my way with that young lady within, say, three weeks?"

Was he kidding? That didn't seem possible. I was about to accept the bet when I saw Kevin staring at me with a Merritt-thinks-he-knows-everything-but-just-wait look. I hesitated.

"There's something you 've been holding back since the summer. You guys did something. What was it?"

"It's so secret that if we told you, we'd have to kill you," Kevin said.

"They got laid during Plebe Summer!" BJ suddenly exclaimed in delighted revelation. He said it so loudly that several nearby families looked up from their own conversations. BJ either didn't notice, or didn't care. "That's got to be a record of some kind," he continued. "Holy Shit! How'd you do it?" Neither Rico nor Kevin answered, but both sported enormous all-knowing smiles.

"No way!" I said, disbelievingly. "It's not possible!" Still neither one would say a word of confirmation.

"Okay," BJ said, "I can see where you might not want to tell Merritt-the-greaser about your techniques, but later you can tell me. Hell, I'll participate next time -- God, will I ever. I'll even buy the liquor with which to ply the young lovelies. I am so horny I'm about to burst." The father of a nearby family chuckled at that comment, and his wife poked him with an elbow. His two small children listened open-mouthed. I shook my head and shrugged at the mother, who also smiled secretly at our plight.

And what was this Merritt-the-greaser crap? Sure I liked it here. And sure I wanted to do well. But I was also one of the guys. I liked a good time too. But there just wasn't any sense in my taking any chances for an opportunity to meet a girl in some dark place. I had Lynda to think about, and I was serious about my relationship with her.

The walk back to the Academy was uneventful. Kevin kept a hand strategically in front of his shirt to hide the grease stain. We still had two hours before evening meal. Kevin decided to organize a basketball game, and several of the youngsters participated. I played, but I'm not so great. Rico Guevarra was good. And Kevin O'Reilly was fantastic. He glided up and down the court gracefully. Several times he made spinning, twisting shots that I would have thought impossible. We played two games of full court against a youngster group and beat them handily in both, despite the fact that we had to use Barton Hardesty as our center. I'm not sure he had ever played any sport before he came to Annapolis.

Barton Hardesty was the most unusual plebe in the Company. At six foot five, he was the tallest of the plebes. And Barton was still growing. He had added an inch in height during the summer. But he could not have weighed more than 160 pounds, even after the intensive training of Plebe Summer. However, he had unusually long arms, and he could jump -- even though he looked like a stork on those long thin, spindly legs -- and he took direction well from O'Reilly, who also proved himself to be a good field leader -- at least on the basketball court.

Barton, was also the least liked plebe in the group. His father was a minister in some splinter-of-a-splinter church in Memphis, Tennessee, and Barton had been taught to believe in a very literal interpretation of the Bible. It was one of those religions that calculated, based on biblical "begetting," that the universe had been created during the last Super Bowl despite all scientific and logical proof to the contrary. Now that was okay with me. Super Bowl Sunday is as good a day as any, and Barton could believe anything he wanted.--Hell, he might be right. -- But Barton made the mistake of preaching his beliefs to every human being he met and being insufferable about them. When he got going on religion, he talked with such a fervency and intensity that he frightened me. There was a deep, abiding fire in Barton's eyes that the Academy was not going to quench. And Barton was frustrated.

Flowery language in particular bothered Barton. He winced at every four-lettered word and descriptive phrase. Even "damn" was a forbidden utterance around Barton. -- except that none of it *was* forbidden at Annapolis and certainly not in the fleet. The system almost seemed to encourage a bit of innovation in the speech patterns of midshipmen. I sensed at times there was almost an ongoing contest to invent the newest colorful invective, and some of the upper-class used off-color language the way a sculptor shapes stone. There was actually "art" in their articulation, and I was amazed and impressed by what I heard.

Language, flowery or otherwise, never bothered me particularly. If you've ever heard a cowboy curse, you'd understand. I wasn't particularly sympathetic with Barton, and he acted as if he had some God-given decree which forbade everybody else to be comfortable. Once during the summer he asked Mike Maxwell to tone down his speech. Maxie told him -- and I'm quoting, "Fuck no!" I was behind Maxie a hundred percent on that one.

Despite the aberrations in his personality, Barton learned games quickly -- especially basketball. He jumped high, passed accurately, and even dunked the ball twice, -- under the careful direction of Kevin.

And Rico, who loved to poke and prod into seeping wounds, yelled at Barton with each score. "Good god-damn shot, Bart!" Hardesty winced repeatedly, torn between reacting to the words or to the compliments.

Evening meal on Saturday again marked my turn again to sit with the Rock and his overzealous buddies. I did my duty with precision and competence as always; however, midway through the meal Dale Micklewski looked up from his merciless grilling of Tommy Poole.

He said to Rock, "It looks as if Mugsy's at it again, Rock. Their table has carry-on."

"God damn!" Stone exploded. "I'm gonna get McGinley before this year is over."

"Just make sure he doesn't get you first," Micklewski said. I wasn't sure what he meant by that, but obviously the trouble in the Tiger Company went very deep, and it was strange that someone like Rock didn't realize. He had all the qualities of a good leader, but his perspective seemed skewed The intensive Tiger-style negative leadership never would achieve success. Its harshness forced failure by ensuring most of the Company would root against the leadership -- even some of the Tiger classmates. That was just plain stupid. I had already submitted a recommended topic for my end-of-term paper in Military Leadership class: *"Tiger Company - Why it doesn't work."* God, there was enough material in Tiger Company on negative and bizarre leadership to fill volumes. Why didn't Stone see that?

I could hear Stone chuckle. "Wait 'til Monday morning. We'll see." Monday morning, huh? I wondered what was up.

Sunday was a repeat of Saturday except that Sunday morning meal was a brunch-like affair with no bracing allowed. I loved Sunday morning meals. I marched to Protestant Chapel at 1030 hours with several hundred of my brethren.

The Academy Chapel is inspiring. Words can't describe it properly. I loved the magnificent architecture. I loved the pomp and circumstance. I loved the wonderful chaplains. I loved the feelings the services evoked. And I loved to sing there, and that may be the most amazing thing of all.

I never liked to sing before I went to Annapolis, my voice stinks. But somehow, mixed with the voices of several hundred other midshipmen and backed by the angelic harmony of the Annapolis Choir, my off-key notes seemed to spring directly and melodically to God himself -- and He was pleased. My favorite song of all time is the Naval Academy hymn. Its words and music *have* to be divinely inspired. I can't listen to it without tears coming to my eyes, and that's some admission for a Texan.

Early Sunday afternoon Kevin O'Reilly, who truly loved to sing, and who in fact had a pretty good voice -- went off to Glee Club tryouts while the rest of us wrote letters home. Mom had promised me a massive care package. She had recruited the help of several neighbors in what she now called her "Cookie Brigade." I couldn't wait. Mom made the best chocolate chip cookies in the known universe.

At 1330, while I was writing a letter to sweet Linda, a very despondent Kevin O'Reilly chopped into the room.

"Well Ringo, how'd it go?" asked Rico. Obviously it hadn't gone well.

Kevin didn't speak. He walked dejectedly to his chair, sat, and slowly sank his head onto his arms outstretched on his desk. He groaned. Rico laughed.

"What's the matter? Didn't they have a place in the Glee Club for an off-key Irish tenor?" Kevin groaned again. Then he raised his head and looked at each of us in turn.

"Okay," he said, taking a slow, deep breath. "This is how it went."

"I like to sing. Everybody knows that. Christ, I'm Irish! My parents and I used to watch *Mitch Miller* together, and I always sang along with gusto. I was in my catholic school boy's choir, and I even had a very short career with a folk singing group. Singing is in my blood. It's a natural part of being a Kevin O'Reilly.

"And I *can* sing. You've heard me bellow in the shower and sing along with the radio. I mean -- I sound great to me.

"I went to the choir loft of the chapel for Glee Club tryouts, visions of field trips and time away from the menace of idiotic upper classmen dancing -- or maybe singing -- in my head. I got there and stood in a long line of fellow plebes -- who also had visions of field trips no doubt. I was nervous, to be sure, but, I can sing, damn it!

"Well, finally my turn came to audition, and I entered a small dark room. Inside, alone at an old piano, was an elderly woman. I recognized her as one of the Chapel organists. She introduced herself, looked me over for a moment, and asked me if I knew how to sing *Swanee River*. 'Sort of,' I replied."

"*Swanee River*?" Kevin yelled incredulously. "I mean what kind of singing test is that anyway? What about *Tom Dooley* or *500 Miles* or *The House of the Rising Sun*? But no, *Swanee River*, she said, and *Swanee River* she wanted." I smiled. Kevin was intense, and he told great stories.

"She pounded on an old upright piano with a brief flourish and I knew it was time for me to show my stuff. I took a deep breath and started in on cue -- but maybe not on key. Maybe that stupid song doesn't have a key. Hell, I don't even know what a "key" is, but I could tell immediately I was "off" whatever key she wanted, and I panicked. 'What am I doing here?' I thought, as I began singing that impossible song." Kevin took a deep breath. By this time he was so engrossed in his story he had forgotten how depressed he had been moments earlier.

"I had started badly," he continued, "thinking I could overwhelm the music with the power of my voice. But as the range of asinine notes shifted up and down, I realized I had chosen the wrong tack. By the time I had finished the first line, even my untrained ear told me I was in deep musical trouble. As the last vibrations of "river" echoed through the small room, I decided to change my plan and show her my vocal versatility. I began to croon, "Far, far, away . . . " He gave us an imitation of Kevin O'Reilly trying to sound like Frank Sinatra. Rico began laughing.

"That didn't work either, because the old bitch wouldn't slow the rhythm enough to let me croon. The second line came out in a slur of words and sounds that didn't sound much better than line one. In fact, it was worse -- far worse.

"Soon she had begun the third line and I reverted to my own version of Irish fortissimo. But that damned "r" at the end of the third line screwed it up again, and insisted on sneaking out my nose rather than my mouth.

"Things were bad, guys -- very bad. And they were gonna get worse. As I began the fourth and final line, I realized with a panic that I hadn't the faintest idea of the proper words. So I faked it. You guys want to hear how it sounded?" We all agreed eagerly.

"Way down upon the Swanee Riverrrrr . . . ,
Far, far, away.
That's where my heart is yearning everrrrr . . . ,
That's where the old folks play."

"The old folks play?" Rico asked incredulously in between laughs.

"That's what I sang. Shit. I have no idea how that damn verse ends, and I knew I had screwed that line the second I sang it." Kevin looked at us, his blue eyes twinkling. I found myself laughing so hard I almost couldn't breathe. O'Reilly was a jewel. He held up his hands.

"But that's not the worse thing," he continued. "Suddenly the thought of my gray-haired grandparents tossing a beach ball down on the bank of an old slow river intruded itself into my audition, and I laughed as I finished. No, actually I bellowed. I couldn't help myself. I'm such an idiot!

"The old lady didn't laugh, though. And I'm sure she hadn't even listened to the last three lines. Somewhere between 'Way' and 'down' she had decided she'd heard enough. She looked up at me as I finished with no expression on her face. I swear she didn't even notice I was laughing. That made me laugh harder.

Kevin hunched over his desk with his hands bent-elbowed in front of him pretending he sat at a piano. He bent his head downward and looked at us over what he pretended was a pair of reading glasses. 'Thank you, dear.' he said in a sweet matronly voice. 'Tell the next applicant to enter on your way out.'" I bellowed. Tears streamed down my face. Kevin wasn't finished.

"You shoulda seen the looks on the faces of the other plebes outside when I departed. It was priceless. I'm sure they wondered what kind of rip-roaring audition was happening in that little room. 'Next!' I said between laughs, and this caused me to laugh even harder."

Kevin took a deep breath and calmed himself. "On my way back to Bancroft, I thought about the experience. Does this mean I can't sing? Is Rico finally right about something? Should I give up my shower performances? And where the hell is this rotten, miserable, Swanee River anyway? When I find out, I'm gonna go there and a take a massive and very satisfying, leak right in that stinking stream."

Kevin paused, which was good because I needed a break. I was crying from laughing so hard.

"Then I had a revelation," he continued confidently. "I have decided that my audition was inconclusive. Never having heard *Swanee River* sung by another human being, I'm not convinced it's even possible. Hell, it's never been done by Neal Diamond, there's no Beatles *Swanee* album, and I don't recall my mother or Mitch Miller ever singing about the 'old folks at play' either. So I believe the test was unfair. And even if it wasn't, I don't really care, and you pukes can kiss my ass. I don't sing for anyone's benefit but my own, and all the critics and criticism in the world can't make me give up singing -- in the shower or anywhere else." With that proclamation, Kevin sat up straight in his chair and glared at us defiantly. I continued laughing.

"Does this mean you didn't make the Glee Club?" asked Rico, bursting into another fit of hilarity.

"Eat shit, Guevarra!" Kevin answered, joining in the laughter.

Following The O'Reilly Show, we all went into Annapolis again for another round of subs. Reb, Jeff, and Tommy went along. Kevin was either very depressed or very hungry. He ate an entire foot-long hamburger sub and a six-inch meatball sub and finished before any of us. Reb ate two foot-longs, but he had a reputation to consider.

I ate evening meal with the squad, and Brandis gave us carry-on, ostensibly because it was the birthday of one of the youngsters in the squad, Chuck "Bull" Brewer, who had requested plebe carry-on as part of the festivities. I loved carry-on, and I was especially attentive to Brandis and McGinley to show my appreciation.

After the meal, Rico, Kevin, and BJ went down to the phones to call their young lovelies. I was tempted to go along to see what they had planned, but decided not to get involved. As I sat alone in the room, glancing over my Psychology notes, I recalled the injustice of the incident with the second-classman. I thought about Leslie Taylor Wallace and how it would be nice to talk to her occasionally. I wished her number hadn't been stolen. She seemed very sweet.

Feeling robbed and cheated, I began to fume. Suddenly I remembered that her number had been special because it had been the numerical transposition of my parents'. I half-shouted out loud. I jotted her name and number in my notebook. Maybe I would call her sometime. Maybe I would call her tonight. After all, the asshole who took her note might call and try to weasel his way into her life. She didn't need that prick, did she? Damn it! I decided to call her immediately and straighten this out! It was the honorable thing to do. Even Lynda would understand.

I hurried to the phone banks, careful to avoid the others. They were piled into a single booth, laughing and telling lies to those poor high schoolers. I pitied them in a way. Leslie was in college at least. I mean *Lynda* was in college. I dialed the number she had given me. It turned out to be a sorority house in the Georgetown section of Washington, D.C. Not only did she have class and breeding, but her parents must have been somewhat wealthy. Leslie came to the phone after a few minutes.

"Hello!" she said tentatively.

"Hi," I said. "It's me, Jim Merritt. We met in the sub shop in Annapolis yesterday." There was a long pause.

"Is this really Jim Merritt?" she asked.

"Yes. It's me."

"Why did you give my number to that horrible person who's been calling here making my life miserable? I'm very angry at you, Jim Merritt." It was cute the way she called me "Jim Merritt" instead of Jim or James or Jimmy.

"Wait," I said hurriedly. "I can explain." I told her about the rules against plebe fraternization and about the second-classman and the confrontation and how the note was confiscated, and how concerned I was about her, and how I had memorized her number. I laid it on a little thick and actually might have implied that the confrontation was with several upper-class that I refused to give up the note, and that they had to forcibly remove the note from my cold dead fingers, etc. Leslie ate it up.

"Wow," she said, "you took quite a risk talking to me, Jim Merritt."

"Some things are worth it," I replied.

"You're very sweet." Yeah, I am. That's what Lynda says all the time.

"Maybe we can see each other sometime?" she asked. See each other? I thought I was here to cultivate someone to talk to? What about Lynda? What was I doing?

"It's very hard for me to get away," I continued, "but we might be able to work something out." How the hell was I going to "work something out?"

We talked for several minutes before she said with genuine regret that the house phone had a ten minute conversation limit and that she had to get her homework done.

"Me too," I said. "When's a good time to call again?"

"Any day after seven in the evening," she said.

"Great! I'll call tomorrow." Tomorrow? What was I doing? But Leslie sure was nice to talk to. And there's no harm in phone calls, is there?

That evening a strange thing happened that I didn't immediately understand. The Plan of the Day (POD) is an official Academy document that publishes the scheduled routine and upcoming events, and lists the Officers who have the duty. Usually the POD is posted several days in advance. When I chopped by the Company Office area to check on Monday's events, I noticed the POD was missing. Without it, I could not find out the meals or the Officers for the next day. On the Bulletin Board was a note: *"The POD will be posted prior to 0600 tomorrow."* Shrugging, I returned to my room.

"No POD yet, guys. There's a note by the Company Office that says it'll be posted tomorrow before 0600."

"How are we supposed to learn our rates with the POD missing?" asked Kevin.

"No idea, but that's the way it is. I think I'll get up extra early and go over to the Main Office and check there. That way we can get the info before anyone else."

"Good idea," Rico said. "But don't wake me when you leave."

That evening The Three Lustkateers plotted a rendezvous with their new-found honeys. Since I had informed them that I wasn't interested in participating, they must have decided not to share any information concerning the actual event. I agreed wholeheartedly. I didn't want to know. The three of them giggled like schoolgirls as they discussed possible scenarios and outcomes. I overheard the words Hospital Point quite a few times during their discussion. Afterward we settled down to study. At nearly 2100 an upper-class entered and we braced. It was the same one who had brought shoes for Kevin to polish last Sunday. Guess what he had in his hand?

He plopped the pair of black shoes down in front of Kevin and said.

"I need them by tomorrow morning." He turned to go.

"No sir!" Kevin said. The upper-class turned to him.

"What did you say?"

"I'm not doing your shoes, sir!"

"Give me 50 push-ups, you bastard plebe!" Kevin dropped to the deck and began pushing-up.

"Excuse me, sir," interjected Rico, "but we have been informed by Midshipman First-class McGinley to report the name of any individual who asks us to shine shoes or perform any other personal service. What's your name, sir?" The upper-class became instantly afraid. He reached for his shoes, just as Kevin stopped his push-ups, jumped to his feet, and grabbed them from the desk.

"Give me those shoes!"

"No sir! Orders! You have to see Midshipman McGinley first. He will tell me if I can release the shoes to you."

"Give me those god-damn shoes, plebe, or there'll be hell to pay!"

"Sir!" Rico continued. "You can see Midshipman McGinley to work out the details for shoe release. Until then, consider them held hostage." Neither Guevarra nor O'Reilly braced, which was an incredible breach of Academy etiquette; but they didn't seem concerned. I felt like a weenie, rigidly watching the drama unfolding before me but afraid to let my posture slouch around an upper-classman.

"Are you disobeying a direct order, plebe?"

"Yes, sir!" Kevin answered, but I could tell from his tone that he was nervous about the position he was in. The stranger sensed Kevin's discomfort and pounced.

"Give me those shoes or you're on report, mister!" Rico saved the day. He walked boldly around to the front of the desk and took the shoes from the wavering Kevin.

"Okay," he said, "that'll be enough in the way of threats. Academy regulations strictly forbid the use of plebes as personal servants, and the example in the Reg Book even concerns shoe shining. You're way out of line. Right now this is between you and McGinley. If you don't get out of this room immediately or if you put anyone on report, I will personally go to Captain Dillingham and report what you did. So cut your losses and beat it!" Jesus! He evicted a strange upper-class from the room. He's gonna be a dead man when Stone finds out.

"Do I get my shoes or not?"

"You do not! Sir!"

"Fine! Then suffer the consequences!" Following that threat the upper-class spun around and left the room. Rico handed the shoes to Kevin.

"You better hustle these down to Mugsy so the final confrontation is between the two of them."

"Thanks, Rico," Kevin said. "I was almost ready to give that asshole back his shoes."

"No sweat, pal." Kevin quickly chopped into the passageway and headed toward Mugsy's room.

"Jesus, Rico!" I said after Kevin had departed. "You took quite a chance."

"Nah. The guy's a pussy. He was only bluffing. McGinley will clobber his ass!"

Kevin returned several minutes later.

"McGinley will handle it from here."

We went to bed without further interruption.

CHAPTER 4

COMEAROUNDS

I have always been a very light sleeper and never had any trouble getting up whenever I wanted. I usually don't even need an alarm clock. Just to be safe, however, I set my small wind-up alarm for 0530 -- the usual weekday morning time. I also mentally willed myself to wake early so that I could check the POD at the Main Office.

I woke at 0508. I double checked the time with the alarm near the bed, smiled to myself at the accuracy of my internal clock, and slipped quietly out of bed. With hardly a sound I dressed in my gym gear, grabbed pencil and paper, and quietly stepped into the darkened passageway. Rather than risk disturbing someone by chopping in the Company area at this early hour, I silently ran on tiptoes, quickly reached the outside door, and exited Bancroft Hall into T-Court. The main office was just to the port side of the rotunda entrance.. I hurried across T-Court and up the wide stairway. It was dark and quiet outside.

At this early hour only the small heavy brass personnel doors that led into the rotunda were unlocked. I pushed one open and went inside. I was nervous about visiting the Main Office because the upper-class on duty there were strangers, and I didn't know what they would say to a plebe visit at this unusual hour. But we needed the information on the POD, so the risk was necessary.

The Main Office was brightly lit, an overpowering contrast to the darkened passageway and rotunda. The occasional sounds of laughter and other activity echoed from the watch staff. I approached the door carefully. A plebe sat casually at a desk near the office entrance. He leaned back slightly in his chair, smiling and joking with another person who was out of sight. I entered the Office, stopped just inside the door, and looked hurriedly around.

Three other plebes sat at various desks around the Office. None seemed particularly busy. In the center of the office two upper-class sat relaxed. The second-class, who had his eyes intently focused on the desk in front of him, was making a paper airplane and telling a joke as his fingers deftly folded the paper. The first-class next to him had his feet up on his desk and leaned backward on the rear legs of his chair, supporting the back of his head with his hands. Judging by the three stripes on his black shoulder-boards, he was probably the Company Commander of one of the other Companies. Everyone looked at me when I entered except the second-class who went on with his story.

"Sir!" I began. "Midshipman Fourth-class Merritt. My Company needs today's POD. May I see yours so I can copy the information?" I waited at attention for a response. The first-class looked up questioningly.

"What do you mean you don't have a POD?" he asked. "The main office sends them out a week at a time. We got one in my Company last Monday, and you're the first to report any missing PODs. Are you sure yours is missing?"

"Yes, sir! Our Company Commander posted a note last evening saying it would be delayed until 0600 this morning. I didn't want to wait that long."

"Good idea, plebe," offered the second-class. "What Company you with?"

"Twenty-third, sir!" I snapped with a bit of pride.

"Ohhhhhh!" the second-class replied with mock fear. "The Tigers!"

"It doesn't seem right that Stone and the Tigers would screw up like this, plebe," the first-class said skeptically. "But what the hell. We're all human, right Smitty?" he said addressing the plebe at the door.

"Yes, sir!" the plebe answered with a casualness I found incredible.

"Okay, Smitty," the first-class continued. "Give your classmate some copies of the POD and let him be on his way. But hurry up! You-know-who will be here soon to start his morning rounds."

I didn't know who you-know-who was, but I wasn't going to ask either. The plebe by the door got up and walked to a large white wooden cubbyhole shelf that stretched floor to ceiling almost from one end of the office to the other. The cubbyholes contained forms, announcements, and bulletins. There must have been hundreds of different papers available, and I wondered briefly what each piece of information represented. I didn't have much time for reverie. The plebe quickly extracted nearly 20 copies of the day's POD and handed them to me.

"Here you go," he said with a smile. I smiled in return, then turned to the upper-class.

"Thank you sirs!"

"Don't mention it," the firstie said with genuine friendliness. Who was this guy, and why wasn't he my squadleader or better yet, my Company Commander? Clutching the PODs in one hand, I hurried from the Main Office and through the rotunda. Before I had gone very far I heard loud laughter coming from the office. They were probably laughing about the Tigers.

The entire trip took only a few minutes. The Company passageway s were still dark when I returned, but lights were on in most of the plebe rooms. I slipped a POD under the door of each plebe room, considering it my contribution to classmate unity. Inside our room everyone else was up and ready. Kevin had the newspaper, and he and BJ were reading articles aloud while Rico quoted Sunday's NFL football scores.

"Here's the POD," I said as I entered.

"Great!" said Kevin. "What's the gouge?"

I read off the menu for breakfast and lunch, then came to the names of the new officers of the watch. I was especially interested in seeing who the duty midshipmen were since they seemed so loose in contrast to our Company leadership.

"Let's see," I said, "the Officer of the Watch is Lieutenant Commander LaPointe, the Academy Personal Services Officer. The Junior Officer of the Watch is Lieutenant Swetland, the Fifth Company Officer. And the Midshipman Officer of the Watch is Midshipman First-class Foley, the Thirteenth Company Commander." Foley huh? He seemed like a pretty good head. I wondered what it would be like to have a guy like him in charge?

At 0555 we hurried to the outside of Stone's room and waited, braced against the bulkhead. I was not looking forward to another morning comearound with Rock Stone. He had been particularly careful never to violate the regulations concerning treatment of plebes during indoctrination, but he ran us mercilessly. But Tommy Poole and Tim Butler fared far worse than the rest of us.

Reveille was precisely at 0600, almost simultaneous with the brightening of the passageway. Rock Stone exited his room quickly, smiling brightly as he had every morning thus far. The strange thing about Stone was that he was completely genuine in his enthusiasm for plebe indoctrination . It was a passion, not a perversion like it obviously was for Micklewski and some others. Stone loved running plebes, not hurting them; and he truly felt responsible to ensue we excelled.

"This morning I think we'll do wind sprints," he said brightly. "All of you go to the far end of the passageway and wait for my signal. Winner bags the push-ups." Shit! That meant O'Reilly wouldn't spend much time on the deck this morning. None of us could beat him in a sprint, even when he wasn't half-trying.

We chopped to the end of the passageway and waited. I could hear Tommy taking quick breaths to oxygenate his blood in preparation for the first sprint. We didn't wait long before the shout of "Go!" thundered down the passageway. We sprinted to a position even with the happily-smiling Stone, turned quickly, and raced back. Kevin won easily, and I dropped to the deck for the standard 20 push-up penalty.

Tommy was last to his feet, and Micklewski yelled a great deal of humiliating abuse. We lined up for the second sprint. Stone shouted "Go!" and we ran again with damn O'Reilly in the lead as usual. I began hoping that Stone would switch from sprints to the more painful bear-crawls so that I could watch Kevin in pain. He hated bear-crawls with a passion.

As we finished the second sprint, the double doors at the far end of the passageway opened. A strange officer entered the Company area and paused just inside the double doors. Even at the present distance of more than 50 yards, I could see the officer wore a sword, which clacked at his hip, and had a blue armband with the letters "OOD" on his left arm. He was accompanied by a plebe messenger, so I knew immediately that this must be the Officer of the Watch. I also knew from the information on the POD he was Lieutenant Commander LaPointe. I felt strangely proud of myself for this instant association of facts. LaPointe adjusted his sword belt, consulted a paper he held in his hand, then started forward. Stone had his back to us and didn't notice. I noted that I LaPointe's bulbous red nose stood out, even at this distance. Rico noticed also.

"Shit!" he whispered fiercely. "Big Nose!"

That comment confused me, but Kevin instantly recognized the danger.

"Big Nose! Oh, Shit! Mugsy!" he exclaimed this quietly from his braced-up position against the bulkhead.

"Shut up down there, you sissies!" Micklewski yelled.

I started to rise. Too bad for Mugsy and anyone else LaPointe caught, but there wasn't anything we could do about it. Of course Kevin had other ideas. He suddenly clutched at his stomach and groaned. Then he ran toward Stone.

"What the hell are you doing?" Stone yelled.

"Sir!" Kevin groaned loudly. "I have to go!" He groaned again, grabbing at his middle convincingly. "Request permission to visit the head immediately!" He said it with such conviction that I believed him. Stone believed him too.

"Go! But hurry back. If I find that you're bagging it, you are in deep trouble!"

"Aye, aye sir!" Kevin turned, straightened somewhat, and ran toward us. The head facilities marked the corner of our passageway starting point. Kevin had a panicked look on his face as he passed us and hurried inside the facility. I could hear a stall door slam, but out of the corner of my eye I saw a form exit from the side door which was out of Stone's sight. I swiveled my head just enough to see. It was Kevin. He sprinted at breakneck speed away from us down the side passageway. I've never seen Kevin move so fast. His feet seemed to barely touch the ground. What the hell was he doing? At the far end of the side passageway, he turned the corner and headed down a parallel side passageway in a blur of motion. Oh, shit! I suddenly realized he was racing The Nose to Mugsy's room. But Mugsy lived on the far side of the Company area, and within about ten seconds LaPointe and his plebe would turn the corner into Mugsy's passageway. He'd see Kevin for sure. I didn't think Kevin could possibly make it, and I groaned inwardly at the thought of what was in store for Kevin if he were caught racing to Mugsy's aid.

"Go!" Stone yelled, interrupting my distraction, and I didn't have time for further concern for Kevin. With him gone there was a definite chance I could win the next couple of runs and save myself the push-ups. I sprinted. As we neared Stone, however, he noticed LaPointe approaching.

"Plebes Halt!" Stone yelled excitedly. I was pissed-off because I had been leading the group. "Attention in the Area!"

We came to a skidding stop, and all activity in the passageway ceased as everyone came to attention. Stone hurried off excitedly toward LaPointe and met him near the intersection leading to McGinley's room. They chatted quietly for several seconds. Stone gave LaPointe animated information. Big Nose nodded and smiled in reply.

The Nose gave a final nod to Stone, turned, and headed quickly down the side passageway toward Mugsy's room, plebe messenger in tow. Stone jogged to us with an enormous, and very smug, smile on his face. Immediately, a loud flushing sound echoed from the head behind us. Kevin exited the head and hurried in our direction.

"Midshipman Fourth-class O'Reilly, sir!" he reported as he caught up with us. Kevin's face was flushed with exertion, and he was slightly out of breath. Stone didn't notice, or may have connected Kevin's physical state with his pseudo-gastric distress.

Stone was in a great mood. He laughed.

"Everything come out OKAY, O'Reilly?"

O'Reilly matched his mood.

"I feel a whole lot better now, sir!"

I didn't see it could have been possible for O'Reilly to have gotten from the head, down the short side passageway, around the corner, down the long back passageway, around a second corner to Mugsy's room, warned him, then returned, in the amount of time that passed. But here Kevin was; and judging by his smile, he had been successful. Amazing! Kevin even let me win the sprint back, which pleased me to no end.

Five minutes later The Nose returned to the main passageway, shook his head briefly and negatively to Stone, and continued on his way quickly out of the area, no doubt on his way to terrorize some other poor unsuspecting Company. Unsuspecting? Wait a minute! The POD is published far enough in advance so that every Company should have been aware that LaPointe had the duty. Only *we* didn't know. How come?

I looked watched the severely disappointed Stone during our remaining sprints. Did he really withhold the POD information to get even with Mugsy? Why? What was wrong with him? Rock seemed to have so much leadership talent. Why would he waste his time attacking his classmates? No one was supposed to punish his own classmates. Classmates were the ultimate give-your-life-for friends, and Company class-mates were even more sacred in the hierarchy. It didn't make sense to me. I didn't have much time to devote to deep thinking, however, as the next few minutes were some of the most painful I had yet experienced, as Stone trod carefully at the very edge of hazing us in his frustration.

Kevin told of his unbelievable success when we returned to the room to prepare for chow. Every muscle in my body seemed to ache.

"I didn't think I would make it!" he exclaimed, still excited by his near brush with severe Academy punishment. "I almost collided with several classmates as I sprinted. And when I got to Mugsy's room, sure enough it was dark inside. I burst in and turned on the lights. They were both still in their racks!" He laughed. "I was afraid to make noise for fear LaPointe or Stone would hear the commotion, so I ran to Brandis and McGinley and shook them both as hard as I could. 'Get up quick! The Nose's on his way!' I whispered to each of them."

Kevin laughed again.

"McGinley tried to grab me when I touched him!" he said incredulously. "He was pissed that I woke him. He thought it was some sort of joke. 'Hurry! Get up! The Nose is on his way!' I said again. I didn't have time to say anything else; I had to get back or Stone might have suspected something. McGinley ordered me to attention as I headed for the door, but I ran out anyway. He yelled and followed me to the door, but by then I was already around the corner."

"Unbelievable!" I said, staring at Kevin O'Reilly with admiration. "You did good, plebe!" I looked at Rico, who was staring at me and nodding knowingly.

"I'd trust my life to this man!" he said putting a hand on Kevin's shoulder. It wasn't the last time I heard Rico say that about Kevin.

Kevin laughed and put a hand on Rico's shoulder.

"You admire me so much that you're gonna set me up with Rosa when you're done with her, right?" Rico laughed.

"No sweat, Kevin. She's all yours! Besides, she already has the hots for you." I watched Kevin smiled dreamily at this comment, and I could completely understand his motivation and his persistence about this. Rosa, Rico's Brooklyn girlfriend, was one incredibly good looking and sensual creature.

Brandis and McGinley were quiet at the start of morning meal, which was fine with me. About midway through the meal Mugsy looked closely at Kevin.

"Was that you in my room this morning, O'Reilly?" he whispered quietly.

"Request permission not to answer, sir!" Kevin said equally quietly while quickly and nervously glancing around the table.

"Why's that?" Brandis asked, his voice also almost a whisper. He too leaned in toward Kevin questioningly.

"Sir, in this case what you don't know won't hurt anybody."

"Weren't you supposed to be coming around to Boner Stoner this morning?" asked Mugsy.

"Sir, I did come around to Midshipman First-class Stone."

"Then how did...?" McGinley began, but Henry Brandis interrupted him by grabbing his arm lightly.

"O'Reilly's right, Mugsy. It's best we don't know." Mugsy stared at Kevin for a long time and returned to his meal.

"I'm gonna kill that bastard Stone!" he mumbled with such fierce conviction that I knew a confrontation was imminent.

That evening immediately after chow Captain Dillingham addressed the Company. He usually did not interfere with the running of the daily Company business; and except for an occasional inspection during noon meal, we rarely saw him. But the Superintendent, Jake 'Supersub' Conrad, had decreed that Company Officers would take a more active interest in Company affairs, particularly in the areas of leadership, honor, and responsibility; and Dillingham had decided to give a series of lectures on various appropriate topics. Tonight's was to be on the subject of *honor,* the most important of the fundamental concepts of the Annapolis credo.

Captain Rusty "Bull" Dillingham was more than the Marine's Marine: he could have been their poster boy. He had been born to be a combat soldier and looked every bit the part. He was enormous -- at least six feet six inches tall -- and weighed more than 230 pounds. Not an once of that weight was fat. He bulged and rippled impressively in his crisply pressed uniform shirts. He also shaved his head, which gave him an even more formidable look. And rumor had it that he polished his bald cranium so that it gleamed like a signal beacon in bright sunlight.

He had almost Cro-Magnon facial features, which gave him a slightly unintelligent look; but we knew that he had graduated number 20 in the class of 1961. His most unusual features were his ears -- which were enormous and stuck out from his head like twin saucers -- and his eyes, which were an almost startlingly beautiful deep blue. I was never going to mention either ears or eyes to Bull for fear of the consequences.

He had a soft, almost melodic voice which could change in an instant to a roar. Another rumor said that during his first tour in Vietnam he had stumbled on a platoon-sized group of Communist Chinese troops who were setting up an ambush. Startled by his sheer size -- and maybe by those enormous ears -- the enemy soldiers hesitated. Standing calmly on the edge of their encampment, Second Lieutenant Bull Dillingham roared his loudest and discharged burst after burst of M16 fire into their midst. The enemy retreated in absolute panic, and it was said in Bull's Infantry Division that they didn't stop their retreat until they had crossed the border into China. When the smoke cleared, the remainder of Bull's platoon found him calmly dismantling booby traps, surrounded by ten enemy dead, all of whom had looks of sheer terror on their faces. I didn't want to imagine what he could do to plebes.

But it was Dillingham of the soft voice and the blue eyes who emerged from the Company Office and stood impressively before us that evening. Since there was no Company enclosed space large enough to accommodate us all, we assembled in the passageway outside Dillingham's office. Stone had instructed us to bring our chairs and had ordained that plebes sit up front -- probably, as Rico suggested, to act as a buffer in case something pissed Dillingham off, and he tried to go for someone's throat. We also were instructed to remind each Company room ten minutes prior to the lecture, and to be in place five minutes early. I looked around once I had settled, and it seemed to me that all the plebes and many of the youngsters were ready early. Tommy Poole winked at me when I looked his way. I smiled in return.

Tommy had been holding up pretty well despite intense attention from Stone and Micklewski. Twice during the evening comearounds Tommy had puked his guts out after a particularly stressful exercise routine. But he always bounced back, and endured despite the pressure, and that frustrated the Tigers.

At precisely the appointed time the door to the Company Office opened, and Rock Stone leapt to his feet.

"Attention on Deck!" he snapped, and we all came to brisk attention.

"At ease!" Dillingham said in his soft voice, and he smiled at us. I could tell that he really enjoyed his job, although at times I'll bet he longed for the excitement of the jungle and the opportunity to kill someone. Maybe I should consider being a Marine rather than a Naval Aviator. I could be a good Marine.

"Gentlemen," Bull said, "the Superintendent has instructed each Company Officer to lecture his midshipmen. The subjects of these talks include a variety of topics not taught formally in class. -- subjects such as duty, honor, loyalty, fidelity, responsibility, courage, and sacrifice. I know these subjects well." I had no doubt of that, judging from that chest full of medals and his supreme sense of self-confidence. "They form the backbone of each of the military services and especially of this Academy. Without these concepts we are nothing and whatever we do here is meaningless."

He paused, and I could see his introduction had been impromptu. He looked closely from man to man before he began again. His soft, compelling, voice was difficult to hear, even from the front row, and I could feel the midshipmen behind me straining forward to catch his words. He undivided attention. He looked slowly down at his two massive hands, then brought them forward so that they stretched toward us, palms up.

"Several young, brave men coughed out their final breaths in these arms," he began. "They didn't want to die, I can assure you of that. And I didn't want to lose them; you can count on that too!" He brought his hands down at held them at his side. "They were good men -- Marines -- the best damn warriors on the planet. And when the end came, and they looked up at me, I could see a question in their eyes. It was the same question every good soldier asks when he knows it's his time. 'Did I do my duty well, sir?'"

"I answered them all the same way. 'You are one damn fine Marine, son.' They knew what I meant. They died with honor -- the way good soldiers always die -- and *honor* is the subject of tonight's lecture." He paused again for effect and stared at us as he waited to continue. The thought of anyone's dying in my arms immediately ended speculation about being "Marine Corps" Merritt. I wasn't ready.

Bull continued, "honor is the one quality you possess that no one can ever take away from you. Every word you speak, every thought you harbor, every deed you do tells the world about your sense of honor. Honor is the most important of the Academy's ideals." He smiled. "You may have noticed that there are no "Duty" Committees and no "Loyalty" Boards, but there sure as hell is an "Honor" System."

"*A midshipman must not lie, cheat, or steal,*" he said precisely and professionally, quoting from the Academy Honor Code. Then he smiled again, and his blue eyes twinkled. "It seems like a very simple concept. Almost every religion teaches some slight variation of the same message. The laws of our nation, and of every civilized country on the planet echo those ideas. It's in our blood. We are born honorable.

"But we have to be constantly on guard to protect our honor, because life and circumstances sometimes try to rob us of our self esteem and at times it can seem the only course of action we have is the dishonorable one." He then raised his voice and stood even more erect than previously. "But without our honor we are nothing!" he said forcefully.

Again Dillingham paused. He shook his massive head in sad disgust and lowered his voice.

"Every year several midshipmen are dismissed for violations of the Honor Code. Do you know what excuses they use when confronting the Honor Committee? They say, 'I lied because I had no choice' or 'I cheated because I didn't want to fail' or my personal favorite, 'everybody else does it.'"

Bull pointed a massive finger at all of us, sweeping his hand from side to side to encompass us, and his voice increased in volume several notches.

"You always have a choice where honor is concerned!" he thundered. "Most people lie because they fear the consequences of the truth. Most people cheat because they are unwilling to work hard enough to succeed. Most people steal because they're too impatient to legitimately earn what they covet. And it's all totally unnecessary. Your honor is too important to compromise.

"Let me say to each of you very clearly -- if you haven't figured it out already -- the system here at Annapolis does not tolerate dishonor, and *you* also must not tolerate it, either in yourselves or in others. There is no flexibility on this point. If you haven't already adopted a strong system of personal honor from your family upbringing or from church or school, then listen and learn from what the Academy can teach you. You will be a far better man for it.

"As you already know, the midshipmen at Annapolis administer the Honor System except in cases of extreme necessity when the Academy itself must intercede. Each Company has an Honor Representative for each class, and an Honor Committee that reports to the Brigade Honor Board. Except in the most severe cases of violation, these representatives treat whatever you tell them with strict confidentiality, and try very hard to temper their decisions with reasonableness." Bull paused for a moment. "Are there any questions?"

Jeff Polk raised his hand immediately and Dillingham acknowledged him with a nod.

"Midshipman Fourth-class Polk, Sir!" Jeff said. "You said we shouldn't tolerate honor violations, but the System doesn't require us to turn in persons we suspect in a breach of honor. What exactly does this mean?"

Dillingham smiled.

"You are correct in that no one at Annapolis is *required* to report a suspected honor violation. That makes our system much more flexible than the one at West Point. We allow you substantial leeway to make your own individual investigation and question the persons involved before you make a decision about what you saw or discovered. But along with that leeway comes a great responsibility. If you feel that the offense was not an actual willful violation of the Code, then you must take no action, but if you *know* that an honor violation occurred, you are honor bound to report it or to ask the violator to report it himself."

Polk spoke again.

"Sir, you said the word 'willful.' I can think of times when a lie might not have been intended as a lie, or where cheating was indirect or unintentional. Am I correct that in those cases no violation occurred?"

"Yes!" Bull answered. "The system has no intention of punishing anyone for an honest mistake. That's why all the facts must be discovered and considered before a violation is reported."

Polk continued his questioning.

"Sir," he said. "Isn't there also a huge difference between violating the regs and breaking the Honor Code?"

Dillingham thought for a moment about this, then smiled.

"Very perceptive," he said. "Yes! Absolutely! For example you can stay up past "lights out" to study, even though that's against the rules. If you're caught, the system will punish you but not for an honor violation. But if you put a towel at the bottom of your door to hide the fact that the lights are on -- something an *ex*-midshipman did last year, but the way -- that might be considered an attempt at deception. Or if you stuck pillows and blankets under the covers of your bed to simulate your sleeping body while you were elsewhere after hours that would definitely get you ejected from this place."

At this point Bull stepped completely out of character. He smiled devilishly and relaxed his ramrod posture, considering something.

Then he continued, "The system also accepts the fact that midshipmen are somewhat overactive young men with enormous egos and hyperactive hormones. Some "games" are acceptable." He laughed. "Don't tell anyone I said this, but when I was a second-class midshipman I had this townie young lady who adored me. Every Sunday after noon meal, I sneaked out the side gate, changed into civilian clothes in a gas station restroom, and she drove me to her place, where we spent several passionate hours in the basement of her parent's house. Theoretically speaking wearing civilian clothes outside the walls was deception, but the Academy would never consider that an honor violation. After all, boys will be boys!" He paused again, remembering something else from the good-old-days.

"I also used to run like hell when confronted by the OOD." We all laughed at this revelation. "That's not an honor violation; although if you choose to run, you had better escape. If the OOD catches you, you're a dead man." We laughed again.

"Any other questions?" he asked, still smiling from his reminiscences.

"Yes, sir!" Rico said. "Where exactly *is* this gas station?" Dillingham laughed.

"You'll have to find out on your own," he answered.

Then Kevin raised his hand.

"Sir. This young lady you mentioned. About how old would she be now, and could you introduce me to her?" Dillingham and the rest of the Company laughed at that suggestion.

"No," Bull answered when he had calmed. "You'll have to find your own townie."

"Well, that about does it for the evening," Dillingham said after a moment. "I would like to close the meeting by nominating the plebe who asked the perceptive questions as the Company Honor Representative for the Class of 71. Any objections, Mister Polk?" Jeff didn't look too happy about that, but he wisely kept his mouth shut. "Good. I'll be in touch with you later on what your responsibilities are." He started to dismiss the Company then had a second thought.

"Oh," he said. "On a lighter note, I want to revive the practice of skit-giving, so beginning next Sunday evening I want each class to stage a short skit. We'll start with the youngsters since they have the most recent experience. The second-class will go next, followed by the plebes, and finally the firsties. We'll do this on an alternating week basis." "And," he said smiling broadly again, "anything goes!" I could hear groans from various places within the Company but no overt rebellion. "Good!" Dillingham said with finality. "Dismissed!"

Tommy Poole was certifiably insane. Twice each day Stone and Micklewski ran his ample butt into the ground. At times his arms were so tired he could not lift his poor body off the deck, and his vomiting in the passageway was getting to be a very unsightly -- and smelly -- habit. He hadn't gotten a complete meal except for what Kevin boldly smuggled from the Sandwich Mess, and what he could eat on the weekend during liberty in town. Although no one but Kevin voiced any outward concerns, we were all beginning to worry about Tommy. Why the hell didn't he quit?

On Thursday night Rock Stone entered our room. As we braced, he called out a "carry-on!" That was so completely out of character, we looked at each other quickly, wondering what was up. He looked us over for a moment. "Merritt, Wilson. I want the two of you in the Wardroom in five minutes!" With that enigmatic statement he turned and departed.

The entire room looked at me.

"I wonder what he wants?" I asked them.

Rico looked at me all-knowingly.

"I'll bet I know," he said.

"What?" BJ and I asked simultaneously.

"Poole. It's got to be about Tommy Poole."

"But why?" I asked. "That doesn't make any sense."

"Sure it does," Rico answered. "I was expecting this. Haven't you been watching Stone and Micklewski? They thought they could run Tommy out of here by now, and he's proven tougher than they imagined. They're frustrated. So now they're going to enlist the help of Tommy's greaser classmates -- and you're going to help them."

"Who says?" I asked, offended by Rico's allegation.

"I do!" he answered. "Stone is your hero. You'll do anything he asks. And besides, you agree with him one hundred percent on this. You don't think Tommy belongs here."

"Come on, Rico. Neither do you!"

Rico quickly held up a hand to stop me.

"I'm not even sure I belong here yet, Jim. No way can I make that kind of judgment for Tommy."

"Christ Jim!" Kevin interjected. "Look at what he's been through -- far more than any of us. And he's hung in there. I'm not sure I would put up with all the crap he does. -- He's our classmate for Christ's sake! Tommy Poole deserves our support."

Kevin's words still echoed when BJ and I left the room and chopped to the Wardroom. We burst inside and began yelling our entrances, but Stone, who waited calmly, told us to carry-on and be seated. Strong, Pirelli, Richardson, and Wojeck were already there. That meant that all the top ranking plebes had been invited to the meeting. But Ramsey and Polk, who were the remainder of Tommy's Plebe Summer roommates, were also there, which told me immediately that Rico had been right about the purpose of the meeting. I sat next to Bob Strong. BJ sat next to me. Stone sat on a table in front of the TV console, watching us. He waited until we were comfortable.

"Gentlemen," he began. "This Company has a problem. Plebe Summer is over. Each of you is now a bona fide member of the Brigade and a participating member of this Company. I've called you here to enlist your help with a serious problem." He adjusted his position on the table and looked at us conspiratorially.

"I'll be frank with you. Today Captain Dillingham called me into his office and asked me why Midshipman Fourth-class Poole and several other of your classmates were still aboard. He doesn't feel they -- particularly Mister Poole -- have the necessary talents to be officers we can be proud of. And, frankly, neither do I. When I was a plebe this wouldn't have been a problem. My first-class would have dead-horsed, rigged, and shoved him out so often that he would have had to have quit. "Quit or die!" that's what he used to yell to those plebes he decided to eliminate." Stone paused and continued sadly.

"But hazing is eliminated and we can't use the same effective motivational techniques on Mister Poole. We're hamstrung us in these situations. And Captain Dillingham is upset with our lack of progress.

"So I need your help. Each of you has either roomed with Mister Poole, -- so you know his qualifications -- or else you've been ranked high enough in leadership skills to appreciate the necessity for his departure. I've called you here to ask for suggestions and cooperation in dealing with the Poole issue. I'll open the discussion."

"Is this a completely open discussion?" Jeff Polk asked.

"Of course, Mister Polk. Completely open. Say anything you want."

"Great!" announced Polk. "Because I don't understand what all the fuss is about. What is it about Tommy that pisses everybody off? He's a nice guy. He's very cooperative. He can march, shoot, polish shoes, and straighten his locker as well as most of us. And he's in better shape right now than some of your own classmates in this Company. Plus he's a certifiable genius. Why run him out?"

A smug look played across Stone's face for an instant. He hopped down from the table and walked calmly to one wall of the Wardroom. For several minutes he faced one of the many pictures that hung there; then he turned to us. He indicated the picture, which showed a past midshipman.

"Do you know who this is?" he asked us. I did. There were nine pictures in a grouping, and one evening during a break in the Sandwich Mess operation I had read the plaques that were attached to the wall under each picture.

"This is a photo of Midshipman First-class Thomas Howell III," Stone began. "Class of 1940 and Commander of the Twenty-third Company at Annapolis during his senior year. Lieutenant Howell was assigned to a Destroyer Squadron during the battle of Leyte Gulf in the Second World War. During that battle Howell's destroyer was struck by a kamikaze pilot just aft of the forward gun turret. Howell was in charge of that turret. During the next two hours -- despite severe wounds -- Howell repeatedly braved the inferno. He ignored the possibility of explosion, and carried six unconscious crewmen to safety. When he returned the final time -- in violation of a direct order from his Commanding Officer -- the turret exploded. Howell was killed instantly. Thomas Howell III received the Medal of Honor for his bravery." I shuddered involuntarily at the mental picture the words invoked

Stone moved slightly to his right and faced another picture. "This is Midshipman First-class Orville Huggins, Class of 1943, Twenty-third Company. Orville was captain of Navy's wrestling team. Second Lieutenant Huggins was one of the first men ashore on D-Day on Omaha Beach, leading a demolitions team assigned to destroy personnel obstacles blocking the deployment of the troops. Twenty-five of the 36 members of his platoon didn't make it to shore. As Orville reached the sand, the top sergeant to his right stepped on a mine, and Orville was blown from his feet by the explosion. Severely wounded, Huggins dragged himself up the beach toward the first set of obstacles. As he crawled, Huggins watched his only remaining demolitions expert cut down just in front of the obstacles.

"Disregarding his own peril, Lieutenant Huggins struggled to remove the pack of explosives from the body of his dead comrade and continue forward. He took two additional bullet wounds as he crawled.

Realizing that his injuries were mortal and knowing that unless the obstacle was destroyed, hundreds of his buddies would be cut to pieces before a beachhead could be established, Lieutenant Huggins rigged the explosives to his own body and crawled the final distance, streaming a bloody trail in the sand.

"When he reached the obstacle, Huggins stood -- in full sight the enemy fire -- threw himself up as far as he could onto the obstructions, and detonated the high explosive charges. The resulting explosion cleared a path to allow the landing forces to punch their way threw the German resistance. For his valor Huggins also received the Medal of Honor." Amazing! The way Stone told the story added life to the incredible valor.

He moved to another photo. "Midshipman First-class Wendel Washington, Class of 1960, also of Twenty-third Company, and one of only two black midshipmen in his class. Wendel also became a Marine. In 1966 Marine Captain Washington led a charge of his platoon on a strategic hill near Khe Sahn in Vietnam. Wounded twice during the charge, Wendel continued forward and singlehandedly destroyed two enemy machine-gun positions. His platoon took heavy casualties but captured the hill.

"Captain Washington personally readied the wounded for air evacuation. But before the remainder of his platoon could deploy, the enemy counterattacked in overwhelming numbers. Wendel, placing himself between the scathing fire and his wounded comrades, held off the first wave almost singlehandedly. The second wave overran the hill, killing Captain Washington. Every member of the platoon was slaughtered except for one wounded lance corporal whom the enemy bastards bayoneted and left for dead. He lived to tell the story. Captain Washington received the Navy Cross, the Silver Star, a Legion of Merit, and has been nominated for the Medal of Honor."

Stone was clearly overcome with the emotion of the stories. So was I.

"There are six other graduates of Twenty-third Company commemorated on this wall, gentlemen. One was an admiral in the Great White Fleet; another was the Lieutenant co-inventor of modern sonar; and another is an active astronaut who has landed on the moon. When you have a chance, read each plaque and think about the incredible bravery and the unselfish devotion to duty each of these individuals exhibited." He paused, then held up his left wrist for us to see. Something dull-silver shone on his wrist.

"You may all recognize this as a POW/MIA bracelet. What you don't know is that the name on this particular bracelet belongs to Navy Lieutenant Jeffrey Smittles, Class of 1964. Jeff was my squadleader plebe year, and he was responsible for changing me from a snot-nosed high school brat into a motivated midshipman. Jeff was shot down last spring over North Vietnam." Stone stared at the aluminum band for a long second before he looked up again. "Jeff was my friend," he said softly and with finality, and I could see tears forming in his eyes. Stone was human after all. It made him more admirable.

Rock took a deep breath and returned to front of the room, but did not sit on the table.

"Now maybe you have some idea why persons like Poole do not belong here. Do you honestly think that Mister Poole would continue returning to that gun turret? Would he bravely throw himself on that beach obstacle? Could he lead a desperate charge up a muddy hill? The answer to each of those questions is a clear no. He could not. The military expects each of you to be ready in an instant to make the ultimate sacrifice. That's what we're here for. If you are unable or unwilling to make that sacrifice, then choose another line of work.

"Poole does *not* have what it takes to lead and motivate men in combat, and he's just not smart enough to accept his own failings. We have a responsibility to help him recognize the futility of his remaining here, and I want each of you to help me in this. Talk to Mister Poole; ask him to quit. Be firm. He already proved his mettle by staying as long as he has, but now it's time for the rest of us to move into more advanced stages of character development. I'm counting on each of you to help me. Dismissed!"

I stood up slowly, more overcome by thoughts of my own future mortality than the suggestion that Poole be cajoled into quitting. Could *I* throw myself on the barricades if faced with that possibility? I honestly didn't know. -- But I also didn't know if Tommy or any other person among us, including Stone, could do that either. So maybe Jeff was right. What was the point in targeting Tommy? I was confused and I left the Wardroom in a funk.

o sooner had I returned to the room and told them what had transpired then Mugsy entered. He was carrying a pair of black shoes.

"Carry-on!" he said, and he went directly to O'Reilly.

"What size shoe do you wear?"

"Ten, sir"

"Try these on," Mugsy offered holding out the shoes to Kevin. Kevin sat in his chair and fitted on one of the shoes. He then stood and walked around a bit.

"It seems to fit, sir," he said looking at Mugsy strangely.

"Good," Mugsy replied. "From now on they're yours. That weasel who had you shine them never came by to pick 'em up. If he does, I'm going to tell him I waited a week and threw them out with the trash -- after I kick his ass, that is. So now you got yourself an extra pair of class shoes. You tell me if he comes around again." Smiling, Mugsy left the room. Kevin took off the shoe, examined them both critically, and shrugged.

"I should probably have them fumigated before I wear them," he said. "A guy that slimy probably has several communicable diseases."

"I know who he is," offered Rico.

"Who?" we all asked simultaneously.

"His name is Jeffrey Riggins, and he's a second-class in Twenty-second Company."

"Twenty-second Company? What's he doing over here?"

"Simple," Rico answered. "He probably figured you'd never find out who he was, and he could keep up the scam all year long."

"What a jerk!" Kevin said. "I'm glad I have his shoes.

Thirty minutes before lights-out, I announced that I was going to visit Tommy Poole.

"I think I'll come along," offered Kevin sadly. "Somebody should be on Tommy's side for the crucifixion."

"No," I said, holding out a hand to stop him in the process of rising from his chair. "It's not what you think. I'd rather do this alone." Kevin looked at me curiously, but didn't protest, and soon I chopped down the passageway to Tommy's room.

The entire group looked up as I entered.

"You too, huh?" Hank Butkowski asked sarcastically after I had entered. George Abbot shook his head in disgust but said nothing. Tim Butler stared dejectedly at Tommy, and Tommy, after glancing at me for a moment, looked pointedly into a text book

"What do you mean?" I asked.

"Another member of the 'Let's-get-Tommy-Poole-to-resign' Brigade?" Hank asked.

"No!" I said firmly. "Not me!" Tommy looked up.

"Good," he said, "because the only people to come in here with any encouraging words were Jeff Polk and Mike Wojeck."

"Kevin and I are on your side too," I said. "Kevin wanted to come along, but I asked him not to."

Tommy smiled. "I always knew Kevin supported me, but I was never sure about you."

"Well, to tell the truth, Tommy, I wasn't sure about me either. You know, I love almost everything there is about this place. I love the uniforms, the exercising, the camaraderie, the academics." I laughed loudly. "I even love the parades. But I've been thinking about things a lot lately, and I've been watching you and Stone during comearounds. Tonight when Rock made his speech I looked at the pictures in the Wardroom and realized that none of those people are any different from you or me. Nobody really knows how they'll react to special circumstances until they face them. And after all my soul searching I still love this place, but I also believe that if there *is* a special formula for the perfect Naval Officer and if *guts* is the main ingredient, you're gonna be one of the best. You've got my total support from now on." I smiled to myself. I had never been good at impromptu speeches, but that one seemed perfect.

Tommy was almost in tears. He nodded and averted his eyes. I looked at Hank and George. They obviously approved. Hank grinned broadly, and George gave me a big thumbs-up. I felt good about myself. Let the rest of the Company go to hell, including Stone. I still admired him, but he was way off base on this. I smiled, turned, and left the room. I had done the honorable thing; I was sure of that.

The next day marked a new intensity in the treatment of Tommy Poole. I hadn't thought that comearounds could get more hateful. They did. Tommy passed out from exhaustion before 20 minutes had elapsed, and Stone and Micklewski yelled at the unconscious form until he recovered sufficiently to run again. That evening ten scummy youngsters, succumbing to upper-class pressure, withdrew their "spoons" from Tommy. Tommy had to brace-up in their presence and calls them "sir" again. This was unheard of. And Micklewski began to visit Tommy's room each evening for several minutes of additional harassment. And the more the pressure continued, and the more Tommy Poole dug in his heels and resisted, the more frustrated and willing to lash out at the rest of us the first-class became. I could feel the pressure mounting. Something had to explode.

Four weeks into the Academic Year, Rico Guevarra and Jeff Polk began a strange ritual that amazed me at first. One evening Rico crossed the room to use the sink, but stopped on his way and stared across the passageway. He watched someone, but from my vantage point behind my desk I had no idea who it was. Suddenly Rico dropped his gym shorts to the deck and stood naked just inside the doorway. With one hand he gripped himself and pointed at the opposite room. Then he laughed loudly, reached down, and pulled up his pants. Kevin laughed. He was never surprised at Rico's strange antics. BJ was shocked, and he looked at me with a disgusted grimace. I shrugged. Rico looked at us.

"It's too bad about Polk," he said.

"What's that?" I asked.

"Poor fellas' got a pecker no bigger than my little finger. No wonder his girlfriend seemed so frustrated during Parents' Weekend."

Kevin laughed out loud, distracting us.

He said in a girl's voice, loud enough to be heard across the passageway. "Is it in yet, Jeffie?" We all laughed at that.

Ten minutes later a penny rolled into our room and loudly struck the side of my desk. This was a signal from Polk's room for us to come to the door. BJ rose and walked to the doorway. What he saw caused him to back off two quick steps. His mouth hung open widely. I stood up and hurried to his side.

Across the hall a trio of naked rears faced our room. It was a hell of a sight! Without seeing the faces, I could tell immediately that the small hairy tush was Jeff's, the larger almost bare one was Willy Simpson's, and the enormous one that stretched almost from one side of the door to the other was Reb's. BJ sputtered. I shook my head in disgust. Rico and Kevin came to the doorway and laughed.

"Is that the best you can come up with, Polk you weenie?" Rico whispered loudly. "You should be ashamed." Sounds of an approaching upper-class quickly broke up the fleshy formation, and we retreated to our desks lest the footsteps be headed in our direction and find us having fun, God forbid.

After Rico sat, he spent a minute examining his private areas critically. I watched surreptitiously. Finally he looked up at Kevin.

"O'Reilly," he said. "I'm horny as hell. I think it's time to arrange something."

Kevin looked up eagerly, and so did BJ.

"With our new friends, or are you going to call on Cindy for service to the fleet?" Kevin asked.

"Cindy's out of the picture for the time being. She's been grounded and can't drive. I think we should arrange a party for the three of us." He looked at me. "Want to make it four?"

I laughed.

"No. I told you guys I have a girl back home. I'm not going to take the risk." Even as I said it, I realized my words had a strange, hypocritical quality. I had been talking with Leslie three times every week. We were getting along famously, and we were planning a rendezvous -- if I could work up the guts to try it.

Rico shrugged.

"Suit yourself," he said. BJ took his chair over and put it beside Rico's desk. Kevin leaned across his own desk toward the two of them, and soon they were plotting quietly. Occasional laughter interrupted their serious planning.

TECUMSEH

Originally the figurehead of the U.S.S. Delaware, Tecumseh has watched over activities in Tecumseh Court for more than a hundred years. Painted for special occasions, Tecumseh cuts a striking and sometimes whimsical pose. The Indian is considered the god of 2.0, and desperate midshipmen throw pennies at his head to ensure passing grades.

CHAPTER FIVE

BLUE AND GOLD

The Naval Academy football team, captained by lefty quarterback John Rightman, lost its first two games of the season to powerful teams from Penn State and Boston College. Those were away games, so the ignominy of the defeats was blunted by distance. But there was considerable worry among the Plebes that Navy would suffer another horrible season, particularly since a Navy football victory meant plebe carry-on beginning at game's end and extending until evening meal on Sunday. Plebes in the Tiger Company relished any carry-on.

The first home game was Saturday, 21 September, against Delaware, a would-be pushover, and spirits ran high in the final days before the contest. Navy needed a victory to get on track for what could be an exciting rest-of-the-season --at least according to the press clippings from the Public Affairs Office -- and nothing gets the blood going and the spirits revved like Annapolis football.

The Friday before the game the Academy had a guest -- none other than Roger Staubach himself, the most famous football graduate of any service academy. He spoke to the Brigade prior to the meal, and I found him thoroughly likable. He was softly spoken, funny, reverent, and completely in touch with the magic the Academy represented. What a guy!

Near the end of the meal I heard a commotion at the staff tables where Roger sat, and soon the entire Brigade was on its feet. From my vantage point facing the center of the Mess Hall I saw a group of six plebes lift Roger Staubach, chair and all, onto their shoulders, and begin carrying him down the aisles for everyone to see. As he bobbed toward us, loud cheers accompanied him in an acoustic wave of adulation. But something else also escorted his progress. Toast! Roger Staubach was being "toasted," -- literally -- as he progressed.

From both sides of the Mess Hall pieces of bread flew Frisbee-style toward the elevated hero. As many as ten pieces of toast were in the air at any one time. It was disconcerting. This was my first encounter with "toasting" quests, and I was initially shocked. What the hell were we doing to our hero? And why?

"Guevarra! Get that bread down here!" Mugsy shouted, plainly excited about an opportunity to pelt Roger Staubach. Rico complied eagerly. Rico and Kevin seemed to enjoy the more unusual Annapolis rituals, many of which I found unprofessional and even infantile. I became more disgusted as Roger approached. This was no way to treat one of Annapolis' premiere graduates, one of my personal heroes and a fellow Texan. I stared in shock, disheartened.

But Roger was a good sport. He caught and threw pieces of toast back toward the originators with incredible dexterity. He clearly enjoyed the experience. As Roger neared, Stone reacted.

He turned toward the Company and snapped loudly and with authority, "No bread throwing from Tiger Company! That's a direct order!" He then turned toward Roger and his entourage, puffed out his Marine Corps chest, and applauded as boisterously as anyone. He admired Staubach as much as any of us; that was clear.

As Roger drew even with our table, Mugsy let loose a quick volley of three pieces of toast with a tremendous yell.

"Yeah, Roger!" None of his shots came near Roger. Stone reacted. He spun.

"Who threw that toast?" he yelled over the din. He looked at Mugsy, who smiled sheepishly in return and shrugged. Stone stomped down the aisle.

"Did you throw that toast?" he asked, angrily.

"Did you see me throw anything?" Mugsy asked confidently.

"Did you throw that toast?" Stone asked again, but with greater emphasis.

"Listen, blockhead," Mugsy replied, calmly. I had to strain to hear him since quite a bit of commotion was still ongoing all around us. "I'm not gonna answer an entrapping question. If you didn't see anything, then you ain't got nothing on me. Go run a plebe!"

Stone turned to the remainder of the table.

"Did anyone see Midshipman First-class McGinley throw toast?" he asked us loudly. No one answered. Stone scowled at each of us inturn. "So, no one saw anything? Is that right?" His eyes lingered on me. I was in a perfect position to have seen the offense. He continued to stare at me. I met his gaze, torn between squad loyalty and my admiration for Stone. What Mugsy did was clearly wrong. But I wisely kept my mouth shut. Stone turned away disgustedly and returned to his table.

After we had reseated ourselves, Brandis turned to Mugsy and whispered fiercely, "Shit, Mugsy! You're in big trouble!"

"Screw Stone!" Mugsy exploded, loudly enough for Rock and his table to hear. Then Mugsy addressed the table. "Listen up, everybody! I'm gonna give you a lesson on Academy traditions." He smiled and leaned forward in his chair.

"Midshipmen have been 'toasting' guests for decades," he began. "It's one of those weird but understandable Academy rituals. And it's got a purpose. I've been told it started during the Second World War when the Brigade chaired several war hero pilots. The younger brother of one of the aces tossed several pieces of bread at his brother and yelled, 'Shoot 'em down, big brother!' The brother and the other aces swatted the bread from the air just like they had swatted the Jap zeros. The game caught on." Mugsy paused to let this sink in. I considered what had happened in this light, and wondered whether "toasting" did make sense.

Mugsy continued, dropping out of character and assuming his philosopher's guise. "But it's more than a game, gentlemen. The entire process is also our opportunity to remind the "high and mighty" that they're really no different from any of us -- to kinda bring them back down to earth. For guys like Staubach it's a coming-home exercise. *He* understands, you can bet on that, and so do a great many of the midshipmen in this Mess Hall." Mugsy paused and leaned even farther forward and nodded toward Stone's table.

"Last year, as some of you remember, there was a minor incident with some Apollo astronauts who were toasted. The Annapolis fly boys understood the tradition, but one weenie-assed Air Force major complained that toasting was beneath his dignity. The Superintendent suspended the practice. Now Stone has decided that Twenty-third Company ain't gonna participate again." Mugsy laughed.

"This is the same Company Commander who believes that dead-horses and shoving-out are character building. That's bullshit! -- Those exercises cause injury; even a sluggo knows that. And I got more news for you. Anybody who really thinks that the number of push-ups a plebe can do determines what kind of naval officer he'll make is just plain stupid!" McGinley laughed. "I can do more push-ups than any first-class in the Company. You think they'll make me Company Commander next set?" The upper-class at the table laughed at this obvious joke.

McGinley lifted an arm and made a muscle -- a very substantial muscle -- for the table.

"It ain't what you got here, guys," he said indicating his arm. Then he dropped his arm and pointed to his chest with a thick thumb. "It's what's here, that counts. Never forget that!" I wasn't completely convinced that what Mugsy said was completely true, but he had his points. I guess there are two sides to every issue.

Friday night the Commandant of Midshipmen, a likeable old-timer named Captain Mack 'Greyhound' Hallahan, acted as the head cheerleader for the pre-game pep rally in T-Court. Mainly plebes attended, since most of the upper-class had liberty in town, and since we were the ones who most desperately wanted a Navy victory. Us and Hallahan that is. Mack put on quite an act, jumping up and down and leading all the cheers and shaking the hand of every single member of the Navy football squad. As the grand finale he led us in a rousing rendition of *The Goat is Old and Gnarly*. I was plenty pumped up by the time the rally ended. Navy just had to win the next day.

On the way back to the room, flanked by Rico and BJ, I found myself bubbling with energy. I wanted adventure. I wanted excitement. I wanted freedom. I wanted companionship. So I called Leslie. Leslie was out for the evening. I couldn't remember if I had said I would call, but it was dammed inconvenient of her not to be there. Then I called Lynda. She was out too. That was odd and highly upsetting. She was supposed to be waiting at home patiently, like a good almost-fiancee. She wasn't supposed to be out when I needed her to be in.

I knew that tomorrow was the big rendezvous day for my horny roommates. I had overheard them discussing their plans secretly so I wouldn't know what they were up to. Secrecy was fine with me. It wasn't that they were afraid I'd turn them in if I found out they were planning a trip over the wall; sometimes it's best not to know too much. Ignorance may not be an excuse, but it's the best defense against an honor violation. Right now, however, I wished I had been included. I needed adventure -- any kind of adventure.

I guess the "energy" I absorbed at the pep rally had also spread to my classmates. That evening we plebes were restless. Since so many upper-class were out on the town, we had some opportunity to "assert" ourselves. Twice BJ was caught in a moon barrage from across the passageway. When he tried to retaliate, Jubal lofted a wet paper towel from his doorway and hit BJ squarely and sloppily on his bare butt -- much to BJ's dismay.

"Don't worry!" Rico said laughing at BJ's predicament. "I'll save the honor of the room." He nodded to Kevin, stood, and walked to the doorway. Carefully checking to see that no upper-class were in sight, he dropped his pants, turned, and watching Jeff's room through his legs, he called, "Jeff! Check this Out!" I watched from my desk, slightly disgusted. Kevin stood behind Rico like a cannoneer. When

Jeff appeared in the doorway, Kevin yelled "Fire!" and slapped Rico on his back. Rico then farted -- loudly and perfectly on cue.

"Blaaatttt!" the noise reverberated "cheekily" across the passageway. Polk didn't react immediately. I think he was too stunned.

"Gross, Rico!" he fiercely whispered. "You're disgusting!" I agreed. This was carrying things a bit too far. Kevin and BJ thought it was great, however. They laughed together for an hour

Later that evening I noticed BJ had borrowed one of Rico's smut books in preparation for tomorrow's adventure. His eyes had a glazed-over look as he half-read, half-imagined the next night's happenings. Instead of pity, I realized that I felt a bit jealous. Being cloistered in Bancroft Hall for weeks on end with no opportunity to socialize was beginning to affect me. I went down to the phones and called Leslie's sorority house, and left a message that I would be calling in the morning -- just to talk, of course.

Saturday morning brought a definite smell of expectation on the cool morning air. McGinley had asked Kevin and me to run with him, and we jogged steadily and contentedly along in the pre-dawn. Mornings were getting a bit chilly as summer sailed out of Annapolis. We had changed the uniform of the day to blues on Monday, and the Academy braced itself for the winter siege. But still it was pleasant in the mornings, and Mugsy hadn't increased the pace as yet to anything sufficiently demanding for Kevin or me dread the experience. The exercises by the Field House were always strenuous but exhilarating -- especially since Mugsy didn't really care how many or how well we did. I was beginning to like Mugsy -- something I never thought would happen. I wondered briefly if I should worry about myself.

After the run we hurried off to our morning classes, which in my case happened to be two hours of fleet exercises on the Severn River aboard the Yard Patrol (YP) boats. The YPs were small, wooden, diesel powered, patrol boats, whose main advantages were their maneuverability, mechanical reliability, and lack of power -- all of which combined to reduce the potential damage to various wharves, buoys, and other vessels when novice plebe skippers screwed up -- something that happened quite often. The helmsman was usually a crusty navy Chief Petty Officer Boatswain's Mate who spent most of the "voyage" worrying about the condition of the boat and fudging his response to our commands to reduce damage. During one of my first Saturday exercises, when one of my more dyslexic classmates ordered a "Right Full Rudder!" the Chief below answered loudly, "Left Full Rudder, aye, aye, Sir!" Left was the correct direction. The embarrassed classmate surrendered the con to another nervous plebe.

Most of the tables in our Company -- except Micklewski's of course -- granted the plebes carry-on at noon meal in preparation for the big football game. Unfortunately, it was my turn to help at Micklewski's table, so I missed that small amount of relaxation. I resented it. I found myself feeling sorry for poor Tommy as I witnessed more unnecessary abuse. It wasn't really Tommy's fault that the Tigers were carrying this plebe indoctrination thing a bit too far. I suffered in silence.

Midway through the meal Micklewski turned to me and asked, "Don't you wish we could get Midshipman Poole to resign, Merritt?"

"No, sir!" I answered loudly. Rock Stone, who was sitting next to me on my left clicked his tongue loudly.

"Wrong answer," he said.

"Come on Merritt," Micklewski whined, waving a fork in the air for emphasis. "Poole's a misfit and he needs to go. Are you telling me you want him for your classmate?"

"Yes, sir!" Judging by his actions, I guess Micklewski thought that was the wrong answer too.

Micklewski shook his head as if to dislodge an irritating idea. He looked quickly around the table. I could hear chuckling from some of the upper class, and Micklewski's face flushed and his dark eyes flashed. He obviously didn't appreciate the idea that he might be ridiculed in front of his peers. And I guess he saw me as the source of the ridicule. Micklewski stood up quickly, his eyes becoming wide in anger. He leaned way over the table toward me, and whispered-spat sputtered loudly in the direction of my ear. Stone leaned forward in his chair to allow Micklewski to get in closer to me. Stone was smiling, anticipating the venom. Micklewski seemed ready to spew. I could feel the heat from Micklewski's breath, and I sensed violence and a tinge of madness in his voice. By the time he began making understandable sounds, he seemed completely out of control, and I became a little bit afraid.

"You're a liar, Merritt!" he spat fiercely enough so that I thought the entire Brigade could hear. "You have no honor at all, and you don't belong here either." I could feel myself heat up almost instantly. I have never permitted anyone to call me a liar, because I don't lie -- ever. In Texas we call those, "fighting words." First-class or not, he had no right to say that. But I stifled my initial anger and allowed him that transgression. After all, he was a first-class and I was only a plebe. But he wasn't finished.

"I feel sorry for your parents," he hissed a bit more calmly but with considerable sarcastic emphasis. "They must be ashamed of you. You're not a man, Merritt you sissy! And I know what's going on. I'll bet you and Poole are fruit-boy homosexuals." He laughed cruelly. "Are you more than friends with Poole, Mister Merritt? Is there something happening between you the Academy should know about?" He laughed insanely and looked around the table. No one else seemed to find humor in what he said. "I think I'll run your homo-butt just like I do your good friend Tommy. Then we'll see how quickly your story changes." With that he reached over and gripped my shirt collar with a meaty hand, and pulled me up slightly from my chair toward him. "I'll force you to turn on your good buddy here, Mr. faggot Merritt, and I'll have you begging me to end your misery. You don't deserve to be here. You're scum and I'll make you pay." The last words came out with a vehemence that left small bubbly drops of spittle on my left cheek. He let my collar go, shoving me away simultaneously. He shoved hard. I was propelled backward sidewards in my seat. I flailed my arms. The back of my head struck the hard back of a chair behind me with a resounding thunk, and I toppled sidewards onto the cold, hard, tile deck.

I lay momentarily in a tangled heap on the floor. Several midshipmen laughed nervously. I was instantly angry. Micklewski had attacked my honor, family, and manhood all in one insane tirade. Not only that, he spit on me for Christ's sake and he attacked me physically. I could feel my face redden and my self-control slip quickly away. I stumbled to my feet. Across the table Tommy looked at me with pleading eyes. He didn't want me to get into trouble on his account. I could understand that. I could also hear both Stone and Salenger quietly asking Micklewski to calm down. They knew he was out of line. But these were serious accusations from Midshipman-asshole Micklewski. I couldn't let them go unanswered. Regulations be damned, I had my personal honor to uphold.

I stood and unbraced, shocking everyone at the table -- myself included.

"Sir!" I said loudly, turning toward the contorted face that still smoldered smugly at the head of the table. I stared hard at Micklewski and said as calmly as I could under the circumstances, "Sir, you are way out of line! You can do whatever you want to me. I can take any bullshit you dish out, no problem. But don't ever call me a liar again or talk about my family, or put a slimy hand on me, or we will settle our problems man to man, or I'll have you in front of Captain Dillingham and whoever else will listen." I paused to get my breath. Micklewski was shocked into silence. His eyes were wide and wild. Stone was also shocked, but I could see him considering what was happening and weighing possible alternatives.

"And another thing," I continued, "Tommy Poole has more guts than any ten of you Tigers put together. He's gonna make it, sir!" I picked up my chair carefully, snapped it into place, and sat. I took a deep breath and slid my rear out onto the end of my chair. I could hear stunned whistles and sharp intakes of breath from several places at the table as I readied myself, but I continued to glare right into Dale Micklewski's beady black eyes. I didn't like what I saw there, but I wasn't about to back down. He seemed certifiably insane. Calmer, I sat, pulled my chair in, and moved my eyes into the boat, resuming my plebe status.

It took a second for my words to sink in. Micklewski's sputtered for a minute and settled back into his chair involuntarily.

"How dare you threaten me, you little, stupid, silly, plebe?" Micklewski shouted. It was a strangely subdued response for a crazy man, but then Micklewski prided himself on the fact that he never used profanity, so his tame choice of words was not surprising. His words had no effect. I caught Tommy's eye across the table, and noticed a combination of pride and fear in Tommy's expression as I faced him. I could also hear several of the upper-class at the table chuckling at Micklewski's harsh words. Micklewski didn't like that at all. He started to respond again. He began to rise from his chair.

From the corner of my eye I could see Stone grab Micklewski by the arm and shove him forcefully down onto his chair. I watched Dave Salenger, who was sitting directly across from me, next to Tommy. His shocked gaze was transfixed on his roommate. Salenger was a halfway decent guy, who played strictly by the rules. Unfortunately for the plebes they were Tiger rules. But his reaction told me that he also felt that Micklewski had crossed the line.

Finally calmed, Micklewski shook off Stone's hand. He leaned over again and spat vehemently in the direction of my ear.

"I'm putting you on report for your insubordination, Merritt. You *are* a liar and a sissy boy. Poole is a fool, and so are you! I'm going to personally kill both of you!"

Feeling the spray from his words and his warm breath on my cheek again, and getting a good whiff of the noon meal's meat loaf meal with every word, I became even angrier than before. This was not at all like the Jim Merritt I remembered from high school, but high school seemed a thousand years away at the moment And how dare this puke call me a liar and then decide to punish me for his error? I reacted, and started to rise.

Rock Stone rose quickly and pushed me down into my chair with surprising gentleness with one strong hand. With the other he did the same to Micklewski. He held me in place for a second and patted me on the shoulder.

"Brace up, Merritt," he said quietly. I did. "Calm down, Dale," he said to Micklewski. Micklewski settled into his chair with a loud moan. "Let's finish the meal with no further conflicts," he said to the table, and, after a moment, the entertainment forgotten, the routine began again. But one uttered a word at our table, or it seemed anywhere in the Company, for the remainder of the meal.

After the firsties departed, several second-class came to the table. Mike Maxwell, who had watched the incident in quiet horror from his place at the foot of the table, talked quietly to his classmates, then he stood and moved to the vacant seat next to me.

"Carry-on, plebes!" he announced.

"What the hell happened, Jim?" he asked, addressing me by my first name for the first time I could remember. I turned to Maxie.

"Sir," I said. "I really love this place, you know that. And I know the importance of obedience to superiors. But I have my personal sense of honor and I will not let Midshipman Micklewski or anyone else violate it. I am not a liar, and I am not a homosexual." I smiled. "And my parents *do* love me." Maxwell laughed while I continued. "I'll play the plebe game as long as it takes to pay my dues, and I'll do it as well as anyone; but when Micklewski or anyone else goes too far, I intend to speak up, no matter what the consequences."

Maxwell stared at me for a long second, smiled, then he reached out his hand.

"I agree a hundred percent, Jim. You took a big risk, pal, and I'm proud of you. Call me 'Maxie' from now on, and come see me whenever you need help or advice." His face then grew uncomfortable.

"Just tone the friendliness down at this table, okay?" I shook his hand, shocked that he had spooned me. "I suggest you avoid Micklewski as much as possible from now on," he continued. "I also think Stone will talk him out of frying you. Just continue being a good plebe, and everything will be fine." After Maxie stood up, several of his classmates also spooned me, including Tommy Battle.

"Nice work," Battle said. "You got balls, Merritt." Last in line was Elroy Shantz. He looked at me with a twinkle in his eye.

"Yes," he said, "you *can* call me Shithead." I laughed, suddenly feeling good about myself. I looked across the table at Tommy. He was proud of me too, but I also noticed that he had been pointedly ignored by all the second-class. Tommy sighed. I smiled at him.

"Hang in there, Tommy" I said.

"Last night my mother pleaded with me to come home," he replied. "Maybe I will."

"No you won't. Hang in there. You can make it."

After meal I raced elatedly to the phones and called Leslie's sorority house. I really needed to talk, and I was overjoyed to find her in. She seemed anxious to hear from me, even though we had talked only a few days previously. It was so nice to hear her voice that I instantly forgot my run-in with Dale Micklewski.

"I can't talk for long," I said. "I have to prepare for the big football game."

"It sounds like fun," she replied.

"It is kind of exciting," I answered. "Next year I'll take you to one or two if you'd like," I said boldly.

"That would be great!" she said sincerely. Then she paused. "Jim Merritt," she said sadly, but sweetly. "Last night I went to a movie and coffee shop with some of my sorority friends and their dates. I was the only person there who wasn't with someone. When are we going to see each other?"

"How about tonight?" I blurted. What the hell did I just say? Tonight?

"I'd love to see you," she answered excitedly. She really seemed to like me, and I found that appealing.

"The problem," I continued, "is that being a plebe I'm not allowed to date openly, and I have to be back in my room by eleven for lights-out." As I said it, I realized how idiotic it sounded. I was a 19-year-old college man with an 11 o'clock curfew on Saturday night. Ridiculous!

"That's fine," she said sincerely. "Isn't there someplace quiet we can sit and just talk face to face, Jim Merritt? You know, I haven't seen those gorgeous blue eyes of yours for weeks." Wow! She liked my eyes! My heart sank for an instant. What color were her eyes anyway? I strained my brain but couldn't remember.

"I would really like to see you again too," I said honestly. "You are one of the most beautiful women I have ever met." I meant that. She was gorgeous.

"Why thank you, Jim Merritt. You're very sweet."

"I mean every word of it -- Texas honor!" As far as I knew there was no such term as "Texas honor," but it sounded good, and she liked it.

"So, Jim Merritt, what do we do?"

My brain whirled furiously.

"Drive into the Academy Main Gate and park just past the Field House in the visitors' parking lot that faces the water. You can't miss it, it's the third parking area on the right. Park as close to the seawall as you can; then walk along the road by the river. I'll be waiting there at eight o'clock. We'll sit on the stone wall and watch the Chesapeake Bay at night. Wear something casual, but bring a sweater. It might get chilly. I'll bring a blanket."

Leslie answered dreamily.

"It sounds romantic. But if I get chilly, Jim Merritt, I hope your strong arms will keep me warm rather than a smelly old blanket." Oh, my! What an effect this woman had on me!

"Don't you worry your beautiful head about it," I answered. "Jim Merritt will take care of everything!" I hoped secretly to myself that Jim Merritt was right.

At 1300 on Saturday the 21st of September the entire Brigade of Midshipman -- all 4,000 men less various football players, watch squad members, cheerleaders, ushers, and the sick and infirm -- formed up in their various outside formation locations and began marching toward the

Navy-Marine Corps Stadium. Drummers stationed strategically along the way provided the beat by which 8,000 black shoes slapped the asphalt streets. At specified locations within the confines of the Academy, large groups of Companies met and merged precisely until as we exited the gates and entered Annapolis proper, all 36 companies were lined up in numerical order. It was quite a sight, especially on the long straightaway leading the final half mile to the stadium. The fabulous Brigade of Midshipman stretched the entire distance. We were a formidable force.

Along the way local police stopped traffic to let us pass. They watched, clearly impressed, as we sang our progress through the city of Annapolis. Crowds also gathered at strategic intersections to watch us and cheer. It was an exhilarating experience, and my confrontation with Micklewski faded into insignificance as we marched. 'God,' I thought. 'It's no wonder they teach us that being a member of the Brigade is so much better than being a student in a stupid civilian college. I mean just look at us! We are the best. God, I love this place!'

The parade was marred by one peculiar incident. As we halted near St. John's College -- an Annapolis hotbed of classical scholars, radical thinkers, and communist sympathizers -- several long-haired and bug infested morons heckled us as we passed. They held crudely-painted signs aloft which announced things like "STOP THE WAR NOW" and "YOU ARE IMPLEMENTS OF DEATH" and "PEACE AND LOVE FOR EVERYONE."

The placards were my first reminder since reporting aboard that there was actual political and social unrest in the country. For me it was a completely unfamiliar experience. Almost no one I knew in West Texas opposed the war in Vietnam; the Annapolis area newspapers gave news of the war but not much about dissent; plebes never had a chance to watch television; and the Academy must have had a policy of stopping at the gates anyone who looked like a troublemaker. Never once in four years did anything even remotely anti-military happen inside the brick Annapolis walls -- unless you consider Jeff Polk's harangues, which I didn't. I was amused at first and I felt vaguely sorry for these poor misguided civilians. They didn't understand about duty, honor, and country.

"Pigs! Baby killers!" shouted a young, chunky girl sporting ponderous, unencumbered breasts and large knots in her scraggly brown hair. She wore a wrinkled, flowered granny dress and shiny black-laced, ankle-high shoes that didn't match the rest of her unkempt ensemble. Her eyes flashed and her face was a mask of anger and accusation.

"Murdering bastard military robots!" shouted one of her long-haired, supposedly male, and equally untidy companions. His dark checked flannel shirt had a large grease stain under the left side pocket. I guessed he probably also had an enormous yellow streak down the middle of his back. I looked at him with contempt.

"Have you no conscience?" shouted another, taller youth. This one wore John Lennon glasses and soiled denim bib overalls. He appeared to be attempting to achieve an intellectual pose. "Why do you hide like cowards behind brick walls and accept the lies the government forces down your throats?" Cowards? Lies? Hide? What kind of crap was this? He seemed so full of left-wing arrogance and accusations that I wondered briefly if he were Micklewski's communist doppleganger. I also wondered which person was more out of touch with reality.

"Mister Stone, sir?" shouted Reb Ramsey in his thickest Alabama accent, breaking my temporary reverie. Reb marched next to me.

"What is it, Ramsey?" answered our obviously pissed off Company Commander.

"Sir! Request permission to break fo'mation to break some heads, sir!" Stone, and many of the Company members, as well as two local policemen who were standing by just in case, laughed at Reb's remark.

"Oh, sure!" the tall hippie shouted. "A violent reaction to a peaceful confrontation. -- How typically military!"

"Take a bath, shit-for-brains!" Reb yelled. "I kin smell you from over he'ah! -- Hippie puke!" Again everyone laughed.

"Screw you! Screw you! Screw you!" the girl yelled vehemently as we started forward and marched out of earshot.

"Well, that was somewhat unusual," said Rico from his position behind me. "I'll bet you anything that young lady dated some midshipman in the past and he hose-bagged her but good."

"You really think so?" I asked.

"Absolutely. You don't get that bitter from reading the classics all day." Rico was probably right. She seemed too intense; too full of hate to be a true flower child.

"Boy. I'd like to have just five minutes alone with that tall son of a bitch," Reb added. He left the remainder of his idea dangling in the air for us to imagine. I could tell from his tone that he meant what he said.

"It wouldn't matter a bit, Reb," Rico said. "His kind doesn't listen to reason." I realized immediately that his analysis applied to Dale Micklewski too. I was beginning to appreciate Rico Guevarra, despite his strange sexual appetite and his gross personal habits. He had a way of seeing through the smoke directly to the heart of issues. He was seldom wrong when he voiced an opinion.

At the stadium, ushers formed a line which would lead us onto the field through a wide under-tunnel. We halted outside the stadium while the band played some Navy tunes and the announcer got the crowd going. From our vantage point as the 23rd group to enter, we couldn't hear anything except in a low rumble. But considerable noise was coming from the stadium. From cars parked nearby, various alumni and friends surged toward the stadium. Many shouted encouragement or waved banners. Even the few Delaware supporters smiled and looked at us with pride as we waited to march on. We may be from different schools, but we midshipmen represent *all* Americans. Every school we played or visited treated us with the same respect.

Eventually the formation started forward again to rousing music from the Academy Drum and Bugle Corps, and we marched through the tunnel, turned right, and followed the edge of the playing field behind the southern goal posts. Just prior to the sidelines, we turned left and marched upfield. By this time several companies had already achieved their final positions. They looked impressive standing proudly on the field. We followed the formation, as company-after-company turned left again and marched onto the playing field. In this manner the Brigade formed nine rows of four companies each, facing the Navy side of the field. We waited at loose attention.

A minute or so after we halted, the Brigade Commander called us to attention. The colors paraded onto the field and band played the national anthem.

Immediately after, the Brigade Commander called out loudly, "Brigade! Go Navy! Fight!" As he announced the word "Navy" every midshipman reached for the bill of his combination cap. When he shouted "Fight!" select midshipmen removed their caps, and the words "GO NAVY" stood out in stark white contrast to the green grass of the stadium ground. Cheers rewarded our effort.

Following this grand spectacle, we marched enmasse directly into the stands. The lowermost middle section of the stadium on the west side had been roped off for the Brigade. There were no rules about where midshipmen sat within those barricades. Those upper-class who had dates wandered off to meet their young ladies in the stands proper. The remaining upper-class sat near the rear of the section, higher up so they had a better view. Plebes sat in the front-most area, although "sat" is a misnomer since I don't remember my skinny rear ever touching the metal bench for any game while I was a plebe. Plebes stood and cheered; but the seats were so low to the stadium field level that we *had* to stand if we wanted to see what was happening.

Twenty-third Company plebes crowded into one small area for self-protection. The crowd began to rumble as game time neared, and I could feel excitement building. Soon, amid a rousing chorus of boos, the visiting Delaware team entered the field. The players looked enormous to me, but I thought it was probably the pads that expanded their bulk to such menacing proportions. After they were in place; limbering and lumbering in various ways, the Navy team exploded onto the field led by our dear mascot, Bill the Goat. Plebes leaped into the air waving caps vigorously and screaming until young lungs hurt and throats burned. These were our gladiators, our blue-and-gold heroes, the champions who by moving that small brown pigskin into the opposing end zone enough times, could lighten plebe year considerably. I loved every one of them, and I yelled as loudly as anyone.

As the announcer introduced the various starting line-ups and I listened intently, I realized that a Navy victory on this day -- or any future day this season -- was not going to be easy. The Delaware team was enormous. Their fullback outweighed anyone on Navy's defensive line. Hell the high school I played for in Amarillo outweighed the Navy team. But that was okay. After all, I *had* played football, and I knew that speed and agility were equally as important as size. We probably had several defensive speedsters who would race unopposed into the Delaware backfield to stop the runners before they could get started. Yes, I was sure that must be the Navy game plan. We would win by quickness and a good passing game. We would dazzle these big, slow brutes with plays of military precision. Navy wouldn't run through them. We would go over and around to victory. Hurrah for my heroes!

Navy won the toss and elected to kick; a strategy so strange it left our side of the field quiet and confused. There wasn't any wind. The sun didn't present a problem. What the hell were we kicking for?

Rico and Kevin looked at me, just as confused as I was.

"Okay Jim," Rico observed. "You were a quarterback. What's up?"

I shook my head. "I have no idea."

"Ah know what they're do'in," offered Reb turning around from his place in front of us.

"Tell us, pray tell," said Rico.

"They're try'in to show Del-e-ware they ain't 'fraid of 'em. Give us yo' best shot and see what happens -- that's what they're saying!" Reb answered with confidence. I nodded and looked skeptically at Rico. He shrugged. Delaware gave Navy its best shot, a six-play touchdown that covered the necessary 75 yards almost as if there was no defense. No Navy speedsters raced unopposed into the Delaware backfield. The volume of sound on the Navy side of the field diminished considerably during those six plays, and I began to fantasize what would happen at evening meal with so many pissed off upper-class at the table. It wasn't a pretty vision.

"Don't tell me, Reb," Rico said sarcastically. "Navy let them score just to get their confidence up so we can plaster them later." Ramsey didn't answer. I could tell he was fuming. He came from a state where football is king and where the major universities fielded powerhouse teams year after year. Adjusting to Navy football was going to take patience.

Midway through the first quarter I realized that another of my Navy football fantasies was a myth. Navy had no intention of running around or throwing over anybody either. The game plan was to ram the football right down Delaware's huge and hungry throats despite that fact that this one-yard-and-a-cloud-of-dust offense would be difficult against a team the same size, much less against the behemoths that lumbered on the opposite side of the line of scrimmage. We watched in silent dismay as the one end sweep Navy tried was stopped by a defensive end, who had come over from the opposite side of the field. No speedsters on offense either, huh? It was going to be a long football afternoon. The punt seemed to be our major offensive weapon. Luckily, Delaware wasn't an offensive powerhouse. The score at half time was 7 - zero.

There were many gloomy plebes in the stands that half-time. Not only were our heroes losing to a supposedly weak team from Delaware, but all around us were upper-class, seemingly oblivious to the fate of the Navy football team, basking in the light of adoration from their many lovely dates. I never had seen so many long legs, short skits, and sweaters straining to the point of structural failure as I did that day. But what an overall shitty time I was having!

Several of us bought sodas and returned to our seats to talk. Rico, Kevin, and BJ seemed completely unconcerned about our pending football humiliation. But they had the evening's festivities to think ahead to. Wait a minute, so did I. To hell with this game and with carry-on tonight. I had my own diversion planned. Reb and I swapped football stories while the Lustkateers plotted and giggled.

Navy returned after half-time temporarily a different team. They actually passed the ball, made good yardage, and scored a touchdown on a sustained 80-yard drive. Life returned to plebedom. Delaware fumbled the following kickoff. Navy recovered deep in Delaware territory but had to settle for a field goal after a wide-open Navy receiver dropped a pass in the end zone. Once in the lead, however, Navy reverted to the three-runs-up-the-middle-and-a-long-punt offense. Thank God we had a competent punter. I loved the tradition, the pomp, and the excitement associated with the football program at Annapolis, but I can describe Navy football in one word. Boring! The philosophy never changed the entire four years I was there.

The only real excitement came midway through the second half when the Delaware cheerleaders -- who were attractive girls rather than the standard homely and hairy Navy male variety -- came to visit our side of the field. As they gazed -- it seemed longingly -- at the mass of studly maleness that inhabited our side of the field, I could hear a cheer go up from the rear, upper-class bachelor section.

"Pass them back! Pass them back! Pass them back!" they chanted.

Several plebes in the front row got the idea and raced off to the cheerleaders. The girls agreed to be part of this historic Navy tradition. Soon five young ladies had been lofted over the heads of several groups of plebes and carried back to the stands, smiling lovely faces pointed heavenward and waving to the cameras.

As they reached the mass of midshipmen, the five bundles began a bumpy, start and stop journey up into the stands, still held aloft by steady plebe hands. A new chant began in the rear of the stands.

"Pass them back! Pass them back! Pass them back!" Deftly the girls moved upward into the stands. In the process of passing from one group of hands to another, the pretty smiles became expressions of surprise as several young ladies experienced both accidental and intentional groping.

"Stop pinching!" I heard one girl yell. I carefully passed the girl that floated overhead, touching only her shoulders. A new, somewhat hungry, chant began in the upper sections.

"Bring 'em Here! Bring 'em Here! Bring 'em Here!"

The nearest girl murmured, "Oh, dear!" As they moved back toward the waiting paws of the upper-class.

I heard one buxom young lady shout. "Hey! Get your god-damn hands off me!" Rico and Kevin laughed, but I felt uncomfortable. The girls lingered unintentionally over the upper section of the stands, then came down again. None were smiling very much on the return trip.

At the bottom, the five girls stood shakily, staring first at themselves, then up at the upper-class. One petite girl adjusted her skirt which was considerably askew. The buxom one glared, then flipped the bird to the entire Brigade. So much for admiration for the military. The cheerleaders trotted off to the safety of the other side of the field.

The game eventually ended with a 10 to 7 Navy victory. I think both teams were tired from slamming at each other in the trenches. Navy's superior conditioning did win out. We sang the traditional *Navy Blue and Gold* fight song after the game. Since liberty commenced immediately for everyone, we were on our own until evening meal formation. A large group of us stopped at the sub shop for a victory snack, and a jubilant Reb Ramsey ate two foot-long hamburger subs in less than 20 minutes. My stomach ached just watching.

WHAT TIME IS IT?

"Sir, I am greatly embarrassed and deeply humiliated that due to unforseen circumstances beyond my control, the inner workings and hidden mechanisms of my chronometer are in such inaccord with the great sidereal movement with which time is generally reckoned that I cannot with any degree of accuracy state the correct time, sir. But without fear of being too greatly in error, I will state that it is about ***XXX*** *minutes,* ***XXX*** *seconds, and* ***XXX*** *ticks past* ***XXX*** *bells, sir."*

From *Reef Points*

CHAPTER 6

LOVE'S LABORS

At 1600 I jogged to the seawall to scout secluded spots for the evening's rendezvous. I found three places where a couple could sit out of casual sight of observers. I memorized the location of each and returned to Bancroft Hall. My excitement built -- along with a certain amount of guilt. Was I really so eager to abandon my commitment to Lynda for someone I had only talked to on the phone a few times? On reflection I didn't think so. After all, Lynda and I had a relationship that went back more than a year. We had mutually a special partnership. We had sacrificed our virginity's jointly not so very long ago, and it was a wonderful joyful experience. No, Lynda and I were a couple. I was only going to see Leslie to talk. Leslie was intelligent and lovely and beautiful, but I didn't need any love interest other than my dear sweet Lynda.

When I returned from my jog, I found several classmates waiting in my room. Most were there to congratulate me on my stand against the Tigers. I think many were jealous that so many second-class had spooned me.

"I'm going to tell Rolando Gomez to kiss my ass!" announced Patrick Mulvaney in his Dubuque drawl. "He's another Tiger who needs to understand his place. He came into my room and took the last of my chocolate chip cookies." Knowing Pat, that was a crime punishable by death. Mulvaney lived an entire year on the cookies his mother sent him, and chocolate chip was his favorite variety.

"Yes!" said Barton Hardesty with typical intensity. A light of spiritual awakening fired in his faraway eyes as he spoke. "And I have had enough of the way Grunt Robinson and Wildman Kopciak curse in my presence. With God's help I intend to finally put a stop to it." He looked to heaven and spread his arms in thanks.

"Ain't gonna happen, guys," said Rico with finality from behind his desk where he was meticulously examining his face in a small vanity mirror. He said it with such authority that everyone turned to him, silently.

"What do you mean, Rico?" asked Chuck Chalmers. Chuck's acne had been acting up ever since the Brigade returned, and his ruddy face was marred by bumps.

"Think about it, gentlemen," Rico began, barely glancing up from his careful facial scrutiny. "Do you imagine that Stone and Dillingham are going to allow a full-fledged plebe mutiny? Not a chance! Merritt got away with it because he faced down one of the true certifiable madmen in the Company. Even Stone knew Micklewski was so far out of line that he couldn't be supported. Sure the rest of the Tigers are pains in our collective asses, but they're bearable. If we rise in protest every time something doesn't go our way, the Tigers will crush us like insignificant plebe scum -- which we are -- and Dillingham will support it fully. My advice is to let it ride and it will all blow over. I'll bet Stone asks his misguided classmates to ease up a little bit from now on. Follow in Jimbo's wake, guys. In a couple months Christmas break will be here, and Plebe Year will begin winding down. Shit! We can do this standing on our heads."

"Yea?" said Chalmers, still unconvinced. "Merritt faced Micklewski down because he had to protect his honor; I understand that. But some of the rest of us are in the same situation, and that's not going to change no matter what Stone asks his misguided classmates. We have to act soon. Wildman treats us like shit. We shine his shoes, make his bed, go for gedunk every night. And he still runs our butts mercilessly. We're like his slaves, and I don't like it one damn bit."

"Listen," Rico began patiently. "Merritt was very lucky. He never should have let an insignificant asshole like Micklewski anger him the way he did. Anger is the first sign of failure." Rico paused for effect like a professor lecturing young students. He chuckled. "You guys still don't get it about this place, do you? There's nothing any Tiger can say or do to you that can really hurt you. It's psychological bullshit and all in *your* heads. Don't listen to their crap when they spout it. Tune them out. Think pleasant thoughts."

"That may be easy for you to say, Rico, but you have it different from us," interrupted Chuck.

"Hey, guys," Rico said again, "I'm coming around to Rockhead Stone himself, and you all know he's another madman. But I'm smarter than he is and won't let him get to me -- and he knows it." Rico stopped and looked at his classmates disgustedly. "Wake up, plebes!" he said. "If they want you to shove-out, do it until you're uncomfortable; then stop. Tell them it hurts your knees and that you'll be going to Sick Bay for treatment. Watch how fast that shit ends if they think what they're doing is going down on an official report. And why would you possibly do a good job making their beds and shining their god-damn shoes? Wise up!

"And," he continued, a devilish smile lighting up his face, "if some asshole forced me to run to the Steerage every night, I'd piss in his soda before I gave it to him. Not enough so he'd notice but just enough so I'd know it was there. Then I'd stir the damn drink with my pecker just to add flavor, and I'd add one or two pubic hairs to every hamburger. You may still have to run for gedunk, but think how sweet the revenge would be."

"That's gross, Rico. You wouldn't do that," said Chalmers.

"The hell I wouldn't! Ask Superplebe Merritt what he thinks."

Everyone looked at me.

"Rico is right about mutiny. It won't work. He's also right about the illegal exercises. They were outlawed because they *do* cause injury." I paused and looked at Rico, smiling. "About the food runs. I have no doubt Rico would do exactly as he says."

All eyes turned to Rico again, who was busy examining a proto-zit on his nose. He looked up at the group and smiled sheepishly.

"I don't care what you say," declared Hardesty. "I'll have no more profanity thrown at me even if I have to complain to God himself."

"You'll get better response from God, Barton," said Rico. "Just ignore them. If you let them know you have a weakness, they'll pound on it until you crack. Trust me."

"No, Rico. I won't! I have had enough!" With that statement Barton stormed from the room, forgetting for a moment he was a plebe. Glancing quickly around he assumed a more dignified plebe pose and glided to the center of the passageway, and continued smartly toward his room.

Rico watched him as he departed, shaking his head sadly.

"Barton's next to go," he announced.

"No shit?" Kevin asked. He had been quiet up until now, smiling and watching Rico lecture his classmates. "What makes you think so?"

"He's too damn self-righteous as it is, and the Tigers need a victory after their continued failures with Tommy and after 'Jim's-Last-Stand' today. If Barton makes a big fuss, they'll crush him until he collapses under the strain. He won't have a chance."

"Should we warn him?" Kevin asked seriously. I had heard O'Reilly remark several times about Rico's uncanny ability to predict events, and thus far Rico had been extraordinarily accurate. I agreed with him about Barton too. He was a man on the edge. But would Barton accept advice?

"Barton won't listen to reason, Kevin," Rico answered. "He's too close-minded. It's a fundamental flaw with zealots. He's out of here, and we should start thinking about which uniform items we want to buy from him when he leaves. Maybe one of you could discreetly find out his clothing sizes."

That afternoon the now recharged plebes handily beat the second-class in the weekly basketball tournament. Kevin O'Reilly was a one-man phenomenon, he pumped in baskets from all over the court, and Barton Hardesty -- despite being constantly badgered by a barrage of second-class profanity expressly aimed at him -- was a rebounding fool. I found myself studying Barton during the match, wondering if his shoes or cap would fit me. I felt guilty about that. I also found myself looking forward to next weekend's game against the firsties. I hoped Dale Micklewski guarded me. I would show him a thing or two.

My unvoiced anxiety about the noon meal incident with Micklewski was quickly brought to a head. At almost 1600 Stone and Micklewski came to our room. Neither was smiling.

"Merritt, you stay!" Stone demanded. "The rest of you get lost for ten minutes!" The others quickly left the room, leaving me to worry about my fate. Stone closed the door and turned to face me.

"Carry-on, Merritt," Stone said, and immediately I knew this was going to be a semi-friendly session. I looked at Micklewski as I relaxed, but he was painstakingly avoiding eye contact with me.

"Have a seat," Stone offered, and I retreated to my desk and sat facing them. Stone sat across the room on an edge of Kevin's desk, Micklewski sat in Rico's chair. Stone smiled at me and my fears lightened considerably.

"Dale and I want to apologize for what happened this morning, Mister Merritt," Stone began. "He and I had a long talk, and Dale agrees with me that he got a bit out of hand and had no right to accuse you of dishonor or anything else." Stone's smile broadened. "Merritt, you're one of the top plebes in the Company. Your classmates look to you for leadership, and thus far your behavior has been exemplary. That one factor has considerably tempered our response to your insubordination." He smiled again and spread his hands out in front of him, open palmed. "We intend to forget the entire incident happened, and we're here to see if you can agree."

"Am I to understand that Mister Micklewski is apologizing to me?" I asked boldly. Micklewski looked up quickly and glared at me, but Stone raised an arm and waved away any comment he might have intended. When he continued, it was in a less-friendly tone.

"Don't put us in a difficult position, Merritt. You can surely understand how the game is played. We're the first-class, and you're a god-damn plebe. There has to be some separation between us. It's the only way the system will work, and that's what's most important here." He pointed to me forcefully with his right index finger and continued.

"Learn to swallow your anger or it's going to get you into serious trouble some day. Continue being a good plebe, Mister Merritt," he said with emphasis. "Continue to play your part in this game. But don't make too many waves or you'll find yourself at sea with no way back to safe harbor. Forget what happened and so will we. Leave it at that. Good day." With that he waved Micklewski to his feet, and they departed.

Almost immediately my roommates returned, accompanied by several classmates.

"Well, what happened?" Kevin asked almost before he was inside the doorway.

"Stone has decided to let bygones be bygones and forget the noon meal incident," I replied.

"And what did Micklewski say?" asked Rico perceptively.

"He didn't say a word," I answered. "Stone was the spokesman." Rico snickered at this.

"What was your answer?" asked Willy Simpson.

"I wasn't given a chance to voice an opinion. I was told that was the way it would be, period," I answered.

"What're ya'll gonna do?" asked Ramsey.

"I think I'll forget it like they suggest. I can't see any value in pursuing this."

"I agree wholeheartedly!" said Bob Strong with emphasis. Bob was another of the plebe whose opinion I valued. He was also ranked in the top group with me. "You won a small battle, but they'll win the war if you persist. Be happy you got away with what you did."

"Well I don't know if *I* agree!" said Jeff Polk vehemently. "Screw Stone! Press the issue! Report Micklewski to Captain Dillingham. Let these asshole Tigers know that certain behaviors are unacceptable."

Jeff and I had similar discussions several times before. He found so much about the Academy system unacceptable, it was a wonder he stayed. And his suggestions were sometimes too radical.

"I don't think so, Jeff," I replied. "I'd rather avoid the confrontation."

"Suit yourself," he answered, shaking his head.

"Does anybody want to arrange a game of cards for tonight?" asked Willy. Instantly the Three Lustkateers looked at each other nervously. Rico answered.

"Ah . . . , no thanks, Willy. We have other plans." Conversation stopped for a moment as the others looked Rico over. Rico showed them a great poker face.

"We don't want to know, do we?" asked Jeff Polk with a twinkle.

"No, you don't," replied Rico with finality.

"What about you, Jim? Cards?" asked Willy.

"Maybe later," I lied. "I was thinking about finding a quiet spot and writing letters, so I won't be around for a while."

"Well if any of ya'll change yo' minds, we're gonna be startin' 'bout eight," Jubal Ramsey said. Jubal was a fanatic poker player despite the fact that he was a consistent loser. He also never did get used to the military time system. "I talked Zimmerman into playing," he continued, " and I'm sure the 'po little rich boy is gonna lose some of his daddy's money tonite." Reb was quite a character, and the quaint way he said things helped endear him to the upper-class.

Soon it was time to prepare for evening meal. Since we had carry-on, and since it was Rico's turn to sit on Micklewski's table, I was away from potential confrontation. Mugsy and Kevin engaged in a lively discussion of ethnic origins, and they discovered themselves to be fervent Irishmen -- much to their mutual delight. McGinley definitely liked O'Reilly and his strange sense of humor, and I think Mugsy would have spooned Kevin if he had a chance, but I could tell he was a bit afraid of Dillingham's reaction. I supposed I would be too.

Immediately after chow the other three roommates began their silent preparations for the evening's adventure. Their lecherous smiles were almost disgusting. I noticed Rico staring at me from time to time. Once, when I caught his eye, he smiled enigmatically, then returned to his meticulous preparations. He even vigorously shampooed his pubic area, "to make it soft to the touch," he said. And he powdered himself all over, "to smell good wherever the adventure leads." Kevin copied his ritual precisely. As the two of them around the room, exotic smells followed in their wakes. BJ hardly prepared at all. I'm sure he was relying instead on his killer good looks to ensure tonight's conquest.

Darkness came at nearly 1930, and the three of them put on their gym gear and trotted into the passageway. Rico was the final departee. Before he left, he stopped and turned to me.

"Be careful," he said, smiling. "Don't get into any trouble tonight."

"I don't know what you mean," I answered, trying to sound honest. I didn't fool Rico.

"Be careful," he said again as he left.

Almost immediately I put on my own gym gear, grabbed a blanket, and checked the passageway for upper-class. I cautiously headed out of the room and quickly exited into Tecumseh Court. Instead of crossing the Court in plain view of any curious upper-class who might question my blanket, I slunk in the opposite direction between the second and fourth wings, keeping to shadows as much as possible. I had scouted out the best route earlier. I knew where to head for protection from prying eyes. My only difficulty would be when I jogged toward the seawall. For nearly a hundred yards I would transit a parking area where many upper-class met their evening's dates. But it was dark, and if I kept to the edges of the buildings, I could remain unobtrusive. At least I hoped so.

Only a few midshipmen waited in that parking area. Most were too interested in their potential dates to notice a lowly plebe slinking by. I made it to darkened Farragut Field without any delays. Cutting directly across the enormous field, I jogged toward the seawall. Street lights on the landward side of the perimeter road provided only cursory light to the seawall rocks. Of the three spots I had selected, the middle one offered the best protection from discovery as well as the most room to stretch out and relax. I set up my blanket down on a level plateau among the rocks and waited, keeping down far enough so that only my head was visible. Very few cars went by as I waited, and I had an opportunity to stare out over the dark, glimmering water and smell the aromas the mild evening breeze brought to shore. Luckily the evening proved warm. Leslie and I would be comfortable.

At 1955 a car entered the Academy and drove slowly along the entry road. It was a light colored, late model Corvette Stingray. The driver's head moved from side to side counting parking areas. From this distance the driver seemed to be female. I stood and moved cautiously along the lower rocks, trying to remain out of sight while heading toward the parking area. The car parked in exactly the place I had suggested, and the driver -- definitely a female -- exited and looked around slowly. The driver looked great, and my heart began pounding in my chest. It was Leslie. I waved almost involuntarily when her gaze swept my way, and she waved in return.

I hurried to the parking area, carefully checking the surroundings. No other midshipmen were anywhere in sight. Leslie waited patiently for me beside the driver's door of her car. I stopped when I was a few feet away and smiled. She dazzled me with a return smile.

"You are a sight for sore eyes," I said honestly.

She wore a lightweight dark blue chain-knit sweater that accented her ample figure nicely and a short, plaid cotton skirt that emphasized her long and attractive legs. Her dark hair and glossy lipstick shimmered in the nearby streetlight. Wow! What a woman!

"And so are you, Jim Merritt," she said sweetly. "Can I have a hello hug?" she asked. "Or is that forbidden?"

I looked around quickly, suddenly afraid; then I looked at Leslie again. God she looked good!

"It's forbidden," I said laughing, "but what the hell!" I held out my arms and she stepped eagerly against me.

"It's good to finally get a chance to be close to you, Jim Merritt," she whispered softly against my chest.

"It is for me too," I answered. And it was. She was so soft and so round and so delightfully feminine, and her hair smelled like wild flowers and moonlight and soft breezes all wrapped in one incredible package. We held each other tightly for a long moment and I found myself reacting to her closeness. She moaned almost imperceptibly as she burrowed against me. I buried my nose in her hair and breathed deeply.

"Wow!" I said. "You have quite an effect on me, young lady."

She broke contact and curtsied.

"Thank you, gracious sir," she said with a wonderfully feminine laugh. I enjoyed her infectious laugh, and she seemed to laugh a lot.

She grabbed my arm in two hands and looked out toward the seawall.

"Where are we going, Jim Merritt? This place looks very romantic. I think I'm going to like it here with you."

"I guarantee you will my dear," I answered and led her off toward the rocks. We walked slowly. Leslie clung to my arm and I pointed out various features of the Academy as we strolled. She seemed genuinely interested. In a few minutes we came to my preselected spot, and I helped her over the rocks and down into the niche where my blanket waited.

"How wonderful!" she said as she settled down on the flat rock shelf and leaned back against another rock face. I sat next to her, and for several moments we stared out over the Chesapeake Bay. Hundreds of lights glimmered on the nearly calm waters, and a full moon, reddened by its closeness to the eastern horizon, brightened the scene.

"It's beautiful, Jim Merritt," she said leaning toward me and resting her head against my chest. I slipped my left arm around her and brought her more closely against.

"So are you," I said.

She didn't answer with words. Instead she turned her head up toward me, and I could see moonlight sparkling in her eyes and on her lips. I didn't hesitate an instant. I kissed her, and she kissed me in return. Not a single guilty thought of Lynda intruded for the next brief hour.

I have always loved the act of kissing. To me there is nothing more sensual and arousing than two perfectly suited pairs of lips pressed against each other. Lynda was a good kisser. My mouth seemed to fit perfectly on hers. I knew it instantly, and I did not want to stop kissing her for even a moment.

Finally she drew away, out of breath and dreamy-eyed.

"Oh my goodness, Jim Merritt. You certainly know how to kiss a girl."

I laughed. 'That wasn't me," I said lightly touching her nose with my opposite forefinger. "That was you," I said honestly.

She smiled up at me. "Maybe that was *us*, Jim Merritt." She tilted her head toward mine for another kiss.

"I think you're right," I whispered in the moment before our lips touched again.

I suppose it's a cliché to speak of bells and whistles and skyrockets, but that's what it felt like for me. Leslie was the only other person in creation and the rocks around us were our private universe. Time stopped.

We kissed wonderfully, then settled on the rocky shelf and stared at the stars together. After a minute of quiet conversation, Leslie rolled gently on top of me and smiled devilishly. I slipped my arm around her and pulled her tightly against me. She closed her eyes, moaned, and kissed me with a great deal of passion -- passion I shared. We began to sway and move together, and I found myself crushing her ample chest against mine.

"Oh my goodness, Jim Merritt. What you do to me."

She pushed on my chest with her two hands and lifted herself upward until she straddled me. She reached inside her sweater, and undid her bra. As I watched, amazed, she lifted her sweater to reveal herself. After only a brief glimpse of heaven, she nuzzled against my face.

After a minute she straightened again and slid downward.

"Make love to me, Jim Merritt. I can't stand it another minute." She grabbed my gym shorts and pulled them down to my knees. Quickly she knelt over me, hiked up her skirt, and for nearly a minute we made delicious love together. Finally she settled against me and moaned softly and dreamily.

We lay together, hugging tightly, kissing, and moaning softly for several minutes. Finally she laughed. It was infectious. I joined in. When she stopped, she looked at me with twinkling eyes.

"What?" I asked.

"I hope you don't think me a hussy for what just happened, Jim Merritt, but . . . "

I quickly put a finger on her luscious lips to stop further conversation.

"Not a chance," I said.

"But," she continued with emphasis. "I've never given myself to a man before." Holy smoke! I was her first?

She became suddenly serious.

"I'm going to fall in love with you, Jim Merritt. I think I'm already there. It's crazy. I don't know how it happened, but there it is. Promise me you'll never break my heart."

She was so sweet and beautiful and wonderful. I smiled in return.

"I'm in love too. You are everything I've ever dreamed about. Don't break my heart either."

"Wouldn't think of it," she said returning to her former gaiety.

"That was the most incredible experience of my entire life," I said honestly. That was the truth. I had never felt anything like what was happening to me at that instant.

"Wasn't it?" she said, amazed. "I never dreamed it could be so fantastic. You are an incredible lover, Jim Merritt."

"It's not me, it's you," I said, smiling and knowing what would come next.

She laughed.

"It's us," we said together.

We arranged ourselves, straightened our clothing, then resumed our prone positions on the rocks. She rested against me while we kissed. I gently massaged her back. I could not imagine stopping. We touched for another hour.

At 2030 I announced sadly that we had to get ready. Leslie whined softly and kissed me a final time. We stood, straightened ourselves again, and headed back to her car. Although several cars had passed during our interlude on the rocks, no one even slowed. Because liberty wouldn't expire for the first-class for another hour, I didn't expect to see anyone here by the seawall. We walked, hand-in-hand, and I felt incredibly good about myself and Leslie and what had happened between us.

"It must have been some kind of fate that brought you into the submarine shop when I was there, Jim Merritt," Leslie observed.

I laughed.

"I was thinking that very thing, my dear."

We paused outside her car.

"A farewell hug?" she asked.

"I'll give you more than that," I said, and kissed her deeply, holding her close and memorizing her contours. "Who knows when we'll have this chance again."

Her face fell.

"I intend to be in this very spot next Saturday. You better be here, Jim Merritt or I'll come up to your room and drag you out. You're stuck with me now."

I laughed.

"I accept my punishment. Wild horses won't keep me away."

"Good," she said pressing a forefinger against my chest for emphasis. "I'm in love with you, Jim Merritt, and you won't get away from me that easily." I laughed again. I really liked this girl. Hell, I think I loved this girl. She stared up into my eyes and I looked down into hers -- which were an interesting pale blue color I would never forget.

"I love you too, Leslie Taylor Wallace." I meant it.

She smiled and reached up for a quick farewell kiss.

"Good," she said. "Don't you ever forget that." I helped her into her car, then she started it and drove slowly away. I stood in place waving until she disappeared out the gate. Glancing at my watch I realized I had 30 minutes before lights-out. I hurried to the rocks and gathered up the blanket. I noticed immediately that the blanket had retained Leslie's wonderful scent. I breathed deeply and smiled. I did love that girl. I hurried back to the room, but I don't remember a single instant of that trip.

At 2245, Jeff Polk crept into the room.

"Where're the wayward lads?" he asked, laying on his New England accent a bit thickly.

"No idea," I answered. "Don't want to know."

"That's an excellent idea, especially since I'm the new plebe Company Honor Rep. I wouldn't want to catch you in an honor offense. You ever lie to me and I'll go right for your Texas throat." He said it with such finality that I glanced up, momentarily startled.

Polk laughed and pointed at me.

"Gotcha!" he exclaimed. I looked at him closely.

"Boy, you really did."

Polk left immediately after that, and I decided to shower and climb into bed. I hurried through my shower, and finished at two minutes before lights-out. I became worried about my roomies; they were cutting it close. I checked the passageway clock. It verified my watch. Hurriedly, I pulled back the covers and climbed into the sack, turning so that I faced away from the doorway, and pretended to be asleep.

I thought about Leslie and about the evening's wonderful experience. As the afterglow faded, thoughts of Lynda began creep into my love-sick reverie. What was I going to do about my sweet Lynda? I lay awake thinking for what seemed like a half hour, but no solution came to mind. I couldn't just dump her. After all, she was my almost-fiancee, and we had pledged undying love not a month ago during Parents' Weekend. And I did feel strongly about her. In fact I loved her too. But how was this possible?

I decided to put off decision-making until my head cleared a bit, and I had just begun to drift off to sleep when the door opened quietly. I stiffened, hoping it wasn't someone checking the room. Judging from the sounds, I decided the Lustkateers had returned. Judging from the giggles, I decided they had had a good time. Judging from the satisfied tone of his voice, I decided that at least Rico had been successful in achieving his evening's goal. The shower went on, followed by the sink lights, and I turned over in bed. Rico and BJ stood beside Rico's desk. Kevin was in the shower.

"When did you guys get back?" I asked foolishly.

"Did anyone come around to check rooms?" asked BJ, speaking with enough of a slur to suggest that he might have been drinking.

"I don't think so," I said. "I would have heard if they did."

"Then we got back just before lights-out," answered Rico, telling me an obvious lie. That was okay with me. If someone asked me, I'd honestly say I went to bed before lights out. What they answered to the same question was up to them.

"Have a good time?" I asked.

BJ looked at Rico, who burst into the widest grin I had ever seen on his face.

"I had all three of them!" he said chuckling in his insufferable and self-satisfied way.

"What?" I asked.

"You shoulda seen Rico! He did all three girls!" BJ laughed loudly. "It was amazing!"

I shushed BJ, then looked at Rico.

"How'd you do that?" I asked incredulously.

"It was the most incredible thing I ever saw," BJ laughed again. BJ was pretty far gone, but he really wanted to tell this story. "The girls picked us up in a secluded spot by the parade field somewhere. We drove to Hospital Point and spread a blanket on a flat spot on the side of the hill up near the graves. But the dumb broads only had this one big blanket. We were so close we were practically touching each other. One of the girls -- I think it was my date, Jeannie -- brought a bottle of Jim Beam, which we quickly finished. Then we started making out, but we kept bumping into each other -- especially that animal O'Reilly, who groped all over the place -- so it wasn't working. Then my date went to the car for another bottle, and by the time we finished half of that one, the young ladies -- and Kevin -- were pretty much smashed and giggling like crazy.

"Then Rico took charge," BJ continued shaking his head in amazement. "He asked the girls to kneel on the bottom of the blanket facing us, and they did. Then he said, 'Okay girls, off with those blouses!' The girls giggled for a minute then took 'em off. It was amazing! Then Rico said, 'Bras next!' Soon we had three bare-chested young beauties staring at us. Kevin laughed his ass off the whole time, which made the girls giggle louder. Then Rico said. 'Pants, ladies!' and sure enough they disrobed. Christ, he had them naked within five minutes, Oh, God did they look inviting! And now Kevin's laughing so hard he's about to piss himself. I think he did piss himself for Christ's sake." I looked at Rico, who continued to smile about as broadly as I have ever seen a human being smile.

"'Okay, men,' Rico continued like some admiral giving orders to the fleet, 'shirts off!' I was out of my shirt in an instant, so was Rico, but Kevin got an arm caught and ripped his shirt in frustration. I almost pissed myself at that one. Then Rico says, 'Okay, ladies. Off with your gentlemen's pants!' and they did. You shoulda heard Rico's date suck in her breath. I could see the other girls look, and they were all jealous. Shit, I felt like a pencil dick lying there next to him.

"Anyway, Rico looks down the line at us and says, 'Straighten up the line, O'Reilly!' I thought we'd die, we laughed so hard. Then he says, 'Girls, one step forward, march!' and the three young ladies perched themselves over us on their knees, giggling like crazy. Oh God, was I horny!"

"So was I," said a very sick-looking Kevin O'Reilly as he emerged from the shower. "I tried to get started right away, but Rico yelled. 'O'Reilly, Halt!' Then he said to the girls. 'Ladies, Seats!' and the girls sat on us. You shoulda heard Rico's date moan."

"It was a moan of absolute ecstasy," Rico said smugly.

Kevin continued.

"Then Rico said, 'Ladies, up, down, up, down!', and the girls went to town on us. It was incredible." Kevin's expression became faraway as he remembered the escapade. BJ had to continue.

"It was indeed incredible. The three of us in a line, humping furiously. I was so horny I finished in under three minutes, so did Kevin. But Rico kept going and going. Jesus, he's a machine! Finally his date had too many climaxes, and she literally passed out and fell off him onto the grass. But Rico was still ready. He looked over at my Jeannie and said, 'Are you ready for more?' I almost shit! She looked at me for permission. 'Go for it!' I said. And she did! Rico did her to death too, and he still wasn't satisfied." BJ howled out in laughter at the memory. We all shushed him.

"Kevin's date didn't even ask permission," BJ continued, poking Kevin in the ribs. "She climbed aboard and had her fill too. Happily, Kevin's little sexpot was able to finish Rico; otherwise I think he'd still be there, moving from girl to girl. We dressed, finished the second bottle, the girls dropped us off, and we hurried back. We would have been back sooner, but Kevin had to stop to be sick." BJ laughed loudly again. We quieted him.

"There's an enormous puddle of Kevin puke in front of Tecumseh. Tecumseh doesn't look too pleased about that." BJ looked at Kevin and laughed again. BJ was pretty drunk. "You're supposed to throw pennies at Tecumseh, not puke, Kevin." We all laughed.

"What a great time!" BJ said as he disappeared into the shower.

"How was your evening?" Rico asked knowingly.

"Not as interesting as yours," I answered noncommittally.

"But interesting, huh?" asked Rico. Kevin looked from one of us to the other, not understanding.

"It was fine," I said with a big smile.

"Kevin," Rico said, turning to his buddy. "Jimbo is one of the bad boys." I didn't like the sound of that.

I called Leslie first thing Sunday morning to see how well she had slept. I found myself excited at the prospect of talking to her. I wanted to be sure she felt the same as she had said last night. I wanted to tell her again I loved her.

"I'm angry at you, Jim Merritt," she said very seriously. I was taken aback.

"Why?" I sputtered.

"I didn't get a second's sleep from thinking about you," she said. "How's it feel to have so captured my heart?"

"Wonderful!" I answered. "I didn't sleep much either." That was not true. I had slept deeply and contentedly the entire night. But Leslie was searching for a metaphoric reply, so I didn't feel the least bit guilty.

"I can't wait to see you again," I said honestly. "I'll call you every night if I get a chance."

"Call me every other night, Jim Merritt," Leslie said, bursting my balloon.

"What?"

"I have to study, Jim Merritt. If you call me every night, I'll never be able to concentrate on my books." I laughed.

"Okay, Leslie Taylor Wallace. Every other night."

"I love you, Jim Merritt," she said as we hung up.

"I love you too, sweetheart." I had never used any cute words with Lynda. She thought they were babyish. However, it seemed to fit with Leslie, and she really did enjoy the attention. I was in heaven all day Sunday.

Who gets the brick? Who gets the brick? Who gets the brick?" The words echoed down the long passageway. Singing in a pious almost-Gregorian chant, a procession of Twenty-third Company plebes moved religiously along the center of the long passageway on Sunday evening immediately following meal. Leading the procession, the plebe high priest of unusual ceremonies, was Jubal Ramsey. In his arms, held out at chest level, he cradled a navy blue silk pillow -- borrowed temporarily from the Wardroom. On the pillow rested a brick -- a simple red paving brick appropriated from one of the many construction sites within the Academy proper. Twenty assorted plebes, all identically dressed in B-Robes and shower shoes -- the acolytes of the ceremony -- followed Ramsey in reverent pairs, arms folded across their chests.

The procession continued down the main passageway and around the corner. In the shorter passageways the words echoed eerily. The procession solemnly passed Mugsy's room and continued around the next corner, chanting slowly and loudly. Behind the procession a large group of curious upper-class followed at a respectful distance, whispering among themselves. I watched as doors opened and upper-class watched our approach with dread, hoping the brick was not intended for them.

"Who gets the brick?" we continued more loudly as we turned the final corner. Ramsey stopped us in front of Room 4051, the home of Midshipmen First-class Harvey Linehan and "Big Jim" Daly. Daly opened the door and immediately laughed.

"Hey, Harvey! Someone's here for you!"

"Ah, shit, Jim!" exclaimed a voice from out of sight. "She's my fiancee, for God's sake!"

"Who gets the brick?" we chanted louder.

"Damn!" Linehan yelled, and he came to the door. He confronted Reb.

"What the hell do you want?" he asked angrily.

"Sir!" Ramsey spouted in accordance with the ritual. "I am the official messenger of the Guardians of the Sacred Brick. The Guardians have noticed that you have disgraced your Company and the Academy by dating a female this weekend who could properly be termed unworthy of a studly midshipman. In fact, according to your classmates, she was a real bow-wow." Reb added that last part in a sudden plebe inspiration. "As a symbol of the displeasure of the Guardians, you must keep this sacred brick as a sign of your public shame. It must stay under your careful watch until the Guardians choose to award it to some other disgraced individual."

With that Reb held out the brick to Linehan who took it reluctantly. Ramsey then led us away from the room.

We chanted as we left. "He got the brick! He got the brick! He got the brick!" Before we turned the final corner toward the Company Office, Linehan yelled, "Stone, you bastard! She's my fiancee!"

CHAPTER SEVEN

IN CHARGE OF THE ASYLUM

Monday brought a return of Plebe Year to Room 4025 and with it severe accompanying depression. On Sunday Kevin and BJ had substantial hangovers and hid all day lest they be questioned about the cause of their condition. They were lucky Monday because they had been picked to run with Mugsy, and he wouldn't care about their condition. Rico and I had our various sexual afterglows, but our fantasy thoughts of love or studdom were rudely shattered by a very vicious comearound to Stone. It was the worse so far, and I hadn't thought that possible.

I could see Stone had two objectives in mind. The first was to run Tommy and Tim until they dropped, and within 15 minutes both had puked up stomach bile in the passageway. Judging from the gleam of self-satisfaction in his and Micklewski's eyes, I would say they were proud of themselves for this double retching treat. His second, even more obvious objective -- the one I resented the most -- was to show me who was the real boss of Tiger Company.

"Come on, Merritt, you sissy!" he yelled repeatedly. "Can't you get your god-dammed ass down the passageway any faster than that? Terrible push-ups, Merritt! Stop bagging it!" The abuse was unrelenting, and Rico suffered alongside me -- not altogether in silence, although he kept his comments very subdued. After one long and exhausting sprint, Rico bent over wheezing to recover, his face turned away from the firsties.

"Sorry, Jim," he whispered fiercely between wheezes, and I watched as he stuck a finger down his throat to induce vomiting. That bought him a short respite -- one I didn't have. I wasn't going to force myself to puke. That would satisfy the Tigers far too much.

"Don't worry about your sissy classmates, Merritt!" Micklewski yelled as I watched Rico heaving. "Sprint down here, now!" I ran as fast as I could, which by this time was no more than a fast jog. I was expending energy at a fantastic rate, and I could feel myself growing weak from exertion. I briefly wondered if this was going to be the morning they actually would run me until I dropped.

"Run, you plebe bastard!" Stone shouted as I passed him. "Be a man for once in your life! Knock 'em together!" I sprinted as best I could to the end of the passageway and turned to race back, but I tripped while turning and fell hard onto the deck. My left knee slammed against the unforgiving tile floor, and I knew I would have a nasty bruise later in the day.

"Get up you sissy! No more bagging it, you puke, or so help me God, I'll come down there and kick your ass all the way back!" That was Stone's idea of motivation. I rose and ran as best I could, limping slightly.

"Plebe, halt!" Micklewski yelled as I evened with him. "Twenty push-ups! Now!" I dropped to the deck and began pushing up as best I could. Push-ups were almost a respite after the torturous running, but my head continued to swim as my body moved up and down rhythmically. I shook it to clear my thoughts. "Keep going, you son-of-a-gun!" Micklewski yelled. "No bagging it!" I finished the 20, and held myself aloft in leaning-rest position as expected, waiting for the next command.

"Stand up, Merritt!" Stone yelled. "Brace up against the bulkhead!" I rose, hurried to the wall, turned, and braced. My head swam dangerously from the sudden rising motion. I didn't feel well at all.

"What's the menu for morning meal, Merritt?" Micklewski asked.

"Sir," I said groggily, "the menu for morning meal is breakfast steaks, scrambled eggs, home-fried potatoes, bacon, toast, butter, and jelly, sir!"

"Are you sure, Merritt?" Micklewski asked, yelling in my right ear.

"Yes, sir!" I had no doubt I was right. I had looked at the POD just prior to comearound.

"Mister Butler!" he yelled turning to Tim, who had only just recovered from his sickness and stood braced against the far passageway wall. "What's the menu for morning meal?"

"Sir, the menu for morning meal is breakfast steaks, scrambled eggs, sausages, home-fried potatoes, toast, butter, and jelly, sir!"

Micklewski spun around to face me, clearly angry. Stone came quickly to my opposite side. "You son-of-a-bitch!" Stone yelled in my left ear. "There's no damn bacon this morning! You screwed up, Merritt -- big time! You make that kind of mistake in combat and you might call in artillery rounds on your own god-damn troops. One wrong number, Merritt, one little misunderstanding, and it's death for good men who don't deserve it. Maybe you're no better than Poole, asshole! In fact, you might even be worse. At least Poole doesn't screw up the simplest of rates like. Maybe you don't belong here either! As of now I'm considering putting you on my farewell list, douchebag!"

Across the passageway I could see Rico, who had recovered and braced, waiting for the next round of abuse. He was smiling broadly at me. The bastard was gloating at my misery. I almost lost control. I started to unbrace. But something in Rico's eyes told me to stop and consider.

"You are a sorry excuse for a midshipman, Merritt!" Micklewski continued. "You have no guts at all. I'm disgusted with you." The words droned on as I watched Rico, and I found myself gradually relaxing. Suddenly I understood his message. I almost smiled at the revelation. It *was* all a stupid game. In fact, it was a crazy game run by insane young men. The Academy was an asylum. Nothing that was happening had any relationship to any real world -- including the military world. Artillery rounds? Bullshit! The key was to stay cool and not fold under the pressure. I remained silent, enduring the droning yells and the meaningless threats, letting them bounce off my psyche and not giving them a resting place in my mind. I had the power to do this. I was in charge, not Stone.

Stone sensed he had lost my undivided attention, and *he* became truly angry now.

"Push-ups, Merritt! Begin!" I dropped to the deck as Stone turned to the others. "All of you!" he shouted. "Push-ups! Now!" Every plebe in the passageway, including those coming around to other firsties and one poor Twenty-second Company plebe sent over for an errand, dropped to the ground and began vigorous up-and-down motions. None of Stone's classmates objected.

Taking a cue from a Plebe Summer ritual we plebes had begun, I began to loudly count cadence.

"One, sir! Two, sir! Three, sir!" I suddenly felt good again. I was back in control. Soon every plebe copied the rhythm, and we shouted push-up numbers loudly together. Stone didn't like our unity of purpose one bit. We hadn't gotten to 20 before he yelled.

"On your feet, you plebe scum! Butler, Guevarra, Poole! Clean up your disgusting messes and return to your rooms!" They stood and began to chop. "Merritt!" Stone yelled. "Brace up against the bulkhead!" I hurried to comply. I could feel the cold pink bulkhead tiles stick to my dripping-wet shirt as I flopped against the wall. Sweat ran freely down my face and dropped from my nose and chin. I stared resolutely straight ahead.

Stone approached me slowly, and I watched his face. He didn't seem to be as angry as he sounded, and that confused me. He stopped when he was a step in front of me and he lowered his voice just enough so that no one else could hear.

"Almost lost control again, didn't you, Merritt?"

"Yes, sir!" I answered loudly.

"But you didn't. You exerted yourself and got yourself back under control." He smiled and continued in a near whisper. "That's good, Merritt! I think there's hope for you yet." He looked me over for a second. "How's your knee?"

I had almost forgotten the spill I had taken. I flexed it slightly. It hurt, but not too badly.

"It'll be fine by evening comearound, sir!" I answered with a slight smile.

"It better be, Merritt. You do understand. Now get back to you room and be ready for formation on time." I chopped down the passageway. When I was halfway to my room, Stone, suddenly the Company Commander again, yelled.

"Merritt!"

I stopped and turned, still a bit wobbly.

"Sir!"

"You had better know your rates at breakfast!" I pledged to myself that I would.

Morning meal was another nightmare. It was my unfortunate turn to sit with Stone. They grilled me mercilessly, and I didn't have a chance to eat a single bite. But I knew my rates cold, and luckily Kevin smuggled me a couple sausages from his table.

Monday night after my call to lovely Leslie I went down to Tommy's room with Kevin. Kevin had legitimate business with Tommy that concerned some obscure molecular bonding characteristics, and for a time I chatted with George and Hank about plebe psychology class. Ten minutes later Stone and Micklewski entered. We all snapped to attention. Stone was pissed to see extra plebes in the room.

"What the hell are you two doing here?" he snapped.

"Discussing academic matters, sir!" Kevin answered boldly.

"Brace up against that locker the rest of you! I want to talk to Poole and Butler." Kevin and I hurried to comply, but Abbott and Butkowski were much slower in their response. "Hurry up, I said!" Stone yelled. They moved faster, but only barely. Stone scowled. For the moment he had forgotten the purpose of his visit.

Micklewski sauntered slowly over to the four of us. He eyed Hank and George.

"God would I love to get you two in my squad," he said longingly. Then he smiled at Kevin. "I can really run plebe asses, can't I, O'Reilly?"

"You're the second-best, sir!" Kevin answered brashly. Why does Kevin continue to ask for trouble?

"Second best! Who's better, you miserable plebe?"

"Sir, Your good buddy Midshipman First-class Stone, sir! He really knows how to run my ass!" Stone laughed, but Micklewski was not amused.

"What are the only three responses permitted by a plebe to any question, O'Reilly?"

"Sir! They are, 'Yes, sir!', 'No, sir!', and 'I'll find out, sir!'" Kevin answered.

"Why do you insist on impertinence, O'Reilly?"

"I'll find out, sir!"

"You don't like me, do you, O'Reilly?"

"No, sir!"

"You think I'm an asshole, don't you?"

"Yes, sir!"

"You'd love to take a swing at me, wouldn't you?"

"Oh, yes, sir!" Kevin answered, verbally stepping slightly out of bounds. Micklewski responded.

"I don't care if you like me, O'Reilly!" Micklewski shouted. "You are insignificant as far as I'm concerned. My job is to train you for the fleet, and that's what I intend to do. You believe me when I say that?"

"No, sir!"

"What?" Micklewski shouted angrily. "You don't think I'm sincere in what I do?"

"No, sir!"

Micklewski immediately assumed the look he had when he confronted me. "You son-of-a-gun, you!" he yelled. "How can you say that?"

"I'll find out, sir!"

"Answer me, you plebe!"

"Sir, there are only three standard answers allowed when a plebe responds to an upper-class," Kevin said using Micklewski's words against him.

Micklewski sputtered. He advanced on O'Reilly, who waited calmly against the bulkhead. "Knock it off, Dale!" Stone said. Up to this point he had been watching Micklewski and O'Reilly with amusement.

Stone's words had no effect on Micklewski. He was over the edge. His eyes were wide and wild, and flecks of spittle sprayed from one corner of his mouth. He grabbed Kevin by the shirt front and pulled back a fist. Kevin stood calmly. I could see him bundle up his stomach muscles for the blow that was coming. "Dale!" Stone shouted, moving quickly toward the confrontation.

The first punch landed on Kevin's lower abdomen area. He was ready, and it did little damage. Kevin puffed out some air but continued standing rigidly, a slight smile on his mouth. Micklewski became even more enraged. He readied a second punch, this time aimed at Kevin's face. The fist never connected. George Abbott grabbed his arm in mid-swing and stopped its forward progress. Dale Micklewski screamed incoherently and began to move against George. George was ready. He growled, stepped away, and pulled back a large fist. Judging by the look on his face, he would have killed Dale Micklewski with a single blow had he continued toward him. Thankfully, Hank Butkowski saved the day by grabbing Micklewski around the waist and picking him up several feet into the air. He swung him around -- away from George and Kevin -- almost as if he had no weight at all. He placed the struggling firstie down carefully in front of Stone, retaining the bear hug.

"You better hold him, sir!" he said.

Stone grabbed Micklewski by the arm, and Hank let go, but still Dale struggled to get free.

"You're all on report for assaulting an upper-class!" he screamed.

"That's not what I saw, classmate!" said a voice from the doorway. Two figures stepped into the room and halted.

Standing in the opening were Jeff Rightman and Lebron Butterfield, both prominent first-class members of the Navy football team. We froze, and I could see a variety of emotions play across the faces of the startled Tigers.

"What the hell just happened here?" asked Rightman. Nobody answered. Rightman walked unconcerned to the center of the room between us plebes and the now subdued firsties. He looked us over. I was still braced against the locker. Jeff was a throwback to the Roger Staubach era. He was no more than 6 feet tall, but he was fearless under pressure and could run the ball and throw with accuracy.

He was personable, he sported a bristly blond crew cut, and had a set of laughing blue eyes. He definitely had charisma.

"Carry-on!" he announced. We relaxed.

"What's your name?" he asked Micklewski.

"Dale Micklewski, . . . !" Christ, he almost added a "sir." Such is the power of Navy football.

"What just happened here, Micklessski," Rightman said, deliberately mispronouncing the name.

"I had a disagreement with a disrespectful plebe." Micklewski had a very uncomfortable look on his face. I could almost imagine the Honor Code dancing around the room as they spoke. The Tigers knew that what Micklewski had done was terribly wrong. It might even be a dismissing offense. But neither Stone nor Micklewski knew what Rightman had seen, so they were afraid to admit anything that might cause serious trouble or might be brought before the Honor Board. They were also counting on the fact that none of us plebes would say a word against them unless directly questioned.

"I could swear I heard body contact," observed Butterfield, who had a slight smile on his handsome black face. "I know that sound well." Lebron was a tall defensive back who had a reputation for relishing hard tackles. "Are you saying that a plebe attacked you?"

"You saw Butkowski holding me. What more evidence do you want?" Micklewski said confidently now that he knew that the two firsties hadn't actually seen any punches.

"I saw an insane first-classman being physically restrained by an alert plebe," said Rightman, "a plebe who is a vital member of next year's football squad and one who doesn't need Tiger insanity in the evenings. Who are you?" he asked Stone.

"Reginald Oliver Stone," Stone answered with pride. Rock's first name was "Reginald?" Why didn't I know that?

"Oh, Christ!" Butterfield exclaimed. "The leader of this damn asylum!" Rightman and Butterfield eyed Stone, who stared at them with equal intensity.

"This shit is going to stop!" Rightman said. "I want your word on that, Stone!"

"What happens within my Company is my business," Stone replied.

"No, actually it's not," said Rightman calmly. "The regulations limit plebe indoctrination to morning and evening comearounds, inspections, and meal times. The hours between evening meal and lights-out are strictly reserved for studying. So unless one of these plebes is in the same academic class you are, you have no right being here, much less bracing them up and playing silly-assed Tiger games. Is this shit gonna stop or not, Stone?"

"I'll decide if it does," said Stone smugly.

"Then you'll decide right this instant, asshole!" Rightman said loudly. "Otherwise tomorrow morning on my first break I'll visit my buddy Captain Mack Hallahan. You probably know him Stone. --

He's the Commandant! And he loves Navy football. He's gonna be plenty pissed to find out what the hell I saw in the room of one of the top recruits Navy has been able to get here in several years." Rightman walked over to Butkowski and patted him on a massive shoulder.

"With a forward line made up of guys like this, Navy could be a powerhouse again." He turned on Stone. "And you can bet the Commandant and every other senior officer in the Department of the Navy -- most of whom are alumni, I might add -- are not going to stand idly by while you screw it up. Did I make myself clear?"

"Butkowski will never have a Plebe Year," Stone answered. "The Academy is responsible to train these people."

Butterfield reacted. He laughed in Stone's face. "Give me a break! Push-ups and wind sprints and reciting rates do not a Plebe Year make. Butkowski works his ass off for hours after class. It's far more exhausting -- and dangerous -- than any comearound you can imagine. He's not only having a hell of a Plebe Year, but he's gonna go through the same torture for the next four years while the rest of his classmates are lounging on the beach or poking their girlfriends. He's a hell of a warrior, Stone, and Jeff and I already spooned him."

"What's your answer, Stone?" asked Rightman impatiently. "I don't have time for this. I've got studies of my own."

Rock Stone was on the spot, and he was really pissed. But it was crazy Micklewski that put him there, not us. He responded honorably, I have to hand him that.

"Very well," he said. "I admit my error. No more evening visits to Butkowski's room. And I'll see that all the firsties understand."

"You realize, Stone" Butterfield replied, "that the regulations apply to *all* plebe rooms. Every plebe deserves the chance to study. Academics are no picnic, and I'd hate to think that any Tiger plebe flunks out because he wasn't given a chance. You better remind the firsties of that."

"Of course," Rock replied.

"Good," Rightman said, then he turned to Hank. "See you on the gridiron, big guy!" He and Butterfield departed. We waited, unsure as to whether to brace up or not. Stone looked at us for a moment, then he came over to O'Reilly. He looked at Kevin with admiration.

"You took that punch well, O'Reilly. Were you going to take the second one too?"

"Yes, sir!"

He smiled and nodded in renewed admiration.

"I don't think anyone would blame you if you make a public incident of this, and I'm not going to direct you to stay quiet. Mister Micklewski is deeply sorry for what he did and I would sincerely appreciate it if you would consider the situation closed. We need to keep some discipline here in this Company; I'm sure you can understand that."

"Request permission to speak freely, sir!" Kevin asked.

Stone hesitated a moment. Kevin had a reputation for speaking too freely sometimes.

"Very well, O'Reilly. Speak."

"Sir, I can take any abuse you guys can dish out. You tell me to run, and I run till I barf. You give me push-ups and I go up and down till my arms give out. I know my rates. I shine my shoes." He looked at Micklewski before continuing. "You can even punch me, and I can take that too. But what's the point now? It seems that once we establish that a plebe can perform under the absolute worst circumstances, then whatever happens afterward is torture not training. I resent having to perform for anyone's sadistic pleasure."

"You think what we do is torture, huh, O'Reilly?" asked Micklewski with a sadistic sneer.

"Sir, I think it's sadistic. You want to test me? Go ahead! But when you inflict pain to watch the results, I think it's time to draw the line."

"You think the pain stops for the troops in Vietnam, O'Reilly?" asked Stone.

"Sir! I'm sure the troops endure great physical hardship and danger. However, the stress isn't constant. They're not caged like we are, and they can go wild on a regular basis. You guys keep up the pressure far beyond any meaningful level."

"Listen, plebe!" Micklewski began. "I'll decide when you've had enough torture!"

"Yes, sir. I know that. I guess that's what pisses me off the most." Kevin was really going now, and he was headed for trouble, I could see that.

"What's that mean O'Reilly?" asked Stone.

"Sir," O'Reilly said confidently. "I can take anything any first-class can dish out, but guys like Mister Micklewski go crazy with no provocation and no regard for the consequences. I have absolutely no respect for people like him at all. What's *he* going to do in the fleet when the pressure's on? Scream and spit? What gives? Don't you think it's time to pull in the reins?"

Stone grabbed Micklewski as he started forward, sputtering madly again. Stone glared at O'Reilly.

"You have a really big mouth, O'Reilly. It's going to get you in trouble some day."

O'Reilly laughed.

"It already has many times, sir."

Stone kept a firm hold of Micklewski's arm. He laughed.

"I like you, O'Reilly. You are one brassy asshole. I'll consider what you've said, but I'll decide when the reins get pulled." He steered the still-enraged Micklewski to the door and turned to Tommy.

"I'll talk to you and Butler tomorrow at comearound, Poole. Let's go, Dale." They left the room.

Hank Butkowski came over and stood in front of Kevin, shaking his head in amazement.

"O'Reilly, you are one crazy son-of-a-gun."

Kevin laughed.

"Don't you get it? I beat them both and they can never get one-up on me again. I just graduated from Plebe Year; watch and see."

"You think so, Kevin?" asked Tommy Poole. "I don't think Stone will stand for any more insubordination -- from you or anyone."

"It doesn't matter, Tommy. I can make Micklewski lose control whenever I want. All I have to do is smirk. He's *my* plebe now." Nobody in the room understood Kevin's logic. The blow to his stomach must have dislodged something in his head. I was beginning to wonder if Kevin O'Reilly liked being abused. But he seemed smug. I kept quiet.

Tuesday afternoon I received a note saying I had a package waiting in the Main Office. I couldn't imagine what would be coming for me, so I hurried down after my fifth period class -- my last class that day. The plebe on duty examined the note, checked my ID scrupulously, then went to an area in the corner of the office where several official and unofficial packages were stacked. He examined each and selected a cardboard box more than two feet square on each side. He lifted it with some difficulty and brought it to his desk.

"You might want to get a friend to help you with this," he said. "It's pretty heavy."

I checked the address on the front of the box. It was a "Care Package" from mom! I lowered my nose so that it just touched the box and breathed deeply. I could smell the heady aroma of chocolate even through several layers of wrapping. My mouth began watering. Still bent over, I looked up at my classmate, wiggled my eyebrows up and down, and smiled devilishly. He laughed.

"Lucky bugger!" he said.

I was in a really magnanimous mood, and I couldn't wait to open that package.

"Do you have a knife?" I asked. He produced a letter opener. I slit the top of the box and removed copious quantities of newspaper stuffing from the inside, along with tin after tin of goodies. There were ten tins in all. I opened one that smelled particularly good.

A neatly penned note sat on top of the brownies that filled the tin.

"Fudge Brownies from Mrs. Pam Wilson," the note said. The Wilsons were our next-door neighbors, and I had played Little League with her son Randal. She was a great cook. I held out the tin to my now-salivating classmate.

"Have one?" I asked. He eagerly selected the largest. Then I circled the Main Office, giving brownies out like party favors, even to the upper-class. The second-class on watch grabbed two.

"Only one to a customer," I boldly said.

He looked at me sheepishly.

"It's for my roommate," he said.

"Why not?" I replied, still elated.

The plebes on duty arranged the tins into two paper Midshipmen's Store bags. These were much easier to carry than the box, and soon I hurried off to the Company Area with my treasure. Most of the Company was off at final class, so I arrived unnoticed -- only to discover that I had another note from the Main Office. There was another package waiting. Puzzled, I hurried back.

The plebe on duty looked up when I entered.

"What's the matter, did your back give out from all that weight? Need a truck to finish the delivery?"

"No," I said, laughing and handing him the second note with a flourish. "I have another package."

"No shit?" He went to the pile again, and extracted another box. This one was much smaller, and didn't have a return address on it. He handed it to me. I started to leave, then turned.

"I'm dying to know," he said.

"Me too," I said, as he handed me the letter opener. I carefully slit the top. Inside was a box that held a large red candy heart. On top of that heart was a beautifully penned "*I Love You,*" It was signed "*Leslie.*" I showed it to my classmate.

"Shit," he said. "You must live right."

"Yeah, I guess I do." I felt wonderful, and Saturday was only four days away. Even though I wasn't supposed to call her tonight, I vowed to do so anyway. What a gal!

Back in my room I inventoried my sweet assets and decided to share them with my classmates and squad. Knowing how greedy midshipmen could be -- I had once caught a classmate hiding packages of jelly under his plate so he could spirit them up to his room for later consumption -- I put together three tins of assorted goodies and hid them in my locker. Those would be my reserve. Then I prepared a tin for the guys across the passageway, another expressly for Brandis and McGinley, one for Mahoney and Clanton, and another for Christenson and Brewer. That would take care of the squad obligations. I thought about making one up for Stone, Micklewski, and Salenger but decided that would seem too much like sucking up. Besides, I was still upset at how things were going in Tiger Company. I also put a tin on my desk for my roommates and classmate visitors.

That evening's comearound was as merciless as Monday's. Luckily for Kevin O'Reilly he was coming-around to McGinley because Micklewski was out for blood. Luckily for Rico and me he was mostly out for Tommy's and Tim's blood.

"God almighty! You two are like girls! Pussys, that's what you are! You walk like girls! You talk like girls! You act like girls!" He hesitated, considering a course of action for a moment, then made up his mind. "Get back to your room and pin a towel around your waists. Then wrap another one around your heads and hurry back here!" Tommy and Tim looked at each other briefly, and ran down the passageway.

"Merritt! Guevarra! Push-ups until they get back. And no bagging it Guevarra. I'm tired of your half-assed attitude!" We began counting push-ups together. Rico was a very strong individual. He could do push-ups all day long -- far more than me. But he did "cheat" on the exercises every chance he had. It was a game to him to see how much he could get away with. But whatever he did was his business. I grunted out my push-ups, determined not to give Micklewski or Stone any chance to complain.

We had reached 56 when Tommy and Tim raced from their room and headed toward us. "On you feet!" Stone yelled. We stood and waited.

Both had pinned white Academy towels around their waists so that they hung to just above their knees. Hand towels covered their heads, Carmen Miranda style. They stopped in front of Micklewski and braced. He looked at them critically.

"Now you look more like the girls you are," he said sarcastically. "Roll up your shirts like halter tops and tie them behind your back. Merritt and Guevarra, help them! Hurry!" Tommy and Tim waited while Rico and I pulled up a shirt each until it was almost level with their chests, twisted the fabric behind their backs, and tied it off. It was not a flattering look, particularly for Tommy Poole.

Tommy, despite the exercise and significant weight loss, still had an unsightly roll of fat around his middle. He bulged where the towel-skirt circled him, and his chest filled the bra-like top suggestively. Tim on the other hand didn't look half bad. He was small and thin to begin with -- more girl-sized -- and his body had no hair to speak of. His facial features were also soft and nearly feminine. And the constant exercising had shaped his legs and tightened his stomach to a point where many girls would be jealous. God, if he had make-up on, I could almost imagine him as a flat-chested girl. It was eerie.

Micklewski also noticed.

"I was right about you, Butler. If you had boobies, you'd be female." He looked at Poole closely. "When you two fool around, who plays the dominant role, Poole?" Tommy wisely didn't answer.

"You two look like shit!" Stone said, clearly disgusted. "I want you to go to every person in the Company right now. Don't brace. Say to everyone, 'Look at us sir. Aren't we as cute as can be?' Brace for the plebes and say, 'Classmate, classmate. Aren't you glad we're your classmates, *sir*?' Say it all in a girl's voice; then curtsey to each person before you move on. Got that?"

They looked extremely uncomfortable.

"And from now on whenever you enter my room, pass me in the passageway, or ask me any question, announce yourselves as 'Latent homosexuals Poole or Butler.' Get going, girls!"

Tim and Tommy both gave loud, "Aye-aye, sir's," and ran down the passageway. Their tight "skirts" prevented them from running very fast. Tommy jiggled, which I'm sure did not endear him to Stone. Butler, whose natural gait was somewhat girlish, moved even more suggestively. Stone and Micklewski noticed. They looked at each other wordlessly, then watched as Poole and Butler performed this humiliating ritual to every individual they met.

"Butler!" Stone yelled. "Why did you skip Midshipman Third-class Brewer?"

"Sir!" Tim answered, forgetting and still using his girl's voice. "He's spooned me."

"I don't give a shit about that, you asshole! Do exactly what I said!" Tim trotted back to Bull Brewer and repeated the routine. Within a few minutes they had disappeared around the corner, but we could hear their voices over the general din of other plebe comearounds. Stone and Micklewski listened. Micklewski had a faint smile.

I must have had a disgusted look on my face. Micklewski saw it.

"Sickening, huh?" he asked me.

"It sure is," I said looking instead at Stone. He met my gaze steadily. Was this one of the advanced forms of Plebe indoctrination he had promised?

Noon meal on Wednesday was extremely interesting. Kevin and I sat at the Squad table, waiting on McGinley and Brandis.

"O'Reilly," Brandis asked, "did you read that article about the seven Georgia football players who are accused of raping a cheerleader?"

"Yes, sir!" he answered.

"What do you think?"

"I think they should all be castrated and sent to jail, sir!"

"The men say she offered them sex and they took her up on it."

"Even so, sir. They have to be lying."

"Bullshit, O'Reilly!" Mugsy interrupted. "There's such a thing as asking for it, you know."

"I don't think so, sir." Kevin didn't sound completely convinced.

"Look, she admits she went back into the locker room of her own free will. She says they passed a bottle around. She says she took off her clothes and danced for them. What the hell did she expect to happen? Polite applause? Women have too damn much sexual power, and they don't want to take any god-damn responsibility for their actions."

"Still don't agree, sir."

"Oh, you're just a plebe," McGinley said. "You don't know shit about women or sex."

"And trust me, son," Brandis added in a fatherly tone. "You might eventually get lucky and get laid, but you'll never be able to figure out women no matter how hard you try." Everyone laughed.

"You guys got dates for Army-Navy yet?" Mugsy asked, changing the subject.

"No, sir," we both answered, although I was pretty sure Leslie would come if I asked. She had hinted that she was free that Saturday.

"Well, let me give you some advice," Mugsy continued. "Forget this 'best girl' bullshit. Find yourselves two honest-to-God hose-bags, rent a room in a cheap hotel, get a couple six packs of generic beer, and screw your brains out. You won't ever have a better opportunity the entire year." Again everyone at the table laughed.

"Who's your date this year, Mugsy?" Eddie Christenson asked, laughing. Mugsy stopped laughing. He squinched up his forehead until his brow furrowed like a newly plowed farm.

"That's a good question," he said. "I didn't exactly endear myself to the local ladies very well last year, did I?" Everyone at the table laughed again.

"You guys have got to hear this story," Christenson said. "Tell them, Mugsy."

"You were there," Mugsy said, chuckling to himself. "You tell 'em, Ed."

"It was great!" Christenson began. "We had rented a suite of three hotel rooms for a Company party. We must have had thirty people there, including Captain Dillingham." Christenson lowered his voice and looked around. "By the way, don't let the Captain near your date if you value your girlfriend's virtue. He comes alone to these things, and he's always on the prowl. I think he snuck off with three inebriated young ladies last year."

"You guys let him?" I asked incredulously.

"Who's gonna stop him?" Mugsy asked. Good point!

"So anyway," Christenson continued. "We drank ten cases of beer in an hour and we were having a great time. Everybody is loaded to the gills, and Dillingham is sweet-talking every skirt. Some of us had rented rooms on the same floor for a little private time, and a few began drifting away from the party. Mugsy and about ten other firsties brought a group of local ladies from Anne Arundel Community College, who were drunk on their co-ed asses. So Mugsy gets up, grabs one girl who's pretty far gone by the hand and says. 'Come on baby, let's have some fun!' He half-carries her out of the room, this big-assed grin on his face, and we laughed our asses off."

"About ten minutes later he came back in the room, dejected -- and he's completely naked! 'I got her clothes off,' he says, 'but she passed out.' Then he starts dancing around the room swinging his pecker at every female."

"Most of whom were severely grossed out, by the way," Brandis said to Mugsy. Mugsy laughed and playfully swatted backhanded at Henry.

Christenson continued, "Mugsy starts grabbing at everybody's dates, trying to get them to go with him, and nobody's having any of that."

"It's that god-awful body hair of yours, Mugsy," Henry interrupted again. "I told you a million times it makes you look like an ape."

"Eugene O'Neill," said O'Reilly out of the blue. I had no idea what he was talking about. Brandis chuckled, and Mugsy pointed a fat finger at Kevin and nodded his head in the affirmative.

"Exactly!" he said.

We all turned our attention back to Eddie, who continued for a third time.

"Mugsy dances around the room for several minutes, drunk as a skunk, and horny as hell. Finally he shrugs, says, 'Oh what the hell. At least she isn't dead.' -- and goes back to his room."

"You didn't?" Kevin asked.

"The hell I didn't," Mugsy replied. "Several times. It wasn't half bad, either. She kind of responded."

"Probably thought she was having a bad dream," said Kevin with characteristic boldness. We laughed.

"Anyway," Brandis added, "Mugsy is now persona non grata with a great many local women."

"Yeah," Mugsy said. "So if any of your hose-bag dates have hose-bag sisters -- or mothers for that matter -- I'm available."

The idea of partying with these guys didn't appeal to me at all. If asked, I decided I would gladly forego that experience.

After meal I doled out the goodies when we distributed the sandwiches. I was immediately the most popular plebe in the Company, and a constant parade of upper-class visited our room to partake in my good fortune. By the end of the evening most of the tins had been emptied, and Kevin O'Reilly had pledged undying love for one of my friend's younger sisters, who had made some incredibly wonderful tiny pecan pie sweets. The fact that she was 15 didn't seem to faze him at all.

Sunday evening after meal, the plebes put on a skit for the Company. The youngsters had done theirs two weeks previously, but it was a weenie presentation roasting the ineffectiveness of the Navy football team. Hardly anybody laughed. Dillingham grunted when it finally ended and obviously wasn't particularly impressed.

The plebe Skit Committee consisted of Kevin O'Reilly, Rico Guevarra, Jubal Ramsey, George Abbott, Pat Mulvaney, and Willy Simpson. They met secretly on several occasions to discuss the script and the stagecraft, and Kevin promised a blockbuster -- one he hoped would set Company skits back many years. I think his plan was to make our show so offensive that Captain Dillingham would never ask the plebes to do another. They kept the script secret from any but committee members; but Rico let slip several times that the script was the masterwork of Kevin's fertile brain, and that he had a *prominent* assignment.

We set up the "stage" in front of our room, which happened to be centrally located for what Kevin termed "the quick getaway." Pat Mulvaney ushered the event, making sure that chairs were placed in the suitable locations and that the right people sat up front. George Abbott had somehow found the electrical breakers for the passageway lighting, and he stood by, ready to dowse the lights on Kevin's signal. There had been considerable controversy in the Committee about who would be the Master of Ceremonies, and Kevin had been elected unanimously -- much to his dismay.

At precisely 1900 hours George turned out the passageway lights, and Kevin stepped forward from the room, illuminated by a bright shaft of light from a desk tensor lamp that George deftly wielded from floor level. Kevin wore the sport coat he had worn when he reported aboard, except that he had about a hundred pencils and pens of various lengths sticking out of his coat pockets. He had also borrowed a pair of reading glasses from one of the upper-class, which he wore down on his nose, and he carried a slide rule in his right hand, using it as a pointer. To complete the effect, he had borrowed a mop from a janitor and frizzed several strands into an Albert Einstein hairdo. He tottered, old-man-style, to the immediate front of the audience and looked around at us while Patrick quickly tacked a white sheet over the doorway.

"Goot Eeefnink," he said, pretending to be a German. He assumed an authoritarian spread-feet attitude and tapped his slide-rule on his opposite hand as he spoke. His fake accent, while not-so-accurate, was affectatious enough to be funny. "To-nacht," he continued, "I vill proof zat der Germans haff a rrrocket program more advanced dann der Yanks or der Ruskies."

George directed a second desk lamp onto the sheet, where Pat had taped a crude, almost childlike drawing which was supposed to simulate a slide. The drawing showed a rocket ship, sitting on large fins at some sort of gantry. On the hull of the rocket a bold swastika was displayed.

"Ziss ist der rrrocket uff der future," he continued with an arrogant self-confidence. "Azz you kann zee, it ist ein German rrrocket." The lights went out on the screen and Pat hurried to attach another drawing. The next time the light on the sheet went on a picture of the earth and a dotted orbital path.

"Vee haff zent dis rrrocket into zpace, und it haz zerciled der earth ein tausend times."

The next slide showed a crude representation of Europe, with the size of Germany exaggerated. "Hier ist ein foto uff der earth von schpace," he continued. He followed that with a drawing of a US satellite and a Russian sputnik. He droned on through several more amateurish drawings until the crowd became restless.

"Achtung!" he suddenly shouted in mock indignation. "Zo, You Vud dout der verd uff ein German Zeintist! Den I vill show you pruff datt vee are better dann you. I haff heir somezing neffer bevor zeen by mann. I haff ein klos-up pictur von der moon."

The passageway darkened again and Pat rustled the sheet for a moment. When the light returned, however, no crude drawing greeting the Company. Rather, Jubal Ramsey's enormous dark-haired butt shone glossy in the spotlight. Laughter and some catcalls followed. Dillingham liked this! He laughed loudly. Holy shit! Kevin had succeeded in mooning the entire company upper class.

Kevin stood in front, smiling broadly. I guessed that was it. The joke soon lost its effect, and the upper class began to jeer and get up to leave.

"Sthop!" Kevin yelled angrily, surprising the hell out of me. "Zo, you arr schtill not convinzed dat der Germans haff beeten you Yanks? Ach! Den I vill show you convinzing pruff. I vill show you vot no udder mann hast zeen bevor."

The light again went out, and there was more rustling in the dark as upper-class settled, and as Pat worked the curtain. I began to get an uncomfortable feeling.

" I vill show you der udder zide von der moon!" Oh Jesus! They wouldn't dare, would they? They would! I now knew what Rico's part in the skit. There was no mistaking him, or at least a certain prominent part of him, illuminated from the waist down.

Several voices yelled at once. Many of the watchers booed.

"Gross!" shouted an upper-class from the rear of the audience.

"Way to go, Kevin!" yelled a nearby plebe. Mugsy McGinley laughed so hard he fell backward from his spot up front on the floor. Pat immediately snapped off the tensor lamps, and Rico disappeared behind the blanket.

Everyone in the passageway waited for the final verdict from the "Bull." His vote was immediate and supportive.

"Fantastic!" he shouted, clapping his hands above his head. "Great job!" Kevin stood in front of the audience, beaming.

"Danka," he said, bowing, -- several pencils fell from his jacket pocket in the process -- and the skit committee hastily departed the scene.

CHAPTER 8

ALARMS AND EXCURSIONS

"You sure struggled with that mid-term exam," Tommy Poole observed as he and Kevin returned to Bancroft Hall following their Chemistry mid-term examination.

"Yeah. Those moles and valences get me confused sometimes. I can't seem to get a handle on how to remember which elements and compounds have how many free electrons."

"Well, if you can visualize the Periodic Table and picture the elements in each valence column, it really helps," said Tommy quite seriously.

"*You* may be able to visualize the Periodic Table, genius boy, but a mere mortal like me has to resort to rote memorization."

"I saw you had trouble with question five," Tommy stated.

"How do you know that?" asked Kevin incredulously.

"I glanced at your paper afterward."

"Which was about a half hour before anyone else," Kevin replied. Then he paused. "You know you could get into serious trouble by peeking at my paper."

"Well, no one was watching. Everyone focused on his own test. And besides I had already turned mine in."

"No," Kevin quickly added with a smile. "I meant you might copy down the wrong answer."

Tommy laughed.

"Not a chance," he replied, slightly amazed at the thought of needing to get an answer from someone else. "I know the material." Then he paused. "You know, the way you tried to balance the equation in number five puzzles me. It was really off the mark. We studied together, and despite what you say, you *do* know the material. How did you get so mixed up?"

Kevin laughed.

"It's easy, genius boy. Sometimes my brain circuits don't function properly on test day. It's always been my bane. Besides, it makes no sense to me why we have to memorize meaningless facts that have no basis in the understanding of the physical principles. Ask me why elements act the way they do, and I can explain all about atomic numbers and electron shells. Ask me what happens when you combine specific elements, and I can explain the process and the outcome. I know *why* chemistry works, I just can't always remember that the valence of potassium is plus two."

"Plus one," Tommy corrected.

"See!" Kevin exclaimed. "I'll bet Neils Bohr had to look in the Table every time he wanted to see how many neutrons there were in Bismuth, North Dakota. So why shouldn't I have the same advantage given to Herr Bohr?"

Tommy laughed.

"You have a good point, Kevin, but the Academy system isn't going to change just to humor you. The system seems to work. You just need to memorize more and not be so tense on test day."

They walked in silence for several paces, contemplating. "Listen," Tommy said, "I have an idea. It's an honor violation to bring any extra material into the test that isn't in your head -- you know, like a crib sheet -- but you can use that to your advantage. You should memorize the columns of the Periodic Table you have trouble with and go over them just prior to the test. Then when the test starts, before you do another thing, write it all out on a piece of paper. That way you could have the Table in front of you, and it wouldn't be cheating. You could do that for any test and I'll bet it would take a lot of the pressure off you on test day."

Kevin considered for a moment, then laughed halfheartedly. "That's a great idea, Tommy. I could trick the system without cheating. I like that idea."

Tommy paused. "Fighting the system is what most midshipmen seem best at, doesn't it?" Tommy replied. "Boy, if they could figure out a way to turn all this creative energy in positive directions, the system could produce some astounding results. But we spend too much time in conflict; caged in our rooms, treated like children, afraid of the upper-classes, hiding from the watch officers, tricking the system, gouging the academics, and competing with each other. It's no wonder midshipmen get crazy."

"Wow, Tommy! That's very insightful. Maybe someday when you come back here as Superintendent, you can change all that."

"No chance of that," Tommy replied, chuckling. "There's too much politics in the Navy for a fat, ugly genius boy ever to make it big. Look at who they pick for these posts. Mack Hallahan - first commander of a nuclear surface ship. Decorated for action under fire in Vietnam. He's handsome, charismatic, well-spoken, charming, and probably could still do more push-ups than I can.

"And how about Jake Conrad, the Superintendent. One-time captain of Navy's football team. Color Company Commander. First man to power a nuclear submarine under the north pole. He's the darling of President himself."

Tommy gave Kevin a see-what-I'm-saying look. Kevin laughed. "You are probably right as usual, Tommy." He paused. "You know, you think too much. Put that brain into coast once in a while. You also have your own troubles to cope with. But thanks. That idea about a memory dump on test day sounds like it would work. I'll improve my performance. Wait until next test, you'll see."

"Got any new sci-fi books?" Tommy asked, changing the subject. Tommy and Kevin shared a passion for futuristic literature and often discussed favorite authors and fantasy milieus. I never exactly understood what they saw in this. My own taste tended to Westerns -- part of my Texas background I suppose. I was constantly going to the Academy Midshipmen's Store to see what new Zane Grey and Louie Lamour works were in.

"As a matter of fact, I do," answered Kevin with a definite brightening of spirit. "My mom sent me part of my personal library from home, and I bought several new paperbacks in town last Saturday. I got some good Heinlein and Simak and the complete Norton *Witch World* series. Come browse."

Kevin O'Reilly had become the Company librarian, at least for the subjects of science fiction and fantasy. He had brought several dozen books with him when he arrived, and had accumulated several dozen more through various deals and purchases. The back part of one entire shelf of his locker -- behind his skivvies -- contained books, which he kept alphabetically by author. Company members visited the room at all hours to check his stock and to borrow books.

Kevin had inventoried his library and prominently marked the inside cover of each book with his name and ID number using his heavy black laundry stencil. He kept a clipboard by the book shelf. A bold note on the clipboard informed anyone who wished to borrow a book to sign it out properly, and added that books could be borrowed for no more than a week. He kept a cross-referenced card catalog in his desk. Kevin O'Reilly was the most organized person I had ever met, and he did not hesitate to chase down missing books, even from upperclassmen.

Kevin's wasn't the only "library" in the room. Once the upper-class found out about Rico's collection of smut, an even greater number flocked to his locker. While Rico wasn't nearly as organized as Kevin, he *was* a businessman -- one who was very protective of his "technical manuals." He normally required some form of monetary collateral or desert payment as the fee for borrowing the book. Nobody seemed to complain. These weren't the kind of books you could get in the Midshipman's Store or anywhere reputable in town. Rico claimed he had an uncle Josè who ran a men's bookstore in Brooklyn, and he got his material from him. He could also arrange to order books and magazines for the particularly horny midshipmen who couldn't wait for Rico's next trip to New York.

Once, at Rico's insistent bidding, I glanced through a Guevarra library magazine, one of several that Rico kept hidden in his desk. Every page gleamed with pictures of sleazy-looking young ladies doing anatomically unusual acts with one or more men or women or with disgustingly hairy animals. I was especially grossed out and quickly returned the magazine to Rico.

"Not my style," I said.

"God," he replied, turning the pages distractedly, a far-away look spreading across his face as he turned, "wouldn't you love to be the male model for some of these picture spreads? All that paradise just waiting to be explored. It's got to be heaven."

"No thanks!" I replied.

"You know," he said, changing the subject deftly. "I'm thinking about becoming a Muslim."

"A Muslim! Why?"

"Because they believe that after they die, God provides them with a harem of females called *houris* whose sole purpose is to satisfy their every sexual desire throughout eternity. That's sure a lot more enticing than Christian harps and choral music."

"Rico," I replied. "I don't know much about the Muslim faith, but I think you have to live a decent life and observe a certain amount of sexual propriety here on earth in order to be granted eternal bliss."

"Yeah," Rico replied dejectedly. "There's always a catch."

"Do Muslims really believe that?" asked Kevin incredulously.

"Yeah," Rico answered. "Or something like that anyway."

"Christ!" Kevin observed. "No wonder they're so crazy. They're doing it for sex."

"Aren't we all?" asked BJ with uncommon insight.

Kevin and BJ didn't have any moral problem with Rico's books or magazines. In fact, they were major borrowers. Rico didn't charge them. The three of them would often sit for hours discussing various aspects of the sex act. I'm sorry to admit it, but I picked up much of my sexual knowledge from listening secretly to their discussions.

Rico was in his element during these lectures. He was like a sexual professor, often spicing his talks with explicit glossy photos from his magazines or with personal anecdotes. I must admit that if I hadn't been personally familiar with Rico and his style, I would have sworn that he was a master liar, but there was too much evidence to the contrary. I accepted Rico's claims at face value and began a mental file of potentially stimulating acts and the locations of unusual erogenous zones.

Midterm exams took up the greatest part of a week. The exams weren't particularly difficult for me, and I was thankful. I was a Naval Architecture major -- not a full-fledged engineer or scientist -- but I still had to cope with the same basic math and science. I had breezed through my classes thus far, and it seemed to me that my academic career was going rather well. I was strangely anxious to see my midterm grades.

Academics were the ultimate obstacle for any midshipman, the last hurdle that could prevent graduation. For the plebe -- who still had the constant physical and psychological harassment to contend with -- academics became almost a secondary consideration. But I knew how to cope with the upper-class, and I was confident push-ups or rates would not cause my downfall. Knowing I could handle the stress and the academics was a major ego boost. It would be confirmation that I *was* going to make it!

On Tuesday night I invited Leslie to the Army-Navy game in Philadelphia. I think the residual guilt about Lynda kept me from the decision, but once I decided it was obvious I had done the right thing. Leslie was overjoyed.

"Oh, I do love you, Jim Merritt!" she exclaimed loudly. "I was wondering if you were ever going to ask me."

"How could I not?" I answered. "I have to take advantage of every opportunity to spend time with you. I am just a bit embarrassed because, being a plebe, I can't go with you to Philly or bring you back. I have to travel with the Brigade on the bus. And I can't stay overnight. Liberty ends at 0100. I feel like such a baby. But I'll arrange a nice hotel room for us, and you can stay there overnight."

"Jim Merritt, you're so sweet," she said. "But I'm a big girl. I'll find my way to Philadelphia and back.

"You know, Jim Merritt, there are several girls in this sorority who would die for a chance to date a midshipman and especially to go to an Army-Navy game. If you have any friends who need company, I might be able to arrange it, and then I'd have company for my trip."

"That's a great idea!" I said enthusiastically. "I'll see what I can do."

I broached the idea with my roommates immediately after I returned to the room. I still hadn't told them about Leslie, although Rico knew for sure something had happened in my love life.

"No thanks," said Rico. "I've got Rosa coming."

"Several times, I'll bet," interjected Kevin. We all laughed.

"How about you Kevin?" I asked.

"I wish you had said something sooner. I just asked Sarah Connelly from the neighborhood. My mom has been bugging me to do something with her for months."

"That's a bad idea, Kevin," said Rico. "You're gonna get drunk and be horny as hell, and you'll be in trouble for the next thirty years."

"Yeah? Well, it's too late now," Kevin said dejectedly. "Besides, Sarah's a nice girl, and I think she likes me."

"That's the worst kind to bring to a Navy football game and party, Kevin," said Rico.

"I don't think so, Kevin," I interrupted. "I'm sure you'll have a great time with Sarah. BJ, are you interested?"

"Sure. I was going to bring a friend from school, but she has exams that week, and her father is taking her on a week-long skiing trip to Europe afterward. In fact," he said brightening. "I was also going to suggest a little party for select classmates in the Sheraton Grand Hotel downtown. My mom knows the regional manager of Sheraton Hotels, and he's offered to let us use three suites for the night."

"The Sheraton? For free?" Kevin asked incredulously.

"Of course for free," BJ said looking at Kevin like he was from another planet.

"What does three suites mean?" I asked.

"My mom says each suite has a living room and two large bedrooms. That's six bedrooms. I thought we could use the central living room as a party and social room. The hotel has promised hors d'oeuvres and complimentary soft drinks, and we could eat our dinner there in their grand dining room. That way we'd be spending some money and not be total leeches."

"Wow!" Kevin said. "That sounds great!"

"Agreed!" Rico added.

"Okay, BJ, you're on. What kind of date do you want?" I asked.

"A beautiful, charming, wealthy, young lady, who'll reduce me to jelly, what else?" I laughed, but that seemed a tall order; and I wasn't exactly sure how to broach the subject with Leslie.

"Who else will we invite to the party?" asked BJ.

"No upper-class, please," offered Kevin.

"I agree," said BJ.

"What about Jeff, Jubal, Bob and Willy?" I offered.

"What about Tommy?" Kevin asked.

BJ ignored Kevin.

"Well, we only have two rooms left. That's a problem. I suppose we could offer a room to Jeff and Reb, and let the rest of them fend for themselves."

"What about Tommy?" Kevin asked again.

"I could ask the hotel to set up cots in two of the rooms. That way the other dates could sleep there, but there'd still be the problem of spending time alone together," BJ mused.

"Don't worry about that," Rico said. "If they want sex, they can work out a hot-rack schedule with whoever their roommate is. But we get private rooms."

"What about Tommy!" said Kevin with finality. He was not going to be denied on this.

"I don't know," said BJ. "If we invite him, we'd have to invite his roommates. Then we'd have too many." There was logic in this, but I knew *that* wasn't BJ's reason for not inviting Tommy. He didn't want to be associated with any source of potential discomfort. He was afraid that if the firsties found out he was partying with Tommy Poole, he would make himself a target for harassment.

"You can put a cot in the common area of my suite," offered Kevin. "She and Sarah can share my room." He paused and smiled devilishly. "After Sarah and I explore the possibilities, that is."

"Kevin," I said. "You are sexually fixated worse than Rico."

"Ain't it great!" he answered enthusiastically.

"Want a prediction, Kevin?" asked Rico.

"Sure!"

Rico wasn't smiling with his normal twinkle. He wasn't smiling at all.

"You're going to get into major trouble that weekend." Rico sounded serious. Kevin was taken aback.

"You really think so?" he asked Rico nodded sagely, and Kevin became unusually quiet.

"Okay," BJ said, breaking the suddenly somber spell. "I'll ask Tommy."

Saturday's game was against Virginia, with Navy expected to win. The team came out of the locker room raring to fight. The midshipmen even passed the ball occasionally and took a 17 to 14 lead into the locker room at half-time. However, the Virginia players must have been in better shape than Delaware. They returned to the field looking for blood and quickly assumed a 31 to 17 advantage, which took the wind out of a thousand plebe sails. Navy rallied however, with a brilliant passing attack, and within ten minutes of the end of the game, the midshipmen had brought the score to within four -- 31 to 27. Virginia fumbled a kickoff near the end-zone, and Navy recovered on the 3-yard line. The Navy fans went wild, and I began envisioning another weekend of carry-on.

Instead of sticking with what had worked so well all game, Navy ran three times directly up the middle, resulting in an overall six-yard loss. I was incensed and wanted to strangle the coaches. Navy settled for a field goal. The score was now 31 to 30, and all seemed lost.

Virginia took the kick-off and marched 50 yards on eight plays to the Navy 30-yard line. But the drive miraculously bogged down, and Virginia's field goal attempt went wide left. Five minutes remained in the game, plenty of time for Navy to get a field-goal. I felt good again.

Jeff Rightman passed the ball and mixed his plays masterfully. Once he waved off a play the coach was sending in -- a run up the middle no doubt. He moved the team steadily down field, eating up the clock with every play. The drive stalled third-and-one, dead center on the 22-yard line, with plenty of time for a field-goal. I was elated. Plebes all around me were going crazy, jumping up and down and slapping each other on the back.

We quieted as Navy set up over the snap. The ball was hiked, but skittered through Rightman's hands into the backfield. We screamed. A running back swiftly approached the ball to pick it up, and I began to relax. No real harm done. But a strange bounce of the ball caused it to wobble-hop to the right side. Unfortunately the runner had leaned left. Thinking the ball would roll past him into open field, the runner panicked and leaped toward the ball feet-first. He hit the ball with the toe of his right foot, and a screaming line drive shot directly between our now-turning center's legs.

At the sight of the fumbled ball, every player on Virginia's team had raced toward the line of scrimmage. When the ball zoomed into the pile of humanity, they all leaped. They scrambled for the ball, diving headlong into the sea of jerseys and padded flesh. Immediately, an enormous mass of humanity was grappling in the pile for the football.

But the ball, shot like a rocket from the running back's feet, hardly glanced off any of the many feet and passed quickly through the pile-up, deep into the defensive backfield of Virginia. Then the confusion began. The clock continued to run. Less than a minute remained in the game.

In the meantime, the football rolled wobbly and tauntingly down the middle of the field toward the end zone. Every person in the stands could see it, and we screamed at our respective teams on the field to turn and get the ball. The players on the field must have thought we were shouting encouragement for their efforts to search the formation, and they fought all the harder. The ball continued to roll. We continued to scream and point wildly, and clock continued to run.

Finally the commotion in the pile-up abated, and the players stood warily. They looked at each other closely, but no one seemed to be holding a football. The crowd noise continued unabated, however, and this confused the players, who stared at each other harder. The officials watched the players, waiting for something to happen. The ball was still in play. One older referee laughed so hard he could hardly stand up. But no official pointed or offered a word of encouragement to the now totally-mystified players. I watched, amazed and incredibly frustrated, as the ball finally came to rest two feet into the Virginia end zone, a potential Navy touchdown if it could be recovered there. Thirty seconds remained.

On the sidelines, the Navy coach and every member of the team, jumped up and down and pointed to the end-zone. No one on the field understood. One Virginia lineman looked down field and saw something brown and out of place lying sedately on the grass at the end zone. Thinking that some pass attempt had failed, he removed his helmet, stomped his foot heavily onto the turf, and began to slowly depart the field. Taking their cue from each other, several players from both sides copied his actions. One alert Navy player looked at the clock, then at a nearby referee and asked him something. The referee didn't respond. The player tried to call a time out, but the referee refused to stop time when the ball was still in play. The player became agitated, thinking that if the clock were stopped Navy might have a chance to win the game with a defensive miracle. Fifteen seconds remained.

In the meantime, a Navy wide receiver had jogged dejectedly to the bench. One of the assistant coaches grabbed his face mask and screamed something we could not exactly hear from our vantage point, but which included several loud and artistic uses of the f-word. The receiver initially thought the coach was angry at him. He hung his head in shame. The coach grabbed him by the face-mask again and screamed all the louder. Ten seconds remained.

I could almost see the light come on inside the player's helmet. He looked at the coach, then at the clock, then at the football almost half a field away. He began to jog, then to run, then to sprint toward that illusive pigskin. The Virginia coaches reacted similarly. They pointed insanely at the Navy player as he raced toward the football. One Virginia player who had remained on the field reacted and began his own sprint. Five seconds remained, but time stood still for 4,000 midshipmen.

The Navy player had at least a ten-yard advantage, which is not much when you are inherently slow -- as most Navy football players seemed to be. But when he saw the Virginia player contesting his race for paydirt, he sped up. For the Brigade of Midshipmen, the universe narrowed to those two players and that damn football. It was an almost cosmic experience. I could see chunks of green turf being chewed up and spit out behind the feet of both players. I could almost count the blades of grass. I noticed that the Virginia player had a small yellow wrist band covering an old wound on his right arm, the wristband had several frayed edges which flapped as he ran. I saw that the Navy player was slightly bowlegged and that the cleats on his left shoe were worn down several millimeters more than those on his right shoe. I could swear I heard the Virginia player fart as he exerted himself far beyond any level he had ever attained. Five seconds remained.

The distance to the football rapidly narrowed. Both players approached the end-zone. Four seconds remained. It was now clear the Navy player would arrive first, and a tremendous cheer erupted from our side of the field. It would be carry-on for sure! He dove at the ball. Three seconds remained.

I saw his hands reach out for the ball. His right thumbnail needed cleaning. He hit the grass and fumbled for the ball as he slid. I saw him begin to bobble it toward him along the grass. The football was an "Official Model" manufactured of genuine cowhide by Wilson Sporting Goods in Korea and inspected by Inspector Number 9. There was a six and a quarter inch scuff just under the laces.

With two seconds remaining, he pulled in his knees to try to cradle the ball -- which he still didn't have under complete control. Five referees watched to ensure his touchdown was official. He smiled and I could see he had recently had a root canal and three fillings, one of which was of silver amalgam. A small piece of noon meal chicken tetrazinni was stuck between his front teeth. Then the Virginia player arrived, diving at the recumbent and still sliding and groping Navy player. Did I mention that the Virginia player was a 250-pound lineman?

The lineman landed with a loud thud just as the now prematurely triumphant Navy player finally gripped the football. That grip didn't last for even an instant. The ball squirted free just as the gun sounded, wobbled mockingly across the end-zone, and came to rest on the endline. The game was over, and Navy had lost. No carry-on. No winning streak. No joy in Mudville. I stared, shattered and angry.

At first I thought with cruel satisfaction that the inept Navy player had been killed, crushed under the enormous weight of a man that outweighed him by more than a hundred pounds. Neither he nor the opposing lineman moved for several seconds. Then the Navy punter screamed -- but not in pain. What echoed across the field was one word -- the same word the coach had used repeatedly to express his own frustration.

The Virginia lineman remained strangely quiet, He had apparently lost his wind. He slowly struggled, rolled over like a beached whale, and groaned.

I looked at my classmates, who were all equally devastated by the turn of events. No one spoke for a long moment. The band rushed through *Navy Blue and Gold*, and soon we began a funeral procession back to Annapolis proper.

I was so depressed I could eat only a half of my meatball sub. Ramsey was so depressed he ate the other half plus two foot-longs of his own. I guess we all show grief in our own ways. But by the time I returned to my room I was feeling better, remembering that Leslie would be meeting me soon.

The Lustkateers would be idle this evening, except for Rico. Apparently their companions from the previous week were angry at being treated as sex objects and had decided to withhold any favors for a couple weeks. That didn't bother Rico because a girl named Cindy had worked off her punishment and was available for his eager company.

"You guys know the real reason your dates didn't want to go out with you?" Rico asked the others as we prepared for evening meal.

"No. Why?" BJ asked.

"Use your head," Rico said glancing down at his crotch. "Why would they ever settle for children once they had a chance to experience Mister Ed?" Rico stared lovingly downward, but neither BJ nor Kevin found that remark particularly funny.

"Want to play cards tonight with the guys across the passageway?" Kevin asked me. "Zimmerman's playing. More easy money."

"Not tonight, Kevin," I answered. "I plan on spending a quiet evening writing letters somewhere secluded." Rico quietly guffawed at his desk while Kevin eyed me narrowly.

"Secluded, huh?" he asked.

"Secluded," I answered, and Kevin knew enough not to ask.

It seemed to me that the entire Brigade was pissed off during evening meal because of that incredible football tragedy. Luckily, I ate with the squad, but even Mugsy was far more surly than usual. I felt sorry for Kevin, whose turn it was to eat with Stone and Micklewski. I could hear the grumbling and the threats all during the meal.

I met Leslie at her car at precisely 2030. She was as lovely as usual, and even more affectionate. We held each other tightly and she whispered, "I love you, Jim Merritt" repeatedly. Although there seemed to be more activity near the Field House this evening, no one directed more than a casual glance in our direction as we walked to our spot on the seawall. Once we settled down on the rocks and Leslie kissed me, I forgot all about possible intrusions.

We made love to each other slowly and deliciously, and snuggled together, kissing and laughing quietly, and planning the Army-Navy activities.

"Oh, I can't wait to be completely alone with you, Jim Merritt," Leslie said huskily. "I know nice girls aren't supposed to think such thoughts, but I want desperately to tear off your clothes and ravage your body for hours and hours."

"I think that's a great idea," I replied. "And I promise to do the same to you." We laughed together for a long minute.

"Do you want a big family, Jim Merritt?" she asked suddenly.

I laughed.

"I hadn't thought about it," I replied, still chuckling. "I suppose so."

"Well I want at least three children, and they all have to have your eyes."

I laughed again, wondering why it didn't seem so strange to be planning a family with a young woman I had only recently met and knowing that almost fours years of military life separated us from the possibility of marriage. It was crazy. But Leslie's enthusiasm was infectious, and she was so darn cute about it, and I did love her deeply.

"I have the perfect companion for your friend, Mr. Wilson," Leslie said when I told her about BJ's offer. "She's blond, extremely attractive, and definitely boy crazy." She paused and, assuming a serious air, jabbed my chest with a finger. "But don't you go getting any ideas, Jim Merritt, because you belong to me and no one else."

I laughed.

"There isn't the slightest chance of losing me to some hussy, my dear. You're stuck with me."

"Good," she said snuggling even closer against me.

"Jim Merritt," she said, changing the subject. "I told my parents all about you, and they want to meet you. Can you come visit my house in Richmond over the Thanksgiving weekend?"

I groaned, feeling a momentary sense of panic engulf me. "I feel terrible, Leslie, but I've already made plans to visit my family in Amarillo. I'm supposed to pick up my tickets next week." Leslie looked so crestfallen I stumbled for something else to do or say. After all, I was in love with this girl, and she wanted me to spend time with her. That was only natural.

"Listen," I said after a quick pause, "I'll cut my visit to Texas short. I'll tell my parents I have to fly back on Saturday morning. If you can pick me up at the Richmond airport, I'll be able to spend Saturday and Sunday with you, but I have to be at Annapolis on Sunday evening. Would that be okay?"

Leslie had tears in her eyes.

"I'm so sorry, Jim Merritt. It's really cruel for me to draw you away from your family when you haven't seen them for so long. You stay in Texas."

She had me going now, and I felt doubly bad.

"No, no, sweetheart. I'll have Wednesday night, Thursday, and Friday with my family. That's plenty of time, and they'll be perfectly happy. Hey, you're important to me too, and I'd love to meet your parents. I'll be in Richmond Saturday morning."

She looked up at me, her eyes still glistening.

"I love you, Jim Merritt," she said, and we made love again for what seemed like an hour. God, it was great being with her! I felt intoxicated with her nearness, and visions of Leslie, our marriage, and our cute little children swam in my head.

At 2230 we strolled to her car, so much in love that nothing else mattered. So much in love that I was thinking about names for our three children and how the girls had better look like their mother, but they could have my eyes if Leslie wanted. So much in love that I didn't notice the official automobile that sat in the parking lot of the Field House or the two occupants who intently watched us.

I said a passionate goodby to Leslie and watched as she drove away. Almost immediately the official car started and drove toward me. I noticed it! I felt a sinking feeling of panic, but at first I wasn't sure what was happening. The car was a white sedan, with the words Official Government Vehicle stenciled on each side along with a Motor Pool serial number. Behind the wheel sat an officer. I knew he was an officer because he was wearing an officer's white combination cap. I knew he was a Lieutenant because he had two large gold stripes on the sleeve of the arm he was using to steer the car. I knew he was trouble because on the upper sleeve of his driving arm was a blue armband with the gold initials OOD, whom I knew from my plebe rates to be Lieutenant Swetland from Fifth Company. Beside him was a midshipman, probably a plebe messenger. I had met my doom.

Thinking furiously and pretending I hadn't seen them, I clutched the blanket to my chest and walked unhurriedly across the road and onto Farragut Field, turning my body slightly away from the automobile. My mind was awhirl. They had seen me with Leslie, and we had passionately kissed goodby in plain sight. I had therefore committed several major offenses. One was called Public Display of Affection (PDA) which would get me 30 demerits. Since I was in gym gear -- an improper uniform for entertaining ladies, but perfect garb when the quick and easy removal of clothing was paramount -- I could get another 20 demerits. Since I was a lower-than-dirt plebe and not allowed to even talk to a young lady, much less grope with her in public, I could rate another 50 demerits.

I mentally added up the score, and I came to a grim total of Annapolis - 150, James Wesley Merritt - dead. I didn't like those results at all. Thoughts of restriction musters every hour for the next ten weekends bombarded my brain, numbing me. Jesus! I would have to tell my parents I wouldn't be coming home for Thanksgiving. I would also have to cancel my Army-Navy plans *and* my weekend with sweet, lovely Leslie. I might also have to stay at school during Christmas leave. And I could definitely forget any ideas about being Brigade Commander my first-class year. Shit! This was almost too much to bear, and all because of some stupid rules that cloistered plebes like monks in a stone prison where crazy people were in charge.

I became quite angry as I awaited the fateful words I knew must come. I heard car brakes squeaking slightly as the OOD slowed behind me. I could hear the car window coming down. Elevator music drifted out into the night from the grim confines of that damn automobile. By now I was almost 30 yards out onto the field.

"Plebe, Halt!" someone barked in a squeaky voice. *Those* were the dreaded words. I stopped. I could feel my shoulders slump involuntarily under the psychic impact of what was to come. My life was ruined. I might as well join Ronald Steinway in the great beyond. What was I going to do? I turned slowly and waited. The OOD opened the door to his car, and he and the plebe messenger exited. A streetlight illuminated their faces. Swetland wore a smile on his smug officer's face. That's what started the calamitous chain of events. Had I known at the time what would result, I would have done the same.

I was too panicked to consider anything but self-preservation when that heinous smile caused me to make a fateful decision. I became angry. I looked closely at the OOD and the messenger. I also knew I had three simple choices. I could either:

1. Wait at attention for the OOD to come out onto the field and put me on report.
2. Hurry to his location and help him put me on report.
3. Run like hell and hope I didn't get caught.

Since options one or two would guarantee more demerits than I wanted to think about, my only rational choice was number three. The civilian Jim Merritt would not have included number three on his list. The Jim Merritt of Plebe Summer would not have either. I realized with sudden clear certainty that one factor demanded choice number three -- Leslie! I would not, could not, give her up for even a moment. She was worth a fight -- any fight.

I could feel a rush of adrenaline as I sized up the situation. I had a 30-yard lead on them, which was good. I was in gym gear and they were in uniforms, which was also good. They had a car, however, which was very bad since it canceled both my distance and uniform advantages. But the car was pointed in the wrong direction, which might be good. And they wouldn't dare bring it out onto the field to follow me-- at least I hoped not -- which was also good.

But it was more than 100 yards to Bancroft Hall, which was bad, and I was carrying a bulky blanket, which I couldn't ditch because it had my name and serial number stenciled on it, which was also bad. So far my analysis came up very short. I continued my rapid mental calculations.

I was standing in the dark, so they couldn't identify my face, which was good. But once I returned to Bancroft Hall, my haste -- and the look of sheer terror which most certainly must be etched on my features -- would immediately identify me as an obvious fugitive who would be fair game for any upper-class who wanted to help in the chase, which was very bad. And I had a lot of Bancroft Hall to cover to get back to the fourth wing, which was also bad. But Bancroft Hall was enormous with many nooks and crannies to hide in, which was good for a resourceful midshipman like me.

These thoughts flooded my brain almost in an instant, and the sum total of my analysis resulted in the chances of escape being far less than fifty-fifty. But I had absolutely no chance if I didn't try, and I simply could not allow my life to be ruined like this. I began hyperventilating and flexing my leg and arm muscles.

Lieutenant Swetland must have sensed something in my stance. Maybe he had had this confrontation so many times that he knew the rules of the game and the resulting probabilities better than I did. Staring intently at me, he held up a hand to halt the plebe who had started around the car. His plebe messenger was like a guided missile in the chase -- once loosed he would follow me relentlessly, and the ultimate race would be to see who had the better plebe training. But the OOD didn't want to expend his best shot too soon. He watched me, trying to gauge which way I would go when I bolted. We both knew the game was afoot. He smiled even more broadly, probably sensing that my chances of escape were not good and knowing that once caught, I would have enough demerits for several lifetimes.

"Don't even think about it, Mister!" he shouted. "You're caught. That's the way it is! Now get your ass over here now!"

I turned almost in slow motion until I was perpendicular to the road. I looked first at Bancroft Hall, then back at the OOD. I repeated this distance-gauging procedure several times inching away from the Duty Officer all the while.

Then the OOD yelled, "Shit! Let's get him!" and broke for his car.

Indecision fled. I found myself flying across the open field. And I was really moving. Momentarily I wished Kevin was running beside me. I think I could have beaten him that evening. I felt momentarily elated. Suddenly the lights of an automobile flashed across my body as the OOD turned his car around, and I had a sinking feeling he would follow me out onto the field. If he did, it would be a very short chase. I still had a hundred yards of Farragut Field to go, and another 50 to get me to Bancroft Hall. It was going to be very close.

But the OOD chose the paved road rather than the patchy grass, and I could hear the car turn off Turner Joy Road and hurry down the road beside the enlisted-mans' barracks in Rickett's Hall. He passed my position awfully quickly and I could see the white car as he reached the corner of Brownson Road, turned right, and headed for the place where I would exit the field. It was going to be very close, but it was too late to worry about anything except escape.

I had been aiming for a walkway on Brownson Road between the tennis courts and the reflection pool, since it was a path to the eighth wing extension of Bancroft Hall, but I decided the OOD would beat me there. I increased my angle across the field, aiming for the far side of Bancroft Hall, and trying to time my exit for a place between street lights so that I could use darkness to help me when I was closest to the point of intercept.

The OOD's car was very near by the time I reached the end of the field. Had I continued straight, we would have collided in a mess of plebe blood, bones, and entrails. At the last instant, however, I turned abruptly left and ran behind his still speeding car. In a few steps I was across the road and on the walkway to Bancroft Hall. I could hear Lieutenant Swetland curse loudly as he slammed on his brakes and tried to spin the car around. He would have to go around the tennis courts to head me off. I was confident I could make it to Bancroft Hall before him.

Lieutenant Swetland was a smart man. He momentarily stopped his car and released his human missile.

I heard him yell, his voice breaking into another squeak. "Get him or you're in deep trouble, plebe!" I felt sorry for my classmate. I could hear tromping behind me, his black uniform shoes loudly clomping where my tennis shoes barely squeaked. There was no chance he would catch me easily. I would make this a chase they would talk about for ages. I headed resolutely for the doorway at the southernmost end of the eighth wing, readying myself for the even greater challenge that awaited me inside Bancroft Hall, where I would potentially confront 8,000 curious and potentially-hostile eyes.

But the eighth wing was also where the OOD headed. I saw him turn around the tennis courts in that direction. Once he sounded the general alarm, my chances of escape would rapidly disappear. I decided not to make it easy for him. I changed direction at the end of the tennis courts and headed east along the outside of Mitscher Hall toward the seventh wing. The OOD could not see this move, so it might buy me some time, even if it put me farther from the safety of Room 4024.

The messenger was not a sprinter. But he was a plebe, so he *had* to be in pretty good shape. Despite my directional change, I could still hear him clomping behind in the darkness. It would have been wonderful to run against a Tommy Poole, but fate doesn't always treat us kindly. The plebe *could* run, but not as fast as a terrified Jim Merritt. I gradually pulled ahead so that I had a 50-yard lead by the time I pounded up the stairs into the lowest floor of the seventh wing.

A wide passageway more than 200 yards long stretched before me. Because of the lateness of the hour and because liberty had not yet expired for upper-class, it was darkened and almost deserted. Immediately to my right as I burst inside sat a plebe duty midshipman. He stared at me open-mouthed from behind his gray metal desk. I put my blanket up in front of my face to block his view. He was clearly startled and unsure how to react, but I didn't waste time on conversation. I sprinted down the passageway, passing several surprised upper-class. One yelled halfheartedly for me to halt, but I continued running, hoping no one ahead of me decided to try to stop my progress.

Before I could reach the first set of double doors the messenger who had been chasing me entered the wing.

He yelled loudly, "Midshipman, Halt!" which immediately alerted the wing to my apparent transgressions. Various midshipmen came to their doors in response to the commotion. One midshipman rushed into the passageway to impede my progress, but I sidestepped him without missing a step. -- I had been a "running" quarterback in high school. The messenger didn't give up, however, and I could hear a "Slap-slide" cadence on the tile floor as he followed.

No one else attempted to stop me in the seventh wing, but I could see my chances fading if I continued down this same passageway the entire distance. I might not be so lucky with my next fake. At the junction of the seventh and fifth wings, I turned left and exited into the enormous central courtyard that many of the wings of Bancroft Hall enclose. The Mess Hall lay before me. Instead of trying my luck with a sprint through the Mess Hall, I turned immediately to my right and raced three-steps-at-a-time up a wide stairway that led to a broad red-tiled patio we midshipmen called the Red Beach. In the summer this area was usually clogged with bodies as studly midshipmen worked on their power tans.

I had hoped to reach the top of the stairs before my pursuer exited the building. I almost made it. He spotted me as I leaped the final three steps.

"Shit!" I heard him yell as he saw the long stairway ahead of him. He sounded out of breath, which I took as a good sign. But I could also hear him starting resolutely up the steps. I sprinted down the now darkened Red Beach. Sounds of rock music echoed in the dark empty space from a room several floors above. It goaded me on. I could hear loud laughter from another room, that I passed. By this time my system was so flushed with self-produced fight-or-flight drugs that I found myself smiling. No damn way were they going to catch Jim Merritt. I yelled a loud Texas battle cry as I raced -- not exactly the smartest thing to do, but rational thought had deserted me when I took that first tentative step away from the OOD.

I reached the next entry doorway and glanced quickly back. The messenger hadn't gotten to the top of the stairs. Smiling, I hurriedly entered Bancroft Hall and chopped plebe-style down the central passageway, trying to seem less obvious. I was now on a higher level than when I entered Bancroft Hall. No one seemed alerted to my flight, and I hoped that my blanket and disheveled condition would not attract attention. I continued along the passageway to the first stairway, and went up another level, thinking that would further confuse pursuit. On the third level I chopped down the center of the passageway trying to calm myself slightly.

I followed the fifth wing, chopping slowly and regaining my breath. At the third wing I was getting closer to home. This was our plebe summer area and I knew it well. Keeping in side corridors, I avoided notice as much as possible. So far so good. Eventually I exited the large double doors into the upper rotunda balcony and slowly descended the stairs toward the main floor. Gym gear was not appropriate in the rotunda, but I needed to exit this way if the final step of my newly-hatched escape plan was to work. At the junction between the first deck and the ground floor I stopped in a panic as I heard a familiar voice squeaking in the rotunda below. It was Lieutenant Swetland. I glanced carefully over the edge railing. He stood in almost the exact center of the rotunda addressing the entire Main Office watch squad.

"I want you to call every mate on duty and see if they saw anyone suspicious who answers the description of our runaway. Try to track his path to see where he's headed. Judging from his haircut and conditioning, I'd say the best bet is that our adversary is a plebe. I want every Company mate on duty, and all the Battalion Officers of the Watch, to conduct an immediate bed check of the entire plebe class. I want to talk to every plebe who is missing from his room regardless of his excuse. I also want another bed check of the entire Brigade at exactly 2300. Begin immediately! Dismissed!"

I hesitated on the landing as they passed below, hoping my breathing would not alert them to my presence. My hesitation saved me.

"Gentlemen!" Swetland snapped at the rapidly departing watch squad. Everyone stopped and turned toward him. "Find that miserable twit for me! He's going to go down big time. And that's the way it is!" He stomped off toward the Academy Staff offices as the Watch Squad passed below me in the direction of the Main Office. Once I was sure they were gone, I hurriedly descended to the rotunda floor, checked the area quickly, and rushed across the terrazzo deck to the exit doors. Outside in the night air, I raced along the left side of T-Court, keeping to shadows as much as possible. There was activity as several upper-class escorted their dates around the darkened campus, but their concentration was mostly on what had or would happen in the dark. I didn't fear discovery by any midshipman whose system was engorged in male hormones.

Remembering how many midshipmen stood duty in the Main Office and how quickly they could alert every plebe mate on duty, I was afraid to enter my Company area through the normal doors for fear of drawing attention to myself. Instead I hurried to a point just outside the window to my room and checked the area. It was dark, and no one was watching. Taking an enormous risk, I climbed up on the guardrail that separated the Court from the utility moat that surrounded Bancroft Hall at this point. The moat was installed to prevent just the thing I contemplated. A distance of approximately seven feet separated me from my room. Below was a potential fall of more than 15 feet into darkness. It would be risky to leap the distance from my perch on the round metal rail, but I felt it was the only choice I had. I quickly climbed to the top rail, took a deep breath, and jumped.

Still pumped sky-high on adrenaline, I made the distance easily, but my arms landed painfully on the wide stone window ledge just as my fingers gripped the wooden window sill. I felt a sharp pain in my arm. Almost immediately my legs and body slammed painfully against the wall, and I momentarily lost my breath.

But I could not afford to stay hanging in the night air for even an instant if I was to avoid detection. I strained my arms and pulled myself up onto the ledge, and into the room proper, bursting loudly through the metal Venetian blinds in the process. Kevin and BJ looked up, startled by the commotion and at the sight of their supposedly prim and proper roommate tumbling unexpectedly into the room and onto the floor.

I landed with another painful bump on the floor beside Rico's desk, and quickly got to my feet.

"Don't ask!" I said with emphasis, and I went immediately to the shower. Turning on the water, I quickly removed my clothing and threw it into the closet, and stepped under the steaming water. God, it felt good to be home.

After a minute of hydrotherapy, I leaned my head out of the shower. Both Kevin and BJ stared at me wordlessly, still dumbfounded at my unexpected arrival.

"What time is it?" I asked.

BJ consulted his expensive watch.

"2255," he answered.

"Where's Rico?" I asked.

"Still out," answered Kevin.

"I hope he gets here soon. I suggest you two get into bed and put out the lights immediately." They looked at me questioningly. "Trust me on this!" I said with emphasis. Kevin nodded, immediately put away "Thuvia, Maid of Mars," and quickly took off his T-shirt. He climbed into his rack and faced away from the door. BJ stared at him for a moment, and looked at me. I nodded, and soon BJ had extinguished the lights and climbed into his own rack.

I quickly finished my shower and dried off. Slipping on a new pair of gym shorts, I climbed into bed and waited. Rico had a minute before lights-out and the expiration of liberty. I silently hoped he made it before the mate arrived.

At 2307 I heard minor commotion in the outside passageway as the Company watch squad, led by Rock Stone himself, moved from room to room, checking occupancy. Rico still hadn't returned, and the sounds of impending discovery approached steadily. Soon I could hear Stone and Hans Roudolph -- the plebe on duty this evening -- enter the third-class room next door. Almost simultaneously with the sound of "Bed Check!", I could hear the rapid squeak of tennis shoes coming down the passageway, and the door to the room pushed quietly open. Rico entered, threw his clothes onto the floor beside his desk, and jumped under the sheets. He hadn't been settled for more than five seconds when our door opened.

"Bed Check!" announced Stone, throwing on the lights. He moved to the center of the room as we bolted from our racks and braced up. I winced. My right arm hurt like hell, and my right knee was terribly sore. Stone turned to Roudolph, who held a clipboard. "Merritt, Wilson, Guevarra, and O'Reilly. All present and accounted for."

He then looked us over.

"You plebes seen anything unusual this evening?" he asked. We looked at each other.

"What do you mean unusual, sir?" asked Kevin.

"Anything out of the ordinary that would warrant reporting to the OOD," answered Stone. I immediately imagined Kevin asking if a terrified roommate flying through an open window counted as unusual or if another roommate coming stealthily back at ten minutes past lights out qualified as reportable. Kevin pondered.

"Sir," he said seriously. "I did see something very strange tonight." My heart sank momentarily, then I caught the lilt in O'Reilly's voice.

Stone became immediately interested.

"What was it?" he asked.

"Well sir, at evening meal tonight, when the pizza came around to me, I noticed that there were actually two pieces of pepperoni left on my tiny slice. Usually Joe Mahoney and Billy Bob Clanton take all the pepperoni so that even the third-class have never tasted this culinary delicacy. I suspect that such a serious breach in Second-class etiquette should be reported."

Stone stifled a laugh.

"O'Reilly," he said, "you are a certifiable nut case. Anything else 'unusual'?"

Kevin pondered again. "No, sir!" he said with finality. "Nothing else unusual this evening." Stone shrugged, and he and Hans left the room to continue their checks.

"I wonder what's happened?" Kevin asked innocently. "Anybody here happen to know?"

"Not me," said Rico innocently. Everyone turned to me for enlightenment.

"Me either!" I said with finality.

"Must be very interesting letters you write, Jim," Kevin observed. "Let me read one sometime." I laughed as we all climbed into our racks for the night.

CHAPTER 9

DEPARTURES

On Sunday after Protestant Chapel services I began to get some idea of the furor my escapade had caused. More than 60 midshipmen had been caught missing from their rooms at the expiration of liberty. Most of them had been upper-class returning late from liberty, so my guilt was somewhat assuaged. Rumor was that heads were going to roll throughout the Brigade for this laxity.

In addition, more than 20 plebes had been called before Lieutenant Swetland to satisfy him as to their whereabouts during the bed check. Most had been visiting the head facilities or checking the Company Office POD. One had been in Sick Bay with gastric distress -- he must have been one of the few plebes in the Brigade to get a full share of pepperoni pizza. One had claimed to be wandering Bancroft Hall, scouting out potential places for a small cannon his Company planned to "relocate" as a pre Army-Navy prank. Two had no real excuses for their absence and would pay dearly. I felt no remorse. They knew the rules, they took their chances and paid the price. That was part of the game.

In our Company two not-so-good things happened. Dennis Hayden -- one of the few decent second-classmen -- missed the bed check. He had been out with his fiancee, Jennifer, at a local movie, but her car had a flat tire on the way back. By the time he returned to his room, the bed check was already finished. Dennis would get 30 demerits and miss the Army-Navy festivities for failing to return on time. I did feel bad about that; but fate, not James Wesley Merritt, determined what had happened to Dennis.

Another unfortunate tragedy visited itself on Tim Richardson, one of my plebe companymates. Tim was a friendly and very feisty Floridian. His father was a Navy Captain, presently Commanding Officer of the Naval Air Station in Jacksonville, Florida. Tim had been visiting his first-class brother in a different Company area during the bed check. Neither his brother's lofty status, nor the fact that his father was the classmate of the Superintendent, could save him. Tim reacted with unusual resolution.

Tim would have received 35 demerits, and missed the big post-game celebrations, but rather than suffer these indignities, he decided to resign. It came as a shock to all his classmates, since Tim was one of the highest-ranked and most popular of the plebes. He had attained somewhat of a hero status after he had even saved us considerable trouble this past summer by boldly standing up to an irate but totally out-of-line Mike Maxwell one interesting summer evening.

In his farewell address to his classmates -- given to the Company plebes after Monday's evening meal -- he said he was ready to quit anyway, that the Navy definitely wasn't for him. He said he was on his way to UCLA, where he intended to study psychology and surfing -- not particularly in that order. He also stated firmly that he hated the Academy's Mickey Mouse regulations and the general insanity of Plebe Year, and he could never figure out why so many intelligent and personable young men would suffer such indignities on a daily basis. Jeff Polk, always the radical, wildly applauded Tim's fervent soliloquy. We wished Tim a heartfelt farewell accompanied by a rousing "Three Cheers" led by Jubal Ramsey. Then we asked him about his uniform sizes.

On Sunday morning I also realized with painful clarity that I had seriously injured myself in my leap to salvation the previous night. I decided to wait until after noon meal and go to Sick Bay and report it as a sports injury. Why not? I was certainly engaged in vigorous physical activity at the time. The cast I wore on my right forearm for the next three weeks kept me out of the plebe training regimen -- except for morning runs with Mugsy McGinley, so there was a bright side to the experience.

I also discovered that I had accidentally created a legend by my exploit. When Jubal Ramsey came to our room after evening meal on Sunday with the real "gouge" on the incident -- which he had heard from the roommate of one of the plebes who was on duty Saturday night in the Main Office -- and I listened what he had to say, I felt reasonably certain no one would ever recognize me as the perpetrator of the event.

According to Reb's story --- which I suspect he spiced up a bit in keeping with his exaggerative personality -- a midshipman now known as the "Passionate Plebe" had openly flaunted a steamy sexual liaison with a rather tawdry young lady. The liaison included bold nakedness and the co-mingling of various body parts in the seawall parking lot. When confronted by the OOD -- a good and decent man whose only wish was to enforce time-honored Academy regulations -- the plebe had brashly announced that the OOD and every watch officer who ever lived, plus their unmarried parents, bastard children, and all pre and progenitors, could all 'Go screw themselves!" The plebe then laughed insanely and ran off into the night. An epic chase resulted.

During the chase the plebe was said to have purposefully caused the OOD to wreck his car twice, escaped the clutches of several hundred midshipmen who valiantly tried to apprehend him, assaulted several innocent second-classmen in the passageway of the Seventh wing, run screaming madly through various portions of Bancroft Hall -- and the Chapel, where it was said he raced wildly around the crypt of John Paul Jones singing *Stand Navy down the Field*. The horrible sounds of his singing were even said to have awakened the Commandant's wife, Sandra, who asked Greyhound Hallahan to personally kill whatever beast had gotten loose.

But the evil plebe could not be stopped. He openly flaunted upper-class authority throughout the chase. Finally, he was rumored to have disappeared without a trace from a dead-end passageway where several plebe messengers swore before God he had chased him. The Passionate Plebe was said to be more than six feet four inches tall and to weigh well in excess of 200 muscular pounds. He had bowled Navy football players over without exerting himself -- a task Kevin felt compelled to remind us happened quite regularly every Saturday afternoon in Navy-Marine Corps Stadium. He could also leap ten wide steps in a single bound. It was even hinted that this plebe actually outran the OOD's vehicular pursuit. Only locomotives and speeding bullets were left out of the description. I egged Reb on, but secretly I chuckled to myself with every exaggeration.

It all sounded very mystical; and as time progressed, every unusual event anywhere on the campus came to be blamed on the "Passionate Plebe." There was still an active "Passionate Plebe" legend when I was a first-class, and no one seemed to mind that the individual in question would almost certainly now be the "Passionate first-class." When I asked Kevin O'Reilly to explain how this could be, he told me that "alliteration sometimes has more power than logic" -- whatever that means.

By Monday evening meal the legend had assumed nearly epic proportions and Brigade opinion ran more than five to one in favor of continued anonymity for the "Passionate Plebe." There was serious talk of a write-in election to oust our present nondescript Class President, Larry Martino, in favor of the more mythic figure. No one except a few of the first-class Tigers seemed anxious to see the offender brought to justice. The Tigers were incensed that someone so lowly had caused so great an insult to authority. They increased their plebe punishment as a result. But I had my cast, so I didn't greatly care. I was getting quite a secret self-important feeling from my easy mastery of the Academy duty hierarchy.

But, as my cast and bruised knees attested, maybe it wasn't so easy, and maybe I wouldn't be so lucky next time.

During the meal, Mugsy McGinley swore he would spoon the "Passionate Plebe" on the spot the instant his identity was revealed. I was smart enough to keep my mouth shut.

Rico discovered he had a persistent itch on Monday night, and he began exploring his nether regions as the rest of us studied and discussed the "Passionate Plebe." I noticed that Kevin O'Reilly watched me closely as we talked , and once he went to the window to examine the sill and gauge the distance to the railing across the moat. He looked at me with a thoughtful squint when he returned to his seat.

"God damn!" Rico said suddenly, startling us. "I'll kill that bitch!"

"What's the matter, Rico?" Kevin asked.

"She gave me crabs! Cindy gave me crabs!"

"How do you know that?" I asked.

"Come here and look!" he said groaning. "There's critters everywhere!"

"I'll take your word for it, Rico," I answered, chuckling at how the mighty had suddenly fallen. "What are you going to do?"

"Shit!" he said. "I'd better get right down to Sick Bay before I infect the entire room. Do any of you itch?" We looked at each other for a moment. I could see Kevin's hand creeping down into his gym shorts, immediately after which I heard a raspy scratching sound. Kevin frowned, and began to examine himself.

"What do I look for?" he asked.

"Tiny white bugs. Up close they look like crabs." Kevin continued his self-examination for a moment, and looked up, smiling.

"No. I don't think so," he said. Then he laughed. "You better get your crustacean infestation down to Sick Bay quickly if you want to engage in any interesting Saturday night events."

"Well," Rico replied, "whatever I do certainly won't be with Cindy until she produces a certificate from the Board of Health."

Actually there wouldn't be any interesting weekend evening events for any plebe until the Army-Navy game. On Tuesday the Academy restricted all plebes to their rooms after evening meal on Fridays and Saturdays until further notice or until the "Passionate Plebe" came forward to confess his sins. The Academy is famous for its reactionary responses. No, I did not step forward!

Leslie wasn't happy about the restriction. I didn't tell her of my confrontation with the OOD because I wasn't sure how she'd react, but the restriction was actually convenient in a strange way. I knew we couldn't meet on the seawall again for a long time, and I was a bit afraid to arrange anything else for a while for fear I'd be pushing my luck. I knew they'd be gunning for whoever was out of his room. Besides, Army-Navy was only three weeks away. We'd just have to wait.

Tuesday was also the day midterm grades were posted. The day of reckoning had arrived. I achieved a grade point average of 3.4, and I was in heaven. I could make the Dean's Academic List and would rate stars on my blue uniform. My plan was still in full effect: I would be Brigade Commander. Hell, I was a secret legend already, how could I miss?

Academics were not kind to several of my classmates. George Abbott, Chuck Chalmers, Rico Guevarra, and Steve Rogers were in academic trouble. Rogers and Chalmers were in such serious trouble that they had little hope of recovery. Abbott's and Guevarra's grades were only slightly unsatisfactory. I was greatly surprised at Rico's academic results since he had attended the Bronx School of Science, which was one of the top high schools in the country, but he didn't seem concerned.

"More time with text books and less with the tech manuals, and I'll be fine," was his response.

Tommy Poole, despite the constant first-class harassment had a perfect 4.0, which Douglas Goto also matched. Wesley Lamont, Hans Roudolph and Tony Delvecchio each earned 3.5, while Bob Strong matched my 3.4. Kevin had a 3.2, and BJ a 2.5. Based on the first quarter's results, it didn't seem that studies would be a problem for most my classmates. It was a great relief to pass this rite of passage.

I was so focused on plebe academics, I had almost forgotten that many upper-class also had problems with the books. During Tuesday evening meal I noticed glum faces at several tables, and I overheard hushed discussions about possible options to improve flagging grades. But the grimmest reminder of the consequences of academics came later that evening when Mike Maxwell dourly entered our room. With no hesitation, he spooned each of us, including Tommy Poole, who was there at the time to discuss Kevin's chemistry progress.

"Guys," he said, smiling, but obviously holding back tears, "I just flunked out." He waited for a moment to let the news sink in before he continued in a sad voice that was completely out of character. "I've had trouble with the books since day-one, and I've been on academic probation since First Semester Plebe Year. My grades this midterm are unsat again, and there's no possible way I can get them up high enough to matter. So I'm leaving before the end of the week so that my semester grades won't follow me into the fleet." He saw us wince at the mention of the word "fleet." What a cruel punishment, although I guessed enlisted sailors felt differently about their status. God, we felt instantly sorry for him.

"I want to thank you for the support you gave me this summer and during the year so far. You've been one hell of a good group of plebes -- the Class of '71 is the best I've seen." He turned specifically to Tommy Poole. "I was hard on you this past summer because you deserved it. You weren't ready to be a midshipman when you arrived, and I wasn't sure you could ever be successful until I saw how you reacted when the Brigade returned. You've done a great job, pal!" He laughed suddenly. "Hell, someday *I* may be working for *you*."

"Can he still call you 'Maxie'?" Kevin asked facetiously. Maxwell laughed.

"Sure, pal," he answered with a smile. "I'll have to call him, sir! Unless he spoons me."

"Anyway," he continued, "I'm convinced you can and will be a fine Naval Officer. Keep up the good work." He shook Tommy's hand again and smiled. "4.0, huh?" he asked.

"Yes, sir!" Tommy said, then paused and smiled. "Yes, Maxie." Maxwell shook his head sadly and departed.

After Maxie left, Kevin looked around.

"Holy shit!" he said. "Even legends can die. I feel sorry now we ever bounced his head on the Yacht Basin pier." We laughed, recalling that unusual night of plebe rebellion when we thought fleetingly we might have killed Maxie Maxwell, and we had each secretly relished his possible end.

In typical Tiger fashion the first-class in Twenty-third Company took the surprise bed checks and the plebe restriction edict to mean that discipline was much too lax at Annapolis. Not only did their harassment of the plebes continue with sadistic vengeance but they decided to export their unusual management style throughout the Brigade.

On Wednesday morning, when Dale Micklewski served as Battalion Officer of the Watch, he and his trusty messenger visited the Twenty-second Company area precisely at reveille. Dale was ecstatic when he found ten classmates and five underclassmen who had chosen to sleep-in that morning. The messenger copied their names from each doorplate. Micklewski then went to Twenty-first Company where he caught an additional 12 sleepy miscreants. He would have visited every upper-class room in the Battalion, but time restrained him.

When he returned to the Company Area he went immediately to the Office and drew a table on the chalk board. The first column he titled "date." The second "initials." The third "score." DM's score that morning was 33.

The furor that erupted when the unsuspecting first-class discovered they had been put on report by a classmate, was especially vehement and lasted the rest of the year. One particularly irate firstie publicly told Micklewski that if he ever ran into him in the fleet, he would personally throw him overboard one dark night when no one was looking. And he meant it. The following week Dick Muller caught 37. Five days later when Rolando Gomez had Battalion duty, he amassed an impressive score of 46. He had jogged the entire distance with his messenger, and according to his fried classmates, he hadn't waited for the bell to stop echoing before he was feverishly copying down names. Gomez's record stood until Finals Week in late May when Dale Micklewski found 68 offenders -- one to match each year of his class, including six plebes. No one was supposed to be watching such things so late in the year, so Dale knew it would be easy to catch the unwary.

Tim Richardson had a plebe yard sale on Saturday just before he departed. He sat behind his desk, wearing the coat and tie he wore on induction day. He had spread his gear on his rack and desk, and had lettered a sign and attached it to the front of his desk. The sign said, "Make me an offer!" Within an hour every item, including his Academy-issue V-neck T-shirts and baggy white boxer shorts, was sold. I bought his white uniform shoes for five dollars. Kevin bought his best combination cap. Captain Dillingham allowed him to eat noon meal with the Company in civilian clothes, and it was strange to see the light gray jacket and red-striped tie amid the sea of blue-black uniforms.

Maxie waited until Sunday to leave, and on Saturday night he staggered into our room at 2100, drunk as could be. In his right hand he carried a flashlight. In his left hand he had a can of Coke, which smelled suspiciously as if it had been cut with alcohol.

"Who am I?" he asked giddily, waving the beam of the flashlight onto our surprised faces. We looked at each other puzzled, and no one answered.

"Come on, pal. Who am I?" He waved the flashlight again. Still, we had no idea.

He laughed.

"You guys ain't so smart. I'm Digitalis, the ancient Greek, and I'm searching for truth in this cruel world."

"Heart medicine," said Kevin, which took Maxie completely by surprise.

"What?" he asked.

"Digitalis is heart medicine, Maxie. Diogenes was the Greek. -- and he never found what he was looking for."

Maxwell stared at O'Reilly for a long, inebriated moment.

"Eat shit, O'Reilly!" he said angrily, turned, and departed. Out in the passageway he stopped and screamed. "Oh, poor Diagonals, you never found truth!" then he staggered back toward his room. We laughed quietly among ourselves.

"Where the hell do you learn that shit, O'Reilly?" BJ asked him.

Kevin laughed.

"If you had a proper Catholic education, by the time you graduated from high school, you too would have about six bazillion useless facts crammed into your head."

Almost immediately Jubal Ramsey chopped across the passageway.

"What was that about?" he asked.

"Not sure," I answered. "Maxie was drunk and searching for truth."

"Truth? In this he'ah room?" Reb asked. "Sheeeeet!"

"Kevin enlightened him, and he left severely depressed," I added.

"O'Reilly," Reb said, "you'd screw up a wet dream." Then he turned to us with his customary twinkle. "By the way. I'll bet I know where he got his 'shine.'"

"No shit?" Rico said, perking up. "Where?"

"I'll have to show y'all," Reb answered. "Jeff and I found it by accident when we were explorin' last weekend. Ah think it's time fo' a plebe party." We looked at each other. I immediately knew Rico and Kevin were game for the adventure. BJ watched to see what I would say. I wasn't much in the mood for risk taking. I was still scared from the "Passionate Plebe" escapade. But what the hell? It was important sometimes to be one of the guys.

"Okay," I said. "I guess it won't hurt to look. But remember, we're supposed to be restricted to our rooms, so this will have to be quick."

Reb signaled to his waiting roommates across the passageway, and Jeff and Willy chopped over. Bob Strong never participated in these adventures. He seemed to have no interest in rabble rousing. He was too damn serious. He'd never be a legend.

"One at a time," Reb began. "Go to the farthest head and meet for final instructions." We chopped individually to the head facilities and waited for the group to assemble. "It's in the basement," Reb said after we had assembled. "Follow me!"

Down an adjacent side passageway was a doorway that accessed a set of circular stairs leading down into the basement level of the Academy. Generally maintenance workers used these stairs, one of many small stairways and passages that connected various parts of Bancroft Hall. This particular one was also a great shortcut to the Field House area, one that I had used to get to my most recent rendezvous with Leslie.

Reb led us down and along a wide corridor that passed several darkened maintenance workshops and storage rooms. A hundred yards later, at a position I reckoned to be somewhere beneath T-Court, he stopped at a doorway which was marked, *Steam Pipe Access* on its frosted wired-glass window. He checked to ensure we were not observed, then opened the door quickly and stepped inside. We entered behind him, hurriedly cramming ourselves into a small anteroom.

Once the door was closed behind us, he walked us through another door, this one solid and metal, and into a cramped network of pipes and conduits. Walkways led in three directions, following the route of the pipes and other utility lines. Reb chose the right-hand fork. We followed, amazed at the complexity and sheer size of the underground utility system.

After a journey of only 20 yards, Reb halted, smiling. Unless I was completely turned around, by now we were somewhere near the statue of Tecumseh. Reb stared into the dark confines of a maintenance crawlway that stretched to our left. He got down on hands and knees.

"I'll be right back," he said and crawled inside.

Within a minute he backed out of the crawlway carrying a paper Midshipman's Store bag, inside which bottles clinked together noisily. Sitting on the concrete floor he reached into the bag and removed a nearly-full fifth of Southern Comfort Whiskey. Grinning up at us, he screwed off the top deftly and handed it to Jeff Polk, who had the honor of the first sip. We settled around Reb on the cool floor. Soon I had taken my first swig and I felt the warm tingle vibrate in my throat and settle happily into my stomach area. It was certainly smooth.

For the next twenty minutes we passed the bottle until it was finished "Okay," Reb said. "Everyone pitch in t' replace the stock." We looked at him strangely.

"This he'ah prob'ly belongs to a maint'nance man. He ain't gonna like our stealing his liquor 'less we make it worth his while. I'll betcha if we put 'nough money in this he'ah bag he'll go out and buy some mo'ah for us. And wouldn't it be nice to have a place ta go and have a sip whenever we like?" We couldn't argue with that logic, although the cold and darkly stained concrete floor of a cramped space that smelled like solvents and motor oil was not my idea of the perfect meeting place for camaraderie. Each of us anted up a buck, which seemed to net the unknown supplier a hefty profit.

"Good!" said Reb. "Now let's get back befo' we're missed." We followed Jeff Polk out to the anteroom, and he carefully checked the corridor before motioning us outside. Within ten minutes we were back in our rooms, each of us buzzing nicely.

"We have to be extremely careful not to do that very often," I said. "And not drink too much when we do. If any Tiger suspects us, we'd be dead -- maybe even dismissed." My roommates readily agreed. Alcohol consumption inside Bancroft Hall was a major offense, although it could be argued sea-lawyer style that basement utility trenches under the campus were not strictly inside Bancroft Hall. However, I would hate to risk my entire career on that technicality, and I think my roommates agreed. It hardly seemed worth it.

I had forgotten about BJ's Army-Navy date until now.

"Oh, BJ?" I said. "I've found a suitable date for Army-Navy."

"Does she meet my specifications?" he asked.

"About the good looks and charm, yes. About the sex, maybe; but you'll have to meet her specifications first."

He laughed.

"Not a problem," he said, and I knew he was probably right. He was handsome and charming. I was sure he could charm the pants off any lady, and I was also sure he was going to keep away from Leslie -- him and Rico both, and, hell, maybe O'Reilly too.

"So," Rico asked, "BJ's date is coming up from Texas with what's-her-face?"

I hesitated. Rico smiled.

"Not exactly," I answered. "She's a local girl."

"But one what's-her-face knew from before, huh?" Rico asked not letting go. Oh well, they would find out that weekend anyway.

"No, she's a friend of a girl named Leslie I met recently. I'm taking Leslie to the game and party." Rico raised his eyebrows questioningly.

"What about Lynda?" Kevin asked, remembering the name. "And how'd you meet anybody?"

"She's just a close friend -- and Lynda is too," I answered breaking the Honor Code with a major lie. Leslie was a whole lot more than a close friend. Hell, I was in love with her. Luckily the Honor Code didn't apply to a midshipman's love life and social exploits; otherwise it would be shattered a thousand times by every student before graduation.

"So you have two 'close' friends?" asked Rico.

"Wait a minute," BJ interrupted. "You don't intend to be an old stick-in-the-mud while the rest of us are debauching, do you? Because my date is going to take her cue from yours, and if you're not groping in earnest, I'm going to have to work my ass off. If you hardly know this girl, Jim, your chances for success aren't so great."

"Oh?" I asked. "What's that mean?"

"You know," BJ said apologetically. "You're a decent looking guy, and you have a nice personality, but you have yet to reach the depths of depravity like true swordsmen. Shit, if you just met her, you probably haven't progressed beyond the hand holding and kissy-face stage. We both might as well plan on keeping safely in our pants the entire weekend." BJ looked severely crestfallen.

"I think Jim's been places with Miss Leslie he has yet to reveal," offered Rico.

BJ immediately perked up and the light went on in Kevin's eyes.

"You weren't seeking solitude the past couple weekends, you dick weed!" Kevin exclaimed. "You were out getting laid! You bastard -- I'm proud of you!" he turned to Rico. "Maybe we have a Dartagnion in our midst?"

BJ clapped his hands together loudly, once.

"All right!" he shouted.

"Rico," Kevin said suddenly. "If my date with Sarah doesn't work out, and Rosa maybe gets tired of you, do you think that maybe . . . "

"Not a chance, O'Reilly! I don't trust you. I never should have told you that Rosa thinks you're cute. You're not getting within ten feet of my Rosa for quite a while."

Kevin then looked at me.

"So where does that leave you and Lynda?" he asked.

"Don't get any ideas there either, O'Reilly," I laughed, "Lynda and I are still close friends."

"Not for long," Rico said, and I was suddenly angry. I think my guilty conscience got me for a moment.

"What do you mean by that?" I snapped.

Rico sensed my anger and smiled his you-gotta-learn-to-control-yourself smile.

"Girls have a sixth sense you don't learn about in high school, Merritt" he said. "They know when something's up, and they know when you're getting it somewhere else. Next time you're home, Lynda's gonna dump you before you have a chance to dump her. No way will she accept the "'two close friends' idea."

"Bullshit!" I said still angry. Rico smiled, and I hated him for his ability to predict things so accurately. I still loved Lynda and I didn't want to consider losing her after all that we had meant to each other. Uh, oh! Did I just think "had?"

Stone and Micklewski continued having Tommy Poole and Tim Butler comearound in 'skirts' and head-wraps despite the fact that neither one seemed particularly perturbed. It gave them an excuse for not sprinting all-out. Tommy Poole practiced push-ups and sit-ups in his room at night, and he had actually progressed to a point where he could exercise with almost anyone in the Company. I doubt that Stone noticed; he was so focused on running them to death.

On Thursday evening Captain Dillingham remained behind to watch the progress of plebe training. As Rock and Dale taunted the group, especially Tommy and Tim, Dillingham became incensed.

"You two act and look like girls!" he screamed. Then, ignoring the fact that both Tim and Tommy were standing not five feet away, he turned to Stone, who straightened impressively and awaited the onslaught. "I thought I asked you to rid the Company of the plebes who couldn't hack it?"

"Yes, sir!" Stone snapped.

"Well why are these two still here this late in the first set?"

"Sir," Stone replied. "They are determined to remain, and standard plebe indoctrination has proven inadequate."

"You're going to have to do better, Stone! Improvise!"

Stone looked at Tommy, plainly wondering whether the Captain considered the "skirts" a part of standard indoctrination. Maybe high heels and makeup were next. "Aye, aye, sir!" he answered.

At evening meal Stone, Micklewski, and Salenger worried about the consequences of Dillingham's impatience. Kevin eagerly listened.

"If every one of us cooperated," Stone said regretfully, "we could run these two girls, and several other unworthy plebes, straight out of here before they even knew what hit them."

"Yeah," agreed Micklewski. "It's guys like McGinley who screw the rest of the Brigade."

Suddenly, Dick Salenger, normally the quiet Tiger, had an idea.

"Poole!" he said devilishly. "Go down to McGinley's table and stare at him for five minutes. Don't say a word no matter what he does. Just get as close to him as you can and stare." He looked at Stone. "Maybe that'll make Mugsy uncomfortable." Stone didn't hesitate. He nodded, and soon Tommy was on his way to our table.

Tommy chopped to a point beside Mugsy but against the wall and stared silently. Mugsy and Brandis looked at Tommy, then at each other, than at Stone's table.

"What the piss is this supposed to be, Poole?" Mugsy asked. Tommy didn't answer. "I asked you a question!" he snapped, but Tommy remained silent. Mugsy started to rise, but Henry put a hand on his arm to restrain him.

"It's another one of Stone's psychological games, Mugsy. Don't let him get to you." Mugsy relaxed, then smiled. He looked at Poole and dropped his voice to a whisper.

"Poole," he began, "nod slightly if I'm right about this. Were you sent here to harass me?" Tommy nodded almost imperceptibly. "Did Micklewski send you?" Tommy indicated a "no." "Stone?" Mugsy asked, and again Tommy shook a "no" answer.

"Dickie boy, huh?" he turned to Brandis. "What's the point here?"

"They wanted you to do exactly what you almost did, Mugsy -- get angry at Poole instead of the real culprits. I heard that "Bully" Dillingham was on the warpath again about who is worthy of midshipman status and who isn't."

"And Tommy here made the cut list, huh?" McGinley asked. Brandis nodded.

Mugsy suddenly turned to me.

"Merritt," he said, "you're a plebe super greaser. You know what's up. Is classmate Poole really unworthy?"

I answered instantly, feeling proud of my reputation, and respecting Mugsy for his apparent trust in my opinion.

"No sir!"

"What's the deal here then?" he asked. "I've seen Poole here during comearounds. He's not a screw-up. He puts out better than some of you greasers. He also knows the entire history of mankind, he's great at sports trivia, and he knows more about math and science than most of my classmates." He looked at Brandis and smiled. "Present company excluded, of course."

"Sir," I said. "I believe Captain Dillingham is behind much of it. He's firmly convinced Tommy isn't officer material."

Mugsy snorted.

"Dillingham's hung up on his own press clippings. He thinks every human being has to measure up to his larger-than-life standards, and he's dead wrong." McGinley looked at Tommy. "Come closer, Poole."

Tommy hesitated and McGinley laughed.

"I'm on *your* side -- sort of -- Mister Poole. Get over here."

Tommy sidled closer to Mugsy.

"Go back to your table and stand behind Mister Salenger. Report to them that I am not pleased by their childish antics. Then stick both of your index fingers in your mouth until they are good and moist, and put one in each of Salenger's ears from behind and shout, "Wet Willie! Wet Willie!"

Tommy's eyes narrowed. Mugsy continued patiently.

"We have to end this somehow, Mister Poole. We'll start with a good gross-out. Now get going!" Tommy trotted off, but he didn't look at all happy, and I couldn't blame him.

We watched as Tommy recited Mugsy's speech, quickly licked his two fingers and inserted his wet fingers into Dick Salenger's ears. Salenger leaped to his feet and turned on Tommy, but most of the midshipmen at the table, including Stone, quietly laughed.

"Don't ever do anything to your own squad members you stupid asshole!" Salenger spat.

"Orders, sir!" Tommy answered sputtering slightly. Salenger stared venomously at Mugsy for several seconds. Mugsy extended his middle finger in answer, and continued eating. Mugsy was right about one thing, no one else every bothered him by sending a plebe by.

The final departure of the week was the most unusual and without a doubt the most spectacular, and it began with a "friendly" game of basketball. At least, it was supposed to be friendly. But I think many of us, plebe and upper-class alike, let the ongoing pressures and emotional build-up of the past several weeks get the best of us.

On Saturday afternoon it was the plebe's turn to play the first-class in the continuing round-robin basketball competition. We had beaten the youngsters and the second-class handily during previous weeks' games, as had the firsties. Our games had no conflicts, but the firsties played extremely physical and emotional contests. The entire Company routed for us to win. We could not allow ourselves to lose to the Tigers.

We were smaller than the first-class by several inches each, but we were much quicker. And we had a ringer in the person of Kevin O'Reilly. The first-class game plan would mean getting the ball under the basket to monsters like Big Jim Daly and Grunt Robinson.

It seemed as if every midshipman in the Company came to the courts to watch the big game. Our lineup consisted of Kevin and Reb as forwards, John Pirelli and Rico at guards -- alternating with me -- and Barton Hardesty as the center. The firsties played Daly at center, Micklewski and Robinson at forward, and Linehan and Dick Muller at guards. Daly and Robinson were both taller larger than any of us, and Muller was a fair shooter.

Daly dominated the tip-off, and the firsties scored first on a quick dunk by Robinson. We came right back with a jump shot by Kevin to tie the score. The game continued in a basket-for-basket fashion for the next several minutes. Then the trouble began. As Robinson was backing in on Hardesty on one play near the basket, he threw an elbow -- maybe accidentally -- which caught Barton on the nose. Barton fell backward onto the asphalt deck, and Robinson scored easily. We called a foul, but the firsties protested and naturally won the dispute. Barton had to sit out while classmates tended to his bleeding nose. On the way off the court, Robinson walked over to Barton and said fiercely. "You're playing with the big boys now, plebe, and you're way out of your league."

Barton looked at him, then down at the mass of blood that had pooled in the palm of his hand, and I could see something snap inside Barton's head. His eyes assumed a demented look that I instantly knew foretold of trouble. Robinson looked at Daly, and the two of them laughed together. Barton stumbled off the court, and I came on, shifting Kevin to center until Barton could recover.

A now-angry Kevin didn't do badly at center. During the next several minutes he stole the ball once each from Daly and Robinson, intercepted a pass, and drove through the big firsties for two easy lay-ups. If the firsties hadn't regrouped, I think Kevin would have single-handedly beaten them.

But Daly called a time-out, and afterwards the firsties played a slower, more deliberate game. Repeatedly they worked the ball down the court, taking no chances, and Robinson scored several easy jump shots close to the basket before half-time. We needed Barton back to even the height and size disadvantage, and at the end of the half, Barton was ready. We should have left him on the sidelines.

As Daly and Hardesty lined up for the tip-off, Daly looked Barton in the eye and said, "You are a real screw up, Hardesty, and I am personally going to teach you a lesson about basketball." Barton smoldered but didn't respond, and Daly smiled.

The first-class strategy was immediately apparent. They teamed up on Barton, forgetting for a time the game that was in progress.

"Check this out, you damn religious twit!" Robinson said as he drove to the bucket over Barton. Barton fell to the deck again.

"Hey!" Kevin yelled. "Offensive foul!"

Robinson smiled at Kevin.

"You're right," he said, handing Kevin the ball. He turned to Hardesty. "Maybe if you asked Jesus to stop me, he could come down to earth and do it for you, shit-head, but as it is, I'm all over you until the game ends."

"You'd better pray for salvation, shit-for-brains!" Daly added. Hardesty started forward toward Daly, but Ramsey restrained him.

Suddenly I saw the plan. Hardesty had been on Captain Dillingham's list since the beginning of the year, and this was their way to try to get Barton over the edge. I grabbed Barton by both shoulders.

"Barton!" I said fiercely. "Don't listen to them! They're trying to get you angry. Shake it off!" I looked closely at Barton's face as he stared down at me. His eyes were filled with rage and near insanity. He couldn't even answer.

I ran to Kevin just as play resumed. "We have to get Barton out of the game. He's completely lost control, and something bad is going to happen." Kevin opened his mouth to call a time out, but my warning had come seconds too late. The firsties had the ball and control of the time.

Parker Fullerton brought the ball deliberately down the court. Daly and Robinson set up on either side of the basket, and Micklewski and Linehan waited near the top of the foul line for the pass. Fullerton passed the ball to Dale who took a quick jump shot, then moved for the possible rebound.

Daly and Robinson converged on the basket from either side, and Hardesty and Ramsey jostled for position with them as Kevin moved to block out the oncoming Micklewski. As the ball arched inward, I saw Robinson grab Barton's arm and shove him into Daly's back. Daly threw an elbow backward, catching Barton on the chin with a loud crack. Judging from the sound, I thought for sure Barton would be knocked unconscious. Instead he fell briefly against Robinson, then jumped on Daly's back with a wild scream.

Everyone froze except Daly and Hardesty -- and Micklewski, who continued forward into the under-the-bucket area. Daly shook Hardesty loose and turned screaming into Barton's face.

"Hey! Piss off plebe!" he shouted. Barton quickly pulled back his right fist and threw a round-house punch at Daly, who was ready for a confrontation. He ducked. Dale Micklewski, still staring intently at the basketball bouncing on the rim -- was not. The blow caught Micklewski dead center on his upturned jaw, and Dale's eyes immediately glazed over as he crumpled to the asphalt. Micklewski was knocked out.

The sight of the fallen Tiger did not take the fight out of Hardesty, who struggled in the grasp of Reb Ramsey, still wanting a shot at Daly. But it provided a strange satisfaction to the rest of us.

Plebes on the sideline cheered madly, and yelled, "Way to go, Barton!" I found myself smiling at Kevin, who beamed at me in return. Even Daly and Robinson snickered.

But the smiles didn't last. Rock Stone quickly entered the court and stood before Barton with an almost regal attitude.

"What you just did, Hardesty, was the utmost in plebe insubordination. There is never a reason for physical confrontation during a sports competition. I'm going to do to you exactly what any Navy coach would do and put you on report for 'Conduct Unbecoming an Officer.' That's a Class A offense, so you better cancel your plans for the next several weeks."

Barton still had the wild light in his eyes, and he suddenly broke free of Ramsey and went for Stone. He managed to get both hands around Rock's throat and drive him backward several feet before plebes and firsties pried him loose. I had a perfect vantage point to observe Barton's face as he applied the pressure to Stone's neck, and I could see Barton smile as he squeezed. Just as his fingers lost their grip and Stone sputtered away, I could swear I saw Hardesty mouth several colorful words at Rock. They were words not even Mugsy used.

Hardesty refused to accept the Class-A offense and instead plea-bargained his honorable resignation. He also didn't want to hang around for any farewell speeches. On Monday morning while we were at class, Barton packed up and slipped quietly away. Later that year I learned from his then roommate Tony Delvecchio that instead of staying in Memphis with his reverend father, Barton had gone off to California -- to preach the Word to the many heathens there, no doubt.

CHAPTER 10

NEAR MISS

"Gentlemen! Saturday is the Army-Navy football game, one of the longest football rivalries in the history of the nation, and a competition suspended only during the Second World War. It's unquestionably the most famous inter-school football competition on the planet, and both services are rightly proud of the long and glorious history of the event." The speaker paused and looked up from the podium. His handsome face, weathered by years of salt spray lashings, stiff sea breezes, and dazzling reflections off boundless oceans, spoke of seafaring, of lonely night duties, of glorious battles blazing across the horizon, and of friends who never came home. His laughing pale blue eyes, which squinted slightly in the stage lighting, held a message of violent storms, exotic ports, and equally exotic women. Today was Thursday, 23 November, two days before the big game.

"What we are not so proud of," he continued with a professional twinkle, "is the shenanigans that customarily happen after the big game. Many upperclass laughed at this remark. The Commandant of Midshipmen, Captain Mack "Greyhound" Hallahan ignored the tittering. As he shifted in place, the bright podium lights sparkled off the incredible quantities of gold braid that lined his sleeve. I wanted a uniform like that someday, and if I played my cards right, I would achieve it. I smiled to myself, thinking of Rear Admiral James "Passionate Plebe" Merritt speaking to the Brigade under similar circumstances. Hallahan continued, interrupting my reverie. "We fully expect that the Brigade of Midshipmen and the Corps of Cadets will behave honorably both during the game and afterwards." More chuckling followed his remarks and he stopped and looked over the audience again. Since this was a mandatory evening lecture, Mahan Hall was packed with every able-bodied member of the brigade. Hallahan smiled.

"Listen up," he said, adopting a one-of-the-guys attitude. "Believe it or not I was young once. I understand what it means to be cooped up in this place for long periods and how necessary some form of release can be." Several midshipmen cheered. "Hell, when I was a plebe, not only were we restricted from any contact with females but we couldn't date when we went home for leave or at for Army-Navy either. They made us stand Shore Patrol duty for the upperclass who were drunk and disorderly. Now that was hell!" We laughed loudly. Hallahan told the best -- if not always the most accurate -- stories about his time as a midshipman and in the fleet.

Hallahan was an incredibly personable individual who had made his reputation during the later days of the Korean War when as a junior Lieutenant Commander he commanded a Destroyer that repeatedly harassed North Korean and Chinese torpedo boat squadrons and shore fortifications. He was said to have been totally fearless, often drinking coffee and giving orders calmly while his ship was in combat and maneuvering violently to avoid enemy fire. Since that time he had progressed meteorically through the ranks and had been given command of several of the Navy's most prestigious nuclear-powered surface attack ships. Hallahan loved the sea and had been destined for the Chief of Naval Operations job. Two years ago, however, a fellow senior staffer at the Pentagon interrupted a morning staff meeting to inform Greyhound privately of the death of his only son, killed when his F-4 Phantom fighter flamed out on final approach to the carrier Oriskany. They never recovered the body. Afterward Hallahan was a more subdued version of his former self, and the Commandant's job would be his last hurrah before retirement. We respected Greyhound. He treated us all in the firm but fair fashion that marks good leaders. He also made us feel as if we had been adopted as his surrogate sons.

"I have in my hand two messages I am duty-bound to relay," he continued. He held aloft two slips of paper. "The first is from the mayor of Philadelphia, who last year you may remember threatened to ban future Army-Navy competitions if any 'incidents' are repeated."

He paused, then despite a supreme effort at self control, laughed loudly.

"There will be no depositing drunk Army Cadets into Hotel dumpsters. One poor fellow was missing from his Battalion for two days." The Brigade roared. "Public fountains will not be used to make wine coolers or for public bathing." We laughed again. "And, above all, there will be no repetition of the co-ed nude football competition in Liberty Bell Plaza." He chuckled again, shaking his head. "Although," he continued, "I caught the last quarter of that game, and I must admit some of the female linemen had rather enormous . . . personalities." We roared again.

"The second piece of correspondence is from the Secretary of the Navy. He writes, 'Saturday, November Twenty-fifth, 1967 brings to America the Army-Navy football game, and I am pleased to be the Secretary of the Navy for this historic event. I remind each and every service member of his responsibility to uphold the highest standards of conduct during and after the game and to strive to bring credit to their institutions. I also remind the Brigade of Midshipmen that the Corps of Cadets is represented by a mule -- slow, stupid, and stubborn -- but that Navy has a goat -- agile, powerful, and headstrong. It should be no competition at all. Therefore it seems only fitting I end this message with a prediction that the venerable goat will -- Kick Army's Ass!'" We jumped to our feet and roared again. Greyhound Hallahan loved it.

Hallahan held both hands in the air for quiet, and his eyes lost their twinkle and became steely. We immediately calmed, sensing that he meant business now.

"I am perfectly serious about behavior after the game, gentlemen. Behave yourselves and act like the gentlemen we expect. If you are caught doing anything untoward, you'll get no protection from me. Is that clear?" There were no titters now. He was telling us in no uncertain terms to be on our best behavior, and that was fine with me. All I wanted after the game was my sweet Leslie.

"On my authority as Commandant," Hallahan continued, "all plebes are now granted carry-on beginning tomorrow, Friday, 24 November at 0001 and lasting until game-time Saturday." Kevin nudged me in the ribs.

"That'll piss off the Tigers," he whispered, laughing quietly. Dale Micklewski looked back at Kevin with narrow eyes, and Kevin smiled at him sheepishly.

"I think we can expect a visit tonight, big mouth!" Rico whispered half-seriously from the other side of Kevin.

"Well," Kevin whispered back loudly. "That visit had better be before midnight, because after that I'm going to stick my chin out so far it might stretch clear across the room." On my other side, BJ nudged me. I leaned toward him.

"Why does O'Reilly step on his crank so often?" he asked. "Doesn't he know when to keep his mouth shut?"

"Hey," I said chuckling, "it's just Kevin's way. No big deal!"

But the Commandant wasn't finished yet, and we settled into our seats again.

"Seriously," he said, assuming his role as 'dad' again. "I want you all to behave yourselves on Saturday. I understand how it is to be a midshipman, and I appreciate the pressures you are under every day. The stress can seem overwhelming sometimes, and you feel as if you just have to unwind. Let me tell you sometime about liberty call in Subic." We laughed.

"But this isn't wartime, and stress or not, there's no excuse for lacking self control in public in a major US city after a football game. I will not be happy if the Philadelphia police or the Shore Patrol or the Commanding General of West Point informs me of any unnecessary hooliganism. I will not repeat myself on this." He said it with such authority that I could almost hear the collective consciousness of the Brigade consider the consequences of things that had been thoroughly planned. Hallahan smiled again, and his eyes crinkled mischievously. "Beat Army! Dismissed!"

We walked slowly back to Bancroft Hall in the dark, nearly-moonless night, borne along Stribling Walk in a stream of young bodies in dark coats. The air was chilly, and a brisk breeze swished the branches of the huge poplar trees, dislodging leaves that hadn't already fallen, and swirling them high overhead. It would have been a perfect night for Ichabod Crane. I peered into the dark foliage and through gaps in the canopy I could see heavy clouds scudding ominously.

"Gonna rain tomorrow," Pat Mulvaney observed, watching the sky like the practiced farmer he was. "I can smell it coming. Better get out the raingear tonight." Midshipmen could not carry umbrellas. Instead we wore a black vinyl cape-like overgarment atop our uniform. This provided some measure of protection to our clothes, and our vinyl-covered combination caps protected our heads. In fact, the water always managed to find a way into the back of my raingear at the neckline, and in stiff rains the back of my shirt usually became soaked after a few minutes. An umbrella or a hooded garment would have been infinitely preferable. But I didn't control the uniform process -- or the weather. I hoped silently Pat was wrong, but Pat could scent a chocolate chip hidden in a metal lock box.

"Carry-on tomorrow!" Tommy Poole exclaimed. "I can't wait! I am so tired of this plebe shit!"

"Me too!" I said, surprising everyone. A Corpsman in Sick Bay had removed my cast at the end of the previous week, and the severe exercising, which returned with an absolute vengeance after a three-week hiatus, had been painful. "Hey!" I said. "You guys think I like being a plebe? You think I enjoy comearounds?"

"Yeah," Rico replied, nudging O'Reilly in the process, "we think you do. You love everything about this place, for Christ's sake. I'll bet you get a hard-on just dreaming about bear crawls." Everyone in the group laughed, myself included.

"So are we going to tone down the party on Saturday?" asked BJ, almost afraid of the answer. I was about to say something about the propriety of the event and about conduct unbecoming a midshipman when Rico answered loudly.

"Hell no!" His opinion prevailed, and I didn't particularly care, since I intended to spend as much time as possible snuggled against Leslie's naked body. I didn't think being drunk and rowdy would particularly enhance that experience.

"Guess what, Rico?" Kevin asked boldly.

"What is it, redhead?"

"I've been talking to Sarah Connelly a lot lately, and she has been hinting that Mister Kevin O'Reilly is going to see some hot action on Saturday night. I think she really likes me."

"Your dad might get a little, Kevin," Rico replied. "But I hope that's the only Mister Kevin O'Reilly who will. You're gonna be in big trouble, lad, especially when virginal Sarah tells her mother what you tried to do." Rico was joking, but something in his voice told me he had deep concerns.

"What's up, Rico?" I asked.

"Neighborhood girls? Friends of the family? Are you shitting me? There's a recipe for disaster right there. But add the Catholic factor and there has to be trouble."

"The Catholic factor?" I asked.

"Sure! You go to school for eight years and all they teach you is that sex is bad and you're gonna go to hell if you even think about it. But you do anyway. Once you're 14 or so, you can't stop from thinking about it. And you get so afraid, you're scared of what you might do if you had half a chance. And when you have a chance, you get lecherous like Kevin here." He paused, chuckling. When he continued, he was far more serious. "For girls it's worse. They hold even their thoughts back until it all breaks free. Some catholic girls, once they get some, can't ever get enough. They'll destroy a man with no regrets at all. If Sarah is one of those, Kevin's in deep trouble."

Kevin smiled up at the clouds.

"We'll see!" Rico shook his head sadly. Since Rico was seldom wrong about these things, I decided to keep a special eye on Kevin.

Stone and Micklewski entered our room at 2030, immediately after we had distributed sandwiches. McGinley's enterprise had become surprisingly successful, thanks to our liberal use of extra slices and thickly applied condiments and Mugsy was turning a hefty profit every week. We snapped to attention and braced-up.

Stone went straight to O'Reilly and stood mere inches from his face. Micklewski copied Stone's pose and posture.

"I understand you made a disparaging comment that disrupted tonight's lecture?" Stone asked in a very serious tone.

"Disrupted? No, sir!"

"You made a derogatory comment about the first-class leadership in this Company, did you not?" Micklewski asked. He had moved to a position on one side of Kevin, his mouth inches from Kevin's ear. He pursed and unpursed his lips in irritation as he spoke so that from my position it almost appeared as if he were preparing to kiss Kevin. I wondered briefly what Kevin would do if Dale Micklewski planted a wet one on his cheek. It was a grizzly idea, and I halted that train of thought immediately.

"Sir," Kevin said calmly, "I made a humorous and whispered comment to my classmates which was not intended for general listening. I meant no disrespect or disruption."

"You are a liar, O'Reilly!" Stone said calmly. "From day one, all we've gotten from you has been disrespect and grief, and we are tired of it! When I return to my room, I'm going to write a report chit for 30 demerits which will restrict you immediately after the game on Saturday." He stood back and sneered at Kevin. Micklewski continued -- they must have rehearsed this scene before coming here.

"That means no date, wise-guy. And no partying with your little plebe friends. And no passion with whatever slut would be stupid enough to be seen with you. You just screwed up big time, you little poop-head plebe."

Kevin's face reddened perceptibly. I could see his muscles tensing. Holy shit! I realized we were going to see a repeat of the Barton Hardesty debacle. What could I do?

"Sir!" said Rico suddenly. "Midshipman First-class Micklewski turned around after the comment was made and could not have possibly seen who made the statement."

"Are you calling me a liar?" yelled Dale Micklewski advancing on Rico. "I ought to be able to recognize his voice -- he has a thick silly New England accent!"

"Besides, Guevarra," countered Stone, "he's already admitted it."

"Sir, that's entrapment! Any of us could have made that statement. We all have accents. We all have senses of humor -- even Merritt -- and neither you nor Mr. Micklewski knew *for sure* who made the statement when you came in here."

Stone turned to BJ who shrugged noncommittally but didn't say anything.

"Brace-up, Wilson. God-damn it!" BJ snapped to rigidity. Rock was mad as hell by what Rico was implying. If he couldn't prove Kevin made the comment, how could he initiate the Report Chit in good faith. Honor was vitally important to Rock Stone, and Rico may have found a way to thwart him. I could almost see Stone's mind whirling in confusion and contradiction. He came to a decision.

Stone moved confidently back to the front of O'Reilly and asked slowly and deliberately, "Is Guevarra correct, O'Reilly?" I knew instantly Stone's plan was to see if Kevin would tell a direct, but possibly unprovable, lie.

"Yes, sir!" Kevin answered without hesitation, then he quickly added with a smile. "Mister Merritt *does* in fact have a sense of humor!" BJ and Rico chuckled, but they were the only ones in the room who found anything to laugh about. Humor was not going to save Kevin this time.

Stone's face underwent several changes of emotion.

"I asked if you had said what Mister Micklewski contends or not. Did you?"

"I'll find out, sir!" Kevin said, coping out nicely. Good for Kevin not to let himself be entrapped.

"One of you said it, O'Reilly you stinking asshole!" Stone growled. "Don't you have enough personal honor to admit what you did? You have to give me a better answer than that. Look at the position you put me in. I'll be forced to fry the entire room, and there'll be no partying for any of you. Are you going to let your roommates take the fall for something you and I both know you did?" Stone stepped backward from Kevin and smiled. "I ask you again, did you say what Mister Micklewski contends he heard?"

Rico started to speak again, but Kevin hushed him.

He took a deep breath and smiled right into Stone's face. "Yes, sir! I did make that statement!" I think Stone fully expected Kevin to disavow the statement, because for an instant I could see genuine surprise on his face. After a moment's silent appraisal, he smiled at Kevin in silent approval, nodded once slowly, and turned to Guevarra.

"Nice try, Guevarra. But if you ever attempt an untruth like that again I'll see you before the Honor Board. Is that understood?"

Rico shrugged almost imperceptibly.

"Yes, sir!" he said, smiling slightly.

"And you had better wipe that smile off your face or I'll wipe it off for you!" Stone yelled. Rico stopped smiling but retained an arrogant glint in his eye. Stone stared at him venomously, and I could tell that Rico had just been added to Stone's list of enemies.

Stone walked to me.

"Tell me, Merritt. What would you have said if I asked you directly if Kevin O'Reilly was guilty or not?" What kind of question was that?

"I would not have answered, sir!" I said loudly.

Stone smiled.

"And how about if I had asked you if you made the controversial statement like Guevarra suggested. How would you have answered?" That question really angered me. It was totally hypothetical, he had no right to ask it, and I wasn't about to answer.

"You'll never know, sir!" I said boldly. Instead of reacting in anger, Stone continued smiling.

"Very good, Merritt! Very good! There's hope for you if these other clowns don't screw you up with their insanity." Stone then turned to Kevin. "I do like you, O'Reilly. You've got balls, and you *are* honorable in your own strange way. Your roommates tried valiantly, but first thing tomorrow that report chit will be sitting on Captain Dillingham's desk. Once he gives it back to me and I send it to the Brigade Disciplinary Officer, your name will appear on the Restriction List. You can forget all the good times on Saturday, O'Reilly, and please think about your attitude as you head to the Main Office every hour while your buddies are partying. But remember, you did this to yourself by opening that big mouth of yours. You have no one but yourself to blame." Stone then nodded to Micklewski, and they both trudged from the room.

"Shit, Kevin! What're you gonna do?" asked a genuinely concerned BJ Wilson.

Kevin shook his head slowly.

"Don't know, BJ. I think I'm screwed." Kevin was definitely upset. It was the first time I ever saw him when a smile wasn't ready to explode on his face. I was angry that they had done this to him. Kevin sat slowly at his desk and buried his head onto his arms. "I need to think about this."

Almost immediately the occupants of Room 4026 entered. Ramsey, seeing Kevin's almost lifeless posture, instantly recognized that a severe crisis had occurred. He raised a beefy arm, stopping anyone from speaking after they entered. He walked slowly over to where I still stood.

"What happened?" he asked quietly. 'We heard some commotion."

BJ jumped in quickly, ignoring Kevin's posture and deflated spirits.

"Stone just fried O'Reilly for that anti-Tiger comment he made tonight at the assembly. Now Kevin's gonna miss the whole damn Army-Navy party. What an asshole!"

"No shit?" asked Jeff Polk. "That's the worst pissing Mickey Mouse outrage I have ever heard about this asinine place! Listen, if I were you, I'd go see Captain Dildo in the morning and tell him what happened. Maybe he'll be magnanimous."

"And if he's not?" Kevin asked sitting up slowly. Were those tears in Kevin's eyes?

"Beg for mercy!" Reb interjected. "It's cruel and inhuman to take away the post-game party just for a silly lil 'ol comment."

Kevin sighed deeply. "Mercy, like the gentle rain from heaven," he mumbled into his sleeve. I looked at the others. They shrugged.

"Aw, it's my own fault! You guys have told me a thousand times to watch what I say. I guess I just went too far this time."

"Come on, guys!" I said loudly. "Brainstorm! How can we save Kevin?"

"Legally or illegally?" Polk asked.

"Both!" I answered, surprising everyone.

"We could approach Captain Dillingham as a group tomorrow and ask that he not forward the Report Chit," offered Bob Strong. "He might respond if we form a common front." That was a sensible idea I could support.

"We could get someone to approach Stone tonight and ask him to reconsider before he submits the chit," offered Willy Simpson.

Jeff Polk blurted suddenly.

"We could go to Stone with a signed list of all the Plebe Year violations that the Tigers have committed and threaten to testify before the Commandant if he doesn't start acting like a god-damn human being! Let's bring their paper empire down around their ears. We could bring this off, guys, and be the heroes of the Brigade." Wow! When Polk got wound up he really was intense. But it seemed that what he suggested was carrying things a bit too far.

"We could kill Stone in his sleep before he delivers the chit!" offered Jubal only half in jest.

"I like that idea," said Kevin, raising his head. "We could do it like *Murder on the Orient Express* and each of us stick a bayonet in his chest. They could never prove which stab actually did it. Manslaughter -- ten years tops. But I'll bet we get off with justifiable homicide. It might be worth it, and I volunteer for the first stab."

Unfortunately we had exhausted our supply of ideas, and I could feel the tension mounting. It seemed as if we couldn't save Kevin, and he could sense our frustration. Kevin rose and walked to the door without a word.

"I gotta take a leak, fellas," he said glumly. "I'll be right back." With that he departed. I looked at Rico asking with my eyes if one of us should go with Kevin, but he shook his head.

"What a damn shame!" Strong said as he and his roommates departed. "Tomorrow let's talk to Stone and Dillingham." I agreed that was the best course of action.

I looked at Rico after the room was again quiet and I could see he was considering something. "You are strangely quiet, Rico. What's up?"

He looked at me with none of his customary levity.

"Fun's over, Merritt!" he said seriously. "From now on this is war." Maybe that bayonet idea wasn't supposed to have been rhetorical. Somehow I felt immediately sorry for Rock Stone, realizing that he had bit off more than he could chew this time. Rico rose without a further word and left the room in a determined chop.

I looked at BJ who seemed genuinely concerned.

"It's just not fair," he said sadly.

"Don't worry," I said. "All is not lost. After we talk to Stone tomorrow, maybe he'll give Kevin a reprieve." BJ didn't look at all convinced. "I think I'll go check on Kevin," I said and chopped from the room.

Since I was in gym gear, my entrance into the head was relatively quiet. I didn't see Kevin immediately at the urinals or the sink area. I paused. Then I heard the faint sound of sniffling and shuddered breathing, followed by a long plaintiff sigh. I bent over quietly to view under the stalls, and from this distance I could see there was only one occupant in any of the booths. The red hair on the two thin legs I saw told me immediately it was Kevin. As I watched, I saw a large drop of something liquid strike the tile deck and splash in a small puddle of homogenous wetness. What had they done to Kevin? Silently I crept from the head, leaving Kevin with his remorseful thoughts.

Instead of returning to the room, I went to Rock Stone's room and knocked loudly on the door.

"Enter!" he yelled. I took a deep breath and hurried inside.

"Midshipman Fourth-class Merritt, sir!" I yelled, bracing against the locker wall. Stone sat behind his desk, studying. He looked at me, surprised and disgusted for several silent moments.

"It's not going to do you any god-damn good, Merritt," he said. He held up a small piece of paper. "Here's the chit. Tomorrow it goes to Dillingham. Period!"

"Request permission to speak freely, sir?"

Stone paused for an even longer moment, considering the implications. Finally he sighed.

"Sure," he said. "And shit, carry-on while you're at it." I unbraced and walked to his desk. His roommate, a varsity rower from Texas named John Gladden, looked at me, sighed, and looked at Rock.

"Plebe shit?" he asked in a Houston area drawl.

"Yeah, Tex," Rock answered. Gladden chuckled, stood, brought his chair around to the front of his desk and put it on the floor next to Stone's.

"Have a seat, plebe, pardner" he said, then he left the room.

I waited until he was gone and turned to Stone.

"You've got to reconsider on this report chit," I said boldly. Stone became irritated.

"Don't tell me what I have to do, Merritt, because I know what I have to do, and this is it." Again he held up the chit.

"I'm not contesting the chit. If you feel he deserves it, it's within your authority to put him on report. But let me add something. I was there. The comment was not disruptive. It was barely audible. And it was said privately to a group of plebes. There was no open flouting of first-class authority, you have my word on that."

"I appreciate your comment, Merritt, but Dale overheard the comment, so it *was* public," Stone replied. "I'd like to help you, but it's out of my hands."

"Let's compromise on this," I said. "Hurrying the chit through the system serves no useful purpose. It's cruel and dishonorable. Good leaders aren't cruel to their troops. Delay the chit for a day, and let Kevin have his party. He'll march his demerits off with the best of them."

"I might do that for a plebe who deserved compassion, but O'Reilly doesn't support us at all. He may be funny, and he may be endearing and cute -- and I honestly like him -- but he's a god-damn pain in the ass. He's got to learn to grow up. Screw him!"

"Kevin O'Reilly is the best plebe in this Company!" I said. Stone started to protest, but I held up a hand to stop him. "He runs faster, answers quicker, and tries harder than any of us, and that's the truth, sir. He spends hours shining his shoes, straightening his locker, and making the covers on his bed taut. He really does love it here, and he really does want to succeed."

"Well, he has the strangest way of showing it."

"Yes, sir! He does. But his weird sense of humor is just his defense mechanism. He is also single-handedly keeping the plebe sanity level as high as it is in the face of the constant pressure. If it wasn't for him, I'd be struggling too. I'm not saying Kevin should be Company Commander when we're first-class, but maybe he will be. All I'm saying is that he's crying in the head right now, and he doesn't deserve that. He deserves a break, and I'm here to ask for it. Let him have his party. It's not going to hurt anything if you do, and it might reap benefits for you in the long run."

Stone looked at me appraisingly. Then he smiled, and for a second I thought I had prevailed. "Nice try, Merritt. I'm very impressed you took such a big risk and came to me like this. You're a good leader. But you have to realize that leadership brings responsibilities. I agreed with my classmate to punish O'Reilly, and I'm honor-bound to do that. I also committed myself to immediate action, and now I have to do that too. Sorry, but my decision stands."

I was very disappointed.

"Sir," I said, "several of Kevin's classmates would like to approach Captain Dillingham about delaying or canceling the chit. We'd like your permission to see the Captain in the morning."

"Permission denied!" Stone said quickly. "You know the rules. If you want an audience with the Company Officer you must submit a Special Request Chit through the Chain of Command."

"Sir!" I said, "I will hand-carry one tomorrow morning."

"Maybe you will, Merritt, but I'm very busy tomorrow. I have a full morning of classes. I probably won't see it until the afternoon. Captain Dillingham *will* see the Report Chit first thing in the morning, and the plebe messenger will pick it up for distribution at 0900. By the time he sees your request, the offense will already be posted on the Restriction List. Too bad, but that's the way it's going to be. Now get out of here. I've wasted enough time on plebes tonight, and I have a Thermo test in the morning." I rose slowly and headed for the door.

"Merritt!"

"Sir!"

"Nice try! Very admirable!" I returned to the room.

Rico looked up as I entered. He had the twinkle back in his eye.

"How'd it go with Stone?" he asked.

"How'd you know?"

Rico gave me another of his swami looks.

"Didn't do a bit of good, did it?"

"No," I said turning to Kevin. "I'm sorry."

"Thanks anyway," he said. "You shouldn't have, but thanks."

"What are you going to do?" I asked Kevin.

"I was heading to the phones to tell Sarah, but Rico said not to cancel any arrangements."

I looked at Rico.

"You never know what might happen," he said, "this is the academy, and things are always going wrong." I immediately knew enough not to ask anything further.

The next morning at breakfast I handed my Special Request Chit to Brandis.

"What's this about?" he asked before reading it.

"Sir, Mister Micklewski and Stone have put Kevin on report for a humorous comment he made last night during the lecture. Now Kevin will be missing the Army-Navy party. I want to talk to Captain Dillingham to see if would delay action until after the weekend."

"Those bastards!" Mugsy said loudly. Brandis read the chit slowly. He became angry.

"That's it!" Henry said, slamming the chit down and storming off toward Micklewski's table.

"Cancel that Report Chit, you slimy son-of-a-bitch!" he yelled in Dale's face.

Micklewski smiled. "Not a chance!" he said. "Besides, it wasn't my chit, it was Rock's."

Brandis turned on Stone.

"Cancel that chit!" he demanded. "You have no right to put one of my plebes on report without consulting me!" Stone's smile echoed Micklewski's, and Brandis immediately saw through the ruse.

"You bastard!" he said loudly. "This isn't about O'Reilly. It's about McGinley and me. You just put one of my plebes on report to punish us for not being part of the asinine Tiger program. That's inexcusable, you prick! You haven't heard the last of this!" As he raved, McGinley walked slowly up the aisle and stood smiling behind Micklewski. When Henry finished, Mugsy stooped over next to Micklewski and touched his nose with a beefy finger. He pushed it first from one side then to the other. Micklewski tried to evade the touch, but Mugsy grabbed him by the opposite ear and held his head firmly in place with a muscular arm.

"Stop that!" Micklewski yelled.

Mugsy pushed his nose to the opposite side.

"I'm just trying to see which side your nose will look worse on after I beat the hell out of you. I like it pointed to the right, and that's where I think it'll end up. Of course, there isn't much science to support that conjecture. Maybe I'll consider it my first-class project. *The Physics of Mangled Tiger Cartilage*. Sounds good, huh?"

"Stop this instant, McGinley!" Stone said firmly. Mugsy stopped and turned to Stone. He examined his face critically, moving his head from side to side while Stone eyed him calmly. Rock Stone was clearly unafraid, but I personally thought that was stupid. Finally Mugsy turned to Brandis.

"What do you think, Henry? Do I see an extra-credit assignment here?" Then all semblance of humor and rationality left McGinley. He looked deeply into Stone's eyes.

"You may be master Tiger, Rock-head, and you may be much larger than me; but I am someday soon going to beat you into an unrecognizable pulp. You are a pompous, arrogant, self-important bastard who doesn't know shit about leadership and duty. You deserve the fall that's coming your way. Stand by, Rock, and be afraid, because I'm going to be waiting around some corner where you least expect it; and when I'm finished, Mister Tiger is going to be a pussycat."

"Are you threatening me, McGinley?" Stone asked, still confident.

"Yes!" With that Mugsy stood and returned to his table. I was so focused on the confrontation I hadn't noticed that scores of first-class from neighboring Companies had stood up to listen. Several had wandered to a position directly behind Stone's table. When Mugsy finished his threat, the spectators erupted into loud applause. Several firsties in Twenty-third Company echoed their cheers. Rock Stone looked around, and suddenly he looked terribly alone. His eyes wandered the area and came to rest on me for a long instant. Why the hell he stared at me I don't know.

Mugsy returned to his seat, seemingly unaware of the commotion he had caused. He and Henry Brandis finished their meals as if nothing had happened. I watched as Micklewski and Stone whispered to each other and occasionally glanced in our direction. I could also see Rico unobtrusively leaning toward them to catch every word as he passed food and drink with plebe-like efficiency. At the end of the meal Brandis handed me the signed Request Chit and offered me support in my efforts to stop the atrocity that was happening to Kevin.

At 0900 a plebe messenger visited the Company area to retrieve mail destined for all parts of the Academy. With quiet efficiency he picked up the correspondence from the Captain's out box, put it into a pouch with other mail, and continued on his rounds to the next Company. That was the last anyone admitted seeing Kevin's Report Chit for the next several days. At 1120 just prior to noon meal formation, Stone called the Brigade Discipline Office to see if the information had been posted.

"What chit?" the first-class on duty replied. "We haven't gotten anything from Twenty-third Company since that douchebag Linehan fried ten of our classmates for sleeping in last Wednesday."

"I sent it out this morning, and I need it to be effective immediately," Stone said.

"Well, sorry, but it's not gonna happen. I have to input into the computer system by 1130 today for it to be effective this weekend."

"I'll send another one or a copy directly to you," Stone offered. "You'll have it in five minutes."

"Not a chance!" the firstie replied. "I've got to be at meal formation in ten minutes. So do you. It'll have to wait."

"It can't wait. Pencil the name onto the report for me."

"Stone, you know better than that. If I don't have the *original* form, signed by the initiator and approved by the Company Officer of the offender, my hands are tied." Rock Stone hung up the phone, incensed and intent on revenge. He called the Main Office and asked that the plebe messenger report to him immediately after meal. During the meal Stone and Micklewski engaged in subdued and animated conversation. Neither was particularly happy. BJ, never as bold as the rest of us where eavesdropping was concerned, could not tell us what they discussed.

After meal the messenger and his first-class boss, the Midshipman Officer of the Watch, John Hergenroeder -- Thirtieth Company Commander -- visited Stone in Dillingham's office. The Captain was still out for his usual noontime two-hour workout. Hergenroeder was a muscular and confident firstie who was captain of the Navy lacrosse team. He stood, hands-on-hips as Stone began.

"I asked you here," Stone said, "because this messenger has apparently lost a very important Report Chit I wanted posted today. Now the Disciplinary Office tells me the offender will miss his punishment this weekend."

"So what!" the Hergenroeder exclaimed in a thickly-accented Mid-Eastern slur. "It's Army-Navy, for Christ's sake!"

"I want to know what happened to that chit!"

"Tell the man, Jerry."

"Yes, sir!" the plebe said. "I picked up all the mail for this Battalion area between 0900 and 0930 this morning. There were a couple items in Twenty-third Company box. I put them in the pouch with the rest of the mail, and went on to Twenty-fourth Company."

"Did you stop for any reason during your rounds?" Stone asked.

"Only to visit the head outside Twenty-fourth Company on my way back," the plebe replied.

"What did you do with the mail while you were in the head?" Stone asked.

"I put the pouch on the sink counter until I finished."

"You left the official mail alone while you were in the head?" Stone asked angrily.

"Sir!" I was in the stall. "You don't expect me to take it in there and run the risk of unpleasant damage, do you?"

"What you did was absolutely irresponsible!" Stone stormed. "Did anyone enter the head while you were in the stall?"

"Yes, sir. One person!"

"Could he have tampered with the mail?"

The plebe hesitated. "I don't see how. He was only inside for a minute."

"I'm going to put you on report for your incompetence, mister!" Stone said. "You failed to properly execute your duties and an important document may have been lost."

"Sir?" the plebe began. Hergenroeder raised a hand and smiled.

"You don't even know if the chit was lost yet, Tiger-man. But you go ahead and write whatever you want. I'll make sure Lieutenant Rockwell cancels it. He's not going to let you mess with my Company." Stone stared at Hergenroeder for a long moment.

"Very well," he said. "The case is closed."

On Tuesday of the following week the infamous Report Chit showed up in the Brigade Discipline Office. It was in an envelope which had been marked "Confidential" for routing first to the Laundry Facility, than to the Enlisted Barracks. It certainly hadn't left the Company addressed that way. The Company Firsties blamed the mistake on the Passionate Plebe. I had nothing to do with it.

When Kevin went to the Main Office after class on Friday and found to his absolute delight that his name was not on the Restriction List, he raced back to the room. Catching Rico around the shoulders in a bear hug, he lifted him in the air and twirled around once. He kissed Rico on the cheek noisily.

"It didn't get posted! It didn't get posted! Hot Damn! Party time!" Kevin danced a vigorous jig around the room, moving from desk to desk as we watched, laughing. Stone entered as he was dancing, but Kevin didn't stop.

"The Report Chit didn't get there in time!" he shouted, forgetting completely his earlier promise to keep his mouth shut. "I don't have to restrict!" Stone watched him dance, fascinated, then laughed with the rest of us.

"You are one lucky bastard, O'Reilly!" he said, still smiling. He turned and left.

"I'm Irish, Mr. Stone, sir!" Kevin yelled at the retreating form. "It comes with the territory!"

MAHAN HALL

One of the original structures on the Academy campus. Named after a famous naval historian, Mahan Hall was for years the home of the Academy Library. The famous clock tower serves as a final impetus for haste for midshipmen hurrying to beat the expiration of liberty.

CHAPTER 11

ARMY-NAVY

Final preparations had been made, dates contacted, and hotel reservations confirmed. Excitement was at a level I had never before experienced. Even though plebe training was suspended temporarily, I woke early on Saturday morning, and so did my usually drowsy roommates. We hastened to get ready for the trip and the party afterward, almost giddy at the upcoming prospects. Morning meal -- run mostly by the also-excited second-class since the firsties had been granted liberty starting the previous night and lasting until prior to the game -- was an interesting affair. Many firsties, including Henry and Mugsy, had opted to travel to Philadelphia last evening for a pre-game party and a good shacking-up; although until Friday evening meal it was unclear whether Mugsy would be able to persuade anyone female to go with him.

The youngsters advised us to eat heartily since we might not have another full meal until after the game. The Mess Hall staff must have anticipated this eventuality. I guess if you do something for a hundred years or more you get pretty good at it. There was more than enough food -- even for plebes -- and I ate my fill, and then some. I think Reb Ramsey would have stayed in the Mess Hall eating if we hadn't reminded him of the bus departure schedule.

The Brigade busses were to depart at precisely 0800 from the parking lot at the Field House. Twenty Third Company had been assigned two vehicles from the Annapolis fleet. The Naval Academy owned nearly 50 modern blue and gold buses which they used for precisely this kind of occasion. The words *United States Naval Academy* splashed boldly on each side. The long line was impressive. The only drawback was that the busses had no toilet facilities. That wouldn't be a problem on the trip *to* Philly, since we were sane and sober enough to empty our various bladders before we departed.

Rock Stone, in typical Tiger fashion, had remained behind to guide us. Initially I figured he couldn't get a date. But I saw him briefly after the game accompanied by a stunning young lady. There's no accounting for taste, I suppose. He marched us smartly to the Field House, while the other Companies meandered lazily. We met mostly-good-natured jeers from several groups we passed. Jubal tried to get us started on a rendition of his favorite marching song, but Stone would have none of it. Not so much because the lyrics to *There's a Skeeter on my Peter* are a bit crude -- they are -- but because there were ladies present, coming to work in the various Academy offices, in the Field House, or waiting in their cars to follow the buses to Philly.

It had rained an absolute gully-washing deluge on Friday morning, soaking me on the way to class; but the storm had passed through quickly, and the weather on Saturday was sparklingly clear and brisk. The forecast predicted strong gusty winds and chilly temperatures in the mid-forties. The uniform for the event was Service Dress Blue, with overcoats. I was very pleased. Despite the inconvenience of having to wield the bulky wool coat, it was going to be downright chilly in the stands, far chillier than this Amarillo boy would like.

The two-hour trip to Philly was uneventful. I sat next to BJ, and we both napped on the way. Rico and Kevin sat behind us, giggling while they plotted the party and the ensuing activity. Rico questioned Kevin mercilessly about Sarah Connelly and warned him repeatedly not to get too excited. I could also hear an undercurrent in Kevin's almost arrogantly self-assured replies that did not bode well. There *was* something about this girl that bothered Kevin, and he was not at all confident about what was to happen. I wondered why. It was only a date and party, and he already knew the girl. What possible reason could he have for his discomfort?

The buses parked in military precision in a section of the Veterans' Stadium parking lot reserved for the Naval Academy, -- on the exact opposite side of the stadium from the West Point buses. I often wondered why the Academies went to such great lengths to separate the services. My impression of West Point cadets was that they and we were in the same club, and we each had mutually-evil systemic enemies. I often wanted desperately to take out my frustrations on anti-war protesters, particularly those who focused their hatred on the military, and especially as the Vietnam War death toll mounted, and the civilian leaders of the nation began a cowardly and dishonorable retreat from the conflict. But I couldn't imagine any sane reason to fight a cadet, who in a short period of time might himself face the prospects of his imminent end in a place nobody wanted to be. Those brave souls at West Point were my brothers-in-arms -- except for one Saturday in November each year. Even then the conflict was limited to 22, under-sized and well-protected gladiators, who faced each other across an imaginary line of scrimmage.

Kick-off was set for 1300, and we had arrived at 1030. We would assemble for the march-on at precisely 1200. For the next several minutes we waited in the lee side of the bus for Stone to discover where and how we were to form up. On Wednesday afternoon the entire Brigade had marched to the Academy parade grounds on Worden Field to practice the march-on, but the set-up here was very different and needed a bit extra preparation time so that we could be perfect. Annapolis accepts nothing less than perfection for these evolutions, and it *is* worth the effort.

Several smart food vendors erected stands near the bus area and did a brisk business selling hot dogs, pretzels, and other energy-deficient snack foods to the milling Brigade. Despite my enormous breakfast, I still managed to consume two hot-dogs with the works -- Reb Ramsey ate five. Wildman Kopciak, unable to find any of his plebes to slave for him, made the mistake of ordering Rico to bring him back a hot dog. Wildman gave him just enough money for the one hot dog, thereby violating the sacred "You fly - I'll buy" rule.

"With the works, sir?" Rico asked sweetly.

"Of course with the works, asshole. Just hurry up!"

Rico waited in line with the rest of us, ordering two for himself and one for Wildman. After he got the order, he went to the condiment cart and loaded up the three dogs. He looked carefully around. Satisfied that Wildman's attention was elsewhere, he spit an enormous ball of phlegm onto one of the hot dogs. Kevin and I stood nearby in complete and disgusted shock as he smeared the offensive green slime in with the rest of the gunk. Rico looked at us, smiling.

"Hey! He asked for the works! This is the Brooklyn works!"

O'Reilly almost doubled over with laughter.

"It's a snot-dog now, Rico!" he howled, and we all joined in the joke. Rico handed us *his* two hot dogs and trotted off to Kopciak with the loaded version. Only O'Reilly could watch as Wildman consumed his snot-dog in about five swallows.

"Ah, great!" he said, and Kevin almost wet himself with hilarity. Somehow I never saw Wildman in the same light after that day.

Stone wasn't happy that we had left the bus area to chow down, but since members of every class including fellow Tigers went for food, there wasn't much he could say. At precisely 1200 we assembled in our designated position along with the other 36 companies. Once the Brigade Commander was ready, he ordered us forward. We marched together toward a large vehicle access ramp that led under the stadium proper, and halted when the leading companies were in place. We waited for at least 30 minutes, freezing our butts as a chill wind swirled through that vehicle ramp. The march-on was similar to the ones we did for every football game, except that the hat trick today spelled *GO NAVY* when we faced our stands and *BEAT ARMY* when we faced the Corps of Cadets. I'm told it looks great on TV.

I had never been in a stadium that held as many people as Veterans' Stadium in Philadelphia. The announcer said that more than a hundred thousand fans would attend, and more than several million would watch the game on national TV and on Armed Forces Television. I was impressed. I was not impressed by the cold weather, however. The wind swirled through the stadium, kicking dust continually into my eyes and attacking every vulnerable opening in my overcoat. And my relatively unprotected and still nearly hairless head was completely at the mercy of the chilly blasts. I lost all contact with my ears and nose after a few minutes and fully expected to see them drop frozen at my feet at any second. I groaned several times during the gusts, and so did Reb Ramsey. Kevin and Jeff Polk, rallying around our discomfort, casually mentioned to each other that this was like a spring day in New England. They talked about shedding their coats and trying to get a tan. Had I been able to stop shivering, I would have come up with some witty remark.

Rico and Jeff saved the day by disappearing for several minutes just prior to the kick-off and returning with two large cups of "soda."

"Here Jim," Jeff said with a smile. "Have a little sip of this. It might help take the chill off."

"Ice cold soda to take the chill off? Don't be ridiculous!"

"Take a sip," said Rico with authority. I did; and immediately after I swallowed I felt warmth spreading down my throat to settle gloriously into my stomach. I looked up wide-eyed.

"How did you . . . ?" I began.

"Met an entrepreneur outside the restrooms below. He's doing an incredible business -- probably be a millionaire before half-time." I took another, larger sip.

"I'll bet he will!" We passed the cups among ourselves, and I found the chill rapidly departing. Then I noticed that several upper-class nearby also seemed to be bending over out of sight on a regular basis. With each bending motion, their usually vapid expressions became more stupid.

The stadium filled with fans, and large banners and signs appeared in several places. Army paraded their mule, and a Black Knight on a huge dark horse galloped around the stadium several times.

"Rico!" Kevin said loudly, "pull down your pants and embarrass that horse for us, huh?"

Navy then paraded "Bill the Goat," and immediately afterward the teams entered the field. The fans went wild. Introductions were made, and I was pleased to hear that the Army team was the same midget-size as ours. Good, now maybe we'd see wide-open, run-and-gun, Texas-style football!

Navy won the toss -- which we loudly applauded -- and elected to receive the ball, which was the appropriate decision. Webster's Dictionary defines 'receive" as "to acquire or take." Navy neither acquired nor took the kickoff. Instead the ball slipped between the arms of the returner and bounced off his left knee. He then promptly and accidentally kicked it violently in the process of reaching down to pick it up. The loose ball squirted through both teams in a colossal screw-up reminiscent of the Virginia game, except that this time it came to rest on the Navy forty yard line where it was promptly attacked by 22 players. They pushed and shoved and stretched and dove at the ball, all to no avail. Pile-up after pile-up resulted, but the ball continually squirted loose, thankfully rolling closer to the Army goal line with each manhandling. As the ball wiggled and wobbled and flounced its way farther down field, I had visions of seeing the only touchdown in history to be handled briefly by every player on the field. I expected Bill the Goat to enter the fray at any second, and maybe that guy in the armor too. God, I'll bet he's cold in that outfit.

Sadly history was not made on that play. An Army Cadet recovered the ball on the Army 40-yard line with no intention of letting go. Eventually the referees convinced him -- by repeatedly blowing a whistle in his ear -- that play had stopped and he could give them the ball and get up. He did, and the now elated Army fans sensed something great was about to happen.

Army-Navy football is one of those national pastime things you either love or hate. If you enjoy watching undersized players wearing oversized padding bash into each other in a one-play-only frenzy of grind-it-out up-the-middle battlefield emotion, then you love it. If you enjoy excitement, precision, and masterful play making, tune in another channel, because you're not going to find those things on either the Army or the Navy football teams.

But I was a plebe, so I didn't care whether Navy scored touchdowns by running, passing, or paying off the officials. All I knew was that if those tiny warriors on the field wearing blue and gold scored more points than the identically-sized warriors wearing gray and gold, I could relax for the next three weeks until Christmas leave. To every plebe in Tiger Company the results were life-or-death vital.

I also discovered as soon as play began that except for the gray uniforms Army could have been coached by the Navy staff. I suspect in a cost cutting measure the two academies must have shared playbooks and probably players as well. Army tried three unsuccessful runs up the middle, and punted. What a surprise! Thankfully the Navy returner called for a fair catch, which he made. Navy started its first drive on it's 30-yard line.

Three unsuccessful runs up the middle later, Navy punted, and Army started their second drive on their 36. Three unsuccessful runs up the middle later, Army punted and Navy started their second drive on their 33. I could now see the ingenious strategy each coach was using. We had gained three yards by punt exchange. If every drive started that much closer to pay-dirt, eventually we would start a drive in the other team's end zone. There'd be no need to even run a play. Automatic touchdown! Brilliant!

Then I made a quick mental calculation. If every exchange gained three yards, it would take 22 more punts to score. I doubt that 22 punts are close to the Army-Navy record; but if each exchange took three minutes, it would take us 66 minutes to get to the endzone, and the game lasted only 60 minutes. I wondered if the coaching staff had made a similar calculation, and I thought about sending them a quick note with my calculations on it, but fate interceded. On their fourth series of up-the-middles an Army runner mistakenly cut away from the impending pile of tacklers and ran sideways around the end. I'm sure this upset both teams. Now players had to chase the runner, and the would-be tacklers.

The runner cleared the line and turned upfield, not to find the customary pile of miniature humanity waiting to pounce but rather to face an empty field. The runner, unaccustomed to open fields, hesitated -- and that's what almost killed him. An unhappy Navy defensive lineman slammed into him from the side and drove him flying out of bounds. If it wasn't for the players standing on the sidelines to bring him to earth, he would have come to rest until at about the sixth row of theupper deck.

Despite the fact that the play gained more than the customary yard-and-a-half, Army learned their lesson and reverted to the up-the-middle offense, which seemed to satisfy both teams. Near half-time the Army strategy actually paid off. A runner finally burst through the middle and scored untouched on a 40-yard run. Army took a 7 to 0 lead into the locker room, and deep depression descended on the plebe contingent of Annapolis. I took several rapid "sips," and Kevin and Reb went for more cold "soda." By the end of half-time, after watching the Annapolis Drum and Bugle Corps toot and poot its usual loud and brassy routine, I almost didn't care who won.

Navy thought they would confuse Army in the second half by changing from the three-runs-up-the-middle-and-a-punt offense to a two-runs-up-the-middle-and-a-wobbly-pass-out-of-bounds offense. Surprisingly it worked, but only because one of the wobbly passes -- clearly aimed at a popcorn vendor in the upper section -- actually hung up in a gust of wind and fell into the surprised arms of a Navy receiver who quickly looked at his coaches for "coaching." As in the Virginia game, clever and articulate use of the "F-Word" could be heard clearly as it reverberated its way up throughout the stadium, and the startled player ran like hell -- in the right direction. The score was tied 7 to 7. I could smell carry-on like a piece of raw and ripe carrion waiting for the predators. I began to salivate in anticipation. We had to win this game!

If I had a weapon that afternoon, I would have gladly killed every player on Army's team one-by-one to allow Navy the opportunity to put a single additional point on the board. But I had serious doubts, even with every Army player dead, whether the five minutes remaining would allow enough time for Navy to get a first-down, much less actually score.

Then all my fears disappeared as Navy actually played decent football, much to the chagrin of the coaching staff. They ran right, they ran left, they passed, they lateraled, and they did delay traps. They even ran a pass play I thought we had invented at Sam Houston High School in Amarillo, the Double-L cut. Jeff Rightman masterfully moved the ball down the field, and Navy scored a field goal with two minutes remaining. Navy was ahead 10 to 7, and I discovered that I had an enormous erection. Such was my inebriation that I almost considered showing Rico and Kevin.

Army received the kickoff and ran it back to their 44- yard line. I didn't like that at all -- 30 yards would put them in field goal range. Then Army ran right and left and lateraled, and I became firmly convinced the two teams shared coaches and playbooks. Army moved the ball expertly, eating up the clock as they marched downfield to the 50, Navy's 43, the 36, and the 30 on four consecutive plays. Less than a minute remained. It was clear they were playing for a tie. Two runs up the middle centered the ball on the 25-yard line with 20 seconds remaining. Suddenly everything seemed lost. Army then threw the mandatory wobbler -- which the popcorn vendor caught one-handed -- and now the lives and well-being of more than 2,000 plebes depended on what Army's field goal kicker -- a fellow with the strange name of Arlo Puthper -- would do in the next several seconds.

That Arlo was a country boy was evident by the bold tattoo on his right forearm of a heart with the word "ma'am" emblazoned therein, and by the six wheat shoots he was chewing as he lined up. And anyone with that many flies buzzing around his head on a cold late November day had to be from somewhere in the Deep South. But that wasn't important. All that mattered was the kick he would send between the center of the uprights for a disastrous tie; a kick that would be followed by three weeks of painful comearounds to the biggest assholes on the planet. I was so frustrated I wanted to kill someone. Arlo would be a good place to start.

I hated Arlo as he stood back, confidently sucking on the wheat shoot and waiting for the snap. I hated Arlo as the ball spiraled perfectly to the holder. I hated Arlo as he rapidly approached the now-perfectly-sited spheroid. Arlo also kicked straight-on -- the old style -- which I also hated. Blasts of hate bombarded Arlo, and I'll bet they weren't all mine. Then it happened.

At first I though that somehow my hate-blasting had developed a manifest physical energy that was going to devour Arlo and every other Army hillbilly -- excuse me, comrade-in-arms. Today meteorological scientists would call what happened next a "microburst," a short, intense blast of air, often occurring in advance of a storm front but possible in any unsettled atmospheric condition. It was a hell of a micro-burst! Arlo kicked directly into a dark and gritty wall of dust, debris, banners, soda cans, and small terrified children. The ball didn't even reach the front line before the wind drove it brutally back, along with both teams of players. Referees dove to the earth, thinking a tornado had come to Veterans' Stadium, and praying, I'm sure, that they didn't wake up to Munchkin music. By the time anyone had sense enough to check, the wind had died and the clock showed the game to be over. And that was fine with me!

Later that week the ABC producers of the game, at the behest of the NCAA, spliced together film from every camera whose operator had not fled outright at the time the wall of air descended. Using a primitive computer simulation, they were able to show that the ball, sucked up into the vortex of the micro-burst, probably exited the stadium about Section BB. Where it came to rest was complete speculation. In theory, since complete confirmation of the whereabouts of that ball are still unknown, the game never really ended. Knowing how cruel it would be to the two Academies -- and the fans and TV audience -- to continue or replay the contest, the NCAA wisely called it a Navy victory.

I watched the scene speechlessly. The wind ended as suddenly as it had begun. Players picked themselves up off the turf and brushed dust, paper, and other players, from their uniforms. A referee somewhere on the field blew a whistle, and the game was over. I looked at Kevin, who was also mute. The Navy band played *Navy Blue and Gold*. We sang loudly, and that was that. We hugged each other.

Kevin, who was somewhat giddy and maybe a bit under the influence at the moment, looked around carefully, then bent way over in his seat and yelled as loudly as he could, "I'll bet this pisses the 'Tigers' off!" No one cared. Our beloved little warriors -- with the timely aid of a small tornado -- had defeated the evil Army machine. We laughed together joyously, and began the descent of the stadium to find our dates.

We had purchased tickets for the girls together in the same section and row and asked them to get acquainted. They were going to be spending the next evening together in rather familiar proximity. They would meet us outside the stadium adjacent to their section. They were ready and waiting when we arrived. I was "ready" and completely sober the instant I saw Leslie.

I recognized her immediately. Her long dark hair streamed out from under a blue and gold Naval Academy souvenir wool cap. She wore a tan wool overcoat, thick stockings, heavy gloves, and a huge dark-brown scarf. Covered as she was, I could see the outlines of her magnificent shape calling to me underneath. She saw me almost simultaneously and stood quickly on tip-toes to wave vigorously in my direction. Her smile warmed me more than the "soda." I picked up the pace.

Leslie was surrounded by other girls. I recognized Rico's Rosa immediately. No one could fail to do so. Like Leslie she was dark complexioned; but Rosa Castillo was Hispanic-dark, and her hair was curly black and sparkly as night. Rosa's eyes also matched the dusky darkness, and her thick and pouty lips were splashed with bright and inviting red. She was tall, incredibly long-legged, and built marvelously to match. She was the second most beautiful woman on the planet.

Jeff's girlfriend, Kate Durban was also there. In contrast to Leslie and Rosa, Kate was a petite clear-complexioned blond, whose long hair matched Leslie's in length and straight style and whose deep blue eyes complemented her perky facial features. I had heard him talk about her often. From what Jeff said, it seemed she was sweet, but very intense about life and politics: a perfect match for Jeff.

I also noticed Sara Bradley, Tommy Poole's girl. She was a brown-haired, brown-eyed intellectual from Flint, Michigan, who was presently on a scholarship to Vassar. She wore glasses and no make-up. She admired Tommy greatly.

There were three girls in the group I didn't recognize. The light-haired girl with the big smile standing close to Leslie must be BJ's date, Jennifer Taylor. The brown-haired girl off to one side matched up with Reb's description of his High School flame, Martha. The third one, who had to be Kevin's mysterious Sarah Connelly, was a striking enigma, and I was immediately taken aback as I looked at her. She was not at all what I expected.

Sarah was the tallest and most developed of the group. She jutted forward provocatively, even from within the heavy overcoat she wore. She had shoulder-length brown hair with lighter hints that sparkled in the sun. Her complexion was pale and reddened by the weather. She had the barest hint of freckles, and even from a distance I could see that her eyes were a green-brown color. And those eyes were fixed boldly, possessively on Kevin O'Reilly. She smiled, and the smile promised adventure, and something else I couldn't define. She was one determined young lady, and now I began to understand.

"Rico!" Kevin said suddenly, drawing backward slightly. "I'm scared!"

"I understand, Kevin," Rico answered. I did too. Some girls are sweet and lovely and you want to be near them -- like Jeff's Kate. Kevin's Sarah was pretty, but she wasn't beautiful. Other women exude erotic magnetism -- like Rico's Rosa. Sarah was robustly sexual rather than overtly sensual. Some few women can make men dream of children and futures and quiet and contented old age, and infinity -- that's my Leslie. Sarah Connelly was not so "innocent" and home-town as Kevin had portrayed. Her body promised passion. She seemed almost overpowering. And I had no doubt she would steal a man's soul gladly. And she wanted Kevin's soul. Kevin was in deep trouble if he didn't watch himself. Had Rico foreseen this?

These observations happened in the space of a few seconds as we hurried up to meet our ladies. Rico didn't hesitate or worry for an instant about PDA. He grabbed Rosa and delivered a kiss that warmed the air as far away as Annapolis. I stared at my beautiful Leslie for an instant, holding her hands at arms length and drinking in her beauty.

"Hello, beautiful," I said softly. She smiled, melting me from the inside out. I drew her into my arms and time stopped.

Finally Leslie whispered to me.

"We have to introduce ourselves, silly." We separated and faced the others. Rico was still kissing Rosa. Jeff and Kate, and Tommy and Sara, and Reb and Martha were chatting quietly but amiably nearby. BJ had already introduced himself to Jennifer, who was obviously impressed by his striking handsomeness and absolute charm.

Kevin and Sarah faced each other silently but intently. Sarah smiled devilishly and offered Kevin her hand to shake. She offered it bent-elbowed almost directly in front of her large chest. Kevin couldn't miss the signal. Kevin stared slightly down as he held her hand tightly. Sarah laughed and locked her eyes on Kevin. Kevin smiled and by force of will averted his eyes so that they looked down at the asphalt parking lot underfoot. He shifted his weight from side to side like a little kid.

"Isn't she something, Jim Merritt?" Leslie asked as she snuggled against me.

"Rosa? Yes she is."

"Not Rosa, silly. Sarah Connelly. I've never seen anyone so brazen. Stay away from her."""

I turned to Leslie.

"No, no! You are much more beautiful! She has no effect on me at all."

"You're sweet," she said. "But that young lady is magnetic. I can see all of you young men looking at her and wondering things. She'll be hard for poor Kevin to handle. But . . . " Leslie lowered her voice to a whisper, " . . . she seems to have set her sights on Mister O'Reilly. She told us she's had a crush on him since she was seven years old and he pulled her hair one day in first grade. I hope your friend Kevin is good ready for her."

I looked at Kevin and Sarah and laughed.

"I don't think whatever happens from this point on is up to Kevin."

Leslie laughed with me.

"I think you're right, Jim Merritt."

We made a quick round of introductions, and decided to get to the hotel and clean up for dinner. Leslie had brought her car, as had Sara Bradley. The girls had met before the game and loaded their things into the two trunks. Tommy, Reb, and Jeff piled into Sara's car with their dates. They would find a liquor store and bring the refreshments. The rest of us went to Leslie's late-model Plymouth.

"I think Kevin should drive," said Rico. "After all, he's the leader of the group, and he's got the best sense of direction." He said it with such conviction that no one questioned him. I knew immediately that Rico said this to ensure he wasn't separated for an instant from lovely Rosa. Rico also knew that Kevin enjoyed the leadership position.

Kevin accepted the assignment with authority, and soon we headed slowly toward downtown, plodding stop-and-start in post-game traffic. Sarah sat in the middle of the front seat between Kevin and BJ. Rico and Rosa huddled together in a corner of the back seat. They didn't come up for air the entire trip. Leslie sat on my lap in the opposite corner, and we kissed and chatted with BJ and Jennifer. Twice I saw Sarah Connelly touch Kevin electrically on the hair and make a quiet veiled comment that caused him to laugh while his neck reddened perceptibly. Poor Kevin. He was in for it.

After a quick stop at a convenience store for snack food, we drove into the downtown area. The Sheraton was easy to find. It took up an entire block and exuded all the splendor of a European palace. We pulled in the valet parking area, and BJ exited quickly.

"Stay here! Let me handle this," he said confidently, and he strode up to the bell captain.

I don't know what he said, but the hotel staff reacted instantly. Bellhops raced for the trunk and the doors, and a senior hotel staffer miraculously appeared in the doorway.

"Mister Wilson?" he asked offering a hand. BJ accepted it. He had now assumed a personality I had only glimpsed briefly in the months I had known him. He knew how to wield power over "lesser" people.

"Mister Geist," he said. "Mom and Dad were absolutely delighted that you offered us this opportunity to relax after such a long time away from the bright lights of a big city. You can't imagine how much they appreciate this enormous favor."

Geist brightened.

"It was the least I could do for the son of two such wonderful people," he replied. It all seemed so shallow that I briefly wondered if they believed their own words. But we had a hotel room and a place to have a great time, and I had my Leslie on my arm. Stand-by, world!

The staff was effusive in its efforts to please. The suites were enormous and the beds silk-sheeted and inviting. We divided into groups, agreeing to meet in the central room in an hour for dinner. I helped Leslie take her bag to "our" room. Within five minutes our naked bodies were cocooned in silky smoothness. Leslie and I made love so passionately and all-consumingly in the next half hour that it actually brought tears to my eyes. Afterward we held each other tightly, drinking deeply the feel of each others' nakedness. Then we showered together -- something I instantly and eternally liked -- and dressed for dinner.

Leslie wore a simple black evening dress with green buttons and trim that almost exactly matched her eyes. I watched her as she dressed, realizing that I had never watched a woman get herself ready before. I was fascinated. The process was even more exacting and elaborate than our preparations for noon meal inspection, but the results were incredible. She *was* the most beautiful woman on the planet. God, was I lucky!

Except for Rico, the others were ready as planned. We met in the central sitting room.

"Where's Rico?" BJ asked impatiently. Kevin laughed.

"Where do you think?"

"Well, we have a reservation in ten minutes," BJ reminded us. "We shouldn't be late after all the trouble the hotel has gone through."

Kevin stood.

"I'll get him," he said, and he left the room. Leslie looked at Sarah Connelly.

"You look lovely, Sarah," she said. I could tell immediately after we entered that Sarah was uncomfortable. Leslie, Martha, and Jennifer were exquisitely and expensively dressed. Sara and Kate had chosen their stylish dresses carefully. Sarah Connelly, while not out of place, had chosen an understated light cotton blouse -- slightly tight to accentuate her breasts, -- a dark green skirt, -- also slightly tight -- and a long-sleeved navy blue sweater. Despite the simplicity of her dress, she really was something to look at, and she stared boldly at Kevin as he departed.

Kevin returned in a minute, leading Rico and Rosa, who made the grand entrance. Conversation stopped instantly. I could hear BJ and Jennifer suck in quick breaths. Even my heart sputtered for an instant. Rosa wore a low-cut black dress that hung on her shoulders so precipitously it seemed at any instant it was going to fall to one side, revealing the deliciousness underneath. The dress was also short enough to expose a great many inches of long and unbelievably sensual leg and tight enough to accentuate the curves of her thighs and derriere. Her make-up consisted of bold deep brown swaths under her eyebrows, and an incredible, moist slash of bright red on her sensual mouth. She was a knockout.

Rico, despite the fact that he wore a uniform identical to ours, was even more of a knockout. He had chosen to unbutton his jacket and loosen his tie, but he had tightly tucked his shirt, revealing the taught musculature and narrow waist underneath. His black wavy hair, which he had grown slightly beyond the regulation two inches, fell onto his forehead in several thick, wayward clumps.

"Sorry we're a little late, guys," Rico said, smiling charmingly, "but Rosa had some last minute adjustments to make."

"Yeah, sure, wise guy!" Rosa replied in her thick Brooklyn accent and poking Rico in the ribs. "Especially after you messed up my make-up when we were ready to leave."

Rico laughed.

"I couldn't help it, Babe. You know what you do to me."

We made it to the dining room on time, and BJ again handled the choreography. He was exceptionally good at this sort of thing, and I could tell that Jennifer was suitably impressed. It was going to be a good evening for BJ.

The service was excellent. BJ ordered wine. The waitress hesitated.

"I'm sorry, but could I see some identification please?" BJ smiled charmingly.

"No need to check. Mister Geist will vouch for everyone in the party."

"He will?" she asked skeptically.

"Please feel free to inquire with him," BJ said smiling diplomatically, and the waitress left.

"We can skip the wine if it's gonna get ya'll in trouble," Reb offered. BJ smiled but said nothing, and the waitress returned almost immediately.

"How many bottles of the Chateau Lafette was that again?" she asked.

The food was exquisite. Conversation was stimulating. And everyone had a great time.

Near the end of the meal while we were all eating a decadent chocolate cheesecake, Rico looked over at Leslie and asked, "So tell me, Leslie, when did you and Jim meet exactly?" I gave Rico a look, but he ignored me.

"Why, Jim Merritt and I met in Annapolis on Saturday, October 12th," she answered sweetly. "I'll never forget that date."

"I see," said Rico. "And have you seen each other very often since then?"

"Only on two marvelous evenings. The Academy restricts its freshman terribly, you know."

"Tell me about it," replied Rico. "Would you happen to remember if the last evening you saw Jim Merritt was the second of November?"

Before I could intervene, she answered, but her voice was a little troubled.

"Why yes it was. Hasn't Jim Merritt ever told you about meeting me?" I frowned. Now Rico had me in trouble.

"Jim Merritt is a very private person, as you know," Rico answered. "All he said was that he had met someone very special whom we would meet today." Leslie brightened. Rico's lie had saved the day, but I still glared at him. He smiled, and white teeth flashed at me.

Then Kevin jumped in.

"November the second, huh? Wasn't it cold out on the sea-wall?" He said that last part with enough emphasis to reveal that he suspected things he was not yet ready to reveal but would use against me later if he could.

"It's never cold with Jim Merritt around," Leslie said sweetly, and I had to smile at her.

"Enough questions about us, guys," I jumped in. "Kevin, tell me about you and Sarah. Where have you been hiding this extraordinary creature?" Sarah beamed boldly and Kevin blushed. She truly realized her power, and so did Kevin, and he was confused.

"Sarah and I have been schoolmates since the first grade in parochial school. Then we went to partner catholic high schools in Boston."

"You went to high schools that were only all-boys and all-girls?" asked Rosa.

"Yes," replied Sarah. "That's the way it's done."

Rosa turned to Rico and shook her head.

"I'm glad I did not do that, Rico dear. I couldn't stand it, and neither could you."

"I think Rico would find a way around the restriction," blurted Kevin. Rico and Rosa laughed.

"Kevin," Rosa said. "I think you're right."

"When did you two start dating, Kevin?" asked Kate. Kevin looked at Sarah uncomfortably, and she swiveled in her chair slightly and put a hand on his arm. Her blouse stretched provocatively. Then she zinged him with a flash of brown eyes and a knowing smile.

"I never told him this," Sarah began boldly, "but I've always had a crush on Kevin -- ever since the first grade. He was such a wild one. Never did his homework. Always in trouble. Always asking embarrassing questions of the nuns. And in high school I thought I'd die every time he played basketball." She reached up and touched Kevin on the cheek, and I knew it was all over for Kevin. It really seemed cute to me. I looked at Rico, and he was scowling fiercely. Something about the Kevin-Sarah thing was bothering him. What was going on?

"Well Miss Sarah Connelly," Rosa said lightly. "I'm mad at you because I fell in love with Kevin O'Reilly when we met in August. If it wasn't for my sexy Rico here, you would have fierce competition." She laughed. "And we Puerto Ricans play for keeps."

Small talk continued until we had finished the desert and coffee, after which, we left.

"I'll put the meal on the room tab, and we can settle up on the way out," BJ said.

The hotel provided ample quantities of aperitifs and mixers, as well as a large fruit basket in each suite. We had previously packed the beer into the refrigerators in the central sitting rooms. BJ brought out the rum and scotch he had bought. Kevin opened several bags of chips and pretzels. After a minute, we assembled in the now-crowded sitting room of the central suite, adding as many chairs from other rooms as we could, but Tommy and Sara, and Jubal and Martha sat on the floor. Leslie and I shared a couch with BJ and Jennifer. Kevin and Sarah sat in separate, but touching chairs across the room. Rico sat next to me in an oversized arm chair with lovely Rosa on his lap. We tuned the radio to a local rock-and-roll station.

I heard Rosa whisper in his ear, "What's wrong Toro Grande?" Rico didn't answer, but I saw him watching Kevin and Sarah, and he didn't like what he saw. Sarah had removed her sweater. She was clearly the most developed woman present. As I watched, she leaned away from Kevin to talk to Jeff, who sat next to her. Turning, she had pointed her legs in his direction so that they almost touched his. Jeff noticed. So did Kate. She laughed in a not-entirely-innocent way at something Jeff said, and leaned across Jeff toward Kate to make a comment. As she did so, her breasts jutted outward. I found myself watching her, fascinated, and wondering what it would be like to . . .

"Jim Merritt?" Leslie whispered to me sweetly. "Now do you see what I mean about that Sarah girl?" I brought my attention back to Leslie, embarrassed, and we talked to each other quietly.

"Kevin!" Rico asked a moment later. "Do me a favor. I think I left my wallet in Leslie's car. Would you get it for me?"

"Hey Rico! You can do that yourself."

"Of course I can, Kevin. But who can get down there and back faster than the wonder-mid? You don't want me to miss any party time do you?" Kevin looked at Rico for a long moment. He knew something was up. A silent signal flashed between them, and he also knew he had to go. He patted Sarah on the arm lightly and smiled.

"I'll be right back," he said.

Leslie looked at me uncertainly. I nodded, and she reached into her purse and handed Kevin her car keys. Kevin hurried from the room.

After general talk resumed, Rico said, "Could Jim and I talk to you a moment, Sarah? Let's go some place private." Rico rose and so did Sarah, but I could see inquisitiveness on her face. She looked at Rico, then at Rosa. I had no idea what was up, but I rose also.

"Can I come, dear one?" asked Rosa. Rico thought for a moment.

"Sure. Why not? You too, Leslie." We followed Rico, who strode resolutely to he and Rosa's room. The bed was an absolute mess, and I could guess why.

Rico was suddenly businesslike. I had never seen him like this before, and I was interested in what he intended.

"Sarah," he said, "sit down, please." Sarah walked slowly to the chair he indicated and sat demurely. She seemed to have suddenly lost her sexual appeal, and for some reason I felt sorry for her. I didn't know why. Rico pulled a chair over until it was directly in front of Sarah's, and he sat facing her. Their knees touched. He reached out and took both her hands in his. I was really interested now, but Rosa didn't seem the least concerned. She watched Rico intently, a slight smile on her beautiful mouth. Leslie looked at me, but I shrugged in reply.

"Sarah," Rico began, seriously. "I apologize for sending Kevin away and for getting you out of the room like this, but we have to talk." Sarah looked at him strangely, and silently looked at each of us. She seemed small and vulnerable. I smiled and shrugged encouragement.

"I don't know how to say this, Sarah," Rico continued. "But let me start by saying that Kevin O'Reilly is the truest friend I have ever had. He is a top quality person, the best -- but you already know that, don't you?" Sarah nodded, smiling slightly and still seemingly unsure of what was happening.

"It seems like you really like Kevin, I can tell that." Sarah nodded sweetly, then blushing, looked down into her lap. She seemed almost virginal.

"But I can't let you ruin him. And that's exactly what's going to happen."

I heard Leslie suck in a breath. Sarah flushed red, but a different shade of red from a moment ago. She was angry. Her brown eyes flashed.

"How can you say that?" she said loudly. "I love Kevin. I have for years."

Rico squeezed Sarah's hands even though she wanted him to let go.

"If you really care for Kevin, then listen to me for a moment, okay?" She calmed and nodded suspiciously, staring at Rico as if he were an alien from another world.

"Kevin O'Reilly is gonna graduate from Annapolis and be one of the best officers the Navy has ever seen. He's gonna fly jets and lead troops and go the extra mile better than anyone ever. That's the way he is." Rico softened his tone. "He'll also be a great husband and father. He won't forget a birthday or anniversary. He'll never be unfaithful. He'll join PTA and coach kids sports teams. Sarah nodded, still staring at her lap. This was quite a speech.

"But, Sarah. You and Kevin are very different -- maybe too different. He's always going to be innocent and vulnerable. And you don't know who you are yet. You have a great many worlds -- and men -- to conquer, and you don't really know what you want or who you want to be with. Kevin wants to be tied down; you can't be.

"Once Kevin decides he's in love with you, he's gonna want to quit this place and marry you and have hundreds of redheaded babies. And that's gonna kill his dream, and he'll go through life always wondering 'what if.' I predict Kevin is gonna walk on the moon someday, but needs to be free to do that." Rico smiled his best killer smile.

Sarah Connelly looked closely at Rico. Suddenly I could see she was sizing him up. She straightened slightly, and her chest swelled. Rico noticed, but didn't react. Instead he stared into her eyes, waiting. Sarah paused a moment, then became demure again.

"What am I supposed to do?" she asked in a near-whisper. "I really like Kevin." She started to cry. I almost cried too. I had never seen such a range of emotion from one person before. I was fascinated and enthralled and enticed.

"Look at me, Sarah," Rico said gently, and she looked up at him. Tears glistened in her eyes. Then she looked directly at me. She seemed so vulnerable I wanted to stand in front of her and protect her. I was sure that was what she wanted. Rico would probably say something hurtful, and that wasn't fair. I leaned in toward her, preparing somehow to act, and Leslie nudged me gently. I glanced at Leslie and she shook her head negatively. Sarah's spell over me snapped, and I relaxed. Wow! Was this purposeful, or didn't Sarah realize what she could do to a man when she wanted? O'Reilly would never stand a chance, I could see that now. Rico continued, still seemingly unaffected by Sarah's charms.

"Go back to the room and party with Kevin. Make love to him later if you want. But Kevin's got to wait four more years before he can think about a family. You have power over him now, and if you give him more than your company, you're gonna have even more power. Don't make him give up his dream. I'll fight you if I have to win him back. Do you understand me, Sarah?"

Sarah nodded twice. Rico stood and helped Sarah to her feet, then he hugged her tenderly and kissed her on the forehead. "Let's go back to the party. I'll tell everybody I found my wallet."

Before we left the room, Sarah looked from Leslie to Rosa and back again.

"Do you think I should?" she asked in an almost distracted tone.

"What's that?" Rosa asked.

"You know. Make love to Kevin."

"Why not! Love him, girl," Rosa said laughing loudly. "As often as you can. But be careful, because I still think he's cute as can be."

"Gentlemen," Leslie said. "We need a few minutes to "fix" ourselves. We'll be back in a minute." With that Rico and I departed.

"What do you think?" I asked Rico as he walked slowly back to the room.

"Same as you," he answered. "I'm dying to see what's inside her blouse." I started to protest, but he waved my comment aside. "Sarah Connelly is a very complicated person," he continued, "she has incredibly manipulative power, and she's using that power to trap Kevin. If Kevin falls into the trap, I don't know if he'll be able to hold out."

Rico suddenly stopped and turned to me.

"And I want to talk to you later," he said.

"What about?"

"This girl Leslie is great. She's a "keeper" and she's in love with you. You shouldn't be messing with her like you did with Lynda."

"Hey!" I said. "I didn't 'mess' with Lynda." Rico only stared at me disgustedly. "I couldn't help what happened," I said in weak self defense.

"That's bullshit! You can always help what happens."

I paused, taken aback. "You're right, Rico. And I'm truly sorry about Lynda. But what about you and Rosa?"

"Rosa knows what it's like with me. We have a relationship, but we're each free to see whoever we like until it's time to decide on a permanent commitment. Once I marry -- no more strange women for me." He looked wistfully at the far wall and laughed. "Unless I can get a job for one of those glossy magazines -- then only in the line of duty." I laughed too. I had to admit that Rico was right. I had been unfair to Lynda, and I decided to be honest with her when I saw her over the Thanksgiving holiday.

Everyone looked at us strangely when we entered. Kevin had already returned.

"Christ, wonder-mid!" Rico exclaimed. "You really are fast."

"No wallet, Rico," Kevin said.

"It's okay. I found it." He winked. "It was hidden deep in the folds of the bed covers. I wonder how it got there?" Everybody laughed. The ladies returned only seconds later, and Sarah looked even more desirable. She went directly to Kevin and sat on his lap.

"Find the wallet, wonder-mid?" she asked only part innocently. Kevin laughed, put an arm around her, and soon the party continued full swing. We moved all the chairs out of the room to dance.

I discovered Rico and Rosa were ballroom-equivalent dancers. They swirled around the small room, avoiding tables, chairs and bodies expertly, showing off their style *and* Rosa's incredible legs. It was a thrill to watch them, and we all applauded when they finished, almost too tired to stand!

I also found out that very different people sometimes lurk behind the outward personalities of even close acquaintances. With a few beers under his belt, Tommy Poole was a different person from the timid bookworm he usually projected. He told jokes, some of which were boldly off-color. He and Sara sang their high school fight song with gusto and in harmony. And he did perfect bladder-busting imitations of Stone, Micklewski, and Dillingham. Jeff Polk, on the other hand, became solemn and morose and frequently lamented the state of the country and its moral lack of direction, despite the fact that Kate continually shushed him quiet.

Leslie and I talked and sipped mixed drinks as we watched the others. Kevin was obviously nervous and displayed a tendency to drink too much too fast. Leslie whispered that I should cut Kevin off after he spilled a drink while balancing Sarah precariously on his lap. Remembering the stories of his puddle in front of Tecumseh, I nodded and slipped across the room. I removed the new drink from beside him. He didn't notice because he was too busy staring into Sarah's deep brown eyes -- and at other prominent places. I substituted a soda in an identical glass with ice. I didn't think he'd care. Sarah saw what I was doing and winked at me as she drank deeply from her own glass.

The party continued unabated until 2200, the unofficial time we had decided to reserve for "other activities." Rico and Rosa quietly slipped away first, followed by BJ and Jennifer. That devil didn't waste a minute. I watched Kevin. I could see he wanted to suggest a departure but was too tongue-tied to ask Sarah.

"Kevin," Sarah said sweetly but provocatively, "would you come with me to see if the thermostat is set correctly in my room. I had trouble with it before." Kevin jumped on that cue perfectly. His smile lit up the room, and soon they were missing. I looked at Leslie and didn't speak. We left the rest of the partiers.

When we entered the sitting room of our suite, we could hear a commotion going on in BJ and Jennifer's room. Apparently Jennifer was a screamer, and she was screaming mightily. Leslie looked at me and giggled.

"Do I sound like that, Jim Merritt?" I laughed and gently steered her into our room.

We undressed each other slowly, savoring the removal of each item. Leslie was lovely and so sensual. We stood pressed against each other, making love that way for several delicious minutes.

"Does this feel good, Jim Merritt," she asked huskily.

"My God, does it ever!" I moaned.

"Good," she said. I was never so happy in my life.

After a few long and wonderful minutes I nudged her toward the bed. Within seconds we lost complete awareness of who and where we were. It felt as if every ounce of energy in my entire system released in an instant.

We lay sweetly in each others' arms, talking and laughing quietly until I had to go. I told her to stay in bed and rest rather than get up and see me to the door. I bent over her contented form and kissed her long and lingeringly before I left.

"I love you Leslie Taylor Wallace," I whispered.

"I love you too, James Wesley Merritt."

We met in the central sitting room -- Rico was there on time -- and descended to the lobby loudly and boisterously. BJ again took charge. He thanked Mr. Geist profusely for his hospitality, and settled the dinner bill, which came to a surprising $10.56 each including five bottles of Chateau Lafette. I didn't complain.

"Wow!" Tommy said. "That's an incredible price for 14 dinners plus wine and deserts."

"No shit, genius boy!" Rico observed. "The hotel probably subsidized about a three hundred percent share."

"Why would they do that?" a still-puzzled Tommy asked. Apparently alcohol could dull the great Poole brain.

"Because," Rico said patiently. "BJ probably promised Geist a guest shot in an episode of *Bonanza* -- and maybe kinky sex with Miss Kitty."

"Is that right?" Tommy asked BJ.

"Well, I figured Geist out right away," BJ replied. "Festus is more his type."

The hotel also drove the seven of us to the stadium parking lot in its stretch limousine, which impressed everyone but BJ. The driver, a thin, elderly black man, watched us as he drove.

"Okay," Rico said to the group as we departed. "Time for a 'Stud check'! How many midshipmen in this car had sex with their girlfriends this evening?" Rico and BJ immediately and proudly raised their hands. Jeff and Tommy followed suit. "Poole, you stud!" Rico shouted and reached over to shake Tommy's hand. Tommy was proud to have joined the club. Rico looked at me. "Merritt, you asshole. I know you did it because I could hear you all the way from my room." The driver laughed.

"That was me, Rico," BJ interrupted proudly.

"You're probably going to have to have those scratches disinfected," Rico observed. Then he looked at Reb.

"Not sayin'. Ain't polite!" Ramsey stated firmly, but with a smile.

"You don't have to say. It's written all over your face." He looked at Kevin, who was quiet.

"Well?" he asked

Kevin smiled.

"Maybe," he said.

Rico addressed the group again. "Who did it more than once?" He and BJ were the only ones who raised their hands. Rico looked at Kevin.

"Maybe," Kevin answered, his smile broader. The driver laughed again.

"Okay," Rico said. "Who had sex in any of the positions that might get prison time?" I had no idea what he was asking, but Rico raised his hand boldly.

Kevin also raised his hand quietly. He was smiling. "I think I rate the death penalty in Texas." Everyone laughed.

Rico looked narrowly at Kevin.

"O'Reilly," he said, "we have to talk tomorrow."

When the limo pulled into the parking lot near the buses and seven plebes got out, it caused quite a stir. A steady stream of midshipmen arrived, checked in with the duty section, and walked to the waiting vehicles. Buses departed as soon as they filled.

We hurried on board and settled ourselves near the middle. The driver counted heads, and soon we pulled away. The drive didn't last long, however. Less than ten seconds later the driver stopped in the dark under several old gnarly trees at the exit from the parking lot. He stood and faced us.

"Okay!" he shouted, Marine Corps style, and I knew instantly we were facing a retired gunny sergeant. "I want every one of you to get off the bus right now and empty your bladders but good over there by those trees. I don't care if your pecker freeze and drop off. Orders are I cannot stop on the way back because last year several midshipmen passed out in the grass at a rest stop and didn't get back until late the next day. And if you're carrying booze, dump it now. They usually have a reception committee waiting to catch anyone who had liquor with him during the ride.

"Also, if anyone feels sick during the ride, *do not* vomit inside the bus. Once that happens every single one of you drunkards will be puking your guts out together. Leave the back row of seats open. If you must be sick, open the last window and puke outside. That goes for pissing too. If you have to go, do it out the back window -- or else. No passing piss cups this year or I'll turn every one of you bastards in. Have I made myself clear?" No one objected to what seemed perfectly sensible rules of behavior. We disembarked under the watchful eye of the driver, and I vouch that every one of us actually did try to empty himself. One conscientious midshipman even dropped his drawers and several other smelly things in the grass beside a big oak tree. I have no idea what he wiped with.

The first half hour of the drive was boisterous but uneventful -- three weeks of carry-on is an intoxicant more potent than the Southern Comfort Jubal bragged about. Tommy Poole repeatedly sang his high school fight song -- off-key this time -- until Reb Ramsey threatened to strangle him if he heard the words "Fighting Friars" again. Tommy hummed quietly to himself for a time, then drifted off into a deep sleep. BJ and I talked about the game and the party.

"Thanks a lot for setting me up with Jennifer," he said. "She was great."

"It sure sounded like it!" Kevin said from the seat behind us, and BJ laughed.

"Talk to me, Kevin," Rico said, and I turned around and knelt on the seat to watch and listen.

"About what?"

"You know what," Rico asked.

"Why didn't you tell us about Sarah Connelly before?" I asked him. "She's a hot number."

"I don't know," Kevin answered. "She seemed like such a little girl until recently, always hanging around and being a pain in the butt. I thought she had a silly crush on me, but honestly guys, she seemed so prissy and unreachable I didn't consider the possibilities, and I only asked her to the game because I didn't have a date, and I knew it would make my mom happy. But to tell the truth, she grew up suddenly since last spring."

"She grew out, too!" offered BJ. "How was that?"

Kevin smiled wistfully. "Not saying."

"So what happened?" Rico asked.

"I don't want to say exactly," Kevin said, embarrassed.

"So don't say exactly," Rico replied.

"Did you see her look at me?" Kevin suddenly blurted. "God she's a sexual animal! I didn't really realize she liked me that much, and tonight we didn't even think twice once we were alone. All of a sudden we were in bed together and neither of us had any clothes on. I can't remember how we got naked. Oh my God was it wonderful! She wanted me to do everything all at once, Rico. "

He stopped suddenly and looked from Rico to me and back again. His eyes sparkled.

"Now I miss her already. What's happening to me, Rico?"

Rico laughed and put an arm around Kevin's shoulder, pulling him close. "It's okay, buddy," he said. "You just got bit real hard, and it's your first time. Sarah would have an effect on any man."

"Not on you, Rico. You've got Rosa," Kevin said.

Rico laughed.

"Rosa is Rosa, and she's incredible, but Sarah is something else. I can tell she's stubborn and manipulative. I'll bet she'll also moody and a real challenge to please. Be careful with her, O'Reilly."

"Hey!" Kevin said, "be careful what you say about my girl." He seemed genuinely offended.

"Kevin, Kevin," Rico replied. "You want me to be honest, don't you? I'm your Jimminy Cricket, you dopey Irishman."

Kevin thought for a moment. "*You're* gonna tell me not to go after great sex?" he asked, laughing. "You can't keep Mister Ed in your pants as it is."

"The only thing better than great sex, Kevin, is great advice."

Within a few minutes, the driver dimmed the bus lights completely, and soon the majority of the occupants slept. The only disruptions came from Jubal Ramsey's incredible foghorn snoring and from the frequent trips to the back row by "gotta-go" passengers. I hoped no one was following the bus too closely during several of the more violent-sounding sicknesses. I settled down into the seat. Using my overcoat as a pillow, I put my head against the window and slept soundly. I had a very nice dream about Leslie that involved a big house, hordes of boisterous children, and a boss that looked and acted suspiciously like Dale Micklewski. The Tigers had invaded my dreams.

The next thing I remember, the driver turned on the lights and shouted at us to get up and get off. Immediately after I sat up, I noticed a distinct and unpleasant smell coming from somewhere nearby. I looked around, and everything seemed fine until I saw Tommy Poole. He was alone in the seat lying on his back with his legs stretched out into the aisle.

Sometime during the trip Tommy had been very sick. Luckily his head faced to one side, so the mess lay mostly beside his head. Unfortunately, his head lay in the mess, and it had caked thickly against him, including in his hair and ear. Fortunately for the bus, and for Tommy, he had used his overcoat as a pillow, so the entire mess was contained in the folds and creases of the dark wool garment. It was not a pretty sight, but Tommy didn't notice his predicament.

The driver crinkled his nose as he too smelled the "accident."

"God damn it!" He shouted and moved hurriedly in our direction. He looked at Tommy for a moment, shook his head, and laughed loudly. "Damn baby-assed mids!" he said. Then he turned to me and pointed. "Get him off this bus without making any more mess!"

I nudged BJ, who was still asleep, and I turned to Kevin and Rico.

"Tommy needs help. Let's get him off the bus."

"Why can't he walk?" Rico asked.

"I don't think he's capable," I replied.

Kevin jumped up.

"Come on Rico. A classmate needs help."

We gingerly lifted Tommy, being careful not to spill the mess from his overcoat. We wiped his head as best we could with the clean parts of his coat. Finally, Kevin and Reb carried Tommy feet first off the bus while I carefully carried the overcoat. Outside it had turned very cold.

Reb and Kevin tried to stand Tommy up against the bus and wake him while I dumped the mess near the gutter. Then I shook out the overcoat as best I could, decided that Tommy was so oblivious he didn't need to wear the coat. I carried it.

Tommy wouldn't wake. Kevin and Reb each put an arm around him and half-carried, half-dragged him toward Bancroft Hall. We hadn't gone two steps before the Officer of the Day approached us. I sucked in a breath involuntarily. The OOD was my "Passionate Plebe" nemesis Lieutenant Swetland. I merged into the background, an act that Rico pointedly noticed. He flashed a sage smile in my direction.

"What have we here?" Swetland asked with a squeak.

"Just heading back to our rooms after a wonderful Army-Navy game, sir!" Kevin volunteered.

"And a party afterward, too, I see."

"Just a wee one, sir," Kevin again answered.

"This midshipman is drunk," Swetland said stating the obvious.

"Oh, no sir!" Kevin said quickly. "Just a bit under the weather. It's probably the flu. They say there's a lot of that going around just now."

Swetland leaned toward Tommy and sniffed. He didn't like the smell at all.

"Jesus!" he said pulling back quickly. "This midshipman is disgusting. He's not even aware of his surroundings."

Kevin then put his left hand behind Tommy's head and grabbed him firmly behind each ear. He then lifted Tommy's head and aimed the still-unconscious face toward Swetland. It was not a pretty sight, and the OOD wrinkled up his nose and mouth disgustedly. Kevin wiggled Tommy's head, and at the same time he spoke out of the side of his mouth, ventriloquist-style.

"Oh, no, sir!" he squeaked, bobbing Tommy's head. "Ha, ha, ha! I'm really fine! I must have fallen asleep in a puddle of somebody else's vomit by mistake. Ha, ha, ha! I'm really sorry, sir! It will never happen again, I promise. Or else my friends here have my permission to leave my smelly and decrepit body on the bus for the driver to violate at his convenience." Everyone, including Swetland, laughed at Kevin's -- everyone except Tommy.

Lieutenant Swetland looked us over closely, and I drew back farther into the shadows. Kevin and Reb pushed back the corners of Tommy's mouth so that it seemed as if he were smiling stupidly. Swetland laughed again, and dismissed us with a wave.

"Hurry up!" he said. "Get him back to Bancroft and cleaned up. He's going to have punishment enough in the morning. And I remind you all that chapel attendance is mandatory. Now get going!" We hastened away, dragging Tommy. I let out a deep whoosh of air, suddenly realizing that I had held my breath when Swetland looked us over.

Rico looked at me closely.

"Close call, huh?" I didn't answer.

BANCROFT HALL

Named after George Bancroft, the founder of the Naval Academy, Bancroft Hall is the home of the Brigade of Midshipmen. It is said to be the largest dormitory in the world. The rotunda, located adjacent to the main office, is breathtaking.

CHAPTER 12

REVELATIONS

Sunday morning came impossibly and painfully fast. Apparently I had a bit more to drink than I suspected, because I found myself unable to move more than an inch at a time on what seemed like a hundred-mile journey from my bed to my desk, where my alarm wailed an unwelcome "Good Morning!" Since mine was the only functioning alarm in the room, I had assumed the un-volunteered-for duty as "room mother," which was fine when we all had to rise and shine at the same instant. I dearly regretted being "room mother" at that post-Army-Navy instant, when none of my body's systems seemed to be functioning properly and when my warm rack was calling out to me plaintively to snuggle back into its warm womb-like recesses.

Only last evening just before crawling into the rack -- at three in the morning as I now recalled -- I had foolishly boasted that I would gladly wake Kevin and Rico for their 0900 Catholic Chapel formation. It was my habit to get up when they did on Sundays even though Protestant Chapel formation wasn't until 1030. I would usually shower leisurely and go down to breakfast early to avoid the later rush. However, last night I was flushed with wonderful afterglow. It was now 0800 in the damn morning; and as my arm painfully inched its way across the desk top toward the alarm, I regretted my bold declaration of camaraderie.

I hit the button on the clock, perhaps a bit too hard or too awkwardly. My blow drove the clock across the desk to land loudly on the floor next to the window. I hoped I hadn't broken the damned thing, but at least the infernal noise stopped. No one in the room had stirred at the sound of the alarm or in response to my commotion. I snorted loudly. If it wasn't for me, the room would have been on report that morning. Leaning heavily on my desk, I made my way slowly, each motion bringing intense pain to every part of my body and unbelievable dizziness to my head. I moaned aloud as I inched along. The distance to Kevin's rack seemed to have stretched to several miles, but I continued resolutely forward.

After what seemed like an hour, I arrived at the foot of Kevin's bed. Slowly and gingerly I reached down -- despite the wave of nausea that engulfed me -- and touched Kevin lightly on the foot. No response. I tried again, but still he didn't stir.

"Kevin, . . . Rico!" I tried to speak, but only croaked. But it didn't seem to matter what sounds I made. Neither of them moved.

I am stubbornly conscientious. Sometimes I think it's one of my major faults. Heaving a large sigh, I moved to a spot adjacent to Kevin and reached down with both hands. I grabbed his shoulders and shook him as violently as I could, which wasn't very hard considering my condition. But that action made me instantly too dizzy to stand. The room spun around violently. I moaned loudly and stumbled backward onto Rico's rack, landing on one of his legs.

"Jesus!" he shouted, bolting up quickly. "What?"

I tried to rise but found I couldn't. I sat with my head in my hands, waiting for the nausea to pass, while behind me I could hear Rico shifting uncertainly until he was seated with his back against the wall adjacent to his rack, wondering what the hell I was doing in bed with him. I raised an arm slowly to signal him that I was about to speak. I opened my mouth. It was painful to do even that.

Head still safely encased in my hands, I mumbled.

"Sorry . . . fell down . . . feel terrible . . . can't move . . . church time . . . get up" or words to that effect. Then I strained, trying to stand and almost falling on the deck in the pain-wracked process. Moaning loudly, I rose uncertainly to my feet, both of which seemed suddenly unwilling to obey my mental commands. In this ungainly manner, I shuffled toward the door. That motion initiated the inexorable process which had been building inside me for the last several hours. Suddenly the most important thing in the universe became my ability to get to the head facilities as quickly as possible. I didn't stop to get my B-robe or my shower shoes or to put on gym shorts or a shirt. At that instant, it didn't matter. If some asshole upper-class caught me in my underwear in the passageway and wanted to put me on report for being out of the room in inappropriate dress, too bad for him. I might just puke all over the bastard, and it would serve him right. No dress code was going to prevent my getting to the toilet immediately.

I had no small amount of trouble pulling open our heavy wooden door in my weakened condition. I had gotten the door almost a foot open when the metal handle slipped from my grasp, and the door closed rapidly -- and especially loudly. Panicky, I grabbed again. I groaned as the sudden physical exertion caused renewed waves of pain and dizziness. I struggled the door open with two awkward hands, and I staggered shakily down the deserted passageway in my skivies. The sounds of my groaning echoed eerily off the bulkheads.

Midway down the passageway I noticed someone exiting the head. At first my eyes couldn't focus on the figure, but after a moment I saw it was George Abbot. Relieved it was another plebe, I continued resolutely forward. George stared at me, obviously recognizing my "condition." He smiled.

"Bad night, Jim?" he whispered, chuckling slightly, as I passed. George had told us he and Dianne didn't partake of alcohol, and that they wouldn't waste a single precious second of their time together doing something silly like partying. George must have been a man of his word because he looked very chipper.

I was angry at George at that instant. I wanted to tell him just what I thought of his giggling, his teetottling, and his precious Dianne. I opened my mouth to speak.

"Beffelsnep!" Don't ask me what the hell I said, because even as I said it, I had no idea what the sounds meant. George laughed louder at my attempt to communicate. I realized, however, that I had far more pressing things to consider. I moaned and hurried forward.

I made it to the head and ensconced myself on my knees in a stall. Calamity overtook me. For the next few minutes I experienced an almost out-of-body sensation. I watched from a far away vantage point as enormous quantities of foul and noisome mess gushed forth. The scientific part of me was amazed the human body could process and utilize such slop. The rational part of my brain told me that eight Budweisers, several shots of some mystery liquor, four hot dogs, countless peanuts, and tons of pickle relish, when added to a fancy but very fattening meal -- with expensive wine and topped off with chocolate cheesecake -- was probably not the ideal diet for robust health and wholesome living. As I floated in the nether-world of my present unstable mental and physical condition, I was convinced my body was telling me something important. -- I decided next time to skip the desert. I wished my body hadn't made that lesson so painful and bad smelling.

After several wretched and retching minutes I managed with some difficulty to pry one of my hands away from the white porcelain life-preserver for a brief moment so that I could flush. I thought briefly about jumping in and following the mess to my certain doom. At that instant I would have preferred death to the prospect of a continued battle with the skull-bursting, soul-paralyzing, headache that replaced the nausea.

I moaned and reattached my hand quickly and tightly to my new best friend -- this American Standard Deluxe Commode -- determined to ride out the sickness in that position, no matter if it took all day. It wasn't really so bad sprawled half-kneeling on the floor of the head. There was plenty of water available nearby if I needed it; I didn't have very far to go if I had to go; and being on my knees made it almost a religious experience. Also, the mosaic tile floor was nice and cool and had many thought-provoking patterns built-in for my entertainment. As I stared half-focused, I could make out the vague outline of the face of Abraham Lincoln, who seemed to be looking up at me with some disgust. I wondered briefly what Abe was so upset about, and I returned to counting my present blessings. I felt snug and secure, and I think I drifted off to sleep for a minute, my face inches from "sea-level."

However, some other midshipman had the abject discourtesy to enter the head just as I was at my most comfortable, and to spill his own smelly guts in a loud torrent on the floor just outside my stall. I screeched weakly as the chunky liquid splashed in my direction and then began flowing rapidly in a large, ever-expanding circle. Rationality again gripped me. I realized that if I did not make an immediate break for freedom, I would indeed be trapped in the stall all day, surrounded by someone else's ocean of stale beer and last night's partially-digested menu.

I rose, despite the staggering pain, and fumbled with the stall door for a moment. Grabbing the handle firmly I flung the door open, only to have it rebound from the wall and close in my face before I could take a step. The noise intensified my headache, but did not for an instant stop the sounds of the torrent gushing from whoever was just outside.

I opened the door more carefully the second time, trying to portray a semblance of propriety. I glanced at the midshipman who had the nerve to make such a mess, but turning my head too quickly caused me to endure renewed waves of room-spinning. I centered my gaze and began to walk, careful to avoid stepping in the mess. During my brief view I noticed that the midshipman was bent over almost completely so that his head nearly touched the deck. I also realized that he looked familiar. With as much dignity as I could muster, I moved gingerly passed the figure. Micklewski! It was that bastard Micklewski! I decided to call the guys to come watch and left the head as quickly as I could.

Rico had fallen asleep sitting in his rack where I had left him. Kevin hadn't stirred. I was semi-functional, so I shook each of them with some authority.

"Come on, slug-a-beds!" I said loudly. "Time to get started or you'll miss chapel and get put on report!" Kevin groaned loudly and rolled over. Rico woke with a start and stared first at his position, then at me. He was silent for a long time.

"Jesus!" he moaned. "I just had the worst dream!" He looked at me. "I just imagined that you had climbed into the rack with me. God, what a horrible thought!"

"Come on, you two!" I said, changing the subject. "Out of bed! Hurry up!"

"Jim," Kevin said groggily. "Do me a favor. Go see if Tommy is up."

"Sure," I replied with more gusto than I felt.

"How the hell do you do it, Merritt?" Rico asked. "I want to die. Hell, I might even ask you to kill me. After a hard party, continuous drinking, hours of passion, and five minutes' sleep, you're full of energy."

I paused at the door and looked down my Texas nose at them. It took an enormous effort to battle the headache.

"You guys just don't know how to hold your liquor. Come to Amarillo and I'll take you partying sometime."

"No thanks," Kevin said. "I've had enough partying to last a lifetime."

I hurried to Tommy's room -- wearing my B-robe and shower shoes this time. I found Tim Butler helping Tommy into the shower. Butkowski was still in bed. Abbott the teetotaler was whistling and getting dressed for chapel. Tim turned to look at me as I entered. "Did you guys get Tommy back last night?"

"Yeah," I answered.

"I took the first bus back. It was so late when you returned I was groggy, and I don't remember much. What happened to Tom?"

"He had an accident on the bus, and messed up himself and his overcoat. Will he make it to formation okay?"

"I'll get him there," Tim answered.

"Are you going to get to formation, party boy?" George asked me with a chuckle. I thought that was a very insensitive and stupid thing to say, and I glared at George. Tim didn't understand. I didn't explain. I left to return to my own room.

"Hey!" I said excitedly when I entered, intending to tell them about Micklewski. Then I stopped dead in my tracks. Everybody was asleep again. It was almost as if I had never talked to them. I went over to Kevin again.

"Okay, party boys" I said very loudly, and stealing George's catchy phrase because my brain couldn't think well enough to manufacture one on its own. "Here's the deal. I've already tried to get you two up twice. This is the last call. I'm going to take a shower, get dressed, and go to breakfast." At the thought of food, however, my stomach turned an uncomfortable somersault, and I hesitated. I swallowed hard involuntarily and didn't like the taste my morning's disaster had left in my mouth. "Anyway," I continued. "I'm not going to get you up again. You've got 30 minutes to formation."

Kevin stirred. He rolled over and sat up in one quick motion. Then he groaned, grabbed his head quickly, and fell backward onto the bed. Rico also groaned as he slid to the side of his bed and put his feet on the deck. He stood, very shakily.

"Come on, Kevin, good buddy," he said. "Don't worry about Master Sergeant Merritt. Rico will take care of you." He grabbed Kevin by the arm and lifted him up off the bed easily. He half-carried Kevin to the shower. Kevin cooperated, but only barely.

"We need the shower first," Rico said to me, and I nodded, trying to appear smug. He reached inside, turned on the water, and pushed Kevin in, shorts and all. Kevin yelled. The water was obviously still cold. A shout and a flurry of immediate motion told us Kevin was alive, if not completely functional.

Five minutes later Kevin exited, still wearing the shorts. Rico handed him a towel then jumped inside himself. Despite their weakened condition they managed to shave, brush their teeth, visit the head facility -- which they said was completely grossed out by some asshole who didn't make it to a stall in time -- get dressed properly, and depart for formation with five minutes to spare. BJ slept through the entire process.

After they left, I decided that breakfast was not a good idea, so I retrieved my alarm -- which still seemed to work -- set it for an hour before my chapel formation, and heeded the call of the covers. Within one bazillionth of a second I was sound asleep.

Waking the second time was marginally easier. I nudged BJ to get him started, and I stepped into the shower. I turned the water up as hot as I could stand it. It was marvelous, and after a few minutes I felt half-way human again -- as long as I didn't make any sudden moves. BJ rose quietly, and without too much difficulty. He showered as I shaved and dressed. Soon we headed slowly to formation, and BJ confessed to being somewhat under the weather also.

Never have I seen so many suffering individuals in one place at a single time as were at Chapel formation that morning. It almost seemed as if we were marching off to our deaths rather than to religious services. Such was the mood that I expected someone to start whistling the theme from *The Bridge Over the River Kwai* at any moment. But no doubt he'd whistle softly. Little did we know that Lieutenant Swetland, archenemy of the Passionate Plebe and therefore of every Godfearing midshipman in the Brigade, had waited for just such an opportunity for nefarious revenge.

Hidden in dark recesses on the far starboard side of the central rotunda of the Academy Chapel is a little-known area affectionately called "Sleepy Hollow." It was a place where, rumor had it, not-so-devout upperclassmen would spend the entire service prostrate, not before God, but rather filling their sacrilegious brains with dream images -- which being midshipmen were undoubtedly lewd and completely without redeeming moral value. I suppose some irreverence should be expected, since the chapel attendance was mandatory. But blatant, lying-spread-out-on-the-pews-in-dreamland was vulgar, and frying every heathen who slept in chapel was fine with me.

Usually those snoozing seniors would force their plebes to sit on the ends of the pews and to intersperse themselves strategically so that they could act as watchdogs who would awaken the offenders if anything significant happened -- devotions, communions, and rousing sermons not withstanding.

An often-told story related that a particularly sneaky OOD had once quietly surprised two plebes in Sleepy Hollow before they could alert their prone first-classman. Under orders from the OOD, the plebes let the firstie sleep after services. He roused several hours later when the small daughter of a tourist family touched his shoe and asked her dad if he was another John Paul Jones laid out for viewing in his nice dark uniform. The firstie was not amused, particularly when the Report Chit arrived at his Company Office the first thing Monday morning.

It was manifestly stupid for any upper-class to sleep in chapel, particularly on the morning after the Army-Navy football game.

Lieutenant Swetland, still glowing from last night's bus rendezvous which netted him a grand total of 47 completely inebriated midshipmen -- why he let Tommy Poole go was a matter of some conjecture -- waited quietly with two plebe messengers in the basement of the chapel. He had removed his sword and sword belt to ensure stealth, and he had instructed the messengers on duty that if they made even the slightest sound before he was ready to spring his trap, they would regret it. For 30 minutes he demonstrated and practiced silent hand signals with the messengers. Ten minutes into the service, when the sounds of snoring threatened to drown out even the heroic efforts of the Academy organist, Swetland and his mates emerged quietly from the recesses of a usually unused stairway behind Sleepy Hollow.

Those plebes who were awake -- very few -- had their attention sluggishly focused on the obvious pathways to discovery, and did not see him behind them. Quietly he used his hand signals to point to each offender and indicate who was to wake whom, and in what order. He turned the messengers loose and watched with a sadistic glint as they moved quietly from aisle to aisle, taking names in wholesale fashion. Heads bobbed suddenly to the surface as startled upper-class -- and one bold plebe who was found sprawled out on the wooden pew foot-to-head next to the firstie he was supposed to protect -- snapped to awareness. Those of us in the main chapel area who were aware, saw the erect population of Sleepy Hollow grow by a factor of three almost instantly. The sudden change in attitude and altitude was apparently too much for one firstie who made a break for the outside in anticipation of the sickness that would follow.

Twenty-nine midshipmen met their downfall that morning during Protestant Chapel. Adding that number to the 47 from the previous evening and the 15 from the earlier Catholic Mass -- I suppose Catholics are either more devout than Protestants, or have a stronger sense of self-preservation -- Lieutenant Swetland's twenty-four hour total of 91 Report Chits set a new OOD record. I suppose they'll put *his* picture and a plaque in some Company Wardroom to commemorate the event. In typical Academy mentality, he might even displace some Medal of Honor winner.

Noon meal, which found the Company reunited less the first-class, whose liberty did not expire until the evening, was the most quiet feeding I had ever seen. The entire Mess Hall echoed, not with the usual sounds of excited voices or stimulating conversation, but rather with the faint clinks of silverware on china and the occasional gurgle of iced tea poured into waiting glasses. I marveled at the silence. It was almost deafening.

Kevin halfheartedly tried to interest us in a basketball game in the afternoon, but no one was in the mood. I think he was secretly proud that he had not gotten sick like so many of our classmates -- I didn't mention my own morning disability. Jubal Ramsey suggested that we all go out for pizza or subs, but that idea also fell on deaf ears. About 1500 I became extremely restless and decided to jog despite the fact that it was wintry outside. I needed exercise and a chance to think. Something bothered me, and I didn't know what. I had to go somewhere to think. I didn't ask for company, and I think my roommates sensed that my pensive mood required solitude.

In gray sweat-gear I ran slowly out to the seawall to a spot very near where Leslie and I had spent those precious hours several weeks ago. I sat for nearly half an hour on the rocks, watching the harbor and the commercial shipping plying the slate gray and white-capped Chesapeake Bay. The weak November sun provided little heat, and the wind coming off the water was brisk and eye-watering. My breath puffed faint vapor clouds that quickly disintegrated in the wind. But I found the cold somehow exhilarating. My mind wandered. I wondered briefly what had brought me to this somewhat remote and uncomfortable perch. Something was bothering me. I decided to focus my thoughts. I looked around in a panorama and as my gaze swept the gray stone walls of Bancroft Hall, I began to feel things become clearer. I shifted my seat so that I looked at Mother B.

I had been too busy with the terrors and routines of Plebe Year and Tiger Company to gain more than a general impression of the last several months. But what things had these past months taught me? I knew I loved the Academy. I knew I greatly enjoyed the military and soldierly camaraderie. And I knew that life in the Navy was definitely for me. But Annapolis was not what I expected. The more considered, the firmer my conviction that something was seriously wrong.

The burning fire of duty and honor and damn-the-torpedoes I had expected to shine from every face was there, but not in the all-encompassing way I had imagined. There seemed to be no sense that we midshipmen were part of a greater purpose. No Grand Unified Theory of naval service, keeping us ready in an instant to man the fleet to stamp out the Communist menace and carry the message of peace and democracy throughout the world. So what exactly were we training for? How had beating the system become more important than adopting it? I pondered silently for several long moments as many thoughts coalesced and new theories emerged from my subconscious.

I had to admit was that the Academy "system" stunk. There were too many petty and completely unnecessary rules -- rules that discouraged pride or partnership with the Navy or the Academy, and alienated us from the institution. I could understand that haircuts and shoe shines and marching were discipline builders, and discipline is a necessary part of the military. I could understand that studies and gaining basic military knowledge was also important. And I agreed that physical training and conditioning were vital. The military is an extremely taxing, sometimes life-threatening occupation, and survival might depend on any or all three of these factors.

But plebes couldn't talk to girls -- why? And plebes couldn't go into town on evening liberty -- again why? No midshipmen could ride in a car in the Annapolis area except in special circumstances -- why? Lights-out was at 2200, but why couldn't I go somewhere and study if I needed to? And who really cares about grabbing a few minutes extra sleep in the morning?

And the comearound system made no sense to me no matter how hard I tried to rationalize it. If physical fitness was the purpose of the exercising, why not introduce a set of sensible standards for *every* midshipman, and test the Brigade on a periodic basis. If a midshipman is already fit, why mess with his conditioning or risk a serious injury during the constant and senseless up-and-down-the-passageway sprints? And surely there are better ways to train a potential officer to respond under pressure than to berate him or yell at him while he's physically restrained by his posture and chin and eye positions?

I had recently learned in psychology that screaming and threats were among the poorest motivators -- even prisoners of war hold up better under torture than when confronted with acts of kindness. Yet the system encouraged and reinforced negative motivators? And a major portion of the Academy officer staff reveled in the role of harassers and confrontation mongers rather than leaders.

And where did Annapolis get some of the officers they turn loose on the midshipmen? It seemed to me that the one place in the Navy for the brightest and best leadership examples ought to be Annapolis, at the very core and centerpiece of everything the Navy holds sacred. But then why did I see so many examples of negative or even bad leadership in the Annapolis officer corps? Who's running this place anyway? Why are they messing with *my* Naval Academy?

My head spun from the thoughts, but I resolutely plowed ahead. As I watched an oil barge chug through the choppy gray sea, an answer came to me. Maybe things were as they were because that's the way they had always been. Maybe *tradition* was really in charge at Annapolis. I laughed quietly. Maybe it was a case of old-timer "when I was a plebe" tradition in conflict with the modern world, and tradition prevailed.

It wasn't that I minded tradition or I felt that routine was bad. On the contrary, I relished the history. I loved the uniforms. I could visit the monuments all day. I enjoyed parades, and formations. And I felt at home eating and sleeping and living as a part of the Brigade. I was already hooked on what the place had to offer. I wanted to be molded and shaped and formed into whatever the Navy needed. But the Navy didn't know what it wanted, or didn't care, and so it fell back on the restrictions of the traditional system. And that was the crux of what had caused my discomfort. My thoughts continued but at a more comfortable pace. I had it figured out and I could use this information to my advantage.

People change. The midshipmen sitting in their rooms today were far different from those who were in the same rooms at the turn of the century. And today's midshipman would be different from those at the beginning of the next century. But by being so hidebound in tradition, the Annapolis system had created a chasm between itself and its charges -- a gap that widened with the years. How else would a young man bridge that gap but with cynicism? What better defense than an "us-or-them," "do anything to beat the system" attitude?

I felt better. Thirty minutes on the seawall and I had figured out the entire purpose of the Naval Academy. I was impressed. Maybe I really would be Brigade Commander someday! Now, what could future Brigade Commander Merritt do with this precious information? Nothing! Apart from including the thesis in a class paper, I could have no conceivable impact on what happened around me for at least three years. I was only a plebe and nobody listens to plebes. When I led the Brigade, maybe things would be different? But I realized that wasn't true either. As Rock Stone so aptly reminded me, upper-classmen don't make policy, they enforce it. So what was left?

I realized with some frustration that I would also have to wait until I was senior enough in the naval service before I could really change things. Then I could work with a vengeance to make the system better. Yes, by God, that was what I would do! But my thoughts paused again. Wait a minute! By the time I *could* make changes in the system, society would have changed too. Wouldn't I then be the old-timer, promoting my own "when I was a plebe" attitude?

I laughed out loud, realizing I was stuck in a "do-loop." I might someday be arguing for automobile privileges but maybe women would be attending and bring with them a wholly different and unfathomable range of problems and considerations. I was back to the original problem. The cycle of change was never-ending, but the system resisted change. Without some inherent flexibility, problems would remain, and midshipman attitudes would always tend to the rebellious. I had made another circle. I knew the problem now, but answers eluded me. Maybe I wasn't so smart after all.

I returned to Bancroft Hall at a much faster pace, more because the wind was at my back than due to the euphoria related to any momentous decision making. Later that afternoon I called Leslie to ensure she had returned safely. She had, and she still loved me -- even more deeply, she claimed. What a gal! Then I called home and told my family about my shortened Thanksgiving plans. I had been reluctant to bring up the changes because I didn't want to hurt their feelings. My parents listened politely and didn't make any negative comments, but I sensed concern. Something was left unsaid. Maybe we would be discussing the subject of James Wesley Merritt and his recent attitude changes in great detail. That was fine. I felt sorry about shortening the vacation and about poor Lynda, but I was dying to tell everyone in the world about Leslie and me -- except maybe Lynda.

Sunday evening meal was far more boisterous. I had the unfortunate duty of having to sit at the Tiger Table. Even though we didn't have to eat braced-up, the firsties continued to bombard us with inane questions and irrelevant interruptions. It was very nerve-wracking. I wanted desperately to speak up, to grab Stone by the collar and shake him and tell him to be logical about what was happening in the Company. I also knew that my revelation would not change a single thing.

Midway through the meal Dale Micklewski bragged to the table that he had partied longer and harder than anyone in the first-class group, and that he absolutely never got sick. I accidentally coughed loudly at that statement, choking on a piece of New York cut steak, and everyone looked at me, unsure if my noise was genuine or a reaction to Micklewski's lie. I didn't say anything, but Micklewski looked at me with narrowed eyes for a second. "Three chews and a swallow, Merritt, you silly plebe!"

I raced through the process of dinner slavery with my usual efficiency, but I felt somehow troubled. I watched the upper-class closely, seeing them in a different light. My recent revelations on Annapolis, leadership, and psychology started my brain working. From somewhere in the deep recesses of my memory a troubling thought suddenly emerged near the end of the meal. I was immediately distracted from my plebeness.--- *I had a major psychology test the next day and I hadn't studied a single lick.* My brain swirled. I began to panic.

"Iced tea, Merritt! Wake up!" Rock Stone, who sat next to me, shouted loudly in my ear, holding his glass in my face.

"Sorry, sir!" I said only partially breaking the sudden feeling of impending doom.

"What did you ask?"

"I said I wanted the damn iced tea, and if it isn't poured in my glass in five seconds I'm going to put you on report!"

"Sorry, sir!" I exclaimed as I grabbed the pitcher and poured deftly, half my brain still whirling furiously, considering the various possibilities of success on tomorrow's test. As I reflected, I remembered that I had fully intended to outline the necessary chapters and prepare study notes on Friday evening before the game. But I had completely forgotten, and that was not at all like me.

"What's the matter, Merritt?" Stone asked suddenly. I looked at him and I could see that he had been staring at me for several seconds. He also looked concerned, which surprised me somewhat.

"Sir," I said. "I just remembered that I have a major psychology test tomorrow that I haven't prepared for. Somehow it slipped my mind, and I'm not sure I have enough time to prepare.

"I thought you had decent grades," said Micklewski with a smirk.

"Yes, sir."

"Then don't worry about it. That's the breaks. Don't mess up, and study harder next time."

"My suggestion, Merritt," said Stone, still sounding concerned, "is that you find a secluded place to study this evening and crack the books. If you want, I'll give you special permission to use the Company Office and stay up an extra hour." He paused and smiled almost humanly at me. "As I remember, plebe psychology is fairly straightforward. I had the highest grade in my class. I'd be happy to help quiz you if you want."

I stared at Stone for a second, not knowing how to react.

"Don't worry, Merritt. I don't bite."

"Except during comearounds!" Micklewski added. Stone chuckled and shook his head. Then he stared harder at me.

"You've got real potential, Merritt -- maybe the best in the plebe company. But you also have an underdeveloped sense of duty and responsibility. I can see you think I'm crazy when I'm running you up and down the passageway. You think I enjoy hurting plebes, don't you?"

"Yes, sir!" I answered a bit too loudly, but Stone only laughed.

"You are completely wrong, Merritt! I'm a human being just like you. I'd much rather watch TV in the Wardroom, read a good book, or study for my own tests. I run plebes because that's my duty, and I intend to do my duty the very best I can. If tomorrow the Academy or Captain Dillingham told me to stop plebe indoctrination and to be your friend, I'd spoon every one of you -- Poole included." He added that comment while turning to look directly at Tommy. "And I'd do it without hesitation," he continued. "You'd swear you had found a long-lost big brother."

"Yeah, Merritt," Micklewski said, interrupting my considerable confusion. "Stone here is a very complicated individual. Me, on the other hand, I run you sissies because I enjoy it. I hate plebes, and I love to watch them in pain. So don't expect any big-brother act from me." He laughed at what he thought was his supreme wit; but no one else laughed, and Dale Micklewski didn't notice.

"Well, what about it?" Stone asked, and I was again confused.

"Sir?"

Stone laughed again. "Do you need help studying or not?"

"Yes, sir!"

"Okay. Look over your notes and chapters, memorize what you can, and come to the Company Office about 2100. I'll review the book and quiz you for 30 minutes. Don't worry, Merritt, we'll keep those grades up for you. I want to be able to brag some day that I trained a Brigade Commander." I frowned. Where was this rumor circulating from? I hadn't told a single soul. After meal I hurried back to my room.

"I can't believe I forgot the test," I lamented loudly to the room as I hurriedly pulled out my books and notes.

Rico smiled at me.

"Who's your instructor?" he asked.

"Professor Stevens."

Rico's face lit up.

"Tim Stevens? Tall guy? Skinny? Blondish hair? Soft-spoken? Slightly unkempt? No sense of humor?" I nodded confirmation. Professor Stevens was one of many genius civilian instructors the Academy hires. He was presently conducting a major study on the psychology of long duration cruises under water for none other than Admiral Rickover himself. "No sweat!" Rico continued, "I have him too." He reached into his pile of notes, extracted a four-page document, and brought it to me. "Here," he said. "Study from this."

"What is it?"

"Last year's third major test. I heard from the youngsters that Stevens is so busy studying bubble-heads that he gives the same tests every semester, except for the final."

"I can't study from this!" I said shocked. "That's cheating!"

"Relax," Rico said. "He always returns the corrected tests. That makes them just another public study tool. Besides, I heard he expects midshipmen to review previous tests. That way everybody gets their grades up before the final exam -- which is supposed to be a killer. He keeps *that* test completely secret and changes it from year to year."

I spent several seconds examining the issue from all directions to ensure I was on firm honor ground. I decided that since the old test *was* public property, it would be acceptable to use it as *one* tool in my preparation. But I would still study thoroughly, just in case. Besides, I now had a rendezvous with Stone. Briefly I was angry. Rico hadn't told me about the other two tests, and I had studied my ass off. I had gotten As on both, but what a waste of time! But come final exam, I would have great study notes while my more-lazy classmates would have only the three old tests.

I studied furiously again. I was a Whirling Dervish of psychological fact finding for the next two hours, and by the time I met Stone in the Company Office I was as prepared as I had been for the other tests. Stone paged through the chapters, smiling to himself as he remembered specific information. I had highlighted the important topics with yellow marker and underlined definitions in black. When Professor Stevens underscored information, I had indicated it with a big red star in the adjoining border. Stone raised his eyebrows as he read.

"No wonder your grades are so good, Merritt," he said. "You really know how to mark the text to illustrate the important info. Are you always this organized?" I nodded agreement. For the next 30 minutes he asked questions. I answered them with complete confidence and accuracy. When he finished, he snapped the book shut with a loud boom and smiled at me.

"Great job, Merritt! Let's have your class notes, and I'll see if anything else jogs my memory." I handed him a pile of papers I had accumulated, and he shuffled through them, asking questions as they popped into his mind. When he saw the test Rico had given me, I felt uncomfortable. Stone's previously smiling look became first confused, then doubtful, and finally suspicious.

"Where did you get this?" he asked.

"I think it's one of last year's tests for the same period," I replied, not giving him precisely what he asked for until I knew what he really wanted.

"Did Professor Stevens give these out?" he asked.

"No, I got it from a classmate this evening."

"And what have you done with it so far?"

"Nothing. I was going to review it after I had studied."

"You haven't read or reviewed it?"

"No, sir!"

"Good! I think you're in the clear on this."

"Clear, sir?"

Stone put the test down and looked closely at me.

"Jim," he said, making me even more uncomfortable by using my first name --almost as if I were suddenly a civilian, a fate I did not want to consider. "Last year we had a cheating scandal here at Annapolis. The press thankfully kept it out of the papers; but for several months while the investigation was ongoing, several hundred midshipmen were very nervous, including the ten or so third-class who were eventually expelled.

"The issue was a previous final exam. One resourceful individual who had a photographic memory had managed to reproduce almost the entire final exam verbatim immediately after he finished the test. He knew from the instructor the same test would be used for the second semester's final, and he decided to help his roommates. His act of misplaced kindness exploded in his face. The test got passed around within the third-class population. Several hundred people eventually had access to that information, and the professor in question became suspicious when the second semester grades were so much higher than the first. One of the youngsters innocently indicated to him that he had seen a handwritten paper which had almost all the questions on it. Naturally the Academy investigated.

"The use of that exam information as a preparation tool was eventually ruled a definite honor violation. The Board could only prove that ten midshipmen actually knew the test information was improper and used it anyway. Those ten are not here today." He shook his head sadly.

"Ironically, the midshipman who spirited the test information away was a Dean's List scholar who scored a legitimate 98% on the test. He said he did it so that his roommates -- two of whom were in academic trouble -- could have an edge. None of them are here today."

Stone held up the test.

"This is a very dangerous practice, and unless the professor himself passed out this document, or announced that it was acceptable to use old tests for preparation, I think an Honor Board could rule that having this provides an unfair advantage to its possessor.

"I'm going to have a talk with Henry Brandis about this." I started to protest, but Stone waved my objections aside. "Not only is he your squad-leader, but he's also the first-class Honor Rep. But if I were you, I'd give this back to whoever gave it to you with a warning that using it might be an honor violation unless he has cleared it with the professor. In the meantime, my advice is to fold this paper up and not look at it." Stone handed me my notes, and I took the old test gingerly, almost as if it were infected with hideous disease germs. I could feel my heart racing, and I wondered what the hell was going to happen next. Stone smiled.

"Don't worry, Merritt. I'm sure you're in the clear, and maybe everybody who used this information is too. But why take that kind of chance? You know the material. You'll do fine."

I stammered for a few moments.

"Thanks," I said finally and with a great deal of conviction, staring hard at Rock Stone. I was confused. Within the course of five minutes, I found that my entire opinion of Stone had changed again. This guy was like a chameleon, and I was having a great deal of trouble figuring him out.

"You don't like me very much, do you, Merritt?"

Again I stammered.

"Sir," I said. "That's not a fair question since I'm a plebe and you're a firstie and there has to be some distance between us because of our status."

"Fair enough," he answered. "I guess a better question is, do you respect me?"

I though about my answer before I spoke.

"Yes, sir! You are one of the most honorable people I have ever met."

Stone accepted my response with a smile.

"That was the best answer you could have given, Jim. Honor is everything." He paused. "You see, Merritt, I don't believe in leadership that undermines authority. I know the majority of midshipmen, including most of my fellow Company Commanders, think that the Annapolis system is a game, and that midshipmen must bend the rules and flaunt authority and the regulations whenever they can.

"But that's not me, and it's not what I believe, and I have no intention of ever being just like everybody else if I don't believe in what everybody else represents. The Academy has been around for more than a hundred years, and I know as well as you do that much of what happens here is nonsense and that the training philosophy is based on outmoded ideas. But it doesn't matter if I personally agree with the system or not. I am expected to perform in a certain way, and I will. That's my duty. All the whining and crying in the world won't change the system anyway, so what's to gain?

"The whole point of training the elite officer cadre at Annapolis rather than recruiting normal college grads is that someday. Merritt, your Commanding Officer may order you straight into the jaws of hell, knowing you're not ever coming out. But you have to go, and go gladly, because that's what honor and duty mean. Those are the special qualities of the best graduates of this school. It's what makes us special, better than anybody from civilian schools or those hokey little pseudo-military establishments. We are the best, Jim. We live twenty-four hour lives of duty and honor; and anyone who can't accept that doesn't really belong here."

I listened, fascinated, realizing that Stone had exposed another side of himself to me -- one he kept successfully hidden from most other people. I wondered briefly why. Stone laughed loudly and shook his head, and I think he himself wondered why he had just bared his soul to a plebe.

"Enough for tonight, Merritt. Finish your studying here if you like, but make sure the door is locked when you leave." With that Rock Stone, suddenly wearing a human face, rose and left. I found myself confused and wondering if all the Academy psychoanalysis I had confidently performed hours ago was accurate after all.

On Monday I received a letter from Lynda. She apologized for the delay between letters and I felt embarrassed that I hadn't noticed any gap. When was the last time I wrote her? I couldn't remember.

She brought me up to speed on the news from home, particularly about our high school classmates, several of whom were now engaged and planning big summer weddings. Good for them, but that seemed awfully soon for such a big step. I wasn't sure when I'd be ready to tie the knot. I had a lot of living to do. Then I chuckled to myself and admitted I'd be ready for marriage exactly one millisecond after Leslie decided *she* was ready.

Lynda said she was sorry I had to rush back to school so quickly after Thanksgiving, but that was fine because she knew how tough classes were at the Junior College where she was studying, and she could well imagine what it must be like for me. She said she was anxious to see me and talk to me about the future. She sounded so sweet I had a momentary guilt attack, which I quickly stifled. Painful as it would be, I had to tell Lynda our relationship was over. I just wouldn't tell her exactly why. I was sure she'd understand. Sometimes people outgrow each other and have to move on.

The extended carry-on left us plebes amazingly lighthearted. Monday night the ritual moon barrages between our room and Jubal's reached an amazing peak when Rico persuaded O'Reilly to ignite an emission in the direction of the enemy. It worked. Blue-green flame leaped outward in an amazing pyrotechnic flatulence display which singed several of Kevin's red leg hairs in the process. It was the crowning achievement of the moon wars to that point, and it left the men across the passageway at a loss. How do you top something like that?

Tuesday night some of the fun was ruined when Stone and Micklewski had a little talk with Tommy Poole in Stone's room. Tommy stopped off to visit us on his return.

"They're never going to give up!" Tommy lamented. "I just spent the last half hour with Rockhead and Micklewski and they told me that they would increase the pressure on me if I didn't decide to quit while I was home in Flint over the holiday."

"Screw 'em!" Rico said loudly. "There's no way they're gonna get rid of you on their own. You're tougher than they are."

"Rico's right, Tommy," Kevin said. "But you have to consider if it's all worth it. It's a hell of a strain on you to suffer this way."

"I just don't know any more!" Tommy said firmly. "Sara and my mom are teaming up on me now, and I'm getting weaker." I didn't say anything, even though I could sense that each of them wanted an affirmation from the future Brigade Commander. This was Tommy Poole's decision.

After Tommy left, we discussed our vacation plans briefly. Everybody mentioned how nice it would be to see their families again, but the real excitement started when we talked about girlfriends and what we intended to do when we saw them again. We had become fixated on women and sex and parties in the last few months, and I wasn't completely sure that was a maleness reaction, a function of our seclusion, or a sign of our tender ages.

"By the way, Rico," Kevin said boldly. "You predicted I would be in serious trouble after Army-Navy, and I'm not. I guess you were wrong on that one."

"Kevin, my friend," Rico replied. "You are in more serious trouble than either of us could have possibly imagined." It was immediately apparent that Kevin didn't like this answer and he became pensive for a moment while the rest of us talked.

"What do you think I should do, Rico?" Kevin asked.

"Dump Sarah!" Rico said with conviction, shocking us all.

"What!" Kevin and the rest of us said simultaneously.

Rico stood up without a word and went over to his desk. We watched as he took out a pad and paper and wrote something down quickly. He folded the paper, brought it to Kevin, and handed it to him solemnly.

"I'll make you a deal, Kevin," he said. "Here's Rosa's phone number. She's already said she wants your bod. I'll break up with her and never see her again after Thanksgiving if you'll give up Sarah Connelly."

"You can't be serious!" I said.

Rico held out the note to Kevin so that it almost touched his nose. Kevin stared nearly-crosseyed at the paper, probably thinking of the things Rico just said he intended to do with Rosa and imagining himself in Rico's place. He smiled, and it seemed that lust, dread, and then enlightenment spread over his face. He reached out, grabbed Rico's hand, and pushed it downward.

"I can't do that, Rico," he said.

Rico smiled at him knowingly.

"See. You're in more serious trouble than you ever imagined." With that Rico pressed the note into Kevin's hand, spun around with a flourish, and returned to his desk.

Kevin opened the note slowly, his face brightening.

"You bastard!" he said, laughing and handing the note to me. On it Rico had penciled, "*Not a chance, Irishman*!" I laughed and passed the note to BJ. I looked at Rico. He shrugged.

"Just hedging my bets," he said.

CHAPTER 13

HOMECOMINGS

The Academy had half-day classes on the Wednesday prior to Thanksgiving to allow everyone enough time to get home that day. My flight left Washington's National Airport at 1700 for Dallas. My parents would wait for my arrival in Amarillo at 2115. I was at National almost two hours early, resplendent in my Service Dress Blue uniform, and I flirted shamelessly with the stewardesses on the way to Dallas. I think one would have taken my bait but she found out I was only a college freshman and several years her junior. The other crew accused her of cradle robbery. I laughed along even though I didn't like the inference.

Amarillo at night is not the most exciting or beautiful of cities. Actually Amarillo during the day doesn't bring a lump to most throats either. But it *is* home, and I hadn't seen the old dusty streets for more than six months. I stepped off the plane, took a deep breath, and looked around before I hurried down the ramp onto the tarmac. I found myself disappointed. I expected more. I had expected the city to have changed in some physical way I could recognize, but it obviously hadn't. In fact it seemed smaller, less lively, and more depressing than I last remembered. I expected momentous changes, but only I had changed. No cheering crowds and brass bands waited for me. There was only my family -- God love 'em -- and a cold West Texas wind.

I rushed inside the terminal. Dad thoughtfully produced a six-pack of Lone Star Beer, which I normally would have relished. But since I hadn't fully recovered from the Army-Navy festivities, I looked at the beer with a bit of anguish. After I performed the required hugs and kisses with Mom, and each of my two brothers and two sisters, dad popped the first one for me. I sipped, pretending the first swallow tasted a whole lot better than it did. After the third swallow I was good again. I could handle *my* liquor. I was a Texan after all, pardner.

During the drive home my siblings pestered me about Annapolis and what went on there. I did at least ten imitations of my best brace-up, and I recited several rates for their amusement. My next-oldest brother, Samuel, who was now in the junior year of high school, thought I was crazy to endure such humiliation. I didn't argue with him, but he was always the pacifist and philosopher of the family. No way would he ever be caught dead in a uniform.

I asked my mom if she had seen Lynda lately.

"Yes, Jim dear. I saw her just yesterday. She came by to chat. She's very anxious to see you again." I wondered briefly why, if she were so anxious to see me, she didn't come to the airport? No matter. Lynda and I needed to chat.

The house was exactly as I remembered except that Mom -- it had to have been her -- had draped an old sheet across the garage door. The sheet contained the words *"WELCOME HOME JIM"* in bold black letters. Depictions of two golden anchors flanked the words. My eyes misted up unexpectedly as I studied the loudly flapping banner. Luckily I was outside in the dark, and no one noticed my momentary lapse of Texas manhood.

All four siblings followed me to the room I was to share temporarily with my youngest brother, Houston, who was 14 years old. Sam had moved into my small room soon after I departed, and I insisted during the last phone call that the room was his now and that I would sleep in the vacant bunk in the other room. The girls in particular looked very closely at me as I unpacked, trying to decide if the James Wesley Merritt that left home six months ago was the one who stood before them now. Monica, the 8-year-old, asked me repeatedly to make a muscle so that she could squeeze my expanded biceps and "ooh" delightedly. Merri, who was 11, wanted to hear me recite rates. I enjoyed the attention, and soon the five of us were rough-housing on the floor of the room, wrestling and tickling and laughing like when we were children not so long ago -- last spring.

While I was putting away my gear, Dad went out for Texas pizzas from a local Mexican restaurant -- a treat reserved for special occasions. The family gathered around the dining room table to talk and reminisce and play a quick game of Yahtzee. I had a great time.

At nearly eleven I called Lynda to see when we could meet, but her mom said she wasn't home yet. I supposed she was at a friend's house studying, and I returned to the table and the family fun.

We talked together until nearly two in the morning, and everyone but Monica and Merri stayed up. I fascinated everyone with my stories of Plebe Summer, the squadleaders, my roommates, the Academy, and the Army-Navy game. I left out a great deal of detail that was better unsaid.

"I'd punch out that son-of-a-gun, Mick-whatever-ski!" Sam announced boldly. So much for the pacifist's philosophy.

"I'm sure James will do no such thing," Mom piped in. "After all, it's part of the training program."

Sam harumphed.

"Anyone ever tries to treat me that way, I'll break his nose. If you want, big brother, I'll come to Annapolis and take care of your friend for you." We all shared a laugh, but I could tell he was more than half serious. We were a close family

The next day I slept in until almost ten, something I had not had the luxury of doing since high school. But I was still up before my brothers. Mom and Dad were early risers. Relatives would be arriving about noon-time for our usual Thanksgiving celebration, and I helped Mom in the kitchen, something she usually frowned on since the kitchen was her exclusive domain. But I don't suppose it's possible for a man to mess up deviled eggs and salad preparation -- the tasks she assigned to me. When I had finished, she pronounced my work "adequate," which was high praise from the master cookie maker.

Sam tumbled downstairs at eleven and together with dad we assembled the card tables and set up the folding chairs. Mom orchestrated this procedure because the table positioning and the number of chairs at each was a vital part of the exercise.

"No, no, Hap, dear," she said. "Put five chairs at the smallest table. That's for Uncle Donald and Aunt Margaret and their family. No one else is going to want to sit there because you know how obnoxious Don gets after he has a few drinks." Mom looked sideways at dad, who smiled sheepishly. Uncle Don was dad's older brother. "And move the bigger table closer to the window," mom continued, "I want Gramma Merritt to sit there and the extra light will help her see everything better. Jim, you'll sit next to Gramma

Merritt, at the middle of the table; and I think all the great aunts will sit at that table. I want them all to get a good look at our James."

I heard a stifled snicker and looked up to see Sam poking Houston on the arm. The two of them quietly laughed and looked at me. They knew I'd spend the day engulfed in massive bosoms and enduring a barrage of cheek-pinching and well-meaning but inane elderly questioning. I groaned aloud, but Mom either didn't hear or didn't want to respond. Oh, well, like Stone said, this was my duty, and I should always do my best, no matter how embarrassing it would be.

When we finally got everything set, the house looked great. More than 50 people would eat with us today, many of whom I had not seen for several years. Most were no doubt coming a long distance expressly to see me -- probably because my mom threatened them with bodily harm if they didn't. At 1130 everyone raced to the bathrooms to wash up and dress, and I amazed the family by being able to shower, shave, and dress -- in uniform because Mom asked me please to wear it for the family -- within ten minutes.

The house had a comfortable, all-weather porch, that stretched completely across the back. Dad had it built when I was a freshman in high school, and he used it as his private haven when things were tense or hectic around the house or at work. I liked it out there. The house backed to forest thick with cottonwood trees. They whistled in the breeze, and the sound filtered into the porch even through the glass windows. It was very restful. After I was ready for the family onslaught, I retired quietly to the safety of the porch and found dad waiting. I think he knew I'd go there. He had even opened two Lone Stars and one waited on the small table next to his upholstered rocker. I sat in the wicker rocker and raised the beer.

I took a large swallow, sighed, then said, "Thanks, Dad. I needed that!"

"I know."

For the next few minutes we filled the porch with small talk, and not very much of that. John "Hap" Merritt was not normally a quiet man. He was warm, outgoing, and incredibly cheerful. He could be the life of any party, regaling everyone with wonderful stories and expertly told jokes. But today he was quiet, which was fine with me. I studied him as he sipped his drink, staring off into the woods.

Hap and Martha Merritt had married late in life, so filled with the joy of each other that we children quickly followed. Dad was in his late thirties when I was born, and had recently celebrated his 56th birthday. I hadn't thought much about it, but I supposed that Dad was getting old. He was nearly bald. As far back as I could remember, he had been bare on top. Now his crown of thinning grey hair was very sparse. He had a slight pot belly that protruded even when he leaned back into his recliner. His ruddy face was round and fleshy, and slight jowls hung below either cheek. His clear blue eyes beamed with intelligence and with humor, but also held the sadness of age and experience. So far as I knew, he had always been a perfect husband and father and employee. He never shirked his duty, always seemed to be in the right place, and was gentle and attentive. He loved Martha and his children, and I felt instantly comfortable whenever he was nearby.

"How's it going for you there?" he asked after several minutes.

"Just fine, Dad."

"No problems?"

"Millions! But I have it under control. I'm doing great." I laughed. "Why just the other day I had a long talk with our Company Commander and he said I was one of the best plebes he'd ever seen." I stopped and took a quick drink. "Don't worry about me, Dad, I've got it made."

"That's good, son," said Mom, suddenly appearing in the doorway. I hadn't realized she had been listening, and I wondered how long she had watched us. Her voice was strangely subdued, not at all what it was several minutes ago when she was the perfect field general direction the preparations for the meal, and not at all in keeping with the spirit of the upcoming festivities. She seemed tired too. She closed the kitchen door slowly but firmly behind her -- something else that was strange. I could see the faces of Monica and Merri peeking from behind the small green-checked curtain that mom hung in that door's window. Their two small faces mirrored something I did not recognize. I was puzzled.

I got up to offer Mom my chair, but she waved me away without a word and pulled over a straight-backed wooden outdoor chair from its usual place beside the door. Smiling at me, she sat, her back to the woods, facing me. Mom was slender and very pretty. Her light hair had no gray that I could see, and her face almost no wrinkles. She had amazingly deep blue eyes, and she carried herself almost like royalty. She was very organized and efficient, and when necessary could command the immediate attention of feuding children.

"Can I get you something to drink, Mom?" I asked. "You look tired. All the preparations must be tiring." Poor thing had probably worked herself almost to death preparing for this event. I started to rise, but again she waved me down.

"I'm fine, James," she said sweetly. "Your dad and I have to talk to you about something important." I looked closely at her, wondering what was up, but her face gave nothing away. "You may think this is terrible timing," she continued, "but most of the family knows already, and we thought it would be best if you heard it from us before the relatives arrive."

I looked quickly from Mom to Dad, trying to pick up some psychic signal. For an instant I envied Rico's ability to pluck truth from vapor. What was going on here? Was something wrong with one of my siblings? Was Dad losing his job? Were they -- God-forbid -- divorcing? I looked at Mom closely again because I knew she'd be the one to say the words. Dad stared silently out the windows into the cottonwoods.

She reached out a hand and touched me on the thigh. I gripped her hand lightly and smiled.

"What's up, Mom?" She smiled in return.

"I haven't been feeling well lately, James," she began. So Mom was sick? She probably had been working too hard around the house. I decided to tell the rest of the kids to pitch in. Everybody has duties in this life. No problem; I'd make sure she got the rest she needed. She continued, "Your father suggested I see a doctor. I had some tests that old Doctor Williamson recommended -- he's been the family physician for years -- and the results came back two weeks ago." I immediately knew it was more serious than just exhaustion, but now that medical science was involved, relief had to be imminent.

"I have a cancer, James," she said slowly and quietly, enunciating every syllable so there could be no mistaking the message. The world stopped! An icy shiver started in my lower back and raced up my spine. I shook and took an involuntary gasp of air. Everything around me began to swim. My eyes widened but I couldn't focus on her face, no matter how hard I tried.

"What?" I croaked, grabbing her hand more tightly. "What? What? What do the doctors say? What can they do?"

"Nothing," she said sadly and with absolute finality. For a moment my heart seemed to stop and I could feel my throat tighten.

"Nothing!" I yelped, half choking. "Of course they can! There's always something! This isn't the Middle Ages!" I tried to stand, but Mom held me firmly down in my seat. She took my left hand and gripped it firmly in both of hers. Her hands felt cold. I shivered again.

"We've already talked to several doctors. The cancer is inoperable. They are going to start me on medication, but it's only a matter of time."

"No, damn it! No!" I yelled, not exactly behaving like a model midshipman.

"James," she said firmly, "I know this is a shock, but I need you to be strong. This has been hard on all of us." I shook my head, breathing deeply and trying to calm, but it was too confusing. I turned to Dad. He'd know what to do.

"Dad. This can't be true," I began. "Tell me . . . " I stopped. Dad stared into the distance above the whistling cottonwoods, his hand clutched tightly onto his can of *Lone Star*. His rocker was completely, and deathly, still. Tears rolled freely down his cheeks, but he didn't shudder or sob. That did it! I lost control.

A violent shudder racked my entire body, and I sobbed loudly. Tears flooded my eyes. Mom gripped both my hands, feeling my anguish -- and also feeling guilty that she had caused me pain. She began to cry quietly. She slipped to the wooden deck, knelt in front of me, and put her arms around my waist and her head in my lap.

"I know this is hard, James," she said in a voice muffled by the fabric of my uniform, "but we need you to be strong, to set a good example."

"What's gonna happen, Mom?" I croaked through the tears as I patted her hair.

She looked up at me. Tears had streaked her eye make-up and made tracks on each cheek. She smiled and patted my leg.

"The doctors say the end should be quick and relatively painless. Apparently the cancer's been inside me for a while. I have six months, no more than a year." It was too much to accept. I sobbed again and sputtered, and suddenly became irrationally and uncontrollably angry.

"But what about me? What about Annapolis?! And how about Sam and Houston and Monica and Merri? What's gonna happen to them -- to us -- to Dad?"

She straightened slowly, still kneeling, and looked me in the eyes.

"You'll survive without me, James. That's the way life works. You can't let what's happened to me change anything for you. You're where you want to be, and you're happy. Dad and the family will survive. There are enough relatives here to make sure they have support, and we're all counting on you to uphold the family honor and name." She reached one hand and put it on Dad's leg. "I've given your dad permission to mourn me and remember me fondly but not to forget to live. I want him to remarry when he's ready. He still has a long life ahead. Above all I want him to be happy." When Mom said that, Dad did sob -- loudly. He looked at Mom and held her hand tenderly.

"No, sweetheart. No one will ever replace you. I'll live alone." Whoa! This was too much, too fast! I gulped down a deep breath.

"I'll stay here until vacation is over!" I suddenly blurted. "I can spend some more time with you."

"No, James. You are going to live your life the way it needs to be lived. I won't allow you to alter your plans. We'll spend time together over the Christmas holidays."

My tears had stopped and I drifted into a state of quiet shock. Try as I might, I still could not focus on anything. Mom rose and brushed some imaginary dust from the knees of her dark slacks.

"Well," she said. "Time to get ready." She looked at the two of us sternly. "Don't either of you dare ruin the party. I planned it for too many months. Stop blubbering and get inside and see to setting the tables." She marched resolutely into the house.

I looked at Dad and found him staring at me a sad smile hanging on the edge of his mouth. Then he laughed suddenly and slapped me playfully on the leg.

"Come on, crybaby!" he said loudly. "We've got work to do." He stood and walked into the kitchen without looking at me. I stood slowly and followed him. I went immediately to the sink where I rinsed my face carefully. In the reflection of the kitchen window I could see Monica and Merri watching me from the kitchen table, where they both huddled together in a single chair. I could see that both of them had been crying. My loud reaction to the news had frightened them. I dried my face and turned.

"I'm okay," I said. "Sorry I made so much noise. I'll bet the whole neighborhood knows now." Without a word both the girls ran to me and hugged me. I held the two of them tenderly, trying desperately not to cry again, and almost succeeding.

Mom's party was a smashing success. I found myself the object of unabashed stares, side comments, and family pride. I guess that's the mystique of a service academy. No disrespect intended to the millions of weenies who are reputable college grads, but almost anybody can get a degree from a civilian institution. Surviving at Annapolis, or West Point, or Colorado Springs, was a far more noteworthy accomplishment.

After the party I showered vigorously to remove the makeup and various perfumes that had been deposited on my face during the party. I changed into jeans and a T-shirt and drove the family station-wagon to Lynda's house at 1930. She hugged me tightly when I entered, and it felt good to have her near me again. I remembered her perfume, the silky touch of her short blond hair against my cheeks, and the familiar feel of her thin but pleasantly rounded frame against me. We held each other for a moment. Then she led me into the family room to greet her parents. They were generous in their praise, but I could tell they knew about Mom.

Lynda and I left soon afterward and drove out to our "usual" spot. I had intended to get right to the point, but Lynda interceded.

"I'm so sorry about your mom," she said sweetly. "She's such a wonderful person, and it's such a shame." I agreed.

Without another word Lynda reclined her seat and pulled her jacket and top off, exposing herself to me. I stared for a moment, remembering the loveliness.

"Shouldn't we talk?" I asked.

"No," she said. "We both need this more." She pulled me down to her, and we kissed for a long time. Her kisses were still exciting, and somehow different -- but I didn't complain. A few moments later she nudged my hands down, and I didn't resist. I rationalized that this was a farewell ritual to ease the pain of our separation. I had never seen her so aroused before, and I found myself enormously stimulated in response.

"Get up, Jim. Quickly!" she said suddenly, and I slid over onto the driver's seat, unsure of what was happening. Deftly she slid off the remainder of her clothes, and I marveled at the sight of her. Tossing her jeans onto the back seat, she reached out to me. "Hurry, Jim. I need you badly this instant!" She helped me yank my jeans and shorts off so quickly I hardly knew what had happened. Soon we were joined, and she moaned deliciously under me.

We made love for more than a half-hour, and it was wonderfully enjoyable -- and therapeutic. Finally we were too exhausted to continue and we slipped quietly into our clothes. She lay her head against my shoulder and sighed deeply.

"I love you Jim," she whispered.

"I love you too, Lynda. But we have a lot to talk about."

She straightened suddenly, turned her head, and stared out the side window.

"You know, don't you?" she asked, leaving me puzzled.

Without waiting for an answer she spun around toward me and reached over with her hands to grab my head. She kissed me tenderly for a brief second; then she smiled.

"This is so hard. But I could tell from your voice on the phone and from your letters that you knew. I'm so sorry." She sighed and settled against the passenger door before continuing.

"His name is John Chavez. He's a junior at University of Texas, majoring in business. I met him this summer at the pool, but we were only friends for a long time. Now we're more than friends, and I honestly don't know how that happened. But I knew I couldn't lie to you about this. I still love you. But I have to be honest and tell you that I can't stop seeing John. He's very special. Please understand!"

I sat silently, emotions warring inside me. She began crying.

"God I'm so sorry," she sobbed. " I didn't mean for this to happen, especially with what you already have to deal with. John told me it would be best to get it out in the open so you could deal with it."

I felt a strange combination of betrayal and relief. My sweet wonderful Lynda had been cheating on me. I had also been cheating on her, of course. But somehow her cheating seemed more a sin than mine. I felt my anger flare. "You're in love with a Mexican?" I blurted irrationally.

She drew back, hurt. "He's third generation, Jim. And since when have you become prejudiced?"

I paused, rethinking my attitude. I had been handed the perfect set-up, all I had to do was act sufficiently shocked, and let her go. She'd be happy with "Juan the Wetback," and I'd still have my precious Leslie. But somehow I found that cutting loose from Lynda was harder than I imagined.

Pride and ego are strange things. I was hurt for no rational reason. I looked at Lynda, but she stared down at the seat, purposefully avoiding my glance.

"When did all this happen?" I asked, sounding more hurt than I intended.

"Last month John invited me to come visit him at school for a weekend. One thing led to another, and suddenly I couldn't deny that I was desperately in love with him. I'm really sorry, Jim. If I could change any of this, I would."

I looked at her more closely and I felt my attitude soften. She was stuck in the middle, caught between her "duty" to me and her love for this greasy and smooth-talking son of an immigrant. It wasn't really her fault. After all, expecting someone who is young and lovely and who has her own needs and desires to wait faithfully through the best years of her life for a dream that was four years away was too much to expect. And I hadn't been the most noble of characters. It was cruel to ask her to stay quietly at home waiting for me. I had to let her go. I wondered briefly if I should tell her how happy I was with my new-found love, but decided against it. I may be marginally understanding, but I'm not the least bit stupid.

"Lynda," I said. " I've had an uncomfortable feeling about us for a while, and I was meaning to talk to you about it. It's okay about you and John. I shouldn't have asked you to wait when I've got four hard years ahead of me. I was going to talk to you about it, but now I think it's resolved. I'll still see you when I come home if you like." I said this, knowing I was hedging my bets. Rico would have been proud. But suddenly I felt like a total cad. "No. That's not a good idea. You have to remain faithful to your love with and not let me interfere. We can talk on the phone, and you can tell me what's happening around here. And please write me and send lots of goodies." She laughed, then began to cry.

"Hey, hey!" I said, reaching out to her. "No tears. Everything is okay."

She slid over against me and I put my arms around her while she cried silently. Then she straightened and kissed me tenderly.

"You are so wonderful, Jim. Make love to me one last time." She drew back and began removing clothing again, and for the next half hour she tried to prove how sorry she was for dumping me. I participated wholeheartedly, again rationalizing the sex as a catharsis -- an intense but pleasurably physical therapy for two bruised psyches -- one of which was only pretending to be hurt.

The next day Mom kept herself so busy with clean-up and other chores that I hardly said a word to her. Every time I saw her she smiled and brushed by me. I offered to help, but she would have none of it. I spent Friday visiting school friends, and Friday night Dad took the family out to the theater. Monica and Merri flanked me in the cushioned seats, and at separate times, each held my hand tenderly. I recognized they were comforting me, and I accepted the attention.

On Saturday morning, Dad and the boys took me to the airport. At the terminal Dad drew me aside.

"Jim, your mother wanted me to tell you that she wants you to concentrate on school and your life and not get hung up on her illness. She knows she avoided you yesterday, but that's her nature in these situations. Accept it. I'll keep you informed if anything changes, I promise." I accepted Dad's word, and departed feeling extremely frustrated and desperately anxious.

THE CHAPEL INTERIOR

Inside the Academy chapel, the architecture is subdued but reverent. The striking stained glass windows are memorials to sea heroes.

CHAPTER 14

LET ME COUNT THE WAYS

I was quiet almost all the way from Amarillo to Richmond, despite the valiant efforts of several cute stewardesses and a sweet old matron lady to engage me in lively conversation. I had an awful lot to consider. I felt as though my life had been strangely severed from its anchor, and I wasn't sure how to react. Maybe Leslie would know what I should do.

When I saw her waiting at the end of the exit ramp, my heart stopped. She was so beautiful, and her smile so warm. God, I loved her! We kissed until it was almost embarrassing to the people around us, but I didn't want to let her go. I held her, maybe a bit too tightly, and she sensed something. She drew back and looked at me closely but with the nicest smile.

"What's wrong James Merritt?"

I steered her toward the exit.

"I'll tell you all on the way to your place," I said. She held my arm tightly as we walked. I could tell she was concerned. I drove her Corvette carefully, and Leslie listened intently while snuggled up against me. While I explained about my mother, she slipped her hand around my neck and lightly stroked my hair.

"Poor baby!" she said lovingly. "I'll do everything I can to help."

"I know sweetie, and I appreciate it." Just telling her lifted the cloud enough so that I was almost normal by the time we reached her housing community -- a place named "Windsor Farms" located in the western Richmond suburbs. The area was guarded by a high brick wall with an electric gate and manned guard shack. The guard recognized Leslie and waved us through.

Her "house" was more a mansion than a dwelling, and the land associated with it must have run to several tens of acres. The front of the property line was defined by a four-foot-high ornate dark brick wall. Brass light standards fabricated to resemble colonial lanterns stood every 50 feet along the top of the wall. Two inwardly curving wall sections and two high brick columns marked the entrance where a heavy fancy-scrolled wrought-iron gate stood open. An acre of pristine lawn fronted the huge white house, which was framed by two enormous old magnolia trees. A long bricked driveway led up to the front door, then on to a detached multi-car garage located in the thick pine trees to one side of the property. Pine trees delineated both property side boundaries, and thick virgin hardwood forest stood in the rear. I could not see neighbors' houses in any direction. It was a wonderfully peaceful setting.

"Wow!" I said trying to take it all in at once. "Your parents must be extremely wealthy."

Leslie laughed.

"I suppose so," she answered. "I never thought much about it."

I parked the car in the garage between a black and silver Mercedes precisely as instructed.

"Daddy is very fussy about order and things lying about," she said seriously. Hearing that I straightened my shirt tuck and instantly wished I had worn something other than jeans. I also decided to sit up straight, brush my teeth after every meal, and not chew with my mouth open. God, was I walking into another Plebe Year here?

I started for the kitchen entrance, but Leslie laughed and led me around the house to the front door.

"The side door is for servants," she informed me with a matter-of-fact smile. The side door looked fine to me, and the front door was almost 50 feet out of our way, but I didn't say anything.

The interior of the house assaulted me in a not altogether unpleasant variety of colors and textures and patterns, almost as if I had stepped onto the glossy pages of a lady's magazine.

"Mom is a very successful interior designer," Leslie said, explaining. I had known that, but I never suspected what living with an interior designer would mean. Nothing of what I saw in the wide entryway or the two adjoining front rooms looked as if it was meant to be touched, walked over, or sat upon. It made me uncomfortable. Maybe the rest of the house was livable.

"My parents are expecting you. They'll be in the library." This house had it's own library? Amazing! I followed Leslie to the left into the middle room on that side of the spacious central hall. Inside were three people. Seated in an easy chair with his legs crossed regally, obviously assuming an I'm-the-head-of-the-house-and-lord-of-all-I-survey pose, was Mr. Wallace. He was a thin aristocratic, slightly balding man. He had been reading the Wall Street Journal. He quickly put it down and smiled as we entered. He had a genuine, but appraising smile, and I felt slightly uncomfortable.

Across the room at a large oak desk sat Mrs. Wallace, an attractive blond woman, who looked almost as young as Leslie. She was marvelously made-up, exquisitely coifed, and wore a tight and extremely short skirt that revealed where Leslie got her fantastic legs. She could have been a movie star.

Standing next to her was a tall, thin, middle-aged black woman, who was obviously a servant. She wore a standard maid's white costume with a frilly apron around her waist, and she stood patiently to one side as Mrs. Wallace reviewed a meal plan, speaking in a light, well-bred Virginia accent.

"Louise, let's have the roast for dinner, but please tell Harriet to cook it thoroughly but not burn it like last time. The potatoes and the green beans will be fine, but no asparagus. You still do not have the Hollandaise sauce quiet right. And I think you should get one of the better vintage wines from the cellar, since this will be a special dinner this evening." They had their own wine cellar? How could anybody afford that? Louise turned to depart, smiling at Leslie. "Oh, Louise," Mrs. Wallace said, interrupting her exit. Louise turned. "Please serve us promptly at seven. Not a minute later."

Louise exited, and Mr. and Mrs. Wallace approached the two of us together. Both of them gave me steady, appraising looks, and the smile Mrs. Wallace presented showed sparkling white teeth and cautious good will. Her glance made me even more uncomfortable then her husband's seemed to, saying in no uncertain terms, "So you're the lowlife who might be slipping it to my daughter, huh? What do you have to say for yourself now that you are confronted by your betters?" I met both gazes steadily as Leslie did the introductions.

"Mr. and Mrs. Wallace, may I present Midshipman fourth-class James Wesley Merritt from Annapolis." So that was how the rich folks handled introductions? Well, la-dee-da. I smiled, and I'm sure a hint of humor embedded itself into my ample dimples.

I extended my hand to Mr. Wallace and he shook it with a very firm grip which I matched. -- I was in the middle of Plebe Year. Anybody who wanted to match strength with me was going to have to be quite studly. He approved of my handshake. Mrs. Wallace also extended her hand, after giving me a bit more scrutiny and apparently deciding that I was in fact a human being, and that I had not brought any vermin in on my clothing or tracked Texas cow-pies in on my shoes. She smiled at me much more warmly, and I decided that I had passed whatever test she had given me. I also noticed by the way she stood and the way she squeezed my hand electrically, that she was now purposefully trying to exude some sex appeal my way. It worked quite well, but Leslie rescued me by taking me by the arm possessively.

"I thought I'd take James on a tour of the city," Leslie said, "and be back by about five this evening. That will give us plenty of time for dinner. Does Louise have the master guest room ready?" Master guest room?

"Yes I believe so," Mrs. Wallace answered, still attaching her gaze provocatively on me.

"Well," Leslie said. "Why don't we leave Daddy and James to chat while we check the room?" Leslie steered her mother from the room, leaving me with Mr. Wallace. But I had already passed his test, and we were buddies now. He waved me to a nearby high-backed leather chair, and took out a pipe. I watched as he meticulously filled and lit it. I assumed this was an upper-caste ritual, and only when he had settled back into "his" chair did we dare begin speaking.

"So tell me about yourself, James," he said. Gray-white smoke curled slowly away from his head toward the high ceiling.

"Well," I began. "First off, you can call me Jim."

Mr. Wallace laughed.

"No, no. You don't understand. Mrs. Wallace is 'Old Virginia' -- a real stickler for formality. She would never approve of using nicknames. Sorry, but you will forever be 'James' in this house."

"Okay," I said. "'James' it is. I was raised in Amarillo, Texas. My father is a mid-level accountant with Standard Oil. I have two brothers and two sisters. I'm the oldest. I played football and ran track in high school. I'm a Naval Architecture major at Annapolis. That's a quick summary."

"And what exactly are your intentions with our daughter?" Wow! This guy didn't waist time beating around the bush. I thought for a moment before answering, and decided honesty was always the best policy.

"Sir, Leslie and I have seriously discussed marriage after I graduate in June of 1971. I know it's a long time to wait, but midshipmen cannot be married." Mr. Wallace stared at me for a second.

"And what about after your graduation? What then?"

"Sir, I intend to fly jet fighters for the Navy."

"And what about Leslie? Will you expect her to uproot herself every couple years and to follow you wherever you go?"

"Well, yes, sir. That's part of being in the Navy. It'll be an adventure, and I'm sure Leslie will like it."

"Maybe. What about her career? Do you intend that she stay home and raise children, even though I'm spending a great deal of money to see that she is educated?"

"If that's what she wants, it's fine with me. But if she wants a career, that's wonderful too." I thought I had given the "correct" answer, but Mr. Wallace harumphed.

"Well I don't believe in married women having separate careers," he said. But before I could say anything, he laughed. "However, as you can plainly see," -- he waved his hand in an all-encompassing gesture to indicate the house and his life in general, -- "Mrs. Wallace happens to agree with you. If you so much as mention Leslie's staying at home to raise children, she will probably slice off your manhood and hand it to you on a plate. And, believe me, she'll enjoy every second of it." I laughed tentatively, not knowing if he were serious.

"And so would James, my dear," said Mrs. Wallace, laughing as she reentered the room. Boy, she had great legs! And she noticed that I noticed. I averted my gaze with some difficulty while she addressed Mr. Wallace. "Really. Is it necessary to use such vulgarity to James on his first visit?"

"Yes," I said interrupting, something I was certain Mrs. Wallace was not used to. I continued quickly. "Please save the vulgarity for my *next* visit. We just won't have time to do it properly this weekend." They both laughed.

"Touché, James," said Mrs. Wallace with a wry smile, and almost immediately Leslie entered, and I caught my breath. Mrs. Wallace noticed my distraction and I believe she was jealous. I reaffirmed my belief that Leslie was the most beautiful person in the world!

She had changed clothes and now wore a tight dark blue wool mini-dress that perfectly outlined her figure and showed off her own wonderful legs. She had tied her dark hair up onto her head in a complicated braid, which looked fantastic.

"Don't you love what Louise did to my hair, mother?" she asked. Mrs. Wallace smiled genuinely. She might be jealous of Leslie, but it was also apparent she loved her.

"It looks just lovely, dear," she said.

"I wholeheartedly agree!" I added.

Leslie took me by the arm and steered me purposefully toward the door.

"Well, we've got to go if we're to be back on time. See you around five."

"Nice to meet you both," I called happily back over my shoulder.

"Drive carefully with our precious Leslie," Mr. Wallace replied.

Leslie took me upstairs to my room, where I had intended to quickly grab a jacket. Instead she kissed me passionately for several long minutes, and I was entertaining thoughts of what the old lady would do if she came upstairs and found us naked on the guest bed. I decided she might want to join in. The thought was interesting, but Leslie had other ideas. She led me out of the room and I waited in the hall while she got her own coat, then we hurried down the wide stairway and out the front door.

As we walked to the garage, Leslie said huskily to me.

"I was about to undress you in the guest room, James Merritt. I could hardly control myself."

I laughed.

"I know exactly what you mean."

"But I have something better in mind," she said, as I raised the garage door.

I walked toward Leslie's car, but she closed the garage door behind her and latched it. I turned and looked at her. She was already removing her coat as she walked toward me. From her purse she deftly removed a set of keys.

"Do you know what these are?" she asked with a devilish smile.

"Car keys," I answered with confidence.

"Not just any car keys, James Merritt. These are the keys to my mother's Mercedes. Did you know that Mercedes have the softest leather seats you could ever imagine?"

"What do you have in mind?" I asked, knowing exactly what she had in mind.

She reached behind her.

"No time to talk, James Merritt. Help me unzip and I'll show you." I helped eagerly, and within two minutes we were totally naked and sprawled out on the back seat of the large black Mercedes. Being naked on leather is not as erotic as I had expected -- too much friction -- but I was not about to complain. I became instantly lost in Leslie's loveliness and passion.

The city of Richmond was not as quaint or Civil War-ish as I expected, but with Leslie leading and explaining in her cute Southern accent, I didn't mind at all. I could have been taking a tour of Saint Peter's, she made it all so interesting. After an hour we stopped for a drink in a small restaurant near the center of the city and reaffirmed our love about a bazillion times. Afterward we sat outside on a cold green wrought-iron bench in the chilly air beside a fountain near the "Avenue of the Generals" and watched the semi-bustle of the Saturday city. A slight winter's breeze surrounded our bench with occasional puffs of frigid vapor.

I noted with particular interest a family of locals who were strolling the downtown much like we were. A young mother herded two small children toward the fountain while an older woman -- obviously her mother from her look and demeanor -- walked at the young woman's side. The two shared a glance, several quick smiling words, and an enormous laugh. It was the laugh that did it -- something about the way the older lady threw back her head and laughed with abandon while gripping the arm of her daughter.

I looked closely at the older woman, but I saw Mom instead. I heard her special laugh piercing the air and turning my heart to jelly. And I thought about how I was never going to hear that laugh again, and how she was never going to be able to walk with me while I herded my own children. With a sudden and vicious vengeance I became overwhelmed by the prospects that awaited Mom and the rest of us.

My eyes misted over in an almost instantaneous salty flood. I sobbed so loudly that I startled the women who only seconds before were cushioned in their own contentment. Leslie was also startled for a moment. Then she quickly grabbed me and pulled me toward her, and I wept on her shoulder like a baby.

"Oh, Mom! Oh, Mom!" I cried out repeatedly, while Leslie stroked my head and cooed sympathetically.

"Why, Leslie? Why Mom?" I asked in a plaintiff sob.

"No one ever knows why until after they're gone. Your mother sounds like a wonderful woman. God will take care of her, James Merritt."

"But what if it's all a cosmic joke? What if we've been kidding ourselves and there's only nothing?"

She laughed slightly, but patiently.

"Then there's nothing sweetheart, and not a thing you or I can do about it. But have faith. There's got to be more, and it must be glorious; and that's what awaits your mom when she's gone."

I started to speak again, but Leslie put a soft finger on my lips and shushed me. She removed a handkerchief from her purse and carefully wiped my eyes. As my own tears stopped and my vision cleared, I noticed that she had also been crying. I sat up straighter and taking the handkerchief, I wiped her eyes. We sat quietly snuggled for several minutes, each lost in our separate thoughts.

I felt much better by the time we returned to her house, so much so that I grabbed her when I helped her from the car and nodded toward the Mercedes with raised eyebrows.

"Are you psychic, James Merritt?" she laughed.

"I love you," I answered. "Does that make me psychic?" She laughed, and we "lingered" in the garage until the leather burned our bottoms.

I wore my uniform to dinner because Leslie said dinner in the Wallace house was a semi-formal affair. I could see that it was going to be an opportunity for Mrs. Wallace to put on a show for everyone, because she was last to arrive. I stood next to Leslie in the large dining room. The thick rosewood table, which could have seated 20, had been expertly set for four. Mr. Wallace, wearing a dark suit and white shirt, stood behind the largest chair at the head of the table. Leslie wore a dark blue evening gown. It was neither low-cut nor gaudy, but I could tell it was very expensive. It looked wonderful on Leslie.

When Mrs. Wallace made her entrance I almost adjusted my opinion about who was the most beautiful woman in the world. Mrs. Wallace was an absolute goddess. Her black gown was clingy and revealingly low-cut, both top and bottom; and what it revealed excited me. She had arranged her hair into a more formal coif. As before, her makeup was perfect and bright enough to be provocative, and I immediately bet myself that the diamonds she wore on her fingers, ears, and around her neck were real. Mr. Wallace hardly noticed the gorgeous creature, but Leslie chuckled slightly and pinched my rear -- not so demurely -- so that I could retrieve my tongue from its present position on the floor. I took that as a cue.

"You look simply marvelous, Mrs. Wallace," I said. She beamed and looked at Mr. Wallace for confirmation. He seemed to see her for the first time. He nodded abstractly.

"Very nice, dear," he said.

Mr. Wallace may not have been complimentary, but he knew his manners. I think that Leslie's mom would have castrated him with a butter knife if he didn't. He quickly moved behind his wife and held her chair as she sat, a move I had already matched with Leslie.

"You look very handsome in your uniform, James," she said. "And the two of you make an absolutely marvelous couple." She turned to her husband. "You know, William, I think I'll talk to Bootsie Hilliard about having James and Leslie pose for a photo spread for that magazine she represents. I cannot imagine a more attractive couple in the entire nation." Mr. Wallace nodded distractedly.

"Spoken like a true mother," I quickly added, and this made Mrs. Wallace laugh.

Dinner was served exactly at seven by Louise and another much larger black woman, who I later found out was Harriet the cook. I instantly liked Harriet -- she had that combination of slight irreverence, conversational ease, and light humor. She would fit into any grouping. She winked at Leslie and me several times, and once, when Mrs. Wallace gave a snapping order she wrinkled up her nose.

"Oh, keep your skirt on, Mrs. Wallace! You know Louise and I are moving as fast as we can. And you won't get a better cooked meal from any other help in Richmond." Mrs. Wallace was obviously used to Harriet's sharp tongue. She laughed.

"Mr. Wallace could run away tomorrow with his tramp of a secretary, Harriet, but if you ever left I think I'd kill myself." That got a big laugh from everybody, Mr. Wallace included, and Harriet came behind Mrs. Wallace and put a large hand on her creamy shoulder.

"There, there, Mrs. Wallace. I've worked here with y'all for more'n 20 years now. Lord, I helped raise sweet Leslie. I won't be leaving just yet, thank you."

After dinner we retired to the library, where Louise served cocktails. I sipped on a scotch and soda, but I found it much too strong for my Texas taste and immediately longed for a cold Lone Star. Leslie's father didn't finish a single drink, but Mrs. Wallace had several. I sat next to Leslie on a settee, and she explained some of the more interesting aspects of the library and the house in general. They had owned the house since the early 1950s, and it was the only one Leslie had known. Mr. Wallace's job was in a stock brokerage in New York, and he came home only on weekends. Mrs. Wallace ran a thriving interior design shop in the central district of Richmond. She consulted for clients as far away as Washington, D.C.. Leslie had grown up mostly on her own but under the scrutiny of Harriet.

I felt sorry for Leslie. Growing up without the perpetual noise and emotional turmoil of a large family and without the constant presence of a mother must have been difficult. No wonder she needed physical contact and emotional connection. Not that I was complaining, because the disadvantage of the large family was that no one child ever received enough singular attention. I needed the physical reassurances as much as Leslie. We complemented each other in this way.

Mr. Wallace sat near a corner window because, as Mrs. Wallace put it, "That smelly old pipe makes me nauseous." Mrs. Wallace, however, sat on a chair near Leslie and me and positioned herself so that I had an unobstructed view of her marvelous assets. For an hour Leslie's parents questioned me about my family, Annapolis, and my future prospects. During that period Leslie pinched me several times to bring my concentration back to earth. I endured the grilling in good humor. They had every right to question their future son-in-law. I found that I liked the two of them. I especially liked the way Mrs. Wallace flirted with me.

At nearly 2200 William Wallace stood resolutely and said to his wife, "Well, dear, let's leave these two young people to entertain themselves." Then he said to Leslie, "You know where the TV and snacks are, dear. Have a nice evening." Mrs. Wallace quickly finished her drink and also stood.

"Breakfast will be at ten, dears. See you then." She smiled warmly at me, and they departed together. Mrs. Wallace looked as great from the rear as she did from the front. Leslie pinched me again, and I laughed.

"I have to talk to Mother," Leslie said after they were gone. "She's absolutely shameless."

I laughed. "She is a beautiful woman, and she does like to flaunt it," I replied.

"I have to tell you something about my parents," Leslie said, suddenly becoming very serious. "They have a very 'strange' relationship. Mom is a beauty; she was Miss Virginia in 1947. She also is extremely intelligent and earned an honor's degree in interior architecture from William and Mary College. She met dad after she had graduated and he was in from New York supervising the acceptance of the First National Bank Building in Richmond. At the time it was the tallest and most modern building in the city. They married six months after they met, and bought this house with every penny they had. Mom refused to live in New York, forcing Dad to commute home on the weekends. They've had separate lives almost from the day they married."

"About three years after I was born Mom suspected that Dad was having an affair with a co-worker. She went to New York secretly and discovered the truth. Instead of making a scene, she waited until he returned to Richmond. They discussed their relationship openly. Each of them knew that staying together would be the best thing for them and for me and that a divorce would mean financial ruin for the family. They decided that their private lives were to be their own, but they also promised not to let what happened outside the family become public or interfere with their weekend relationship. As far as I know, they've held to that promise."

"I think it's been hardest on Mom. She doesn't like the deceit, but as you can see she is a very sensual woman, and with Dad gone so much she finds herself restless for companionship. She drinks a bit too much. She's had several men to the house for dinner and whatever, mostly when I'm away; and sometimes she stays in town overnight. I don't ask her what she does, and she doesn't offer to explain. But I do know that she has a need to be desirable, and it's something she has very little control over.

"I'm saying this James Merritt, because if you are to be a permanent part of my life I'm sure there will come a time -- probably soon -- when Mom will try to seduce you. I've already seen the look in her eye. I'm not saying I will hate you if you give in to her, because I know how overpowering a woman she can be and I also care about her happiness. But I don't want us ever to have the relationship my parents do. I intend to love you forever and as often as I can, and I want you to turn to me whenever you need comfort and compassion. And I'll go wherever you want me to go." I watched her eyes tear up. I reached out and held her gently.

"Your mom is beautiful, Leslie, but you are far more so. Besides, she can't really be interested in me, I'm young enough to be her son." I laughed, but she didn't even smile. "Anyway, I'm your man. I'll resist."

Leslie sat up straight and looked closely at me with a frown. She shook her head.

"How naive men are. If mother wants you in a physical way, I doubt there will be anything you can do to resist. You really don't understand the power women wield, James Merritt."

I was really confused now. "Then what am I supposed to do, Leslie. If you want, I won't ever come here again, and I'll stay a million miles away from your mother. All I want is you." Leslie smiled at me, considering the alternatives, then I had a sudden brainstorm. I laughed aloud.

"What?" she asked.

"Leslie, dear, I have the ultimate, solution for this situation, one that will satisfy you, me, your mother, and a certain person we both know."

"What?" she asked again.

"Rico!" I answered with happy conviction. She didn't look convinced. "Trust me on this, Leslie Taylor Wallace. Rico is the answer to all our prayers."

We changed clothes and met in the family room, a place I instantly loved. A large, fancy, television and entertainment center adorned one interior side wall. An enormous stone fireplace completely filled another. A huge picture window arrangement offered a great view of the forest on the third side. The remaining side led to an enormous screened-in porch and sunroom. Comfortable couches were arranged so that the fire, the view, and the TV could be enjoyed equally. I could envision myself lord-of-all-I-surveyed in this room -- with Leslie as my wife and consort, of course.

Leslie checked to ensure the house was quiet and returned with two cold beers. It wasn't Lone Star, but at least I knew there was some semblance of civilization here in the Wallace mansion. We sat quietly together and sipped the beer. Then Leslie locked the door and we made quiet love on the largest couch.

"I want to sleep next to you tonight, James Merritt," she said sweetly.

"Ah, do you think that's a good idea?" I asked. She giggled.

"As long as we don't sleep in too late, it'll be okay. Daddy never gets up before nine, and Mother sometimes misses breakfast entirely."

"If you say so, that'll be wonderful."

"Good," she said with a twinkle in her eye. "Let's give the remainder of the family a chance to fall soundly asleep. Leave your door unlocked, and I'll be visiting about one o'clock. Set the alarm next to the bed for eight so we wake in time."

"Who says I'm gonna let you sleep?" I asked. She laughed.

"Sounds wonderful," she said huskily. God was this woman ever sensual.

I had been lying naked in the dark bed under the soft satin covers, recounting the events of the day and of the holiday when she entered. The naked part was a surprise for Leslie, who I had expected in about fifteen minutes but who obviously couldn't wait. Good, neither could I.

For a brief instant as she pushed the door carefully closed behind her, her marvelous figure was outlined against the dim hall light, clothed in only a short lace nightie. Wow, what incredible breasts she had! They seemed even larger than I last remembered. Now that was strange. I didn't realize that breasts could get bigger in just a matter of an hour or so. And Leslie must have cut her hair too, because it was a whole lot shorter then when we parted. And I could hear the tinkle of ice in a glass. I began to panic.

Oh, shit! I couldn't believe that what I thought was happening *was* happening. What the hell was I supposed to do? Obviously I would have to firmly but politely resist. But I also had to be nice because this was, after all, my future mother-in-law. The figure slowly approached, and through the dappled patterns of faint window light I could see more of what Leslie's mom had flaunted before, during, and after dinner. What legs! What breasts! What a wonderful curve to her pelvic area and the darkness centered there! What the hell was I thinking? She drew nearer until she was next to the bed.

Should I pretend to be asleep? Should I act startled? Should I wet myself? Should I try to concentrate on stopping the involuntary reaction that was quickly lifting the sheets? I realized two things immediately. First, Leslie was absolutely correct. When faced with something this primitively sensual and determined, there was no way even the pope himself could resist. I was about to be seduced and enjoy every moment of it. I decided that I was an absolute shithead for thinking I should throw in the towel so quickly.

She stared at me for a second or two and I watched the rise and fall of her delicious chest. She must have been able to see that I was awake.

She put her drink on the nightstand, leaned over, and whispered, "James?" Oh, my God, what a view!

I croaked a "yes" and waited.

"Are you awake?"

Was I awake? Was every nerve in my body on fire? Was my heart about to explode? Hadn't I erected a suspicious tent?

"Sort of," I answered, telling an absolute lie. I was awake all right. She reached over and lightly touched my chest. I tingled and I burned. She patted my chest area and rubbed her fingers in my sparse but completely sufficient light hair.

"Good," she said. "I want to talk to you."

"About what?"

"James, I won't lie. I find you enormously attractive in a wholesome and virile way, and I can completely understand why Leslie is in love with you. But I also know that you find me attractive, and I know that young men your age are capable of sharing their love." She paused and removed her hand.

"William and I have not shared 'love' for several years, and it's been a very lonely time for me. You can feed a mature older woman's ego by responding to her advances. I promise you the experience will be worth the effort, and I also promise that I will never let on to Leslie that we had did anything."

She sat down on the bed next to me, leaned over, kissed me softly on the forehead, and whispered huskily, "I want you, James. Make love with me." God almighty, what a sexy voice she had!

Her breasts brushed against my chest, igniting more fire inside me. I raised my right arm, intending to hold her away for a moment so I could collect my thoughts. She took my hand, slipped it inside her nightgown. Then she kissed me with a great deal of passion. I didn't remove my hand, although I thought about it briefly. She had pressed against me in such a way that I might scratch or injure her if I moved my hand. I couldn't do that could I? I could feel her responding to my finger pressure, and I didn't want to stop that either.

I had kissed her for less than a minute before I began to come to my senses. I ended the kiss, realizing uncomfortably that I was ten seconds away from complete abandon. I wanted this woman.

"Stop for a minute," I whispered.

She sat up and gently rubbed my cheek while she held my hand to her chest.

"Nice kiss," she said.

"Listen," I continued quickly, taking several deep breaths. "I can't believe this is happening. We've got to stop."

"No we don't," she said sweetly. "William sleeps like a log." She chuckled in a throaty fashion that excited me even more, then she began to lean down toward me again.

"It's not William I'm concerned about," I said quickly. She paused and tilted her head, puzzled.

"Leslie will be here in two minutes," I said. I didn't know if revealing Leslie's imminent arrival to Mrs. Wallace was a good idea or not, but it seemed the best way to end her advances, and if they didn't end soon, Leslie would find the two of us when she came in.

Mrs. Wallace sat up straight and looked down at me, keeping her one hand on my chest.

"Leslie is coming here?" she asked.

I looked at the clock. "In exactly two minutes," I said. I found myself torn between relief that the crisis was resolved and surprising anger that Mrs. Wallace hadn't timed her visit better. Why couldn't she have visited about 30 minutes ago. I still wanted her, and I had to strain to rein in my desires.

She laughed.

"That little she-devil," she said with genuine fondness. "I didn't realize. But then again," she said, leaning down on me once more and running her hand along my flat belly. "I can completely understand."

She kissed me quickly and whispered, "Some other time then, James." She quickly stood, straightened herself, and chuckled.

"I must have a motherly talk with little Leslie. See you tomorrow, James dear." Within a few seconds she had slipped quietly from the room.

It was almost too much for me to handle. Plebe Year, the Tigers, Stone, Poole, Lynda, poor Mom, sweet Leslie, and now this incredible sexpot of a future mother-in-law. It all swam confusedly around in my head for several minutes. Then the door opened quietly again and I could tell from the silhouette that the visitor was my wonderful woman. For the next several hours we made love to each other in as many ways as I could think of and until we were both worn out to the point of exhaustion.

"Wow, James Merritt. You are like a big, strong, loving machine, and I love every cog and gear and piston." I didn't tell her that her passionate mother had stoked the flames and gotten me revved up. Leslie and I slept in each other's arms the rest of the night. I had never before slept with someone else, and I decided that I liked it. Leslie touched me tenderly during her dreams, and the smell of her perfume and shampoo and womanliness aided in my contentment.

Mrs. Wallace made it to breakfast and never once alluded that she knew anything about Leslie and my sleeping arrangements. And even though she was sexy as hell in her leather riding outfit -- she was off to the stables after the meal -- and she continued to flirt at me, she didn't so much as hint at what had almost happened. I admired her for that. I also quickly stifled a regret that but for fifteen minutes I would have experienced the promise that awaited the chosen few inside that tight outfit. I wasn't at all sure I could have handled it.

Leslie and I sneaked out to the garage as part of her tour of the grounds, which included 25 acres of virgin forest threaded by narrow trails, a large stream with freshly running water, a magnificent riding meadow, and several wooded knolls. I fell in love with Leslie's Tara.

At 1400 we departed for Annapolis. I drove, and we chatted until Leslie fell asleep with her head against the far window. I stayed quiet and let her sleep. The drive took two uneventful hours, and Leslie didn't wake until we neared the outskirts of the city.

"Why didn't you wake me?" she asked, still groggy, as she stretched and tried to bring blood to her extremities.

"It's okay," I said. "You needed the rest. And besides, you still have an hour's drive back to Washington." Leslie changed places with me and drove through the gate. This was an authorized vacation and plebes were allowed to ride in cars, but not drive them. It was impossible amid the bustle of the returning brigade to say a proper farewell, but we made plans to try to see each other next weekend. If not, Christmas vacation was only three weeks away, and I would be visiting Leslie on the front end of that period for five glorious days, during two of which we would have the house to ourselves. I could not wait.

I waved goodby to her as she drove away, feeling suddenly sad and alone. As I turned toward the fourth wing, I found myself completely dreading my return to Tiger Company, despite the carry-on that awaited. I trudged the distance slowly, watching other midshipmen and wondering if everybody's life was as complicated as mine.

CHAPTER 15

HOME AGAIN - HOME AGAIN

Kevin was already there when I returned, and he didn't look too happy.

"What's up, O'Reilly?" I asked.

"I broke up with Sarah!"

"No way! Why!"

"Because she's trying to run my life, that's why! She wouldn't leave me alone for a minute."

"Maybe she loves you, Kevin," I said thinking about Leslie. "What could be better than that?"

"Well maybe too much love is bad!" he blurted. "She came to Thanksgiving dinner at the O'Reilly house, which was okay, and we had a nice time afterward." He paused and smiled, suddenly remembering something. "Her parents were away for the weekend, and her monster big brother was visiting his friends in Dedham all day and most of the night. We had a great time -- the best I've ever had. We did things I only read about in Rico's tech manuals."

He looked at me and shook his head.

"I think she really does love me, but she wants to possess me, and it makes me afraid. Hell no, it pisses me off; that's what it does! She objected when I said that Friday night I wanted to go out with my friends. Tell me what's the harm in that?" I didn't answer, and he really didn't expect an answer. "I went anyway, and she wouldn't talk to me on Saturday, even though we were supposed to go to a movie. I guess she expected me to come crawling to her, but I didn't. Mom told me she had been fuming all day today and that she told her mother she was stupid to behave like she did. But she didn't tell *me* anything, so I left without saying a word."

"Why didn't you at least call her and tell her what bothered you?"

"Because that's what she wants, that's why! I remembered on Saturday the big reason why I never tried to date her previously. She's too damn insecure. She'll want me to constantly prove my worthiness. Marriage will be a test of love and loyalty, so forget the whole thing. I'll find someone else."

"It sounds like a poem I read in high school," I said.

"Yeah, *The Glove and the Lion,*" he replied.

"But you love her, Kevin!"

He smiled at me sheepishly. "Yeah. I think so! But I still threw the glove in her face. I won't have a relationship that's one-sided and sucks the life out of me."

BJ was next to arrive, and he was in a bad mood too.

"Damn I hate this place!"

"What's up with you?" I asked.

"There's so much to do in New York. The city is so full of life and energy -- and beautiful women. But I'm a plebe, and it's driving me crazy."

Rico arrived last, only 15 minutes before formation, which would have presented a problem because it was our room's turn to do chow calls for the week.

"Sorry guys," he said gaily-- At least he was smiling. "Rosa wanted a quickie in the car before she'd let me go. I had to comply, but it was hell finding an appropriate spot."

"You had Rosa drive you all the way from New York?" I asked incredulously.

"I have my reasons. She's taking the bus back, so she'll be safe."

"Bus? What about the car," Kevin asked. Rico beamed.

"That's the reason for the bus."

"You didn't?" BJ almost exploded. Rico smiled devilishly. "Guevarra, you've got bigger huevos than any amigo I have ever heard of."

Rico smiled at us.

"Party time, gentlemen!" That perked up Kevin and BJ considerably. We couldn't think or talk further, as it was time to chop to our positions at the corners of the passageways and scream out the rates of the day -- the upcoming meal menu, the names and jobs of the officers of the watch, the movies in town, and the days remaining until Christmas leave, Hundredth Night, and First-class graduation. Since it was the first formation following a vacation period, everybody was interested in vacation stories, and no one bothered us.

The meal was casual, but then I was on Brandis's table, and I had the impression that they had already abrogated Plebe Year. I could hear shouting from Micklewski's table though. They were after Poole and Butler again. This was getting tiresome.

I had brought back a supply of homemade cookies and we distributed them to select clientele as part of the sandwich mess deliveries.

"Goodwill is good business," BJ said repeatedly. He was probably right because orders were way up and Mugsy was happy as a pig in poop. I saw a Corvette catalog on his desk one evening when we handed over the proceeds.

On the Tuesday following Thanksgiving life took another nose-dive in Twenty-third Company when Captain Dillingham visited the Company for a noon-meal inspection and luncheon. He sat with Stone at Micklewski's table. Unfortunately it was my turn to sit there also.

"Did everybody have a good vacation?" Dillingham asked the table and received a chorus of nods and affirmations in answer. "How about you, Mister Poole? Was your vacation enjoyable?"

Tommy looked straight across the table at the Captain.

"Yes, sir! It was great!"

"Did you tell your parents about the possibility of your coming home soon, Mister Poole?"

"We talked, sir, but I decided to stay," Tommy answered in a very subdued voice. Had Dillingham actually instructed Tommy to tell his parents he was leaving? Bull took a deep breath; and although I sat exactly next to him, and did not dare turn his way, I could tell by the way he expanded his chest that he was not pleased.

"Mister Poole, I am about to lose patience with you. I told you that you did not fit the physical and character standards of a proper midshipman and that I did not want you to remain here. I asked you also to tell your parents that you will be coming home. Why didn't you do that?"

"Sir, I still don't understand what it is about me that upsets everyone so. I feel I do meet the uniform standards, and the academics, and the physical requirements. I may not be the best athlete, but I'm not the worst either, by a long shot."

Dillingham sighed, plainly exasperated.

"I'm not used to having my orders disobeyed, Mister Poole, but I'll give you one more chance. You will re-discuss what I said with your parents when you go home at Christmas. Is that understood?"

I could see from Tommy's face that he was plainly upset.

"Aye, aye, sir!" he finally answered, then quickly asked, "Request permission to speak, sir?"

Dillingham, always the good democrat, answered smiling.

"Of course, Mister Poole."

"Sir, what is it that convinces you that I am not a fit midshipman?"

Dillingham, clearly relishing his role as lecturer and protector of the sacred Annapolis image, smiled again at the group before he continued.

"It's really quite simple, Mister Poole. You don't fit here. You stand out in the group like a sore thumb, and you draw unnecessary attention to yourself, which in turn distracts the rest of us from our mission. You're like a third tit -- an interesting curiosity, but neither relevant nor welcome -- and I'll bet everyone at this table agrees." He looked around seeking confirmation, which came quickly from the firsties and second-class. I was dreading what might happen next.

Dillingham turned to me.

"Mister Merritt, do you agree with me on this?"

"Sir," I said diplomatically, "Tommy Poole is my classmate and friend." I knew that wasn't an answer, but I didn't want to jump off the fence just yet. Stone watched me closely.

"Yes! I understand that, Mister Merritt. But that's just the point? If Tommy here is really your friend, you need to tell him how out of place he is and how uncomfortable he makes you feel. That's what a good friend would do."

I looked at Tommy. His look told me to say anything I wanted and he would understand but not to get into trouble on his part.

"Sir," I said. "I'm just a plebe. I have almost no experience with officers and what it takes to make a good one. I'm not qualified to comment."

"Come on, Merritt!" Dillingham said loudly. "What do you really think?"

To hell with it!

"Sir. I am not personally embarrassed by Tommy Poole. I think he will make a fine naval officer." I looked directly at Stone as I spoke. He smiled at me, I think pleased at my taking a moral stand even though he didn't personally agree with my position. Dillingham was not pleased.

"Damn it, Merritt! What kind of attitude is that? Look at Poole! He's dumpy, he's funny looking, and he's feminine. He will *not* make a good officer -- except maybe in the Nurse Corps." Dillingham laughed deeply at his own humor, and unfortunately, too many of the table's occupants joined in. I began to feel myself losing my temper. It wasn't right to treat Tommy this way in a publicly humiliating fashion. To hell with my attitude, what kind of *leadership* was that? I noticed identical please-keep-your-big-mouth-shut expressions on the faces of Tommy Poole and Rock Stone, and they noticed each other simultaneously.

I calmed.

"Again, sir. I'm not qualified to say whether Tommy should quit." I knew that immediately I had been put on Dillingham's mental list of potential subversives and agitators. I would have to walk softly around him from now on.

Dillingham looked at Tommy and seemed to come down from his self-erected heroic pedestal.

"I really don't have anything personally against you, Mister Poole. In fact, like Merritt here, I admire your guts. You'd make a great doctor fighting to save lives, or an attorney rescuing desperate clients, or a scientist working tirelessly to find a cure for acne or hangnails." Again too many people laughed. "But this isn't a question of guts, it's a question of more than a hundred years of tradition and service and honor. In my very professional opinion you will not be an effective naval officer. Your troops will not respect you. Your peers will avoid you. And you will make your superiors damned uncomfortable. My job is to recognize this inadequacy. If I can't convince you that what I say is true, I'm very sorry, but I have to follow my convictions. You cannot remain here, Mister Poole," he said very firmly. "Tell your parents you are coming home." I became instantly afraid for poor Tommy.

With that Dillingham changed the subject almost as if nothing had happened. To the Captain, Tommy and every other plebe in the Brigade no doubt, were almost inconsequential elements in the grand scheme of Annapolis training. But, judging from the determined look in his eyes, I had the feeling that Tommy Poole was not about to let Dillingham's beliefs convince him to depart. I decided to take some action to support Tommy.

That evening I passed the word that I wanted to have a closed meeting of the plebes. Stone had agreed that we could use the Wardroom if we kept the meeting to under 30 minutes. He never even asked what the meeting was about, although I think he knew the subject must be Tommy Poole.

Most of the plebes arrived on time and seated themselves in various places and positions around the Wardroom. We had not had a plebe-only meeting since the summer, and I immediately realized it would be a benefit for us to meet on a monthly basis to discuss problems and progress. I decided to broach the idea with Stone. I though he'd agree.

I had purposefully not asked Tommy to attend and also instructed his roommates not to let on what was happening, so we began the meeting Poole-less, and somewhat restless as well.

"Okay, Merritt," Danny French blurted. "What's all this about? Some of us have studies and papers to work on." I never liked French. He was a stuck-up jerk about most things. I ignored him.

"I want to talk to everyone for a minute about Tommy Poole," I began. Loud moans erupted. Many of my classmates were tired of Tommy, and the trouble he caused, and some saw him as the main reason the firsties hadn't loosened up on the rest of us more. Quite a few of the plebes agreed with Dillingham and Stone.

"Hold on," I said. "Give me a chance to speak." Everyone quieted except French. He stood and walked to the door.

"Poole is useless!" he said loudly. "Let them run him out. I don't care. If you called me in here to support some 'Rally Round Tommy' campaign, forget my participation. In case you haven't heard, my grades are marginal. I have other things to worry about." Not waiting for further comments, he departed. I shook my head in disbelief after he had gone.

"French is a dick-head!" Jeff Polk said loudly. Many of our classmates, myself included, laughed.

"Okay," I said. "French's position is obvious, but I don't know where the rest of us stand on this, and it's important because after what I saw at lunch I would say that Dillingham himself is fed up and will take some action after the holidays to get rid of Tommy -- if he doesn't quit on his own." I paused for a moment, collecting my thoughts.

"I have had a chance to watch Tommy during the last six months. He was my roommate during the summer. Forgetting for a moment where he started, right now he performs as well as many of us. I believe he needs our support, both directly and indirectly. We hurt him by supporting the upper-class in their humiliation and jokes. I really believe he deserves to graduate with the rest of us. So let's get some ideas on the floor about what we can do."

Hank Butkowski stood. "Tommy Poole is a good guy. Actually he's a pretty funny . And he's helped me a number of times with my studies when he had better things to do. I say we need to stand behind him."

Mike Wojeck spoke up next. "I'm not completely convinced that Tommy is the best midshipman in the world, but nobody says he has to be the best. So long as he meets the minimum standards, he should be allowed to stay. But even more so I detest everything the Tigers stand for. They are completely wrong in how they run this company. Anything I can do to hinder them is okay with me."

Tony Delvecchio raised his hand. "Danny French is my roommate . . . " he began.

"French is a dickhead!" Polk interrupted.

Delvecchio laughed with the rest of us.

"Yes, maybe. But he has a point. All the shit the upper-class feel about Tommy gets dumped onto us too. Because of Tommy we all suffer."

"I don't agree!" Bob Strong piped in. " Without Tommy they'd just focus on someone else. French is completely wrong."

"French is a dickhead!" Polk said again.

Then the door burst open and Tommy rushed in.

"What's this all about?" he asked.

"We're having a meeting, Tommy," I said.

"About me!"

"How did you know?"

"Danny French came by the room and told me!"

"French is a dickhead!" chanted five plebes in the back row in unison. That really got a laugh, but Tommy was not pleased.

"Why are you meeting?" he asked challengingly.

"Tommy," Jubal said. "It's okay. We're thinking up ways t' help y'all." Tommy looked closely at Ramsey, who had been almost violently opposed to Tommy's status during the summer period. "I mean it Tommy. You should stay."

"Well, I don't think you should meet without me."

"Tommy," I said, "use your head. How could we have an open discussion with you present? We have to thrash out the pros and cons."

"Well, maybe, but I want to know what you decide."

"Go home, Tommy!" said George Abbott. "It'll be okay." Tommy stared hard at George, turned, and departed. George stood and quietly walked to the front of the room. I had never heard George say more than five words together before. I stepped aside for him. He turned to the group.

"Okay," he said. "I know what's up with Tommy. I know why he's here, and why he can't quit. And why we have to help him." That really piqued our interest because the subject had been the root of much speculation.

George began again.

"I happened to fly back to Annapolis with Tommy on the airplane from Chicago on Saturday. I was visiting relatives there for the holidays. Tommy and I talked the stews into letting us sit together. He had already had a few drinks, and he had a few more on the plane."

"I hope you covered yourself with towels before he puked!" Jubal blurted.

"No, no. He was fine -- tipsy, but fine. Midway back he started talking about his older brother, who died when he was younger. He was really close, and apparently they used to dare each other to do things that were challenging. He talked a lot about this kid. Well, one of their biggest bets was to see which one would be first to fly a jet plane. It sounds crazy, I know, but they loved these challenges; and Tommy really loved his brother. They both talked about joining the Air Force and learning to fly someday. Poole picked Annapolis because he figured that carriers would be harder to land on than nice flat runways. He wants to fly over the graveyard where his brother is buried and dip his wings in tribute."

George paused while we digested this information.

"That doesn't seem rational," offered Doug Goto, the analytical member of the group. Douglas was a Japanese American from nearby Baltimore who was tall, athletic, and very friendly. He was also a consummate team player.

"Dreams often aren't," said Kevin with typical confusing poeticism.

"It all does make a kind of sense now," said Wesley Lamont in his deep and wonderful islands accent. "Tommy has a mission that surpasses even that of the Tigers. It will be impossible for them to beat him." He laughed delightedly. It had almost a musical quality. "They never had a chance!"

The meeting seemed to have ended with that, but instead Tim Butler stood tentatively.

"Tommy is my dearest friend," he said with great emotion. "He's brave and strong and wonderful. You just have to get to know him like I do. He's the closest friend I've ever had." Tim's voice, normally quiet and unpretentious, sounded naturally girl-like. Even though the content was harmless, the undercurrents of what he said made every one of us uncomfortable. We were all silent for a moment. Butler's speech did not help Tommy's cause as much as he had hoped.

"Great!" I said. "So do we have agreement?"

"For what?" asked Pat Mulvaney.

"To help Tommy however we can," I answered.

"Of course," Pat said. "What else would we do?"

We returned to our respective rooms.

"That was nicely done, Jim," Kevin said. "I think Tommy will make it for sure now that we're all behind him." Rico laughed.

"O'Reilly, you're almost as naive as Merritt and the rest of the greasers."

"What's that mean?" I asked.

"You people are all hung up on duty, honor, and loyalty, and you forget that those terms are vague. It's honorable for us to support Tommy, but it's just as honorable for Stone to support Dillingham. So who's the bad guy? And all Tommy's had to deal with is the Tigers, and they're mostly paper. Wait 'til Bull gets his two cents in after Christmas leave, then the whole ball game changes."

"Are you saying Tommy isn't going to make it?" Kevin asked.

"I don't know," Rico answered. "Let's just say the jury's still out." That statement sounded especially prophetic, even coming from the great Swami.

"Damn it's cold outside!" Kevin complained as he threw his rifle onto his rack. "I swear icicles were forming on my nose." It was Saturday after noon meal and Kevin had been marching off his demerits. Stone's Report Chit had resulted in 20 demerits, and from 1300 to 1500, Kevin and nearly 50 other midshipmen of various grades, had marched under the not-so-observant supervision of a first-class who was also on report. Each hour of marching reduced the demerit total by five. Unfortunately for Kevin, the marching had taken place in 26 degree temperatures and in the middle of a series of blowing snow and rain showers.

Kevin looked miserable, but that was all the marching he would have to endure today. From now until 2100 he would instead report to the Main Office every hour in service dress uniform for a muster. Every hour of this restriction would reduce his demerit total by one additional point. By the end of the day Kevin would have six demerits. Tomorrow he would march again for two hours, completely erasing the penalty for his disrespect to Micklewski. I asked Kevin if it seemed worth it.

"With icicles hanging from my nose? Hell no! Next time I'll just kill the bastard. Then it's a nice cushy prison cell for me."

No one went into town that Saturday, although Kevin begged us to get him a submarine.

"No damn way, O'Reilly!" Rico said, and that was final.

I waited until Kevin was mustering and BJ had gone to the head before asking Rico the big question. I had no idea how to broach the subject, so I tried the direct-indirect approach.

"Rico!" I said.

"Yeah," he said, looking up from a tech manual.

"How would you like to come to visit Leslie's house for a few days at the beginning of the Christmas holidays?"

Rico looked at me suspiciously.

"What's the matter, can't BJ come to schtup Leslie's friend?"

"No, it's not Leslie's friend I'm thinking about for you."

"Then who?"

"I'd rather not say. But I can promise you more pleasure than you ever imagined."

Rico laughed and held up the latest book. The hero, stripped to the waist, was riding a camel in some desert kingdom, blazing happily away at a group of Arabs who were chasing him. A scantily clad and robustly chested young lady clung to him with one hand and held a pistol in the other.

"I don't know," he said, chuckling. "I can imagine an awful lot."

"Trust me on this, Rico. I promise you will not be disappointed."

"What about Rosa?" he asked.

"Better!"

"No way!"

"I swear before God! Better!"

"Jesus, Merritt! You've got my interest piqued now! When would this be?"

"The first three days of the vacation."

Rico looked at me.

"Better huh?"

"I swear!"

"Okay. You've got a deal. We can drive down in my car." Rico was an easy sell when sexual adventure was in the offing.

"Don't say anything to the other guys," I added. "Kevin would be mad because he's broken up with Sarah. But to tell the truth neither he nor BJ could handle it."

"Merritt, my mouth is watering already. This had better be legit!" Legit? Interesting question, but I'll bet after getting one look at Mrs. Wallace it wouldn't matter a bit if the opportunities were "legit" or not.

The days leading to Christmas vacation passed quickly, but the time was marred by a serious incident in the life of Tommy Poole. I suppose the "best buddies" speech by Tim Butler put an idea in some plebe's empty head and he talked to an upper-class, who talked to a firstie, who talked to Stone. By the time the rendition of what Tim said had reached Stone, it had been twisted all out of proportion.

"Merritt," Stone asked me on a Tuesday evening immediately after meal. "What do you think about homosexuality?" He had called me to his room for this "private" conversation.

"I hadn't thought much about it, sir," I said, wondering what the heck was up. I wasn't being propositioned was I? Surely not by Stone? How could anyone with the name 'Rock' be funny that way?

"Do you think homosexuality should be tolerated in this institution?" he asked me.

"No, sir!" I answered. It was an honest answer. I didn't see how midshipmen could live comfortably among others who might be interested in doing strange things in the shower.

"What if I were to tell you that we suspect some of your classmates are not everything they pretend to be?"

Why was he asking me this?

"I don't know, sir."

"Would you help us ferret them out?"

"That depends, sir."

"On what?"

"On who it is, what kind of evidence you have, and what you expect me to do."

Stone paused for effect.

"We have reason to believe that Midshipmen Poole and Butler are having a homosexual affair."

"Tommy! No way sir! I've seen him with his girlfriend."

"Homosexuals hide what they are sometimes, Merritt. Quite a few get married to normal women and fool around on the side. Some even have children." We both shuddered involuntarily at this thought.

"Still, sir. Not Tommy!"

"Look," Stone said, "I just want you to ask around and see what you can find out. No matter how brave he is, you must surely see that if the rumor is true, he has to go."

I pondered the implications.

"Yes, sir," I said quietly and reluctantly.

Immediately after returning to the room, I broached the subject with my roommates.

"Tommy, a fag? I can't believe it!" Kevin said.

I looked at BJ.

"I've know plenty of out-and-out flamers," he said, "they're all over the entertainment business." "Most are actually very nice, conscientious, hard working people, and perfectly harmless. Tommy? -- I don't think so."

"I'll be honest with you guys," Rico said. "I get very upset by the very idea of homos. It's probably my Catholic upbringing and my Latino machismo. But I'm sure as I can be Tommy is not that way." Somehow hearing Rico say it lifted my spirits, I decided not to investigate any farther.

"But Tim, on the other hand . . . " Rico continued, then let the idea drop.

"Now wait a minute, Rico!" I said. "Sure he's a bit feminine, but Tim Butler seems completely uninterested in other guys. Don't you think someone would have noticed by now?"

"Not really. I think we're all focused on other things."

"While Tim is focused on *our* things?" Kevin asked. We chuckled. I could understand the humor. Tim Butler was the most unthreatening of midshipmen.

"Besides," I added, "Suspicion is one thing. Even if he is 'different', so what? So long as he keeps it to himself, shouldn't that be okay?"

"No, it shouldn't!" said Rico forcefully. "If he is, he doesn't belong here. There's enough pressure on us already without adding the possibility that a classmate might be looking up your gym shorts during gymnastics, or coping a feel during wrestling. Sorry, Jim, but I don't agree!"

"But you think Tim is homosexual?" I asked.

"All I'm saying is maybe," Rico said. Rico was so seldom wrong that I decided to shift my attention to Tim for a while, which was easy since I had to sit at the meal table with him on a rotating basis. The more I watched him, the more uncomfortable I became, particular in the way he related to Tommy. I began wondering what to do.

Three days before Christmas vacation Tim Butler came to the room just after evening meal. I don't think he had ever been there before. I couldn't remember ever having an honest conversation with him prior to that day.

"I have to talk to you, Jim," he said. Then he looked at Rico and Kevin. "In private, please."

"Ah, okay," I answered. "Let's go to the Company Office. I think it should still be open, and Dillingham's usually gone by now."

We went slowly and quietly down the passageway. I secretly watched Tim. I could sense he was troubled. Stone was in Dillingham's office.

"Sir," I said. "May I use the office for a few minutes for an official conversation?" Stone looked from me to Butler. He must have remembered our conversation of several days ago. He nodded.

"I guess so," he said. "But make it quick. I have a Company project I'm working on for the Captain." He quickly departed. I closed the door, and Tim and I sat on chairs in the anteroom facing each other.

"What's up, Tim?"

He hesitated, obviously unsure how to continue. I watched as he unconsciously jiggled his legs and shifted in the seat. Finally he looked up.

"I heard about the rumor Stone is spreading about me and Tommy."

"What's that?"

"Oh, you can stop the act," he said quietly. "I know you're in on it too."

"Well, why don't you tell me what you think, Tim, and I'll fill you in with the truth."

"The rumor is that Tommy and I are homosexuals."

"That's only a rumor, Tim. How did you find out?"

"It doesn't matter. I told Tommy and he laughed about it. He just shrugged it off. Called it ridiculous." Suddenly Tim Butler became very angry. His eyes flashed as he brought them to bear on me. I felt uncomfortable.

"Tommy Poole is not a homosexual!" he almost shouted. "He is the finest human being I have ever known. He's kind and generous and sincere. In fact he's more a man than anyone in this Company!"

The words came out in such a rush that he was out of breath when he finished. He was also out of anger. Almost immediately he calmed and became distressed. I could see tears building up in his eyes.

"You have to believe me, Jim. You're the best of all of us. Tommy is a real man!" Tears splashed on the tile floor as he sobbed.

I reached over and touched him on the foot. "It's okay, Tim," I said softly. "I know Tommy's okay."

He looked at me closely.

"But I'm not okay, Jim." Shocked at the implication, I almost pulled my hand back without thinking. Thankfully I held my position.

"What do you mean, Tim?"

"Tommy's fine. I'm the homo! And I think I love Tommy Poole. But I love him as a brother and I never said or did anything funny. Do you believe that?"

"Yes, Tim, I do." I continued to pat his foot, proud of myself for my compassion and for my open-mindedness. "But what are you going to do now?"

"Actually," he said, "I'm glad I told someone. I guess the next move is up to you."

I did pull my hand back at that.

"No Tim. It's not. I won't turn you in because you *say* you're different. You admit you haven't done anything, and you might be trying to sacrifice yourself to save Tommy. I don't want that on my conscience." It was my turn to pause, uncomfortable. "I've never known anyone who was different like that, Tim, so I'm at a personal loss here about advising you. But the regulations are clear about sexual preferences at Annapolis and in the Navy. If you are what you say, it's your responsibility either to turn yourself in or to resign quietly." I paused again.

"You'll make a good officer, Tim. With a little more forcefulness in your personality, you could be very good. You have a feeling for people that I'm sure your subordinates will respect. But still, rules are rules, and we need to remember there's more involved here than any one individual. Do you really want to compromise *your* personal ethics as well as the system's Honor Code? Living a constant lie is not good for you or Annapolis. But I respect you, and I'll keep mum about whatever you decide, I promise."

"You'd let me stay knowing I am a homosexual?"

"It's only you that says that, Tim. I don't know that for a fact. You say you haven't done anything. I don't care to know. This is your decision, but you do have the option of resigning without bringing any more unwanted attention on Tommy."

"Do you think Tommy would be blamed if I announced myself?"

"Knowing the Tigers? Of course he would. If you want to protect Tommy, either keep everything to yourself and continue as you are or resign quietly."

"Should I tell Tommy how I feel?"

I was shocked.

"Wow! That's up to you too. I personally think he'd understand, but I also don't think he's capable of returning your affection. It's a no-win situation for you. But it's your decision."

Tim stared at the deck for several seconds, plainly at an emotional loss. I reached over and patted his foot again. Finally he looked up and put one of his hands over mine. There's this thing in American male culture that repels us from physical contact with other men -- even casual contact. I felt a rush of that revulsion as Tim touched me and I wondered briefly what that touch meant. I had to force my hand to stay where it was.

"Thanks Jim," he said. "You're the best!" Somehow I didn't feel that way then. Tim stood and quietly left. I hurried out after him, not wanting to discuss the meeting with Stone.

Later that evening,, Tommy came to the room.

"Jim," he said, "can we talk in private?" I agreed, and we went to the head facility.

"I just want you to know I discussed quitting with Dillingham and Stone privately and I promised them I would talk to my parents seriously during the holidays."

"You can't quit Tommy," I blurted.

"Yes, I can! I'm sick of the pain and humiliation! My mother begs me every phone conversation to leave. Sara wants me closer to her. I just don't know if I can handle months more of this abuse." I started to talk, but Tommy held up a hand and turned to depart.

"I just wanted to let you know," he said as he left the head.

First semester left me drained. I realized that clearly as the final days would down to Christmas vacation. Classes and formations and meals passed in a blur, and soon two glorious weeks of relatively stress-free living stared me lovingly in the face. I was ready to get the hell out of Dodge, so to speak, and so were my classmates. So was every midshipman. There's something about the time leading up to Christmas that touches the American psyche and mellows even the staunchest soul. As the music and the spirit of the season increased in volume, even Dale Micklewski did endearing things -- although not to Tommy. Two nights before we departed for home and family and special friends, Captain Dillingham called another Company meeting.

"Gentlemen. Christmas leave is almost here, and there are several very important things I need to discuss with you before you go racing off to the four winds." He paced the passageway in front of us, flexing my muscular arms which were clasped behind him. I could see his chest muscles ripple as he walked. This was really one imposing guy.

"The first thing concerns the period itself. You all are aware of the duration of leave. Every year midshipmen cut the margin too close and end up late because of flight delays or car breakdowns. You'll get no sympathy from the system except in the gravest of circumstances, so plan your return carefully and conservatively.

"Second. While you are home or visiting friends, for God's sake be careful. Every year we lose several good men to traffic accidents. Do not drive when you have been drinking, and do not think that because you are in good shape you can drag race your car or take unnecessary chances with your lives. We want you back in Mother Bancroft's safe warm bosom." We chuckled.

"Third. Those of you who are behind academically had better take some books,--- ***and study***, damn it! When you return, you'll only have three weeks before finals, and it'll be too late then.

"Fourth. Since the first-class will soon be concentrating on Service Selection and their hopeful ultimate graduation, I will begin turning some of the leadership responsibilities over to the second-class."

"However, fifth and last. Plebes will not return complacent, because it ain't over yet, guys! Plebe Year *will* continue unabated until Hundredth Night -- and maybe beyond in some cases." Hundredth Night occurred on the evening of the one hundredth day prior to the graduation of the first-class. On that night the plebes and firsties switched places during the comearound, and the plebes were allowed -- expected -- to run the firsties' asses as hard as they themselves had been run. Since Hundredth Night also marked the semi-official end of Plebe Year, it was a night I was anticipating the event, even though it still seemed impossibly far away.

Dillingham continued, "I also think some of your classmates will not be returning after Christmas leave, and I want to wish them well and thank them for their participation." He looked directly at Tommy when he said that. Tommy returned his gaze.

"I've been able to observe plebe training thus far," he said gleefully, "and I'm pleased; but I want to see a Hundredth Night that will set Academy records. Is that understood?" The upper-class seemed to understand; but never having seen or participated in a Hundredth Night, I wasn't sure about the significance of the comment. And I didn't particularly care either, because leave was only three days away, and I wanted to erase all thoughts of Annapolis, Plebe Year, Tommy Poole, and Rock Stone as quickly and completely as possible so that I could get on with my real life.

I departed on Christmas vacation two days later, happily lounging in the front seat of Rico's 1966 Oldsmobile, thinking dreamily of Leslie, and whistling Christmas tunes in time with the songs on the radio. Rico stopped at a liquor store between Annapolis and Washington and produced some fake ID which got him served. We sipped from a six-pack of cold National Bohemian Beer as we drove, and hardly spoke as the concrete miles passed beneath the wheels. We were each very content with our temporary freedom.

Midway between Washington and Richmond, Rico turned to me with an enormous smile on his face and asked, "Better than Rosa, huh?"

I smiled.

MACDONOUGH HALL

Macdonough Hall, named after Commodore Thomas Macdonough, the victorious commander at the battle of Lake Champlain in 1814. It houses the Department of Physical Education where midshipmen train in gymnastics, wrestling, and boxing.

THE HUNDREDTH NIGHT

A NOVEL OF THE NAVAL ACADEMY

HANK TUROWSKI

USNA CLASS OF 1971

THE HUNDREDTH NIGHT

CHAPTER 1

THE ACADEMY

Last night's snow had accumulated several wet and slushy inches. The storm had been brief but intense, rattling the substantial windows of his dormitory room and waking him several times during the night. But last night's snow and wind were a welcome relief after two weeks of overcast and oppressively dismal days and sub-freezing nighttime temperatures. The forecast called for sunshine and a warming trend.

The morning definitely held promise. The sky was the deepest blue possible with hardly a cloud to mar the color, and the early sun blazed beautifully as it rose just above the tree-line of the far opposite bank of the Severn River. Patches of thin river ice glistened brightly on perfectly calm water, and the snow that covered the grass of Dewey Field and the wide lawns of the mansions across the river sparkled in pristine white. The air was almost startlingly still after last night's blow, and every slight hint of a breeze dislodged large clumps of wet snow from drooping tree branches, dropping wetness and slush-melt onto students who trudged to first period class.

For a brief moment the scene reminded him of the countryside near his home in Derry, New Hampshire. Weeks ago when he was home during Christmas vacation, a day-long snow had covered the farmland and gently rolling hills with a similar blanket. If he had the time to appreciate the scene, Jeff Polk might have smiled. He loved winter. He loved real New England winter that is, not so much this cowardly, cold-one-day-warm-the-next Maryland climate. This late in January the ponds near Derry would be thickly frozen and his friends and family would be skating and playing hockey every afternoon. Today's forecast for Annapolis promised just enough warmth to melt the snow and turn the near-frozen ground to mush. Sissy Maryland winter! Too many clouds. Too much rain. No excitement! No wonder his fellow students called this period the "Dark Ages."

Looking briefly toward the far end of Michelson Hall, Jeff watched several students who had braved the dirt path near the construction area between the main campus and the Severn. This shortcut, which midshipmen had named the "Ho Chi Minh Trail," was usually a time saver to the farthest academic buildings. Today it was a quickly-worsening quagmire, and even the thick black rubber galoshes they wore over their uniform shoes would not protect them from the cold, the wet, and the mud.

Jeff had a first period class in Sampson Hall, one of several older academic buildings that rose in a cluster of dark stone near the library. Being New England smart, he had wisely elected to remain on the brick paths that crisscrossed the campus. Maintenance crews had yet to begin clearing the snow, and patches of deeper slush frequently slopped over his own galoshes and sloshed a mixture of frigid liquid, dirt, and ground-up leaves into his shoes. He still had a distance to go, and he was almost late. He sighed a great cloud of white frost, mumbled an incoherent and disgruntled sentiment, and trudged onward.

During a snow storm last winter in Derry, while he was attending a local Junior College, Jeff had begun a frigid trip to his snowbound college chemistry class. Before he took ten steps in the snow and blowing cold, he balanced the prospects of wet feet, pneumonia, and frozen facial extremities against the hunger for knowledge, turned, and retreated to the warmth of the Student Union. He spent the morning drinking hot chocolate and chatting with his friends. He fervently wished he could do the same thing today, but neither Jeff nor any other student comrade-in-misery had the luxury of taking a "cut" -- today or any other day.

Jeff Polk and 4,000 other students were "special." They were midshipmen -- student naval-officers-in-training at the United States Naval Academy at Annapolis. Classes -- like parades, meal formations, chapel attendance, and lights-out -- were mandatory. Being late or missing a military evolution resulted in demerits and painful or annoying punishment. Jeff hated being controlled by the system -- another New England characteristic -- but he also knew he would have to obey the rules or face the consequences. Jeff consulted his watch and grunted. He had only five minutes to get to his military leadership class or be reported tardy. He picked up his pace, ignoring the slush that filled his shoes and rested with frigid discomfort in the arches of each foot. He shivered, but there was no time to worry about physical nuisances now. He should have allowed more time to get to class instead of finishing his letter to Kate after morning meal. The thought of Kate and her sweet smile and sunny disposition warmed him -- everywhere but his feet.

Jeff hurried past the Macedonian Monument with its four old brass cannons; each topped with several inches of wet whiteness, and each pointed precisely to a nautical compass point. He hesitated at the small parking area near Sampson and Mahan Halls, eyeing the conditions. His feet skidded slightly as he jumped from the relative safety of the brick walkway as far as possible out into the snow-covered asphalt to avoid a deep puddle in the gutter. Some of the midshipmen hurrying near him were either not so observant or not so athletic. Loud splashes and colorful obscenities pierced the morning quiet. The impassive monuments and the impressive old buildings ignored the sudden commotions. They had witnessed similar midshipman haste and confusion for more than a hundred years, and nothing would disturb their dignified repose. The Naval Academy teems with history, tradition, and pomp. The campus bristles with old weapons, imposing monuments, and displays of Naval aircraft and technology, all carefully designed and situated to impress students, faculty, military dignitaries, and the hordes of visitors who flock for a brief glimpse of life within the stone-walled campus. Sometimes -- although he never admitted it aloud -- even Jeff Polk was thrilled to be a member of the Brigade of Midshipmen.

Jeff chuckled as he hurried up the wide stone stairs of Sampson Hall.

"If the visitors only knew what really happens here," he thought, "I'll bet they'd see midshipmen and naval officers in a different light." Jeff turned left after he entered the wide brass door, and hurried up a flight of narrow terrazzo stairs to the second deck. Running all out down the wide passageway, he reached the door of the class just as the instructor was closing it. He entered the classroom slightly out of breath. The instructor hadn't looked pleased as he pressed his way inside.

To maintain the expected studly midshipman image, Jeff purposefully forced himself not to wheeze or show his exertion in any way, even though his fellow students were all plebes like himself and probably had more important things on their minds. Jeff was certain that, to a man, none of his classmates would consider showing the slightest weakness. They were trained that well. He watched carefully to ensure the class monitor marked him present, and took his seat in the middle far left aisle near the window.

Even accepting that this was a military institution, it amazed Jeff how "uniform" everything was at Annapolis. Every student in the class wore identical black pants, shirts, and shoes. Every student had identical brass belt buckles and gold-lettered name tags sewed to the shirts above the left pocket. Every student wore the same thin black tie, held in place at precisely the correct angle by a strange metal-and-spring device called a "spiffy." Yet even though he expected all the students to dress alike, Jeff also found an underlying, unnerving, almost tribal sameness to the students themselves. It went far beyond the clothing and the haircuts. Almost every student was athletically thin and lean in the face. Almost every student sat erect and attentive. And the eyes of each classmate held identical fervent intensity. Robots! Most of them were like robots and wind-up toys! It frightened Jeff to think about what he saw -- or didn't see -- in many of the faces around him.

Military Leadership was a three-credit plebe class designed to introduce first year midshipmen to the challenges and expectations of life as a military officer. It was a complimentary course to the human psychology class he completed first semester -- his only "A" to highlight an otherwise lackluster academic performance. But he had passed all his courses and achieved a 2.4 cumulative point average, a feat that was laudable considering the tough 18-credit load and the multitude of mandatory Academy-specific courses, as well as the odious military requirements. All in all, he was satisfied. Next year when he could study properly, he would surely do better.

Annapolis has an extremely rigid hierarchical structure, stricter even then many other military organizations. Plebes are the freshman and the new-comers. They are the very bottom of the power structure. Their entire existence and the continuation of their attendance are at the deference of the system and of their fellow midshipman.

The price of admission as a full-fledged member of the Brigade of Midshipmen, and for eventually being able to wear the heavy gold Academy ring that marks alumni as the elite among college graduates, is the completion of a grueling ten-months of physical, emotional, and psychological testing known as "Plebe Year." At Annapolis, Plebe Year is said to be the crucible from which the elite center of the Navy's officer corps is molded. But after seven months of plebedom, Jeff wasn't sure about the accuracy of that sentiment.

To Jeff, Plebe Year at Annapolis would be a normal person's worst nightmare, exceeded in physical pain, mental anguish, and emotional distress only by political prisoners, inmates on Death Row, and cadets at West Point. The inmates and the cadets rated no sympathy from Jeff: he had his own survival to consider, and months of difficult plebe indoctrination were yet to come. Jeff felt he could handle the physical and psychological pressures. What bothered him were the inconsistencies. To Jeff, Plebe Year seemed to be a haphazard and inconsistent effort by other midshipmen -- in particular seniors and juniors -- to visit needless pain and suffering. What was the point? The great majority of the first year students were young men who were already passionately motivated to succeed. Why the sadism? Why the humiliation? Why the needless suffering? Those were the questions he had asked himself repeatedly during the last several months. Answers did not come easy.

Early the past summer, when most of the Brigade was participating in training cruises and enjoying vacations, the plebe class of 1971 reported to Annapolis for the first phase of midshipman training, a three-month torture test known as Plebe Summer. During Plebe Summer, 36 groups of 30 or more plebes were "motivated" by a pair of second-class (junior) midshipmen. For Jeff and his classmates it was a time of intense emotional transition that demarcated the difference between Jeff-Polk-the-civilian and Jeff-Polk-the-proto-naval-officer. During the summer Jeff had learned how to march in a straight line; how to sail; to handle a rifle; to wear the various uniforms; to shine shoes, belt buckles, and cap brims -- and especially how to look, act, feel, and *be* a typically cocky midshipman.

During the summer Jeff also had his first experience with the misery of "comearounds," exercises in physical and psychological intimidation used almost brutally by the upperclass to establish in no uncertain terms who was superior in the chain of command. Jeff and his classmates had been exercised to the point of total exhaustion -- and often beyond it. They had also demonstrated the inane ability to memorize and recite senseless "rates" -- reams of military, administrative, and social information -- while being loudly and abusively berated. They had learned to perform such painful and totally useless exercises as "bear crawls" and "crab crawls" and the forbidden and even more painful "shoving-out" and "dead horse" positions. Plebes did this in the name of dues-paying, ticket-punching, and plebe indoctrination, but Jeff suspected that upperclass tyranny was the real reason for most of the stupidity he had experienced.

Plebe Summer whittled the number of classmates in Jeff's Twenty-third Company from 32 to 25. In September, Jeff and the other plebes confronted the 3,000 members of the Brigade and the start of the first semester of Academic Year. Second semester had begun three weeks ago, and the number of plebes remaining in Jeff's company was now 21. The latest casualties were Steve Rogers, who flunked out near the end of the first semester, and Tim Butler, who resigned under suspicious circumstances immediately following completion of his first semester finals. Jeff doubted that Steve and Tim would be the last to go. Both Chuck Chalmers and Willy Simpson were in academic trouble in a system that was unforgiving of failure. And Jeff's ex-roommate Tommy Poole, who was at best a marginal midshipman and military man, but who was a bonafide genius, was the top name on the upper-class' and Company Officer's "discard" list. Tommy's future was in serious doubt.

"Okay, gentlemen," began Lieutenant Austin, breaking Jeff's reverie. "Let's have your attention so we can get started." Austin was a junior Naval Aviator from the Class of 1965. He had been assigned to Annapolis as a tension-relieving reward after three successful Vietnam deployments as an A-7 Intruder Naval Flight Officer. His uniform jacket flashed with colorful ribbons that silently certified his many hours on the edge. And his normally-playful blue eyes assumed a haunted look at the mention of Vietnam. That look told the students he didn't really want to talk about the experience. Sam Austin had "been there."

Vietnam was a much discussed topic at Annapolis during 1968. Not all the talk was pro-military. Jeff Polk himself was one of the sub rosa minority of students who verbally opposed the United States's involvement in Southeastern Asia, something many of his classmates and fellow midshipmen neither appreciated nor understood. Jeff kept quiet around the officers, particularly the war veterans; but he enjoyed watching his classmates wilt under blast after blast of his irrefutable anti-war logic.

"You were supposed to read last night about basic leadership characteristics and be ready to discuss your opinions on what it takes to be a good or a poor leader, and what you see here at Annapolis that fits your opinions. Who wants to start?" Austin looked around the class with a smile.

Jeff found Austin an interesting study in leadership. Lieutenant Austin was not particularly tall, had thinning blondish hair that was always slightly unkempt, was almost pencil thin, and seemed reserved and almost bookish. He certainly didn't fit the image of Naval Aviator and jet jockey that the media loved to portray. His soft voice, somewhat loose attitude, and abundant sense of humor also missed the leadership model by quite a large margin. A plebe at Jeff's right in the front row spoke up.

"Sir. I'm confused by the concepts of positive and negative leadership. The term 'negative leadership' sounds bad, and negative leaders certainly irk me, but the text says that negative leadership is sometimes best. How come?"

Jeff chuckled to himself, losing track of Austin's reply. Being a member of the Twenty-third "Tiger" Company, he knew a great deal about negative leadership. His Company upper-class had a Brigade-wide reputation for their purposeless attitudes and harsh, almost perverse, discipline. His

Company Officer, Captain Rusty "Bull" Dillingham, was a certifiable Marine Corps madman. No other company in the Brigade took its responsibilities with such painful seriousness as the Tigers. His own squadleaders, "Big Jim" Daly and Harvey Linehan, were full-fledged sadists, priding themselves on the viciousness of their demented punishment. But they were two of the more reasonable of the firstie Tigers. Twenty-third Company was negative leadership at its best -- or worst.

"Anybody want to share any good examples of negative leadership?" Austin asked the group.

"How about 'Big Nose,' sir?" asked Kevin O'Reilly from his seat next to Jeff's. Kevin and Jeff were Company-mates and fellow New Englanders whose rooms were separated by a wide passageway -- a passageway that might have represented an ocean for all the differences between them. Kevin had grown up in Irish South Boston, and he was known in the Company as the outspoken plebe with the "strange" sense of humor. Jeff thought, "bizarre" might have been a better word. To add to Polk's confusion, O'Reilly loved the system without reservation and accepted the military routines and Annapolis stupidity with inane enthusiasm -- a fact that Polk found both illogical and irritating. Kevin had turned down a partial scholarship to MIT to attend Annapolis, something else Jeff found unbelievable. The class laughed loudly at Kevin's question.

"Brian 'The Nose' LaPointe" was a crusty Lieutenant Commander -- a non-alumnus -- who had attained commissioned officer status during the Korean War. His job at Annapolis was as Personnel Officer, and he was notorious for his blatant scorn of all midshipmen and his personal crusade to punish as many as possible each time he had the duty. "The Nose" was most famous for his incredible proboscis, which was a massive, bulbous lump of frightening contours, deep red veins, and enormous hideous pores. Yet "The Nose" wasn't the only staff officer to take strange pleasure in putting midshipmen on report, something Jeff also found amazing.

Jeff chuckled along with the other plebes, remembering vividly the one time he had seen this "nemesis of midshipmen" close up. "The Nose" had been after one of his favorite targets, a firstie in Twenty-third Company named Mugsy McGinley. Mugsy, who had been Kevin's first semester assistant squadleader, was about as bizarre and out-of-place a midshipman as could ever be imagined. That particular morning an obviously disappointed "Nose" had missed catching Mugsy -- much to the chagrin of Mugsy's own Tiger Company Commander, another bizarre first-class named Rock Stone. What a screwy place!

"Okay," said Austin, chuckling slightly. "What's so negative about Lieutenant Commander LaPointe?"

"Well, for one thing he's sadistic about his punishment," began Kevin.

"Are you sure he's sadistic? Maybe he's just conscientious!" asked Austin.

"He goes out of his way to find offenders," said Kevin. "What's the benefit?"

"It keeps you on your toes, doesn't it?" countered Austin with a chuckle. Many in the class laughed.

"It instills fear and generates a lack of respect among the Brigade," countered Kevin. "I mean, look at him. He's made himself an object of ridicule with his attitude and that hideous nose."

"This isn't a country club," Austin replied. "And it's not a civilian college or a part-time ROTC program. We don't do things halfway. Despite what you may think, the staff is here to ensure Annapolis graduates are the very best in the world. Maybe LaPointe is truly dedicated. About the nose, he really can't help his looks can he?"

"Maybe his nose is cute after all, but what about his need to punish people?" Kevin continued. "I read the text last night, and punishment is the least effective form of motivation and leadership." Kevin leaned back in his seat and smiled, thinking he had scored some points.

"And what would you do if you were in his position?" Austin asked.

"I wouldn't seek out trouble for one thing, and I'd probably assume a counselor's role when I found it."

"You'd counsel midshipmen for sleeping in or for wearing sloppy uniforms in public? What about for public intoxication? How about missing formation? Being over-the-wall? Hair length? Where do you draw the line? When you consider it from both sides, the discipline issue is not easy."

"Okay," Kevin replied. "Rules are rules. You may be right in general. But when all you do is punish, you miss genuine opportunities to sprinkle in some gentle rain from heaven. According to the text, that's the best motivator there is." Austin frowned.

"I don't understand your comment about rain," he began.

"Okay," Jeff Polk interrupted, fidgeting in his seat and frustrated that the conversation had completely missed the point, "granted that some offenses may rate severe punishment, but surely anyone who's been around as long as Lieutenant Commander LaPointe can see that most of the rules here are unbelievably Mickey Mouse and have no basis in reality. No wonder there's so much midshipman rebellion with all the idiocy around us. Isn't the Academy itself guilty of practicing gross negative leadership?"

"Excuse me," replied Austin, "but I was a midshipman not so long ago. Every Academy rule, no matter how silly it seems, has a fundamental basis, most of which is rooted in an honorable and proud tradition. You had better get used to rules and restrictions. This *is* the military, you know. What else would you expect? You may not believe this, but the fleet has even more rules and regulations than this place, most of which ensure the safety of sailors and civilians. Someday obeying every silly little rule may save your life."

As Jeff watched, Austin transformed from a smiling, lecturing instructor to a war-weary naval officer with memories he would rather avoid. His eyes fixed on an "infinity" somewhere in the rear of the class and he winced almost imperceptively. He paused, took a deep breath, and shook his head vigorously to dislodge an uncomfortable thought.

"Believe me," he continued, "if you ignore even the smallest regulation when landing on a moving carrier deck on a moonless night, you'll be a dead man. If you deviate from your attack flight plan by so much as a millimeter, you may end up killing one of your best friends. War is serious damn business, and so are the regs! You guys are only naval students. You don't understand what the fleet's about, and you haven't lived with death like so many of the alumni. Rules are essential, and the ones here may seem Mickey Mouse, but they serve a purpose." The light returned to Austin's eyes. He smiled. "Besides," he said, "if the Brigade isn't constantly afraid someone in authority will find them out, the place would be no more than a glorified civilian institution."

"What's so bad about that?" Jeff Polk piped in. "Treating the Brigade with some respect and privilege could go a long way."

"Privilege?" asked Austin with a laugh. "You already have that. Don't forget where you are and who you are! This is one of the most prestigious schools in the entire country. When you graduate you get to protect democracy for the whole damn planet. That's a hell of a burden, my young and naive protégés, and it's my responsibility and the duty of this Academy to train you to do your duty honorably." Austin laughed again. "And besides, you've got it a whole lot better than I did. My God, when I was a plebe . . " Instantly the plebe contingent moaned.

Lieutenant Austin had just uttered the most feared phrase any lowly plebe could ever hear. It was the ultimate conversation stopper. It seemed to Jeff that every grad felt his personal Plebe Year was the worst -- which meant the best -- and that no one could ever equal his pain and suffering, and consequently his studliness and his worthiness to lead men. Most graduates of Annapolis were more proud of the abuses they had to endure Plebe Year than of their academic triumphs, their achievements as a naval officer, or their victories over enemies in battle. Jeff frowned and looked away as Austin droned on about push-ups over sharpened bayonets, gauntlets of rifle butts, and blanket parties that sent classmates to the hospital.

Jeff chose a seat on the side of the class next to the wide windows. Sampson Hall was an older building, erected during the early history of the Academy. The interior incandescent lighting was inadequate for good studying. From his seat by the window Jeff could take advantage of the natural outdoor light. He could also enjoy staring outside at the activity on the quiet campus. It was very restful. The view was a perfect inspiration for daydreaming.

Today the view was picture perfect. The sun glistened brightly on broad virgin patches of snow and on the clumps of whiteness that still clung to the canopy of the enormous Annapolis trees. From his vantage point Jeff could see patches of several long brick walkways peeking through the branches. Already the sun was warming some spots to near-dry redness, and large globs of wet snow continually fell from the branches. Jeff watched a lone officer trudge his way toward Bancroft Hall, carefully avoiding the slush piles and the falling snow bundles. He had pulled the collar of his overcoat snugly against his neck, and clouds of whiteness accompanied each breath. At the lower limit of his vantage point Jeff saw a crew of Public Works employees begin the process of clearing the walkways prior to the second period rush. The work crews at Annapolis amazed Jeff. They kept the grounds and buildings in immaculate condition with hardly a disruption to the normal schedule. The campus really was a showplace.

Rising just over the trees at the far end of the main walkway, Jeff could see the gray stone upper two floors and the verdigris roof of Bancroft Hall, the midshipmen's dormitory. He smiled at the thought of that amazing building. Jeff's *Reef Points* -- a compendium of totally useless but absolutely essential plebe survival information -- stated that it was the largest dormitory building in the world. Its eight five-story, interconnected wings spread over several dozen acres, and housed more than 4,000 students plus the administrative offices of the various staffs. It was mind-bogglingly enormous.

To Jeff's right, rising grandly above the stately trees was the copper dome of the Annapolis chapel, one of the most remarkable of the many imposing architectural marvels on campus. The chapel was a cross-shaped display of devotional grandeur. The huge and colorful stained glass windows depicted seamanship, valor, and ultimate duty. Jeff, being typically New England reverent, relished the pomp and ceremony of religious services in that building. To Jeff's left were Michelson and Chauvenet Halls, newly constructed academic buildings devoted to mathematics and the sciences. The design of these two facilities was so similar to the remainder of the campus that they blended in with the surrounding architecture.

But Annapolis certainly didn't dwell on tradition where studies and academic qualifications were concerned. Several years previously the Navy had wholeheartedly adopted the principle that the Academy must train officers who not only could lead men into battle but who could also cope with the rapidly changing technology of modern warfare. Jeff's class would be the first to graduate with nationally accredited degrees; and all graduates, whether engineers or management majors, still had to pass tough course work in advanced mathematics, physics, basic engineering, and electrical and weapons science. Jeff liked the idea that his education was not as limited as it might have been in another university, but there were still many things a good university could teach Annapolis about learning and about respectful treatment of students.

"When I was a plebe, they still allowed hazing," Austin continued to the now-only-half-listening audience. "I used to have to 'rig' full pitchers of iced tea and 'shove-out' during every meal. It was murder, believe me! But none of that is allowed now. And my left knee got screwed up but good when my squad-leader kicked me during a 'dead-horse' on the day right before 'Hundredth Night.' Can't hit or kick plebes now either. It was absolute hell being a plebe in my class. Christ! It almost *is* a country club for you guys. Any more relaxation of the rules and they might as well take away the uniforms and call the place 'The Annapolis College of Liberal Arts.' That's all this country needs, more liberal sissies pretending to be warriors."

Jeff twinged. He was strongly opposed to the war in Vietnam, and in many ways he was a typical New England-style liberal, but he certainly was no sissy. As a matter of fact, he was having a heck of a Plebe Year. Austin chuckled.

"But enough of that. Let's talk more about leadership. Give me more examples of the positive and negative variety."

O'Reilly's hand shot into the air.

"Sir, I'm in Twenty-third Company. Have you ever heard of the 'Tigers'?" Groans of sympathy erupted from the other plebes. Tiger Company had a reputation for strict, almost insane, discipline. More than a few of Jeff's company classmates regularly discussed the option of dropping out, simply to save themselves the unnecessary pain of continuing plebe indoctrination. Jeff was absolutely convinced that the first-class in Twenty-third Company would have celebrated wildly if they could run every plebe into resignation. It didn't make sense Jeff or to most of his companymates.

"Don't like the physical aspects of the training, huh?" asked Austin.

Kevin laughed loudly.

"Give me a break, sir! I can outrun, out fight, out love, and out think every firstie in Tiger Company. None of their Tiger baloney can break me or most of my classmates. But it still doesn't make any sense. Physical intimidation is the refuge of the weak minded. It's counter productive. I love the Academy and the Navy, but I'm not in the least bit motivated to fight on for the glory of the Tigers. Every one of them can kiss my butt!" Kevin paused, realizing that his big mouth may have gone too far again. He reddened. "Excuse me, sir!"

Austin smiled in a fatherly way at Kevin.

"You say it's stupid now, Mister O'Reilly, but watch what happens during your first-class year. You'll find yourself looking back on the experience and remembering how the physical and mental stress made you a far better midshipman. You may even be "Tigers" when you have your own plebes."

Kevin quickly leaned over into the aisle and made a loud retching sound that caused the class to laugh. Then he looked up.

"Oh. Bite thy tongue, sir!" he said. He looked around the class and announced, "Every one of you has my personal permission to hunt me down and kill me like a scurvy dog if I ever so much as hint at becoming a Tiger!" The class laughed again.

"Good, O'Reilly!" Austin said. "I'll guess it'll be my job this semester to convince you that there is sometimes logic and necessity for Tiger-style leadership." He faced the class smartly and assumed his lecturer pose. "Setting aside stereotypical positive and negative leadership for a moment, remember the other things the text says. No one style of leadership is effective in every situation. Life isn't static, gentlemen. You have to learn to be flexible and to adapt your leadership to the situation of the moment; otherwise you'll never make it in the fleet."

The walk back to Bancroft Hall at the end of third period was certainly better than the pre-first-period slog to class. The sun was up and rapidly warming the air, no more snow pelted unsuspecting midshipmen, and walkways had been cleared of slush by the efficient work crews. Even so Jeff had to hurry. His room had the "Chow Call" responsibility this week, and he must get ready and be out in the passageway reciting rates ten minutes prior to the 1130 formation. That left him only 20 minutes to get from Michelson Hall to his room on the first level of the fourth wing. As always, as he neared the doors that separated the relatively stress-free external campus from the insanity of interior Bancroft Hall and the Company area, Jeff began to feel a nagging and chronic discomfort.

He entered the building and chopped quickly toward his room. This chopping action was accomplished by assuming a rigidly-erect posture, staring nowhere other than directly ahead, keeping his head absolutely vertical and his chin "braced" tightly against his neck, and running in short "chopping" steps in a straight line down the very center of the passageway. Every direction change was precise and military and accompanied by a loud, 'Beat Army, sir!" When Jeff entered his room, Willy Simpson and Reb Ramsey were already there and mostly ready. Noon meal was a formation that required a perfect uniform. Midshipmen never wore their best uniforms to class -- too much opportunity for an accident to destroy the crease or the shine. Jeff hurried to his locker, stepped out of his class uniform, and removed his "grease" uniform from his locker. It was identical in every physical respect to the one he wore to class except that it was perfectly pressed, dust-free, and brilliantly polished. Bob Strong entered as Jeff examined the immaculate uniform for microscopic flaws before putting it on.

Carefully Jeff slipped on his black shirt, buttoning each button with care to ensure that no loose threads -- "Irish Pennants" -- escaped into the open air where they would be spied by some observant upperclassman and result in derision and punishment. He slipped his perfectly-tied black necktie over his head and centered it, and adjusted his spiffy to the correct angle. Next he stepped into his black pants and socks and carefully removed his grease shoes from their cloth protective womb, never once touching the glass-like polished surface in the process. He held each shoe up no more than six inches from his eyes and rotated it to observe with critically exacting precision how the room lights reflected off the brilliant leather. Satisfied with the quality of the shoe shine, Jeff slipped on his shoes. He meticulously tucked his shirt, grabbing the loose material at each side firmly and pulling the front panel material backward, at the same time thrusting the back panel material under the front with his thumbs. Holding the tuck tightly, he pulled up and fastened his pants without losing the taut tightness of the tuck. Jeff was ready.

"Two minutes to Chow Call!" announced Bob Strong with his usual authority. Bob had assumed the leadership of the room, a fact which the other three roommates reluctantly accepted. Jeff sure didn't want to take on any other responsibilities, Willy Simpson lacked the talent and motivation to take charge, and Jubal Ramsey spent a great deal of time concentrating on his studies. But Bob seemed to revel in the leadership role.

Bob Strong was actually one of the better company classmates -- in Jeff's opinion. He was light-haired, stood just under six feet -- several inches taller than Jeff -- and weighed an athletic 160 pounds. He came from San Diego, where his father worked as a foreman in a ship repair facility for the Navy. He had played second team on the Annapolis plebe soccer team, which recently had completed the first-ever undefeated season in Academy history. Because of his soccer abilities and the team's success, Bob had eaten with the jocks and had missed the first semester's idiotic activities at the Company meal tables. Jeff didn't envy this; he liked Bob. Bob was the calmest and most sensible of his classmates. Jeff had never seen him rattled. And Bob was also rational and patient -- a highly practical quality when dealing with their other two roommates.

Jubal Hunter "Reb" Ramsey came to Annapolis from High Point, Alabama. Reb was light-haired but not blond. He was as tall as Bob Strong; but at nearly 200 pounds, Reb was much larger than the rest of Jeff's roommates. He had played football for his high school in High Point and for a season on the freshman team at the University of Alabama before coming to Annapolis. He was the son of a West Point graduate who had been killed in Vietnam two years previously. Although he originally wanted to attend the Military Academy, his high school grades hadn't been adequate. During his year at 'Bama Reb decided the Marine Corps suited him better than the Army, and he selected Annapolis instead of the long gray line.

Jeff found Reb an interesting personality study. He was a consummate team player, never failing to participate wholeheartedly in any plebe activity. He was a practical joker of enormous proportion, always ready to lighten the stress level with some new and unusual prank on one or several of his roommates or on the "doofs" across the passageway. But Reb had a secret and somewhat dark side that neither Jeff nor any of the other roommates could penetrate; and when he was morose, it was best to stay far away from him. Jeff knew better than to discuss his opinions of the war in Vietnam when Reb was around. Because of his sad personal loss, Reb could not see past his own pain to the reality of the Vietnam situation, and Jeff had learned during one violent outburst several months ago it was better to avoid the subject when Reb was nearby.

The final roomie was Willy Simpson, who came from the hills around Greenville, South Carolina, and who brought a slow Southern drawl to match his steady, always-smiling, totally unflappable personality. Willy was tall, very thin, and highly likable -- maybe the best-liked of all the plebes. He was fair-haired and country-boy attractive; and to complete his "image," he played guitar quite well. His father was the chief of police in Greenville.

Jeff had tried repeatedly to involve Willy in his political arguments, but Willy simply didn't care about politics or about the abuses of the Academy system. Willy was in some academic trouble, so maybe he had ample reason to concentrate on things other than hazing and stupid rules. Jeff wasn't sure that even if Willy had a 4.0, he would care too much about plebeisms. Still, Jeff liked Willy. He had begun tutoring him in the subjects he felt comfortable with. He didn't want to think that Willy might not make it.

At eleven minutes prior to formation Jeff and his roommates chopped into the passageway and headed to their positions at various strategic locations throughout the Company. Once in position, the plebes faced the required directions and waited. The many clocks in the passageway had been precisely synchronized and every 60 seconds the minute hands simultaneously jumped forward with a loud "click."

At 1120 the clocks clicked, and the four roommates began a loud yelling chant.

"Sir, you now have ten minutes until noon meal formation! The menu for noon meal is fried chicken breasts, mashed potatoes, gravy, green beans, crisp garden salad, fruit-filled Jell-O, dinner rolls and butter, iced tea, coffee, cream, and milk, sir."

Taking a deep breath they continued, "Sir, the Officers of the Watch are, the Officer of the Watch is Lieutenant Commander Glowacki, the Academy Training Officer; the Junior Officer of the Watch is Lieutenant Junior Grade Peach, the Assistant Honor Officer; the Midshipman Officer of the Watch is Midshipman Commander Thompson, the Second Regimental Commander, and the Battalion Officer of the Watch is Midshipman Lieutenant Pera, the Tenth Company Commander." Another quick breath.

"Sir, the movies in town are, at the Capitol, *The Magnificent Seven*. At the Town, *Never on Sunday*. Sir, the days are, 34 days 'til Hundredth Night, 77 days until Spring Vacation, 120 days until the second-class Ring Dance, and 123 days until first-class graduation, sir! You now have nine minutes until noon meal formation, sir!"

Immediately after the announcements, Jeff and his roommates chopped hurriedly to their room.

"God, I hate doing that!" Jeff announced. "Every time I do Chow Call I feel like a circus animal performing a trick for my masters."

"No sweat," Bob said. "We've done so many we could do them in our sleep."

"Well, I've got better things to dream about," replied Jeff.

At six minutes before formation the crew returned to their stations. The five-minute Chow Call required a recitation of only the meal menu, which took just a few seconds. They remained braced in place. At four minutes they recited the Officers of the Watch, at three minutes the movies in town, and at two minutes the "days." By this time most of the Company had exited their rooms and headed for formation. The final recitation ended with a loud, "Sir, you now have one minute until noon meal formation! Time, tide, and formation wait for no man! I am now shoving off! You have one minute, sir!"

Jeff hurried down the center of the passageway to the inside formation location just outside the Company Officer's office. He liked inside formations because they were much easier to get to than the ones outside in Tecumseh Court, and they were significantly warmer this time of year. Besides, the fluorescent lighting in the passageway hid most shoe shine and cap brim flaws. Jeff slid into place in the middle of the middle squad of the third and final platoon and waited at attention.

Jeff hadn't been pleased when the squads had changed just after Christmas vacation since nothing had essentially changed in Tiger Company. Instead of the big shake-up as promised, the Tigers had simply switched the first set squadleaders with their assistant squadleaders so that for Jeff and his roommates Harvey Linehan was now in charge instead of Big Jim Daly -- big whoop-dee-do! The second-class, Marion Weatherby and John Phlegler, were still the same dolt and imbecile, as were the helpful but incredibly boring third-class Jim Daly, Paul Romanczyk, Dave Saul, and Larry Merkousko. Jeff secretly wished he could have ended up in a more reasonable situation for second set, but there wasn't anything he could do about it now.

The new Company Commander, Sidney Littleton, had replaced Rock Stone with an ostentatious flourish which didn't really change anything for the Company. Both firsties were assholes of the highest magnitude who believed in the full range of Tigerness. Jeff had at least respected Stone for his consistency and resolve. Littleton was a diminutive twit and a pompous ass who wielded his power unscrupulously. It was a swaggering Littleton who addressed the Company.

"Company! A-ten-hut!" The Company responded with a snapping of shoe heels.

"Close interval -- dress right -- dress!" Every member of the Company quickly slid his left arm up onto his corresponding hip and stretched it toward the person on his left, snapping his head to the right, lining up his feet with the others in the line, and shuffling until he came into contact with the elbow of the person on his right side. In this manner each squad member assumed a straight-line nearly-equal distance from his neighbors.

"Ready, to!" Littleton shouted, and everyone dropped his left arm and snapped his head forward simultaneously. "Cover!" Littleton shouted, and the middle and third squads adjusted their positions so that they were exactly lined up with the corresponding member of the squad in front of them. The Company was now ready for inspection. For the next five minutes various first-class moved down the lines of their squads and inspected their charges. Linehan checked his squad over but didn't say anything to Jeff or the other plebes.

"How could he?" Jeff thought. "I'm already perfect!" Soon the Company was inspected and ready for announcements.

"Gentlemen," Littleton said with a smirk as he looked calmly from first to second to third platoon. "I have only one announcement to make today, and that concerns the 'Hundredth Night' festivities." He looked at the squad directly in front of him. "Guevarra! How many days until Hundredth Night?"

"Thirty-four, sir!"

Littleton smiled.

"That means that within the next four days each plebe must select a firstie and ask them to comearound. That will give the firsties 30 days to run the plebe to death before the tables are turned on Hundredth Night. Captain Dillingham wants this to be an occasion to remember, so I expect full participation in the event. Four days, gentlemen!" With that Littleton announced, "Company! Right . . . Face!" The three platoons turned as one.

"Forward . . . march!" The Company headed to toward the Mess Hall for lunch.

CHAPTER 2

CHOW TIME

The Annapolis Mess Hall is an enormous T-shaped and column-less building completely nestled within the embrace of the high stone wings of Bancroft Hall. The crosspiece of the "T," which is almost 200 yards long, is attached to an enormous kitchen which occupies one of the sub-levels of Bancroft Hall. The leg of the "T," which is itself more than 100 yards in length, bisects the inner courtyard. *Reef Points* calls the Midshipman's Mess Hall the largest eating facility in the world, and anyone who has ever eaten there would agree that it is indeed formidable. Four hundred solid wooden, 12-man tables sit along the arms and leg of the Mess Hall in precise pairs extending perpendicularly from the walls. A 30-yard wide center corridor allows easy table access for both the flood of students and for the many meal service personnel and their accessories.

Three times every day a uniformed sea of midshipman motion -- dark or white depending on the season -- surges into the Mess Hall seconds after meal formation ends. Each Company marches loosely to its assigned area, where each midshipman quickly disperses and waits patiently behind his seat. The Academy Administrative staff and Watch officers file quickly inside and assume their places at a large table in the center of the hub. A thunderous din fills the Mess Hall as upper-class banter with each other or scream at plebes. After a long moment of confusion, the entire Brigade lapses into total and utter silence as the Midshipman Brigade Commander steps to the raised podium near the Staff tables and calls the Brigade to attention for prayer and announcements. Usually this formality lasts only a minute, after which the Brigade Commander barks the greedily-anticipated command, "Brigade . . . Seats!" and midshipmen scramble into their chairs to await the meal.

Company tables at mealtime are absolute demonic bedlam for plebes, where time exists only in the moment and where reality narrows sharply to the immediate stress-filled environs of the meal table! Words cannot accurately describe the constant, darting, amoebae-like motion of food service; and the rapid-fire and boisterous verbal response to rates and other queries. A feeling of intense physical and emotional strain engulfs every plebe at each of the almost 400 ten-man table microcosms. The entire process is an amazingly choreographed, precisely controlled bedlam. For the upper-classes the eating part of the process is worth the wait. The food at Annapolis is first rate, consistently better than at home, although few midshipmen would dare admit that to their parents.

Every Company occupies ten of the large wooden tables -- one for each of the nine squads, and an extra table for staff and overflow. The first-class sit at the head of the table, the second-class at the foot, and third-class occupy the middle. A pair of plebes usually sits as near as possible to each end of the table and between the various upper-classes. The primary function of plebes at mealtime is to ensure that the upper-class are adequately fed. The primary function of the upper classes in Tiger Company is to eat their fill and harass the plebes mercilessly.

At precisely the same instant, more than ten sets of double doors open in the various scullery and kitchen areas beside the Mess Hall. Crews of enlisted stewards hurry into the Mess Hall proper, each pair pushing a large stainless steel cart laden with trays of wonderfully-smelling food. The carts stop at prearranged locations in the wide corridors and the stewards immediately deliver trays to the waiting plebes. Plebes off-load the trays quickly, and pass the food to their tablemates in order of rank -- serving themselves last. By the time any plebe gets a chance to take even the first tentative bite, the stewards have already collected the empty trays, returned to their stations in the center of the aisle, and stand waiting for the inevitable calls for second helpings.

As eating continues, the plebes ensure that upper-class glasses and plates are filled to capacity and that seconds are ordered when needed. For a plebe, mealtime is a constant, energy consuming process which leaves little time for the actual eating. The process is further complicated by several physical restraints, all of which Jeff Polk found ridiculously silly and completely unnecessary.

All plebes eat "braced" during the meal, sitting rigidly with their backs and heads perfectly straight and their chins tucked tightly against their necks. They must also sit on the very edge of the chair so that their taught plebe rear ends precariously touch only the last three inches of the seat. Plebes can stare nowhere but "eyes-in-the-boat" straight ahead.

Every plebe eats a "square-meal," an excruciatingly slow process where every bite of food rises vertically then turns a sharp ninety degree angle into the waiting mouth. And plebe bites must be Lilliputian. Every morsel must meet the "three-chews-and-a-swallow" rule. Annapolis meals were without a doubt the most frustratingly miserable experience of Jeff Polk's young life.

"Simpson!" barked Big Jim Daly almost immediately after everyone sat and just as Willy readied himself to receive and distribute the food. "Keep your god-damn eyes in the boat or I'll lean over and pluck them out with my butter knife." He picked up his knife as he talked and toyed with it, running his finger along its dull edge.

"Aye-aye, sir!" answered Willy in his slow mountain drawl. For this meal Willy unfortunately sat in the chair next to Daly. Big Jim was very attentive to his plebes. Big Jim loved to torment. And Big Jim was always hungry.

"What's the main course for this circle jerk, Simpson?" Daly growled. His dark brown eyes narrowed as he squinted slightly in Willy's direction. Daly was by no stretch of the imagination a handsome man. To Jeff his coarse features and unpolished demeanor seemed better suited for tree-swinging and knuckle dragging than for life on the boundless main. Daly was an enigma.

Jeff glanced sidewards toward Big Jim on the pretense of checking the location of the water and iced tea pitchers and caught a glimpse of the thickly-clumped blond crew-cut as it bristled like a glistening antenna focused on Willy Simpson. From across the table Jeff watched Daly's wide prominent jaw as it jutted aggressively forward with each clipped word. The jaw sported an enormous Kurt Douglas dimple that seemed at times to function as a third eye, always alert and watching the plebes. Jeff feared that pseudo-psychic dimple more than any other physical aspect of Big Jim Daly. He shivered and quickly returned his gaze to straight-ahead infinity, glad the dimple hadn't caught his brief out-of-the-boat lapse.

Willy Simpson drew back slightly before he answered.

"Sir, fried chicken, sir!"

Daly was a large individual who had been recruited for the Navy football team. He had done fairly well as an outside linebacker for two seasons, but had been unable to continue playing after a disabling knee injury the previous season against Notre Dame. The loss of BMOC status made him somewhat bitter and remorselessly vindictive. Daly considered the upcoming meal for a moment, and Jeff could hear Big

Jim's big stomach rumble in anticipation.

"You hungry, Simpson?" he finally asked.

"Yes, sir!" Willy answered loudly just as a tray bearing several serving bowls of fried chicken arrived and Willy passed it quickly to the head of the table. Jeff's mouth started to salivate in anticipation as he caught a whiff of the aroma.

"Tell you what, Simpson . . . " Big Jim said as he meticulously chose the largest remaining piece of chicken and passed the tray to Jeff for its journey to the second-class at the foot of the table. Daly took a large chomp, moaned in ecstasy, and continued -- no qualms about speaking with food in his mouth. "Since I'm in a really good mood today, I'll let you "carry-on" this meal if you give me your chicken." Willy's eyes brightened immediately. "Carry-on" was a temporary relaxation of the plebe restrictions. It meant no chin painfully squashed against the neck, no ridiculous square meal mechanics, no staring stupidly into infinity, and -- best of all -- being able to sit back in the chair and relax. Normally plebes in Tiger Company would gladly kill a stranger for a meal's carry-on, so Willy hesitated slightly before answering. But there was one other thing in a Tiger plebe's life worse than bracing during meals, and more important even than eating. Willy Simpson, even though he acted like a true hayseed, had a great deal of Southern savvy.

"Sir," Willy replied in an exaggerated drawl, smiling slightly as he passed the salad to Linehan, "I'll give you my chicken this meal for no "comearound" this evening." "Comearounds" were the twice-daily exercises in run-until-you-puke physical motivation that were a constant, chronic, and debilitating part of plebe life. Every Tiger plebe would kill a close relative to save himself the pain, humiliation, and potential injury of a single evening comearound.

Daly thought it over quickly. His stomach rumbled again loudly as he took another large bite. His predatory teeth pulled loose a large flap of skin from the thick chicken breast, and it slapped against his chin, temporarily depriving the third-eye of sight. Big Jim hurriedly plucked the skin into his mouth and wiped his chin, frowning.

"Hey, great! A negotiation!" he answered. "Okay! Here's the deal. You order seconds. I eat my fill. I ask you rates all meal. I stuff my face. You don't eat. I take your piece back to my room and eat it later." Daly paused and smiled. "But hey! Since I'm a nice guy. My original offer still stands."

Willy didn't answer immediately. Jeff watched him surreptitiously as he glanced down at his waiting chicken breast, then to a point just above Jeff's head. Jeff had by now served himself and was ready to dig in, although he knew the chances of eating in peace were very small.

"Time's almost up on my offer, Simpson," announced Daly several seconds later, after his own chicken breast was consumed. He drank an entire glass of iced tea in a single gulping swallow. "What's your answer?" Jeff grabbed the iced tea pitcher and refilled Big Jim's glass. Naturally Daly didn't notice.

Willy struggled for a reply, torn between his hunger and his exhaustion. Finally he sighed audibly.

"I'll keep my chicken sir." Willy quickly raised one of the now-empty chicken bowls high into the air to signal the waiting stewards that the table needed seconds.

"Maybe," Jeff thought, "seconds would satisfy Daly."

"Suit yourself, asshole! Daly angrily answered as he stared at Simpson's chicken breast. "Your chicken's mine! I think I'll eat it while I'm running your ass this evening. How's that sound?"

"Not so good, sir."

Big Jim glanced toward Jeff's plate.

"How about you, douchebag? Want to trade your chicken for carry-on?"

"No, sir!"

"The shit on you both! That'll be two pieces I'll eat later."

"How's the cow, Ramsey?" barked Harvey Linehan, warming to the action. Linehan was a mostly quiet, totally unassuming, and almost forgettably nondescript individual who was terminally meticulous about uniform appearance, class and formation schedules, and plebe indoctrination. He was medium tall with a thinning crop of dark hair, unusually thick lips, and slightly bugged-out blue eyes that gave him a distinctly fish-like appearance. He was so incredibly organized and exact, that Jeff thought he would make a good auditor or banker, but Harvey intended to be a submariner on a missile boat. It was his dream. Jeff could well imagine meticulous Harvey, submerged in the dark cold ocean for six months at a time with no contact from home or the outside world. Nary a stray idea would intrude on Harvey's structured thoughts, and he would practice like a concert pianist, his organized fingers dancing over the buttons that would send fire and death to cities and facilities half a world away. Harvey talked almost continuously about missile boats, and about their ultimate and final destructive duty. And when he spoke of megaton yields and multiple warhead spreads, a strange and satisfied gleam entered his eyes. Linehan was a very good student of naval warfare, but he definitely excluded the human factor from his equations.

"Sir!" Reb intoned from his place at the far end of the table as he picked up the nearest Blue-and-gold Naval Academy Dairy milk carton and hefted it slightly. Then he began the time-honored, traditional, but totally ridiculous plebe response: "She walks. She talks. She's full of chalk. That lacteal fluid extracted from the female of the bovine species is highly prolific to the *fifth* degree, sir!" Reb had just informed Harvey in his thickest Alabama accent -- which he seemed to save for mealtimes and comearounds --that he estimated there were *five* glasses of milk in the carton nearest him. Why Harvey or any other first-class cared about milk or cows, except for their harassment value, was a mystery Jeff never did understand. Jeff tossed the annoyance aside as he passed additional green beans Big Jim's way and refilled his iced tea glass for a second time.

"You look hungry, Polk," Big Jim said with false concern. "Want some mashed potatoes?"

"Aye, aye, sir!" Jeff reached for his fork.

"No Polk! Grab a handful." Jeff knew what was coming. He reached over and grabbed a palm's worth of mashed potatoes and held them out in front of him. Daly chuckled.

"Whammo, Polk!" Big Jim yelled, and Jeff slammed the entire handful of potatoes into his mouth and began chewing furiously. Daly and Linehan both laughed.

"Poole, you stupid son-of-a-bitch!" shouted Dave Salenger from the next table. Dick was Tommy's new squadleader, a marginal improvement over last set's total shit-for-brains, Dale Micklewski. Salenger was a short, balding, little clone-of-Napoleon, whom Jeff would gladly like to run into in a dark alley sometime. Salenger represented everything that was wrong with the Academy system. Outwardly he seemed perfectly sane. He was an accomplished tennis player. He laughed and joked with his classmates. He had a keen intelligence and perception. But he was arrogant to the point of insufferableness, mindlessly submissive to the system, and devoted to plebe indoctrination to the point of cruelty. Jeff smiled to himself slightly. But Salenger was still better than Micklewski, who was not only sadistic but certifiably crazy. Salenger would probably do well in the fleet, but Jeff wouldn't trust Dale Micklewski in a row boat, much less in command of a hundred-ton vessel plowing the sea lanes in support of national defense policy. Micklewski at the helm was a very scary thought.

Jeff leaned microscopically forward in his chair to catch the conversation at the next table -- an act that didn't really make sense considering the substantial volume of the exchange -- and watched the action while pretending to stare into infinity.

"I asked you to tell me why you still haven't resigned," Salenger continued, his voice on the very edge of hysteria. "I'm not interested in how big and brave you are, or whether you think you can hack it here, numb nuts, because you *can't* hack it! You do not belong here! You're a fat slug! You're repulsive! And you're a disgusting pussy!"

Not to be left out, Micklewski interrupted Salenger. Dale had an irritating nasal whine that Jeff had come to hate.

"Your homo boyfriend quit already, Fat Tommy, so why don't you?"

Tommy Poole, who was a great deal smarter than any individual at his table -- probably than anyone in the Company, and maybe than anyone in the entire Brigade -- did not answer. Jeff knew he wouldn't. Tommy wouldn't let anyone as insignificant as Salenger or Micklewski force him to lose control. Tommy had been incredibly good about keeping control despite the enormous abuses he suffered for the last eight months.

Salenger quieted, leaned forward, and pointed a small finger toward Tommy Poole's face. His finger touched the side of Tommy's nose, and Salenger pressed, causing Tommy to push against the finger so as not to let his head shift from its straight-ahead position. The nasal tug of war went on for several seconds, until Dave lowered his finger, wiping it on Tommy's uniform shirt before returning to his lap.

"From now on, douchebag," Salenger said more quietly, "the only answer I want to hear to any question that concerns your future at Annapolis is, *'because I'm stupid, sir!'* You got that, Poole?"

But Tommy was *not* stupid, and he wasn't about to let his personal pride stand in the way of his staying at Annapolis -- something Jeff and several other classmates had occasional trouble with.

"Yes, sir!" he yelled loudly in return.

"Okay, Poole. Now, why won't you quit?"

"Because I'm stupid, sir!"

"Very good, Poole. You are *incredibly* stupid."

"You know, Poole, you sissy," continued Dale Micklewski in his own soft and sissy-like whine, "Captain Dillingham has had several meetings with the first-class about you. You were supposed to quit over Christmas leave. You promised him you would, and you didn't. He's mad as heck and out to get you now, Poole. You're as good as dead." Micklewski paused. "Why did you lie to the Captain, Poole?"

"I did not lie, sir!"

"You told him you would quit and you didn't. That seems like a lie to me."

"Sir, I told Captain Dillingham I would seriously discuss it with my parents. I did. They told me it would be fine if I came home. I told them I wanted to stay. That was fine with them."

"That was very stupid, Poole," Micklewski said. "You think you've had it badly so far? Your pain hasn't even started yet."

"Polk! Wake up, god-damn it!" Big Jim shouted in his ear, startling Jeff out of his reverie. "I've been waving my iced tea glass in the air for almost an hour. Fill it and add another ten comearounds to your list, douchebag!"

"Aye-aye, sir!" Jeff answered, hating the Tigers with renewed vigor. What good was adding comearounds when he already owed enough for ten years? Sheer stupidity!

Daly noticed Simpson. "Were you always stupid, Simpson?" he asked.

"No, sir," Willy answered quickly.

"So this is a recent phenomenon?" asked Linehan to the delight of the upperclass at the table.

"No, sir," Willy answered, but not so quickly this time.

"How about you, Polk? Were you always stupid?" asked Daly.

Jeff had not eaten any food since his whammo of potato. Daly's question came just as he had closed his mouth around three green beans. Quickly and with exaggerated jaw movements, Jeff chomped three times, then swallowed.

"I'll find out, sir!" he answered. Theoretically plebes were only supposed to answer a direct question with either the correct factual information, or with the response, 'Yes, sir!', 'No, sir!', or 'I'll find out, sir!'

"How are you going to find that out, shit-for-brains?" asked Daly.

"I'll find out, sir!" Jeff answered again with a slight sigh. There was food on his plate getting cold and he had eaten only a single bite of potato and beans, but what else was new? He reached for his fork.

Linehan stared hard at Jeff.

"All this plebe shit pisses you off, doesn't it, Polk?"

Jeff put down his fork, put his hands in his lap, and answered, "I'll find out, sir!"

Daly shook his head in disgust.

"You got to get into the spirit of Plebe Year, Polk. You're no fun at all. Comearound!"

"Aye-aye, sir!"

There were penalties when a plebe didn't want to play the game by upper-class rules.

"Polk!" Linehan barked as Jeff tried again to pick up his fork.

The fork clattered to the plate.

"Yes, sir?"

"Tell me about the progress of the war, asshole." Jeff paused. That was a foul! Usually recitations of the news were a morning meal routine. Harvey was obviously upset at Polk's attitude and responses.

Jeff sighed openly in frustration, which also wasn't wise.

"Sir," he said. "Air operations on enemy supply lines throughout the North continue. The battle for Hill 236 near Que Sahn goes on. To date 131 Americans have been killed in the operation and 419 have been wounded. American intelligence estimates enemy casualties at more than 3,000 the past week."

"What's the kill-ratio, Polk?" asked Daly. Ever since General Westmoreland had publicly announced that in this kind of guerrilla war, a ratio of ten enemy dead to every American casualty was an acceptable rate of loss that would guarantee US victory, plebes in Twenty-third Company had been required to calculate the kill-ratio for every ongoing operation.

"Thirteen to one, sir," Jeff answered with little outward enthusiasm.

"What the piss is wrong with you, Polk?" asked Linehan. "Aren't you happy that we're killing so many of the enemy?"

Jeff paused, considering his response carefully.

"Request permission to speak freely, sir?"

"Request denied, asshole! Answer the question!"

"Then, I'll find out, sir!" A sinking feeling immediately settled into Jeff's stomach. He had just broken a cardinal plebe common-sense rule and unnecessarily drawn attention to himself. Oh, well, he thought, too late now to un-say anything.

"Jesus Christ!" yelled Linehan loudly enough to alert every table in the Mess Hall. "A commie sympathizer!" He turned toward the other Company tables and yelled again. "Rock! Get over here!" Rock Stone, last set's Company Commander, was the undisputed head Tiger and a soon-to-be US Marine. He rose from his seat three tables away and swaggered toward them. As he watched him approach, Jeff had to admit that Stone was an impressive son-of-a-bitch. Standing several inches over six feet tall and weighing close to 200 completely muscular pounds, he was an imposing young man. He was ruggedly good looking, naturally intelligent, and completely personable when necessary. He sported the almost-shaved crewcut required of combat Marines.

"What's up, Harvey?" he asked, putting a large hand on Linehan's shoulder.

"Did you know that Midshipman fourth-class Polk apparently doesn't agree with the US involvement in the Vietnam War?" Linehan asked sarcastically.

Stone paused, then leaned down toward Jeff.

"What's this all about, Jeff?" he asked in a big-brotherly tone.

"Request permission to speak freely, sir?"

"Sure. Go ahead!"

"Sir. Talk of the War in Vietnam and things like 'kill-ratios' make me uncomfortable. I never have understood why we're involved in the internal affairs of another nation, and I'm not happy about the deaths of other human beings -- communists or otherwise. I'm not a communist, and I don't think I'm unreasonable, sir!"

Stone frowned and shook his head.

"Mister Polk," he said patiently, "did you listen during Captain Dillingham's last Company lecture?" At the direction of the Commandant, every Company Officer talked to his midshipmen monthly on subjects such as honor, responsibility, loyalty, and duty.

"Yes, sir," Jeff answered.

"What was the subject of the last lecture, Mister Polk?"

"Duty, sir!"

"And what is your duty regarding the War in Vietnam, Polk?"

"To obey the lawful orders of the President and my superior officers, sir!"

"Good!" Stone said smiling. "Are you going to participate in that conflict if so ordered?"

"Yes, sir! Reluctantly."

Stone became immediately angry.

"*Reluctantly* may get you or some undeserving comrade killed, Mister!" said Stone loudly. "You are a military officer. You either support what you are told to support wholeheartedly or you do not belong in uniform."

"But, sir . . . "

"No god-damn 'But, sirs!', Polk. You're either a good soldier or not. And this nation does not need a bad soldier, especially now when the media dotes on traitors like Jane Fonda and portrays us as mindless baby killers."

Stone paused.

"Nobody wants to die, Polk, and no good soldier wants to kill if it can be avoided. I don't know anything about politics, and I don't really care. As a good officer you have to trust that smarter men than you are making the right decisions. All anyone expects is for you do your duty with honor. If you can't accept that, then your presence in this institution is a fraud. Think about it seriously, Polk. If you can't accept your duty, resign now and save the lives of men who may perish because you lack resolution."

"Ramsey!" Stone said, smiling and looking down to the other end of the table.

"Sir!"

"What do you think of today's kill-ratio?"

"Too damn low, sir!" Reb yelled delightedly in his thickest accent. Everyone at the table, including Jeff, laughed.

"Good man, Ramsey!" Reb answered with a loud Marine Corps "Ooh - Rah!"

Stone rested a huge hand on Jeff's shoulder for a moment.

"I like you, Polk. You have guts and talents. But if you can't do your duty, you have no place here. There are plenty of young men who would die for a chance to be in your shoes. Either accept that the military has a sometimes bloody job to do -- and then do what you are told -- or let someone take your place who will do that duty." With that pronouncement Stone turned and swaggered back to his table.

Linehan stared hard at Jeff for a moment.

"Pretty stirring speech, huh Polk?"

"Yes, sir!"

"Makes you want to go out and kill commies, doesn't it, Jeffie?"

Jeff paused.

"Doesn't it, Polk?" asked Daly.

"Yes, sir!" answered Jeff halfheartedly.

Daly leaned toward Jeff and poked him in the side of the head with a big meaty -- and greasy -- finger that smelled of fried chicken. Big Jim laughed.

"You're a miserable liar, Polk, but at least you're showing some common sense for a change." Jeff sighed as he wiped the grease from the side of his head and boldly reached for his own chicken.

"Polk!" Linehan barked. The chicken returned to the plate.

"Free shot?" asked Harvey Linehan, holding up his balled up napkin and taking aim at Jeff's glass of nearly-full iced tea.

"No, sir!" Jeff answered, daring Harvey to try a shot and make it. Tradition was that a plebe could refuse the request of an upper-class to take aim at his drink glass with his napkin. If the upper-class tossed the napkin into the glass, the plebe had automatic permission to dump the contents of the glass onto the upper-class. But the upper-class, if he made the unapproved shot, would hightail it for the exit to avoid the dousing, and any chase could only continue to the exit doors. Free shots added an element of comedy to the usually deadly serious meals, particularly when a frightened firstie went fleeing past the Company tables with a plebe, glass at his side, in hot pursuit.

Most Tigers did not participate in the free shot game. Linehan was an exception. Almost every meal he asked one or more of the plebes for permission to take a shot. Each time he had been refused, and usually he did nothing. Occasionally he shot anyway. His aim with the napkin was exceptionally bad, and none of his tosses had even come close.

Jeff tensed himself in case Harvey took the shot and it went in. Harvey glanced briefly from Jeff's glass to his face.

"You really wouldn't, would you?" he asked.

"Try me, sir!" Jeff answered. Linehan laughed put the napkin down, and got up to leave. When Jeff's attention wavered, Harvey picked up the napkin and shot. Startled, Jeff saw the napkin bounce off the rim of the glass. The upper-class at the table "oohed" at the effort.

"Tough luck, Harv," Daly said. "Maybe next time."

Things were not much different at any other table in Tiger Company, except maybe in Mugsy McGinley's squad.

Mugsy McGinley was the first-class enigma. He was distinctly anti-system, loudly anti-military, and fervently anti-Tiger. He was a lonely individual in each of those regards. However, neither Mugsy nor his almost-equally-rebellious roommate Henry Brandis particularly cared about their pariah status. Being outcasts did not affect their plebe indoctrination efforts, except to focus them in different directions.

"Come on, Guevarra!" yelled Mugsy in delight. "Who the piss was it who Rocky Marciano beat for the heavyweight title, and what year was it?" Mugsy McGinley had been the Brigade middleweight boxing champion for the past three years, and he seemed primed for a fourth title. His dark, swarthy features and his ample thick black hair -- inherited from his Sicilian mother -- gave him a distinct Mediterranean appearance. His aggressive personality, his passion for conflict, and his ability to party longer than any of his classmates were traits that came from his fiercely Irish father. His flat, too-many-times-broken nose and the scars on both eyebrows came from three years in the Academy ring. McGinley was a remorseless competitor who was known throughout the Brigade for pounding his opponents into a jelly-like mass before he would consider letting up on the force of his blows.

McGinley also was strange for a Tiger in that he participated in plebe comearounds. Three times a week, despite the weather or the status of academics, he took his squad for a five-mile morning run; and in the evenings he ran up and down the passageway alongside his squad members and matched them push-up for push-up. Except for BJ Wilson, the other plebes in the squad could match Mugsy in the morning runs, but no one except smooth and handsomely-swarthy Guevarra could handle the exercise load that McGinley dished out. Guevarra, a Puerto-Rican American from the Brooklyn area of New York City, was a physical -- and sexual -- machine that few people could match. Mugsy had grown to like Rico. Mugsy also liked the flamboyant Kevin O'Reilly, more because of Kevin's inane Irish sense of humor and public irreverence than his ability to impress or outperform him.

"Sir, Rocky Marciano beat Jersey Joe Walcott in Philadelphia in September 1952. Marciano retired undefeated."

"Exactly, Guevarra. Nobody could beat the son of a bitch, and they hated him for that. Ya see, Guevarra, nobody likes Italians. This country blames us for everything. That ain't fair, is it?"

"Sir," Rico quickly relied, grinning broadly and looking directly at Mugsy despite the fact that he was supposed to be braced. "You're asking that of a Puerto Rican? Italians run New York City; Puerto Ricans pick up the trash."

McGinley laughed.

"Yeah! But you guys deserve it. You got no brains about America, Guevarra. You people live in tenements and love it. You segregate yourselves. You don't try to blend in, and the American dream *is* blending. You spicks are really dumb. Italians run New York because they were smart enough to figure out the system."

"Guevarra," McGinley asked, changing the subject abruptly, "I hear you have quite a reputation as a ladies' man. How many times can you make your girlfriend get off in an hour? I got this friend who says female sexuality is all a myth. He says most girls are like guys, and once they get it, it's turn-on-the-TV time."

"Sir," Rico said with a superior air, "that definitely is untrue!" Rico was an authority on ladies and anything to do with sex -- if you asked him. He had an extensive library of smut books and magazines he rented out to horny or inquisitive midshipmen. Not only was he well-versed in matters of physical intimacy but he also had the most sensual and sexual Puerto Rican girlfriend who freely and wantonly admitted to his studliness.

"As a matter of fact," Rico continued, "I recently met a woman who actually can outdistance *me* between the sheets, and that's saying something. Although," he added with an enormous, sparkling white grin, "she really has to work hard to do that."

"Is this that young lovely from the barrio I've heard so much about?" Henry Brandis asked. Quiet and non-threatening Brandis was the complete opposite of dark, brooding McGinley. Henry was a short, thin individual who looked like the intellectual he was. He had regulation brown hair that he combed down over his very high forehead -- when he remembered to comb his hair at all. Had the regulations allowed it, he surely would have combed his hair over his truly enormous ears. There had been much discussion in the squad and throughout the plebe Tiger contingent as to how it was possible for a human being to have ears that stick out from the head at the 90-degree angle that Brandis' achieved. The consensus was that his ears violated some law of physics and that Brandis purposefully slept with them folded over -- kind of as a living, fleshy pillow -- or that he had a mechanical winch-and-pulley device at his desk that stretched the ears forward while he was studying. Another school of thought declared that Henry used those enormous ears as a kind of antenna to suck knowledge from the ether. He seemed to be a veritable storehouse of facts and theories. He had maintained a near 4.0 academic average every semester he was a midshipman and was a prime candidate for a Rhodes Scholarship come graduation.

"No, sir! This is a new woman I met recently."

"Yeah?" McGinley said. "Who is it?"

"Sir," Rico replied staring down the table at Jim Merritt, "I'm not at liberty to discuss that." Merritt glared back at Rico, not at all happy.

"So. You gonna dump your Spanish beauty? What say you dump her in my direction?"

"No sir! He will not!" interjected Kevin O'Reilly quickly, and with typical boldness. "She's been madly in love with me from the very instant she laid eyes on me -- and who can blame her? In fact, lover-boy himself has already conceded defeat and promised her to me. She'll be resting safely in these Irish arms before the year is out." Kevin smiled and huffed in Rico's direction. "And she won't find me two-timing her like a certain greasy cucaracha across the table from me has."

Rico and Mugsy laughed.

"O'Reilly," Rico said. "I didn't want to tell you this for fear it would shatter your fantasy, but Rosa is far too hot for you. She's going to be so frustrated, she'll probably grind you down to a useless nub, and be desperate for me. I feel sorry for you, my friend." Everyone at the table laughed, despite the incongruity of the scene. Plebes semi-relaxing during the meal, and entertaining the table with their banter? Unheard of in "Tiger" Company. Even more amazing, to the other plebes at least, was the fact that the members of McGinley's squad actually ate a reasonable meal.

"Does this new lady of yours have a friend who might be interested in an all-night free-for-all?"

Again Rico looked at Jim before he answered.

"No sir! She does not."

"Too pissing bad!" Mugsy exclaimed. Then, changing the subject with rapidity for a second time, he added, "Hey guys! About this 'Hundredth Night' horseshit. Any of you thinking about asking me around?"

No one answered immediately; then Kevin blurted, "Sir. I'd love to run your ass into the ground, but I was thinking about easier prey. What would you think if I went for the big guy himself?"

"Stone?" exclaimed Mugsy and Brandis almost simultaneously.

"You must be crazy," added Henry Brandis. "Why would you do that?"

"For the challenge, I suppose. Stone doesn't scare me."

"He should, you idiot!" Mugsy added. "Stone takes this plebe shit far too seriously, and 'Hundredth Night' is a great excuse for pushing the limits. He'll kill you!"

"I don't think so, sir," Kevin answered. "I think he likes me. I *am* irresistible, you know. Besides, think of the when-I-was-a-plebe stories I'll have."

"You fool!" Brandis interrupted. "Do you think any of those Plebe Year stories are real? We all make them up as we go." He laughed loudly. "Shit, McGinley and I didn't do a single push-up the entire year, did we, Mugsy?"

"Henry," Mugsy said, "we know *you* didn't have a plebe year. You were too busy being an altar boy or going to squash practice or tutoring the upper-class. But I had my ass run the entire year, and I still have a scar from where that homo Charlie Swift kicked me with his god-damn combat boots. He made me slip in my own vomit. I lost a wind sprint to shit-for-brains Wildman Kopciak." Mugsy looked at Kevin seriously. "Forget that idea, O'Reilly. Stone had a great Plebe Year, believe me. He'll kill you!"

"I'll think about it, sir!" Kevin answered, obviously unconvinced.

Mugsy heard a commotion from one of the other tables and looked up, momentarily forgetting about Kevin.

"Wilson!" he said suddenly but quietly. "Micklewski is getting out of control again. Go give him a big 'Wet Willy' from me."

"Aye, aye, sir!" BJ answered and quickly stood. Noting where Dale sat, he chopped quickly down a side aisle, keeping himself out of Micklewski's sight. At the next table he turned, chopped to the center aisle and approached Micklewski from the rear. Standing momentarily behind the firstie, he put his two index fingers into his mouth and wet them. He thrust the two fingers into Micklewski's ears and wiggled them around, shouting "Wet Willy! Wet Willy! A gift from Midshipman First-class McGinley, sir!" Micklewski tried to shake the fingers loose, but could not. After a few seconds, BJ withdrew his fingers, turned, and chopped back to the table. Midshipmen at neighboring Companies cheered this insult to the craziest Tiger.

Dale Micklewski was incensed. He started to rise, saw that the plebe belonged to Mugsy, had immediate second thoughts, and wiped his ears with his napkin, glaring at Mugsy all the while. Dale's roommate and squad-mate, Dick Salenger, hardly noticed. Salenger was squadleader this semester, and he intended to use every indoctrination second to full advantage.

At Salenger's table the Reign of Plebe Terror continued unabated. Dick Salenger was one of the more fervent Tigers. He was a short, brown-haired, rapidly balding individual who had piercing blue eyes and a slightly hooked nose. He attacked life with an unbelievable intensity.

"Well, Abbott!" Salenger shouted. "What is the menu for morning meal?" George Abbott was confused.

"Sir," George said, "that's tomorrow. We're only supposed to know the menu for today's meals."

Salenger rose from his chair angrily and leaned over toward George.

"That's a god-damn lie, Abbott, you sack of shit! You're supposed to know the menus for the next three meals. This is noon meal; therefore, you should know tomorrow's breakfast."

"Aye, aye, sir!"

"Poole!" Salenger shouted. "What's the menu for tomorrow breakfast?"

"Sir, request permission not to bilge my classmate!"

"Bilge him, Poole!" Salenger shouted.

"Sir, the menu for morning meal is, grilled breakfast steaks, home-fried potatoes, assorted cereals, fruit, toast, butter, and jelly, sir!"

"You see that, Abbott! Even a no-load scum-bag like your classmate Poole knows his rates. This isn't Training Tables, and I don't give a shit if you're the next Kevin Dolan." Dolan was Navy's last full-fledged All-American soccer player. "Don't you ever come to meal unprepared again. You got that?"

"Yes, sir!" George stammered.

"Fat Tommy," Dale Micklewski continued calmly, now somewhat recovered from the Wet Willy incident, "why did you just bilge your classmate?"

"Midshipman First-class Salenger ordered me to, sir!"

"Comearound, Fat Tommy."

"Aye, aye, sir!"

"How many comearounds does that make now, Fat Tommy?"

"Six hundred fifteen, sir!"

"You know what the biggest pisser of that is, Poole?" asked Salenger.

"No sir!"

"There's not enough time left for you to sweat them all out. Time is going to cheat us out of the satisfaction of having you serve your full punishment for being the worthless smack you are. Isn't that a shame, Poole?"

"Yes, sir," Tommy lied.

CHAPTER 3

COMEAROUNDS

After each meal Jeff and his roommates relaxed briefly studying in earnest. There was safety for plebes in the evenings: the Academy having decreed studying to be sacrosanct and undisturbed except under the most dire of circumstances. Only truly dedicated Tigers risked punishment getting caught in a plebe room during study hour.

Jeff liked the size and functionality of the Annapolis accommodations. Each plebe room held three or four single midshipmen's beds -- always nestled in alcoves against the far walls -- and the same number of large, gray metal desks in the open center of each room. Every room had a shared walk-in closet, a small sink area, a shower, and at least one window. Some rooms afforded spectacular views of the Severn River, the Chesapeake Bay, or the Annapolis harbor; many more had interesting views of the activity in other midshipman rooms across open courtyards. Every midshipman had his own seven-foot tall by five-foot wide built-in locker, complete with sliding wood doors. In the winter a beastly heating system pumped steam to wall radiators located under the windows and kept the rooms pleasantly warm. In the deep and humid Maryland summer, midshipmen sweltered with neither breeze nor air conditioning.

Despite the physical comfort, the daily nervous confusion bothered Jeff, and he longed for the time when he would rate the relative peace of a two-man room. Four people could generate too much background noise and tense energy. Often Jeff could feel emotions swirling in the room. Tonight Jeff tried to ignore the distractions as he sat quietly at his desk, sorting his notes from the past three weeks of Military Leadership in preparation for the next test. Annapolis academic standards were high and the Academy recently had qualified for full accreditation. That made Jeff's course load grueling, even without the mandatory military courses, physical fitness standards, parades, formations, and athletics.

While he was home for Christmas leave, Jeff had initiated several good-natured and usually beer-induced discussions with his civilian university friends concerning the true nature of the typical service academy. Despite all his patience, enthusiasm, and persistence, Jeff found himself unable to convince them how extremely difficult it was to be a midshipman -- much less a scum-sucking-douchebag plebe. Since most of his friends' New England political leanings were far to the left of Joseph Stalin, they readily accepted Jeff's word about the stupidity of the system and the mindless robotics of the Tigers. But when Jeff talked about the intense brother-in-arms camaraderie and about the spirit and sense of loyalty, his friends -- all except his sweet Kate -- looked at him as if he were the reincarnation of Joseph McCarthy. He was sure his friends thought he exaggerated the loyalties and the difficulties for their benefit, and Jeff had come to accept that the Annapolis experience could only be defined by first-hand experience.

His friends often interrupted his stories by asking, "If it's so damn tough, why don't you just quit? Who needs that shit anyway?" It was a reasonable question, but no reasonable answer came immediately into his mind. Resignation was the single topic -- next to sex -- that most occupied the minds of his classmates. Why were any of them staying? What kind of invisible hold did the place have on them? Jeff had returned to Annapolis in January determined to find out.

Bob Strong sat across the room facing Jeff, checking the homework assignments for his six classes. Bob was an aeronautical engineering major who carried a full load of pre-engineering classes including chemistry, calculus, and strength of materials, as well as English literature, world history, and psychology. With 21 semester hours, he had the heaviest workload in the room. But Bob was an incredibly intelligent and precisely organized individual who scheduled his daily activities and evening study time almost to the minute. Jeff knew why Bob was at Annapolis. He intended to use naval aviation as a ticket into the astronaut corps and the ride of a lifetime into the great beyond. Jeff envied Bob's ability to focus on the bigger picture and the grander goal. Often he wished he had that same ability.

"Well, ya'll," Jubal said, pausing in his ritual inspection of his black shoes prior to returning them to their chamois protective sleeves. "Who's it gonna be?" Jubal "Reb" Ramsey, like Jeff Polk, was a management major with a technically less-demanding load than Bob but with almost as many credit hours. Thus far Ramsey had managed to bull his way through the coursework -- barely and with significant help from his classmates. But Reb had passed the first semester, and he was elated that he might be able to compete with the bigger brains that surrounded him.

Jeff knew why Reb tried so hard to be a model midshipman. Reb had to fulfill a promise he had made to Lieutenant Colonel Joshua Ramsey, West Point, Class of 1948 -- his father -- now lying in Arlington National Cemetery, far beyond the reach of promises. Reb held a fierce pride and love for "The Colonel." Sometimes it threatened to consume him. Jeff wondered if Reb had vowed to avenge his loss by leaving behind a pile of dead and wounded bodies in tribute -- or in payment. Reb talked continually about the war; and when he did, his eyes blazed. Jeff pitied the Vietnamese who got into Reb's line of fire. Jeff wondered how high the pile of bodies would have to be to satisfy Reb's blood lust.

"For what?" Bob Strong asked Reb in reply, not looking up from his planning calendar.

"Hundredth Night? Who ya'll gonna ask?"

Bob raised his head quickly and stared at Reb.

"I think it'll be Linehan for me," he said. "Plebe Year is a great character builder and everything, but it's also getting very tiring. I'll bet Linehan takes it less seriously than Daly."

"Absolutely Linehan for me, guys," offered Willy Simpson with a chuckle. Willy was also at his desk reviewing assignments with a frown. Willy was a political science major. While his workload was similar to Reb and Jeff's, his coursework required a great many more papers, preparations, and reports. "Shucks, guys!" he continued, "Daly is a crazy son-of-a-gun, and I don't want to get myself hurt this late in the year. It's hard enough keeping up with the studies without risking my life." He indicated a pile of books he had brought back from the library in Mahan Hall and groaned.

Why was Willy at Annapolis? Jeff wasn't sure. Willy Simpson didn't seem to belong in a naval uniform. His father had never been in the service; he wasn't brought up near the sea; and he had little or no fascination with wars or great battles or personal notoriety. Willy was almost boringly hayseed and down-to-earth; not exactly a characteristic of a great leader. Whenever Jeff asked him the reason for coming to Annapolis, Willy always looked puzzled for a moment and answered, "Because I was accepted" -- as if that provided some deep insight. Jeff didn't understand, but he let it go.

Reb turned to Jeff Polk.

"How about you?" he asked.

Jeff thought for a minute.

"You know what's so sad?" he answered. "There's not a single one of the Tiger bastards I'd trust for a second to behave with any honor doing this Hundredth Night shit. So, hell, it might as well be Daly himself."

Reb hurried over and pounded Jeff on the back with a meaty hand.

"Hoo-rah, Jeff! Me and you little buddy! We' gonna run the bastard's ass come Hundredth Night. We're gonna need a bucket to collect the puke that's gonna come from inside that sorry-assed maggot." Jeff didn't look at all convinced.

"You know who's gonna be sorely disappointed come announcement time?" Jeff smirked to no one in particular. "Stone -- the bastard! No plebe in his right mind will ever ask "Rockhead" around. Stone's gonna be one sorry shit when Hundredth Night arrives, and all his Tiger classmates are getting their jollies bleeding in the passageway, and he can't share the fun." Jeff glanced at his roommates, but none looked particularly sympathetic to Stone's plight.

"Well, that's too bad for Stone," said Reb Ramsey.

"I feel really sorry for Tommy Poole," offered Willy. "He's gonna have to ask either Salenger or that dick-breath Micklewski."

"To hell with Tommy Poole!" Reb offered. "He shoulda quit three months ago and saved himself the pain and suff'rin. He's really in fo' it now that Captain Dillingham has him marked for revenge, and I ain't got the time ta worry 'bout it."

Jeff started to speak, but Reb waved a big hand in his direction.

"I know. I know. He's our classmate and 'yo personal hero, and he walks on water, and he's braver than any plebe who ever lived, and he has my personal support an all that. But he's still one stupid son-of-a-bitch!"

Jeff shook his head sadly and moved toward the door. A loud blatting, originating in the doorway of the plebe room directly across the passageway, stopped him dead. He looked.

"Shit!" he moaned in disgust. "Rico just broadsided me." Jeff was referring to the now tiresome and increasingly gross game his room played with the room across the passageway. The game had started early in the academic year when Rico Guevarra had dropped his drawers and pridefully exposed himself pridefully to Jeff and Reb. The two of them -- too embarrassed to expose their own deficiencies in response -- had resorted to a period of multiple "moonings" of Rico and his roommates.

The battle escalated over the next several months. Rico's room achieved a four-man moon-pyramid that was suggestive to Jeff of a stack of hairy catcher's mitts -- with legs. Then during the week prior to the Army-Navy game Jeff and Reb had simultaneously farted in the direction of an outraged BJ Wilson. Not to be undone, Rico had coaxed the always naive and easily impressionable Kevin O'Reilly into lighting off a massive post-bean-casserole gas emission in Willy Simpson's direction. The results were an impressive flash of blue-green pyrotechnic flatulence -- as well as a patch of raw, bare pink Irish bottom where the flame burned the hair surrounding Kevin's butt. Jeff and his roommates had howled with laughter for several minutes while O'Reilly screamed in pain and embarrassment, and Jeff took secret satisfaction in watching Kevin wince each time he sat the following week.

But Rico's noise was now small potatoes and did not deter Jeff from his intended trip across the passageway through Tiger territory. Plebes were generally safe in their room during study hours, but anyone caught in the passageway at any time was fair game. Some of Jeff's grosser and more timid plebe classmates resorted to relieving themselves in the sinks or showers of their rooms during the early evenings so they could forego a trip to the communal head facilities. But Jeff wasn't about to be cowed by the Tigers.

Jeff clearly remembered the moment of truth that set him apart from the Annapolis plebe system. It happened late one evening two weeks into Plebe Summer as he lay in his dark bunk, near tears from the exhausting physical and emotional pressure. Without conscious thought, Jeff had realized that his tears were stupid and his fears groundless because there really wasn't anything the upper-class could do to him that he didn't empower by his own acquiescence. The Tigers wanted him to have a miserable Plebe Year -- which in their terms meant a great one -- but they had no real power over him. Every time he wind-sprinted until he vomited, it was because *he* pushed himself to beyond his limit Whenever he stood rigidly braced and withstood the screams and howls of his tormentors, it happened because *he* allowed it. And every chopping step he took, every tiny square bit he ate, and every rate he recited he did of his own volition.

"To hell with the Tigers!" he decided. "I'll decide just how good a Plebe Year I have." From then on Jeff was able to tailor his response to the upper-class pressure, and to keep just a little bit in reserve. So far he had been able to hide his revelation from the upper-classes. If they thought for an instant he was bagging it, he'd be under more pressure than he wanted to face -- willingly or not.

But if he wasn't willing to play the game 100 percent, why was Jeff at Annapolis at all? The answer, he realized only recently, was simple. Originally Jeff had believed the recruiter's propaganda that Annapolis was a holy, military shrine where only the most decent and noble of human beings were allowed to worship, and that each midshipman was an integral part of a far greater universe of goodness and justice and honor. The recruiter could not have been more right, or more wrong.

Jeff found the abject cruelty and the petty and unreasonable restrictions -- the real basis of the Annapolis system -- disgusting and disheartening. He would have quit at the end of the first week but for one very important thing: -- He was no quitter. -- And Annapolis counted on that! Once safely within the cold womb of Bancroft Hall, Jeff and many of his classmates accepted their various fates as a test of their manhood: a severe, mostly nonsensical test for sure but a test nonetheless. Jeff never shirked when it came to proving his mettle. Despite his misgivings, Jeff would survive simply because it *was* tough and because so many of his peers had collapsed under the strain. He'd show the Tigers and the system that he could handle whatever they could dish out.

Smiling, he chopped into the passageway and hurried across enemy territory into what had to be the strangest room in the history of Bancroft Hall.

"You must be slipping, Rico," Jeff said as he entered. "Moons are passé now. Besides, there's no way we can ever top your setting a classmate on fire! We concede victory!" Kevin O'Reilly laughed the loudest of the four, reaching back and rubbing his behind tenderly.

"That really smarted!" he announced. "And I'm still tender. I'll probably be denuded on my poor freckled rear for the rest of my life. But it was a great gag, wasn't it!" Everyone laughed and agreed that Kevin's trick would be hard to match.

"What can we do for you, Jeff?" Jim Merritt asked, flashing his usual captivating smile. Jim Merritt smiled a lot. He always acted like he knew something the rest of the Company didn't. Merritt, unlike Jeff, tried hard to be the perfect plebe and the consummate midshipman. No wonder he smiled a lot; Merritt really knew his shit. He never screwed up or hesitated or got into trouble the way the rest of his classmates sometimes did. Jeff always felt he was addressing a potential admiral when he spoke to Jim. To further piss Jeff off, Jim Merritt was a very nice person and a consummate team player. In fact, there was little Jeff could dislike about him. It was the presence of so many young men like Jim Merritt -- those with the highest moral and ethical qualities -- that proved that the recruiters had been right about the bright side of Annapolis.

Merritt was the undisputed leader of this crazy room. Probably, Jeff thought, because none of the other no-loads wanted the position. Maybe they recognized Merritt's leadership talent and were content to let him do what came naturally.

Jeff both admired Jim Merritt *and* felt sorry for him. He was an interesting dichotomy. Jim had been one of Jeff's Plebe Summer "Goon-Room" roommates. He had shown a great deal of talent for persuasion and peer motivation by defusing many potential confrontations between Jeff and Reb, and Reb and Tommy Poole. But he had also displayed an almost unwavering acceptance of the Academy system, despite its many cruel inconsistencies and ridiculous idiosyncrasies. That frustrated Jeff greatly. It seemed grossly hypocritical for Merritt and the other plebe "greasers" to condone the insanity. Merritt not only embraced the system but he brushed away the disturbing aspects of life at Annapolis like so many pesky flies and pressed his roommates and classmates on to greater plebe efforts -- all for the good of the Academy and its traditions.

But Merritt wasn't being molded into a mindless cretin like the Tigers had hoped. He was perfectly capable of independent thought and action, and he openly defied the first-class methods of discipline when they didn't meet his own strict standards. Once he had boldly challenged Dale Micklewski to a fist fight during noon meal when Micklewski had called him a liar in front of his squadmates. For that act of bravery Merritt had won the undying love of his classmates and the reluctant admiration of several of the Tigers, including Stone himself.

"I came to ask a question of genius-boy O'Reilly," Jeff answered. Kevin O'Reilly, the Boston Irishman, was the greatest human conundrum Jeff had ever encountered. Kevin had flaming red hair, deep blue eyes, multitudes of freckles, a twinklingly infectious smile, an incredibly bizarre sense of humor, and a keen and perceptive intelligence that dwarfed most of his classmates. O'Reilly was a rebel, but not a flaming member of the Academy counter-culture like Jeff. O'Reilly was a sincere humanitarian who spoke out more loudly than any other plebe against injustice and cruelty -- two things that abounded in Tiger Company. And Kevin had suffered severely for his occasional insubordination.

But O'Reilly always endured and bounced back from whatever revenge the Tigers inflicted, and he had never failed to laugh in their faces and ask for more. But like Jim Merritt, Kevin O'Reilly really loved Annapolis and everything it stood for, and he passionately hated whatever tarnished its sacred image. Jeff had seen him become teary-eyed listening to the choir sing the *Navy Hymn* during chapel, and he knew that neither O'Reilly nor Merritt would ever support the systemic lobotomy that he himself knew Annapolis needed.

Jeff went to Kevin's desk, where the Irishman sat entering information on several newly-acquired science fiction books into the card catalog he maintained for his personal library. O'Reilly's lending library was the most popular in the Company, and he had organized a system so that anyone could check out a book, a week at a time. Kevin kept track of who had borrowed which books and when they were returned. He even sent occasional written reminder notices to Company members, including upper-class, who were overdue in returning books. The library made Kevin popular with the forward thinkers and dreamers in the Company but not among the Tiger power structure.

"What can I do for you, my poor unenlightened friend?" Kevin asked. "Come to borrow a book? Seeking sexual advice? Or perhaps you want the "gouge" on Austin's class?" The "gouge" referred to the rumored absolute Bible-truth concerning what the professor expected from his charges. But "gouge" was a slippery term. Sometimes getting the gouge could infer obtaining information the professor didn't intend anyone to have -- copies of previous tests, instructor notes, or sometimes actual test questions provided by a classmate who had to take an exam early for emergency or health reasons. As the Company Plebe Honor Representative, Jeff had observed several Academy Honor Boards as they confronted the wide, gray, and often fuzzy line separating an unquestionable honor offense from an honest mistake or misunderstanding. The system was neither sympathetic nor forgiving to blatant honor offenders, and Jeff fervently hoped he'd never have to investigate any of his classmates for an Honor violation. It wasn't so much that he shirked from the responsibilities, but rather because he had no sympathy for dishonor.

Jeff frowned at Kevin.

"What's the gouge on Austin?" he asked hesitantly.

Kevin immediately assumed a serious look.

He leaned in close to Jeff, looked around the room cautiously, and whispered loudly, "Study hard!" Jeff laughed.

"Sure, Kevin," Jeff replied. "Now what about next week's test. Do you want to study together this weekend?"

"Well," Kevin replied, "I do have several hot dates lined up, but I'll see if I can fit in a little study time.

"Date, hell!" Rico piped in from the adjoining desk. "Kevin hasn't even looked at a woman since he broke up with Miss Sarah Connelly -- and good riddance to her. Rico referred to Kevin's Army-Navy date who was a dark-eyed, bold and buxom young lady who seemed to adore Kevin."

Jeff was taken aback.

"I thought Sarah was pretty hot," he said. "And she seemed perfect for you, Kevin. Why did you break up?"

"She just wants to control me like a puppet; and to top it off, she acts like a little kid." Kevin sat back smugly in his chair and put his freckled arms behind his head. "As my dad always says, "Women are like streetcars. There's one along every couple minutes." I'll just wait until I capture another heart. It's inevitable when you're Irish."

"This isn't exactly Grand Central Station, you redheaded sack of shit!" Rico exclaimed. "And in case you've forgotten, you're an insignificant plebe not allowed to even think about girls. How do you intend to find another woman?" Kevin smiled, and began furiously scribbling on a small piece of paper.

"I'm going to use the Rico Guevarra secret note method," he said holding up the paper. "See, I've already written down my initial approach. I'll slip it sleight-of-hand-style to the first long-legged beauty I see in town this weekend." He passed the note to Rico, who read it and burst out laughing. Rico waved it in the air, still chuckling, and announced, "The note says, '*Hi, I'm Kevin -- twelve-inch - O'Reilly. Let's get naked!*'" Everyone laughed at this, and Rico handed the note back to Kevin.

"It'll work!" Rico exclaimed. "Don't change a word."

"I want to watch from across the street," Jim Merritt offered, "so I can witness you getting your Irish ass kicked."

"Speaking of asses getting kicked," Jeff asked Kevin, "how are you and Tommy Poole doing in the organic chemistry class?"

"Tommy's doing okay. I'm heading to his room right now to ask him something chemical. Want to come along?"

"Sure, why not?" Jeff replied. The two of them chopped into the center of the passageway, Kevin in the lead, and turned the corner toward Tommy Poole's room, each sending an equally loud "Beat Army, sir!'"reverberating off the pink tile walls.

Tommy and George Abbott were studying when the two classmates entered. Hank Butkowski, their enormous football-playing roommate, had gone to the library earlier in the evening.

"Hey, guys!" Tommy said cheerily as they entered, "how's it going?" To Jeff, Tommy Poole was the biggest Company enigma. More than Willy Simpson or anyone else Jeff could think of, Tommy Pole was out of place at Annapolis. He would never be an ideal midshipman or an ideal naval officer.

Tommy was moderately short -- much shorter than most of his classmates. He had to look up into the eyes of his tormentors. He was considerably homely -- with an oversized head, a wide lumpy face, a very weak chin, an enormous gap between his two front teeth, and oily patches of pimples which constantly sprouted on his forehead and cheeks. He was also terminally pear-shaped, despite six months of the most extensive exercise regime a human being could endure. As if that wasn't enough, his thin brown, nondescript, hair -- which Tommy never seemed to be able to comb properly -- receded slightly at each temple, giving him an old-before-his-time appearance. His pale brown eyes were almost listless, and seemed ready to pour forth tears at any instant. Rico aptly called them Bambi eyes.

But Tommy Poole was a certifiable genius who had maxed every section of the Scholastic Aptitude Test and who had achieved a 4.0 grade average the first semester despite a 20-credit load and constant tormenting harassment. Tommy had indisputably more guts than any other plebe in the Company. Nothing the Tigers did deterred him from his goal to finish Plebe Year and go on to be a Navy pilot. Tommy had taken every conceivable physical and emotional bruise and trundled back for more.

"Hey," he continued, not letting them answer his question. "I just got a letter from Tim Butler. He says he's doing fine and that he'll be starting classes at Berkeley next semester. He also adds that if anyone is passing through Modesto this summer to look him up."

"I can't think of any reason to visit Modesto," replied Kevin. "Even its name conjures up images of strange smells, ugly buildings, and utter boredom. If there were anything redeeming about it they would have called it "Good-o" or "Excite-o." I'll pass. Besides, I know you liked Tim, but he gave me the creeps. I could never decide if he was normal -- if, you know what I mean."

Jeff did. A persistent rumor -- started by the Tigers during the first semester -- intimated that Tim Butler was a homosexual and that he and Tommy Poole were secret lovers. Jeff sincerely doubted Tommy would have participated, but he had to admit that Tim *was* different. Not that Jeff had anything in particular against homosexuals, as long as they left him completely alone. At a time in his life when sexuality was the primary motivational factor, Jeff contended that he did not want to be confronted with anything unusual.

"I can tell you for a fact that Tim Butler never made any advances toward me or insinuated any thing," said Tommy firmly. "And I really liked him. He was a very nice person, a great listener, and extremely easy to talk to."

"I second that about Tim!" George Abbott added with a touch of belligerence. "He was okay in my book." George's opinions were not something to trifle with. He was a large, swarthy, soccer defender from New Jersey who had the dangerous look about him. The subject of Tim Butler's sexual preference was closed for George.

"How's life-without-training-tables, George?" Jeff asked.

"Not so damn good!" George said frowning. "Salenger and Micklewski are really running my ass. I can't decide which one I hate more."

"Be like me," Kevin announced, smiling, "and hate them both! Say, who are you guys going to ask around?"

"I'm going for Micklewski!" Abbott said with vehemence. "And come Hundredth Night, I promise he'll suffer the most excruciating pain a first-class ever endured." No one doubted George's sincerity in this regard.

"Yeah," replied Jeff, "but until then he's gonna run your ass."

"Shit, Jeff! Wise up!" George replied. "He's doing that now. I might as well get some punishment in later."

"Good point!" said Kevin, considering. "How about you, Tommy?"

Tommy paused and looked from classmate to classmate before answering.

"You guys are going to think I'm crazy, but I'm thinking of asking Rock Stone around."

"No shit!" exclaimed Jeff. "That's crazy, Tommy! He'll kill you!"

"Maybe," Tommy answered. "But like George says, it'll be no better or worse for me with Stone in charge than it is now. Stone is tough, but at least he's not crazy like Micklewski or some of the other Tigers."

"I was thinking about Stone too, Tommy," Kevin said. "Would it interfere if I also ran his ass?"

"No, not at all!" Tommy said laughing. "It might even help. Since I'll be embarrassing you in the sprints and push-ups, Stone will concentrate on your inadequacies instead of running me so hard."

Kevin laughed.

"Sorry to disappoint you, Tommy, but plebe basketball practice will keep me out of the evening comearounds. You'll only get to kick my ass in the mornings."

Tommy sighed loudly, making what proved to be a not-so-bad muscle. He stared at it for a moment, surprised that he was seeing himself pumped up like he was.

"Oh, well," he continued, "I was so looking forward to watching you wilt in the presence of my superior manliness." Everyone laughed, but loud upper-class laughter in the passageway outside the room interrupted their fantasies.

"We better get back to our rooms," Jeff said. "We have a combined comearound with Kevin's room in the morning, and I need my rest. Running against O'Reilly and his cohorts means I'll end up doing push-ups until my arms fall off." Jeff and Kevin waited near the door until the upper-class passed and quickly returned to their respective rooms.

"Move your god-damn ass, Ramsey!" Linehan screamed as Reb ran past him on his way down the long passageway. "Beat them! Beat those bastards, or so help me I'll kick your fat ass all the way down the passageway during the next sprint." Rock Stone, who stood smugly nearby, laughed at Harvey's frustration. It was early the next morning -- 0600. Linehan had just ordered the first wind sprint of the morning's comearound. Big Jim Daly watched silently while leaning against the bulkhead outside his room. Big Jim was not a morning person and rarely participated in the dawn indoctrination activities. But every evening Daly transformed into a monster who seemed to derive a special satisfaction from watching plebes exhaust themselves into gut-emptying masses of protoplasm. So Linehan took charge in the morning and let Big Jim run plebes in the evening. They were a great plebe-killing comearound tag team.

The main passageway outside the Company Office of the Twenty-third Company was more than 50 yards long and 10 wide. Every morning and evening for the last five months -- except for Sundays and holidays by Academy decree, and during the period between the Army-Navy game and Christmas vacation because Navy had been victorious -- Jeff and his fellow plebe squad-members and plebes from almost every other squad in the Company, raced up and down that passageway like a desperate tide of sweating and fearful cattle, urged on by the insane prodding screams of the squadleaders. This physical exertion was ostensibly in the name of character-building, but Jeff was never sure whether the plebe or first-class characters were being torture-molded by the experience.

Today they ran against Merritt's room, which meant that Jeff and his roommates would have to do a great many push-ups, the penalty for losing the wind sprints. Both Willy and Reb were downright slow, and he and Bob could barely beat BJ Wilson. That meant that Rico, Kevin, and Jim Merritt always came in ahead of his entire room -- to the dismay of Harvey Linehan. Nobody in the Company, plebe or otherwise, could catch Kevin O'Reilly. Kevin won every single sprint. For the past several weeks the squadleaders had used a sliding scale of push-up punishment. The winner -- always Kevin -- did none. The second place finisher got ten push-ups. Third place got 15, etcetera. For Jeff, this meant at least 20 push-ups after every sprint, and sometimes they sprinted more than 20 times during the half-hour comearound. His arms ached thinking about it.

Jeff wasn't sure why his room ran against Kevin and the gang so often recently. Apparently Stone and several other firsties were angry that Mugsy and Henry gave such easy comearounds that nobody ever puked his guts out. Rumor said they had petitioned Captain Dillingham to let Stone, who had no squad of his own, indoctrinate their room in the evenings and on alternate mornings. Today was one of the alternate days. As Jeff finished his third set of 20 push-ups, he wished it was Tommy Poole's squad he was pitted against. He knew he could beat that whole damn room in the short frenzied races.

But it never paid to whine or dwell on the impossible during Plebe Year; survival required maximum attention. Jeff grunted out the push-ups, stood quickly, and waited for the next race. As he waited rigidly, he glanced over at Kevin O'Reilly. The bastard was smiling. Shit, Kevin wasn't even winded. Then Jeff shifted his gaze down the passageway and was immediately outraged by what he saw.

In groups of three and four, plebes suffered the indoctrination process. Lacking true direction, plebe training at Annapolis consisted of learning how to march, how to maintain and wear the various uniforms, how to keep military property properly stowed, and how to achieve the proper cocky proto-officer swagger and attitude for which midshipmen are famous. But these were things mastered during the first week of Plebe Summer. Afterward, the potential usefulness of the entire training process disappeared as the upper-class fell into a historic -- Jeff would say stupidly traditional -- pattern of plebe motivation hallmarked by constant and senseless screaming, ridiculous run-until-you-drop physical exercises, or questionable, demeaning, or humiliating psychological stresses. The upper-class insisted that the physical and emotional degradation let each plebe test himself and extend his personal limits in order to develop the strength of character that would eventually provide graduates with a distinct advantage over their non-Academy comrades. Even though a part of Jeff disputed this "crucible-of-manhood" assumption, Jeff had to admit he was a different, more confident, and stronger person as a result of Plebe Year training. He hated the idea that the system might be right, but the facts were inescapable. Even his mom had remarked on it when he was home.

Along the bulkhead just outside Micklewski's room, Tommy Poole and George Abbott stood -- already sweating profusely -- braced and motionless while Dale screamed something incoherent. As Jeff watched, George dropped to the deck and began easy push-ups. To make the exercise more difficult, Micklewski placed a foot in the middle of Abbott's back and applied pressure against his rising. The foot on George's back did not deter Micklewski from continuing to yell almost directly into Tommy Poole's ear. Dick Salenger stood on the opposite side of Tommy, yelling something entirely different at Tommy with equal intensity and volume.

On the other side of the passageway but further from Jeff's vantage point, Rolando Gomez -- another certifiable Tiger loony -- ran alongside Patrick Mulvaney and Wesley Lamont as they bear-crawled on hands and feet down the passageway. Gomez yelled a continuous stream of Filipino obscenities at the two of them as he jogged. It was rumored that Rolando was related to General Ferdinand Marcos and that he might eventually be in line for the military leadership of that island archipelago. The thought of Gomez leading an entire nation -- when the only words Jeff had ever heard him say were, "You betta do betta push-up, you Fucka!" -- was very scary indeed. John Pirelli, the remaining member of Gomez's squad, was doing pushing-up under the watchful eye and the continuous screaming motivation of the other squadleader, Sheldon Bloodworth.

Scarier even than this, were the events happening in the side passageway to Jeff's left, where Grunt Robinson and Wildman Bill Kopciak motivated their plebes. Grunt had lined up Chuck Chalmers,

Danny French, and Tony Delvecchio at equally-spaced intervals in the center of the passageway facing Jeff. Grunt moved quickly from plebe to plebe, demonstrating karate-style body blows to Kopciak. The blows were not gentle. Tony doubled over and fell to his knees, winded by the fist that slammed into his midsection.

"Get back on your feet, you little pussy!" Kopciak screamed, and Tony scrambled up, still slightly bent over and sucking air desperately into his lungs. On his way down the line from the rear, Robinson kicked the backs of each plebe's knees, sending them one-by-one to the hard tile deck, much to the delight of Wildman who hooted his approval. Direct physical abuse of any kind was strictly forbidden by the Academy regulations, but many of the Tigers didn't care about that particular restriction. After all, they had suffered egregiously under the painful tutelage of their Tiger firsties, and they didn't want their own plebes to miss out on any of the fun.

"Go!" Harvey yelled, starting the next sprint and catching Jeff completely off guard. By the time he was moving, Reb and Willy were several long strides ahead of him.

"Polk, you lazy bastard!" Linehan screamed as Jeff neared his position. "Halt right here!" Jeff hurried to a squeaking stop and stood braced in the center of the passageway.

"I'll take care of this," Daly said loudly, leaning against the bulkhead. "Get over here, Polk!" Jeff hurried to Daly's side, arriving just as Kevin O'Reilly streaked by on his way to another victory. Daly glared at Jeff. "You stinking puke!" he said. "What makes you think you can bag the sprint?"

"I'll find out sir!"

"Hit it for a hundred! And count them out loudly, Polk. I want my classmates in the seventh wing to hear you. Got it?"

"Yes, sir!" Jeff yelled as he dropped to the deck and began screaming out numbers in response to his up-and-down motions. Daly shifted his position slightly so that one massive foot rested under his chest. As Jeff rose and fell, he could feel Daly's big toenail rake painfully against his side as Big Jim held it lathe-style in a position where it was sure to come into scraping contact with Jeff's body. Jeff endured the pain and continued counting. By 50 the pain in his side was considerable. As he finished 70, he glanced down and saw that he was bleeding.

"Keep your god-damn eyes in the boat, Polk!" Big Jim yelled. Jeff continued his count, the pain becoming excruciating. At 90 his pace faltered and he began to strain. His arms tired quickly now, and he paused momentarily at the top of the push-up position to shake out the fatigue from each arm before continuing. At 100 he grunted as he raised himself and paused in the leaning-rest position. His arms ached, and his spine had begun to arch downward toward the floor.

"Straighten up, you douchebag!" Daly shouted. Jeff managed to pull his body momentarily into a straight line, but he could feel his strength giving out quickly despite his best efforts. He moaned, fighting with all his strength to stay in the air. Ten seconds passed, then twenty, then thirty. The time between each instant seemed to grow exponentially. Jeff cursed as his back sagged again, and he could feel his arms shaking.

"Straighten up!" Daly shouted again. Jeff tried valiantly but could not move his backside any higher into the air. "Straighten up!" Daly repeated. Jeff sagged further, angry at himself that he could not do any better.

"You stinking son-of-a-whore sissy! My mother could do better than that! You're another goddamn plebe girl! What's the matter, Jeffie? I give you too many push-ups to do? Shit, what a disgrace you are to the uniform!" Jeff's anger grew.

"Say, Harvey," Daly said suddenly, confusing Jeff with the abrupt change of subject. "Did you see *Cool Hand Luke* this past weekend?" As he said this, Big Jim turned toward Linehan and walked away from Jeff. As he departed he "accidentally" nudged Jeff's left arm, which immediately collapsed. Jeff had no time to react. His forehead came into painful contact with the unforgiving tile floor. He groaned loudly.

"Oh, shit!" Daly wailed. "Look what I accidentally did to my poor little girl plebe. Jeffie, are you hurt? Should I get something for the boo-boo? Maybe I should carry you to Sick Bay on my back? Would you like that Jeffie, you faggot?"

Jeff's head swam. He pushed himself off the tile and sat up slowly. Contact with the floor had broken the tear ducts in both eyes and caused a split in the skin just above his left eyebrow. He reached up and felt something warm and sticky, but he could not decide what it was. He withdrew his hand and stared at the redness for a moment, still considerably disoriented.

"Get your ass back on that deck, or I'll beat the living shit out of you!" roared Daly. "Who gave you permission to sit up?" Jeff shook his head to try to think clearly, and droplets of blood flew in all directions. One of them landed on the top of Harvey Linehan's foot.

"Jesus Christ! Polk! You bastard!" he screamed. "You bled on me!" Linehan and Daly advanced on Jeff simultaneously. Harvey bent down and stared at Jeff, his face a mask of terrible retribution. "You cock!" Harvey yelled. "I'll kill you for this!"

Suddenly Big Jim's face appeared beside Harvey's. He stared at Jeff, smiling.

"Wait a minute, Harvey," he said with mock concern. "I think the little girl's hurt. Look, she's crying. Maybe we should help her to her room before she gets really mad and tries to scratch our eyes out." Linehan laughed loudly at this.

Jeff stared at Daly, still groggy from the fall. He saw the big grin, he heard the words, and he felt the insults. He reached up slowly and dabbed his fingers in the blood that was now running freely down the side of his head. He stared at the redness; then with perfect calmness he flicked several drops of blood from his fingertips directly into Daly's face.

"Comearound on Hundredth Night, you ignorant prick!" Jeff announced loudly, "I'll run your fat ass into the ground. You're mine! Sir!" Daly had drawn back away from the flying blood and had tripped over his bathrobe in the process. He now sat on the tile deck facing Jeff. Two bright blood drops stood out starkly on his left cheek. The passageway was suddenly silent. Daly stared at Jeff for several long seconds. Then he laughed loudly and clapped his two huge hands together.

"This is great!" he yelled. "Jeffie, you little faggot. We're gonna have such fun, you and me; and since you asked me around early, it's only fitting that we start early." He paused and became deadly serious. His eyes narrowed and focused on Jeff menacingly. Jeff shivered slightly, suddenly afraid. Daly continued, his hand reaching for his face and the blood drops that glistened there. "Tonight I'm gonna give you my special comearound, douchebag, and you're gonna wish you'd never been born."

CHAPTER 4

POOLE'S CONFLICT

A tall hulking figure loomed unexpectedly in the doorway of Tommy Poole's room. George happened to be looking in that direction, and Tommy had been staring into space above George's head, contemplating chemical bonds and the relationship between various compounds. Tommy could see a momentary fear on George's face as he bolted to his feet

"Attention on deck!" George Abbott yelled. Hank Butkowski and Tommy Poole jumped to attention. Tommy could not see who had entered, but he realized by George's reaction it was someone formidable. Unable to turn, Tommy remained rigid.

"At ease!" a soft familiar voice announced, and Tommy immediately realized with dread that Captain Dillingham had come to visit. He drew a quick, deep breath and steeled himself into his seat as a sick feeling began in the lower parts of his stomach. He turned slowly and stared. At first it seemed a monster blocked the doorway. Marine Corps Captain Rusty "Bull" Dillingham, frightening though he may have been, was not a monster, at least not in the classic sense.

Standing more than six feet six inches tall and weighing in excess of 230 pounds, Bull Dillingham was imposing. He was also an Academy larger-than-life legend. Tourists and midshipmen alike stopped to gape whenever the "Green Giant" passed. Being a consummate Marine and an zealous weight lifter, Bull worked hard each day to ensure that not a single ounce of his weight was fat and that the muscles that adorned his impressive body were awe inspiringly over-developed. His body rippled and flexed involuntarily under the cotton fabric of his uniform shirt as he moved purposefully about his business.

Bull also shaved and polished his enormous head so that it glistened brighter than the brims of most midshipmens' combination caps, and his prominent facial features and oversized teeth stood out in stark Cro-Magnon relief against the subtler background of the merely-human young men who surrounded him. In sharp counter-point to his fierce appearance Bull sported a set of ears which stuck outward from his glossy head and which would have begged instant ridicule on lesser men. However, no one in the entire Academy dared mention Bull's aberrant appendages in a derogatory or humorous fashion for fear of God-knew-what reprisal. Six rows of brightly colored combat ribbons on Bull's chest attested to the fact that Bull had been places Tommy did not ever want to go and had done things in the name of victory and glory that Tommy did not want to know about. Tommy tried to stop himself from staring at that decorated chest, but he couldn't help himself.

Size and fearful visage aside, two more mundane physical aspects of the Bull's personality affected Tommy Poole the most. First were Bull's eyes, which were a deep, intelligent but constantly-sad blue, and which fixed on Tommy with an intense and mesmerizing stare. They were old and troubled eyes, eyes that had seen too many frightening and bloodthirsty acts committed in the name of war. They were eyes that lived with painful memory images fused permanently on the retinas. Tommy fervently hoped he would never see those eyes in his own mirror.

The other amazing aspect of Bull's personality was his soft, almost-feminine voice, which -- while completely out of character with his other physical features -- managed to capture the absolute attention of his listeners. That is not to say that when Bull roared he couldn't be heard 20 miles away. He could. Tommy stared up at Bull and swallowed again. Bull returned his glance. None of the plebes could remember ever having seen Bull blink. It was a subject of considerable plebe controversy.

After what seemed like hours, Bull averted his gaze slowly from Tommy and shifted it to Hank Butkowski. He smiled broadly, oversized teeth flashing.

"How is everything with you, Hank?" he asked. Hank was the only person Tommy personally knew that rivaled Bull in sheer physical size, but Tommy knew Bull would easily win a ferocity contest.

"Fine, sir!" Hank answered, grinning broadly. "Track practice is going well. I set a new plebe shot-put record yesterday."

"Great!" Dillingham replied, turning to George Abbott. "How about you, George?"

"Fine, sir!" George answered, not at all convincingly. Bull turned to Tommy.

"And you, Mister Poole?" he asked.

"I'm doing well, sir!" Tommy answered.

Dillingham appraised Tommy critically. His eyes lingered on Tommy's ample waistline, settled on his pimple-laden face.

"That's good to hear, Mister Poole," Bull said softly. "After all, we're almost in the middle of the Dark Ages. Hundredth Night is just around the corner, and Plebe Year is winding down. You probably figure you have it made."

"No, sir!" Tommy answered firmly but smiling. "I definitely *do not* have it made!"

"But you're still convinced you're going to make it through the year, aren't you?"

Tommy hesitated. Being pointedly resolute with upper-class midshipmen was expected from the best plebes, but Tommy knew Dillingham didn't want to hear resolution from him.

"Sir," he answered, "I have been able to withstand the punishments and pressures so far, but it has been extremely difficult."

In the passageway just outside the room Wesley Lamont began yelling out a chow call. Dillingham glanced at his watch. Noon meal formation was only ten minutes away. He stared again at Tommy silently for several seconds and began speaking quietly in the midst of the din. Tommy strained to catch the words.

"Come to my office after your final class today, Mister Poole, so that we can talk about your remaining time at the Academy."

"Aye, aye, sir!" Tommy answered. With that Dillingham turned sharply and strode from the room.

"Shit!" said George Abbott fiercely. "I'll bet I know what that's gonna be about."

"Yeah," Hank Butkowski added with a frustrated sigh. "Another motivational talk about your quitting, Tommy."

Tommy remained quiet for a moment.

"It's getting serious now, guys. For the first time I'm beginning to have reservations about whether I'm going to make it to the Herndon Monument come June Week. Dillingham is the one person who could easily get me discharged, and he's really pissed at me for staying despite all his brotherly advice to the contrary. Shit, I don't know what to do!"

"Just hang in there, Tommy," offered George. "You've got our support one hundred percent. The year is almost over."

Tommy looked at each of them gravely. He sighed loudly and shook his head.

"Thanks guys."

As he sat quietly in the anteroom of the Company Office that afternoon, textbooks in a neat stack beside his chair, Tommy Poole was confused about the his situation. He was in big trouble, and he knew it. He had not expected the ferocity of Captain Dillingham's response when he returned to Annapolis after Christmas leave. But he couldn't understand what it was about him that so many upper-class midshipmen hated. He understood he would never be a model midshipman; that he didn't project the proper macho, arrogant, Academy image. But he had made tremendous improvements, and he could now excel both physically and professionally. Why didn't that count?

Tommy chuckled, remembering the morning he had arrived at Annapolis early last June. He had been grossly fat and in terrible physical condition. It made him an immediate target for the upper-class at the very time when it was most important not to stand out in any contrary fashion. Despite the negative attention he had attracted during the summer, he had survived, and even flourished. Tommy smiled again and glanced briefly at himself. Today he could do as many push-ups as most of his classmates, and he could run practically all day long -- two feats he would not have thought possible scant months ago. During Christmas vacation his parents had been awestruck by the physical changes he had undergone, and he was secretly proud at how the muscles in his arms and legs bulged.

He worked diligently to become a model midshipman, excelling in the mundane aspects of life at Annapolis. His locker and rack were always immaculate. His uniforms were invariably crisp and precisely aligned. And he could polish shoes better than anyone in the Company. He could march as straight as the rest of the plebes. He could command the Yard Patrol Boat maneuvers expertly. And he had qualified as "expert" with both the rifle and pistol. He had even maintained a 4.0 academic grade average despite the best efforts of an army of upper-class to destroy him. As far as he could tell, he performed his military duties as well as any plebe, except maybe for Jim Merritt and Bob Strong. But Tommy could tell Jim and Bob were destined for future greatness. He just longed for the feel of the joy stick and the roar of the jet engines.

The stigma of the "fat-and-ugly" Tommy Poole seemed impossible to erase, no matter how hard he worked or how well he performed. And once the relentless Academy system, in the person of Captain "Bull" Dillingham, officially decided that he was of questionable quality, events proceeded almost of their own accord. Every upper-class in the Company had been given the word to run him out, and they had accepted the assignment with a vengeance. Life had been pure hell for Tommy Poole, far more than for any of his classmates in Tiger Company, and maybe worse than for any other plebe in the Class of 1971. He was physically, mentally, and emotionally exhausted. He shook his head sadly. How could he convince Captain Dillingham that he *was* Annapolis material and especially that despite the harassment, he loved the Academy and everything it stood for?

He had discussed the vengeance of the system and his own constant punishment with his parents, and they had urged him to consider attending another school. Mom hated the thought of his being abused, despite the obvious physical benefits and his new-found aggressive self confidence. Dad, always pragmatic, knew that he would do well at any of the many universities that had eagerly sought his attendance. "Go somewhere they appreciate you," he said. But Tommy had remained firm that he was going to stick it out. He'd get a seat in the cockpit of a Navy fighter no matter what the Academy said to the contrary.

The door to Captain Dillingham's office opened, and Bull emerged, interrupting his reverie. He smiled at Tommy, but the smile did not look at all genuine.

"Come in, please," he said, standing aside to allow Tommy into the inner sanctum of Company administration. Tommy entered hesitatingly, surprised to see that Rock Stone already was seated at one side of the Captain's large wooden desk. Rock also smiled at him, but his smile was more genuine. Tommy suspected that Rock admired his spunk.

The office was a Marine Corps and "Bull" Dillingham memorial with the Marine Corps getting second billing. A huge wooden desk sat in the rear center of the room facing the door. A large window directly behind the desk provided ample light and backdrop. On the center-front of the desk was a brightly polished brass pen and pencil holder featuring small flags of the United States, Vietnam, and the Marine Corps. Several papers sat precisely in a stack on the right side of the desk, but no in-out box or blotter marred the pristine polished surface that shone with reflected sunlight. A large glass display plaque of crossed military swords -- Navy and Marine Corps -- mounted on bright red velvet adorned the wall to Tommy's right. Beside it on both sides were framed pictures of men in combat uniforms, posing, arms on each others' shoulders, beside various pieces of field equipment and military aircraft. "Vietnam" shouted from every picture. The "Bull"was prominent in every pose, but Tommy could see the vapid smiles of recent combat veterans cemented onto each tired face.

On the opposite wall were Bull's Naval Academy diploma and Certificate of Appointment as an Officer of the United States Marine Corps. Tommy had been surprised to discover several months ago that Bull had ranked within the top ten percent of his class and that he had received a degree in advanced mathematics. Bull certainly did not look or act the part of an intellectual.

Across the very top of the wall facing the desk and continuing above the entry door were a series of colorful wood and metal organizational plaques designating every military unit Bull had served with during his brief career. Beneath those were framed copies of certificates of achievements and awards. There were a great many of those. In the very center of this display, completely out of place and attached to the wall by a single silver-headed thumb tack rather than by frame and nail, was a poor photostat copy of a drawing of a vulture sitting on a dead tree branch. The vulture stared backward at the observer with a grim expression, and a caption underneath said. "*I'm having a bad day. I think I'll go out and kill something!*" The paper looked incongruous in the midst of all the precisely placed military memorabilia, and Tommy shuddered to think what it might say about the inner Bull Dillingham.

Tommy stared fascinated at the walls for several seconds as Bull walked passed him and seated himself behind his desk. Finally Bull cleared his throat, and Tommy snapped back to reality. Bull indicated a straight-backed wooden chair that sat directly in front of the desk.

"Please be seated, Mister Poole," he said.

Tommy sat, and stared at Captain Dillingham, and looked at Rock Stone. Rock returned his stare, but his face gave nothing away.

Dillingham placed his two enormous arms on the desk in front of him and leaned forward toward Tommy. His Academy ring, its red stone shining brightly, banged loudly and unintentionally against the wood.

"Mister Poole," he said, "we have to have a very serious discussion, you and me, and I'll get right to the point.

"The motto of this institution," Dillingham began, "is *duty, honor, and loyalty.* Those words are the foundation by which this nation has become and remained great. A member of the Armed Forces must always do his duty, no matter what the cost. An officer must always act with honor. And a good military leader must be loyal to his nation, his service, and his Commanding Officer.

"In order to ensure this institution produces men who can and will embrace those concepts, the requirements for entrance and continuing attendance at the service academies are extremely strict. No other schools in the nation turn away or wash out so many bright candidates. But no other schools command the same respect and admiration of the general population of the nation."

Bull paused and looked at Tommy closely. Tommy could see by the fire that blazed in his eyes that Bull meant every word he said.

"It's our responsibility to live up to that respect, Mister Poole! It's our responsibility to show the nation every day of our lives that their trust is well-founded! It's our responsibility to be ready and willing to pay the ultimate sacrifice in the service of the citizens!"

Dillingham's voice rose in timbre as he spoke until he almost shouted the last words. Realizing he had been preaching, he smiled and his voice quieted.

"For more than a hundred years the service academies have produced leaders who have led this nation in peace and war. Men of honor -- loyal men -- men who will do their duty without fail. The tradition must be upheld."

Again he stared at Tommy. His eyes became sad.

"I like you, Mister Poole. I really do! You have guts, and brains, and ambition. You've lasted far longer than any one of us could have imagined. But it's time to face the facts, and the facts are clear to me that you do not meet the standards this institution sets for its graduates." Bull pointed to Tommy.

"Look at yourself, Mister Poole. You've been running and exercising almost constantly since the first day of Plebe Summer, and you're still a sickly-squishy lard-ass. You can run and exercise and do an adequate number of push-ups now -- nobody denies that -- but what happens when you're not faced with the constant pressure to perform? Without proper motivation, you'll revert to your former self within a few months. We can't risk that.

"Consider your leadership abilities, Mister Poole. You have been consistently ranked last in the Company by the first-class and by your own peers. Who's ever going to follow you cheerfully into battle? The nation needs leaders, and this place is supposed to train them. Frankly, I find you untrainable in that regard.

"Finally, you are a genius -- no question. But the services need more than brains to operate. They need smart men of courage and conviction and compassion. You lack those qualities. The thought your finger on the button someday, Mister Poole, frankly scares me to death. We can't have that either.

"We can't allow you to graduate, Mister Poole," Bull said with startling conviction. "We have to get you out of here as soon as possible. It's far better for everyone, yourself included, if you go now; so I'm asking you a final time to resign honorably. Give up, Mister Poole. Recognize what we have been trying to convince you of for the last eight months. You don't belong! Quit! Resign! Go home!"

Tommy had stared at Dillingham as he talked, trying to fathom what motivated the "Bull's" attitude; and for the first time since he arrived, he became physically afraid. He realized that Dillingham -- and probably every Tiger -- considered it his absolute jihad duty to drive him out. He faced military zealots, and they had all the power. Tommy felt sudden intense depression. He sighed and for the first time hesitated. Then he remembered his brother, and his promise to the family that he would make it through no matter what. He pushed aside the fear. He had meant that promise, and he fully intended to keep it, despite anyone's insane devotion to duty, despite the continued cruelties inflicted by Dale Micklewski, and despite Captain Rusty "Bull" Dillingham himself. He would make it. Dillingham was just another obstacle.

"Sir!" Tommy said boldly. "I'm sorry, but I can't quit."

Dillingham slammed his right hand down on his desk with a suddenness and violence that shocked Tommy and frightened him again. The booming noise the huge flat palm made as it contacted the wood reverberated through the office, visibly shaking the glass panes in the window behind Bull. Tommy heard something shift position on the wall behind him. Out of the corner of his eye he thought he saw Stone flinch slightly. For several seconds Dillingham said nothing; then he sighed.

"Why are you doing this, Poole? What motivates you to suffer so much pain and humiliation? There are a hundred colleges out there where that brain of yours could thrive in academic freedom." Dillingham waved a huge arm in the air. "You don't need this, Poole. You could join an ROTC unit at the university of your choices, and still be a part of the Armed Forces after you graduate. Hell, you could accelerate your studies and graduate earlier than your classmates and outrank them in the field." He shook his head. "Why are you staying?"

Tommy paused before answering. He looked from Dillingham to Stone.

"Sir, your logic is perfect; and if someone had told me this at the beginning of the summer, I might have quit. I was very confused and unsure when I arrived. I wanted to resign every single day during the summer. In fact, I almost did several times."

Tommy paused again and looked beseechingly from Stone to Dillingham.

"But since Plebe Summer I've changed." He pointed passed Bull out the wide window where midshipmen went about their business. "I love this place, sir, and I really love what I've become since I first put on the Academy uniform. Never before in my life have I been such an part of something as fulfilling. Nowhere have I felt so much at home. And no one has cared for my well being and success as much as my classmates in this Company." Tommy laughed. "I think some of them love me more than my parents do. We've sweated and bled and struggled together. My classmates here are the truest bunch of friends I have ever had. I owe it to them to finish."

Tommy smiled at Bull.

"No matter what anyone does to me, I'm already a full-fledged midshipman. I've passed every test the system's faced me with, and look what it's done to me." He held up his right arm to flex his biceps for Dillingham. The muscle that flexed would have impressed the average American but was hardly worth mentioning on the Dillingham scale. Dillingham dismissed the muscle show with a contemptuous wave of his hand. "I *am* a midshipman to be proud of, sir," Tommy continued. "And I'll never let anyone down either on the job or in combat." Tommy leaned across the desk toward Bull.

"I like you, sir. You are an impressive leader. And I like and admire Mister Stone also. But you're both wrong about one important thing. I *have* to make it. I can help the Navy and the serve the country. I deserve to graduate."

Tommy settled back slightly in his chair while Bull digested his words silently. Tommy looked at Rock Stone, who calmly returned his glance.

"Leave us, Mister Poole," Dillingham announced. "Midshipman First-class Stone and I have some things to discuss. I'll call you back here if I have anything further to say to you on this matter."

Tommy felt slightly dejected. He had expected an immediate decision, so he could know how to react; but the Captain's face told him none was forthcoming. He rose, turned, and departed without a further word. Before he left the Company Office, Tommy glanced at his watch. He would have to hurry. He had only fifteen minutes to change and be down on Worden field for a Company intermural football game against Sixth Company.

At Annapolis every midshipman participates in a varsity or intramural level sport in every one of the three sports seasons. In the fall Tommy had played on the Company soccer team, where he had an undistinguished season as a second team defender. This winter he was doing better as an interior lineman on the Company football team. He found himself relishing the physical contact -- something that surprised him greatly. He had received several compliments from upperclassmen for his bruising blocking abilities. Bookworm "Fat Tommy" Poole looked forward to the competitions. He smiled broadly as he hurried to his room to change. Sixth Company had better watch out. "Fat Tommy" Poole was going to crunch someone today.

During the later part of evening meal that same day, most of Tommy's classmates, as well as a great many upper-class, thought he had gone completely insane. In the middle of the usual intense grilling from Micklewski and Salenger, Kevin O'Reilly suddenly appeared unbidden behind Tommy's chair.

"It's time, classmate!" he announced loudly, and Tommy rose from his seat without permission.

"Sit your fat ass back down, Poole!" yelled Salenger. "I'm in the middle of doing something with you." Tommy ignored him and he and Kevin chopped to the table headed by John "Tex" Gladden, where Rock Stone functioned as assistant squadleader. Tommy and Kevin each took a position behind Rock, one on each side of him.

Gladden looked up at them, smiled, and shook his head. John was a proud Texan and a varsity rower in the fastest of the Annapolis four-man sculls. His scull had captured the Eastern Regional Championships last year, and that made John a potential rowing All-American. He was one of the few genuinely nice firsties in Tiger Company. It was common plebe knowledge that he didn't have much use for Plebe Year and that he had asked Rock to ease up a bit on his lucky plebes, who happened to be Doug Goto, Mike Wojeck, and Elliot Zimmerman.

"I think you got company, Rock", Gladden said with a Texas chuckle as Tommy and Kevin paused behind Stone's chair, braced and obviously ready for some action.

"Oh, really," Rock said, turning. Seeing Kevin nearby did not surprise him at all. O'Reilly was always mixed up in some sort of mischief. But the fact that Tommy also stood waiting caused him to raise his eyebrows slightly.

"What can I do for you gentlemen?"

Kevin looked at Tommy, and both of them began reciting together,

"*We think no one has ever known,*
A midshipman uglier than Stone.
His face a fright, his teeth all hairy,
Classmates say he's still a cherry.

He fusses and struts and thinks he's a wit,
But all he is, is a load of shit.
He's never had a good idea,
We wouldn't follow him to the head if we had diarrhea.

Hundredth Night is fast approaching,
Pardon us classmates for our poaching.
It may be dumb, it may be crass,
But we want to run his sissy ass.

So Mister Stone our loser buddy,
We're gonna turn you into putty.
We're gonna run you like a comet,
Come Hundredth Night, we'll make you vomit!"

With that both Tommy and Kevin leaned over on each side of Stone and yelled in his ears simultaneously. "Come around on Hundredth Night, sir!"

Everyone at Gladden's table, and at most of the surrounding tables laughed loudly at Kevin and Tommy's joke on Stone. Even Stone chuckled. He rose and turned toward them, still smiling.

"That was really funny, guys." He reached out and put a large hand on each of their shoulders. "Thanks. I appreciate the opportunity you've given me here." He looked at Kevin, who was grinning broadly. "O'Reilly," he said loudly, "you are one of the biggest smacks I have ever come across. I'm going to run that silly-assed smile right off your face."

"I'll find out, sir!" Kevin yelled in reply, confusing Rock momentarily. Rock turned to Tommy.

"Mister Poole, I've had the wonderful pleasure of running you for the last several months, and I've enjoyed every blessed minute of it. But everything that happened up to this moment was solely chicken-shit motivational exercising. Now the fun starts." He squeezed Tommy's shoulder. "Get ready to die, 'Fat Tommy' Poole."

"Aye, aye, sir!" Tommy answered, a slight hesitancy in his voice.

Keeping his hand on their shoulders, Stone smiled and leaned in close to the two of them. Then he whispered so that only Kevin and Tommy could hear.

"Thanks a lot, guys. This means a lot to me." He straightened and looked them both in the eye seriously.

"Get back to your seats, assholes," he announced loudly, "and pray that you die before tomorrow morning!" Tommy and Kevin chopped back to their seats to the accompanying cheers of neighboring Companies who desperately wanted to see Stone and his Tigers suffer in reparation for the hundreds of demerits they had passed out to classmates and under-classmen alike.

"That's plenty gutsy of them isn't it, Jeffie?" Big Jim asked Jeff soon after the commotion had died down.

"Yes, sir!" Polk answered.

Daly leaned across the table toward Jeff.

"Just like it was gutsy of *you* to ask me around. I'm not a pussy like classmate Linehan, am I?"

Jeff paused. He knew that no matter how he answered that question he was going to be in trouble. He improvised.

"Mr. Linehan is not a pussy, sir," he yelled, "and I defy anyone to say so to my face!" Linehan smiled. Daly stared at Jeff.

"Quick thinking, Polk. But you and I both know that Harvey Linehan is a pussy. Christ, you'd have to be pretty desperate to date that dog he calls a fiance. Don't you agree, Jeffie?"

"I've never seen Mister Linehan's girlfriend, sir!"

"Well that's good for you, Jeffie. It's not a pretty sight."

Through the whole thing, Harvey Linehan smiled at Big Jim.

Finally he said before Daly could add anything else, "you're just jealous, Daly, you wimp." Harvey turned to Jeff and said quietly. "You know what his problem is, Mister Polk?"

"No, sir!"

"Daly is a pervert. Nobody has ever seen his girl, even though he claims to have one back on the farm in Iowa. I think Jim here is really engaged to his right hand, and that will be the closest he ever comes to a decent relationship."

Polk didn't answer, but Big Jim chuckled loudly.

"Good one, Harv. I like that!"

Saturday morning at precisely 0800, immediately after morning meal, Captain Dillingham and Rock Stone entered Tommy Poole's room unannounced. Jeff Polk and Reb Ramsey were there discussing options for the afternoon's liberty call in town. The sun had driven the chill away temporarily, and the morning brought promise of a perfect day.

"Attention on deck!" Hank Butkowski yelled, and the plebes snapped to attention. Jeff could tell from the demeanor of the two visitors that something was seriously amiss. Bull offered no friendly greetings to the jocks, none of the usual Marine Corps kidding with Reb. His posture, normally stiff and formal, was ramrod straight. Rock Stone seemed uncomfortable. Rock carried a clipboard to which was attached a Room Inspection chit.

"Good morning, gentlemen," Dillingham announced in an unusually curt voice. "In keeping with Academy policy to ensure that midshipmen maintain proper military decorum, I have decided to institute a policy of surprise room and personnel inspections. Today I will start with Midshipman Fourth-class Poole."

A visible shockwave coursed through the room, and everyone was quiet for several seconds. Rock Stone focused on something outside the bright winter window.

"Mister Poole," Dillingham snapped. "Please prepare you locker, desk, and rack for inspection.

"Aye, aye, sir!" Tommy yelled smartly, but it was clear to Jeff that he was as confused as the rest of them. Surprise inspections were a constant threat to any plebe, but thus far those had been conducted by the squadleaders only. Company Officer inspections had always been announced in advance. This clearly did not bode well for Tommy.

Tommy opened the drawers of his desk stair-step fashion, and quickly moved to his locker, where he opened the port side door fully to expose the hanging items inside. He turned and, standing at rigid attention beside his locker, announced, "Sir! Midshipman Fourth-class Poole prepared for inspection, sir!"

Dillingham nodded curtly and proceeded to Tommy's locker, Stone trailing behind him. He glanced briefly at the hanging items, which according to regulations were spaced a uniform one-half inch distance from one another. He glanced down at the shoe formation and immediately spied Tommy's class shoes, which he had worn to Friday's afternoon classes but he had not polished. Normally he would not be expected to have them ready for viewing until the following Monday. The shoes were slightly scuffed, and a residue of leftover mud -- from where Tommy had unsuccessfully traversed a puddle as he hurried back to Bancroft Hall for Friday evening comearound -- marred the heel area of the right shoe.

"Disgraceful!" snapped Dillingham as he pointed down at the offending shoes. Rock dutifully recorded the item on the chit. Dillingham opened the starboard side of Tommy's locker and examined the folds and alignment of his stowed gear. He shook his head.

"This definitely needs more work, Mister Poole," he said as he reached inside the locker and pulled the undershirts and boxer underpants out with a sweep of his arm, leaving them in a crumpled heap on the floor. Stone recorded this as well. Next Bull swept the socks and belts aside to join the other items on the floor. Behind the belts Dillingham spied Tommy's collection of books. He turned.

"Is this the proper place for books, Mister Poole?" he asked.

Tommy hesitated. Academy regulations were silent about stowage of personal items like books, but in every plebe and upper-class room personal books were kept in exactly the same location.

"I'll find out, sir!" he replied.

"Do that, Mister Poole!" Bull pulled the books down onto the floor.

Within five minutes no item remained on any of Tommy's shelves, his desk had been emptied onto the floor, and his immaculate bed had been pulled apart and the sheets thrown on the floor. Dillingham turned to Stone.

"Did you get all that?"

"Yes, sir!" Stone answered smartly. Then Bull turned to Tommy.

"I am very disappointed in you and your entire squad, Mister Poole. It's too late in the year for such haphazard attention to detail. I can see that your superiors have slacked up too much." He paused and stared at Tommy with a glare that would have melted a polar icecap. "I have decided to take a personal interest in your training, Mister Poole. From now on I will inspect your room and locker on a random basis. And I will do so until everything is ship-shape or until there is no longer any necessity for my attention. Is that clear?"

Tommy stammered. "Yes, sir!"

"Good." Bull turned to Stone. "What's the tally?"

"Twenty-five demerits, sir!"

Dillingham clapped his hands together loudly and smiled.

"Excellent!" He then turned to Tommy. "That will be all for now, Mister Poole." With that he led Stone from the room. Rock hesitated before leaving, staring at Tommy. His eyes said nothing.

"Holy shit!" Hank exploded once he was sure the Captain was out of earshot. "I can't believe I just saw what I did."

"Me either," added George emphatically.

"I'll get some help," Jeff offered, putting a hand on Tommy's shoulder. Jeff chopped from the room and went directly to Jim Merritt's room, where he enlisted Kevin and Jim to help Tommy straighten his things. He then went across the passageway to his own room and recruited Willy and Bob. Together the nine plebes quickly and expertly folded and reassembled Tommy's gear, taking slow and special care to stow each item precisely in accordance with the regulations. Jim Merritt had gone so far as to bring a ruler with which he meticulously measured the dimensions of each folded item and identified its precise location on the locker shelves with a small pencil tic.

"I'll keep your books safely in my room until this blows over," Kevin offered.

"*If* it blows over," Tommy added sadly. "I'm really worried guys. This may mark the beginning of the end of Tommy Poole the Midshipmen."

"Not a chance, Tommy," offered Jim. "We'll cover for you. We'll see you make it through. Bob and I will organize the rest of the classmates to help with your locker and gear. By tomorrow there'll won't be a single thing anyone can find wrong. And we'll make sure you look 100 percent before formations." Jim turned to the others, a troubled look on his face.

"This is war, guys, and I intend to see we win it."

Tommy looked from classmate to classmate and he eyes teared up.

"Thanks," he stammered. "I won't forget this."

"It's our duty, Tommy," added Bob Strong. "We won't let you down."

CHAPTER 5

BATTLE LINES

Saturday afternoon a large contingent of Twenty-third Company plebes took liberty in the town of Annapolis. Annapolis is about as quaint and comfortable as any small town in America, and its proximity to the Chesapeake Bay and the Naval Academy make it a popular tourist stop. Many of the narrow streets retain the cobblestone charm of the last century, large old trees abound, it has a picturesque harbor, and the small shops reflect a determined desire on the part of the locals to retain a small-town hominess. Even the midshipmen grant the city a grudging respect, something most other towns-outside-the-base never receive, but some of that respect no doubt results from the fact that the city usually teems with lovely young women eager to meet, mate, and marry future naval officers.

All midshipmen -- other than first-class on an authorized overnight absence -- wear the uniform of the day when on liberty. It's an inconvenience, but better to suffer an inconvenience and be free than remain potential targets inside Bancroft Hall. For most of the year the uniform for liberty in town was Service Dress Blue, a sharp suit-like uniform consisting of black shoes, dark pants, a white shirt with black tie, a matching dark jacket with ribbons, and a white-vinyl-covered combination cap. Jeff always felt more connected to the navy in his Service Dress, and he also knew he looked impressive.

Despite the slight chill and a steady freshening breeze from the west, the sun blazed brightly, and the city of Annapolis bustled. Although few sail boats braved the harbor and channel, many people sat boldly along the water's edge, enduring the breeze and the chill as they watched the water and the activity in the far off Bay and listened to the multitudes of seagulls that soared overhead and screamed for attention from nearby pilings. January sun sparkled on the water and reflected brightly off the brilliant white paint of several of the boats' hulls and from the many polished brass fittings. People in heavy-but-open-fronted coats hurried from shop to shop or strolled aimlessly along the busy streets, intent on enjoying the brief warming trend. Tonight a predicted storm might return Maryland to a cold and wet wintry grip.

The large group of Twenty-third Company plebes on liberty in Annapolis included all the occupants of Jeff Polk's and Jim Merritt's rooms, as well as Tommy Poole, Hank Butkowski, Wesley Lamont, and Patrick Mulvaney. The group strolled purposefully to the local submarine sandwich shop the Company had adopted as their preferred food source away from Mother Bancroft. But not all the plebes in the group were intent on the culinary aspects of their trip to town. Kevin, Rico, and BJ Wilson openly discussed the attributes and potential of every female they passed. Kevin was plainly excited, and Rico and BJ would never turn down a chance for companionship, even when so much as talking to a female in public was strictly forbidden. Jeff had heard Rico and BJ brag about the various rendezvous and sexual encounters they arranged during the first set. Setting aside midshipman bravado, Jeff knew they spoke mostly the truth.

Jim Merritt might have joined in the never-ending search for fulfillment, but he had found a darling of a girl named Leslie Taylor Wallace, who attended a college near Washington, D.C. She visited him every other weekend. Jeff had met her during the Army-Navy festivities. He had to admit that if he were in Jim's place, he would take huge risks to spend time alone with Leslie. Jim also seemed to have found a companion for Rico Guevarra, but neither Jim nor Rico would talk about that arrangement, which was strange considering Rico's boastful nature.

"What do you guys think about that one?" Kevin asked Rico and BJ, indicating with a nod of his head a pretty blonde girl standing on the corner across the street.

"She's already taken," announced Rico.

"How do you know that?" asked Kevin.

"You can tell by the way she's standing. She's not in the least bit interested in fishing. I'll bet her beau is an upper-classman."

"How can you tell *that*?"

"She checked us out casually when we first approached, like she was expecting someone in uniform; but when she saw the bare sleeves on our jackets, she decided we were beneath notice."

"Okay," Kevin asked. "How about that one?" He indicated a dark haired and rather buxom young lady who had just emerged from a souvenir shop. Rico studied her.

"Nah," he said, "she's too hot for you. Not your type at all."

"How do you know?"

"Body language, my Irish friend. She's had a great deal of experience and is willing to share it; but she's looking for a good time, not a life-long commitment."

"Hey!" Kevin exclaimed. "I like a good time as much as the next person."

"O'Reilly, you sack of shit," added BJ. "You don't know anything about a good time. You fall in love too easily to ever fall into lust. You'd probably be talking marriage before you had your pants off." Kevin pondered what BJ had just said.

"So you think I should just learn to go after the cheap stuff all the time?"

"No, Kevin! They do *not* mean that!" interrupted Jim Merritt. "You should stay just exactly the way you are. That's part of what makes you attractive. You couldn't pull off the Don Juan role like Rico and BJ. Find a nice girl and settle down with her for a while. That..." he said, indicating the young lady across the street who could tell they were discussing her and who now had her eyes focused on the group,"...is not for you."

"Rico?" Kevin asked referring to the expert on all things sexual.

"For once I agree with Jim. You stay away from women like that, and you'll be far better off."

While Kevin pondered Rico's advice, BJ Wilson broke formation and headed across the street toward the woman in question.

As he stepped into the street, he said over his shoulder, "Don't worry about me boys. I'll sacrifice myself so that poor Kevin stays uncorrupted. I can handle this. -- Foot-long pepperoni please. Pay you later." Rico and Jim laughed. Kevin wasn't sure if he had been had or not. Rico put a brotherly hand on Kevin's shoulder and steered him toward the sub shop.

"Leave *those* women to the experts," he said gently.

With their load of subs in tow, the group found an open spot near the Annapolis Harbor quaywall, sat down on several green metal benches, and prepared to eat. BJ Wilson joined them soon afterward, boldly displaying a hastily-written note which contained the girl's name and phone number.

"Maybe I'll get lucky tonight," he said as he sat.

"Tonight?" asked Bob Strong.

"Well," BJ said, "it just so happens that she wasn't doing anything, and -- surprise, surprise -- neither was I. So I'm going to call her a little later, and she just may be up for a little Hospital Point action this evening."

"Wilson, you're one lucky bastard," Willy Simpson observed.

"It's not luck, hayseed," BJ answered. "Skill, daring, and a glib tongue is all it takes."

"Yeah," Rico added. "That and being the heir to a million-dollar fortune."

BJ laughed.

"You're right. That doesn't hurt either."

As they opened their bags and peeled back the waxed paper wrapping, glorious smells snapped into the cold breezy air. For Jeff, hungry after another week of not being able to eat a decent meal, the experience was almost religious. Moans of gastric ecstasy rumbled with every enormous bite. No three-chews-and-a-swallow rules applied in town. As usual, only Reb Ramsey had the boldness to order more than one entire foot-long sub. His quick devouring of the first meatball sub amazed even his perpetually hungry classmates. When he started on his second, Hank Butkowski interrupted him.

"Where do you put it all, Reb? I'm a big guy, and I thought I had an appetite; but I can't eat nearly as much as you."

Reb smiled as he chomped down an enormous bite. A string of sauce-covered onion hung briefly from the side of his smile until he pushed it eagerly into his mouth.

"It's easy," he mumbled. "All it takes is practice. Ah figure that if ah consume enough on the weekend, ah don't have ta worry 'bout what ah can't eat durin' the week."

Hank Butkowski frowned at this thought, then quickly brightened.

"You know, Reb, you should try the cannonball test. I'm sure you could get classmates to volunteer their assistance." The cannonball test was a standing pledge from the upper-class that any plebe who could successfully consume 12 of the large apple-fritter desserts in one sitting could have carry-on for the remainder of the year. Jeff hated the heavy, sauce-covered, globs of bulk. "Cannonball" was an apt name. But Reb was the only human being Jeff knew who might have a chance eating 12.

"He'd probably even enjoy the experience," Jeff thought.

"Hey Reb!" Jeff said. "You know, if you figure that the size of a cannonball is about equal to half a foot-long, you'd have to eat the equivalent of six subs to win the test. I'm sure you could eat three subs with no problem whatsoever, but I'll bet you could eat six! Hell, you might have a shot at it!"

Jubal Hunter Ramsey sat quietly for a moment, pondering the feat. He looked at his second sub, one of the hamburger variety. He lifted it, weighing it carefully. Then he patted his stomach, obviously trying to gage the space available inside his huge frame.

"You know what?" he declared. "I think I could do it." The group cheered loudly -- all except Kevin O'Reilly, who was busy eyeing a young girl who sat with her parents several benches away. The girl was smiling sweetly at Kevin, who was obviously pondering how to approach the young lady with her parents nearby and without any of the many upper-class in the vicinity being aware of his actions. The penalty for a plebe caught fraternizing with a female was 20 demerits, which this time of year meant four hours of heavy-duty marching in the freezing cold.

Rico leaned over and whispered something to Kevin, who looked at the girl and nodded his head toward the shops across the street. She looked in the direction he indicated, and back to Kevin with a puzzled expression. Kevin stood, turned resolutely, and headed across the street toward an antique store. It was the same store Rico and his charges had used earlier in the year to lure several other young ladies to eventual debauchery. The girl watched Kevin for a moment, said something to her parents, stood, and followed him across the street. She entered the shop just behind Kevin.

"Go for it, Kevin!" Rico said loudly to the retreating form; then he looked at the remainder of his classmates. "Hey," he said, "he's my protégé. I taught him everything he knows. His success is my success."

"So who's your newest flame, Rico?" asked Jeff suddenly.

"I'm dying to tell," Rico answered, smiling, but he looked at a frowning Jim Merritt and said. "But I promised to keep *mum*." He laughed at his private joke, which no one else understood. Jim Merritt was plainly uncomfortable. "And I still love my sweet Rosa," he continued.

"Can we see her picture?" asked Pat Mulvaney.

Rico removed his hat carefully, first checking to ensure no upper-class were watching. The penalty for being uncovered in public was ten demerits. Inside a clear plastic pocket in the wide vinyl upper support, in a spot intended for an ID card, was a glossy modeling photo of the startlingly attractive Rosa Gomez. He quickly removed the picture and snugly replaced his cap on his head, then he passed the photo around the group.

"Don't grease it up, gentlemen," Rico warned as the picture made the rounds.

The entire group, Jeff included, sighed and drooled with jealous anticipation at the sight of Rosa Gomez.

"This is my one sweet love," announced Rico. "My present female distraction is very interesting, but I'm still committed to my Rosa, and she to me." He sighed dramatically and stared lovingly at the picture. "And who can blame her?" he added.

"How about the rest of you?" Jeff asked. "Let's see your girls."

Heads turned in various directions to survey the surroundings, and everyone in the group doffed hats and removed the pictures inside. Most were copies of high school graduation photos. All showed sweet young women smiling brightly for the camera, looks of graduational anticipation evident in their gleaming teeth and shining eyes. While they were sharing photos, Kevin returned. He sat with a loud sigh. He seemed clearly disappointed.

"Too young!" he declared.

Rico laughed. "That didn't stop you Parent's Weekend," he said referring to an incident at the very end of Plebe Summer when the plebe brother of a young lady punched Kevin for fooling around with his 15-year-old sister. Kevin swore she had told him she was 18, and Jeff believed him. Kevin didn't lie. He was an upstanding midshipman. But that still didn't mean any of his classmates would let him off the hook for his little social gaffe. His split lip had been a topic of conversation for several weeks.

"Well, I won't make that mistake again," Kevin said, indicating the young girl, who had returned to her parents' side still smiling sweetly at Kevin. "She's only 16. Too young!" He reached into his pocket, pulled out a piece of paper, and held it up. "But just in case -- I got her number."

"O'Reilly, you asshole!" BJ said. "Throw that away. She's jailbait! You're gonna get into serious trouble!"

O'Reilly looked over at the young lady. He waved.

"But she sure is cute," he said.

"Let's see the picture in your hat, Kevin," Jeff asked him.

Kevin looked uncomfortable in the moment before he took off his hat, and passed around a photo of Sarah Connelly.

"She seems sweet, Kevin," Tommy added. "I don't understand why you split up."

"It's a long story," Kevin replied, looking at the concrete under his feet. "I'm thinking about changing the photo, but I'm not sure who to replace Sarah with. After all, there are so many possibilities." Everyone laughed.

"Sure, Kevin," Jeff said.

Kevin pondered for a long moment as classmates finished their sandwiches.

"You know," he finally said, "there *are* a great many possibilities."

"Yeah," added Pat Mulvaney in his Iowa drawl. "Just like Hundredth Night."

"You know what?" Rico said. "You guys are all insane about this Hundredth Night bullshit. You should be like me and ask around one of the somewhat reasonable firsties. Hell, I asked Henry Brandis, and do you know what we agreed? He won't run my ass too hard from now until then, and I'll let him off easy come the big night. It's a great deal for both of us, and it makes me a shoe-in to finish Plebe Year in one piece."

"Brandis agreed to that?" asked an incredulous Bob Strong.

"Of course," Rico replied. "He's no fool, and besides, he's got an academic record to uphold. He can't afford to get himself injured senselessly this late in the game."

"You lucky bastard!" Mulvaney said. "Who did you ask, BJ?"

"Brandis!" BJ answered, smiling broadly. Everybody looked at Jim Merritt.

"Mugsy!" he said. "I felt sorry for him and I didn't want him to feel left out after his favorite plebe asked Rock Stone." He indicated Kevin with a nod of his head.

"Hey, guys," Kevin observed. "Somebody has to have some balls in this outfit besides Tommy Poole, and he's hanging tough despite the demerit campaign Captain Dillingham has begun."

The group simultaneously looked at Tommy, who glanced nervously at the concrete paving.

"How many demerits today, Tommy?" asked Jim Merritt.

"Thirty," Tommy answered, "but they won't appear on the Restriction Listing until next week. This will be my last free weekend for God knows how long."

"Boy, I feel sorry for you!" exclaimed Kevin. "When Micklewski put me on report, he and Stone tried to prevent me from attending the Army-Navy party. They tried to push the chit through the system like lightning to make sure I was restricted. Luckily the chit was lost, and I had my party, but those hours I marched in the freezing rain were the worst of my life."

Tommy frowned.

"Yeah. I know. I'm sure they won't be slow about getting the paperwork processed for me either. Then it'll be my turn to march in misery."

"Yeah," added BJ slyly. "But maybe he'll save the chits and submit everything as a Class-A Offense so that you have to appear before a Disciplinary Board."

Tommy's frown deepened.

"Oh, God!" he said. "I hadn't thought of that."

"Well, I'll bet that's what happens!" said BJ smugly. BJ always seemed to take a strange pride in the discomfort of his classmates. For that reason and for several others BJ Wilson was not the best liked of the Plebes.

Rico smiled at BJ.

"Then again, maybe not," he said. The plebes respected Rico's uncanny ability to predict events and people's reactions. Everyone looked at him.

"I have a feeling that Stone -- bastard that he is -- objects to Dillingham's interference. It's not that he's particularly fond of Tommy or any other plebe. I think he resents the implied lack of confidence and wants Dillingham to back off."

Kevin smiled at Tommy.

"But, black as the pit may be, Tommy, it's good you have at least one weekend off before the bludgeons of demerits ruins your social life." Kevin was trying to be philosophical again, and Jeff sighed.

"Hey!" Jim Merritt added. "Let's not get too maudlin. With each of us pitching in, we can keep Tommy's demerit level way down."

Rico laughed.

"Get real, Jimbo! If 'Bullshit' Dillingham wants to fry Tommy out of here, then that's exactly what he'll do."

For several long minutes everyone was quiet, except for Reb, who greedily devoured the remnants of his final submarine. The wind had picked up in intensity as they sat, and massed clouds began to blow across the sky. A dark shadow passed over them suddenly, and the temperature dropped perceptibly. Jeff shivered and looked up at the sky.

"Weather's changing," he observed, trying to sound New England perceptive.

"Rain soon," added Pat Mulvaney, not to be outdone.

"What we need," burst Willy suddenly, "is a Passionate Plebe incident to take the Captain's mind off Tommy." The group laughed, recalling the excitement in the weeks following an incident in which an apparent plebe, caught in an illegal -- some say immoral -- encounter with a lovely female near the seawall, led the Officer of the Day and his entire squad of plebe watch messengers and mates on a chase throughout the grounds, passageways, and ladders of the Academy. It was an epic chase, and since then rumors had abounded about the identity of the Passionate Plebe. Every unusual or boldly anonymous act had been credited to this mythic figure.

Rico looked briefly at Jim Merritt and said. "I think the Passionate Plebe has retired temporarily."

"Yeah," added Jeff, also glancing at Jim, "but he might be encouraged out of retirement by the right circumstances." The group stared at both Rico and Jeff, but neither spoke further. Jim Merritt chose to look across the harbor.

"Well," said Willy with finality, "we need some sort of action, Passionate Plebe or not. What're we gonna do?"

"Why don't we counsel his big white muscular ass to death?" offered Wesley Lamont, smiling his best, most handsome smile, which caused his sparkling white teeth to stand out starkly against his chocolate brown face. Wesley was the only black member of the Company, a recruit who had come from the American Virgin Islands and who had perhaps the most mellow personality of all the plebes. He was a topnotch athlete who excelled on the gymnastics parallel bars. God, could he do push-ups!

Everyone frowned, unsure what Wesley intended. Wesley spoke in a wonderful British-Islands accent. Jeff smiled. He loved hearing Wesley Lamont speak. It made Jeff think of swaying palm trees, steel band music, and peaceful island rhythms.

"You know, man," he said, "each of us could use up the Captain's time requesting his help on personal problems. Advice about classes or careers. Help with our parents and homesickness. Or give the stud-monster the sex talk. He loves that, man. We could keep him busy 24 hours a day."

"How 'bout if he asks why we don't just go ta our squadleaders?" Ramsey asked

"No problem Jubal, man," answered Wesley with a grace that indicated he took no offense. "We can just tell him that we would be embarrassed speaking to other midshipmen, and that we need a real man's advice. He'll eat that up, man."

"That might work for a while," said Bob Strong. "But we need a better plan if we're going to keep him occupied full time."

"Well, maybe we could challenge another Company to some friendly competition that would include the Captain and Tommy?" asked Hank Butkowski.

Jim Merritt perked up.

"That's a great idea, Hank! We could go to Dillingham as a group and suggest a competition. We could do it on successive weekends to spread it out as much as possible. What events?"

"A race to Hospital Point and back," suggested Kevin O'Reilly with a broad smile. Several of the plebes, aware of Kevin's racing prowess, cheered boldly, startling several passersby.

"Push-ups?" added Rico, flexing his muscle for the group. More cheers.

"Tug of war!" suggested Hank, and everyone enthusiastically agreed.

"A cannonball contest!" suggested Reb Ramsey to the delight of his classmates.

"Chess?" added Tommy timidly, when the response to Reb's idea had died down, and everyone paused in their enthusiasm.

"Chess?" asked Jubal with some sarcasm. "That's for girls!"

"Never been beaten," added Tommy with a sly smile. More cheers.

"This is great!" interjected Jim. "We could pull this off as a way to beat the Dark Ages blues. "Let's organize tomorrow and present the idea on Monday."

"We should also start some other controversies that will occupy the Bull," added Pat Mulvaney, "'cause this may not be enough."

"Like what?" asked Bob.

"I don't know yet," Pat answered, with a huge smile, "but we'll think of something." Looking at Jeff pointedly he added, "I think we better head back. Storm's coming in earnest."

They all looked at the now-rapidly-darkening sky. Jeff shivered and wondered if that were a prophetic statement. The group looked carefully at each other as they quietly rose and set off for the safety of Mother-B. Jeff was sure he wasn't the only one who made that connection.

Very early the following morning a darkly-clothed figure slowly opened the double door that separated the inner passageways of the academy from the darkened rotunda. Outside in Tecumseh Court steady, heavy rain beat against the windows and dull thunder rumbled almost continuously. Occasional lightning briefly and starkly brightened the night. The figure slipped quietly into the rotunda, closed the door, and paused, studying the Main Office area and the surrounding rotunda. A louder rumble of thunder echoed from the rotunda dome.

Finding no one about, the figure slipped noiselessly across the rotunda, crept slowly toward the office door, and waited in the passageway just outside the Main Office. The clock on the bulkhead indicated 0308. The figure paused, then moved to the heavy brass personnel doors that led to the outside. He pushed open a door and the wind and rain-spray briefly engulfed him and drove him backward. He let the door close behind him and faced the windows of the Main office. He took a deep breath and waited. It was very cold. A lightning flash suddenly lit up Tecumseh court, and the figure let out a loud, bloodcurdling scream, turned, raced inside, and ran noiselessly to just outside the Main Office door.

The occupants of the Main Office had reacted to the scream and jumped to the large windows to see what had happened.

"What the hell was that?" someone said loudly. At the window, rain obscured their vision. A plebe messenger wiped his hand across one window pane and stared outside. The figure in the passageway peeked briefly into the office to ensure everyone faced the window, then bent way over in a crouch, and hurried passed the office door and down the passageway. He stopped at the Main Bulletin Board and its adjacent Staff Roster Display case.

The glass case displayed the photos and identification of every staff officer in the Academy. Quickly he found the photo he sought. The case was not locked. He smiled. Gingerly he gripped the door of the case and pulled it toward him. The door stuck for a moment, then came loose all at once. An impossibly loud screech filled the passageway.

The figure pushed the door so that it barely contacted the case, and retreated silently across the passageway to the sample midshipman's room. He opened the door, slipped inside, and paused in the opening, waiting, the door slightly ajar.

"What's going on?" said a loud voice in the vicinity of the Main Office. The figure retreated farther, and listened intently. Scuffling feet sounded in the passageway just outside the Office.

"Janvrin! You and Openshaw get your rain-gear on and check Tecumseh Court. Lorenz, check the passageway and find out what made that second noise." At the sound of approaching footsteps the figure closed the door completely and turned the latch. He waited. The plebe on watch stopped at each of the display rooms along the passage and tried the doors. All the other rooms were unlocked, and the plebe checked inside each room quickly. He came to the sample room, and found the door locked.

"Mister Dolan, Sir!" the plebe shouted down the passageway. "Is this door supposed to be locked?"

"I don't know," came an irritated answer after a pause. "There's a key ring on the bulkhead by the OOD's office. Get your butt down here and get it." The messenger hesitated then slowly walked away. The figure immediately unlatched the door and glanced hurriedly outside. The departing plebe was just feet away. Watching the messenger, the figure silently returned to the display case, opened the door quietly, and deftly removed a photograph. Pushing the door slightly to, he silently hurried behind the still retreating plebe. He could feel his heart pound. The original plan had evaporated with the door screech. He would have to adlib.

The messenger unfortunately did not reenter the office, and instead waited in the doorway facing the interior of the office. The figure pulled his black Navy watch cap farther down over his ears, hunched his shoulders, took a deep breath, and readied himself for a sprint passed the plebe. He counted to three to himself, and began moving as quietly as possible toward the rotunda.

He hadn't taken a single step before the upper-class who had gone to get the keys -- a three-stripe firstie -- reappeared in the doorway. He spied the stealthy figure behind the messenger.

"Hey!" he said loudly.

Then there was no time for anything but gut reaction. The figure changed direction midstride, bent his head so it was hidden behind the plebe, and quickly headed toward the office doorway. The plebe began his turn. The figure's outstretched arm caught the plebe in the small of his back, shoving him. The messenger wasn't expecting physical contact. He yelled in surprise. The glancing blow threw him off balance and he stumbled forward into the arms of the surprised first-classman.

The dark figure sprinted passed the two of them and headed for the rotunda. As he neared the rotunda, two plebe messengers reentered through the heavy brass personnel doors. Their rain-gear dripped with moisture and left substantial puddles as they walked. The plebes saw the dark figure. He paused.

"Plebe Halt!" yelled a voice from the vicinity of the Main Office. Sounds of pursuit came from the rear. The two returning plebes became instantly alert. Chances of escape dimmed. The figure began to sprint across the rotunda and the plebes moved to intercept him. The dark figure changed direction, heading instead toward the wide stairway that leads to Memorial Hall above. The plebes moved to cut him off. The sound of pursuit behind was louder. But the fugitive knew there was no escape from Memorial Hall.

The figure put a foot on the bottommost step and pushed off, changing direction again. He turned a complete circle and headed toward the outside doors. The plebes in their wet raingear had gotten to the center of the rotunda but had difficulty with the direction shift. One slid on the terrazzo deck and fell to his knees cursing. The other kept his balance by placing a hand on his companion's shoulder.

The messenger coming from the office did not have the same trouble. He moved to cut off the fleeing figure at the doors, smiling in anticipation of revenge for the shove. Instead of continuing to the doors, the dark figure changed direction again at the last instant, heading instead toward the Main Office. The seeming stupidity of the change confused the pursuit momentarily. The plebe messenger could not reverse direction quickly. He yelled a curse, skidded slightly, and the fugitive fled passed his outstretched arm.

The figure moved toward the office passageway. Now only the firstie and a single remaining messenger had a chance to stop him.

"Plebe Halt!" The firstie yelled loudly as he himself halted. The figure knew from his rates that this must be Midshipmen First-class James Dolan, the Commander of Thirty-sixth Company. The fugitive smiled. Dolan must be crazy to think he was going to stop now. He wondered briefly if Dolan had ever bucked the system himself.

The figure did not halt. He picked up speed and moved forward purposefully. Faking to one side, he passed the firstie and his mate, and turned again, this time sprinting for the stairs that flank the rotunda on both sides. As he reached the stairs, a second-class and two additional plebes emerged from the Main Office. The second-class did not look happy.

"Halt, you lowlife bastard!" the second-class yelled. The panicky figure screamed a psychotic laugh, and taking the steps three at a time, raced upward. He did not stop at either the first or second decks.

"Catch that plebe reprobate!" yelled a loud voice as the figure began the race upward toward the third deck, and the rustle of rain-gear and the scuffling of uniform shoes followed on the steps behind him. He ran to the double doorway that led onto the third deck of the fifth wing and slammed his hands against the doors noisily. They flung open before him. The passageway was dark and deserted. Instead of entering the fifth wing, the figure soundlessly raced up another flight of stairs and moved quickly to the walkway that connects the fifth and fourth wings on the fourth deck.

He heard someone below him say loudly, "He must have gone in here!" He could hear the double doors on the third deck opening, the sound of several people pushing inside.

In the rotunda someone yelled out, "I'll notify the OOD and sound the alarm." Still, the figure waited. His breath came in raged gasps, but adrenaline still coursed through his bloodstream. He found himself elated.

When the sound had died completely, the figure moved quickly onto the open bridge-like walkway, in plain but shadowy view of anyone below.

"There he goes!" shouted someone, and he glanced down. Midshipman First-class Dolan and the messenger he had shoved stood below. The plebe pointed directly at him and glared.

Dolan, standing hands-on-hips, suddenly held up an arm to silence the messenger. He leaned backward slightly and smiled widely, which caused the figure to pause, then come to a complete stop. He looked down at the scene, clearly puzzled. The rotunda was silent again except for the sounds of rain and his rapid breathing. The figure spoke.

"What?" he asked quietly.

Dolan chuckled. Then he saluted the dark figure dramatically.

"Well done, bold one!" Dolan said with a dramatic flourish. "You have earned an escape this evening. But beware! I'll will be watching for you!" Then he saluted. The figure paused, still confused, returned the salute smartly, and turned, but suddenly paused again and leaned down toward the others.

"Everyone okay?" he asked quietly.

The messenger glared, but Dolan smiled again and laughed.

"Yes, my good friend! We are well indeed. Hurry back into the dark, and the night. The alarm is given. Your luck is fast running out." The figure smiled, nodded, and prepared to go.

"Hey, are you the Passionate Plebe?" the plebe messenger asked, the shove suddenly forgotten. The figure smiled in the shadows but said nothing. He ran across the remainder of the bridge and quietly opened the doors onto the fourth deck of the fourth wing. Silently he slipped inside and began noiselessly running tiptoed down one side of the darkened passageway. As he ran, he removed his wet cap and sweatshirt. At the first head facility he slipped inside and removed his still damp sweatpants. These he stuffed into a ball which he placed carefully under his arm. Checking the passageway, he slipped out of the head and headed for a small usually-unused stairwell that led to the Twenty-third Company area, four decks below.

Once safely in his own area he headed quietly for his room. He could hear the company plebe messenger in Stone's room as he passed. No one saw him the entire way, and he didn't think that his own roommates even knew he had left. He put the wet gear under his desk, and the photo under his pillow. He was asleep within minutes, and the bed check marred his dreams only slightly.

On Sunday, 20 January, the inevitable conclusion of Plebe Year for the Twenty-third Company Class of 1971began. Outside, the day was dark and miserable. Freezing rain pelted Bancroft Hall, driven by an intense wind that gusted at times to almost 40-knots. Chapel formation had been inside Bancroft Hall, and the march to services was a hurried affair which soaked every midshipman to the skin. The entire Brigade seemed irritable. Early in the afternoon Tommy Poole found a plain white envelope on his desk. Inside was a note folded around a photograph of Captain Dillingham.

The note said, *"Here's your new sweetheart! Destroy this note immediately!"* Tommy stared from the photo to the note and smiled. Cutting the edges from the photo so it would fit properly, he slipped it into his cap atop the picture of his girlfriend, Sara. Because of the rain, most plebes did not take liberty in town. However, Strong, Ramsey, Simpson, and Polk briefly visited a hardware store. Reb talked them into stopping at the submarine shop. They consumed their sandwiches standing on the premises watching the storm rage outside.

Immediately after chapel, Jim Merritt asked Rock Stone for permission to use the Company Wardroom at 1400 for a plebe class meeting. Stone readily consented, but Jim agreed that they would vacate the room at 1500 when the first-class began television viewing. Jim and Bob passed the word during noon meal formation that all plebes were expected to attend. Most did.

Peer motivation is the most difficult of leadership skills. Since there were no appointed positions of authority within the plebe ranks, and since most midshipmen -- plebes included -- considered themselves to possess the very pinnacle of leadership skills, group meetings often became posturing sessions. Jeff wondered briefly if this meeting would be any different. Rico must have agreed because he boldly switched on the television so that he could watch the Dallas Cowboys play the New York Giants while the rest of the group concentrated on the matter at hand.

"What the shit is this meeting all about, Merritt, and what gives you the right to call it, anyway?" asked Danny French in his usual belligerent tone. "I've got plenty of things to do, and this evening we all begin comearound sessions with our Hundredth Night firsties. I really don't need any bullshit meetings." French was a handsome but extremely arrogant wrestler from Chicago. His father was a city councilman. Danny was the least agreeable of the plebe classmates and the one who could not be counted on to pitch in to help a buddy. Jeff wasn't even sure why Merritt had invited him to the meeting. He always started trouble when things infringed on his time or attention.

"Why are you here then, asshole?" announced George Abbott from the back of the room. French spun around to answer, saw the dark look on George's face, then turned back toward the front of the room and mumbled something incoherent.

"Go, Roger Dodger!" said Rico a little too loudly as Dallas made a first down. Merritt sighed, moved to the shelves, and switched off the set. Rico looked hurt.

"It wasn't just me who decided we needed to have a meeting," said Jim Merritt patiently Bob Strong and Mike Wojeck stood nearby. The remainder of the classmates sat on various seats and furniture throughout the room. Kevin stood just inside the door, reading for the thousandth time the inscriptions under the many photos that lined the wall. Each photo showed a former member of Twenty-third Company who had distinguished himself in battle or in outstanding Naval service. Most had died in the supreme performance of their duty. This display was impressive, even to the usually-against-the-military-grain Jeff Polk.

"There are some things happening we need to discuss and act on," added Bob.

"So *you* say!"

Jim ignored him and continued.

"Yesterday several of us discussed options to get Captain Dillingham to ease up on Tommy."

"Not that shit again!" exploded French. He turned and stared at Tommy, rising from his seat. "No offense, okay, but I'm really tired of everybody asking me to come to *your* defense. I've got problems of my own trying to cope with the bullshit I get from Kopciak."

"Nobody is asking you to do anything, Danny," said Hank Butkowski from the rear of the room next to George.

"Good, because I'm all tapped out." He started for the door, brushed passed Kevin, and left without another word.

"Danny French is a dickhead!" announced George Abbott with finality. Several of the classmates chuckled, remembering earlier sessions where French had disrupted the group with his outspoken independence.

Jim stared at the now-vacant doorway for a moment. He pulled a note card from his pocket and addressed the group.

"As you all know Captain Dillingham inspected Tommy's locker yesterday and tore it apart unmercifully -- which is his right if it's not up to standard. But Tommy has the best locker of any of us. Dillingham gave Tommy 25 demerits. He intends to continue the unannounced inspections until he fries Tommy out of here.

"We think it's possible to have an effect on Dillingham if we distract him from his focus on Tommy. Yesterday we discussed options and decided on several. Number one is to divide into a duty section whose responsibilities are to help Tommy be perfect at every meal formation and to ensure every item in his locker is properly stowed. The second is for each of us to engage the Bull one-on-one for counseling as often as possible -- to try to get him thinking about things other than Tommy.

"Third, we thought it would be a good idea to have the Bull sponsor a sports challenge with another Company. We could do it over the next three weekends to take up Bull's Saturday time. Fourth we thought we could reinstate the prank-pulling that made us so famous last summer.

"Guys," Jim said looking from face to face. "Plebe Year is almost over. We worked hard, and we're going to make it -- so should Tommy. It's time to pitch in again to help him out of this terrible mess. And, in case you haven't heard," he added smiling, "the Passionate Plebe is back." Most of the plebes in the room cheered.

"If everybody agrees to help out," asked Mike Wojeck, "I'll set up a duty roster. He's got to be perfect, guys, so let's not bag this duty a single iota. Everybody agree?" No one dissented. Tommy turned to the group from his seat on the front couch.

"Thanks, guys," he said genuinely. "If it were just the physical and mental harassment, I could handle it, but Dillingham has raised the stakes and I'm not sure that we will pull this off. But I really do appreciate it."

"Okay," Merritt continued. "Wesley and Pat will coordinate the counseling. Make it sincere, guys, or else he'll suspect we're up to something." Wesley raised a hand.

"I'll be around to see each of you sometime this evening," he said, grinning broadly.

"Kevin and I will plan the sports challenge and it will include at least one event that will showcase Tommy to the Captain," added Jim. Kevin turned to face the group.

"It will be memorable. I promise," he said with an enormous, toothy grin.

"Ramsey and I will work up a prank routine," chuckled Mike Wojeck, "and we'll call on each of you to help. We've already been discussing it, and we hade some great ones planned."

"Okay," Jim asked, "anybody have any other ideas?"

"Is there some way we could remove either Tommy or the Captain from the picture temporarily?" asked John Pirelli.

"What do you mean?" asked Jim.

"Tommy could get admitted to the hospital, or maybe Dillingham could be so involved with something important he doesn't have time to spend around the Company," offered John.

"The hospital's out!" said Tommy emphatically. "If somebody wants to admit Dillingham into the psycho ward that's fine, but I'm not going to desert my Hundredth Night obligation. I intend to run Stone's butt!"

"So how else can we distract the Bull?" asked Bob, "And remember that anything we do has to look accidental or coincidental."

"Go over his head?" asked Tony Delvecchio. "We could get our parents and friends to write the Commandant and say they heard about Tommy's predicament and don't understand why he's being persecuted."

"Well, remembering what happened with Nathan Spielenberg last summer," replied Bob, referring to an incident where a former classmate's mother had tried to intercede with the Commandant. Swift and remorseless retribution resulted. Her hapless son was no longer a midshipman. "I'm not sure that's a good idea."

"We can appeal as a group to the Captain's decency and sense of fair play," offered Jeff with not a little sarcasm.

"Yes," said Bob Strong, ignoring the sarcasm. "Let's do that. Maybe he'll listen if we approached him as a group on this. I'll ask Stone tomorrow for an audience with 'his holy jarheadedness.'"

"Could we intercept the Report Chits before they get into the system?" asked Rico with a smile.

"Too obvious. He'd find out right away and be back at Tommy with a vengeance."

"We could knock Bull unconscious and drown him in the Yacht Basin," offered Rico, only half in jest. "If we can figure a way to explain the chains around his neck and weights attached to his ankles, we might be able to make it seem like an accident."

"Chains and weights and a January swim in freezing water can be explained?" asked Hank.

"He's a Marine," replied Rico. "They'd call it a recreational accident."

It was clear that all the viable ideas had been exhausted. Jim must have thought so as well.

"Well he said, consulting his watch. I think we've just about covered it all. If anyone can come up with another *reasonable* idea . . . let me or Bob know." He looked at the chuckling Rico, who smiled sheepishly back. "Let's get out of here." The plebes rose almost as one and chopped from the Wardroom, squaring every corner perfectly and yelling a string of "Beat Armys!" as they headed for the relative safety of their rooms.

THE CORNERSTONE
The cornerstone of Bancroft Hall.

CHAPTER 6

HONOR BOUND

"Midshipmen are persons of integrity:
They do not lie, cheat, or steal."

The second weekend of the Company competition, each Company could choose an event of its own devising. Twenty-second Company chose a six-inning fast-pitch softball game. The only Tiger stipulation was that only three team members from each class could play. They set this restriction knowing that Twenty-second Company had seven very good second-class players and that their softball team always led the Brigade. Still, Twenty-third Company was distinctly disadvantaged.

Jeff, Chuck, and Rico Guevarra represented the plebes, and they were the only team members to safely hit the Twenty-second Company's lightning-fast youngster pitcher. But three hitters do not a team make, and Happy Houseman, the only pitcher in the Company, was bombed early and often. The final score was 20 to 5, and the Captain was not pleased.

The Tigers chose a push-up contest. Each class selected ten members, who would do regulation push-ups without stopping until their arms could no longer support their weight. The Company with the highest total push-up score would win. Twenty-third Company produced more than 4,500 push-ups from its 40 contestants, almost a thousand more than the competition. Dillingham was happy again, but he did take time to inspect Tommy's room, which, despite the best efforts of 21 frustrated plebes, still resulted in 10 demerits.

Saturday night in Jeff's room was mostly quiet. Across the passageway, Rico and Jim had secret love plans. Apparently Rico's new-found sex kitten had money because he overheard Rico boast to Kevin that he would be spending the evening in the cozy warmth of a hotel room bed rather than the frigid dark of Hospital Point. Kevin and BJ stayed behind, both plainly unhappy about their unattached status. Jeff didn't care much for BJ Wilson's pompous and sexist attitude, but he sincerely hoped Kevin found a decent partner soon.

Across the passageway Jeff could see BJ staring out the dark window, his back to Jeff. Jeff quickly pulled his gym shorts down around his knees and whistled. Just as BJ turned to see what the noise was about, Jeff squeezed out a popping flatulence, which caused BJ's face to darken.

"Eat shit, Polk!" he said fiercely. Jeff laughed and pulled up his shorts but found no satisfaction in the act. It was just too damn easy to get BJ to fall for the crude humor. Jeff returned to his study area, picked up a paperback novel he had been reading, sat down at his desk, and lost himself in the pages.

At 0010, long after the four roommates had fallen asleep, the door to Jeff's room opened abruptly and the lights flashed on.

"Attention on deck!" Bob Strong yelled from across the room, and Jeff and his other roommates leapt out of bed and stood at braced attention beside their racks. Two persons entered, but from his position facing the exterior wall, Jeff could not see who they were.

"Okay, plebe bastards!" said a slurred voice. "Up against this locker! Now! Move it!" Jeff hurried. Within five seconds the roommates stood rigidly against the lockers, facing outward. The two visitors were Harvey Linehan and Big Jim Daly. Both were dressed in rumpled civilian clothes and fresh from an evening in town. Judging by the way they stood shakily and slurred their words, Jeff decided the two of them were undeniably drunk.

Possessing alcohol within the confines of Bancroft Hall was an offense punishable by immediate dismissal, but drinking elsewhere and returning intoxicated was quietly accepted so long as it didn't exceed certain unwritten behavior standards. It was also a major offense to harass plebes after lights-out. The two firsties took an enormous chance. Jeff wondered why.

"How's Plebe Year treating you so far, gentlemen?" slurred Harvey as he swayed in front of them, trying not to appear drunk. "Any complaints?" He bent over and giggled uncontrollably. The four plebes were smart enough not to answer.

"You know what pisses me off?" asked an even drunker Daly. His words came out in a rumble that Jeff had to strain to understand. But Daly didn't wait for an answer. "This Hundredth Night shit, that's what!" He leaned in closer to the four of them, almost falling down in the process, and put a big finger squarely on Jeff's chest. "I'm not allowed to do anything interesting. Christ Harvey, do you remember when that bastard Paul Kackleman prepared us for the big night? Jesus, the things that bastard had us do! I've still got scars." Daly looked disgusted. "None of this wimpy, pussy-assed, crap for us, huh Harv?" Linehan seemed to nod agreement, but Jeff wasn't sure if he actually heard Big Jim.

"Simpson!" Daly commanded, pointing a shaky finger at the deck. "Get your ass down into a dead-horse for me. I want to show you what I mean." He giggled as he wobbled. "Just for demonstration purposes, you understand?" Willy dropped to the deck and rolled over onto his back. Quickly he lifted arms and legs straight into the air and waited. Daly went into the closet and removed one of the room's M-2 rifles, which he handed to Willy. "Hold this up!" he demanded. Then he looked at Strong.

"Get me some masking tape!" he demanded. Bob hurried to his desk and returned with a wide roll of tape. Using the tape lavishly, Big Jim taped Willy's wrists and hands to the ends of the rifle, which Willy continued to hold aloft. "Getting tired, douchebag?" Daly asked with a sarcastic sneer.

"No, sir!" Willy yelled loudly, although Jeff could see strain on his face, and a vibration beginning in his arms and legs. Jeff had done the illegal dead-horse several times, and he was always amazed at how quickly arms and legs tired without occasional relief by shaking or stretching.

"Hey! Hey!" replied Harvey in a fierce whisper. "Keep it down! Do you want to get us into trouble?"

"Yes," thought Jeff. "I would sincerely love to get you in trouble for this."

"No, sir!" Willy answered in a halfhearted whisper, his arms now visibly shaking.

Daly again went to the closet, and this time returned with plebe bayonets. He smiled.

"This is the fun part," he slurred. "Hang in there, Simpson. Don't ruin the demonstration."

Big Jim gripped the rifle firmly, took the tape, and firmly attached a bayonet, point-down, to the middle of the rifle. He taped the other bayonets alongside the first so that only a few inches separated the points, which now poised, slightly more than a foot from Willy's chest. Daly let go, and Willy's eyes widened slightly. The added weight immediately affected Willy's strength. The rifle dipped visibly. Daly chuckled.

"See, fellas?" he asked. "This is motivation. I'll bet he can keep this up almost all night." Jeff didn't think so. Willy's arms were shaking again and his legs had fallen down onto the deck. Neither Linehan nor Daly noticed. Daly turned to Reb with a grin.

"Think you're tough, Ramsey?" he asked.

"Yes, sir!" Reb answered fiercely.

Big Jim moved to the front of Reb.

"Tighten your stomach, you fat Southern sow!" Reb pulled his abdominal muscles taught. Big Jim smiled.

"We'll start with a love tap," he said and hit Reb a solid blow, which Ramsey absorbed with a grunt.

"Good! Good! Now another." A second time Daly hit Reb. This time was visibly harder. Reb grunted loudly, but did not double over.

"This is great, Harv!" he said, turning slightly toward Linehan, who had a stupid grin on his face. "Ramsey's a real stud!" Without any further warning Daly hammered three quick hard punches into Reb's midsection. Reb was not prepared. He lost his wind with the first. The second bent him over violently. And the third drove him backward against the sliding locker door. The door slammed against its stops with a loud boom, and the wheels bent their aluminum tracks, causing the door to wedge in a half-open position. The noise was almost deafening in the small room.

None of the plebes cared about the noise or the door. Reb had toppled sideways onto the deck, sucking mightily for air. Strong and Polk broke their bracing and came to Reb's assistance.

"Polk, you stinking bastard!" Daly boomed. "Brace up! It was you I saved the best trick for." Jeff hesitated. Seeing that Bob was taking care of Reb, he reluctantly returned to the locker. By this time a straining Willy Simpson was just barely keeping the four bayonet points off his chest.

Almost immediately the door opened again, and Sidney Littleton entered, officiously garbed in a West Point bathrobe he had won at this year's Army-Navy football game.

"What the hell's going on in here?" he asked loudly.

"Beat it, Sid. We're giving our plebes additional indoctrination!"

Littleton looked around with a scowl.

"You know it's not allowed, Jim. This has to stop."

"Eat shit, Littleton! What're you gonna do about it, you little twit?"

"Stop this now or I'll see Dillingham personally," Littleton said with a whine and a smirk, still trying to stay in a superior position.

Daly smiled crookedly, and staggered slowly toward the Company Commander who, seeing something he did not like in Big Jim's eyes, backed away until he was up against another locker. Daly closed the distance and towered over his classmate. He put a finger on Sidney's chest.

"What's the matter, Sidney," Daly said with a sarcastic sneer. "Rock Stone not here to protect you? Are you afraid, Sidney?" Big Jim laughed loudly and his voice turned evil. "Listen dick-face," he said, pounding the finger into Littleton's chest with every phrase. "You so much as hint to anyone about this, and I'll beat you so bad you'll be in a body cast come graduation. I'm tired of your bullshit, Littleton you little turd, and I mean business!" He stepped backward, looked down at the tile floor, and pointed with his toe to a joint in the flooring.

"You're my enemy, Sidney," he said. "You and I both know that. And I don't like you or trust you. If you so much as think about crossing this line, I'll kill you tonight." Daly tapped the floor with a toe again. "Stay on the other side of this line. I mean it!" With that Daly turned shakily and looked at the plebes. Willy strained with the bayonet, the blades only an inch from his chest. Reb had recovered his wind and sat on the deck holding his stomach and glaring at La Master. Bob had returned to the locker and braced next to Jeff. Big Jim smiled and staggered across the room, patting the still-inebriated Harvey Linehan on the head as he passed. Harvey looked incapable of thought or action, and Jeff doubted that Harvey felt the touch.

Daly went to the sink and opened the doors to the cabinet area underneath. Smiling, he removed a large paper bag and opened it. The bag had holes cut in it for the eyes and mouth and a residue of masking tape around its bottom. Daly smiled and held the bag up for Linehan to see.

"Look, Harv! Seems like this room has troublemakers! Think we should tell pervert Micklewski we found one of the ski instructors?" He brought the bag to Jeff. "This yours?"

"I'll find out, sir!"

"Let's see if it fits," Big Jim said, lifting the bag over Jeff's head and adjusting the holes so that Jeff had partial sight. Daly leaned in closely and peered into one eye hole. Jeff could smell the cloying stench of stale beer and onions. Daly smiled. "Seems like a perfect fit to me."

Big Jim turned to Harvey. "Think we should turn him in, Harv?" he asked. Linehan didn't answer. Daly returned his gaze to Jeff. "Maybe not. I'm in a generous mood." He leaned inward, and fumbled in his pockets.

"In fact, I'm going to help you out of this mess, Polk. And I'm going to teach you a lesson at the same time." He stopped fumbling and glanced down at something in his hands. Jeff heard an unfamiliar metallic click-snapping sound. Big Jim smiled at Jeff through one of the eye holes.

"Here's the lesson, Polk," he said, and an almost-evil glare came into his eyes. "Always destroy the evidence!" Immediately Jeff heard a raspy metal sound and within seconds he felt heat and saw a great deal of reddish light near the bottom of the bag. He glanced down. The bag was on fire! Things happened quickly.

"Jesus!" Bob Strong yelled.

Feeling the heat rising along his chest and neck, Jeff screamed in absolute panic. Smoke swirled inside the bag. Jeff took a deep choking breath, twisted his head away from the flames, and grabbed the sides of the bag with his hands. He pulled the burning bag from his head with a jerk and threw it. The bag struck the stuporous Harvey Linehan in the center of his chest. Sparks flew outward. Harvey moaned and fell backward onto Willy Simpson and the bayonet. Willy screamed.

"Shit! Jesus! Willy!" Bob screamed. Ramsey struggled to his feet, kicked the still-smoldering bag to one side, and dropped to his knees beside Willy. Jeff felt sharp pain on the side of his head and smelled a rope-burning odor. Suddenly Bob Strong was patting his temples fiercely. He turned to Bob.

"Your hair was on fire!" Bob said, his eyes wide with shock. Jeff shook his head fiercely, and turned toward the two bodies struggling on the floor.

"Willy!" he shouted, just as a shocked Sidney Littleton started forward.

"Stay there Sidney!" shouted Daly, "or so help me God, I'll beat you to death!" Sidney looked around in a panic. Daly started toward him. Sidney retreated to his place against the locker, his mouth working furiously in protest but no words coming out. By then Reb Ramsey had pulled Harvey to his feet by each arm. Everyone looked at Willy.

Harvey's tumble had knocked the rifle downward away from Willy's chest, which may have saved his life. But during the follow-up rolling about, Harvey had pressed the blades of the bayonet forcefully against Willy's torso and caused them to slide and slice. Willy's Academy T-shirt was torn severely in three places. One rip neatly severed the Annapolis logo just above his heart. Jeff could see a great deal of blood on Willy's chest and shirt front, and he felt a sudden hollow-stomached fear.

"Oh, shit!" said Ramsey loudly.

Bob Strong deftly and gently lifted Willy's shirt. Willy had screwed his eyes tightly shut, afraid of what he would see if he looked.

Jeff patted Willy on the arm and said soothingly, "You're gonna be okay, Willy!"

They stared at the wounds for a second. Luckily for Willy, his arms had naturally twisted as they were forced down, so that when the blades scraped at a very acute angle. But even so, three bloody gouges and several minor scratches snaked their way from Willy's chest and upper abdomen to near his navel. A fourth blade which had not been securely taped into place and its connection had come loose sometime during the tussling. That bayonet lay on Willy's upper chest, the blade pointed toward his chin. The scratches were obviously superficial, but blood seeped outward steadily and ominously from the three rambling gouges.

Bob examined the wounds. Sidney looked, but Big Jim Daly continued to glare. Jeff removed the tape from Willy's wrists. Harvey, shaken by the fall and the tumbling, stood beside Reb Ramsey moaning loudly. He leaned over and put his hands on his knees for support, and the moaning continued.

"Get me a wet towel, Reb," Bob Strong asked. Reb went to the sink.

Jeff looked up at the inebriated Linehan.

"You guys were way out of line tonight, Harvey. Somebody's gonna pay for this." Jeff heard Littleton gasp suddenly, and a big fist crashed into the rear side of his head. He winced and fell over on top of Willy. Willy shouted in pain and confusion but still did not open his eyes.

"Are you threatening me, you son-of-a-bitch?" Daly shrieked wildly. Bob Strong had never seen anyone so angry before. Jeff whirled around and tried to get to his feet. Bob grabbed him by the arm and pulled him down.

"Not now, Jeff," he said.

"Not *ever,* you slimy bastard!" Daly sneered. "I'm no reg book sissy like Stone or Littleton here. Turn me in if you want. If you can't hack a little plebe indoctrination," he said with emphasis, "that's too damn bad for you!"

Reb returned with the wet towel and began to clean Willy's wounds. A wipe revealed that none of the wounds had punctured more than the skin's upper surface, but two looked jagged and very nasty.

Bob Strong spoke.

"Sir! You were very lucky nobody was killed tonight."

"Kiss my ass, Strong!" he replied, "Polk knocked Harvey down, not me."

"Tell that to Dillingham, shit-head!" Jeff announced starting to rise, "because first thing Monday that's just what I'm doing. No more comearounds! No more plebe indoctrination bullshit! Start packing your bags! You're gone!" Big Jim advanced toward Jeff who struggled in Bob's grasp.

A rumbling gurgle interrupted the confrontation. They turned, just as Harvey Linehan lost control and vomited all over the still-shocked Willy Simpson. Harvey wet Willy, the nearby floor, and everyone's feet. Willy opened his eyes, looked down. Seeing the mess of blood and vomit, Willy moaned loudly and his eyes rolled up into his head. Bob held him by the shoulders to steady him.

A sudden wave of compassion overcame Daly, and he immediately forgot about Willy's wounds and Jeff's threats. He stepped forward, not trying to avoid the mess, and grabbed Harvey by the arms.

"You okay, Harv?" he asked sincerely. Linehan gurgled and vomited again, this time getting Bob Strong on the side of his shirt. Daly steered Linehan slowly toward the door.

"I know, I know," he said sweetly as he guided the shaky Harvey Linehan from the room. "Plebes make me sick too." Sidney Littleton watched the pair until they had departed. He stepped officiously away from the locker and surveyed the situation briefly.

"Maybe you should get him to Sick Bay?" he asked tentatively.

"Sure thing,,Sidney," answered Jeff. "Go back to sleep, okay? We'll handle this. But I'll see you and that douchebag Daly on Monday in Dillingham's office." Sidney stared at Jeff for a moment, shrugged, and hurried from the room.

In seconds the room was quiet. Bob looked at Willy, who now sat up as Reb removed the remainder of the tape from his hands. Willy stunk of Linehan's vomit. Pieces of it sat in a puddle on his belly, and chunks hung from his hair.

"Start the shower, Jeff," Bob said, "and bring me another wet towel."

Jeff stood slowly and walked toward the shower. He had a splitting headache, and he could feel an intense pain on the top of his left ear. He stopped at the sink to check his wounds. His ear was blistered, and his hair singed.

"He's gonna pay for this!" Jeff said quietly as he reached into the shower and turned on the water for Willy. Bob and Jubal took towels and used them to swab the messy floor. Jeff trudged slowly to his chair and sat. He sighed loudly and put his head on his arms at his desk hoping the pain would subside.

Following the shower, Bob and Reb escorted Jeff and Willy to Sick Bay, where a corpsman examined their wounds, dressed them expertly, and sent them to bed with an admonition to stay out of the local bars because some of the river-born crabbers were mighty tough characters. The roommates were too tired to explain what had happened.

Before they climbed into their racks to sleep, Reb Ramsey spoke up.

"Listen, guys," he said in an even slower than usual drawl. "We need to think about what we do 'bout this he'ah inc'dent. We ain't none of us really hurt. Maybe we should jist let it all pass."

"No damn way, Reb!" Jeff exploded, and his headache returned with a vigor he regretted. "First opportunity tomorrow I'm going to report this to Stone."

"Shouldn't that be a joint decision, Jeff?" asked Bob Strong.

"I don't give a shit what any one of you do!" Jeff said forcefully. "I won't let them get away with this!"

"Think about it for a couple days, please, Jeff," implored Bob. "This could have serious repercussions."

"For asshole Daly? Yes it could!" Jeff turned to Willy. "What do you think about this?" he asked.

"Don't know yet," Willy answered. "I'm still in pain."

"All the more reason to act!" Jeff said triumphantly. "You'll see. This is the right thing to do."

"Maybe so, Jeff," said Bob. "But remember that whatever you do will effect the rest of us too!"

Sunday noontime marked the next event in the Company competition: a prearranged chess match between Twenty-second and Twenty-third Companies. Tommy Poole, who had defeated the best of the upper-class in under five minutes, represented the Tigers. Tommy brought his own "lucky" chessboard, and the Tiger overflow table was prepared for the event. Captain Dillingham sat at the head of the table, and Lieutenant Keith Spencer sat at the foot. They would eat during the match. Tommy sat in the middle of on side, and his opponent, a thin second-class who sported Navy-issue glasses and Dean's List Academic stars, sat opposite him.

The board was red-and-white marble: the pieces were red and white onyx. In order to speed up the match, anyone who took more than a minute to make a move automatically lost. Rock Stone would keep the time. Tommy confidently eyed the board and the upper-class who sat across from him. Tommy's opponent looked more confident. Bull and Bob started on their salads, and the match began.

Within a minute a crowd had gathered. Plebes from Twenty-second Company began to cheer.

"T-O-M, Tom!" and Tiger plebes replied with "Tommy, Tommy, Tommy!"

"I just found out that Tom Gross is the president of the Academy Chess Club," Rico whispered in Jeff's ear. "I hope Tommy's as good as he says." Jeff frowned. Poor Tommy. Would anything ever go his way?

Three moves into the contest the Twenty-second Company opponent looked up at Tommy with a smirk and deftly moved a bishop to an open space. Tommy didn't flinch. He immediately countered with a blocking sweep of his queen. The opponent frowned, then quickly smiled as he moved a rook to a square that threatened Tommy's queen.

Tom Gross sat back and said smugly, "Your move, Tiger boy."

Tommy smiled and countered with a move of a pawn. The upper-class voiced a loud grunt of approval, attacked and captured Tommy's queen. The noise on the Tiger side of the table diminished considerably. At first Jeff thought Tommy was purposely throwing the match.

"Even I know that wasn't a very smart thing to do, Mister Poole," said Captain Dillingham, frowning. Tommy ignored him. He slid his second bishop nearly across the board to a protected position within the opponent's pieces. Tom Gross stared at the board, then looked closely at Tommy. Jeff could almost hear Tom's brain working furiously, trying to calculate the possibilities of Tommy's move. He hesitated, his eyes darting about the board.

"Ten seconds!" Rock called, and the Tiger side came alive again. The second-class reached for a piece, changed his mind, reached for another, changed his mind a second time, then quickly moved the rook back to where it had been before the capture.

Tommy sat straight in his chair and grinned enormously. Gross studied the board desperately. Boldly Tommy removed a roll from the stainless steel serving bowl and took a leisurely bite.

He examined his fingernails closely, looked around thoughtfully, spied Kevin O'Reilly, and asked, "are we still going out to the sub shop this afternoon?"

"Sure, Tommy, sure!" Kevin replied in a panicky voice.

"Ten seconds!" Stone announced.

"Are you going to get a cheeseburger sub or one of those steak ones?" Tommy asked Kevin.

"Cheeseburger, for Christ sake, Tommy! Make a move, quick!"

Tommy stared at Kevin.

"I think I'll get my usual meatball sub, foot long." Kevin gasped in frustration. Then Tommy deftly spun toward the board, slid his rook over one space, and called "Checkmate!" Tom Gross slumped dejectedly into his chair and Tiger Company cheered. Tommy smiled, grasped the chicken bowl, and served himself two pieces in clear violation of table etiquette. Holding up the bowl, he boldly asked. "Anybody else hungry?" Lieutenant Spencer laughed loudly and applauded.

"Great work, Mister Poole!" Captain Dillingham stood and turned to the remainder of the Company. "Carry-on for all plebes for the remainder of the day!" The plebes grabbed Tommy, hoisted him up onto their shoulders, and paraded him around the Company area. Only Mugsy McGinley was bold enough to throw toast at Tommy. Tommy loved it!

The plebes returned Tommy to the table and put him down. As he pulled out his chair to prepare to sit, he looked down and winced. Reaching downward he picked up his combination cap, which is usually kept under the seat, but which, in the commotion had been shoved to one side and stepped on. The pristine white cover was scuffed in several places. He groaned.

"How bad is it, Poole? asked Dillingham.

"I'll need a new cover, sir," Tommy answered.

"Let me see." Tommy handed the cap to Dillingham, who examined it critically and glanced inside. He paused, and a look of surprise flashed across his face. He held up the cap so that Tommy could see the photo inside.

"What's this, Poole?" he asked.

Tommy hesitated.

"Your photo, sir," he said weakly.

"Why is it in your hat?"

Tommy hesitated.

"I'll find out sir!" he answered.

"Is this the photo that was stolen from the Academy Information Board several weeks ago?"

"I'll find out sir!"

"You don't know?"

"No, sir!"

"Come on, Poole. Be honest! Did you take the photo?"

"No, sir!"

Dillingham became immediately more angry and frustrated.

"Then who did?" he demanded.

"I'll find out, sir!" Tommy said slowly.

Dillingham slowly handed the cap back to Tommy.

"Leave that photo exactly where it is for the time being, Poole. I'm going to discuss this unfortunate discovery with the Company staff and get back to you."

"Yes, sir!" Tommy stammered, his self-confidence deflated. Lieutenant Spencer stared at Dillingham for several long seconds, shook his head, then returned to his salad.

Sunday afternoon immediately following Tommy's glorious victory and abrupt defeat, Jeff Polk chopped to Rock Stone's room and knocked on the door. John Gladden answered, allowing him to enter. Jeff hurried inside.

Both John and Rock were preparing for town liberty. Jeff braced just inside the doorway.

"Midshipman Fourth-class Polk, sir!" he announced. Stone paused and stared at him. It was plain that Rock had expected a visit, and it was equally plain that he had dreaded this encounter. Gladden stared at Rock, his face hard and unsmiling as he washed his Texas A&M coffee mug in the sink.

"What is it, hippy?" Stone asked, trying to force lightness into the situation.

"Sir," Jeff began. "I'm here to report an incident that I feel must be handled by the appropriate authorities."

"Why not report to Mister Littleton?" Stone asked. "He's the Company Commander."

"Sir, Mister Littleton was directly involved in the incident, and I feel it would be inappropriate to report to him."

Stone stared hard at Jeff for a long moment.

"At ease, Polk," he finally said, and Jeff relaxed. Rock indicated his chair with a wave. "Have a seat and tell me all about it."

Jeff sat in the proffered chair. Gladden stopped his preparations and sat down at his desk to listen. Stone remained standing. Jeff took a deep breath and began.

"Last night just after midnight, Midshipmen First-class Daly and Linehan visited our room in a drunken state. Daly had Willy do the dead horse with a rifle rigged to his arms and bayonets taped point-down to the rifle. Daly also assaulted Reb Ramsey and knocked him to the ground with punches. Then he put a paper bag over my head and set fire to it. Willy Simpson has several deep gashes on his chest." Jeff turned his head so that Stone could see his ear. "My hair and ear were burned as you can see. Mister Littleton personally witnessed the event." Jeff paused and extended several sheets of paper to Rock. "Here is my statement about the event. Reb, Bob, and Willy will have theirs ready before tomorrow." Stone took the three-page document, examined it briefly, and looked at Jeff.

"You sure you want to do this?"

"Yes, sir! Last night carried Plebe Year much too far."

"Harvey and Jim were drunk. They may not have been rational."

"Makes no difference," Jeff said with a smirk. "This is Tiger Company. Rules are rules. Besides, someone could have been killed. Last night wasn't a cute, character building exercise; it was insanity."

Stone looked momentarily at Jeff, then glanced at John Gladden, who shrugged. Rock nodded.

"Okay, Polk. Your complaint has been received and noted. I'll discuss this with Mister Littleton, and we'll present it to Captain Dillingham on Monday. Ask your roommates to be ready to tell their versions as soon as the Captain is briefed." He looked down at the document in his hand, then up at Jeff. "That'll be all," he said, and Jeff left the room.

All Sunday a parade of classmates and upper-class visited Jeff's room to hear about the incident and to see the broken locker and scorched floor. By evening meal Jeff was tired of recounting the event but still too angry to concentrate on his classwork. All evening he sat quietly at his desk fantasizing how he would teach Daly a proper lesson. Rico and Kevin stopped by at nearly 2100.

"Let's see your scars, Willy," Kevin asked gaily. Willy hesitated, then raised his shirt to expose the bandages. It was an impressive sight. "God, Willy," Kevin said. "You're a bonafide hero!"

"What do y'all mean?" asked Reb.

"This is the blow that ends the Tiger empire. Once Daly is kicked out of here, the rest of the idiots will be too afraid to do anything. We can cruise from here on."

"That's only Kevin's opinion," added Rico with his usual prognosticative smugness. "The book isn't closed yet."

"What do you think will happen?" asked Jeff, suddenly concerned.

"Look," Rico said patiently. "Daly's been here for nearly four years. The system has got to give him every chance to graduate. It's only fair. And getting drunk and messing with plebes isn't normally a dismissal offense. I think he stays, and I think he'll be pissed at the plebes who turned him in."

"Shit, Rico!" Jeff said loudly. "He could have killed someone."

Rico chuckled.

"You'll get no argument from me. But does he really need dismissal in disgrace?"

"Absolutely!" said Jeff, insulted that Rico would assert such insanity.

"Well, whatever . . . " Rico answered. "Time will tell."

Almost immediately a worried Tommy Poole entered. He looked nervously around.

"Jeff, I need to talk to you."

Kevin and Rico excused themselves and departed. Tommy looked at the other roommates.

"This needs to be a private talk. Can Jeff and I be alone for a few minutes?" Reb and Willy exchanged glances.

Bob Strong stood.

"Okay guys. Let's visit the girls across the way." The others followed Bob on his chop across the passageway. When they had gone, Tommy sat at Reb's desk, directly across from Jeff. He put both hands in front of him on the desk and immediately began wringing them nervously. Jeff noticed the bear-crawl scars on his left palm.

"I think I'm in trouble," Tommy said, "and you may be the only person who can help me." Jeff considered this silently for a moment, watching Tommy's homely face transition through a range of emotions as he waited for Jeff to answer.

"Okay," Jeff said hesitatingly. "What's up?"

"It's about noon meal and the photo in my cap," Tommy said with dread. "Dillingham thinks I stole the picture, and he's going to try to initiate an honor offense against me."

"How do you know that?" Jeff asked with some skepticism.

"A gut feeling."

"Christ, don't tell me you're practicing voodoo like Rico. Did you steal the picture?"

"No! Honest! I found it on my desk a couple weeks ago day. It had a note attached that indicated I should put it in my hat."

"Well," said Jeff smiling, "if you didn't steal it, don't worry."

"Except . . ." Tommy quickly jumped in, "everybody was talking about a missing photo of Dillingham two weeks ago, and I even showed everyone the photo last weekend in town. Could I be judged guilty of accepting stolen merchandise or aiding in a crime?"

"I don't think so," Jeff answered considering the possibilities.

"But you don't know, do you? I think the Bull could use this as an opportunity to have the system get rid of me once and for all."

"Well, there's nothing anyone can do if Bull initiates an honor violation report. If he does, it would be very difficult to get the review boards to endorse something so vague. I still think you're going to be fine. Don't worry."

Tommy sighed.

"You didn't see Bull's eyes," he lamented.

Monday morning's comearound to Big Jim Daly and Harvey Linehan was no different from Friday's. Linehan yelled, although not quiet so loudly, and Big Jim observed the torture in silence. Several times Jeff caught Daly staring at him with a mixture of curiosity and contempt. By noon meal nothing had changed in the Company. But tensions were extremely high.

Jeff and his roommates were summoned to the Wardroom at 1530 after classes. Linehan, Daly, Stone and Littleton were there, seated on the sofa in front of the room. Captain Dillingham sat on a wooden stiff-backed chair facing them. Linehan and Daly looked extremely uncomfortable. Jeff smiled secretly. The Captain seemed very contemplative. The plebes braced as they entered, and no one invited them to relax, so they remained standing rigidly for almost a minute while the Captain stared into space.

Finally Bull turned to the four and spoke.

"You may stand at parade rest during this procedure," he informed them, and they instantly converted their stances appropriately and waited.

"This meeting has been called to announce the repercussions resulting from an unauthorized visit to Room 4025 on Saturday night. I have heard the facts of the case from the accused and I have read each of your reports, and I am frankly very angry -- *with everyone*. As I understand the facts, Midshipmen First-class Linnehan and Daly entered a plebe room illegally after lights-out and ordered the plebes to perform blatantly unauthorized acts which resulted in bodily harm. I also understand that the Company Commander observed the acts and did nothing." Littleton started to protest but Dillingham waved his hand sharply to cut him off. The Captain stood slowly, and his usually quiet voice hardened.

"Haven't any of you listened to me when I've been lecturing you for the past year?" he demanded. "Didn't you hear a word I said about duty, honor, and responsibility?" The question was of rhetorical, and no one answered.

"Midshipman First-class Daly, for entering a plebe room after hours, for ordering acts you knew were in violation of the regulations, and for nearly causing serious harm to the troops entrusted to you, I am submitting a Report Chit to Academy Administration recommending that you be awarded 500 demerits. That's the most I can award and not simultaneously recommend dismissal. You will forfeit all liberty and muster at the Main Office for restriction every weekend from now until June Week. I do concede that you may return home during Spring Break if you so want." Daly looked extremely crestfallen for a moment; then he looked at Jeff and glared. But Dillingham wasn't finished. "You will also forfeit your position as Squad Leader, which will revert to Midshipman Second-class Marion Weatherby as of tomorrow morning.

"Midshipman First-class Linehan, for also entering a plebe room after hours and for allowing these illegal acts to continue without protest, you will be awarded 300 demerits, but keep the right to Spring Break. Your duties will revert to Midshipman Second-class John Phlegler." Linehan looked near tears.

"Midshipman First-class Littleton, what the hell were you thinking? I put you in charge of this Company to act in my stead after hours. Not only did this happen while you were in charge, you saw it and allowed it to continue. I am awarding you 100 demerits, and removing your responsibilities as Company Commander, which will revert immediately to Midshipman Stone." Littleton kept quiet.

Captain Dillingham then turned to the plebes and his voice rose another octave.

"Plebe Year is almost over, and I'm wondering if any of you listened in leadership class or observed what goes on here. Do you have any idea of what the Annapolis Honor System is all about?"

Jeff became angry and started to protest.

"Don't say a damn word!" Bull roared. His eyes filled with fire, and he began hyperventilating. He began speaking in a rush. "You obeyed blatantly illegal orders! You allowed a drunken disgrace to place your comrades in physical danger! You stood quietly by while a roommate was beaten, another was stabbed, and a third was burned! Have you no sense of honor or responsibility? Despite the risks you should have stopped this travesty before it got out of hand."

Captain Rusty "Bull" Dillingham paused for breath, still glaring at them. Jeff's head swirled. What was going on? How could the Captain blame them? He almost spoke again, but Dillingham continued loudly.

"Since you have already suffered physically, I will not put you on report for your disgraceful behavior, although believe me, I considered it. However, as of today the four of you will revert to the bottom of the leadership ladder in this Company. None of you will move upward until I am convinced that you have learned the lesson of this incident."

Dillingham turned and addressed everyone, looking directly at Rock Stone. "If anything like this happens again I will not be so lenient. Is that clear?" Everyone quickly answered in the affirmative. "Good!" he said with finality. "Stone. Get Mister Poole and bring him here. Polk, you remain. You others, get out! You disgust me and remind me of what a terrible failure I have been!"

Jeff stood at parade rest near the door while Stone went for Tommy. The Captain did not say a word during the wait. He walked to the window to observe activity in the yard. Jeff watched fascinated as the late afternoon sunlight reflected of the Captain's polished skull and sparkled whenever he turned his head slightly and a different lump or bump broke the line of reflection. It was almost hypnotic.

Less than three minutes later Stone and Tommy Poole arrived. Tommy glanced hurriedly at Jeff as he entered. He was frightened. Tommy snapped to attention. "Midshipman Fourth-class Poole reporting as ordered, sir!"

"At-ease, Poole," the Captain said without a hint of humor in his voice or on his stern face. Judging by what he had just seen in the way of justice, Jeff suddenly began to worry about Tommy's chances of avoiding confinement at Fort Leavenworth.

"Mister Poole," the Captain began. "I have given the photograph in your hat a great deal of thought and I cannot truly decide if what you did was an honor violation or not." Tommy visibly relaxed a fraction of a percent, but the Captain was not finished. "However," he continued, "I cannot in good faith let the matter drop. We must not tolerate any dishonorable behavior." Jeff could hear Tommy suck in his breath quickly.

"I have decided to recommend that the Company Honor Board review the facts and make a recommendation. Midshipman Fourth-class Polk will represent you. I have asked Midshipman First-class Stone to convene the Board to begin hearings on Wednesday evening, lasting as long as is necessary to reach a consensus." Dillingham paused. "I find I am beginning to like you, Mister Poole, and I truly do not want the disgrace of an honor trial to mar your record or to follow you for the rest of your life.

However, if the Brigade Honor Board finds you guilty of theft, I will support their recommendation for dismissal."

Dillingham stared hard to Tommy.

"Good luck, Tommy. Dismissed!"

THE NAVY HYMN

Eternal Father strong to save.

Whose arm hath bound the restless wave.

Who bidd'st the mighty ocean deep.

It's own appointed limits keep.

Oh, hear us when we cry to Thee.

For those in peril on the sea!

From *Reef Points*

CHAPTER 7

THE BUILD-UP

Kevin O'Reilly had been partially right about one thing: Plebe Year changed considerably in Tiger Company after what later came to be called the *Monday Massacre*. Except for Mugsy McGinley, who didn't sweat what he called "the plebe shit" anyway, almost all the first-class became subdued and cautious, particularly in how they treated the plebes in the Company.

Rather than face the humiliation of having two more-junior midshipmen run mealtimes in their presence, Linehan and Daly abrogated their seats on the squad's meal time table and chose to eat at the Company overflow table. Company comearounds became precisely structured and much less vicious and humiliating. Illegal exercises ceased completely, threats disappeared from the first-class vernacular, and nobody vomited in the passageway. But Jeff experienced no feelings of power or accomplishment. Incredibly, it seemed that when the screaming stopped in Twenty-third Company, so did the caring. A strained and aloof politeness pervaded every aspect of the plebe-firstie relationship. Jeff and many other plebes felt unsure of their place in the Academy system. Many classmates voiced displeasure, irritated they were missing something vital from the experience. Jeff began to feel depressed and less confident.

Even Dale Micklewski calmed considerably. Rumor was that the Bull had informed "Dickhead Dale" personally that if he stepped even a single toe out of line, the punishment for him would be so severe that he might be watching his classmates from the stands on graduation day.

An injured Willy Simpson graduated from Plebe Year. The doctors in Sick Bay who examined his wounds on the Monday following the bayonet incident strongly recommended that he not participate in physical activity for the next two weeks. Willy could cruise to Hundredth Night without so much as doing another push-up. But Willy shared the unspoken depression. He asked permission to participate in the comearound activity. Linehan politely refused.

Strangely, Tommy and Kevin were more "fortunate" than the other plebes since the only firstie who retained any semblance of his tigerness was Rock Stone. Rock always played by the rules and didn't need to alter his pre-Hundredth Night behavior to stay legal. But it was clear that even Rock had lost some of his enthusiasm. In Twenty-third Company, the Dark Ages became darker.

"What the hell's going on in this Company?" Jeff asked Tuesday evening while he visited with Kevin and Rico. "I don't get it."

Jim Merritt spoke up, and it was clear to Jeff that the room had been discussing the events of the past week and their repercussions.

"No one wants to think that they've gotten through three and a half years of hell only to be dismissed for violating the plebe system. It's natural for the firsties to clam up and calm down."

"I think it's great!" burst Kevin, who immediately eased his enthusiasm. "At least I think it's great. Stone sure didn't get the word about easing up. His comearounds are still a royal pain in the ass, but it's all mechanical. He calls me a douchebag just like before, but I can tell he doesn't mean it. Am I nuts, or is it normal to *want* to be run into the ground and humiliated?"

"You're definitely nuts!" said BJ Wilson enthusiastically. "But it's less than two weeks to Hundredth Night. Plebe Year is all downhill."

"Not for Tommy Poole," said Jeff. "His Company Honor hearing is tomorrow." Everyone became quiet.

"Plebe Year isn't over for us either," added Rico suddenly from his position near his locker, where he was uncharacteristically straightening his gear. Rico never folded laundry, yet his locker was always perfect. That was because Rico had a system. During the first several months of the training, when classmates were dropping like flies, Rico had bought -- at a substantial discount -- a second set of almost every item of clothing and paraphernalia. He placed one set of gear in his locker exactly according to the regulations, ensuring that the creases were precise, the dimensions of the stacks were perfect, and that placement matched the pictures in the Midshipman's Manual. He never once touched those things the entire year, and his locker was always commended for excellence. In fact, except for access to his smut book library, he could have covered the face of the shelf side of his locker with glass and used it as a shrine to scamming the system.

For daily living Rico kept two laundry bags hanging in the closet. One contained soiled clothing to go to the Academy Laundry; the other held the clean items he used on a daily basis. When he needed clean underwear or socks, he reached into the clean bag and pulled out whatever he wanted. Living out of a laundry bag didn't seem to bother Rico at all.

Rico Guevarra only made his rack one time during the entire year. But when he made his bed, he made it perfectly and then immediately attached small bungy cords to the underside of the tucked-in sheets and covers to keep them taut. Every evening he snuggled up with his pillow on top of the made-up bed and used only his USNA wool blanket for warmth. In the morning, after a 10-second straightening of the sheet and cover edges, he was ready to go to class. He told everyone that he had once calculated that his systems saved him a precious five minutes a day. Jeff chuckled to himself when he heard this because Rico usually used whatever spare time he had to read or ogle material from his "library."

"What do you mean, Rico?" asked Jeff.

"Think about it, Polk," he said as he straightened his skivvy stack to perfection. "You guys just screwed up the lives of 20 first-classmen. You defanged the Tigers and took away their wet-dreams. They prided themselves on being assholes, and now they have to be normal. They're plenty pissed. You can bet your ass they won't roll over and die. The fun is just starting."

The room was silent for a moment.

"I don't get it, Rico," said BJ. "I mean, what can they do?"

Rico picked up a black uniform sock ball and examined the precise vertical run of the material that was folded inside the ball. He put the sock down and laughed.

"Plenty! If I were you people, I'd make sure that everything I do from here on is precisely by the book."

"No way!" exclaimed BJ. "If they get crazy, Captain Dillingham will slap them down again."

Rico sighed and turned toward the room.

"Listen up people! Captain Dildo is just as upset as the Tigers. He isn't gonna do a damn thing about protecting plebes when they violate the regulations. He's mister duty and honor, for Christ's sake. Wait and see. Plebe Year ain't over yet by a long shot!"

Kevin moaned loudly.

"You're such a optimist, Rico. Can't you predict something good for a change?"

"I only call 'em as I see 'em, you Irish twit!" Rico said playfully. "And Jimbo . . . " he said addressing Merritt. "No more secret meetings with your sweetie if you know what's good for you. Too many people suspect, and if the firsties get wind of it, you're dead meat. We all have to tread very carefully from here on. As a matter of fact, I'm taking my car back to New York during spring break. I'll have Rosa drive it down again before June Week." Rico Guevarra was probably the only plebe in the history of Annapolis to have the balls to keep an automobile handy for his clandestine over-the-wall escapades. Cars were strictly forbidden to any but first-classmen and then only after spring break. Rico also enjoyed more liberty out in town than most firsties, and he knew the secret ways in and out of the Academy yard better than anyone in the Brigade.

"Jesus, Rico!" said BJ. "Giving up your car? You *must* be serious." Rico nodded and returned to the careful examination of his sock balls. Jeff felt a dull aching in his stomach; a wonderful companion to accompany his sudden headache and general depression.

"Don't you think it will change after Hundredth Night?" asked Jeff, not wanting to imagine Plebe Year torture continuing until June Week.

"I think tradition will force most of the firsties to let go after that, but I think Big Jim and Dale Micklewski cannot be trusted at any time. And 'Jerk-off' Daly is going to be snooping around the Company area every single hour on every weekend from now on. He's going to remember who put him on permanent restriction," he continued, staring hard at Jeff. "And it wasn't Dillingham, my friend."

"Hey, asshole!" Jeff said, becoming very angry. "Daly deserved whatever he got! And besides you heard how Dillingham read him the Riot Act. Bull agreed!"

"That's bullshit!" Rico said emphatically. "Wake up, Jeff! Captain Dildo isn't at all happy. You forced him to act, and if you think for a single second he'll come running to your protection if you step an inch out of line, you're crazy. Look what he did to Tommy."

Everyone was quiet for a moment considering what Rico had said.

"Eat shit, Rico!" Jeff said harshly. "I'm glad Daly got nailed! And it's just too damn bad if it screws up your weekend sex-capades!"

Rico laughed.

"You'll change your mind before too long."

"And your horse, Rico!" Jeff shouted. "You're not always right."

"Hey! Jeff, Jeff!" Jim Merritt interrupted with a smile. "Calm down! What's done is done. I completely agree that we *all* need to be very careful. But let's not go at each other's throats."

"And Jeff," Kevin interrupted, "Rico is never wrong in these things."

"Kiss my ass, O'Reilly!"

By Wednesday evening Jeff was extremely nervous. He had read every piece of documentation he could find on the Academy Honor System and had shared the information with Tommy. He still wasn't sure what to do. Jeff had never been particularly fond of public speaking. Luckily, his part in the preliminary proceedings was minor, but whatever he did might affect the disposition of the hearing.

The hearing had been set for 1900, immediately following evening meal, and the proceedings were closed to everyone except the Company Honor Board, the defendant, and his representative. The plebe alternate honor representative, John Pirelli, sat in for Jeff on the Board. Tommy and Jeff arrived at the Wardroom door precisely on time, dressed in their best Service Dress Blue uniforms. They waited at braced attention for the Board to call them in.

While they waited, Grunt Robinson and Wildman Kopciak wandered up and started to enter the Wardroom. Grunt paused, one hand on the door.

"What's up, Polk?" he asked derisively.

"Company Honor Board, sir!" Jeff answered.

"Shit!" Kopciak said. "No Star Trek!" He glared at the two plebes. "That really pisses me off. You guys are more god-damn trouble then you're worth." He then turned to Tommy. "Are you guilty, asshole?" he asked.

"No, sir!"

Kopciak leaned in close to Tommy.

"Well, I hope they run you out anyway. You should have quit a long god-damn time ago. You're never going to make much of a Naval Officer. And look at all the trouble you've caused. If it wasn't for you, none of this shit would have happened." He pulled away and smiled. "I've got my fingers crossed Poole, that you get your fat ass honor-offensed out of here." Kopciak turned to Grunt Robinson. "Come on, Grunt. Let's go to the Steerage for a soda." He turned to Jeff. "Can't send any plebes 'cause we might get into trouble." The two firsties pulled back and stared at Jeff and Tommy. Wildman looked up and down the passageway carefully and back to the two of them with disgust. Without a further word he spit on the floor directly in front of them. Jeff flinched.

"Turn me in for that, you miserable weenie!" he said with a sneer.

Grunt laughed.

"Come on, Wildman," he said, putting an arm on Kopciak's shoulder. "Let's get that soda." They sauntered arrogantly down the passageway in the direction of the rotunda.

"Shit!" Jeff whispered fiercely without moving his head, remembering Rico's warning. "These guys are certifiably nuts!"

"Tell me about it," Tommy replied.

At 1907 the door to the Wardroom opened, and John Pirelli emerged. He looked at the two of them closely. His face was unreadable.

"The Board is ready," he said. "Please enter."

The Wardroom had been converted. It was ominous. The wooden chairs were stacked to one side. The large leather couch was pushed against the upholstered chairs behind it to serve as seating for the Board members. The low coffee table was covered with a dark blue Academy blanket. A yellow legal pad and a desk tensor lamp sat precisely in front of each board member. The only light came from the tensor lamps. Facing the sofa, just in front of the TV and book shelves, were two wooden chairs. The accused's chair sat alone in the very center of the room. The advocate's chair sat to the right next to a small end table holding a desk lamp and paper.

Jeff and Tommy chopped into the room and sounded off simultaneously. The Board Chairman, Sheldon Bloodworth, spoke.

"Gentlemen, please take your seats and we can begin." Jeff and Tommy moved to the indicated chairs and sat. The four Board members were identically dressed in Service Dress uniforms, and each was quiet and stone-faced as Jeff and Tommy fidgeted.

Bloodworth began. He lifted his yellow pad and read from his notes.

"This is an official meeting of the Twenty-third Company Honor Board to review the facts of the charges of theft against Midshipman Fourth-class Thomas Henry Poole. My name is Midshipman First-class Sheldon Edward Bloodworth the Third and I am heading this preliminary investigation. The remainder of the Board comprises Midshipman First-class Richard Horace Muller, Midshipman Second-class Thomas Alva Battle, Midshipman Third-class Charles Zachary Brewer, and Midshipman Fourth-class John Paul Pirelli. Midshipman Pirelli will act as recorder, and Midshipman Fourth-class Polk will be the advocate of the accused." Pirelli scribbled furiously as Sheldon spoke.

Bloodworth looked at Tommy, then down at his penciled notes.

"Midshipman Fourth-class Poole. You are charged with the theft of an item, namely an official photograph of the Company Officer, Captain Dillingham, from its assigned bracket in the Academy Roster Board at the Main Office. You are also charged with the subsequent display of the photo in your uniform cap. How do you plead?"

Tommy answered immediately, "not guilty of the theft. However, I did have a photo of Captain Dillingham in my cap."

Bloodworth looked at Tommy.

"Your plea is so noted." He reached down to a paper bag under the table and pulled out a combination cap. The cap had several scuff marks on it. "Is this your combination cap?" he asked. Tommy rose and took the cap from Bloodworth, careful not to touch the shiny black plastic brim which he had spent so many hours carefully polishing. He looked at it closely for several seconds, turning it in different directions while he looked.

Finally he returned the cap to Bloodworth.

"Yes, sir. That's my cap."

"So noted." Bloodworth said. Turning the cap around so the inside faced Tommy, he said, "do you recognize this photograph?"

"Yes, sir!"

"Who is it of?"

"Captain Dillingham, sir."

"And how did the photo get into your cap?"

"I put it there, sir!"

Bloodworth put the cap down on the table.

"Please be seated, Mister Poole." He turned to John Pirelli. "The Board notes that Midshipman Poole recognizes the cap and the photo and admits placing the photo inside his cap." Pirelli scribbled again furiously.

Bloodworth settled backward onto the sofa and picked up his pad.

"Very well," he said, "the facts concerning the evidence are presented. Now we'll begin general questioning." He tapped the pad several times with his pencil tip, studying his notes, and looked up at Tommy.

"How did you come into possession of the photograph of Captain Dillingham?"

"Sir, I found it on my desk one day along with a note saying that it was a picture of my new "sweetie." I thought it was a funny idea, and I put the picture into my cap, on top of a picture of my girlfriend."

"And where is the note that came along with the photo?"

"I tossed it out, sir."

"And you have no idea who could have taken the photo or who put it on your desk?"

"No, sir!"

"And when did you discover that this photo had been taken from the Roster Board?"

"Sir!" interrupted Jeff, "no one has proved that this is the photo from the Roster Board."

Bloodworth looked hard at Jeff for a moment.

"Give the Board credit for some brains Midshipman Polk. There is only one Roster Board, and no place else this photo could have originated. However, let me rephrase the question." He looked at Tommy. "When did you discover that *a* photo of Captain Dillingham was missing from the Roster Board?"

"Several days later, sir, when one of my classmates -- I don't remember who -- mentioned that he had seen a gap in the Board where Dillingham's photo should have been. After that everyone in the Company seemed to know about it."

"Did you then consider this photo might be stolen?"

"In truth, sir, the thought never crossed my mind."

Bloodworth stopped writing and stared at Tommy; then he put down his pencil and turned to the others.

"Anyone else have any questions to put to Mister Poole?" he asked.

"Yes, I do," said Tommy Battle. Battle had been one of two Second-class squadleaders who had trained the plebes during Plebe Summer. Jeff knew that he was very tough but also extremely fair.

"If you knew that a photo was missing," he asked, "why didn't you consider you might have the missing photo?"

Tommy paused.

"Sir," he said addressing Battle, "I thought the photo was indeed the missing one, but I never considered it stolen."

"I don't understand that, Mister Poole," said Bloodworth. "Explain to me how you could not have considered it stolen."

"Sir, the photo seemed an inconsequential thing, borrowed in jest. I figured that the Main Office must have a million of them and that one would not be missed. Revealing that I might have had the missing photo would have caused unnecessary trouble to me and my Company-mates."

"How come you say company-mates, not classmates?" asked Chuck Brewer.

"Because I originally thought the photo might have come from an upper-class. A plebe slinking around the Roster Board would have been noticed far more easily than an upper-classman who could pretend he was on official business."

"I see," said Bloodworth. "And why did you put the photo in your hat instead of just disposing of it along with the note?"

"Why not?" Tommy asked.

"Sir!" Jeff interrupted. "I don't see that Tommy's putting the photo in his cap has any bearing on whether or not a theft occurred."

"It might," added Bloodworth.

"I don't understand," said Tommy.

"You didn't do your homework, Mister Polk. According to the Honor Code, a thief doesn't have to steal money or anything valuable. Having a use for the photo may have given you a reason for taking it." Tommy looked confused while the Board considered what Bloodworth had just said. The room became still as everyone considered what had been said thus far.

Bloodworth ended the silence.

"Okay, Mister Poole. We have reviewed the case against you. Do you or Mister Polk have any questions or statements to make before we deliberate?"

"I absolutely did not steal the photo!" Tommy said with conviction. "And I did not consider it *stolen* when I put it in my hat."

"Sir!" Jeff added. "All the evidence is circumstantial. Nothing links Mister Poole with taking of the photo, and nothing identifies that as the missing photo. I would also like to remind the Board that the item in question is a three inch by five inch black-and-white photograph of inconsequential value and that no harm was done to anyone. This is clearly not an honor violation, and I recommend no further action be taken on this matter."

"Thank you, Mister Polk," Sheldon Bloodworth said with not a little sarcasm. "When you are Chairman of this Board, you can make recommendations for dismissal. But you are not chairman, and recommendations are *my* function." Bloodworth then addressed Tommy. "Mister Poole. As you know, the Honor System has a clear purpose, and the policing of the Honor Code falls to the midshipmen themselves. We do not tolerate lying, cheating, or stealing; but we must also be very sure of ourselves before we recommend an honor dismissal. In order to protect you, it will be necessary that a full majority of the Company Board members vote to send the case forward to the Brigade Board." Jeff glanced at Tommy, who was looking with concern at each Board member.

Bloodworth continued.

"You and Mister Polk are to leave the room immediately and wait at attention outside. The Board will discuss the facts briefly and then vote on disposition. Our vote will be secret, and when we have finished you will be called inside to witness the opening of the votes and to hear our recommendation before I present it to Captain Dillingham in the morning." Tommy and Jeff rose and went to the door. Before leaving, Tommy turned to the others and stared at them silently for a second.

"I didn't do it!" he said with conviction. He turned and followed Jeff outside.

The discussion and vote took less than ten minutes. John Pirelli came outside to get them, his face dispassionate.

"Come in, please," he said. They returned to their seats and waited.

Bloodworth addressed them.

"The voting is finished," he announced. "And I will count the ballots in your presence." Four folded-over pieces of paper sat on the blanket-covered table. All other items had been removed from the tabletop. "First I want the Board members to confirm that these are in fact the Board ballots." He looked at Battle, Pirelli, and Brewer, who each nodded silently. "Very well," he said. "I also want to remind every person in this room that the discussion of this case and the questioning of the accused, as well as the results of the balloting are strictly confidential. Disclosure of any information may result in disciplinary action. I will now open the ballots."

With a flourish he folded back the first paper and examined it.

"The first vote is for forwarding the case. He displayed the ballot so that Tommy and Jeff could plainly see the *Forward for Further Disciplinary Action* box marked with a bold *X*. Bloodworth opened a second ballot. "The second ballot recommends dismissal of the case." Again he held up the ballot for them to see. Bloodworth picked up another ballot. "The third ballot recommends dismissal." Jeff began to relax a bit. All they needed was one more acquittal vote and Tommy would be off the hook.

"The fourth ballot recommends further action," announced Bloodworth, and Jeff became aware that he had begun to sweat profusely. He fidgeted in his seat. Sheldon picked up the final ballot with a great deal of dramatics. He opened it. "The final ballot recommends further action," he said, displaying the vote. Jeff heard Tommy gasp audibly. Jeff felt cheated by the verdict.

Bloodworth turned to Pirelli.

"Please record that the Board has recommended the case of a possible honor violation by Midshipman Poole be forwarded to the Brigade Honor Board by a vote of three to two." He then turned to Tommy.

"Mister Poole," he said. "Annapolis Honor Boards have been meeting and considering cases for more than 100 years. At one time, midshipmen guilty of egregious crimes or unpardonable honor violations were taken aboard the largest training vessel available at the time and keelhauled by members of the graduating class. None of the offenders survived. Until 50 years ago the Academy secretly condoned a drumming-out ceremony that included a gauntlet of classmates whose purpose was to physically injure and humiliate the offender. Even as late as 20 years ago the Academy publicly disgraced guilty parties in the center of Tecumseh Court during a Saturday noon meal formation."

Bloodworth smiled.

"We are more civilized now, but that doesn't mean that we value honor any less. The Brigade Honor Committee is extremely fair. I have personally seen it in action. You have my word that they will carefully consider every fact and opinion and come to a reasonable decision. You will be given every opportunity to defend yourself, and you can present a personal statement to the committee before final deliberations. I sincerely wish you the best of luck. God go with you, Midshipman Fourth-class Poole. These proceedings are closed!"

Jeff looked at Tommy, who sat in shock. Jeff touched his arm.

"Come on, Tommy," he said. "Let's get back to our rooms." Tommy rose slowly and followed Jeff. Together they chopped to Tommy's room, where Hank and George anxiously waited. They read Tommy's features.

"No way!" George Abbott exploded. "How could they do that?"

Jeff shook his head.

"I don't know, George. It just happened."

"What's the next step?" asked Hank.

"Well," Jeff answered, "the Brigade Honor Committee meets the first Monday of every month to discuss offenses and agenda. Most cases are usually heard on the Monday following the regular Committee meeting. March first is the next first Monday, which means the case will be heard on the eighth. That gives us almost three weeks to prepare. I'll need to gather evidence and character witnesses."

"Count me in!" said Hank and George simultaneously.

Jeff put a hand on Tommy's shoulder.

"Don't worry too much, Tommy. I still think we have a good case."

"I can't believe he did it!" said Tommy with a great deal of disbelief. Jeff was puzzled.

"Who?" he asked.

"Pirelli!" Tommy replied. "He voted to forward my case!"

"John Pirelli did? How do you know that?"

"Because the one vote for dismissal was written in pen, and everyone except Pirelli took notes in pencil. No one else had a pen anywhere near them."

"Holy shit!" exclaimed George, his voice getting agitated. "Pirelli could have saved your ass, and he chose to sell you out. That rotten bastard!"

"Easy, George," said Jeff. "Pirelli is intense, but he's okay. He must have had his reasons. And the balloting is supposed to be secret. We can't let on that we know what he did."

"Maybe not now," said George, "but when Plebe Year is over, Mister Pirelli and I are going to have a long and painful discussion about what it means to support a classmate who is being railroaded by a group of assholes."

Almost immediately Rock Stone appeared in the doorway. If he had heard George's outburst, he didn't let on.

Before anyone could yell for attention, he said. "Carry-on!" He went immediately to Tommy Poole and looked him over.

"I just heard," he said, "and I came to offer my support. I wasn't there, so I don't know what was said or asked. I don't want to know. But if you need a character witness, I volunteer to speak before the Committee for you." With that he turned and walked from the room.

"Holy Shit Squared!" said George, his mouth hanging open. "That was unbelievable!"

Revenge started -- as Rico predicted -- on the following Monday when John Phlegler and Marion Weatherby inspected Jeff's room while everyone was at class. The roommates returned after third period to prepare for noon meal formation and found Report Chits on each of their desks. Each of them had been given 10 demerits for various petty infractions.

"My desk was disorderly?" exclaimed Jeff. "What the piss about my desk is disorderly?"

"Damn it!" Reb interrupted, "y'all can't complain. This he'ah," he said, showing his own Report Chit, "says my skivvies ain't lined up right." Reb laughed. "My skivvies gonna make me march this weekend."

"Shit, Jeff," Willy said quietly. "We shoulda kept quiet."

"Hey!" Bob interrupted. "It's too late for that now. Let's not cry about what we should have done and instead let's concentrate on surviving. If we start fighting among ourselves, we're sunk."

"Well, maybe so," added Reb, who was now staring hard at Jeff. "But I don't like being whooped up on to satisfy Polk's moral outrage. From now on, Polk, keep yo' damn hippy conscience to yo'self! Or else!"

"Or else what?" Jeff asked angrily.

"Come over he'ah and find out, Yankee!"

Jeff started across the room toward Reb, who stood confidently waiting. Bob tried to grab Jeff's arm, but he shrugged aside the grip. Reb moved out from behind his desk toward Jeff. Before Reb could get close enough to grab him, Jeff hit him quickly with two right-hand jabs above his left eye. It didn't even slow Reb. Ramsey grabbed Jeff in a bear hug, lifted him off the floor, and squeezed. Jeff groaned and almost lost consciousness. Reb threw him to the ground beside Willy's locker, fell on him, and pummeled a groggy Jeff for several seconds before Bob and Kevin O'Reilly -- who came to the rescue from across the passageway -- could subdue him. The still recovering Willy Simpson could only stand helplessly by and watch, yelling at the two combatants to stop.

The noise alerted the ever-vigilant Tigers, and within 20 seconds a smug-looking Dave Salenger stood in the doorway.

"Fighting in Bancroft Hall isn't allowed, ladies," he said sweetly. "And it appears you won't be able to make meal formation either. Too bad, huh? I'll have a report chit written for the two of you by the time you get back from classes." Salenger stared at the scene silently for several seconds, beaming broadly before he turned and walked away.

Jeff Polk had suffered a bloody nose, a rapidly-blackening eye, and several bruised ribs, as well as the ignominy of having Reb's blood splattered with his own all over his uniform shirt. Risking his own demerits, Bob Strong helped them both to Sick Bay, and Willy reported to Stone why the three would be missing noon meal formation. Jeff and Reb received ten additional demerits for their formation absence. Bob was excused for general humanitarianism.

That afternoon, when Bob, Jeff, and Reb reported to Harvey for comearound, Linehan surprised them by inviting them inside. He asked them to carry-on. The three plebes reluctantly relaxed.

"Have a seat," Harvey offered, suggesting the desk and chair opposite his own. Big Jim was not aboard. Jeff stared curiously around the room and settled himself on top of Daly's desk. The room looked remarkably sane. Jeff saw a photo of Big Jim's rather attractive girl friend set in a brass frame on one side of the desk, and a similar-sized photo of his family back home set in a matching frame on the opposite side. His parents looked nice, and his younger sister was blonde and stunning.

Along the top of the bulletin board on Daly's side of the room was a collection of silk trophy panties of various styles and colors. The board displayed glossy game photos of the Minnesota Vikings football team. Big Jim seemed to have a particular fondness for Fran Tarkenton. In the very middle of the board was an action picture of Big Jim himself taken during last year's Army-Navy game. In it Daly is delivering a bruising tackle to an Army runner, lifting the hapless cadet off the ground and sending him flying backward. Jeff could see a smile on Big Jim's face. His old Navy jersey with a large number 52 was stapled to the wall next to the bulletin board.

Across the room Harvey Linehan's side seemed stark in comparison. His bulletin board contained Academy notices and class schedules, and his desk held only a single photo, which Jeff could not see from his present position, but which must be of the young lady whom Big Jim continually referred to as "Linehan's hose-bag."

Linehan gave them a moment to adjust to the strangeness before he spoke.

"I decided it was time to have a man-to-man talk with you. I asked Jim to contribute, but he's still very angry." Daly was angry? So what! Jeff was angry too. What right did Jerk-off Daly have to be angry?

"We Tigers are the last of a breed at Annapolis. We represent the old ways: tight discipline, by-the-book, and death-before-dishonor. But that's all changed now. It started during our plebe year when the system "officially" banned hazing and restricted plebe indoctrination to a short list of specific exercise-related activities. The following year the list was further restricted, and last year it was cut even further. Now, of course, there is hardly a thing we can do. It almost isn't worth having a Plebe Year."

"Excuse me, sir," said Jeff, interrupting, and Reb growled. Jeff hesitated, then continued, "but I don't consider running up and down the passageway until I puke any picnic. How can you say we're not having a Plebe Year?"

"Polk," Linehan replied. "I have serious doubts about you. If I had known how deep your rebellious attitude went, I would have ensured you were run out early in the year."

"No, sir!" Jeff said boldly. "I can hack it!"

"No you can't, Polk. You already proved that. I guarantee we could make your life so miserable that you would have been gone in two weeks."

"Pride in pain and suffering is idiocy, sir!" Jeff replied, miffed that Harvey, who was no John Wayne by a long shot, was ridiculing his abilities. "It doesn't matter a bit in what kind of officer you become."

"That's *your* opinion, Polk. Mine and a great many other peoples' is different." Harvey stared hard at Jeff before continuing. "When you're a first-class, Mister Polk, you can run your plebes or not. That's your business. But this year the Class of 1968 is in charge, and it's *our* responsibility, to decide what is right and what isn't. Your responsibility is to do what you're told and learn."

Linehan stood, walked to the window, and waited for several seconds with his hands clasped behind his back. Then he turned slowly to face the three of them again.

"Do you want to know what makes Jim and me the most angry about the incident the other week? It isn't that we did something stupid. It isn't that we're restricted until the end of time. And it isn't that we almost hurt any of you. No! It's that you showed no loyalty to the squad." Linehan breathed deeply and continued pacing. When he continued, his voice became louder and more angry.

"For the rest of your lives you're going to work for people you consider assholes. That's an unavoidable fact of life." He spun on Jeff, walked to within a foot of him and put a small finger on the center of his chest. He taped strongly against Jeff for emphasis as he continued. "But here's another fact of life, buddy boy," Harvey said. "Your personal and professional success will depend on how well the organization does, so you had better always support the organization."

Jeff started to protest.

"I don't mean you should be head cheerleader. You don't have to suffer abuse for the good of the group. And you certainly don't need to stick your nose up the boss's ass either, Polk. But you have to do something! Either lead, follow, or get out of the way." Linehan stopped poking and laughed derisively. Jeff looked around, but the faces or his roommates offered no support. He began to feel uncomfortable.

"It's easy to sit in the background and complain about the insanity of the system, and how you're being treated so badly, and about what stupid idiots we Tigers are; but once you're in charge, you'll see that it's not so easy being a good leader, just like it's not so easy to be a good follower." He turned away from Jeff and again addressed the room.

"And that brings me to the point, which is that none of this would have happened if you had been good followers." Again Jeff started to protest. Linehan's face darkened. He stamped his foot loudly and raised a hand to stifle him.

"Shut up, Polk! You whine too damn much! It's time to listen." Jeff wanted to protest, but kept quiet.

"What Jim and I did the other night was stupid and unfortunate, but what you did was even more so. If you ever graduate and find yourself flying an attack mission or leading troops into battle or navigating in a crowded channel, you had better be willing to speak out and come to the rescue when the boss is about to do something stupid, even if it means punishment. You don't ever let your flight leader fly into a danger you can foresee, or your Company Commander lead your comrades into an ambush, or your skipper run the ship aground. And you should *never* let your Annapolis Squad Leader put himself into a position where he threatens your physical safety. Each of you had the responsibility to speak up when you saw what was happening. Each of you had the duty to disobey an order that grossly violated the rules. Each of you had an obligation to protect your squad members whether they are first-class or classmates. You did not do that and therefore you obeyed dishonorably. And that's what upsets the first-class in the Company more than anything else."

Harvey paused to let that sink in.

"And then by making an issue of the situation *after* it was over, you compounded the problem. You attempted to invalidate the entire leadership arrangement in this Company. What you did was to mutiny. It doesn't work that way, gentlemen, and, frankly, I have no intention of restricting unless I can see your shiny faces alongside my own."

"You will see in the final analysis it's still the Tigers who have the power."

"Surely there must be some way to compromise on this," offered Bob.

"No, Strong. What's done is done."

"How 'bout if I take Mister Polk up to the roof and drop him over the edge?" asked Reb, only half in jest. Harvey laughed.

"As attractive as that sounds, it wouldn't do any good at this point."

"Are you going to renege on the tradition of spooning us after Hundredth Night?" asked Bob.

"No. We're Tigers. Honor is important."

"This is all bullshit!" said Jeff loudly. "You don't know what you're talking about. You guys screwed up and now you expect us to grovel and apologize. No way!"

"I'll grovel, sir!" said Reb with a smile. Harvey laughed again.

"Part of the mystique of this place," Harvey said again after a pause, "a part that applies only to graduates, is the ability to look back when it's all over and say, 'Wow! Look what hell I went through! If I could handle that, I can do anything!' Polk here is never going to be able to say he endured the worst. The best you can say is that when it got really tough, you put your tail between your legs and scampered behind the reg book. I feel really sorry for you. No matter what happens from this point on, you failed Plebe Year."

Jeff sat back stunned and noticed that Reb was smiling smugly at him. He remained quiet while Linehan and Ramsey stared.

THE JAPANESE BELL

Located in Tecumseh Court near the entrance to Bancroft Hall, the Japanese Bell is more than 600 years old. It was brought back from Japan by Commodore Perry during his voyages. The bell rings the Navy score following a Navy football victory over Army.

CHAPTER 8

THE WEEK BEFORE

By Saturday, 18 February 1968, every plebe in the Twenty-third Company restricted -- except Jim Merritt and his roommates. But Rock Stone inspected their room on the previous Wednesday and gave each plebe 15 demerits for general untidiness. Mugsy McGinley was outraged. He questioned Kevin O'Reilly during noon meal formation the following day, after he heard about the inspection from several classmates -- who told him strictly for the purpose of starting trouble.

"What the shit is this about your room being fried by Stone?"

Kevin hesitated not wanting to cause additional trouble within the Company. Mugsy McGinley had a reputation for physical violence that was legendary. No one messed with McGinley, not even Stone, who was far more muscular and outweighed Mugsy by 20 pounds.

Even in a nicely starched uniform Mugsy was a genuinely frightening individual. He had a swarthy, Mediterranean complexion, a solid body, large bony hands, and the thickest growth of facial and body hair that fair-skinned, red-haired Kevin had ever seen. Despite the fact that he had developed an almost brotherly relationship with Mugsy, Kevin felt fear when he saw the anger flair.

"Sir," Kevin said, hesitating and choosing his words carefully, "it's true we were put on report. But it's no big deal! Can we I talk before you do anything?"

"Kiss my butt, O'Reilly! I'll decide what to do about this!"

"Come on, Mugsy," Kevin said, dropping his plebe-to-upper-class demeanor, and speaking to Mugsy on a brotherly basis. "This could be some really serious shit. No need for you to get involved." Kevin looked around briefly, and lowered his voice. "Besides," he whispered, a twinkle creeping into his eyes, "whatever you do to Stone, he's just gonna kill my ass in retaliation."

"Enlightened self interest, huh?" asked Mugsy, chuckling. Despite his gruff, uncultured behavior and appearance, Mugsy, like all midshipmen, was an intelligent, well-educated individual.

"Damn right, sir!" Kevin replied. "Remember when earthly power is liketh God's." Kevin and Mugsy had an ongoing contest of quoting Shakespeare. Each of them enjoyed their Elizabethan erudition. Kevin had purchased a two-volume set of *The Complete Works of William Shakespeare* in the Midshipman's Store for $9.95, a major investment for an underpaid proto Naval officer.

McGinley chuckled.

"You mean I should show mercy on you when I mete out justice to Stone? We'll see, O'Reilly. I'll talk with Stoner the Boner to see why he did what he did. What's the harm in that?

"Nothing, I guess."

Near the end of the meal Mugsy stood, placed his napkin carefully on his plate, and sauntered to Stone's table. Since it was so close to Hundredth Night, the Mess Hall buzzed with incredible activity. At almost every table plebes and first-class engaged in the sometimes-playful, sometimes-serious activities that portend a big event. It was almost as noisy as the first weeks after the September return of the Brigade. As Mugsy's unspoken purpose became evident, the localized din quieted, and many heads swiveled to watch. At Stone's table everyone, including Stone himself, looked up with a bit of dread as Mugsy approached. Mugsy tapped Tommy Poole on the shoulder. Tommy had the "duty" this meal at Stone's table.

"Go finish the meal with the overflow, Poole. I have to chat with Mister Stone."

Tommy hesitated and glanced briefly at Rock, who only nodded. Tommy departed quickly, carrying his plate and utensils. Mugsy sat and put his two beefy arms on the table in front of him.

"Rock," he said, "You inspected my plebes' room and put them on report. I have serious problems with that." He chuckled and nodded at his table. "That pussy O'Reilly made me promise to behave about this, so I'm going to explain myself professionally -- this time. Listen closely. First, I don't want anybody in my plebes' room without first telling me about it. Second, I want to be there whenever someone inspects. And third, I'm in their room often enough to know what the conditions are, and there's no way they could have rated demerits."

Mugsy smiled broadly and made a gesture of supplication with his two big hands. "See, I can be calm when I have to." His smile faded.

"Stone," he continued, "you pride yourself on being the best at going by the book. But what you did was unprofessional. *You* skipped the chain-of-command and undermined my authority. That's a no-no, and I can't allow things like that to continue. So what's going on? And I don't want any bullshit answers. This needs to be man-to-man, Stone."

Stone looked around the table and then back at Mugsy. He paused, clearly considering his next words carefully, then smiled.

"What you're asking is an inappropriate topic for open discussion. According to the book . . . I suggest that you come by my room after class today."

Mugsy smiled.

"Fine, Rock," he said sweetly. "I'll be there. But hear this -- and I don't care who's listening -- the next person who inspects, grills, or otherwise harasses my plebes without my approval or a very good reason gets a challenge to three rounds in the ring. I won't be a gentleman. Pass the word, okay?"

Mugsy stood and balled a napkin Tommy had left behind. He turned to the far end of the table.

"Free shot?" he asked Danny French, who had just returned to Company tables with the end of the winter wrestling season and who had the duty on the second-class end of the table. French looked down at his half-full glass of iced tea and smiled at Mugsy.

"Yes, sir!" he said, beaming.

Mugsy pulled back his right arm, took careful aim, and threw the napkin forcefully across the table, where it struck against Danny's forehead with a soft thud and fell onto his plate. Danny looked bewildered.

"You god-damn smack!" Mugsy said with derision. "Never give anyone permission to take a free shot at your drink." With that, Mugsy turned to Stone and said, "I'll take plebes I train over ones you train any day, Stone." Mugsy then snorted, turned, and departed the Mess Hall.

Monday evening during comearound, the entire plebe contingent of Twenty-third Company engaged in uniform races. Supposedly the drill trains midshipmen to quickly prepare for any shipboard or crisis contingency. In fact, the drills were far more useful in the daily Annapolis race to get from the final morning class -- which often seemed to be in a building halfway to Baltimore -- to noon meal formation without sweat or panic.

The exercise started out professionally. Daly ordered a change from gym gear into Service Dress Blue. Two minutes later the plebes returned to Daly's room dressed appropriately. Big Jim looked them over, grunted, and said, "Okay. Next is White Works Alpha. Go!"

After three such changes it was clear to Jeff that Big Jim and Harvey were tired of the exercise, but plebes all around them continued to scurry about in a uniform frenzy. Daly's eyes twinkled.

"Harvey," he said, "what if the Academy decided that we should dress more formally during physical training? We should make sure these guys are ready for any contingency, shouldn't we?" Linehan smiled.

"You're absolutely right, Jim." Harvey turned to the group. "Gym gear, dress black shoes, combination cap, and neckerchief. Go!" When the three of them returned, dressed as ordered, Big Jim looked them over critically.

"That's an interesting uniform, Harv." The two of them chuckled for a moment. Then Linehan saw Jeff's feet.

"Polk, you idiot! You can't wear black socks to gym class. It's unsanitary. Twenty push-ups, please!" Jeff dropped groaning to the deck, knowing that the exercise would ruin the shine on his good shoes.

When Jeff finished, Linehan suggested, "What if they reported to the Commandant immediately following last class, Jim?"

Jim considered.

"Absolutely. That could happen. Service Dress Blue under Working Blues. Carry the jacket. Go!"

As he was carefully buttoning his black class shirt over the white one, Jeff exclaimed, "What the piss is all this about?"

"Shut up, Polk, and do what y'all 're asked!" Reb exploded. "And ah don't want ta hear any of yo' bullshit!"

"This is stupid!" Jeff countered.

"Stupid or not," Bob offered patiently, "play along please!" Jeff rumbled but said nothing further.

"Harvey," Daly said when they had been inspected by the two firsties, "what if there was a drug scare here at Annapolis, the Administration knew for certain that some plebe in Twenty-third Company had smuggled in heroin, and they searched all the rooms but couldn't find anything? The Academy would require a total body cavity search."

"And what if there was a storm raging at the same time?" added Linehan, laughing out loud.

"Yeah," Big Jim said chuckling. He turned to the three plebes. "Prepare for a body cavity search in a rainstorm. Go!" The plebes returned wearing only jock straps, gym shoes and socks, all covered by raingear. For the remainder of the evening, the strangeness continued.

Two events remained in the Company competition. The cannonball eating contest would be held on Wednesday at noon meal when the dreaded deserts were next served. The other event was a Saturday afternoon long-boat race across the Severn River and back in celebration of Washington's birthday. Only first-class could participate. The winning boat would have to cross the River and beach on the far side. The Company Officer would symbolically plant the Company guidon while the ten-man crew switched sides. Then the boats would race back. The winning boat would be first to touch the Santee Basin seawall on the Academy side. The Tigers reluctantly agreed that John Gladden could not participate, but he could coach.

"Come on cowgirls, Stroke! Stroke! Stroke!" Gladden urged the Tiger team to row in rhythm, although what they were presently rowing was an imaginary boat which they set up outside the Company office. Every evening for the past week, two identical rows of five desk chairs had been placed in the passageway with an eleventh chair in the rear for the Company Officer. The ten Tigers sat in the chairs facing astern. Each rower carried his rifle, which he set on his lap, butt end out. On John's command the rowers pretended to pull toward the far shore.

"If you can get a good rhythm going, pardners," Tex announced, "I calculate you can reach the far shore in 300 strokes. That shouldn't be so bad, especially since the wind will be with you on the way over. Coming back into the stiff afternoon breeze is gonna mighty cold on the prairie, so don't overdo it on the way over. Six hundred strokes at a slower pace will get you back."

"That's almost a thousand strokes!" moaned Grunt Robinson. "And we have to pull two-ton Dillingham. Jesus!"

Gladden laughed.

"Hey, that's about ten times fewer than I do every day at practice, pardner. You can hack it!" He laughed again. "You'll hack it; otherwise Dillingham will make steers of you!"

Jubal Ramsey stared at his plate with genuine relish. He smiled, rubbed the palms of his hands together, and looked at the group that had gathered around him. To Jeff, he looked hungry -- maybe hungry enough to pull this off. All that aside, Jeff smiled. Jubal Hunter Ramsey loved to put on a show, and now he had an audience.

"Umm . . . umm," Reb moaned delightedly, gazing with affection at the brown tennis-ball-sized desert that sat alone on the pristine, gleaming white, Naval Academy plate. Jeff and many of the other observers stared also, but not so lovingly. The Brigade had aptly named the not-so-appetizing object a "cannonball" not so much because of its shape, which was generally round, but more because of its consistency and deceptive mass. No light-and-fluffy thing was the cannonball. In fact, it was an entire baked apple covered with several layers of thick, underdone crust and soaked in a thick, sweet, goo of syrup and brown sugar. Despite the fact he had gone most of the entire year with an empty, please-feed-me, feeling in his stomach, Jeff had yet to finish one. Remembering that Reb secretly admitted he didn't much care for the taste either, Jeff reassessed Jubal's chances.

There were only two plates on the table, one in front of Reb, the other in front of a beefy blond third-classman from Twenty-second Company. The Third-classman was sarcastically named "Jumbo" Jim Hernandez, and according to rumor, he was an eating machine who had beaten the challenge of eating twelve of the gastric monstrosities. Jumbo Jim didn't seem concerned.

In the center of the table sat a huge stainless steel platter piled high with cannonballs gladly donated by classmates. The platter required two midshipmen to safely lift and carry. Captain Dillingham sat in the chair to Jubal's right side; Lieutenant Spencer sat to Jumbo Jim's right. While the remainder of both companies ate the standard noon meal fare, the two cannonball competitors would concentrate solely on the desserts.

"I just have to remember to pace myself," Jubal told any classmate who would listen. "If I eat steadily, I can eat all day." Unfortunately, as Jeff reminded him, Jubal wouldn't have all day. The contest would end at precisely 1245, giving the participants time to return to their rooms and prepare for afternoon classes. Whoever consumed the most cannonballs without mishap would be the winner.

"What are the current odds on Ramsey?" Linehan asked Jeff as the meal started and the supply of cannonballs in the huge tray began to diminish.

"Ten to one, sir."

"You room with him," said Daly. What do you think of his chances?"

"Sir, Reb is an incredible eater, but I've heard Jumbo Jim is a phenomenon."

"I'll bet you five dollars Reb doesn't finish ten," Daly offered.

Jeff considered the offer. Ten was quite a few.

"Sir, make it eight and you've got a bet."

"Eat shit, Polk! I could eat eight!"

"Bet you five dollars you can't, sir!" Jeff had intended that comment as a bit of light banter, but Big Jim, still angry at Jeff for his perpetual restricting, reacted loudly.

"Get your chins in, Polk, and slide your ass out onto the edge of your chair! Any more verbal funny-boy screw-ups and I'll add a pile to your demerit total on the spot."

"Aye, aye, sir!"

"Simpson, want to take my bet?"

"Yes, sir, I do!"

Daly nudged Linehan and laughed.

"You heard him, Harv. That'll be an easy five dollars." Big Jim thought for a second. "Hey I got a moneymaking idea!" He rose and walked to the next table and repeated the bet. Pat Mulvaney took the bait. Daly went to the next table.

By the time he reluctantly approached Mugsy McGinley's table, Big Jim had amassed 50 dollars in bets and he was feeling pretty good about himself. At the challenge table Reb had just finished his third cannonball and was still going strong. Jumbo Jim was on number five.

"What do you want, Daly?" McGinley growled. Big Jim ignored him.

"Any of you plebes want to bet me five dollars that Ramsey can't finish ten cannonballs before time runs out?" he asked.

"Go away, shithead!" McGinley growled again. "Leave my plebes alone!" Daly hesitated.

"Excuse me, sir, "Kevin interrupted. "How many is that again?"

Daly brightened.

"Ten!"

"Oh, is that all? Pardon me, but that's not a very smart bet on your part. I'd just be stealing your money. I tell you what, why don't we make the wager more interesting?" Kevin asked.

"How?" Daly asked, genuinely confused.

"Well, I'll bet you 25 dollars Reb can eat 12."

Daly brightened, then looked at Kevin cautiously.

"Why do you say that?"

Kevin assumed his professorial pose, and his blue eyes twinkled.

"Sir, I did come research. The average cannonball weighs approximately eight ounces, the average meatball submarine weighs twenty-five. Saturday afternoon, in preparation, Reb ate two-and-a-half subs in well under an hour, which is the mass equivalent of 9.4 cannonballs, which almost puts him past the goal of ten without straining. However, according to the Medical Encyclopedia in the Library, the average human body digests food at the rate of ten ounces an hour. This equates to one cannonball in a 45 minute period. And Reb certainly has a higher-than-average metabolism, which means that counting the digestion factor, Reb has to eat only nine cannonballs to consume the mass equivalent of ten. In addition, the hourly calorie consumption for a man when eating is 350, which also equates to one cannonball. But you can see from the way Reb fidgets and jiggles his legs while he's eating that he is basically a nervous person, which means that he consumes an additional 50 calories per hour, which equates to the mass equivalent of another half cannonball. All this means that he only needs to eat eight cannonballs to consume the mass equivalent of ten, and as I said, I personally saw him eat the equivalent of 9.4 cannonballs last Saturday. You can't win that bet."

Daly stared at O'Reilly totally dumbfounded for several seconds. Kevin didn't blink.

"If it's such a sure thing, wise-ass, than why didn't you take me up on it immediately?" Daly asked, a very nervous look beginning to settle on his face.

"Sir, accepting the original bet with the foreknowledge that you had to lose would be tantamount to theft. We plebes have to be very careful these days. I want a bet that has some risk to it, and I calculate that Reb has a 60 percent chance of eating twelve, so the odds are still in my favor."

Daly drew back and considered.

"Wait a minute," he said, genuinely perplexed. "He only has to eat eight cannonballs to actually consume ten?"

"Feel free to check my math, sir. And like I say, he's a shoe-in for 9.4." Kevin stated this with such categoric finality that Daly had an instantaneous vision of 50 dollars floating out of his wallet and into the pockets of the plebes he hated.

"Shit!" Daly growled. Then he spun quickly around and returned to the last table he had visited. "The bet's off!" he announced boldly. "You guys were trying to cheat me." As Big Jim moved out of earshot, repeating the same denouncement at every table, Rico broke out laughing.

"That was brilliant, O'Reilly! You are amazing!"

Mugsy and his roommate Henry Brandis stared at Kevin for several seconds.

"All bullshit?" Mugsy asked incredulously.

"Of course, sir! I didn't want Mister Daly stealing my classmates' money." Kevin answered with a twinkle. The two firsties chuckled.

"You're a kick, O'Reilly," Henry observed. "How do you think of those things?"

"I'll find out, sir!" he answered, "but I'll tell you one thing: Sometimes I scare myself."

By the end of the normal mealtime, Reb had finished seven of the apple-beasts while Jim was working happily on number ten. Even though it was clear to all the observers that Reb hadn't a ghost of a chance, he plowed ahead, but he was clearly in gastronomic trouble. His pace had slowed after number six, a particularly massive lump of gunk-covered apple. For the first time in his life he actually felt as if his stomach was filled to capacity. As the physical discomfort increased, his face reddened, he began to sweat uncontrollably, and his chewing slowed to near imperceptibility.

Jeff noticed another sign of distress. Reb's table manners -- usually impeccably Southern -- began to suffer. At cannonball five he sighed and had begun peeling back and eating small sections of the layers of thick batter using his fingers instead of a fork. By number seven apple, he had bitten the apple directly from his large hands.

As he stared at cannonball number eight, Reb's face was a sticky, brown, shiny mess. The sauce left a curious ring around his lips, which he was too preoccupied to wipe, and beads of sweat rolled freely down his cheeks and mixed with the sauce residue on both sides of his mouth. His eyes were wide and showed a kind of surprised expression. In fact, Reb Ramsey looked like hell. Seeing Reb, and sensing imminent defeat, the upper-class of Twenty-third Company slunk passed the table on their way to their rooms. Captain Dillingham, usually faithful to the bitter end, feigned an appointment and departed early. As the clock neared the pre-determined minute, only fellow plebes and Rock Stone remained to cheer Reb on.

Halfway into number eight only a minute remained. Reb moaned with every bite, and his chewing became labored. Jumbo Jim, on the other hand, had finished 12 and smiled at Reb as he reached for number 13. Reb hesitated, stared for several seconds at his cannonball, and pushed the plate away with clear distaste and a final moan. The Twenty-second Company cheered, and several companymates pounded Jumbo Jim on the back in celebration. He continued to eat, oblivious to the accolades, as the back pounding and jostling continued.

"Do you concede defeat?" asked a smug Lieutenant Spencer, who waved his Company into quiet. Reb stared at Spencer as if it were the first time he had ever seen him, and didn't comprehend the question.

A loud liquid honk interrupted Reb's contemplation. Everyone turned to the source of the noise. Rico Guevarra and Kevin O'Reilly stood almost next to Jumbo Jim. Rico had just blown his nose into a white handkerchief. As everyone watched, he peeled open the cloth and peered inside.

"Jesus, Kevin!" he exclaimed. "What the hell do you think that is?" With a nod of his head he indicated something inside the hanky.

"I don't know, Rico," Kevin answered. "I've never seen anything so slimy and gross in my life. Maybe you should see a doctor?" As Kevin spoke, Rico slowly lowered his handkerchief so that just a glimpse of the mess inside peeked at the watchers, Jumbo Jim included. His eyes became wide and his lips pulled back in a repulsed sneer.

Suddenly Kevin reached down and grabbed a napkin from the table in front of Jumbo Jim.

"I think whatever you've got must be catching!" he said suddenly as he himself sneezed wetness into the napkin with loud dramatics. Kevin examined his mess. "That's gross! Maybe we have a communicable disease!" he exclaimed.

Jim's eyes got wider, and a change washed over his face. He looked up at his now-quiet companymates apologetically, and his face turned a greenish-pale shade. He yelled incoherently and threw his arms backward to move midshipmen out of the way of what was now inevitable. Those in the crowd that didn't scurry immediately to safety watched in silent anticipation. Jeff could hear Jim's stomach rumble from the far side of the table. Lieutenant Keith Spencer, sensing the the impending disaster, hurriedly stood, pushed midshipmen to one side, and moved quickly upstream.

Jumbo Jim made a loud involuntary gurgle, and his eyes grew incredibly wide. He looked down at his ample stomach momentarily as if to question his betrayal. Then he gushed, and a sickening brown chunky puddle formed on the middle of the table in front of Jim. It smelled really bad.

Jeff Polk reacted first.

"He puked!" Jeff yelled jubilantly. "Reb wins!" The Twenty-third Company plebes began cheering and jumping around, and Reb, still pale, began to smile.

"Now wait a minute!" interrupted Lieutenant Spencer, watching in open-mouthed amazement as Jumbo Jim continued to discharge. "Your man was ready to concede defeat!"

"Yes," agreed Rock. "I'll grant you that, sir. But vomiting is automatic disqualification, so Reb would have won anyway." Keith Spencer considered while enlisted Filipino stewards from all parts of the Mess Hall began to congregate nearby in the wide center aisle, jabbering rapidly in Tagalog and pointing to the table and the mess.

As Reb later remembered, it was the smell that did it. As Jumbo Jim had gotten ill, Reb settled in his chair, feeling bad but not physically ill. He tried to stand, but the lethargy of his food load caused him to slump back into his chair. Jumbo stopped but the odor did not.

Suddenly Reb's face underwent a transformation. He moaned. Every voice in the immediate vicinity became hushed, and all eyes focused on Reb.

"Don't you dare!" warned Rock Stone, pointing forcefully. Jubal Hunter Ramsey looked at Rock with wide and pleading cow-eyes. Jeff could sense the inevitable. So did many others

"Thar she blows!" yelled J. P. Feeney, the Company Commander of Twenty-second Company with genuine happiness, and his companymates began chanting. "Puke! Puke! Puke! Puke!" Reb didn't need any encouragement. He rumbled and gurgled and let loose.

Lieutenant Spencer spoke first, staring at the incredible mess with clear distaste.

"Well, this contest is a draw. The competition comes down to the final event. Good luck Saturday on the river, Mister Stone."

"Thank you, sir!"

The midshipmen spectators rapidly left the Mess Hall, careful to avoid the overflow puddles on the terrazzo deck. Jeff and Willy helped Reb to the room. He decided to forgo afternoon classes and went instead to Sick Bay, feigning the flu. Although Reb Ramsey consumed two foot-long subs at the very next opportunity, he never ate another cannonball.

That evening at nearly 2000, eleven plebes waited outside the doorway that separated Twenty-third from Twenty-second Companies. Each plebe carried an office chair equipped with caster wheels they had borrowed from various offices throughout the Academy. Rock Stone poked his head inside the Twenty-second Company area, carefully checked the passageway, and found it mostly deserted.

"Set up quickly!" he commanded, and the plebes filed into the passageway. Quietly they set their chairs into ten pairs facing the doors and a single chair facing forward. They waited. Butkowski and Abbott were the lead pair, followed by Kevin and Jim, Bob and Willy, Chuck and Tony, and Doug Goto and Mike Wojeck. The plebe in the final chair, Pat Mulvaney, carried the Company guidon.

"Ready?" Stone asked as Mulvaney settled into place. The plebes nodded affirmation. Stone smiled. "Good," he said pushing the doors open. "Then get going!"

Pat Mulvaney held the guidon forward so it extended over the pseudo-boat, and the ten other plebes extended their arms in front of them pretending to hold oars. "Stroke!" Pat yelled, and they group pushed off with their legs while simultaneously pretending to stroke with their arms. The "boat" glided ahead, and the plebes sang as they rowed.

"Row, row, row, your boat, gently down the Severn,"
"Twenty-second will never win. Never! Never! Never!"

The plebes repeated the verse loudly and repeatedly as they stroked. Soon the passageway filled with onlookers who hooted and cheered derisively but who did nothing to interfere.

J. P. Feeney -- a much looser fellow than Rock -- emerged from the Company Office to observe the commotion. Feeney was an interesting character who used the fact that his Company had won last year's Brigade-wide color competition to proclaim himself the "Color Midshipman." It was an often-repeated joke which he enjoyed playfully rubbing in the Tiger noses. He watched the plebes for a moment, smiling, and glanced up the passageway at Stone. He waved and saluted Rock, who returned the greeting.

Once they reached the end of the main passageway, the plebes grabbed their chairs and disappeared into a small side passageway, returning to the Company area by a side route.

Twenty-second Company retaliated much later that evening. Midshipman Lieutenant Feeney and twenty of his charges quietly entered Tiger country loaded with loosely-balled newspapers, which they dumped in the Wardroom doorway until the pile completely blocked the entrance. On the door to the Wardroom they left a large poster board sign.

WE HOPE THAT WE WILL NEVER SEE
ANOTHER COMPANY LIKE TWENTY-THREE.
THEY THINK THAT THEY WILL WIN THE RACE,
BUT THEY'LL ONLY MEET DISGRACE.
TIGERS IS LIKE TIGERS DOES
AND TIGERS NEVER WIN BECAUSE
THEY'RE ONLY BAGS OF SMELLY GASSES,
AND LOSING, "BULL" WILL KICK THEIR ASSES!

Good Luck Saturday
The Color Midshipman

Thursday night the anticipation of the Hundredth Night activities hung excitedly in the air. No one could sit still, and the moon battle between Jeff's room and Jim Merritt's room continued with renewed passion.

Although Jeff understood and accepted that streaking, mooning, and other tidbits of exhibitionism were the current rage, he was never a wholehearted participant. However, during the past year an amazing contest of one-upmanship had developed. This evening the fireworks were spectacular as Rico again goaded Kevin into lighting his flatulence in retaliation for a Ramsey noisy barrage.

BJ Wilson had been "gotten" by this more often than anyone else in the past year, and it had been a constant source of frustration to him. He pledged revenge, but his retaliation -- even though he strained so hard at times that his faced turned red -- was never more than a fizzing disappointment.

Thursday evening meal was Mexican bean casserole. An hour after dinner, BJ was uncharacteristically calm and smug.

"Just wait," he told the room. "This is the night for revenge! I can feel myself brewing." He patted his stomach in anticipation, while Rico and Kevin exchanged smiles and raised eyebrow glances.

"I think this thing has gotten out of control," observed Jim Merritt, looking up from a chemistry text. "I hope we all grow up soon and get on with more important things."

"Yeah!" said Kevin. "Like being able to go on liberty again and meet some sweet things in town. I'm gonna burst!"

"Be careful, Kevin," Rico offered.

"What?"

"What you have is a common condition for young men in our situation. If you don't do something about it, your gonads can actually expand until they drag on the floor. You end up stepping on yourself every time you try to walk. -- Very painful!" Kevin and Jim laughed, but BJ was not amused.

Jim could hear BJ's stomach rumble as he shifted in his chair to face Rico.

"You must suffer as much as I do, Rico," Kevin replied.

"Yeah," he said. "And my hand isn't large enough." Everyone but BJ laughed. Jim noticed that BJ was smiling but not at Rico's joke.

BJ concentrated intently for a moment, smiled, rose from his chair, and smugly walked to the door. Turning toward his roommates, he bent over in the open doorway, and pulled down his shorts.

"Not again, Wilson!" Rico laughed. "Give it up!"

BJ looked up at Rico and smirked.

"You'll see," he said. He then leaned completely over, peering at the room across the passageway through his spread legs, and aimed his bare cheeks carefully at Jeff's room.

"Hey, guys!" he whispered loudly, "Look what I have!"

Jeff and Willy responded to his summons. They came to the doorway and looked.

"Big deal, Wilson!" Jeff replied, and started to return to his studying, but something made him hesitate. He and Willy faced the action and waited patiently. "Hey, Reb, Bob!" Jeff said, "Check this out! BJ's trying to pop." Both Ramsey and Strong came to the door to watch.

"What ya'll do'in, Wilson?" Reb asked laughing. "Tight asses like ya'll cain't cut no breeze."

BJ didn't listen. Instead he was concentrating intently. He began to grunt loudly with effort. One, two, then all three of his roommates appeared in the far doorway to watch. He continued to strain.

He puffed, he grunted, he pushed. The part of his face that showed between his legs turned beet red. Reb laughed.

"Jesus, Wilson! Ya'll gonna have a heart attack!"

Finally BJ's plumbing system let go with a loud and satisfied "*POOOOT*" sound, and a small, brown, fecal projectile lofted out into the passageway to land with a plop on the tile.

"Oh, Jesus!" BJ said, quickly pulling up his pants.

"My God!" Reb shouted, "Wilson 'jis shit in the passageway!"

Everyone except BJ began laughing so hard that it was almost impossible to hold water. Before BJ could get to his unfortunate mistake, the doors to every plebe room had opened, and heads poked out.

BJ took his washcloth from the sink and raced into the passageway. Ignoring the potential penalty for not chopping or bracing, he fell immediately to his knees and wiped the mess vigorously. When he returned to the room, he washed the washcloth thoroughly in the shower. Jeff's entire room came to visit.

"That was great, BJ!" Jeff said. "I wish I had a camera."

"All of you can eat shit!" BJ exclaimed while wringing out the washcloth.

"Are you serving?" asked Rico bursting into a fit of renewed laughter.

"Piss off!" BJ announced and never spoke another word about the incident. When Jeff and his roommates had returned to the safety of their own room, Jeff decided that his participation in the moon wars was over.

Friday evening was the final comearound in preparation for the big Sunday night event. Jeff and Reb arrived at Daly's room dreading the pain that would surely follow. They waited nervously outside the room for the two firsties to emerge.

Exactly on time the door to the room opened and Linehan poked his head outside.

"Inside, quick!" he said, and held the door open for them.

Jeff and Reb exchanged a curious glance as they hurried inside and immediately braced against the nearest locker.

"Carry-on! Carry-on!" Daly said in a very friendly voice, and the two plebes relaxed, but only barely.

"Well, fellas," Linehan began, "this is probably the last time we'll be able to give you any physical indoctrination. It's a sad event, and Jim and I were talking about it just now. We thought, what the hell, why not just end this plebe-firstie shit right now. I mean, what's the sense in prolonging the inevitable even for a day. So Jim and I hereby offer you our spoons." He held out his hand to Reb and Big Jim did the same to Jeff.

"Let's let bygones be bygones," said Daly with genuine good humor. "Shit, we already spooned Merritt's room."

Jeff stared at the big hand that stretched before him and he glanced at Reb. Their eyes met for an instant, and Jeff could see a definite warning in Reb's glance. He turned back to Daly and smiled.

"Not a chance in hell, sir!" he said. "I'm gonna run your ass!"

"Damn right!" Reb echoed.

Daly laughed.

"Maybe there's hope for you yet, Polk, you scum-sucking douchebag! If you had reached for my hand I would have ripped off your god-damn arm and slapped you silly with it -- no matter what the Captain would have done. Now get your ASSES into the passageway and prepare to puke your guts out!" That comearound was the hardest Jeff ever had to endure.

Saturday dawned bright and sunny but exceedingly chilly. By the end of noon meal the temperature was up to a frigid 25, and a stiff breeze was flowing steadily from the west as Tex Gladden had predicted. Two long, white wooden rowboats that had been used by midshipmen for life boat drills more than 30 years ago, had been brought into the middle of Tecumseh Court where they waited while a tide of curious visitors flowed around them. At 1300 the teams assembled.

Twenty-third Company was well represented by muscular monsters like Big Jim Daly and Rock Stone, who were the biggest of any of the competitors. In addition, the Tigers selected Wildman Kopciak and Grunt Robinson, who were also athletic heavyweights. Dale Micklewski, Sheldon Bloodworth, Dick Muller, Harvey Linehan, and Dave Salenger also competed. The final competitor was Mugsy McGinley, probably the best athlete of the entire group. Kevin had asked Mugsy why he volunteered to compete for the Tigers he hated so much.

"O'Reilly," he answered, "I think most of my companymates are genuine assholes; you know that. But they're also my mates, and when all is said and done, you have to support the unit no matter what you think about its leadership. I'll give them 100 percent and they know that. Sometimes you suffer the slings and arrows; sometimes you oppose them." Mugsy looked closely at Kevin. "Why did you ask Stone around anyway?"

"I wanted to show the worst of them that I was better than they are."

"Exactly, O'Reilly!"

The Twenty-third Company competitors wore identical sweatgear with watch caps, over which they wore a white T-shirt. On each shirt front a plebe had stenciled the bold number "23." Across the back were identically-sized letters which spelled "TIGERS" in block capital letters. Twenty-second Company wore a conglomeration of outfits which included one firstie in bright red ski gear and another in wool Arctic parka. The two Company Officers each wore sweatgear and carried a guidon. They looked uncomfortable at the thought of braving the river in this freezing weather.

Lieutenant Al Wyatt, the Twenty-fourth Company Officer, stood nearby in his Service Dress Blues, smiling at the thought of the pain and discomfort that awaited his officer cohorts. Almost every member of both Companies surrounded the competitors and the boats, leaving only a narrow lane for their race to the Yacht basin.

"Ready, gentlemen?" Lieutenant Wyatt asked with a wry chuckle. The competitors answered loudly in the affirmative. "Very well. Line up and grab the gunwales of the long boat with one hand." The two Company groups aligned themselves along both sides of the boats with the Company Officers in the rear. Lieutenant Wyatt checked his stopwatch.

"On my mark, gentlemen. Five, four, three, two, one, Go!" Both Companies reached down with the second hand and hefted the wooden boat overhead. The boats started forward with the Tigers in a slight lead. A substantial crowd had gathered, including a reporter and photographer with the local Annapolis crab-wrapper newspaper. The boats surged ahead, to loud cheering.

The Tigers jogged across the remainder of Tecumseh Court, Bull counting cadence so that their feet would not get tangled. The Tigers loudly chanted "Tigers!" with alternate steps. Puffs of white frosty breath accompanied their motions. They were an impressive sight. The Company observers jogged along behind at a respectful distance, and not a few of the spectators followed at a walk. Children scampered to the fore of the boats, delighted to be a part of this strange ritual and the beautifully cold afternoon.

At the bottom of the stairs near the Midshipman's Store parking lot, Twenty-third Company was in the lead by ten yards and jogging steadily. On the flat parking lot the Tigers yelled louder. It was adrenaline-inducing. Jeff found himself yelling "Tigers!" in time with the firsties and most of the other company members. He looked at Kevin, who ran next to him. Kevin grinned broadly, as did most of his plebe classmates. Jeff briefly wondered if Kevin and the others had finally sold out, but soon he was swept up in the emotions and yelled as loudly as the others.

The teams reached the Yacht Basin with the Tigers in a 25-yard lead. Deftly the Tigers launched the boat, and Rock and Mugsy pulled it snug against the small wooden pier while the port side rowers boarded and readied their oars. Once they were settled, the starboard side boarded while Dillingham himself steadied the boat. Finally all was ready, and the Bull stepped quickly into the boat and stood in the rear in front of his seat.

Yelling a huge Marine "Ohh Rah!" he held the guidon aloft and waved it as the Tigers pushed off and surged forward. Twenty-third Company had stroked 20 times before Twenty-second Company cleared the pier. Jeff could see discomfort on some Twenty-second company faces.

"Come on, color-boys!" yelled JP Feeney. "Do it for the Color Midshipman!"

When the boat left the protected harbor for the more open waters of the Severn River, Captain Dillingham sat and held the guidon between his legs. The Company nonparticipant followed the long-boat's progress along the Basin, cheering, until the boat stroked into the open water.

"Now the hard part starts," Gladden announced with a Texas twinkle.

With the steady breeze at their backs, the Tigers made good progress out into the river. At the request of Lieutenant Spencer, the Academy had requested the Navigation Department to man several of the large Yard Patrol motor boats and escort the competitors at a discreet distance. Each YP craft carried additional crew, a supply of life preservers, blankets, and a corpsman, just in case. The Annapolis newspaper reporter and photographer rode in the final YP, along with photographers from the Lucky Bag Yearbook and the Public Affairs Office and several senior officers from the Academy staff.

"Stroke! Stroke! Stroke!" Bull called out loudly as the Tigers pulled water.

Despite the breeze, the river was surprisingly calm, and the run across to the far side was cold but undeniably easy. Twenty-third Company touched ashore on the sandy beach of a private property, which, judging by the size of the house which sat on the hill some 50 yards inland, was owned by a wealthy family. No one had thought to clear the event with the people across the river. As the first rowers jumped ashore and pulled the boat up onto the sand, the back door opened, and an elderly man came running down to the beach, bundled in a heavy woolen jacket and carrying a thermos. He was somewhat short and paunchy, but he smiled mischievously.

"What are you doing, Navy? What are you doing, Navy?" he yelled as he approached.

By this time all the Tigers were ashore, and the boat was completely beached. Dillingham planted the flag forcefully in the cold sand and looked at the man defiantly.

"Academy competition!" he answered. "We'll be out of here in a moment."

The old man ran up to Dillingham and saluted smartly.

"Captain Joseph O'Donnell!" he yelled. "Retired! Class of forty-two!" Dillingham returned his salute and the man opened the thermos. "Here, pass this around!" he said. "You're off the grounds, and it's no fit day to be at sea."

Dillingham took a swig, brightened and passed the thermos to the nearest Tiger.

"Thank you, sir!" he said, beaming. Then he turned and looked seaward into the wind. Twenty-second Company was 50 yards offshore.

Rock Stone moved up alongside the Captain.

"Shouldn't we start, sir?"

Dillingham waited until each of the Tigers had a healthy pull from the thermos. He saluted the old man.

"Good day to you, sir!" he said. He turned to the Tigers. "Get Aboard!" he yelled, and the Tigers launched and boarded the boat. Soon they stroked into the wind. As they passed Twenty-second Company, Bull stood, waved his guidon, and screamed another Marine Corps yell. Keith Spencer laughed at Bull and playfully extended his middle finger at the Tigers. Bull roared.

Despite the stiff breeze and the oncoming chop, the Tigers rowed with enthusiasm. Lieutenant Keith Spencer, once ashore and faced with the choices of either the near-impossible task of catching the Tigers or lingering with the thermos, elected to allow his troops two slugs before reentering the frigid waters. The "Color Midshipman" heartily agreed

Rock Stone heard the Twenty-third Company cheers from midway out into the river. He looked back briefly into the wind and was amazed at the throng that lined the seawall. Nearby, the Patrol boat with the photographers hovered to starboard, cameras snapping. Seagulls wheeled overhead, loudly calling their defiance.

"Ship your oars!" Dillingham yelled, and the Tigers stopped rowing and settled the oars into the boat beside them. They looked at the Bull, who smiled and pointed toward the Patrol boat. "Smile for the camera, Tigers!" he commanded. Bull stood and waved the guidon high overhead. It snapped in the stiff wind. All heads turned to starboard to pose for the photo that would grace the Company Wardroom for years to come.

After a minute the Captain yelled again.

"Okay, slackers. Let's make up that lost time! Stoke like your lives depended on it!" the Tigers complied. The gulls cheered them on.

With nearly a 200-yard lead, the Tiger long-boat cleared the Yacht Basin and stroked for the pier. The crowd noise was deafening. Bull, sensing the moment, removed his cap, sweat shirt, and his undershirt, exposing his massive bear-chested torso and his shiny bald head. As the boat approached the pier, he stood and waved the guidon overhead in two huge arms. The crowd responded even more loudly. Then Bull thrust the guidon skyward and yelled his loudest battle yell. It was a yell of absolute take-no-prisoners victory. It was the scream of the ultimate warrior. It was a sound certain to make Viet Cong wet their pants and run North. On the sea wall Jeff shivered, and it wasn't from the cold.

CHAPTER 9

THE 'PASSION' RETURNS

"Cover for me for a while guys!" asked a worried Jim Merritt after he returned to his room Saturday night following a phone conversation with his fiancee Leslie Taylor Wallace. "Leslie will be here in 40 minutes and I'm going to meet her out on Hospital Point."

"You horny bastard!" Kevin chuckled. "Can't you wait for next weekend?"

Jim's face was troubled. "This meeting was her idea. She said it was an emergency. I asked her what it was all about, but she said she didn't want to discuss it over the phone." He looked at his watch. "It's 2000. She'll be here at 2030. I better get ready." He began to dress in gym gear and sweats.

"It's cold as hell outside," observed Kevin after Jim had slipped on a thin wool stadium jacket over his sweats. "You better bundle up better than that."

"I'll be fine," Jim replied.

"Where do we say you are if someone asks?" asked Rico.

"I went for a jog around the yard to clear my mind. That's partially true."

"No sweat, we'll cover!" Kevin said. Jim Merritt had been feeling low the past several weeks. His mother had been diagnosed with cancer in November, and the doctors had not held out much hope. Each time he talked to her she sounded more weak and prepared for the end. Jim was terribly frustrated. It wasn't like his mother to just give up in a difficult situation, but he had decided she must have known something about her condition he did not.

Because the cancer was terminal, Mrs. Merritt had elected to forego the hospital and stay at home. A day nurse cared for her and administered essential pain medicine. During the evenings Jim's father and siblings pitched in, but as his dad explained it, she hardly ever asked for anything even though she was in obvious pain. Jim's mother was a trooper about those things. Every evening Jim prayed secretly that she'd be able to return to Annapolis during June Week and see him climb the Herndon Monument in a final delirious celebration of the end of Plebe Year. She promised she would do her best to be there, and Jim could always count on her promises. In a strange way Jim was thankful for the Tigers because the daily stress of survival took his mind off his mother's illness at least a little.

"If I'm not back by 2200," he continued, "and there's a bed check, absolutely don't lie for me, okay? I'll take my chances. If I'm caught, I'll restrict."

"No sweat, Jim," Rico said again, only half sarcastically. "Go get yourself laid and forget about the rest of us."

Fifteen minutes later Jim departed the Company area and scampered across Tecumseh Court. It was not unusual for midshipmen to be exercising after hours, even this late on a frigid February evening, so his presence outside wasn't particularly noteworthy to the many midshipmen who hurriedly transited the area on their way to and from the library or various research projects.

He jogged steadily, the icy air stinging his throat and lungs. His path took him directly across Tecumseh Court and down the wide outside stairs to the parking lot of the Midshipman's Store. He then crossed the parking lot and turned northward toward Hospital Point, keeping far out onto Dewey Field where he might not be noticed. Fortunately he was the only jogger who chose to brave the cold and the dark, and as he plowed forward he found himself alone with his thoughts and the sound of his footfalls as they crunched the frozen field.

He crossed the footbridge, almost losing his wool watch cap when a gust of winter caught him near the center. As he topped the bridge, he could see Leslie's car parked in the shadows.

"She must have been flying to have gotten here so quickly," he thought as he sped up. Soon he was smiling, thoughts of impending nearness to the most beautiful woman in the world overriding his concerns and the discomfort of the cold evening.

The lights were out in Leslie's large plush Buick -- a car her mother encouraged her to borrow in the cold icy weather -- but Jim could tell from the shadows that she was sitting in the back seat, waiting. He began to become excited. God, how this woman affected him! Quickly he opened the rear driver-side door and climbed inside. Leslie smiled at him from the far side, and it was plain that she was upset about something.

"I love you Jim Merritt," she said sweetly after he had removed his jacket and settled into the plush seat.

"And I you," he replied.

Leslie looked around outside the car for a moment, then reached for his clothing. "Make love to me, Jim Merritt. I need you badly." Jim smiled. Soon they were coupled.

"Oh, God, I love you!" she said, as her passion mounted. She pressed herself against him and Jim could feel a rippling wave of spasms as she kissed him deeply and moaned repeatedly.

After another minute she broke off their kiss and smiled.

"You are the devil himself, Jim Merritt, and I'd love to do this all night, but we have to talk. " She became immediately serious.

"I have to leave the United States in two weeks to go to London," she said. Jim knew that her father, an important banker from Richmond, often had business in Europe, so he wasn't especially concerned.

"When will you be back?" he asked.

"Not until the summer," she moaned. "Daddy has decided to move to London permanently and he wants Mom and I to follow him. We're going to keep the house in Richmond but only use it when we visit."

"What about your studies?" Jim asked a bit perplexed.

"Dad has signed me up at an exclusive school in London. I'll finish my degree there."

Jim felt nervousness creep into his voice.

"What about us?"

"I still love you, silly," Leslie answered with a girlish giggle. "We'll see each other as often as possible. Maybe you can come to visit in London this summer?" But as she spoke, Jim could detect something in her voice that sounded different to him.

"Your mom agreed to this?" Jim asked skeptically.

"Yes," Leslie answered a bit uncertainly. "She told me that she and Dad had discussed it, and they've decided a move like this might save their marriage."

Jim laughed.

"Rico sure won't be happy."

Leslie echoed Jim's humor.

"Rico will manage without Mom. Besides, I wasn't comfortable with that arrangement. I didn't like being party to her infidelity."

"But that's the way your parents both wanted it," Jim observed.

"Yes, that's what they said. But I never believed either of them."

"What about us really, Leslie?" Jim asked with more seriousness. Leslie looked down at the floor of the car.

"I know what you're asking," she replied. She looked up at Jim, and tears welled up in her eyes. "It's going to be so hard. I don't know. I just don't know."

"Jesus, Leslie! I thought we were going to be married when I graduate?"

Leslie reached out and touched Jim tenderly on the cheek. She smiled.

"We still may be. But that's three years away. A lot can happen."

Jim felt an overwhelming sense of panic. Too many things were going wrong in his life. He needed Leslie and her wonderful and loving stability. He suddenly felt his throat constricting and his heart racing. He seemed to be lost and drowning at the same time, and his sense of control deserted him for the first time in his life.

"Leslie, don't go!" he pleaded in an uncharacteristic squeak, not believing the words he spoke as they came rushing from his mouth. "I'll quit the Academy and we can be married immediately. We can pick a school and live and study together."

Leslie sighed. She twisted and sat facing him.

"No!" she said firmly. "I have to go to London, Jim Merritt. But I promise I'll do everything I can to stay in love with you. You are everything I want right now." Then she straightened. He could see from the vague glistening that broke the darkness on her face that she was crying again.

"Neither of us knows what we'll want in three years," she continued. "We have to agree to try our very best to stay connected, but if it hurts either of us too much, then we have to separate. It's the only fair way to treat each other."

The finality of the words and the terrible empty feelings they brought on, caused his head to spin. He became suddenly desperate and he felt his own eyes well up with tears.

"How could you do this to me, Leslie? I need you!" He tried to hold back the tears, but he found himself blubbering uncontrollably. Almost immediately he felt a simultaneous flush of embarrassment and a wave of anger. Then the most incredible arousal engulfed him, and he reached for Leslie and drew her close. She hugged him tightly as he wept, but Jim found himself beyond the emotions of the moment.

He gripped her panties with one hand and pulled them toward her knees. Without her cooperation the silk material balled up. Leslie became confused and resisted.

"What are you doing Jim?" she asked.

"God I need you!" he said, pulling harder, which only tightened the ball of material. Leslie pushed him away. Jim felt his panic increase.

"No, Jim!" she said firmly. "Not now!"

"Why not?" he pleaded. "I need you so badly," he said. "Please!"

She pulled away quickly.

"No! I can't!" she said in a surprised voice. Jim felt himself became even more desperate. In a flash he could see Leslie and his dreams of their future slipping away, and he didn't know what to do to stop the pain.

"For the love of God, Leslie!" he said in a high-pitched voice that was not his own. "Don't leave me like this! This is happening too fast!" Again he pulled her toward him. This time she pushed herself away with both hands and almost yelled.

"Stop! What's gotten into you?"

Jim moaned and threw his head backward on the seat. Tears flooded down his cheeks. Acutely embarrassment overcame the other conflicting emotions. He took a deep breath and felt a flood of shame. He turned toward Leslie, who had moved toward the far side of the car. She looked frightened. He opened his mouth to speak.

A loud banging on the outside of the frosty window startled them.

"Okay! Open up! Is everything all right in there?" During the emotion and frenzy of the past several minutes they had forgotten to be alert. All the windows of the large Buick had become fogged. The only thing Jim could see outside was a vague shadow of a man standing beside the door.

"It must be the OOD," he whispered fiercely. "Climb into the front seat and start the car, hurry!" Leslie stared at Jim wide-eyed for an instant, then clambered into the front seat, where she immediately began fumbling with her purse. Jim heard her keys jingle reassuringly.

"Hurry up in there!" the voice demanded. "This is an unauthorized area for after hours parking."

Leslie started the car, turned on the lights, wipers and defroster, and started forward slowly. Jim saw her leaning forward, straining to see the road in front of her. In the back Jim quickly wiped the rear window to get a better, if still somewhat blurry, view of the activity outside.

"Stop that car!" a voice yelled, and Jim could now see that the voice indeed belonged to the OOD. He had driven his Government sedan to a position just opposite Leslie's car. The sedan had its motor running and its lights out. The blurred figure of a plebe messenger stood shivering on the road beside the OOD.

As Leslie pulled away, Jim slid to the passenger side of the car and wiped the remainder of the back window furiously in a nearly vain attempt to observe what the OOD was doing. Through the frosty blur he could see figures headed quickly toward the sedan. A chase was beginning.

"What do I do, Jim?" Leslie asked from the front seat, desperation creeping into her voice.

"Don't worry, sweets," Jim said, suddenly feeling uncontrollably elated. He laughed loudly. "I've done this before. Danger is my middle name!"

The road along Hospital Point turns a ninety-degree angle westward almost at a point even with the wooden footbridge.

"Don't touch your breaks!" he said. "Once you get around the curve and out of sight, let the car slow down some!" Leslie looked back at him for a moment. He smiled again, feeling suddenly and inexplicably wonderful. When the car was out of sight of the now pursuing OOD sedan, Jim opened the door. A blast of frigid air entered. "Once I'm out, don't worry about me! Drive straight to the gate. Don't stop for anything. You'll be fine." Judging the speed of the car and his own ability to keep his balance, he leaned outside, checked to see that the OOD was not in sight, then he looked at Leslie.

"I'm terribly sorry about tonight!" he shouted. "I'll make it up to you, I promise! I'll love you always!" With that he leaped from the moving car with a Douglas Fairbanks flourish, slamming the door behind him as he flew out into the dark night.

Jim Merritt was an excellent athlete, but the Buick was traveling at more than 20 miles an hour when he jumped, and the instant he touched the asphalt, he felt his legs give way beneath him, and his right ankle snapped over painfully. Luckily he had the presence of mind to tuck and roll as his momentum carried him along the road, and within a few seconds he came to his feet and scampered, not across the road where he was sure to be seen by the now dangerously close OOD, but rather up the hill on the far side of the road, heading for a convenient tree midway to the top of the steep bank.

He ran up the frozen grass, slipping when he had hardly gotten three steps, and watched Leslie's now-speeding car to ensure that his escape door had closed. It had. Then he checked the curve in the road. He was only midway to the target tree when the OOD's sedan barreled around the curve. Luckily the headlights swept the far side of the road. That fact gained him the several precious seconds he needed. He reached the tree just as the sedan evened with the footbridge. Jim watched with dread. The car slowed. If the OOD suspected he was still on this side of the bridge he was as good as dead.

Over the drone of the engine Jim heard the window of the sedan come down and muffled conversation from inside. Suddenly he caught his breath. In the dull light from a street lamp directly across the road, he saw the path of his uphill flight set out distinctly against the frosty earth. Every step he took stood out in stark darkness on the glistening rime. A large dark smear indicated where he had stumbled. Quickly he looked around. He had better find another hiding position if he was to have any chance of escape at all.

The tree he stood behind and several similar ones had been planted on a slight terrace midway up the hill. He moved out from behind the tree, jogging cautiously along the terrace and working his way back toward the curve in the road. Still the OOD hesitated, and Jim was puzzled. He increased his pace until he was even with the footbridge; then he moved cautiously behind another nearby tree.

One of the rear doors of the sedan opened, and a plebe messenger stepped out into the cold. The plebe wore his thick overcoat, and as Jim watched, he pulled the collar up and tucked his head down into the warmth. White puffs of breath marked every exhalation. The plebe leaned into the sedan, obviously getting instructions, then closed the door with a loud slam, and the OOD hurried off in pursuit of Leslie. Jim fervently hoped by now she was safely within the city of Annapolis, where the Academy Security forces had no jurisdiction.

Jim watched the plebe for a moment while he caught his breath and prepared for the next sprint, which would be much more difficult. The plebe hunkered down into his overcoat, staring at the departing taillights until the sedan turned northward onto the main road and headed toward the gate. Seemingly alone, the plebe checked the footbridge 20 yards away, then made a slow sweep of the area. His gaze circled steadily then stopped when he saw the dark sliding patch on the hill. The messenger stared for a moment, looked quickly down the now empty road, and started toward the upward trail.

Jim moved to the side of the tree away from the messenger, carefully checked the path he would be forced to take, and sprinted downhill. His desperate slip-slide progress made far too much noise in the dark and mostly quiet night. He heard a shout, and almost simultaneously lost his footing on the slippery frost. His feet flew out from under him and he fell onto the frozen ground in a heap, landing on his back. Luckily he had a great deal of downward momentum, and he continued sliding rapidly toward the road in a prone position.

As he slid, he saw the plebe messenger move hesitantly in his direction. Then he paused, and deducing Jim's escape plan, the messenger ran forward not toward Jim, but rather diagonally across the road toward the bridge.

"Halt!" the plebe yelled, but Jim wasn't about to take orders from a fellow plebe, not when his future freedom was on the line.

At the bottom of the hill Jim gathered his feet under him in a quick motion and stood. Without hesitation, he sprinted across the road toward the bridge, deciding immediately that it was going to be very close, but realizing also that he didn't have much choice. The penalty for a plebe being out on Hospital Point with a female during non-liberty hours was too severe to consider. The penalty for all of the above plus running from the OOD was worse. But penalties only mattered if he got caught. If Jim could escape successfully, he avoided all the demerits.

Jim had felt a similar rush of excitement the previous October when he had escaped the clutches of the OOD after a clandestine meeting with Leslie on the Severn River seawall. That time he had led what seemed to have been every member of the Academy watch organization and several asshole volunteers on a merry chase throughout several wings of Bancroft Hall. He had won that encounter, but only barely. It had cost him a broken wrist and a severely bruised knee. That incident had also started a series of completely blown-out-of-proportion stories about the *Passionate Plebe*, the hero of every midshipman and the nemesis of the Academy system. He laughed loudly as he realized that he would get to the bridge ahead of his pursuer.

In seconds he was at the entrance to the bridge, skidding slightly on a slick patch of ice. His pursuer, slowed by the overcoat and uniform shoes, arrived an instant too late. Jim let out a loud yell of relief as his first foot thudded on the wooden planks. He was going to win another battle with the system. The legend of the Passionate Plebe would be reborn! He was invincible!

Two steps later Jim heard a startled, desperate yell and a loud splash, and his self-satisfaction evaporated in an instant. He stopped, skidding on the wood and almost falling.

The messenger, his slick uniform shoes slipping on the same patch of ice that had momentarily inconvenienced Jim, had overrun the entrance to the bridge and had tripped and tumbled headlong into the icy water. Jim had no idea how deep the water was, but with a heavy overcoat and uniform on, his classmate would in serious trouble. Jim retraced his steps, sprinting to the end of the bridge. A streetlight illuminated the scene. It was not encouraging.

The water was deeper than Jim had imagined, and he could see the plebe struggling fiercely to make his way toward shore. Jim surveyed the situation and realized that he could not reach the plebe from the sea wall. However, Jim noticed that the underside of the bridge was supported by piling which was cross-braced in several locations. He took off his wool stadium jacket, discarded it beside the bridge, climbed down onto the nearest crosspiece, and straddled the member. He was only two feet from the water's dark and forbidding surface. Patches of icy slush floated everywhere. The light and the waves caused by the messenger's struggles made the slush twinkle and whisper eerily.

"Over here!" Jim yelled, and he leaned outward toward the struggling classmate.

The plebe saw Jim and reached in his direction, slapping the water desperately with repeated frenzied motions. Their hands were only inches apart, but the plebe seemed to be rapidly losing his strength and getting no closer. Gripping the freezing timber firmly with one hand, Jim stretched out to the limit of his reach. He grabbed the classmate firmly by the left wrist and pulled him toward the bridge. The plebe moaned in agony as Jim clamped his hands on the timber.

Jim knew he had to get the plebe out of the water quickly, but he also knew that he could never lift him and his soaking wet clothes. Deftly Jim began unbuttoning the overcoat. The final five buttons were under water and Jim had to dip his hands rapidly and repeatedly into the icy water to get them undone. With much struggling the overcoat came loose, and Jim grabbed the sleeve and tugged. The classmate, sensing what Jim was doing, groggily shrugged off first one sleeve, then the other. He moaned as each motion brought a wave of icy water washing against his face. Jim lifted the wet coat out of the water and hefted it with two hands onto the seawall where it landed with a dull splat.

Without the bulky overcoat, the plebe was much lighter. Balancing himself on the timber and gripping the deck with one hand, Jim grabbed the plebe by the wrists again. Straining mightily, Jim lifted the plebe far enough out of the water so that he could straddle the timber on his belly. Next Jim pulled each leg up out of the water, and for the moment the plebe was safe from drowning. The messenger was almost incoherent from the frigid dunking. Jim looked around quickly. No help was in sight, and the Hospital was several hundred meters away up the hill Jim had only recently vacated.

Slowly and painfully Jim lifted the almost completely helpless classmate and hoisted him from behind onto the bridge deck. The effort took several minutes, and when he had finished, the classmate lay on his stomach, hardly moving. Jim was almost completely soaked by the effort and he began shivering violently as he stood above his classmate deciding what to do next.

He grabbed the plebe by the shoulders, spun him over, and removed his wet uniform jacket, shirt, and undershirt. He tossed those into a ball beside the overcoat. The bare-chested classmate moaned again and shivered fiercely. Jim went to the end of the bridge and returned with his wool stadium jacket. He wrapped the warm, dry jacket around the classmate, zipped it tightly up to his neck, and pulled the wool hood up around his head and ears. Strangely, he noticed that the plebe smelled distinctly of stale salty water. It was not a pleasant smell. Jim laughed. The messenger's eyes were partially open, but he didn't react.

"You stink, classmate!" Jim exclaimed, laughing again. "But don't worry. I'll get you help!"

Jim hefted the plebe into a sitting position against one of the guardrail posts and worked the body upright until it leaned against the guardrail. Completely exhausted and in shock, the plebe was almost no help. Next Jim let the body fall forward over his right shoulder, and straightening, he lifted the plebe into the air. Grunting, Jim started forward as rapidly as he could, following the road. The distance to the Hospital Emergency Room was considerably longer if he followed the winding road, but Jim doubted he could negotiate the steep hill in his condition.

His progress was slow but steady, and the effort of the motion kept him somewhat warm. Several times Jim tried to talk to the plebe, but all he could discern were mumbled, incoherent replies. Jim kept up the talk as he struggled along the Hospital Point Road and turned north onto the Hospital Complex entry road. He wondered briefly why the OOD hadn't returned, but dismissed that thought. He really didn't want to confront authority in his present condition.

The hilly entry road leading to the Hospital seemed impossibly long and steep, but Jim didn't hesitate. One-foot-in-front-of-the-other he struggled upward, his shoulder aching desperately. Midway up the hill he began singing *Stand Navy Down the Field*. He had no idea why. He arrived at the entrance to the Emergency Room after what seemed like hours, almost totally without energy. His body steamed from the effort.

As he bumped open the glass door with a shoulder, he could see several nurses joking behind the reception desk. They looked up, startled, as he lumbered inside. The nearest, a pretty blonde, reacted first.

"What happened?" she asked coming rapidly in his direction.

"Fell . . . in water . . . by bridge," Jim struggled out the words.

"Put him on the floor, quickly!" she said. Jim leaned over to comply, but he stumbled as his legs gave way. He moaned loudly and he and his classmate fell to the deck. As he fell, he managed to reach an arm under the plebe's head, saving it from damage, but yelped as the plebe's head and his arm struck the deck.

Rolling onto his back, his arm still under the classmate's head, Jim lay still. The ceiling swam around him. He could sense activity within inches as nurses ministered to the classmate, and at one point he noticed that his sweat pants and shorts had been removed and that he was covered with a blanket from the waist down. But he could not stay focused on what was happening.

Corpsmen and nurses lifted him onto a stretcher and carried him away. Someone -- he thought it must have been a doctor -- took his temperature, examined his eyes, felt his extremities carefully, and ordered additional blankets. For the next several minutes, Jim drifted into and out of consciousness, unsure where he was.

After 20 minutes his brain came slowly aware, and he realized that he had recovered sufficiently to take stock of his condition. His feet and legs were severely chilled but rapidly warming. His hands were mostly numb and stung with the feeling of a hundred needles piercing the skin. When he raised his hands, he noticed wooden splinters embedded in both palms, as well as several deep scratches, and an ugly slice across his left palm. He had no idea how he had cut himself. He began rubbing his arms vigorously to restore circulation and found that his right shoulder ached with every motion.

After another few minutes he felt well enough to sit up in bed and begin fumbling with the exposed splinters. He looked at his watch, -- it was almost 2300. If there was a bed check, he would be in serious trouble. He realized that he needed to return to Bancroft Hall before anyone asked too many questions. He slipped his feet over the end of the bed and put his two bare feet on the tile floor. Steadying himself with one hand on the bed, he tried to stand. His legs were incredibly tired and would not function correctly. Leaning backward so that he half-sat on the mattress, he shook first one thigh muscle then the other to remove the lethargy. He then stood with some difficulty and looked around.

The first thing he noticed was that he was naked under the light green cotton hospital gown. How had they gotten his taken off without his noticing? Where was everyone now? Remembering everything that had happened more clearly, he began to panic. He moved to the curtain that separated his bed from its neighbors and carefully peeked out. The room was more than 30 feet square and illuminated harshly by banks of overhead fluorescent lights. The room contained several pieces of medical gear as well as three other partitioned spaces, all of which were uncurtained and unoccupied. He could hear considerable activity in a neighboring room, but he was presently alone. He looked around quickly but did not see any storage locker where the staff could have put his clothes.

Cautiously he moved to the main door and peeked into the passageway. Again he saw no one, but the activity next door was hectic. He could hear voices, and the clank of instruments, and the scuffling activity of people moving quickly about their business. He moved into the passageway, heading for the reception desk, thinking he could bluff his way back into his clothes and out of this place.

The only person on duty in the entry lobby was an older Lieutenant nurse who read from a paperback novel. He walked cautiously to the desk, his feet making almost no sound on the tile floor. The nurse didn't notice him.

"Excuse me ma'am," he said, leaning on the counter and trying to sound professional. The nurse looked up startled and hurriedly put down her book.

"May I help you?" she asked smiling.

"Yes," he replied. "I need my clothes so I can get back to Bancroft Hall."

"Aren't you the man who brought in the near-drowning victim?" she asked puzzled.

"I suppose so," he answered.

She smiled again. "Well I'm sure Doctor Schuerholz doesn't intend to release you until tomorrow."

"Well, I'm fine now," Jim replied, "and I really need to get back."

The nurse glanced over his shoulder and spoke.

"He wants to leave us already, Carolyn." Jim turned his head to see the cute blonde nurse he remembered from earlier standing at the passageway entrance. She had an enormous smile on her face and her eyes sparkled with mischief. Jim wondered briefly why she was staring so intently, and suddenly remembered his physical status.

"Oh, shit!" he said, grabbing the back of his gown and spinning around in one motion. The blonde nurse laughed.

"You're not supposed to be out of bed yet," she said half scoldingly, coming in his direction.

"He's ready to go home," the desk nurse announced.

"Well that'll be for the doctor to decide," said the blonde, and she walked up to Jim, took him by the arm, and steered him back toward the passageway. Jim noticed from her shoulder-boards that she was an Ensign. Jim glanced back at the desk nurse and used one hand to hold the back of the gown in place as he walked away. She laughed.

As they passed the room where all the activity was ongoing Jim paused.

"How is he?" he asked.

"He'll be fine, thanks to you," she answered. "Did you really singlehandedly fish him out of the inlet and carry him all the way here on your shoulder?"

"Yeah," Jim said hesitatingly. "I guess so."

"Was it also you that removed his wet clothes down by the bridge, and gave him your jacket?"

"Yeah, . . . I mean, yes ma'am!"

"Well," she said, laughing and squeezing his arm while steering him again toward the examining room. "You are a hero. You most probably saved his life."

"Ah, has anybody been by to check on him? He's probably on duty, and somebody will wonder what's happened?"

"The Academy Officer of the Day has been notified, and so has the Office of the Superintendent. Doctor Schuerholz has put off any visitors or questioning until tomorrow."

"What about me, ma'am? If I don't get back, I'm going to be in serious trouble."

"Already taken care of," the nurse replied. "Your Company Officer was notified. He'll be here in the morning when we release you." She smiled again devilishly. "Unless there are complications and you have to stay another day."

Jim laughed.

"The thought of avoiding Plebe Year for a single day is almost too much to consider, but I really do need to get back. Tomorrow is a special day. Couldn't I just bug out of here now, ma'am?"

The nurse, whose black and yellow name plate announced her name as Horne, looked disappointed.

"Listen," she said, "I've only been commissioned for a few months, and I definitely don't bite. You can stop the ma'am stuff. I don't like it, and beside, you and I are nearly the same age." She steered him back to his bed, and he climbed in, careful to face away from her when he did. She laughed again and patted him on the arm.

"You should be proud of yourself," she said. "What you did was incredible. I'll tell the doctor you're up and about, then I'll be back later to tuck you in." She winked, turned, and departed quickly.

Doctor Schuerholz proved to be a good-looking, dark-haired young internist who was brought up in nearby Baltimore. He arrived at Jim's bedside minutes later.

"Well, well," he said. "The hero lives! It was a great thing you did. You probably saved that young man's life."

"Yes, sir," Jim said. "About that . . . " The doctor patted him on the arm and laughed.

"Your devotion to duty is commendable," he said. "But you're going to stay here for observation until tomorrow, so settle back and enjoy the attention. Is there anything we can do for you?"

Jim thought for a moment, then smiled.

"Yes, sir. You know, it was such a frightening experience. I'm still a little shaken. Do you think you could send Nurse Horne back to keep me company for a while?" Doctor Schuerholz laughed loudly, revealing perfect white teeth and a devilish smile.

"Yes, I think we could arrange that." He paused and winked at Jim. "I think she'll insist."

The next morning the day nurse woke him at 0600 at his request. Carefully ensuring that no one was watching, Jim dropped to the deck to perform his morning workout. Because of the pain in his hands and the stiffness throughout his body, he was not able to do more than 50 push-ups and 100 sit-ups. When he finished, he felt refreshed and went in search of a nurse and the shower.

At 0700 Jim had a breakfast of tasteless hospital food and put on the sweat-gear he had worn the previous night. The clothes had been laundered by the nursing staff, and they smelled sweetly of fabric softener. One of the day nurses escorted him to a small conference room. The only other occupant was the plebe messenger he had saved the previous night. The classmate brightened as he entered.

"How are you doing?" Jim asked as he reached out a hand in greeting.

"Still picking pieces of seaweed from my hair," he replied. "And I'm not sure my body will ever function again."

"Maybe you should tell the nurses," Jim answered. "They might be able to help."

The classmate, a small dark-haired midshipman, laughed loudly and introduced himself as John Schuyler from Connecticut. They had hardly exchanged greetings when visitors arrived.

The entourage was led by the Officer of the Day, who happened to be the infamous Lieutenant Commander LaPointe, commonly known around the Brigade as "The Nose" for his outrageous and bulbous appendage. LaPointe did not look at all happy as he glared at Jim and tossed his hat on the conference table in front of him. Captain Dillingham and Rock Stone followed LaPointe into the room. They both smiled and greeted Jim warmly. No one sat before Doctor Schuerholz entered from a different doorway escorting a smiling Lieutenant Commander Jim did not recognize. Introductions were made quickly, and everyone settled around the table. Jim found himself flanked by Rock and the Bull and facing LaPointe. Doctor Schuerholz sat at the head of the table, and the other officer -- who when he introduced himself to Jim, studied him particularly closely -- was named Hanes. Lieutenant Commander Hanes was the Commandant's Chief-of-Staff.

LaPointe glared at Jim for a long moment before beginning officiously.

"This is a preliminary investigation into the causes of the accident which occurred on the evening of 25 February 1968, in which a Messenger of the Watch, Midshipman Fourth-class John Delano Schuyler, was knocked overboard into Dorsey Creek and almost drowned. I will determine the preliminary facts and make a recommendation for further disposition to Academy Administration. Since this is potentially a serious offense, my recommendation may be for a full Courts Martial.

"What!" Captain Dillingham exploded. "Are you out of your mind?"

LaPointe looked calmly at Dillingham.

"I will remind you, *Captain,* that I am a senior officer, *and* that I am in charge of this investigation."

"Yes, sir!" Bull said, his eyes narrowing, but not in the least bit calmed. "I am so reminded!"

"Very well," LaPointe said, addressing Jim directly.

"Were you on Hospital Point last night when I came searching for illegally parked individuals?"

"Don't answer that!" Dillingham shouted to Jim, then he turned to LaPointe and Lieutenant Commander Hanes. "That's entrapment. If you didn't catch him or recognize him, then you don't know who it was. No one, not even a plebe, can be forced to incriminate himself in this Navy."

"He was out parked on Hospital Point poking a young lady, "LaPointe continued sarcastically. "I caught them. They sped away. He tried to escape over the footbridge and knocked my messenger into the water -- perhaps on purpose -- almost killing him."

"Excuse me," Doctor Schuerholz interrupted loudly, "but this midshipman braved sub-freezing water to rescue another human being who surely would have drowned. He risked his life, pulled that person from the water, ministered to him, then carried the unconscious and person more than 300 yards in the freezing cold and dark, uphill to the Hospital. What the hell is happening here?" The doctor looked crossly at Lieutenant Commander Hanes, who remained silent, but intently listened.

"If he hadn't struggled with the messenger, none of that would have happened," LaPointe said. "I'm glad he has a conscience, but it came just a bit too late for me. I think we're dealing with attempted manslaughter."

"You must be out of your mind!" Dillingham exploded again. "I won't stand for this!"

"You have no choice!"LaPointe stated calmly. "The rules are clear."

"This is an outrage!" Bull shouted, this time aiming *his* words at Hanes.

'Excuse me, sir!" Midshipman Fourth-class Schuyler interrupted, "but that's not true!"

"What!" LaPointe shouted, turning on the plebe.

"I did not struggle with anyone! I slipped on a patch of ice and fell into the water on my own. Classmate Merritt came off the footbridge to rescue me." Jim stared at John Schuyler, who did not return his gaze, but instead stared directly into the glaring eyes of Lieutenant Commander LaPointe.

"You're lying!" LaPointe shouted. "Are you telling me that this . . . " he said indicating Jim with a contemptuous wave of his hand, "is not the person you were sent to watch for?"

"Sir, I have no idea if he is or not. The back of the car in question was steamed and I couldn't see anything. I also did not see anyone get out of the car. And Midshipman Merritt came to my rescue from the Academy side, *not* the Hospital side."

"So you're convinced this is not the person we were chasing?"

"Sir, I cannot say for certain!" Schuyler stated boldly.

"There!" Dillingham barked. "That proves it! He's not the person you want."

But LaPointe wasn't finished. His face turned dark and his eyes flashed at Schuyler, who after all had seen thousands of such rages during Plebe Year and wasn't particularly afraid or impressed.

"You damn midshipman are all alike!"LaPointe exploded. "You think this is all a game! All of you are willing to sacrifice your personal honor and break the sacred code of Annapolis just to save a buddy. I won't stand for this!"

"Midshipman Merritt did not shove me or push me into that water, Commander!" Schuyler boldly shouted. "That's the truth!"

"Bastard!" LaPointe spat out the word, then he looked at Merritt.

"Were you the person in that car, Mister?"

"Don't answer that!" Bull commanded.

LaPointe stood and leaned over the table toward Jim.

"Were you in that car?" Jim stared into LaPointe's eyes.

"Sir, even if I were, I would not answer."

"I think this case is closed, Commander," Hanes said with finality, grabbing LaPointe gently by the arm and sitting him back down.

"Son," he said addressing Jim, "I heard your story from the Medical staff, and I went down to the footbridge to see the scene of the rescue. Frankly, I am amazed you were able to do what you did. I am recommending you for a bravery award -- probably a Navy Commendation Medal. Congratulations!" He held out a hand, smiling broadly at Jim. Confused, Jim took the proffered hand and shook it.

"You're a bonafide hero, son!"

"I won't stand for this!" LaPointe said boldly. "This is a mockery of the Honor Code."

"Well, I'm glad that's finished!" Doctor Schuerholz announced standing. "Midshipmen Merritt and Schuyler will be released at 1300. I'll have our duty driver take them to Bancroft Hall and deliver the Medical Reports to Administration." With that he left the room and everyone else stood.

"Great job, Merritt!" Bull said pounding him on the back. "Are you sure you don't want to be a Marine?" Jim and Rock Stone laughed. Rock held out a hand to Jim.

"What the hell," he said. "Hundredth Night is only a day away, and you'd be my first choice for spooning anyway." Jim took the hand and shook it firmly. "Good work, Jim. You're a credit to Tiger Company."

John Schuyler remained behind after the others had departed, and he and Jim chatted briefly.

"So," Schuyler said after a few minutes. "Are you the mythic figure we've been hearing about all year?"

"Huh?"

Steve smiled. "You know exactly what I mean," he said. "Are you the 'Passionate Plebe'?"

Jim laughed.

"Can't say," he replied.

"It doesn't matter," Schuyler replied. "I can tell from the twinkle in your eyes."

As they passed the front desk on their way back to their rooms, the duty nurse looked up.

"Excuse me," she said. "Which of you is Midshipman Merritt?"

"I am!" Jim replied. The nurse took an envelope from the desk and handed it to him with a smile.

"Nurse Horne asked me to be sure to give this to you," she said.

"Thanks," Jim replied, opening the envelope. A note inside, written in fancy script, said, *Carolyn Horne 577-0987. Please call!!!!!!* Jim laughed and suddenly felt a smugness and sense of well-being he didn't think he would ever feel again after the previous night. Life was certainly strange, and he seemed to leading the most charmed existence he had ever imagined. He tucked the note into his jumper pocket and turned to Schuyler. "I'm a very luck guy, Johnny boy. I must live right!"

THE MISSION OF THE UNITED STATES NAVAL ACADEMY

To develop midshipmen morally, mentally, and physically, and to imbue them with the highest ideals of duty, honor, and loyalty in order to provide graduates who are dedicated to a career of naval service and have potential for future development in mind and character to assume the highest responsibilities of command, citizenship, and government.

From *Reef Points*

CHAPTER 10

THE BIG EVENT

Jim Merritt returned to Bancroft Hall on Sunday afternoon half expecting a hero's welcome, but the word of his adventure hadn't spread as yet. After he had regaled his room about the events of the previous evening -- leaving out of course the part about his ungentlemanly conduct, the car chase, and hiding on the Hospital Point hill in the dark -- what he received mostly was sympathy.

"Gee, Jim!" Kevin said. "I'm really sorry about Leslie. You two were such a good couple."

"Well," Jim said with far more enthusiasm than he felt, "things can still work out."

"Not a chance, Merritt!" Rico interjected. "Face it! She's got money, an important father, a well-bred education, and she's hot as a pistol. I hate to be the bearer of bad tidings, but you're history. Some effete son of a viscount who wears expertly tailored suits, plays polo, and lives in some drafty, moss-covered castle his great-great-grandfather stole from the peasants, is gonna latch onto her, charm her into the sack with stories of the royal family and vacations on the Riviera, and she'll be Mrs. Viscount. Shit! Some poor boy from middle class Texas family ain't got a damn thing to offer her that she can't get in spades in Merry Olde England. I'm really sorry buddy, but it's over, and you might as well accept it."

Jeff studied Rico for a long moment. Rico had a painful sense of honesty that sometimes grated on his nerves, but Rico was seldom wrong about matters of the heart. Both Jeff and Jim knew instinctively that Rico was right. What the hell did Jim have to offer someone like Leslie? She'd never be happy married to a Navy pilot and moving every couple years. Even so, Jeff felt sorry for Jim, and even happier that he had sweet and faithful Kate.

A weight seemed to lift from Jim's shoulders. He realized that Rico's words and the freezing water had accelerated the grieving period, and he felt much better. Jim smiled slowly at Rico, reached dramatically into his pocket, and removed the note Ensign Carolyn Horne. He handed it to Rico.

Rico read it quickly and beamed.

"Right on! Merritt there's hope for you yet!" Rico handed the note to Kevin and BJ, then pounded Jim on the back in celebration.

"Is she a nurse?" Kevin asked.

"And an Ensign!" Jim replied smugly.

"You lucky bastard!" BJ added. "Does she have any friends?"

Well wishing was short-lived, however, because ten minutes later Kevin reminded the room that it was time to get ready for restriction marching. Jim Merritt, like every plebe in Twenty-third company except Willy Simpson, was restricting for the foreseeable future. Despite Mugsy's strenuous protests and threats of physical violence against his classmates, Captain Dillingham had wholeheartedly endorsed a first-class policy of bogus room and uniform inspections for every plebe, Jim and his roommates had accumulated more than 70 demerits each. They were a lucky room. Across the passageway Jeff and his roommates were each nearing 120 demerits. Hundredth Night seemed the only hope for plebe salvation.

To reduce the demerit total at Annapolis, offenders restricted on weekends or holidays. The demerit total lessened by five-per-hour for Main Office musters, and ten-per-hour for the twice-a-day 60-minute afternoon marching detail. Restriction started promptly during liberty hours at 1300 with the first marching exercise, followed by another march at 1500. Afterward restriction musters were every hour in the Uniform of the Day in front of the Main Office.

The weather on Dewey Field was sunny but extremely cold, and a stiff breeze flowed from the west with stinging vigor. Jeff Polk hefted his rifle onto his shoulder in unison with the other Tiger plebes, and waited for the leader of the restriction exercise -- himself a restrictee -- to begin the punitive marching. Because there were so many of them -- and as additional humiliation for the Tiger Company -- the Twenty-third Company plebes formed their own marching platoon separate from the other restrictors. Daly and Linehan, marching unhappily with the lead of the three platoons, and no doubt fuming over their restrictions, hardly acknowledged their presence. Jeff waited at loose attention, his rifle sitting haphazardly on his right shoulder, facing the biting wind and the First-class in charge. As he waited, Jeff found an involuntary wind-induced tear rolling down his cheek. He shrugged his shoulder against his chin to wipe it away.

"Okay, fellow restrictors!" snapped the firstie, a tall, thin individual who obviously didn't want to be out on Dewey Field in the bitter cold any more than the rest of them. "Before we start, I will relate to you a painful lesson I learned several weeks ago. It's one you underclass should carry with you into first-class year. It's this: If you're ever *really* drunk and almost late getting back from liberty, don't think you can park your car -- which you're not supposed to have yet -- on the brick walkway in front of Tecumseh thinking you'll just move it in the morning and nobody will notice." He laughed at his own foolishness. "I guarantee you *will* be discovered!" The restrictors laughed with him.

"Okay," he continued. "Everybody pull up your collars and snuggle down into your coats because in the next 40 minutes the Academy expects us to freeze our asses off."

He spun around so that he was also facing the wind. He shivered.

"Shit!" he exclaimed over his shoulder. "Let's get this circle jerk rolling so we can warm up. Last hour we marched up and down Dewey field in a north-south direction, which was murder. This hour I'm going to exercise my ample leadership abilities and march up and down Dewey Field in an east-west direction which will also be murder. Damn I hate this!"

With that he waved an arm in the air and yelled cavalry style, "Forward, . . . Yoooo!" The groups surged forward, stumbling slightly at first, but gradually spacing themselves correctly and attaining the trudging rhythm of reluctant men under considerable strain. The firstie counted cadence for several paces, then he yelled over his shoulder, "One of you Tiger plebes continue the cadence please!"

Reb Ramsey, who was a cadence master, having learned several interesting ribald marching rhythms from his Army Lieutenant Colonel father and from life on military bases around the country, immediately began a loud sing-song counting chant. After 50 yards Reb started a marching song which had been his father's personal favorite. It was one Reb always sang with gusto.

"Oh it's beer, beer, beer, that makes me want to cheer,
in the Corps, in the Corps.
Oh it's beer, beer, beer, that makes me want to cheer,
in the Quartermaster's, Quartermaster's Corps."

The Tiger plebes, already familiar with the words, joined Reb, and soon some small measure of the chill departed Jeff and his classmates as they warmed to the melody. Immediately after the first verse had finished, Kevin O'Reilly yelled out, "Whiskey!" and the plebes began the second verse.

"Oh it's whiskey, whiskey, whiskey, that makes me feel so frisky,
in the Corps, in the Corps.
Oh it's whiskey, whiskey, whiskey, that makes me feel so frisky,
in the Quartermaster's, Quartermaster's Corps."

The first-class in charge drifted backward toward the Tiger plebe platoon, grinning. "I like it so far," he said loudly. "Any other verses?"

"Rum!" yelled Patrick Mulvaney, and the plebes continued.

"Oh it's rum, rum, rum, that makes me want to come,
to the Corps, to the Corps.
Oh it's rum, rum, rum, that makes me want to come,
to the Quartermaster's, Quartermaster's Corps."

After the sixth verse Rico Guevarra yelled out, "Hot roast duck!"

"Oh it's hot roast duck, that makes me want -- a sandwich,
in the Corps, in the Corps.
Oh it's hot roast duck, that makes me want -- a sandwich
in the Quartermaster's, Quartermaster's Corps."

The firstie laughed when the plebes had finished, and resumed his marching leadership. By this time the platoons had completed two laps of the field and were headed again into the teeth of the breeze. A brisk gust of winter caught them as they turned east, and the firstie yelled, "Damn!" Jeff could see him look quickly around and come to a decision. Instead of marching downwind he led the platoons toward the rear side of Michelson and Chauvenet Halls. A broad stairway led down from the wide patio that connected the two buildings. Here at this level were the well-equipped student research labs. More importantly, the restrictees were hidden from sight. Since today was Sunday, no instructors were in the facility, but the doors were open to allow midshipmen to conduct after-hours research.

In the lee of the academic buildings the weather was much less hostile.

"Platoons Halt!" the firstie yelled, and the three groups came to a stop near the stairs. "Left Face!" The platoons turned toward him. "Port arms!" Every midshipman removed his rifle from his tired shoulder and held it loosely with two hands at his chest. The firstie then turned to the Tiger platoon.

"First rank of plebes, front and center!" he barked. Hank Butkowski, Hans Roudolph, and Doug Goto ran forward, carrying their rifles. The firstie looked them over. He pointed to the far northernmost corner of Chauvenet Hall. "One of you march to that corner and post so you can see if anyone approaches from the north." He pointed in the opposite direction. "One of you post at the far southernmost corner of Michelson Hall and watch for intruders." He pointed out onto Dewey Field. "The third plebe will march on the field 20 yards away and watch above us on the patio. Each of you sound off if anyone in uniform heads this way, and return to your place in ranks. Got that? I'll send reliefs in five minutes." Hank, Hans, and Henry chopped away.

Once the three plebes were stationed, the firstie addressed the first platoon, which was composed entirely of upper-class. "Okay, break formation and huddle together for warmth in the entryway to the labs, but stay close by in case we have to form up quickly." The upper-class cheered and ran for the doors and the comfort of the interior. The firstie then addressed the remaining two platoons -- one was composed of assorted plebes from the other Thirty-five Companies, and the other was the Tiger platoon.

"You guys stay in loose formation and at ease, but stay alert." He turned to the Tigers. "Relieve your companymates every five minutes. If there's any hint of detection, start marching and inform me immediately." He grinned. "Meanwhile, I'll be inside." He winked at them. "After all, the first platoon is my responsibility too, and I need to check up on them to make sure they don't wander." With that he turned and headed down the stairs and into the waiting warmth.

The Tiger plebes maintained ragged ranks while crowding together for warmth. Jeff stood next to Jim Merritt as he related his self-edited story of the rescue.

"Well, wait a minute," Jeff asked. "What were you doing jogging out to Hospital Point on a Saturday night anyway?"

"Staying in shape?" Jim answered with a smile.

"Yeah, right!" Jeff answered sarcastically. "So, you were running on Hospital Point in the freezing cold. Something happened. A plebe messenger *mysteriously* fell in the drink. You pulled the poor classmate out, and now you're a hero? That doesn't make any sense!"

"It didn't happen that way," Jim said cautiously, "and I'm not admitting anything further." Jeff Polk was after all the Plebe Honor Representative, and it was best, just in case, that he knew as little as possible.

"Is The Nose gonna fry the messenger for lying?" asked Jeff.

"He didn't lie!" Jim stated firmly.

"Well, it seems as if he didn't exactly tell the truth either," Jeff replied. "It's still an Honor offense."

"Hey Jeff!" Kevin interrupted. "Jim saved the guy's life. What do you expect?"

"I honestly don't know," Jeff answered. "But it sickens me how people play pretty fast and loose with the Honor Code."

"The Honor Code's bullshit!" Rico stated loudly. Every plebe was shocked to instant silence. The Honor Code was the sacred creed by which all midshipmen and Naval Officers are expected to model their lives. *"A midshipman shall not lie, cheat, or steal!"* Jeff recited the Code to himself as he pondered Rico's remark.

"What do you mean?" Jeff asked him cautiously.

"Every midshipman violates the Code. It's all a matter of interpretation. The Code is too black-and-white when life is absolutely gray and fuzzy!"

"I don't lie!" Jeff said firmly. "I believe in the Code!"

"Bullshit!" Rico replied. "I saw you copy Kevin's class notes to help you prepare for the last leadership test."

"So?" Jeff answered indignantly. "Copying class notes is allowed."

"You copied the notes because you didn't do them yourself. That's against the regs."

"I had notes!" Jeff answered fiercely. "Mine weren't as good as Kevin's."

"But you still copied Kevin's because it gave you an advantage you didn't have on your own," Rico observed.

"But that's not illegal!"

"Oh, yes!" Rico replied. "In the strictest sense it is. Listen, two months ago Henry Brandis asked me the menu for a noon meal and I screwed it up by substituting the evening's vegetable for the noon one. I did that because I had only glanced at the main course and assumed that the vegetable would be the same. Brandis asked me if I had studied my rates, and I said I had. You could say I lied just a little, but I wasn't going to admit it. I took my punishment for the screw-up, but telling the exact truth would have been incredibly stupid and you better believe that I check the menu thoroughly now. Should I turn myself in and risk expulsion for a misstatement?"

Rico looked at Jeff very hard for a moment, then he laughed.

"You know Jeff, you're enthusiastic about your Honor responsibilities, and that's great. But don't miss the big picture. Open your eyes. Life is full of lies, and honor is strictly a matter of degree. There is no perfectly honest man anywhere." Jeff started to protest, but Rico waved a hand to stop him. "There isn't! Trust me! Just think about it, and you'll agree."

Rico turned to Tommy Poole, who had been almost deathly quiet for the last week as his particular honor fate approached.

"There isn't a plebe in the Company who thinks Tommy Poole is dishonorable and that this photo-in-the-hat incident isn't the most bullshit thing in the world. But there are plenty of upper-class and officers who might genuinely disagree with our opinion. Who's right? Nobody! Everybody!"

Rico was on a roll now. As he boldly continued, every plebe listened carefully.

"Honor *is* a game. We believe that liars, cheaters, and thieves do not belong in our club. And when we hear about violations, we are disgusted and cheer the expulsions. We love to keep our image clean. But inside we're just happy we weren't caught because every day we live on the very edge of dishonor ourselves." The plebes remained quiet for a long time, pondering Rico's words.

Jeff answered smugly.

"Well, the Honor System may be confusing for you, Rico, but I'm convinced of my own ability to recognize violations and to stay honorable."

"Then you better put that rifle back on your shoulder, buddy-boy, and march your ass out onto the field!" Rico blurted. "And I guess that means you're also gonna have to turn in the entire restriction group *and* all your companymates for honor offenses." A general din arose among the plebes. Rico continued "Because I for one have no intention of speaking up when the firstie reports to the Main Office that we served our time this hour. We restricted all right, but we ain't marching, are we butt-head? And if you don't think that's not just a pubic-hair this side of dishonest, then you need to examine your own hypocritical -- but honorable -- standards."

Jeff pulled back slightly and considered what Rico had just said. He could also see several of his companymates looking around nervously and fingering their rifle barrels, obviously wondering if they were in deep trouble. Many of the remaining plebes stared hard at Jeff, and he knew they were worried that he *would* report them like he had Linehan and Daly. He saw Ramsey eyeing him.

"Don't you even think about it!" Reb said with vehemence. But Jeff continued to ponder.

What Rico suggested was silly. They weren't marching because they were following orders, and if they were caught they would be at the most guilty of bending the regulations. This wasn't an honor violation, was it? Jeff found himself unsure. He looked at Rico, who smiled enigmatically.

The final restriction muster on Sunday, 26 February 1968 was at 1700. The Tiger plebes lined up eagerly outside Main Office waiting for the first-class Midshipman Officer of the Watch to call the roll and release them.

"Well, well," the firstie said in a thick Texas accent. "This looks like a mighty anxious group of plebes. What's the matter boys, something going on? How many days to Hundredth Night anyway?"

The Tiger plebes answered with a roar.

"None, sir!" The firstie laughed.

"Well I can surely understand your eager attitudes. Got some asses to kick?"

"Yes, sir!" the plebes bellowed. He laughed again, and taking the Restriction Muster clipboard, he rapidly called out the names of the Twenty-third Company plebes.

"Okay, pardners," he said after he had finished, and obviously laying on the accent a bit too thickly. "You better hightail it outta here!" As the plebes headed rapidly for the Company area, he called out. "Good luck! Don't kill anyone! I hate doing official reports."

Back in his room, Jeff quickly prepared. Most of the plebes had elected to remain in their restriction uniform of Service Dress Blue, since it was the same uniform for the upcoming meal, but Jeff elected to undress and put on his purple-blue Academy bathrobe. Since injured Willy could not participate, he was the designated photographer.

At precisely 1730 Big Jim Daly and Harvey Linehan showed up outside the room. Reb, Bob, and Jeff burst outside in unison and immediately began yelling at the firsties, while Willy Simpson hefted the camera. The passageway teemed with third-class and second-class spectators, and the atmosphere was a mixture of gaiety and anticipation.

"Jesus Christ!" Reb screamed, "Pull those god-damn chins in!" The two firsties hastened to comply.

"Foreheads back, you pussies!" Bob yelled. "What do you think this is, a summer camp?"

"Yeah!" Jeff added vengefully. "It's pay-back time for you assholes!" The three plebes had discussed several times how they intended to run the comearound, but could not agree on what they should do. Jeff was all for making Daly and Linehan run until they puked, but Bob wanted them to remain sensible.

"Listen," he had said patiently to Jeff, "none of us care for Tiger leadership style. If we imitate it the first time we have a chance, then we're no better than they are."

"Can the fatherly advice!" Jeff replied. "I want their asses on a platter!"

"Ah think we should run 'em," Reb had offered. "But ah want ta have some fun with 'em. Let's make 'em sweat, but let's show 'em we're better than they are."

"You guys are crazy!" Jeff had said. "I'm gonna kill the two bastards!" They left it at that.

"Wind sprints!" Reb screamed playfully. "Start by the head. And no bagging it or so help me I'll murder you." Harvey and Big Jim chopped to the end of the passageway.

"Ready, go!" Bob yelled, and the two firsties started off. Neither was particularly fast, but it was clear to Jeff that they weren't moving nearly as quickly as they could.

By the time they passed the plebe room, Jeff screamed at them. "Move your asses, you sacks of shit!" The firsties continued along at the same unimpressive pace.

As Jeff watched them reach the turnaround point and head back, he also noticed that the rest of his classmates were equally active. The main passageway was a noisy, congested riot of comearound madness. Across the passageway, Kevin O'Reilly had chosen to don gym gear and run alongside Rock Stone, taunting him and remaining a step ahead of the Company Commander in the sprints despite Rock's best efforts to catch up. Tommy Poole yelled disparaging comments from the doorway. Rico and BJ had Mugsy McGinley on the deck doing push-ups. Jim Merritt was inspecting with utter dissatisfaction the "uniform" Henry Brandis wore which consisted of a jock, gym socks, and his gray metal lock box. Even though he was braced, Jeff could see that Brandis smile and drop awkwardly to the deck for 20 push-ups, one hand still clutching the metal carrying handle of the lock box. Mugsy had passed 100 push-ups and didn't show a sign of strain. Willy worked his way up the passageway laughing and snapping photos.

From around the corner by the head facility Jeff heard yelling than saw Grunt Robinson and Wildman Kopciak emerge doing bear crawls and wearing only jock straps. They were doing something Danny French called the "Greyhound Races." Robinson was out in front by several yards. French, Delvecchio, and Chalmers ran alongside them. As they passed, Jeff noticed that Grunt had a large quantity of cotton balls shoved into the crack of his rear and that Wildman wore a second jockstrap over his nose and mouth.

"You better move faster, Robinson you rabbit bastard!" French yelled at the lead firstie.

"You better be sniffing cotton before this race ends, greyhound!" Chuck yelled at Wildman. Willy got several pictures.

Down the passageway Rolando Gomez was doing a dead horse while Pat Mulvaney called him colorful names. Several were in Tagalog. Gomez laughed, and Jeff wondered where Pat had done his Hundredth Night research. Sheldon Bloodworth was braced against the bulkhead as both John Pirelli and Wesley Lamont yelled in alternate ears.

Worst off of all was Dale Micklewski. George Abbott ran him unrelentingly in short intense wind sprints back and forth across the passageway. Within minutes Jeff could see that Dale become disoriented. Abbott yelled louder. To his credit, Dale Micklewski *was* trying his hardest.

Big Jim sprinted passed on his way back to the starting point, slightly behind the plodding Harvey Linehan.

Jeff yelled, "Faster, you slimy bastards!" They didn't improve their paces.

"Come on, you two!" Bob yelled. "Run!"

Jeff suddenly found himself angry. Linehan and Daly were cheating him out of his Hundredth Night revenge. He ran hurriedly to where the firsties waited to begin their next sprint, his shower shoes making angry slapping sounds on the hard floor. Reb stepped aside when he saw the fire in Jeff's eyes.

"Push-ups! Both of you! Now!" he yelled. La Master and Linehan dropped to the deck, but not nearly at the speed they would have expected from Jeff and his roommates.

"What are you waiting for?" Jeff yelled. "Begin!" Big Jim started first and set the pace, while Harvey matched his motions. They counted numbers together.

"Faster! God damn it!" Jeff yelled. He slipped down on his belly on the tile floor next to Big Jim and screamed insanely. "Move your asses! You're bagging it, you bastards! Put out! Put out!" He slapped a hand down on the tile next to Daly's head. "You sissies! You can do better than that!" He slapped the tile again as they counted their way slowly passed thirty.

"Get up!" Jeff yelled disgustedly. "Hurry!" The firsties rose and stood half-braced waiting for the next order.

"Bear crawls! Down to my room and back! Last one does 20 push-ups! Go!" La Master and Linehan got on their hands and feet and started forward with almost identical slow loping gaits. Jeff chopped alongside, yelling at them to speed up. As they neared the plebe's room, Jeff could see that Reb and Bob were more interested in what was happening with the other groups than with what Big Jim or Harvey did. What was wrong with Reb and Bob? Time was running out on his only opportunity to crush these hateful bastards! Jeff became even more angry.

"Halt!" he yelled insanely as they evened with his room. "Push-ups! Begin!" The two firsties began moving up and down again as Jeff continued to yell, stamping his feet and waving his arms with every invective.

"Put out! God Damn it! You douchebags! You're not trying!" Flecks of spittle sprayed from his mouth as he yelled, and Jeff could feel the blood pounding in his temples. The bastards were trying to get away with not doing their best -- after everything they had put him through. He wouldn't stand for it! He leaned toward the two firsties and opened his mouth to yell something else.

"Linehan!" Bob Strong yelled from the doorway. "Get over here!" Harvey jumped to his feet. Jeff looked up at Bob, angry that he had missed an opportunity to keep pressing Harvey. Then Reb stepped in too.

"Daly! What's the menu for evening meal?" Big Jim stopped push-ups and began reciting for Reb. Jeff opened his mouth to speak, but someone touched him on the shoulder. It was Willy. The camera dangled from its strap around his neck, almost hitting Jeff in the head as Willy leaned down.

"What?" Jeff yelled.

"Let Reb and Bob have a turn," Willy said calmly.

"But the bastards are bagging the whole thing!" Jeff said loudly.

"Let Reb and Bob have their fun."

"This isn't fair!" Jeff said emphatically. "They tried to kill me! I want revenge!"

"It's not about revenge, Jeff" Willy said with unusual insight. "Hundredth Night is supposed to be fun."

"Fun? Bullshit!" Jeff said. "I want revenge for everything!"

"Look around, Jeff," Willy said with a smile and a nod of his head. "It's not like that at all." Jeff sat up and observed the incredible near-turmoil. The passageway was a swirling confusion, and the din of screams and pained responses was almost overpowering. Yet, except for Dale Micklewski -- who seemed ready to die, not so much because George was pressing him so hard, but because he intended to be the best plebe he could for this one evening -- everybody else was smiling and having a relatively good time. Even stoic Rock Stone grinned as Kevin and Tommy did push-ups alongside him and said "interesting" things about the sex lives of Jarhead Marines. Jeff heard a sudden click-click noise and looked up quickly to see that Willy had snapped a picture of Stone's amusement. Willy was also amused.

Nearby, Mugsy McGinley was still doing push-ups with Rico, but Rico was straining while Mugsy laughed and continued to crank them out.

"You bastard!' Rico moaned as he strained out his number 200. "How do you do it?"

"Unlike you, sir" Mugsy answered with a smirk, "*I* had a Plebe Year."

"That's because my squadleader is a pussy!" Rico answered, and fell exhausted on the deck. He rolled slowly onto his back while Mugsy calmly continued his up-and-downs. A deep sweat stain was evident on Mugsy's back and a puddle of water accumulated where perspiration dripped from his forehead and nose onto the tile deck. There was just a hint of strain showing in those hairy muscular arms. Willy gleefully snapped another picture.

Around the corner came Robinson and Kopciak again, this time doing Tony Delvecchio's choreographed impression of the Rockettes. Still jock-strapped they kicked their way in unison down the passageway, singing, *"How ya gonna keep 'em down on the farm, after they've seen Mother-B!"* Jeff smiled. Willy took several pictures and hurriedly changed film.

Less than a minute later Dale Micklewski bent over at the waste and vomited loudly. George Abbott cheered, then made Dale do push-ups over the puddle. Just as Dickhead Dale was about to sag uncontrollably into the mess, George grabbed him by the back of his shirt and yanked him clear. Willy got that on film too.

Jeff, still numbly observing the activity from the deck, sat back on his heels and watched Hundredth Night surge in a blur around him. He forgot about Big Jim and Harvey for the moment. What was happening? This was the night he had waited for; the big event that marked the winding down of the plebe indoctrination process. After tonight, every plebe in the Company would be considered a member of the club, and 100 days from now, when some member of the Class of 1971 removed a cloth Dixie-cup cap from the top of the Herndon Monument, Plebe Year would officially end. Every plebe would be a third-class midshipmen. But Herndon was symbolism. Tonight saw the real end to the misery. Then why was he so miserable?

Slowly Jeff stood and walked toward his room. Before he reached the door, he was interrupted by a tap on the shoulder. He turned slowly. Rock Stone stood impressively before him, stripped to the waist and rippling muscularly.

"Excuse me, sir," Rock said, flexing his ample biceps, "I need career advice." Immediately he changed to a slouching posture and said in his best imitation of a girl. "Do they allow pansies like me in the Marine Corps?" With that Rock smiled, put a finger under his chin, curtsied sweetly to Jeff, and hurried off to greet the next plebe.

Jeff smiled, turned slowly, and entered his room without a word. In the passageway the frivolity continued unabated. Jeff went directly to his desk, sat with a sigh, and stared out the window into the adjacent courtyard and the rooms that faced his own 20 yards away. In starkly framed microcosms throughout the fourth wing he could see feverish activity and hear the sounds of intense laughter and relief. But somehow Jeff wasn't satisfied. He continued to stare until his roommates entered and announced with whoops of glee that it was time to prepare for meal.

Evening meal formation was the loosest Jeff had even seen. All around him midshipmen discussed the evening's comearound with fervent hilarity. Reb Ramsey nudged him playfully, something he never would have done this afternoon, when the pain and humiliation of the restriction marching and musters was still vivid.

"That was the best time I've ever had with my clothes on!" he exclaimed quietly. "It was great!" Jeff didn't respond. Reb nudged him again, ignoring his brooding silence. "Here they come!"

Big Jim Daly and Harvey Linehan strolled down the squad chatting amiably with various upperclassmen. They stopped in front of Willy Simpson first. Daly stuck out his hand.

"Great work, Willy," he said. "It's been good having you in the squad." Immediately afterward Harvey also shook Willy's hand proudly.

"If you need help with your studies, let me know," he said.

The firsties continued down the line stopping next in front of Bob Strong. Daly beamed at Bob when he stuck out his hand.

"You're one of the best plebes I've ever seen -- maybe even better than I was." He laughed as he shook hands with Bob, and again Linehan followed suit.

Jeff was next plebe in line, but the two firsties skipped over him and stood instead in front of Reb. Daly laughed as he stuck out his hand.

"You're a barrel of laughs, Ramsey," he said. "And a credit to the outfit!"

"So are you, Jim," Reb answered.

Harvey also quickly shook his hand.

"My offer of academic help stands for you also, Reb." Ramsey thanked him.

Jeff had been fuming at the firsties exclusionary actions. Did this mean he would not be spooned in accordance with the 100-year-old tradition? He wondered what the next three months would be like if he remained under the watchful wrath of the squadleaders. He'd probably be the only plebe still coming around, the only one being inspected at every formation, and almost certainly the only one in constant trouble. The thought was not at all heartwarming.

But the first-classmen did eventually stop in front of Jeff. Daly displayed none of the smiling banter he showed the other plebes, and Harvey Linehan showed a poker face. It was Harvey Linehan who spoke up.

"There's something wrong with you, Polk," he began in a low whisper. "But I can't quite put my finger on it, and that bothers me. Even after six months of close observation I'm still not convinced you belong here. You have a holier-than-thou attitude. You think you're the only midshipman who knows the divine truth. And you're convinced that anyone who displays even the slightest enthusiasm for the system is stupid. You openly disdain the rules and regulations even to the exclusion of the mission, your classmates, and companymates. Based on what I've seen so far, I personally don't think you'll make a good naval officer unless you have a fundamental personality change." Linehan paused and stared at Jeff intently. Jeff returned his gaze steadily.

"But your story isn't all bad, Polk. You have brains and personality, and you don't quit when things get tough. Believe it or not, every midshipman agrees with you that some idiotic things happen at Annapolis. And it may come as a surprise to you that several of my fellow Tigers are personally uncomfortable about the war in Vietnam. Despite what you think and say about us, nobody wants to be a robot." Harvey paused and smiled to himself before he continued.

"Some of my classmates even have occasionally accused me of arrogance, Polk, a trait you can identify with. So, frightening as it may sound, maybe you and I aren't so far apart philosophically.

"Jim and I talked about what to do about you after tonight. I'll tell you in truth, it was not comfortable talk. We're still Tigers, you see -- no matter how stupid that may be to you -- and we take our responsibilities seriously. So our decision did not come easy. What finally swayed us were two factors. The first was something Jim inadvertently said when we were really going strong in our Jeff Polk discussion. He looked at me with his squinty-eyed ugly face and said, 'That douchebag Polk is an immature baby!' He's right! That's what you are, immature. Maybe if you get the proper training and counseling, and you're smart enough to observe the Academy during the next couple years, there might be hope.

"The final and most important factor -- and you may hate this because it's a Tiger thing -- is that we decided the tradition of Hundredth Night demands that the firstie spoon the plebe after the big event. And we believe in this Academy and its tradition."

Harvey stuck out his hand to Jeff. Jeff hesitated, his brain swirling with the implications of Linehan's speech. He shook his head to clear it and realized that Harvey's hand was still extended. Harvey smiled and raised his eyebrows questioningly. Jeff quickly grabbed and shook the proffered hand.

"Sorry," Jeff said. "That was quite a speech!"

"Don't let me down, Jeff," Harvey replied. Jeff nodded absently, looking at Big Jim to see what he would do. Jim stuck out his hand.

"Whatever he said, I agree with, Polk. Don't screw up or I'll personally kill you!"

Jeff took his hand and shook it.

"Sure, Jim." Daly didn't look convinced.

CHAPTER 11

THE LET DOWN

Sunday evening the plebes tallied their "spoons" and took renewed stock of their personal situations. For Jeff's room the news was mixed. Strong and Ramsey were ecstatic, having been spooned by every firstie in the Company. Willy had also done well, lacking the friendship of only the Tiger-most of the firsties. Jeff however had shaken hands with his own squadleaders and with Henry Brandis and Mugsy McGinley. He was being shunned for his anti-Tiger stand. As Jeff watched wistfully -- and resentfully -- from his desk as firstie-after-firstie paraded into Jim Merritt's room to offer handshakes and friendship to the occupants of that room, he began to worry.

As Jeff watched the gaiety across the passageway, Tommy Poole arrived, and Jeff felt guilty he had forgotten that for Tommy Hundredth Night might prove a hollow victory. The worst thing that could possibly happen to a midshipman might be ahead.

"Hi, Tommy. How's your spoon total coming along?"

Tommy smiled.

"A whole lot better than I expected," he answered, smiling broadly. "Only Micklewski and Littleton haven't spooned me. Dale told me he decided it was more important to show support for Captain Dillingham, but that he had abdicated his squadleader responsibilities to the second-classmen, who already have spooned me. I should be okay."

"What about Stoner the Boner?" Jeff asked sarcastically.

"He didn't spoon me, but he came by the room. He said he had been ordered by Dillingham not to relax until my honor case was heard. He also repeated his support at the Hearing."

"Ah think ya'll gonna be fine, Tommy," Reb offered. "They got no case 'ganst ya'll."

Tommy wandered over to Jeff's desk and sat on it.

"Well," he said. "I certainly hope so, but I'm still worried." He turned to Jeff. "We have to work hard to ensure the best possible defense."

"I'll do my best, Tommy," Jeff replied, suddenly feeling himself a bit hurt that he had not accumulated as many offers of friendship as Tommy Poole. Not so long ago opinion against Tommy was nearly universal even within the ranks of the plebes.

Tommy handed Jeff a page of notebook paper.

"Here are some ideas to help you prepare."

Jeff took the note and glanced at it quickly while he talked.

"Thanks, Tommy," he said. "The committee will meet a week from tomorrow to discuss the case. The formal hearing should take place on 13 March. That means we have almost two weeks to prepare." Jeff paused in his reading. "Since you're here, let's talk."

Tommy sat on the window sill beside Willy's seat and looked at Jeff. Jeff picked up a pencil absentmindedly and tapped it on Tommy's note paper.

"The way I see it, in order to expel you, the Brigade Honor Committee has to be convinced that you either stole the photo or accepted a stolen photo. There is no direct evidence -- except that you had the photo in your possession."

Jeff paused.

"We know you didn't steal the photo. It appeared on your desk on 16 January, a Monday. We should investigate whether anything suspicious happened the previous weekend near the Roster Board. We can question the plebes from the Companies that had Main Office duty. Can you verify your whereabouts?"

Tommy didn't hesitate.

"I've already considered that. I can account for large segments of time during that weekend, but there are still several periods during which I could have taken the photo."

"Reb," Jeff asked, "can you visit the Roster Board and work out how *you* would take a photo if you wanted to?"

"Sure!" Reb answered. "Ah'll do it tomorrow."

"I suppose someone could eventually come forward and admit that he took it," offered Willy. "That might get Tommy off the hook."

"I hope no one does!" said Tommy emphatically. "He would open himself up to his own honor offense, and it still wouldn't clear me from possibly accepting stolen property."

"But is it really theft?" asked Bob Strong. "Maybe you could convince the Committee that an innocent prank doesn't violate the Code."

"Good point!" replied Jeff quickly jotting down a related note.

"And how can it be theft. Doesn't stealing have to be willful?" asked Bob.

Jeff wrote some more.

"And maybe Tommy's photo isn'tthe one that was removed from the Board."

"That's a very shaky point," Jeff answered, "but we'll use it anyway. Someone on the Committee might believe it."

"And, as I admitted to Rock," Tommy added, "at first I thought the photo had been given to me by an upper-classman. Maybe I was only following orders."

"Shaky, but we'll try that too," Jeff replied.

"How about character references?" Bob asked. "Who is going to defend Tommy's honor?"

"Well, I think his two roommates are obvious choices. Both are jocks, and can handle questioning without being intimidated. I thought I'd ask Micklewski and Salenger to testify about his honesty, sprinkle in some other classmates as character references, and finish up with Stone as the high card. I think we have a good case in support of Tommy's honorable personal qualities."

"How about the Committee? How will they present their case?" Tommy asked.

"Well," Jeff said, trying to remember exactly how the one and only case he had ever observed had gone. "I think on Monday the Committee will appoint one of their number -- probably the plebe representative -- to present the evidence against Tommy. He'll stick to the two points fairly closely and make his argument based strictly on the circumstantial evidence." Jeff paused. "But circumstantial evidence can sway the Committee, and I think it'll all boil down to whether the committee members believe Tommy."

"What do you think my chances are?" Tommy asked quietly.

Jeff stared hard at Tommy.

"I can't be overly optimistic, Tommy. The Brigade takes the Honor Code very seriously. I'd say your chances are no better than fifty-fifty." Tommy's eyes dropped despondently to the top of Jeff's desk and he shook his head slowly. The four roommates watched him silently.

"God!" Tommy Poole said fiercely. "To think that I could have come all this way and lose everything because of lies and false accusations."

"Yes, Tommy," Jeff said. "That could definitely happen."

Monday during noon meal Captain Dillingham approached Jim Merritt, who along with his roommates was enjoying a loose carry-on at the squad table.

"Mr. Merritt!" Dillingham announced, beaming broadly and patting Jim on the back as he spoke. "I have some good news for you. I just talked to Lieutenant Commander Hanes, and the Superintendent has approved an award for your bravery. You're going to get a Navy Commendation Medal tomorrow during noon meal. The Commandant is going to present it himself here in the Mess Hall, and the entire Brigade will witness the ceremony." He pounded Jim again. "Congratulations!"

Jim swelled with pride as Dillingham sauntered away.

"What a stud!" Rico observed. Jim had to admit, he sure felt like one.

Captain Dillingham also got a surprise that noon meal. At a signal from Lieutenant Spencer plebes from the Twenty-second company lifted the seated and cheering Marine over their shoulders and carried his around the company tables. Normally this would be an opportunity to "toast" the chaired individual by throwing bread Frisbee-style at the elevated target, but earlier in the year Dillingham and Rock Stone declared that Tigers did not toast.

As Dillingham toured Twenty-third Company tables, Rock glared at Mugsy McGinley, but Mugsy held both hands aloft to show Rock he was "unbreaded." After the Twenty-second Company plebes had returned Bull to Stone's table, he gave both companies his best Marine Corps "Ohhh Rah!"

Monday evening in the company Wardroom, as Jim and his roommates prepared sandwiches for Mugsy's Company Sandwich Mess venture, Kevin paused. He walked to the Wall of Honor to view the photos of distinguished Twenty-third Company graduates. Most of the ten men honored had performed selfless acts of heroism. Many had died in the commission of those acts.

Kevin pointed to a spot on the wall next to the most recent photo. It showed a Vietnam War air ace from the Class of 1960 who had been shot down and killed while attacking an anti-aircraft missile battery.

"Right here!" Kevin said indicating the bare spot.

"What?" Rico asked.

"This is where they're going to put Jim's picture and plaque," he answered.

Merritt laughed.

"Knock it off, Kevin. I didn't really do anything so brave."

"Yeah," Rico added. "But if Jim had drowned saving the classmate, that would be a different story. They don't honor the living the same as the dead."

"Why is that?" Kevin asked.

"It's because dead men don't have to make speeches that show how stupid they really are or won't embarrass themselves later by shacking up with somebody else's wife or by getting drunk in the O'Club. Once they're dead, all the bad and embarrassing things heroes do get forgotten."

"You mean Marc Anthony was wrong?" Kevin asked.

"What the hell does that mean?" Rico asked, clearly annoyed that Kevin was about to quote.

"The evil that heroes do does *not* live after them. We bury it with their broken bones and only remember the good."

Rico looked pensive for a moment.

"Yeah, Kevin," he said. "That's right!"

"Come on guys," Jim said. "Let's make the deliveries so I can study for my chemistry class." Jim picked up his stack of sandwiches and Mugsy's delivery list, and started for the door. The others did the same.

A familiar figure waited in the passageway. Jim stopped abruptly and braced up. The others collided with him, almost dropping their loads.

"What the hell!" Rico yelled, then became quiet. "The Nose" LaPointe and two plebe messengers waited in the passageway. He and his nose seemed genuinely excited to see Jim -- almost as disheartened as Jim was to see him.

"Well, well!" LaPointe exclaimed with glee. "What have we here? Why it's my soggy friend Mister James "Big Hero" Merritt and three cohorts. Why aren't you braced and chopping?"

"Sir," Jim answered. "Hundredth Night celebration was yesterday. Our Company Commander has given all plebes carry-on in the Company area until further notice."

"Oh, has he now?" The Nose asked with dripping sarcasm.

"Yes, sir!"

"And where might I find the fierce Tiger Company Commander?" LaPointe asked.

"Sir, his room is 4040!" LaPointe looked closely at the four of them. Suddenly his eyes focused on the bag Jim held in his right hand and the list he held in his left. His nostrils expanded visibly and LaPointe sniffed the air.

"What's that you have there?" he asked with a growing smile. Even his nose seemed happy.

Jim hesitated fractionally.

"Sandwiches, sir!"

"And does your Company Commander allow food in the Wardroom?"

"Sir!" Kevin burst in, trying to charm LaPointe. "In Tiger Company the need for after hours refreshment is recognized. We provide a humanitarian sandwich service to our hungry companymates. If you'd like, I can whip you up one of my special blends? You want salami? pimento loaf? or maybe one of my baloney specialties?"

The Nose was not amused.

"No thank you, Mister Wiseguy." He faced Jim again. "So under whose authority do you provide these sandwiches? Who's responsible for this plebe servitude."

Again Jim hesitated.

"Midshipman First-class McGinley runs the Sandwich Mess, sir! But there is no servitude. We are paid in food, sir!" However, Jim was not sure LaPointe heard everything. At the mention of Mugsy's name, LaPointe smiled and his hateful nose lit up like a beacon.

"You do this for Donald E. 'Mugsy' McGinley?" He smiled and looked toward heaven. "Oh, there is a God!"

By this time the upper-class had noticed that "The Nose" was in the Company area, and someone had gone off to find Rock Stone. Rock trotted up.

"Midshipman First-class Stone, sir!" he reported.

"You the Commander of this abortion?" LaPointe asked.

"Yes, sir!" Rock said with pride, ignoring the insult. "I lead Tiger Company!".

"The Nose" snatched the bag of sandwiches from Jim's hand.

"What's this?" he asked, holding the bag in Rock's face.

"Deliveries for the Company Sandwich Mess, sir!"

"Sanctioned by Captain Dillingham?"

"Yes, sir!"

Jim Merritt sneaked a quick glance at Kevin O'Reilly who was shocked into silence. Since it was inconceivable Stone would lie, Dillingham knew about the Sandwich Mess and hadn't stopped it.

"You realize that this is completely non-regulation?"

"Yes, sir!"

LaPointe fumed.

"Yes, sir? That's all you have to say?"

"Sir, every Company has midshipmen who provide personal services for their Companymates. There are Tiger barbers, several lending libraries, a second-class photographer, another second-class who can draw quite a fanciful sketch of almost any woman, a third-class who mounts ribbons or frames awards, as well as a first-class who runs the Sandwich Mess."

"All of which are illegal!"

"All are essential nonetheless for good order and discipline," Stone boldly replied.

"Well," LaPointe replied with a harsh laugh, "it's admirable that you feel so strongly about free enterprise and about protecting your troops, but I don't care about barbers and artists. I do care about Mister Donald McGinley. I intend to visit him this very instant and tell him the wonderful news about his new status as restriction king of the entire Brigade. I'm certain that will make him so happy he'll just shit in his pants!"

"The Nose" turned to Jim.

"Lead the way, Mister plebe Tiger Hero!" He pointed to Kevin. "And you with the big mouth can come along to watch your squadleader beg and whimper. It'll be a good object lesson."

With that LaPointe turned and marched down the passageway. His two plebe messengers trailed closely behind. Jim hurried to catch up, but Kevin lagged behind. He put his hands on his hips and swaggered as he strolled behind LaPointe. Several of the observing upper-class laughed loudly and

"The Nose" whipped around. But Kevin was too fast. He instantly reverted to an erect plebe-like stature. LaPointe stared at O'Reilly for a moment, then hurriedly turned around. Soon the entourage turned the corner toward Mugsy's room. At the corner, Kevin deftly spun in a circle, smiled at his "audience," bowed, and followed the group down the smaller side passageway.

At Mugsy's room, Jim stepped aside to let "The Nose" take charge. LaPointe did not hesitate. He burst inside, followed immediately by his messengers. A thoroughly surprised Mugsy leapt to his feet.

"Midshipman First-class McGinley, sir!" he shouted.

"Where's your roommate?" LaPointe barked.

"Library, sir!"

"Just as well," LaPointe snickered. He held up the paper bag of sandwiches he had carried after his encounter with Rock.

"What's this?" he asked.

"A paper bag, sir?" Mugsy answered without hesitation.

"What's inside the bag?"

"I'll find out, sir!"

"Don't give me any of your wiseass crap, McGinley!" LaPointe roared. He dumped the contents of the bag onto the floor. "These are sandwiches! Your sandwiches! From your Sandwich Mess! That just happens to be an illegal activity. Plebe servitude is also illegal!" LaPointe smiled. "You're in big trouble, Mister!"

"Sir!" Jim blurted. "We were compensated for our efforts. There is no plebe servitude!"

LaPointe whirled on Jim.

"Listen to me, you snot-nosed little ass!" he yelled, advancing on Jim until the famous nose almost touched his chin. LaPointe's dark eyes narrowed and fixed on Jim's own. Jim noticed that one of the lumps on the left side of the famous appendage seeped a mixture of blood and clear liquids.

"You've lied to me once too many times, you spineless jellyfish!" LaPointe yelled. "One more word from you and I'll give you so many demerits you'll have to restrict until you graduate." Jim quieted but returned his stare steadily. The oozing spot glistened in the fluorescent lighting.

LaPointe spun around and glared at Mugsy. "What is it about midshipmen that makes them protect each other? Why would anyone protect a low life like you?"

Mugsy returned LaPointe's stare.

"You didn't graduate from here, did you, sir?"

"The Nose" became instantly angry.

"No, asshole! I didn't! What's that supposed to imply?"

"No offense intended, sir, but unless you had, you just cannot hope to understand."

"That's ring-knocker bullshit!" LaPointe said loudly, and turned to Kevin.

"How about you? Are you a ring-knocker, or do you want to be the only honest plebe in the Company? Admit that Mister McGinley was using you as slave labor!"

Kevin laughed.

"We're all slaves after a fashion, sir, but I worked for Mister McGinley for two main reasons. First because I wanted to. Despite all that ugly hair and that gruff personality, Mister McGinley is a genuine humanitarian and an excellent leader of men. But second -- and more important -- I do the Sandwich Mess thing because I happen to make a great baloney masterpiece." Kevin waved his hands as he spoke, illustrating. "You see, the secret is that I put mustard on one side and mayonnaise on the other. Then I take two slices of baloney, one on each side, and put a slice of fresh Swiss cheese and four large dill pickle slices in between the baloney." LaPointe watched Kevin as he waved his hands in demonstration. Jim could see momentary confusion. Kevin noticed also.

"But the piece-de-resistance," Kevin added, "is that I add a single thick slice of juicy, red, and fresh tomato right there with the pickles. God, it's great! I have one every night, and frankly it's the one thing that's kept me going through Plebe Year." Kevin paused and stared at LaPointe. "Tell you what, sir! Come on down to the Wardroom and I'll make each of you one of those masterpieces right now. Believe me, you'll love it! You'll come back every night for a Kevin O'Reilly specialty." Kevin moved to the door and held it open, still smiling broadly.

LaPointe continued to stare at the smiling Kevin for several seconds. McGinley smiled and shook his head quietly. Jim, used to Kevin's strange antics, watched "The Nose" closely. LaPointe's eyebrows worked slowly up and down, and as he tried to understand what it was he had just experienced. A plebe messenger started chuckling, then laughing loudly when Kevin opened the door. LaPointe became distracted. He looked at the messenger.

"What's so funny?" LaPointe demanded.

The messenger pointed to Kevin, still laughing.

"He is, sir!"

"The Nose" looked at Kevin.

"Are you always so strange, Mister?"

"Strange, sir? No, I'm just me. Now how about that sandwich?" The messenger laughed loudly as Kevin gestured out the door.

"No thank you," LaPointe replied politely, still confused by Kevin. The messenger tried to stifle a laugh and snorted, startling Jim. The other messenger began to laugh. Mugsy's twinkle increased.

"Stop!" LaPointe shouted. "Stop this immediately!" The laughter almost at once.
"You!" The Nose said to O'Reilly, "get your ass out in the passageway and wait."

"Aye, aye, sir!" Kevin replied, and started to close the door. Then he paused and turned back toward "The Nose."

"Sir, can I eat my sandwich while I wait, sir?"

LaPointe laughed briefly, which started the messenger laughing again.

"You!" LaPointe said to the messenger. "Wait in the passageway with Jerry Lewis."

The messenger moved toward the door and Kevin held up his bag.

"Baloney or salami?" he asked. Everyone laughed again.

After they had closed the door, "The Nose" stared at Mugsy then indicated with a nod of his head the now-departed Kevin O'Reilly.

"He's an idiot, isn't he?"

"Most first-class in the Company would tell you he's the best plebe we have," Mugsy answered with a chuckle, surprising Jim.

"Then it's no wonder this Company is so screwed up," LaPointe answered. He smiled at Mugsy. "It looks like Mister Hero plebe and his cohorts are going to lie for you, McGinley. Why? I can't imagine. I guess I can't get you for plebe servitude like I'd hoped. But you know very well that private enterprise in any form is strictly prohibited. Since you are in charge of the Sandwich Mess, it's *you* I'm going to fry. Guess what? -- It's a Class-A offense. That means you should be restricting until June Week. No car. No weekend liberty. No beer parties."

"The Nose" moved closer until he was standing almost directly in front of Mugsy. Without the nose to distract him, Jim noticed for the first time that LaPointe's face sagged with age and that he had deep lines at the corners of both his eyes and mouth. He also had a prominent mole just behind the ear on Jim's side of his head. From the very center of the mole sprouted a single thick dark hair, which stood out in stark contrast to the almost-white thin hair that showed around the edges of his uniform hat.

"I've been waiting for two years to get you, McGinley. I had begun to think that I'd fail because I didn't have much time left. I'll be retiring immediately after the school year ends, so you and the Navy have almost seen the last of me. And, believe me, I'll be glad as hell to get away from it all and especially from you sneaky, lying, midshipmen. The Navy's changed a lot in the years I was with the fleet, and honor is one of those things that's been lacking lately, and this school is the reason."

LaPointe smiled and leaned over toward Mugsy until their noses almost touched. McGinley didn't even flinch.

"I'll bet you never suspected why I hate you so much, did you?"

"Oh, I know why, sir!" Mugsy answered surprising everyone in the room.

"You do?" LaPointe asked, surprised and disappointed.

"Yes, sir. It all goes back to the Brigade Boxing finals in 1965. I was a plebe. You had reported aboard that past winter, and already had a reputation as an OOD to avoid. Your first month, you caught three of my firsties with booze in Bancroft Hall and had them expelled. Do you remember that incident? One of them had put the bottle in his overnight bag by mistake and was too drunk to remember. He discovered it just before you walked in. The other two were involved only by accident. They tried to explain it was a mistake, but you didn't listen. Three good men left because you didn't listen.

"I had already qualified for the Finals at that point. My opponent was a first-class from 9th Company. I didn't know him, but he had a reputation as a good technical boxer. He was a jerk who had half the Brigade pissed off because he felt the need to fry every single minor offense he found. It didn't matter if it was in his squad, his Company, or anywhere else in the Brigade. His name, as I recall, was Nathan LaPointe.

"A few days before the event a strange firstie came to my room and told me that Nathan was your son. He was supposed to keep you a secret so that no one would accuse him of getting any special treatment from the system.

"I knew then I had a mission. Half the Brigade wanted me to win just because Nathan LaPointe was a jerk. I decided to pulverize him because of what you did to my first-class squadleader -- who didn't have the booze, and who was one of the finest people I had ever met. When the night of the fight arrived, I found out that Nathan was a good technical boxer all right. But I never cared much for technical things." Mugsy laughed loudly. "Nathan seemed surprised that I would gladly walk right into his best punch for the opportunity to deliver one of mine. Mine were far more potent. I knocked Nathan out in the beginning of the third round. He took quite a bit of punishment before he went down, and it was my first knockout. I have to admit it was a sweet feeling."

Jim found that his mouth had opened widely. He exchanged quick glances with the other messenger. What was Mugsy doing? The Nose was going to kill him.

But LaPointe didn't react. Instead Jim saw the beginnings of tears forming in his eyes. When he spoke, his voice had lost it's bold timbre.

"You didn't just beat him, McGinley. You destroyed him! That beating look the heart out of him, and he was never the same afterward. He's still a Lieutenant Junior Grade when his peers are all Lieutenants. He's serving as the Assistant Administrative Officer on a destroyer in San Diego, and the chances are he won't rise much higher. I asked his skipper what the problem was, and he told me that Nathan had no spirit."

As Jim watched, a tear rolled down LaPointe's face. His voice trembled.

"He *had* spirit, you bastard! He *had* guts, you son-of-a-bitch! He stood up and spoke out for the things he believed in, and he had life by the throat. You destroyed all that when you beat him that night. I was watching from the rear of the hall. You had the fight won in the second round. But you didn't let up. You kept at him until both his eyes were swollen shut and his mouth was a pulpy mess. It took him weeks to recover physically . . . but he never recovered his soul."

LaPointe sniffed back another tear and his voice rose in volume to a shriek.

"You took his spirit, McGinley, and I'll never forgive you for that!"

"The Nose" shook his head and voiced an unintelligible moan of pure rage. He pulled back his right hand and balled it into a fist. Jim was shocked. The OOD was about to strike Mugsy! As Jim watched he saw LaPointe shake violently and Jim started forward. Mugsy stopped him with a quick glare, and suddenly Jim was confused. LaPointe struck with a sweeping blow that caught Mugsy on the side of his face and knocked him sidewards sprawling against his desk. LaPointe moved to the bent-over figure and began raining rapid punches along Mugsy's back and arms as Mugsy curled into a protective cocoon. Papers and books fell from the desk in a rain of debris. The framed photo of Mugsy's parents toppled to the deck and broke loudly.

"You destroyed my only son!" LaPointe yelled as he continued flailing. "You destroyed my only son! I hate you for that!"

Despite Mugsy's warning, Jim moved forward, grabbed LaPointe, and pulled him away from Mugsy. "The Nose" screamed.

"Let me go! You're on report for interfering with an officer! Let me go!"

Things happened quickly. Kevin burst into the room with the sound of the screams. He came to Jim's side and helped control the raging Lieutenant Commander LaPointe. One messenger stood in front of LaPointe to block his path to Mugsy.

The other peeked inside, saw the turmoil, and shouted, "I'm going to the Main Office for the Junior Officer of the Watch!"

It took almost five minutes for Brian LaPointe to calm, and whenhe did, he sagged almost lifelessly. Jim nodded to Kevin, and they led the officer to Henry Brandis's bed and sat him down. LaPointe buried his head in his hands and began to sob. Within seconds the door opened, and Jim saw an enormous crowd gathered in the passageway. Heads craned in the background as Rock Stone entered, leading a Lieutenant, who Jim knew from his rates must be Lieutenant Schwirtz, the Seventeenth Company Commander. Schwirtz was a tall Nuclear Power submariner in his first year on the staff.

"What happened here?" he demanded. No one spoke.

"I asked a question!" he repeated. "What happened here?"

"Sir!" Mugsy said straightening up from the desk with a stiffness that indicated to Jim that not every punch LaPointe landed had been ineffectual. "Lieutenant Commander LaPointe came here to question me about the Company Sandwich Mess. While he was questioning me I became excited. I think I slipped, fell against my desk, and hit my head. I'm confused and can't remember exactly. Someone sent the messenger for help."

Schwirtz stared at Mugsy who looked sufficiently groggy that his story could be true. But Schwirtz suspected that what Mugsy had just said was not the exact truth. He hesitated; then he turned to LaPointe.

"Perhaps it would be best, sir, if we sorted this out in the Main Office? Shall I bring all the involved parties and witnesses there?"

"The Nose" continued to sit with his head in his hands. He had stopped crying, but now he was deathly still.

"Sir?" Schwirtz asked.

With a wave of a hand, LaPointe dismissed him.

"Clear the crowd, Lieutenant, and return to the Main Office. We'll discuss what to do when I get there." Schwirtz hesitated. LaPointe looked up at him, anguish plainly etched on his tired face.

"I'll be okay, Lieutenant. Get moving!"

Schwirtz hesitated briefly and looked at each of the occupants of the room in turn. His gaze dwelled suspiciously on Mugsy. He turned and beckoned the messengers to follow.

"You heard the Commander, gentlemen. Let's disperse that crowd and return to the Main Office." The two plebes hurriedly left, glad, Jim was sure, to be away from the insanity they had witnessed.

LaPointe sat still for several long moments, staring across the room at Mugsy, who returned his gaze. Jim saw that Mugsy had suffered a considerable welt under his left eye where LaPointe's Navy Fleet ring had connected with his upper cheek. Mugsy also had an ugly red scratch across the lower part of the same jaw. Blood ran from the scratch and hung in a red drop at the edge of Mugsy's prominent chin. Mugsy made no move to tend to his wounds.

When Lieutenant Commander LaPointe spoke, his voice was calm but resolved. No spirit remained behind his words.

"You just told a direct lie to the JOOD, why? More midshipman nobility?"

"Sir," Mugsy replied. "I am truly sorry about your son. I was just a plebe. If I had known what might have happened, I would not have beaten him so badly. You have my word on that. I'm also sure if you had time to consider, you would not have hit me tonight. It's over between us. You need to retire and get on with your life, and I need to graduate and get on with my career. I have no intention of pursuing the matter, and I hope you agree that's the best course of action."

"What about the Honor Code?" LaPointe asked.

"Sir, in a case like this, there is a more profound personal Honor Code that governs."

LaPointe considered for a moment.

"What about the Sandwich Mess violation?"

Mugsy smiled.

"I operated the Mess knowing I was taking a risk. I was caught, and I'll take my punishment like a man. I ask that you not give me special treatment because of tonight's incident." LaPointe nodded slowly and started to stand, but his legs were weak. He almost fell backward onto the bed. Jim and Kevin grabbed him by an arm each and helped him erect.

"Let us help you down to the Main Office," Jim offered. LaPointe shook away their arms gently, and smiled at them.

"No, thank you," he replied. "I need to salvage some dignity. I'll be fine." He took a deep breath, followed by a tentative step, and paused. He stared hard at Jim.

"I still don't understand exactly why you didn't tell the entire truth about the incident on Hospital Point, but your act of rescue was very brave." Jim nodded.

LaPointe looked at Kevin. "You are a very strange person, son," he said with a smile. "But you're also very funny, and I appreciate what you tried to do." Kevin returned the smile.

Taking another deep breath, Lieutenant Commander Matthew LaPointe left the room. Jim turned to Mugsy.

"Anything we can do?"

"No," he replied sadly.

"So what's the lesson here?" asked a confused Kevin O'Reilly.

Mugsy didn't hesitate in answering.

"Power corrupts," he said.

"And absolute power corrupts absolutely . . . ," Kevin answered quizzically. "How does that apply?"

"I knew I could beat Nathan LaPointe after the first ten seconds," Mugsy replied. " I let that power affect my actions. I didn't need to kill the guy to win that fight."

"And 'The Nose?'" Kevin asked.

"He let the power of the system corrupt him. Officers are almost gods here and he thought he could use his position to exact a personal revenge. It almost cost him his career."

"Why don't you turn him in for what he did? It was borderline insanity," Jim asked. "Shouldn't he be punished?"

Mugsy laughed. "What's the point of that? He did what he did, and I'm sure he regrets it as much as I regret what I did to his son. Everybody makes mistakes, guys. Most honorable people learn from them and become better people. Do you think it's honorable to ruin his life over a physical outburst? I don't!"

"What if he decides to turn you in for lying?" Kevin asked.

Mugsy looked briefly concerned, then he smiled.

"If he does, he does. It'll be a 'slings and arrows' thing."

"Well," Kevin answered, "if you need help taking arms, you know where to find us."

"Thanks," Mugsy replied. "Now leave me to my thoughts." Kevin and Jim exchanged glances and moved toward the door. "Oh," Mugsy added, "and don't let this get out, otherwise it may become an incident we can't control."

Noon meal the next day found Twenty-third Company strangely subdued by the previous night's events. Despite pleadings from Jeff and the other plebes, Kevin and Jim remained quiet about the details of the incredible encounter with "The Nose." Jim wore his best set of Service Dress Blues to the meal. Dillingham wore Marine Corps Dress Blues as well. He looked incredibly military and imposing. Just after prayer, the Midshipman Brigade Commander, who was Midshipman first-class Thomas Abernathy, moved to the podium.

"Brigade, attention!" he called smartly, and everyone rose to their feet. "Midshipman Fourth-class James Merritt, front and center!" Jim took a deep breath and looked at the beaming Dillingham who gestured him to the center aisle.

"Go for it, Jim!" Kevin whispered nudging him in the side. Rico smiled proudly and nodded from his place across the table, and BJ reached over and shook Jim's hand briefly.

Jim moved to the center aisle and stood next to Captain Dillingham facing the staff tables which were more than 50 yards away in the center of the Mess Hall. Hundreds of eyes watched him as he waited.

"Forward, march!" Dillingham said in a low voice, and the two of them strode identically forward. Jim could see the Bull nod and smile to the other Company Officers at the various tables they passed. The Captain was obviously in his glory, but still Jim felt subdued.

Near the center of the Mess Hall, Bull said, "Ready, halt!" They stopped precisely five yards in front of the podium facing the Superintendent and Commandant, both of whom had moved to positions on alternate sides flanking the podium. Civilian photographers and reporters milled about on both sides of the Academy leadership, and the flashing of camera strobes assaulted Jim's eyes briefly. A staff officer standing next to the Superintendent held a small dark blue case and a thick dark vinyl letter-sized folder. Rear Admiral Jake Conrad smiled at Jim, then looked at Midshipman Abernathy.

"Read the citation, please," he said, and the camera flashes stopped.

Midshipman Commander Abernathy took a deep breath and read.

"For outstanding gallantry on the night of 25 February 1968, the Secretary of the Navy takes great pleasure in presenting the Navy Commendation Medal to Midshipman Fourth-class James Wesley Merritt of Twenty-third Company. Jim looked at the senior staffers. Rear Admiral Conrad watched impassively. Captain Mack Hallahan smiled in a fatherly way and winked at Jim. Lieutenant Commander Hanes whispered quietly to the newspaper attendees.

"During the evening hours of Saturday, 25 February 1968, while jogging near the Hospital Point footbridge, Midshipman Merritt heard the cries of a fellow midshipman who had fallen into College Creek. At great personal risk, and despite the sub-freezing temperatures, Midshipman Merritt braved the elements, climbed precariously down onto the footbridge structure, pulled the struggling comrade from the water, and lifted his nearly unconscious body several feet onto the seawall.

"With no regard for his own comfort, and despite the fact that he himself was soaked from the effort, Midshipman Merritt removed his comrade's wet over clothes and gave him his jacket. Upon seeing that the classmate was near death, Midshipman Merritt administered first aid and lifted his classmate onto his shoulder, carrying him more than five hundred yards, a journey that was mostly uphill, in treacherous footing to the Naval Hospital Emergency Room.

"Midshipman Merritt's actions almost certainly saved the life of his comrade and are in keeping with the highest standards of the Naval Service. He is a credit to his uniform and to the proud institution in which he serves. Go Navy!' Midshipman Commander Abernathy looked at Jim.

"The citation is signed by the Secretary of the Navy."

Rear Admiral Jake Conrad and his aide moved forward smartly to a position directly in front of Jim. The aide opened the case, exposing a large bronze medal suspended from a green and white triangular ribbon. The Superintendent took the medal and held it aloft. Smiling at Jim, he pinned it onto his shirt just above his other ribbons. Cameras flashed, and the Brigade roared its approval. When he had finished, Rear Admiral Conrad reached out a hand. Jim shook it vigorously. "

Congratulations, son," the Superintendent said over the shouting. "That was one hell of an effort. I visited the spot yesterday afternoon with Mack Hallahan, and we retraced your steps. Unbelievable!"

"Thank you, sir!"

"This is one hell of a plebe you have here, Captain," he said to Dillingham.

Dillingham beamed.

"Yes, sir! I know! He's a Tiger, no doubt about it!" Jim had no time to consider. Soon he was shaking hands with Captain Hallahan and the other staffers.

When it came his turn, Lieutenant Commander Hanes leaned in close and whispered.

"Don't worry about Lieutenant Commander LaPointe. I already squelched his protests."

"Thank you, sir!" Jim replied, beginning to relax. "I talked to him yesterday, and everything is fine now."

"Really?" Hanes said, surprised. "That's great! Now smile for the cameras and act like a hero! You're representing the entire Brigade. Enjoy your fame!"

CHAPTER 12

THE HONOR COMMITTEE

During the week following Hundredth Night, Jeff and Tommy prepared for the Honor Committee meeting. After reviewing the preliminary information, and the list of potential witnesses, the committee had decided that Tommy's case was complex and would require two evenings of meetings. On the first evening the committee would examine the evidence against Tommy and hear testimony from selected witnesses. The second evening Tommy and Jeff could present their defense. As the first meeting neared, Jeff became extremely nervous and not at all confident about the outcome.

The Honor Committee met in the Superintendent's Conference Room, a 50-foot by 30-foot, spacious, richly paneled showpiece room in the staff office area of Bancroft Hall beside the Superintendent's office. The Superintendent and Commandant used the room for large staff meetings and for entertaining groups of dignitaries. The Honor Committee used the room for more serious venues.

Jeff and Tommy arrived thirty minutes early. The room had been laid out for the meeting. Jeff's first impression was of the table which was an enormous, highly-polished dark oak oval. The side of the table facing the entry doors was prepared for the Honor Committee, which consisted of a first-class Chairman, and first-class, second-class, third-class, and plebe representatives. Each Committee member would have an equal vote which could recommend either dismissal of the case, or dismissal of the offender. Blue-and-gold placards designated where each class representative would sit.

Directly across the table from the Honor Committee were two seats, one designated for the accused, and the other for the Honor Advocate. A staff officer chosen randomly from the Academy Administration and not directly involved in the case would sit at the head of the table near the entrance to the Superintendent's office. The Recorder, a plebe Committee member whose functions were to record the testimony on an electronic tape recorder, to identify speakers, note the time sequence of the Hearing, and identify all evidence presented, would sit adjacent to the observer. The Recorder would produce the official Committee report which would be approved by each member of the Committee and presented to the Commandant of Midshipmen for ultimate approval. Jeff had learned that Commandants almost always followed the Committee's recommendations.

One chair sat at the foot of the table. It was for witnesses and those giving direct testimony. Every other conference table chair had been removed to an adjoining storage room except those for potential witnesses. Those chairs lined the outer walls of the room. In order to ensure some semblance of privacy, the meeting was closed to all but those midshipmen and officers directly involved in the proceedings, and all participants swore to maintain the secrecy of the testimony.

The room itself was the ultimate in Naval decorum. The expensive chairs were upholstered in a plush navy blue fabric attached to a dark oak frame by large, bright-gold-colored tacks. The dark blue customized carpet featured a gold Naval Academy seal imprinted onto the fiber just inside the doorway. Several large original oils which depicted famous sea battles and naval triumphs of different eras lined both long side walls. A huge display case along the wall at the foot of the table housed a painstakingly-detailed model of one of John Paul Jones' early ships of war. Spot lighting and subdued and recessed provided the illumination. The room gave the distinct impression that loud speech would be illegal, but Jeff was willing to bet some very heated discussions had occurred around this table.

Once they had taken a moment to orient themselves, Tommy pulled back his chair and sat with a huge sigh. Still taking in the nautical splendor, Jeff patted his shoulder absentmindedly.

"It'll be okay, Tommy. Tonight is just round one. We meet the committee and size them up, and they'll do the same to us. Then we'll hear a rehash of the evidence. Before the meeting adjourns for the evening, you'll have to admit that you understand the charges and will present evidence that will support your innocence. When you speak, speak plainly and without emotion. First impressions are very important. Don't waver, sound upright and honorable. We need to convince three of the committee members that this is all an unfortunate mistake." Tommy nodded but did not voice any reply.

The meeting was scheduled to begin at 1930. At 1915 several midshipmen entered, followed quickly by the Twenty-third Company witnesses. The group included Kevin O'Reilly and Jim Merritt, as well as Tommy's two roommates and several other plebe companymates. Jeff greeted them and told them where to sit. A minute later a somewhat unkempt and harried-looking Lieutenant entered and hurried to a chair at the far end of the room near the display case. At 1920 Rock Stone and Captain Dillingham entered and immediately choose witness seats against the wall directly behind Jeff and Tommy. Dale Micklewski followed several seconds later, and Henry Brandis entered soon after him. At 1925 Jeff allowed himself to sit for the first time in his chair to Tommy's left. He nervously arranged and rearranged his papers as they waited for the committee to arrive.

At precisely 1930, the wall chronometer clicked the minute, the door to the conference room opened, and six midshipmen and a Lieutenant entered. Five of the midshipmen assumed seats directly across from Jeff and Tommy. The Lieutenant went to his place at the head of the table, and the remaining plebe sat quickly in the recorder's seat where he immediately played with the equipment and readied it for the beginning of the proceedings. The Committee Chairman, a first-class named Homer Smith, watched closely as the recorder checked the gear. When the recorder nodded that all was ready, Homer looked calmly at Tommy and Jeff, and Jeff could feel his stomach immediately tighten.

"Let the record show that the Brigade Honor Committee of the United States Naval Academy met at nineteen thirty on 6 March 1968 to consider the conduct of Midshipman Fourth-class Thomas Henry Poole. Present this evening are Midshipman First-class William J. Hilderbrand, Midshipman Second-class Brian John Lehre, Midshipman Third-class Richard David Cellon, Midshipman Fourth-class Steven Alan Miller -- each of whom represent their various classes -- and finally myself, Midshipman First-class Homer William Smith, the Committee Chairman."

Homer looked to the far end of the table and continued. "With us this evening is Lieutenant Ronald Edward Powell, the Thirtieth Company Officer, who will be the staff observer for this Hearing, and . . . " he said looking to the other plebe, "Midshipman Fourth-class Andrew W. Dunloy, who will be the recorder."

Homer then centered his gaze on the two plebes across the table. "Also present at the Hearing is Midshipman Fourth-class Jeffrey Alan Polk, who will serve as Advocate for the accused."

Homer paused, and for the first time smiled at Tommy.

"I can see that you're very nervous, Mister Poole, and if I were in your position I'm sure I would be too." He then assumed a formal posture and demeanor. "Let me assure you at the beginning that we take the Honor Code very seriously. That means two things. First, of course, is that if we find that you willfully violated the Code, we will recommend expulsion without hesitation. But second, and far more important, the Board will never recommend dismissal without convincing evidence that an honor offense occurred. If we are not absolutely swayed by what we see and hear than any recommendation for your dismissal would be dishonorable on our part. So rest assured that we will give this case the fullest attention it deserves."

Homer continued, "This committee functions similarly to the Company Honor Boards in that all members may pose questions to you or to any witness and that the voting will be private; but the vote counting will be witnessed by the committee, the Accused and his Advocate, the Staff observer, and the Recorder. If the committee recommends dismissal, your expulsion is still not automatic. The Commandant of Midshipmen must review the Committee's report and provide his concurrence before any administrative action is taken."

Smith paused and consulted his notes.

"Until such time as the report is approved, you will retain all rights and privileges of any midshipman of comparable rank, and I remind everyone that the proceedings are confidential. Only personnel with a direct need to know can be allowed access to the information presented in this room."

Homer then looked around the room.

"Is everyone here present either a witness or a participant in these proceedings?" he asked. Everyone nodded confirmation. Then he looked at Tommy and Jeff. "Are there any questions before we begin the proceedings?" Both plebes shook their heads. "Good! Let's begin." He consulted his notes.

"This is Hearing Number USNA23-1-68. The defendant is accused of violating the Honor Code in that he did willfully remove a photograph of his Company Officer from the Main Office Roster Board and that he then inserted that photo into his combination cap, thereafter using it to ridicule a superior officer."

"Midshipman Fourth-class Thomas Henry Poole? Do you understand these charges?"

"Yes, sir!" Tommy answered boldly. Jeff mentally congratulated Tommy for his self-confidence.

"How do you respond to the charges, Mister Poole?" Smith asked.

"Sir," Tommy replied with equal boldness. "I did *not* take the photo from the Roster Board. I do not know who took the photo. I do not even know if the photo in my cap is the same photo that was taken. I *did* put the photo into my cap, but I never ridiculed my Company Officer."

"Excuse me, sir!" Jeff interjected. "No disrespect intended to Captain Dillingham, but I don't understand how ridicule applies to an honor violation."

Homer Smith looked at Jeff for a long second.

"It applies in that it provides a possible motive for an alleged theft, Mister Polk."

Jeff paused. "Okay, I see, sir."

Homer continued. "Any other questions?" Both Tommy and Jeff shook their heads negatively.

"Very well," Smith continued, "for the first witness, the committee calls Midshipman First-class Kevin Sean Dolan." A firstie Jeff had never seen rose, moved dramatically to the witness chair, and seated himself with a great deal of panache. He seemed to relish the goings-on, and he leaned forward with both hands folded in front of him on the table as he waited for the first question.

"Midshipman Dolan, is it a fact that you were assigned Main Office duty on the evening of Saturday, 21 January 1968?"

"Yes, I was there all evening."

"In what capacity?"

"I was the Midshipman Officer of the Watch that night, the MOOW, representing 17th Company."

"Did anything unusual happen that evening?"

Dolan laughed. As he began speaking, he lifted his hands from the table and waved them dramatically in rhythm with the story. It was clear to Jeff that he had practiced and retold this tale several times since that particular evening. It was also clear that he enjoyed performing for an audience. He leaned forward toward Homer Smith.

"As a matter of fact, it did. It was a dark and stormy night," he began with a broad smile. "About 0200 hours Sunday morning a loud bloodcurdling scream from the vicinity of Tecumseh Court interrupted my meditation." He paused and the upper-class present chuckled, knowing he meant that he had been napping, a watch activity frowned on by the Administration. Dolan continued.

"I sent two messengers out into the cold and dark to investigate. Almost immediately after the messengers departed, I heard a loud scraping sound in the passageway outside the Main Office." He paused again and looked down the table at Lieutenant Powell. "It sounded like a coffin lid being lifted, the nails screeching in unholy protest." Jeff chuckled. Dolan was a good storyteller, though a bit dramatic.

"I asked another messenger to investigate the new sound," he continued, "and I stood guard near the doorway to the office, ready to repel boarders." Everyone chuckled and Dolan warmed to the attention. Dolan continued with renewed flamboyance.

"The second plebe checked the passageway carefully." He paused dramatically. "No one was there, and every door was locked! But, as the second messenger was returning to the office, a figure, hooded and sinister, rushed past, pushing the messenger against me. We gave chase! The culprit had expected to scamper across the rotunda and disappear into the bowels of the fourth wing, but he hadn't counted on the first messengers returning from Tecumseh Court at that precise moment. We nearly trapped him in the rotunda, but he deftly eluded us in a marvelous display of athleticism."

Dolan paused again, then resettled his hands onto the table. "Immediately afterward, when I checked the passageway to see where he could have been hiding, I noticed that the door to the Roster Board was slightly ajar and that one photograph was missing." Dolan smiled dramatically, waiting for the inevitable next question.

"Which photograph was missing?" Homer asked.

Dolan continued with a distinct flamboyance.

"The photo of Captain Rusty Dillingham, the Twenty-third Company Officer."

Homer paused, jotted a note, and smiled at Dolan.

"Thank you, Mister Dolan. I just have one further question. What Company areas are directly in the path of the mystery thief's intended line of flight?"

Dolan smiled.

"Twenty-second and Twenty-third Companies!" he said with gusto.

Smith noted this.

"Are there any other questions from the Committee?" he asked. There were none. "You may be seated, Midshipman Dolan, or you may leave, however I remind you that you must be here tomorrow evening at the same time in case there are defense questions."

"I'll stay and watch," Dolan said as he retreated to his chair.

The plebes who had been messengers verified their boss's story, but both of them elected to depart after they gave testimony.

Smith consulted his notes.

"Next I'd like to hear from Captain Russell Dillingham," he said. Bull rose immediately and strode imposingly to the table. He smiled at Jeff and Tommy before he sat. Jeff was somewhat taken aback by the smile.

"He's the cause of this mess," he thought. "How can he smile when Tommy's future is on the line?"

"Captain Dillingham," Smith asked. "Are you familiar with the charges against Midshipman Fourth-class Poole?"

"I am!"

"Did you initiate those charges?"

"I did!"

"Can you tell us the circumstances that led to this case being formally reported?"

"On Sunday, 5 February 1968, I witnessed a chess competition between our top player, Midshipman Poole, and the best player in Twenty-second Company." Bull smiled and indicated Tommy with one large hand. "Tommy clobbered the enemy player. It was a brilliant game! After the match I noticed that in the victory excitement someone had stepped on Tommy's uniform cap, scuffing it badly. I asked to see the cap. During my examination I looked inside and saw that my picture had been inserted over the photo of his girlfriend. I had been informed that a photo of myself had been reported missing from the Roster board, and I asked him where he had gotten the photo. His answers were unsatisfactory, so I decided an investigation was in order. I asked the Company Commander to initiate an Honor Board to decide whether an honor offense had been committed. They recommended the case be forwarded."

"You say his answers were unsatisfactory? In what way?"

"He was very nervous. He didn't admit taking the photo. He said it mysteriously appeared on his desk along with a cryptic note, which he conveniently destroyed. I felt uncomfortable with his answers."

"Thank you, Captain. I have no further questions." No one else on the Committee wished to ask anything further, and Bull Dillingham rose smartly, put a hand on Tommy's shoulder and squeezed it gently, and returned to his seat.

Again Smith consulted his notes.

"The Committee next calls Midshipman First-class Dale Wayne Micklewski." Jeff had no idea why Micklewski had been listed for testimony. He picked up his pencil, anxious to take notes on what was said. Micklewski was a tall, dark-haired man with flawless skin and almost feminine features. He spoke in a slow, precise soft voice.

Smith began.

"Midshipman Micklewski, are you aware of the accusations being investigated in this case?"

"Yes, I am."

"Can you add anything to the facts presented?"

"Yes, I can! Several weeks ago, before the honor investigation had been initiated, I was feeling a bit of an upset stomach. I was using the head facilities when two midshipmen entered and went to the urinals. I recognized George Abbott's voice. He's one of my plebes. He began talking to his companion, whose voice I did not recognize. He said, 'Hey, John, did you see Tommy's hat?' John replied that he had not. George laughed loudly. 'It's really great!' he said. 'He's got a picture of Bull-shit' -- excuse me sir -- 'Dillingham inside it where his girl's photo was.' The other plebe said, 'So?'

"'He said somebody stole it from the Main Office, and now every time that . . . 'excuse me again sir, 'asshole Dillingham, shits on him, he just glares at the photo and gives it the Hawaiian Good Luck sign. I think it's great revenge!'" With that Micklewski settled back into his chair slightly and waited.

"Those were Midshipman Abbott's exact words?" asked Smith.

"Yes, they were, almost exactly. I remember them because when I heard George speak, my ears perked up." Smith looked at the Committee. Brian Lehre spoke.

"Are you positive he used the word "stole" when he referred to the photo?"

"Yes," Dale replied. "I heard the word distinctly." Lehre nodded. There were no further questions, and Dale Micklewski returned to his seat.

"The Committee next calls Midshipman Fourth-class John Pirelli." John Pirelli was a short, thin but sharp individual who usually ranked near the top of the group in leadership standings. Until the incident of the negative vote, Jeff had considered him one of his most capable classmates. Jeff was unsure of what to expect. Pirelli strode smartly to the witness chair, sat erect, and waited.

"Midshipman Pirelli," Smith began, "are you familiar with the conversation that Mister Micklewski just referred to?"

"I am, sir!"

"Did that conversation happen as he described it?"

"Yes, sir. It did!"

"Including his reference to the theft of the photo?"

"That's what he said. Yes, sir!"

Smith looked at the Committee.

"You're sure he said 'stolen'," asked Lehre.

"Yes, I am!" Pirelli was dismissed. Tommy hastily scribbled a note to Jeff and slid it across the short distance between them. "*Now I understand his negative vote in the Company Hearing!*" the note said. Jeff wasn't sure he agreed.

"The Committee next calls Midshipman Fourth-class George Abbott!" A brooding George approached the witness chair and plopped defiantly into the seat.

"Midshipman Abbott, can you confirm the conversation Mister Micklewski refers to?"

"I remember the conversation vaguely," he replied cautiously.

"Did the conversation go as stated?"

"In general I think so, but I can't remember my exact words nearly as well as Dale Micklewski or John Pirelli."

"But you did hear Mister Poole bragging about the photo in his cap, and you did in fact see that photo?"

"Yes! Tommy didn't keep the photo hidden."

"Do you remember if he referred to the picture as stolen as alleged?"

"No, I don't!"

After George, Smith and the various Committee members consulted their notes for a few moments before Homer looked at Tommy again.

"Okay, Mister Poole. Now it's time for the Committee to ask questions based on the facts presented. Answer each question as completely as possible. My first question is whether you understand the testimony presented thus far?" Tommy agreed that he did.

"Good! You still insist that you did not take the photo from the Roster Board?"

"I do, absolutely!"

"Can you tell us in your own word how you happened to come into possession of the photo?"

"Yes, sir! I found the picture on the center of my desk on Monday morning, 22 January, after I returned from classes. I was the only one in the room at the time. The photo was in a sealed envelope along with a note which said something to the effect that this was a picture of my new sweetheart and I should use it appropriately. I thought it was a great idea, and I immediately put it into my cap."

"And you still insist you did not know it was the photo from the Roster Board when you put it in your cap?"

"Yes."

"When did you hear that a photo might have been taken from the Roster Board?"

"Several days later," Tommy answered. "I don't remember exactly."

"Did you think that the photo in your possession might be the missing photo?"

"I suspected it might."

Lehre asked the next question.

"Did you joke with Midshipman Abbott or any other person that the photo was stolen?"

"Stolen? No! I never considered the picture stolen."

"Why didn't you return the picture?"

"There was no reason to. Another photo replaced it in the Roster Board almost immediately."

"Why did you keep the photo in the cap when you knew it might be stolen?" asked a skeptical Steve Miller. By the tone of the question, Jeff immediately knew he might have trouble convincing Miller of Tommy's innocence.

"I never considered the photo stolen! I kept it in my cap because it was like having a secret advantage over Captain Dillingham."

"Why do you need an advantage over your Company Officer?" Rich Cellon asked.

Tommy hesitated, then chuckled.

"Let's just say he's been *personally* concerned with my progress this year." Jeff could hear Bull laugh loudly at this. He looked around briefly. The Captain seemed to be taking it all marvelously well.

A brief silence followed while Homer looked to the other Committee members to see if they had any further comments. There were none. Jeff looked at his watch. Almost exactly one hour had elapsed.

"Very well!" Smith said. "This concludes the presentation of evidence and testimony. We will reconvene tomorrow at precisely 1930. I remind each of you that the discussions you have heard are confidential. Thank you!" With that the Committee and the staff observer rose and departed. Once they left, the other witnesses headed for the door. A sheepish John Pirelli remained behind and approached Tommy Poole.

"Sorry about the testimony, Tommy," he said.

"Don't be," Tommy replied. "You are only telling the truth."

"If you hadn't voted against Tommy in the company hearing, none of this would be taking place!" burst George Abbott. John was taken aback.

"How did you know my vote?" he asked.

"We just do asshole! That was no way to support a classmate."

"Listen," Pirelli said. "I voted my conscience. What else am I supposed to do?"

"You might have signed Tommy's death certificate as far as his staying here is concerned," George replied.

"It didn't seem that way at the time. I had no way of knowing how the other members were going to vote. Besides, classmate or not, the Code is clear; and if he violated it, he must be dismissed."

"Well," George said. "The Code may be clear, but Tommy's offense sure isn't. What the hell's gonna happen when you're in the fleet, shit-for-brains, and you don't protect your shipmates when there's a shadow of a doubt?"

"I did what I though was right!" Pirelli said with finality. He turned toward the door and departed.

"You're still an asshole!" George replied to the departing figure.

Tommy waited until John was gone, then he turned to Jeff.

"So what do you think?"

"It's still fifty-fifty. It seems that Lehre and Miller are going to be the hardest to convince. The others looked open-minded. Cellon was downright sympathetic. Everything depends on how we present the defense tomorrow."

The mystery Lieutenant who had chosen the seat in the far corner had been waiting patiently nearby. He was a shortish, somewhat chunky and unkempt instructor with deep blue intelligent and laughing eyes. His uniform was wrinkled and dusty and several pencils and pens protruded from the jacket pocket. His thin red hair was far too long to be regulation in any Navy, and was combed strategically over a balding area. Tommy noticed him for the first time.

"Bill!" Tommy said enthusiastically. "I'm really glad you could come!" Jeff was greatly surprised that Tommy actually referred to an officer by his first name. That surprise lasted only a few seconds as Lieutenant Bill Harlan introduced himself to the group. "Bill is my instructor in advanced physics," Tommy informed them.

"Actually Tommy has been teaching me a few things," he said enthusiastically. "The guy is a certifiable genius. And please call me Bill. I hate the military stiffness." Bill then looked at Tommy quizzically. "This is all about a three-by-five photograph?" he asked incredulously.

"No!" Jeff replied emphatically. "The photograph is inconsequential! This is about theft! This is about honesty! This is about a sacred Honor Code!"

Bill snorted loudly.

"It can't be too sacred if it might get Tommy here expelled!" Then he looked seriously at Tommy. "You should be at MIT anyway. They'll appreciate you up there, and you can take any pictures you want from the walls. Believe me, they won't mind." Tommy laughed, then Bill handed Jeff a written note. "Here are some questions you can ask me tomorrow, along with my suggested responses, and why I think they might help Tommy's case. I'll be here on time and ready to do battle with the crazies."

"The crazies?" George asked.

"Yeah!" Bill replied. "What's happening in this room is silly and a bit insane, but you guys are so wrapped up in the system and this so-called Honor Code that you can't see it from the perspective of an outsider like me."

At almost exactly 2100 that evening a messenger from the Main Office arrived at Rock Stone's room. He spoke to Rock for a brief moment, handed him a note, and hurried happily away from Tiger Country. Rock studied the message for a long time, and called Captain Dillingham. After informing the Captain, Rock went to Jim Merritt's room. Everyone was studying for the next day's classes.

"Jim," he said after he entered. "Can you come down to the Company Office for a minute? I have something to discuss with you." Jim agreed, and soon after the two of them were seated in the small anteroom.

Stone held up the note.

"A messenger brought this to my room a few minutes ago. I already informed the Captain." He paused and looked closely at Jim. "The call was from the office of the Red Cross in Amarillo, relayed through the Public Affairs Duty Office in Washington, D.C.." Rock could see Jim take a deep breath and wait for the news. Rock continued.

"The doctors say that your mom is near death, Jim. She has apparently taken a turn for the worse today, and she's in the hospital. She's asking that you come home to her before it's too late. The Captain has authorized emergency leave starting immediately, but I don't believe there will be any flights until morning from either Friendship Airport in Baltimore or from National in D.C.. The duty section in the Main Office is calling now to find the next available flight. Pack up and be ready for the Academy civilian messenger service van to drive you to Washington. Get a good night's sleep if you can. You may have to leave before dawn."

"Jim," he continued. "I'm very sorry about this. I lost my mother when I was much younger, so I know what a terrible shock this can be. Let me know if I can do anything."

"I can't go!" Jim said loudly.

Stone was shocked!

"What's that?" he asked.

"I can't go just yet!" Jim replied pleadingly. "I have to wait until after the Honor Committee Meeting tomorrow evening."

"Jim," Stone said, "your family comes first. You have to go immediately!"

Jim looked at Stone with troubled eyes.

"I can't go, Rock! Tommy's case may depend on how well I present my information -- and what I have to say is vital. If I desert my friend and comrade now, I'll never forgive myself."

"But what about your mother. She needs you, Jim!"

"Mom would understand most of all. I'll call Dad immediately and tell him I have to stay one more day but that I'll be back as soon as I can after tomorrow night."

"It might be too late, Jim!"

"Mom will understand." Jim looked near tears as he faced Rock. "I have to do this for Tommy. He'd do it for me."

Rock looked into Jim's eyes for a long moment.

"Okay, Jim," he said. "I'll go down to the Main Office and make the travel arrangements personally so that you can leave immediately after the meeting tomorrow." Rock stood and stepped over to Jim. He put a hand on his shoulder reassuringly. "I understand, Jim," he said. "I really do!"

"Rock?" Jim said as he prepared to return to his room.

"Yes?"

"Don't tell anyone, okay? Let me handle this on my own."

"Sure, Jim."

Jeff didn't get a bit of sleep that night. From 2000 to 2200 he discussed testimony and questions with the various witnesses. Afterward he sat in the Company Office and listed the questions he would ask of each non-plebe witness. He followed that with the counter-questions he would ask depending on each possible response they could give. The permutations soon began to overwhelm him, but he kept doggedly at it. By 0200 he had finished preparing for the questioning, and he returned to his room. But he lay in his rack and fidgeted for the remainder of the evening, wondering what he might have forgotten. Twice he pulled back his sheets and went to his desk where he scribbled notes at the window by the light of the full moon. By morning he was as prepared as he thought he could be.

For Tommy Poole the night was just as hectic, but Tommy suffered even greater anxiety. At 2100 he went to the phones and called home. He had told his parents everything he knew about the upcoming case and the possibilities for success, and they were incredibly supportive.

"Sounds like everything went very well," his father said after Tommy related his account of the evening's testimony. "I don't see how they can possibly convict you of anything with so little evidence to go on."

"This isn't a court of law, Dad," he patiently explained. "The committee members will vote based on their impressions and feelings about the case."

"Well that doesn't seem fair to me," his dad replied.

"It's not criminal justice, but the honor system has worked successfully for more than a hundred years, and you can't fault the quality of the people who graduate, so something about the process must work very well."

"All the same, it isn't possible they could find you guilty."

"It doesn't seem like it to me either, dad, but it could happen. Jeff Polk says my chances are still no better than fifty-fifty."

"That can't be right, son. But you listen to me. No matter what the outcome, you have your mom's and my complete support. If they say you have to quit, come on home. You can go to school anywhere you like. I'll bet all the scholarship offers are still valid."

For a moment Tommy's eyes teared up.

"Thanks, dad. I know I have your support in this."

"My son a thief! Ridiculous! Boy is my Congressman going to hear about this!"

"Don't do anything just yet, dad. Let's see what happens tomorrow."

"Okay, Tommy. I understand."

When he hung up, he called his girlfriend Sara who gave him her support as well as promises of undying love. It was just three months ago during the party after the Army-Navy game that he and Sara had shared their first act of physical intimacy, and Tommy still felt the afterglow. The once-chubby bookworm from Flint Michigan, the shy introvert who had studiously substituted academics for dating all during high school, had found that he had a great deal of passion, and his new sleek, well-tuned body gave him the stamina to exploit that passion.

"How did everything go?" Sara asked.

"About as predicted," he replied.

"Oh," Sara said, obviously disappointed. She was a budding attorney who had hoped that the entire case would be dismissed based on lack of concrete evidence.

"But it's okay," Tommy replied. "Tomorrow I get my turn, and Jeff and I have worked up quite a show. If *we* plebe Tigers can't convince the committee, no one can."

"That's what I'm afraid of, sweetheart. But just remember that I love you and whatever happens I don't for an instant believe that you stole anything except my heart. No matter what I'll be waiting."

Tommy accepted her support gratefully and returned to his room. Hank and George were there when he returned.

"Well, Tommy," Hank said, "I don't know about you, but I'm really confident the case will be dismissed tomorrow. There's no way they could find you guilty."

"Yeah, Tommy," George added. "We're gonna blow them all away tomorrow night. Once they listen to what we have to say they can't help but dismiss the charges. Hell, they'll probably even give you an official apology when it's all over.

"Maybe so," Tommy replied. "But win or lose, I'll be glad when this is over. It's been hell on earth."

Tommy's room went to bed on time that night, but like Jeff, Tommy slept badly. Repeatedly he imagined what civilian life would be like. It seemed to him that without the constant activity and incredible sense of belonging that Annapolis had given him he would be lost. He really liked the Academy. During the last eight months it had become a vital part of him. He loved the campus, the uniforms, the formations, the instructors, the intramural sports -- even the lousy football team -- and he knew instinctively that he would never be so close to anyone ever again in his life as he was with his fellow plebe companymates. He didn't want to leave, and he decided that if a fight is what Dillingham and the Academy wanted, then, by God, they'd get the best one they'd ever seen from Thomas Henry Poole.

THE INTERIOR OF MAHAN HALL LIBRARY

The interior of the old library is elegant. Oil paintings and the busts of famous people frame the wide marble stairs.

CHAPTER 13

DRAWING THE LINE

"Mister Poole," Homer Smith said calmly, "are you ready for the questioning phase of this meeting?"

Tommy took a deep breath and stared boldly at the Committee Chairman.

"Yes, sir. We are!" he asserted. Jeff smiled slightly. Tommy exuded calm confidence in the middle of the most critical crisis of his young life. He had obviously had an excellent Plebe Year. Jeff wished he could feel as confident as Tommy Poole sounded. No brilliant flashes of inspiration had come to him during the night. During the day's classes, he could not concentrate on the instructors. His mind kept returning to the ugly possibilities and the great responsibility he had reluctantly assumed. He sighed. He'd just have to stick to the plan he and Tommy had drafted.

"You may begin when you are ready," Homer said, and he and the other committee members settled into their chairs to listen.

"First we would like to recall Midshipman First-class Dolan, sir." Smith nodded. Dolan approached the witness chair with relish. He smiled broadly at both the committee and at Tommy. Jeff began the questioning.

"Mister Dolan, sir . . . " Dolan interrupted.

"Please, no need to stand on formality with me. Call me Kevin. I'm not a stern taskmaster like some of my more celebrated classmates." With that he glanced toward Rock Stone, who returned his smile. "I've spooned every plebe in my Company," he continued.

"Very well, Kevin," Jeff continued. "That'll make things easier. Let's continue." He consulted his notes quickly.

"You say that the mystery plebe you encountered in the early morning hours of 22 January headed across the rotunda toward the doors to the fourth wing?"

"Yes, he did. And with great haste, I might add."

"And you say that Twenty-third Company is one destination immediately adjacent to those doors?"

"That's also correct."

"Isn't it also true that those doors provide access to every Company in the Second Regiment? Every Company from Eighteenth to the Thirty-sixth?"

Dolan pondered dramatically.

"The thief could have continued through those doors to any of the Companies you mentioned, that's true!"

"So according to the laws of probability, there's only a one-in-eighteen chance that the destination was, in fact, Tiger company. That calculates as less than 6 percent. Those aren't very good odds, are they?"

"Probability not!" Dolan replied, beaming delightedly. Jeff and several others laughed.

"Okay," Jeff continued. "Let's talk about the mystery thief himself. You say he shoved a messenger and almost knocked him down; then he eluded three of you in a chase through the rotunda?"

"He didn't actually knock the messenger down, just sent him slightly off balance -- and he actually eluded five of us."

"Five of you? That's very impressive! Would you say this mystery thief was an athlete?"

"Of no small measure!" Dolan chuckled. "If he had been running back kick-offs during this past season, Navy might have had a bowl opportunity."

"That good, huh?"

"He darted one way, then another, keeping us off balance the entire time. He spun around, headed up the stairs toward Memorial Hall, turned, leaped down at least ten steps to the floor, darted again, and finally went up the side stairs four at a time. Not one of the five of us even touched the man. Then he faked us out again by pretending to exit the stairwell on the third deck third wing. Instead he slipped quietly across the rotunda to the fourth wing by way of the personnel bridge on the fourth level. It was altogether an amazing feat of daring, cunning, and panache."

"It sounds to me as if you admire whoever it was."

"I do. I personally believe the Navy needs more daring-do. I witnessed incredible bravery and seat-of-the-pants initiative. It was a privilege to see him in action."

Jeff leaned toward Tommy and whispered to him. Tommy stood and faced Dolan.

"Mister Dolan, . . . Kevin," Jeff said, " I know you only saw him fleetingly. But could this possibly be the person who challenged your entire Watch Section that evening?" Dolan made a show of studying Tommy's face and physique.

"Not a chance!" he said with determination.

"If things were as hectic as you describe," interrupted Midshipman Lehre, "how can you be so sure?"

"I got a very close look at his face twice. First when he pushed the messenger in my direction and second when he ran past me up the side stairs. The man who eluded us was much taller, more athletic in appearance, and ran like the wind."

"In a chase situation you could be mistaken, however," added Homer Smith.

Dolan chuckled. He had been waiting for such a comment.

"The person I encountered had red hair and freckles, and spoke with a New England accent!" he said with a dramatic flourish.

"What?" Lehre exclaimed. "How do you know that?"

"I'm a thespian. My avocation is studying people, and it's very hard to hide a well-freckled complexion and the ruddy glow and red eyebrows indicative of a red-haired man. Also I talked to the person briefly as he was departing the rotunda four floors above."

Jeff turned and looked quickly at Kevin O'Reilly. He could see suspicious stares from the Committee in Kevin's direction. Kevin's face had turned bright red, and he slumped down slightly in his chair. Tommy Poole chuckled, but didn't look at Kevin.

"You say you talked to him?" Smith asked. "What did you say?"

"It was he who spoke," Dolan replied.

"Then what did he say?" Smith asked.

Dolan laughed.

"He inquired of our health. He seemed concerned he might have injured us in our mad chase. He was a swashbuckler and a complete gentleman."

Homer Smith looked directly at Kevin O'Reilly. He addressed Dolan.

"Midshipman Dolan, do you see the individual in this room?" Jeff and Tommy both turned and looked at the witnesses. Dillingham and Stone stared boldly at Kevin, who was desperately trying to look un-Irish. Unfortunately the more attention he received the redder and more Irish his countenance became. He smiled sheepishly at Dolan.

Dolan assumed a totally blank face as he looked from person to person. His gaze fastened on Kevin for a long moment.

"The individual I saw looked somewhat like that plebe," he said, pointing dramatically in Kevin's direction.

Jeff's heart immediately sank.

"Jesus!" he thought. "This could mean that Kevin would be up before the Honor Committee like Tommy. Two honor offenses in one group of plebes. That was a very bad record."

"But," Dolan continued. "The person I saw was bigger, more larger-then-life. His freckles seemed more pronounced. His hair more flaming red. His eyes more alive with passion. I don't think this is the one."

Lehre wasn't convinced. He consulted his witness list and addressed Kevin.

"O'Reilly, isn't it?" Kevin nodded affirmation.

"You are a Company-mate of Mister Poole's?" Again Kevin only nodded.

"You're here to present testimony as to Mister Poole's character?" Kevin nodded, and it was clear he had no intention of speaking unless forced to. Lehre smiled, then added.

"Where are you from, O'Reilly?"

Kevin smiled in return, then using his best imitation of Reb Ramsey, said, "Ahm from Ballston, suh!" Everyone in the room, Lehre included, laughed. Dolan actually applauded.

"Well done!" he said in congratulations. Kevin smiled sheepishly and reddened even more.

"Okay, okay," Smith said. "Enough sidetracking. Let's return to the case at hand. Please continue Mister Polk."

"Mister Dolan, you say the photograph of Captain Dillingham was missing immediately after your encounter with the unknown person in the passageway. Did you notice that the person who eluded you carried anything with him?"

"No. I did not!"

"Did you see any person at or near the Roster Board?"

"No again!"

"Then you don't know if the person you chased actually took the photo, do you?"

"No, sir. I do not!"

"Is it a requirement of the Watch Section to check the Roster Board for contents?" Jeff asked.

"No, it's not!"

"So you checked the passageway because the fleeing figure had come from that direction, and you saw that the door to the Roster Board was slightly ajar and a photo was missing, but you have no idea when the photo was taken. It could have been that night. It could have been the night before. It could have been weeks earlier."

"That's correct!"

"What did you do when you discovered that a photo was missing?"

"I made a note to discuss it with the oncoming Midshipman Officer of the Watch, a Midshipman First-class Charles Schreiner from Second Company. He showed me a storage cabinet in the Main Office where a supply of the photos are kept."

"And what did you do?"

"We had a plebe messenger replace the photo."

"How many copies of Captain Dillingham's photo were in that cabinet?"

"At least a dozen."

"Could anyone in the Main Office who knew where to look get into that cabinet and remove a photograph?"

"The cabinet is always unlocked so far as I know. The answer to your question is yes."

"So again, it then seems logical that the photo in Tommy Poole's cap could have come, not from the Roster Board, but from the files?"

"It's possible, yes."

"That also means," interrupted Lehre smugly, "that Tommy Poole himself could have sneaked into the cabinet during watch and taken the photo at some other time prior to that evening. It may now be possible that Mister Poole wasn't the person the Watch Section chased that particular evening, but somebody took the photo from the Roster Board, and the photo in his hat had to come from somewhere. So it's still possible he took *a* photo or accepted a stolen photo."

Jeff looked at Tommy.

"Have you ever had duty in the Main Office, Classmate Poole?"

"No, I have not!"

Jeff returned his gaze to Dolan.

"Are you an honest man, Mister Dolan?" he said, switching tactics.

Dolan's features narrowed slightly and his faced clouded over. When he answered, the humor had left his voice.

"I believe I am completely honorable."

"Yet you practice an avocation based on deception. Every time you act, you try to convince the audience of a lie."

Dolan hesitated only slightly, then smiled at Jeff.

"Yes, that's true. Otherwise there would be no entertainment in acting." Dolan's voice rose in timbre and became more British and passionate as he spoke. "If I stood before you and recited Hamlet's great soliloquy, you would hear the princeliness in my words and feel my anguish and know that I was greatly wronged." He dropped his eyes and his tone. "Otherwise, my act would be a failure."

Jeff applauded.

"Well done! So sometimes it's acceptable, even preferable, for a midshipman to be a good liar? And that does not violate the Honor Code in the least."

"For me, unquestionably!" Dolan replied with a smile.

"Thank you, Midshipman Dolan. That's all I have." Dolan rose.

"We probably won't be needing you this evening, Mister Dolan," Smith said. "You may leave now if you wish."

Dolan smiled. "No, I think I'll stay! This is great entertainment!"

Jeff consulted his notes as Dolan returned to his seat.

"I'd like to question Captain Dillingham, please." Bull rose and took the witness chair.

"Good evening, Captain!" Jeff said. "Sorry for the inconvenience, but I have a few questions for you about what's been said so far."

"Ask any question you like," Bull replied.

"Okay," Jeff began. "First let's talk about the photo. You say the first time you noticed it was in Tommy Poole's cap?"

"Yes, it was."

"What was the occasion of that incident?"

Bull settled back in his chair slightly and smiled.

"My Tigers had challenged Twenty-second Company to a series of contests. One of the events pitted the best chess players in each Company against each other. Tommy Poole represented the Tigers."

"How did the match go?"

Bull's smile increased and his eyes twinkled.

"Poole murdered the son-of-a-gun! He was brilliant!"

"I don't know much about chess myself," Jeff admitted. "Why do you use the word murdered?"

"I play a little chess myself," he said. "Just a little, but enough. I watched Tommy's moves carefully. He set up the opponent and toyed with him. Had him thinking Tommy was a rank amateur. When the poor fool pressed a supposed advantage after Tommy purposefully lost his queen, Poole pounced. In two moves the opponent knew he was in deep trouble. I could sense the fear in his face." Bull laughed. "On the last move Poole waited calmly, even though time was running out. He even asked questions unrelated to the match. Damn! He had me nervous. At the last possible instant he slipped his rook into the final position, announced '*Checkmate*', and that was that! What a show!"

"Good huh?"

"Better than good! It was great!"

"Then you saw his messed up cap and noticed your picture? What was your initial reaction?"

"I was upset!"

"Why?"

"The compartment in the combination cap is traditionally for the photograph of a girlfriend, not a Company Officer. I thought it was inappropriate for him to display my picture."

"Why do you think he had your photo there?"

"I have no idea."

"What's your relationship been like with Tommy Poole?"

"Perfectly professional!"

"Do you think Tommy is a good midshipman?"

"He will never have a great deal of physical stamina. His uniform appearance is barely adequate. He has little in the way of personal charisma. He exhibits questionable battlefield leadership skills. And he has been consistently ranked near the bottom of the grease ladder by the upper-class and the plebes in Tiger Company."

"That doesn't sound so good," Jeff observed. "Would you be happy to see Tommy Poole leave the Academy?"

"For months the company leadership and I have agonized over Mister Poole's prospects. For a time I was convinced that he would not make a suitable naval officer and that his departure would be in everyone's mutual interest."

"That's very interesting," Jeff replied. "Yet I saw you smile at him and squeeze his shoulder encouragingly yesterday evening after you testified."

"Yes!" Dillingham said with gusto. "Despite my professional opinions, I like Tommy Poole. He has guts and a strong competitive spirit."

"I'm confused," Jeff said slowly. "It almost sounds to me as if you've changed your mind about Tommy. Has your attitude toward Tommy's character and potential changed recently?"

"Based on what I've seen recently, Tommy Poole seems to be making great strides."

"And how would you rank him among his peers right now?"

Bull considered.

"I would say he's moved into the middle third and is gaining ground quickly."

"So maybe he deserves a chance to stay and to graduate?"

"I'm beginning to think so," Bull said nodding his head slowly and looking directly at Tommy.

"Tell us more about the Company competition? Tell us about Tommy's part in the race to Hospital Point?"

Bull laughed and turned toward the committee.

"Another great performance!" he announced. He paused and stared again at Tommy, still smiling. "Although he didn't finish in the top five, he wasn't last either."

"What was Tommy's condition when he finished?"

"He had a bloody nose and a sore abdomen."

"From a foot race?"

Bull laughed.

"Apparently the competitors took some liberties with the rules when they were out of sight. Tommy was slightly injured, but he still managed to aid our runners, recover from a beating, and pass the final two opponents on the way back. It was glorious!"

Homer Smith interrupted, tapping his pencil rapidly on his yellow notepad.

"What's the purpose of this questioning, Mister Polk?"

"Sir, I'm trying to establish the fact that Tommy Poole has a very strong sense of what's honorable and that he will do his duty when many of us would quit. I'm also trying to show that for a person like Tommy theft is inconceivable, that if he did accept a photo and put it into his cap, it was only for its motivational value, not to ridicule the Captain or to dishonor himself. And that especially, Tommy Poole would never violate the Honor Code."

"Well," Smith continued, "the committee concedes the enviable character of Midshipman Fourth-class Poole, but the question as to whether the photo was stolen and used with foreknowledge of its theft remains open."

Jeff consulted his notes again.

"Captain Dillingham, you're a war hero, aren't you?"

"I have served my country in combat on several occasions."

"You are also an advocate of the Honor Code, sir?"

"I believe in death before dishonor, if that's what you mean."

"That's a noble code of conduct. Tell me, is it honorable to lie to the enemy?"

"I don't know what you mean?"

"You know, to deceive the enemy with false troop movements, or camouflage, or deceptive messages?"

"Of course!"

"So it's still honorable to lie as long as it's to an enemy?"

"If that deception saves the lives of my troops, you're damn right!"

"What about to the Russians? Can we lie to them? Hide our plans? Give them false leads and information?"

"Absolutely!"

"But we're not at war with the Russians."

Dillingham harrumphed loudly.

"We may not be in a shooting war with the communists right this instant, but judging from the political climate, we well might be. Therefore, it's in the best interests of the country not to be open."

"And even to be deceptive?"

"Of course!"

"What about internal politics? Say for instance the press corps. Would you deceive a member of Jack Anderson's staff?"

"If I was convinced it would save one brave warrior from a senseless death, I'd slit Jack Anderson's throat myself with a dull bayonet. The press seeks conspiracies where none exist. Half of them hate us like we're the reincarnation of Adolph Hitler. 'Baby Killers!' they call us. To keep the knowledge of the disposition and movement of my troops from the press I'd lie to my own mother."

Jeff pressed on.

"What about Congress."

"Dishonorable pimps! Kill the lot of them! They've cost more American lives than the enemy!" Dillingham paused, his face red and the veins in his temples protruding.

"I've seen Congressmen in Vietnam," he continued, pointing to his chest-full of ribbons. "One even pinned on my last Purple Heart and Silver Star." Bull laughed loudly again. "Those fat-assed empty-smilers supposedly come to 'find facts', but all they do is drink booze, pose for pictures, and play hide-the-sausage with their female staffers. If just one of them had to face down a Russian Kalashnikov or a Regiment of Chinese regulars which had come across the border a few days previously, he'd be screaming either to provide additional support for the poor troops in the field, or to pull every American out so we could go home and raise our kids in peace."

Bull paused and lowered his voice, but continued to speak with conviction. "There is no honor in Congress! They are elected based on lies! They represent money not voters! And their only interest is self-interest! Yes! I'd lie to Congress if I thought it meant one fewer body bag!"

"But what about the Honor Code!"

"That *is* the Honor Code, Polk!" Bull said, becoming loud again. "Listen up! When this nation gives you responsibility for the lives of other men, you had better be willing to do whatever it takes to protect them and return them to their families. This nation may well hate its Armed Forces and wish them all dead, and they may turn out in the millions to protest Vietnam. But so long as we wear the uniform, we must not violate the sacred trust of the President and the men under us. The rest is all bullshit!"

During Dillingham's speeches no one in the room had moved so much as an inch. Bull had that special way with words, particularly when he was excited and his usually-calm voice rose in volume. Everyone relaxed and let out a collective sigh. Jeff knew that what Bull had said was the general sentiment at the Academy -- probably at every Academy -- and he could understand it up to a point, but sometimes the fervency and single-mindedness of the military sentient frightened him. He shuddered involuntarily as goose bumps raced up the middle of his back.

"Thank you Captain Dillingham," Jeff said after a slight pause. Bull then glared at the Committee almost challengingly, but no one had anything further to ask.

"Next I'd like to call Midshipman First-class Micklewski." Dale approached the chair tentatively and sat almost plebe-like on its very edge as if waiting to dart for the door at the first sign of trouble.

"Mister Micklewski, yesterday you mentioned that you distinctly heard Midshipman Abbott say that Tommy said the photo had been stolen. Knowing that the fate of a fellow midshipman may rest on the accuracy of what's said in testimony, are you absolutely certain that Abbot said that Tommy said the photo was 'stolen?'"

"Yes," Micklewski said smugly. "He said stolen."

"Not missing, or borrowed, or taken, or removed? You're certain he used that particular word?"

"Yes, I am!"

"Well, we all know that what George says he heard is hearsay. Not everybody can remember things accurately. George could have been mistaken about what he heard Tommy say, isn't that true?"

"All I know is what I heard!"

"But what you heard may not be what Tommy actually said. You would have to allow for that wouldn't you?"

"I suppose it's possible."

"That's the problem with hearsay evidence and the reason it's not allowed in a court of law. I learned in psychology class last semester that everybody filters what they hear and experience and that several people can recall the exact event in different ways, sometimes even totally different ways. So what you say that George said about what Tommy said isn't really worth anything."

"I reported what I had heard." Dale said indignantly.

"Well, yes you did," Jeff replied calmly. "But if I may ask, when did you report that hearsay conversation?"

"I don't know. I told Captain Dillingham about three weeks ago."

"Wasn't that several weeks after it had occurred?"

"I suppose so."

Jeff looked purposefully puzzled.

"Why did you wait so long to report it?"

"Once I realized that the Captain had asked for an Honor investigation, I realized that the information might be relevant."

"Yes," Jeff said assuming an even-more-puzzled voice. "I can understand that. But what I can't understand is that if you heard George tell someone that Tommy had a 'stolen' item in his possession several weeks earlier, why didn't you report it immediately? Wouldn't that be what the Honor Code requires?"

Micklewski paused in a panic. It was clear he had not considered those implications.

"I wasn't sure he had anything that was stolen. I didn't see the photo until long afterward."

"But surely you should have approached Tommy and confronted him with your knowledge?"

Dale Micklewski paused for a very long time considering what to say next.

"I didn't consider the photo as actually stolen," he said slowly.

"But it was supposedly taken from the Roster Board, and Tommy supposedly admitted that it was stolen. How could you not consider it stolen?"

"It was only a three-by-five photograph. Sometimes midshipmen move things for fun just to annoy the system. At first I figured as much."

"When did you decide that an Honor offense might be involved?"

"I told you. When Captain Dillingham initiated the investigation, I reconsidered."

"So until you thought Tommy was in trouble with the Captain, you didn't personally consider him in trouble at all?"

"No! I don't suppose I did."

"Yet here Tommy sits, accused of an Honor violation. So I guess not reporting immediately was a small mistake on your part?"

The always volatile Micklewski looked quickly back and forth between the Committee and Jeff Polk, then exploded in anger.

"Yes! A mistake! Okay? I admit it!"

Jeff continued soothingly, "Well, that's great! It takes a big man to admit his mistakes." Then he paused and looked at Dale Micklewski closely, still with a broad smile on his face. "Now, since you were unsure initially about the supposed theft, and you now admit you made a mistake, surely it's possible you also could have erred about hearing George use the word 'stolen?'"

Dale Micklewski looked hard at Jeff, realizing that Jeff had opened a door that could release him from his involvement in the entire process. Jeff knew Micklewski was also considering Captain Dillingham's new-found respect for Tommy Poole. He took a long time to consider his reply.

"It's possible I am mistaken," he said slowly.

"So maybe you didn't hear the word stolen?"

"It's possible!"

"Thank you Mister Micklewski." Jeff beamed and Tommy leaned in toward him smiling.

"Good work!" he whispered.

"But it's also possible you *did* hear the word stolen, isn't it?" Brian Lehre asked as Micklewski began to rise from the chair.

"I can't say for sure," Dale answered and hastily departed the conference room.

"Next I'd like to question Midshipman Fourth-class Pirelli." John strode to the chair and quickly sat.

"Mister Pirelli, you just heard Midshipman First-class Micklewski admit that he might not have heard the word 'stolen' when George Abbott was describing Tommy's statement. Is it possible you are also mistaken?" Pirelli looked closely at Tommy as he spoke.

"Sorry, Tommy," he said. "But George did say that you said you had a stolen photograph."

"Could George have been mistaken about what he heard Tommy say?"

"Of course he could," John replied, slightly irritated. "I had the same psychology course. George was excited and he might have misspoken."

"He might also have said the word but not referred to an actual theft?" Jeff added.

Pirelli paused and considered.

"I'm not sure I follow you," he replied.

"I mean you can steal a base, or steal a heart, or steal a kiss, but none of those incidents actually describe Honor Code theft do they?"

"No, of course they don't."

"So if Tommy or George said the photo was stolen, they could have meant that it had disappeared from its previous location, or that it was borrowed, or that it was misplaced. They didn't necessarily have to be referring to the actual commission of a crime."

"That's true!"

Jeff consulted his notes again.

"John, you're an alternate member of the Company Honor Board. What does the Honor Code require when a midshipman suspects a theft?"

"It should be reported immediately to the Company Honor representatives, or the thief should be approached in private to discover his motives. Before any Honor offense is reported, the reporting individual must be absolutely sure of the facts."

"That's very true," Jeff replied encouragingly. "But you didn't report Tommy Poole after you heard George Abbott say he had a stolen item. How come?"

"It seemed to me initially that George was mistaken, that the theft was more a prank than an actual offense. I exercised my duty to ignore what I had heard."

"But you came forward later? Why?"

"Well, Jeff, I'm just a plebe like you. Once the Captain initiated the investigation, I thought that maybe I had been mistaken. Since the Board needed to examine all the information, I came forward."

"You still don't think what Tommy did was theft?"

"I don't personally think so, but this is one for better heads than mine to sort out and decide." No one had any further questions for John Pirelli.

"George Abbott, please!" George strode defiantly to the witness chair, seemingly more confident than the previous night.

"Midshipman Abbott," Jeff began, "about your statement to John Pirelli in the head. You still are uncertain about your exact wording?"

"Yes, of course I am!"

"Do you think Tommy Poole stole the photo or accepted and used it knowing it was stolen?"

"Absolutely not! He'd have to be stupid, and stupid is one thing Tommy Poole definitely isn't."

"Can you explain that please?"

"Sure! Tommy had the photo in his cap. But if he thought it was stolen, then why the hell did he show it off to so many people? He'd have hidden it somewhere and not said a word. This is Annapolis, after all, and we do live by the Honor Code. I can't even figure what this whole thing's about. There's no way Tommy stole anything!"

"Thank you for your opinion, Mister Abbott," Homer Smith interrupted sternly. "But I think the committee is perfectly capable of deciding whether there has or has not been an Honor offense committed. Leave that to us, please."

Properly chastised, George replied in a more sedate tone.

"Aye, aye, sir!" There were no further questions of George Abbott.

After George had time to settle back into his seat, Jeff again consulted his notes.

"Mister Chairman," he said, "I have finished my questioning of yesterday's witnesses. I would now like to make a couple brief comments concerning the evidence."

Homer answered almost immediately.

"You may do so."

"Thank you, sir!" Jeff rose to his feet and consulted his notes again. Facing the committee, he began. "Gentlemen, there are really only two indisputable facts that have been presented in this conference room. The first is that a photograph of Captain Dillingham was missing from the Main Office Roster Board, and the second is that Tommy Poole had *a* picture of Captain Dillingham in his cap. That's it! Everything else is accusation, hearsay, and conjecture. We don't know who took the photo. We don't know how a photo got onto Tommy's desk. We don't even know if the photo in Tommy's cap is the photo from the Roster Board.

"On the face of it, that's pretty flimsy evidence. Certainly this kind of case would never get to trial in a civilian court." Jeff hesitated before continuing, and before Homer Smith could interrupt. "Now, I know that this isn't a court of law, and I also know the Honor Code is sacred for every midshipman. We cannot allow dishonor. As the good Captain has indicated, the honor of our nation depends on it. However, we also can't afford to loose a midshipman of the caliber of Thomas Henry Poole, who obviously didn't lie, cheat, or steal, and who is an excellent midshipman."

"Therefore, if I may, I'd like to suggest that we take a quick recess and that the committee discuss the case in private and take a preliminary ballot, as is their right. If the consensus is to dismiss the case, then let's dismiss it immediately. Otherwise I am ready to present new testimony, character witnesses, and convincing supporting evidence that this case has been undeniably a waste of the committee's time and energy."

Homer Smith looked at the other committee members who each nodded. Then he addressed Tommy.

"Mister Poole," he said. "The committee will take a 20-minute recess and discuss the case. Afterward we will take a preliminary ballot. If the result of that balloting is for dismissal, we will recall the witnesses and yourself and formally vote in your presence. If the results are inconclusive, we will hear addition testimony before casting the final ballots. Do you understand what we intend?"

"Yes, sir," Tommy said.

"Very well," Homer announced to everyone. "All persons except the committee, the staff observer, and the recorder will please leave the room. The committee will reconvene in 22 minutes at precisely 2100." Everyone rose and filed from the room.

In the passageway George Abbott rushed over and congratulated Jeff and Tommy. "Great work! There's no way they will vote to continue this abortion."

"I hope so," Tommy answered slowly, and not at all confidently. "I hope so!"

HOW LONG HAVE YOU BEEN IN THE NAVY?

All me bloomin' life , sir! Me mother was a mermaid, me father was King Neptune. I was born on the crest of a wave and rocked in the cradle of the deep. Seaweed and barnacles are me clothes. Every tooth in me head is a marlinspike; the hair on me head is hemp. Every bone in me body is a spar, and when I spits, I spits tar! I'se hard, I is, I am, I are! Sir!"

From *Reef Points*

CHAPTER 14

LAST PLEAS

"Thank you all for returning so promptly," Midshipman First-class Smith announced after the room had settled again. Jeff could see at once that he was deadly serious. "Before I announce the results of our preliminary vote I want to read a quote from *Reef Points*."

He picked up a worn copy of *Reef Points* and continued. "*It is by no means enough that an officer of the Navy should be a capable mariner. He must be that, of course, but also a great deal more. He should be as well a gentleman of liberal education, refined manners, punctilious courtesy, and the nicest sense of personal honor.*" Smith put down the *Reef Points* carefully, on the table. He looked at the group and smiled.

"Whenever I get confused about how to judge a supposed honor offense I always return to that quotation. It tells me that the conduct of Midshipmen must be above that of any other group of college-aged students. It tells me that Midshipmen are special, elite, and must withstand the closest scrutiny of the system and the nation." Jeff felt a sudden sinking feeling. He could hear fidgeting behind him, so he knew his discomfort was shared.

Smith continued. "This Committee has a very serious responsibility. We fully realize we are deciding the fate of another human being, and never make a decision rashly or based solely on emotion or hunches. We must be absolutely sure before we cast a guilty vote." Smith paused and looked directly at Tommy Poole. "At this point, Mister Poole, there are insufficient members of the Committee who are convinced that the charges against you are insupportable to allow me to go to a final vote. We want to hear the rest of the testimony." He glanced at Jeff. "Therefore, Mister Polk, I ask that you continue your presentation of the defense." A chorus of groans erupted from the witnesses and observers.

Jeff looked at Tommy. Seeing that Tommy's face was slightly clouded over with worry, he patted Tommy gently on the arm.

"No sweat," he said gently. "We've got a great defense lined up. We'll knock 'em dead!" Jeff consulted his notes. "For my first defense witness I would like to call Midshipman Fourth-class James Wesley Merritt."

As Jim walked to the witness chair, Jeff spoke directly to Homer Smith.

"Mister Chairman, calling this witness is slightly out of sequence, however, the Red Cross has asked that Midshipman Merritt return home as soon as possible. The Academy has a driver waiting to take him to the airport immediately after his testimony. So if it's okay with you, I'd like to present his testimony first."

"It's fine with us, Mister Polk," Homer said, then he looked at Jim. "Welcome to the Honor Committee, Mister Merritt. You wear the new ribbon well."

"Thank you, sir," Jim replied.

"Mister Merritt," Jeff began, "how well do you know Tommy Poole?"

"About as well as I know anyone in our Company. He was a roommate during Plebe Summer."

"Would you consider him a dishonorable person?"

"Absolutely not!" Jim said with conviction. "Never once in the time that I roomed with him or since have I ever seen or heard him perform a dishonest act. He is a top-rate individual." Jeff continued.

"Midshipman Merritt, can you give any examples to back up your opinion?"

"I can cite several, but I think the most telling information is unrelated to isolated acts of bravery." Jim smiled at the Committee and touched his left chest. "I look at this award every day, and I can't honestly understand why it's there. The Academy says I did something brave and worthy of recognition, but I'll tell you truthfully that what I did happened without conscious thought. Instinct ruled my actions. I didn't feel like a hero at the time, and I don't feel like a hero now." He smiled winningly. "Although I must admit this ribbon sure looks good, and it makes me feel wonderful.

"But this hearing is about Tommy Poole, who is one of the finest individuals I have ever met, and a far bigger hero than I am. The reason is in Tommy's character. Tommy's not the world's best athlete, and in Tiger Company that's a big negative. He's also not the most military of Midshipmen. And he's certainly not cut from the same cookie-cutter image mold like many of the rest of us. But, despite these drawbacks, he has persevered. He's been run unmercifully by the Tigers, but every single comearound he does his absolute best. He's been taunted, ridiculed, shamed, and harassed; yet he's still here, and he's still wearing the uniform. He's as proud to be a Midshipman as any one of us -- maybe even prouder.

"I'm not sure I could have survived the abuse he's suffered. -- I'm not sure I would have wanted to. But he endured, gentlemen, and that says something special about Tommy Poole and his qualifications to be a midshipman and naval officer. And it especially says something about his sense of honor. I am absolutely convinced he would never steal anything. If he is dismissed, the Honor Code will have failed."

Homer Smith stared at Jim Merritt. It was clear from the spark in his eyes that Jim meant every word he said, and Homer obviously respected that.

"Well said, Mister Merritt. I promise that this Committee will do its absolute best to interpret the Honor Code and whether it has been violated." As Homer was talking, the door to the Conference Room opened slowly and an enlisted sailor entered tentatively. He looked around confused. Rock Stone gestured to the vacant chair to his right. Rock and the sailor whispered together for several seconds.

Jeff continued. He smiled at Jim. "Are you a firm proponent of the Academy Honor Code, Mister Merritt?" he asked.

"Absolutely!"

"What's your opinion in this particular case?"

"I think it's clear that Tommy Poole neither stole anything nor accepted and used anything he considered stolen. If he had cheated on a test, if he had uttered a direct lie to a superior officer, or if he had taken something of value that did not belong to him, then I would agree the recommendations of the committee would be clear. But in this case the only ***honorable*** course of action is to give an innocent man the benefit of the doubt and to dismiss the charges. Tommy Poole has suffered enough this year."

"Mister Chairman!" Rock Stone interrupted. "The driver is here to take Midshipman Merritt to the airport. He must leave now or he may miss his flight." Homer didn't hesitate.

"Of course," Homer said. "Mister Merritt you are excused. Good luck, sir!" The fact that a first-class chose to call a plebe "sir" was significant. Jim smiled, stood briefly at attention, nodded to the committee, and walked toward the door. On the way out he turned to Tommy.

"I'm certain you'll be exonerated, Tommy. I'll see you when I get back and we can celebrate."

"Right," Tommy answered. "After Restriction Muster we can go to the Steerage and have a milkshake." Jim laughed, patted Tommy on the shoulder, and hurried from the room, trailed by the Navy driver.

After Jim had gone, Jeff consulted his notes again.

"Next I'd like to call Midshipman Fourth-class Enrique Jose Guevarra." Rico strolled to the witness chair and sat. He smiled handsomely to the committee, straightened his tie, leaned against the rear support of the chair, and spread his leg slightly out in front of him. He looked completely relaxed.

"Midshipman Guevarra, several weekends ago you made a statement about the Honor Code that shocked everyone who was listening. Would you repeat that statement for the committee?"

Rico smiled devilishly, and looking directly at Homer Smith said, "I announced that the Naval Academy Honor Code was bullshit!" The Committee took the statement even less well then did Rico's fellow Company plebes. All five Committee members jerked visibly and leaned forward in their seats. Five sets of very angry eyes regarded Rico.

"I hope you have an explanation for this, Polk!" Lehre said sternly.

"Yes, sir! I do!" Jeff replied. He turned to Rico. "Midshipman Guevarra, you went on to explain what you meant. Would do that for the Committee?"

Rico smiled at the still-glaring Committee.

"Actually it's quite simple. The Honor Code says clearly that a Midshipman will not lie, cheat, or steal. That's a broad and sweeping statement, but the Code doesn't really mean what is says."

Homer interrupted.

"Yes it does, Mister Guevarra, and you insult this committee with that assertion!"

Rico smiled again and continued.

"No sir, it doesn't!" Rico replied, then quickly raised a hand to stifle protests, "and I'll explain why." Rico paused dramatically and stared at each member of the Committee in turn. "It's not an Honor Offense when I tell my kid brother there's a Santa Claus. It's not an honor offense when I tell a police officer I didn't realize I was going over the limit. It's not an honor offense when I tell a woman I just met that I'll respect her in the morning. It's not an honor offense when I sneak out of the Academy grounds to visit a young lady. But in the strictest sense, each of those examples is dishonorable."

"My padre says it best," Rico continued, then he chuckled. "He's a great guy! A real Latin from Puerto Rico who runs a grocery store in Brooklyn. Every time I'm home and my parents are going to a friend's house or to church, my mama always inspects herself critically just before they go out the door. She always asks him if he thinks she's too heavy." Rico chuckled. "Now my mama is a sweet lady, but she does tend to carry a little bit extra around hips. Papa always winks at me before he answers, and he always says the same thing, '*No dear, you're not fat at all!*'" Most of the committee members had settled down slightly, but none of them laughed at Rico's story. However, there was a great deal of chuckling from the witness chairs. Rico continued. "I asked my papa why he told such fibs and he answered that sometimes you have to bend the truth if you want to be able to live with yourself.

"He's right, you see," Rico continued. "The truth isn't always the most honorable course of action. Now, don't get me wrong on this. The Honor Code is a wonderful guide. It just doesn't apply always and forever to what happens in real life. In fact it only applies to what happens inside the walls on the Naval Academy and within the context of military duty. I could lie to my roommate about my sexual prowess -- not that I do, mind you -- and that wouldn't be an honor offense. I could cheat a patsy classmate at a poker game." He looked at Jubal Ramsey. "I don't though -- and that would be between him and me.

"So what the Honor Code really says is that a Midshipman should never lie, cheat, or steal *while in the course of carrying out his official duties*. And that's where Tommy Poole's case falls apart. He had a picture of Captain Dillingham in his hat. So what? Tommy used that photo for motivation, to remind him of the task at hand, which for every plebe is to survive the year. The photo was taken as a prank, gentlemen. There was no harm done. Having that photo helped Tommy survive and grow, something our good Captain would agree was beneficial."

Rico paused again.

"So when I said the Honor Code was bullshit, I meant that any literal, black-and-white interpretation is dangerous. Life is very gray. There was no Honor offense committed here. Please don't use the Code to expel a Midshipman of the caliber of Tommy Poole."

Brian Lehre spoke up almost immediately.

"Interesting speech, Midshipman Guevarra, but if we followed your logic, we'd never convene a single Honor Hearing because not only is life sometimes gray, but so are the honor offenses themselves. Like this one. Someone has to interpret the gray."

"For us," Homer Smith continued, "honor often comes down to personal opinion and gut feeling. We sometimes have to decide based on what we feel. You may think that's unfair, but that's the way it has to be. We *must* protect the reputation of the Academy and we must prosecute whenever we feel the Code may have been violated. It may be unfair to you, and certainly it will seem unfair to Tommy Poole if we recommend dismissal, but the Naval Academy will nonetheless endure without Thomas Henry Poole. It will not endure without an Honor Code."

The room was quiet for several seconds. Rico continued smiling then stood, still facing the Committee.

"Tommy is one of the most honorable people I've ever met. He deserves to stay, amigos. Don't screw him for the sake of the system." With that Rico retired to his chair.

"Next," Jeff announced, "I'd like to call Midshipman Fourth-class Kevin Patrick O'Reilly." Kevin bounced to his feet and hurried to the witness chair.

"Mister O'Reilly," Jeff began. "You've heard the evidence and testimony presented thus far. What do you think about the case?"

"There's not a chance in the world that Tommy Poole committed an Honor offense," Kevin replied. "It's just not in his nature."

"Well," Jeff continued, "it seems to me the committee is very concerned about the missing photo. After all it was removed from the official Roster Board. I can understand why removing something from its rightful and official place might be considered theft, can't you?"

"Of course!" Kevin relied. "But the committee isn't seeing this in the right light."

"Oh? It what way?"

Kevin chuckled.

"At the end of last summer a small group of the more playful members of our Company got up late one night and "borrowed" the guidons from more than 15 Company areas." We chuckled again, leaning toward the Committee conspiratorially. "We planted the guidons in the flower garden at the entrance to Tecumseh Court. They made quite a display. Until this very instant no one official knew who pulled that stunt. Last November another group of us removed one of the Army cannons from its stand by Dahlgren Hall and wheeled it into the Rotunda. Pre Army-Navy spirit! And only a couple weeks ago some dastardly individuals temporarily adulterated the brave statue of Tecumseh so that it looked more 'Tiger-ish.' Would anyone consider prosecuting those incidents as Honor offenses? Not a chance! Why? Because there were pranks, harmless stunts designed to increase morale or harass the bureaucracy. The system encourages those kinds of activities.

"What Tommy is accused of is nothing more than another prank. A photo is not a cannon, true, but the act is still a prank. Believe me, his having that photo in his cap *did* improve the morale of the plebes in Tiger Company -- something we desperately needed at the time." Kevin laughed at his last statement, then became immediately serious.

"In case you people have missed it, we're Twenty-third Company Tiger plebes. I can't say that I agree with the way plebe indoctrination is managed by some of the firsties in our Company, but plebes don't have much of a say here, do they? So we have to endure or else quit. I hated going to bed every night hungry and waking up every morning with a knot in my stomach. People under stress tend to grab diversions and attack free time with a frenzy. A photo in a cap may seem like a serious matter to you gentlemen, but it was no more than a fun way for Tommy to show that he's got something to knock together despite the harassment. I think it was a great idea, and I'm going to encourage my own plebes to invent that kind of diversion to help them survive the year."

"So," Jeff asked, "you say it should all be considered a prank, a joke, a silly diversion?"

"Absolutely!" Kevin exclaimed with emphasis. "What else could it be?"

"Okay," Jeff said. "Thank you!"

"Wait!" Kevin said suddenly. "There's more!"

Jeff looked at his notes momentarily, then looked at Kevin with raised eyebrows. "More, huh?"

"Yes! Absolutely!"

"Then continue, please," Jeff offered.

"Mister Smith," Kevin said. "Earlier this evening you read us a quote from John Paul Jones about the qualities of the Naval Officer. I'm a plebe, so naturally I memorized that quotation last summer and I've had to recite it about a bazillion times since then. But I think you missed something when you recited."

"Really?" Homer replied. "And what was that?"

"John Paul was setting a standard for naval officers -- but let's face it, none of us is really a naval officer. I'm an eighteen-year-old naval student. -- Just a kid who wants desperately to become a fine naval officer. I have a great deal to learn not just about ships and academics, but also about myself and maybe even about honor. I'm certainly not qualified to take the Oath of Commissioning yet, but I'll get there." Kevin looked at each committee member in turn.

"If I take a test and miss a question or two, my grade is reduced and maybe I don't make the Superintendent's List. If I play basketball and miss a critical shot, the team may lose. If I screw up while reciting a rate to my Tiger firstie, I get my butt run off. Great! Those are the rules, and when I endure punishment, I'm more motivated to do better next opportunity. But why is it that Honor is a black-or-white offense with the only recourse dismissal? Why can't an 18-year-old be allowed a small mistake or two in the learning process? How else do we develop that "nice" sense of personal honor?

"I guess what I'm saying is that even if you are convinced that Tommy committed an Honor offense -- no matter how inconceivable that is to me -- think about what this particular offense is and the consequences. Should he be dismissed for a prank? Is a photograph -- even of a genuine war hero -- worth this? Bull laughed loudly.

The usually devilish Kevin paused, seriously considering his next words.

"You know," he continued, "one of my favorite authors is William Shakespeare, and something he said in the play *Othello* about mercy has always stuck with me. If you wish, I could paraphrase the words.

"No need!" said a voice in the witness area. Kevin Dolan stood. "I know that particular quote well." He looked at Homer Smith, who nodded. Dolan continued in a Shakespearean voice, *"And earthly power seems like God's, when mercy seasons justice."*"

Kevin O'Reilly applauded and Kevin Dolan sat, happy to have been able to put on another show. O'Reilly stared straight into the eyes of Homer Smith.

"Remember John Paul Jones' words, and consider Shakespeare when you deliberate. And remember also that your decision will affect the lives of not just Tommy Poole, but every person in this room. Don't make a mockery of *my* Honor Code but using it to destroy a decent human being like Tommy Poole!"

Homer Smith returned Kevin's stare for a long second then nodded almost imperceptibly. None of the other Committee members had questions for Kevin.

"Next I would like to call Lieutenant William Archibald Harlan," Jeff said. Harlan moved purposefully to the chair and sat.

"Lieutenant Harlan," Jeff began. "What's your relationship with Midshipman Poole?"

"He's a student of mine in a special advanced physics class I teach."

"How many students are there in that class?"

"Five!"

"All plebes?"

"No!" Bill said smiling. "All firsties except for Tommy Poole."

"Wow!" Jeff said. "Tommy is the only plebe in the advanced physics class? That's pretty impressive. What kind of student would you say Tommy Poole is?"

"The best in the class. On every test so far he developed some new and interesting way of solving very difficult problems. He's even shortened several to where they're more understandable than the solutions recommended in the text."

"Would you say that Tommy Poole would be a definite asset as a naval officer?"

"He has a unique way of grappling with situations that would make him valuable in any organization."

"Would you say he has leadership qualities?"

"No question about it. If you could see him lead the class discussions and help the other students with the more difficult material, you'd have no doubts about his potential. He'll make a fine leader someday."

"Lieutenant Harlan, you've listened to the facts and testimony. What do you make of the case against Tommy Poole?"

"Ridiculous! I've worked closely with the boy and found him completely honorable. In fact, I think the direction this Honor Committee has taken is indefensible."

"Really? In what way?"

"Everybody agrees that the Naval Academy should weed out every potential officer who may be dishonest. If I were to catch a student cheating on a test, I would not hesitate to turn the matter over to the authorities. But when students in my classes give the wrong responses, that doesn't make them liars. When they guess an answer on a quiz, that doesn't make them dishonorable. This photo thing has me very concerned. It reminds me of the witch trials that were held in Salem Village in the early days of the colonies. There are accusations and a great many people acting strangely, but no facts. The charges against Tommy are they're deceptive, and when I try to examine them rationally they disappear in a puff of smoke. Nothing was stolen, nobody was hurt, and no dishonor committed."

Bill paused and cleared his throat before continuing. "Direct lies, cheating on a test, taking someone else's property, they might rate dismissal. But for God's sake when the charges are vague and the evidence weak, you have to decide in favor of the accused, who in this case is one of the best examples of a Midshipman I have ever had the privilege to instruct."

"Thank you, Lieutenant Harlan," Homer Smith said. "Trust me when I say that we will carefully consider your statements before we decide the disposition of this case."

"Next I'd like to call Midshipman First-class Reginald Oliver Stone." Rock stood slowly and began to walk toward the chair.

"Reginald?" Kevin asked as he passed.

Rock smiled devilishly.

"Why do you think I choose to be called 'Rock?'" he whispered.

"I wish I had known sooner," Kevin added.

Rock laughed.

"I purposefully kept that information from the plebes."

"Yeah," Kevin answered. "Who would follow "Reginald" if he were leader of the Tigers?"

"Excuse me," Homer said. "But it's getting late. Can we get on with this?" Rock nodded and continued to the chair.

"My questions to you will be brief, Mister Stone," Jeff began. "Really all I want you to do is to share your opinion of Tommy Poole."

Rock leaned forward and folded his hands on the table and began.

"When Mister Poole first entered the Company after Plebe Summer and for several months thereafter, I was convinced he would be a washout. He was grossly out-of-shape, he looked horrible in a uniform, and he had no force of personality. I enlisted the assistance of all my classmates to help convince Tommy it would be best to depart quietly.

"But that was before he endured everything we threw at him. He resisted even the staunchest of the Tigers. He proved his mettle under the harshest possible circumstances. Tommy Poole is a Tiger! He has guts and character and someday he'll make a fine leader. I believe it would be a shame to lose his talents. Most of the first-class in Twenty-third Company agree with my assessment wholeheartedly. So unless you are absolutely convinced he violated the Honor Code, I'm here to ask that you quickly dismiss the charges and let him get on with the tasks at hand."

Homer Smith raised his eyebrows, knowing this was high praise coming from the Head Tiger.

"Thank you, Rock," he said, and Stone returned to his seat, smiling at Kevin on the way.

"Thank you, Reginald," Kevin whispered loudly, and the mood in the Conference Room lightened considerably.

"For my final witness I would like to recall Captain Rusty Dillingham," Jeff said. Homer nodded agreement.

The Captain again settled impressively into his seat and waited while Jeff consulted his notes.

"Captain, you're the final person to testify for Thomas Henry Poole. Yours is the last voice raised in defense. And you may well be the only person who can really save Tommy now. I'm just going to ask you a single question which will tell the committee how you really feel about the plebe that stands accused of an Honor violation." Jeff paused and looked directly at Captain Dillingham.

"You brought these charges against Tommy, but if you were in combat and you needed someone to pull you out of a deep mess, would you trust your life to Thomas Henry Poole?" The room became quite. Jeff found himself staring at the rows of ribbons on Bull's chest. Most of the others did also.

Captain Dillingham looked at Tommy closely. He opened his mouth. In a loud voice announced, "You're God damned right I would!" The power of the statement and its clear intent brought quick tears to Jeff's eyes. He blinked them back hurriedly. Dillingham meantime rose like a giant and faced the committee.

"I make it a point never to interfere in the internal affairs of the Brigade," he said slowly, "so I won't tell you how I think you should vote." Then he smiled his most predatory smile and leaned across the table toward the committee, balancing his weight on his enormous arms. "But the fate of one of my best troops hangs in the best balance here, and I have been known to become violent in defense of my troops." He flexed an arm muscle and twisted his neck menacingly "You people better do what's right here because Tiger Company won't be the same without Tiger Poole." He straightened, spun around, and returned to his seat, patting Tommy on the shoulder as he passed.

It took several moments for the Committee to recover. Homer Smith addressed Jeff.

"Do you have a final statement?" he asked.

"Yes, sir. I do!"

Jeff took a deep breath and stood up. He smiled at the Committee.

"Forgive me," he said. "I'm a little scared. This whole honor thing, it's an awesome responsibility. The stakes are so high it's frightening, isn't it. I mean, here we are, all the testimony is given, all the facts and suppositions presented, and where are we? We're right back where we started this thing. Did Tommy Poole steal a photograph and did he use it knowing it was stolen?

"For me, it's open-and-shut case. Tommy Poole is an extremely honorable person, therefore he could not have stolen anything, and besides, the whole thing was a prank, and the photo was used to enhance morale, so no Honor offense was possible.

"I recognize it's not so easy for the committee. The only facts are that a photo was missing and that Tommy had a similar -- maybe identical -- photo in his hat. But none of the facts presented *prove* that Tommy did anything wrong, so you have to decide based on your feelings. That's hard too because none of you know Tommy Poole. Is he honorable or not? How can you tell?

"Listen to the testimony presented tonight. You heard classmates sing his praises. An instructor told you he's a model Midshipman. The Commander of the toughest Company in the Brigade stands behind his character. And a many-times-decorated combat veteran would trust his life to the Midshipman who sits before you. That says it all, gentlemen. You can't get higher praise and testimonial that Thomas Henry Poole has just received.

"Therefore, I am confident you will reach a quick conclusion and each vote to dismiss the charges against my friend and classmate. I rest my defense."

The entire room seemed to breathe a collective sigh. Almost immediately Homer Smith looked to the other committee members and spoke.

"Thank you for presenting an excellent defense, Mister Polk. You served your friend and classmate well. The committee will now review the testimony and call you back inside when we are ready to vote. Please depart and remain in the passageway."

Again the group rose and filed from the room. A crowd formed around Tommy Poole congratulating him in advance of his victory.

"Please," he said. "I'm worried to death. Let's wait until they vote."

Fifteen minutes later the Midshipman Dunloy pushed open the heavy door and beaconed everyone inside. Jeff's heart raced as he took his place. He couldn't imagine how Tommy felt. When everyone was seated, Homer spoke.

"We are ready to vote and I have passed out the ballots in the presence of the Staff Observer. Gentlemen," he said to address the committee, "cast your ballots, please!" Jeff watched as each committee member marked a box on the sheet in front of him, folded the ballot paper over, and handed it to the Chairman. When all five ballots sat in a pile, he looked at Tommy.

"I will now read the votes," he said. He opened the top ballot.

"The first ballot is Not Guilty!" He displayed the paper so that every witness could see the sheet. He passed the ballot to Midshipman Dunloy and selected a second ballot.

"The second ballot is Guilty!" Jeff felt his heart sink. How could anyone vote to convict Tommy based on that flimsy evidence? He looked at the Committee and saw that Brian Lehre returned his stare boldly. Homer selected the third ballot. "Not Guilty!" he read, and Jeff began to feel better. One more vote would do it. He could feel his pulse pounding in his neck as he waited for Homer Smith to read the fourth ballot. Smith opened the paper.

"Not Guilty!" Homer said loudly, and with an enormous smile. Pandemonium! Jeff leapt to his feet and whooped. He wasn't the only one.

Captain Dillingham grabbed Tommy out of his chair and hefted him into the air as classmates danced around the pair. Tommy spread his two arms and raised his eyes skyward in a prayer of thanks as Dillingham spun around in circles.

The elation continued for a long several moments while Homer and most of the committee looked on. Finally the room quieted enough for Homer to be heard.

"The fifth ballot also recommended dismissal. The record shows that the case of Midshipman Fourth-class Thomas Henry Poole is dismissed by a vote of four to one. I want to thank each of you who participated for your interesting and enlightening testimony. The methods of justice may sometimes seem unfair at Annapolis, but the system has worked successfully for more than a hundred years. I hope it will continue for several hundred more. This case is officially closed, the Company Officers of all concerned as well as the defendant and the staff observer will receive a copy of the final Committee Report once it is endorsed by the Commandant. I again remind everyone that this hearing is classified as confidential. Good night to all. Beat Army!"

A second celebration followed in the passageway. Hank Butkowski and George Abbott hefted Tommy up onto their shoulders and carried him to the Company area while the rest of Tommy's classmates paraded alongside. Inside Tiger Country the news of Tommy's victory was greeted with elation. Mugsy even let Tommy have a free sandwich from the Mess, but he had to pay for an extra slice of cheese.

Naturally Tommy's parents took the news well, and Sara was overjoyed. Tommy realized that up until that evening the rest of his life had seemed unfocused. Now he could plan for Spring Break and June Week, and things began to come into focus. Although it was well after midnight before he finally fell asleep, he slept as well as he had at any time in his life.

For the plebes in Twenty-third Company life assumed a different and much-less-intense routine. They still studied rates, polished shoes, and passed the food during meals, but comearounds were forgotten, as were square meals, chopping in the Company area, bracing up, and the constant terror that had marked the previous nine months. For the first time all year most plebes actually ate a full meal and had sufficient study time. The ceremony on Herndon Monument was still three months away, but Plebe Year had, in effect, ended.

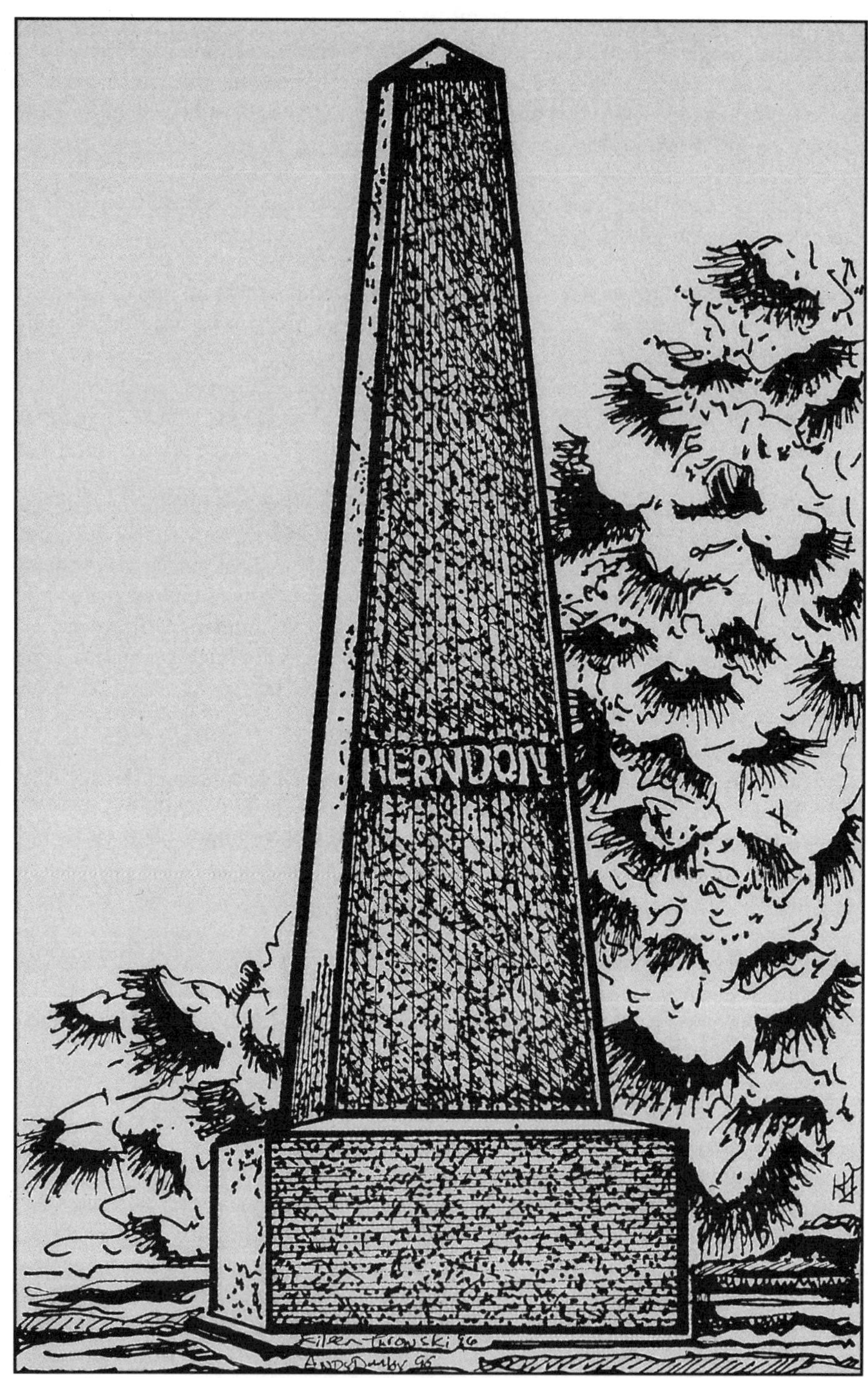

HERNDON MONUMENT

Herndon Monument is a 15-foot stone obelisk located on the campus across from the chapel. It is the site of the final act of the Plebe class when they remove a cap from its top signifying the end of Plebe year.

CHAPTER 15

EPILOG

The critical care room of Saint Jude's Cancer Ward was cool and brightly lit and smelled of liniments and medicines and other unfamiliar odors that Jim immediately hated. It was not a place for a Midshipman full of life and vigor and fresh from a whirlwind race halfway across the country. Jim had arrived downstairs only minutes earlier. Impatient, he had sprinted up the four flights of stairs, his feet hardly touching the concrete steps. When he opened the door to the ward he wasn't physically stressed, but his heart pounded nonetheless. He slowed involuntarily and took an enormous breath before continuing down the white-tiled corridor. The last 50 feet were the hardest distance Jim had ever crossed. The room swam with familiar faces.

He was still greeting his subdued relatives when he heard a raspy voice squeak his name. He had not as yet approached the bed and the quiet bundle that lay there. James Wesley Merritt -- hero of Hospital Point Inlet -- was more afraid then he had never been in his life. Every eye in the room focused on him. He looked around briefly, almost in a panic.

The enlisted driver who had taken Jim from Bancroft Hall to Washington, D.C., had far exceeded the speed limit because he knew the reason for Jim's departure. The drive had been unusually quiet because the driver also respected Jim's plight and knew he would want to be alone with his thoughts in a similar situation. Jim had arrived at National Airport only ten minutes before the departure of his flight. Hurrying to the gate, he found several smiling attendants waiting nervously for him. Within five minutes he was settled into a first-class seat American Airlines had suddenly opened up. He knew he was getting special treatment and he appreciated it, but he had found himself unable to voice his gratitude. Despite the obvious flirtations of several rather attractive young stewardesses, he remained quiet, staring bleakly at the dark night sky during the entire flight to Dallas.

In Dallas he had taken time for a quick call home. No one answered. He assumed everyone was at the hospital, even at that late hour, and within 40 minutes he had boarded the small commuter plane for the one-hour flight to Amarillo. He landed in the tiny airport at 0200 and had taken a cab directly to Saint Jude's Hospital -- to join the death vigil.

His aunt Jane's hand lingered on his arm, and he looked briefly into her troubled eyes before beginning the reluctant journey across the room. He hadn't yet seen his mother's face, but he could feel the tears welling up in his eyes as he approached the bed. He walked slowly and resolutely, and he could feel every eye follow his movements. He felt renewed panic. He realized he wasn't prepared. His parents had been so protective and reluctant to let their far-away son feel pain, that they had kept the full horror of the truth from him. Looking around briefly at all the tired and tortured eyes, he knew the truth was unimaginable. His heart threatened to explode and his neck throbbed with every pulse.

His first feeling as he approached the bed was relief. For a fleeting moment he felt certain there had been a terrible mistake. *This* person was not his mother. His mother was strong and tall and full of energy, a dynamo of psychic and emotional power that never seemed to wind down. What lay before him was shriveled, powerless -- and almost -- lifeless. A large tear rolled down his right cheek, and he silently cursed his weakness.

Across the bed, his father, John "Hap" Merritt, sat on a straight-backed wooden chair holding one of his wife's hands lightly, and rubbing her arm gently with his other hand. He looked up as Jim approached. Hap Merritt, usually the life-of-the-party, smiled weakly. Jim could see from the red and swollen eyes that he had been crying recently -- very recently. Suddenly a pair of cold tears traced identical paths down Jim's cheeks. In one corner of the room by the dark window, his siblings sat huddled in a single oversized arm chair. His youngest sisters, Monica and Merri, only seven and eight years old, cried quietly. New tears chilled paths along Jim's face and nose.

Jim took a deep breath, swallowed hard, and moved closer to the head of the bed. He realized that the entire family had been waiting for this moment, that his arrival had triggered an unvoiced signal, and that the person who would ultimately respond to that signal was his mother. He looked down and his eyes met hers. His vision immediately clouded, and wetness ran dripping onto the sterile white sheets. Mom didn't say anything, letting him have his little cry while she waited patiently. A box of hospital tissues miraculously appeared in front of him and he took several. The sound of his somewhat loud sniffling broke the silence and caused a great deal of sobbing from other persons in the room.

Jim Merritt took a deep and ragged breath and reached down to hold his mother's other hand. She tried to squeeze, but her grip was weak. He squeezed gently for her, and she winced. Jim almost let go of her hand until he realized she was feeling some inner pain he had no control over.

When his vision cleared, he found his mom smiling. That puzzled him out of his grief temporarily.

"What?" he croaked, a smile cracking his frozen features.

"Your father tells me you're a hero," she answered in a quiet whisper he had to lean over to hear. Another slight wince accompanying her exhalation.

Jim smiled again and looked down at his uniform where the new Commendation Ribbon still blazed in shiny green glory. His mother tried to reach up to touch the ribbons but her hand would not rise more than a few inches. Jim took her fingers and placed them against the ribbons.

"No big deal, Mom." His mother knew differently.

"Sorry about Leslie," she continued as he gently returned her hand to the bed and held it lightly.

"It's okay," he replied. "These things happen."

"She sounded lovely."

"She was," Jim said, looking at her more closely. "How are you doing?" It was of course a stupid question, and Jim knew that immediately, but somehow it seemed appropriate. Mom didn't mind.

She smiled.

"I'm very glad you could make it, Jim." She paused and struggled to take a breath. A more substantial flood of pain momentarily stopped her. "Even if the circumstances aren't the best." Again she paused and took several shallow breaths while she composed her thoughts. Jim could see that the sickness and the medicine were making her on-again-off-again groggy but that she was struggling to keep lucid. "Your father and I have already made the final arrangements," she croaked. "Your Aunt Jane is going to stay at the house for a few weeks until things settle down." That long statement came out in a rush that must have exhausted her. Jim saw her eyes swim lazily, then turn upward into their lids, and she settled into a peaceful doze. Final arrangements? Jim felt panic again. He looked at his father.

Hap Merritt looked down to assure himself that Mrs. Merritt was asleep, then he gently released her hand and whispered to Jim.

"Let's talk outside." Jim nodded and together the two of them retired to the relative seclusion of the corridor.

They moved several yards down the dimly lit passageway, passed several darkened rooms, and stopped when they were out of sight of the relatives -- and the room. They faced each other. Hap Merritt suddenly grabbed Jim's arm tightly and leaned against him. Sobs racked his father as Jim slipped his arms around the older man and held on gently.

"Oh, God!" his father whispered. "I love that woman! It's so hard!" Jim patted his dad's back for several minutes until the sobs stopped, then his dad drew away sniffing.

"Sorry, son," he said.

"It's okay, dad. I'm here now. I'll help all I can."

The night physician had visited Mrs. Merritt's room while Jim and his dad were in the hall. He approached the two of them tentatively. To Jim he seemed incredibly young to already be a doctor.

"Mister Merritt," he said in a sad and tired voice.

"Yes?" the two of them answered simultaneously, which caused Hap Merritt to giggle, then to laugh almost hysterically. Jim and the young doctor joined in, although not with the fervency of the elder Merritt.

"Mister Merritt," the doctor said, this time addressing Hap. "I'm Doctor Godwin. I take it this is your son?"

"Yes," Jim answered. "I'm Jim Junior."

"Jim," the Doctor Godwin said, offering his hand. "Your mom is quite a woman! When we admitted her two days ago, I wouldn't have thought she would live out the first night; but she insisted she wanted to see you one last time and that she had to wait until you came. I'm glad you're here. She's been in terrible pain but she insisted that we hold off on the strong medicines until after you arrived. I've asked the nurse to administer some morphine. She'll rest comfortably between now and the end." The last two words struck Jim with almost physical force, and he sucked in a deep involuntary breath.

Jim looked from doctor to dad. "How long, doc?" he asked with a sigh, feeling the tears well up again.

"Tonight. Tomorrow at the latest. I'm really very sorry to tell you this, but we did everything we could. Sometimes everything just isn't enough."

"Thanks, doc," Jim answered, and Doctor Godwin drifted quietly away.

Hap Merritt grabbed Jim's arm again.

"Come on," he said. "We'd better say goodby while there's still time." Together the two of them entered the room and moved resolutely to the bed.

An elderly nurse had propped Martha Merritt up in the hospital bed and was administering an IV as they approached. She taped the tubing gently to his mother's arm, carefully fluffed the pillows, smiled at the two men, then walked away without saying a word. Jim looked down.

His mother's breath came in short ragged gasps, and her face pinched slightly as waves of pain swept her body. Only vaguely aware of what was happening, her eyes moved slowly about the room until they met Jim's. She focused instantly. She wet her lips. Jim looked deeply into the sad blue eyes. Behind the pain, at the edge of her consciousness, Jim could sense she wanted to share something, but couldn't push the sounds past her dry and chapped lips except in a vague mumble. Jim felt her frustration. She knew her time was rapidly ebbing, and she wasn't able to say vital, final, cosmic things.

Jim felt a flush of sudden anger. His brain whirled furiously. He looked around for a medical person. He wanted to cry out, "Wait a minute! Give her a chance! Let her speak!"

He calmed almost immediately. He leaned over the bed and whispered gently, "I love you, mom." Martha Merritt smiled, and Jim sobbed loudly, which caused every one of his siblings to burst into simultaneous sobs of grief. He turned his head toward the window. Suddenly Jim felt a feather touch of soft fingers on his cheek. Through the tears he saw his mother looking at him. As he watched, she gathered her strength for one final effort. She took a slow deep breath, opened her mouth, and struggled desperately to speak, all of her physical power focused for a last effort at communication. Jim leaned down close to her face, tears dripping, wetting the sheets.

Determined and concentrating, she whispered softly, almost imperceptibly, in his ear, "A kiss." It was her final message. Her head sagged into the pillows and her eyes rolled into her head. She settled into sleep.

Jim kissed her cool forehead and gently wiped his tear drops from her cheek. His fingers lingered on her cheek, remembering how soft and comforting they had been. He leaned over and smelled her hair, remembering the scent of her shampoo. He lifted her hand and traced each finger slowly. He leaned down one final time.

"Goodby, Mom." He must have said it louder than he intended. Behind him several relatives wailed. The sounds caused shivers to course his body, and the hair on his neck to stand on end.

Jim straightened, wiped his salty face vigorously with several tissues, and smiled at his father. He walked slowly around the bed to the chair where his brothers and sisters waited. Their eyes pleaded with him, but he knew he couldn't tell them what they wanted to hear. He motioned for his sisters to get up, and he took her place on the chair. The two girls crowded onto his lap and cried with him. Samuel, standing to the left, gently rubbed Merri's shoulders. Houston, on the right, patted Monica's head absentmindedly. They comforted each other for several minutes while Hap said his goodbye.

The nurse had been waiting patiently by the door for Jim's father to finish. She now moved into the room and gently steered the relatives out into the corridor.

"She needs her rest," she said to Jim as she stood before him. Jim nodded, picked up the youngest and held her against his shoulder, where she promptly fell asleep. The nurse herded the rest of the family from the room. The hospital had allowed Dad to stay the evenings with his wife, and they would soon bring in a cot for him. In the meantime Jim led his Aunt Jane and his siblings to the car and drove them home.

Before he had time to get them all settled for the night, Aunt Jane handed him a note from his mother.

"She gave this to me several weeks ago," she said. "She wants you to read it at the funeral." Jim opened the envelope hesitantly. Inside was a single piece of paper. Written in his mother's sweeping handwriting was a poem, titled "*Remember*," she had copied from a library book. The ending of the poem was underlined in red ink. It said:

"And if you should forget me for a while,
and afterwards remember, do not grieve.
For if the sadness and corruption leave,
a vestige of the thoughts that once I had.
Better by far you should forget and smile,
than that you should remember and be sad."

LOVE, MOM

Jim cried again.

On a flight winging its way eastward high over the Atlantic, two women exchanged smiling glances. Both were stunning, almost movie-star in their perfection. The older woman exuded an overt sexuality that automatically caused every male within a hundred yards to drool and fantasize. She lounged in the comfortable first-class seat, totally at ease with her dramatic beauty, her legs crossed above the knees and extending to impossible lengths from her short skirt. Even though she didn't acknowledge the attention, she knew that the flight crew had made several trips into the first-class cabin solely for the purpose of seeing her. She also noticed but didn't acknowledge the envious stares of even the perkiest and most lovely of the stewardesses. Mrs. Wallace shrugged the attention away. She was used to it. She had even come to expect it.

Next to her sat a much younger woman, equally attractive in a more wholesome and innocent way, and equally as heart-stopping, but in a take-her-home-to-mother way. The older lady clearly relished the attention focused on the young lady beside her. This was her daughter, Lesley Taylor Wallace, soon to be of London, England. Lesley didn't look happy.

"What's the matter, dear?" Mrs. Wallace asked, leaning toward her daughter and brushing a dark lock of hair from her face.

"I really miss him, Mom," Lesley said.

Mrs. Wallace patted her daughter reassuringly on the shoulder.

"I know, dear," she said. "But you'll meet other young men in London, and eventually you'll forget about Jim. It's all part of life."

"He would have made such a wonderful husband and father," Lesley said with a sigh.

"Yes, I'm sure of that, dear," her mother answered, "but you would have grown tired of moving from place to godforsaken place, living in tiny houses, and always worrying if his next fiery flight into the heavens would be his last. It's not the life I want for you, dear."

Lesley considered and turned to her mother, tears in her eyes.

"I really loved him. I won't ever love anyone the same."

Mrs. Wallace tenderly wiped a tear from Lesley's cheek.

"I know dear. But sometimes we have to be practical."

Jeff Polk approached the door hesitantly. He was wearing his Service Dress Blues, having returned from a Restriction Muster not ten minutes previously. He had been mulling over a possible course of action ever since the Honor Committee meeting, but until this moment was unsure of what to do or how to do it. He knocked loudly.

"Enter!" Big Jim's voice boomed, and Jeff walked inside.

Harvey and Big Jim both looked up as Jeff entered, and their expressions drooped almost simultaneously.

"Whadda you want!" Big Jim asked gruffly.

"I've come to apologize for turning you in," Jeff said.

"A little late for that, huh?" Big Jim asked. He started to say more but Harvey interrupted.

"Hear him out, Jim!" he said. Daly looked at Linehan gruffly, then nodded.

"It took me a long time to get over the anger and the feeling of abuse. I couldn't understand why so many people were mad at me for doing what I thought was the honorable thing. The Honor Committee changed all that. As I listened to Captain Dillingham and Rock Stone and every one of my classmates describe what honor meant to them, I realized that I had been seeing it all from the wrong angle. Up until last week I was an outsider watching the Academy from the safety of detachment. From the outside my decision seemed perfectly correct.

"But now I'm an insider. I'm a real Midshipman. I'm one of you. And I can see that I was wrong. You guys were out of line, but you're also comrades, companions in this asylum, and it was *my* responsibility to handle the problem rather than turning you in. I know there's nothing I can do now, but I really am sorry."

Harvey Linehan stood and looked at Big Jim.

"See! I told you he'd come around."

Jeff laughed.

"Oh, no! No more comearounds, thank you!"

"It's good to see you again, Kevin," Sarah Connelly said sweetly. "I'm glad you could come over." Sarah Connelly was a desirable young lady, tall, big-chested, long-legged, and overtly sexual. This evening she had chosen to wear a very tight skirt and a bulky white cable-knot sweater that accented both her robust femininity and her dark hair perfectly. She was stunning, and both she and Kevin knew it.

Sarah and Kevin had a stormy relationship that started during the Army-Navy festivities, and had continued stop-start during Christmas vacation and ever since. Kevin had returned to Boston with no intention of even speaking to Sarah during the short Spring Vacation. That was what Sarah said she wanted, and Kevin had made it a point -- despite his mother's insistence otherwise -- to avoid Sarah during the first two days.

Kevin looked down at the floor of the Connelly living room momentarily.

"Yeah," he said. "Well you said you had something important to talk about."

"I do, Kevin," she said, adjusting her position slightly so that her breasts jutted forward provocatively in her sweater. "It's about us!" Rico had told Kevin that girls practiced those poses to confuse young men, and Kevin believed him. Rico had told him a great deal about women, and he had been especially keen to have Kevin watch out for Sarah during this vacation period.

"She's trouble, Kevin!" he had said repeatedly. "Take my word for it!" Rico Guevarra was seldom wrong.

"What *about* us?" Kevin asked suspiciously.

"I've missed you, Kevin," she said, smiling disarmingly. "I don't know what got into me when we fought last time I saw you, but I was wrong, and I want to apologize." Kevin perked up at this. Last time they talked Sarah had loudly sworn she was completely right and said she would never apologize. Kevin looked at her closely for a moment as she continued to pose for him. He found he couldn't remember what it was they had fought about.

"It's okay," he said, smiling. "I forgive you."

"Wonderful!" she exclaimed, laughing and leaping into his arms. Suddenly she was pressed against him -- something else Rico had warned him about. He found himself responding, -- another Rico warning sign. As the embrace lingered, Rico's words drifted farther and farther from his conscious thoughts. Sarah sighed and whispered against his shoulder. "My parents are shopping in Deerfield and won't be back until after nine."

"And . . . ," Kevin asked devilishly.

"And," she said looking up at him coyly, "if we run upstairs to my room right this minute, I could make love to you a hundred times before they get back." Kevin agreed.

As they headed toward the stairs, Sarah asked sweetly, "Will you take me to see a movie tomorrow night?"

"Darn!" he replied. "I can't! I already promised Jim and Wally I'd go with them to the quarry in the afternoon. I want to show them how well I swim now. We won't be back until almost eight in the evening." Sarah stopped in her tracks, one foot poised on the stairs.

"But what about us?" she asked.

"We can go on Saturday night," Kevin offered nudging her upward with a laugh.

"But I can't go Saturday," she said sweetly, resisting his gentle shove. "I have to watch my little brother while my parents go to an American Legion Dance. It's got to be tomorrow."

" I already arranged everything with Jim and Wally," Kevin replied, "and Wally's working Saturday." He nudged her again. "We can catch the Sunday matinee. No problem!"

Sarah spun around, her face red with anger.

"No!" she screamed. "Tomorrow or never!"

Kevin looked at her closely, then smiled. Rico had warned him about this too.

"You're trying to control me with sex," Kevin said. "It won't work. The last time we talked you yelled at me for half an hour and said you never wanted to see me again. I thought you meant it. I've been home for two days and I've already made plans. I'm sorry, but you can't expect me to drop everything just because you decide I have to. I won't do it!"

"Then get out!" she spat hatefully. Kevin paused, nodded, turned slowly, and started for the door. "I lied, you know," she said as he slipped on his jacket. "I'm not sorry. I meant every word of what I said last time we argued." Kevin nodded, zipped his jacket, then moved to the door.

Sarah suddenly ran ahead of him and blocked the way. She pressed her backside against the door, spread her legs slightly, and spread her arms across the doorway. The pose made her skirt ride up her legs past mid-thigh, and her breasts strained the sweater fabric. Kevin moaned quietly. He faltered.

"Wait!" she said, her voice a mask of fright and confusion. Her green eyes flashed. "Don't go! I *am* sorry. I promise if you take me out tomorrow night, I'll never act stupid again."

Kevin took a deep breath and tried to picture Rico. Rico looked disappointed.

"No Sarah! Stop this! I'd love to take you to a movie, but I already have plans tomorrow."

She flared again. She inhaled deeply.

"If you walk out the door, you'll never see me again!" she said dramatically, still baring the way.

Kevin walked closer. He could see her eyes regard him smugly. He reached out for the door handle.

"If that's what you want," he said, "that's the way it'll have to be." He opened the door, but it nudged gently against her backside. She stared at him for several long seconds, not moving. Looking straight ahead, she pulled her arms to her side and walked away from the door toward the stairs. She walked with a practiced motion Kevin recognized. Her legs and backside enticed him. He thought of Rico.

"Close the door and take off your jacket," she said sadly without turning. Rico's face evaporated.

"What? Why?"

She stopped with her right foot poised on the first stair tread, exposing more leg to sight.

"If that's all I'm good for," she said disgustedly, removing her sweater with one swift motion, "let's go upstairs and get it over with. You can forget all about me tomorrow when you're with your stupid friends." Kevin hesitated, his hand still on the knob.

"Come on!" she said, reaching behind her to unfasten her bra, "we don't have all night!" She dropped her bra and sweater on the stairs and started upward without looking back. Within moments Kevin could hear the door to her room open, and the sounds of sheets and blankets being swept from the bed. He hesitated, staring up the empty stairway, momentarily unsure what to do. The thought of Sarah's nakedness brought warm memories that aroused him. Kevin groaned. He toyed with his jacket zipper and closed his eyes. Rico's face startled him. Rico flashed the all-knowing half-smirk he always used when Kevin was about to do something stupid. Kevin O'Reilly smiled, opened the outside door, stepped outside into the cool spring air, and shut the door firmly behind him.

"All right, Kevin O'Reilly," he said aloud, smiling broadly. "You *did* have a Plebe Year!" He decided to brag to Rico about his new-found moral fiber.

Eight weeks before Graduation, on Service Selection Night, Rock Stone -- who graduated number 107 in the Class of 1968 -- moved resolutely to the front of the special table. "Special" because this one advertised itself in a bold yellow-and-gold sign that it was for Marine Corps candidates. Captain Dillingham and the senior Marine at Annapolis, a crusty old Lieutenant Colonel named Eldridge, looked up as he faced them.

"Good Evening, Midshipman Stone," the Colonel said. "I've heard a great deal about you. Think you're ready for my Corps?"

"Yes, sir!" he replied loudly.

"Good!" The Colonel said. "Sign here!" Rock signed, then after a brief discussion, selected the earliest possible Officer Candidate School slot at the Quantico, Virginia, followed by assignment to the Second Marine Division. Rock Stone would meet the Division in Qwang Tri Province, Republic of Vietnam.

Six weeks before Graduation Mugsy McGinley drove his brand new automobile to his assigned parking place along the Farragut Field sea wall. It was a fire-engine red Corvette he nicknamed Mugsy's Mess. More than 20 second-class volunteered to take over the sandwich concession the next year, but Mugsy left it all to Kevin O'Reilly. He did make Kevin pay for the leftover baloney and condiments.

Two weeks before Graduation, in the middle of Finals activity, Harvey Linehan felt pretty good. He had just taken -- and surely passed -- his first-class thermodynamics course, the last hurdle to Graduation. All during the meal he had talked excitedly about what he suspected life would be like in the fleet. Harvey was elated.

At the very end of the meal he stood, balled up his napkin as was his custom and looked to the far near side of the table, and called out.

"Hey, Reb?"

Jubal "Reb" Ramsey had been regaling the table with a story about Alabama life when Harvey interrupted.

"Yeah, Harv," Reb answered.

"Free shot?" he asked.

Ramsey looked down at his nearly-filled glass of tea.

"No way!"

Harvey sighed, turned toward the doors, then lofted a hook shot toward Reb without looking. The napkin ball arced lazily, bounced off the unsuspecting Reb's nose, and landed with a plop in his iced tea glass. Reb looked down, surprised, grabbed the glass, and jumped to his feet.

"Jesus, Harvey!" Big Jim laughed. "You finally made one!"

Harvey, who had continued to saunter toward the doors, looked back at the table, and saw Reb Ramsey, an enormous smile on his face, coming full steam around the end of the table, holding the iced tea glass out in front of him.

Linehan let out a startled cry and stumbled slightly as he began running desperately toward the exit. Big Jim Daly let out a whoop of pure delight and stepped aside to let the ecstatic plebe by. Ramsey rumble passed, yelling loudly. His yells excited Linehan to greater efforts and Daly to louder encouragement.

Near the exit, Thirty-fourth Company was entertaining a group of prospective athletic candidates who might decide to join the Brigade as plebes next year. They looked up as the commotion of the chase distracted them and watched a desperate Harvey Linehan race by on his way out the doors, followed closely by the screaming and obviously delighted Reb Ramsey.

The firstie who had been lecturing the candidates on the wonderful life within Bancroft Hall laughed at the pursuit.

"The guy being chased made a free shot!" he announced. When he saw the puzzled expressions, he continued, "If you come here, you'll understand." The candidates laughed, and one tall, bright-eyed high school junior turned to his neighbor and said.

"Plebe Year sure seems like a lot of fun!"

Tommy Poole stood back to survey the frantic activity. The tall thin obelisk named Herndon Monument had been covered in a layer of motor oil and Crisco more than an inch thick, giving it's normal light gray gloss a blotchy and lumpy and sick-looking whiteness. Around the monument hundreds of members of the Class of 1971 pressed themselves, arm linked to arm, around the structure until they were several plebes thick. One plebe Tommy had never seen before stood near the mass of sweating and soon-to-be-Criscoed young men, extolling them to pack themselves tighter.

"Okay!" he said. "One more bottom layer; then let's start on the second tier!"

Tommy watched fascinated as his classmates performed a choreography of ultimate teamwork. Larger plebes -- he could see both Hank Butkowski and George Abbott in the crowd, backs pressed firmly against the marble -- made a human chain for classmates to climb to form a second, not so massive, layer, which in turn would become the base for a third even smaller layer from which a classmate would ultimately wrest the Midshipman's cap from its glued-down position atop the monument.

"You should get the cap, Tommy," Jeff Polk offered. "God knows you probably suffered more than anyone else this past year." Tommy glanced down at his now-muscular bulk and shook his head, laughing.

"I think I'll save my classmates the pain of having to support my mass," he said, "and let some smaller plebe get the cap down. Besides, I'm tired of standing out in the crowd. If I never have a single second's worth of attention the entire rest of my career, it'll be fine with me."

"We need more human bracing along the bottom row of the north side of the monument!" shouted the plebe in charge in a worried voice. Tommy and Jeff exchanged quick glances, and Tommy, laughing, plunged delightedly into the mass of plebeness. The Class of 1971 was only seconds away from officially being recognized as third-class Midshipmen, and life would never be the same again.

THE CLASS CREST OF THE CLASS OF 1971

Every graduating class at Annapolis designs its own crest, which is included on the class ring on the side opposite the Academy seal. The ring is worn on the left hand and the crest side is turned outward following graduation.

litional copies of the ***Plebe*** trilogy can be obtained from the publisher

ease Send [ ] copies of ***Plebe***
nclose **$29.95 each** ($26.95 plus $3.00 postage and handling)

ME ______________________________

DRESS ______________________________

TY ______________ **STATE** ________ **ZIP** ________
(No cash or COD orders please)

e number of copies available is limited. Price subject to change without notice.
ease allow four weeks for delivery.
il your check and order blank (or photocopy) to:
radigm Press, PO Box 5248, Kent, Washington, 98064-5248

---

lditional copies of individual ***Plebe*** trilogy artwork can be obtained from the publisher

ease Send [ ] copies of ***Plebe Artwork in*** 8 1/2" X 11" or 11" X 17"
nclose **$12.99 each** - 8 1/2 X 11print or **$16.99 each** - 11 X 17 print.

AME ______________________________

DDRESS ______________________________

ITY ______________ **STATE** ________ **ZIP** ________
(No cash or COD orders please)

IOTE CARDS AND OTHER ART WORK ARE AVAILABLE FROM THE PUBLISHER
lease allow four weeks for delivery.
rice subject to change without notice.
lail your check and order blank (or photocopy) to:
aradigm Press, PO Box 5248, Kent, Washington, 98064-5248

NO. PAGES	PAGE	SIZE

Additional copies of the ***Plebe*** trilogy can be obtained from the publisher

Please Send [ ] copies of ***Plebe***
I enclose **$29.95 each** ($26.95 plus $3.00 postage and handling)

NAME ______________________________

ADDRESS ______________________________

CITY ______________ **STATE** ________ **ZIP** ________
(No cash or COD orders please)

The number of copies available is limited. Price subject to change without notice.
Please allow four weeks for delivery.
Mail your check and order blank (or photocopy) to:
Paradigm Press, PO Box 5248, Kent, Washington, 98064-5248

Additional copies of individual ***Plebe*** trilogy artwork can be obtained from the publisher

Please Send [ ] copies of ***Plebe Artwork*** in 8 1/2" X 11" or 11" X 17"
I enclose **$12.99 each** - 8 1/2 X 11print or **$16.99 each** - 11 X 17 print.

NAME ______________________________

ADDRESS ______________________________

CITY ______________ **STATE** ________ **ZIP** ________
(No cash or COD orders please)

NOTE CARDS AND OTHER ART WORK ARE AVAILABLE FROM THE PUBLISHER
Please allow four weeks for delivery.
Price subject to change without notice.
Mail your check and order blank (or photocopy) to:
Paradigm Press, PO Box 5248, Kent, Washington, 98064-5248

NO. PAGES	PAGE	SIZE